OF ANCIENTS UNBOUND

THE BLADEBORN SAGA, BOOK SEVEN

T. C. EDGE

COPYRIGHT

Previous book in the series:

CONTENTS

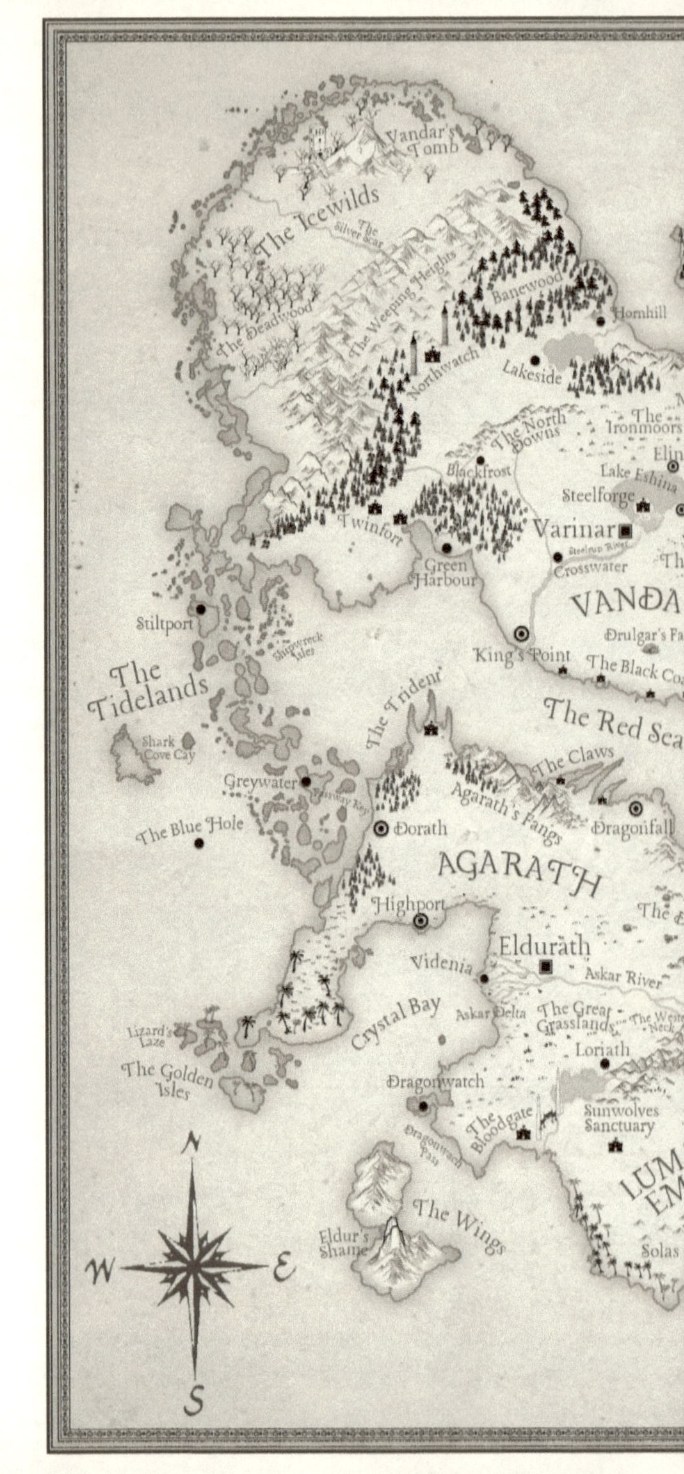

Vandar's Tomb
The Icewilds
The Silver Scar
The Weeping Heights
Banewood
Hornhill
The Deadwood
Northwatch
Lakeside
The North Downs
The Ironmoors
Elina
Blackfrost
Lake Eshina
Steelforge
Twinfort
Varinar
M
Green Harbour
Steelrun River
VANDA
Crosswater
Drulgar's Fall
Stiltport
The
King's Point
The Black Coas
Shipwreck Isles
The Tidelands
The Red Sea
The Trident
Shark Cove Cay
The Claws
Greywater
Fairway Reef
Agarath's Fangs
Dragonfall
The Blue Hole
Dorath
AGARATH
The Dr
Highport
Eldurath
Videnia
Askar River
Lizard's Laze
Crystal Bay
Askar Delta
The Great Grasslands
The Western Neck
The Golden Isles
Loriath
Dragonwatch
The Bloodgate
Sunwolves Sanctuary
Dragonwatch Pass
LUMA
EM
The Wings
Eldur's Shame
Solas
N
W
E
S

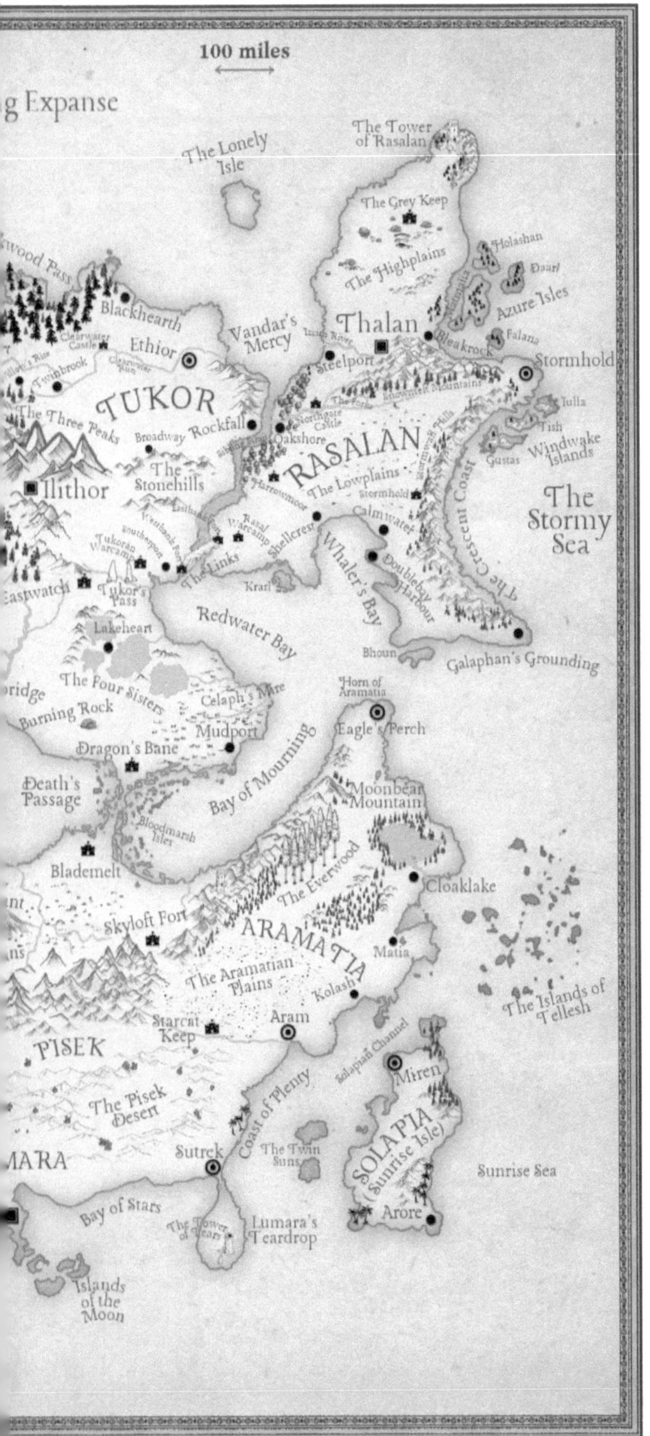

100 miles
g Expanse
The Lonely Isle
The Tower of Rasalan
The Grey Keep
The Highplains
Holashan
Daarl
Azure Isles
wood Pass
Blackhearth
Vandar's Mercy
Thalan
Clearwater Castle
Ethior
Indie River
Bleakrock
Falana
Stormhold
Twinbrook
Clearwater Run
Steelport
TUKOR
Broadway
Rockfall
The Forks
Snowmelt Mountains
Iulla
The Three Peaks
Northgate Castle
Tish
Oakshore
RASALAN
Gustas
Windwake Islands
The Stonehills
Harrowmoor
The Lowplains
stormheld
Ilithor
Easthaven
Rasal Warcamp
Calmwater
The Crescent Coast
The Stormy Sea
Westbank
southport
Shellcrest
Tukoran Warcamp
The Links
Whaler's Bay
Doubleby Harbour
Eastwatch
Tukor's Pass
Krarl
Lakeheart
Redwater Bay
Bhoun
Galaphan's Grounding
bridge
The Four Sisters
Celaph's Mire
Horn of Aramatia
Burning Rock
Mudport
Eagle's Perch
Dragon's Bane
Bay of Mourning
Moonbear Mountain
Death's Passage
Bloodmarsh Isles
Blademelt
The Everwood
Cloaklake
nt
Skyloft Fort
ARAMATIA
Matia
ns
The Aramatian Plains
The Islands of Tellesh
Kolash
Starcat Keep
Aram
PISEK
Solapian Channel
Miren
The Pisek Desert
SOLAPIA
(Sunrise Isle)
Sunrise Sea
MARA
Sutrek
Coast of Plenty
The Twin Suns
Bay of Stars
The Tower of Tears
Lumara's Teardrop
Arore
Islands of the Moon

PROLOGUE

King Ethin stood alone outside his grandfather's forge, looking out across the wonders of his country.

It was beautiful. The white city, the great valley crossed with all its twinkling streams, the flowering meadows and lush little thickets where the deer and wood fowl roamed. Above him, the summer's warmth had driven the snow right up to the very tips of the mountain peaks; he could see a fine glittery mist blowing off from them when the wind came just right, and that was beautiful too.

It is all beautiful, he thought. *All of it.* Beautiful and wondrous, and that was why he didn't come here. Seeing the great city his grandfather had built. Thinking of all the wonders he'd performed within his forge. The structures he'd designed. The magic he'd devised. The armour and the weapons he'd made. *He shattered the heart of a god up here,* Ethin reflected. Was there any greater magic than that? To unmake Vandar's almighty heart and remake it anew into five bladed shards, each with a unique power of its own?

Ethin had heard the stories from his father, King Varyth. He knew the dark magic it took to break the heart, and he knew of the sorceries and potions Ilith had conjured in order to shape and empower the blades. It was unthinkable. Impossible. Something only Ilith could have done. And that was why Ethin chose to stay away, why he had shut the forge and abandoned the mountain. It only reminded the king of his own limitations and inadequacies. *I am just an echo of him,* he thought, bitterly. *Nought but a pale imitation forever doomed to live in his long shadow.*

Ethior, he thought. That was his only true triumph as king, the pretty stone city he'd raised astride the Clearwater Run, but even that was no more than a poor cousin to Ilithor. *It is to Ilithor as I am to Ilith,* Ethin thought. *A lesser version, and greatly so.* He turned his head now, hearing foosteps coming up the stair. *And here comes another... Just another echo like me.*

The king went over to await her at the top, straightening out his long green cloak over the fine brown jerkin he wore. He made himself smile; it would not serve to greet her grumpily. No. Last night at her welcome banquet, Queen Thalina had told him she had a gift for him, and that she wanted to present it to him up here, at the old forge, and that was the reason he had come. *I must smile and be thankful,* he told himself. *Accept the gift with grace, whatever it is she gives me.*

So that's what he did. He forced a smile onto his lips as the young queen crested the top of the stair and arrived upon the plateau to join him. He dipped his head. "Your Grace. Good morrow. I hope the journey was not too arduous?"

"By no means," she said to him, smiling demurely. Thalina shared somewhat in the look of her famous grandmother, and somewhat in manner as well, though in much the same way as Ethin was no more than a reflection of his grandfather, so Thalina was of Thala, and the reflection was blurred. She had several men with her, guards and servants who followed behind bearing what was surely the gift she had spoken of. It was large, flat, and rectangular, wrapped up in linen and bound in string. It looked like it was probably a painting, so far as Ethin could tell. He had heard the young queen liked to paint.

"Is that…?" he began.

"Your gift, yes. Can you tell what it is?" Her blue eyes twinkled with amusement. "I think you should hang it up here, Ethin. Somewhere inside the forge. There are living quarters at the back, I have heard. You should find a place for it in there."

Ethin frowned. "My lady. I daresay it would go ignored up here. No one comes here now, Thalina. I have not visited in many years."

"You can leave it for your descendants to enjoy, then. I'm quite sure this forge will be restored to use one day, Ethin. It might take many generations, centuries, even…but *someone* will enjoy it eventually."

She is a strange one, Ethin thought, smiling awkwardly. He'd heard the same of Thala, though he had not known the Far-Seeing Queen himself. Always with the riddles and the mysteries, the things she'd seen in Rasalan's Eye. Ethin had to wonder if Thalina had seen something as well. Did she have that same power? Was Rasalan showing her visions too?

The queen waved her men toward the forge. "Inside," she said. "Ethin, shall we?" She strode away in her sky-blue cloak sewn with many small golden discs. Ethin followed, stepping quickly after the younger monarch as she went right through the open mouth and into the forgotten forge.

It was much as the king remembered it, much as his father Varyth had kept it when he would come here himself during his reign. And that was often. Ethin's father had not been burdened by ambition as his son was. Perhaps that was merely a matter of proximity. Seeing Ilith in his work had likely humbled King Varyth to the point where he knew he would never match him, and did not develop the instinct to even try. Ethin, once removed, grew up with a different drive. *And that is my curse,* he thought. To reach so far and fall so short was the ruin of all ambitious men.

The forge was covered in a film of dust that coated every surface. The anvil, the ovens, the bellows and the benches were all grimy and the tools and instruments had not been moved since the last time King Varyth set them down. The queen looked around, smiling serenely. "Where is the Hammer of Tukor, my lord? Is it not here?"

"No. I keep that in my own forge near the palace, Thalina." Ethin used it often when making weapons and armour for the Bladeborn who came to his lands. That was another success of his, he would admit; during his reign, he had lured many disaffected Bladeborn over from Vandar to settle in his kingdom, in the hope their children and grand-children would grow up Tukoran. Besides the lands and titles he granted them, he would often present them with suits of godsteel armour and swords as well, all of his personal forging. Ethin was very eager to make sure that Tukor was not always reliant on Vandar for protection. Especially now that hostilities with Agarath had been renewed by King Amron. *That warmonger will drag us all into his crusades eventually*, Ethin though. He really did not like the one they were calling Amron the Bold. *The fool thinks himself Varin, but he is not. He's just another echo like us…*

"I will see it later, then," Thalina said. "If you're willing to show me?"

"I'm sorry, my lady?" His thoughts had run off with him, as they were prone to do.

"The Hammer of Tukor. I would like to see it."

"Yes, of course. Though it really isn't much to look at."

The same could be said of this forge. There was little that was grand or visually arresting about it to those uninterested in such things. More the memory of what happened here. Therein lay its wonder. Thalina looked around a moment, poking about the stacks of scrolls and books, the armour that sometimes sat up against the walls or hung from pegs and nails. Once she'd satisfied her curiosity, she looked over at him. "Will you show me to the living quarters, Ethin?"

He nodded. "Very well."

The door at the back led into the mountain, where Ilith had built out his personal apartments and storerooms. "I've heard it said your grandfa-ther would often stay weeks up here," Thalina said, as Ethin showed her around. It was all quite plain as well, really; Ilith was always the most humble of the demigods, in his manner of living at least. In his achieve-ments he was profoundly more successful than the rest of them, Ethin believed. Though admittedly, he was rather biased.

"Yes," he answered. "My grandsire had the habit of letting his projects consume him, my lady." He showed her the kitchens, a store-room filled with armour, another with weapons, another with old wine jugs and other liquid refreshments, a snug library and a small and simple bedroom with hardly more than a little bed and desk inside it.

She paused here, looking around. Then she nodded. "Yes. Here, I think."

Ethin was not understanding this woman. If it was his gift, surely he could put it where he pleased.

"There, on the wall above the desk," she said. Her men came in, carefully manoeuvring the wrapped painting through the door. "Unwrap it and hang it. The king will show me the presentation chamber while you do so."

Will I? This young queen was becoming increasingly impertinent. *She could be my daughter, my granddaughter almost. Whatever happened to respecting your elders?*

He led her on anyway, not wanting to make a fuss of it, taking her along the corridor to the very rear where Ilith was said to have arrayed the five Blades of Vandar for Varin when he first came here to see them. That was hundreds of years ago now, yet the weight of the event still lingered in the room like an old smell that wouldn't drift away. Ethin had loved that scent as a boy, but it soured to him as he got older and more bitter, as he came to see how far beyond him Ilith was, how insignificant they all were compared to their godly grandparents who had built and shaped and changed the world.

"Here we are," he said, emptily. He waved a hand at the presentation table.

Thalina moved over, touching the stone, turning her eyes across the chamber. It was roughly circular and devoid of any furnishing but for the plain stone table at its heart. "This is where your grandfather presented the blades?"

Ethin nodded. "Right here, yes." He looked around the room. "He had this chamber made for that purpose alone. It has been empty ever since."

"Ilith understood the importance of that day," said the queen. "And so it proved, and will continue to do so. Those blades have a large part to play in the future, I think."

Think or know? Ethin looked at her and wondered. But that was it; he did not ask, because if she knew anything she wasn't going to say so. *Echoes*, Ethin thought. *Thala was the same with Ilith.* He knew of some book Thala had written, a diary of sorts, filled with visions she'd seen in the Eye. It was said to be passed down her line, only taken up by the new king or queen at the death of their predecessor. Perhaps that's all this was, then. Perhaps Thala had seen many things and written them into this book, and thus was Thalina now endowed with such knowledge. He nodded at that. It made more sense, and in truth it made him feel better. *She is a pale reflection, like me.* He did not like the idea that she might be closer in her gifts to Thala than he was to Ilith. No, no, he didn't like that at all.

"Well then," the queen said, smiling at him. "I think they'll be ready with the painting."

He led her back through to the bedchamber. Thalina's servants were just coming out with the string and the linen wrappings. Ethin let the queen enter the room first and took a moment to cast away his brewing bitterness. *Be grateful,* he thought. *Tell her how wonderful it is, whether you think it's true or not.* He drew a smile onto his face in preparation, then followed her inside.

The painting was astonishing.

Not, perhaps, in the manner he was used to. It was not a work of singular aesthetic appeal, and the detail and devotion to realism that Ethin favoured in art was not there. No, it was astonishing in how *chaotic* it was, in the sheer abundance of scenes and characters that twisted and bustled across the canvas. He stood back a moment, trying to puzzle out its meaning, if there was one. There must have been twenty or even thirty separate events being depicted at once, all pressing up against one another and spilling over the edges.

He saw an eagle bearing in its talons a bag with a shining light within it, a face that was both frightening and beautiful at once, a line of misting men standing before a black storm. There was a cloaked man who bore a hammer laughing in utterable joy as the shadows scowled around him, a youth with black hair enshrouded all in darkness with a bat painted inside his skull, a pair of enormous winged creatures tumbling and twisting down from a great height amid shadow and a rain of steaming blood. In some cases the details were remarkable; in others everything was bizarre and abstract, and Ethin could hardly tell what they were. In the centre of the painting stood an old man with a young one, both smiling, looking very much alike as though grandson and grandfather. There was something very familiar about them both, and the figures seemed to be staring straight out of the painting at him as all else whirled around them.

He was not quite certain how long he'd been staring at it when he finally broke from the spell and looked at Queen Thalina. "My lady, it is…quite wonderful," he said.

"I'm glad you like it, my lord."

"I do. Very much." He took the back of her hand and kissed it. "Thank you, Thalina. It is a fine gift, truly. It must have taken many long hours to paint."

"I painted it in my sleep," the woman told him.

That took him aback. "You…I'm sorry, my lady? You…?"

"Strange, I know. But true. I painted it in my sleep, Ethin. It is a depiction of my dreams, stories my grandmother told me. She was there, I recall. Thala told me many tales in the dream, and I do suppose that's what you see before you. When I awoke, the painting was complete. And I had only the faintest memory of a lingering instruction in my head."

"And what is that, my lady?"

"That the painting was for *you,* Ethin. That this was where it must be…here in this very room."

This room, Ethin thought. *This plain little room that my grandfather used to sleep in.* His mood began to sour again at that thought. *We are but echoes,*

echoes and imitations. Even after the departure of the demigods, they were still poking around and trying to interfere. *Their time is done. Done,* he thought. He wondered if he might put this painting aside once Thalina left, even cast it down the mountainside, but he was not so petty as that. Perhaps there was some importance here to be unveiled at a later time. He would not let it be said that *he* interfered with such things.

So he simply said, "I will keep it here always, Thalina. Perhaps one day it will inspire someone."

"It will," she told him. "One day, it will." She looked at the figures at the heart of the painting, the old man and the young one who seemed to be staring back. They really did look very alike, almost like they were the same person. "Them, I think," Thalina said. "I think it will be them."

1

Elyon

3110 Years Later…

He found the ship long leagues from its companions, drawn off on a northwesterly wind.

About it the seas were white-capped and rough, the gusts fierce, the skies a swamp of grey-black gloom from one horizon to the next. Before too long dusk would set in and thin the light yet further. Elyon Daecar wanted to be back before then. He had a fearsome need to rest.

Men spotted his approach, calling out words he could not hear, many stopping in their work to look up. *Wild Raven* had suffered from the stormy weather, several of its sails torn down and shredded, its mainmast cracked and broken. Carpenters and sailmakers were milling about the decks making repairs, others scrambling up the rigging or manning the gunwale scorpions, searching the seas through narrow, frightened eyes. After the kraken attack, Elyon could not blame them. *Just don't fire at me,* he thought. He'd been mistaken for a dragon often enough before and these men were clearly on edge.

He flew a slow pass over them, circling, showing them he meant no harm, and then softened the flow of wind around him and came down to land upon the quarterdeck. The captain of the vessel was a man by name of Duke Murdock, a one-eyed seaman of fifty winters with a scraggle of brown beard on his long thin chin and a wonky spear of a nose who plied his trade out of Blackhearth. A decent captain though he was, he was Tukoran, not Rasalanian, and bore no Seaborn blood. Most of his crew were the same. The best of the Seaborn sailors were aboard the prince's flagship *Hammer*, Elyon knew.

"Your name is Murdock," he said, stepping toward the captain at the helm. He thrust the Windblade back into its sheath and looked into the man's working eye. The other was no more than a gaping hole. The sight was not a pretty one, and this was not a pretty man.

"That'd be me," Duke Murdock confirmed, gruffly. He gave Elyon a scan up and down. "And you'd be Elyon Daecar, unless I got my princes mixed up." He sniffed through his sideways nose, the sort that had been broken badly once too many times and never healed straight. "To what do we owe this pleasure, m'lord?"

"I bring word from the other prince. He wishes to reassemble his fleet and I offered to help." Elyon looked around. "I'm told Sir Colyn Rowley commands the men?"

"The soldiers, aye. The crew are mine. You want to talk with him?" When Elyon nodded, Murdock barked for a boy to fetch Sir Colyn and the lad scampered off through the press of men, wriggling down the stairs and across the main deck, hailing the Emerald Guard with a high-pitched squeak of a voice.

A few moments later the knight was marching up the stairs to join them wearing a loose-fitting jerkin and an Emerald Guard cloak that looked a size or two too big for his slender shoulders. His face was gaunt, forehead blistered, hair bleached blond by the harsh southern sun. Yet his smile was bright and his eyes yet brighter. "Sir Elyon," he exclaimed, upon seeing him. "Gods be good, you're a sight for sore eyes." He took Elyon's forearm in his leather-glove grip, shaking firmly. "Good to have you with us."

"I won't be staying long, Sir Colyn. I only came to report on the prince." Elyon knew the man but barely, having met him during the siege of Harrowmoor half a lifetime ago, or so it felt. Sir Colyn had been in the service of Prince Rylian back then and had looked rather different as well, thicker of face and darker of hair and not near so slim as he was now. His days at sea had made a wreck of him.

The knight did not appear to be aware of his prince's fate. "So *Hammer*...she was not taken down, Sir Elyon? The last we saw of her, that kraken was coming up from the sea...and we had thought... feared..."

"*Hammer* is safe," Elyon assured him, and the other men listening. There were at least two dozen of them gathering around now, ragged bearded men who all looked as fleshless and wild as Rowley did. Small wonder. Elyon had heard about their trials at sea, how *Wild Raven* had been becalmed out in some windless void for a full dozen days and nights with barely any rations to go around. It had driven some men to madness and inflicted illness upon a great many more. "And Prince Robbert as well," he went on. "I arrived in time to help drive the kraken away, though there is a small chance it may return. If it does, your prince and I agree that you'll all be safer together."

"Safe? There's no ship safe from that thing," blurted a man. Elyon could not say who said it, such was the crowd about him now. "It'll kill us all."

"Was Lorin's Bane, I heard," called out another. "That one what dragged the king right down to Daarl's Domain. If the king couldn't kill it, how can we?"

"We?" snorted a third. "What you gonna do to it, Morkin, moan it to death?" A gale of laughter blew across the deck.

The man Morkin did not care for it. "More'n you will, Tallard," he came back. "I saw you before, soiling your breeches when that kraken crawled out o' the water. Might want to change 'em." He wrinkled his nose. "Can still smell the stink from here."

More laughter. Sir Colyn cut them off. "Silence now. Be quiet." He waved them down from their bickering. "Damn you all, let Prince Elyon talk."

Elyon waited for quiet before continuing, talking loudly so all could hear. "If the kraken does return I will do what I can to drive it off, but right now you're too far away. I cannot watch over both you and *Hammer*, and as you will know I must prioritise the flagship. You must make your own way back to her." He looked down the ship and addressed Duke Murdock. "I see you're having trouble with your mainmast, Captain?"

The man grunted bitterly. "Spot of bother, aye. Second snapped mast in as many weeks." He snorted and spat to the side.

"Can it be repaired?"

"We hope," Murdock muttered. "Might take another hour or two, but we'll see it taped up. Just have to hope it stands fast if these winds pick up again." He checked the skies, scowling. "Seems to be easing off to me, but you never know these days. How far is *Hammer* from here, m'lord?"

"About twenty miles, I would say. Set a westerly course and with luck you'll intercept her come dawn. If I don't see you by first light, I'll fly back over to find you."

"And if the Bane comes back by then?"

Elyon answered the question with one of his own. "Do you have beacon fires you can light? Torches atop the crow's nest?"

"Once we've got the mast back up, aye."

"Then light them if you're in trouble, and perhaps someone will see. If so, I will fly to your aid. But otherwise you're on your own."

He neglected to tell them that his aid would be limited without the storm. That the lightning was responsible for driving the Bane away and without it Elyon would be relying on the edge of his blade alone. Against a squid of such scale a simple sword would have its limits, and in truth he would be wiser to avoid such a foe. *One good hit from one of those swinging tentacles and I might drop the blade*, he thought. If the Windblade was lost to the depths to drown, their hopes would drown along with it.

The men were not liking the thought that the kraken could return. There were a deal of worried voices about him now, all muttering and murmuring their concerns. One man was so struck by alarm at the thought that he stepped in and grabbed Elyon by the arm, eyes widening as he stared up at him. "Tow us," he said, in a begging voice. "Please, milord. We can tie ropes to the forecastle and you can tow us back to *Hammer*. If we don't get the mast up, we'll never make it. Tow us, milord. *Please*. You must."

Others seemed to like the notion. Shouts of 'tow us' fogged in the frigid air.

Elyon would not hear of it. "I can't," he said, firmly, shaking the man off. "I don't have the strength to pull a vessel this size." He hadn't tried, in truth, but wasn't going to submit to the attempt. He was, quite simply, far too exhausted. *And I am only borrowing this blade,* he told himself. He needed to get it back to Saska as soon as he could. It was critical that she bond to it quickly, and frankly the fate of *Wild Raven* was of little importance when considered as part of the broader picture, cruel as that might be to say.

"Mayhaps lead *Hammer* to us, then?" cried another man, over the clamour. "If she's strong and seaworthy, then…"

Elyon was not going to listen to this any more. "I've said what I came to say. Now step back and give me room." He moved the nearest men aside with a sweep of the arm, forming a space about him. "West, Captain Murdock," he called to the one-eyed seaman. "And make haste. I hope to see you again come the dawn."

Murdock nodded. Elyon gave Sir Colyn Rowley a parting look and then drew the Windblade from its sheath, firing a propulsive blast of air from its edge to drive any remaining men back from him. Once he had space enough to take flight, he shot forth into the turbid skies without delay and swung west, flying beneath the wet grey clouds in an eager bid to return to *Hammer's* decks before the dark became too dense.

In no time at all *Wild Raven* was a distant spec on the water behind him and *Hammer* was appearing ahead, a blurred brown smudge on the horizon. Just beyond it, another smaller blot revealed itself; *Blood Bear*, the third and smallest of Prince Robbert's vessels. They had lost sight of *Hammer* briefly too during the attack, though managed to find their way back shortly after the kraken had fled.

Elyon made for them quickly, weary beyond all reckoning. It had been a long two days since he'd received that cryptic message far to the north at the Tower of Rasalan…a message delivered not by crow or rider but by an Aramatian eagle no less. The king's horsemaster Rodney had taken the scroll from the eagle's leg when it landed on his arm, and handed it to King Sevrin. "For you, m'lord," he'd said. But when Sevrin broke the seal and opened the note he had only said, "It's not for me," and handed it to Elyon instead.

The words written within had brought him here. Words of a man who called himself the *First Elder*, an ancient Lightborn living in the mysterious Everwood of Aramatia. He had written that Saska was setting sail from Eagle's Perch in a small fleet and that she would face terrible danger along the way. He had not said exactly what, or exactly where the fleet would be found. Only that Elyon must find her, and with all haste. And so he'd put all thoughts of flying to Rustbridge aside, and King's Point, and the Twinfort and Varinar too. He had a need to visit them all, to seek out his father again, and Lythian, and his sister Lillia, and Borrus Kanabar and his bastard brother Jonik, but this new mission was of a higher priority. So tucking the scroll into his cloak, he'd bid the Rasal king farewell and taken flight at once to the south.

It took him all day to fly across the kingdom, and by the time he reached the southern shores the pall of dark was descending. Much as he had wanted to fly all through the night, he had instead stopped for a few short hours on the island of Bhoun, sitting alone on a high crag atop a windswept strand, his eyes trained out to sea. Sleep had not come to him. It *would* not come. He had only sat and waited for the herald of dawn, watching the eastern horizon until the first faint line of light appeared. Then he stood and stretched and soared again, crossing beyond the beach and out over the open sea, searching through the storm-racked skies for her, for Saska, the girl in silver and blue.

It had not been easy and it had not been quick. Visibility was poor, the gales were fierce, and the rain had spat relentlessly into his face. A dozen times he'd spotted ships beneath him, but when he plunged down for a closer look they were never the right one. Some were traders, others whalers, he'd seen some hardy fishermen here and there and a warship sometimes too, from Aramatia and Agarath and further afield still. For hours he'd searched, flying back and forth, calling upon his reserves of strength. Twice or thrice he sensed dragons, moving just beyond his sight, shadows in the fog. It made him think of the first time he'd slain a dragon. Ezukar, with the long snout and lashing tail, who had hunted him in that storm. *Then the Windblade saved me*, he'd thought. By instinct he had raised it high and the lightning had done the rest.

It was strange how things went. Because even as Elyon had that thought, so he sighted in the distance the ships. There, out there in the storm, he saw the shadow of whales beneath the waves and the rising black arms of the kraken. One vessel was a wreck, sinking, two others drifting away. Yet the biggest of them was in the grip of the beast. The bulbous body. The long glistening limbs, each armed with ten thousand jaw-like suckers. A monster it was, colossal. And Saska, he knew, was aboard.

So he had flown over there, and it had happened again. He'd raised the Windblade up to the skies and the lightning had done the rest.

After, once the great kraken had slithered away, he'd presented Saska with the blade of her fathers. *She* was the heir of Varin, he had discovered in another letter, a letter given to Sevrin's sister Cristin by her uncle Godrin when she was a child. In it Godrin had written a story, a story he told Elyon through time. Of King Lorin's love and romance with Atia, Godrin's sister. Of the child they sired named Thalavar, who was raised in secret on the Lonely Isle. Of Thalavar's escape and capture at the hands of slavers, who brought him to Aram to be sold at market when he was nought but a boy of sixteen. Of Safina Nemati, the Grand Duchess, who was instructed by Godrin to find him and take him into her service, to watch over him, so that Thalavar could live and work in the palace and fall in love with Safina's daughter, the princess Leila Nemati...and sire a child of his own...

Her, he thought. Saska was that child. *Gods, it was always her…*

For months he'd wondered who this heir of Varin was; he had discussed it with his father and Lythian and Rikkard and many others. If Lorin had sired a secret son, they imagined, he'd have been kept in secret and trained with sword and spear so that one day he might reveal himself, stepping from the shadows to bear the Heart Remade. What a stirring story that would have been, and yet nothing was ever so simple. In the end, Thalavar, named for Thala and for Varin, was never the prophesied heir.

It was her, Elyon thought again. *Her. It was always her.*

The flagship was right beneath him now, men milling about the decks. He scanned in search of Saska but could not see her. Most likely she'd gone below. It had been only hours since he'd presented the Windblade to her and since then they'd had little chance to talk. As soon as the kraken had been driven away all efforts went toward helping the men in the water. There were some hundreds out there, Elyon had seen. From the ship *Blackthorn* mostly, sinking to the depths, but scores had been sent tumbling from the decks of *Hammer* as well by Lorin's Bane's lashing arms.

Robbert Lukar had rushed right up to him. "Will you help us, Elyon?" he'd asked, desperate. "My men…" His eyes flashed over the water. "They'll drown before the rowboats get to them."

Elyon nodded at once and reached to his hip, only to find that the Windblade was no longer there. Just an empty sheath. "I…I'm not sure what…"

"Take it back," Saska had said. She was there as well, listening. Straining, she lifted the Windblade and hauled it across the deck. "Please…take it back, Elyon. I can't use it yet, I don't know how."

"My lady…that isn't…it's not mine any…"

"Take it," she urged. "I don't want to deprive you. We can share it. You *have* to help them."

Robbert was staring at him through his one good eye. The other was patched, for reasons Elyon didn't know at the time. "Elyon, *please*. You don't have to give it all up at once. Help them. I'm asking you, as a prince."

Elyon nodded. He was right. "I'll…do what I can," he'd said, taking the Windblade back from Saska only moments after giving it away. "I need a net," he told them, calling out. "Give me a net for them to cling to." It was done. Flying too close to the waves was too risky, he knew, so he'd merely hovered above the drowning men instead and let them pull themselves up. Many times he flew back and forth, hauling as many as five or six of them from the water each time and depositing them onto the decks, shivering and spluttering. Only once the rowboats were out fetching the last of them did Elyon take a short rest, during which he met some of the men, Robbert's and Saska's, and heard a little of what they'd all been through. But it was in snippets only, and by then both *Blood Bear* and *Wild Raven* had long since drifted out of sight, so Robbert came to him with another request. To fly out and find them, bring his broken fleet back together. Elyon had nodded wearily. And so the hunt began again.

But his work was done for now. Below him, the men of *Hammer* raised their voices in salute at his return. A chant of 'Elyon Daecar' went out, a chant to cheer his heart as he came down to land on the deck. He wanted so very badly to collapse right there and then, but thought the better of it. Instead he dropped to a gallant dismount, then stood, sliding the Windblade into its sheath. Prince Robbert Lukar was there at once. "So? Did you find them?" He looked south. "We see *Blood Bear* out there, but not *Wild Raven* as yet."

Elyon took a moment to catch his breath. He was so weary he felt like he might faint. "They're fine, Robbert. *Wild Raven* has a broken main-mast and some sails that need stitching, but repairs are coming along well. I told them to head west. Gods willing, we should see them by first light."

Robbert gripped his arm. "My thanks, Elyon. I appreciate it. Truly." He turned his head and called for Sir Lothar Tunney, who strode over to join them. The man was exceedingly tall and slim, a green cloak tumbling from his wide square shoulders like a banner from the wall of a fort. It took him about five strides to cross from one side of the ship to the other. "Tell Droyn I want him in the crow's nest," Robbert said. "*Wild Raven* is heading our way, and I want to know as soon as she's spotted."

Sir Lothar bobbed his head. "I'll tell him, Robb. You want him up there right now? He's sleeping, I think."

"Give him another hour, then wake him." Robbert returned his attention to Elyon. "I'd like to talk to you about what's happening in Vandar when you have a chance. We've heard reports of savage fighting in the Marshlands, and my brother....I'm told he is there, leading an army. Is there any truth to that?"

Elyon nodded. "Raynald was at Rustbridge the last I saw of him. He commands thirty thousand swords."

Robbert seemed greatly enthused by that. "*Thirty thousand?*" He retreated for a private thought, rubbing at his chin, then said, "How long ago were you there?"

"Some weeks. They may well have come to battle by now. There was a great Agarathi horde in camp nearby. And forces from the empire as well. I..." He shook his head, closing his eyes, opening them. A deep pang of fatigue thickened in his blood. "Robbert, do you mind if we pick this up tomorrow? I've been flying almost non-stop for two days, and..."

"You must sleep. Of course. I am in remiss, Elyon. We'll talk when you're better rested."

And how long will that take? Elyon felt like he could sleep for a week. "My thanks." He looked around. "Is there somewhere quiet I could go?"

"Quiet? Here at sea? I doubt it." Robbert smiled handsomely. He had diverged somewhat in looks from his twin brother, owing largely to that patched eye. The hair had also grown longer, and more curly, and he had begun to grow out a short brown beard, tinged red like his father's. "I can't promise quiet, Elyon, but *private* I can do. Give me a few minutes and I'll find a cabin for you. Lady Saska currently occupies my own, but…" Something awkward festered in his eyes. "Well, I'll find somewhere else for you. We're rather cramped aboard, as you can see, but I'll see that you have a room."

"Anywhere will do," Elyon told him. "Just a bunk would serve."

Robbert Lukar would not have it. "Nonsense. You're a prince and will be given quarters appropriate for your station. Or the best we have, anyway. Lank, with me. Let's go and turf out some miscreants, what do you say?"

"Plenty of those aboard to choose from." The stupidly tall knight grinned and together the pair strode away.

Elyon let out a long breath, then drank in a full gulp of cold salty air. There was a great deal of activity around him and the damage to *Hammer* was significant, if mostly superficial. On either side of the vessel, the huge muscular arms of Lorin's Bane had shattered the gunwale walls, sweeping clear the harpoon guns and tearing down several sails. Though the mainmast and foremast were still standing stable and erect, the mizzenmast had been ripped free of the quarterdeck and thrown out to sea. Men moved past him bearing hammers and pots of nails, lengths of sailcloth and buckets of tar. The repair work had been going on for long hours and would continue all through the night, he knew. *Let's hope Robbert finds me a cabin away from all this hammering.*

Elyon saw a young midshipman passing by and hailed him over. "You there."

It was a boy, redheaded and chunky of build. He smiled and strode over jauntily. "What can I do for you, Your Highness?" the lad chirped.

"I'm a little lost," Elyon said.

"Lost? On the deck of a ship?" The boy found that terribly amusing. "Where are you trying to get to?"

"Prince Robbert's cabin. I am told Lady Saska is there."

"Oh, you mean the heir." The boy nodded to himself, very proudly. "I thought there was something more about her. She's got good sea legs, I told her only earlier today. Knew she had some Seaborn blood. And strong stuff too. Now we find out it's from Princess Atia. She was King Godrin's youngest sister, you know, and daughter to King Astan. I'm told I'm distantly related to them." He smiled a freckly smile.

"What's your name, boy?" Elyon asked.

"Finn Rivers."

"Well, Finn, you're clearly a perceptive lad. Perceptive enough to see that I'm cataclysmically tired and not in much of a mood for a history lesson. So, Lady Saska. Take me to her, please."

The boy took no offence to that. "As you say, my lord. She's right down here. Follow me." He led him across the main deck, all but whistling a tune.

The royal cabin was to be found beneath the quarterdeck and down a long damp corridor with smaller cabins to either side. The door at the end was ajar, voices coming from within. Outside stood two of Saska's men, sellswords from the Bloody Traders. Elyon did not know their names yet and didn't care to learn them right now. That would come later. "Thank you, Finn." He patted the boy on the shoulder and stepped inside.

There was a conference going on at the heart of the cabin, several of Saska's captains gathered around her. On the far wall, a large breach had been crudely patched over with lengths of planking and strips of sail-cloth, the wind billowing and rustling outside. Elyon had been told that Lorin's Bane had smashed a tentacled arm right through the window, swatting aside some of Saska's men as they hacked and heaved at the meat, though by some miracle none of them had been killed and were nursing only minor injuries. The stink of kraken-blood was thick in the air. It had a horrid acrid reek to it and came out all black and oily. There were patches of it on the floor and soaked into the planks. Evidently, an effort had been made to clean it up, but there was only so much they could do.

Saska was the first to see him. Her eyes lit up when she did. "Elyon… you're back."

He nodded and looked around. "I hope I'm not interrupting."

"Not at all. No." Saska vacated the circle at once and stepped over to him, smiling. Gods, it was a beautiful sight. "How did it go out there?"

"Well." Elyon repeated what he'd told Prince Robbert, then said, "He is just finding somewhere for me to rest. I wanted to give you this first." He unbuckled his swordbelt and handed her the Windblade and accompanying scabbard. "You should sleep with it beside you. It will help you build the bond."

She looked at it, drew a breath, and then nodded. "Thank you. I will." She still had her doubts, Elyon could see that clearly enough, but those were natural. *When she learns to fly she'll soar beyond them.* There was no better sensation in the world. *She will feel like a goddess up there…and will need to become one if we're to stand a chance.* "Do you mind…putting it there." She gestured to the wall near the door, and Elyon stepped over to prop it up. "We're discussing where to go next," Saska told him, when he turned back around. She glanced over her shoulder. "Sir Ralston thinks you should just fly me to the mountain refuge. To Ilith. He thinks I'll be safer there."

"You will," Elyon agreed. He linked eyes with the Wall, a steel behemoth of a man, and nodded in accord. "It would be the wise course, Saska. I have the harness. I could fly you there tomorrow."

She looked uncomfortable with the thought and gave a stubborn shake of the head. "I don't want to leave my men. I can't just hide while all the work is done for me."

"What work?" Elyon asked her. He wasn't sure what she meant by that.

"The other blades," she explained. "Gathering them. That's my task. No one else's."

The Wall shook his boulder of a head from side to side, bald and burned and scarred. He wore his armour from heel to neck, his greathelm clutched in the crook of his arm, a dour bland cloak hanging from his back, torn and frayed and stained with the blood of men and monsters both. "Your task is to wield the Heart Remade," he said to Saska. "Gathering the shards is not your burden."

"It is," she insisted. "I have to learn to bear them. All of them. Not just the Windblade."

"The boy can bring them to you," said one of the sellswords. He was big and horrifically scarred, a Bloody Trader captain Elyon had overheard as being called the Butcher. "This windy prince who killed the kraken. He can fly and fetch them for you."

"He's not some messenger boy," the girl Leshie snapped at him. "He's a *prince*, and do you even know what *windy* means?" She looked at Elyon, admiring. "I don't think he's the 'windy' sort."

"That would depend upon what I eat," Elyon said, raising a smile.

Leshie smiled back at him, staring a moment, then blinked. "And anyway…that kraken's not dead, dummy," she said to the Butcher. "It just slithered off is all."

The sellsword shrugged. "Dead or not it makes no matter. The squid is afraid and will not come back. Of this windy prince, yes, and of *me*. It knows I will cut it again if it returns. Again and again. I am the greatest sellsword in all the world and I will kill it." He thumped his chest, tattered cloak rippling.

Leshie scowled at him. "No one wants to listen to your empty boasts, Parapet. We'd all be dead if it wasn't for Prince Elyon. Even Coldheart. None of us could have killed that thing."

"The red girl speaks true," said the man with the white teeth and golden spectacles. He was missing an ear and had hands the size of hams. Thick brown hair twisted off his muscular forearms. *The Baker, this one*, Elyon recalled. He was brother to the other he'd heard, though he hardly believed it. They looked nothing alike. "The prince did save us all, this we know. Now we are discussing what more he can do for us." He pushed the spectacles up his nose and smiled. "We hear that your father holds one of the blades, is this so? The cold one, that shoots ice from its tip. Is this still the case or has someone taken it from him?"

"He bore the Frostblade the last I saw of him," Elyon confirmed.

"The last. Ah, the way you speak…it has been a while since this time, no?"

"Weeks."

"Weeks? Oh, weeks is not so long. And he is Amron Daecar, the greatest swordsman for a hundred years. There is no man who will take that blade from the Crippler of Kings."

Elyon liked this man, he realised. "I agree," he said.

"And he wields it well, we can surmise?" That question came from the plain-looking man with the empty eyes and neat brown hair. On his chest was a cross-belt full of knives and scalpels. *Surgical instruments,* Elyon thought. He could guess who this man might be. "Your father has taken well to the Frostblade, true?"

"What do you think?" Elyon had little interest in dawdling to some conclusion. He would lay it out for them quick and clear. "My father has mastered the Frostblade and has been using it to great effect. He killed the dragon Zyndrar the Unnatural with it and together we battled the Dread." He felt a pang of grief as he thought of Vesryn and his valiant death. "But it was not enough. Not nearly enough. My father has known for long months that the blades must be combined. He will be willing to give the Frostblade up when he must."

"That time is now," the Butcher declared. "Tomorrow. You can fly to him tomorrow and then return the next day with this Frostblade."

"No," Elyon said, coming close to losing his patience. This Butcher was especially insolent. "I would never be able to carry it so far. Not without bonding it first."

The Surgeon slid a finger along one of his thin sharp blades. "Perhaps it would be wise for you to fly Lady Saska to your father's safe-keeping instead, using this harness of yours. She could train with both blades, then, and benefit from the tutelage of Amron Daecar. Who could be better?"

No one, Elyon knew. He was certain the King's Wall had done what he could to prepare her, but fearsome as he was he did not know what it was to bond and train with a Blade of Vandar. The suggestion was not the worst one. And selfishly, Elyon would much sooner return to his father's side than remain here aboard this ship.

But the Whaleheart shook his head again. "Amron Daecar may well be in battle. There is no sense in taking such a risk at this point. No. She must go north. To this refuge."

"I'm not going to the refuge," Saska said, in a tired voice.

The Wall looked at her sternly. "You are not thinking straight. Or at all. Why do you resist so much?"

"I've told you why. I can't leave you all."

"You can. We will follow and join you later."

"I'm not leaving," Saska repeated. "Stop asking me to go. I'm not going anywhere, all right? Now can we drop the subject, *please?*"

"No. Not until you present a good enough reason."

"I've said…I've said a hundred times…"

"This is about the cat," the giant rumbled. He paused and stared down at her, impassive. "I told you it was a mistake to bring her. I warned you it was folly, and yet…"

"You know nothing about it," Saska snapped at him. "It's not only about Joy. It's about everything. Del, Leshie, even *you,* Rolly." She looked around. "All of you. You've been with me for far too long for me to abandon you now."

"You would not be abandoning…"

"I never told you about Alym, did I?" she went right on. "Ranulf told me he died in a sinkhole. Him and all the rest of his men. After everything they did for me they went to sleep one night and that was that. They woke to the world crumbling down around them, and then nothing. They were all dead. For me. I won't let that happen again."

A short silence followed. Elyon did not know who this man Alym was, but it seemed he was well-liked. "That is a great shame," the Baker said, sombre. "Sunrider Tantario was a good man."

"A good man," Saska agreed. "Who never complained once to me, not once, even when I refused to help his people. He heard their pleas a hundred times and waved them off because of me. And my duty. And after all that he only died anyway."

"That wasn't your fault," the King's Wall told her. "You cannot let his death cloud your judgement."

"And if it happens again? To you this time?" She looked around. "To *all* of you?"

Leshie's youthful face was twisted in a frown. She gave her bottom lip and chew and said, "I don't understand. What do you think's going to happen?"

"The same thing," Saska said, letting out a sharp breath. "If I fly away the ship will sink. Or Lorin's Bane will come back, or a dragon or something else. You'll all die. All of you. Robbert and Lothar and Lord Gullimer as well, everyone on this ship will die. I know it." She shook her head. "I just know it in my bones."

The giant took a short pace toward her and the planks creaked beneath his weight. "Saska. That isn't going to happen. But even if it does….everyone here…all of us are expendable."

"No, you're not. Not to me. You're not expendable to *me*, Rolly."

"Saska…"

"No. I've made my choice. It's made, Ralston. *Enough.*" She would hear nothing else on it. Turning her eyes to Elyon, she said, "So…tomorrow, then?" Her eyes flitted to the Windblade by the wall. "We'll get started tomorrow, when you're rested?"

"Tomorrow," he agreed. "But tonight…keep it with you, as I say. Hold the haft and try to get used to its weight. This isn't the Sword of Varinar. It's not as heavy as that, but it's more complex. The others are too. With the Sword of Varinar it's simple…once you can bear the weight and swing the blade, then it becomes more or less a regular sword. But these others…" He shook his head. It would take specialist training, he knew. He could help hasten her learning with the Windblade, but the others would require different tutors. *My father will help her*, he told himself. *He'll help her with the Frostblade when the time comes.* The Sword of Varinar would not be a problem, not with Lythian currently acting as its guardian. *But the others…*

The sound of footfall interrupted his thoughts. Elyon turned to the doorway and saw Prince Robbert Lukar enter. "Elyon. Finn said you were here." His eyes glanced briefly over the others. "Your cabin's ready when you are."

"Now," Elyon told him. "I'm ready now, Robbert." He said his good-byes and did so quickly, promising Saska he would see her tomorrow, and then left. Robbert led him only a few doors down the corridor.

"Here," the prince said. "Bernie had this one…him and another unwashed oaf so you'll have to excuse the smell." He smiled at his own jest and opened the door. The interior was plain, but private; a narrow bed to either side, small table fastened to the floor in one corner, trunks for clothes and armour. Elyon could not have hoped for anything more.

Robbert followed him in and shut the door. *So much for privacy,* Elyon thought. "Are we sharing this cabin, Robbert?"

"No. It's yours and yours alone. I just wanted to ask…about Saska."

Elyon removed his cloak and threw it on a bed. "Yes? What about her?"

"Well….this whole Varin's heir thing. How did you know about that? And find us? How did you find us all the way out here?"

Elyon reached to unfix his shoulder clasps and escape his stifling armour. *Gods, I'm almost too exhausted to undress.* "Help me with these and I'll tell you."

Robbert obliged, stepping forward. As he helped Elyon out of his armour, he spoke briefly of the last few days. The letter given to Princess Cristin when she was just a girl. The words of her uncle King Godrin, telling her that one day a handsome prince would come to visit her and when he did, she must give him the letter. He spoke of the contents of that latter, which told the story of Saska's birth and lineage, and the one he'd received at the Tower of Rasalan as well, written by an ancient Lightborn called the First Elder who told Elyon that Saska needed his help, that he must find her, train her, support her, and aid her in her quest. He even told Robbert briefly of the Eye of Rasalan, of its theft in Eldurath, and of Eldur, and Drulgar, and the short battle they'd fought at the coast.

The younger prince listened all the while, quiet as a windless sky, working to release Elyon from his armour as he spoke. Elyon found it cathartic, despite his fatigue, to unload it all on a fellow prince. He had always liked Robbert Lukar, as he'd liked his brother Raynald.

"Well, it seems you've had quite the time of it, Elyon," was Robbert's pithy summation when he was done. He deposited the last of Elyon's armour into the trunk by his bed. "And here was me thinking *I'd* been through the wars. Well…there's this…" He pointed at his patched eye. "And my uncle's treacheries with Sunlord Krator, but frankly not much else. Oh, the storms were bad, I suppose. The one that splintered my fleet in particular. We battled a manator as well that night. Bloodhound was a miracle in the way he outmanoeuvred and outwitted it. We'd all be dead if it wasn't for him. And now you as well. I owe rather a lot of life debts, Elyon."

"You don't owe me anything, Robbert."

"Oh? *I* ought to be the judge of that, wouldn't you say?"

"No, I mean…your father. I was partly to blame for what happened to him. Everything with the Windblade…being put in that cell. Your father was the one to release me and then your grandfather…"

Robbert waved it away. "No. Forget all that. You're not to blame at all."

Elyon was taken aback. It was hardly the reaction his twin brother had given. A light scolding though it had been, Raynald *had* scolded him. Robbert only seemed to want to dismiss it.

"Whatever happened, happened. There's no point dwelling on it and, frankly, it seems it's all been for a reason. If you hadn't taken the Windblade that night, then how would you be here now? Saving my life. And Saska's, more importantly." He frowned, looking down, thinking about all that. "Strange, isn't it? You're a prince now and I might even be a king, and yet *she's* the important one. This servant girl from North Tukor."

"She's more than that, Robbert. And always was. Even if she never knew it."

"I know." He nodded for a time. "I could see that from the moment I met her in Aram. The ancient dagger at her hip…the mixed heritage. It's been a puzzle I've been trying to put together for a while, and now here you come, flying in with the final piece." He smiled again, half in wonder. "Gods, the way she lifted that blade. I don't suppose even you raised the Windblade like that on your first try."

"No," Elyon admitted. He tried not to feel sour about it. "Well, she is of Varin's direct blood, so…"

"Do you think she'll learn to fly as quickly as you did? And the rest of it. That lightning…"

"Was more luck than anything."

He laughed. "I don't believe it. You're just being modest."

"Modest? Try *honest*."

"Well, in the spirit of that, I'm just going to say it." He paused, then all but blurted out, "We kissed. Saska and I. It was nothing really, more of a misunderstanding than anything, but…well, I thought you should know."

Elyon raised one eye, half in bemusement, though there it was, a stirring deep in his chest; a flinch of jealousy at the thought of it. "Why should that concern me?" The words came out a little harder than he'd anticipated.

Robbert saw right through him. "Because of Harrowmoor. I was there, Elyon. That was Saska in your tent, I know that. You two…you share something. It's obvious, I can see it. When she looks at you and you look at her, and the way you're reacting now." He ran a hand through his hair. "Well, it's different with me. I'll not lie to you…I liked her, still do, but…"

"But we don't need to talk about it," Elyon cut in. He did not quite know how they'd ended up here, in this small little ship cabin, talking about a girl. It was almost like it used to be, back in Varinar, when he and some fellow highborn prancer had designs on the same young lady at the banquets and balls. "None of us should be thinking about any of that right now, Robbert. What's the point? We might be dead in a day."

"Or an hour. Or less. That's the thing about krakens. They do tend to come out of nowhere, don't they?" The prince chuckled lightly, then stood, letting his cloak fall down his back. "I'll leave you to rest. I can see I've outstayed my welcome and maybe even touched a nerve, so…" He gave a grin. "We can talk more tomorrow, Elyon. There's still much I want to hear. Of the war, in particular." He opened the door. "Rest well, then. And thank you again. For everything." He nodded in gratitude and left Elyon alone.

And at last he could rest. Collapsing into the nearest bunk, Elyon Daecar pulled over a rough woollen cover, shut his eyes, and let the motion of the seas rock him off into a deep and dreamless sleep.

Ranulf

"She does not like this cold," Talasha Taan complained. "She hates it. And so do I."

Ranulf Shackton had never imagined a dragon could *shiver*, but that's just what Neyruu was doing, trembling as she sat there, furled in her wings, looking like the most miserable dragon to have ever drawn breath.

"Her fires will not burn properly here," the princess went on. She tugged her heavy cloak tighter. Every ranting word came out with a puff of mist. "If they go out she may die, Ranulf Shackton. Believe me, that is a fate you will share. I do not care who you think you are, if she dies up here then *you* will too. I will make sure of it, the fate of the world be damned. Do you understand me? She must eat to replenish her energy. Every forge must have its fuel."

Ranulf smiled to try to placate her, though she took it the wrong way.

"A smile? You would give me a grin at this time? Think yourself lucky I am half frozen, Ranulf, else I would slap that look right off your face."

The slap was not required. The smile slipped away without it.

"Better. Now tell me where we will find some food for her. You said there would be mountain goats up here, many of them, but we have seen no sign of horn nor hoof. Where are they all?"

"I could not say, my lady." They had been flying over the Three Peaks, the jutting range of mountains that speared off the greater Hammersongs in the west of Tukor, and Ranulf knew from experience that mountain goats were common up here. "I scaled the Three Peaks only a few years ago," he explained, by way of explanation and sincere apology. "They were thick as crows on a corpse back then. I suppose the cold must have driven them away."

"Then they are smarter than we are. This is folly. We will have to fly lower and look for livestock. Or deer. There must be deer down there in the woods." She peered through the icy winds to the valleys below. All was white beneath them, save the occasional ledge of cliff or hill, the glimpse of green in thickets and woods and sometimes a tower or keep, rising from the shroud in the midst of some half-buried town. "This place is a wilderness. If this is summer here, then I dread to think what winter is like."

Ranulf's blue lips twisted into a smile. "We'll fly lower, as you say. The winds will not be so sharp down there, and with good fortune we will find Neyruu some food. And maybe some cover to rest the night." To the west the changing light told of the swift coming of dusk, and they would do well to sleep before continuing on their journey. If it was this cold by day, Ranulf did not care to dwell on what frosted horrors the coming of night would bring.

"Where do you suggest?" Talasha asked, folding her arms. She had a particularly demanding way about her today. Fear had done that to her, Ranulf knew. Fear for Neyruu. She was not wrong about those furnace fires going out and the harm it could do to a dragon. "Are there any caves we might take shelter in? A large barn, perhaps? These are your lands, Ranulf. I do hope you know where you're going."

"Well...I am not Tukoran, my lady, but..."

"You are *northern*. And an adventurer who has travelled all over the world, including this region as you have said yourself. They are *your* lands. Now where will we stop to rest?"

He did not have an adequate answer for her. He knew of no caves, no great barns to fit a dragon. There might be some stone halls down there spacious enough for them all, but Ranulf had to doubt whether the resident lords of this land would be happy to accommodate them. Agarathi were rarely welcome guests around here. Dragons rather less so. "I do not know, Talasha. We'll have to find somewhere. An area of woodland, perhaps? It is summer, no matter how it looks, and the canopies will be thick. They should offer us some cover and concealment."

She clenched her jaw, then nodded. "Fine. But we *must* build a fire and hope Neyruu is able to light it. We shall do so once she's eaten. This is our first priority, Ranulf. Yes? Do you agree?"

"I agree, my lady."

"Good. Then let us go." She turned sharply and picked her way across the icy rocks toward the dragon, fur coat tugging in the wind. "Cevi," she shouted over the bluster. "Come out now. It's time to go."

The grey webbing of Neyruu's wing rippled and Cevi poked her head out from under it. She looked cold and miserable. "I was just starting to get warm," the girl complained pitifully.

"You are only stealing Neyruu's heat. Now out. It is unpleasant, I know, but we have no choice." When the handmaid hesitated, the princess strode forward and grabbed her with a leather-gloved hand, tugging her out into the cold. Neyruu stirred and rumbled, wing flopping back down to cover her side. "Don't get comfortable," Talasha said to the beast. "We are going to find you something to eat below. You'll feel much better after."

They took a moment to get mounted up and strapped in. The saddle itself had been custom-built in the Everwood, the skilled men and women of the Calacania carving and cutting it into shape during Talasha and Cevi's short time there. Before then, they had used a dual saddle, meant for two, but that would not serve. This one was designed to seat all three.

A strange three, to be sure, Ranulf reflected. Talasha, rich in Fireborn blood though she was, had never expected to be a dragonrider, and it was not often that a lady Fireborn chose to bring her handmaid along for the ride. That Ranulf Shackton was with them made the trio all the more unlikely.

He took his place at the back, his slim rump settling into the cushioned seat, the harness snug about his shoulders and chest. He gave the straps a tug to be certain they were properly fixed and called, "Ready," at Talasha's asking. In front of him, Cevi called the same, and without further ado Neyruu widened her wings and flew.

The wind hit him in the face at once, and his stomach gave its customary lurch as Neyruu reached the edge of the mountainside and plunged down in a steep descent. The flight had not been pleasant for Ranulf Shackton thus far, the early part in particular when they'd left the dusty lands of Aramatia behind and soared northward over the sea. Above the waters of the Three Bays the winds had been wild and fierce, buffeting Neyruu as she flew, and the motion did not agree with him. Several times he had retched, and not always were those retches dry. That was the benefit of being at the back, however. Talasha had been wise to put him there.

The sea crossing had been hard on Neyruu as well. The bigger dragons did not suffer so in stormy weather, but Neyruu was sleek and swift, lighter than many of her kin, and those winds had disrupted the elegance of her flight somewhat. So they had decided to land and rest a short while, descending to a long and lonely strand on the island of Krarl, a rather dour and barren rock that lay just off the south coast of Rasalan.

Ranulf knew it to be thinly inhabited, a stony place where crops did not grow but where crabs scuttled about in great abundance. A few lords had taken up residence over the centuries - all bearing crabs in their sigils, of course - raising their grim stone keeps a little inland from the shore. On the beach where they landed, Ranulf could see one such place in the distance, no more than a blur to his eyes. But not *Kamcho's*.

He'd given a whistle, and off the eagle went, screeching and soaring, to get a better view. Ranulf closed his eyes to look, shifting to the eagle's vision. A strange sensation still, it was, to see the world through Kamcho's eyes. Ranulf had Elder blood in him, he had learned during his long days in the Everwood. Some two centuries ago, his great-great-great-grandmother had travelled to the Everwood, and there she fell in love with the Eighth Elder of that time. He seeded a son in her: Edmond Shackton, Ranulf's great-great-grandfather who had become a famed adventurer himself. Ranulf's grandmother had told him stories of Edmond when he was just a boy, of his quests and travels and the places he had seen, the kings and heroes he had known…but never of the Elders, never of the Everwood. That was a secret that his great-great-great-grandmother had kept, a secret only unveiled to Ranulf Shackton when the First Elder had deemed it time. *So you may see through Kamcho's eyes, as we do*, he had told him. *And use this power in your downward quest.*

He was using that power now. Peering through the eagle's sight as he flew toward the fort. The castle bore tattered banners from its lichen-covered walls, showing a crab with bladed claws, the Swiftwater crest. There were some old men on the crumbling grey battlements, a defence of greybeards peering away to the distant shore. No doubt they had seen the dragon come down, though none paid any notice to the eagle.

When Ranulf opened his eyes, withdrawing from Kamcho's sight, he found Talasha looking at him. She was in a slightly better mood back then, earlier in the day, before they reached the snow. "So? What do you see?"

"Nothing of concern. The castle is one of Lord Harry Swiftwater's. They originated from here. Though are now very rich and powerful."

Talasha knew the name. "Shellcrest is their seat now, is that right?"

"It's so. A fine city. Lord Harry does not come out here anymore, though likes to keep his old castles garrisoned. He is still the power here on Krarl, such as it is. A few other minor lords and knights pay him fealty."

Cevi was listening in. "The war hasn't come here, then?" she asked. She looked around. The island was flat, featureless, and positively infested with crabs. Even now they were scuttling underfoot, small ones mostly, though there were some larger ones here as well, Ranulf knew. "I don't see any ships or armies. Only these crabs." She knelt down to inspect one as it scaled a nearby rock, giggling. It had one small claw and one much bigger one. The proportions seemed to amuse her greatly. "This one's so silly, look. It's like it's got one of your arms, Ranulf, and another from the King's Wall." She laughed again, louder this time, and Talasha laughed along with her.

"You are terribly slight, Ranulf," the princess agreed. "There really isn't much of you, is there?"

"No, my lady. And a good thing too, else Neyruu would have a great deal more trouble bearing the three of us on her back." Ranulf let them giggle themselves out, then added, "I daresay Eldur has scant interest in the island of Krarl, Cevi. Not unless he has a great hunger for crabmeat, of course."

The girl stood up and looked around, smiling. "I bet the people here *never* go hungry. There are *so* many of them. You could feed the world from here if you wanted."

"Ah, one might think. But as with many things, the gods like to give with one hand, and take away with the other. Regrettably, many of these crabs are inedible and poisonous. And not the ones you might think either." Ranulf pointed out a particular crab. "You see that one. Plain and brown, large enough to give a bit of meat. It looks harmless enough, does it not? And perhaps it is…or isn't. You see, there is a variety here that is very tasty…and one that looks exactly like it that will kill you with a brush of your fingertip on its shell. The locals here can tell the difference, but only them, and even they can make mistakes sometimes. It is part of the reason why so few live here. It may not look it, but Krarl is a most perilous place, Cevi."

All of a sudden Cevi was looking around in dismay, hopping aside whenever a crab came near.

Her mistress smiled at her. "I do not believe you are in danger with those boots on, Cevi. They can only harm you with contact to the skin, is that not right, Ranulf?"

Ranulf nodded. "The one I mentioned, yes. Though others are perfectly fine to handle…but will cause great upset should you eat them." There were others still he did not care to mention. Much larger varieties with thick hard armour and great pinching claws that lurked in the waters just offshore, waiting to pick unknowing fishermen away to drown and let their flesh go soft so they could feast on them at their leisure. Some even spoke of the legend of a crab the size of a kraken crawling about down there, but he decided to keep that one to himself as well.

They stayed on the island only long enough for Neyruu to take some rest, an hour or so in the end, during which Ranulf built a fire of dried moss and seaweed on a base of stones and put a pot of soup on the boil. "I do hope you're not taking our lives in hand with that broth, Ranulf Shackton," Talasha remarked.

He had caught some crabs for the soup, though only ones he was certain were safe to eat. A pair of the red ones, as it happened, that might look poisoning but were, in fact, quite harmless. "I'll be sure to have the first taste, my lady," he said.

"A royal taster. Yes, a fine job for one such as you." She smiled and perched on a smooth rock beside him. "Though in truth it should be me doing the tasting for you. This secret in your head…it's truly the formula for combining the blades?"

He nodded, throwing in a sprig of wild thyme he'd found up the beach and giving the pot a stir. "Unless I've forgotten or misremembered something. If I have then we're all doomed, my lady, so we had best hope my memory is still sharp."

"As sharp as those swords they're trying to gather, yes." Talasha looked out to sea, pondering for a long moment. "The crossing will not be pleasant by ship, even one so strong as *Hammer*," she said. "The waters look rough out there, Ranulf. I do hope they'll make it safely."

Hope. It was a tonic half the world was drinking. "The prince's fleet faced worse before, my lady, and lived through it."

She gave him a look. "That fleet was thirty ships. Now it's four."

"Seven," Ranulf said. "Or ought to have been, had Lord Huffort not abandoned them." Still, he took the point. Seven surviving ships from thirty was a poor return, though the superstorm Prince Robbert's armada had endured out near the Telleshi Isles was a truly savage thing. It was unlikely they'd face anything so fearsome here, leastways not from the winds and waves. "*Hammer* has survived worse," he assured her. "And she's blessed with a worthy captain. Ash Burton is as fine a sailor as I've ever known. He'll steer them safe to port, my lady."

The soup was about ready to be served by then, so Ranulf did the honours. Tasting it first himself he declared it a tad bland but edible. "It could do with a bit more spice, but it won't kill us," was his review. He spooned Talasha a bowl and she ate it eagerly. Cevi did not partake, not after what he'd told her. She had taken refuge on the summit of Neyruu's back, to be as far from the skittering creatures as possible, and refused to come back down.

They ate in silence, each retreating to the sanctuary of their thoughts. Ranulf listened to the wind howling across the island, the seas hissing as the waves hit the stony shore. He had spoken to give Talasha comfort, though his own fears about Saska were ripe. More than once he had spotted menacing shapes in the water as they flew, and further to the north the threat of dragons would become more constant.

She has Bloodhound, he thought, *and a fine Seaborn crew.* Their task was to see Saska safely across the water. After that she had her knights and warriors to help protect her on her onward journey north, the Whale-heart and the Bloody Traders, Leshie and Joy. He only wished that Robbert Lukar might join her too. Yet from what he could glean, the boy was intent on marching to war. *He is a king now, in truth. And a king must lead his people.*

"We should go," Ranulf heard Talasha say. He looked over as she stood, striding down to where the water lapped at the shore, cleaning out her bowl. "Here, give me yours." She took his and cleaned that too. "Get everything packed up, Ranulf. The sooner we reach this refuge of yours, the sooner we can return." She looked out to sea, their thoughts aligned. "Saska may need us. And she may take a while to find."

He nodded in accord, stood, and did as bidden. Five minutes later, they were on their way.

The next stretch of their journey was less windy, but more wet. As they crossed the bleak and barren island, the rains started to come down from a slate-grey sky; a cold rain, hard and relentless. Such as they were, they obscured the view below, as they crossed the mainland, near the Links, and soared over the Sibling Strait. Beyond lay Tukor, its southern-most reaches drenched and sodden, yet before too long the rain turned to snow and Talasha's mood began to sour.

That was long hours ago. And now here they were, flying through the blizzard, searching for something for Neyruu to eat. Ranulf moved his eyes around as they flew, though his pitiful range of sight was unlikely to bear reward. Instead he turned to Kamcho again, instructing the big blue and gold eagle to fly away and conduct a search. Talasha gave

Neyruu free rein to hunt as needed and the three passengers hunkered down and hoped.

Somehow, Ranulf slept.

Or he must have, anyway, because all of a sudden his eyes were ripping open as he jolted awake, harness straining, the wind howling loudly in his ears and stabbing at his eyes. He raised a hand to shield them, peered forward past the dragon's long slender body, and saw the ground rushing up toward them, swift as an arrow from a bow.

A panicked noise erupted from his lips, somewhere between a scream and a squeak. Cevi laughed ahead of him, twisting her neck back. "You're awake then!" Her hair was whipping wildly, a broad smile on her cherubic face. "Knew that would wake you. You were snoring!" She laughed again.

Snoring? Ranulf was still gathering his bearings. *Did they do that just to wake me? Is this some cruel prank?*

No. He spotted movement below, something large charging across an open field and toward a stand of trees. The world was dull white down there, black everywhere else, no moon to light the sky, no stars to be seen at all. A few flakes drifted but the snows had waned for now. Ranulf squeezed his eyes into a squint against the rushing air. Faintly, he glimpsed Kamcho shooting along beside the dragon, giving chase as well.

What is that thing? It was no deer, that was obvious, no cattle of any kind. It ran on all fours, forelegs longer than the rear, a lumbering, powerful stride. Thick fur covered its broad muscular body, dark and shaggy. Snow and clumps of blackened soil flew behind it as it ran.

"It's a bear," Cevi shouted. "I've never seen a bear!"

It wasn't a bear, no common bear at least. By the size and shape Ranulf judged it to be a grimbear, greatly larger and more fearsome than its younger cousin. Its claws were long and razor-sharp, its hide a great carpet of skin that moved over the meat and muscle of its body like a protective blanket, tough as layers of beaten leather. It was a big one too, he saw. *If it turns and lashes out with those claws…*

He had no time to contemplate it. Neyruu was nearing, thrusting forward with her talons like an eagle hunting a vole, wings tucked and streamlined, then suddenly spreading to slow as the claws reached down toward the flesh of the grimbear's back, digging, gripping. The beast roared, bursting away to the left. Tufts of thick black hair flew, scattering to the wind. Neyruu hissed, flapping her wide wings, twisting to give chase.

"It's too big," Ranulf shouted forward. "That's no normal bear, Talasha! There must be easier prey."

She did not heed him. Or perhaps she had no control. The dragon was all in a lather, snarling and snapping as she flapped and kicked up from the snowy ground, wild from the scent of fear and meat. Somewhere deep inside the beast Ranulf could feel the forge-fires trying to spark, the steam issuing through her teeth, misting through vents in her grey plate armour. But they would not catch. She gave a screeching roar of rage, half running and half flying in pursuit as she took to the air. The woods were near, the protective shield of the trees. Two hundred feet and no more. The grimbear was closing.

There was motion from beneath the branches. Ranulf glimpsed shapes bursting out of the woodland, the shadows of men, a score of them at least. They bore swords, axes, spears, wore heavy frosted cloaks in black and brown. Thinly he heard them shouting, calling out to one another, spreading to enclose the bear. *Local men,* Ranulf thought. *Villagers.* They likely lived around here, had come to drive the bear away. *Or kill it for meat.*

They had not yet noticed the dragon.

The grimbear charged them. The bravest lurched in its way, driving spears up into its chest as men do when defending a cavalry charge. Tips gouged deep into its layers-of-leather hide, shafts snapping and breaking off. The bear bellowed, rearing, lashing out with a forepaw to knock several spearmen aside. It tried to run off but a rope came flying over its shoulder, hooked iron claws digging into the flesh. On the other end men held on, five of them, tugging hard to slow it. More hooked ropes flew, more men clung on. Axmen charged in, hewing and chopping at the bears legs like woodcutters felling trees. Spearmen surged and thrust, driving for the face and neck.

Then someone saw Neyruu.

The cry pierced the air. "Dragon! *Dragon!*"

Others turned to look, saw the shadow descending. Axes stilled as they swung, spears quivered in trembling hands. The men holding the ropes lost their grip and the grimbear burst away, long hempen snakes trailing from its shoulders and back as it crashed through the villagers and into the trees. The men scattered, screaming, as Neyruu swept down from the black skies, snapping at the air the grimbear had left. The beast was gone, hurtling through the boughs to the song of snapping wood, bloody footprints in its wake. The dragon gave out a savage wild roar and Talasha was shrieking, "No! Not *them!* No, Neyruu, no!"

"Run," Ranulf Shackton cried out to the men. "Run! All of you, run!"

They did not need to be told. Most were fleeing for the trees, vanishing into the dark. The stragglers followed, some tripping on roots and rocks in their haste. Neyruu's eyes snapped upon one, long neck twisting. Her wings flapped, stirring the snow into a billowing white shroud. Talasha was screaming but the dragon would not be tamed. Her talons reached out, grasping. The man on the ground could do nothing but raise a hand to ward her…and then the claws snapped shut, crushing the life from him.

Cevi screamed. Talasha was shouting and kicking out at the dragon but she paid her no mind. The last of the men were gone, fleeing into the forest. Echoed shouts rang out from the wood as Neyruu lay the dead man down and began to eat him.

There was nothing they could do to stop her, nothing they could do but sit there and listen to the crunch of bone, the rending of flesh, the deep rumble of pleasure in the dragon's chest as she feasted. When she was done her neck swung around, nostrils flaring at the scent of blood. Another man lay unconscious nearby, maybe dead they could not say, knocked aside by the grimbear's paw. Once more Talasha's screamed commands went unheard. Once more the dragon ate.

She knows the taste of man now, Ranulf thought.

A shiver went up his spine.

3

Emeric

Emeric Manfrey clutched at the prince's hand, telling him he wasn't going to die.

"You're strong, Raynald, like your father. Do you want to see your sister again? Your mother?" He tightened his grasp. "Hold on, just a little longer. Can you do that for me? Can you do it for Tukor?"

"For Tukor," the boy prince rasped, blinking to try to stay awake. His skin was bloodless, pale as curdled milk, the light fading from his green-brown eyes. The wound in his gut was as bad as Emeric had feared, the flesh torn open in a six-inch gash and it was all he could do to try to keep the lad conscious. *If he sleeps, he dies,* he thought. He would not let that happen.

The exile stood and marched over to the cabin door in which they'd taken refuge. Two men had the guard of it. Another pair were desperately trying to light a fire using whatever dry wood they had found outside and scrounged from within the shanty. "You," Emeric said to one of the armsmen. "Keep the prince awake. Slap him if you must, but keep him awake. And get that fire going. We need to staunch the bleeding and keep him warm."

The man nodded. Emeric strode outside. There were a few more Tukoran soldiers there, watching the trees for signs of foemen. Some others were away in the woods in a frantic search for herbs and healing plants. There had been none in this huntsman's cabin, chanced upon in their rush to flee the fighting, but a natural herb called *bloodnettle* grew in these parts, Sir Ernold Esterling had said, and he'd taken off with some of the men to try to find it.

"Any movement?" Emeric asked the guards.

They shook their heads, silently peering out into the fading light. It was dim beneath the trees. Swirls of smoke moved between the boles of beech and the thin branches of alder, coming from the south where the larger forest was burning. What was happening out there right now

Emeric could not say. *Chaos*, he thought. He knew that much. When they'd fled the battle, the fighting had been spread far and wide, the fortress of Rustbridge aflame, tens of thousands lying dead and dying for miles across the field. By now his friends might be dead, all of them. Turner and Jack and Braxton and the others. Borrus, Torvyn, Mooton, Rikkard Amadar, Marian Payne, he knew nothing of their fates. But he could not think about all that right now, or give any thought to returning to the fray. He had to try to save his prince first and foremost. Exiled or not, it was his duty as a man of Tukor.

"Any sign of Sir Ernold?" he asked.

One of the guards pointed. "I saw him out that way, m'lord. A few minutes ago. Heading east."

"Keep watch. Guard the prince with your lives. If there's trouble, blow your horn." Emeric marched away in a fierce step, moving his eyes around as he plunged into the dark of the trees. He reached a shallow gully, scrambled down and up the other side, passed a swollen muddy brook and heard voices ahead. A few moments later he found Sir Ernold Esterling and one of his men hunting about the base of a clutch of huge ash trees that stood imperious beside a spread of soggy bogland. "Sir Ernold. Any luck in your search?"

The man looked up, scowling. "Not as yet. These blasted rains have rotted all the bloodnettle away. It's all useless mulch, drowned and dead." He kicked hard at the nearest tree, chips of bark flying from the toe of his steel boot. "How's the fire coming? If we can at least cauterise the wound…"

"They're working to get it lit. But it's taking time. Most of the wood is too damp."

"The rain again. This cursed rain!" Sir Ernold looked around, shaking his head. His hair was thinning on top and sat wet and lank against his scalp, rainwater dripping from his salted brown beard. "There's small good you being here, Emeric. You'll be better served staying at the cabin and protecting the prince."

"He's well protected. If there's trouble we'll hear a horn blast and return."

"Fine. Then help us search. Bloodnettle likes to take root around the base of ash and oak, so that'd be a good place to start."

They set back to the task. Of ash trees here, there were many , and bloodnettle too, but all they found were dead and useless. Once and twice and thrice more Sir Ernold Esterling cursed the rain, but it made no matter; their search still yielded nothing and no amount of cursing the weather or the gods would help. When five minutes turned to ten and ten turned to twenty they were all but ready to give up the search. "There's nothing here we can use," Esterling grunted. "The fire will serve. They'll have it lit by now and if not I'll have their…"

A bustle of movement interrupted him as one of his soldiers came rushing through the trees, panting and wheezing. He wore a bloodied brown cloak and godsteel breastplate, the rest good castle-forged steel supplemented with studded leather. "Benithy," Sir Ernold said, seeing him. It was one of his men-at-arms, another who'd gone off hunting for herbs. "You found bloodnettle? Tell me you bloody did."

"No, my lord, not…not bloodnettle…but we found something better." Benithy put his hands to his knees, breathing hard. "Davney…he came upon some dead Lumarans just off…off outside these woods. Half dozen or them, my lord, and one of them carrying supplies in a satchel."

Sir Ernold's eyes lit up. "What sort of supplies?"

"Bandages, balms, ointments and such. Even needle and thread, my lord."

"Needle and thread? The gods are good! Where is Davney now?"

"On his way back to the cabin. Might be there by now…"

"Then what are we bloody well doing here?" Sir Ernold Esterling sped back toward the cabin without delay, the rest following behind. Inside they found the man Davney - another man-at-arms of thin Blade-born blood - emptying out the supplies onto an old butchering table as the prince groaned on a bed of cloaks. The men were still trying to keep him awake, talking to him constantly, getting him to talk back. *He's strong*, Emeric thought. Most others would have succumbed by now but Raynald Lukar was made of sterner stuff.

They had managed to get the fire lit too, a meagre thing puffing out dark smoke that rose up toward a smoke hole in the pointed thatch roof. "Get outside and help keep watch," Sir Ernold told Benithy. "You as well Davney. You see anything, you come tell me straightaway." The men departed. "We need that fire hotter," the knight went on, shouting at the two men coaxing it to life. "You throw yourselves on if you need to. See it done, I don't care how."

He marched to join Emeric at the table as he picked through the medical supplies. All the jars and pots of medicine were written in Lumaran, but thankfully it was a language in which Emeric was fluent. It was a fortuitous find. "This'll serve," he said. "We've been lucky here, Ernold."

"Only if the boy survives," the knight said. He looked over the contents of the satchel. "How are you with needle and thread?"

"Fair to reasonable."

Esterling gave a bark of laughter despite the desperate circumstances. "You're a humble man, Manfrey. Fair to reasonable? Guess that means you're skilled as a seamstress. *You'll* be sewing the boy back together, then. The rest of us can't stitch a wound worth a damn."

Emeric saw no reason to argue with that. He had some experience fixing up cuts and cleaves during his days in the south. Minor accidents were common enough on the estate, though this was something alto-gether more serious. "We'll have to cut and cauterise the flesh first to stop the worst of the bleeding," he said. "And to stave off infection." It was a dragon tail-spike that had torn the prince open and oft as not they could leave deadly infections in their wake. "We'll need a dagger, common steel. Godsteel doesn't hold heat well enough."

"I'll see to it." Sir Ernold marched off, calling for a man to yield up his dagger. They had a mix of Bladeborn and common soldiers here in their small company, so finding one oughtn't be a problem. It wasn't. The knight returned a moment later and plonked the blade down on the table.

"Get that into the fire," Emeric said. "The needle as well, to sterilise it." He handed it over and Esterling saw to it. When he returned he asked about the medicines. "This one's from a herb called *alarilia*," Emeric explained, plucking up a small stoppered pot with a purplish-blue liquid inside. "Take a bit of this with water and works as a strong painkiller. Apply it directly to a wound or injury and it causes a mild numbing effect." He handed it over. "Mix a few drops into a water cup and give it to the prince. Then add a more generous sprinkling to a cloth and dab it around the wound. It'll help him manage the pain."

Sir Ernold took the pot, nodding.

"We'll use this after," Emeric went on, picking up a larger jar wound up in a coat of thick brown leather. "They call it *juice of the snakevine* and it works the same as drakeshell powder, as an antiseptic and healing accelerator."

"Juice of the snakevine," Esterling repeated. "Another medicinal plant?"

"Yes. From the Hollowhills of Aramatia. The vines grow down from the cave ceilings like snakes hanging from the branches of a tree. Their heads are shaped somewhat like snakes as well and the 'juice' is extracted from them like venom. They have teeth, these vines."

Sir Ernold made a face. "Serpent vines with teeth. Well, now I've heard it all. So long as it works, that's good enough for me."

The knight moved away once again to administer the painkiller to the groaning prince. By the time Emeric went over to join them the fire was blazing brighter and the steel of the dagger was turning red hot. Esterling had peeled away the bloody bandaging and was rubbing the alarilia extract into the flesh about the wound.

Emeric went down to a knee and withdrew his godsteel dagger. Prince Raynald Lukar's skin was clammy, shimmering with sweat, his eyes going cloudy. "Raynald. How do you feel?"

"A little…a little better," the boy said, in a rasping voice. "The pain isn't so bad now."

"Good. I'm going to cut at some of the ragged flesh. We need to strip it off before we sear and stitch the wound. There will be pain, Raynald. Try not to scream if you can avoid it."

The boy nodded defiantly. Emeric turned the godsteel blade at once and began shearing away a few loose strips of flesh in a bid to neaten the gash. A man had to go about and hold Raynald down as he squirmed, but to his great credit, he did not cry out. Once that was done Emeric wiped down his dagger and sheathed it, then called for the searing blade to be brought forward. "This will hurt worse," he warned. "Sir Ernold, find something for him to bite down on." The knight dashed outside and returned with a suitably sized stick, dripping wet, and placed it between the prince's jaws. He took his place behind him, propping him up a little, taking his hand. "Hold him firm. Try not to move, Raynald. And take a deep breath. It will all be over quickly."

The next part was the most unpleasant, the hiss and stink of searing meat as Emeric pressed down with the flat of the blade against the bloody flesh. The smell was horrid, the sound as bad. Raynald bucked and lurched in agony, biting down hard on his stick. It cracked, then snapped between his jaws as Emeric turned the blade over and pressed again, and this time it was all too much for the boy. His eyes flickered and rolled over and he passed out limp. "Check his pulse," Emeric commanded at once. "Make sure he's still breathing."

The boy was alive, but his heart rate was weak.

"Sir Ernold, fetch the juice of the snakevine. Drip it on the seared flesh. You there, bring the needle and thread."

The man at the fire rushed to hand it to him and Emeric went to work, stabbing and pulling, drawing the burnt flesh together as Ernold administered the antiseptic. It was not the cleanest set of sutures that Emeric Manfrey had ever stitched, but did the job. When he was done with that, he took the snakevine venom from Sir Ernold and applied it more liberally across the wound and the flesh that bordered it, letting it sink down in to work its magic.

"Let's clean and bandage him up," he finished. "Hopefully that will stabilise him."

Once the blood was wiped away and the new bandages were wrapped about him, they placed the boy down near the fire and set two men to watch him. Emeric cleaned his utensils and set the medicine back on the table, to be reapplied when the boy awoke. How long that would be he couldn't say. Now all they could do was wait.

The world had gone true dark by the time Emeric Manfrey stepped out of the cabin, an inky blackness enveloping the woods in a mantle dark as death. It was silent. Nothing but the occasional hoot of an owl or the rustle of some small creature in the brush, the movement of the men on watch, dotted here and there. Emeric took his godsteel dagger in his grasp and listened for the sounds of battle far away, but there was nothing. No faint ring of steel at the edge of hearing. No screams and cries of dying men. Not even the roar of a dragon screeching in the skies or the bellow of a raging moonbear.

Sir Ernold stepped out of the cabin to join him, firelight momentarily bathing the woods as the door was opened and closed. "You did well in there, Emeric," he said, resting a hand on his shoulder. "You have my thanks. That's a steady hand you've got."

Emeric dipped his chin. "We were lucky with the supplies."

"And you. None of us would have had any idea what any of it was. Might have sewn him up at a pinch, but the rest…" He shook his head, surveying the trees through a set of tense and weary eyes. "It's gone quiet," he noted, gaze narrowing. "That unnerving sort of quiet. Makes you wonder what's lurking out there, just beyond our sight."

"More trees," Emeric said. "Let's hope it's nothing worse than that."

"Indeed." Esterling allowed a smile to break the tension. "I'd imagine the battle's over by now…for the most part at least. Our forces will be trying to regroup at Rustbridge and we'd be wise to try to join them."

Emeric wondered about the wisdom of that. "We both saw the fortress, Ernold. It was still burning when we entered these woods."

"The *towers* were burning," the Emerald Guard corrected. "We can't know what's become of the rest of it until we go there and find out. Tomorrow at first light we'll send out a small scouting force. If the fortress is still standing, we can consider taking the prince there."

"And if not?"

"Then we'll have to think of something else. It might be that the fort is overwhelmed and the remains of our forces have retreated across the river. If so we can be certain that the bridge will have been collapsed." He turned to look at him. "You know about the failsafe, I trust?"

Emeric nodded. Rustbridge was both city and fortress in one, with the city spread out upon the western banks of the Rustriver and the fortress built upon its eastern shore. If the city was ever under threat of falling into enemy hands, the bridge that spanned the river would be collapsed so that the enemy couldn't cross. It was a possibility, yes, but Emeric doubted it had come to that. From what he'd seen the fighting had been largely kept to the open field; so far as he knew the Agarathi foot had not made their way beyond the walls and past the gates and until that happened, there was no reason for Lord Lester Pentar to order the bridge to be brought down.

Evidently Ernold Esterling thought the same. "It is a last-ditch measure, to be initiated in the very gravest of circumstances. Circumstances that have not yet come to pass, I would hope. We shall find out on the morrow when you lead the scouting party there."

Emeric raised a brow. "Me?"

The knight gave a firm nod. "You're the finest sword here and seem to have a good nose for this sort of thing. A multi-skilled man you appear to be, Emeric Manfrey." He clapped him on the arm. "I'd join you as well if I could, but my place is with the prince. I trust you to lead on in my stead."

Emeric had no issue with that. "Who will come with me?"

"I'll send Benithy. He's a reasonable scout and a more than useful sword. Daveny as well. Three should serve, don't you think?"

"Three is sufficient," Emeric agreed. He did not know these men well, but from what he'd seen both Benithy and Daveny could handle themselves in battle. Both had helped to fight off Avar Avam's men and fought with both purpose and pride.

"Good. Now by my reckoning we're about six or seven miles away from the fortress here, and half of that distance through these woods. It would be best if you range westward to the river first, rather than returning the way we came. Follow its course near the shoreline and observe Rustbridge from a distance. If the skies are clear we'll know at a glance whether our men still hold it."

Emeric agreed with every word of that. "I can leave shortly," he said. "No sense in waiting for first light."

The Emerald Guard shook his head. "I would prefer you stay here for now. To observe Raynald a little longer, should he take a turn for the worse. And to let things settle out there." He looked to the trees. "If we suffer no unwanted surprises, then you can leave an hour or so before dawn. Happy?"

"With that, yes. Not with much else."

Ernold gave a soft bark of laughter. "You're a droll fellow, my friend. Now wait here a moment while I check in with the men. I'll be back in a minute or two."

He stepped away from the cabin and across the small clearing, thick with thornbushes and long wet grass, and moved quickly beneath the branches of the trees. In short order the knight was out of sight. Emeric could hear only the soft squelchy tread of Sir Ernold's boots, the rustle of vegetation, the low words of his thrumming bass voice as he went from man to man to take report. He could hear the faint crackle of the fire inside the cabin as well, the sound the wind made as it sighed eerily through the trees. All that would be prone to make a man feel sleepy, but Emeric had cause to doubt whether sleep would come to him tonight. He was on edge, his pulse thick and heavy, his muscles coiled up like bundles of rope. It had been a long day, a frenzied day, a day in which he'd slain his first dragon and claimed vengeance on a sunlord and senior Patriot of Lumara…a day when two hundred thousand men and mounts had clashed beneath the dawn.

Borrus, what did you do? he thought. *How could you let Vargo Ven goad you like that?*

It was a head in a bag that did it. The head that doomed ten thousand souls, or more, many times more than that. Lord Wallis Kanabar, so beloved, had been tortured, beaten, burned and mutilated…and then at last beheaded. A dragon had dropped his head over the fortress in a bag and when Borrus saw it…when the bag was brought to his command pavilion and he saw his father's lifeless face gazing up at him…Gods, Emeric still recalled the way the man roared. The roar that spread all through the ward, and then the horns were blowing, and the drums were thumping, and the men all rushed to mount their steeds and into the bloody dawn they charged.

Now here they were, broken, divided, their army a shattered wreck. How many of his friends were dead? How many had made it through? Did Borrus himself still draw breath? Had he sought his vengeance on Vargo Ven, as he'd sworn that he would do? What of Rikkard, who'd been fighting with Emeric for a time, before that dragon came? The heir of House Amadar was knocked aside by the dragon's lashing tail and then Emeric fought it alone, killed it alone, and got trapped beneath its huge great bulk when it collapsed and died atop him. By the time he crawled out, the light had changed, the battle had spread, and Rikkard Amadar was nowhere to be seen.

That tail may have torn him open the same as Raynald, Emeric thought. *And Mooton…what of Mooton?* Did he fall defending the door to the tower? The last Emeric had seen of him, a great tide of foemen were pouring up the hillside toward them. He had wanted to turn back and fight alongside him, but he couldn't. He had to help the prince. *I had to. I had no choice. Tomorrow. On the morrow I'll find out what happened to them…*

A soft rustle of movement intruded on his thoughts, coming from the trees to his left. He turned his head, peering into the black, through the shadows of branches and boles. Among those shadows he saw something that didn't look right, a shape in the gloom, still as a statue, glaring out with silver eyes. It was a glimpse, no more. Then in a sudden dash the creature was gone, slipping silent as a spectre away and into the thick dark of the night.

Emeric's heart thumped a steady hard beat. He listened and listened hard for the approach of an unseen enemy, somewhere further off, drawn by flame-light and smoke from the top of the cabin. But there was nothing. Just the faint murmur of Sir Ernold's voice as he checked in with his guards. The crack of twigs and soft press of sodden leaves as the knight went from one to the next.

The man returned to him a few moments later to report that Benithy and Davney were to rest soon in the cabin and he must do so as well. "You need to sleep if you're to leave before dawn, Emeric. It's been a long day and I won't have you…" He trailed off, seeing the look on Emeric's face. "What's the matter? Is something wrong?"

Emeric was only half listening. His eyes were still trained on the woods to their left, where he'd seen the shadow.

The Emerald Guard took his arm, squeezing. "What is it? Did you see something out there?"

Emeric nodded slowly. His voice was a whisper when he said, "Starcat. It came and went quickly, but…"

"You're certain it was a starcat?" Ernold's fingers clenched harder.

He nodded. "I've spent years around them and know how they move. It was a starcat, Ernold."

The man let go and looked out. "Was there a rider?"

"Just the cat. Its rider may have died during the battle. Or it was sent ahead to scout."

"*Scout?* You think…" Esterling looked uneasy at the notion. His eyes darted around. "If that cat leads an enemy host here…they may be out there now, closing on us as we speak. What happened when you saw it?"

Emeric was confused by the question. "Nothing. It fled."

"At once? It fled at once?"

"Yes, but…"

"Then it knew it was spotted. Damn it," the man cursed, closing a fist. "It's going to lead them here, sure as summer follows spring." He turned to the door of the cabin. "We'll have to leave," he said. "Go deeper into the woods. There's a brook not far from here, wide enough to walk two by two. If we go upstream in the water we'll leave no trail."

I should never have said anything, a part of Emeric thought. "The cat may not be a scout, Ernold. Or even an enemy."

The knight snorted. "How'd you figure that? It's a *starcat*, Emeric. It didn't wander all the way north by itself now did it?"

"Not all of the empire's forces are against us," Emeric told him. "Mooton Blackshaw said he saw Moonrider Ballantris lead a southern charge against the Agarathi earlier during the battle. And you saw how Ballantris and Tathranor killed that dragon. They're divided, Ernold. If that cat leads some of Ballantris's men here they might be able to help us."

"*Help* us? What help do we need but the help they've already given? Those supplies are good enough for me." He made for the cabin. "We need to go."

Emeric breathed out. "If you move him now he could die. He needs to rest and stay still. How do you intend to carry him upriver? Over your shoulder? The stitches will break."

"We'll make a stretcher from the table. Break off the legs and carry him. Or we stay here and hope for the best. Is that what you'd advise?"

He had him in a corner. The prince's safety must be the first priority. They'd done the first part by stabilising his wounds, but they were a long way from being out of the woods. Did the cabin make much of a difference? Only to half-conceal the flames and keep him dry, but elsewise no, it was a beacon not a buttress and offered no real defence. If there was a chance, small though it might be, that an enemy force might hunt them down, they had no choice but to flee.

"Fine," Emeric said. "We'll go, if that's your command." Sir Ernold Esterling was a senior knight among the Emerald Guards, a sworn protector of the prince, and these were his men. Emeric could only advise, not order. He had no recourse here. "Gather your men then, Sir Ernold. I'll see about that stretcher."

The knight nodded and paced back into the trees. The men inside the cabin did not seem particularly pleased when Emeric told them what was happening, but submitted all the same and began stamping out the fire. They left only some fading embers for them to work by as Emeric withdrew his godsteel dagger and cut off each of the four table legs where they joined the top of the wood. Then he gouged handholds into the tabletop to make carrying it a little easier. "Let's get him on."

Together they lifted the prince gently aboard, setting him down into a bed of cloaks to cushion him. Emeric took a moment to gather up the medical supplies and return them to their satchel bag, then threw it over his shoulder. By then Sir Ernold was stepping back inside. The door creaked hauntingly as he pushed it open and one of the men almost jumped. "You're skittish as a kitten, Willard," the knight said. He looked down. "Good work with the stretcher. Is he ready?"

"Is this truly necessary, my lord?" asked the other soldier, an older man-at-arms, grizzled and grey. "Lord Manfrey said he saw a cat, but…"

"A cat? Don't be a bloody fool, Lambert. He saw a *star*cat, and that's an important detail. Now come, the others are gathered outside. I'll help you lift him." He stepped in, slipped his fingers through the handhold, and together the four of them hefted the prince through the door.

The other men were waiting for them. Sir Ernold ordered for Benithy and Willard to go ahead and scout the way to the stream. Lambert was sent to their left flank and Davney their right. Each man slipped away into the trees out of sight, shields on their backs and armour dripping wet from the drizzle, horns hanging from their sword-belts. They were told to blow only if in dire peril. "But don't go blasting your horns for nothing," Sir Ernold said. "You get spooked by a squirrel and give our positions away, and I'll kill you before the enemy does, be sure of that."

The rest of the men were to remain with the prince, a force of only eight, Emeric and Ernold included. They were a mix of weak-blood Bladeborn and common fighting men, mostly Tukorans under Sir Ernold's charge with some Vandarians spicing the mix. During their escape from the battlefield some waifs and strays had joined them, having lost touch with their own companies. One was a Riverlander, a big bearded man with a trout and godsteel gutting knife for a sigil, not one that Emeric knew. There was a pair of Marshlanders who'd served under Lord Rammas, and one of Sir Rikkard Amadar's soldiers in his pink and pale blue cloak, a sapling of a boy who had the look of a squire about him. In the rush of it all Emeric had not yet learned all their names. He had barely had time enough to look them in the eye, in truth, hectic as the last hours had been.

They kept as quiet as they could, picking their way through the stands of beech and alder. The ground was even enough underfoot, but here and there were rocks and roots that might trip them if they weren't careful. Two men walked ahead to test the ground and detect any hidden perils, the men carrying the stretcher just behind, the rest making up a small four-man rearguard. Before long the cabin was a hundred metres behind them, nothing but a distant memory. Emeric grumbled a silent lament for the warmth of that fire, the cover of that roof. Most of all he misliked moving the prince in this dark, when it wasn't just the perils underfoot they had to worry about. *That wound will carry a stink*, he thought. *The gods know what might come sniffing after it.*

They came upon the river soon after, a flowing course of water that might not have been here a month ago. At the very least it was swollen beyond its natural shape, like a slim young man turned thick and gouty in his dotage. "Runoff from all these rains," the big Riverlander declared. He waded into the waters to test its strength, as their resident river expert, and gave a nod. "We can walk in this."

"Lead on, then," Sir Ernold said. "You." He pointed at the Amadar boy. "Go with him. Make sure the ground is flat enough for us to walk. Warn us of any hazards."

The water was cold, sloshing around their shins and as high as their thighs sometimes when the river ran deeper. In places it plunged through natural gulleys, creating shallow pools that went up to their navels. They were careful all the while to keep the prince dry, laying cloaks over the top of him to shield him from the drizzling rain, replacing them if ever they got too wet. The going was slow, steady and silent but for the sounds they made as they went. Any talking was quickly shut down by Ernold Esterling with a hissing rebuke of, "Shut up, all of you. We don't know who might be listening."

Emeric held his tongue for as long as he could, but after an hour of wading upriver he had to know. "How far do you intend to go, Sir Ernold?" he asked in a low voice. They'd heard no sign of any pursuit, nothing to suggest that starcat might herald a chase.

"Further," the knight only said. "Until we find somewhere dry to stop for the night."

The night might be over by then. "Every mile we go is another we must travel on the way back."

"If we go back."

Emeric turned to look at him, the width of the stretcher and the unconscious prince between them. Water splashed about their ankles, the wind keening through the trees like some grieving mother weeping for the loss of her babes. Emeric didn't like this wood. It was dark, wet, cold, and dangerous. It didn't sound right and didn't smell right either. "*If?*" he asked. "I thought we had agreed to return to Rustbridge."

"We agreed to scout it from afar and see how it lies. We still may, tomorrow, or the next day. Or some days after if it comes to that. Rustbridge isn't going anywhere, Emeric. I have to think first of my prince."

"Raynald will be safer when he's returned to the men."

"He may. Or he may not. That would depend on what we find back there, and when we left it wasn't looking good. Even if the fighting is over it'll take days for our forces to reassemble. Those days might be better spent hidden here in these woods, giving the prince a bit of time to convalesce. This juice of the snakevine. You said it works well?"

Emeric nodded, somewhat curtly.

"Then a few days of its healing effects will greatly help. Once Raynald's gut is knitted back together, and he's got a bit of strength back in him, maybe then we'll return."

Maybe? *Maybe* they'd return? The man was prevaricating, his language unsure. But Emeric was. "I've done what I can to help you," he said. "The prince is stable, and you know how to use the medicines. If you wish to remain in these woods, fine, that's your choice. But I have my own obligations to keep."

"More important obligations than to your prince, and perhaps even more than that?" Ernold gave him a demanding look. "His brother Robbert is long away and we must doubt his return, his father is dead, his grandfather as well so far as we have heard." He cast his eyes down at the boy as he groaned beneath his blankets. "This may very well be your king. Your obligation is to him, and no one else."

Emeric disagreed. "I'm an exile." *An exile due to the scheming of Raynald's very own grandsires*, he decided not to say. "Until such a time as my lands and titles are restored, I owe fealty to no one but myself."

"And yet you're here. You helped to save his life not once but twice. Don't lie to yourself, Emeric. You're a man of honour. You will not abandon him until he is safely recovered, no matter these other *obligations* of yours."

Emeric ground his jaw. The man seemed to know him rather too well already. *A man of honour, yes. And that damnable honour will compel me to stay with him.* He knew that all too well. "Fine," he said, with a measure of reluctance. "Perhaps you're right in that. But I would still entreat you to scout the state of Rustbridge at the first available opportunity. If the army should move, we would be better to be with them. Alone, we will be vulnerable. We must seek the sanctuary of a larger force as soon as we can."

"We will," Sir Ernold said, and that was the end of it.

They kept on up the river for a while longer, another hour or so passing before the elevation began to gradually climb. The trees started to thin a little, the woods spreading to become less dense and brambly, the ground growing drier and more stony, tumbles of rock appearing here and there. A further twenty minutes later they came upon what they were looking for; a cave of sorts, more a wind-carved recess in a stumpy granite cliff, too shallow to shield them all from the wind and rain, but enough to accommodate the prince.

"This'll do," Sir Ernold declared, to audible sighs from the men. The cave faced south, back the way they'd come, and offered an adequate vantage over the woods they'd passed. "We'll be able to see if anyone comes from here. Ben, Lambert, I want you on watch. Climb the scarp above us and take position there. And no fire," he said, sensing the ask was coming. "You light a flame and we'll be surrounded come daybreak."

"Or we'd just be warmer," grunted one of the Marshmen, shrugging and pulling up his cloak.

Sir Ernold chose to ignore that. "Davney, Torret, take the western flank. Will, Burk, you have the east. Find a pair of tall trees to climb and sit tight. Take it in turns to watch and sleep if you can. If there's trouble, blow your horns."

"I don't have a horn," said Burk. He was bald, stout, with a large axe strapped to his back. An ugly scar ran down the left of his lips, making his mouth into a perpetual scowl.

"Willard does. When he takes his rest, he'll give you his. Torret, you and Davney will do the same." Sir Ernold looked over the other men, wondering how best to deploy them. "The rest of you will stay to guard the prince. I'll…"

A sound rang out through the night, somewhere distant and away to the south. It had the distinctive tone of a sunwolf, half-howl and half-roar, like a common wolf crossed with a lion. Everyone froze at the sound. For a moment even the rain seemed to cease. Then the pitter patter came again and Sir Ernold's voice came with it. "They're still on our trail," he said. "Damn it, we have no choice. We're going to have to keep moving."

"No," said young Willard, despairing. "Sir Ernold. It was just a wolf…"

"A *sun*wolf. Emeric will tell us as much. He knows how they sound and that one sounded big." He looked around, shaking his head. "I like this no more than you do, Will, but if they've got our scent…"

"Then we stand and fight," declared Lambert. Like Davney and Willard and Benithy he'd been recruited from Sir Ernold's knightly lands and wore the Esterling sigil on his cloak. He was tall, lean, hard, old, a man who'd fought as many battles as he'd seen winters and bore the battle scars of both. "We defended the princeling from that sunlord before. If they're still after us we'll kill the rest of them."

Emeric had not considered that as yet…that they were being hunted down by Sunlord Avam's men. All of a sudden he had to wonder about that starcat. Perhaps it *was* one of Avam's after all, sent off to sniff them out. It might just be that Sir Ernold Esterling had the right of this all along.

"That isn't an option," the Emerald Guard said. "Not without knowing their strength."

"We have the high ground here," said Torret, who had a missing front tooth and spoke with a lisp. "We should fight, I say."

"I don't care what you say. Your opinion counts for nothing. I said we keep going and so we keep going."

"But my lord…"

"No buts, Willard. Damn it, I have made my decision." He stamped back over to the prince and took his place at the stretcher. "Emeric, Ben, Lambert, help me carry him. Quickly. We'll have to move at pace if we hope to lose them."

For a moment no one moved, not even Emeric, but only a moment. After a brief pause he stepped over, sighing internally, and the others stirred and followed. The stretcher was lifted, the rest of the men grumbling as they were ordered back into position. Then off they went, back into the wind and the rain. Through the long cold hours of the night.

4

_____

Amron

They took dinner together as a family, just the six of them, enjoying the quiet warmth of the small dining hall high up in Blackfrost Castle.

Outside the timber-frame windows, white flickers of snow danced against the darkness, drifting down from a starless sky, and beyond, spread out through the city proper, men milled in their thousands, their tens of thousands, filling the squares and streets of Blackfrost as it had never been filled before.

It was loud down there, Amron knew, in the great camps that had been raised both within and without of the breached and battered walls, but not here. Up here it was quiet, peaceful. Here and there came servers bearing plates of food and jugs of mulled wine, the only sound the slosh of liquid and whisper of slippered feet, the soft murmur of old Artibus's voice as he expounded on some theory, Lillia's sweet high giggling as she sat with Jovyn, the pair thick as thieves, basking in their youthful affection. Cousin Gereth was something of a pebble in his shoe, true, always trying to talk about the war, but here in this hall Amron did not want to discuss it. He wanted to sit and enjoy a simple dinner with his family. He wanted to recall a simpler time.

Amara was sitting at his left, lost to some deep thought. She had barely spoken a word since they'd sat down and hadn't had a sip of wine. That was most unlike her, though Amron knew the cause. He reached out and took her hand, squeezing, retrieving her from her trance. "You can have one cup, you know," he said quietly. "Artibus said it was all right."

"I know." She smiled, a rare innocence in that look. She was wrapped in grey wool, her hair greying too, the gold turning to silver in strands. She was a beautiful woman, Amara Daecar; tall, elegant, with a touch of green in her cool blue eyes to mark her Lukar blood. "I'd just… rather not risk it, Amron," she told him. "All that drinking…I suppose I

44

was making up for something, trying to fill a void." She cradled her belly with a long slim arm. "I never thought…believed…"

He squeezed tighter. "You deserve it, Amara. After everything you've been through."

She gave a soft huff of self-reproach. "What have *I* been through, truly? I had a finger cut off, a few nails ripped away, a spot of torture, and yes…I lost my husband. But others have lost a great deal more. You, Amron. You've lost a wife, an infant son. And your eldest…"

"Was dear to you too."

She nodded. "But not mine. Not my son. That's not a pain I know."

"And you won't," he promised her. He was adamant about that. Amron adored his good-sister, much as she did vex him sometimes, and was fiercely protective of her. Now even more so. *Greatly* more so. "Your child will grow tall, Amara," he vowed. "Tall and strong and *old*. You won't outlive him as I did Aleron, that I promise you."

She smiled at those words and clutched back at his hand. "*Her*," she said, after a moment. "Outlive *her*." She dipped her eyes. "It's a girl, I think. Something Vesryn said, in a dream. Just a dream, I know, but… 'Take care of her' he told me. 'Promise me you will'. I thought he was talking about Lillia, but now…well…you know about the curse. It lifted when he died a hero, restoring his honour. His death paved the way for this life." She thought on that a moment, a line across her brow. "It's hard to know what to make of that. That he must die so our daughter might live…"

"Will live," Amron assured her.

"You don't know that for sure. There's every chance…"

"She will live," Amron repeated. He saw no sense in believing otherwise, letting that worm of a thought wriggle into her head, that doubt fester and grow. He wanted her strong, in body and mind.

She nodded, stiffening her resolve. "I'll have to start thinking of names," she said, with half a smile. "We used to talk of it, Vesryn and I. When we were first wed. What we'd call our son or daughter if ever…if ever it happened." The pain of his passing with still fresh in her eyes, the wound yet to scar over and heal. "I'm told you were there with him, at the end. Did you have a chance to talk…to make up…before he…"

"We did," he said, gently. "We came to terms, in the short time we had. I was there when he spoke his last words."

She looked at him earnestly. "What were they? Something poignant, I hope. He didn't say anything foolish, did he? That would be so very like him." She made a nervous face, waiting.

"He spoke of Aleron," he told her. "He said…he said he would give Aleron his seat."

"His seat at Varin's Table?" She looked a little confused. "Is that possible? To swap places like that?"

"It isn't thought…"

"He would, you know. Vesryn would do it if he could. He'd be happy just being there, Amron. After everything he did, he feared the Long Abyss, so to even sit at that Table…"

Amron nodded. He knew she was right. *He'd have swapped if he could, but he wouldn't be allowed, and I saw him in my dream, ascending in triumph.* It was only a dream, but there was truth in dreams they said. He cleared his throat of the lump that was forming. "Aleron would not have swapped in any case. He wouldn't have felt worthy without earning it."

"And Vesryn would? A slash or two at Drulgar the Dread and suddenly he's Varin's best chum?" She gave a snort. "It's all rather silly, I've always thought, how these placings are handed out. When we're dead, let's all just wander around some other hall together, how about that, find a table of our own? *That's* the only table that matters, the one where family gather. *Family*, Amron, not some long-dead lords and knights who happened to win some acclaim once upon a time. Who would you rather spend your afterlife with when you're gone? Your beautiful wife or a bunch of fusty old men boasting endlessly about their deeds?"

Amron chuckled and had a sip of wine. It was a succinct dismantling of the nature of the Steel Father's Table, to be sure. "I daresay Varin would take umbrage with being called a fusty old man, Amara."

She flicked a wrist. "He's been sitting in that seat for three and a half thousand years, and only the gods know how long he lived *before* then. If that doesn't make one fusty and old, I don't know what does. Goodness, how his arse must ache. I do hope they have cushions on those chairs up there…else the *piles*, gods forbid! Are there such things as piles in the afterlife, sweet brother?"

More laughter ruffled through Amron's lips, a chortle overdue and much needed. This was the Amara Daecar he loved so well, quick of wit and sharp of tongue. The gloom did not suit a woman of such spirit. "I'll be sure to make inquiries when I ascend, Amara. Just for you."

"You want to do something for me? *Don't die.* Let's delay that ascension of yours for now, shall we? If you fall all hope is lost."

He fought the urge to huff. "I'm not the saviour, Amara."

"I beg to differ. I keep hearing all this about some heir, some hidden hero prophesied to bring balance and end the war, but I prefer my heroes to be *seen.* So here you are, right here before us all, killing dragons and leading armies and saving cities from swarming hordes. That's my sort of hero, Amron. Believe me, when the time comes it will be you who deals the killing blow, not some last-minute usurper come to steal your crown. Varin's heir? I prefer Varin *Reborn*, thank you very much." She sat back and folded her arms.

Amron only smiled an inscrutable smile and hid behind another sip of wine. Were it not for the coming of the Snowfist and Lord Robert Borrington and the great force of tribesmen and rangers and commonfolk mustered from the north, Amron might well have died, and the battle would likely have been lost, the city swallowed, Amara and Lillia and everyone else in the mines chased down and slain. That did not make him feel like Varin Reborn, and still he dreamed of Amron the Bold telling him he'd not earned the name. *King Amron the Broken,* he thought. *Varin Reborn in the body of a cripple, more like.*

He put those misgivings aside. The Frostblade was at his hip, resting against the chair in which he sat, there to ease his ails if he needed it. He was trying not to touch it…and failing in that as well. His pain was becoming more acute, and he did not want Lillia in particular to see it, to ruin this dinner, though in truth she was barely aware of him. *She only has eyes for Jovyn, that one.* It made him smile, and it made him sad, because there was every chance that Jovyn would die. He had fought well during the battle, he had heard, defending fiercely at one of the breaches beside Sir Connor and Sir Penrose and some of these Knights Assorted whom Amara had picked up on her travels, but it was one battle among many, and there would be more to come, and in each of them the boy would be tested.

As we all will, the king knew. He'd had his reprieve, and others had too, but many good stout men had fallen two days ago, some noble knights and lesser lords among them. Dependable Sir Harold Conwyn, a leal Borrington man, had been killed by a dragon, and young Sir Trystan Spencer in his bright golden armour had been dragged from his horse and overwhelmed by dragonknights. Of Amara's knights had fallen Sir Hockney Barrow, a cousin of Lord Barrow whom Amron had left with Lythian in King's Point, and Sir Gobert Fuller of Tukor. Lord Styron Strand had lost many of his own defending the city, chief among them Lord Victor Manson, known as the Valiant, and his brother Sir Gervis the Unshrinking. Both brothers had perished when the Agarathi poured through a breach, proving their names as they stood at the front lines, facing the tide which eventually drowned them.

Others had been wounded, sometimes badly, and their fates remained uncertain. Sir Marcus Flint had taken a spear to the flank, and Lord Mantle of the bat-wing cloak and sigil was crushed by a fall of mortared stone when a portion of wall tumbled down atop him. When his men dug through the rubble to release him they found him breathing, his armour protecting him from the worst of the weight, but he'd snapped an ankle and cracked several ribs and would not be battle-strong for a while.

The same was true of Sir Taegon, the greatest loss of all by Amron's judgement. The Giant of Hammerhall had taken a wound to the knee that would not heal anytime soon. The prognosis was uncertain, according to the surgeons, though they dare not tell Taegon that. *He might become a cripple like me and Gereth,* Amron thought. *Another limper, shambling along.*

A spasm of pain moved through his right thigh, and he winced in his attempt to beat it away, tensing the muscle. Sometimes these waves could last a while, a rhythm of agony that built like an ocean swell before subsiding. He dropped a hand beneath the table, reached forward, and pressed at the place where the Nightblade had cut him to the bone, digging his fingers into the meat, rubbing. The pain was lessened, but barely. The waves came, one and then another, building, and he could feel the heat on his neck, the shimmer of sweat on his brow, a droplet forming, falling, snaking past his eye and down his cheek like a tear. He reached and wiped it away, closing his eyes and clenching his jaw, and at last the pain began to fade, as a retreating tide that would come again, stronger and more furious each time.

"That was a bad one," Artibus observed.

Amron looked to his right and saw that the old man was watching him, as ever he did. He didn't miss much. "I can handle it," the king said. "I must, Artibus. This is a pain I will have to live with soon."

"Yes. Once you hand over the Frostblade, as you claim."

It was not a claim. It was a truth and one Amron Daecar was set in. He nodded.

"And when this happens, what will you do? Without the Frostblade, how do you expect to fight?"

"With another blade. How else?"

Artibus paused to frown at him. "You are being defensive, Amron. I am only asking a question, and a fair one at that. I was referring to your physical state. The Frostblade heals you. Another blade will not. How then will you fight with a limp in your right leg and debilitating pain in your left shoulder?"

The debilitating pain was not limited to his left shoulder. It often centred around his right thigh as well, though there was no point in quibbling over that. "I will bear it as best I can. Why else do you think I leave the Frostblade untouched in private or when in trusted company? I am learning to handle the pain, Artibus. I have told you this already."

The old man continued to study him. "You have told me other things, Amron. For example, you told me that when you dropped the Frostblade during the battle, the pain was so severe that you almost passed out, and that it was all you could do to remain conscious. And you're to tell me you can fight in this state?"

Amron didn't like this conversation. This was not the relaxing dinner he had hoped it would be. *Perhaps I was naive to expect it.* "I'm learning to, yes."

"To bear the pain?"

"Yes."

"And the limp? The poor movement and rotation in your shoulder? How will you combat these….limitations?"

"By fighting ahorse," Amron said. "I'm just as good in the saddle anyway, and there's no steed more fierce than Wolfsbane. Don't forget I bear my blade in my *right* arm." That was a small mercy. Had his bastard son hacked through his right shoulder instead of his left, his fighting days would be all but done.

"That won't be enough if you're under threat of passing out. We must do more to combat the pain and free you to fight without such constraints. I am devising a new potion that will help you. For when the time comes."

Amron did not want to take any potions and tonics, but he knew the old man was right. Without some form of medication, he would be severely limited in battle, and that would not do if he intended to lead. "Fine."

Artibus had a sip of his wine. "We can consider more permanent solutions when the war is over. There are new surgeries we may try. I know you will say they did not work before, but I have come upon a new technique that may yield better results. And failing that, there is the possibility of visiting a seamage also."

"A seamage?" Amron snorted. The old man was clearly desperate. "You don't believe in that sort of thing. Never have."

"A man can change. Times are strange, Amron, and much I never believed before has been proven to be true. I just don't want you to lose hope and do something foolish."

"Meaning?"

"Meaning give your life away needlessly. Sacrifice yourself, thinking there will be no joy for you following the war. You can still live in comfort when it's done. Trust that, Amron, and do not lose hope."

It was too late for that. "You seem to have mistaken me for a reckless man, Artibus." His eyes moved down the table. "You see that young girl there. She is my daughter, I am certain you're aware. Yes, I have much to live for."

Artibus did not enjoy the sarcasm, though took the point, and truly it was starting to feel like a family dinner now with all this bickering. *I ought to be more careful what I wish for in the future*, the king reflected. But he was done with it for now. "I heard you speaking to Gereth of some theory earlier. Only snippets. Perhaps you'd like to share it with me as well?" The old man liked nothing more than regaling others of his theories and Amron hoped it would be enough to divert him.

"Ah, well I'm glad you asked." Artibus's white-whiskered lips pulled up into a wrinkled smile. He sat back, suitably distracted, folded his fingers together across his slim waist and began right into it, proposing to Amron that the world was slowly dying, rotting and decaying from its outer edges inward and that before too long almost nowhere would be inhabitable. The weather events proved it. The heavy rains and flooding in the southern swathes of the continent. The unending snows in the north, called the *End Fall* by Stegra Snowfist and his people. Such events would be unfolding in the southern continent as well, Artibus claimed. Sandstorms, typhoons, tornadoes, blistering and unbearable heatwaves, earthquakes and sinkholes and volcanic eruptions. "It is almost as though we are being driven together," he said, "the walls of the world closing in to force us into conflict. Not just man, but beast as well. How will we all fare when we're fighting to inhabit the same land? What will be left if these snows and rains do not stop?"

Amron had no answer for him but to say, "These events will stop when the war is won. There will be a new dawn."

"A world of harmony," Artibus said, nodding. "North and south combined as one." He pulled on his wispy beard. "I never put much stock in these beliefs of other continents beyond our own, but now…well, perhaps they are worth consideration. There may be other lands that have already suffered the same fate as we are experiencing, cataclysmic wars that have rendered them broken and uninhabitable…or renewed and reborn. The Aramatians say there are paradises out there…along with the battlegrounds. Is that the precipice at which we stand, Amron? To retain our footing and turn back to restore our world…or fall to oblivion, and the ending of it all?"

"It would seem so, Artibus."

The old man nodded, sad and thoughtful. "How sobering to bear witness to these final days. To think this world might perish, where there may be lands of peace and beauty out there, just beyond our fingertips…" He gave a deep sigh. "I wonder…"

A deep powerful rumble interrupted him. A great rending sound that shook the very table at which they sat in a sudden violent shudder. Plates rattled, cutlery clinking and dancing on the wood, chalices toppling, spilling water and wine. At once Amron was on his feet, kicking his chair aside. "Get under the table," he shouted. "Now!"

"Is it an earthquake?" asked Lillia.

"Now," Amron repeated. "Jovyn, get her under. Amara…" He looked at his good-sister, but she was already in motion, tucking herself past the tablecloth. Artibus groaned about his age and did the same, Gereth standing and looking around.

The world shook again, a fierce jolt, and Amron heard one of the serving women scream. He spun to the sound, saw her drop the clay jug she'd been carrying to shatter on the floor, twisting her ankle as she fell. He staggered over, wincing through the pain in his thigh, and helped her up, taking her to a sturdy doorframe as a chandelier came crashing from the high ceiling, shattering right where she'd fallen.

"Thank you, m'lord, thank you, thank you," she breathed. Her eyes were ripe with fear.

Amron held her shoulders. "Stay here. Don't move." He marched back to the table, snatched up the Frostblade and cinched his swordbelt about his waist. Jovyn was climbing out. "No. Stay," Amron commanded. "Stay with them, Jovyn. Gereth, on me."

He marched from the room, his physical strength restored. Rogen Whitebeard was at his place outside the door, fully armoured in his scratched grey steel the colour of smoke, a plain black cloak hanging from the pins at his shoulders. Amron had invited him to join them, but he'd refused. He would not be Rogen Whitebeard if he hadn't. The ranger's eyes were dark. "Drulgar," he said. "You don't think…"

"I don't know." The Frostblade was not swirling as it might if it sensed the Dread approach, and he did not feel that primal thrumming in his veins like last time. More likely Lillia had the answer. "Have there been earthquakes here of late, Gereth?" he asked his cousin.

"Not for long years, no. There have been rumours of others further away, but not here."

Amron turned, marching hastily down the corridor toward the spiral stair that led up to the castle watchtower, *Blacksight* as it was known. It was the highest point in the city, though not so high as it had been. During the battle a dragon had given it a good mauling, and the top third had come tumbling down, but what remained was tall enough. The king picked past the debris on the stairs, the chunks of broken stone and shards of timber, climbing the tight narrow passage until he felt the wind coming down the tunnel, stirring through his hair. It was biting cold, snowflakes capering. He paced briskly to the top where a subfloor had been made into the new tower summit.

Sir Torus Stoutman was there on watch with several others, one stocky leg up on a broken section of wall that had formed a sort of jagged parapet. He wore a heavy fur cloak and his beard draped down his chest like a thick wiry blanket, stirring in the breeze. A rosewood pipe dangled from his lips.

"Torus," Amron said, stepping out to join him.

The dwarfish knight looked over. "Steady on your feet there, Amron. It's a tad unstable up here." His eyes returned to the ranging view. "No sign of the Dread, if you're wondering."

"Where's it coming from?" The ground was still shaking occasionally, though it felt further off now, weaker, somewhere to the southwest if the king was any judge. He clutched the Frostblade, enhancing his sight, the darkness receding, yet the snow still obscured his view. "I can't see anything."

"Earthquakes don't tend to be visible," the knight said to that. "Not certain what you expect to see."

"If it *is* an earthquake." Amron continued to scan, searching for distant shadows, movement, but saw nothing. Only the faint flicker of fires below, the spread of the encampment raised beyond the walls. "Well, keep watching the skies, Torus. If you see anything, blow a long low note. One for dragons. Two for the Dread."

"Aye, will do." The small knight gave his warhorn a tap. For all his diminutive size, he had lungs the size of a blacksmith's bellows and knew just how to use them.

Amron turned to step away again, eager to find out if the tremors had caused any further damage to the city below. Gereth limped at his side to the strains of his walking stick, *clack clack clack*.

They wended down through the castle and into the frozen streets, snow-topped, furrowed with lanes and trenches. The pretty timber shops and inns that clustered shoulder to shoulder either side of every lane were garbed in cloaks of snow, thick and white, and there were icicles dangling from every doorframe and sill. Here and there a building had been burned and scorched by dragonfire during the battle, but those were few. The fires could not catch for most of them, and even when they did, those white cloaks offered protection.

The lanes were thick with soldiers, every tavern occupied to full capacity, private shops and homes given up for the men to sleep in out of the cold. Firelight burned through a thousand windows, and shadows moved through smoky rooms. Gereth called out to the city captains he knew, demanding reports. The tremors had toppled a building or two, and men were quickly sifting through the rubble to save anyone trapped within, but that was the worst of the damage.

They continued down toward the city perimeter, where the fighting had been fiercest. It was a world of blackened stone and tumbled towers, smashed scorpions and broken walls. The barbican was rubble, the gate a twisted heap, and the crenellated fortifications had seen much better days, pitted and scarred from one end to another, where the walls curved to meet the mountains. Some command pavilions had sprung up like mushrooms after rain within the main courtyard, predominantly of the Strand host who arrived first, but for the most part the men were in camp beyond the walls. Outside or inside, it made no matter. The snow was tumbling all the same, a constant barrage that had men shovelling night and day to clear paths and prevent pavilions from being over-whelmed and buried.

"It's not getting any lighter," Gereth observed. "Your friend the Snowfist may be right, Amron. These snows may bury us all."

Amron shook his head. "They weaken further to the south, according to the latest reports." *Where they meet the rains*, he thought. Those too were still refusing to cease. He spared a thought for Lythian, rooted to the ruin of King's Point. By now the city might be all but underwater, the Red Sea rising to swallow it whole.

"I fear we will not be able to stay here long," Gereth went on. "There are too many mouths to feed and our reserves of food are already stretched." It was the subject he'd been trying to dig at all night and now he saw his chance. "Amron, what are you thinking? Will it be the Twin-fort or Varinar, or do you intend to split your strength?"

He had no answer for him just yet. "We are still gathering our dead, Gereth. Once that is done I will make my decision."

"When?"

"Soon. I'll convene a council in the coming days."

He marched away from the discussion, continuing through the tents and trenches, passing a shattered breach and out into the world beyond. The lands here were churned from the fighting, still freckled in corpses, most of them Agarathi. Their own had been gathered to be burned in large part, though some were still being loaded onto the carts and barrows to be heaped and set to the flame on enormous wooden pyres. There were many patches now where dozens of men had been burned at once, leaving behind only charred remains of bone and wood, some still smouldering and sending up trails of smoke.

To the northeast were the camps, raised outside the walls. Amron's own men had taken up there, along with the spillover from the Strand forces and the great militia army under the command of Lord Robert Borrington. They numbered over twenty-five thousand in sum, most of them hailing from the Vandarian northwest, out of Lakeside and Hornhill, Tallfort and Windswatch, even the little towns and villages scattered throughout the Banewood. There were soldiers among them, and watchmen from the cities, hardy mountain men and woodsmen who knew how to hunt and kill…yet for every man who had been taught to fight with sword and spear and axe were half a dozen more used to hoes and nets, hammers and tongs, common men and even women who'd taken up the call to fight.

"We heard all sorts of grim tidings from the south," Lord Robert had told Amron after the battle, when the king summoned him and Stegra Snowfist to his solar. "I gathered the local lords at Northwatch and told them to put out the word to muster whatever able-bodied and fighting men they could. Our plan was to gather at Northwatch and then hurry on down to help defend the western gate…heard whisperings you were heading that way, but you've saved us that journey, Amron." He laughed, as he liked to, smiling all through his story. "Well, then these cursed snows started to fall. Came down hard just as we were assembling at the castle, and then I get word that a pair of my best rangers are coming back from the Weeping Heights. And not alone, I'm told."

The Snowfist had nodded at that, taking up the tale. "It was me," he said, as though Amron hadn't realised that already. "Me and my tribe, for we are *one tribe* now." He proceeded to tell Amron his story. Of the End Fall and the signs; of Verner, now called the Herald, who had seen the Ember of the Red Storm in the skies. That had precipitated a great gathering at the Hall of Orthrand, a holy place to the people of the Icewilds, where the bear titan Orthrand had perished fighting the Dread. The ember was a dragon, Amron found out, and a sign of the Dread's return, as foretold by an ancient woods witch called Shrikna who had observed the great bout many millennia before.

At the conclave, Stegra had persuaded the other tribal leaders to join him and march south, lest they be buried beneath the snows forever. Only the Wild Weepers had refused, and so it came to blood. "Blood-Eye slew Kusto Crowbane," Stegra said, with a snarl. "He was the Wildest Weeper, this Blood-Eye, most hated. I say *was*, because I took off his head for it. For Kusto. I killed Blood-Eye and my men killed many others, but there were more of them who escaped, and hundreds who never answered my summoning. If they have stayed in the mountains, they will be dead, or will die soon. But I fear not, Lord of Daecar. These Wildest Weepers may be ugly and cruel but they are not stupid. They will have gathered under a new leader and crossed south, into your lands. Here, they will do as they do best."

Rape, pillage, murder, steal. Amron didn't need to be told. It was yet another problem he could do without. "How many tribespeople do you have, Stegra?" the king had asked him.

The big Snowskin dug fingers into his huge white beard, scratching. "Numbers...I do not know numbers. Some died during the journey across the mountains. From the cold. From snowslides and rockfalls. A few were taken by Weepers and there were some creature attacks as well. The creatures, Steel Lord...they left like we did, to flee the snow. Many will be prowling these lands now. It is the old world, awakening. A world we tribesfolk know."

Amron knew that all too well. He pressed the man on the numbers again and the makeup of his host.

"Thousands. There are thousands of us, Lord of Daecar, that is all I know. Or is that King of Daecar now? Steel *King*, should I be calling you?"

"Call me what you wish, Stegra. I am still the same man you knew."

"No, you are bigger now. A bigger man, wearing many cloaks. Cloak of father to your girl, yes, and champion to your people. Cloak of lord and cloak of king and I hear whispers of cloak of saviour too." He smiled and went on before Amron could deny it. "We are many tribes made one, and each tribe has its leader...but above them all I stand as the one who brought them together." He listed the rest of them out all the same. "The Crowmen are led by Narek, son of Tarek, who was killed by the Ember when it attacked our camp at Orthrand's bones. A great many died there, but at last we drove the Ember away. This was done mostly by the Stone Men, and their leader Hraka the Great. He proved this name that day. His spear was the one that hit the Ember in his neck. A powerful throw it was, Steel King. You have seen these Stone Men. Many make you and I look like children." And he laughed.

Then he went on. "The Deadcloaks are ruled by Black Merryl, of Shrikna's blood her people say. She helped to drive away the Ember as well, with her sorcery. She is a powerful creature, that woman...and will make a powerful ally, or a dangerous foe. I am still unsure of which. The Mole men less so. They are small and afraid. And the people of the Scar as well...the river folk. They are timid also."

"And the men of the western shores?" Amron had asked him. He had recognised their whale-bone clubs and shark-tooth swords and spears, the cloaks of sealskin they wore.

"Yes, these ones came as well, in large numbers," the big tribal leader said. "The Walrus Lord was their master, but he died in the mountains." He shook his head. "A great loss. He was old...as old as you and I combined, and then add a little more. He wanted to see his hundredth year, but a landslide took him and many of his kin. It was a bitter day, yet the Walrus was slowing us. His death may have saved others, in the end. This is the truth of it."

Amron allowed a short silence in respect of his loss, then asked, "Who leads them now?"

"His grandson. One of many of them. This one they have raised up with the name of Orca Lord. They all have different names, these lords of the coast. Walrus suited the Walrus Lord, for his size and great moustache. And Orca suits this new one. He is a killer, King of Daecar. Cunning and cold. You will see. Soft spoken, but ruthless. And ambitious, yes, ambitious."

"In what way?"

"Your way. You steel men, with your lands and honours. He likes this way. He wants lands and honours too."

"If he serves me well, he'll have them."

Stegra's eyes narrowed. "We respect you, King of Daecar, but our service is to ourselves. We will fight with you, not for you." He looked at Borrington. "I have told him this."

Lord Robert confirmed it. "He has. The tribespeople are quite adamant they not be under any obligation to follow orders, Amron. Certainly not from me."

Nor me, it would seem. Amron addressed the Snowfist again. "We are of the same purpose, Stegra. I would be honoured to have you as our ally. But the command of the tribespeople will remain yours."

The Snowfist dipped his head. "You are a brother to us, King of Daecar. A brother. And brothers fight together." He closed a fist. "Now, I must return to them. There are men to burn and shelters to raise and sickmilk to drink. This most importantly. Do you remember sickmilk, Steel King?"

Amron smiled. "Not fondly."

"Well, you must come and drink with us. The other leaders wish to speak with you." He took his shoulder and shook him. "When you have a chance."

"I'll come soon," Amron promised.

Stegra had nodded gruffly and stamped toward the door, leaving Amron and Robert Borrington alone. For the next hour they discussed the war. Robert told Amron more of the troubles he'd faced in the north. Many beasts had prowled out of the Weeping Heights, he'd said, picking off villagers and travellers on the road. "But they're getting bolder, Amron," he'd told him, drinking deep of a cup of wine. "Gods be good, they might even be working together, some of them. Leastways that's what it sounds like from the stories."

Amron listened to them. It was all more of the same. A battleground, that was the sum of it, a world terraforming back into the hellscape that Agarath and his puppet Eldur wanted to make it. He ground his jaw as he listened, wishing only that he could muster all his strength and march south. Perhaps now he could, with this new militia? Did they have the numbers here? Might they take the fight to the enemy, cross the Brindle Steppe and the Tidelands and march right up to Eldur's door?

He put the notion aside. They had won a great victory here, but this was no time to be reckless. *We must consolidate*, he thought. *And count our losses.* Now, two days later, he was thinking the same thing. Consolidation, not confrontation. *Be Ayrin the Wise, not Amron the Bold*, he told himself. *He was always the better king.*

There seemed little disruption beyond the walls from the rumbling felt a little earlier. Amron strode out across the battlefield, Gereth limping at his side. The stink of death was growing ripe, though the cold did enough to spare them the worst of it. Men were heaping a barrow nearby, picking through the Agarathi dead to find some of their own. Amron went up to them and drew their attention. "That rumbling just now. Did you see anything?"

They were some of Lord Strand's men, common soldiers, and young. "No m'lord…nothing," said one, blinking up at him. Another was staring at the Frostblade and two more were just gaping.

"None of you?" Amron asked them.

They shook their heads, silent. The first one spoke again. "It were a quake, we all thought. Felt like one, m'lord, an earthquake, so it were." He pointed to one of the gaping men. "Bratson said there were a quake up north, some months ago. On Lord Strand's lands. Said it felt the same."

The youth called Bratson was a pimply lad. There was one particularly large group of carbuncles to the right of his long sniffly nose. He gave the nose a wipe and said, "Aye, m'lord, felt similar, it did… though…"

"Though?"

"Well." He scratched at that area of pimples with a gloved finger. "Last time it were more…more constant, like. Worse at first, then better, if you follow me?" He scrunched his face up, searching for the right word. "Rhythmic. That's it. Was a rhythm to it. This was all over the place. Felt like something big moving. Burrowing, even. Underground, like."

Amron rubbed his chin. He'd had that sense as well. "Thank you, Bratson." He gave them a nod and walked out a little further, Gereth still with him, Rogen Whitebeard keeping several paces behind. Soon enough they were beyond the carts and corpse-gatherers, out where there was no fire or light. Only darkness reigned before them. A troubling darkness that felt more dangerous than ever before. Once, Amron had known what lurked in his kingdom, but now that wasn't the case.

"I want a scouting party arranged," he said. He gestured for Whitebeard to come forward. "Rogen, gather your best men and search for the source of these tremors. Take Sir Quinn with you, and a strong host of men-at-arms. There are still thousands of Agarathi unaccounted for out there and I'd prefer you travel with an escort."

"Scouts don't need an escort," the ranger rasped. "But if that's your command…"

"It is." Amron looked out into that thick impenetrable darkness. "You can muster them to leave at daybreak. In this light you'd only risk falling upon some unseen peril."

"As you say, my lord."

There was nothing else to be said. Amron wrapped his fingers around the Frostblade, listening to the faint hissing whispers of Vandar's shattered heart. Oft as not he could perceive the approach of dragons in those whispers, and sometimes the coming of some other malevolent force. Yet somewhere deep within the blade he felt only the whisper of approval, and excitement, of some other force rising, a force perhaps allied to their cause.

Something is stirring out there, the king thought. And he suspected he knew what it was.

5

Lythian

Lythian woke sharply, eyes widening, memories flooding his mind in a sudden violent surge.

He tried to sit up, felt the pain flare in the small of his back, and gasped, flopping back down. A hand came to touch his shoulder. "Easy, my lord. Take it easy now."

He blinked, vision clearing, and the seamed old face of Ralf of Rotting Bridge came into view, standing over him. There were others in the tent, a large tent, not his own, a blur of movement and noise all about him. He glimpsed beds, stretchers, men bleeding, dying. Sir Storos Pentar was crouched over a figure nearby, his red cloak and silver armour spattered in mud and blood. Daylight leaked in through the tent flaps, wan and sickly, the rains still falling outside. They swayed open as another man was brought within, moaning loudly, the lower part of his left leg cut off and wrapped in linen, blood dripping from the sodden bandaging.

Lythian swallowed, his throat dry as bone. There was a fearsome ache at the back of his head and his jaw was throbbing. He reached up, felt the cut, the blood. He recalled being tripped as he fled through the back of his tent, the cobbles rushing up to smack his chin. The boot that came down on his back, pressing, the savage impact at the base of his skull. Sir Symon Steelheart's voice, hissing in his ear. *You've had your day, Lindar. But it's over. And you're done.*

He'd feared it was true. That he'd never wake again. But he had. *I'm alive.*

He reached up and gripped Sir Ralf's slim arm. "The Sword of Varinar. The blade, Ralf. *Where is it?*"

The old man shook his head, easing him back down. "You need to rest. You're badly concussed, and your back…"

"*Where,* Ralf?" he demanded, raising his voice. Pain flared in his head, spots dancing in his vision. He blinked, fighting to stay conscious. "Just…just tell me. Tell me where it is, Ralf." His heart rate was soaring, smashing at his chest. "Where….I need…I need to…to know…"

And then darkness rushed in from the edges of his sight and the old man's face was gone.

When he woke again the world was quieter.

Voices murmured about him, low grunts and groans of pain, men whispering as they stood and moved about the wounded, doctors and healers inspecting. Firelight glowed from braziers, shadows pooling in between. Another shadow lurked closer, right beside him. Lythian moved his eyes. A man sat on a camp stool next to his bed, hunched forward, jaw clenched. "Sir Oswin's dead," he said, in a dark voice. "Those bastards…they cut him down when he tried to stop them. I'll kill them all…all of them, Lythian. *Cowards*. They're treacherous cowards, every one."

Lythian tried to clear his throat to speak, but his mouth was too dry. Sir Storos noticed, reached out and took up a cup of water. "Here. Let me help." He lifted his head gently and dribbled the water through Lythian's parched, cracked lips.

"How long…" he began to rasp. "Since…"

"Three days," Storos Pentar said. "The doctors say you'll be fine. In time. But you need to rest. There's no permanent damage to your back."

"I've rested enough." Lythian grimaced as he shifted to sit up, his back stiff, head fuzzy. There was a tension about his head; a bandage, he realised. The cut on his chin had been stitched shut, the wound tender. A grimace warped his face. *Three days. It's been three days*. "What happened, Storos? That night. There was fighting…I heard…"

"Deserters," Storos grunted. "Hundreds of them, all at once." He spoke bitterly, spitting the words out. "Seems Sir Fitz Colloway was more well-liked than we thought. Or else they just used his execution as a reason to go. Either way, they left. Almost all the Rosetree men under Colloway's command, and some others too; Barrows, others from lesser houses, freeriders, some feckless sellswords. The men you posted weren't enough to stop them, and we came to blows." His eyes moved darkly through the pavilion. "A few dozen of our own died. Twice as many of theirs. I'd hoped Oswin might pull through, but…"

"So he…"

"Died by the hand of *deserters*," Storos growled. "He was too good for that. He didn't deserve it, Lythian. That man had earned a noble death and some Rosetree cur shoved a dirk in the back of his neck. Where is the justice in that, I ask you? Where?" The grief was plain in his eyes.

Justice, Lythian thought. *Justice. Vengeance*. His dreams had been dark and vivid as he slept. The harbinger of dread and doom, hunting deserters for their crimes, a shadowed menace, merciless, unrelenting…

He shifted to sit up straighter, moving his legs over the edge of the bed to plant his bare feet on the floor. The motion made him feel nauseous. He took a few deep breaths to steady himself, picked up the water cup and drank some more. He had thought Storos was referring to others when he said Oswin Cole had tried to stop them…to Sir Brontus and Symon Steelheart and their band of treasonous thieves, but clearly not. He needed to know at once what had happened to them. Another breath, deep and long, to make sure he would not pass out again. Then he asked the question. "Where is the Sword of Varinar, Storos? Did Brontus escape with it?"

"*Oloran.*" The man's features twisted in disgust. "So *that's* who it was. We all suspected so."

Lythian frowned. It was not the response he'd hoped for. "No one caught him? Even *saw* him?"

Storos shook his head. "The fighting proved a distraction. And the storm. It was fearsome that night. No doubt Oloran chose his timing wisely. He may have been lying in wait for days, hiding." He narrowed his gaze, centred it on Lythian. "What do you plan to do?"

"Go after him." Lythian stood, regretted it, and sat back down. Another wave of nausea washed over him, his stomach cramping from lack of food. He breathed in, out, in again.

"I'm not sure you're well enough yet," Storos observed. "Ralf said this would be your reaction. And that I was to tell you to do nothing rash if you woke."

"Rash? Doing nothing *is* doing something rash, Storos. I *have* to retrieve that blade, as well you know." He did not need to tell the knight why; he knew well enough what was at stake. "Has anyone gone out to hunt for a trail, at least?"

Storos gave an indecisive nod. "Efforts have been made, though they've yielded nothing of value. With all the desertions it's been hard to keep track, and hundreds more have left over the last two nights. I fear to say it, Lythian, but after three days Oloran could be anywhere. With all the chaos out there, finding him…"

"Is not a choice," Lythian cut in. "It's a need and an obligation." His gut was a nest of twisting snakes. He had failed, and was sick with shame. *I had one duty. One purpose. I was meant to guard that blade…and I failed.*

He would not let it end like this.

"Summon Ralf to my tent," he told Storos Pentar. "And Lord Rodmond as well. I'll need food, Storos. Bread, cheese, salted meat. For now and the days ahead. See that I'm well provisioned."

He did not wait to hear the knight's response. Rising, he steadied his feet and staggered out into the rain.

There were several guards on duty outside, Sir Adam's men of the Pointed Watch, those who had remained loyal to Lythian's command as the rest began to turn against him. Two stood at either side of the flaps, a few others taking cover beneath canvas awnings or sitting on stools with their spears resting beside them, sharpening blades and conversing in murmurs. They stood to attention as they saw Lythian pass through, giving out mutters of, 'M'lord' as he went. They all looked at him with dubious eyes as though unsure whether they should try to stop him. Most likely Ralf and Adam had commanded that they do just that, but if any of them had a mind to try, the look on Lythian's face made them doubt it.

He laboured on through the yard, moving stiffly past the sagging tents of deserted knights and lords. Water pooled in their canvas roofs and some had collapsed into heaps of wood and tarp, half submerged in growing puddles. The rain was falling heavily, tumbling down from a sky as black as a raven's wing, moonless, starless, a sky without light or warmth. The water soaked through his robes, his hair, his bandages, chilling him to the bone, but it was bracing. The cold gave relief to the ache in his back, the deep bruising in the flesh either side of his spine.

They could have killed me, he thought, as he went. He remembered how Brontus had said he didn't want him dead, that they had served for many years together and that was never his intent, that he had come only for the blade. *They spared my life, and were merciful,* he reflected, *even Steelheart and that big bearded one too.* Brontus had staggered off with the Sword of Varinar by then and they might just as easily have made sure he never woke up. *But they didn't. They let me live, the fools. They think I'm still Lythian, noble Knight of the Vale. They do not know what I have become...*

He closed a fist, knuckles whitening. They would not live to regret it.

No guards were on duty at his tent. He passed inside, turning his eyes around. It was cold, the braziers unlit, the wind blowing through the tear in the rear wall where he'd cut through the canvas to escape. The table had been put back in its proper place after that burly bearded brute had thrown it aside, and the chest in which he'd kept the Sword of Varinar was still open, nothing within it but shadow and shame.

His armour and weapons were set on his mannequin, misting in the gloom. He stepped over and took the hilt of his dagger, felt his blood-bond ignite, the warmth and strength flood through him. He sighed from the relief it gave him, the sensation of power, driving away some of the stiffness in his back, the throbbing ache that pounded in his head. There was still wine on the sideboard table, perhaps the same sour stuff he'd been drinking that night. He gulped a cup, and another, to help dull the pain, then set about dressing in his armour, pulling on his padded under-clothes and fastening his godsteel plate, sliding the segments together, sealing his frail flesh from the dangers of the world.

He was almost done when the flaps drew aside and old Ralf stepped within, dressed in his worn leathers and cloak with the rotting bridge of his house stitched in fraying thread. He took one look at Lythian and shook his head. "This is folly. You're weak as a kitten, Lythian. Stop and think. You'll do no good to anyone dead."

"I don't intend on dying."

"You didn't intend on losing the Sword of Varinar either. But you did."

Lythian paused in his dressing. "You would scold me for that?"

The old man checked his words and shook his head. "No. It was not your fault, but…"

"It was," Lythian told him. "Where else does the blame lie if not with me? I let down my guard, even when I knew I had enemies here, and paid for it."

"You *had* guards. Two of them. Two of Sir Adam's best, but they were outmatched and overwhelmed." Ralf gestured to two bloodstained patches on the plank floor. "They were killed before they could raise the alarm, their murder masked by the storm. Sir Brontus," he said, shaking his head. "You could not have known that he…"

"I *should* have known. I should have slept in my armour that night, and been ready. I should not have drowned my misery in five cups of wine, Ralf. I made mistakes, and now the blade is gone." He took his swordbelt, girding his waist, the familiar weight of blade and dagger on opposing hips giving him comfort. Something stirred in him, some excitement to be leaving. "I'm going to go out there and bring it back. And seek justice against those who took it."

For once Sir Ralf looked his age, the skin sagging about his eyes, thin wrinkles branching out. His gaze was tired, pleading. "Lythian, see sense. In time the blade will be retrieved, but it does not have to be you. When Elyon comes back…"

"I cannot put that burden on him. This is my duty, Ralf."

"And your duty here? To the men. Amron left you in command of this army."

"A role another can fulfil. Sir Adam has the loyalty of the Pointed Watch and Brockenhurst men. The rest are Taynar banners, under the command of Lord Barrow and Lord Rodmond. I'm not needed."

"Lord Barrow is unwell. His cough…it has taken a bad turn and laid the lord low. He is abed and there are fears he may die…"

"Along with thousands of others," Lythian said. He had a flash of memory, of Lord Barrow looking at him as he collected the Sword of Varinar from his chest that night. That look. Was he part of it? Did he tell Brontus Oloran where it would be and how to get it? He could not say for sure and that was one reason he wanted to go. He could not take it anymore, the doubt and paranoia, never knowing friend from foe. Lythian Lindar was not built for this world of shadows and lies. "Lord Rodmond can take command of his men if Barrow dies," he went on. "He is the senior lord in any case. A greatlord, Ralf. I will not be missed."

"You will. By many you will."

Lythian valued the old knight greatly, appreciated his counsel, but in this he would not be turned. "I trust you will help Rodmond when I'm gone, as you have me?" He did not wait for the man to respond; he knew he would do what was needed. Turning, Lythian went to fetch a cloak from a hook. It was not his First Blade cloak, but a plain mantle of brown wool, warmer and waterproofed. It suited him better. He had never truly been First Blade, after all. "I suppose the curse is real," he said, once the cloak was fixed in place. "That blade leads to nothing good. Amron, Vesryn, Dalton, now me. It makes cripples and corpses of us all. I will ensure the same is true of Brontus."

Ralf of Rotting Bridge closed his tired eyes and sighed. "And if he has learned to wield it? Sir Brontus Oloran is a brilliant swordsman. With the Sword of Varinar he will be lethal."

"Then I'd best track him down before he becomes too proficient," Lythian said. "And enough of the sir. He is no knight anymore."

A shadow moved outside and the flaps swayed open to admit Lord Rodmond of House Taynar with Sir Storos trailing in behind him bearing a bag of provisions. He set it down at Lythian's feet. "Enough for two," he said. "If you're to leave, I'm coming with you."

Lythian Lindar was opposed to it. He shook his head at once. "I would sooner be alone. There is no sense in you risking yourself as well, Storos. You're a fine swordsman and can still contribute to the war."

"I'll contribute by helping you get that blade back. It's critical, you said it yourself. And besides, I've had enough of this cursed ruin. We'll be safer as a three."

Lythian looked at him flatly. "Three? And who is the third?"

"Nathaniel. He's packing a bag as we speak."

"Tell him to unpack it. Nathaniel is Brontus's cousin. If it comes to a clash of steel, I cannot trust him to act." He shook his head, adamant. "And I might remind you that he is a traitor and an oathbreaker besides. He has done well to restore his honour, yes, but that is a stain that cannot be so easily washed away. A man with that weakness inside him is at risk of relapsing."

Sir Ralf interjected. "I see the value in it. Nathaniel has worked both tirelessly and without complaint ever since he entered your service. He is a gifted swordsman, courteous and dependable. If you are indeed set on this path, you will need such men to help defend you. He may even be able to talk his cousin down. Who better than kin to make a man see sense?"

No, Lythian thought. There was no sense in Brontus Oloran anymore. He needed no one, wanted no one, with him. Yet he knew that they would not be swayed by his words, and so he only nodded and said, "Fine. Have it your way if you must. We'll leave at daybreak, Storos, the three of us. How long until the dawn?"

"Four hours, give or take," Ralf answered, looking at him with a squint. "The haste with which you've dressed in your armour, Lythian...one might think you were about to leave at once."

This old man misses nothing. He shook his head. "I was caught unarmored once, and will not be caught again. I'll remove it once I have the Sword of Varinar back in my possession, and not a moment sooner." He moved his eyes to Storos again. "Get some sleep and tell Nathaniel to do the same. Ralf, you're well acquainted with the remaining horses here. Choose three of good breeding, strong and swift. We would be better travelling by horseback and must assume Brontus will be doing the same."

"That would seem likely," the old knight said. "How many did he have with him? Were you able to take a count?"

"There were four that I saw," Lythian said, scowling as he remembered. "Oloran, Steelheart, and two others I didn't know. I killed one, as you'll have seen. There were more outside. How many I couldn't say. A handful, I would guess. Brontus would want to travel quick and light."

"He'll make for Elinar," Lord Rodmond declared confidently. "His lord uncle Penrith has always yearned for a First Blade in the family, same as my grandfather did. He'll be protected there."

Storos disagreed. "Penrith Oloran is at death's door and might already be feeding the worms for all we know. I doubt Brontus would take that risk. He'll find somewhere safe to hide while he trains and then go out and seek acclaim. He'll want to kill dragons, not cower from them. This is about Varin's Table. He's trying to secure himself a good afterlife, seeing that the world is ending."

"Varin doesn't look fondly on traitors, Sir Storos," old Ralf said to that. "Though that's not to say that Brontus considers himself a traitor. More a liberator of the blade. He believes himself to be its rightful bearer, and has sought justice by taking it back. There is a parallel here with Prince Elyon and your uncle Dalton," he said to Rodmond. "To most, Elyon's heist of the Windblade was just, but not all. Some considered it theft, a dishonourable act. In the end it is a matter of perspective. I have little doubt that Sir Brontus believes he is doing the right thing."

Lythian ground his jaw, misliking the notion there, though he could not deny the point. "The same can be said of most betrayers and usurpers and wrongdoers. That Brontus's sense of probity is skewed and warped will not save him."

"No," agreed Sir Ralf. "I am not suggesting it will. Yet without a first crumb to follow, where do you intend to start?"

Lythian had a vague thought on that, though didn't share it. "We will learn more when we go upriver," he simply said. "Whether to Elinar or elsewhere, he will have gone north from here, to escape the rains. Someone will have seen him. We'll find a crumb beyond this ruin."

Speaking of crumbs reminded Lythian that he still had not eaten. He would get to that in a moment, but first he looked at Rodmond. "I'm told Lord Barrow is abed with a cough."

"Alas yes. He is bringing up blood, I regret to say. Even Lord Warton looks at him with pity. Should it become any worse he will likely perish."

"So Ralf told me. A shame." He spoke without tone or caring. "I trust you'll lead his men in his absence, Lord Taynar?"

"I will do my best. With luck King Daecar will return here soon. Or some other relief will come. I have wondered if we might retreat to Crosswater, given these rains. Soon enough the entire coast will be underwater."

Lythian would leave it to them to puzzle that out. He was done with it. *Done.* As Steelheart had said. "My lords, if I may ask for some privacy. I must eat and take some more rest. Please, see to your duties. If any fresh reports should materialise by dawn, we can discuss them before we leave."

"I'll go ask some more questions," said Storos. The way he said it made it clear they would not be spoken gently. "Someone knows where Oloran went, I'm sure of it. A few broken fingers might have them talking."

"Make sure they're not their sword hands," Lythian said. "They may still need to fight." Elsewise he had no problem with it. "Go."

They left, though Sir Ralf lingered for a final word. "Who do you want to perform the executions when you're gone? There are some wounded men, attempted deserters… they are being kept alive only to be killed at the right time. By you, we thought, once you were strong enough. Though now…"

"Let their commanding officers take on the duty. As is done at a thousand towns and castles across the north. I bore that burden long enough, Ralf. And spare me the judging eyes. I feel guilty enough as it is." He waved him away, and the old man bowed and left.

Lythian refilled his cup of wine, drinking to the bitter dregs, then dug into the bag Storos Pentar had brought. He filled his stomach with meat and cheese, then removed half the contents, lightening the load, tucking the bag beneath the folds of his cloak and stepping out into the rain. The darkness veiled his journey toward the River Gate, where he found some more of Sir Adam's men on duty. "Fetch me a strong horse. I wish to visit with Vilmar the Black."

It was done without question. Only those doubtful eyes, glancing at one another.

"I will be back within the hour, if anyone should ask," he told them. "Watch for my return." That ought to hold them a while.

He climbed into the saddle of the jet black gelding they'd given him, an ageing beast but hale and swift, a good match for him, and kicked the spurs.

Beyond the gate, the lands were more waterlogged than ever, the mires deep and thick and treacherous. He took a wide route around the worst of the bogs, the hooves of his horse splashing and sucking as he went, the lights of the broken city dwindling at his back. Soon enough the roar of the Steelrun River could be heard, thrashing down from the north, strengthened by a thousand swollen channels. When last he'd come three days ago, the night of the theft, the bridge had been clotted with debris and runoff, but tonight he found it clear. He hastened over the planks, the water rushing up past his horse's fetlocks, crossing to the other side and into the woods.

The old huntsman was in his usual place, sitting by the fire fletching arrows. "You again," he said, without looking up. That was always Vilmar's way; he'd likely heard Lythian coming a mile off. "You don't usually visit on a horse."

"I have need of one tonight."

"That iron I smell in the air?" The man's scarred nose wrinkled and his dark eyes moved to observe him. "Aye. Nasty gash. Cut yourself shaving did you?"

Lythian ignored the remark. He'd not come for pithy banter. "I see the gruloks cleared the bridge, as I asked."

"Well spotted. Guess whoever did that to you left your eyes intact. What happened?"

"The Sword of Varinar was taken." Even saying it…giving it voice. His anger flared, and his shame along with it. "It was stolen from my tent."

The huntsman sat back and put the arrow aside. "Aye. Thought as much." He thumbed behind him. "This lot. Fair few of them been looking out north. Don't usually do that. It's south and west they look. Not north."

That confirmed Brontus's direction, at least. The gruloks were drawn to the Blades of Vandar, so often looked west toward the city, where the Sword of Varinar was being kept. South was where their enemy lay; Eldur, Drulgar, Agarath, so they liked to look that way as well. "Do they know how far it's gone?"

"I haven't asked."

"Can you?" Lythian stared at him. "This is important, Vilmar."

"I can see that." He stood on thick strong legs, an old bull of a man, wrapped up all in black with a beard as tough as wire coiling densely about his weathered face. "So, who stole it? One of these lordlings who's been plaguing you, was it?"

"Brontus Oloran," Lythian said.

"I know that one. Watched him lose to Dalton Taynar that day at Crosswater. Still sour about that, is he?"

"Sour enough to commit treason." Lythian looked into the trees. "Is Hruum awake this time?"

"Far as I know."

"Good." Lythian swung a leg and dismounted, tying his gelding to the branch of a tree so he did not wander off. "Take me to him."

The huntsman was infuriatingly truculent most of the time, but for once he made no complaint. "Come, then." He led him through his little camp, the cookfire, hammock, chopping block he used to hack up meat. Beyond the line of trees the gruloks were spread out across a wide area, most sleeping, indiscernible from boulders until they moved. Several were standing, still and straight as if they were carved rock figures, looming over twenty feet tall, shadows in the night. Two of them were gazing in a northerly direction, where the woods thickened along the eastern shores of the river. Some others were gazing out south, to the sea.

But Hrumm was looking right at him.

The grulok captain's eyes were small, primordial, like tiny chips of ice, clear blue, shining from that giant rock face. Blunt features gave the vague expression of man; craggy chin, a sloped wedge of nose and ridge of brow, a small and narrow mouth. The head rested upon a stumpy neck which spread into a thick body, shorter in the leg than the arm, which trailed almost to the ground. The gruloks all shared the same general form, but as with men some were taller, others broader, some more thin where others were more stout, and where some had weapons carved from the rock of their limbs, others bore weapons in their three-fingered grasp.

Hruum had both. His right arm took the form of a long savage spear; in his left he held the godsteel greatsword that Amron had given him, a huge blade seven feet long, edges misting, yet no more than a shortsword in his grasp. *A Bladeborn grulok*, Lythian thought. *How many of these will it take to bring down the Dread?*

He bent his back into a low bow, as he knew to do, showing respect. Hruum watched him all the while, judging. There was a frame to his face, a slight twist to that ledge of brow. *He is disappointed in me*, Lythian knew. *I was weak, I failed, and he can smell it.* "My lord. I have a question, if I may?"

Hruum's head dipped, just slightly, to the sound of grinding stone. A rumbling noise echoed from his chest.

"The Sword Varinar…as you know it is no longer here, in the city. Someone has stolen it from my safekeeping and I need to find out where." He glanced to the pair of gruloks looking north. "Can you judge its distance from this location?"

The captain's eyes were unblinking, impenetrable. He stared a long while and then rumbled, "Far," in his rockfall voice.

"Far," Lythian repeated. "Do you know *how* far, Hruum?"

Hruum stared at him. He did not give answer.

Vilmar spoke in his stead. "He won't answer that," the huntsman growled. "They don't know distance like we do. Like time, it means nothing to them. Might be ten miles or a hundred or a thousand for all we know."

"The first of those, let's hope," Lythian said. He looked at Hruum again, gesturing to the north-facing gruloks. "This direction they're look-ing. Is the Sword of Varinar directly in that path?"

The captain's ridge-brow twisted a fraction lower, and he nodded. Some words rumbled from his primal aperture-mouth, but Lythian could not understand them. He turned to Vilmar, hoping he did.

"He says the blade's out there," the huntsman confirmed. He looked up through the canopy; above, the skies were still deep black and starless. "No stars to guide you," he grunted. "Shame. Though perhaps you shouldn't have let the blade be stolen in the first place."

"I brought this on myself. I know." Lythian did not care for these reprimands. He logged the vague direction of travel from the gruloks, judging it to be north by northwest, into the Wandering Wood. There were ten thousand places to hide in there, the forest comprised of a hundred separate swathes of woodland over a vast land of valleys and hills. If they were looking to hide, as Storos claimed, they could do a lot worse. And if they were making for Elinar, and the safe harbour of Lord Penrith's keep, they were heading in the right direction for that as well.

It gave him somewhere to start. A crumb, at least, to follow.

"I should go," he said. It was not his intention to stay here long or let Brontus Oloran extend his lead. "I take it the gruloks have made no move to follow?"

"Follow Oloran? No. They're drawn to the blades, aye, but *honour* too. That knave's got none of that."

He did once, Lythian reflected sadly. *Before that blade cursed him like it did me.* "Stand fast here, Vilmar. Watch the seas as you've been doing, and if you see any dragons…"

"Hruum says the big one's awoken," the huntsman broke in. "That lot looking south. They're waiting for him. He'll be coming back soon."

Lythian's heart gave a powerful thud. A cold ripple slithered up his spine. "*Here?*"

"North. Mayhaps south as well. Far as I can figure it, that big one's got a few scores to settle. So does Hruum. He fought him once himself, he says. During the old wars. Might be five thousand years ago now, more even. Eight, ten. Makes you feel small, doesn't it?"

"Insignificant," Lythian agreed, looking at Hruum, trying to imagine the giant of rock and rage battling the Dread with his kin. He had seen Drulgar in the flesh, and big as the gruloks were, they were tiny against his bulk. *How many?* he wondered again. *How many to take him down?* There were more than twenty of them here now. *Would that be enough to defeat him?*

He gave the grulok a parting bow, grateful for what small help he had given, and turned to move back through the trees and into Vilmar's camp. The gelding was munching on some wet grass at the base of an oak. Lythian patted his neck and untied the rope, then climbed up into the saddle. He looked down to find that Vilmar the Black was stuffing items into a bag, swinging it onto his back, fixing his waist with his weapons belt, fitted with axe and dagger and flaying knife. "What are you doing?" Lythian asked him, as the huntsman took up his bow and quiver, plucking up a sheaf of arrows, fletched and unfletched, and dropping them inside.

"What's it look like? I'm coming with you."

"No," Lythian said at once. "You have to stay with the gruloks. If you leave…"

"They're smarter than you think," Vilmar cut in. "They're not going anywhere, and I'll grow roots if I sit here any longer. You're sick of that ruin? I'm sick of this camp. I need a hunt, Lythian, and you're going to give me one." He swung his quiver over his shoulder and looked up at him. "No arguments. You're a knight, not a tracker, and you'll never find them without me." He slid out his blade and picked at his teeth, flicking away a bit of bone. "How many we after, anyhow?"

"I don't know. Three, at least. More likely several times that number."

"Good. The more men, the bigger the trail. Three days, was it?"

Lythian nodded.

"Then we'd best get moving. And don't get too attached to that horse. It's not going to last too long in there."

The huntsman said nothing more. Swinging about in his great black cloak, he stalked away into the dark of the trees.

Lythian sighed and followed.

6

Amara

Amara Daecar had spent time with many odd people in her past, but this particular group might just be the queerest of them all.

She looked around the animal skin pavilion, not quite sure who was the most interesting. The barrel-chested giant with the bone armour and huge rock club? The beak-nosed raven of a man with the cloak of crow feathers and greasy black hair? Perhaps it was the wild-haired woods witch with the moss-green eyes who wore a dark mantle of many-coloured pelts stitched together from a dozen different creatures? Or the tall, quiet, dreadfully handsome man with the hard narrow gaze and black-and-white whale-hide armour made from the skin of an orca that he had slain with his very own spear, or so she had heard.

Truly any of them might have cause to claim the title, but the most arresting was surely the Snowfist himself. His skin alone was astonishing, almost translucent in its quality, and the snow-white mane and bushy thicket of beard only made him all the more prepossessing. Amara found his snow-bear cloak rather dashing as well, she had to admit.

"He is a fearsome-looking fellow, isn't he?" she whispered to Sir Connor Crawfield as they stood at the side, observing.

"Indeed," the knight said, stiffly. "The hood grants him a menacing aspect, my lady."

That hood had been made from the head of the bear he'd killed, a roaring maw that encircled his face complete with fangs jutting down past his temples. "He is a menacing fellow, Connor. A nightmare to his enemies, a dream to his friends. That sort of fellow. The sort we very much need."

Sir Connor nodded. "I am told he has some Bladeborn blood. And his son as well."

"That is typically how bloodlines work, Connor." The son was named Svaldar, Amara knew, though he was absent from this gathering. Only the appointed tribal leaders had come, so they might meet with the

Vandarian king and get the measure of the man they were allied to. Amara's presence was purely out of curiosity. She had requested she be allowed to observe from the side, and Amron in his great generosity had permitted it. *Or more likely he didn't want to come alone.* The king was not entirely comfortable in this company, it seemed to her, and looked rather keen to get it done.

Right now he was being urged to have a drink of sickmilk. "You said you would, King of Daecar, so you will," declared the Snowfist forcefully. "He drank much of our sickmilk when he travelled with us," he told the others. "He pretends he does not like it, but he does. Do not believe him. He is a liar, yes, a liar!"

The woods witch called Black Merryl sniffed at that. She had a haunting, whispery quality to her voice that made the hair on the back of Amara's neck stand on end. "We should not be allying ourselves to a liar, Stegra. We were told this man was noble."

"He is, yes, he is very noble, Merryl. The noblest of all the noblemen in this land of the noble steel lords. He lies only about his liking for sickmilk. The rest he says is truth, yes. All else is truth that passes his lips."

Amron smiled uncomfortably. "I consider myself an honest man, my lady," he said to the witch.

"Lady?" Stegra gave a hoot of laughter. "We do not use these terms, King of Daecar. I told you this already. Lord. Lady. No. She is Black Merryl. Or just Merryl, sometimes, with her friends." He grinned at the witch. "We are very good friends, Merryl and the Snowfist. The Witch and the Fist they call us."

Amara doubted that anyone called them that, based on the blank look the woman gave him. "Black Merryl will do, Lord Daecar. But if you lapse into calling me lady I will not be offended. I know it is your custom here."

"Lord, lady, black, white, all just words," said Stegra loudly. "We will hear more words soon, but first the sickmilk, yes. It must be drunk, King of Daecar, to seal the bond between us. We all must drink it. But you most of all."

"Very well," the king told him. "I will have one cup, Stegra, but no more. I must keep my wits about me. I know how strong it is."

"Sickmilk improves the wits," the Snowfist claimed. "All the best Snowskins fight better with some sickmilk in their blood."

He sounds like an East Vandarian, Amara thought. The men of the rivers and marshes in particular were fond of drinking before battle, the Lakelanders less so. *Turn that hair from white to black and he'd make a good Riverlander himself.* She had a fun little thought about Stegra Snowfist and Mooton Blackshaw facing off in a drinking contest, alternating between rounds of sickmilk and thick hearty ale. Mooton liked to drink as much as he liked to fight and he was half a barbarian besides. That was one contest she should like to witness. The duel of cups and flagons was always more interesting to her than those of sword and spear.

The Snowfist served the sickmilk himself, pouring from a large jug into cups carved out of pinewood. The liquid had a pungent stench to it, sour and acrid, though all the same Amara might once have liked to sample a taste. Not in her present condition, though. *If I'm to break and enjoy a cup of something, it won't be sickmilk,* she thought. A nice spiced wine would serve her much better during these bitter cold days and nights.

When the cups were handed out the Snowfist raised a toast. "To the ending of the Endfall," he called. "To the death of the Red Storm. In this fight we are all one tribe now. We will march side by side with the steel men. Together, we will prevail!"

The sickmilk was drunk. Stegra and Hraka, mighty leader of the Stone Men, threw theirs back with relish. Narek son of Tarek, new leader of the Crowmen of the Crag, seemed less fond of the liquor, but drank it all down anyway, while Black Merryl and the Orca Lord sipped with more reserve. Amron had to fight to keep his down. Dignity intact, he smiled gamely and put his cup aside. "Delicious. And well put, Stegra. Now, I must be away. There is much else I need to attend to today, and…"

"No." The Snowfist put a hand on Amron's shoulder. The two men stood at a height, splitting six and seven feet, though Hraka the Great still towered over them both. "You cannot be going yet, King of Daecar. I know you, yes, we are as brothers you and I, but these others…" He swung an arm out to his fellow tribal leaders. "They know nothing of you except what I have told them, and have questions to ask, yes questions you must answer. So sit. Sit right here for a while and we will talk. Your other duties will wait."

Amron bit his tongue. He was not fond of being dictated to, Amara knew from long experience, though every good shepherd must make time for the whole of his flock. These were black sheep, true, but had their value all the same. "Very well. I can spare a few minutes." He stepped over and sat down on the assigned seat. "So, what do you want to ask me?"

The tribal leaders took turns to ask their questions. Amron answered them as best he could, sometimes giving full responses, at other times being rather more curt. In particular the questions of his past were uncomfortable for him. The many names he'd accumulated. The battle glory and triumphs. The Orca Lord was interested in his famous duel with Vallath and Dulian, asking him to recount it in detail. Amron gave him only a sketch. Narek son of Tarek was more interested in hearing of the king's encounter with Drulgar the Dread, who they called the Red Storm. Once more, Amron refused to enter into detail when discussing the Dread, though allowed that the giant dragon god was a formidable prospect, unfathomable in size and fury, and not to be taken lightly."

Black Merryl sniffed at that and said, "My ancestor Shrikna saw the Red Storm bring Orthrand to his knees. She watched the dragon you call the Dread cast the great bear down into the valley, watched the fountain of blood explode from his neck where the dragon had breached his armour. It rose a thousand feet high, Shrikna said. Where Orthrand fell, the land was shattered and forever changed. We have all seen this land many times, and many times have we stood beneath Orthrand's bones. No, Lord Daecar, we will not take the Red Storm lightly. That is why we have all come here. To help end the Storm, and the Endfall with it, and bring the dawn that Shrikna foresaw."

Amron awarded that a nod. "Pardons, Black Merryl. I did not mean to be flippant in my choice of words. Drulgar the Dread is also known here as the Great Calamity. It will take all of our combined might to overcome him…and the god who holds his reins." He held her gaze a moment, then looked around. "Now, who is next?"

More questions were asked and answered. The Mole Men leader, a tiny little shrew of a man called Kintrett, squeaked of finding somewhere nice and warm and ideally underground for his people to live in until the time came for them to return beyond the mountains. "We are not fighters," he said, in a high-pitched voice. "I have some…maybe some who will fight…but the rest would only be in the way. We joined Stegra to escape the snow, but…but…"

"There are other ways you might serve," Amron told him. "Not every man is born to wield a weapon, but you and your people are skilled diggers, I know, with knowledge of building and securing tunnels. I am sure we will find a use for you."

"And what of the rest?" asked Narek harshly. "We have many dependents with us. Those too old or too young to help. What will happen to these?"

"That I leave to you. Tend to your people as you see fit. But those who are able to serve in some way will be required to do so. We must bring our skills together for the common cause."

"My people are strong," declared the Orca Lord. He stood tall and straight as a spear, very noble in the form of his posture. Even his voice had a highborn crispness to it. *Put him in a velvet cloak and you have a ready-made lord right here*, Amara thought. "I will not have my people sit idle. They can sew clothes, sharpen weapons, build and tend fires and shelters. If you need longboats, we can carve them. If you wish to fish the water, we are experts in this as well." He raised his lean, clean-shaven chin in a gesture of pride for his people. As with the rest of these tribal leaders he was pale as bone, his hair so black it was almost blue, wavy like the wild open ocean. His eyes were a deep blue-green and it was said his daughter was just as beautiful, a stunner from a world away who he no doubt hoped to wed into power and wealth. This was a forward-thinking man, planning for beyond the war. *Perhaps he doesn't realise quite how bad it is here?* Amara wondered if any of them did.

"We will make use of these skills," Amron said. "Tell me, how many warriors do you all have?"

The tribal leaders each spoke of their individual strength in arms. Amron listened, nodding to himself here and there, no doubt wondering how best to deploy them in battle. The men of the western shores were skilled spearmen, the Orca Lord said, especially when throwing at moving targets. Their armour was tough and hard to pierce, and they had the cunning of the whales after whom he'd taken his name. The Crowmen of the Crag were brilliant bowmen, battle-hardened and brave, while the Stone Men, small in number though they were, were brutally powerful warriors with their stone clubs and bone garb. Amron rubbed his chin, pondering perhaps whether these tribesmen might be willing to accept superior armour. Amara could see that well enough. *He is thinking about how to make them better*, she knew. *They are dull blades and he is the whetstone.*

Black Merryl's Deadcloaks were hunters, the witch said, men and women who spent their lives tracking and killing dangerous prey. Some of them used magic, as she did, though to a lesser degree. Her own powers she did not speak of openly, but Amara had the sense this woman would be an asset. The Mole Men less so. And the river folk of the Silver Scar as well. They were represented by a young woman called Grella who wore a throwing net at her hip and held a fishing spear in her grasp. She seemed fierce enough, and spoke confidently, but admitted that most of her kin were not the same and tended toward a peaceful existence. They spent their lives fishing the river, moving from place to place and generally avoiding the other tribes. "We do not fight them for territory and hunting grounds," she said. "We avoid conflict and always have."

"Ha!" laughed Stegra. "Yes, this is so. But do not believe everything she says, King of Daecar. There are many killers who live on the river. They move silently, yes, and kill with poison. If they feel threatened they can be lethal."

Grella did not deny that. "We do what we must to keep our people safe. But killing is never our first choice."

"Nor any of ours," said Narek. "We fight through need not desire. It is only the *Weepers* who take pleasure in killing." He spat to the side. "They're inhuman, all of them. From the womb they're made wrong and they don't get better with age."

The Orca Lord agreed. "Many of our people were attacked and killed by them during the crossing. They are here, now, in your own lands, King Daecar. As many as hundreds of them. I would advise you mount a force to hunt them down and kill them."

"I have already sent out scouts to try to find them," Amron said. "I did so as soon as Stegra spoke of this threat."

"And have any of these scouts returned?"

"Not as yet."

"Then they may be dead."

"I would doubt it. I sent them out in pairs, all of them rangers supplied by Lord Borrington. They spend their lives watching for threats like this, and each has prior experience of the Wild Weepers. When they are found they will be dealt with. As things stand they are no threat to us here." The king stood up from his chair. "Now, unless there is anything else that you wish to discuss, I must be getting on. I have a pressing engagement with Lord Strand and he is not a man to be kept waiting."

He looked around; no one seemed to have anything urgent to ask. "Well and good. It has been a pleasure to officially meet you all. I hope that I will get more time with each of you in the coming days and weeks." He gave a noble dip of the chin and then strode at once from the tent.

Amara slid out after him, with Sir Connor at her side. The day was bright, the sun shining down through an open patch in the clouds to reflect dazzlingly off the snow. Amara lifted her arm to shield her eyes as they crossed through the tribal camp and back toward the city. "You seem very eager to get away, Amron," she said, pacing to keep up. "I wasn't aware you were meeting with Styron?"

"Nor is he. But it's high time we came to a decision about what to do." Amron stopped and turned. "Sir Connor. Once you've taken Amara back to her chambers, send word for my cousin and Lord Borrington to join me in Lord Strand's pavilion. I'll want their counsel on this too."

"Yes, my lord."

"And I want to see you in my solar later," the king went on. "Come at sundown. I will be waiting for you."

Sir Connor frowned. "Yes, sire. Might I ask…"

"Later," Amron cut in. "Amara, I'll have you present as well." He looked out to the south, across the snow-heaped lands. "I would hope to hear back from Rogen and Sir Quinn today. Make sure a close watch is kept for them, Connor. Have them admitted to me at once if they should return while I'm with Lord Strand."

The knight nodded. "Of course, my lord. Will there be anything else?"

"No. Just see to my cousin and Lord Robert. Then keep a watch from the walls."

Amara had no intention of returning to the boredom of her own quarters. Amron liked to keep her there in her present condition, but Amron was overprotective, and sweet as that was she preferred to remain active. So once her good-brother had marched away from them and into the city, she told Sir Connor she would go up to the battlements instead. "The men will be there," she said. "Return to me when you're done."

Amara climbed the stair behind the gatehouse, watching her step on the slippery stones. On the barbican above she found them; Carly, Sir Penrose and some of her other Knights Assorted all gathered together on one section of blackened, pitted wall, snowdrifts heaped to either side. Sir Talmer Hedgeside, Sir Montague Shaw, and Sir Ryger Joyce were sat on a heap of broken stone, muttering among themselves. Sir Hugo Dain was sitting away from them, oiling his longsword in long clean strokes while Brazen Ben Rivers and the Three Bees, Baxter, Brandon and Ballard practised their swordplay nearby to the sound of grunts and heckles and the clear strains of ringing steel. Penrose Brightwood stood at the parapet looking out through the shattered crenels. Carly was with him, perched atop the battlements with one foot propped up on the stone, the other hanging freely over the edge.

"Must you sit like that, Carly?" Amara asked as she strode to join them. "It makes my palms sweaty just to look at you there."

The girl leaned back and smiled, red hair shining in the sun. She had no fear of heights at all. No fear of anything really. "How'd it go with the barbarians?"

"They're not barbarians. Not *all* of them, anyway. The Orca Lord seemed rather refined to me." She turned to address her men. "So, how are we all this afternoon?"

"Cold. Hungry. Bored." Sir Talmer Hedgeside shrugged. "But nothing new there, my lady."

Amara smiled at the gruff old soldier, then performed her rounds. She liked to speak to each of her men individually to further secure their bonds of service. First she went to Sir Hugo Dain and gave him a favourable compliment concerning the fine gleam of his blade. "Who needs a mirror, Sir Hugo, when you have a blade like that?" The man was very vain and didn't care to hide it; no doubt that was a large part of his motivation when keeping his blade to such a shine. Next she asked of Sir Montague's arm; he'd taken a cut there during the battle, a deep slash to the meat of the shoulder, but it was healing well he told her. "Master Artibus has been very attentive, my lady." The old man had sewn the wound himself and been very generous with his healing potions.

"And how are you, Sir Ryger? Have you spoken with your brother yet?"

The man growled something she didn't quite get. She took that as a no. Or perhaps they had exchanged words, but not pleasant ones. "Well. Time is a great healer, they say," was her nugget of wisdom. "I'm sure he'll come around." Sir Lambert Joyce was Ryger's younger brother and had joined Amron's service when the king passed through Green Harbour. He had believed Ryger dead for many long years, while in truth he'd merely languished in the service of the Seal King at the hidden heart of Lake Eshina and had never sent word of his whereabouts. Lambert was no doubt sour about that, Amara knew.

She wandered over to Brazen Ben and the Three Bees, watched them at their swordplay for a few minutes with some of the other sentry guards, applauding some of the better strikes and sharing the odd encouraging word with her men. Then she completed her circuit by rejoining Sir Penrose and Carly.

"One day you're going to slip and fall," she said to the girl. "I really would prefer it if you sat less recklessly."

"This isn't reckless, my lady. You forget I grew up climbing about the palace in Ilithor." She wiggled her legs over the edge, grinning broadly. "And in snowy conditions like this too."

Amara only sighed. "I thought you were helping train Lillia," she said to the flame-haired sellsword. When she'd left to visit with the tribal leaders, Carly and Jovyn had been engaging Lillia in her daily routines, along with Sir Daryl Blunt, who had continued in his role as her escort and protector.

"I was. Until I wasn't. There are some sorts of *training* I'm not involved in, my lady." She grinned improperly.

Amara didn't like that. "Carly, please. Don't be smutty."

"Just saying." The girl shrugged and swung her legs around to face her. "The thrill of battle…fear of death. Those things tend to get the blood running hot, my lady. Jovyn's fifteen. Lillia's a year younger. Doesn't take a genius to work out what they're getting up to."

"Within limits." Amara was certain the pair were exploring the *outer* bounds of their youthful lust, though nothing toward the *centre* as yet. Jovyn would not take it so far as that, not without getting the proper consents and permissions. "Tell me how she's progressing. In her training," Amara said.

"Which training? I'm not privy to the private stuff. If you want I could put an ear to the door, but…"

"*Carly.*" Amara was not in the mood for this. "Her swordplay…"

"Which swordplay?" The girl was incorrigible. "I've seen Jovyn's broadsword often enough, but not the blade he carries between his…"

"Carly! For the sake of the gods, and my own bloody sanity, would you please just answer the question!"

The Flame Mane's grin was far too mischievous to dislike. Amara would forgive the girl almost anything, in truth. "Sorry, my lady. I couldn't resist. But as to her *proper* training, it's going well and she's improving every day. If a fight comes her way, she'll be ready. She's fierce, your neice. I don't think she'll have a problem taking life."

Amara wasn't sure whether she should be proud of that or not. Snuffing out the essence of another person wasn't something everyone could withstand without psychological repercussions. *Men are born to take life. Women to make it.* She'd read that somewhere, she recalled. A tad reductive, yes, but there was a kernel of truth in there all the same.

Still, she was glad to hear Carly's report. "Does she have a favourite form?"

Carly laughed. "I'm trying to get her to like my sellsword stances, but she seems more drawn to Strikeform."

There was no surprise there. Elyon was a master of Strikeform, having learned it during his time as Lythian's squire, and the Knight of the Vale was the preeminent proponent of the stance, most agreed. Elyon had gone on to teach Jovyn, and now Jovyn was teaching Lillia. It all lined up, neat and tidy. "And her Blockform?" Amara asked.

Carly's shoulders went up and down. "She doesn't care for Blockform. Calls it *Boreform* and I agree. It's dull, my lady. Strikeform's exciting."

"Yes. But Blockform is the foundation of a good defence." Amara looked to Sir Penrose. "Back me up, Pen."

The household knight nodded. "All knights learn Blockform first," he agreed. "Her father is unbeatable in that stance. And her eldest brother….they didn't call him Aleron the Immovable for nothing."

"He got that name from tourneys and duels," said Carly. "I doubt

Lillia will ever fight in any arena. She's a girl, light and quick and the nimble forms are better for her. When I get her to loosen up and learn how to fight like me, she'll be lethal. If that girl had been born with something swinging between her legs, she'd have been just as good as her brothers."

Sir Penrose shook his head doubtfully. "In skill, perhaps, but there are certain physical attributes that she'll never have. Women are rarely the match of men in combat."

"Because women are rarely trained. When they are, they're just as good." Carly hopped down from the parapet and spun quickly around Sir Penrose's back. In an instant she had the edge of her dagger kissing the skin of his neck. "Say we're just as good. Say it, Penny, or I'll give you a big red smile."

"Unhand me." Penrose Brightwood struggled in her grasp, but she clung on like a limpet. "I'm just speaking the plain truth."

"Say it," Carly insisted. "I'll do it, don't think that I won't."

"You won't. Of course you won't. This is an empty threat."

She pressed harder. Amara could see a thin line of blood leaking from the knight's neck. That was enough for her to call an end to it. "You've made your point, Carly. Now get off him."

The sellsword drew her blade back, spun it between her fingers and stabbed it back into its sheath. Just like that she was back on the wall again, quick as a cat. Penrose lifted a hand to his neck, wincing as he saw the blood. "You cut me."

"A scratch. Don't be such a baby."

His eyes narrowed. "A baby? A bit more force and you could have opened my throat."

"Penny, you'll know it when I want to use force. I've half a mind to force you into bed, how about that? A handsome man like you…"

He swatted her hand away as she reached to touch his cheek, reddening. Penrose was terribly stiff in matters of intimacy, Carly rather less so. *Well, she was born in a brothel,* Amara thought.

The sound of footsteps interrupted any further squabbling, heralding the return of Sir Connor Crawfield. He exchanged nods and words of greeting with the other men as he came. "My lady." He gave Amara his customary bow, frowned at the blood smear on Sir Penrose's neck, and then went on. "Sir Gereth and Lord Borrington are both heading to join the king now. I found them both in the castle and decided to visit Blacksight while there to check in with the watchmen. Sir Bryce is on duty. He said he spotted the return of the scouting party just before I arrived. They had entered a small wood, so I couldn't see them myself, but they ought to be arriving back here shortly."

That was good news. "Sir Bryce is certain it was them?"

"Yes, my lady. Quite certain. I will go down and await their return at the gates, if it please you?"

"No. I'd sooner ride out and meet them."

"My lady? Are you sure…"

"Quite sure, Con. I'm eager to hear what they have learned." The prospect of finding out before Amron did was also of some appeal to her, so she hurried on down into the yard and had her mare saddled at once.

It was nice to feel the wind in her face, biting cold though it was. With Sir Connor and the bickering pair of Penrose and Carly in tow, she crossed beneath the gate and out over the frosted lands, the thick snows already hardening underhoof. Corpses lay everywhere, stiff and frozen. Perhaps some of their own might still be out here, hidden under heaps of Agarathi dead or concealed within the snow, but there would be no getting at them now. Before long the city and the sprawling encampments raised outside the walls were behind them, and ahead lay a great white expanse of open plains and fields of scree, frozen streams and little woods armoured in cloaks of ice. From one such thicket, a host of men were riding on horseback. They had left three mornings ago beneath a snowy dawn and so far as Amara Daecar could tell, their numbers had been depleted.

"I was told two dozen men had ridden out," she said. "I count no more than twenty."

"Yes, my lady," Sir Connor confirmed. "They must have taken casualties."

"Do you think they came to blows with the Agarathi?" asked Carly.

It seemed the most likely course, though there was no sense in jumping to any conclusions. "We'll let them tell us themselves," Amara said. She put her heels to her horse and galloped away as quick as the snow would allow.

They came together by the banks of a small river where a stone bridge spanned its frozen flow. Sir Quinn Sharp led his men-at-arms onward, Rogen Strand had command of the scouts. It was the Varin Knight who spoke first as he came trotting across the bridge. "Lady Amara," he called. "I had not expected to see you here."

"I am not a patient woman, Sir Quinn. I wanted to be first to hear your report."

"Before the king?"

"The king is engaged in an important session of council. Tell me, what did you find?"

Sir Quinn was a broad-faced and rather homely man, but had become a hugely dependable asset for Amron these last long months. He turned his destrier and pointed back the way they'd come, his Varin blue cloak draped proudly at his back. "We found the source of the disturbance a little way north of the Greenwood, my lady. A great rift in the earth, leading to an underground burrow."

"A burrow, did you say? Then this was not a natural formation?"

"It did not seem so. The earth was freshly tunnelled and broken, and there were tracks leading further to the southwest. Where they met the Greenwood, the trees were toppled and trampled. Something colossal emerged from the earth and moved into those woods, my lady."

"Brannatar," she said, suddenly breathless. "The giant boar." Artibus had spoken not long ago about a great miles-long chasm that had opened up in the Heartlands. There were rumours that the boar titan had awoken, as Drulgar had, and this seemed to be further confirmation. *Goodness, could it be true?* Her heart gave a powerful thump. "How far did you follow these tracks, Sir Quinn?"

It was Rogen Whitebeard who rasped an answer. "They are being followed as we speak, Lady Amara," he said. For once the name Whitebeard suited him; his black and grey whiskers were coated in hoarfrost and his breath came out in puffs of mist as he spoke. Patches of frost clung to his black cloak like spots of nitre on the walls of a cave. "I commanded that two of my best scouts follow them into the woods. Sir Quinn supplied two of his own men to go with them."

That explained the depleted numbers. Amara did not imagine that any tracks made by a giant boar titan would require skilled trackers to follow, though. *A blind man would have no trouble*, she thought. "So you didn't suffer any losses?"

"No, my lady," said Sharp. "We met no resistance. If there are any Agarathi within leagues of here, we didn't encounter them. Most likely they have reassembled to retreat back across the Brindle Steppe and return to their ships at anchor."

"And go where?"

"Back to the Trident to lick their wounds. Or they may seek to invade at another port. Our coastline remains sorely undefended in great swathes, I regret to say. There are many places they might land to strike at us again."

Amara nodded. These Agarathi were nothing if not persistent.

"My lady. I must report this to the king," Sir Quinn stressed. "You mentioned a session of council. Is he in the castle?"

"Lord Strand's pavilion," Sir Connor answered. "I will lead you to him, sir."

Not for the first time, Amara found herself rather pushed to the side. She followed behind with Rogen Strand as the party made back for the city, probing for more information from the ranger. He offered little, but when was that not the case? Realising she would be better speaking to Amron directly later, she set aside her enquiries and waited for sundown, when it came time to meet the king in his solar.

She arrived with Sir Connor Crawfield in tow. The knight seemed strangely nervous. "Do you know what this is about, my lady?" The skies were still broken, coloured in the shades of sunset. Rich reds and purples warmed the western horizon through the windows, saturating the white world below. It had snowed through most of the afternoon, though the evening was clear and crisp and beautiful.

A beautiful night for a foul command, Amara thought. Was Amron going to send her and Lillia away, tuck them off somewhere safe as far from the war as he could find? Why else would she and Sir Connor be here? *He'll captain my escort*, she thought. *And he'll do so uncomplaining, even as he hates it.*

"I'm afraid not, Con," she merely said in answer, as she raised her knuckles to the door and knocked.

It opened a moment later and Rogen Strand was there, dressed in his scratched, smoke-grey armour overtopped with his black wool cloak. The frost had long since melted away and he was Whitebeard to her eyes no more. "Lady Amara. Sir Connor. The king awaits you." He stepped aside and then out, shutting the door behind him.

Amron was seated behind his great pine desk as his father and grandfather had done before. He had some papers and parchments before him, a fat tallow candle burning down to the wick and leaking wax onto the table. The hearth was burning warmly, giving out that comforting crackle Amara had always liked. She looked over at the drinks counter; she'd always liked that as well. By instinct she was halfway there before she realised those days were done. She checked herself and said, "Would you like a drink, Amron? Connor?"

"Not for me," the king said. He shuffled some papers into a stack. "Connor, by all means partake."

The Captain of the Daecar Household Guard shook his head. "Thank you, my lord, but no." He stood at attention before him.

Amron leaned back and studied him. He looked increasingly kingly these days as his hair took on a bit more grey and his beard grew out well salted. "I've always liked you, Connor," he intoned. "You're something of a dry fellow, there's no denying it, but by the gods there's no one more dutiful. Please, do have a drink. I insist."

"As you say, my lord." Amara served him a small cup of red and he sipped with great reserve. Connor Crawfield had never been a big drinker. *He drinks as little as he laughs and smiles, and that's little enough.*

"Have one too, Amara," Amron said. "A small cup won't hurt."

She shook her head. "Not tonight."

"But another night?"

"When there's cause for celebration, perhaps."

"Then have one," the king repeated. "And…fine, I'll have one too. We'll all drink together."

He waved her to the counter and she relented, wondering what this was about. *Is there cause for celebration?* When she handed the king his cup, she asked him how it went earlier with Lord Styron. *Perhaps that was it?* "You've decided what to do, then?"

He nodded and set straight into it. "We're to return to Varinar. With these snows, there seems no other viable choice. From there we can regather and consolidate our strength." He looked at her. "Gereth will remain here, Amara, with his men. I will lend a small supplementary force to enhance his garrison should the Agarathi return, but I don't think it will come to that."

She moved forward to sit, folding one leg over the other. "And if this snow keeps falling? The city could be buried, Amron."

"Gereth knows the risks. They have the mines, should their need become desperate, but so long as the snow does not come down any more heavily, this city will remain liveable. We think we've seen the worst of it."

It would be snowing in Varinar too, no doubt. Though not so heavily, they must but hope. "And the rest of us…we're all to go? The tribes? Lord Robert's militia from the north?" She met his eyes. "*Everyone?*"

"Everyone, yes. Pending what we learn of Crosswater, I may send more men there on the way. And to King's Point as well to join Lythian's command."

She nodded. "And us? Lillia and I?" She paused. "You're not planning to send us away?"

"Send you away? No. Why should I do that?"

"To keep us safe. I thought you might send us north somewhere."

"North of here is hardly safe. Not with this snow." He leaned forward. "Amara, I want you and Lillia near so I can protect you. Varinar may have fallen on some troubled times, but there's still nowhere safer in the kingdom. You told me that yourself."

She sighed, relieved. "And the Twinfort? If the Agarathi retreat back toward the Brindle Steppe, they might assault Lord Randall's garrison as they pass. You told me he only had a small force there now. You would let them keep that foothold in the realm?"

"Let them? There's nothing I can do to stop them. Tens of thousands of men fled the battlefield, and I don't know how many dragons. If they try to occupy those strongholds, Randall's men will soon be overwhelmed. I hope it doesn't come to that." He tapped a finger on a piece of parchment. "I sent riders after the battle. To flank the enemy with all speed and reach Randall Borrington before the enemy does. I commanded them to instruct Randall to let the enemy pass without a fight."

"And will he?" Amara knew Lord Randall Borrington well. Even lying abed with a wound in his neck, he would take umbrage with letting the enemy pass his gates like that, whether in retreat or not.

"If he doesn't, he and every one of his men will die needlessly. I do not think the Agarathi want to occupy the Twinfort, Amara. They tried to kick through the western gate and they failed. So they'll go back and try another way." He sipped his wine. "I'm told you think Brannatar has returned."

The sudden change in subject had her reeling. "Yes. From what Sir Quinn said, it sounded like…"

"I agree with you. In fact I thought that the very night we felt those tremors."

She blinked at him. "You did? Why didn't you say anything?"

"I wanted confirmation first. Now I have it." He turned his eyes to the door. "Rogen sent men to track him, as you know. I believe Brannatar has been summoned by Vandar to help us in our fight. It was Vandar who made him. As Agarath made Drulgar. They will clash, we can be sure of it. I would like to know where."

Amara swallowed. Her throat felt suddenly very dry. A sip of wine helped settle her. This was terribly exciting stuff. "Rogen said the tracks led into the Greenwood," she managed to get out. "Perhaps Brannatar feels the trees will grant some cover to spring an attack?"

"Trees burn, Amara. And the boar is big. I'm not sure he'd find too many places to hide in there."

"There are deep valleys, high ravines. Places even Brannatar could lie in wait."

"And wait for what? Drulgar to happen by him?"

"Be drawn to him. He will sense his return as well. Brannatar will want to battle on his own grounds, and he'll know the dragon will come to him. He won't be able to stop himself."

"He's arrogant, yes. A trait of his master." Amron leaned back in his chair and had a drink of wine, thinking. He gave a shake of the head. "We may be wrong in all this. A creature that size…he might be as much a threat to us as Drulgar. If he should rampage through some city…"

"He won't. If not Drulgar he'll be hunting the Agarathi. He may attack their armies just as Drulgar attacked yours."

"I told you about King's Point, Amara," Amron pointed out. "Drulgar killed *indiscriminately*. His rivers of flame were not directed at us alone, so why should Brannatar be any different? These titans come from a different time, before the birth of man. We're nought but ants to them."

"Not all. Not you."

He shook his head. "I'm not the saviour, Amara. How often must I tell you?"

"As often as you like. It won't stop me believing it." She unfolded her legs and leaned forward. "So what are you to do? If Rogen's men find Brannatar, what then? Will you ride to fight alongside him? Will you send out word to King's Point, to Lythian, to command the gruloks there in your stead?"

The king's jaw gave a ripple. He did not seem to have an answer.

"Or perhaps you'll do nothing, because there's nothing to be done. Drulgar could come at any moment, and we'd have no time to react. For all we know they have already fought and we don't have to worry about going hungry anymore."

He frowned at her. "That's not something to jest about. If Brannatar falls…"

"He'll feed us all." She sipped her wine. "I've never tasted titan, but I bet it's good. We must make use of what we have, but that's not the point I'm making."

"Then what is?"

"That these creatures are beyond us. They're from another time, as you said. Let them stamp about and battle as they once did. And in the shadow of their conflict…*prepare*."

He stared at her a moment, mulling on that word. "Prepare," he repeated, tasting it on his tongue. "Yes. Perhaps you're right. If nothing else this may grant us time. Time to gather our strength and make our plans." He nodded again and then smiled at her. "And you think I would send you away? Gods, Amara, what would I do without you?"

"At last you're realising it." She smiled back at him. "You said to drink when there was cause for celebration, Amron. Is it this news of Brannatar you wanted to toast?"

"No." The king turned his attention to Connor Crawfield, still standing silent to the side of her chair. "I said there's no one more dutiful than you, Connor. Let me add that you're loyal, brave, and proving yourself increasingly skilled in combat. You fought courageously during this island coup Amara told me about and here defending the city as well, I am reliably informed. You have been a constant reassurance to my good-sister, a presence she has come to rely on, and for that I could not be more grateful."

"I'm…just doing my duty, my lord." Connor glanced at Amara. "Serving the Daecars has been the great honour of my life."

"But not enough. You wanted more, once." The king pushed back his chair and stood, turning to a trunk at the side of the room. He knelt down and opened it. When he stood he held in his grasp a brand new cloak, rich in blue, emblazoned on the back with the seal of Vandar wrought in silver thread. He stepped forward. Sir Connor's face had gone pale. "Years ago you applied to join the Varin Knights. You faced the selection trials and were deemed to be unready, but that is no longer the case. I need men I can trust, Sir Connor. Men who will never back down in the face of mortal danger. You've proven yourself such a man. Kneel," the king said.

Sir Connor Crawfield knelt before him, trembling. Amara watched on, tears misting her eyes as Amron fixed his cloak, wondering if anything would change. Connor had been the head of her household guard for years, but now…what now? She did not give voice to such concerns. The man deserved it, by the gods did he deserve it, and now and forevermore he would have a place at Varin's Table. This was not just about his service here on earth. It was about the afterlife. And Amron had the power to grant him one greater.

When the king was done fixing the cloak into place, he took a step back, withdrew the Frostblade from its sheath, and anointed the man with a tap on each shoulder. "Rise, Connor Crawfield," he said, smiling. "Rise, a Varin Knight."

Sir Connor rose to his feet, his new cloak falling resplendent down his back. It was a rare day indeed when an ancient titan awoke.

And just as rare a day…when Sir Connor Crawfield smiled.

7

Saska

It was only her second flight.

The first had been in the saddle behind Talasha, soaring through the skies on Neyruu's back above the dusty brown Aramatian plains. Now those browns had turned to greys and blues, and the surface below was a deal more wet. Her steed was somewhat different too. *The dragon becomes a handsome prince*, she thought. She smiled in glee as they soared.

"Are you ready to take the reins?" Elyon shouted in her ear. He was flying slowly, gliding a soft circuit around the ships below, which were making a steady course north across the choppy, wind-ruffled waters toward the coast of Rasalan. It looked close from up here, reachable within the hour but the ships would still take the rest of the day to make it.

Saska twisted her neck to look up at him. It wasn't comfortable, or easy. The harness had her strapped up with her back to his chest, and for all her flexibility, she could not turn her head fully around. "Are you sure I'm ready?" she called back at him, over the gusty wind. "It's only been a few days, Elyon."

"It's fine. I'll be here."

She had her doubts, a good many of them. "I don't want to drop it. It's still heavy for me to hold for long, and the winds…"

"If it's too heavy, tell me, and I'll take it back. I'll have my hand there all the time."

And the flying bit? The command of the winds? She had only started training with him three mornings ago, and that was proof enough that she was far from ready for this. So far, that training had been kept to the forecastle deck, consisting of the basics of wind manipulation, take-off and landing…and had all been done in full view of the men. Elyon at least had the luxury of training out on the Bloodmarshes when he first got started, but Saska had no such fortune. No soft soggy marshland to cushion her falls, of which there had been many. No privacy to practice away from prying eyes…and there were many of those as well. Dozens of Bloodhound Burton's sailors and deckhands were always bustling about, many of Robbert's soldiers were constantly on deck too, and of course the sellswords had wanted to watch and lend her their 'emotional' support. A lot of that was just heckling, though to be fair when she did manage to achieve some minor triumph her efforts were awarded with cheers. Those were nice. And she *had* made progress. But enough to fly? She could propel herself up off the ground a half dozen metres, and once or twice she'd even floated a bit when the air whizzed and spun around her, but *flying?* Flying was another matter entirely.

It all ran through her mind in an instant. "I'm not ready for this, Elyon," she fretted. "You told me you just wanted to take me up in the harness to get me used to being in flight. I never really expected…" She shook her head. "We'll just plummet straight down to the sea. It's stupid. Let's give it a few more days."

"We don't have a few more days. We have here, and we have now."

That made no sense to her. "Of course we have days. We have weeks, months. If we don't, how else do you expect me to…"

He cut her off. "Are you afraid, Saska?"

"Of course I'm afraid. I'm afraid I'll *drop* it. If I do…"

"We're all lost," he finished for her. "Use that. Use that desperation. You drop it, and it sinks, we die. All of us. So don't drop it. *Fly.*"

He reached forward with his spare hand, grabbed her wrist, and pulled it up toward the Windblade's haft. "Take it," he shouted in her ear, and she did so despite herself, wrapping her fingers around the hilt, clutching tight. "Good. Now I'm going to let go. Fly or die, Saska. Fly… or we *all* die."

She had no time to think about it. Elyon was good to his word. As soon as he felt her take the weight, he opened his fingers and let go, just like that and she felt the heavy strain. Her arm dropped at once, but she tensed and held firm, holding the blade outstretched, and somehow… *somehow* the winds continued to spin about them, a vortex of air swirling as they soared. Her fear became joy in that sudden moment, a smile tearing open on her lips. *I'm doing it,* she thought, both befuddled and elated. *I'm actually…I'm actually doing it…*

It was premature. *Of course* it was premature. A mere moment later the winds began to wither, weakening, guttering out like a dying candle-flame in the midst of a raging storm. She frowned, hard, trying to concentrate and stir the winds back to her will but her panic was over-whelming her. *Fly,* she could only think to herself. *Fly. Fly or die!* The winds spluttered and stuttered, swirling, fading, holding them for a few more moments and then all at once they were abandoning her entirely and both prince and heir were falling.

"Take it back," she shouted. "Elyon, take it back!"

His hand was hovering near. "No. Not yet. Fly or die Saska. Fly or die!"

Damn him, what does he expect from me? They were plummeting straight down. "I can't! I don't know what I'm doing!" The wind rushed in her ears and below, on the ships, she could see the men watching on worriedly, pointing and calling out.

"Fly, Saska. I know you can do it. *Fly.*"

She tried. She *really* tried. But it was no use. The white-capped waters were coming right up to meet them and Elyon Daecar saw no other choice. He reached out, snapped fingers about the handle, and they swung at once into an elegant arc and soared back up to a relieved chorus of cheers.

Saska was irate. Her heart was hammering at her ribs. It took her a good few moments to calm down before she twisted her neck and snapped up at him. "What was *that*? Are you *trying* to get us all killed?"

She could see him smiling. A carefree look. Strands of black hair whipped against his forehead and his eyes were twinkling with amusement. "You did better than I thought you would, actually."

"Better? I did *nothing*."

"Are you sure about that? We flew for a little bit there. Before we, you know, fell straight down. That was all you."

She shook her head. "It was nothing. Just residual airflow from you, that's all."

"You're wrong. *You* stirred the winds…believe me, I should know. I've been doing this longer than you have." He lifted them into a pleasant glide so they could speak freely and clearly, without the wind blasting in their ears. Nothing worse than a fine rain was falling from the wan broken skies, and there were even a few shards of sunlight, here and there. "Look, I know that was tough and frightening, but time is not on our side. We have to speed up your training and these sorts of things can help. It depends on the person. You told me once that Lady Marian used fear to help you build your bond to godsteel when she first trained you. So, I thought I'd try it myself. And it worked. So expect some more of it from me."

She sighed. He was right, damn him. Lady Marian *had* employed the use of fear to put her and Leshie and Astrid on edge many times during those early days. Picking those dreadshrooms in the Darkwood. Climbing the ship masts when they crossed Vandar's Mercy on the caravel *Nancy*. Forcing them up onto the forecastle when that storm had raged, wild and rough, with waves lashing across the decks. In that state of heightened consciousness, they either excelled or broke, and Saska had typically excelled.

Fear she was used to. She'd lived with it for most of her life. The fear of the whip and the dark of her cell in Keep Kastor. The fear of Lord Modrik's plodding step, approaching outside the door. Most of all she feared the day he would come and take her chastity. A fear that grew so ripe within her that the night he tried, she killed him. But still that fear lingered on, rearing its ugly head again when Lord Quintan tried the same. *And I killed him too,* she thought, remembering how his eyes had swelled and opened as she punched his own blade through his gut. She had gone on the run after and still did not know what had come of Master Orryn and Llana. Now she feared that *they* were dead, as she'd feared for Del as well. Fear had always walked side by side with her. But even before Marian, she'd learned to use it, harness it. *And now I must do the same.*

Her anger fled her all at once, and she drew a deep long breath. "You're right," she said, turning her head once more to look back at him. "It was just a shock, is all. But you're right. I thrive in fear."

"I know you do. You'd never have made it this far if you didn't." He sketched a smile and then turned his eyes around, moving things on. "You said Princess Talasha exposed you to some acrobatics when she took you up on Neyruu. How did you find it?"

"Exhilarating," she said. *If a little stomach-churning*, she left out. "Neyruu's the quickest dragon in Agarath, Talasha told me."

"But not the most agile," Elyon asserted. "The smaller ones are typically the nippiest."

"Neyruu is small. As dragons go."

"Compared to a Garlath or Malathar, yes, but there are much smaller dragons out there. I should know, I've fought all sorts. The little ones we call crow-killers. That's all they seem to do; kill crows to disrupt communication. They may not have the straight-line speed of a dragon like Neyruu, but by Varin they're *lively*. My point is I've had to learn to chase them down and the turns of speed can take some getting used to. Best we start with that."

"Sharp turns?" Saska asked.

"And bursts of speed. There's no dragon that can match the Windblade for sudden acceleration. More times than I can count I've had one snapping at my heels, and only a sudden burst of speed has got me free of them."

He should keep the blade, a part of Saska was thinking, as she listened. She could hear the passion in his voice, the sense of pride as well. He was self-taught and never had anyone to guide him. *He did this all on his own, and now he has to hand it over.* She didn't much like it, but that was the way it must be, so there was no use complaining or lamenting her fate. *And I'm lucky to have him teach me*, she knew. Everything Elyon had gone through would help her and she couldn't much imagine a more pleasant tutor. She just had to hope the others were just as accommodating; Elyon had already told her that the best way for her to learn would be to get specific tutelage from the men who'd mastered the blades. In some cases, that might prove troublesome, he'd admitted. Saska knew all about his Shadowknight brother and the idea of Jonik teaching her how to wield the Nightblade did not exactly fill Elyon with relish.

But that was all for another day, or week, or month. Right now it was just Elyon and the Windblade, and she'd not have it any other way. "So…" she shouted, putting all that aside. "You're going to subject me to some quick turns and gut-twisting acceleration, is that it? Please tell me you're not intending to hand over the blade while you do."

She heard him laugh behind her. He was so close she could feel his warm breath at the nape of her neck. It sent other memories through her. Of his tent, his bed, his body up next to hers…

"Not this time no…you can rest easy. But we'll get there soon enough. Ready?"

"When you are."

"Then hold on tight. And if you start to feel queasy, just wave a hand. I won't be able to hear when the wind starts roaring."

It was only her second flight…and by the gods was it more chaotic than the first. Elyon was not lying about the sudden acceleration and he did not go easy on her either. When he fired them forward, he did so with such sudden speed that it felt like her eyeballs might just burst through the back of her skull, and when he shot left or right or up or down, the turns were so sharp they turned her insides inside out. It was all Saska could do not to pass out from the force of it, the world blurring and rushing about her in a wild grey-blue frenzy. Once she thought she might have fainted, though couldn't be sure, because her eyes snapped open just as quickly, and the world all looked the same. Sea, sky, the glimpse of ships beneath them…

And then she saw the dragon.

It was off in the distance, away to the west, but drifting in their vague direction. She raised a hand and waved, shouting, "Dragon!" as best she could against the rushing, surging air.

Elyon slowed at once, pulling to a bone-jarring stop. He gathered a cushion of air around them so they could hover in place over the seas.

Saska gasped, catching her breath. She pointed. "Dragon…do you… do you see it, Elyon?"

"I see it." He was not gasping for breath or breathing heavily at all. His voice was perfectly calm and even. "It looks like it's hunting, don't you think? Well, *fishing*. A dragon's got to eat."

The way he spoke…so utterly relaxed. Saska took a few more gulps of air then reached down to clutch her Varin blade. She kept it at her hip always now, hoping one day she would feel worthy of it. Her sight was enhanced and the beast came into clearer focus. "It's big, Elyon. Not huge, but…"

"It's middling size, don't worry. It's not a great threat to us."

"And the ships?" She turned her eyes in search of the fleet and found that it was a little way off. Rolly would no doubt be displeased about that. He had, of course, requested that they remain close. "What if it attacks them?"

"It won't."

"How do you know?"

"It's fishing, not spoiling for a fight with a trio of warships. *Hammer's* a massive vessel, Saska. It'd be a fool to get near it alone."

Saska wasn't so sure about that, but had to submit to his experience. So far as she saw it, *Hammer* was badly weakened, her mounted scorpions mostly smashed and broken, half her harpoons and throwing spears still lodged in the thick hide of Lorin's Bane like spines on a great black hedgehog. When the kraken had been driven off by Elyon's lightning strikes, it took a good proportion of their armoury with it, and another attack might prove fatal.

But Elyon did not seem concerned. So they waited, and they watched, as the dragon continued to float serenely over the sea, webbed wings fluttering like banners caught in a breeze. The long neck was moving left and right and the head was trained down, eyes on the water. Elyon was indeed correct. The beast was fishing, there was no doubt, and it seemed to have spotted something moving down there as it turned once more, circling like an eagle, and plunged suddenly down, talons outstretched, reaching for the waves.

When it hit the water and rose again it had an eel lodged between its claws. It was large, long, thick, greyish blue in colour, squirming and lashing with a broad flat muscular tail. There were some sort of spines protruding from the tail, Saska saw, long and deadly sharp, which struck hard at the beast's hindquarters, punching through scale and sinew. Blood rained down as the dragon flapped up, snapping with its maw to kill the eel, but its prey was not so easily defeated. The tail kept swinging, *punch punch punch*, the spines cutting deep, blood flowing freely. Saska perceived some churning beneath the water. The choppy surf turning white, bubbling. Something else was down there.

"He's going to have to give it up," Elyon observed. "That tail could kill him."

"What is it?"

"I don't know. Some cousin of the manator I'd guess."

The giant eel was still thrashing, blood flying from the tail-spines as they slashed fearsomely at the dragon's flank and rear leg muscles. The beast flapped skyward in a frenzy, snapping and biting at the eel's head but somehow it was still alive. "The wing's torn," Elyon said. "On the right. You see? The webbing's been caught by those spines. It won't be able to fly properly now."

The dragon at last saw a failing cause and tried to give up the meal, but the eel seemed too enraged to let it lie. It had clamped its own jaws down on the dragon's wing arm and was still swinging with its tail, coiling about the body of its foe, constricting it until the dragon could fly no more. Then they went down together, twisting and thrashing and hitting the water with a great white splash. Saska could hear the dragon screaming as it fell.

Yet as they hit the waves, the *monster* appeared. It came up so suddenly and fiercely it took Saska's breath away. The air caught in her throat as the enormous form came soaring vertically out of the surf, breaching several dozen metres above the water before twisting and crashing back down, sending huge waves spreading in all directions. The jaws were gigantic, wide and ringed in rows of triangular teeth as long as a man's forearm. The lips were pulled back, as though the beast was grinning, great slabs of meaty gums glistening pink and bloody red. Both the eel and the dragon were caught in that gaping nightmare as the monster dragged them right down into the depths.

Saska was at a loss for words. It happened so quickly, so violently. "That was a…a…"

"Greatshark," Elyon said. "I never knew they could get that big."

"It was as big as a great*whale*," Saska breathed. She turned her eyes around again; the ships were heading in that direction. "We need to warn them. There might be more of them down there."

Elyon agreed. "We'll call it for today, then."

It took no time at all for news of the greatshark to spread across *Hammer's* decks. Then it spread across the decks of *Blood Bear* and *Wild Raven* as well after Elyon flew over to report to them. There was a nervousness in the air, a rich tang of concern, a general sense of disbelief that they might suffer the attentions of a bloody *greatshark* so soon after being molested by Lorin's Bane. Elyon rejoined Saska on the quarter-deck, with Prince Robbert, Lord Gullimer, Rolly and Bloodhound Burton. That had become the core leadership group when smaller councils were called for.

"They're suitably warned," Elyon reported, as he unhitched the Windblade and handed it to Saska. She took it without question, fixing the sheath to her swordbelt and then wrapping her fingers about the hilt. It was important to continually build the bond whenever she had a chance. If there was trouble, Elyon could easily take it back, but until that time it would remain with her. "And I took a quick pass to where we saw the shark. Nothing left in the water but a few dragon scales and trails of blood. With luck it's satiated for now."

"Aye, let's hope," Captain Burton agreed. "If not we may be in a spot of bother. Plenty of men aboard these ships, and these sharks can smell 'em, be sure of that. If it wants a snack, they'll know where to find us."

Saska misliked the sound of that. "Don't you have any countermeasures against them?"

"Against greatsharks? Aye, same as all the rest. Harpoons and spears and scorpions."

All lacking, Saska thought. She didn't like this one bit. "Won't you come ashore here, Robbert?" she asked, turning to the prince. He still planned to sail across the Redwater Bay and make for the Vandarian coast, as far as she knew. That was hundreds of miles of open water, thick with threats armed with fin and fang. "If you're set on making for the Marshlands, you can march there instead."

Robbert Lukar did not consider that an option. "It could take weeks to get there, longer if we don't find horses for all the men. I can't wait that long. My army needs me. And my brother."

"They need you *alive*," Saska said. "Not dead."

"They need me *now*," Robbert came back, adamant. It was clear his mind would not be changed on the matter. "Crossing the sea is much the quicker route. And one I'm set on." He gave her a strong look to deter any further protests and then turned his eyes to Elyon. He opened his mouth to speak, then thought the better of it and said nothing.

Elyon prompted him. "What is it, Robbert? If you have something to say…"

"Just a question," Robbert said. "Well, a request, really. But one that comes too late now. It's nothing. Forget it."

Elyon was too intrigued to let that pass. "What request? Tell me."

The prince sighed and said, "I was going to ask that you fly west from here, to the Marshlands and Rustbridge. I'd hoped you might be able to update me on how things are there. You said there was battle brewing, and I'm eager to know if it's come to that or not. But that's not a request I'm going to make anymore. It's too late for that, I know. You have other priorities."

Saska could see the conflict on Elyon's face. He had grown used to being able to cross vast distances quickly, bringing news to the news-less, checking on the fate of family and friends all across the north. Yet for the last few days he'd been here, with Saska, ship-locked. His priority was training her, he had said. He could not be flying off on these errands anymore, much as he might want to. *And he* does *want to*, she knew. *He wants to find out what's happening. In Rustbridge and further west as well.* His father. Sir Lythian Lindar. They were two of the bearers and must be told what was happening.

But Elyon was shaking his head. "If I fly there, there's no knowing what I might find. I can't be drawn into any battles that might risk me harm, not right now. If I'm injured or killed…if I lose the Windblade…" He shook his head. "Only recently, I dislocated my shoulder, and I couldn't fly properly for over a week. What if that happens when I'm a thousand miles away? If I can't return to Saska for a week, or two, or longer?" He did not seem overly happy about it, but he was resolved in it all the same. "Her training *must* be the first priority right now. I hope you understand, Robbert."

"I do. I understand." Robbert Lukar smiled to show he truly did. "It's fine. We'll find out more when we get there."

Elyon gave a stiff nod. Behind his eyes Saska perceived the thoughts running through his head. His uncle Rikkard was at Rustbridge. As was Borrus Kanabar. Elyon had a pressing desire to see them, Saska knew, and she'd even heard that Lady Marian was there as well. *If I could fly, I'd want to go there as well,* she thought. Maybe she would, when she was better trained? Maybe they could fly there together, in the harness, taking it in turns to hold the Windblade? That thought gave her some solace and it would still take Robbert a good while to reach Rustbridge anyway. Even when he reached the Vandarian coast, he'd have a long march ahead of him.

The discussion turned to the prince's onward plans. A coastal port called Winslow Point was his intended destination. It was the closest harbour in the Marshlands, some fifty miles or so north of Mudport, though there was a risk it was under enemy occupation, Elyon said. "Every major stronghold and city across the Marshlands has been razed. It's possible Winslow Point will be garrisoned, though if so the enemy forces will likely be small in number there. Most of them were drawn up into Vargo Ven's orbit."

"If the town is occupied, we'll de-occupy it," Prince Robbert said defiantly. "A part of me hopes it is. I've been longing to wet my blade with Agarathi blood."

"Be careful what you wish for," cautioned the apple lord. "We still have many sick and wounded in our company, Robbert. We would be better off avoiding any fighting for now."

"I did only say a *part*, Wilson. The rest of me is wiser than to want battle just yet."

"You may not have a choice," warned Elyon. "There may still be Agarathi patrols in those marshes, and other things besides. It will be dark there, wet, and dangerous. If you can, seek guidance from any locals. They'll know the safest routes."

"I will," Robbert said.

Saska wanted to try to talk him out of it, to suggest he make port further north and avoid that mire entirely, but she didn't. She had a bad feeling in the pit of her gut. She'd heard terrible stories about that mire and wished he might reconsider. But she knew he would not heed her.

So later that day, with dusk falling and the ships dropping anchor off the Rasalanian coast, she invited the prince to join her for a private farewell. He stepped into the royal cabin he'd vacated for her and looked around. "Del said you wanted to see me, my lady?"

She nodded. The cabin had been cleared and neatened and tidied as well as she and her men could manage, to make it suitably liveable for the prince once again. She was alone; all her men were up on deck, preparing to depart. "I wanted to give you this."

He stepped forward, curious. "What is it?"

She opened her palm; in it she held the piece of coral that had called to her, the totem that told of her Seaborn side. She'd had it set in clasps to make a crude necklace. "I know how it must look. Just an ugly piece of rock, but…"

"I cannot take it," he said, shying away. "I know how much that means to you."

She stepped in. "That's why I want you to have it. I've nothing of value to give you…nothing like the armour you gave me, but in this rock is a piece of me. I would not be alive if it wasn't for you, Robbert. You saved my life in Aram, and you granted me safe passage on your ship. I hope…I wonder if some of the fortune that has followed me will go with you if you take this rock." She reached out. "I want you to have it."

"My lady…I'm not sure…"

"Please, Robbert, take it. It's all I have to give you." She could not give up her Varin dagger, and her other trinkets didn't carry the same meaning. But the coral was special. She would miss moving it between her fingers, feeling the pits and grooves...miss how it made her remember the day she found it, that warm lazy afternoon on the reef with Captain Rikki and Little Billy Bowen and Old Hob and all the rest. It had been precious to her ever since, a piece of the puzzle of her past, and a great part of her did not want to let it go. But that's why the rest of her did. Because it was hard. And it meant a lot to her. And maybe, somehow, it would help protect him. It was a fool's hope, a vain hope, but a hope all the same. "Take it," she said again.

And this time he did.

The prince took it carefully from her palm and looked it over with a smile. "I'll keep it with me at all times," he promised, turning it between his fingers, inspecting it like it was some fabulous glittering jewel. It was to Saska, a jewel beyond price, and it touched her that he paid it that due respect. "Thank you, Saska. Truly. It means a lot."

"It's nothing really. Price*less* in a bad way. Try to sell that at market and you'll be laughed away, but to me...to me..."

"It means a lot," he repeated. She met his gaze; his eyes were sincere. "This is more valuable to me than any gemstone."

She smiled at that, hoping he didn't read more into it than she was trying to say. *He won't,* she knew. They were past all that now, whatever that had been. *Friends,* she thought, *but more.* Nothing romantic, no. A deeper connection, brought together by something greater. Two paths not quite aligned, but intersected, crossing here and crossing there but always going in the same direction, moving forward toward a brighter dawn. Saska hoped they would cross again soon. She hoped the destination would be the same as well; victory, and a long life beyond this war. Just the thought of it made her smile. And Robbert, she knew, would make a wonderful king.

She told him so and he lowered his chin humbly. "I hope so. After my grandfather, the gods know Tukor deserves one. A righteous king who will act first and foremost for the people. My father...he'd have been a magnificent ruler, but in his stead I'll do what I can. A pale reflection, I'm sure, but..."

"You'll be just as great as he was, Robbert. Don't doubt that. Never doubt it."

He smiled, just a flash on his lips, then said, "I might say the same to you. Not to doubt who you are or who you need to be. *Embrace* it, Saska. You are...unique. And I mean that in the best possible way. The way you've taken so quickly to that blade..." He looked at it, at the Windblade at her hip. "Believe in that, if nothing else. Believe that you were born to bear it, and the rest...the rest will come."

They were wise words. And kind ones too. "I'll fly and see you... when I'm better trained," she promised. It was something of an empty promise; finding him out there would not be easy, and who could say if she'd have the chance, but she said it anyway and hoped it was true.

"I'd like that," he said. "We'll have more stories to share by then. And perhaps you'll be bearing another blade as well."

She only nodded, never quite sure how to talk about all that, then stepped in and hugged him, a prolonged embrace to show him what he meant to her. It was the best way to say goodbye, with some affection. She'd never been so good with words.

Nothing else needed to be said. Together they returned to the decks, stepping out into a russet-drenched world. To the west the skies were almost clear of clouds for once, and colour saturated the sea from one horizon to another. On *Hammer's* starboard side a clutch of rowboats were being lowered into the water, to ferry Saska's men and mounts to shore. They were a paltry few in sum; just the Bloody Traders and Leshie and Del, Rolly and Joy and Jaito. Robbert went over to say his goodbyes, to the Whaleheart, Leshie, Jaito and Del principally - he had no great liking for the sellswords - and even knelt to give Joy a scratch under the chin. Saska smiled to see it. Not many could approach Joy like that without getting a hiss or snarl or judgemental glare, at the very least. It seemed Robbert had been accepted.

"She's a good judge of character," Elyon said, coming over to join her. "I'm not quite sure she trusts *me* yet."

"She will. Give her time, Elyon. You've only just met her."

The sellswords were climbing down into the skiffs only two or three to a boat, the horses being lowered in harnesses to be taken over one at a time, steadied and calmed by grooms. With their armour and weapons each of her men weighed a lot and those boats could only bear so much without sinking. "Best if we fly," Elyon told her. "Shall we get you strapped into the harness, or do you think you can manage the flight yourself?" He grinned at her. The shore was still over a hundred metres away, much too far for her to cross alone.

Saska wouldn't justify it with an answer. "I have some of my own goodbyes to make," she said. "We'll go over when I'm done.

She stepped away, speaking short farewells to the few men she'd come to know a bit while in Robbert's company. Sir Lothar quipped of coming with her, so as to avoid heading back out onto the open sea, which he greatly misliked. Sir Bernie said quite the opposite and seemed perfectly happy to see them all gone, so as to avoid sharing a ship with the Wall. The two were hardly friendly, not since their bout in Aram. "He's just not used to being around someone who's twice as big as him," Lothar confided, leaning down to her. "It makes him feel emasculated."

Lord Gullimer told her she was doing the right thing by remaining with her men. "They've earned that much from you," he said, in his clean and noble voice. "Your decision to stay is the right one, my lady."

She liked that coming from him. "Thank you, my lord. I welcome your support."

"My support counts for little, I fear. But you have more powerful men behind you now. Prince Robbert is loyal to you, as is Prince Elyon as he has made clear. That is quite the cohort you are gathering, Lady Saska. A cohort that fits you well."

She blushed at those words, and he bowed and moved away.

A few others came to her, some kneeling, others speaking words of faith. Some saw her now as a saviour, though not everyone by any means. There remained much confusion among the men as to just who she was, why she was so important, how *she* could possibly be Varin's heir. This nineteen-year-old girl from the wilds of Tukor, with the tan skin and southern heritage? How could she have the direct blood of Varin and King Lorin flowing in her veins? Few knew the truth of the tale and that left them hopelessly confused. And doubtful, that as well. Not all believed in this coming of an heir or the need to remake the Heart of Vandar at all…and those who did said that another would be the one to wield it. Amron Daecar was the name on most lips. Some others claimed that another true heir was out there still, just waiting to be unveiled, while others still declared that Elyon would bear the Heart himself. They'd seen how he'd driven off the kraken, seen him up there in the skies, wreathed in wind and lightning and that had been enough to convince them of his credentials. Then there were the old grizzled veterans who still had faith in Janilah Lukar. They waved off these stories of his death and said that he was the only one who could win the war for good and all. It was his life's work, they reasoned. Only the Warrior King could complete it.

To Saska it was all just words. Words and wild speculation and she could do nothing but let them talk. But there was a danger in that as well. Her secret was well and truly out now, and Rolly did not much like it. He had even used it as a pretext to try to persuade her to go straight to the refuge again. "The enemy will soon know who you are, and when they do they will hunt you relentlessly. Ilith can protect you. You *must* go to him, Saska. The rest of us will follow."

She denied him again, and tried to make light of it. "The enemy has no idea who I am. I'm just a girl, Rolly. A southern girl with olive skin. Do I *look* like the heir of Varin to you?"

"You look like who you are. And when they find out…"

"Then I'll have you to protect me. And the others. And now Elyon as well." *And myself, most of all,* she was starting to think. Wasn't that the point of all this training? To make it so that she didn't need all these protectors and could protect herself instead? Even protect *them*? Wasn't that the person she was meant to become?

The Wall came up to her now, a shadow blotting out the last of the sun. "The sellswords are almost all ashore," he said. He pointed them out. In the waning light Saska could see them on the shingly beach, corralling the horses and heading a little inland to make sure the coast was clear. Quite literally, in this case. The shore here was empty of settlements, a quiet strand a little way east of the island of Krarl, and much further along than they might have been. The original intent had been to disembark north of Bhoun, but the winds had been favourable enough for them to sail quickly across Whaler's Bay instead, from its eastern coast to its west, saving them weeks of travel around the coast. Robbert had been very accommodating in that regard. It was yet another thing she was thankful for. *And all I had to give him in return was an ugly hunk of coral...*

"I'll travel in the last boat alone," the Whaleheart went on. That made sense. The Wall weighed as much as at least two or three full-armoured knights combined. Right now Leshie, Del, Jaito and Joy were in a skiff nearing the shore, while another was approaching *Hammer* having deposited the Tigress and the Surgeon onto the beach. Elyon was helping to ferry the horses ashore, transporting them in nets much as he'd saved those men from the sea. He was flying over with Bedrock now, Rolly's gigantic mount; all the rest had been deposited on the beach. The Butcher and the Baker were preparing to step aboard the approaching skiff. They were the last of her men to depart but for Rolly.

Saska felt a little stir of emotion in her chest. She smiled wistfully. "We first met near here, do you remember? At Shellcrest. It isn't so far to the north."

"A hundred miles or so," the Wall rumbled. "I remember the day well."

So did she. She recalled how the knight Sir Cleon Marsh and his men had surrounded her and Lancel and Barnibus at the docks. How Sir Ralston had appeared from nowhere to butcher them one and all. *He picked me up and leapt aboard the Steel Sister,* she thought, *just as she was pulling from the docks.* Later, the Wall had declared himself her guardian and protector, presenting her the blade of her forefathers, a gift from King Godrin, and he'd been by her side ever since while others came and went. She wondered what had come of Rikki and Billy and the rest. Whether Barnibus was still alive. Elyon had told her his friend was missing in the Marshlands, and Lancel...poor Lancel had perished fighting at Dragon's Bane against Vargo Ven and Malathar the Mighty. Elyon vowed to get vengeance for that and had met Ven in combat twice since then. *And if they meet for a third time?* Saska wondered. *Will Elyon battle him bearing the Windblade or some other lesser steel?*

She turned to Sir Ralston. "How big is Malathar the Mighty? Did you ever see him during the last war?"

He frowned at the change in topic. "Once, yes. He is very large, Saska. Blunt-nosed and thick-bodied. A brutish dragon. Second in size only to Garlath."

"And Drulgar," she said.

"I do not count Drulgar," the giant told her. "He is no normal dragon, but a titan of another age."

And just as the histories describe, Saska thought. Elyon had told her all about the staggering scale of the beast. "But...Malathar *is* killable, isn't he?" she asked. "Using regular godsteel, I mean?"

"Of course. Every dragon is killable." He peered down at her for a moment. "You're worried about Prince Elyon? You feel guilty for taking away his blade."

She nodded. "I try not to, but…"

"The prince himself seems quite content with the arrangement."

"Because he has to be. I'm sure he'd rather it wasn't this way."

"But it *is* this way. Saska, you're doubting yourself again. We've spoken of this…"

"I know. And I'm trying, but sometimes it's difficult." She glanced down at the blade; her fingers were tight about the haft, the bond building, strengthening. Tiny wisps of wind rose up from the top of the sheath, turning in silver circles, whistling softly. "I'm starting to hear the whispers," she confessed, in half a whisper herself. "Elyon warned me about them…that they might try to sow conflict in me. And stir my doubts."

Rolly understood. "A part of it yearns to remain with its former bearer. They are sentient, in their limited way. They seek to remain free."

"They don't want to be combined," Saska said. "Elyon told me that. He told me all about the feelings of obsession and addiction. They can stir anger, fear, resentment, and other emotions. With me the whispers will say I'm not worthy. They'll try to dissuade me, Rolly, discourage me, so I give the blade up and abandon my duty. I can't let that happen, I know that. But sometimes…my doubts…"

"We're here to support you," her guardian said. He put a hand on her shoulder. "All of us are."

She nodded, smiling at him; it was all she needed to hear and those simple words…they helped. She hoped in time she would master the voices; Elyon had spoken of that as well. Dominating the blade through force of will, driving those whispers so far into the depths that they could no longer be heard or affect her. Killing with it would help, he'd said, and being true to its inception and intent. "The Blades of Vandar were made for war," he'd told her. "Ilith…he used dark magic to shatter the Heart and some of that darkness is wedded into them. They all seek blood and battle, Saska, and unless we give it to them…they grow restless."

He had not exactly said it outright, but she'd understood his meaning. When she was ready, she would need to kill with the Windblade to fasten it to her. It was not like regular godsteel. Blood would help to seal the bond and the blood of the enemy in particular. *No wonder he didn't want to kill that dragon earlier*, she reflected. That would only give the Windblade further cause to remain with *him*. *He knows it's me who needs to do the killing.*

The Bloody Trader brothers were halfway across the water now, and the last skiff was returning for Rolly. Saska could see Joy loping about on the beach, pouncing on bits of seaweed as they floated in and out on the surf, careful not to get too wet and dashing off when a bigger wave rolled in. Leshie had grabbed Del by the hand and was twirling him in a dance. Saska smiled as she watched them. "They seem happy to be ashore," she observed, as the last rowboat came up toward the ship. "You'd best go join them, Rolly, make sure all's well. I'll see you over there in a minute."

He nodded - "As you say" - and climbed down toward the skiff. Saska turned in search of Elyon. He was done with his duties and talking with Robbert Lukar on the forecastle, sharing some final words. She went over to join them. "It's time, Elyon."

"So it is." He reached out and took Robbert's forearm, the Tukoran Prince doing the same. They gripped and shook. "Thank you for the blade, Robbert. I hadn't thought to bring a spare."

"Think nothing of it." Robbert had given Elyon a longsword, it appeared, now sheathed and fastened at his hip. Another ripple of guilt slithered through Saska's gut but she didn't give it voice. "Good fortune for your onward travels, both of you. I'll hail you if I see you in the skies."

The young princes drew back their hands and there was nothing else to be said. Saska had already given her farewells; she merely smiled at Robbert as he dipped his head and stepped away, joining Captain Burton on the quarterdeck. It seemed they would not be staying the night or seek to make repairs at a larger port. "They're heading straight back out to sea," Elyon told her, as he began strapping her into the harness. "Captain Burton feels confident the weather will blow them quickly to the southwest." He completed his work, tugging at the straps to make sure she was safe and secure. "Ready?"

She slid the Windblade from its sheath and handed it to him. "Ready."

"Then let us be away. Rasalan awaits."

They took off slowly, lifting and turning and gliding the short distance across the purpling waters toward the nearby shore. The men gathered to watch at the gunwales and Saska was certain she could hear the mutters of disappointment to see Elyon Daecar leave. Every man aboard felt safer in his company and they would be sad to see him go. She did not imagine they minded seeing the back of the sellswords so much, or Joy, or even her. But Elyon Daecar had become a hero to them. *He is his father's son.*

Soon they were above the beach, the pebbles glistening beneath the last of the light as the waves lapped against the shore. She could see several of the sellswords setting camp a little inland; someone had apparently judged it safe for the night and she wasn't going to argue. Others were gathering driftwood for a fire and Joy was now racing off into the hills, hunting no doubt.

Elyon brought them to a stop above the strand, a dozen or so metres high. He shifted the winds so that their legs hung down and there they floated, suspended in mid-air.

"Why have we stopped?" Saska asked.

"Because you deserve to take us down," Elyon said. "This is what you've been waiting for. To return to the north. So I want you to land."

She took a breath. It was higher than she'd been so far and her doubts were swirling, swirling, but she ignored them. She *had* to ignore them, every time. "Fine. Good idea." She reached out her hand. "Hand it over, then."

He handed her the Windblade and she didn't give it any further thought. No thought of falling embarrassingly. No notion of tumbling right down to the ground to howls and jeers from the men. She let her natural instincts take hold and calmly, assuredly, she kept the surge of air spinning about them and slowly lowered them down.

When her feet touched northern soil, she smiled.

And from the ships, she heard the cheers.

8

Talasha

The morning dawned crisp and clear, and the air was freezing cold.

Talasha crawled out of the ditch that she'd slept in, huddling beside Cevi like a mole beneath the mud. A thick cloak had been stretched across them to shield them from the snow, but it seemed to have stopped overnight. *For now, at least.* No doubt it would begin again soon to further disrupt their search.

The princess lurched sleepily away around a nearby pine tree, breath frosting, pulled down her thick wool breeches and stockings and squatted to make her water. *Imagine if my mother could see me now,* she thought, sighing, as the hot steam rose about her. *Pissing up against a tree like a dog.* In truth this was nothing particularly new to her; Talasha had spent much of her youth hunting and hawking on the Askar Delta and had emptied both bladder and bowels in this fashion often enough. *Never in front of Mother, though,* she reflected. She had never quite approved of her daughter's great fondness for the outdoor life, much as it was serving her well now.

A crack of twigs sounded to her right and a figure moved past the tree, the pale morning mist parting to reveal the form of Ranulf Shackton. "Do you mind, Ranulf?" the princess said. "You're rather intruding on my privacy."

"Oh, Talasha." He averted his eyes at once. "My apologies. I didn't realise you were here."

"You might want to be more observant," she offered, still squatting. She raised a hand and stifled a yawn. "I am sure I left tracks. Or did you not see them?"

"No, I…not in these mists, no." He took a step away. "I'll leave you to…"

"Finish?" she chuckled. "No need. I am quite done." She completed her necessities and stood, pulling her breeches back up to cover herself. "You seem uncomfortable, Ranulf," she observed. "Now surely in all your years adventuring you've seen worse than a woman squatting by a tree?"

"It isn't a case of worse, my lady. But propriety. You are a princess…"

"Who must make her water from time to time, just like any other woman." She laughed at the man's discomfiture and lifted her gaze toward the thin canopy above them; the trees here were tall, great noble pines and towering sentinels, well spaced apart, and the ground was draped with frozen ferns and huckleberry bushes armoured in ice. "The snow has stopped," she said. "And the skies are clear. Perhaps today is the day we'll find this secret fortress of yours, Ranulf?"

The small adventurer nodded, rubbing his hands together. "We must hope, my lady." Ranulf was rather unremarkable in countenance and remarkable in character, interesting and entertaining in equal measure. If she was to endure this grim white wilderness, she was thankful it was with him. "I would suggest we get moving as quickly as we can," he went on. "As soon as the clouds close in again, we will be blinded. If we're lucky, we may have a few hours before that happens."

"Since when have we been lucky?" Talasha asked. "It's been snowing heavily on and off for five days." There was another issue to confront as well. "And Neyruu is still away hunting," she added. "We cannot go anywhere until she gets back."

"Yes, I had noticed that." He rubbed his scruffy beard, perhaps wondering just *what* she was hunting. "Can you not reach out to her? Summon her, if you will?"

"No. She is too far away. Do not mistake me for Kin'rar Kroll, Ranulf Shackton. My bond to Neyruu is not nearly so strong."

"I have never met Kin'rar Kroll, my lady."

"And you're not likely to, now that he is dead." Sometimes, Talasha still felt Kin'rar's presence within the dragon, a part of his poor fractured soul left behind after Ashun Klo slew him. But that voice was fading now, as her own bond to Neyruu evolved. That made her sad and somewhat ashamed, as though she was partly responsible for killing off what remained of him. She gave a sigh. "He was a good man, Ranulf. I daresay this would all be going much easier if he was here with you instead of me."

"My lady, don't say that. I should doubt even Kin'rar Kroll would have been able to do anything about this weather."

"The weather, no. But Neyruu? You've seen how wilful she is with me, Ranulf. Those men…" She clamped up a bit just to think of it, her throat tightening. "I shouted at her to stop, you heard me…but she just went and ate them anyway. She'd never have done that with Kin'rar. *Never*." She knew that in her bones.

Ranulf made a soft and sympathetic sound, then said, "My lady, do not blame yourself. Neyruu was driven mad by the cold, that is all. If she had caught that grimbear, those men would have been spared. But when it fled…what choice did she have? Her hunger was rampant, and if her fires had gone out…"

"She would have died, I know." And that would have left them stranded too. Somehow it did not make it easier, though. *She's a man-eater now. There's no going back from that.*

It was time that Cevi was awoken. Talasha excused herself and stepped back over to the shelter, drew back the snow-covered cloak and looked down into the ditch. The handmaid groaned at the sudden wash of light and raised a hand up to her eyes. "Time to get up, Cevi," Talasha told the girl. "Get everything packed up so we're ready to leave."

"Now?" she croaked. "I just overheard…Neyruu, she's not even here…"

"She'll be back shortly."

The girl drew her big fur cloak up to her chin. "Can't I stay in here until then? It's cold, my lady, and…"

"We're all cold, Cevi. Now up. You'll feel better when you get your muscles moving."

Reluctantly, the handmaid crawled miserably out of the shelter, went off behind a tree to relieve herself, and then set about packing up. Ranulf was busying himself with his maps, unrolling one that depicted the High Hammersongs over a fallen, snow-encrusted log to consider just where they were, and where they must go. Occasionally, he would shut his eyes for a few moments, then open them and resume his work. Talasha knew he would be peering through Kamcho's gaze. She walked over to join him. "Where is he right now?" she asked.

"Watching," Ranulf said. "For Neyruu's return. And other dangers." He gestured her closer and pointed at the map. "I think we're about here, my lady. You see this peak, and that one there." His finger prodded at the two locations. "This second one is the *Witch's Crook*. You see how it's drawn on the map…like a finger, slightly bent."

"The crook of a finger," Talasha said.

"Yes, exactly. That's how the peak is shaped, roughly. It is stark and sheer, quite unclimbable. I should know, I've tried before. Legend says a witch once had her home atop it, hence the name, though if that is so she must have used magic to scale it. Anyway, it's close. Not so far to the northwest of here, and the direction of the crook urges one further north. To the Shadowfort, some like to say. If we fly in that direction and keep as high as we can, we should be able to spot it."

"And Ilith's seals? You told me the fort was protected, Ranulf. Was it not designed to be that way? To hide Ilith's people from the enemy's eye?"

"It's so, my lady, though I daresay we aren't the enemy."

"We are riding a dragon." *And a man-eating one at that.* "Will these magic seals be able to tell the difference?"

He did not have an answer for that except to say Ilith's magic was complex and highly sophisticated, and he would hope that *he*, at the very least, would be able to see through his charms. "That being said," he added, "we must keep our eyes peeled. As you can see from the map, there are hundreds of separate peaks in the range and hundreds of valleys between them. The Shadowfort could be nestled among any number of them, and with as much snow as we've seen, the black towers may not be so black."

"You think they will be buried?"

"The tallest towers, no. But much of the rest will likely be covered. But so long as this weather holds, we ought to be able to spot it."

*And if the snow starts to fall again…*Talasha didn't want to think about that. It had blinded them for too long now and she would not let this opportunity pass by. *Neyruu, where are you? Get your leathery arse back here at once!* She sent her will out into the world and hoped the dragon would hear it.

It seemed, for once, the gods were with them. Only a few short minutes later, she felt Neyruu's presence grow, swelling within her, and at about the same time, Ranulf smiled and exclaimed that Kamcho had spotted her too. It was rather humbling for Talasha to know that her connection to Neyruu stretched only so far as the eagle's sight, but she was not going to dwell on that now.

It appeared the hunt had been successful. "She is holding something in her talons," Ranulf said, eyes closed tight as Kamcho wheeled high overhead. "I cannot be certain what, but it looks large…" He paused a moment, and Talasha's heart was in her throat. Large. A large *man*? Would Neyruu be so cruel as to bring back such a catch? But Ranulf put that fear to bed, and she could hear the relief in his voice as well. "It is a boar, I think. Yes. A large boar, my lady." He opened his eyes and smiled broadly. "Perhaps she'll be willing to share it?"

The boar was as large as Ranulf had said, a great barrel-chested brindle beast with long sharp tusks and a thick fat hide. Neyruu came crashing down through the thin spindly branches, thumping her wings in triumph as twigs and kindling rained down all around them. She threw the carcass into the snow with a great white puff and raised her head, screeching.

"A large boar indeed," Ranulf Shackton observed, as the dragon began ripping at the flesh. "Will she not cook it first? Dragons prefer to roast their meat, I know."

"Once her fires return," Talasha said. "She needs fuel first. Just wait, Ranulf."

Cevi was standing with them, watching hungrily. Her eyes were large, her mouth half open. "What sort of boar is that Master Ranulf?" she asked.

"Ah, well I do believe that is a greatboar, Cevi. Though of the smaller variety. The ones in the Greenwood and Wandering Wood of Vandar come much larger."

"A greatboar?" Cevi had never heard the name. "Is that just a name for a big boar?"

"In essence, yes, just a larger variety of the more common boars that roam the north. But many would say the greatboars derive from Brannatar as well, as direwolves derive from Fronn, and snowbears from

Orthrand." He smiled at the young handmaiden. "Do you know these names, Cevi?"

"I think…I'm not sure." She bit her lip. "Who are they?"

"Ancient and colossal beings, called titans and even lesser gods by some. The greatest of the gods made them to fight in their wars, the same as they made other creatures. Though these were much larger and more powerful."

"Like Drulgar," Cevi said. "Agarath made him, from the rock of the *Kruhn'din*, the Ash Mountain."

"The Ashmount," Talasha corrected. "That's what they call it here, Cevi."

The girl nodded. "Are they still alive, these other titans?"

"No," Ranulf said. "Most are long dead. Fronn and Drulgar fought four times, thousands of years ago, before the wolf eventually fell, and Drulgar killed Orthrand as well. His realm was beyond the Weeping Heights, in the lands now known as the Icewilds. Yet Drulgar flew there and defeated him anyway."

Talasha frowned at him. "You sound almost impressed, Ranulf."

"Are you not? To go there, to a land so foreign to him, where the great bear's power was at its peak…that is an astonishing feat, my lady. When a dragon and moonbear fight, it is most often the moonbear that comes out the victor, unless it should be greatly overmatched in size. Most of the legends say that Orthrand was just as large as Drulgar, and much the stronger of the two. I would say it was his greatest test and triumph."

Cevi interrupted. "Look," she exclaimed excitedly, pointing. "Neyruu's fires are back! She can cook for us, my lady!"

And warm us, Talasha thought, feeling the blaze of heat as the fire chugged and puffed from between Neyruu's teeth, weak at first and thick with black fume, then clean and clear as a bright orange lance. Exulting, the dragon raised her head and shot a spear of flame skyward, causing the snow caught among the branches of the trees to melt and fall, the bark to blacken and burn. Steam rose from her body as the inner furnace grew hot, thawing the snow around her. Then, bathing the carcass in flame, she cooked, and ate, and ate some more, gorging herself until her belly grew so swollen she looked like a snake with a deer lodged halfway down its length. Cevi giggled at the sight. "Can we eat now, my lady? Has she had enough?"

"I would say she's had plenty, yes." Talasha stepped forward, drawing out her knife and began cutting off strips of fatty charred meat and handing them out to the others. Large as the boar was, there was more than enough to go around. Neyruu made no complaint.

It was a veritable feast, and more delicious than she could say. Cevi made moaning noises as she chewed, oily fat dribbling down her chin, and Ranulf emitted a deep and satisfied sigh. Talasha ate with more dignity, but filled herself up all the same, then decided it would be wise to take as much of the meat as they could with them. "For us and

Neyruu," she said. "We can wrap it in linen and tie it in hempen string."

Ranulf thought it a sensible idea. Together they set about butchering what remained of the carcass, as Cevi went to fetch the linen and string. The girl came shuffling back and plonked the supplies down in the snow. "My lady. I think Neyruu is going to sleep."

Talasha turned and saw. The dragon was lumbering away through the trees in a walk the princess recognised. She was going to find somewhere snug to bask in the sun and digest all that boar, and when a dragon slept, it could sleep for days. "Neyruu, *no*, we have to find the refuge. You can't sleep yet."

A huff of smoke swirled from the dragon's nostrils. She kept on going.

She'd never do this with Kin'rar. "Neyruu…" Talasha stepped after her. "You're tired, I know, and full. I'm sure the hunt was wearying and that boar put up a fight, but the sky is clear and we *have to go*. A few more hours is all I ask. Once we find the refuge, we'll be able to go south again. South, where it's warmer. Wouldn't you like that?"

The sleek grey dragon stopped, the plate armour of her underside shimmering colourfully as the sun reflected off the snow. Steam rose from her body. Her neck twisted, and she glanced back. *I have her,* Talasha knew, then. A dragon loved nothing so much as warmth.

They were on their way shortly after, though Neyruu's take-off lacked its usual grace. Heavily laden by all that boar, both inside and out, she struggled up into the skies, wheezing as she climbed like an unfit oaf forced into an uphill jog. Talasha patted her neck, finding it rather amusing. *Gain some height,* she thought to her. *Then you'll be able to glide.* It would be smoother that way, she knew.

Up they went, rising through the foothills, past stands of pine and thrusts of rock, soaring over frozen rivers. The Witch's Crook came and went, a good name at certain angles, Talasha judged, if not others, and Ranulf called out other mountain peaks he knew.

"That one there is the *Manticore's Tail,*" he said, gesturing to a large, curved spike of a mountain veiled in bands of mist. "And there, you see the one with the flattened top?" That top was somewhat obscured among the high floating clouds, but yes, she did see it. "They call that one *Mount Headless*. It's like a man without a head, you see, the shoulders and…"

"I understand, Ranulf." She pointed. "And that one?" Further on, and right ahead rose a great thick brute of a prominence, dominating the skies. Most of the other peaks were dwarfed by its size, though further off the ranges and massifs appeared to go even higher. *Gods, these mountains go on forever.* The Hammersongs were not nearly as long as the Scales that sliced right through the southern continent, splitting the realm of Agarath from the nations of the empire further south, but here at their most northern point they widened and broadened, spreading out to the east and west like the crossguard of some colossal greatsword.

"That is the *Grey Sentinel*, my lady," Ranulf called forward, from the back. "It looks out from here in all directions, and once called home to a great watchtower at its summit. Ilith raised it himself, to watch for threats coming from the south. Dragons, principally. Those who might come looking for his refuge."

"Like us," Cevi said, muffled in her furs. She was a pair of eyes only, peeking out from her wrappings of wool. All of them wore several layers on top and bottom, with three pairs of thick socks and two pairs of gloves, caps and hats and heavy hoods, scarfs for their necks and another on top to be drawn up over their faces, of which Cevi was making good use. "Is this watchtower still there, Ranulf? Will people see us coming?"

"It is there, but only as a ruin now. When Ilith died, many of his plans died with him. His refuge was never used as a sanctuary and this watchtower was never truly manned. Over the centuries, it fell into disrepair. By now it will be little more than dust and rubble."

Cevi pulled down her face scarf. "And now Ilith is alive again. What will happen when we find him?"

Ranulf gave a soft chuckle. "I should hope we'll find out today, Cevi. I will bring him the formula, for a start. After that...well, I don't know. He may have another task for us, or he may not. We will have to wait and see."

The Grey Sentinel grew ever more colossal as they approached, swinging in a great high arc around its craggy cliffs and walls. Snow covered it from base to peak, yet here and there the grey of the rock poked through, and Talasha could see frozen waterfalls tumbling down from its lower bluffs in countless icy shards. Then just as quickly they were beyond it, and the great heart of the crossguard opened out before them.

"It's somewhere in there," Ranulf called. "I have not been permitted to visit these ranges before, though I know from Jonik a few details of the fort's location."

Jonik, Talasha thought. The Shadowknight, former-bearer, and bastard son of Amron Daecar whom Ranulf had travelled with once before. He had given up the Nightblade now, they knew, and ventured out to help find the others, though his current whereabouts were unknown. Even the Elders had limited sight, and that sight was growing dim.

"My lady, make for that peak there..." Ranulf was going on. He leaned forward, pointing so she could see. "That one with the jagged top amidst that central massif. I have a feeling we'll find it among those passes. The fortress is built atop a plateau, with a valley sweeping southeast beneath it, and a mountain at its back. There is a great deep rift just outside its walls, crossed with a short stone bridge. Look for those features. And the black towers rising through the drifts. The stone may shine in the sun."

Perhaps that would have been so, but alas they would never know. A short while later, the winds picked up, and the clouds began to roll in, and the lands below were bathed in shadow. Talasha inwardly cursed at their luck, and spared a curse or two for the gods as well who would tease them with this fine bright weather, only to take it away so suddenly.

But Ranulf was unperturbed. "It's all right," he called, to keep up their spirits. He had to shout louder now. The winds were beginning to knife through them, the cold slicing deep into their bones. "We still have enough light. Just so long as the snow does not fall, we will find it. I know we will."

The snow began to fall.

It did not happen at once, but as they drove hard toward the heart of the range, moving past and around the snowy mountain peaks, they saw the first flakes capering by. "No matter," Ranulf said. "We can manage a light fall. We must all train our eyes now and watch closely. Kamcho will do the same. We will find it. A gentle fall is not a problem."

The snow began to fall harder.

The flakes bred and grew into giants, tumbling down one and then the next. Before very long at all the entire sky was overrun and the mountains were no more than murky shadows in the shroud. Ranulf's positivity was undimmed, if growing desperate. "It will weaken, fear not. We need but wait for it to thin and pass. Beyond this squall the skies will be clearer."

Talasha had heard enough. The man was living on blind hope and the cold was becoming dangerous. "Neyruu cannot sustain flight in this weather, Ranulf," she called back to him. "Nor can we. We have to turn back."

"My lady, no. We may not have another chance for days. We *must* reach the refuge."

"And how will we do that? We are flying blind."

"Go lower, Talasha. If you fly a few passes through these valleys, I'm sure we will find it."

"Fine." She wanted to find it as much as he did, and the thought of abandoning their search again made her want to scream. But they had time now at the very least. Neyruu had eaten and eaten well, and that should keep her fires burning for a while. They had taken extra rations and could return to the foothills to the southeast if needed. Cold as it was there, it remained liveable. If they must go back and wait for another clear day, so be it. She wasn't going to die here chasing a lost cause.

The high peaks haunted their way. Each one was like some great spectral giant, looming above them as they passed. *We are flying through a land of gods,* she thought. *Are these the ghosts of the titans Ranulf spoke of? Fronn and Orthrand and Brannatar and a dozen more.* Some took strange forms to her eyes, of creatures and man, twisted and misshapen. It was her imagination, she knew. The cold was in her, warping her thoughts. How far had they gone from the pinewood now? Which way were they flying? North? Still north? *Have we turned east or west?* She could not see the sun, only snow and shadows and sometimes a deeper darkness sweeping by below as they passed some bottomless rift.

Cevi was whimpering behind her. "My lady, I'm afraid." She was speaking in their native tongue, which she always did when frightened. "We can't see anything. I am so *cold*. I cannot feel my hands," she whined.

Nor could Talasha, she realised. She tried to close a fist, but her fingers would not work inside her gloves. And her feet. She was losing feeling in them too. "Wiggle your toes, Cevi, and your fingers. You must get the blood moving."

"I can't. They're frozen."

Ice was crusting on their cloaks, armouring them in frost. Already Talasha could feel the warmth in Neyruu waning. She was prioritising her internal organs, she knew, whipping her tail and flapping her wings to prevent herself from becoming too stiff. Talasha's eyes wandered the white wilderness below, but she could see little through the tumbling snow. They might be flying right over the Shadowfort and would never ever know it. *We are blind*, she thought. *Blind and freezing.* "We're going back," she called.

Ranulf barely heard her. "My lady?" His voice was thin, swallowed by the roar of the wind.

"We're going back," she repeated, louder, turning her head. "This cold is going to kill us. We have no choice." She looked around. "Which way, Ranulf? I have lost my bearings. Which way is south?"

He did not know either. "If we keep on going through this squall, we may…"

"No. We must go *south*." She took matters in hand and commanded that Neyruu turn. The dragon screeched and swung, flapping against the snow, plunging to gain speed, rising again. Talasha pressed herself down, the others doing the same. A wide mountain rose up before them, cast with great black cliffs all caked in snow. Neyruu turned left, wheeling suddenly away, then dipped and tucked beneath a great stone arch that spread across a sweeping valley. Ranulf shouted something from behind her, but she didn't hear. Beneath the shadow of the arch they went, crashing through the crystal icicles of a frozen waterfall with a sound of shattering glass. Neyruu banked as another frozen fall shimmered before them, twisting, turning, rising, bursting beyond the arch and back into the wide white skies.

Then she heard Ranulf's voice again. "*Hundrar's Bow*," he called. "I think that was Hundrar's Bow, Talasha. We're close, my lady. Jonik, he said…"

A shadow shivered by, sleek and black. *What was that?* Talasha turned her head, trying to follow its motion, but it was gone, vanishing into the void behind them. A tension gripped at her, and Neyruu too. *Another dragon*, she thought. *Could there be another dragon out here?*

Ranulf had seen it as well. "We're not alone," he called out. His voice was edged with fear. "Kamcho saw something. Behind us. It is behind us."

The eagle flew at Neyruu's side, sometimes easing back to ride in her slipstream, sometimes plunging for a closer look at something below or shrieking as he flapped up high, but never straying far. Kamcho was a strong, noble bird, and both eagle and dragon got along well. Sometimes they even seemed to communicate, in their limited way, bypassing both Talasha and Ranulf as they did. That happened now. The dragon rumbled and the eagle cried, swooping down to land on her back. His talons hooked into the grooves between Neyruu's scale armour, blue and gold plumage fluttering in the wind as he braced and peered back behind them. *He is watching our rear,* Talasha knew. She craned back to look and saw that Ranulf's eyes were closed, watching too through the eagle's sight.

Neyruu banked hard around a jutting bluff, cutting through bands of mist. Faintly the princess could see woodland on the lower slopes, flashes of green and brown amid the white, spreading down toward a broad valley. *Lower,* she thought. *Take us lower, Neyruu.*

They plunged. Behind her, Cevi was sobbing and clutching at her arm with a frozen claw, murmuring some unheard prayer. Talasha turned back, teeth chattering. "Ranulf," she called. "Do you see it? Are we being followed?"

"I am not sure, Talasha."

"Was it a dragon? Could there be another dragon here?"

"A dragon? No. I think…"

His words were cut off by a sudden piercing shriek that overwhelmed all other sound. It felt like a thousand tiny daggers were stabbing inside her ears. She made a noise, between a groan and a whimper, and tucked her head right down between her shoulders, cringing against the terrible din. On it went, on and on. On and on and on before at last it withered away, leaving behind a ringing, a dreadful ringing in her ears. Muffled voices called behind her: Cevi crying, Ranulf shouting.

She felt a presence above them. A shadow lurking in the shroud. Her eyes flashed up, saw a veiled shape and shadow. *Not a dragon,* she thought, in horror. It was tail-less, its neck short and stubby, head squat and broad. Great wings spread down the whole length of its body from shoulder to foot. Dark eyes stared, gleaming with hate. *Spawn of the Nightmare,* she thought, breathless.

And then she heard Ranulf's voice. "Greatbat," he bellowed, his voice clearing. "It is one of Brexatron's brood! Cover your ears, both of you! Your ears! Cover your *ears!*"

That high-pitched shriek whistled out across the world again. Talasha let go of her handles and slapped her hands down over her ears, pressing hard to muffle the sound. Neyruu bucked her head, twisting in pain, fingers of smoke and flickery fire pouring from between her teeth as she arced away.

The greatbat gave chase, haunting her every move, staying behind and just out of sight. The air was thick with a sudden sense of malice, the snow falling hard, mountains shadowed about them, looming, leaning. Wingbeats sounded, *thump thump thump*; the bat was close, right there at their heel. It would scream and scream and scream some more until

Neyruu crashed into some mountain bluff, disoriented, then dive in for the kill. Long needle-like fangs curved horribly around its mouth, able to pierce and puncture a dragon's scales and drive deep down through its flesh. A bite to the head would finish her. Once staggered and dazed, she would have no defence.

They swung hard about the edge of a jagged sheer bluff, their harnesses straining as they were thrown to one side. Talasha clenched against the motion, tightening her gut, but the turbulence was too much for Ranulf Shackton and she could hear him heaving and retching behind her, bringing up bile and chunks of half-digested boar. When Neyruu straightened out again, Talasha realised there was a cliff on the *other* side as well, another high sheer one, and they were flying down some bottomless gorge that seemed to tighten and close in as they went, each side rising high above them and going down so deep only the gods knew where.

We're trapped, Talasha thought, in half a panic. *It's chased us here on purpose.* She could feel the dark menace closing in, feel its raging spite and anger. It was a feud ten thousand years old. *This creature was born of shadow and hate.*

The canyon rang to the sound of shrieking, a sound pitched so high it felt her head might explode. *My ears are bleeding,* she thought. They felt warm, wet inside her hood. Neyruu was twisting and hissing; every time she attempted to turn back or fly lower or higher another shriek split the sky and she would be forced to keep on going. *She's being herded,* the princess realised. *But where…where…*

Then she saw it. Through the shroud the end of the canyon appeared, a sudden great cliff face rising right up before them. *Slow, Neyruu, slow! Slow!* The dragon did not need to be told. She jerked upward into a fierce near-vertical ascent, thrashing at the air as her claws scrambled against the face of the rock. Talasha's head swam, the snow rushing down to blind her. She squeezed her eyes shut and tucked her chin and hoped for the best…

…and then suddenly Neyruu was levelling out again, flying flat and straight, and she opened her eyes to see that they'd cleared the top of the cliff and were soaring now over a great white open plain.

The bat gave a shrill shriek of rage behind them. It had expected them to crash. Talasha winced, craned back and saw it, the gleaming black eyes and squashed ugly face, the grotesque, overlarge ears and maw full of clustered needle fangs. Something dripped off them, thick and sticky, blood or poison or something else she could not say. Revulsed, she swung her eyes back around, and then, just then, she heard the *sighing* sound, then a low *thud* and last of all, a *grunt.*

The grunt was from Neyruu. Talasha felt a stab of shared pain and looked down. There was an arrow lodged in the dragon's shoulder where it met the base of her long slender neck. A dozen more arrows flew by, whistling past their ears. "Men," Ranulf called, in a heavy splutter of a voice. "There are men down there…behind that ridge."

Neyruu screeched and swung around toward them, hissing. *No, no, leave them, ignore them!* She could hear voices shouting below. Thin calls of nock and draw and fire, and another flight of arrows came bursting from behind the ridge. "Get down!" The princess threw herself low against Neyruu's neck, hoping the others were doing the same behind her. The arrows missed, most of them. But one caught Neyruu flush in the breast and another drove into her trailing right leg, and she shrieked again, tucked her wings and plunged upon them.

The men broke and ran for cover, rushing away, all but one. Forward he came, unsheathing a misting blade from his hip, throwing his heavy cloak over his shoulder and brandishing it two-handed. His hood flew back, golden hair whipping in the wind.

Neyruu screamed and went for him. The man threw himself to the side, rolling through the snow, surging back to his feet caked in white as Neyruu wheeled around. *Stop! Leave him!* Talasha's commands went unheard. The dragon was all in a lather, gouts of blood trailing from her wounds. As she came back around another flight of arrows flew out toward her; she glimpsed the blond man hefting a spear. Several of the arrows struck and pinged harmlessly away, but one...there was a wet *thump* and a choked scream and Talasha turned back and saw it driven deep into Cevi's thigh. *No...no...*

A spear-tip flashed in the sickly cold light, a throw strong and true. Misting it came, right for Neyruu's neck. Inches from striking, the dragon twisted at the last and lost control, her balance gone, and went reeling to the ground. There was a white explosion as she crashed down into the snowfield, her body and wingtips drawing ruts in the frozen earth. The whole world jarred as they came to a juddering stop. Talasha heaved for breath, half-winded, blinking. She could see the men running for them, some with swords and some with bows and some with spears, all cloaked against the cold. "Ranulf...tell them...you have to tell them who we..."

Then all of a sudden the men stopped and turned. There was a shout from somewhere, confused voices, and the men with bows swung them up and nocked arrows, drawing and loosing as the greatbat screamed and soared by. Several of the nearest men threw down their weapons and fell to their knees, cupping their gloves against their ears. Others only turned their heads, cringing, and a few seemed immune to it, hefting their spears and throwing them out into the shroud. Talasha could not say if any hit the creature. A moment later it was gone, swallowed up by the swirling snow.

"Ranulf," she wheezed. "Climb down. Tell them...tell them who we are..."

The man was struggling to undo his harness, his fingers stiff and frozen. Cevi moaned softly behind her, blood leaking out from the arrow in her leg. "It'll be okay. It's all going to be okay." Talasha closed her fists, opened them, closed them again and opened them to get her fingers working. It was enough for her to work her harness free, then twist around and unstrap Cevi as well. By then the bat was passing again, and the men were shouting and firing as it ghosted by. She glimpsed it plunge down and pluck one away with its queer clawed feet, saw it snap out and sever another top from bottom with its long needle teeth. Patches of red stained the pristine white plain. The blond Bladeborn was shouting orders, turning with the bat with blade brandished high, trying to call it down for a duel. It would not work, not with that demon.

At last Talasha got Cevi free, pulling the leather loops from her shoulders. "Come. Quickly. We have to climb down."

The girl was crying, mewling in a plaintive voice. "But…we have to flee. My lady, that thing…that *thing*…my…my *leg*…"

"Down, Cevi. I'll help you." Talasha stood from the saddle, hooked an arm around her handmaid's waist and pulled her up onto her feet. The girl gave a yelp of pain and buckled. "You have to be brave now. Be strong." She hauled her to her feet again and commanded Neyruu to lower her wing, and together they staggered out onto it, sliding gracelessly down into the thick snow and landing in a heap.

The snow was plenty thick enough to break their fall. Talasha scrambled back up at once, white winds blowing about them, turned her eyes around and saw that Ranulf was already out and on his feet, staggering away toward the men, waving his arms and shouting. "We are friends… *friends…*"

The greatbat passed overhead, a shadow of death coming and going from the shroud, screaming and snatching at the men with fingers and fangs. A dozen of them looked to be dead now, scattered bloodily across the snowfield. *It will kill them all. And us as well.*

Talasha turned to Neyruu. The dragon was shivering, but not from the cold. Her head swayed on her long neck, following the bat through the valley. Hate boiled in her gaze, and flame brewed in her chest. Burdened with three passengers on her back, she had not been able to fight it. *But now…now…*

"Go," Talasha said, growling. "Kill it."

Neyruu snorted flame. She flapped her wings and soared.

9

———————

Amilia

It was not how she remembered it. Not how she remembered it at all.

"Much has changed, my lady," Lord Morwood told her proudly, as he led her on through the vast, echoing chambers of Ilith's refuge. "Day by day I see it take shape as more people come through the portal. There is light here now, and life and music." He smiled, the great bristly jowls that hung from his cheeks lifting, and turned his head toward one corridor that branched off through this endless maze. "Listen? Do you hear it, through the halls? The people are singing Your Highness. A pleasant sound, is it not?"

It was pleasant enough, Amilia Lukar would not deny it, and a far cry from the eerie silence that haunted these halls once before. She had not returned since her short time here with Jonik and his men, when only the mages had stalked these rooms and corridors, along with what remained of the order they oversaw. Now there were thousands, tens of thousands, even, and thousands more were flooding in by the day. "Very pleasant, yes. How many settlers are there now?"

"We passed forty-five thousand inhabitants just this morning," Morwood told her. "With the numbers coming in, we expect to cross fifty thousand by the end of tomorrow."

"And a hundred? When will you reach that vaunted number?"

"At the rate we're going, roughly a fortnight from now. Unfortunately, we can only process so many people in a single day. You saw it yourself. There are bottlenecks in the tunnel systems and it takes time for some to summon the courage to enter the portal. Our daily record is three thousand, four hundred and five, I do believe. Perhaps we could increase that to above four thousand, but any more would be difficult with our current resources."

"Do you need more men?"

"Men? No. I have access to the entire city guard, and many other volunteers besides. It is simply a matter of time. Hours and minutes in the day, and all that. I'm sure it is possible to squeeze out a little more efficiency from our systems, but those changes will be minimal. At first we were taking names and details upon entry to the refuge, but my scribes now do that as they wait in the tunnels. That helped, to be sure. But as to other changes, I…"

She put a hand on his arm. "You're doing a wonderful job, Trillion. Truly. Everything was running very smoothly, that I saw."

She had journeyed through the tunnel systems herself that morning, moving along among the masses as they made their long dark pilgrimage. Like the refuge, now full of noise and motion and life, the tunnels had changed dramatically as well. When Amilia took that journey with Jonik, the route was treacherous, lightless, frightening. Now torches lit the way, and bridges had been built across the chasms, and the narrow tighter passages had even been opened out by Morwood's men, who'd cut them wider with their godsteel blades and reinforced them so they did not collapse.

It was an impressive operation. Along the way she'd passed wagons and carts bearing additional supplies, and even some donkeys and goats were being herded in. Cloaked she'd gone, and cowled so as not to be recognised, her guards all cloaked and cowled as well. Once or twice someone looked at her like they knew, but in the dimness, always shuffling and moving toward the portal door, they never had a chance to confirm it or raise a stir.

And the portal was different too. Morwood's men had built a lintel and frame around it, so it was not so unnerving as it was before. And there was a screen as well, so that those waiting further back down the passage did not have to see their friends and loved ones vanishing from sight as they entered. That was the strangest thing about the portal. The suddenness in the way a person was swallowed up like that…there one minute, gone the next, blinking out of existence. It took away much of the fear, Amilia knew, to be spared seeing that. Morwood had been very wise to make it so.

The big lord was smiling at her, touched by her praise. "That is kind of you to say, my lady. Yes, smooth enough, I hope. There are troubles, of course. This is a large endeavour and such displacement has its challenges…but yes, I like to think everything is going well enough for now."

He led her onward toward a chamber she had seen before, with great pillars and statues depicting ancient gods and mighty heroes. Now hundreds of men and women and children had joined those stone behemoths, laying down their blankets and furs and pallet beds to make nests about the bases of the statues. Some had brought tents with them, or raised shelters and crude lean-tos against the walls, and it seemed to Amilia that a tavern of sorts had even sprouted up within a larger pavilion, complete with barrels and stools for people to sit on. A fiddler was moving about singing some jaunty song and a few rowdy men were raising cups and joining in.

Amilia was quite bemused. "I thought the people were not allowed to bring any furniture in with them? How on earth were those barrels smuggled in, my lord? Are men strapping them to their backs and pretending to be hunchbacks?"

The heavyset watch commander chuckled. "No, these barrels have come from the official stores and supply rooms. We arranged to bring them here ourselves with the help of local taverners and innkeeps from the city. As part of the bargain, we permit them to continue their operations, in these *tent-taverns*, as the people are coming to call them. There are many throughout the refuge now."

Tent-taverns, she thought, wondering how quickly some of those establishments might find themselves becoming *pavilion-pillowhouses* instead. In her experience, where there were places for men to drink, *other* services soon began to follow. "So I take it money is still changing hands, then?" She could not imagine any of these proprietors were giving out their ale for free.

"Yes, in a limited form. We are trying to recreate a regular life here… with restrictions, of course. Some items are still for sale, and we have set aside certain chambers to be used for markets. They will open bi-weekly, once we've settled on the details. All very strictly overseen by my men, you understand. To prevent the spread of crime."

Slow it, more like. There was no chance of stopping it entirely. The cynic in Amilia suspected that right this very moment there would be looting, thievery, beatings, rapes, and even murder going on within the mountain. That was war. That was *people. And there are almost fifty thousand of them here now. What chance of them all being peaceable and pleasant?*

But that was not for her to concern herself with. Lord Trillion Morwood had been Commander of the City Watch for long years. He knew best how to run this refuge.

The tour continued. In several other chambers, Amilia saw other tent-taverns and signs of trade. A cobbler and his son had set up a stall and were mending a pair of shoes as they passed. Another old man was offering a service to patch holes and rips in clothes, and a group of washerwomen were busily scrubbing the filth from a great heap of rags, charging a half sickle per sack of items. Morwood explained that their drinking water was coming from the snow. "I have men coming and going constantly from the fortress outside," he said. "They bring in the snow and melt it down in great vats inside the doors. Some of that water is used for washing as well." He waved to the washerwomen. "Like them."

As they wandered along, it started to become apparent to Amilia that a social hierarchy was forming, and that kith and kin were staying together. Smallfolk from White Shadow here. Merchants from Many Markets there. The city guards from the Sentinels were being housed in a sequence of chambers of their own, with barracks set up for them to sleep in, all very orderly of course. Amilia proposed they change their name to 'refuge-guards' and that made Morwood chuckle. "Yes, the distinction might help," he agreed. "Half of my men are still in Ilithor, after all. Though gradually I expect they'll join us here as the city empties and the refuge fills."

There were many Vandarians here as well, Marshlanders in particular, but those from the lakes and rivers too who had fled northward from the war. Amilia could often spot them from afar, if only for the look in their eyes. Haunted was the word. Lost. Broken. Many of them had lost loved ones, their homes, their livelihoods, everything. They had witnessed horrors and atrocities that had scarred them. Some sat staring vacantly as she passed, as though their very own souls had been ripped out from them, while others rocked back and forward or sobbed into their hands. Sometimes they would rise and stumble toward her, reaching out to her as if she was some sort of saviour. "They thank you for letting them through the gates," Lord Morwood told her. "Many are here because of you, my lady."

There was some truth to that, she supposed. It was by her own decree that the Vandarians were being treated equally to the Tukorans; all who wished to come to the refuge were permitted to do so, she had said.

In another chamber, a crowd gathered around her, shuffling forward to speak to her, or just get a good close look at the Jewel of Tukor. *Stay back*, she thought. *I shine brighter from afar. Look close and you'll see the cracks…*

Her guards were quick to cordon her off from any advances, but she waved them away. "Let them come closer," she commanded. "I would speak to them." She set her eyes on one young woman dressed in brown roughspun. She had a babe at her breast and another small child hiding in the folds of her skirt. "And what is your name?" she asked the woman.

"D-Daisy, m'lady." She did a clumsy curtsey. "And this is Wilt," she added, "and Oscar." She bobbed the baby up and down on her bosom.

"Lovely names," Amilia told her, smiling. She knew to say that from the many public engagements she'd done before. Whether she believed it or not wasn't important. "And where did you come from, Daisy? Were you in the city? Among the refugees outside?"

"White Shadow, m'lady. Mudmucker Lane. Though not much mud or muck there now. It's all snow."

Others murmured agreement. "We're all o' us from Mudmuckers," a little old crone said. She leaned heavily on a walking stick and had a thin moustache on her rumpled upper lip. Kind of face she was, but terribly ugly. Amilia had to look down to find her; she could not have been much more than four and a half feet tall. "We came here the day you spoke to us, m'lady. All o' us are here 'cause o' you."

More murmuring. Amilia saw many brown smiles and nodding heads about her. "You heard me speak?"

"Aye. Mudmuckers is right down near Pissman's Yard…well, maybe you remember it, maybe you don't…I know you been goin' all about the city…that's a lot o' good you're doing, a lot o' good Your Highness…but anyhow, you came down to Pissman's about eight, nine days ago I think it was and gave a mighty fine speech. Most o' this lot gathered their things and went to the tunnels that very same day."

Amilia smiled politely at the woman, who had about four teeth that she could see, trying to remember Pissman's Yard. True enough, she'd been all over the city, and on some days she visited a good dozen different places to address whatever people were there. Then it came to her. *Pissman's, yes. The rather grubby little square beset by grubby taverns on all sides where men would freely relieve themselves on the cobbles as they drank.* That was how it got its name, Amilia supposed, though by the time she went there the cobbles had been covered in snow, and, blessedly, all the drunkards had taken their pissing off elsewhere lest their manhoods freeze in the act. "I remember Pissman's Yard," she said. "Forgive the delay. I don't know White Shadow near as well as I should."

"No need to apologise. Some of these here might say you're too high and mighty for that, but I know different. You're your father's daughter, a woman o' the people. And you came at our time o 'need." She put her wrinkled hands together in a gesture of praise and prayer.

Amilia smiled again. All this praise was wildly overdone, but it did not serve to say so. She was about to ask the crone whether it was fear of the demigod, the giant dragon, or the snow that had motivated them to leave, before a voice at the back shouted out, "You might have said something about the *black door*, though!" in an angry, bitter voice.

Amilia looked around, trying to find the man.

"I heard you speak too," he went on loudly. "Lots of pretty words about a safe haven, but that door? That black magic door? You never once warned us about *that*."

She raised a dainty hand, still trying to locate him, and decided to just address the crowd. "I understand it can be a frightening experience, but it's perfectly safe, I assure you."

"Safe?" Another voice this was. A different man, somewhere behind her. "My cousin broke his leg when he came through. That sound safe to you?"

Morwood spoke up at that. "There were some injuries at the start, yes, but…"

"*Injuries?* I heard some people *die!*" the first man shouted again. "They're spat out the other side inside out, all blood and gore, or never come out at all. Dozens are dying every day! Every day! Dozens of them! That's the *Long Abyss* inside that portal. Hundreds are getting sucked right into that hell."

"Then they deserved it," someone else spat at him. "Murderers. Rapists. We don't want their sort in here."

"Then how'd *you* get through? I hear you've raped a dozen girls."

A brawl broke out, just like that. One moment the two men were shouting at one another and the next their fists were flying and teeth were pinging across the floor. A dozen others joined in on either side and the chamber rang to the sound of grunts and screaming and scuffing feet.

Amilia felt a hand on her back. "My lady, best go. My men will break them up."

Morwood ushered her away the way they'd come, her Emerald Guards going with her, hands on the hilts of their blades. When the chamber was far behind them, the watch commander gave a sigh. "I'm sorry, my lady. We get those responses about the portal quite often, I'm afraid. Some people don't like that they were deceived."

Necessarily, Amilia thought. No one was told about the door until they were committed to entering the tunnels, lest knowledge of the portal spread beyond the city. If it should be overheard by the wrong ears, there was a possibility that the refuge itself might come under attack, and well protected though it was, it was far from impregnable from certain ancient threats.

"Has there been a lot of violence over it?" she asked.

"Some, yes, but nothing we can't handle. Mostly from family and friends of those affected."

"Those affected? So what he said about the deaths…"

"Nonsense, mostly. The portal has no connection to the Long Abyss, I'm assured, and everyone who goes inside comes out. And not *inside out*, like he said. There was one youth who exited rather bloodily, I fear to say, but that was his own fault."

Amilia raised her eyes, waiting for elaboration.

"He entered in a spinning leap, my lady, against the instruction of my men. You must have heard them…they tell everyone to walk in slowly, and calmly, so that they come out the other side the same. But if you jump in spinning, you may very well come out spinning as well, and so it was. An unpleasant business, to be sure, but a rarity. We had a broken neck or two early on as well, but nothing much worse than a twisted ankle since we raised the net."

The net was a new safety feature erected to catch those coming through. A crude thing, but effective. "And Lord Ilith?" She looked around. "I take it his presence here is still being closely guarded too?"

"As best we can, yes, but I am told that rumours are starting to circulate. I have spoken with him myself, and he seems unconcerned, even eager to walk among the people and show his face. But Fhanrir remains the voice of reason in this. Until Lord Ilith has completed his duty, it is best no one knows he's here."

Completed his duty, she thought. *Combined the blades.* It was the demigod's last great purpose…a purpose paved in blood. Bladeborn blood and the blood of boys. *Auntie Cecilia's blood…and mine.* Amilia placed a hand on her belly, below her navel, remembering. *I never wanted the child anyway*, she told herself. *It was Hadrin's seed, Hadrin's son, and I'd killed a hundred of them before.*

She had not wanted to return here, not after all of that. The day she'd left she vowed to never come back, but somehow, mysteriously, Amilia Lukar had decided to give up her life of hedonistic pleasure and do her duty instead. *Damn Elyon for that*, she thought. The bloody man was so infuriatingly tireless and driven in his efforts to save the world that he'd shamed her into action. And seeing Thalan lost under all that snow…hearing King Sevrin speak of families entombed in their own homes, frozen in each other's arms…well, how could she *not* act?

So she'd decided one day to leave her bedchamber and the comforts of the palace and wander among the people, to help cheer them as a princess should and give them her royal succour…and soon during those wanders she found herself stopping, and speaking, and then crowds would gather, and she would tell the tale of Thalan, *both* tales in truth, for she had two to speak of.

One felt like an age ago now, when Eldur the Eternal had assaulted the city with his dragons and stolen the Eye of Rasalan and her rat-king husband along with it. *I saw his eyes. His red, red eyes…* The second was much more recent, when Elyon flew her to the city to meet with Hadrin's cousin Sevrin, the new king. *That* story involved the endless snow and the iced-over harbour, the buildings hidden beneath the drifts and all those morbid reports of frozen families. One city, two tales, and before very long at all Amilia had told them both a hundred times in squares little and large, and in firelit halls, and from the tops of walls and stages with crowds gathered below, and even outside the city as well in the sprawling refugee camps.

And all because of Elyon, she thought, clenching her jaw. *That noble bloody bastard.* Why couldn't he have just left her alone to drink her wine and sit by the fire and roll beneath the sheets with Mallister Monsort or Gifford Gold-Tongue? *Why deny me, Elyon, why?* All she'd wanted to do was await the apocalypse with a handsome man between her thighs and a goblet of Solapian red in her grasp, but no, no, that damnable *hero* had to ruin it.

The tour was not quite over. "Let us continue," Morwood said, and they did. Next, he showed her the store and supply rooms, some way distant from the vast settler quarters and nearer the front of the refuge, where the great doors gave access to the Shadowfort beyond. Amilia saw the great line of vats and tanks where the snow was being melted, saw the men coming and going with handcarts piled high and shovels slung across their backs. Others were carrying wood, big burly lumberjacks employed to keep them well stocked with firewood and kindling for the ten thousand torches and fires and braziers now burning all through the mountain. Morwood followed one of them to the relevant storage chamber nearby, and Amilia was impressed by the amount they'd gathered. "Oh no, this is only the overflow," the lord said. "We have another larger room full of good firewood, my lady. Not all the credit goes to us, I must add. A large stock was already here, gathered by the men of the Shadow Order."

The same went for the food. Several huge chambers were filled with barrels of beef and salted pork, casks of smoked herring and cod, several hundred enormous hams, bags of barley and wheat and oats in enormous quantity, dried peas and beans and lentils, figs, walnuts, raisins, almonds, jars and pots of preserved fruits and pickled vegetables, and a great deal else besides.

"We brought it all through as we built out the tunnels," Morwood explained. "And there's more, my lady, elsewhere. They have ice cellars here they use to help preserve their meats, cut deeper in the mountain, and we have made use of those as well." He leaned in. "It turns out, they were already better stocked than we knew, Amilia. There is a lot of food here. Much more than I could have hoped."

She was not aware of that. "I suppose they knew something we didn't, Trillion."

"Indeed. They may very well have foreseen all of this and been preparing accordingly. I still intend to ration strictly, but it is a weight off my mind, to be sure."

A *clacking* sound interrupted them, and a shiver went up Amilia's spine. She turned around and there he was, the creature Fhanrir in his moth-eaten robes. His face was grotesque; a terrible visage, eaten away by time and the scouring of his soul. The dark sorcery had made him this, the blood magic. *All to keep Hamlyn the Humble alive,* she thought. *So he could raise Ilith in the body of his heir.*

"A sweet sight," the mage said, peering up at her from the dark of his hood. He kept his face in shadow almost always, to spare men the sight of him. "I said you'd come back, didn't I?"

She grew stiff in his presence, stiff and defensive. "I don't mean to stay. I only came to see the refuge."

"Did you? Or is there someone else you want to see?" He smiled, and she saw the rotten stumps of teeth, the broken, purply-black lips. The shadows did only so much to conceal them. "I know he misses you too. Ah, young love. Such a sweet thing."

Morwood cleared his throat. "My lord. I am glad you're here. There are matters I have been meaning to talk to you ab…"

"Later." The mage flicked a skeletal hand in dismissal. "First I bring news. We have guests arriving."

"Guests? What do you…"

Fhanrir quietened Morwood with a hiss, then looked at Amilia. "Good timing, you coming here today. *Fate,* maybe? Though I know you hate that word."

"It's just a word. I have no feelings for it either way."

"Yes you do. There's no lying to me, girl. Was fate that led you here and fate that stole your son. We were only ever its tools and vessels. Or do you still hate us for what we did?"

She kept her face perfectly calm. "There's only one person I hate, and he's dead."

"I'm not dead yet."

"Not you."

"I know. Can a mage not make a jape? You're talking about your husband. I know what he did to you, I know it all. The bedchamber, the bedposts, your wrists all bound in rope. The guards standing there in the shadows, watching. That pretty lover of yours not so pretty anymore, hanging in chains on the wall."

Morwood made himself large. "My lord, that's enough. There is no sense in being cruel."

"Who's being cruel? I sympathise with the girl. What that man did was monstrous, though necessary in the end. He had to put his seed in her somehow, didn't he? How else was she to get with child?"

Morwood was aghast. "You are condoning rape…"

"Am I? Is that what you're hearing? I'm saying what he did was monstrous, but that it had to be done. That's fate right there, all wrapped up neat and tidy. Horrific things done for greater ends, and I should know, just look at me." When they both turned their eyes away, his voice went foul and guttural. "*Look at me*, I said. You see what *fate* has done." He pushed his face forward to show them, and into the light it was cast. The sloughing flesh and gaping abscess in his cheek, the thin grey strands of meat that crossed his jaw. Bone moved beneath it, brown and stained and dying. "Handsome, aren't I? That's the face of fate."

Morwood made a discomfited sound. "The things you've had to do…"

"Unspeakable things. Inhuman things."

"Yes, but…without them…as you say…"

"Evil things. Abominable things. Things to make soft men squirm in horror." He snorted and drew back, pulling his hood lower. "And necessary, yes, to pave the way. So I did them and would do them again if I must. But why talk of it? It's done. Now come, follow me."

He turned and shambled off, clacking at the stone with his walking stick. For perhaps the first time Amilia felt some small pity for the creature, for the long foul existence he'd lived up here. She'd feel more if he wasn't so unutterably unpleasant all the time, though she supposed that was the point. His life had made him into this, and it wasn't pity he craved, especially not from the likes of her. *He's from an older time*, she reminded herself. *He grew up among the gods.* She might be a princess to her people, but to Fhanrir she was nothing. Just mortal flesh and bone, pretty for a blink or two and then old and dying and gone, and just as quickly forgotten.

No further words were spoken until they reached the doors to the refuge. The men were still filling the vats and tanks with snow, melting it down for drinking water, others hauling in their stocks of wood. Fhanrir stopped near the exit and turned to them. "Morwood, you wait here. Girl, with me. I'll take you down myself."

She wasn't understanding. "Where are we going?"

"Outside. Not far. We'll be the welcome party, you and I. A mage and a princess…that ought to impress them." He snorted as though he didn't care.

"Impress who?"

"You'll see." On he went through the doors, clacking with his stick, *clack clack clack*.

Amilia saw Morwood give her a reassuring smile as she pulled her cloak tight about herself and stepped out into the blistering cold. The wind was blowing in gusts, stirring her cloak as she went. They went past some of the snow-gatherers and lumbermen, defiantly battling the conditions as they marched in and out through the doors. Amilia dared ask where the wood was coming from, and Fhanrir honoured her with a plain response. "There are some trees a little way down the valley. Good wood, though needs drying. Morwood's got these men going up and down all night and day. And he calls *me* cruel." He laughed.

"And the ice cellars? Trillion was telling me there are stores of food here. I wasn't aware you had any."

"No food? Now where'd you hear that? Or do you think we mages don't eat?"

"No, but…there's a lot, he says…"

"And less each day the way you're all eating. Best get this war done and won or else everyone's going to starve."

He didn't want to discuss it, that was obvious enough. She said nothing more as they worked through the tall trenches the men had made, moving down the steps through the upper ward, along narrow alleys between black stone buildings buried in snow, and into the lower yard encircled by the curtain wall. Most of the snow had been cleared away for drinking water here, though the walls were heavily burdened and great drifts climbed up about the towers. It was misty, snowing, but she could see that the gates were open, and outside of them the short bridge that crossed the deep chasm was cleared of snow as well, so the axmen and woodchoppers could pass on their way down into the lower valleys. She could see a path working away to the left and out of sight, see the shadows of men moving along it.

"Is that the way down into Tukor?" she asked.

"We're in Tukor."

"The lower foothills, I mean. The route the Shadowknights would take when they went out on their contracts?"

"Knights, masters, apprentices, aye. Even us mages would leave every now and then."

"But not you?" she asked. "I was told you stayed here…all the time." The thought of it made something tighten inside her. Millenia trapped here in this godsforsaken place, fettered to an abhorrent duty. Her pity was swelling, bit by bit. "It can't have been pleasant."

"What's pleasant got to do with it? We went through that just now. It was my task, and it's done."

"And now? Why not leave, see some of the world?"

He craned to look up at her. "You mean well, I can see, but you say another witless thing like that and I'll see you never speak again. I can, you know. One word from my mouth and yours will close forever."

She ignored the threat. "I'm serious. You've done enough. Why not go…"

"*Enough.*" The word shut her up, her jaw locking tight. "I've seen the world, girl, and back when it was *worth* seeing. You think this is a good time to go out for a wander? Pack me up a little sack and go whistling from town to town? There are enough monsters out there without subjecting people to the likes of me. No. I've got work to do here. Ilith needs protecting and guiding, and more so each passing day. You haven't seen him since you left. He's aging, and quickly. That body he's in…the boy Tyrith…that's mortal flesh and can't sustain him. Ilith's essence is like a fire burning bright and Tyrith's body is the fuel. It's not going to last. No. Unless…"

He stopped, snorted, and gave a sour shake of the head. "But Ilith doesn't want *that*, oh no. Enough boys have died, he says, to get us here. And you know what I say? I say we've come this far and can't stop now. He needs to be strong to hammer those blades together, the same as he was when he tore that heart apart. If the blades were all here now, fine, maybe we'd not have a problem, but they're not, and we do." He looked at her again, eyes shining in the shadows of his hood. "You been helping in the city, haven't you? Going about telling everyone to come here where it's warm and safe. So you're familiar with duty. Yes? You've given up the drinking and the philandering, all that?"

She would not call it philandering, exactly, but for the most part, yes, she had refocused her efforts elsewhere. *And the gods damn Elyon for that. The bastard.* "Yes. Mostly."

He nodded. "Good. Then how about I give you another duty to perform? One that runs in the family." He waved a hand behind them. "Go in there and find me some young Bladeborn boys for blooding. We might be needing them soon enough."

She shook her head at once. "No. I could not be part of…"

"I gave your auntie the same duty. And your cousin. I needed three boys, and they gave me three. Jonik knew what was needed, Cecilia did too. Does that make them evil like me?"

"I never said you were evil."

He snorted. "Maybe I am. I don't know anymore. Once I used to care more. Those first boys…can you imagine how that was for me? I had to take their blood, take their lives, feed their youth into Hamlyn. Horrific. I felt sick every time. That lasted years, decades. But after a century or two, I got used to it. I'm a once-soft hand grown hard with callus, a tool of terror and I know what I am. So aye, if I need to blood some boys so Ilith can live a little longer, I will. But you'll not help me, will you?"

She had no answer for him. What could she say to that? Was he testing her? Was any of this true? Ilith had seemed youthful and radiant when she'd left and that was not so long ago at all. *A fire, burning bright.* She looked away out into the world, away from his hard gaze. "The blades…" she said, changing the subject. "How long before they're brought here, do you think?"

"I don't know. No one does. But it's not just about the blades, girl. The process of reforging them…well, that's a long-lost secret that's on its way here as we speak, but there's more to it than that. We'll need certain ingredients, and some not easily found. One in particular…" He looked up, sighing. "And in this snow…"

She was not following everything he was saying, though the gist was clear enough. *Layers beneath the layers*, she thought. Gathering the blades was not enough, it seemed. *Was it ever going to be so simple?*

Through the mist beyond the fort she could see figures now, cloaked figures approaching the bridge from the white shroud beyond. Everyone looked the same in a snowstorm from this distance. Whether king or commoner they were just shadows bound in fur and she could not make out one from the next.

But the numbers she could. About a dozen were approaching, men for the most part by the size of them, soldiers with swords at their hips and clutching spears in their grasp. The biggest had someone on his back, she saw, a smaller figure, most likely a girl who was either injured, unconscious, or exhausted from the trek. How the newcomers had come to be here, she could not hope to say. The only way to this fortress was through the portal. Crossing the mountains by foot was surely impossible now.

Only when they reached the bridge and narrowed to cross it one by one, did she recognise the man at their head, leading on from the front. A smile lifted on her lips. *Young love*, Fhanrir had said, and for Sir Mallister at least that was true…or *had* been. For Amilia young lust would be more accurate, though she had wondered if she was starting to love him as well. She never seemed to know, not with Jeremy, not with Mallister, not with all the others gone before.

Only Aleron, she reflected. She was sure it was love she felt for him, before it was taken away. But even that was growing less certain. A part of her wondered if she was even capable of love. *I'm too selfish. Too broken. And everyone I care for seems to die.*

Still, she missed her beautiful blond knight. She missed him in her bed and she missed looking at him as he slept, at that honed body and perfect jaw, the high cheekbones and kissable lips. Sometimes she *did* kiss him when he was sleeping, unable to stop herself, and that would often stir him awake, and he would draw her legs apart and make love to her all over again. But that was all over now. *He only brandishes his steel sword these days, not that other one for me.*

Sir Mallister Monsort stopped once he'd crossed the bridge, waiting to make sure his whole party was safely over before leading them on. She had not seen him for weeks, not since he'd come here to the refuge and taken up in Ilith's service. But she heard the reports from Morwood. Mallister had over a hundred men under his command now, all sworn to protect the refuge from what monsters might lurk in these heights. He had bloodied his blade already, she knew, battling a great pack of mountain wolves and direwolves and fighting off grimbears and icecats as well. Had he been fighting now? There was blood on his cloak, it looked like, and some of his men as well.

She watched as they approached, curious. All were Mallister's men, but three - a man, small of stature, scholarly of face, a tall beautiful woman of dusky visage, and the girl on the soldier's back, who was tan of skin as well.

"My lord." Sir Mallister stepped toward Fhanrir, and gave a bow. His eyes glanced at Amilia, though he did not smile. *He hates me,* she thought. *He knows I took Gifford Gold-Tongue to bed. But only because I missed you,* she wanted to say. "Did you receive my message?"

Fhanrir snorted. "Good thing you're useful with that sword, boy, because you're witless as a worm. Aye, I got your message. Why else would I be standing out here in the cold?"

"Yes. Right." Mallister looked at Amilia again. "Your Highness. I had not expected to see you here."

"I came to see the refuge." *And you.* The mage was not wrong in that. "Lord Morwood requested I visit, and so…"

"You two can catch up later," Fhanrir interrupted. "We have guests." The dusky woman was looking at the mage with a great deal of interest, and he returned the favour. "Your Highness," he said to her. "You're the first Agarathi ever to come here. How is your dragon? Not too badly injured, I hope."

"She is resting," the woman said. Her voice was smooth as silk. "She took the shadow's lair after she killed it."

"Killed it? You're certain?"

"I have men climbing down to its carcass as we speak, my lord," Sir Mallister said. "The greatbat slew many of my men, but the dragon… Lady Talasha's dragon, she was able to kill it in return. It fell into a ravine, difficult to reach. But my men will get there, in time. They will retrieve what we need."

"Good. That's one less thing to worry about."

The small scholarly man moved forward. There was something about him Amilia recognised. He bowed to the mage, very low and polite. "A great pleasure to meet you, Lord Fhanrir," he said, in a Rasalanian accent. "I have something in my possession that I must deliver at once to Ilith. It is of the highest importance that I…"

"I know what you have, Ranulf Shackton," Fhanrir cut in. "And I know who you are. You'll say your reputation precedes you, but it's not that. It was a *letter* that preceded you, brought from one of those." He jutted his wreck of a chin at the large blue and gold eagle that perched on Ranulf's shoulder. Amid all the queerness, that was another oddity that Amilia could not figure out. *Just what on earth is happening here?*

"Ah." Ranulf Shackton gave a smile. "Then the First Elder sent word of our coming?"

"Aye, he did. And we've got much to discuss." The mage clacked his walking stick on the ground, *clack clack,* and turned back toward the refuge.

10

Jonik

He could confirm what no one in history had ever cared to know…

Geckantula did not taste good.

"Perhaps I roasted it too long," Jonik muttered to himself, as he tore at the tough stringy meat with his teeth. He chewed hard to soften it, working the flesh around his dry dusty mouth until his jaw was sore from the effort, then swallowed, forcing it down with a grimace. The taste was as foul as one might expect from a scuttling subterranean spider-lizard with too many legs and *far* too many eyes, and this one Jonik had found dead besides. *But fresh enough,* he had decided, when gingerly poking at it with his finger. He'd concluded the risk was worth it. It was that or starve to death.

Still, death might be better. Already he could feel the meat roiling about in his stomach, churning in acid and unleashing an unspeakable gas. *At least I'm alone,* he thought. That was one benefit of being only-the-gods-knew-how-far beneath the ground, down in the depths of this otherworldly pit, hopelessly and helplessly and irretrievably lost…

He sighed, drawing the carcass back to his lips, but his gut gave another twisting heave and he could not take another bite. Disgusted, he gave a flick of his wrist, tossing the remains out into the dark. "You have it," he said. The sound of skittering feet awoke in a surge of noise as the creatures plunged toward the kill. Jonik was not quite as alone here as he might have hoped, in truth. He only wished it was Gerrin and Sir Owen alongside him. Not these skittering, murderous snakes-with-legs that would eat the flesh off his bones if he let them.

"Eat up," he called to them. "And share it evenly. I've got nothing else to give you."

The creatures chittered excitedly in the gloom, a heaving mass that had pursued him for days. They'd been nearby ever since he'd tumbled down that underground river and been spat out into this humid hell… ever since he'd fallen down that craggy hill and awoke in the Mistblade's light. Gods, what a feeling *that* had been. To find the blade. To have it save him. By then the last light of his armour was fading out and the creatures were closing in, crawling and clambering all over him. *The Mistblade saved me,* he thought, looking at it glowing beside him. *It saved me and now I must save it.* He firmed his jaw and nodded. *I must find a way out of this maze.*

It was hard going, though. He'd been wandering aimlessly for long days now and had no true notion of how much time had gone by since last he'd seen Gerrin and Owen. *Are they looking for me? Did they return to the surface?* With any luck the latter was true and they'd gone back the way they'd come, following the trail of maple leaves they'd left to take them back to the main cavern into which they'd first descended. Maybe they'd even find Harden still waiting at the surface and then…well, *what?* Would they gather more men and mount a rescue? Spelunk back down into this vast and endless underworld to try to find him? Jonik hoped not. It was too big, this place, for them to reasonably locate him and that river had dragged him a long way besides. *Miles,* he suspected, though how many he couldn't say. And deeper too, there was no doubt there. *Right down to the very roots of the world.*

The fire was crackling down low, throwing warped shadows across the rock floor. Sometimes a shift in the light might unveil one of the *murder-pedes,* as he liked to call them (given their resemblance to giant centipedes and penchant for murder) but never for long. The light *burned* them, Jonik had discovered, and they would only squcak and chitter and scuttle back away into the dark if ever it touched their chitinous armour. They were waiting for it to go out, so they could rush in and have their meal. "You'll be waiting forever," Jonik rasped out at them. The fire would soon dwindle and die out, but the Mistblade's light was inexhaustible. "Just go and leave me alone. Find someone else to torment."

It was time to keep on moving. He stood, kicking out the last of the flames with his boot, killing off its orange glow. That left only the light of blade and armour, both brilliant in ethereal blue. His armour did not originate the light as the Mistblade did; nay, it simply *drank* and radiated it, the light soaking deep into the steel to reflect from the plate. A gift of Ilith, that had been. It was Tyrith who had forged the armour at first, but Ilith had augmented it when he awoke in the body of his heir, milking out a little of the Nightblade's power to infuse into the godsteel. Now Jonik could brighten and darken his armour at will, turning it from night-black to dazzling blue with nothing more than a thought. Here in the dark that helped him tremendously. It was as if Ilith had known.

The cavern in which he'd stopped to rest and roast the geckantula was one of the smaller ones he'd passed. Most of the chambers down here in the depths were vast, each as large as a hundred greathalls and all linked together by massive doorways and huge, open passages. Sometimes it took him an hour to cross a single chamber, and he would wonder if he had truly entered a boundless place, a room without walls or ceiling or end. This was not the same as the maze of tunnels and caves and great open chambers that he'd traversed with Gerrin and Owen. No, up there above him there was life and light, colour and sound. Bioluminescent vines hung down from the rock ceilings and moss glowed upon the walls. Even the patches of nitre had given off a glow, and some of the creatures too. Water dripped from many of the chambers and glittered on the walls of the rock. He would hear the rush of rivers moving through the earth like blood through the flesh of a body.

Not so here. Aside from the waterfall that had spat him out into this dead and barren underworld, he'd heard no rushing rivers and seen no glistening rock. But for these pursuant murder-pedes there had been almost no signs of life at all. Above him, sometimes, he would glimpse shafts that led up to the caverns overhead. When he'd been travelling up there with Gerrin and Owen they'd been careful to avoid those shafts, lest they trip and fall in and end up gods-know-where. Well, he had to wonder no more. Those shafts led *here*, down into this immense and unending nether-realm, and those shafts and fissures had become his only salvation, delivering to him what he needed to survive. The dead geckantula had fallen through one such crack. He had found enough dried vines and scraps of moss as well to make a fire. There had been occasional puddles from where a few drops of rainwater had dribbled down this far, but those were few and small besides. His mouth was parched, and he cursed that he had not returned to the waterfall to fill his waterskin.

I was a fool, he thought. He had mistakenly believed it would be easy to find a way back out and up, but no, he'd been wrong. The ceilings here were high, glimpsed only at the edge of sight or not at all, and he'd found no passages or tunnels that led upward. It was like a separate world, unattached from what lay above. Sometimes when he looked upward and saw one of those thin scars in the faint rock ceiling, he would wonder if Gerrin and Owen were there. Or whether it was a place they had passed before. The three of them had gone down so deep… hundreds and hundreds of metres beneath the surface, and yet this place was *so* much deeper still. He might be a mile underground by now, or more. *If I dig a little, perhaps I'll break through to the other side?* The southerners spoke of other lands out there, beyond their own. *Is this one way to reach them? Will I find a shaft that goes even deeper…a portal to another world?*

His mind swirled as he walked, plodding aimlessly through into a greater chamber that had no visible ceiling or walls. How many of these had he passed? Ten? Twenty? A hundred? He stopped, moving his eyes around, lifting the Mistblade high like a torch. Its light spread and reached out as far as it could…yet still he saw no sides. Only the murder-pedes, buzzing and cheeping as they rushed away from the light in a wriggling, writhing tide.

Jonik looked around. "Where to go?" he asked himself, as he had come to do down here. He found comfort in hearing the sound of his own voice, echoing out through the gloom. It made him feel less alone. "Straight on? To the right or the left?" There was no knowing which way might be best. Or whether it mattered at all. *Could there be no way out of this place?* That fear gnawed at him daily, hourly, a growing fear that pursued him like these creatures. Could fate have played on him a terrible trick? Had he been brought down here to find the Mistblade…only to die with it in his grasp. He shook his head to tell himself no. He would not…*could* not…let himself believe that. "Just keep on walking," he told himself, driving all other thoughts aside. "Reach the far wall and search for a passage. And if there's nothing there, keep going."

He nodded and did his own bidding, waving the Mistblade side to side as he went. He could bear its weight well enough now, a task made simpler by his former mastery of the Nightblade. The second was easier, it was always said. Bond one Blade of Vandar and the second becomes no problem at all. That was so, he had found. In carrying it at least. Training to use and deploy its powers…well, that was another matter.

Thus far Jonik had refused to bend to that desire and he managed his bond accordingly, keeping it strong enough so he could heft the steel… and yet weak enough so that he could keep the corruption at bay. To him the Mistblade was cargo only, a package to be delivered to Ilith so he might hammer it together with the other four shards. So long as he could carry it, why bother with the rest? To train with it would only expose him to the whispers and open up old wounds. As of now he could hear them, but only quietly, a soft faint hissing that he kept shut and barred behind a door. *But if I should train, let that door be opened…*

"No," he told himself, out loud, the word echoing into the gloom. It spread forth, repeating, *no, no, no,* and he nodded at the validation. "You see," he said to the swarming murder-pedes. "They all agree with me."

He smiled at his own silliness and walked on, wondering how long it would take him to go insane down here. Thirst would do that, and hunger too, and that was to say nothing of fear and helplessness and this interminable dark. But Jonik was strong, and he had a mission to fulfil. *Reach the surface. Bring the blade to Ilith.* That was his task, his one true drive. Right now nothing else mattered in the world.

The chamber took a long while to cross; perhaps as much as an hour or even more. Then a high rock wall rose up before him, a towering cliff of ancient stone with cracks and little fractures running through it. Many of the walls were like that, soaring high and straight, more uniform than he'd have thought. It made him wonder how natural these chambers truly were. Had some ancient civilisation once lived down here? Was this where the gods were born and raised before they emerged to shape the world?

He gazed up at the cliff, turning his eyes to the left and right to try to spot a passage. Nothing. He turned right and began walking along it; another twenty minutes must have passed before he saw the wall end abruptly, a colossal doorway opening into the next chamber, another that bled out into the thick of the darkness, another of unfathomable size.

"Just keep going," he said. "Don't think. Just walk."

The hours passed by as he wandered through this lost land of giants and gods and other ancient things. Chamber after chamber passed by with them. The creatures crawled along after him, their claws clacking and clicking at the stone as they went. Not all the chambers were so neat and uniform, and increasingly so he found. Some had uneven, craggy floors with pits and scars running through them. He saw walls of the same, not sheer but pitted and broken, and across the floor were great boulders of tumbled stone and blocks of shattered rock, collapsed from some wall or fallen from the ceiling he could not say for sure. He passed places where high pillars and columns rose like giant stalagmites, soaring beyond his sight. Some had fallen down and crumbled, others were close to doing the same, thinning at the base as though something had gnawed and chewed and scratched at them over hundreds or thousands of years.

Jonik paused and looked up, wondering if he might climb one up to the ceiling, but their tops were not visible, each bleeding into the dark above, and whether they reached the ceiling or not was impossible to know. Most likely, they ended in a void of open air, and even if they did take him to the top, what then? Could he cut himself a path upward? Slash his way to salvation? Perhaps, but that led to other questions. How thick would the ceiling be? Might it crumble and collapse as he hacked at it, knocking him back down to the floor to be buried under a thousand tonnes of stone?

His grandfather had perished that way, so far as Sir Owen said it. Jonik did not much want to emulate him in how he died…..*No more than the way he lived,* he thought.

He put the notion of climbing aside, for now at least. Into the next chamber he went, passing beyond the hall of craggy columns and pitted pillars, the air growing hotter with each passing step. Sticky and close, it clung to his skin, and ahead he saw steam rising up from the floor, squeezing through vents only a few thin inches wide. The chamber stank of sulphur, a putrid rotten stench suffusing the air, which boiled with a fiery glow. Before long he was sweating, and that would not serve. He was dehydrated enough. "Perhaps I should turn back," he wondered to the watching eyes. The murder-pedes were still with him, trailing his every step. "What do you think?" he asked them. "Have I gone too far?"

He got the usual response of chittering, and decided they'd be no help. "Fine. I'll go on a little further, but if it gets any worse, I'll have no choice but to turn back."

Decision made, he kept on going, passing onward through the hot orange mists. Massive rock formations rose up to his left and right, emerging from the dark to draw his gaze. One had the shape of a giant chair, a throne perhaps forged by some ancient god. It made him think of Tukor. Had the Forge God made some lair down here? Is this where his Hammer was born?

Soon enough, the vents were behind him, the air cooling enough to be bearable, and only a vast spread of darkness was ahead. He had the vague sense that the ground was sloping upward—not much, just a little, but enough to give him hope.

Could this be it? he wondered. *The end of my purgatory?* His mind fluttered with the thought that his fortunes might be on the rise, that this path would lead toward a passage, and that passage would wend and rise up through the bowels of the earth, and take him right back up to the surface. He even smiled, thinking of the cool bracing air that awaited him, the wash of rain on his skin. Gods, how he missed it. The wet and the cold and the sight of open sky. The feel of the wind in his hair and the rich green colours of the open plains. It felt sometimes like he'd been down here half a lifetime. *I'll climb out an old man with an aching back and creaking joints, but I'll be out and that's what matters.* He set his face, determined, and paced on.

When the ground levelled off only a few minutes later, something died inside him. It was the curse of hope, the folly of fantasy. Before him more darkness ruled, and to the left and right and above him too. It might just be the largest chamber of them all, the chamber that bled out into a void of never-ending nothingness. *Not even the gods came here,* he thought. *They made the world…right up to this point. Then they wiped their hands and said, 'enough', and turned back the way they'd come.*

He wondered again if he should turn back too, but grim duty spurred him on. Into the everlasting dark he went, bone-weary and cramping from lack of water. His insides were a nest of snakes, twisting and writhing from the foul meat of the geckantula. Putrid gas leaked out of him from high and low, and a sudden urge took him to empty his bowels and vomit all at the same time. Stinking and soiled he soldiered on, and even the creeping chitinous creatures seemed now to hold back. Was it the smell? Did they not want to eat him now? Or was something lurking here that only they could see?

He walked on heedless. The earth became less stable underfoot. There were breaches here, ruts and gouges torn through the rock. A frown tightened on his brow as he walked around them. These did not look natural either. They seemed almost like claw marks to Jonik, as though something monstrous had torn the earth open in a rage, scattering rocks and bits of stone all across the chamber.

He turned around, waving the Mistblade high overhead. In the spread of light he saw that his companions were nowhere to be seen. *What frightens them?* A faint unease was climbing his spine. His arm was growing weary now, so he thrust down, planting the Mistblade into the rock to unburden himself of its weight and the whispers hissing wildly in the dark. *The blade fears something,* he thought. *There is something here…*

Breathing.

A deep low sound of breathing was coming from somewhere to his left.

His hand was clasped around the hilt of Mother's Mercy in an instant, the fine two-handed bastard sword he'd named for his mother Cecilia. Double-fullered and double-edged, it was as good a godsteel blade as one might hope to own, forged by Tyrith with the Hammer of Tukor. Slowly, he drew it from its sheath, ready to fight if he must. With a thought his armour dimmed, the light leeching out of the metal to enshroud him in a shadowy dark. He stepped away from the Mistblade, away from its light. If something was coming, the blade would draw it. Bleeding into the gloom, he waited and he watched.

The minutes ticked by, one and another and more. He listened for the chittering of the creatures, listened for the scratch of their claws on the stone, but there was nothing. They were gone, turned back to whence they'd come. There was only the breathing of the beast, the menace beyond his sight, slow and rhythmic and it soon dawned on him the truth…

It's sleeping, he realised. He could tell from the slow smooth cadence. How far away he could not tell, though it sounded monstrous, a creature of colossal form. The air thrummed and vibrated around him with each breath, drawn in and out of massive lungs. He had no notion of what it could be, what ancient terror might be lurking down here. Could it be something unseen, never known by the mind of man? Something that predated them, unwritten in history and myth?

He shuddered in his skin, waiting some more to ensure the thing was not moving. Then as quietly as he could he crept back toward the Mistblade, carefully placing his footsteps. He reached the blade and slid Mother's Mercy back into her sheath. He could hear the Mistblade's whispers hissing and screaming behind the barred door in his head, but he dared not open it. *They will corrupt me, lead me astray. Ignore them,* he told himself. *Ignore them.*

Carefully, he wrapped his fingers around the haft and withdrew it from the stone. The scraping sound it made was like the tumble of an avalanche to his ears, and he cringed, praying the thing did not awaken, waited, listened, and breathed out, slow and steady. It slept on. Perhaps it had been sleeping for centuries, even thousands of years. If so, a scrape of stone ought not be enough to awaken it, but still…still…

His heart was hammering in his chest. He felt lightheaded from the fear…and lack of water…and the horrid foul churning in his belly and bowels. Gingerly he turned his eyes around, wondering which way he had come and which way to go. *Away from the creature,* he thought. That seemed a sensible plan.

The light of the Mistblade could not be dimmed in the same way his armour could. It was eternal, constant, yet he could sheathe it to hide its light. He stopped to do so, gently withdrawing Mother's Mercy once more and swapping the two blades over. The sheath was not made to fit the Mistblade but was good enough to douse its glow. All that remained was a soft mist of light drifting from the scabbard's lip, barely enough to see by. Jonik restored a dim glow to his armour to balance it out, focusing on the front of his breastplate. The rest of his armour he left lightless. Specific segments of his plate could be prioritised to shine the light where it was needed most.

He crept forward, chest aglow, watching his footing, treading lightly to muffle his step. He no longer wore leather boots over his sabatons, nor gloves atop his gauntlets. Those he'd taken off when he'd awoken beside the waterfall so that his armour could shine more brightly. Foolishly, he'd not gone back to retrieve them. He wished now that he had, wished he had a layer of leather between steel and rock. He could hear the stone grinding as he went, feel the gentle *thump* move through the rock with every pace he took. He concentrated so hard his head started to ache and grow dizzy. His guts roiled and churned with the foul stinking flesh of the geckantula and he could feel his palms growing clammy with sweat. He needed water. He needed food, proper food. He needed away from this place. Step by step, on he went. The Mistblade was screaming... screaming in his head...

"Be quiet," he found himself hissing, a grimace twisting his lips. "You're as bad as your brother. Just shut up. I'm taking you back to Ilith and that's that."

The whispers were a chaos of unheard words. He refused to heed them or try to unravel their meaning, refused to let them in. The blade would feed his fears, he knew. It would break him down and take him for its own, replacing its former partner. *Perhaps it even knows I'm his grandson,* he thought. *Perhaps it can sense my weakness.* He cursed again that Gerrin wasn't here. *He might have carried it and spared me the burden. I could have monitored and supported him instead. But this...this...*

Run, he heard.

He paused, tensing. The whispered screams were creeping out, squeezing beneath the heavy barred door.

Run, run...RUN!

Jonik stopped, listening for movement behind him, turning to stare back the way he'd come. Blackness. Foul deep blackness and the stink of ancient things. He heard nothing. Nothing. No movement. No...

Breathing.

The sound of slow rythmic breathing was gone.

The hair stood up on the back of his neck and prickled along his arms. At once he sucked all light from his armour, blinking out like a candle in a storm. He still wore his cloak, torn and stained. He swung it across to hide the faint glow of light rising from his scabbard. Crouching, he went as still as stone. He could feel the blood thumping in his neck.

Even the Mistblade had gone silent. There was nothing...no sound here at all. No light, no sense of space or time. For what seemed like an age he stayed there hunched low.

And then...suddenly and from the depths of the chamber came a terrible, chasm-deep groaning, a deafening rumble like the waking of a god. Something colossal was rising, stretching, and from its lungs was emitted an unearthly screech. It grew in pitch, higher and higher still, a sound unlike anything he'd ever heard. Pebbles and pits of rocks jumped on the floor and from above him came a rain of grit and dust, the whole chamber shaking, trembling, vibrating...

And then it stopped, fading away, leaving behind a ringing like the pealing of bells. Jonik cringed against it, wincing, but gradually that ringing faded as well. And when it did, he felt the rumble. The tremors in the ground and breaking of stone. The creature was moving toward him.

Run. Run…RUN!

Jonik's heart was in his throat. He rose from his crouch on cramping legs, turning in retreat as another screeching roar rang out, and there was a sudden *thwumping* sound, like a blast of giant wings, and he felt the rush of air come storming across the chamber, stirring at his cloak and hair. The force was so powerful he almost stumbled and fell forward, but he kept his footing and lit up his left gauntlet, pointing it at the ground so he could see.

The noise the monster made went through him like a thousand knives at once. The pain was excruciating, a violent storm of daggers stabbing inside his skull. Spots danced before his vision. He stumbled onward, tripping on a jut of rock, landing heavily and with a reverberating *clang*. If it was not aware of him before…now it was.

Run, the voice was screaming at him. *Run, run, run, run, RUN!*

Jonik stood. He could feel blood in his mouth, hot bile rising up his throat. There was nothing for it now. In a sudden blaze his armour exploded with light and he reached down to tear the Mistblade from Mother's Mercy's sheath. More light was added, light on light, so bright the creature shrieked out once more behind him, somewhere further back, but he dare not turn to look, he dare not stop…

He ran, as the blade was urging. Desperate and driven by his destiny, he ran.

For his life and the saving of all the world above, Jonik of the Shadowfort ran.

11

____

Robbert

"The gods are with us," Sir Lothar declared in a voice of profound relief. "This damnable voyage, Robb…it's almost at an end. When I get ashore I'm going to kiss the earth, see that I bloody well don't!" Lank smiled so broadly it looked like the skin around his mouth might split apart. "Gods, it feels like it's been a lifetime, doesn't it?"

"Two," Robbert Lukar said, holding his own elation. He would not be happy until they were all safely ashore. "Two lifetimes, Lank. You might even make an argument for three."

"One, two, three, it's all the same. Gods, the whole world's turned upside down since we left. But we're back now. We're _back_, Robb!"

They were…or what was left of them. They'd disembarked from the southeast of Tukor with hopes of glory and conquest…and come crawling back north with their tail between their legs, battered and beaten…but not quite broken. _We have men left to make a difference_, Robbert told himself, as he had a hundred times. _And there's an army out there, waiting for me. My brother and his thirty thousand swords._

His little fleet was still intact and their crossing from Rasalan had gone smoothly. Three ships they were - _Hammer_, _Wild Raven_, and _Blood Bear_ - three ships down from thirty, but he'd make the best of what he had. The winds had been with them for the last half week. No long days languishing in some breezeless void. No fight against strong headwinds either. They'd seen shadows in the water and shadows in the sky, but so far nothing had attacked them with anything more than curiosity. That greatshark that devoured the dragon had not come, there had been no run-ins with grumpy leviathans or ill-mannered manators either. And most blessedly of all, Lorin's Bane had not returned.

Perhaps the great kraken was dead, after all? It was possible those lightning strikes had killed it, or at least weakened the beast enough to make him vulnerable. _Those greatwhales_, Robbert thought. _Maybe they finished the job._ But whatever the case, it made no matter. The kraken was long behind them now, and lest it rear his bulbous slimy head over the next half mile, they were free of him for good.

The coast was less than a thousand metres away, a blur of rock behind bands of mist. The seas rocked them onward, cutting the distance with every leap. Many of the men had come up from belowdecks to watch, and the relief in the air was palpable. They were chattering excitedly, shaking hands and hugging and raising their fists as *Hammer* rode the waves, straining and groaning like a weary old man stumbling onward on his last legs. *Blood Bear* was to her left, *Wild Raven* to her right; together they inched toward salvation.

Lord Gullimer stood with them on the forecastle, along with Sir Bernie Westermont. The apple lord's usually handsome face was drawn and dour and he was not sharing in the joys of the men. "We still have a long journey ahead of us," he said in a mirthless voice. "These men are acting like the war is won. It isn't. Most of them are still going to die."

Sir Lothar frowned down at him. "They're happy to be home, is all. You wouldn't begrudge them that, would you?

"This isn't home. It's Vandar. Tukor is five hundred miles from here and none of them are going to see it."

"None? Gods, Gullimer, since when did you get so grim? You've been brooding about decks for days now. Ever since we…"

Lord Gulimmer did not wait to hear his next words. Abruptly, he spun, marching away from the deck.

Lank was at a loss. "What…did I say something, or…?"

"It's not you, Lank," Robbert told him. "He's just…grieving. His son died."

The knight's mouth opened and closed. "Sir Jeremy? He's *dead*?"

"Yes."

Since when?"

"Since Thalan," Robbert told him. He'd heard a great deal from Elyon Daecar, but not everything had needed to be shared. This of Sir Jeremy Gullimer's death was one such detail he hadn't discussed with them yet, to spare Lord Gullimer their sympathy. He didn't want it, Robbert knew. He just wanted to get on with the job and focus on his duty as men must do when losing loved ones in war.

"Did he die in the attack?" Bernie Westermont asked. "He was in Thalan guarding your sister, wasn't he?"

That they *did* know about. How the Rasal capital had been sieged by a score of dragons the same night as Dragon's Bane fell. Eldur himself had been there and had stolen away both the Eye of Rasalan and Amilia's weaselly little husband. There was much more to that as well, but it wasn't for Robbert to worry about.

"He died a short while before, I'm told. Hadrin had him killed for showing Amilia too much attention."

"A little too much *affection*, you mean." Lothar shrugged his absurdly wide shoulders. "For all his faults, it's hard to deny Jeremy's looks. Just the sort your sister likes, Robb. He was probably caught between her legs and…"

"Enough." Robbert looked up at the much taller man. "I've warned you about that before, Lank. My sister is not a harlot."

"No, Robb, course not. That's not the word I'd use, anyway."

"And what word would you use?" The man did not respond, wisely. "Talk ill of her again and I'll have you thrown overboard. I mean it, Lank, I'm sick of you casting these aspersions."

"Sure, Robb, I hear you. Consider me all casted out. No more aspersions from me, I promise."

Somehow Robbert doubted it, though there were rather more important things at stake than his sister's honour. He gave a sigh. "Just get the men ready to disembark. I'm going to speak with the captain."

Robbert marched away to the rear of the ship, climbing the steps to the quarterdeck where Bloodhound Burton manned the helm. "Anything?" he asked.

Burton knew what he meant. That nose of his was singularly sensitive to the approach of sea monsters, and he always seemed to know when something was lurking nearby. The captain shook his head, bristly jowls wobbling. "Nothing. Worry not for them sea beasties, princeling. Best turn your thoughts to those on land."

Those on land I can handle, Robbert thought. With firm earth beneath his feet he could fight them, but that wasn't the case here. "I want you to sail north when you leave us, Bloodhound. You're to take our injured and infirm back to Tukor under the command of Sir Tamber Rickson. See them deposited at a safe harbour of your choosing and Sir Tamber will take them on from there." To Tukor's Pass, Robbert had told the knight, where they might convalesce beneath the great statue of their god. If and when they were ready to rejoin the war, they could march south from there. But right now he could not bear them as a burden and there were still some three hundred men in his company who were far too weak to travel, let alone fight. Sir Tamber was one of them. He had wounded his leg during the attack by Lorin's Bane and was an old man besides. Sad to say, but he would not be missed. The prince wanted only fighting men in his company when he marched inland from here.

Bloodhound gave a nod. "And the ships? You want them docked near the Links?"

"Yes. There may come a time when they are needed again. I would keep you on, if I can, Ash. Though I know what you're like and I sense you'll be seeking another challenge. If you wish to return to Rasalan, that is up to you. I know there are many lords there who could use you."

Burton gave that some consideration. "I'll decide on the way," he said. "Might be Lorin's Bane's still out there, and I wouldn't mind another crack at the kraken. A strong host of Rasal warships ought to be enough to claim my vengeance. Mayhaps I'll drum up some interest from Lord Swiftwater or Lord Merrymarsh. Those two have more ships than they know what to do with."

Or did, Robbert thought. Who could say what had befallen their fleets now? "As you will. And if you happen to pass Lady Saska and Prince Elyon on the way, do give them my regards."

Burton gave a growly chuckle at that. "Aye, I'll do that if I see them. Was that their plan? Crossing the Links?"

Robbert didn't know, in truth. "They were expecting to decide along the way," he said, which seemed to be the case for everyone these days. It was hard to plan ahead too much when you didn't know what might be awaiting you over the next hill.

There was a call from up in the crow's nest, and both prince and captain raised their eyes. "Yes, Droyn? What do you see?"

"Light, my prince. In the castle. It looks like there's someone home."

Robbert searched forward through the shifting fogs. The coastal town of Winslow Point was spread out across a broad stretch of shore with a sizeable castle fortress looming on the rocks to its northern side. True enough, firelight was flickering through some of the high windows but elsewise all was still and calm. The town itself looked deserted and there was a small harbour facing east, no more than a half dozen short stone jetties enclosed within a rough-hewn rock sea wall. A few boats were tied up there, half submerged in the murky surf as the waters sloshed across their blackened hulls. Scorched masts poked up through the waves like withered grasping fingers and Robbert could hear a bell ringing eerily as it caught in a keening breeze.

"Is the water in the harbour deep enough to accommodate us?" Robbert asked the captain.

"Aye. I've landed here several times before. Never had trouble and the tides are in." He scratched at a jowl. "Those wrecks will hinder us, though. Doesn't look like there's space for all three of us to moor, so we'll have to take it in turns to unload the men."

"We'll go first," Robbert said. "Have that relayed to the other ships." He let Burton take care of that and turned his attention back to Kester Droyn. "Do you see any banners, Sir Kester? Any colours?"

"Nothing, my prince."

"Men on the ramparts?"

"No, my lord, no sign of anyone as yet."

Robbert nodded. He had to be wary of an Agarathi ambush, and supposed if the enemy had such designs, they'd have taken in their banners and hidden themselves away, so as not to reveal their presence. The fact that fires were burning inside suggested they were dealing with friend, not foe. Even so, Robbert would not count on that until he knew for certain.

He called for his captains to join him on the quarterdeck and they came quickly to his summons. "We're going to land first," he said. "Bernie, I want you off the ship at once. Take some men and go straight to the castle. I want to know who lit those fires."

Bernard Westermont nodded. "I'll see to it, Robb."

"Lothar, Wilson, send your men through the town and see that there are no surprises awaiting us. It looks abandoned to me, but we'd best be sure. And search for food," he added. "Whatever you can salvage. There may be hidden cellars beneath the rubble. And if you can get into those half-sunken ships, perhaps you'll find something there as well."

By then the waters were flattening out as they cruised on past the sea wall and into the quiet of the harbour. Sir Kester came scrambling down the rigging to join them. "My prince. I saw flashes of movement through the windows. No knowing who they are, but they've seen us, we can be sure of it."

There was never going to be any avoiding that. "I take it the gates are barred?"

"That I could make out, my lord."

"Any breaches in the walls?"

"Not that I could see."

"Very well. Go with Bernie to the gates, and knock loudly. I won't be far behind."

The ship was brought to a safe mooring a few minutes later, the crew climbing to the jetty to tie her up to the iron stakes. Sir Bernie did not wait for the gangplanks to be slid into place, but leaped to the docks at once and set off toward the fort. Sir Kester and some of the other men rushed to follow.

Lord Gullimer and Sir Lothar Tunney went off shortly after, scouring through the town with twoscore men apiece. The rest were set the task of unloading what provisions they had, mostly their last supplies of food and spare weapons, tents and portable shelters.

As all that was happening, the prince picked his way up the path that wended toward the fort, a stout square structure with four towers at its corners built upon a shallow headland overlooking the town to the south and the sea to the east. The light was withering as late afternoon set in and a fine rainfall was coming down. Elyon had said to expect as much. Bernie Westermont and Kester Droyn were awaiting him at the gate. It remained barred shut. "So? Who are they?"

"Don't know," Bernie muttered. "No one's answering, Robb."

The prince looked up toward the keep, set behind the walls within the inner bailey. The fire that had been flickering was now doused and all was dark.

"They put out the fires when they saw us coming," Droyn explained. "I guess they hope we'll be on our way. The other men are searching for another way in."

"What about the postern gate?" Robbert asked.

"Barred as well. The locks don't seem to be godsteel, though, so we could cut through if we need to. We were waiting for you to decide on that, my lord."

Robbert pondered it a little longer. "Could this be a trap? Elyon warned us there might be a garrison here."

"Doubt it," said Bernie. "Just some frightened townsfolk holed up in there, I reckon. You know what these peasants are like. They're sheep, most of them, and see wolves at the door. Doesn't much matter whether we're northern wolves or southern wolves, we've got teeth and can bite and they fear us all the same."

It was a fair summation and likely true. "Try again, Bernie. Smash that big fist of yours on the door and tell them that Prince Robbert Lukar is here. If that doesn't get them moving, then we'll have to cut our way in."

Bernie did as bidden, smashing with his godsteel gauntlet and making an awful racket. His thunderous bellows about their royal guest went unanswered, however. The other men returned as well and reported no breaches or easy ways in, so the postern gate it would be.

They walked around the back. "Bernie, if you will," said Robbert.

The big man unsheathed his greatsword. "With pleasure."

The small rear gate yielded easily enough; a few well-placed swings and the locks were cut and the door kicked open.

There was a small area of overgrown gardens beyond, with a stable bereft of horses. They rounded to the front of the fort, passing a dusty armoury and several storehouses, which they briefly checked on the way. They found nothing but rats and spiders. The keep was set within a moat, overflowing with rainwater and choked with old corpses that had now rotted right down to their bones. Much of the colour had drained from their cloaks, but the sight of red and black was unmistakable. "Agarathi," Robbert said. "They must have fallen storming the keep."

"The drawbridge is down," Bernie remarked. "You'd think they might have raised it."

They couldn't, Robbert saw, owing to a broken chain. That had not stopped them from lowering the portcullis gate on the other side, however. Bernie saw to that as well, swinging clean through the iron bars with his greatsword and carving them a way through. It was simple iron, not even steel, and no barrier to a godsteel blade. Beyond the portcullis was an inner ward with the keep standing proud at its centre. More bodies lay here, both Agarathi and Vandarian. Robbert stepped through them and up the steps and, of course, found the door to the keep barred shut.

He banged with his fist. "You inside. My name is Robbert Lukar, Crown Prince of Tukor. We have broken through your postern gate and cut the bars of your portcullis. Must we shatter this door too? Open it and spare us the trouble."

He gave them a few moments to submit, then turned to Bernie for the third time, sighing. "Go ahead. Let's get this done." The big man was midway through hefting his blade when they heard the sound of the bolts sliding on the other side. The door pulled an inch open with a plaintive groan. An eye peered out, suspicious and old. Robbert smiled at that eye. "Ah. There you are. So you heard us at last, did you?"

The eye narrowed to a squint, moving from Robbert to the others behind him. "Prince Robbert Lukar, you say?"

Robbert nodded. "Last time I checked."

"Thought you were dead."

"Not quite yet, no. I lost an eye, but still draw breath. Now are you going to let us through or not?"

The old man relented, grumbling, and pulled the door open. The interior was cold, dark, and stunk of death. "Who are you?" Robbert asked him. "Someone from the town?"

"From the castle," the old man said. "I was the steward here, to Lord Denison."

That sounded about right. He had the look of a steward. "And where is Lord Denison now?"

"Dead. Fell defending the keep with the rest of his men." The steward gestured out through the door to all the corpses littering the ward outside. "We brought the good lord down into the crypts, but couldn't do that for everyone. Not so bad now that they're all rotted away. The stink was awful at first."

It was still bad enough so far as Robbert was concerned. "I know the reek of death well enough. And your name?"

"Bartus"

"Well, Bartus. Tell me…how is it that you're still alive when all these others are not?"

"Because I hid. Me and some others. When the heathens came. Down in those crypts I just mentioned. There's a place at the back, a secret door. The firefolk didn't find us in there."

Sir Kester Droyn stepped in. "Were they here long?"

"Just long enough to kill everyone. And steal most of our food." That suspicious squint returned. "We don't have anything to give you," he told them, with a bite to his voice. "Only what we need for ourselves and there's nothing going spare."

Robbert Lukar wasn't overly fond of the old man's tone, but supposed he'd let that pass. "We're not here to steal from you. I take it you've scavenged the town as well?"

The steward's head shifted left and right. "Nothing to find there but charred wood and corpses."

That wasn't an answer. "Have you searched through the town or not?"

"No. We've been here behind these walls."

Then clearly they have a good bit of food squirrelled away, Robbert thought. If they were desperate they'd have risked leaving the castle. Still, he wasn't going to take it from them. There were probably only a few people here and he had well over a thousand. Any food they plundered would make little difference. "How many of you are there?"

"A dozen. Maids, a cook, Lord Denison's lady wife. Mostly women." The squint grew harder. "And don't be getting any ideas about that either. You've been long away, I know. But these women aren't to be touched."

Robbert's patience was at an end. "First you accuse us of being thieves and now you insinuate that we would take your womenfolk for our pleasure? Do I have that right?"

The old man did not back down. "I know the stories of that uncle of yours and I know what men are like returning from war. Not saying you'd dishonour yourself, my lord, but your men…can you say the same for all of *them*?"

No, was the gods' honest truth. There was always the possibility of finding a rotten apple in the basket, but Robbert would have no such behaviour from his men. "Any man caught molesting a woman against her will will be suitably punished," he promised. "But if you fear for them, by all means keep them away from us during our stay. Where exactly are you situated?"

The steward lifted his eyes. "Up in Lord Denison's quarters. And the adjoining servant cells."

"All of you?"

"Yes."

"Then keep them there while we're here and there will be no trouble. We will only stay one night and then we'll be out of your hair." It was a figure of speech. The old man was bald as a melon. "My men will want to get out of this rain, so they'll find what space they can in the feast hall and whatever large spaces you have to accommodate them. The rest will remain in the lower bailey."

"And you, my lord?" At last the man was showing some deference. "I can have a room prepared for you. We have some guest chambers at the top of the castle that might serve."

"If it's not too much trouble. Prepare as many as you can for my lords and captains. I'll be calling upon you for tidings later, Master Bartus. There is much I want to know."

He left the old man at that, returning to the ships to find that *Hammer* had been replaced by *Blood Bear* at the docks and her men were pouring ashore beneath the grey and rainy skies. Lothar and Lord Gullimer came to him with their reports. A bit of food had been found here and there; two casks of salted port, some pickled herring, a few bags of potatoes and grains and several large wheels of cheese, even some stoppered barrels of ale and some old clay bottles of whiskey and wine. "We'll keep that for ourselves," Lothar said, with a grin. "We can toast our return home later."

Once *Blood Bear* was fully unloaded, *Wild Raven* took her spot, weaving through the tangled ships half-sunken about the harbour. Sir Colyn Rowley disembarked at their head and stepped right up to Robbert. "My prince. Captain Murdock and I sent men to search the shipwrecks while we waited. There are two merchant vessels out there that I'm told were carrying provisions of food. It is a reasonable bounty, my lord." He listed what they'd salvaged so far and added that some of the holds were completely submerged and hard to reach.

"Send word to Bloodhound," Robbert told him. "Tell him to send his Seaborn over to help."

"Very good, my lord." Sir Colyn barked orders and men went off in a rowboat. Others were coming in with the bounty salvaged from the merchant ships and it was turning into a good day. *The gods have blessed our return,* Robbert thought. He hoped such blessings would last, but doubted it. More likely they'd face some other disaster on the morrow, but for now he raised a smile and declared it an auspicious return.

It was dusk with he returned to the grumpy old steward, the last of the light leeching out of the world and bringing with it a deeper chill. The man met him at the keep door, as before, and led him up a winding stone stair and into a private audience chamber. The hearth had been lit. From the windows Robbert could see the town down the hill, the ships in the harbour, the black vastness of the sea. A harder rain was falling now and the men were coming up the hill to take refuge for the night. "Does this rain ever cease, Master Bartus?" Robbert asked him.

"Now and then. But never for long. It's been like this for months, my lord. We hear much of the land is waterlogged."

"These are the Marshlands," Robbert said to that. "Isn't that normal?"

"Not like this. The bogs and marshes aren't prone to change so dramatically. Near the coast the waters rise and fall a bit through the year, but nothing we're not prepared for. You've heard of Timbertown, I take it? It's a stilt city not so far inland from here, and all the plank roads leading in and out for miles are raised up over the marshes to make bridges and walkways. Once every decade or so the waters might rise high enough to threaten to spill across them…but they almost never do. In my long lifetime there's been maybe one occasion where a raised road was submerged, and that for only a day or two and during a particularly bad season of storms. Now half of those paths are under a foot of water, and much of Timbertown is drowned as well. If your intention is to cross these lands you're going to have a hard time doing it."

"We're used to hard journeys, Master Bartus." Robbert turned from the window and took a seat on a reinforced chair, strong enough to support him in his armour. "I was told Timbertown had been destroyed."

The steward gave a sagging nod. "Along with Castle Crag, Mudport, Fort Bleakmire, and others. Might be a few survivors lingering among the ruins like we are here, but for the most part the people have fled north. I've seen many groups of them, my lord, escaping from Mudport and the Crag and every town and village south of here. From Lord Denison's rooms the view to the west is ranging and I've spent much time observing them. It's been a sad charge, in all truth. Watching these lands I love burned and abandoned."

Robbert was starting to feel a shred of pity for this old man. "Did you ever think to join them?"

"Lady Denison forbade it. She reasoned we'd be safer here so long as we did not make a sound, and she's had the right of that so far. But how long that'll last…we have some food, but not much. And searching the town…the lady forbade that as well, though I've tried to counsel her otherwise. She fears a trap, my lord, that some band of marauders will come rushing through the gate if ever we open it. Ever since her lord husband's death she's been fitful and anxious. It's been hard getting through to her. And our stocks are starting to dwindle."

Robbert Lukar had come here to hear tidings from the west. All of a sudden he was a shoulder for this old steward to cry on and wasn't certain how that had happened. Still, he had a solution for him if he would take it. "My ships are to rest at anchor here for the night, but will be leaving on the morning tide. You have that time to convince your lady to leave with them, Master Bartus. They will be sailing north for Tukor along with hundreds of sick and wounded. I would advise you go as well."

The old man nodded briskly. "That is kind of you, my lord. Yes, I will speak to the good lady at once."

Not at once, Robbert thought. "You owe me tidings, Bartus. Tell me all your news."

The old man bobbed his head and bustled over to a hidden side-board. Robbert hadn't seen it at first, concealed there in the wall. Inside was a secret store of refreshments. The steward had a look of mischief on his face as he said, "Lord Denison liked to have a tipple when he met his guests in here. Might I offer you one as well, my lord? It is not often we entertain a prince."

Robbert thought it would be rude to say no. He chose a rich Solapian red and sipped it slowly as they spoke, savouring every mouthful. The tidings the old man gave him were nowhere near so rich. It was watered wine, the thinnest of thin gruel and did little to sate him. But what could he expect? The steward had been holed up here for months and the news was as old and stale as he was. Most of what he said Robbert had already heard from Elyon. The old man knew nothing of what was going on at Rustbridge, hadn't even heard that Robbert's brother was there, and wasn't aware either that Borrus Kanabar had reappeared to take command of the Vandarian host.

"Borrus Kanabar? Truly? I was quite sure he was dead."

Robbert sighed deeply. *It's me sharing tidings, not him.* "He is Lord of the Riverlands now, and Warden of the East. Your own Lord Rammas has been deposed."

"Oh, Rammas won't mind that. No. He's always paid homage to the Kanabars."

"So I hear." Robbert was most disappointed by this. "Tell me more of the route to Rustbridge. The Mudway is the most direct path, I'm told."

On the lay of the land, the old man proved more helpful. He fetched a detailed map for Robbert to take with him, pointing out the best way forward and pondering which sections might be submerged. He spoke of the sundry perils that lurked in the bogs and mires, the ghouls and grem-lins, bog lizards and marsh serpents that liked to pluck unknowing men from the road and eat them as they still drew breath. Staying to the centre of the road was always sensible, he said, though with large sections swamped in murky water that wasn't going to be possible. He also pointed out which parts to avoid, possible diversions and detours they could take, and told Robbert in no uncertain terms that it was sensible to avoid travelling by night at all costs. After all that, Robbert had a much better idea of where to go, and how he might lead his men safely on, or near enough. It would not be a straight road, but it would be a less dangerous one.

And then the old man gave his final warning. "I told you before that I spent a lot of time watching from Lord Denison's rooms. All those poor souls drifting north. Well, I've seen more than that. Dragons…well, we all see those these days, that's nothing new, but only a week or so past I saw something else. It was late…late and dark and the rain was coming down, so I didn't get a good look, but what I saw out there…out there in the marshes…" He paused to take a swallow of wine. "Something big is out there, my lord. Something monstrous and ancient, stirring from its slumber. I saw it…I'm sure I did. I saw *her*."

"Her?" Robbert asked.

The old man gulped down another portion; he seemed to be getting a little drunk. "Celaph," he murmured. "This is *her* mire, my lord, named for her and owned by her and we've only ever been her lodgers. Ever since man settled here, we've known this isn't our land. Not truly. It's *hers*. And if you're to pass through, you'd better beware. She may take exception to that."

Robbert smiled and finished his wine then set it aside on a table. "Thank you for your counsel, Master Bartus. I will bear it in mind." He stood and dipped his chin. "Now, you said you were going to prepare a chamber for me. I do hope it has a featherbed."

It did. A nice soft one, most welcome after a hard long voyage. There was a fire crackling softly in the hearth, and outside the rain made a soft soothing sound as it washed down against the old stone walls. Yet for all that, Robbert Lukar did not sleep well. The terrors of the deep were behind him now, but ahead lay the terrors of the mire. They were out of the frying pan…were they into the fire?

Robbert drifted, dozing, wondering…

12

Elyon

The winds were fierce, loud and roaring. Above him, Saska was suspended in a swirling cushion of air, working hard to defend against the buffeting gusts. Her face was a picture of concentration, fixed and focused.

"Good," Elyon called up to her. She had not faced gusts this strong as yet, but her air cushion was holding well. "Now I want you to fly, not float." He turned his eyes around, searching for an appropriate target. "There, you see that spire of rock shaped like a finger? Fly there and back again, then land right here in front of me. Do that without falling and I'll be impressed."

He was impressed enough already, but it didn't always serve to say so. Each student needed a different carrot and hers was not constant praise, the Whaleheart had told him. According to the giant, Saska learned quickest when she felt she had something to prove. "Be spare with your kindness and compliments," he'd said. "She'll thank you for it later."

Fear and lack of praise, the prince thought. *Deliver plenty of the former and deny her the latter and she'll soar.* It was a potent mix, though not always easy. Every time she did something well, the first thing he wanted to do was tell her, but he had to deny those impulses as best he could.

The stone spire stood a little inland up the windswept coast. Bands of wet grey mist blew across a land of scree and stone and old dead trees, twisted and gnarled. To the southwest the waves were crashing angrily against the rocky strand and beyond the sea was rough and white. Elyon could see an old trading galley caught on a submerged sandbank out there, and closer to land a crabman's skiff had been snagged and gutted during the crossing from Krarl, the crab-isle. There were more wrecks than working vessels to be seen these days, Elyon had come to find. *The monsters have reclaimed the sea,* he thought.

Saska was judging the distance to the finger, and not much liking what she saw. "That's got to be two hundred metres from here, Elyon," she called down, uncertain. "It's too far. I won't make it in these winds."

Ah, the familiar doubt. She still wore it like an old cloak. Elyon was trying to swap it for one finer; a cloth-of-gold mantle of certainty would suit her better, he knew, but that was a garment that would take time to tailor. Mastery, he knew, was the solution. *When she can soar she'll leave her doubts behind, and the Windblade's whispers will fade along with them.*

He smiled up at her. "You've flown a hundred metres, Saska. Two hundred really isn't so different."

"It's double," she said, deadpan. "And I only flew a hundred metres *yesterday*…and in calmer weather too. These winds…"

"Are better," he insisted. "I know the gusts make it feel more challenging, but truly they make it easier. They're *yours* now, Saska. The winds. The squalls. The storm. All yours. *Use them.* Be like Bloodhound Burton out there on the ocean. You're the captain of those skies, and they're there for you to dominate. So go dominate."

He gave her an urging look and then settled down on a rock to watch, waving a hand toward the spire as if to say, 'go on then, let's get on with it'. After a short hesitation, she firmed herself up and set off, angling her body horizontally with the Windblade thrust forward in the direction of the spire. Her progress was steady and determined, her speed of motion sedate. Speed was not their goal here today. She had learned the basics of take-off and landing, could form a strong current to shield and support her, and could fly alone and unassisted over short distances. When Elyon took her up tandem, he guided her through different drills, displaying a full range of acrobatics and getting her used to the fierceness of high-speed flight. Sometimes he would hand her the blade and let her lead, always knowing he was there should there be a problem. But when flying alone, no, the fundamentals must come first. He would not have her risk injury by going too fast and losing control, not until she was ready. That was a sure recipe for a crash.

In her own good sweet time she reached the stone finger, circled around it, and returned. Elyon observed happily, proud like a parent watching their child learning to walk. The brutal gusts were making life hard for her, shoving and pushing her around, but like all cowardly bullies, they must be stood up to. So she stood up to them, as he had hoped she would, beating back their sallies and attacks, and calmly, assuredly, flew back to where he waited.

When she landed before him, she had a hopeful smile on her face. "So? How did I do?"

Wonderfully. You are wonderful, Saska, a large part of him wanted to gush. Instead he rubbed his bearded chin thoughtfully and nodded. "Well," he simply said. "Yes, that was a reasonable effort."

"Reasonable?" He didn't like the way her face dropped at that. She looked at him with a small frown creasing her smooth and perfect brow. "Do you…have any advice? I'd like to be better than *reasonable*."

He considered a moment. "Go again. That's the best way. Repetition to build confidence. The more time you spend in the air in this weather, the better."

"Fine."

"And a little faster this time, I think. That was very slow."

Her frown hardened. "I thought the whole point was to take it slow."

"Not that slow. A snail would have gotten there and back faster." He smiled, to take the edge of the insult. She had in truth gone just the speed he had hoped for, but he was looking for ways to keep her on edge. *Complacency is a killer.* That was another thing Sir Ralston had said, though Elyon did not take Saska Varin for a complacent person. To the contrary, she was determined, hardworking, and driven to the point where she risked overtraining. Elyon could not imagine a better student, in fact. *And here I am, damning her with faint praise.* "Perhaps go at one and a half that pace this time," he offered.

"The speed of a turtle, then?"

He laughed. "Just that. A turtle's pace. After, we'll have you flying at the speed of a lame-legged hedgehog. And following, a small and incontinent dog that must stop regularly to…

"Yes, I get the point." She looked at him flatly. "When will I be soaring like an eagle and swooping like a swallow? Surely we'll be better served mimicking the speed of birds, not woodland mammals and molluscs?"

"In time. Control comes first, then speed. I'll be the judge of when you're ready." He sat back on his rock and looked inland from the beach. "That finger is looking awfully lonely, Saska. Go ahead and let it give you another tickle. Nice and controlled. That's what I want to see."

She showed him just that, flying to the spire and returning once more to land before him. He withdrew a heel of old bread from his pack to chew on in the meanwhile, then judged her performance on her return, before sending her off again. A half dozen times he had her fly the same circuit. Each time her control improved, and the bullying assaults of the winds were soon reduced to minor annoyances and no more. Her speed increased as well. "That was the incontinent dog speed you wanted," she said when she returned for the last time.

He laughed again. "I rather think you passed that speed already. No, that was more of a squirrel running up a tree sort of pace."

"Then we're *really* getting somewhere." She gave a shallow scoff and dismissed the winds, her cloak settling back down at her back. She kept her long brown hair tied up when in flight to stop it whipping and getting in her eyes, but now that they were done, she unlooped and undid it, and down it came in a great flowing cascade. It was much changed from when Elyon had first known her, back at Harrowmoor. She had worn a disguise then, using Rasal ointments and potions she'd learned when studying spycraft and the art of deception in Thalan to subtly alter her appearance. Her hair had been short and so dark it was almost black, her eyes turned a warm hazel brown by an elixir she had taken. They were blue now, though, a dazzling and prepossessing blue, a true blue for her royal Vandarian father. Gods, he had thought her the most mesmerising beauty back then, but now….*now*…

"Do I have something on my face?" she asked him. "A bug, maybe? Did I fly into a bug, Elyon?" She rubbed her cheek, and it came back clean. "Then why are you staring at me like that?"

He smiled. He *had* been staring, there was no lie there. "I'm reminiscing," he said, as coolly as he could. "About Harrowmoor."

She gave him a look. "Which part, exactly?"

You know which part, he thought. Saska had spent a week in his tent, but that *first* night…the night Cecilia Blakewood sent her to him to take his seed…Elyon had to admit, that night had passed through his mind many times since their reunion. He was here to train her, though, not court her, and mixing duty and desire could make for a dangerous brew, so he'd tried his best not to dwell on it.

"I'm just remembering how you looked back then," he said instead. "The eyes. The hair. I suppose your skin tone is about the same…"

"That's the Aramatian sun, Elyon. It's bronzed me. When we met at Harrowmoor I was using balms to darken my skin tone. I'd gone paler living in the north."

I like the bronze, he thought. Her natural colouring was warm and glorious, like her hair. He wondered if the colour might fade a little now that she was here, back in the bleak northlands where she'd been raised. There was little sun to speak of, certainly. *Just rain,* he thought. *And snow further north.*

She was thinking the same thing. "I'll get paler again now, so long as it doesn't become summer all of a sudden. *Real* summer, I mean. Not this cold wet twisted version. That's probably for the best, don't you think? For me to look as northern as possible?"

She's worried about being accepted. The Wall had told her that, and Leshie, and some of the others sellswords too. It was a natural concern, though not one she needed to worry about. She had the support of Prince Robbert, who was likely now the King of Tukor, and Elyon could quite safely say that his own support could be counted on. *Father will accept her too,* he told himself. *And Lythian and my uncle Rikkard, and Killian will as well. Maybe Borrus? Rodmond will, and he's a greatlord now. Even my grumpy old grandsire might come around…*

Well, *that* one seemed unlikely, but the rest would accept her, he knew.

He said as much to her now. She nodded and smiled innocently. "I wouldn't blame them if they disapproved. I'm half Aramatian and a woman besides. Hardly the champion they expect."

"Not many are expecting a champion at all," Elyon said. "They're just trying to survive. Food. Shelter. Somewhere safe for their families. That's what the smallfolk are thinking about."

"And the rest? All the soldiers, lords, knights…"

He shrugged. "Everyone's got their favourites, Saska. Let them look to my father and others to lead if they please. That isn't your duty."

"I know. I'm just…a *weapon*, I suppose. A special spear to be thrust into the enemy's heart."

"You're more than that."

"Am I? I'm hardly going to be made Queen of Vandar if we prevail, and I wouldn't want to be either. Nor Grand Duchess of Aramatia. When this is done…"

"We'll figure it out." He took her hand, a clasp of steel on steel. "Later. *If* we make it that far. We'll figure it out then."

She nodded, and her face went determined. Thinking ahead only served to overwhelm her, she had admitted to him, and it was a trap she was trying to avoid. It was the here and now that mattered. One step in front of the other, forward progress, a road toward mastery that would lead her to a suit of mental armour that no doubts and hissing whispers of a long-dead god could penetrate. Then she would become unstoppable.

A goddess, Elyon thought.

The day was growing old. They had spent the last two hours training alone, but now the others were nearing, fording a shallow pebble-bed stream that wended out of the rugged plains and into the sea. It was common for the two of them to fly a few miles ahead, finding somewhere where they could train undisturbed and away from watching eyes. Elyon had done just that when he'd trained with the Windblade at Dragon's Bane, and sensed Saska could do with the same courtesy. This long stretch of coastland provided many such places; it was a broad and open land and the people here were few, living across a smattering of little fishing villages and crab-huts along the shore, and very much kept themselves to themselves.

Still, Sir Ralston did not much like it when they went too far ahead. "I lost sight of you," he complained, when he rode up to them on Bedrock, his monstrously large warhorse. The beast was snorting mist from his nostrils. Well, both beasts were.

"Did you?" Saska did not seem concerned. "Sorry about that, Rolly. We'll try to do better next time."

She smiled to placate him, though the giant could smell the insincerity. "I would prefer it if you did not try, but delivered on your promises. You go beyond my sight too often, Saska. What if something should happen?"

"I have Elyon with me. He's killed lots of dragons and drove Lorin's Bane back into the depths. I should think I'm well protected."

Elyon felt obliged to come in at that. The giant was right, as far as he saw it. It was no use having a man like Sir Ralston Whaleheart in your company, along with a host of savage sellswords, if they were too far away to fight should some sudden foe come upon them. "We'll remain closer next time," he assured him. "I would not want to deny you your duty, sir."

The Whaleheart bowed his boulder of a head. "My thanks, Prince Elyon. I am glad you understand."

Saska gave a light scoff. It seemed to irk her that her guardian spared Elyon any reproaches when they went too far ahead. She looked at Elyon as though he was some teacher's pet, shook her head at him, then turned her eyes over her company as they came trotting along in ones and twos. All the sellswords were strange to look upon in their own ways, though the simple sartorial choice of a large dark cloak was oft enough to make them look like nothing but common travellers from a distance. Even the Butcher had finally closed his cloak and spared them the sight of his horribly scarred chest, thank the gods.

At the rear, Del and the Aramatian archer called Jaito were riding with the spare horses; Saska's chestnut mare and the courser that Robbert had provisioned for Elyon to use when not in flight. All the company were accounted for except for Leshie, who appeared to have taken herself off from the main column and ventured down to where the water crashed and spumed against the rocks. Her horse was waiting nearby as the girl picked her way across the slimy stone, searching among the rock pools.

"What's she doing?" Saska asked. "Looking for clams or something?"

"Crabs," the giant rumbled. "She says she saw a large one crawling about the rocks and wanted a closer look."

"How large?"

"She didn't say."

"A small dog," put in another voice. The Surgeon moved up to join them on his gaunt stallion, the Tigress at his flank. "There are crabs of that size here, come across from Krarl. They can grow very large there, and very bold. She ought to be careful."

"She has her armour," Saska said. "I know of no crab that can pinch through godsteel."

"Ah. But what if the girl does the pinching? Or prodding, perhaps? Some of these crabs can be poisonous, Serenity. If she removes a gauntlet and handles the wrong one, oh, it could be fatal."

Saska frowned. "Did you tell *her* that?"

"Sometimes it is better for a person to learn by experience, I have always thought. It speeds one's growth to make mistakes."

"Death is not a mistake one can grow from, Captain." Saska sighed and shook her head. "I'll go talk to her. Elyon, you'll want to scout ahead I presume?"

He nodded. "I should try to find somewhere to stop for the night." He looked up. "There's only an hour or two of daylight left."

"Here, then." She handed him the Windblade as the others rode up to join them: the Butcher, the Baker, and their two men, Umberto and the cadaverous and unspeaking man they called the Gravedigger. Behind rode the Surgeon's remaining swords: the wedded pair Savage and Scalpel, followed by the witless blond lookalikes Gutter and Gore. "The rest of you, stay here," Saska commanded. "I'll be back in a few minutes."

She strode away, mounting up as Del handed her the reins to her mare. The lanky boy rode off with her, Jaito too. Joy came bounding in from the plains to follow as well, leaping from rock to rock. She appeared to be in a manic phase. *She is a cat, to be sure,* Elyon thought.

When they were gone, the Surgeon withdrew a scalpel from his cross-belt and started twirling it between his fingers. "We are making poor time," he declared, in his toneless voice. He was a plain man, cold-eyed and small. His drab appearance was in rich contrast to the Tigress, who was astonishingly tall and peculiar. Little of her could be seen within her cloak and cowl but those cat-like eyes, burning like twin coals in the darkness, always staring. "We have walked and wandered since we set foot on this land, when we should be riding hard. This coast may seem free of peril, but no, it is not. I can smell malice in the air."

"Malice?" laughed the Butcher. "And what does malice smell like? I smell sea salt and the stink of rotting fish and seaweed. Natural smells, yes, and dead ones. There is nothing here but rocks and waves."

The Tigress gave a soft hiss, and the Surgeon nodded his head. "She says that not all threats are seen. It is the unseen we must be wary of."

"This woman hisses in riddles," the Baker said. "Speak plainly. What concerns you?"

Elyon agreed. Riddles were of no use to them. "Does she sense something we do not?" He knew the Tigress to have mage blood in her, and the people of the Unseen Isles were mysterious enough as it was.

"She sees what we see," the Butcher dismissed, waving a hand. "My eyes are as good as hers and my hearing is better. Do not doubt it. The Butcher is the greatest sellsword in all the world." He thumped his chest, but got no reaction. His bluster could be tiresome, Elyon had found.

"I daresay Prince Elyon has the best vantage of us all," the Wall rumbled, atop Bedrock. "I do not doubt the Tigress's prowess, but she cannot see from a mile high. Talk of shadows and unseen threats is useless. We can only fight what we know is there."

The Surgeon smiled an empty smile. "Something unseen can quickly become seen, Sir Ralston. A dragon from the clouds. A devil from the surf. A horror from its hole. We must remain wary, always. And make haste. We have lingered on this coast too long."

"Do not concern yourself with distance," Elyon said, quite bluntly. "That is not how our progress is measured. Rather how quickly Saska is learning to master the Windblade. That is the only metric that concerns me."

He was done with the debate. Turning, he left them and took flight to scout ahead, wishing and not for the first time that he and Saska might leave for good, just the two of them. He still would prefer to fly her to the refuge if she allowed it, but no, that was a dead horse that needed no further flogging. So here they were, crawling up this coast.

The skies were wet, and the rain was starting to spit. In no time at all he was a quarter mile above them, threading through bands of cold pale mist. Visibility was reasonable, though there wasn't much to see. Some more wrecks scarred the waters off the bay, and inland he could see some stony roads crossing the land. To the west, the coast rose up into cliffs. Much of the coast of Rasalan was as such, a good natural defence against invasion, and he could see watchtowers raised in the distance as well.

At the base of a far cliff, he sighted a port within a narrow bay. It was one of Lord Swiftwater's, no doubt, used to ferry his men back and forward to Krarl. The Swiftwaters began life there, on the crab-isle, before growing in power. As far as Elyon knew it, they still had landhold-ings out on that rock.

Perhaps we could stay in that port? He squinted to the distance. Too far, he realised. Not for him, no, but the horses would take hours to get there at the pace they were going, and the place might be populated too. They were trying to avoid people as much as they could.

He scanned below him, floating smoothly on the wind. Something caught his eye: a path that led right up the edge of a shallow bluff that rose stark from the sea. He flew lower and saw that the path ended in a rough-hewn stair, cut into the rock, leading down to a small settlement built into a hollow in the cliff. Well hidden, he might have missed it had he been ahorse. He flew closer, cutting an arc out to sea to get a better look inside. Within, he saw a cluster of homes and hovels packed into the rock where the work of wind and wave had opened out a large recess. A low parapet wall had been built to protect them from the elements. He could see no movement beyond it, no light. At a glance it looked aban-doned, but it was hard to be sure with the people here. They were a timid and watchful sort, not fond of strangers. If anyone had seen him they may have rushed to hide at once.

On closer inspection, he had the truth of it. The place had been deserted, perhaps some weeks or months ago to look at it. Flying past the low storm wall, he landed within the cave. A large communal fire pit between the hovels was dry as dust, long since unused, and half the homes had been stripped bare of belongings; clothing, food, trinkets all taken. Below the cave, the waters sloshed and frothed some ten metres beneath them, rising and falling on the rocks. There was a battered skiff down there, tied up on the water. Another vessel, a small sailboat, was moored in a watery alcove to the right. Some stairs led down to it, he saw. That was how they accessed the water. There were some rusted iron cages too, bolted to the rock on lengths of coiled rope. Elyon supposed those would be lowered when the tide was up to trap crabs and other crustaceans, maybe even fish.

It seemed a good spot for them to stop, quiet and secluded and out of the rain, so he flew back to the company to give his report. "Good find," Saska said, nodding. "How far away is it, Elyon?"

"Three or four miles. The coast becomes more cliffy further on." He pointed that way; already the rising bluffs could be seen, white chalk against the grey and dreary skies, growing higher into the distance. "We'll be there in no more than an hour at this pace."

"And the horses? Is there any way in for them?"

Elyon had half forgotten about the horses. It had been a while since he'd ridden them regularly; the sky had been his steed. "No. It's accessed via a stair and there isn't space for them anyway. We'll have to hobble them above and put a watch so nothing happens."

"I will create a rota," said the Wall. "Are there trees above? Any cover?"

"There are some rocks," Elyon said. "It should provide some concealment."

The Butcher rubbed his hands together. He wore gloves over his gauntlets, his breath misting as he spoke. "This cave…it will let us build a fire, yes? No one will see from the top."

"Someone out to sea would see," said Leshie, who had not perished by crab poisoning, it turned out.

"Let the fish enjoy the glow of the flame, then. I'm cold." He pulled his hood up, shadowing his scarred face. "Very cold. I want a fire to warm me."

This man isn't going to like the coming weeks, Elyon thought. This was not cold…not compared to what was to come. "There's a storm wall at the mouth of the cave. And some of the hovels are built in front of the fire pit. If we keep the flame low, it shouldn't be a problem."

"I want to see it," Leshie blurted suddenly. "This cave. Someone should go there and make sure it's safe before we arrive."

Elyon wasn't sure what she was trying to get at. "I've just said…"

"Fly me there. Squire, you can lead my horse, can't you? If Prince Elyon flies me there?"

Del nodded.

Elyon had agreed to no such thing. "It's only a few miles. There's no need to…"

The redhead would not hear of it. "I haven't flown yet. Princess Talasha said she'd take me up on her dragon, but she's gone now. *Again.* And hasn't come back. And you won't let Saska take me up either, in that harness, so it's down to you. Fly me there," she repeated, insistent.

Elyon did not know what to say. He looked at Saska, who was chuckling at the exchange and giving him an urging smile. That was enough for him to concede; if it made her happy, who was he to argue? "Come on, then. I'll take you up for a twirl."

Leshie was much less enthusiastic than he had expected her to be. Once airborne, she did not whoop and holler and scream out with her hands spread wide to catch the wind. She was not laughing, hooting or otherwise crying out in joy. Instead she turned her head to him almost at once and called, "Don't worry about the acrobatics or anything. Maybe another time. Just fly me to the cave. I want to talk to you alone."

Elyon's interest was piqued. "About…"

"When we're there." She turned her head forward again, disengaging.

Frowning, Elyon wasted no time in getting her there, cutting clean through the rainy skies and swooping in to land within the protective wall. As soon as he unstrapped her, she turned around with a face of thunder. "Gods," he recoiled, seeing it. "Did I do something to offend you?"

"Is your name Sir Ralston Whaleheart?" she demanded, bewilderingly. She stepped forward and prodded at his breastplate. "Is that a cold heart in there, Prince Elyon? Or a warm one? Are you dead inside?"

He was at a loss for words. "What are you…"

"Are you the King's Wall? Saska's Wall? Coldheart? Big Butch?" Her eyes bored into him. "*Are you Sir Ralston Whaleheart?*"

"No." He thought a plain answer might yield some light on this. "What on earth are you talking about?" This must be some silly jape. The girl was fond of her japes.

"I'm talking about *you*, Prince Elyon. If that *is* your real name." She squinted at him, suspicious. "Because I see a small version of the Wall before me, hard and mean, not the dashing prince I'd heard about. Why are you treating her like this? Why? That's what I want to know."

The penny dropped. "This is about Saska."

"Of course it is. What else would it be about?" She was frowning at him like he was some appalling lackwit, her freckly cheeks flushed red. The girl was relentlessly direct. Apparently she'd spent enough time around royalty to feel she could speak to him in this way. "You're being too cold with her," she accused. "Too distant. That's not what she needs. Not from you. You're not the Whaleheart. Or are you?" She squinted at him again.

"No." His voice flattened out, though he was starting to see what she was getting at. "Sir Ralston insisted I be spare with my praise. She learns better that way, he told me."

"With *him*, maybe. She's always trying to prove to him that she's strong and capable, but with *you* it's not the same. You're trying to get rid of her doubts, aren't you? Build her confidence? Help her become who she needs to be? Yes? Do I have that right?"

He nodded, saying nothing.

"And yet when she does something well you only shrug and say it was 'reasonable'. How does that make *any* sense? Please explain it to me, because I don't understand." She folded her arms and waited.

It sounded a little perverse when put like that, Elyon had to admit. He floundered for a suitable explanation. "I don't want her becoming complacent," was the best he could come up with. "Sir Ralston says…"

"Forget what he says, most of it's rubbish. You need to listen to me. *Me*. There's no one who knows Saska like I do…I've been with her since the day she found out she was Bladeborn, and I'll tell you right now, you're going about this all wrong."

He nodded slowly, willing to hear her despite her hostile approach. There were some old sitting stones arrayed around the central fire pit. He went to sit, smoothing out his cloak. "So," he said, once he was suitably settled. "What am I doing wrong? Tell me."

"Everything." She was still standing, arms folded, frowning.

"*Everything?*" That sounded a little unfair. "I'm training her, aren't I? Her progress has been good."

"Then tell her. Give her better support. You think she doesn't need that, but she does. All she's had are hard taskmasters. Lady Marian. Coldheart. Even her grandmother could be grim, before she got ill. Ranulf's barely been around, and Talasha…she was good for Saska for a while, but she's gone now too, and there's no knowing when she's coming back…"

She looked him right in the eye, judging him. "And now we have *you*. A mini-Wall. A slightly less-cold-Coldheart. You make a quip and have a pretty smile, but at the end of the day, you're not giving her what she needs. Something no one else can give her."

"And what is that, Leshie?" He thought he knew already, but asked anyway.

She snorted. "You want me to spell it out for you? Don't be dim, my prince, it doesn't suit you. I've seen how you look at her, and I've seen how she looks at you, and I know all about your time in Harrowmoor. Or have you forgotten? I know she hasn't. You're her first and only, did you know that? I'll bet she's just another conquest for you."

He took umbrage with that. "You have no idea how I feel about her."

A triumphant smile rose on her lips. "Well…good. Some passion at last. So, how *do* you feel about her? Tell me." She went to sit, rain glistening on her fine, red plate armour.

Elyon found his tongue tied up. A muscle rippled in his jaw, and he said nothing.

Leshie laughed. The sound echoed through the cavern. "How very *Vandarian* of you," she mocked. "You people have no idea how to talk about your feelings. Just tell me, Elyon." Her eyes narrowed on him. "Do you love her?"

He clenched up like a clam, turning away. He was not willing to answer that, not here and not with her.

"You're struggling, I can see. It's a big word, I know. Not a long one…but packed with meaning." She leaned forward on her stone, peering at him with those unyielding eyes. "She loves you, I think. She hasn't said it, not so plainly, and Saska's not great with her feelings either, but still…I can tell. That's a power I've got. I always know how people feel about one another."

His eyes lifted. "You think…she…?"

Her laugh was softer. "The gallant prince becomes a lovestruck boy," she said, chuckling. "How is it that you can fly about slaying dragons and fighting demigods atop the Dread, yet one mention of love has you turning as coy as a maid?" She chortled again, then her face was serious. "Just what is it you're afraid of? Are you worried about getting too close, in case you lose her?"

Yes, he thought, at once. He had loved and lost with Melany, and this…this would be a whole lot worse. It was often easier to shut that door entirely. "I don't want to distract her," he decided to say instead. "She needs to keep focus on her training. The rest…"

"Is important too. The pressure on her is mounting and if she doesn't have an outlet, some light in the dark, she might break. You say you don't want to distract her? Well, too late. You've been a distraction ever since you flew back into her life. There's no hiding from that. And the longer you keep her at arm's length, the more she'll come to resent you."

Well, that didn't sound very nice at all. *She's wiser than I gave her credit for*, he thought. *She has me all figured out, damn her.* "You're very forward, you know. Not many people would talk to a prince like this."

"People are cowards, then. You're a person, aren't you? Why shouldn't I speak my mind?"

He supposed that was fair. In truth he found her forthrightness refreshing; there were too many lickspittles in this world already. He looked out through the mouth of the cave, thinking about what she'd said. Could he deny that he'd thought about that night with Saska a thousand times since their parting? Had she not been in his thoughts ever since, this girl in silver and blue?

But she is more now, he told himself. *So much more than the girl I knew.* He still was not sure it was best to take that other path with her, not now. The Wall would not like it, he suspected. He would tell Elyon to focus on the task at hand, and not deviate, but of course he would, he was wedded to duty and had lived a life of celibate service. Leshie was different. She might look young and innocent, but the girl was a voracious lover, he'd been told, and even on this trip he'd spotted her emerging from tents that were not her own.

But Saska? He had no answer to that riddle right now…and to him it *was* a riddle, not near as simple as Leshie was making it out to be. Intimacy oft led to arguments, and challenges they'd be better to avoid. Why risk it? Would Saska even want to cross that line again? Did she truly love him like Leshie said? *I'm her first and only*, he thought. *It only makes sense.* He knew how young maids could grow besotted with the man who took their virtue; oh, Elyon had experienced that more than a few times before. Or was he being unfair? Had he and Saska not bonded beyond the bedchamber, during their long nights alone in his pavilion? That first night was special in so many ways, but in truth the ones that followed were fonder to him, when they would read together, and laugh together, and share their secrets and dreams and fears together in hushed, whispered tones. But since his return, there'd been none of that between them. It was all business. All training and travelling. The serious matter of the war.

And it has to be, doesn't it? Shouldn't all else be put aside until that war is won?

His head was hurting from the effort, and when he looked up he realised Leshie was no longer sitting before him. She was nosing around one of the old hovels, peering inside to check the contents within. She smiled over at him, catching him looking. "You were deep in thought. I decided not to disturb you. Seems that doesn't happen too often, so…"

She grinned. "Did you make any progress in that complex noggin of yours, then?"

"Some," he said, though in truth he'd been going in circles. She'd sown the seed, but in stony ground. Who knew if it was fertile? "What are you looking for?"

"Anything we can use. Not much here, though." She gestured to a couple of other huts; apparently she'd looked inside them already as well. Then she drew her shortsword, stepped over to one of the smaller hovels, and began hacking at the wooden foundations.

Elyon couldn't figure this girl out. "What are you doing now?"

"The others will be here soon, and I'd sooner make this place more habitable for their arrival. For Saska, mostly. You see, I'm *always* trying to make her life better."

It wasn't much of an answer. "You're only making a mess…"

"I'm making a fire. This is good wood, and dry, and there are plenty of shelters to go around. Now are you going to just sit there, or help? It's bloody cold in here."

13

Saska

She had the watch.

If her men were to sit up here on this bleak and windy clifftop, she would as well, and she'd told Rolly so. Del was with her, perched atop a boulder amid a cluster of rocks forty yards from the edge, looking out into the darkness.

He isn't much of a lookout, Saska thought, smiling. Del was no Bladeborn and had regular vision, so could not see well in the dark. To Saska the plains and open ocean were lit a faint silvery green, as though moonlit, despite the thick and overcast skies. To Del they would be dark and foreboding, the waves crashing and roaring beyond his sight, every whisper of wind promising the coming of an unseen enemy, set to pounce upon him from the gloom.

Saska had said he did not need to take the watch, but he insisted he would anyway. She was glad for his company, though. Del had grown a lot, in stature and in strength, but he still remained the shy boy she knew from the farm, reminding her of a simpler, happier time.

They'd been talking of Willow's Rise again. Speaking in quiet tones as the horses munched on the grasses that grew about the base of the boulders. Summer was the subject. How they would be frolicking in the river at this time of year, hunting quail and pheasant in the fields and woods that took root in the shadow of the mountains. How Llana would be dressing herself up all prettily for the solstice, and Master Orryn would go off to Twinbrook to buy supplies for the village celebrations.

"She'd be teasing me," Del said, his smile faint in the dimness. "Llana always teased me more during special occasions. She always thought she was so important, do you remember? Like some lord's daughter. When she was just a farmer's girl."

"Orryn brought her up well," Saska said. "Not the teasing part, maybe. I think that was all Llana."

Del's head bobbed up and down. "I miss it, sometimes. The teasing. Strange, isn't it? I never liked it at the time."

"You don't miss the teasing, Del. You miss *Llana*." She did as well, when she took a moment to think of her. Master Orryn too. They were the only family Saska had ever known, still the closest version she had to knowing a normal life. Ever since she'd gone on the run, her life had been a whirlwind, a spinning vortex that only grew faster and faster as the months passed by. *And now I can make a vortex of my own*, she reflected, holding the hilt of the Windblade at her hip. Life was strange, sometimes. So strange she'd half forgotten what normal was.

Del was looking away to the north, a wistful expression on his long horsey face. "Do you think they're still out there somewhere? Llana and Master Orryn?"

The last either of them had seen of the pair was the day of Lord Quintan's coming. The pompous Lord of Twinbrook had taken Del off for the war, and shortly after Saska had taken his life. Both their paths had changed that day, to twist and turn and eventually bring them back together. Of that at least Saska was thankful. "I hope so, Del," she only said.

He nodded. "They could still be in Willow's Rise, do you think? Would they have stayed in the village?"

"I don't know, Del," she told him. "Most likely they'd have left and gone somewhere else, a bigger town or city. Maybe not at first. But with all the snow Elyon's told us about, they'd have had no choice."

"Right. The snow. I forgot about the snow."

They would have a bleak reminder of it soon. When flying that day, she'd seen it, away to the distant north. Just patches of it, true, upon the sloping hills, but further up the Lowplains it would be thicker and deeper, and further north of that it would be even worse. Elyon had told them it was coming down heavily in Ilithor when he was last there, and Thalan was half buried in it. And north of *that* was a white wasteland, more ice than snow now.

Del's brow was furrowed in thought. "They might have gone to Clearwater, then, or Ethior. Maybe even Blackhearth…"

"All those are north of Willow's Rise, Del. It'll be just as bad there."

"Even in the cities?"

"Even there."

He thought some more. "They'd have gone south, then, wouldn't they? Away from the snow. Do you think?"

I think they are likely dead, Saska thought, though it didn't serve to say it. After she'd put that blade in Lord Quintan's gut, there was no knowing what had happened to them. *I killed him in Master Orryn's own bedchamber, in his very own house.* The old farmer might have been executed for that, even Llana as well. Quintan's men might have butchered them when they found their master dead, or at least taken Orryn off to be put in chains. He could have been forgotten in some dungeon, left to starve or freeze to death, and Llana…who knew what might have happened to Llana. She was a plump, pretty girl and the world was full of monsters. Saska did not think she would ever see either of them again.

"Saska?" Del urged. "Would they have gone south, then? To Ilithor, maybe?" His eyes were big and brown and hopeful, still just the boy she knew. "People are being let in there, Prince Elyon says. They're all going to this refuge. It'll be safe there, won't it? If they've made it." The youth was more enthused by that notion. His horsey face went up and down. "We might find them, when we get there. Or in the city, even, waiting for their turn to go through?"

"We might," Saska said, allowing for that. "If they went there."

Del was thinking about it hard, his brow all twisted up like a rope. "And that's still the plan? For us, I mean. To get to Ilithor, and go through this portal?"

She nodded. "As things stand." It was the quickest way to reach Ilith's refuge, save flying, and she still remained adamant she stay with her men. They had discussed how to get there. Crossing the Links would take them by the surest road, but Rolly preferred them to travel by quieter paths if they could. That meant ranging inland to the northwest, and finding a place to cross the Sibling Strait somewhere south of Harrowmoor. Saska knew those lands well enough, having travelled them with Marian and her men. There were places where the Strait was crossable by boat, and if they couldn't find one, or the waters were too rough and treacherous, Elyon might be able to ferry them across by air instead, one at a time. After that they would be back in Tukor, and would need only travel south of the Stonehills, then cross the open plains to Ilithor, tucked up among the mountains.

"How long will it take to get there?" Del asked. "Ilithor, I mean. If we go that way, like you planned."

Not my plan, she thought, but said, "I'm not sure. A few weeks, maybe. Though could be a deal longer if we stay at this pace."

"But…when you're trained…when you can fly properly, I mean, over long distances…" He bit his upper lip. "I wonder, could you…fly me there? Maybe? To Ilithor? So I could look for them? Orryn and Llana, I mean?"

She had not expected him to ask her that. "I didn't realise you wanted to go, Del."

"I don't. Not really. I don't want to leave *you*, or anything. It's just… Master Orryn and Llana, and maybe the others from the village as well. All this talk of them…" He looked out into the darkness, peering as though trying to see, but to him all would be black and sinister. *There is nothing out there,* Saska thought, seeing the open plains roll out before her. *But he cannot know that.* She forgot her own powers sometimes. Forgot what it was like not to have them. "I'm not Bladeborn, Saska," Del said, as though she needed reminding. "I didn't even finish my training with Master Sokari, and now he's dead with Sunrider Tantario and all the rest. I don't want to be a burden, or get in the way. I know…" He glanced at her, then looked away. "I know you worry about me, and you've got enough to worry about already. I think…I think it will be easier for you if I'm gone."

No, she wanted to say. *No, you're my brother and I love you and I want you by my side.* But nothing he said was a lie. She *did* worry about him terribly, as she knew she would, and would feel happier knowing he was safe. She cared deeply for some of the others as well, but they were Bladeborn, armoured in godsteel, and could protect themselves where Del could not. If they died they would die fighting, and perhaps she could accept that, but it would not be the same with Del. He would not be able to protect himself, so others would have to do that for him. *And if he dies…if I have to watch him die…*

She grimaced at the thought. "I can talk to Elyon," she said, deciding. "Tomorrow. He might be willing to fly you there. We're getting closer to Ilithor every day, so…"

"Elyon? But I thought…"

"I'm not ready, Del," she told him. "And won't be for a while. Elyon would be better anyway. He knows Princess Amilia, and she rules the city now. Along with a lord called Morwood. They'll be able to help you find Llana and Orryn, if they're there."

The tall youth was hunched forward in his cloak, long black hair framing the sides of his face. He chewed his lip. "I…I don't want to be any trouble. He's a prince…and a *Daecar.* They're such an old house…"

Saska almost laughed. *Mine is older,* she thought. *And take your pick.* Sometimes Del seemed to forget just who she was now. It made her glad, in truth. She was getting used to commanding her men, even Rolly, and Elyon seemed to be letting her take charge as well when they made any final decisions, but with Del she just wanted to be who she'd always been to him. *I want to be his sister, nothing more.*

"He won't mind," she assured him. "Elyon has reason to go to Ilithor besides taking you, you know." While there, he could learn of any recent tidings, and perhaps even visit Ilith as well, to update him. He could find out if Ranulf and Talasha made it too, and whether they had left to search them out once more, as Ranulf had promised they would. *Maybe they would even know what is happening in the west, with his father? Or tell him that the Mistblade has been tracked down and recovered?* The more she thought on it, the more set she became. "I'll talk to him tomorrow," she repeated, nodding to herself. "If I ask him, he'll fly you there, I know he will."

The youth's eyes were in a frown; he seemed very unsure all of a sudden. "And…you're sure he won't mind? I don't want to be thought of as a coward or anything. By the others. For leaving, I mean. I'm not a coward, Saska."

"I know you're not. We all know how brave you are, Del. You've been through a lot. And you're not Bladeborn, as you say. There's no shame in it."

"Jaito isn't Bladeborn either."

No, but I don't care about Jaito. Saska liked the archer plenty enough, but he was a soldier in her service now and would be given no special allowances. "I could see if Elyon could take you both, but I would doubt it's possible. Jaito was born and raised a soldier. He'll want to stay, I think."

The boy lowered his eyes. "Not just because of that. He'll want to stay for Leshie too." He glanced over at her, head low. "I heard them, the other night. She was in his tent…and not to talk."

It did not surprise her much to hear that; Leshie did like to get around and didn't care who knew it. She could see Del was not so happy about it, though. Ever since that night they'd all bathed in the river, and Leshie stripped right down to her skin in front of him, he'd looked at her in a different way. He was jealous, that was clear. *He wishes Leshie had chosen him instead.*

"I wouldn't worry about all that, Del," she said, to give him comfort. "Leshie is like a magpie, always looking for the next shiny thing. She'll soon get bored and move on, you'll see."

He shrugged, playing like he didn't care when it was painfully obvious he did. It made her smile. Del had always been an open book to her. "They can do whatever they want…it means nothing to me. I just… they woke me up, is all. And Jaito…he's always sniffing after her now. He's not the same as he was."

Saska was barely aware of any of this. She'd been too caught up in her own affairs to notice. "I didn't realise things had gone sour between you," she said, feeling guilty. "You still ride together a lot."

"Yeah, but when we do he's distracted. And he thinks I don't know… about him and Leshie. But I do. So it's awkward."

"Maybe you should talk to him? Clear the air."

He shook his head briskly. The notion seemed to horrify him. "There's nothing to say, and it's none of my business. I shouldn't…I shouldn't have said anything. You don't need to hear all this."

"I want to, Del. You can talk to me about anything."

"Not this. It's not important. I'm just being stupid and I don't want to talk about it anymore."

"Fine. We don't have to…if you don't want."

He nodded, turning his eyes away over the darkened plains, and went silent. Saska thought better than to interrupt his brooding; who was she to lecture him on love and lust anyway? Those were subjects she was poorly versed in. *I'm as green as he is, almost,* she thought. Elyon was the only man she'd ever been with, and that night was hardly normal. *He took my virtue because he had to, and I begged him,* she reflected. If he hadn't, Lady Cecilia would have sent her off to some other man, a less gentle man, to break her in and make her a woman and so Elyon had been given little choice. Saska wasn't even certain how much he recalled of it; they hadn't spoken of it, certainly, and barely talked of their time at Harrowmoor either. No, it was all training now…as it should be. *I am his student, and he my teacher, and that's all there is between us…*

They sat in silence for a time, brooding on their own troubles, as the wind whispered around them and the waves rolled in from the sea. After a while, Saska felt the presence of Joy returning, bounding in soundlessly from the open plains. Saska had made sure to keep the starcat closer at hand since landing in the north, by day especially, but still let her roam freely enough during the night, so she could hunt for prey, just so long as she kept well away from people.

Tonight she'd caught a hare. Like all good cats she brought it back as a trophy, and dropped it down at Saska's feet in a bloody heap of torn flesh and tufty fur. Some of the horses shied away from her, catching her scent and the smell of blood, whickering and flicking their manes.

"What's wrong with them?" Del asked, looking over from his rock. Joy was so dark and hard to see at night, the boy hadn't noticed her. "Oh," he said, when he did. "I didn't realise they were still frightened of her?"

"She just spooked them, is all. Give them a moment and they'll settle."

The starcat was waiting for Saska's permission to eat. She gave her a good long scratch under the chin, then nodded. Joy opened her jaws and leaned in to rip at the carcass…then immediately raised her head again, stretching her neck high, and stared out over the sea.

Saska frowned. *Trouble, girl?*

The cat's hackles were rising, and her lips pulled back to bare her long canine teeth. When she hissed, the horses stamped their feet and backed away. Del was staring in confusion. "What's got into her? Why is she hissing like that?" His eyes swung to the sea. "Does she see something out there?"

Saska stared out over the ocean. It took her a moment, then she saw it. The water was churning, a little way out from the shore. White froth rose and boiled on the surface, as though some great underwater vent had opened up on the sea bed. She stood, curious, and paced toward the cliff edge to get a better look.

Del rose and followed. "Is something wrong? I can barely see, Saska. What's out there? Why is Joy so angry?"

She did not answer at once. Clasping her Varin dagger, she peered toward the frothing water. There was a shadow there, something dark beneath the waves. It rose, growing lighter, turning black to coal to a lighter grey as it broke the surface, shimmering in the faint light. It was gently curved, but rough, as though an enormous boulder had risen from the bottom to float with its top just breaking the surface. There it stayed, as the bubbles popped and fizzed around it.

"Saska? What…what *is* that? I can see something out there. There's something in the water."

The boulder *lifted*, just a little, and a long craggy ridge appeared along its front. At the centre were two short thick poles, moving independently, topped with a pair of gleaming black orbs. *Eyes,* Saska thought, open-mouthed. *Gods, those are eyes.* They turned, looking and searching, and all of a sudden they snapped right at her, one and then the other. For a moment the two eyes stared, fixed and unmoving.

Then just like that, the thing was gone, vanishing silently back into the bay.

Del's voice was a choked whisper. "It's gone," he breathed. "Has... has it gone, Saska?"

For a moment it seemed like it might have. Then she saw the shadow again, moving with the motion of the sea, saw the water rising up into a growing wave before it. It was moving quickly. Quicker and quicker still. *The cave*, Saska thought. *It's going for the cave.* She opened her mouth and shouted out, "Up! Everyone, wake up! Wake up!"

Then she was running, dashing to her right to where the stone stair worked down from the clifftop. She waved Del back when he made to chase, commanding Joy to stay with him. The way down into the cavern was not far. She leapt from step to step and crashed inside past the storm wall, tripping right into a shelter as she went. Someone was sleeping within it. She heard a meaty grunt and the sound of snapping wood, and pushed herself back up to her feet, shouting.

"Get up, all of you! Up! Up! Up!"

The creature was closing, no more than two dozen metres away. A great white wave rose before it, swelling and looming. She had barely enough time to shout out again before it hit the rocks at the base of the cliff and rose up to surge inside, crashing right over the storm wall to drown the whole cavern in saltwater and seaweed.

At once the fire hissed out, plunging the whole cave into darkness. For a moment Saska was submerged; all was blurred sounds and burning lungs, the churn of seawater swirling around her. Then the wave hit the back of the cavern and broke, sloshing side to side, and began emptying back out past the wall, dragging with it bits of debris. Saska broke the surface and filled her lungs, gasping. All around her the sellswords were crawling from their sodden shelters and hovels, retching and spluttering in confusion.

"What is this fresh madness!" the Baker was saying, slipping as he scrambled to his feet. "I was having a nice dream!"

"A tidal wave," Leshie cried out, from somewhere. "It's a tidal wave. What else could it be?"

"It's that kraken come again," bellowed the Butcher. "He wants another go at me...I will kill it...this time I will make sure I..." Another wave swallowed his next words. He shouldered through it, the water parting against his brawny scarred frame. The Surgeon was shouting about unseen things becoming seen and she could hear the Wall thundering about trying to find her in the dark.

Then Elyon was at her side. "What is it?" he asked. He was astonishingly calm, his silver-blue eyes peering out past the storm wall. She gave him a quick look up and down; he wore breeks and nothing else, his honed body wet and dripping. Water ran down through the contours of his muscles. "Is it Lorin's Bane?"

She opened her mouth to speak, but the low groaning sound cut her off. A deep rumble that came from the water beneath them, outside the cave. "It's not the kraken," she managed to get out. "It looked…it looked more like a…"

"Crab!" Leshie screamed.

Everyone looked to the mouth of the cave. A huge greyish-blue pincer was rising up and reaching in, clicking and clacking, a claw as big as a rowboat all covered in nubbly studs and horns and barnacles. Long strands of green seaweed hung from the serrated teeth between the pincers and there were rags there too, caught on snags, the rags of dead sailors and seamen.

The Butcher roared and charged. "Foul monster!" He was naked, bearing only his blade, manhood swinging side to side as he went. He made it a few feet before the Whaleheart thundered in and shoved him aside, knocking him out of the way, to stand before the claw. He was armoured from head to heel; even his greathelm was on. Rolly was never not armoured. Rolly was always prepared.

"Everyone get back," he bellowed from within his bucket helm. "I know what this is." He turned his head and caught Saska's eye. "Back, I said. Get up to the surface."

They couldn't. The giant crab creature was too close to the stair, and there was no back door to this cavern.

"Back, all of you," the giant thundered. "None of you are armoured. I will face this foe alone."

Saska would not allow it. She was armoured too, and this creature was here for her. *Like Lorin's Bane*, she thought. *All dark things are drawn to me.*

She stepped forward. The pincer was a few metres from where Rolly stood in Blockform, clicking and preparing to engage. Beyond, she saw the long ridge at the front of the crab's body rise up, saw those *eyes* again, staring at her. They seemed to dilate, ripening as they saw her, the mandibles of its maw twitching in anticipation. *It's here for me*, she thought again, as the huge claw snapped forward, moving straight past the Whaleheart to try to get at her. The giant grunted and threw himself into it, smashing it aside in his heavy godsteel plate. "Get back," he roared, as he tore a greatsword from his sheath, swinging down in a single swift motion. The blade bit deep into the thick carapace armour, but not through it. "Get back, I said! Get *her* back!"

Someone reached out to take her arm, Elyon or another she could not say. She pulled away and drew the Windblade from its sheath.

"Saska, no…" That *was* Elyon, she knew.

She ignored him, pacing away across the flattened drowned hovels and floating black logs from the fire. A foot and a half of water still splashed and sloshed at her legs as it drained out past the wall, roiling with debris. The *other* Wall was ripping his second greatsword from its sheath, even as he tore the first from the crab's claw. One sang out to a song of steel, the other with a crack of carapace plate and in a brutal attack both came down again, one and then the other, hacking and cleaving. The shell cracked and shattered, chips flying everywhere, and the great demon crab gave out a shuddering roar that vibrated through the inside of the cave. Saska could feel the tremors moving up through her feet. Even the water seemed to bounce and tremble.

Then she saw the *second* claw.

It was even bigger than the first, wider and thicker, reaching up from the other side of the cave mouth. "Rolly!" she shouted out, as it came in behind him. His back was turned and he was not going to see it in time. "Rolly, look out!" He heeded her, but too late. The claw reached out and closed around him, the huge serrated pincers snapping down and crushing at his breastplate. There was a sickening screech of steel, the sound of Sir Ralston bellowing a curse as he tried to shift and swing, but the claw had one arm trapped and pinned to his side, the other raised high, unable to strike with force. The claw was dragging him away, out toward the water.

"Saska!" Elyon shouted right behind her. A hand reached out. "The blade! Hand me the Windblade!"

He was unarmoured. *No.* If the creature got him in its claws it would snip him right in two. She shrugged away from him and took three quick paces forward, set her feet and mustered the winds and swung. A powerful pulse of swirling air went flying, sucking up water and debris as it went. The whirlpool struck the crab in the bigger claw, momentarily stunning it. The pincers opened just enough for Rolly to shift and struggle free.

He surged backward into the cave, a greatsword in each hand, defending the way in. The claw had left fresh scratches and dents in his armour, Saska saw. Much more and it might have been able to crush or cut right through the plate. There was a deal of shouting and calling behind her as the others snatched up their weapons, swords and spears and bows, voices echoing. The Wall bellowed for them to stay away again, and Saska was calling the same, but they did not listen. At the yawning maw of the cave the enormous crab was all in a rage, smashing at the rock with his larger claw as though trying to bring the roof down atop them. His other claw was a wreck, the bottom pincer hanging loose on long wet strands of pulpy pink meat, blood spurting everywhere.

Sir Ralston roared and charged in to finish the job, dual greatswords swishing in a grey blur. Before Saska could rush to follow, she saw the Butcher stamping past her, still nude as a newborn, the Tigress with him. Astonishingly, she was undressed as well, her scourged back and breasts all torn and horrifically scarred. The two made quite the pair. From another part of the cave Gutter and Gore were screaming madly and charging as well.

The entire cave was shaking. Bits of rock came lose from the ceiling, splashing into the water and crashing into the hovels. Saska saw movement to her right. Someone was trapped inside one of the collapsed shelters, screaming as they tried to fight their way out through tangles of animal skin and broken wood. It was a woman's voice, and must be Savage. Most likely Scalpel was in there too. She began toward them, rushing to help, but only made it a handful of steps before the crab smashed its huge claw at the cliffside again, and a larger portion of the cave ceiling gave way, tumbling and crashing down atop them. She came to a shuddering stop, heard the screaming end abruptly. A hand grabbed her and tugged back and she turned and saw Elyon there again. He bore a sword, the sword Robbert had given him. But he wanted the other one. "Saska…let me have it."

"You're unarmoured." She pushed him in the chest. "Get away. I can't lose you."

"You won't lose me."

She didn't wait to hear more from him. This monster was going to bury them all if she didn't try to stop it. Bursting to the front of the cave she gave in to desperate instinct, swinging hard with the Wind-blade, buffeting the beast with powerful pulses of swirling air. The huge body was there, scrambling on the rocks outside the shattered storm wall, long segmented legs reaching out to either side to cling on to the wet glistening stone as it reached inside with its pincer-claws. She swung again and again and again. The giant crab reeled, its long pole-eyes swivelling wildly. The sellswords were mustering about her now, leaping and hacking at the claws. Some had rushed out down onto the rocks to cut at the long spindly legs, trying to dislodge the beast, driving it away.

Then suddenly it was scrambling higher, up above them, its huge bulk rising up onto the clifftop. Water cascaded down from its grotesque underside, streaming off seaweed as it rumbled and crashed away, bits of stone and soil tumbling loose from the brink. *Del*, Saska thought, panicking. *Joy…*

The men scrambled for the broken stair, giving chase, but Saska had a quicker way. She swung the Windblade forward and flew out of the mouth, twisting in a quick upward arc, soaring right up and over the surface. She took the measure of the scene in a glance; Del, standing horrorstruck as he stared at the approaching monster, bow in his grasp, Joy at his side, coiled and hissing, the horses screaming and tugging at their ropes in blind terror. One or two had gotten free and were bolting away over the plains. Del took a step back, fumbling to nock an arrow to his string, stumbled on a rock and fell. Joy leapt in front of him, as though ready to pounce but she was powerless against this foe.

"Run!" Saska screamed. "Run!" She shot down from the skies like a lightning bolt, faster than she ever had before, much faster, flying straight for the creature's stalk-eyes.

Blind it, she told herself. *Cut them off and blind it.* The eyes swivelled right around, seeing her. *Look upon your death, monster!* She swung and swung hard…and only then realised her mistake. When she flew, she flew where the tip of the Windblade pointed. She hadn't yet learned how to swing it in flight, hadn't learned aerial combat. Her body lurched suddenly away as the tip swished to the side, pulling her that way, and she lost all control and balance, casting herself out over the plains. The winds deserted her and she crashed into a scatter of rocks, driving a deep rut through the earth.

She spat dirt, wheezing as she got right back up to her feet. Her armour had taken the brunt of it, yet she felt unsteady, dazed. She'd lost the Windblade on landing. Turning, she saw it lying on the rocks nearby, and staggered to fetch it, fighting for breath. She could hear the monster crashing across the clifftop, roaring, hear the voices of her men shouting out as they climbed up the broken stair and gave chase. When her fingers closed around the Windblade's hilt she felt strong again, and stood tall and straight, filling her lungs. She'd flown further than she realised when she lost control; seventy metres in the distance she saw the great shadow of the crab, the men like insects chopping at its legs. The beast was turning this way and that, surrounded, lashing out with its enormous claws and stabbing legs. The giant form of Sir Ralston Whaleheart did not look so giant against this foe, yet he stood against it all the same. Stepping in closer than the rest would dare he thrust and plunged at its underside with his two long mighty greatswords.

Saska could not delay. She pulled a final breath into her lungs and swung the Windblade upward. Desperation drove her and the winds obeyed. Distantly, she could feel Joy's presence and knew the cat was still with Del, defending him as Saska would have. *He is safe*, she told herself. *They're both safe.*

She flew back into the fray, the chaos becoming clearer as she neared. One of her men was down, she saw, punctured through the chest by one of the crab's long spindly legs. Fear bloomed when she thought it might be Elyon, but no, it was Gutter or Gore, lying dead in a pool of spreading blood. The other rushed to kneel over him, trying to shake him awake but it was no use. His shriek of wild grief rang out through the air.

Enough, Saska thought. She pointed the tip of the Windblade between the creature's stalked eyes; the brain would be in there somewhere, she thought. *Puncture it. Puncture it and kill it.* She flew hard at her target, clos- ing, closing…but the monster was moving, twisting and turning, and she dare not swing the tip as she had before lest she lose control and crash. Cursing, she missed her mark and was forced to fly over the top of it, turning in a wide arc, swinging around to face it again.

The men were still prodding and poking, getting only as close as they dared. Twice more Saska flew for her target and twice more she had to bail out as the monster moved at the last moment. When she came around for a fourth attempt she saw that another of her men was down, dead or injured she could not be sure. Only Rolly stood up before it, chopping and fending at the larger claw as it snapped out, trying to grab him. Stinking steaming filth was leaking from the beast's underside and its smaller claw was a mangled mess of pulp and shattered shell. From a weapon to chop it had become a weapon to crush, a bloody hammer spraying blood and gore across the field. *Turn to me*, Saska thought, as she flew toward it. *Me. Look at me, damn you!*

Then suddenly she saw Elyon there, racing across the rocky clifftop. He came up close to the monster, calling and waving to it, slashing out with his blade at one of its skinny segmented legs. The beast turned to him, kicking out and stabbing, and Saska's heart was in her throat. The prince danced back and away, nimble as a mountain goat. A strange bellowing roar rumbled out of the beast and it surged toward him, bashing Rolly aside. It did not run sideways like a common crab, but forward, its many legs tearing out chunks of soil as it thundered after the prince. *What's he doing? Damn it, Elyon, run!*

He did run. He turned and ran…right in her direction, and the crab gave chase, and she realised what he was doing. *He's leading it toward me, keeping it on a straight course.* She would not waste the chance. Setting her sights on her target she flew fast and fierce, the air rushing past her ears, the beast lurching and scrambling, Elyon leaping away. In a blink she was upon her foe, and this time her aim was true. The stalk-eyes saw her, and she saw in them the strange fear, but it was too late. The Windblade struck.

It drove deep, plunging through hard thick carapace shell and right into the soft wet meat beneath, right up to the curving cross guard. Saska's arm juddered to a halt as she swung her legs forward and landed with her feet between the eyes, pulling hard to withdraw the steel. It didn't budge. She pulled again. Nothing. The colossal crab was quivering, the stalk-eyes jerking. A deep low hissing sound poured out of its hideous mouth, spitting a stinking white froth, and the legs were giving way beneath it, scrambling wildly and in all directions as though each had a mind of its own. It lurched sideways, as if a common crab after all, nearing the cliff edge…

No, Saska thought. The blade was still stuck. She tugged harder, reached down to grab the hilt with both hands and bent at the knees, pulling with all her strength. The earth was crumbling at the precipice, the monster about to go over. Below, the sea raged, crashing against the rocks below.

"Get off, Saska!" Sir Ralston was bellowing. "Get off now! You will have to jump!"

But the blade…she could *not* leave without the blade. She gave a final desperate heave and felt it *move*, the steel shifting, sliding up and out… and all of a sudden the entire length of it was bursting free, lacquered red, just as the creature tumbled over the cliff and into the sea.

She leapt, propelling herself just high and far enough to land in a rolling tumble at the top of the cliffs. She could hear the colossal crab crashing and landing below, hear the monster giving out a final low groan as it struck the rocks and splashed through the waves. It sounded dead. She hoped it was dead. *Please be dead,* she thought.

The Wall strode past her, a looming steel shadow, fog steaming through the vents of his faceplate. He went straight to the edge and looked down, paused a moment, then returned to stand above her. "It's dead," he rumbled. "Dashed on the rocks."

She breathed out in relief. "You're sure? It might still take itself away to heal, or…"

He shook his head to cut her off. "I told you to get back, Saska," he admonished. "To *not* engage. You could have gotten yourself killed."

She blinked up at him, astonished. A reproach, after *that*? Weakly, she got up onto a knee and then stood to face him, craning her eyes up to meet his. "I didn't have a choice," she told him, more hurt than angry. "It was dragging you to the water. What was I to do? Let you drown?"

"Yes. If you must. I am not important. *You* are."

She vented a breath, exasperated. She was bone-weary of his constant need to keep her from harm. It was his duty, and it touched her that he cared, but she was weary of it. "The others…" She looked over the plains. "How…how many…?"

"I'm not sure. Several."

"Del? Leshie?"

"They are uninjured. Your brother was well away from the fighting, with the cat." He made no mention of Leshie's participation as Elyon approached from the gloom, still wearing little more than a breechclout, filthy with mud and blood.

He went straight to Saska and put his hands on her armoured arms, looking her worriedly up and down. "Are you all right? Are you hurt?"

"I'm…fine, Elyon. Just…a little shaken." She looked into his eyes, silver-blue and beautiful. "You…you led it to me. You knew what I…"

"I saw your intent." He nodded, once and twice. "That was smart, going for the brain. I'd have done the same thing in your position."

He would, she realised, *and more quickly than I did.* He might have flown straight out of the cave and ended it all at once, if she'd handed the blade over. That realisation wounded her. *Men are dead. They're dead because of me.* "I should have given you the blade. I was just worried…because you weren't armoured. But…"

He put a hand on her cheek; there was a look in his eyes, like he wanted to kiss her, she thought, but he only smiled and said, "You did great, Saska. Truly," in a soft and encouraging voice. "I only wanted to help, that's all, but you…don't second guess yourself. You made the right decision at the time."

She began shaking her head.

"You did," he insisted, more firmly. "One hit from that thing's claw and I might have been knocked out to sea, Windblade and all. In your armour you were better placed to act, and it was a good test…a more advanced one than I'd want you to have at this point, but you excelled. And what you did…those propulsive blasts." His eyes were big. "I haven't taught you that yet. How did you…"

"Instinct." She shrugged. "And desperation. Like you said happened with you…with the lightning in the storm. The blade did all the work, not me. It was more luck than anything." She could tell he was about to deny that, tell her it was all her doing, but what use in talking about it now? Some of her sellswords were dead, up here on the plains and down in the cave as well. They needed to count their losses and bury their fallen. This was no time for back-slapping, she knew.

The next hour was grim and solemn. The Surgeon had suffered most grievously from the attack, losing Savage and Scalpel, as Saska had feared, as well as both Gutter and Gore. When they picked through the rocks in the cave, they found Savage so horribly crushed as to be unrecognisable, though Scalpel was still breathing. They might have tried to save him, but when he was told that his wife was gone, he only croaked that he would go with her. "Kill me," he whispered, a tear rolling down his bloody cheek, and his master the Surgeon saw to it, withdrawing a scalpel from his cross-belt to see him to his end. *A scalpel to kill Scalpel,* Saska thought. It was grimly fitting.

Gore's manner of death was fitting also, gored by one of the crab's long legs. He had been the one Saska saw after her crash: Gore lying dead, Gutter rushing over to him, bellowing out in bloodcurdling grief. What she hadn't seen was Gutter's maddened dash to try to slay the crab himself. "He got too close," the Baker told her. "I tried to pull him away, but he was in a frenzy of pain. He was crushed by the broken claw, smashed to death. And I have lost my spectacles," he lamented. He shook his head and sighed. "It has been a difficult night for us all."

As dawn rose, it rose bloody, and with a line of fresh graves dug beneath it. Her company had been reduced to fewer than ten, and she wondered if she had erred in giving her coral away to Robbert Lukar. *Have I handed over my luck? Are we all to be picked off, night after night, by one foul creature or the next?*

If that was so, she would not let Del be one of them. Once the dead had been honoured with their rites and words and their armour and belongings fetched from the cave, Saska took Elyon aside. She had said she would wait until the morrow, and the morrow had come.

"I have a request to ask of you, Elyon," she said as a rare spear of sunlight crossed the plains. It seemed to point in the direction of Ilithor, so far as she could tell.

"Anything," he said, earnest.

He left that very same day.

14

____

Emeric

Sir Ernold Esterling was pacing side to side, moving between the lichen-encrusted walls of the small broken hillfort in which they'd taken refuge. The rain fell outside in a cold constant patter, the winds buffeting and howling at the door like some ghostly wolf trying to claw its way inside.

"That blasted noise…I can't take much more of this infernal racket," grunted Burk, scarred lip twisting. "All this rattling day and night. Another gust like that and I'll kick that door right off its hinges."

"You'll do no such thing," Sir Ernold Esterling said fiercely. "You can't take the noise? Stuff some wool in your ears and spare us your carping. It's trying my nerves."

Tensions were running high. They'd been here for days now, three, four of them, and the accommodations left much to be desired. Small, damp, and filled with broken stone, it was evident no one had been here in long years. Weeds grew up through cracks in the stone, while moss and creeping vines had taken dominion over one of the walls. It was a grim place, old and cold and uninviting and the rain dripped ceaselessly through little holes in the ceiling above them to pitter and patter and drive a man half insane. There were some arrow-slit windows that looked out over the wooded hills, and here Emeric Manfrey stood, at the south-facing window, watching for the return of the scouts. Watching for days.

They're not coming back, he thought. *They're dead, or lost, or captured.* Either way, it amounted to the same thing.

"We have to think about moving on," he said, turning from the window. Esterling was pacing, the rest of the men sitting hunched and miserable here and there. "It's been too long, Ernold. We can't wait here forever."

"Another day. We'll give it another day."

"*You'll* give it another day," grunted Ronson, the hulking Riverlander. He was a forester by trade who'd swapped his woodchopper's axe for a battle-axe when he was mustered for the war. "Not me." He stood up from the block of stone he'd been sitting on. "I'm sick of this place. I'm going home." He swung toward the door.

"Stop," commanded Sir Ernold. "No one is to leave this tower."

"Says who? You?" Ronson didn't stop. He plodded to the door, reaching out to pull across a rusty bolt. "You're Tukoran, Esterling, and your orders are piss to me. I've been rotting here too long. Got a wife back home, kids. You stay with your dying prince if you like, I'm done with him. Done with you all." He pulled across the second bolt.

"You pull that last bolt, Ronson, and…"

"And what? You'll kill me?" The man barked mocking laughter and pulled the last bolt and the rotting door flew inward, the winds howling inside, stirring his cloak and his unwashed hair. "Anyone else wants to come with me, they're welcome," he shouted over the gale. "I'd sooner take my chances out there than wait in here to starve to death." He gave the men a passing glance. When no one moved to follow, he grunted a curse at them and stamped outside, swinging the door shut behind him.

A moment passed. Then another. Emeric could see the shade of red rising up Sir Ernold's neck. His lips flickered. Then he stamped to the door and pulled the bolts across, one, two, three, each with a rusty scrape. "He'll not get far. Home? He'll never make it on his own." He swung around again and resumed his pacing, a hard angry step from one weatherbeaten wall to another.

For a while no one spoke. Back and forth Ernold Esterling went, back and forth, back and forth, while the rest of them stood and sat around, silent and unmoving. Prince Raynald was swaddled beneath the cover of his blankets and furs, murmuring occasionally. The young Amadar squire Harey was with him, mopping at his brow with a cloth and keeping a close eye for any changes in his condition.

The prince hadn't stirred, not once, since Emeric had sewn and cauterised his wound. The fever was in him, a constant menace that threatened to spread and overwhelm the boy. Emeric had intended to leave with the scouts when they returned to Rustbridge. Benithy and Davney had gone and Emeric was meant to be the third, but the prince's condition had taken a turn for the worse and Esterling had asked Emeric to stay. "I need you here," he'd said. "You're the best healer we have."

So Emeric had remained, and the Marshlander Cuthbert had gone off in his place. That was days ago. They'd intended only to get within sight of Rustbridge, to determine what had come of it, whether the battle had been won or lost, and then return with their report and men and medics, a strong escort to bear the prince back. But they hadn't. They were still missing and it should not have taken this long. They were maybe a day and half walk from the city, and much less if they made good time.

Dead, Emeric thought. Or they might have become lost; that was a possibility too. These fogs and rains made navigation difficult and the skies were never clear of clouds. Getting to Rustbridge would be the easy part. They would need only reach the river and head south, but finding their way back here…that was another matter.

"Maybe that sunwolf got them," said Torret, in his lispy voice. "The one that chased us out here."

Burk grumbled something under his breath.

Esterling rounded on him. "What was that, Burk?"

"Nothing. I said nothing."

"You're going to curse me for leading us out here again, are you? For prioritising the safety of our prince?"

"No. I'm just cold, is all, and tired."

"And *bitter*, yes," Ernold snorted. "I'm bitter too, Burk. You think I want to be here? You think I like all this waiting? You think I'm enjoying watching our noble prince suffer like this?" He didn't wait for or expect a response. "No. I want to return him to Rustbridge so he can be properly tended, to where he'll be safe, but I cannot very well make that decision until we know the city remains ours. The scouts *will* return," he insisted. "Tomorrow, I am sure of it. They will return to us tomorrow with good tidings and we'll be able to go back to the rest of the men."

The rest of the day passed like a slow funereal procession. There was no laughter here, no conversation. Sir Ernold did not allow for a fire to be lit and the rain did not relent. The light was never more than sickly and grey, and when the sun sank away in the west the dark was as impenetrable as pitch.

By midnight the weather had worsened, lashing and thrashing against the walls of their sanctuary in a raging tempest, the wind roaring a dreaded song as it swirled and blustered outside. Thunder crashed and lightning raged, but never did a flash unveil the return of the men. Once or twice Emeric thought he heard the *thwump* of wings, something enormous moving in the air above them, but through the windows all was black. Was it Drulgar? Had the Dread come again? The hair went up on the back of his neck to imagine the dragon god up there.

The rain did not abate all through the long hours of the night. By morning it still fell hard and straight from a slate grey sky, patched black with stormclouds great and grim, and no men were spotted approaching. "They'll never find us in this weather, even if they're alive," Burk said, looking rougher than ever after a poor night's sleep.

Lambert agreed. "My lord. We'd best make a choice before this tower comes down. It doesn't feel so stable to me anymore." Some stones had come loose during the night and the earth was weakening underfoot from all the rain. The old armsman pressed his foot down on a pavestone, water rising and bubbling up through the weed-strangled cracks. "The winds pick up again and they might just blow us over. We can't say here, my lord. When the rain calms we have to move."

Sir Ernold's jaw was hard as rock. Clearly he had expected his men to come back. "We'll give it one more day. If they're not here tomorrow…"

"You said that yesterday," Burk snorted at him. "Maybe Ronson had the right of it all along…"

Sir Ernold stamped over and struck him with the back of his hand, turning the man's bald head aside. "That scarred lip not enough for you, Burk? Speak to me like that again and I'll tear the other side open, do you hear me?'

The gruff soldier stood, wiping blood from his mouth. His scowl twisted harder than ever, though whatever was going through his head never made it past his lips.

Sir Ernold turned his head. "Tomorrow," he called out to the rest of them. "I know I said that yesterday, but this weather changes things. I'm sure the tower will stay standing for another night, Lambert. It has stood here for centuries and hasn't fallen yet. One more evening will not hurt."

"The straw that broke the camel's back," mumbled Burk, unable to hold his tongue. "Guess you never heard that one, milord."

"Careful now, Burk, or it will be *your* back breaking, not a camel's. This is your last warning. Another word from you and I'll have your tongue out."

Burk heeded the unseemly warning, scowling as he went back to stand at his place by the window. Emeric could feel the tension, thick in the air. They'd been almost a week cooped up in this broken tower and something was about to give.

He found himself praying that day, speaking whispered words under his breath in petition to some unseen god. *Let them come,* he said. *Let them come back and tell us all is well. Let them bring knights with them, and horses, to speed us back to Rustbridge. Let the army be intact, and my companions alive. Even Borrus, the fool, who led so many to their deaths. Let me tell him that to his face. And then embrace him as a brother and smile.*

His prayers went answered, as they always had. When morning came and Emeric awoke from a brief sleep, he found Sir Ernold staring out into the dreary coming of dawn. "They're not back," he said, in a dour listless voice. "I'd thought…hoped…" He shook his head. He looked pale, bedraggled, old. He'd aged years in a week, the skin thinning and growing winkled about his eyes, patches sagging and darkening. "We'll have to continue north. Are you with me, Emeric? Do I still have your faith at least?"

"I'm with you, Ernold," Emeric said. "Raynald is my prince as well as yours." The knight had not been wrong about that. The prince must be his priority now.

They left an hour later, abandoning their dilapidated little refuge and all hope of the scout's return, striking due north beneath the cover of a cold wet sky. The rain was still falling, though lightly now, hardly more than a faint mist suspended in the air. Their party had shrunk by a third; there were only eight of them now. *Eight,* Emeric thought grimly, as the mist swallowed them whole. Eight would not be enough should some ancient menace come upon them, and in this grey-white world it was hard to know what lurked out there, hiding just beyond their sight, stalking them through the trees.

The fort had been on a hilltop, true, but that hilltop wasn't high. The land here went up and down in a gentle gradient, wooded mostly, though the trees were sparse. The trunks appeared like ghostly apparitions in the fog, their branches swaying and leaning, leaves rattling eerily overheard. "It's like they're coming closer," young Willard said, looking around uneasily. "Like they're listening to us."

"Trees have no interest in the conversations of men," Sir Ernold said.

"It's not the words they're listening for, my lord. It's our heartbeats. Our breathing. They crave our fear."

Esterling gave a laugh. "Ridiculous superstition. Now where'd you hear about that?"

"My grandmother. She used to tell me all about the things that lurked in the woods. We lived near the Darkwood before my father moved us south. She'd wander there herself, my grandmother. Brave woman. The things she saw…"

Emeric had heard these sorts of tales before. Oft as not the things people saw in the Darkwood were due to the Greengill mushrooms that grew there, called dreadshrooms by the locals. They had spores that awoke a man's nightmares when disturbed, brought to life his darkest dreams. No doubt that's all it was. Emeric was open-minded to the weird and wonderful in this world, but he'd never heard of trees that feasted on a man's fears before.

Willard was still going on, recounting the various creatures his grandmother had encountered. "…she hid from a grimbear in the trees, once," he was saying. "Had to climb up into the canopy to escape it. Stayed up there for hours until night came and it fell asleep. Then she crept down and escaped, but not before taking a tuft of its hair as a keepsake."

Burk snorted doubtfully. "Sounds like she was having you on, lad. She found that fur snagged on a branch or something. And from a common bear too. She never saw a grimbear."

Willard shook his head. "We had a huntsman confirm it. Man called Vilmar. He used to stop in our village when he went into the woods on his hunts. He said the fur was genuine."

Another scoff from Burk. "Never heard of him."

"Which means nothing," dismissed Sir Ernold. "Vilmar the Black is a famed hunter, Burk. Have you heard of Amron Daecar, perchance? Does the King's Wall ring a bell?" The knight laughed loudly, disturbing the eerie silence of the waterlogged wood. "You'd forget your own name if people stopped calling you by it."

The squat soldier scowled at him. "I'd never. Just haven't heard of that hunter, is all."

Sir Ernold laughed again. He seemed more relaxed now that they'd left the cramped confines of that tower. Or perhaps he was just hiding his unease by being more jaunty. That seemed just as likely. "So, what else did your grandmother encounter, Will? Other than grimbears and talking trees."

"I never said the trees talked, my lord. Just that they have more senses than we know."

"Fine. Fine." The knight waved a hand. "Come, what else? Anything exciting?"

"Well…" Willard scratched his long chin. "She did see one of Brexatron's brood once. Flying over the Darkwood Pass."

That won an appreciative nod from the knight. "That's nothing to scoff over. Even you'd be impressed by a greatbat, Burk."

"I would if I believed it."

"Ha! Ever the cynic. We wouldn't have you any other way, you miserable old fool."

"What was it like?" Torret asked Willard excitedly. "The bat? Was it as big as a dragon like they say?"

"It *was* a dragon, most like," Burk said. "All of Brexatron's brood are long dead."

"So was Drulgar. And Eldur. And a thousand other creatures that have come crawling up from the bowels of the earth." Sir Ernold's expression turned sour. "Never much believed in this talk of a Last Renewal, but seems we're right in the midst of it. You say all of Brexatron's brood are dead, Burk. I say maybe Braxatron himself is still alive."

Burk snorted loudly. "Aye. And where's he been hiding these last ten thousand years?"

"The Darkisle," said Torret. "Somewhere there. That's where he went when Agarath cast him out."

"No." Old Lambert shook his head. "He went into the High Hammersongs. Up in those mountains. That's where he made his brood. Forged them from his hate."

"And Drulgar killed them," Burk said. "He swore vengeance against the bat after he tried to kill their father. Battled him over the mountains and cast him down into some bottomless pit. They're dead, all of them. All this talk is nonsense."

"Just cause you don't like it, doesn't mean it's nonsense. But let's put it aside for now." Sir Ernold looked out into the trees. "All this chattering isn't so smart out here. Look lively, lads. Eyes peeled on the woods and no talking for a while."

The men heeded his command, each watching the woods for signs of movement as they continued through the valley. Heavy as the prince was in his armour, the four remaining Bladeborn were required to carry the stretcher; Emeric and Ernold holding the front with Willard and Lambert at the back. The Marshlander Woodruff and Amadar squire Harey walked behind them, forming a rearguard of sorts, with Burk and Torret leading from the front, a dozen or so paces ahead.

With all talk ending, the tension was at once restored. Suddenly every wisp of mist took on the form of some spectral malice, each tree trunk appearing from the wintry shroud mistaken for a perilous threat. Several times someone called out that they'd seen something shifting through the fogs, and the prince would at once be lowered to the ground so the Bladeborn could fight if needed. In each case they would wait, and watch the woods, and sometimes Ernold and Emeric would go out together to see if there was something in the trees. Over long hours this sequence of events was repeated. But never was anything seen.

The gloaming soon came upon them. It felt like the day had passed in a blink. With the feeble light fading, the forest only grew more close and sinister, and they began to wonder on the wisdom of leaving behind the fort.

"We'll have to find somewhere to make camp," Sir Ernold said, though it was easier said than done. All of a sudden they could see no more than ten paces in front of them, and were forced to creep on, slow as a glacier, fretting over what lay ahead. There were sudden gulleys here, and raging rivers surging loudly and unseen, thick tarry bogs clotted with mud into which a man could stumble and sink. They needed more eyes watching their flanks, so decided that they'd have to leave the carrying of the prince to only two men at a time, which slowed them further. Will and Lambert took up the burden at first, leaving Ernold and Emeric to walk ahead, their night-eyes helping to spot hidden threats. When the men-at-arms grew too exhausted, they would swap, and Willard and Lambert would take the lead instead.

It must have been about midnight when they heard the sound of howling. It came from the left of them, from the right, from ahead and from behind. "They're everywhere," Torret fretted, raising his bow, turning it here and there. "Must be dozens of them out there."

"Are they sunwolves, my lord?" asked the Amadar squire. His eyes were ripe with fear.

"No," said Emeric. "They sound like common wolves to me."

"A super pack," said Lambert. "Must have found safety in numbers."

"Then they're scared," Burk said. He sounded scared himself. "They're scared of something out here."

Sir Ernold ordered that they close ranks about the prince. "Tighten up," he said. "Two men to each side." They set the prince down on his stretcher and took position, the Bladeborn forming an outer guard, the rest of them standing behind them. "You see a wolf, Torret, you fire an arrow down its throat. Make them see we're not messing about."

Emeric disagreed with that. "You might only provoke a larger attack if you do. Hold fire, Torret, until they show their intent."

Torret looked at Esterling for confirmation and the Emerald Guard gave a nod. "So be it. But soon as any of them get too close, you let fly. Understand?"

The wait began. The howling got closer and soon turned to growls, low and menacing and hungry. Emeric clutched his godsteel dagger, eyes roaming the nearest trees. They were spread here, tall and thin, brambles and ferns clustered between them, the earth uneven, busy with rocks and roots. A river was bashing away somewhere nearby, and closer was the tinkling of a stream. Shapes began to appear, dark shaggy shapes with glowing eyes, moving through the boles and bushes. All was rustles and growls and the pacey breathing of the men.

"Hold," Emeric said, fearing one might break. "Don't draw your weapons until they attack. They may yet go away."

They didn't. More of them came, and more, until there seemed to be at least fifty of the beasts prowling around them, concealed within the dark of the bushes and bracken. *They're waiting*, Emeric thought. *The alpha will decide.* And then he saw him, the leader of the pack, no common wolf this one, but a brute of an older age. *A direwolf,* he thought at first glance, before realising, *no, the proportions are off.* The direwolf was shaped as a common wolf, but much larger, yet this creature moved in an ungainly way, hunched in the back, its rear legs crooked and forelimbs long, elongated body hanging with a long coat of ragged black fur. The face was wrong, the snout shortened and blunt, eyes big and round and soulless. Emeric's mouth twisted at seeing it and the others saw it too.

"What…what *is* that?" whispered Torret, in horror. "It ain't no wolf, that thing."

"Fellwolf," said Esterling.

"And a big one," growled Lambert.

Sir Ernold turned his head sharply and linked eyes with Emeric. "We take it together," he whispered. "The pack will scatter when it's dead."

Emeric nodded; it was the right course he knew.

"The rest of you, protect the prince. Will, Lambert, I'm counting on you."

Willard slid his sword out half an inch, to make sure it hadn't got stuck in the cold. "We're ready," he said.

And then the whole world burst into motion.

Sir Ernold was the first to engage, surging forward from a standing start to where the fellwolf stood among the bushes. The creature snarled and bounded away, scrambling up into the branches of a nearby tree with its long forelimbs, crashing loudly through the foliage above.

"Cowardly bloody creature!" Sir Ernold roared. A dozen other wolves were slinking forward, snapping and snarling. One came for Emeric as he raced after Esterling. He spun, swung, cutting the beast down with a yelp and spray of blood, Lambert and Willard fighting back several others as Torret nocked and fired with his bow.

A sudden crashing heralded the return of the fellwolf. "Look out," squeaked Harey, seeing it emerge above them. The boy threw himself aside as the beast leapt down atop Woodruff the Marshlander, who saw it too late. A spear thrust missed, and the fellwolf was upon him, its maw opening unnaturally wide to close upon the Marshman's head. A sudden scream was cut short, a crunch of bone, and Woodruff's skull exploded inward with a burst of blood and brain.

Torret screamed, Harey scrambled back in terror. "It's mine," bellowed old Lambert, stepping forward. "Get back, boy. Behind me!" The man-at-arms was an experienced swordsman, skilled in the forms.

He swung his cloak over his shoulder and met the menace blade to claws, sparks flying as the fellwolf slashed and snarled, spitting saliva from its fang-cluttered jaws.

Emeric surged in behind, stance in Glideform, light-footed and sleek, but the creature heard. Its humanoid face whipped around at him, half man and half wolf, black eyes swimming with malice. "Together," Emeric shouted. He sensed Sir Ernold closing in too. Lambert roared and together they charged, but the beast leapt again, scrambling for a tree, long hooked claws tearing away chunks of brown bark as it clambered back into the night.

Emeric Manfrey wouldn't have it, not this time. Anticipating the move, he darted for the tree trunk and swung with a clean true strike, slicing the alder in a diagonal arc and kicking at once at the bole. The weight of his godsteel armour went through the trunk, sending it tumbling, crashing, the fellwolf howling in alarm above. It tried to scramble away, leap to another tree, but down the alder came, smashing to the forest floor. And the Bladeborn followed it in.

The fellwolf died right there where it landed, tangled among the branches, Emeric's blade driven through its shoulder and neck, Ernold's its spine, Lambert's its gut. When it had gurgled its last Esterling looked at it in disgust. "Always heard it had a face like that." He spat right at it. "Ugliest beast the gods ever made."

"Dhatar was responsible for this one," Emeric said, giving the creature's hindquarters a kick to make sure it was dead. He glanced through the glade; the rest of the wolves were racing away, as expected, Willard and Burk forming a cordon around the prince. Several more of the wolves were dead. "He never had much skill at life creation."

"He was a battle god. Should never have been making life in the first place."

Emeric had another look at Raynald. "That was close, Ernold. Too close. If it had leapt down on top of Raynald and not Woodruff, our prince would be dead, and all this for nought."

The man clenched his jaw and nodded. "We need to at least get him somewhere where he can rest up to heal a little longer."

"Then where would you suggest?"

The knight thought it through a moment. "We have no map, no notion of where we are. None of us are local to this land and the man who was…that damnable Riverlander…only the gods know where he's gone. Most likely he made a good meal for this pack, and that's the least that he deserves. Woodruff…perhaps he'd have known, but he won't be much use without a head. We're all strangers to this land, Emeric."

And me more than most, the exile thought. It had been a dozen years since Emeric Manfrey had visited Vandar, and never here. The lands were alien to him, the same as all the men. "We'll have to find a road," he decided. "One that tracks north. With fortune we will happen upon a traveller who can help us. But right now I would suggest we keep moving. A dead fellwolf is sure to draw a crowd and not of the sociable sort."

As they continued on through the night, they did so to the sound of howling, as though the wolf pack were lamenting the death of their brothers. Emeric found himself walking ahead with Lambert, Willard and Ernold carrying the prince. The old man had a frown on his long grizzled face, grey hair hanging lank to his scalp. "Odd, don't you think? Common wolves following a fellwolf like that?"

"Lesser creatures bow to power," Emeric said. "That howling might just be joy for all we know. They're glad to be rid of him."

"They might have slain it if they'd teamed up."

"Might. But in the attempt how many would die? Sometimes it's better to be ruled by an enemy than die by his hand, Lambert."

No good shelter was forthcoming that night, so once the howling had died away into the distance they made do with what they had, settling down beneath the tangled branches of a deadfall where they might steal some rest. "You look tired, Ernold," Emeric said. "I'll take the watch tonight. You've done enough."

The man was too weary to argue for once. He chose two men to take turns accompanying Emeric, first Torret and then Willard, who he deemed to be younger and better rested than the others, then curled up in the muddy little shelter to sleep. The night passed without further incident. By the time the faint light of dawn began to leak through the trees, the rains had eased off for the first time in long days. There were even some blue patches in the sky, shards of sunlight breaking through to cast the woods in a golden light, raindrops glittering like jewels upon the leaves. They passed through the wood and into a wide grassy vale, dew dancing in a sea of sparkles, and into more woodland on the other side. The birds were twittering their morning songs, the insects buzzing as though true summer had finally come. *Do they sense something we don't?* Emeric wondered. *Is this the end of these interminable rains?*

A short time later the strains of a woman's voice filtered through the woodland. The sound was sweet, a soothing comfort to the soul. "There's a woman out there," Willard said, smiling. "Can you hear that, Sir Ernold?"

"I hear it, Will."

"She's singing," said Torret, with that gap-toothed grin. "Maybe there's a village nearby? They could feed us. Like…proper food."

They'd barely eaten in days, scavenging what they could as they fled north. The pickings had been slim and during their time in the abandoned hillfort Sir Ernold had not permitted them to hunt. A trap had brought home a hare once and Torret had managed to shoot a plump quail through a window, but that was the only meat they'd had. Elsewise it had been berries and roots and not much else, and the prospect of real food was enticing.

"I could do with a mutton steak," said Will. "A side of buttery potatoes…maybe some steamed greens as well."

"And milk," added Torret, nodding. "A nice warm cup of milk…

nothing better." He smacked his lips and sped his pace. "I'll go ahead and check, m'lord? Make them know there's nothing to fear from us."

"Hold off a moment there, Torret," Ernold said. "There's a woman singing out there, is all. Let's not go jumping to conclusions." He peered ahead. "I'll go. Will, you come with me. Harey, you too. Never hurts to have a boy to show we mean well. Emeric, Lambert, hold back with the prince. Burk, make yourself scarce. One look at you and you'll send that woman running."

The knight laughed and marched off with the squire and the young man-at-arms, drawn on by the sound of the woman's voice like a fish caught on the end of a line. Emeric was not certain he'd ever heard a sound so sweet, though something in the air felt off. The sunshine, the singing, the birds and the buzzing bees, could it all be too perfect?

He glanced back behind them, into the wide vale they'd passed; the lands there were falling back into shadow, the skies curdling and clotting anew. Yet when he looked forward all was bright and sunny, and the other men were smiling, old Lambert and Torret and even grumpy Burk...*even* Burk was smiling as they wandered on deeper...deeper... deeper into the trees.

Emeric was drawn along with them. Doubt tugged at him, insistent but weak; a stronger force was pulling him onward. *I am hungry, that's all,* he told himself. *Hungry and paranoid. There is nothing to fear here.*

Then suddenly a figure was approaching. Ernold and the others had not long vanished ahead before she came, stepping toward them through the trees. Her hair was golden, bright as the high summer sun, her dress the colour of early spring, the soft green of blooming leaves. She had a glow to her skin, a lustrous shine. Her lips wore a perfect, radiant smile, and from her mouth came a voice as smooth as a silken scarf.

"Good morning to you," she said to them. "Come...come with me. Join your friends. They're just through here." She opened an arm to the glade.

The other men stepped eagerly onward without so much as saying a word. Emeric was carrying the rear end of the stretcher, Lambert the front. The old man quickened his pace and Emeric too was forced to follow, unable to slow or stop or speak a warning, to give voice to the doubts in his head.

And then about him all seemed to blur and ripple, as though he was moving through a veil, entering a dream. He did not recall much more of what happened next. Just a sensation of the sun disappearing behind the clouds, of the warmth of the world stolen away. The rain, falling. The storm, rising.

A cabin of horrors. And death.

15

_____

Pagaloth

Rhok swung a large fist into the fire priest's gut. The man spluttered, wheezing, and his chains rattled through the gloom of the cave.

"More? Do you want more, priest?" Rhok was a hulking man with big sloping shoulders, a barrel chest, a heavy gut and equally heavy voice that boomed when it bounced off the walls. Tattoos were inked about his eyes to record all the men he'd killed during the last war and the long black braided beard that hung down to his waist had been thrown over his shoulder so it did not get in the way. "More?" he said again, when the priest did not answer. He gave a nod. "Yes, more I think."

He swung his meaty fist again, driving what little air remained out of Jerek's lungs. Gouts of blood spat out with the burst of breath. Then Rhok slapped him, a fierce _ringing_ strike that reddened his already red, raw cheek. The priest had come in for much punishment already, slaps and strikes and kicks, even the occasional use of a blade when the big man felt the urge to mix things up. He had taken his right nipple, the lobe of his left ear, and had prised off most of his fingernails by now. The dark bruising around his neck spoke of one of Rhok's favourite techniques; the big man liked to strangle him until he almost lost consciousness, but not quite. As with his other methods of torture, he seemed to know just how far to push.

The treatment went on for a few moments longer. Pagaloth stood away in the shadows behind the big Agarathi, observing. It did not make for particularly pleasant viewing, though that was part of the point. _My pity for him will weaken me and make me more vulnerable to the voice._ The others had all built up a strong immunity to it by now, but not so Pagaloth. He was still relatively new here and must work to increase his resistance.

With one final assault, Rhok finished his work, kneeing the man in the nethers, swinging an elbow into his chin, then headbutting him right in the bridge of the nose. There was a crunch of bone and flow of blood, raining down into the fire priest's mouth. Rhok laughed. "Your nose breaks at last. It took long enough." He gave another blistering slap, spat in the priest's face for good measure, then turned and marched away to meet Pagaloth in the shadows. His face went deadly serious as he joined him, "He's yours," he said, in a low voice. "I will be outside, just in case." His eyes glanced back. "Be careful. He is angry, very angry. The voice will be strong."

Sir Pagaloth nodded his understanding.

"Call if you need me." The big man put a paw on his shoulder and then departed, squeezing out through the thin scar in the rock wall and into the rift beyond. The dragonknight waited a moment, bracing himself with several long deep breaths, and then stepped inside the cell.

The priest's head was hung low, eyes staring at his feet. He was trembling, and not from cold, Pagaloth knew. This was rage, a deep thrumming bottomless rage and a hate that went as deep as this great chasm they'd taken for a home. A thick menace saturated the air about him. He was breathing raggedly, blood leaking from two dozen little wounds scattered across his spindly body. The red robes he'd worn had been reduced to rags.

"You're hurt," Pagaloth said. He stepped toward him, reaching out. "You need attention, Jerek. My *friend*, you are not well."

The word had its desired effect. He saw the man's upper lip give a twist, a half grimace. "Friend," the priest rasped, his voice bitter and hoarse. His eyes stayed down, staring at the blood-spattered stone at his feet. A few chips and fragments told of the teeth he'd lost. "You would call *me* friend?"

"We could be…if you like," Pagaloth said. "You need only join us, Jerek. Commit to our cause and all your troubles will go away."

Low growling laughter bubbled up from within him. His eyes flashed up, red and wild and hateful. "*Join* you? Commit to *your* cause? There is only one cause, Kadosk, as well you know. The righteous way of Eldur the Eternal, Master of the World."

"Agarath the All-Father, you mean," Pagaloth corrected him. "Eldur is a slave, as you are. Agarath is the true power."

"You dare? *Dare!*" Jerek raged within his chains, pulling and jerking, but there was nowhere for him to go. The fire priests were predictable creatures. Any word against their lord and master was plenty enough to spark their ire. "Eldur is the Fire Father, the will and force of Agarath on this earth! He serves by choice and duty. Slave? *Slave!* You dare call *him* slave!" The fetters rattled in a ringing chaos. Bloody white spittle frothed and slavered from his mouth.

Pagaloth only watched, waiting for the inevitable. This man was no true man anymore. He was an ant in a colony, driven by instinct alone and had no capacity for critical thought. *A hive*, Pagaloth thought. That was how Dragonlady Adelle Kazaan had called it. She'd said that Eldur was the hive mind and these priests were only his vessels, sent out to spread his will and take all Agarathi back under his wing. There were dozens of them, perhaps scores of them now creeping about these lands and perhaps further afield across the north, and each was a cinder of a larger flame that must be stamped out. It was part of their purpose here; to hunt and kill these priests. But not all, Pagaloth knew. Some were brought here to be chained and stripped and beaten, their rage and hate enhanced, the voice unleashed.

Pagaloth knew it was just a matter of time before he heard it. Whoever this priest Jerek had been in his previous life, he was not that man anymore, He may once have been a good man. A holy man. A man who led groups in prayer and listened to their sins, who worked with the sick and the poor. But that man was dead now. Eldur slew him the moment he empowered him to spread his will, making him nought but a tool to do his bidding. An'zon Graz had even told him their memories were wiped when Eldur filled them with his poison.

"They don't remember who they were or where they came from," he'd said. "Not until they break free, as we have." He'd gestured to Ulrik Marak and Adelle Kazaan, to Rhok and the other man here called Angrar, who'd all been seduced by Eldur's voice before breaking free of his spell. "Our memories were blurred once too. There is a fog, Pagaloth, that does not lift until the fingers of the Fire Father are withdrawn."

Pagaloth had not experienced that himself. He wondered if these priests could be saved, as the others had been.

"No," was Ulrik Marak's flat answer. "It is not the same. We were enslaved by Eldur, but not given a part of his power. These creatures speak with his voice. They are a part of him, as Lady Adelle has told you. They must all be killed, no matter who they were. But first, we extract what we can from them."

That had been long days ago now, when he'd first arrived. In the time since then, Pagaloth had visited Jerek several times to test himself and grow stronger. By now the Voice of Eldur did not claw at him as it had. He did not recoil from it, nor cower from it; he did not throw himself down and plead for mercy or bid himself Eldur's undying servant and declare himself his man for all time. At first, he'd felt the dark pull of those responses. Several times Rhok or Angrar had been required to step in and strike the priest in the jaw or gut to stop him, lest Pagaloth fall, but that risk had withered now. *I am not to be made a weapon*, he thought. He was here now only to harden his resistance. To armour his mind against what was to come.

The chains were still rattling in the gloom. Jerek's voice twisted and deepened, but it remained his own, not yet the tongue of his master. "You say join you," he rasped. "Join *you*? You do not see, Pagaloth, do you? Do cannot see the truth."

"What truth is that, Jerek?"

"That this world must end. It must end and be renewed. This is all the Fire Father craves, a chance to sweep clear the festering filth and begin again."

Pagaloth had heard these lies before. "That is not what Eldur wishes," he said. "Not truly. That is the will of Agarath. Destruction is his only desire."

"No, no! This world has grown fat and soft and weak, but soon… soon…"

Pagaloth stepped in and slapped him. "You're a fool, Jerek. A lamentable blind fool cowering at the toes of a madman." He snorted. "Pathetic. You betray everything the *true* Eldur stands for. Everything he once fought to build."

"No, no!" the man cried again. "That was the others…Varin and Ilith and Thala and Lumo…they forced him to a peace he never wanted. Agarath never wanted it. So Eldur did not!"

Pagaloth was growing weary of listening to him. He was not here to debate the topic with Jerek. He was here for the voice, and the voice alone. He struck him again, harder this time, then closed his fingers around his neck. "A land where the strong survive," he said, putting his face right up close to him. "An eternal battleground of chaos and war. Tell me, Jerek, where would your place be in this world?" He looked him up and down in contempt. "You are weak. Frail. You'd die within a day."

He closed his fingers tight so the man could not respond. His eyes bulged, bloodshot and baleful, his hands quivering in his iron manacles. Pagaloth held on, and on, and on, watching the hate grow fierce. He could sense it…feel it…rumbling up from below, a torrent of loathing and fury and disdain rising…rising…

At last he let go, and so out it came…the Voice of Eldur exploding from within.

"*YOU!*" Jerek hissed. The world coiled itself through the air, snapping and biting, spreading through every corner of that dark and damp stone cell. "You *will* join us, Pagaloth Kadosk! You *will* do as Eldur bids you!"

Pagaloth felt the first tug, a sharp jerk against his will. He held firm and turned his head, flinching against it. "No," he declared, standing back tall. "*Never.* I will never join you."

The air seemed to fill and enshroud with a swirling black-red fog. Laughter rang out through the gloom. In the mists the forms of figures appeared, moving and writhing and taking shape, tens of them, hundreds, now thousands and thousands and thousands more. He was in the midst of a battle all of a sudden, fog figures hacking and cleaving in combat, dragons screeching overhead, steeds of horse and wolf and cat leaping and charging. He lifted above it all, seeming to float over the battlefield, watching as a great army of steel-clad men poured forth, slaughtering a host in red and gold and black.

"These are your people," Jerek hissed in Eldur's voice. "Look, your people, they are dying, dying…"

The sound of bloodshed and butchery filled the air, the screams of horses and dying men, the ring of steel on steel. Pagaloth could hear his name being called out by someone, a dull distant voice echoing out through the fog. Other voices joined it, each shouting for him to avenge them. He frowned, turning through the mists, looking for them…and then he saw…down on the battlefield he saw them all, his father and his uncles and his brothers were all there, desperately trying to fight off a storming charge of northern steel. Then a monstrous man marched imperiously toward them, knocking all others side, a great misting blade in his grasp. He swung and swung and swung again, roaring laughter as he cut them all apart. *Borrus*, Pagaloth thought, watching in horror. It was Borrus Kanabar. He turned his head and cringed.

"You helped him," the voice said, accusing. "This man who killed your kin. You *befriended* him, and guided him, this man who *ruined your life.*"

"No, I…"

"Your mother died because of *him*," the voice went on, scathing. "This man murdered your family, your father, your brothers. Your *mother*," it hissed. "He murdered your mother."

"No." Pagaloth tightened his jaw and shook his head. His mother had killed herself from unbearable grief from the loss of her husband and eldest sons, but that was never Borrus's fault. *He was a soldier*, Pagaloth thought. *And he killed them in combat, some of them only. It was fair and just.*

"He murdered her," the voice repeated, as though reading his thoughts. "Through time and trial, *he* murdered her. He murdered them all. And you served him."

"I never served him," Pagaloth found himself saying. The fog was thickening around him, disorientating. He turned his eyes this way and that and could no longer see the walls, the way out. The spread of the battlefield blurred and swirled, changing, coalescing once more into the shape of a single figure, sitting before him on a giant throne. A cloak of red fell from his shoulders and from his sleeve came a hand, white as bone, clutching at a tall black staff. He saw the Bondstone fixed atop it, saw the great rising cloud of smoke and ash and dread billowing from the orb, rising high above the throne, spreading out into a form of ancient and unutterable malice.

Agarath, he thought, flinching away. He could see a face take shape in the swirls of black storm, red lighting flashing and forming features. The face was staring at him, judging. Pagaloth could feel his boundless power, his ageless hate. He took another step back, and turned, but there he was again, Eldur in his throne, Agarath rumbling in the storm above. Again Pagaloth turned, and again and again, but no matter where he looked, he was there, always there.

Eldur's laughter rang out through the cavern. "Why resist, Sir Pagaloth? You will return to us eventually. If Jerek does not get you, another will. Did Ten'kin not say that to you once before?" A smile twisted his lips. "You had best heed his words."

Ten'kin. The name made Pagaloth close his fist and grimace. "I'll find Ten'kin," he began, growling. "I'll find him…and when I do…"

"You'll kill him. Or *Ulrik* will. Sa'har Nakaan meant more to Ulrik Marak than he did to *you*, Pagaloth Kadosk. They flew together for decades, as wing-riders and brothers. Sa'har was a great man once before, and Ulrik Marak…is anyone in Agarath greater? But you? *You?*" His voice descended into a sneer. "You are nothing but a traitor to your people. A steel-lover. You bring shame upon your house."

Pagaloth's doubts swirled about him. This was his own conscience speaking, just a vision, a mocking vision of his mind. It was not truly Eldur, he knew. *He cannot see me,* he told himself. *This a trick and nothing more.*

"Your house fell when Borrus Kanabar slew your family," the voice went on. "You should have killed him in the Drylands, in vengeance. But no, you guided him instead, and served him. This man who toppled your house…"

"He did not topple it. My house lives on." Pagaloth turned and faced the shadow, lifting his chin. "I can still restore it."

"You? *You?*" The laughter came again, thick with disdain. "You are nothing, nothing, a dragonknight and no more."

"No," Pagaloth said, firmly. "I am a dragon*rider* now. And we will never submit to you, Echo of Eldur. You are the spectre of him, *and no more.*" He stood before the ghostly apparition, proud and tall, and when the voice raged on, he did not submit. Like skin growing hard with callus, he let it buffer and beat against him, parrying every attempt to ensnare him. And he knew then that he would never yield or wilt. He had passed the test. *I am ready,* he thought.

He stepped in closer toward the throne. "I am done with you," he said, casting the voice aside. The shrouded figure shrank back and the dark clouds rolled away, and then once more there was only Jerek, poor Jerek, a beaten slave hanging in chains.

The man sputtered for breath, wheezing raggedly. The voice took much out of him, sapping his strength, and left him each time a wasted form. Pagaloth never felt such pity for him as he did right after. He was a tool to be battered until blunt and spent of use, and Eldur, his Father of Fire, did not care.

"Rest," Pagaloth said. "Food and water will be brought to you."

He left him there and moved through the scar in the wall. Rhok was sitting on a smaller rock outside. The big man peered up at him through his heavy beetled brow. "Sounded intense," he rumbled. He stood and stretched his back. "You are doing better?"

"Better than better. I'm doing *well.*" Pagaloth drew a long deep breath to freshen out his lungs. There was a tingle in his blood, and the thrill would take a while to leave him. Such as it always was after these sessions.

He could see that Lord Marak and Lady Kazaan had not yet returned, though An'zon Graz and Angrar were both sitting beside the fire in their little camp of tents and shelters. He went over to them, leaving Rhok by his rock. Graz looked up at him with a smile. "I heard a voice," he said, "and not a pleasant one. Sounded rather like Eldur to me." He unleashed a grin; the man was rarely serious. "So, how was it? Rhok didn't need to go in and save you this time?"

"That only happened once." It had been his first session with Jerek, the day after he'd arrived. Alone with the voice and with no guidance on how to repel it, the priest had got his claws into him, and Rhok had been required to pull them out.

"Once with *Rhok*," An'zon said casually. He was a handsome man, and knew it, slim and athletic and still youthful enough, with thick black hair that fell in waves to his shoulders and brown eyes that were always smiling. "Angrar had to save you once too, I recall." He looked across at Angrar, who was stirring a pot of steaming broth. The gaunt man looked up, nodded, and returned to his work. Angrar did not talk, Pagaloth knew. Not since his tongue has been torn out, anyway.

"Fine. Angrar had to help me once as well," Pagaloth admitted. "But since then I've needed no aid." He took a seat on a stone seat by the fire, enjoying its crackling warmth. Angrar ladled out some bowls, handed one to Graz and one to Pagaloth, then took one over to Rhok before returning. Pagaloth tipped the bowl back and had a good long swallow, then wiped his mouth with the back of his sleeve. "I saw Eldur and Agarath," he said. It was only a vision, but visions could be traced with truth, it was known. "They were in the heart of the Ashmount, I think."

An'zon's lips curled down. "The Ashmount? You think Eldur's there? Not in Eldurath?"

"It would make sense. The Ashmount is a primary source of Agarath's power." Pagaloth had another gulp of soup. It was more delicious than it had any right to be, well spiced and salted and with plenty of chunks of meat. "Venison?" he asked. There were some root vegetables too, a bit of turnip and carrot, all told a hardy meal. Angrar had been a cook before they put a spear in his hand. Now he was a cook again. *And a dragonrider besides.*

"*Happy* caught a deer," Graz confirmed. "He was kind enough to let us share it." He glanced up to a nearby rock ledge where his dragon *Hapthanor* had made his roost. His scales were a mottled mix of greyish-white and lime green, a match for An'zon's chequered cloak.

Several other dragons were resting on their own private ledges and shelves on either side of the rift walls above them. Others were missing from their nests, flying patrol in the skies or hunting for game in the woods. Pagaloth could not see *Lendrathor* on his perch. *He will be stretching his wings*, he thought. His dragon was a restless sort, and rarely slept for long. *He is much the same as I am in that…*

An'zon's voice pulled him back from his thoughts. "We might want to consider an assault," he said, musing as he set aside his soup. "We have ten dragons here now, and six riders. If we are clever about it, we might be able to get close before they detect us. End this war in one snap of a dragon's maw." He clipped his fingers.

If only it could be so easy. Alas no, that would not work. But Graz was nothing if not optimistic. Pagaloth had always been more pragmatic. "We'd be seen before we get within a hundred leagues of the mountain. We would do better to weaken Eldur first before we consider any strike."

"By killing these priests?" Graz asked.

It was a possibility. "If Eldur has given them the power to deploy his voice, then killing them may weaken him, yes."

And if not, they would be ridding the north of the Fire Father's pernicious presence and preventing more Agarathi from being drawn back beneath his shadow. Sir Pagaloth only had to remember Sir Hadros and the rest of the united host for that. He only had to remember Ten'kin, and how he'd infiltrated their ranks and turned all the Agarathi deserters against them. He'd even gotten into the head of Sa'har Nakaan. Sa'har, who had cut his own throat rather than be enslaved once more. *He told me to run, and I ran,* the dragonknight thought. *He knew if I was taken they'd make me into a weapon. Send me into the heart of the northern cause as a friend…only to unleash me as their foe.*

Lord Marak knew that as well. It was why he wanted to be certain Pagaloth was immune to the risk of enslavement before he let him return to King's Point so he might seek the counsel of Captain Lythian and the king. The dragonknight was keen to fly back there to report on what had happened and hear of their latest tidings. He alone was a trusted link to the northern cause and dragonrider or not, he remained Lythian's man by oath. *We should be working together,* he knew. *Our purposes are now aligned.*

The blanket of fog that hung above them was darkening, dusk falling in the world beyond. That shroud was curiously thick, helping to keep the worst of the cold at bay and shield them from sight. Pagaloth could hear a distant thumping of wings out there, a shriek ringing through the skies. A moment later the fog billowed and parted and a dragon cut right down into the rift, scales glistening in shades of royal red and copper, to land upon his private perch. Pagaloth smiled to see him, then stood and turned to An'zon Graz. "I'm going to see about taking a short flight, before it gets too dark. I still have much to learn."

"I know. I have seen you fly, Pagaloth. Much to learn indeed." He grinned. Graz had a great repertoire of smirks and grins and winks and laughs that he deployed with great regularity.

Pagaloth did grow weary of him sometimes. "I do not have the same connection to Lendrathor as you do with Hapthanor," he said. "You were tethered by the Bondstone. You can sense each other's thoughts."

"Yes, true, and I don't always like it. Happy is not always happy, Pagaloth. He has dark feelings and they do not sit well with me." He shook his head and frowned dramatically.

Pagaloth walked away from him. He crossed the craggy plateau until he was right beneath Lendrathor's high perch. A soul-bonded Fireborn rider would merely be able to summon their dragon with a thought, but that was not so for Pagaloth. His dragon was as a horse to a knight, a giant flying steed and the depth of bond was much the same. Once before such riders were known as rogues.

Lythian spoke of such, he remembered. The captain had wondered if he might catch and cage a few dragons, then find some willing men with Fireborn blood among the Agarathi prisoners to fly them, men who might become loyal to his cause. He wondered how those plans were going. It made him smile to think of their reunion now that he was a rogue rider himself.

Still, he had work to do on that. As a horse can be hard to break in, so could a dragon, and it was dangerous work besides. A rider bonded by the Soul of Agarath need not concern himself with such fears; they were soul-bonded from that moment on, and would never do each other harm lest they do harm to themselves. But wild horses could bite, and wild dragons could bite *harder*. The dragon had chosen him, true, the day Pagaloth first arrived, but that did not mean he made it easy. No, he preferred to make it difficult. Lendrathor was stubborn, spirited, and not one to follow commands. And so he proved now, as Pagaloth did all he could to summon him.

Calling him down did not work. Whistling certainly didn't. "Do you want me to beg, is that it?" he even found himself asking in desperation. The dragon only peered down at him through a set of keen purple eyes, unmoved.

Across the shelf he could hear An'zon laughing. "You need to climb up there and show him who's boss, Pagaloth. He is just a big puppy, that's all. He needs to be trained."

A big puppy who could end my life in an instant if he so chose. Graz was being typically facetious, as was his way. But still, his advice had some small merit, he would admit. *I must be firm*, he told himself. *I must assert myself to build the bond.* "Lendrathor," he shouted. "You are tired, I know, but there is work that must be done. *You* chose *me*, remember. You bear the colours of my house. Honour that choice and take me up to fly. I ask for only ten minutes. Then you may rest."

The dragon continued to stare at him from over the lip of his ledge, much as a cat might do. He was a handsome beast of above-average size, not bulky in the way that Garlath was but strong and quick for all that. A trio of dark copper horns, rather like the triple-pronged beard Pagaloth once wore from his chin, jutted down from the bottom of his jaw. It was an unusual feature, but elsewise he bore the hallmarks of a classic dragon, broad-winged and slim in the body, with a fine long tail that ended in another three-pronged spike. He looked down for what seemed like an age, as though testing Pagaloth to see if he might lose his patience and give up, before at last he shifted and stood, unfurling his wings, and gave a short, acceding screech.

Pagaloth breathed out silently and held his smile. It was a win. A small one, yes, but progress.

With a thump of his wings the dragon rose and then fell, landing with a rumble before him. Pagaloth gave a bow to show his thanks, waited for the wing to drop, and then climbed up into the saddle that Ulrik Marak and Rhok had made for him, a harness of tough vines and leather, simple but sturdy. Lendrathor did not wait until he was fully strapped up, nor did he wait for the command to go. He just went of his own accord, leaving Pagaloth to hastily strap and tighten his restraints as the beast soared skyward through the thick wet blanket of fog and up into the dusk-drenched skies.

The air rushed past his cheeks and through his hair, stirring the lengthening bristles of his unbraided beard. Sir Pagaloth was not like An'zon Graz; he was not one for smiling quickly and often, but now he did, and his smile was broad. He took the reins in hand, holding tight, ducking low as he'd been taught. Many years of watching other Fireborn riders in flight had given him the basics of knowledge, yet Lady Kazaan and An'zon Graz, and Ulrik Marak in particular, had been there to help steer his course.

All the same, it was different for them. They were linked to their dragons by soul and mind, their feelings entwined, and in time became as one. Pagaloth had no such shortcut. He could see the sunset blazing to the west, a rarely pretty sight and he wanted to enjoy it. "Right," he shouted, over the rush of wind, tugging the reins that way. "Come, Lendrathor, let us look at the sunset together. No…north? Why are you taking us *north*?"

He could not understand the dragon's answer or decipher his rumbles and roars. So far they had flown together only a dozen or so times and their pairing was still very new. It would take time, he had been told, for them to learn to trust one another.

"Lendrathor, the light is beautiful, look. West…will you not take me west?" He tugged at the reins again, and kicked with his heel, but what good would that do with a dragon? It was his instinct of riding horses all his life, but those instincts must be unlearned.

Your voice, he thought. *Use your voice.* Dragons were a great deal smarter than most horses and he would understand almost everything he said. He drew a breath and called out, "Remember what we just said below? You chose me, Lendrathor, and our colours are the same." Pagaloth had even named him for his uncle Sir Lendroth, who he'd trained under as a squire. Perhaps the beast did not like that, being named? If so he had not shown any leaning one way or the other. "Come, I am not trying to control you. We are here together, you and I…and the sunset, I only wish to see the sunset, Lendrathor."

The dragon ignored him completely. Pagaloth muttered something under his breath and consoled himself with the fact that he'd managed to stir him to flight at all. They continued north, for what reason the knight could not say. *Is he being defiant for the sake of it? Has he caught the scent of something he wants to kill?*

He didn't have to wonder for long. A half second later the dragon was dipping his head and tucking his wings and plunging in a fierce descent. Pagaloth gasped for air, squeezing his eyes to slits against the onrushing wind. They pierced a wet grey cloud and at once the vast woodland came back into view below. And then he saw it; the lake, shimmering like beaten silver. "*Don't go under*," he called out, suddenly aware of the beast's intentions. "*Don't*, Lendrathor. This…this isn't funny."

It seemed to be to the dragon. Was that a rumble of laughter thrumming through his chest? Pagaloth could not say for certain, but he was certainly suspicious. He braced for impact, ducking down low. And then the water rushed up to meet them and with a great splash, in they went.

The world turned to a blur of bubbles and froth and half-heard sounds, but only for a dozen heartbeats. Then the dragon was thrashing at the water once more, breaking the surface, beating fast and furious back up into the air as glittering streams cascaded off his wings, lit by the light of the setting sun.

Pagaloth gasped once again, sucking deep. He was soaked to the bone and chilled to the marrow, but somehow…somehow he was laughing. "Damn you…" he managed to splutter. "You think I deserved that, do you? For…for disturbing your rest!"

He could almost see the dragon grin as he turned his long slender neck back to look at him. *Am I mad? Or are we starting to get to know one another?* Then the bastard ducked and dived again, deeper this time, gliding through the lake with astonishing grace. He broke the surface, flapping skyward. Pagaloth wheezed and sucked air. Then they plunged again.

"Enough!" Pagaloth managed to cry out, when they rose a third time. "Please, enough!" He was laughing again, laughing as he fought for air. "Lendrathor, you've made your point." He did not know what point that was, but it had been finely articulated. "Now can we not go see that sunset? I'm clean enough…" - *perhaps that's the point he was trying to make?* - "…I don't need another bath!"

It seemed that Lendrathor had had his fun. With a twisting barrel roll he shook off the water from his scales, then rose and flapped away toward the west. He was rising up toward the low scuttling clouds when Pagaloth sighted another dragon in the skies, soaring along smoothly beside them. The sight was enough to startle him until he saw who it was. "When did you get here?" he shouted out, to An'zon Graz.

The man must have followed him right out on Hapthanor. "You know Lord Marak doesn't like it when you fly alone, Pagaloth," Graz called back. He looked annoyingly good in the saddle, half standing and half crouching, his chequered cape flapping in the wind. Hapthanor was smaller than Lendrathor, sleeker and quicker, very much as Neyruu had been in fleetness and agility. Lythian had said that Princess Talasha now flew Neyruu, having heard that from Elyon Daecar. Pagaloth wondered if he would see her sometime, up here. He would like that very much, for her to join their rebel flock.

"I do not need a chaperone."

"Marak says otherwise. And I'm not here to chaperone you. I'm here to watch how you fly and laugh at you." He grinned. "Maybe offer you some pointers too."

"I need no pointers from you, Graz," Pagaloth shouted back. The two dragons were close, flying wing to wing. "I'll take tuition from Lord Marak and Lady Kazaan. You're almost as green in the saddle as I am."

"Adelle is no different. Eldur bonded her to Tundrath the same time as he bonded us." He gave Happy a slap on the flank.

That was true. But Adelle Kazaan had been wed to the skilled Skymaster Lord Rhukar Kazaan and somehow that made a difference. Graz was a storied and rich house, but An'zon only hailed from a lesser branch and had spent his life womanising and working the Eldurathian social scene. He never even attempted the trials at the Nest, Pagaloth knew. *And here he is, claiming to be some expert.*

It vexed him a little, it had to be said.

"Anyway," Graz called out, "none of that is the truth. I'm not here to chaperone you or give you pointers, not on this occasion. I'm here to tell you that I saw Lord Marak and Lady Kazaan returning from the south, and I thought you might want to hear their tidings. So, shall we go? We can race on the way back."

"Fine." Pagaloth had grown up with brothers. He'd always been competitive. "Let's race, then."

And they went. It seemed Lendrathor was competitive also. As soon as Hapthanor shot away, the bigger dragon raced right after him, losing ground at first due to Hapthanor's acceleration, but then slowly catching up as they reached their top speeds.

It was not enough, in the end, and they lost, but it was close. "You've got a good dragon there, Pagaloth," An'zon admitted once they'd returned and undone their restraints, dismounting from their saddles and sliding down their dragons' wings. They walked together toward the camp as the beasts flapped back up to their perches to rest, rumbling at one another as though discussing the race as well. "I didn't think Lenny would be so quick."

"Hapthanor is quicker."

"In short bursts, yes, but over a longer distance I think Lenny would have him."

The sound of voices echoed through the air ahead. Lord Ulrik Marak and Lady Adelle Kazaan were sat together at the fire, enjoying warm bowls of soup, talking quietly between themselves. The dragonlord wore his Body of Karagar armour, a near impervious suit of scales in rippling shades of red and black, the same colours as Karagar's father. The Fireblade rested beside him, sheathed and steaming from the top of its scabbard.

"You were gone longer than expected," An'zon called, striding over. "Did you have any success?"

Marak looked up at them. He appeared weary from his days away, so too Lady Kazaan. Both Garlath the Grand and Tundrath had already fallen asleep on their roosts.

"We killed three more priests," Marak told them, as the two men sat down by the fire. Pagaloth welcomed the warmth after his dips in the lake. "And took another." He gestured to the scar in the wall that led into the cells. "Rhok is stringing him up as we speak. And disposing of the other."

Pagaloth felt a sharp prod in his chest. "You're to kill Jerek?" He was not sure how he felt about that. A part of him still pitied the man, enslaved as he was, and wondered if he could be saved.

"We have no further use for him." Marak spooned a measure of soup into his mouth, hunched forward on his seat. He was a very large man, Ulrik Marak, still thick with muscle even at his age. "Rhok told me about your session today. The voice was fierce, he said, and it has drained him. Jerek is spent, and will not likely be revived. The chasm will take him off our hands."

Graz chuckled. "We ought to feed him to the dragons instead. Save them having to hunt."

"No. It would be best that they do not get a taste for the flesh of man. We cannot have them hunting people, An'zon."

"Depends on the people. There are a few I could think of who'd make a fine feast for them, my lord."

"I said no. Wild dragons may hunt man, but not ridden ones." He turned back to Pagaloth. "You look wet. Was it raining in the west?"

Pagaloth felt slightly ashamed to report the truth on that. "Lendrathor flew me into the lake," he said. "The one to the north of here."

"Hunting for fish, was he?"

"No. He…"

"Was having fun," came in Graz. "Trying to build the bond."

Marak nodded. He was not a man for fun, but seemed to understand. "Lendrathor is a willful dragon. He will test you from time to time, to see how you react." He had a bit more soup. "You're growing closer?"

Graz spoke up for him again. His praise was welcome, if unexpected. "They're working well together, Ulrik, and Pagaloth flies well. It seems to me that he and Lenny are starting to get along."

"Do *not* call him that," sniffed Lady Kazaan. She was a hard old woman, the dragonlady, not one for Graz's pithy ways. "And do not call Hapthanor 'Happy' either. A dragon should not have a pet name."

"But he likes it. It makes him happy."

Kazaan's stern lilac eyes bore into him. "I regret returning so soon, Ulrik. We should leave again on the morrow to continue our hunt."

"But you've only just returned, Adelle." An'zon leaned over, as though to clutch her hand. "I have missed you so."

She snatched her fingers back from him, and might have slapped him had he not withdrawn, laughing.

"We will hunt again soon, I assure you." Lord Marak was pondering something, looking up toward Lendrathor as he settled down to sleep on his shelf. "Does he obey your commands yet, Pagaloth?"

The dragonknight felt compelled to tell the truth. "Not as such, no. He is still defiant, my lord, but it does feel like we're finding some common ground, as An'zon says."

"Enough for him to fly you to King's Point?"

Pagaloth wished he could give a positive answer to that, but he was nothing if not honest. Too honest, sometimes. That sense of candour had led him to speak out of their plot to assassinate Prince Tavash, once before. It had gotten him into trouble too when he stood before Alrus Pentar in Redhelm and admitted his part in his brother Tomos's death by unveiling the aforementioned plot. Tomos had perished in the Pits of Kharthar due to that betrayal, torn apart by malformed pygmy dragons, and so Alrus had declared he be hanged at once as Lythian struggled and watched on from the side. Then Elyon Daecar had flown down to save them both. *Another reprieve*, Pagaloth thought. One day perhaps he would have a chance to return the favour.

His answer was as forthright as ever. "I would not trust him to obey me, my lord. King's Point is many leagues from here, and there is a chance Lendrathor would be distracted along the way. He could easily take me off somewhere else, or refuse to go at all."

Once more the voice of An'zon Graz came in. "If I may, my lord…if *I* were there too, I'm sure Lendrathor would be more compliant. Happy and Lenny get along well and were friends back on the Wings, Happy says. If we go together, we should reach King's Point easily enough."

Lady Kazaan sniffed again. "Are we sure we want to unveil ourselves to the Vandarians, Ulrik? We still have much work to do here." She looked at An'zon Graz doubtfully. "And *him*? I'm not sure he's the best person to represent us."

Graz shrugged. "I don't see why not. People like me. I'm likeable, Adelle."

"You're a child, An'zon. A pampered child and I do not think a man like Amron Daecar would take you seriously."

"He does not need to," Marak said. "Sir Pagaloth is known and trusted by the Vandarians, and will be the one to do the talking. We have been here in hiding long enough. It is time we declare to them our support."

Kazaan remained unsure, but she was a skeptical and wary old woman who had lived long in distrust of the northmen. Her husband had been killed in the last war and she'd lost two sons to northern steel besides. Her eyes were narrow, mouth puckered. "If you're sure," she managed to say, reluctantly. "My husband always trusted you, Ulrik, and so must I." She dipped her sharp chin. "So be it."

"Then you'll leave in a couple of days," Marak said to Pagaloth and An'zon Graz. "Take the time to build your bond, Pagaloth, and test yourself with our new captive. His voice is strong, we found. He will make a worthy replacement."

And as he spoke the words, the man he was to replace was dragged out from the scar by Rhok, who held him by the scruff of the neck. The fire priest had no strength left in him to fight, or struggle, or speak. Like a carcass he was hauled over the rough rock shelf, body bouncing over juts and snags, until Rhok reached the edge of the chasm. He looked over at Marak, who gave a nod.

And just like that, Jerek was thrown unceremoniously into the void.
He never even made a sound.

16

Ranulf

He watched the *Hammer of Tukor* rise and fall, and felt the great *thrum* move through his body as it crashed down upon the anvil. Up the hammer went, and down and up, down it went and up and down, up and down, strike and spark, working the steel, beating the blade.

It was a wonder to witness, another to add to his list, and perhaps one to top them all. *I am a lucky man,* Ranulf Shackton thought, as he observed the demigod at his work. His life had been exciting enough when he was a mere adventurer and scholar, a student of the arcane, but now…now…

Ilith slammed the hammer down again, and the whole forge seemed to shake. A thrill ran right through Ranulf's body at the godly sound it made. Sweat dappled the demigod's sinewy arms and his golden hair had turned dark from his toil. He wore a leather vest and breeches and thick hardy gloves, the simple garb of a blacksmith. *Just like in the frescoes and the paintings and the sculptures,* Ranulf thought. Not *all* depicted the World-builder that way, of course, but many did, and that was how Ranulf had always thought of him; Ilith at his anvil with the Hammer of Tukor in his grasp, working another wonder to life.

The hammer rose and fell, rose and fell, and Ranulf watched trans-fixed. Sparks flew at each mighty strike, flashing as hammer met steel. With his heavy tongs Ilith turned the blade, striking again and again, up and down, flattening the godsteel, folding it, reheating it and repeating the process all over again. *How many times has he folded it now? How long have I been watching?* It might have been a minute or ten or an hour or two; here time seemed to stand still. *I could watch him work forever.*

The blade was not to be completed today, it seemed. Once folded and refolded several dozen times over to drive all impurity away, Ilith placed it into his forge oven and worked the bellows, heating it anew, then buried the glowing metal into a bed of ashes for cooling. Ranulf was not especially familiar with the process. "Will you not quench it in water or oil, my lord?"

"Only once the blade is complete, Ranulf. This method of slow cooling is called annealing. It helps to soften the blade and reduce internal stress, which might have built up during the folding process. In turn that makes it easier to shape and fuller, and create a perfect edge." He smiled, removing his gloves. "Once I've done that, I will quench and temper it. But that all takes time. I will continue when I'm better rested."

Rested, yes. That was important, to be sure. There was a time when Ilith could work at his anvil for days on end, even weeks the legends said, but this was not the same Ilith of old. Ilith in spirit, but not in body, and the mortal vessel was not as strong as it was. According to Fhanrir, Ilith had been bright and radiant shortly following the transference, but some of that light was starting to dim. "I worry he won't have the strength to hammer the heart back together," the mage had confided to him in his rough and rattly voice. "He can make these lesser blades all day long, but none of them are going to matter. There's only one that does. He needs to be strong for it. He needs to see *sense*."

But Ilith seemed unconcerned about that. Or perhaps he was simply burying his head in the sand in the same way he'd just buried that blade in those ashes? Ranulf had been here less than a week, but true enough, if ever he heard Fhanrir raise the subject of Ilith's ageing, of the quick diminishing of his spirit and strength, the demigod would only wave it away and tell his friend not to worry.

He is much as the histories say in that way as well, Ranulf reflected. Ilith of the silvery voice and quick smile, the wit and wisdom and stubborn defiance, yes, that too. It was said that Varin the Steel Father had pled and begged and demanded that Ilith remake the Heart of Vandar a hundred times over, but not once did the Worldbuilder wilt. Would he wilt to Fhanrir's pleas, then? Ranulf had to wonder.

The demigod was humming a tune now, filling the forge with the divine wonder of his voice as he wiped himself down with a cloth, cleaning sweat and soot from his arms and forehead, scrubbing the dirt from his hands. It made Ranulf think of the stories of Ilith at his forge above Ilithor, where the Blades of Vandar were said to have been made. *He would sing as he worked,* he thought. *Hammer and song as one.* It was how the Hammersong Mountains had first been named, or renamed from some older name they'd had during the time of the gods. It was said that you could still hear Ilith's voice ringing out softly when the wind was right, accompanied by the gentle thud and strike of his hammer. *And now here I am, standing witness to a private verse.* Ranulf felt like the luckiest man in all the world.

The demigod broke from his singing and looked over at the adventurer. He had a smile on his face; rarely did he not. "So…how did you find that, Ranulf?" he asked him in that pleasant, silverly tone of his. "I hope it wasn't too dull for you?"

"Oh no, my lord…quite the opposite," he gushed. "I have seen weapons forged before once or twice, but never quite like that. The precision of the strikes, the flow and the rhythm…" It was almost like a dance, or some ritual motion, one performed countless times to the point of perfection. He said so and Ilith laughed modestly.

"You are too kind, Ranulf, but no, I am still working to remove some rust. Tyrith's body…it does not have the same ingrained knowledge as mine did, you see. A sort of muscle memory, you might call it. I still must hone my skill so I'm ready for the final forging, when the time comes."

He smiled and paused for a brief moment, as though engaging in a short internal dialogue. Ranulf had been somewhat unnerved at seeing that the first time, but now he'd grown quite used to it. *He is speaking to Tyrith*, he knew. *Sharing some private word.* The heir still resided within the same body, Ranulf had been told, though as a fragment only it did seem to him, an observer and little more.

After a brief moment, Ilith nodded and said, "Tyrith is keen for me to tell you he spent his entire youth and early adulthood forging weapons and armour as well, in my old forge above Ilithor. And with the Hammer of Tukor, once he'd learned to wield it. That has made my own task easier, of course. He is a gifted blacksmith, as I have told him many times before, but he lived only a quarter century, less than half of that with the Hammer of Tukor in his grasp, where I…well, best not tell you how old *I* am, Ranulf Shackton. It would only sour my mood."

He chuckled and threw aside his cloth, then went to a peg on the wall, removed a light wool cloak, and threw it over his lean glistening shoulders. "Come, let us escape this heat. Walk with me, Ranulf." He strolled from the forge.

Ranulf followed him out, feeling as though he was caught in a lucid dream. They moved slowly, languidly, wandering side-by-side through the quiet of the refuge, and here it *was* quiet, unlike the sprawling settler quarters, with the busy tent-taverns and market-chambers, the bustling cavernous rooms and corridors and hectic chaos of the entrance hall where thousands still poured through the portal each and every day. Ranulf had spent much time wandering those rooms and speaking with the people, but here it was very different. This part of the refuge was private, a quiet sanctum away from all that noise that was used only by Ilith and those in his close council, of which Ranulf Shackton, astonishingly blessed as he was, had found himself a part.

"Tell me, Ranulf," Ilith said as they walked, "what is the feeling like among the people? How would you say they are finding life here? Is there fear? Discord among them? Do many of them want to leave?"

"Leave, my lord?"

He nodded. "Lord Morwood has explained to me that many feel deceived, and would not have come if they'd known about the portal door. There have been injuries, I am told, even deaths."

Very few of them, so far as Ranulf was aware. And a small price to pay for bringing so many here to safety. It vexed him a little that anyone would cause a fuss over that. "I would ignore those people, my lord. It sounds to me that they're being ungrateful."

"Then you haven't heard any grumblings yourself, Ranulf? I daresay Lord Morwood is something of a cautious man. Perhaps it's not as bad as he makes out?"

"I have heard very little complaint or protests," Ranulf told him. "Yes, there is a certain…tension among the more fragile souls, but that can only be expected. For the most part the people are very thankful to be here."

They walked on a moment, entering a great open chamber full of statues. A shaft of light lanced down from the ceiling, illuminating one; a great monument to Varin, it was, looming some twenty feet high and cast in a pose of great glory and triumph with blade brandished high and cloak stirring at his back. The detail was astonishing. Ilith stopped to look at it, smiling in admiration, though for the demigod friend he knew or the skill of the work Ranulf could not say. "I wonder, Ranulf…what if *I* were to walk among the people? Would they not benefit from knowing I was here?"

When Ranulf did not give an immediate answer, Ilith turned to him. "Your silence is telling, Ranulf. You agree with Fhanrir, is that not so? He tells me that there is no sense in putting me at risk. Not until my task is complete."

"He…may be right, my lord. It would be better to keep your presence here a secret."

"Then I am Hamlyn, the Steward of these halls. Kept alive for a single duty, only to perish when it is done." He looked away down a long dim corridor, sighing. "He died so I could live again, and I never even got to see him. You are a scholar, Ranulf. You know our history, I trust?"

"I know you and Hamlyn were very close, my lord."

"As brothers, yes. He was at my side always, and helped me shape this world. Hamlyn the Humble, I hear you called him. An apt name. Never did he seek acclaim." He looked at the statue of Varin again and gave a soft little chuckle. "Another brother, but so very different. Varin never liked to shun the light. Tell me, Ranulf, of his grandson. I never had the chance to meet him."

Ranulf frowned. "You're referring to Amron the Bold, my lord?"

"There are some accounts here I have read of him. They say Amron was much as his grandfather; a seeker of triumph and acclaim, imperious on the battlefield. But he lacked a certain wisdom. A brutal king, some call him, even a tyrant. Would that be fair to say?"

Ranulf considered that, then shook his head. "No, my lord. That term would suggest an oppressive king, cruel toward his own people. I have heard it used to describe him before as well, though those who do so tend to argue that his wars were senseless and driven by bloodlust, that his people suffered as a result, and thus he was tyrannical. It is a roundabout way of reaching that conclusion and flawed, I feel. But brutal? Yes. He was a brutal king to his enemies, of that there can be no doubt."

Ilith nodded thoughtfully. "More like his grandfather than this father, then. I knew both of them very well."

Ranulf still struggled to imagine it. *I am standing here with Ilith. Ilith who built the world.* Not in his truest form, perhaps, but his memory seemed to be intact. And his spirit, yes. He could feel the ancient wisdom in him, the knowledge, the great depth of his years. And the sadness, that as well. Much as he did smile and chuckle there was a deep sadness in him too.

"And what of his namesake? Tell me of Amron Daecar, Ranulf. I have heard he is both hawk and dove, a complex man, peerless with the blade and as a leader both. Is there truth in that?"

Ranulf gave a nod. "It's an apt description. He rose to fame during the War of the Continents, when he slew the dragon Vallath and crippled Prince Dulian, his rider. Many legends surround that day and he won many names from the duel, and the war at large. But principally, that battle served as the beginning of the end of the war. Many thank Amron Daecar for bringing the conflict to a close."

"And after? When the peace was agreed."

"He became more like King Ayrin," Ranulf said. "Officially, Vandar was ruled by Ellis Reynar, whose father, King Storris, was killed at the Burning Rock, along with Amron's sire. But unofficially, Amron and his younger brother Vesryn ruled the kingdom, and Amron in particular. He presided over the regrowth of the realm as king in all but name."

"A peaceable man at heart, would you say?"

"It is said, yes. Though I have not met him myself. He is a man to end a war, but not to start one, my lord. That is what they say of him."

"The very sort of man we need, then." Ilith stroked his narrow chin, green eyes glimmering thoughtfully as he looked at the statue of Varin. "One of these names he won during the war. Men call him Varin Reborn, is that so?"

"It is one of his names, yes."

"And a good one, I think. If not to be taken quite literally, of course." Something twinkled in his gaze and he said nothing more, but only turned and wandered on. Ranulf stepped after him, never quite sure if he should walk at his side or just behind to show deference, but in this case it did not matter. On leaving the chamber, Ilith turned a corner and they were met by a pair of figures cloaked and cowled. The demigod stopped and smiled. "Dear friend," he said to the smaller of the pair. "You are developing an uncanny ability to appear from nowhere in these halls."

"I learned the secrets of teleportation in your absence, Ilith," Fhanrir rasped. He made a noise that was probably a laugh, and Ranulf supposed he must be joking. "Came to report on your seals. We're doing what we can to strengthen them, but these others have no great power like you do." He flicked a hand at his companion. "Vottur. Agnar, Dagnyr. Even me. None of us are *you*."

"You were always a great mage, Fhanrir. I'll not hear you say otherwise."

The other ancient snorted. "Aye, I had my moments. Making that whole town think I was Varin was a highlight. Bunch of fools, they were. The king was long dead by then, but they still all went down on their knees as though I was the Steel Father himself come down from his Table." Laughter rattled in his throat." Served on me hand and foot for a fortnight before Hamlyn came along and spoiled it."

Ilith made a tutting sound. "That will ill-done, Fhanrir. What did you expect? To rule over them forever as Varin's ghost?"

The little mage bobbed his shoulders. "Was just a bit of fun, and I made them all forget it after. Always did like a spot of illusion, you know that. Used to be good at it too."

"Yes, rather too good." Ilith turned to Ranulf. "There was a time when one need only turn their back for a moment, and when they looked at Fhanrir again, he'd have them gazing in a mirror. Most Shadowcloaks take time to study a subject to mimic them properly, but Fhanrir always had an uncanny eye for detail. He was even able to deceive the divine."

Fhanrir grinned. "Aye, that's true. Was no one could see through my illusion when I put my mind to it. Had Thala thinking I was you once, you remember Ilith? Reckon that was my proudest moment, you know, deceiving the Far-Seeing Queen."

Ranulf smiled, trying to picture it. "Do you still practice the art, my lord?"

"You think I'd go about looking like this if I did? No. Good illusion takes focus and I don't have the fuel to spare on that sort of sorcery. Speaking of which…" He rounded on Ilith again. "We need to talk again about the boys, Ilith. You've aged a decade since we awoke you, and if you continue at that rate…"

Ilith raised a hand.

"No," Fhanrir said, "you'll not silence me on this. You can't keep avoiding it. Or do you want your seals to keep on weakening? You want us to be exposed?"

"The seals are holding, Fhanrir."

"For now. But not for much longer. You know what the First Elder wrote in his letter. The power of Aramatia is fading down in that wood of his and soon the enemy will find them. It's no different here. All we can do is paper over the cracks, and those cracks are getting wider. It won't be long before they break down completely, and when that happens, we'll be vulnerable. Only *you* can mend them, Ilith. Only *you* have that power. It'll drain you, aye, and age you quicker, and leave you unable to reforge the blades. So you'll *need* rejuvenating, like Hamlyn did. He kept the seals strong all these years in your stead and I saw what it did to him. He'd go from young to old in a matter of months, but I was always there to make it right, as was my duty. The boys…"

"Have suffered enough."

"*Fool*," Fhanrir growled, sudden as a whip-slash. His eyes flashed with anger. "This is Tyrith speaking, not you. The Ilith I knew would never have been so weak."

have been so weak."

"This is not weakness, Fhanrir. Nor is it folly. There may be choices before us you do not yet see."

"Then what use are they to me? I know only what I know. There are Bladeborn bastards here in this refuge right now. You only need to say the word and I'll have them rounded up for choosing." He waited, eyes shining darkly within his hood. A long silent moment passed and then he snorted through his grotesque dangly nose. "Damn you, then. Why am I still here? Thought I'd die with Hamlyn, but no, Tukor's still keeping me alive and for what? This is all I know."

"My friend, another purpose may await you." Ilith put a hand on his shoulder.

Fhanrir shrugged free. "The girl...she asked me why I don't leave. Go off wandering into the world, see a bit more of it while I can. Well maybe she was right. What am I doing here if you won't let me help you?" He did not wait for an answer. Abruptly, the mage turned and shambled away, his walking stick *clack, clack, clacking* on the cold stone floor. His great-grandson Vottur lingered a moment, then turned to follow when Ilith gave him a nod. Some silent instruction seemed to pass between them that Ranulf was not privy to.

Once the two mages were gone, Ilith gave a distressed sigh. "He was always very headstrong," he murmured, in a sad voice. "It grieves me so that he has been cursed by this life. As a boy he had such a vibrancy to him. Always smiling, laughing, playing his pranks. That one he spoke of, when he mimicked Varin...it was one of a hundred he played during the long peace following Eldur's fall. And why not, Ranulf? The world was scarred and needed healing and Fhanrir brought to us much joy back then...though yes, sometimes he went too far." He smiled melancholically. Tears glistened in his eyes. "To see him become so hardened and cold...so changed from the sweet man he was. In many ways he was as a son to me, where Hamlyn was a brother. And as I slept through the last three thousand years, he was here, forced to endure the unthinkable. And look how it has corrupted him." He blinked the tears from his eyes.

A cruel fate makes a cruel man, Ranulf thought, not quite knowing what to say. Perhaps Ilith did see another way to revive himself? Perhaps he didn't, and was merely avoiding the inevitable for now. But one way or another, he must be strong when it mattered most. Ranulf had watched him for hours at his work, seen the passion and the precision, the dedication to his craft, but that was in the forging of nought but a common godsteel blade. Hammering the Heart of Vandar back together would be altogether different.

I have given him the formula, but that is just one part. In that hidden message to him written by King Godrin in the Book of Thala, Ranulf had learned the secret to combining the blades, the precise sequence of events and instructions Ilith must follow to successfully reforge them. It was a gap in the demigod's knowledge, now restored, but the rest...the depths of dark sorcery he must conjure, the strength of both body and will he must possess to master the shards of Vandar's broken heart... those things remained in grave doubt.

And there was another thing too. Something Ranulf was eager to know more about. He cleared his throat, shuffling his feet. "My lord," he said. "I wanted to ask...about the list."

Ilith turned to him, escaping some old memory. "The list, Ranulf?"

"Yes. These, um, *ingredients* you need. For your sorceries. To reforge the Heart. I have asked Fhanrir of them, but beyond the greatbat hair and fang, he seems unwilling to tell me more. Are there many that you require? Rare items, I mean to say?"

"Are these trinkets from the brood of Brexatron not rare enough for you, Ranulf?" Ilith smiled that warm avuncular smile of his, the laughter lines spreading from his eyes. "Curious, isn't it? That the same day you arrive here bringing to me my lost formula, you should encounter such a rare creature...and one essential to our needs."

Yes, Ranulf thought, *and Neyruu's stirring defeat of the bat made it all the more providential.* He had glimpsed only the first exchanges of the battle before the two winged creatures had surged away out of sight, first fading off into the thick of the snowstorm before plunging through the valleys and duelling about the bluffs. He only knew that because he could still hear them, the great ringing shriek of the greatbat in particular as it tried to disorient its foe. Only when that shrieking went quiet did they dare hope that Neyruu had won.

Ilith smiled and went on. "Sir Mallister was out hunting the greatbat that day, did he tell you? We knew there was one here, lurking in these mountains, and we knew it must be slain for certain parts to be retrieved. A difficult task for common Bladeborn, even one as skilled as Mallister Monsort. Dragons may be drawn down into a duel, but that is not so for Brexatron's brood. How do you slay a creature if it refuses to engage, Ranulf? And one that has been blessed with wings? Quite the challenge, I'm sure you'll agree. If you had not come that day, the bat may very well have fled, never to be seen again. Instead it was drawn into a duel of its own, a feud ten thousand years old, and it paid the ultimate price." He put his hands together. "We owe Neyruu a great debt of gratitude for laying the greatbat to waste. With the hair from its wing and a chip of its fang I will now be able to brew *Essense of Nightwing*. Have you heard of it, Ranulf? It is a very rare elixir."

"I think...it rings a distant bell, my lord. I may have seen it written in an old tome on arcane potions."

"It takes very powerful sorcery to brew," Ilith told him. "A steady hand and the right incantation, spoken in the right tongue and in the correct tone and rhythm. There are issues of timing in these spells. Delay too long between two words and the sorcery can wither and die before it comes alive. Get a word mixed up with another, and you may veer down an even darker path. Spells can be extremely volatile, Ranulf. When mixing ingredients, great care must be taken. Add the hair before the chip of fang and you may fill the air with a noxious fume or see the chamber burst with flame. Delay but a moment and you may look upon not triumph, but ruin. Men do not understand the courage these incantations require. They are a battle in their own…one wrong step and you may miss your parry and see the flash of steel as it comes for your neck. There was a time when being a mage was the most perilous life path of all. Some spells, no, they are simple and harmless…in the same way a knight faces no harm when duelling with wooden swords in the training yard. But swap the wooden blade for a godsteel one, remove your armour, and face a foe who wants to slay you…then you'll know fear. Such is the life of a mage who works with powerful magic. Every spell and potion that pushes at the edge of their limit is a blade that can kill them…and many have died."

Ranulf had never heard it put in that way. Nor fully appreciated the risks. "And this…Essense of Nightwing. Have you brewed it before, my lord?"

Ilith smiled at him. "Once, yes. It is an elixir of my own making, Ranulf, one I designed for a special purpose, long ago, when Varin brought to me Vandar's Heart. His instruction was quite clear. "Break it," he told me. "Make from it the greatest weapons that man will ever know." I was rather struck, of course, that he would have befouled his god like that, but he assured me it was Vandar's will. So I trusted him, and set to the task, and when I had the idea of forging from it five blades, I knew I would need five elixirs."

"So there are four others? Besides this Essense of Nightwing?"

"Four, yes. It is often said I shattered Vandar's Heart beneath the Hammer of Tukor…an evocative image, I am quite sure, and one used in your artwork, your statues and paintings…but never quite accurate I fear to say. Rather, I used these elixirs and certain dark incantations to slowly reshape one into five. To give each blade life and power, tone and shade. Black is Essense of Nightwing, Ranulf, and black the blade it made. The others also have corresponding colours. White, blue, silver and gold. For frost and mist, wind and soul."

"Soul? You mean…the Sword of Varinar?"

"So Varin named it the day he first came to visit me, once the blades were complete. When he set his eyes upon the Five Blades, it was naturally the one that drew his gaze. And small wonder. Larger than the others, and glowing gold, I did rather suspect it would appeal to him." He gave a chuckle. "And so it was. I had given its name as the Soulblade, to reflect the very essence of Vandar's strength, but alas he elected to choose another. There was a god's soul out there already, he told me. The Soul of Agarath. And he did not want his blade to share that word." Another smile touched his lips. "There is an elixir to be made for each of the blades, Ranulf. Essense of Nightwing I can now brew, and with it I will be able to soften the Nightblade, turn it pliable, compliant. Only in this state will it be willing to reunite with the others…as only in this state was I able to first pull the heart apart."

"And…" Ranulf moistened his throat. The enormity of the task was beginning to dawn on him. "The other elixirs…"

"*Dew of the Mistmeadow. Seed of the Windwillow. Tears of the Frostshade. Light of the Soulstar.*" The demigod smiled. "Fair-sounding potions, I'm sure you'll agree. Though the ingredients required to make them…" He shook his head. "Some I have already, here in these halls, though each elixir is complex and requires a varied blend. Certain elements will be hard to find, Ranulf, and dangerous to acquire. And there is one, one last piece of the puzzle that must be retrieved as well…a thing most rare and one of a kind that we will need specialist help to obtain."

Specialist help? Is he asking… "My lord." Ranulf Shackton went down to a knee before him. "Tell me what you need and I will do everything in my power to find it for you. I have knowledge gathered over decades of learning, and…"

"And you are here for a reason, Ranulf Shackton," Ilith said. "Or so one may be led to believe, if they were so inclined." The demigod smiled and touched his shoulder, bidding that he rise, and he did so. "Yes, there may be something you can help me with. This particular ingredient… I'm afraid it is beyond your reach. But others…yes….I have something in mind for you. Come, Ranulf, let us start by showing you the list. It is right along here, just down here in my chambers."

They had been walking for only a few moments longer when they heard the sound of *clacking* behind them. Murmuring voices and the sound of slippered feet and pounding boots accompanied the noise. "Ah," Ilith said, pausing. "I daresay Fhanrir is coming to intrude on us again, Ranulf."

"Perhaps he is coming to clear the air, my lord?"

"I would think not. Fhanrir's moods are famously long. Much like his nose." He gave Ranulf a playful wink.

A few moments later the mage reappeared, shambling and *clacking* along with his walking stick and the burly form of Lord Morwood now at his side. "Found this lumbering fool on my way through the halls," Fhanrir muttered. "He's got some news for you. Thought I'd best bring him."

"Thoughtful as ever, my friend." Ilith addressed the watch commander. "And what do you have to report to me, young man?"

Morwood bent low into a bow. His cloak was chequered green and brown and his barrel chest was wrapped tight in a fine wool doublet showing the crest of Tukor on the breast. By the rosy tone of his jowly cheeks he'd paced rather hard to be here. "My Lord Ilith," he said. "I just came from the portal door. Another guest is shortly arriving, I am told, in the company of Her Highness Princess Amilia. A man was sent ahead to inform us."

"And now you've been sent ahead to inform me." Ilith smiled at him. "Who is this new guest, Lord Morwood?"

"Elyon Daecar, my lord. He's come here with a boy."

Ilith smiled - "Wonderful," - and put his hands together at his waist. Then he looked at Ranulf with a knowing little grin. "Most rare and one of a kind, Ranulf. And here comes our specialist help."

17

Talasha

They had come to her requesting she return to the refuge, and her thoughts had gone at once to Cevi.

"Is she not well? Has the wound festered?" she asked.

"No, Your Highness," the messenger reported to her. "Your hand-maid's condition hasn't changed."

"Then what is it?"

"You're needed in a session of council, my lady. I don't know more than that I'm afraid."

Talasha turned to Sir Mallister Monsort. "What could this be about?"

The knight was sitting on a rock near the fire, running a whetstone along the long length of his blade to the sound of constant scraping. He'd been the one to accompany Talasha here, along with half a dozen of his men, taking her on the short snowy trek through the mountains southwest of the fort. "I would not want to speculate, Lady Talasha. They may only be inquiring into the health of your dragon."

"Her name is Neyruu, sir."

"Yes, my lady. I did not mean any offence. Neyruu. Of course. I will remember next time."

He's a beautiful man, this one. If a little dim. How hard was it to remember a name? She'd said it often enough. "Well if that is the case," she said to the messenger, "please return and report that Neyruu is fast on the mend. Thank them for their healing balms and hospitality and tell them I will be leaving soon."

Sir Mallister set his whetstone aside. "How soon, my lady?"

He is fed up of escorting me out here, she thought. She could not blame him for that. Over the last six days Talasha had gone to the refuge only a handful of times, and those to visit Cevi in her sickbed. The rest of the time she spent here, in the grim mountain cave that the spawn of the nightmare had taken for its lair, and each time she needed strong men to come with her. Noble-born as he was, and an Emerald Guard of noted skill, Sir Mallister Monsort had been given that charge. *He is bored to the back teeth*, she thought. *He wants to be out there with his men, defending the passes and patrolling the plains. He wants to be battling monsters.*

Well, he would be able to do all that soon enough. "A day or two, maybe three," was her answer. "By then Neyruu should be quite ready to fly and I'll be out of that lovely blond hair of yours."

The knight frowned at the remark. "My lady, I hope you do not consider yourself to be an imposition. You are royalty, and it seems to me you may even be a queen. I am honoured to be your escort."

Words as handsome as he is. The man was chivalrous, there was no doubt. "You are kind, sir. But I'm sure you have better things to be doing than sitting in this horrid cave with me." And horrid it was, full of old bones and rags and strips of hide from all the men and beasts the greatbat had devoured. A stink of death suffused the air, and a lingering malice as well. Talasha had urged Neyruu to find somewhere better to convalesce, but the dragon did not seem interested. She had won this lair fair and square and perhaps even got a little kick out of being here, in the home of her fallen foe.

But it was big, that was true, and the fires helped to cover the stink and beat away the chill. There was space enough for the men to find nooks to sleep in and even a high rock perch above them at the back of the cave that Neyruu had taken as her roost. That was good. It kept her just far enough away from the others so they did not feel unduly uncomfortable sharing this space with a dragon, and Sir Mallister had been so kind as to chisel a ladder of sorts into the rock so that Talasha could climb up and join her if she pleased. Which she did, and often. By night she liked to sleep at Neyruu's side, and often by day she would sit with her as well, enjoying the warmth that came off her scales as she slept for long hours at a time.

"My lady," the knight said. "You must stay here as long as you please. I will remain with you until released from that duty, and happily. That goes for us all."

Talasha glanced around. The other men under his charge did not seem to share his view. "A day or three, as I say. I think we all have better things to be doing, Sir Mallister. And better places to be."

"Indeed. Yes. That may be so. And if I may ask, my lady…where do you plan to go? When you leave us, that is?" He took out his oil cloth and gave his blade a good long wipe. There was something almost sensual about the motion, Talasha had always thought. *These knights so love their swords.* Her sweet captain was much the same, always tending his blade Starslayer whenever he had a spare moment, before he went and lost it down in Eldur's tomb, never to be seen again.

Her answer was ambiguous. "South, for a start. This cold does not agree with me. Neyruu even less so." She was not certain how much the knight knew of Saska Varin, and even if he knew it all, she could not say that of his other men. So she decided to leave it at that. "And you, Sir

Mallister? Is this your war now, here in these mountains? Or do you plan to add your blade to the battles further south?”

“Ilith must be protected, my lady. And the people. There may come a time when the rest of the world is dying and we are the last bastion of humankind to remain. Until I’m commanded to some other station, I will be here, defending our future.”

There was a cough to her side, and Talasha remembered the messenger. “My lady. Are you to come with me, then? I understand it is of some importance that you are there. In council, that is.”

She smiled up at him. “You’re being so terribly patient. How could I possibly say no?” She stood up from the comfortable seat that Mallister Monsort had carved for her from a rock. Firelight flickered from the pit before her and burned on torches jammed into cracks in the walls. There were two either side of the cave mouth, their orange light giving shape to a pair of guards posted there. “How is the weather looking?” Talasha called to them.

“Cold, m’lady,” said the old one called Gunter, “but nothing new there.” The other laughed. “There’s a white wind blowing, but that oughtn’t trouble us. Visibility ain’t too bad.”

The messenger interjected. “We made it here easily enough, my lady, though the weather was worsening as we drew near. I would suggest me make some haste.” He gave Sir Mallister Monsort an urging look.

“Very well. We’ll leave at once.” The knight called an order for his men to make ready to depart, rolled his whetstone up in the oilcloth and rose, sheathing his blade and cinching his swordbelt around his slim athletic waist. After all that sharpening and oiling the longsword slid into the scabbard beautifully. “Rufford, add some more wood to the fire so it burns long and bright. We would not want Neyruu to get cold.”

Talasha smiled at him. That was thoughtful. “I may want to return after this council session,” she said. It felt only right to warn him.

“Then we will return, my lady. Whatever you need.” He inclined his head at her and turned, going between his men to make sure each was ready. “Check your weapons,” he said, voice echoing against the blood-stained walls. “Make sure they’re oiled so they don’t stick. Cloaks tight. Stick-Jym, Darron, I want you fifty hards ahead when we reach the bottom of the ridge. Watch for wolves. I heard them howling last night and they may still be prowling these heights. Simcock, Gunter, you’ll be the flanks. The rest stay tight.” He turned to the messenger. “How many men did you bring?”

“Four, my lord. Besides me. They’re waiting below.”

“Mine?”

“Yes, my lord.”

Mallister nodded. He had a hundred or so men under his charge, and more were still being recruited. “I want us setting a good pace,” he called out. “Rufford, that’s enough wood I think. We don’t want to smoke Neyruu out.” He looked to the perch where the dragon slept, a slim shape curled up in the dimness above them. Her eyes shone down like two little lamps, the only thing to say she wasn't sleeping. "My lady. Will you take a moment with her before we go?"

Talasha saw no need. Neyruu had been in pain and distress during those first days, but the worst of that had passed now and she seemed perfectly content. She told Mallister no, and he led her from the cave. The way was rough and perilous. First came the short climb down from the cave mouth, a near-vertical thirty-foot cliff that ended upon a narrow, wind-beaten plateau. As with Neyruu's perch, Mallister had cut hand and footholds into the rock with his blade so they could come and go more easily. He held out a hand to help her down as she reached the bottom. The others were all gathered. "All well, my lady?"

She nodded.

"Then let us continue."

The next section was the worst. From the plateau fell away a gaping chasm that swept into a boundless valley. In the white mists Talasha could see the shadows of other mountain peaks out there, but they were far away, and the valley floor was beyond the reach of her sight. To the right ran a stony path that hugged the mountain wall, before opening out into a steep and narrow ridge with plunging descents to either side. In a line they had to go, picking their way carefully across the rocks, each trying to step where the man ahead had stepped before. Sir Mallister went behind her, ever on hand should she trip and stumble, burly Rufford just ahead. "Just step where Ruff steps, my lady. I'm right here, if you need me."

Eventually, the ridge began to open out, growing flatter and wider in the middle, and a little way down the slope she could see four cloaked men awaiting them. Before very long the two groups were merging where the slope settled into the mountain plains. A great snowfield stretched away before them here, rutted with a newly trodden path made by the messenger and his men. Already the falling snow was starting to fill it in.

They paused to share brief greetings, and Sir Mallister also took the time to check that all was well with her, as was his wont. *He has a compulsion toward courtesy, this one.* She only smiled and told him what he wanted to hear, and then they continued on their way.

It was another hour and a half before the Shadowfort came into sight, by which point she was cold, tired, and rather dreading the return journey. The wind had picked up as they'd gone, and the snow was falling harder, swirling about on the blustery air and blowing right into her eyes. Sir Mallister scrutinised the skies. "We may need to wait until this weather passes, my lady," he told her, calling over the gale. "It would not be safe to return to the cave in this."

She had anticipated that. "Do you think we'll have to stay the night?"

"Unless this squall should blow over, yes, I think that would be wise. I will make sure your lodgings are cleaned and prepared, my lady, and a bath drawn for you. I'm sure you will welcome the comfort."

She only nodded, silent. There was little in the way of comfort about this refuge, though to be sure, she would not object to a steaming bath.

Down the slope toward the fort they went, and across the short stone bridge and through the gate. In the yard beyond, men were shovelling snow from a mountainous drift, piling it into a series of handcarts. Others were hauling firewood. She glimpsed a cloaked figure away atop the eastern walls, looking out across the valley. He had his hands raised high above him, pale fingers splayed, his wide black sleeves flapping in the wind. Faintly she could hear the man reciting some incantation, repeating a sequence of queer words over and over in a strange singing tongue. "One of the mages," Sir Mallister said. "I'm not sure which."

"Vottur," said Gunter. "Looks like Vottur to me. He's the tallest."

"What's he doing?" Talasha asked, peering up at him through the falling snow.

Mallister Monsort shook his head. "I could not say, my lady, and best not to ask. I prefer not to trouble myself with mage-business."

They hastened on. In Talasha's previous visits here, she had sensed a certain disquiet toward the mages, not quite a distrust but close. They did not mingle with the men, she had been told, and rarely did they speak. Even Ranulf had struggled to get to know them, and that rather said it all.

The man himself was nowhere to be seen when they scaled the steps toward the great door that led into the mountain. As always it was open, wide enough for the carts to be drawn through, and the snow was drifting in from outside to settle on the smooth stone floor. The entrance hall was vast. To left and right a pair of mighty stone knights rose up, astonishingly lifelike, guarding the way, and along one wall two dozen great vats and tubs were melting snow for drinking water, fires burning constantly beneath them. Several men shuffled down the line, adding wood and bits of kindling, stoking the flames with pokers and bellows. Others were removing the water with buckets for cooling, and there were scribes as well with books and ledgers in hand, scribbling their accounts, directing where the water needed to be taken or recording how much wood was being brought in.

It was busy here, always busy. Busier still away in the settler quarters, but of course Talasha had not gone *there*. Her presence would only cause discord, she sensed, and perhaps even open riot. Even the labourers and soldiers here in the entrance looked at her with a certain suspicion.

She ignored those looks as best she could, turning her eyes over the organised chaos in search of Ranulf. Nothing. That was unexpected. He always came to meet her when she returned, and Sir Mallister had sent two men ahead to report that they were on their way. *He must be in this council meeting,* she thought. *If it's still going on.* She'd be damned if she had trekked all the way back here just to miss it.

"This way, my lady." Sir Mallister led her on, leaving the others to stay behind. "They're meeting in Ilith's personal chambers, I'm told. Have you been there before?"

"No. Are they nice?"

"Modest, like the man. But comfortable. There are lots of books, stacked high, and old wooden desks. It's rather like a library, in truth. And there's a threadbare armchair he likes to sit in, I've seen. It was his favourite before his death."

Death. That's what they called it, for want of a better word, though much like Eldur, Ilith had only been lying in stasis all those years.

"I heard a story from him about that chair," the knight went on. "He told me he was sitting in it during his final days when Queen Thala paid her last visit. She gave a book to Hamlyn, the Steward. Ilith said he never knew what it was back then, that book, but…"

"You're talking of the Book of Contracts," she interrupted. She knew all about that, of course. Ranulf had told her, and she had discussed it with Amilia Lukar as well. *The Book That Doomed a Thousand Souls*, the Jewel of Tukor had called it, with a bite to her voice. That was understandable. She had lost her unborn child to the very last contract written within it.

The thought made her skin crawl. *Is that why I hate it here so much? Because of things like that?* It was part of it, she had no doubt. But there was more as well. There was something in the air, something alien to her senses, a mist of old magic perhaps that made her feel uneasy. *Lythian felt the same at the Nest*, she recalled. *And down in Eldur's Tomb as well.* Maybe this was the same. No Bladeborn was ever meant to visit those places and no Fireborn was meant to come here.

Mallister was going blithely on. "The Book of Contracts, yes. The entire purpose of the Shadow Order was to carry those contracts out, though it was built under false pretences and lies. The men here never knew about Thala's involvement and foresight, or how important the order truly was. Only the mages did. I don't know why that was kept from them."

"Because men cannot be trusted, Mallister. It really is as simple as that." She was starting to feel a little queasy as he led her deeper into the refuge. "How far is it? Or must I endure another two-hour trek?"

He frowned at her sudden disgruntlement. "No, my lady. It's…right along here." He turned her down another short corridor. Past another almost identical and empty, lifeless chamber they went, and into a smaller anteroom with an oakwood door at the end. It was hanging ajar and she could hear the voices coming out from inside. *They're still going, then. They must have plenty to discuss.*

She let Sir Mallister stride ahead and announce her, knocking and entering and declaring her arrival. Then he stepped aside and she strode right past him. The familiar faces all looked at her. Ilith in the body of his heir, sitting in that armchair Mallister had just mentioned. The crookbacked mage Fhanrir lurking at his side, face hidden in the shadow of his cowl. Lord Morwood was present. He was the man who ran the refuge, big and jowly and barrel-chested. Ranulf was smiling amiably, and Amilia Lukar was smiling at her too, very demure. Talasha had found her somewhat tart-tongued, but agreeable, and very beautiful in her soft northern way. She wore green samite and her eyes glittered the same colour. And last, Elyon Daecar. He was the only real surprise.

"Princess Talasha, be welcome." Ilith stood from his chair to greet her. "We have been awaiting you. How was the trek through the mountains?"

"Windy and cold." She bowed to him, but could not come to feel comfortable around him as these others did. *There is too much fire in my blood.* "Lord Ilith, might I know what this is about? The messenger you sent did not seem to be aware."

"It's about you." Elyon stepped forward and bowed to her. He wore full plate armour and blue Varin cloak. His hair was longer than last she'd seen it and he had a scar through his right eyebrow now as well, a wound won during some battle she did not doubt, and at his hip he bore the Windblade still, the mists swirling and rising from the scabbard. That made her frown. In the letter the First Elder had sent to Ilith, he had described many things, not least the fact that he had sent a letter to Elyon Daecar as well, instructing him to track down Saska Varin and aid her in her task. Talasha had hoped that would have happened by now. *Apparently not, if he still bears that blade.*

She smiled at him all the same, remembering the day he saved her from the palace in Eldurath. She would forever be thankful for that. "Prince Elyon. I daresay your presence here surprises me. How are you?"

"Well, my lady. Tired." He smiled back at her. "I might say the same to you. This is no normal place to find an Agarathi princess."

"What is normal these days, Elyon?"

He gave a weary laugh. "Quite. It has become trite to say it, but these times are nothing if not strange."

A rattling voice spoke. "You two done? You want to play catch up, do it later. We have business to discuss." The mage Fhanrir was in a fearsome mood it did seem. "Talasha, we want to know about your dragon. How is she? Strong enough to fly?"

Is that it? The messenger could have asked me that. "She will be in a day or two…"

"And how much weight can she haul?"

"I don't know."

"You don't know?" He glared at her impatiently.

"No." She had little time for this mage and his mean-spirited carping. "The most Neyruu has carried before is three individuals of middling weight and some provisions in her saddlebags." She waved a hand. "I'm referring to Ranulf, Cevi, and myself, of course. Feel free to guess at our collective weight and that should give you some idea."

Fhanrir did not seem to like her tone. Did he like anything, this mage?

"Could she carry more, my lady?" Lord Morwood asked her, more pleasantly. "A heavier burden, if you will? And over a reasonable distance?"

That was far too vague for Talasha Taan. "What burden? What

distance?" She looked around at the faces in the room. "Who exactly am I to be carrying? You, Elyon? Are you to leave the Windblade here?"

"It's not a person you'll be carrying," Fhanrir told her. "It's a blade. And it's folly, I say, rank folly."

"Now Fhanrir, do be calm, please." Ilith smiled at the man in that everything-will-be-all-right way of his. "We've heard your protests, and at great length besides, and do not need to hear them again. Elyon considers this a sensible course, given the circumstances."

"Elyon? And you'd listen to that swaggering whelp over me?"

"In this instance, yes. Nothing we do is going to be entirely free of risk, Fhanrir. Come, my friend, you know that as well as anyone."

"Aye. But risk can be mitigated. That girl needs to be bought *here*. We should *not* be bringing the blades to her."

Elyon groaned. "She won't come, I told you…"

"Then *make* her, damn you! Knock her out and carry her here if you must. It's madness leaving her out there. She should be here. Not there. *Here*."

"You're talking about Saska," Talasha said, looking between them. They must be. Who else could they be discussing? "Then you *have* found her, Elyon?" She looked at the Windblade again. "I had thought…"

"I've been with her for weeks, my lady. Training her to use this." He tapped his fine silver hilt. "But certain new information has come to light and I will have to go away for a while. Not at once, but soon." He glanced at Ilith. "When I do I will have to take the Windblade with me… it is the only way of getting where I need to go. That would deprive Saska of it, so…"

"So you want to bring her another blade to train with in its place." Talasha Taan was quite able to puzzle out what was going on here. "The Nightblade," she said. It was the only other Blade of Vandar here, she knew. "You want Neyruu to carry it to her."

Elyon nodded. "If I could I would fly it to her myself, but without bonding it I'd be unable to bear the weight. Neyruu is a large and powerful creature and I believe she will be able to manage it; she has carried godsteel before, after all."

Talasha thought a moment, remembering. "Lythian," she said.

"And Borrus. The day they were to be executed at the Pits of Kharthar, Neyruu brought them both their blades, carrying them in her talons. She had flown all the way from the Western Neck, Lythian told me, a not-inconsiderable distance to haul such a heavy load. The Nightblade will be a deal heavier, this is true, but I think she can manage it."

Talasha had heard that tale from Lythian as well, her dear sweet captain. She was sensing they wanted her reassurance that Neyruu could indeed manage the weight, though that was not something she could possibly answer. She had no idea how much the blade might weigh. "How far is Saska from here?" Knowing that would be a start.

"In the southwest of Rasalan," Elyon said. "On the mainland north of Krarl."

"Krarl? The crab island?" Her eyes found Ranulf. "We stopped there briefly when we flew here."

"It is far, I know," Elyon said, "but I will be at your side the whole time, and we can stop as often as we must."

"And what chance the dragon drops it along the way?" Fhanrir came in, in his foul voice of doom. "What if it falls into some river or down some shaft? What if the dragon realises she doesn't want to carry it after all…or worse, betrays us…"

"She wouldn't," Talasha bristled. "Neyruu has chosen her side."

"She slew the greatbat," Ilith said calmly. "Without her we would be lost."

"And you think she did that out of the goodness of her scaly heart?" Fhanrir's rotten laughter filled the chamber. "That bat attacked her, and she attacked it back. She's a dragon, Ilith. No dragon can be trusted."

"I'll hear no more of this," Ilith said, with a harder edge to his voice. He had a power in that voice when he wanted to deploy it, a growing, spreading sound that caused Fhanrir to shrink away. "You will be the death of me, my friend. The decision has been made."

"It's folly." Fhanrir's voice was smaller. "Let *me* go, Ilith. I'll make the girl come here instead. Just one word from my lips and all this goes away."

"No," Ilith said. "I will not let her free will be undermined."

"So the world dies because you won't tamper with a bit of free will…"

"Fhanrir!" The word was an explosion of sound, crashing from wall to wall. Talasha stepped backward. A pulse of light and power erupted from the demigod, then just as quickly shrank away. And all went quiet. "Enough," he said. His voice was now barely a whisper. "That is enough, Fhanrir. Please, let it lie."

A silence followed. There was an awkwardness in it, and Talasha saw worried eyes. *He is weakening*, she thought, daring to look at Ilith. He seemed suddenly exhausted, suddenly old. Suddenly pale where once he glowed.

At last, Fhanrir spoke. "Aye, my lord. As you command." The silence lingered on like a rotten smell. Eventually, the little cloaked mage put his beady eyes on Talasha, shining in the shadows of his hood. "You'll have to ride Neyruu alone," he told her. The bitterness was gone now; his voice was plain. "No excess weight. Your maidservant. She'll have to stay here."

Talasha accepted that. In Cevi's state it would do no good to take her from her sickbed.

"And Ranulf too," the mage went on. "He won't go with you. He's got a new duty now."

"Oh?" Ranulf had been very quiet thus far. "And what is this duty, Ranulf? I thought you considered it your sole and sacred duty to return to Saska Varin? To help support her and guide her. Or did I get that wrong?"

The adventurer looked a little ashamed by those words. "My lady, there is something more important that I must do. For Lord Ilith. And the final forging. Saska has enough wise heads about her already. She has no need of me."

"And what wise heads are these, exactly? The sellsword with all the scars? The cat-woman who talks in hisses?" She looked at Elyon again. "Who is with her now? Did Prince Robbert choose to accompany her?"

"No, my lady. The prince set sail to the west, to join the war." He listed those who remained in Saska's company and it was just about as Talasha had expected. "She will welcome your return, my lady. Saska...I know she valued your guidance."

Talasha made no comment on that. She was not certain if she would return to Saska at all. Flying a protective escort for her in Aramatia was one thing. Doing so here in the cold harsh north was another. *There are other dragons hereabouts*, she thought, *and I am not much loved by my people.* When they'd crossed Eagle Lake, the big dragon Paglar had tracked her down, and might have attacked and tried to kill Saska if Neyruu had not drawn him away. *She is too important,* Talasha thought. It seemed as though she had a small company now and was trying to travel discreetly. Having a dragon circling above her may only draw attention. *The Wall will not want that. And nor do I, in truth.*

There wasn't much else to be said, but to confirm that she would help them. "I will return to Neyruu when the storm passes and assess her condition. It may require some coaxing before she agrees." She had carried godsteel, yes, but they were talking of a Blade of Vandar. That was different. "I will see what I can do."

Ilith put his hands together. "That is all we ask, my lady." He smiled pleasantly, then moved his eyes to Ranulf. "It would also be wise for you to begin making your preparations, Ranulf." He waved a hand toward the shelves and bookcases. "Take what you need from my collection here; whatever you think may help. Sir Mallister, please help him. You will be accompanying him when he leaves."

The poor young knight looked stumped. "My lord? I swore an oath to protect Lady Talasha..."

"An oath you have executed with great commitment and courage thus far, Sir Mallister, and one you will continue to fulfil until such a time as she departs. Only then will you swear a new oath, to Ranulf. Where he is going, he will need men of fortitude to protect him. You will select such men to accompany you."

Mallister Monsort had a dutiful look on his face. "Yes, my lord. And...where we are going?"

"Not the Icewilds," said Elyon Daecar, puzzlingly. He gave a snort. "Think yourself lucky you don't have to go *there*, Mallister."

"The Icewilds? I..."

"North," said Ilith, in answer to the knight's question. "And beyond the border of this land. There is something that must be fetched for me, Mallister. And it is only to be found on the Darkisle."

18

The Elder

He was the First Elder, the tenth of his line, the Tenth First and he would be the last.

It is time, he thought, knowing the end was near. His eyes were closed, yet his sight was *clear.* Through the eyes of *Elethro,* oldest of all his eagles, he could see *him* coming, approaching from the west, a great winged host pouring forth from the black storm in a blaze of smoke and flame.

He opened his eyes, returning to *himself,* to the great green glade in which he had lived all of his three hundred years. The others were with him, gathered on the holy ground between the Twelve Trees, for this their final council. Before he spoke, they knew. They could see it in his eyes. "He is coming," he said, to confirm all their fears. "We all knew this day would come."

The others murmured worriedly, fidgeting and looking at one another as they sat upon the grass. They formed a circle, evenly spaced apart, beds of rare flowers blooming about and between them. Scented candles burned in little wicker baskets, filling the air with the aromas of lemon and lavender. To the First Elder's right sat the Second, the Third to his left. In numbers even and odd they spread to the Twelfth, perched opposite him, men and women, young and old, all blessed with Lumo's Last Light.

The Ninth was the first to speak. "Will Calacan come to save us, Great Elder?" She was the youngest of them, the twenty-fourth of her line, beautiful and radiant and pure in her heart. Her big eyes looked at him, trying to stay strong.

"I fear Calacan is too far away, child."

"He cannot help us," rumbled the Sixth, agreeing. He was a large man, and fierce, a warrior to look upon him with big hands and a great brown beard. His bonded eagles were big and strong as well; the most powerful of them, *Brathro,* was capable of bearing a rider in flight, as the ridden eagles of old. "I saw him through the eyes of *Pralarrio,* flying south out to sea beyond the Twin Suns. Something dark draws him there. He would never make it back in time."

"Something *dark*? What could be darker than…than *him*." The Twelfth was fretful, thin and tall, a man of caution and tender heart. "If the Father of Fire truly comes, Calacan *must* turn back to protect us. The Trees hold Aramatia's holy light. They are children to her, her power on this earth, fed by her Spring." He looked around. "If they burn. If they die…"

The First Elder raised a wrinkled palm to calm him. His long white beard fell like a waterfall to the ground, where it pooled between his legs as he sat cross-legged upon the grass. "You must not panic, child," he said. "Clear heads are needed, and we must all remain strong."

"But Great Elder…if you would but try…"

"Try? There is no trying the impossible. You know that Calacan is beyond my power to command. If he should sense the coming of the Fire Father, he may return, but it will be too late. I fear the damage will already have been done." He looked at them all, one and then another. "Our home will not survive. But the people can. Lead them, as you have led them for long years. We have prepared our sanctuaries, and now we must go."

The Twelfth sat before him, open-mouthed, and the eyes of the Ninth were moist with fear. Yes, they had prepared, and the Calacania knew this day might one day come, but that did not make it any easier. *They have all lived in hope we would stay hidden forever. Nothing can truly prepare them.*

"How much time do we have?" asked the Seventh, a woman old and wise.

"Not long, I fear. Elethro soars above the Smokeplains west of Skyloft and our enemy moves with speed." He thought a moment and shook his head. "We may have little more than an hour."

"An *hour*?" repeated the Twelfth. "Then we must *evacuate*…we must evacuate at once."

"Yes," the Tenth First agreed. "We must. Blow the horns, my friends, and return to your trees. Tell your dwellers the time has come. Have them gather water from the Spring before it fouls. It will be needed in the days to come." He looked around at them, connecting with the eyes of one and then the next, sharing what strength he had left. "The Light of Lumo go with you all. Go. There is little time."

The council disbanded quickly, the Elders rising in their feathered cloaks and hurrying away to their trees. Only the Second remained behind. "Are we certain he is coming here?" he asked. "We have not been discovered *yet*, Great Elder. Aramatia's power still protects us."

His head shook slowly, forlorn. "Her power wanes, my friend." There had been sightings of dragons over the woods for months; some Calacan warded away, others he slew, but the beasts were growing more daring. Empowered and emboldened by the dark strength of Agarath they flew over the Greater Everwood, searching for their secret glade, forever hidden and concealed by Aramatia's ancient seals….until now. "I hoped we would have more time," he admitted, "but it isn't so." He put a hand on the Second's feathered arm. "You have been my closest friend and wisest councillor for long years," he told him fondly. "Can I trust you to lead the others in my stead?"

"In your stead? But Great Elder, if he is truly coming, then…"

"Then I must stay and meet him." He smiled at the other man; it was the last time he would ever do so. "Go, take the others to our havens. Send word of what has happened here, and help our allies however you can. I leave that with you, my friend. Be strong for them. We will not meet again."

It was the hardest thing he had ever had to do, turning and leaving the Second standing there behind him, but turn and leave he did, and not once did he look back. He lifted his eyes up toward the vastness of the First Tree, looming five hundred metres above him. About the colossal trunk the steps spiralled, thousands of them leading up and up, through the canopy toward his high eyrie above. *I still have time*, he thought. *I must be quick. I must be there when he comes.*

It was a beautiful morning, and how cruel that was. Sunlight pierced the great glade in ten thousand sparkling shards and the laughter of children filled the air as they splashed among the streams. He could see women weaving fishing baskets and hammocks by sparkling pools, smiling and chattering, men carving out homes from the great Everwood nuts that grew upon the branches. In the Fourth Tree, a huge communal prayer nest was being made by a dozen men with branch and vine. The sound of hammering rang out from the Sixth as rope bridges and platforms were repaired. The people lived on as they had, praying the day they dreaded would never come. *And I have prayed for that myself*, the First Elder thought. *For three centuries I have prayed for it. But now that day is here.*

And then the first wood horn blew, a low deep call that the people had always feared. All other sound stilled for just a moment as the Calacania stopped to listen. And then just like that their peace was shattered, and at once the tranquil mirth that had long filled the glade was stricken…and in its place came the sounds of panic. Baskets were thrown down as the women ran to collect their children, their innocent laughter curdling into cries and sobs of fear. The men at work cast aside their tools, the hammering and ringing replaced by the rush of their footfall as they hurtled across the bridges and walkways to rally their families to flee. They were prepared. They knew what to do. But time, long their ally, had now deserted them. *Be quick, my people*, the First Elder prayed. *Oh, be quick. He is coming.*

He reached the bottom of the spiral stair, his long beard trailing and tripping at his feet. Not oft did the First Elder run, but run he did. The great roots surged and bulged up around him like bark-covered boulders as he tucked his beard into his belt and began the climb. Eagles long bonded to him flapped and circled, shrieking and whistling as the wood horns began to bellow out across the glade. It was a journey he'd taken countless times before. Each step was as an old friend to him; he knew the wear of them, where each was chipped and scarred, where best to place his feet from the first to the very last. There were thousands, many thousands, and he must be quick. Barefoot he went, circling the great bole. Each circuit took him higher, higher. He could see his people panicking below, hear the horns and the cries and the chaos. *They will live on*, he told himself. *They will find a new peace beyond the glade.*

Such was his sure-footedness here on the spiral stair that he closed his eyes as he went, looking again through the eyes of Elethro. The old eagle was soaring high on a wind current, watching and trying to keep up with the dragons, but already they were outpacing him. Soon he would lose them, and he must not overstrain. *Calm, Elethro,* he called out to the bird. *You have warned us. You have done enough.*

Before long he was panting from the climb, his old legs weakening. He paused to look up; he had a long way to go. *Help,* he called out, summoning aid, and at once two of his eagles came to him, *Plitho* and *Bruco*, their strong talons clasping his shoulders, wings flapping as they sped him on. The Tenth First let them take him, his legs barely touching the hard surface of the steps as they danced from one to the next. Around the colossal trunk of the First Tree he went, around and around and up past the great branches, into the thick canopy, on and up and up…

When at last he reached his eyrie, the winds were picking up. Gasping, he staggered across the high plateau toward a table of woven branches, pouring himself a cup of water taken from the Spring of Aramatia. It gave him strength, renewing him. He filled his lungs and went to the edge, looking down, his feathered robes pulling and tugging at him as though urging him over the edge. Plitho and Bruco were still there, holding him steady, wings flapping in his ears. Far below he could see his people leaving, great columns of them fleeing from the glade. The wood horns rang out distantly now and a hum of panic buzzed faintly in the air like a swarm of angered wasps. From each tree the dwellers flowed like channels to a larger river, joining and swelling and rushing into the Greater Everwood. *Be swift, my people. Run. He is near…*

He turned his eyes to the western skies. The dragons had long since outflown the sight of Elethro, but that made no matter now. He could see them. The blur of them, in the distance, growing larger, nearer with each passing moment.

Time was running short, but he must act…he must *try*. He hurried back to the heart of his great high perch. "Plitho, Bruco, Maguto, Tallarnia, Jirtaro, Fullisia," he said, "take these. Come, quick." The six eagles swept down to the table and took up the dozen circular wood vessels he had prepared, clasping them in the curl of their claws. "Break them when I say. Now go. Hide below, among the branches. Do not be afraid, my friends. Go. I will be with you."

The eagles flapped and plunged away into the canopy beneath him, leaving him alone. Not long ago he had dozens of bonded eagles to call upon, each watching over the world. Not so now. He had his six here, and Elethro, and scant few others beyond the border of these lands. So many had died, too many, each a new scar in his old withered heart, slain by fang and flame by the dragons that hunted them. *And soon all the rest will be free of me,* he thought. *They must make their own way now…*

There was nothing to do but wait. He had minutes only, his last minutes on this earth. He turned back again to look down at his people, willing them to rush and flee. His heart clutched at what he saw. *Too many,* he thought. *There are too many still in the open.* He should have seen this earlier, should have given them more time. *I waited too long. They will never get away in time…*

The wind was growing hot, furnace gusts blowing and biting at his skin. A premature dark was falling as black clouds gathered and rolled in, and the last beautiful morning here felt no more than a distant memory. The blur of dragons separated now, each becoming distinct. *So many,* he thought. *Good Aramatia, there are so many…*

Yet he must not lose heart. He knew of the prophesies, yes, and he knew of his *role.* He was sworn to watch, as his ancestors had watched, to gently correct the course of time with a nudge here and a nudge there, as the Far-Seeing Queen had required. *Mother Lumo gave her light for us to see,* he thought. *And we have seen. We have watched and done what we must to shape the path. We have done as we've been asked. And here today our watch ends.*

Information had always been their power. The gathering of it, the sharing of it, so they might shape and influence the world. They had no Book of Contracts, not like the poor souls of the Shadow Order. *Where we were asked to watch, they were asked to kill.* He had always pitied them for that, this holy order that was so scorned, and the ancient mages most of all. Lurking in that darkness for century after century, dealing their blood magic, cursing their souls. It was all for the greater good, a need and duty and not a choice. They were two sides of the same coin, the Shadow Order and the Elders of the Everwood, two hidden and holy sects formed to help mould the world. *We are the light, they are the dark. We use whispers and they use knives, and yet…and yet…*

He looked to the skies. The dragons were screaming, spitting out gouts of flame, exulting now as they saw the Twelve Trees rising before them. *They see us,* he knew. *They see right through her spells and charms.* Aramatia's ancient seals were broken, withered away by the darkness filling the world. Once before they would see only a simple woodland here, plain and green, but no longer. The veil had been drawn back and the towering twelve rose up before them, and they would burn them down, root and branch and bole, burn them and kill them as the Twelfth Elder had said…

The Tenth First watched them come. He was a vessel of light, and the use of violence was not his tool. He knew the prophesies, he knew all too well of the heir of Varin. He knew it was not his place to interfere here, and yet…and yet…

He saw him now, the Father of Fire, standing tall between the shoulders of a broad-winged dragon, horned and hellish with grey scales all veined in red. It was not a dragon he knew, a dragon corrupted by Agarath's Soul. The Tenth First had not glimpsed Eldur since he'd descended into the Ashmount, since the great black-red storm that was Agarath the All-Father had exploded and spread from its summit, hiding all from the eyes of his eagles. Yet he knew what he was doing. He knew what power lurked in there. *A bastard form of creation,* he thought. *A wicked way of twisting life.* He had seen it himself, through Elethro's piercing eyes. Seen the Sunlord enter the mountain with his sunwolf…and seen the beast leave, *changed…*

Before he knew it the dragons were above him, spreading out and fanning like the fingers of an open fist, diving and swooping through the trees. He could hear their roars ringing out across the glade, feel the heat of their fiery breath, hear the screaming far below. Hundreds were still down there, thousands. Their voices rose up as one in a chorus of terror as though Aramatia herself was screaming.

But he did not look down, what good would it do? He held his eyes upon Eldur the Eternal, turning with him as his grotesque and malformed dragon flew in a wide arc around his eyrie. A pair of red eyes glowed, trailing light as the aberration flew by, and from the top of his tall black staff the soul of his master throbbed and swirled. One circuit he flew, and a second and a third, studying him, watching him, before at last he spoke.

"You are the First," he said, a thundering whisper that reached out from afar. "The Tenth First. But still a child to me." Laughter rumbled, rising, crackling. "I have found you, child, you and your little haven. Your goddess can hide you no longer. She is weak. She was always weak."

The First Elder stayed his tongue. His beard and cloak of many-coloured feathers stirred in the hot swirling wind.

"I knew her," the Eternal went on. "I knew all the gods, great and small. Aramatia was always so quiet, so at peace, so *above* us. This world was never right for her." He flew around him as the First Elder turned, trying not to look down toward the other trees as they caught flame, trying not to listen to the wailing of his people. He could do nothing for them now. They would die and the trees would burn and there was nothing he could do.

"But she had her eagle," the dark demigod went on, his blood-red cloak rippling behind him. His skin and hair were bone-white against it. "Calacan…oh, he *was* powerful. Powerful enough to repel the Dread, once before, with that blinding *light* of his." He smiled, circling. The old man turned with him. "But that light will fade too. I see your trees, *child.* I see the light leeching from the leaves. Is it not so for Calacan? Is that not why he hides?"

The First Elder gave no answer. He only turned and watched, turned and watched.

The Fire Father did not like it. "*Where is he?*" he asked. The voice was rasped, violent. "Tell me. Tell me and I will spare your tree."

My tree, he thought. *The first seedling that Aramatia planted here, to grow grander than all the rest.* Nine First Elders had come before him, each watching over this sacred grove. *Could I save just this one? Might the others regrow, even flourish as they once had, should the First's great power remain?* He could feel the heat rising around him, see the shroud of orange light below, see the black smoke curling up like dead fingers to scratch at the guts of the sky. The other trees were burning, their leaves of light withering to die. The grief in his heart was overwhelming. His haven had turned to hell. He opened his mouth to speak…

…and closed it just as quickly.

The Eternal's eyes blazed bright. His dragon wheeled toward him, claws reaching forward as though to pluck him from his perch, but at the last moment he thumped his wings and landed with a great crash, woven branches cracking beneath his weight, the entire eyrie trembling. His head swung forward, and down the spine of his neck Eldur walked, through the jutting red-veined horns that grew at odd angles from the dragon's head, past the sharp high ridge of his skull, to his long pointed snout as the hellbeast tipped forward, delivering him smoothly to the ground.

He stopped five paces away. The dragon drew back, hunched and strange, a nightmare form of his kin. The First Elder set his eyes upon Eldur and held his gaze, refusing to wilt, to tremble. Sweat ran from his forehead and down his back, hot and cold at once, but he did not look away. The demigod towered above him, as grand as he'd been of old, taller than the First Elder had last seen him before he vanished into the Ashmount. His flesh was like that of a statue, seamed and cracked and worn. A shower of brittle white hair draped the sides and back of his head, framing those crimson, pupil-less eyes.

"You have been watching me," he said. His voice was withdrawn now, a common voice and no more. The cloak was the colour of new-drawn blood, stirring gently at the hem.

For the first time the Elder spoke. "I have seen your rise."

"And my fall? Is that not what you wish to see most?" He smiled, skin cracking, breaking…and reforming as the smile was drawn back.

The old man would not deny it. "Yes. You are a blight on this world."

"I am saving this world. Restoring it."

"Killing it."

"All things must die to be reborn."

"This world needs no rebirth."

That smile again, coming and going. "You are old, First Elder, yet I am ancient. And Agarath…he is *ageless*. He made this world and decrees it must end. Do you think he is alone in that? Do you think Vandar wants it saved?" He laughed. "Vandar, whose heart refuses to be remade. He cares not if the people of Varin prevail." He raised an arm and flicked a wrist, long fingers pointing. "Vandar is gone, as the others are gone. They play their games elsewhere now, and more than you can imagine. Oh, the things the All-Father has shown me. You think *you* have seen, Tenth of the Firsts? *My* sight pierces far beyond this world."

Agarath's sight, the First Elder thought. "Then leave this world and be gone," he said. "Go to another if you so please."

"Please? It pleases me to obey my master, so here I am, his humble servant." He gave a bow, and above and about him a crack of black thunder shook the sky. "They are all at different stages, these lands. Some are primitive, others at peace, others still have seen ten thousand years of battle and bloodshed and still there is no end." He tapped the butt of his black staff to the ground; fire fizzed and cracked, burning the floor of the eyrie, but with a flick of his hand he dismissed the fledgling blaze. "You call this the Soul of Agarath, but truly that is just a name. The gods do not have souls, First Elder. No more than they have hearts. They are beings beyond our understanding; they can splinter and part and reform as they please, and their power spreads out across this boundless world. This orb is but a part of Agarath's spirit, a part he left to me. Do you think he is confined to this land alone? Do you think any of them are? We are but an island in an ocean and there are many others out there, raised and felled and raised again, and on each the gods take on a different name..."

He drew forward, looming closer, laughing. "Does that make you feel *small*, child? Do you not feel so very insignificant now? Even you who have held such power in your grasp. You who sit up here on your high hidden perch, watching. You who twist the knife from the shadows so you might keep your hands clean of blood. Oh, I know what you have done. A letter here, a coded message there, and thousands die by the things you unveil. You have turned wars on a word and sat kings upon distant thrones. You have forged empires and broken them apart. Is that what dear Lumo would have wanted when she gave your ancestors her *light*? You stand there and look upon me like I'm a monster, but who is the true evil here? How many men have died in battle because of you? How many women have been raped during the sack of cities? How many children taken into bondage? I would see this world free of such iniquity. I would see it made fair again."

He stepped in and took the First Elder by the throat, lifting. Clawed white hands curled and tightened about his neck, choking the life from him. Up the Elder went, up and up. "It was Thala, was it not? It was she who set your sect into motion?"

He could not speak, could not breathe. The demigod loosened his grip and the Elder sucked a ragged breath. "She is a step ahead of you... always," he managed to get out. "Even in death she defies you."

"*Rasalan* defies me. Where is his Eye?"

"I do...not know. I have not seen it."

"You lie. It was taken from me. By the boy..." His scarlet gaze was aflame. The First Elder could feel the hairs of his beard singeing, the feathers of his robes curling, blackening. The Fire Father was looking deep into his eyes. He drew him closer, closer, and delved into his very soul, reading his heart. His lips curled in a hideous smile and the First Elder fought to repel him. He knew things. Things he must not see. He twisted his thin neck, but Eldur moved a finger and snapped him back, and his eyes were red and glowing, growing, and the darkness was all around him…

It was time. He could not delay any longer. Faint cries rose from below, a blur of sound at the edge of hearing; all the world was fire and ash and horror, a glimpse of what was to come. But his eagles were ready, perched about the edges of the eyrie. The hell dragon had not seen them. He was looking away toward the glade below, to the trees as they went up in a blaze, as though wanting to join and spread his flame. Distracted, he would react too late. And the demigod's back was turned.

The First Elder closed his eyes and called out to them. *Now, my friends, now is our only chance…*

The flap of wings sounded suddenly to left and right, cinder and smoke eddying as the six eagles came. The First Elder looked into the eyes of Eldur, right there beyond the tip of his nose, and in them he saw no fear. Only something *knowing*. Only a dark light of amusement. *No*, he thought…*no*…He tried to call out again to his bonded birds…*go back, he knows…go back…fly away*…but it was too late. They flew over the head of the demigod, crunching down on the orbs in their talons, and from each came a liquid substance, misting and spreading into a green and purple fog.

The shroud enveloped them both. The First Elder felt the poison surge at once down his throat and into his lungs, burning. His skin blistered, the hair of his beard darkening, dying. He gasped and struggled in agony…but Eldur did not let go. He only stared at him as he choked and died. And there was a smile on his lips. A little broken smile. "Did you really think that would work?"

Laughter rippled out across the eyrie and the Soul of Agarath pulsed, sending out a wash of light to drive the poison fog away. The First Elder heard the screams of the fallen within it, the thousands, hundreds of thousands, millions that had died by his hand. *I was a fool. Such a fool…*

"A violent man you are, Tenth First. I thought you only killed from afar, with quill and ink?"

The birds had escaped the shroud, flying away into the rising smoke. The First Elder could hear them, feel them, wheeling around, their sharp curved claws stretched out before them as they plunged down toward the demigod to try to save him. *No, no…go back, you're free…*He had only moments left to live, but his birds, his birds…

The Fire Father tapped his staff. A bloom of flame spread out, an expanding bubble of fiery death that set the eagles ablaze. The First Elder screamed, writhing in their pain, and Eldur laughed, he laughed aloud in thunderous joy. "In the new world, the *weak* die, Tenth First. You are weak, as your goddess was weak, and your people…these *people*…all are weak." His lip curled, and turning his head he shouted out, "Kill them all," in a great spreading voice. "Burn down the woods. Put out their light. I want the Elders taken…kill the rest…"

Tears ran down the old man's cheeks as Eldur threw him to the floor. He spluttered, gasping for breath as his eagles landed about him, aflame. He reached out to them as they twisted and shrieked, dying as he died, their fates entwined. His whole eyrie was catching light, smoke roaring and swirling skyward, and from the branches below, the First Tree was burning…

And there amidst the flames *he* stood, Eldur the Eternal, looking out upon his work. And on his lips was an exulting smile, and through them came a spreading roar as he laughed, loudly, and he laughed again. "Kill them all, kill them all. They are *weak!* Weak! Kill them all!" Rough laughter thundered out across the glade.

It was the song by which he died.

19

Jonik

He fell to his knees and pressed his lips to the stone, slurping eagerly at the brown standing water like a hound after a long hot hunt.

It was a quarter inch deep, no more, a puddle that could barely be called a puddle, but was enough to save his life. He drank and sucked and licked until every last drop of it was gone, then sat back against the hard rock wall and sighed in sweet blessed relief. Hunger he could handle; if he must he could go weeks without food, but water was a more troublesome foe. For the last few days he'd been down to sucking moisture from rocks and even turned to drinking his own urine. He hoped never to have to cross that line again.

More, he thought, panting against the wall. *I need more. I must have more.*

He stood back up as far as the ceiling would allow, head hunched low and he lurched onward. He'd entered a series of smaller caves and passages, honeycombing through the rock like some enormous insect hive. Something had tunnelled and built this place, he knew. He'd seen fragments of them, bits of head and leg and chitinous armour scattered here and there. What they were he could not say. Giant ants? Overgrown termites? Those horrid beetles he'd fought with Gerrin and Owen, with their thick sticky blood and long pincer-legs and soulless beady black eyes?

Whatever they were, he prayed that none were home. He was hoping to use this nest to climb higher, get back to the maze of caves above him and be free of this wretched netherworld for good. If he did that, he'd be able to find a way back to the surface. He *must*, and soon, because he was not alone down here. Giant insects and murder-pedes were one thing. The colossal menace that still lurked down in these depths was something else entirely.

He'd been lucky to escape it that first time. The monster had awoken to chase him through the dark, and by the good grace of whatever gods were still with him, Jonik had come quickly upon a door. It was enormous, a passageway several times as large as the largest city gate he'd ever seen, and yet the colossal creature could not follow him through. He could hear it shrieking as he fled it, ripping and smashing at the stone in a torrent of wrath and fury. He'd wanted to glance back, wanted to see it, but there had been no time before the doorway collapsed behind him and the ceiling crumbled down.

He heard the deafening din of stone tumbling, heard the creature screaming that high-pitched, ear-bleeding sound that caused his vision to dance with spots of white light and his brain to thicken and swell in his skull. Was it dead? Crushed by all that stone? He had no time to think about it. He just ran as fast and as far as his legs would take him, through another great chamber, and another and another until his thighs were turned as weak as weeds and he fell down to his knees on the hard rock floor with a ringing *clang* of steel.

Distantly, then, he heard the world trembling far away behind him, and knew the creature was not dead at all, but trapped, trapped behind all that fallen rock. "Keep going," he'd urged himself, trying to stand. "You need to keep going," he rasped out loud.

But he couldn't. He was spent, done. It was all he could do to stay conscious as the desperate fear and thrill leeched out from his blood, sucking away the last of his energy. He fought the urge to pass out, but in that he must have failed, because the next thing he knew he was jolting awake, not knowing how much time had passed, and the tremors were closer, and the world was shaking, and he could hear the terror getting nearer…nearer…

The rest of it was a blur to him now. He had stood and run and fallen and stood again. He had driven the Mistblade into Mother's Mercy's sheath and held the bastard blade in his grasp, and when that got too heavy he'd thrown it away…and then he'd stopped almost at once and turned back to retrieve it. He would *not* leave it, not on any account. Discarding it had been but a moment of desperate folly, but it was his blade now, the blade named for his mother, the blade made with the Hammer of Tukor. He would carry Mother's Mercy into battle. He would kill with it and save with it and die with it in his grasp. So gripping it tight, he'd staggered on. For hours and days he'd staggered on.

And now here he was, broken but alive, crawling through this honeycomb hive and praying it would take him higher. The monster of the deep was still out there, he knew. Occasionally he would feel a shudder through the rock, or hear it screaming its dreaded song somewhere in another chamber. It was hard to know where, or how far away it was. Sound did strange things here as it moved through this world and Jonik had learned not to trust it.

He trusted only himself. Trusted his desire and his drive to keep on going. He could feel the meat melting off his flesh every day, feel himself growing thinner, weaker, gaunt of cheek and lean to the bone. But life in the Shadowfort had prepared him for this. It had always been an ascetic existence, a hard cold life of hunger and hate where boys grew up living alone in their cells, friendless and angry and afraid.

He was all that now. All that and more, but he could bear it as others could not. Down the passage he went in a crouch, searching for a tunnel that went up, eyes roving all the while for any glinting puddles on the ground, collected in holes and hollows. Above he could hear a faint trickling sound, as though water was being fed down into the rock. Had this hive been built for that? To draw down moisture to feed the creatures who made it? Hope flared in him. He came to a small interjoining chamber, a dozen ways branching off to left and right, up and down. One veered up steeply to his right and his hope flared brighter. He scrambled at once into it, going down onto his hands and knees to crawl and then climb his way up. A little ahead he saw the lip and reached up to pull himself into another branching cell.

He looked around. Two other tunnels ascended from here, he saw. And there too…another puddle! He threw himself to the ground to lap and lick once more. When he could get no more moisture out of the stone, he pressed down with his cloak to try to soak it in, squeezing it into the little holes and cracks, then sucked at the wool to extract it. Refreshed, he rose again and made quickly for the nearest up-slanting tunnel, scrambling inside. It widened further on, enough for him to crouch, curving around and delivering him into a much larger chamber.

There he paused, staring forward. It appeared to be some sort of central room, a great hollow at the heart of the hive. Perhaps this was where the creatures once gathered their food or hosted their queen. Jonik knew enough about the sorts of creatures that lived in structures like this to know that a queen was often the senior figure in the colony. *And larger than the rest*, he thought, moving his gaze around, wondering. His eyes scanned for anything moving, anything living, but it seemed to him that this nest had long since been abandoned.

He breathed out, stepping to the heart of the chamber. Many more ways led in and out. He performed a circuit, searching for the best route to take. There was a structure here that he liked, a structure that he could trust. Above, when he'd been with Gerrin and Owen, oft as not a tunnel could rise sharply or descend suddenly or narrow so tight they could go no further, forcing them to turn back around. They were natural formations, largely, made over millennia by the movement of the earth, by rock and water, but not these. These were purpose-built; bug-built. When a tunnel went up, he knew it would keep going up until it took him to another chamber.

He climbed eagerly onward. He was getting closer now, every tunnel taking him higher. Soon he'd be free of these depths and this darkness. There would be bioluminescent moss and vines and light, plants that he might chew on, great pools of water from which to drink. He might even hunt something to eat. *Another geckantula,* he thought. *Why not? So long as I kill it myself this time and don't find it already dead.*

He was sweating now, panting from the climb. His breath came out ragged and worn. Rasping and heaving, he pulled himself up into another room. There were more insect remains here, but he paid them no mind. The next climb was harder, almost vertical. He went up with his back pressed against one wall, his hands the other, his feet split and driving him upward. It was hard going after so long without food, but he made it, dragging himself exhausted over the edge to sprawl out and catch his breath.

He was still breathing heavily when he felt the tremor.

No, was his first thought. *Damn you, not now.*

The second tremor was worse.

If the first was a nudge, this was a shove. The entire hive seemed to rock on its foundations, walls splitting from the force of the impact. Jonik cursed aloud, surging up to his feet. The monster was near, its thunderous footsteps getting closer. The whole world was shaking. Jonik turned his eyes around, searching for a way out. Bits of rock were coming loose from the ceiling. He saw a tunnel that led further up and dashed inside, scrambling up on all fours as bits of stone came tumbling down toward him. One *pinged* harmlessly against his breastplate. Another ricocheted into his cheekbone, cutting a gash. He crawled on, led by the light radiating from his armour. It stretched only so far and the rocks came out of nowhere, rushing from the blackness ahead.

His eyes widened as he saw a much bigger block of stone clattering loudly down the passage, bashing violently from wall to wall. There was nowhere for him to go. He braced, making himself small, and it struck him a hard glancing blow in the shoulder, the same shoulder that had been torn and shredded during his tumble down the river. He felt a spike of pain, wincing as the rock tore a fresh wound open and kept on going. But more stones were falling, cascading in a thickening flow.

"Damn you," Jonik shouted, scrambling up as quick as he could. "Damn you to this infernal hell!"

The monster was nearby, though he knew not where. Was it after him? Was it just passing through? He could not say whether the creature cared for him at all or whether it was just trying to escape this place the same as he was. It didn't matter. He needed to get out. The walls were disintegrating around him. As he entered a new chamber the floor gave way beneath his feet and he had to leap forward to keep from falling. He clung on, climbed up into another tunnel, kept on scrambling. *The top. I have to reach the top.*

The Mistblade was hissing incoherently. Jonik refused to listen. The whispers grew louder when the monster was near, and that told him this beast was not of Vandar's making. *A dragon,* Jonik had thought, when he'd first heard the *thwump* of wings and felt that hot blasting rush of air behind him. Could it be so? Another ancient dragon of colossal size? Jonik did not know of any. Only Drulgar the Dread and why would he be here? Unless…*how far did that river take me?* Could it have rushed all the way to Agarath? *Am I beneath the Ashmount even now? Or somewhere far beneath the Scales, far beneath* his *Nest?*

It was madness. How could a river have taken him so far unless some twisted magic was involved? *Only Ilith can build portals,* he thought, *and he only built the one.* No. He was in Vandar still, deep beneath the Riverlands somewhere. Or perhaps he'd gone as far as the Lakelands or Marshlands by now, but it was Vandar, East Vandar, of that he had no doubt.

The hive was still shaking, loose stone falling and crumbling about him. The air filled with dust and grit and he gasped and coughed as he went, snatching out his godsteel dagger to slash at any larger rocks that came near. There was a sound of wind above him, air moving, eddying down through the tunnels. His legs burned as he drove on upward. The top was near. And then…and then…

A savage tremor struck the hive.

For a moment Jonik was suspended in midair as the world gave way beneath him. He managed to reach out just in time to grasp at a lip of rock…but then *that* crumbled and collapsed as well. He tumbled, flailing for something, anything. There was nothing to grab onto. Nothing but the rock that was falling with him.

His back smashed suddenly against solid stone, punching the air right out of his lungs. He gasped for breath as a rain of pebbles and rocks as big as fists fell down upon him, pinging and ringing against his armour. Turning, he flung his cloak over to cover himself, holding his gauntlet over his face. The rock kept coming. There was still no breath in his lungs. Wheezing, he peered past his arm and saw a flood of falling rock that had no end…a flood that would bury him if he did not move.

Twisting at the core, he rolled aside and lurched back up to his feet, kicking and scrabbling away. The whole top of the hive was coming down around him. The noise was deafening. He could hear the creature tearing at the rock, shrieking its high-pitched otherworldly roar. Jonik wanted nothing more than to cover his ears, and shut his eyes against the pain, but he couldn't. He had to keep going.

He saw another passage ahead, leading to the far side of the hive. It looked more stable there. He was on his feet and running in an instant, dodging chunks of falling stone. Another struck his injured shoulder. He grunted, blinking the white spots from his vision. Others rattled and pinged off his left-hand gauntlet as he kept it raised above his head. He had his helm looped through his belt but there was no time to put it on. In ten paces he was at the tunnel. He saw that it went *down*, not up, but damn it what choice did he have? He threw himself inside, doing all he could to keep his feet as he hurried back down into the chamber below. He made it just in time as the passage folded in on itself, an explosion of dust and rocky splinters blasting out behind him.

The whole world seemed to be coming down. He glanced back through the crumbling hive; amid the chaos he glimpsed an immense black creature moving, a part of its flank or arm he could not say. His heart almost stopped. This was a demon from another time. The thing was tearing at the rock above it, screaming as it ripped at the ceiling, trying to dig its way out. *It wants to escape,* Jonik realised. *It's trying to reach the surface, the same as me.*

And then the glimpse was gone, and all was rock and stone as the walls and ceiling came down, blocking out his view. He turned on his heels and sped the other way, thinking of his grandfather, his mad king grandfather who'd died just like this. He imagined the terror of being trapped and crushed, kept alive by his armour, dying slow. If he did not get out, that fate awaited him. *It's not my fate,* he thought, insisting. *It's not my fate. It's not…*

And then he was at the far side of the hive. A wall gave way before him and he could see an open black space beyond, another great chamber stretching away beyond his sight. The ground rocked, shifting, about to crumble beneath his feet. He looked out into the darkness. The bottom was there, far below…far enough to kill him if he did not land right, but he had no choice.

He leapt.

20

Lythian

The huntsman was kneeling on the ground, running his fingers over a patch of wet earth. He took a handful of sodden mulch, raised it to his nose and gave a good long sniff, then jabbed out his tongue like a snake to taste it. He spat, snorted, tossed the detritus aside and stood, pulling his scuffed leather glove back on over scarred and callused fingers.

Lythian watched him all the while. "Well?" he asked, when the man did not speak. "Anything?"

Slowly, he nodded. "They passed this way," he said, in his growling voice. "Two days gone or thereabouts." He pointed. "Northeast heading. I'd wager they stopped to make camp somewhere up ahead. Passed here near dusk, so far as I can figure, and would have looked for somewhere to rest."

Lythian stared at the man in astonishment, and not for the first time. *All that from a sniff and lick of mud?* "You're a rare breed, Vilmar, truly. One day you'll have to teach me your tricks."

"Wouldn't bother. You don't have the knack."

Lythian sighed and went over to his horse. He drew a sheepskin map from his saddlebag, unrolling it against the horse's flank. The Black prowled over to join him and together they leaned in. "We're about here," Lythian said, as much to himself as anything. No doubt Vilmar knew exactly where they were and had no need of maps. Even under these endless rains with not a scrap of sky to show them the stars, he seemed quite able to navigate. "There's a shallow valley here that might have made good cover. So long as it's not too waterlogged. Perhaps they rested there."

Vilmar grunted under his breath. "Hills are better than valleys. Less chance of a flood and better for keeping watch too. They'd have sought higher ground."

"Fine." He was not about to argue with the man. Oft as not that only won him scowls and scoldings, and they tended to do things Vilmar's way in any case. *This is my purgatory*, he thought, *for all my crimes and failures. Being chastened night and day by this grim old huntsman.*

He continued to scan the map. There was a small village a dozen or so miles ahead, built at the conjunction of several smaller forests. That was all the Wandering Wood was, a series of smaller woods and thickets, copses and coppices spread over a vast hilly land of low peaks and shallow valleys. "They may have passed through there," Lythian said, gesturing. He peered, trying to read the name, but the ink was too faded. This was a very old map. "If they're running low on provisions, they'll want to restore them any chance they get. Someone might be able to tell us where they went."

The hunter snorted. "No better than my nose will. I'd trust that more than the word of some stranger, but very well, have it your way. If we pass that village, we'll stop in and ask. But first we find their overnight camp. It'll tell us which way they went."

They continued through the wood, Vilmar leading, Lythian following behind with his horse. Large old oaks loomed around them, interspersed with knots of thorny bushes and great glistening puddles that rippled beneath the rain. That rain had not abated since the day they left King's Point. Sometimes it fell hard, sometimes soft, sometimes it slanted sideways or squalled around them and sometimes it fell straight down, but never did it stop. The days were gloomy, the light strangled by a swamp of thick grey clouds, the nights black as tar and moonless.

Lythian had learned to live and operate in such conditions - in that he had no choice - but Vilmar the Black had been born to them. "Was birthed under a sky as dark as Dhatar's heart," the grim old hunter had said. "Thunder and rain so loud it drowned out my mother's screaming. I ripped her open to come into this world and she bled out right there on the grass. My father stood over me, judging me ill. He took up my mother's body and left me there to die in that storm. And it was stormy too when I killed him."

Lythian had known nothing of that. The huntsman's past had always been mysterious to him. "How did you survive if your father left you? You were only a newborn babe."

"A newborn babe with a heart of thunder."

"But a babe all the same," Lythian said. "So…"

"Woodsman found me," Vilmar told him. "Old man, blind in both eyes. Took me in and raised me for a time, fed me, gave me a place to lay my head in his hut. When I was five years old he was killed by bandits. After that it was just me, alone in that lonely old cabin. The woods became my father then. They were my mother, my siblings, my protector and my guide, and they made me what I am."

It was quite the tale. One Lythian would not have believed had it come from anyone else, but Vilmar was indeed a rare breed. Even watching him now, Lythian could see it. How at home he was here in the wild, how at one with the natural world. Crotchety and sour-tempered as the old man was, he would be hopelessly lost without him. He knew every plant and animal, every bird call and buzzing insect. His nose picked up ten thousand scents and sifted through them all in an instant. If there was a creature nearby, he knew it, no matter how small and sneaky. He would smell it, hear it, long before Lythian saw it, and the shroud of rainfall was little hindrance to him. Sometimes that's all Lythian could hear - the rain as it hit the leaves and branches and came crashing down onto the forest floor. The patter and rumble and thunder of it blotting out all other sounds. But not Vilmar the Black, no. His ears cut through both wind and rain and perceived what lurked beyond.

The man was a shadow in black, a beast himself, stalking onward in that silent step. No matter what lay underfoot he barely made a sound. And the huntsman was no small figure. Powerfully built, he soared several inches taller than Lythian in height and had much broader shoulders too. How he walked so quietly the knight could not say. Mud did not seem to squelch to his tread, twigs gave out no crack. *He could walk across a field of autumn leaves and not one would crunch beneath him.* Lythian had always fancied himself a light-treader, able to creep and sneak with the best of them, and perhaps in another setting that would be so. But here in the wild the huntsman was king. And he liked to remind him of it too.

"Keep up, Lindar," he grumbled now. "I've seen turtles move faster than you."

Lythian was quite literally right behind him. "I move any quicker and I'll step on your heels. You want to go faster? Then go faster. I have no trouble keeping up."

The hunter scoffed. "It's that horse. Picking its way along like that. Told you not to get attached, didn't I? Knew it would slow us down."

Those were two different things. Two wrong things. Lythian wasn't attached to his steed and the horse was not slowing them down. In fact he was helping bear the burden of their provisions and the complaint was thus utterly groundless. "You're in one of your moods again, I see." They came on suddenly, these moods. Vilmar was grouchy at the best of times, but sometimes, for no reason Lythian could fathom, he would start assaulting him with baseless insults and objections. "You have an addiction to cantankerousness, Vilmar. You really ought to lighten up."

"Me? You should hear yourself when you sleep, boy. The things you say."

I shouldn't bite, Lythian told himself. *Don't respond. Just ignore him.* He managed about five seconds. "What things?" he asked.

The huntsman turned his head and smiled like a wolf. "Oh. Wouldn't you like to know?"

Damn him. "Forget it." He could guess easily enough. His dreams were dark and full of death as he roved the lands, slaying deserters. *No doubt I mumble about that sometimes. And Talasha, maybe.* He dreamed of her as well, every once in a while. Though those were different dreams, softer dreams, dreams from which he wished he never awoke. He hoped he made no noises during *those* dreams. *Do I mumble sweetly? Do I say her name?* The huntsman would never let him live that down.

He put it from his mind, navigating his horse around a particularly boggy puddle, following as much as he could in Vilmar's tread. The land ahead was steadily rising. Rills ran down from the higher ground like veins, twisting and wending around rocks and roots. Sometimes they would gather to form a larger stream or raging river. Sometimes they would pool in some valley, giving life to ponds and lakes. It was a deluge beyond reckoning, apocalyptic and never-ending. *These lands will soon be drowned,* Lythian thought sourly. *We'll have to rename it the Wandering Sea instead.*

Still, it was better than being in the city, presiding over that rotting ruin and all its shadows and ghosts. Dark as his dreams still were, he felt lighter in his heart than he had. He was not required to behead deserters out here, nor did he have to concern himself with the dark eyes of staring men, watching him from beneath their hoods. *Amron should never have left me in charge. He should never have given me that blade.* Lythian's place was at the king's side, fighting at his flank. *I was born and bred to walk at his heel. Ruling…no, I was never made to rule.*

The huntsman had stopped a few paces ahead of him, kneeling down to inspect something in the mud. His face twisted in a grimace as he stood, and Lythian didn't like that look at all.

"What is it?" he asked, glancing around. His horse gave a nervous wicker and pulled on his rope. "Is there something out there?"

"There's plenty out there. This whole wood is like a maze, boy. There's a devil down nine of every ten paths…and some of those we'd best not tangle with."

It was an exaggeration. But Lythian took the point. "You've done well to guide us from trouble thus far, Vilmar." For the most part, anyway. Their journey had not been *entirely* without incident.

His compliment only won him another grunt from the man. "I'd sooner guide us *toward* trouble, so you call it," Vilmar told him. "There are some creatures here I've been longing to hunt, monsters not seen since an age before man. Damn you for making me clean up your mess."

Lythian stiffened his jaw. He'd had it up to here with the man's reprimands. "I was trying to be nice and you respond with another rebuke. But for me you'd be stuck with Hruum and the gruloks. A dull charge, you said it yourself. You ought to thank me for letting you come."

"Letting me?" A glint of yellow teeth showed behind the black of his beard. "You need me, boy. Same as I needed that woodsman who raised me. You're just a babe out here, same as I was…but I hear no thunder in *your* bloody heart."

"No thunder?" The accusation stung more than anything he'd said. "You have no idea what I've done."

"You lost the blade you were sworn to guard. I know *that*. What else matters?"

Lythian opened his mouth to bite back, but nothing came. He only looked away and dipped his eyes. "You're right. I lost the blade. I…"

"Need to stop apologising for it," the big huntsman said unexpectedly. "I know what it takes to wield those blades. And I know how they can corrupt. You sat in that ruin with nothing to do but rot, and it got into you. No shame in that."

"There is," Lythian said. "I failed my king."

"We all fail," the huntsman said. "That's life, yours and mine and everyone's. Failure. And a lot of it. With a bit of success scattered here and there. Aye, the blade was taken from you. But you're here trying to get it back and that says a lot." He stepped in and took his arm. "Here's the deal. I'll stop beating you up about that when you do. Agreed?"

Lythian looked into the man's dark eyes. They seemed sincere enough. "Agreed."

"Good. I'm getting bored of that anyway. Only so much pleasure to take from kicking a man when he's down." He grinned and released Lythian's arm. Then he gestured up the slope. "The camp's ahead. Can smell the old ashes from here."

The Black was right about that as well. A little further up they found the remains of a campfire. There were some old charred bones among the cinders, a rudimentary spit collapsed to one side. Vilmar told Lythian to hobble the horse and prepare them a dinner ration while he did his checks. They would stop here the night, he said. With the last thin rays of daylight leeching from the woods, it seemed sensible, and Lythian made no complaint.

Their ration was old cheese, hard bread, and salted pork. Sir Storos had even been good enough to add a bottle of whiskey to Lythian's pack. No doubt he had expected to share that between the two of them and Nathaniel Oloran, but Lythian had other ideas, and here he was with Vilmar instead.

They handed the bottle back and forward as they ate, taking small sips each time to make it last. The cheese was pungent, the bread like edible rock, the pork chewy as old leather, but at least here they were dry. Oloran had chosen a great old oak under which to camp and the choice was wise, its canopy thick enough to keep off all but a few drops of rain. Vilmar spoke of what he'd found. "I counted nine tracks leading north toward that village of yours. Might be they had a map of their own and knew of it. If we're lucky, they'll still be there. But we're not that lucky and they won't be."

Lythian took a sip of whiskey, pondering. Its warmth was much needed on another cold and dreary day. "The village may very well be deserted like the others." They'd passed two already and found them abandoned, though neither of those was on the map. That this one was suggested it would be a more substantial settlement. "If not, someone might be able to help us. You have your nose, I know, but it can't tell us who we're hunting."

"We know who we're hunting. Traitors and thieves. Oloran. That Steelheart dandy. The other one you saw…"

"And six others," Lythian said. That night in the tent there had only been four; Brontus Oloran, the Knight of Nine-Hearth, the big bearded soldier and the one that Lythian had slain. It seemed a further six men were waiting outside, and they could be anyone. "A smart swordsman wants to know who he's fighting before he enters the duelling circle. To know his weak points and vulnerabilities. Isn't that true of you, Vilmar? Do you not want to learn all you can of the creatures you hunt before you close in on their lair?" He did not wait for the man to answer; both knew the truth in that. "We know three of them," he continued on. "I'd like to know more about the other six. How well armoured they are, what weapons they're carrying, whether they're men I know so I might better judge their prowess. Are they spearmen? Swordsmen. Bowmen? Are they younger, older? Are any carrying injuries or wounds. If it comes to a straight fight, we'll be badly outnumbered. The more we know about them, the better."

His speech elicited a grunt of acknowledgement. "Fine. If that'll make you less jumpy." The huntsman thrust his chin toward the dead campfire. "That's the first fire we've seen. And those the first bones. You know what they are?"

Lythian peered forward. "I'd only be guessing. Pheasant, perhaps?"

"Close." Vilmar picked up a bone and crunched down on it with his teeth. "Woodcock," he said. "They're smaller. Might feed two or three men, but not much to share between eight. It tells a story, that. Says they're hungry, growing desperate. They've travelled all the way from the Twinfort. Would have packed good rations there, maybe scavenged some more on the way, but who knows how much they've got left. That they're stopping to hunt and cook, and a meal as paltry as this…"

"Paltry? Or poultry?" Lythian's lips parted in a grin. "Sorry, couldn't resist."

The hunter snorted. "You taking this seriously or not? The woodcock isn't even poultry. It's a migratory game bird, part of the sandpiper family."

"Right. Fascinating. Not poultry, but paltry. I understand." Lythian smiled.

Vilmar scowled. "Are you done? I'm saying they're slowing. They're hungry, tired, and maybe letting their guard down now that they're this far from the city. Might be looking for somewhere to rest a few days. Somewhere to use as a base while they hunt, while that traitor trains with his shiny new blade."

Lythian sipped the whiskey, turning more serious. "This village might offer them the sanctuary they need. If it's abandoned, they could do worse."

The hunter took the bottle back. He drank, wiping his bearded lips with his long black sleeve. "Somewhere off the map would be better. They'll stay hidden if they're smart. Is he a fool, this Oloran?"

"Not in my experience."

"Then they'll find somewhere else. Unless they think they're out of reach. I doubt they counted on someone like *me* tracking them. No one else would have kept their trail. No one." He drank again.

The man was not short of the occasional boast. "We'll know more tomorrow," is all Lythian said. He desperately hoped one of the villagers might know…*if* there were any. Just as likely the place was abandoned…or Brontus had put them all to the sword…or he'd taken his crew on north after all, and hadn't stopped, and this woodcock in the fire was nothing but a tasty treat after many long days on the run and they were reading too much into it. It was all speculation and neither man had much patience for it. So they put the matter aside, finished their food, decided on the watch, and another day in these woods was done.

The night passed without incident, which wasn't always the case. They had been required to fend off the attentions of a pair of large direwolves that had designs over Lythian's horse, and only two nights ago a huge greatboar had come swaggering past them with an intent to root about their rations. Lythian had been on watch at the time, though somehow Vilmar saw it first. How that was possible the knight wasn't sure. Even in his sleep the huntsman seemed to cast a net of sense around him, as though the very roots and leaves of the trees relayed to him what they saw.

Together they'd fought the beast away, a great crashing battle that had ended when the greatboar took one too many wounds and decided to call it a day. "A shame we didn't finish it," Vilmar had growled. "There's enough meat on that beast to feed half a city."

"I tried," Lythian said, deadpan. He'd cut the monstrous boar at least half a dozen times, but its thick hide and dense layers of muscle and fat were too deep to wound it mortally. "Next time I'll cut us a few steaks before it runs away, how about that?"

"Next time you'll die if you fight like that. It almost skewered you three times."

"Almost is different to did. I can live with almost."

"Aye. And one day you'll die with did. This is the wild, not the sparring circle. You still fight like a knight. And it'll get you killed out here."

Lythian didn't care to listen to that. "I'm here to kill Brontus Oloran - a knight. And his companions - knights and swordsmen. Believe me, my fighting style will serve me well then. They teach no forms for slaying greatboars, Vilmar. If you're such an expert, you take care of the next one."

The morning dawned sickly and pale, a shade brighter than the days before. As Lythian packed up, Vilmar set into his morning routine. First he peered out into the woods for a long while, ears taking in the sounds of the world. Then he sniffed long and deep, detecting scents both old and new. Lastly, he licked his finger, raised it to the breeze, waited, waited, and then thrust it back into his mouth, sucking like a toddler sucks his thumb. Lythian watched on, mildly put off, but the technique was an effective one he'd come to see. After the huntsman was done, he gave his report. "Rain's gonna thicken, then die off," he said, glancing to the skies. "Not completely. Well, course not. Never does here. But it'll go lighter for a while. Should be nought but misty drizzle by the time we reach the village."

That was good. Vilmar's weather forecasts were accurate for the most part. "Anything else?"

"Another greatboar passed nearby overnight, few hundred metres down that hill. Not the same one. Bigger. A female. Likely the mate looking for vengeance. They're all about vengeance, these greatboars. Get that from Brannatar. He was said to never let a feud lie, that one. His kin are all the same."

Lythian withdrew his sword. "Is it too late for steak?"

"Put that away," Vilmar growled. "A vengeful female's nothing to joke about. That'd be twice the battle as before, and she'll have tusks that can skewer your plate."

He resheathed the blade. "I thought only the males had tusks."

"No. Both. And the females are bigger. So let's be on our way."

Vilmar the Black led them on. The slope continued upward a little longer before levelling out into an open hilltop. The greatboar had ventured off west, Vilmar went on to add, and he was keeping an ear out for its approach should it catch their scent and follow. "Even *you* might hear that one coming," he mocked. "Big old sow like that."

Lythian ignored the comment. Acute as his senses were, he had long since realised that out here he was most assuredly second best. "How big do they get? The females?"

"Can be double the size. But that's rare. They're more aggressive too, especially when they got some little boarlings running about."

Lythian didn't imagine these boarlings would be so little. Even fresh from the womb they'd be almost as large as regular boars. "Well, if this charming lady should catch up to us, I'll stand back and observe your technique this time, Vilmar. Let's see if you don't 'almost' get skewered as well."

The Black withdrew his savage hunting knife so quickly Lythian barely saw. "This is all I need, you'll see. I may not be as quick as I was, or as strong, but this counts for more than that." He tapped his temple with the flat of the blade. "I know how these creatures think, how they move. I see what they'll do before they even know it themselves. I know where to strike, how deep and how hard. One thrust or throw is all it would take."

"I should like to see that, Vilmar."

"You will. When the time comes, you will."

They passed the grassy knoll atop the hill. The vantage permitted them a ranging view, though in truth there wasn't much to see. Just a sky cloud-choked and grey, a land of green and brown spread out far as the eye could see. Water glistened everywhere, puddles and ponds and lakes newly made, and the roar of rushing rivers was never too far away. Vilmar stopped to look around, sniffing, listening, then carried on across the field. They plunged back into another wood on the other side.

It was long past midday when the village reared into view, appearing from beyond the trees at a crossroad between the woods. There was a dirt road running through it, furrowed and filthy, its edges thick with weeds. Another pair of side tracks broke off from the main path, and to either side of all of them were lined a series of shacks and shelters and cabins. Lythian saw a ten-stall stable, a traveller's tavern with a broken sign, several pigpens and sheepfolds spreading into a muddy field. At the heart of the village the road parted to permit the placement of a statue, though from here he couldn't see of what or whom. Where the statue stood was formed a village square of sorts. Opposite stood the largest building in town: a log-walled longhall with a double door banded in iron and a curved thatched roof. A trail of smoke was rising from the chimney hole.

"Someone's home," growled Vilmar the Black.

"There are horses in the stable too," said Lythian. He could not see inside from here, but had heard a whiny or two.

The huntsman drew deep, nostrils flaring. "Several of them. Three, maybe four." His narrow eyes scanned from the dark of the trees. The rain was falling lightly as he'd said, and bands of mist moved through the village like the ghosts of long-dead men. "I smell death here, plenty of it. Sheep. Pigs. *Men*." He clutched his godsteel hunting knife, though didn't seem to need it to enhance his senses. "Might be your friends have taken up residence after all."

Something stirred in Lythian's chest. Anger, excitement, nerves. "We'd best be sure before we act. If all nine are in that longhouse, we'll have a hard time facing them head-on."

"Hunters don't fight head-on lest they have to. We're smarter than that." He picked at his teeth with the point of his blade. "We'd be wise to split them up. Start a fire or two, cause some panic once it's dark. That's how I work best. Hunting from the shadows."

"You'd have made a good assassin, Vilmar. Did the ranks of the Shadow Order never tempt you?"

The man gave a deep grunt that passed for laughter. "They came for me once. Those bandits who slew the woodsman…who d'you think *they* were?"

Lythian took that for a jest, though could not be sure. "Then I suppose they didn't think you had the right stuff. Or they'd have taken you."

"They tried. Even at five, I was lethal." The huntsman's grin was that of a beast. His gaze moved over to the stables nearby and doubt showed in his eyes. "They don't smell right, them horses. Oloran and his crew would need Bladeborn-bearers, but these…they smell like common stock."

Lythian frowned. "You can tell?"

"Near enough. My eyes will tell better. Come."

They left their horse tied up to a branch and crept as close as the trees allowed, peering for signs of people as they went. The village seemed deserted, the buildings shuttered and closed. Some doors hung off their hinges; others were broken or missing entirely and many windows had been smashed. Several cottages were half-burned, though the rain had stopped the fire from spreading, and the traveller tavern looked to have been ransacked from the glimpses Lythian saw inside. But when they reached the stables, it was clear these were not Brontus's horses. Vilmar was right…again. They were common breeds, workhorses and hobby horses, and not capable of bearing Bladeborn men.

"It doesn't mean they're not here," Lythian said. "They may be keeping their mounts elsewhere…in the woods or even in the longhouse with them. They'd be safer there together."

"So would the villagers. With this much death, they'd have herded themselves in like sheep. That longhouse is the stoutest place here. You want my guess, they've barred themselves inside."

Lythian gave a reluctant nod. Most likely he was right, but they wouldn't know until they checked. "Those log walls look easy enough to climb. If you get up onto the roof you might be able to get a look inside through the smoke hole."

"Why me? I'm two decades older than you."

"And ten times lighter without armour." Lythian wore full godsteel plate beneath his cloak and would not remove it until he had the Sword of Varinar back in hand, as per his vow. Vilmar wore only leather and fur and an air of disgruntled rage. "That roof would never hold me."

"Nor me. That thunder in my heart weighs a lot." The hunter scowled down the road. "Fine. I'll do it. Let's just get this over with."

The man was as skilled a climber as Lythian had expected. He clambered weightlessly up the wall like a great black insect, rain dripping from the fur of his cloak as he went from log to log. When he reached the roof, he tested his weight, then crept carefully toward the smoke hole. Lythian listened for voices all the while. There were men inside, that was clear, but whether Oloran and his cronies he couldn't say. There seemed to be some sort of an argument going on, men talking in heated debate, voices rising. Then all of a sudden he heard movement, the stamp of footsteps, and the double doors flew open. Smoky firelight poured out from inside and an old man emerged, grunting and shaking his head. Then another followed, younger, and another and another. Beyond, many more people were gathered inside the hall, all murmuring and talking and arguing.

Lythian stepped out of the shadows. "A fine afternoon, good sirs. Might I trouble you for a word?"

The men rounded on him at once, snatching weapons from their crude leather belts. They were simple blades, a bit of steel and iron. One bore a scythe, another a chopping axe. Two of the men were carrying wounds by judge of those bloody bandages about their shoulders and thighs.

The oldest of the villagers stepped forward, the first man to emerge from the hall. He was north of fifty, slim as a lance, haggard jaws spotted with sparse grey stubble. Grey-black hair grew thinly on his scalp. "Who are you?" he demanded roughly. "Are you armed? Show your weapons."

"Remove the cloak," one of the other men shouted.

"It's cold," Lythian said. "But very well." He removed his cloak and unveiled his misting armour.

"Bladeborn!" someone yelled. "Another one."

More men were rushing out from inside the hall, weapons being pulled from their cloaks.

Lythian raised his hands. "I mean no harm." His eyes moved between the emerging men. There was not a Bladeborn among them, no true soldiers, yet they were still dangerous if they attacked as one. *The Bladeborn knight has no love for two things,* a wise man had once written. *Deep water and the mob. And he'd best beware them both.* History had proven both to be true. Not so long ago Sir Edwyn Huffort of Janilah's Six had been torn apart by the mob in Ilithor. Lythian would not have his own life end the same way. "I have come only to hear tidings of a man who passed this way. He led seven others, some of them ahorse. I am seeking him in the name of the king."

Not everyone heard him, such was the noise, but the haggard man did. "You're talking about Brontus Oloran."

Lythian's eyes lit up. "I am. Tell me…when did he pass?"

"Two days gone." The man spat to the side. "They stole everything they could carry and left. We fought them off such as we could, but what could we do against men like that? They cut down Arry and Den and Mutton, Pearson and Lamberry too. We captured one, knocked him out in the heat of the fighting." He laid a hand on the shoulder of the young man at his side. He had the look of his son. "My Jethro got him, brave lad. Got the bugger chained up inside."

Lythian looked at the hall. "He's in there now?"

"Well he's not out here. We've been discussing what to do with him. Half would have me throw up a gibbet and hang him, others say he's worth a bit of coin. Not that coin's worth much these days. The world's dying, so we hear."

Lythian took a pace forward. "I would speak with him," he said. "I must know where Brontus Oloran went. It is a matter of urgency."

"Why? What'd he do to you?"

"He stole something of great value. It must be retrieved."

"By you and who's army?" The man frowned and scratched at his cheek. "You're here alone, are you?"

"No." Vilmar the Black prowled out from the gloom like a spectre. Several men shuddered and drew back at the sight of him, fumbling for weapons. A woman screamed and a young man shouted, "Grimbear… grimbear…" pointing. Vilmar's response was to snort and say, "I killed a dozen grimbears before. Believe me, boy, I'm much worse."

Lythian addressed the growing assembly. "This is my companion. He means no harm." Slowly, the panic settled. "I must speak with your prisoner. He may be able to speed our hunt for justice." He looked around. "For all of you. Justice for the men you lost. I'm sure they were dear to you."

"They were," shouted a woman's voice from the throng. "Arry was my son! My son and they slaughtered him like he was nothing. Nothing!"

Others called out as well. Each man had been a son, a brother, a father and a friend and the grief and anger in the air was palpable. Lythian could see very well why they wanted this prisoner hanged, and they were welcome to do so…once he'd had his word. He waited for the crying and caterwauling to die down before repeating once more that he must speak with this man at once. The haggard man scratched his chin as his close companions whispered about him. At last he spoke, raising a hand to silence his people. There was a febrile, ragged energy in the air. A dangerous energy if Lythian didn't play this right. "You want to speak with him…then you'll do something for us first." He looked at Vilmar. "You have the look of a hunter."

"And you have the stink of a pig farmer. What of it?"

The man smiled thinly. "That sense of smell serves you well in the wild, I'll wager. Was a pig man once, but now my pigs are all dead. There's a creature that's been plaguing us. Out in those woods. It's killed two dozen pigs and sheep and has started to take people too. We've had sentries go missing. Women taken as they muck out the pens. Been going on long before Oloran came and that bastard only made it worse by killing our best fighting men." He paused as one of the others leaned in to say something to him, then nodded and spoke again. "Derik says he recognises you. Captain Lythian Lindar, is that so?"

Lythian had no choice but to nod.

The pig farmer smiled. "The Knight of the Vale, companion to the great Amron Daecar. What an honour to have you here in our humble little village." He put himself into a bow. "We all know you here, Captain Lythian. We've all heard of your great deeds. They say you're the most noble knight in all the realm. That you take your oaths more seriously than anyone."

Once, Lythian thought. *Yes, once that was true.* He kept his silence and said nothing.

The pig farmer went on. "A knight's duty is to protect the weak," he said, loud enough for all to hear. "To fight for those who cannot fight for themselves. You swear all that when they give you your spurs. Not all follow those oaths… we know that well enough, but you…*you* do, don't you, Captain Lythian?"

Lythian sensed an ask was coming. He had him neatly cornered here. "I try to, yes."

"Then you'll help us," the man said, getting to it at last. "In exchange for a meeting with our prisoner back there. This beast…" He looked at Vilmar again. "Won't be much of a challenge for the likes of you."

"I'll be the judge of that," the huntsman growled. "You describe it to me. Then I'll tell you what we're dealing with."

"Be glad to." The pig farmer rubbed his hands together. "Let's sit down out of this cold, how about it? I'll tell you all I know."

It was the whereabouts of Brontus Oloran that Lythian wanted to know. Not some creature. "My mission is of great urgency. What's to stop me forcing my way into that hall and speaking to the prisoner right now?"

"Your honour. As previously referenced. I reckon some of these lads would try to stop you and you'd have no choice but to cut them down. And besides, the prisoner would be dead. You make a move to get near him and I'll have his throat cut. His secrets will die with him."

Lythian silently cursed the man. "Your negotiating skills are admirable," he said. "I don't suppose it would matter if I told you what Brontus had stolen?"

"The Sword of Varinar would be my guess. He wasn't caring to hide it."

Lythian closed a fist. "Did he use it?"

"No. Kept it sheathed at his hip. Was his men who did the dirty work."

Lythian nodded and leaned in to Vilmar for a quiet word. "Do we have a way out of this?" he whispered.

"Not unless you want to bloody your blade."

"We could just leave. Forget this prisoner. He might not know anything anyway."

"Or he might. Best we sit down with this pig farmer first, see what else he's got to say. If this creature keeps on coming back, it'll have a lair near here. A day, two tops, and I'll have its head mounted above that longhall's hearth."

Lythian Lindar wasn't seeing much of a way out. "Fine. We'll talk to him. But I want you to be honest with me, Vilmar. If this creature he describes is one you deem to be too dangerous, we can't go risking our lives. Understand?"

"More than you do. I'm deep into my sixties, boy. I haven't lived this long being reckless."

That was good enough for him. He turned back to the pig farmer and raised his voice. "We agree to your proposal. But I'll want to see this prisoner first to confirm you're telling the truth."

The man conferred with his men a moment, then a pair of them rushed inside the longhall. "If you'll follow me," he said. "I'll give you a look at him, but no more than that. He'll be gagged the whole time, so no talking. But I have a good feeling you'll recognise him anyway. He's one of yours, after all."

"One of mine?" Lythian wasn't sure what he meant. "You mean he's a knight? A *Varin* Knight?"

The man smiled. "Come. See for yourself." He turned and led the way, Lythian following, wondering all the while who it could be. Sir Symon? No, Brontus would never leave him behind, and he was not a Varin Knight in any case. Had Brontus recruited Sir Marcus Flint before he left the Twinfort? The Flints were Oloran bannermen. Would that be enough for the man to desert his post? Lythian doubted that as well. Sir Marcus was too honourable for that. More likely this prisoner was not a

Varin Knight at all. Just a common household knight blindly loyal to Oloran's cause.

He did not have to mull on it long. As the pig farmer led Lythian into the longhall, a man was being led out from an iron cage at the rear. He was dressed in rags with a bag on his head, spindly as a sapling, all gristle and bone. His wrists were tied behind his back, his ankles fettered together with a foot of rope between them, causing him to shuffle along. The two men walked either side of him, prodding him forward.

"That's far enough," the pig farmer said, stopping a dozen paces away. The prisoner was driven down to his knees. Around him all manner of men and women and children were crowding and huddling, dogs and goats moving among them. A smoky peat fire burned at the heart of the hall, supplying the only warmth.

"I'm going to need to see his face," Lythian said.

"Of course. It's a nasty one, you'll see." The farmer waved. "Remove the bag."

He was not wrong. A nasty face that Lythian had never much liked, mean-mouthed and cruel-eyed, though one he'd served with for long years. His lip curled up in disgust to see him here, wondering how it was so. The last time he'd seen this man, he'd been deserting from the battle at King's Point, abandoning the side of Lord Dalton Taynar. He was no ally of Brontus Oloran - nay, the two had never gotten along - but somewhere along the way, they must have joined forces. *The enemy of my enemy is my friend,* Lythian thought, and his face was in a scowl.

"I know that one," a gruff voice growled behind him. "Sir Ramsey some-such, no? Didn't know he and Oloran were friends."

"They're not," Lythian said. "And he's no knight anymore." He turned to the pig farmer, firming his jaw. "Tell us about this creature and we'll kill it for you. And after..." He turned and pointed at Ramsey Stone. "That one there is mine."

21

Elyon

He groaned as he rolled his left arm over in its socket, mouth twisting in a grimace of pain.

"Problem?" Talasha Taan asked, peering at him across the fledgling fire. "You look in some discomfort, Elyon. Would you like me to give you a massage?"

"No, my lady, that…won't be necessary. I dislocated my shoulder not so long ago…in a death duel with Sir Mallister, if you'd believe it. It can grow stiff, sometimes. Especially so in the cold."

"And from bearing the weight of *that*, no doubt." She gestured toward the long bundle of linen resting against the inner wall of the abandoned stone barn, a stout little sanctuary beside a small frozen river on the outskirts of a deserted village. It was quiet here, very quiet and calm following the unending bluster and roar of the flight. Now the only sounds were the soft soothing crackle of the flames and the whistling noise the wind made as it squeezed through thin gaps in the stone.

And the whispers, Elyon thought. They were always with him too, and loud and insistent today especially.

He gave his shoulder another stretch. "Yes," he agreed. "I'm sure that contributed." If it was only a bale of linen there would have been no issue, but *within* the bundle was a certain ancient black blade, and a fiendishly heavy one at that. Elyon had spent the flight so far helping Neyruu bear its weight, and it had taken its toll.

Before they'd left the mountains that morning, Elyon had deemed it wise and prudent to tie a length of rope to the swaddled Nightblade to tether to him while he flew. The theory was simple; Neyruu, being a dragon of middling size, noted more for her speed and agility than her strength, would struggle to bear the weight for long when they lashed it to her back, and the journey would thus be in fits and starts and might even threaten to overwhelm her. "I can help to carry the blade," Elyon

Daecar had thus declared. "A problem halved is a problem solved. Together we'll be stronger."

So with the blade bundled in linen and safely fixed between Neyruu's shoulders, Elyon had tied to it a robust hempen rope, tethered the other end to his swordbelt, and taken flight above her. Almost at once he'd realised his folly. The dragon did not fly as he did. Her movements were different, each pulse of her wings causing her to rise in sudden jerks, and the air currents and gusts affected her too, forcing her to constantly turn and weave between them. Where Elyon mastered and controlled the winds, Neyruu merely sailed upon them, and her form of flight wasn't always so smooth. He had consequently found himself tugged and pulled along with her, struggling to maintain the right height above the beast so the rope was taut and he was actually, well, helping in the way he had hoped.

After a while, they came down to land in the midst of an open snowfield bordered by shadowed peaks. "It's not working," Elyon had admitted, already untethering the rope from his belt. "I'll have to hold onto it instead, my lady. With my spare hand. As I fly."

She'd frowned down from her saddle, breath fogging through the scarf that covered her mouth. "Won't you only lose your grip and let go?"

That was the point. Better to let go than be dragged and tugged about and risk losing his grip on the Windblade instead. *That* would be a disaster for them all. "I will hold on *tight*," he assured her. "If I let go I will fly down and retrieve the end. And as many times as I must, my lady. I will not let Neyruu carry it alone." It was the best compromise he could give her, and so for the rest of the day that was how it went.

Now, hours later, his left arm was weary beyond all reckoning and he felt like his shoulder might just pop back out of its socket if he put it through any further strain. He stretched it for a little while longer, parrying Talasha's further invites for a massage, then drew a breath and said, "I ought to take a look around the village, my lady. Are we good for firewood?"

Talasha glanced over at the pile that Elyon had cut when they first arrived. "We should have enough for the night, I think."

He nodded and went to the door, drawing across the rusted bolt that fastened it, and pushed out into the chill afternoon air. The sky was largely clear, and sunset remained an hour or so away. "Best lock this behind me, my lady, to be safe. I'll knock when I return."

Stepping out, he closed the door behind him and took a moment to drink in the purity of winter, false winter though it was, looking out over the peaceful lands. It was eerily quiet, still and tranquil. The river that would normally be trickling and splashing softly was frozen solid and silent. No birds were to be seen in bush or tree or sky, nor could he hear their calls. No insects clicking and buzzing. No frogs croaking among the reeds. The stone barn in which they'd taken up residence for the night was part of a larger grouping of buildings. Nearby stood a handsome farmhouse, some pens for cattle, a vegetable garden and open fields for grazing. There were no animals, however, no cows or sheep or goats, no pigs in the pig pens or chickens in their coops. The accompanying sounds of life on a farm were absent. It was as though everything here had just vanished from existence.

One animal did remain, however, a newcomer though she was. Neyruu had taken up in a large open-fronted haybarn, curled up beneath the snow-draped awning like some enormous grey cat. Steam rose off her armoured plate to fog the air above her, and she appeared to be sleeping, so far as Elyon could tell. And well deserved that sleep was. The dragon had worked very hard today and written some new history all the while. *The first dragon to bear a Blade of Vandar,* Elyon thought. Added to her victory over the greatbat, she was becoming quite the star.

The village was a short walk away, a small settlement on the banks of the river. Elyon knew neither the name of the river nor the name of the village and had not found it on his map. It was too small to note a mention, clearly. There was a traveller tavern at the far end, a cluster of fishing huts built along the water, a small church and not much else. A pair of rowboats sat tied up on posts outside two huts, and he saw a jetty and a river barge as well, close by the tavern. It was a ferry crossing, and a crude one. The river was not particularly wide, but it was too deep to wade through, and there were probably few places to ford nearby.

He started with the church, stepping into the dimness within. It was small, low-ceilinged, far from grand. If anything of value had once been here, now it was gone, stripped away like all the people. In a room at the back he uncovered a floor hatch leading down into a dusty old under-croft. There he found some stacks of old religious texts, a crate of clay bottles filled with spoiled, vinegary wine, a few bits of broken and discarded furniture, wonky pews and a worm-eaten lectern, nothing to interest or excite him. And spiders and rats too, yes, plenty of those.

Exiting, he wandered northward to the tavern situated at the far end of the village, poking his nose into a few of the fisher huts along the way. In one, he found a bucket of dead, half-frozen fish, though the smell suggested they were beyond the point of being edible. In another, a variety of insects and lizards, birds and small mammals were laid out in a display case and across a scarred, blood-stained table. Some were intact, others dissected. It looked like a biologist had lived here once, or at least some hobbyist interested in anatomy. Like the farmer and the ferryman and the priest, however, he was gone with all the rest.

In the next hut he encountered his first people, but both of them were long dead. The scene was sweet and tragic; an old woman and an old man, lying together in their bed with their wrists opened up in what looked like a mutual suicide. *They saw the end was coming,* he thought, *and wanted to die on their own terms.* Wherever the rest of the village had gone - Ilithor far to the west or Rockfall much closer to the east - this old couple had preferred to die where they had lived.

He found a blanket to place over them and left them there in peace.

When at last he came to the inn the eastern skies were beginning to darken. Opposite, just across the rutted road, the ferry barg was stuck in the ice and the glow of sunset gleamed off the frozen river. Beside the tavern was a four-stall stable with a dead horse inside. A broken leg seemed to be the cause. The snow had grown so heaped and heavy that one side of the stable had collapsed. There was an outhouse too, expect-edly filthy, a hitching post and what would once have been decorative plant pots filled with flowers to make the entrance to the inn more invit-ing. The flowers were dead, though, black and wilted. Several of the pots had cracked and long icicles stretched down from the lintel above the door.

Elyon looked at the sign. It showed a picture of a giant stone man with a boulder for a head, his rock face split and tipped back in laughter as he splashed about in a river. *A grulok?* he wondered. His experience of the colossal stone sentinels was limited, he would admit, but they were not much for laughing that he had seen. Then he saw the sign and remembered. *The Laughing Lugabor*, it read. Thinly he recalled the tale of a huge stone man who wandered about beneath the rivers in these parts, snatching up children from the banks when they got too close. Sinister as that sounded, the Lugabor never meant any harm and only ever wanted to play. He'd read that in one of his old monster books as a boy.

He spent a short time moseying about the inn, searching the kitchens and the common room, the cellar and the loft, checking each of the four bedchambers upstairs. His mind wandered as he went, moving between myriad topics. He thought of his father, and he thought of Amara, and he thought of Lillia and he thought of Lythian. He wondered where his bastard brother Jonik was now. Dead? A part of him would not weep at that news. Another part would feel cheated that he did not have a chance to confront him himself. Not kill him, no. He'd made a godsteel oath to Amilia that he wouldn't kill her cousin, but that did not mean he couldn't confront him in *other* ways.

Mostly he thought of Saska, though. One way or another, she was always on his mind. They had flown some two-thirds of the way back to her now and stopped just north of the Stonehills. Tomorrow they would cross over the Sibling Strait into Rasalan and rejoin her, he hoped, and he would present to her a *second* blade.

Two of five, he reflected. He wondered how quickly she would bond it. *The second is always simpler, yes.* He nodded. That is what people said, and yet bonding it was only part of the battle. With a strong blood-bond she'd be able to wield it only, not harness its power, and only his bastard of a Shadowknight brother had mastered the Nightblade. Only *he* could teach her to use it.

The thought made him snarl. He wanted Jonik nowhere near her. *She will have to discover its mysteries on her own,* he told himself. *I learned to master the Windblade by myself, so she can do the same.*

He stamped from one bedchamber to another, a hard bitter step that caused the reinforced boards beneath him to crack. *Or not*, he thought.

Why master that blade at all? There had always been a dishonour to the Nightblade, he thought. *A good warrior should face his foe head on, and not creep upon him unseen.* Elyon would never wish to deploy such a power. *Even if I were to battle Eldur himself, I would not use it. I would fight him fair, man to mage. And if I should die, so be it. I would die with my honour intact.*

He closed a fist, opened it, and let out a long slow breath. Thinking of the Nightblade only raised his ire and he would admit he had a bias against it. How could he not? It was the blade that had crippled his father. The blade that had ensnared that Shadowknight bastard and driven him to kill their brother. He could feel a darkness and an anger in that cold black steel and in truth he wanted to be nowhere near it. And sometimes…sometimes when he'd been flying today, clinging onto that rope, he had wanted to plunge down suddenly and slash the Nightblade free from Neyruu's back, to pull on the rope and tug it away and cast it down into some bottomless chasm never to be found again…

But he hadn't.

Of course he hadn't.

It was only the Windblade's influence, he told himself, urging him to do it. The Windblade hated its brother even more than Elyon did his and had begged the prince endlessly to fly far away, to soar beyond this continent, beyond this world, to fly out to unknown lands where they both might live together in freedom.

We could be gods, it had told him. *Gods in another world.* The whispers might once have clawed at his fear and paranoia, but Elyon was strong enough to repel them now. *But Saska?* he wondered. *What of her?* How was she going to cope when she had *both* the Windblade and the Nightblade in her head, whispering and arguing at one another down there in the dark and driving her to the brink of madness?

He mulled on that as he poked about in a bedchamber, rifling through a wardrobe and finding nothing but roughspun rags. Ilith had said that the divergent will of the five Blades of Vandar would matter not when they were hammered back together. That a single sentience would re-emerge that would seek only the destruction of its enemies, united to them in their cause. But until that time the five fragments would continue to desire their own independence. They would thrash and scream like spoiled children and must be forced by strength of will into line.

For that Saska must be resilient. She must be strong and single-minded and well-supported too. Elyon had a new task that only he could see done, a task that would take him far to the west with the Windblade in his grasp, but he needn't complete that task yet.

I will stay with her, at least until I know she's ready. She still needed to complete her training with the Windblade so she was able to fight in flight, and that would take some time. *A week, two, maybe more.* He would remain at her side until then, and saw no need to tell her anything more. *If she knows I'm going to leave, she will only fret and worry.* Why bother her with that distraction? *No,* he decided, *I will not tell her. And nor must Talasha. I will have to make sure she…*

He heard a screech outside, and froze.

The sudden, high-pitched cry of a dragon.

Neyruu, he thought, spinning at once to the bedchamber door. He was moving in an instant, hurrying past the threshold and down the stairs into the common room. More sounds came to him as he went. Wingbeats. The shouting of men in a blunt rough tongue. The raging roar of a much larger dragon...

He rushed to the exit and kicked out into the twilight, drawing the Windblade from its scabbard. The light had gone deep red and vermillion, saturating the western skies. Elyon's eyes surged downriver to the farm at the edge of the village, some two hundred metres away. A dragon had landed in the yard outside the haybarn where Neyruu had been resting. It looked strange, *wrong.* A chaos of twisting purple spines and curving green horns, uneven segments of ugly plate armour bulging from its oversized shoulders. Its neck was thick, its head enormous, and from its rear a great long tail curled and whipped, out of proportion with the rest of its body.

It had a structure on its back, a troop-carrier of sorts akin to those Elyon had read about from the olden wars. On either side of its spine ran two long benches. Dragonknights were unstrapping themselves and dropping to the ground on ropes, crimson cloaks fluttering. There must have been a dozen of them on either side and two other figures sat harnessed in a saddle: a Fireborn rider, a woman broad-shouldered and strong, armoured in purple scale with a light green cape trailing down her back. Behind her sat a middle-aged man, his head shaven bald except for the twin sideburns that he'd twisted and oiled and shaped into a pair of black-red horns that curled out from the sides of his head like a demon. His flesh was pale and his robes were red.

Fire priest, Elyon knew at once. *Like the ones Talasha spoke of...*

The Fireborn rider was shouting orders. Her voice was deep and powerful. She thumped a hand against the side of her deformed dragon, *thump thump thump,* as she bellowed out words Elyon could not understand. But he didn't need to. He knew their meaning. The dragonknights were fanning out to check the buildings, pulling their blades as they went. Half of them were marching his way toward the village, a dozen men clutching at dragonsteel swords and spears, crimson cloaks stirring as they strode down the track.

The prince slid back inside the tavern and out of sight. *They have not seen me yet.* He closed the door very quietly, resting his back against the wall in the shadows, waiting. Sliding the Windblade back into its sheath, he withdrew his dagger instead, reached to take up the helm looped around his belt and realised he'd left it in the barn.

So be it. He would go without. He could hear the voices getting closer, the men spreading to kick down doors and check the fish huts and the church. Senses heightened, he knew where they all were, heard their footfall as they drew nearer. Four were making for the tavern.

He filled his lungs, remaining perfectly still and calm. As the four drew close an order was barked and one moved away to check the stable and the outhouse. The other three reached the door and someone kicked it in. It swung with a wild crash and a man appeared, stepping forward into the dimness, blade brandished before him, swinging it from side to side…

Elyon Daecar emerged from the darkness. The man had not a moment to react before the prince opened up his throat. The dragonknight's head tipped back in a gushing red fountain and he staggered back clutching his craw, knocking into the men behind him. Elyon surged, bulldozing all three out into the snow. He pounced and drove his bloody dagger into one's heart, spun and swung to take off the other man's leg just above the knee. A scream ripped out through throat and air. The man tumbled back snatching his leg as the blood spurted thick and red.

The fourth dragonknight was appearing from the outhouse as though he'd just emptied his bowels. Perhaps he had by that look on his face. Wide-eyed, he let out an echoing howl and lowered his spear to charge, but Elyon was already on him, ghosting through the dusk to plunge his dagger through his gut. He twisted, slashed, opening up both breastplate and belly as his guts spilled out like steaming pink snakes to splash onto the snowy ground.

There were shouts behind him and Elyon wheeled about. More dragonknights were charging his way from the huts and holy house. He looked right past them through the gathering dark and heard the sounds of struggle, a woman screaming, Talasha being dragged from the barn. The fire priest had reached the ground and was standing awaiting her with his hands clasped together at the navel. Neyruu was curled and coiled, hissing, ready to spring at the other dragon, but Talasha seemed to be calling to her, holding out her hand and saying no…

It was all he saw. Then the knights were upon him. Another six, seven, eight of them in their black scale armour and crimson cloaks, the red flame of their forging glimmering in their dragonsteel blades. Elyon re-sheathed his dagger and withdrew the Windblade as they moved to surround him.

"Have you come for her or me?" he asked.

"Her," shouted one of them in his barking tongue. "The traitor. *He* will take her."

"He? Your priest?"

"He is a vessel of the Fire Father. He is a strand of his will. His web will cover the world. He…"

"Will die like all the rest of you."

Elyon swung the Windblade. A propulsive blast met the man hard in the chest and sent him flying back off his feet, grunting and rolling through the snow. The Prince of the Skies took a small moment to lament that this might be his last time doing battle with the Windblade in his grasp, that he would soon be land-locked again, fighting such foes blade to blade without the wondrous power he'd wielded and won and learned to master all by himself. A small stab of bitterness cut at him, but he ignored it. *I will give it up. I must. I must.*

He smiled to let some light from his soul and drove all his misgivings away. *If this is the last, so be it. It has grown too easy now anyway.* These men stood no chance against him.

They charged him all the same, three driving spears from his left and his right and behind him, the others closing in with their swords. *A classic dragonknight pincer attack,* he mused, as he flicked the Windblade up and surged skyward beyond their reach. Dragonknights were trained to fight Bladeborn in numbers, surrounding them and closing in as one in a bid to find weak links in their defences and armour. Fighting the Master of Winds was different, though. *They are nothing to me now. Nothing.*

Above them now, the men cursed and growled like the primitive beasts they were, and a pair of them hefted their spears and threw. Elyon shifted sideways in a misting blur as one flew by; the other grazed harmlessly off his right pauldron and away into the river to land quivering in the ice.

"Craven!" someone shouted.

"Fight ground," roared another in a garbled effort at speaking the common tongue. "Fight ground with us! Fight even!"

Elyon smiled. "There is no fighting even with insects." He slashed his blade again and again and again, and with each swish sent blasts of air at his enemies to separate and scatter them. The snow billowed into a white cloud and he shot down through it, kicking out at a knight as he landed, knocking him back and plunging the Windblade through his sternum. A man came in behind him, slashing in a downcut. Elyon ripped out his dagger to deflect the strike, pulled the Windblade from the dead man and turned, slicing. The steel made it about halfway through the man's ribcage before juddering to a halt, but that was plenty to kill him. Another he slew with a hack to the head and a fourth was made legless and left to bleed out. That was enough for the final three. They broke and ran, shouting out as they fled back toward the farm.

Elyon gave chase, flying to cut them down. Beyond, he could see Talasha being held before the fire priest. She was on her knees, her head held so she could not turn away. The priest was murmuring something, reaching out to cup her cheek with his palm. There was a twisted smile on his face, a twisted grimace on Talasha's. Neyruu was screaming. Pinned down by the bigger dragon and screaming.

Then suddenly the big woman rider turned and saw him coming, alerted by the screams of the fleeing men. She stood up in her saddle and tore a cruel curved dragonsteel blade from her sheath. "Stop!" she bellowed. "Stop or the dragon will die!"

Elyon slowed, the threat giving him pause. He looked to Talasha. The princess had tears in her eyes, her face contorted in an agonised grimace as though battling some inner demon. The priest was standing with his hand on the top of her head now, stroking softly. His eyes were on Elyon Daecar. Red eyes, and soulless. "The Lord of Storms," he said, in a spreading whisper.

"And you are?"

"Rah'kin, a Voice of Eldur. One of many, *many many*, yes. We spread his *voice* and we spread his *will*. North we spread it. And far to the south." He smiled. "We are the new watchers of the world."

The new watchers. Those words were enough to disquiet him. During his time in the refuge he'd seen the letter the First Elder had sent to Ilith. In it the ancient Lightborn had spoken of the fading light of Aramatia, his fears that they would soon be found. Have they? Are the Elders dead, their eagles with them?

The priest was going on. "We did not expect to find you here, Master of the Wind and Sharer of the Skies. We accept you now, as *airborne*. The skies are the dominion of dragons, yes, but you…you have proven a worthy foe. Great Eldur in his benevolence allows you to fly them untroubled. Go, now, and you will not be harmed. It is only the woman we want."

Elyon gave no answer. He drifted another foot closer, and another.

The priest's red eyes darkened. "I grant you free passage, Son of Vandar. By the righteous will of Eldur the Eternal and the divine right of Agarath the All-Father, almighty above us all. Your silence is spit in the face of this clemency." He flicked a pale hand to the corpses lying in his wake. "You have taken your share of life and spilt your share of blood. Let that be enough. You have no right to interfere."

Another foot. Another.

"No right!" The priest screamed out, in a thunderous voice. Elyon barely cringed. He had met the true Eldur, had fought him face to face. What was this pale shadow next to him? "We trespass on your lands, you will say. You will say we are not welcome here. *I* say we have come only to catch this *traitor*. She is the Fire Father's own blood and must be returned to him. What business is that of yours? Why are you even here?"

Elyon ignored the questions. He asked one of his own. "How did you find us? I am curious to know."

The priest snorted. "No answers from you. None from me."

"Was it the power of this blade that drew you?" He flicked the Windblade upward and a pulse of air blew off him to stir every cloak and cape. Several men backed away. The priest's eyes glazed a moment. *They fear me*, Elyon knew, then. *They all fear me. They know what I am.* "I was hunted once before," he went on. "Ezukar, a famous dragon to your people. Do you hunt me still?"

"No. It is the woman…"

"You are lying to me." The Nightblade was still in the barn, Elyon sensed, and they'd found it there when they found Talasha. Both blades in one place must have sent out a beacon, a combined power that Elyon had been unable to suppress or shield. Had it drawn them here to investigate? Was finding Talasha nought but coincidence?

He would consider the ramifications of that later. For now he was done, and it was time to act.

"Lying?" the priest was blaring. "No, there is no lying here! I speak with the Voice of Eldur and the Voice of Eldur does not lie. It is truth he tells, truth I tell. The woman is all we want. Her blood drew us, yes, the Blood of Eldur. Keep your blades of Wind and Night. You keep them. We do not want them!" He pointed a shivering finger in Elyon's direction. "Go, now! Go and we will spare you. Do this thing not and we will…"

Elyon Daecar had heard enough. "Silence!" he bellowed, in a ringing voice of his own. "Silence, priest! My lady, *get down*!" And he unleashed the full breadth of his power.

The wind-blast that surged from the swing of his blade was like a pyroclastic cloud flowing down from a volcano. With a deafening *crack* it spread out in a great pulsing wave, picking up snow and stone and debris as it blasted into everyone around him. A nearby pig-pen exploded, chicken coops were blasted apart. The nearest men to him went flying off their feet and out toward the river, snapping necks and limbs as they landed. Those further away were merely knocked back off their feet, the priest and the princess among them. She'd been on her knees, crowded by a group of dragonknights. That ought to be enough to shield her. He hoped…he hoped…

A roar pierced the air. He turned, saw the dragon lumbering toward him through the gritty white-grey shroud. Twisted and deformed, the beast scrambled over the dead and dying to reach him, its wings widening and flapping as it came. Thin black veins spread through the webbing pumping dark corrupted blood. The woman on its back screamed and brandished her curved blade aloft. She was no known rider, this woman, just some upjumped cow in a cape. Eldur had made her, Elyon Daecar knew.

I will unmake her, he thought.

The Prince of Vandar shot left as the dragon snapped at him with its huge broad face, a great sagging mass of scaly flesh swinging from the bottom of its neck. He was far too agile for it, far too quick. Slashing, he cut at that immense wattle, shaving off shards of plate armour. The beast made a bizarre sort of bellowing noise and twisted, the air *whooshing*, snapping at him again, but it was slow. It bit down only on air; Elyon was gone. From the other side he cut, drawing a thin black line along its right flank as blood began to leak from its bulk. It was a scratch only and would take a thousand more to kill it.

Away toward the river, he could hear the men shouting in confusion as they struggled to work out what had just happened. Some were screaming in agony, from twisted knees and broken arms. Others were silent, dead. Through the cloud of grit and blowing snow he glimpsed the princess further back toward the stone barn. Several dragonknights were sprawled about her, the priest as well, lying prone on the ground. Slowly they were waking, trying to stand.

Elyon blasted himself over to them. A dragonknight rose to his feet unsteadily, fumbling to draw his blade. Elyon cut him down, heard a noise behind him, saw another running at him screaming and took off his head in a single clean strike. A third surged through the murky air, hacking down at him. Elyon swung his spare arm to parry the blow, kicked with his boot and sent the man tumbling back. Before his foe could rise he leapt upon him, stamping down to crush his spine, then spun.

The priest was wheezing on the ground nearby, his red robes torn and soiled, trying to crawl away. Elyon stepped over and pressed the tip of his blade through the back of the man's neck to kill him. *One less strand of that web,* he thought. Further back, he heard the chaos of roars and hisses as Neyruu rose up to join the fray. She would not stand long alone against the other dragon. He marched over to the princess. "My lady, are you all right?"

She was on her knees, hunkered low, her hands raised up to cover her face. When he saw the blood leaking out between her fingers a terrible fear clutched at him. "Talasha. You…"

"Go." The word was weak. Her voice sounded brittle and strange. "Help her, Elyon. Please…"

"But my lady, I need to get you somewhere safe…"

"Save her," she whispered. "Forget me. Save…her…"

Unnerved, he backed away, pausing to look at her a moment longer before wheeling about and taking flight. Not far off the world was a chaos of steam and claw and fang. Blood hissed out from several savage gashes in the demon dragon's neck as Neyruu flapped above her, wild and enraged, clawing at her like a crow. The brute swung here and swung there, snapping out and missing. The farmhouse shattered as it lumbered right through it as though it was nought but a miniature shed.

"For Vandar!" Elyon Daecar roared. He set his aim at the dragon's red eye and flew forward at shattering speed. The big woman glimpsed him coming and screamed like a little girl. It was enough. The dragon shifted at the last moment, and the Windblade struck it three feet beneath the eye, juddering to a halt deep down in the bone.

There was a moment, then, almost of sudden calm, as Elyon hung there, right there on the head of his foe, clinging to the hilt of his blade, watching the dragon's great eye grow wide and wet as it saw him. *Fear,* he knew. He could see it. It was ripe. He snarled, reached to his hip, ripped the dagger from its sheath and slashed out. The huge eye split open like a runny red egg and the dragon bucked, bellowing, blood pouring from the socket in a thick black spray.

Elyon tugged the Windblade out and pulsed backward. The monster roared in rage and went for him, snapping, but Elyon surged away, up and over the beast, landing before the woman in the saddle.

Her face was a pale puddle of terror. "De…devil…" she managed to splutter. She raised her curved blade, but feebly, shivering.

"There's only one devil in this world." Elyon whipped the Windblade so fiercely it snapped her neck, bone bursting out through flesh and sinew as the dragon jerked and roared again, a terrible sound as half its soul went dark. Then it was flapping its wide wings in frenzy and running, one beat, two, three and four and five, trampling through the village as it took flight. Elyon swung and followed after it, swerving past the long thin tail as it whipped and lashed at him. "For Vandar!" he was roaring. "For Vandar! For the king!" He heard a screech and Neyruu plunged down, snapping her jaws about the tail, gnawing and ripping at it. Their foe thrashed its wings yet harder, climbing. Neyruu pulled back on the tail, stripping off scale and flesh. Blood was pouring off it, steaming as it rained to the snow.

The dragon arced west into the last of the daylight, a thin band of red on the horizon. Long fingers of smoke were trailing up and out from between its jagged teeth, causing Elyon to cough and splutter. He ducked low and into the clear air beneath it, then surged upward, swinging with a wind-enhanced strike more powerful than a common cut. The strike was true, cleaving through plate and flesh. The blood and gore that gushed out was black and smoking.

The dragon lurched, kicking out with a trailing leg. Elyon spun away, barrel-rolling, shot for the wing and cut through the webbing as easy as though slicing a sail. The split wing blew like a torn banner caught in a gale and the dragon faltered, losing height, and suddenly it was plunging down in a fierce descent, roaring, smoke and flame gushing up through its maw as it flapped wildly to recover, failing, falling faster, down and down and down and right into the side of a rocky hillock.

The earth bulged and broke, stone shattering, as the beast drove through and burst out the other side. The impact was thunderous. Elyon whipped his blade and swung around, ready to strike down at it again, but he saw at once there was no need. The dragon lay in a twisted wreck, its right wing-arm snapped back and broken, a sharp spire of stone lodged in its massive neck. Blood oozed out of it in a black steaming river. The only sound was the slow deep rumble as it took its final breaths. The thick thud of the heart as it failed.

Elyon drew a deep breath, panting fiercely from the thrill. He hovered above it, watching. A plaintive, almost soft sound rang from the dying beast's jaws and he felt for it a moment of pity. The men of the north were taught to hate and demonise dragons, but Elyon saw in them a nobility too. *Even this one*, he thought, watching it die. *It never wanted to leave the Wings. It never wanted to be turned into this.*

By the time the dragon had breathed its last, the skies had gone dark, and a pale pink moon was rising. Elyon swung back to the south and returned to the princess. A cold sweat licked at the back of his neck as he approached. He found her close to where he'd left her, crouching by the frozen river, its surface gleaming with reddish moonlight. There was blood on the reeds around her, Elyon saw. Blood on her hands and dripping down her neck.

"My lady," he whispered, stepping up behind her. "The dragon…it is slain. We are safe, for now."

She nodded, just once, saying nothing.

"The rest of the men are dead, my lady. Or fled. Some are not accounted for. I saw them running from here, to the south. I will chase them down, but…" He swallowed, fearing what he would find when she turned to him. "We had best see to your wounds first, my lady. Your face…I…" He caught a glimpse of her reflection in the river and winced at what he saw. "Talasha, I am so sorry. I never thought…expected…I was only trying to…"

"To save my life, I know. And you did, Elyon. You did." Something in her voice made him wonder if she was glad for that. A long silence stretched out as she stared at herself in the river. "There are medical supplies in Neyruu's saddlebags. How…are you with a needle?"

He did not know what to say. "My lady. Rockfall isn't so far. You would do better under the attentions of one properly trained. I…"

"I am not going to Rockfall, Elyon. I am not going anywhere." Her voice was weak, numb. "Fetch the needle and thread, and do the best you can. In the end I don't…I don't know that it'll make much of a difference."

He swallowed. His heart was breaking for her. "Very well, I…I will do what I can, my lady."

She nodded again, and did not turn to face him. Stepping away, Elyon sank into shame. And softly, so softly, he heard her weep.

22

The Sunlord

He had always hated the Glass City.

It was beautiful, magnificent, a sparkling wonder, the jewel of the south…and he hated it.

It was the city where empires were seeded and born, where emperors and empresses were raised up and crowned in crystal to walk as gods among common men, ruling over all their subjects from the Bloodgate to Eagle's Perch…and he hated it.

Time and again the Lumaran Empire had sprouted up from the disparate nations of the south…only to collapse and fall back into the dust ten or twenty or a hundred years later, and always it was *here*, in *Lumos*, where their capital was proclaimed, always Lumara from which the ruling bloodlines were drawn.

And Elio Krator *hated* it.

It sprawled before him now, this city of empires and gods, splendid in its superiority, a marvel of glass and polished silver stone, of rare architecture and gardens so sweet to look upon they would make a grown man weep. Within the high curtain walls palms grew in pretty groves, standing attendance around glittering pools where the people of the city would bathe, and tall domed towers rose up into the bright azure cloudless sky, banners cast out from long thin poles, rippling in silver and gold. He could see men on the walls, but few. Most were hiding in the shade, out of the blazing sun, and he could almost *feel* the city sweating. It made him smile, to think of them all baking in there, trapped. *This is what comes of their arrogance*, he thought. *They have brought this on themselves.*

"My lord, the Moon Gate is opening." Mar Malaan was at his side, soft and pink in silk and satin. He stank, did Malaan, a heady mix of perfume and sweat, but he remained his staunchest supporter. For that Krator continued to honour him. "A lone man, it looks. A herald of Her Eminence."

Eminence. Krator scoffed at the word.

"Do we send an envoy of our own, my lord?"

"In time," the sunlord said. "Let him stew in the sun a while first."

It was morning, the day yet young, the sun climbing the eastern sky above the glittering waters of the Bay of Stars. The heat was already intense, and would only grow worse in the hours to come; this was an unnatural heat, Elio Krator knew, a *killing* heat, and they would be feeling it behind him, the great legions gathered at his back. A strong host it was, of man and beast both, and more than he would need. *Her greatest defenders have been sent away,* the sunlord thought. *Today I claim my rights.*

He let the wait go on, watching as the herald stood alone beyond the great city gates, draped in his heavy ceremonial robes. He cut a sad and lonely figure and bore a tall staff in his grasp. A white flag blew from its summit, a pathetic gesture of parley, but Elio Krator would honour it all the same. *The strip of white fabric will protect* him, *at least,* he thought. Of the rest he would make no promises. That would depend on *her.*

His command shelter was raised at the front of his army. Open-walled, it permitted a gentle breeze to pass through and shielded them from the worst of the sun, but in truth that did little. The air was debilitatingly hot, even this early in the morning, and his captains were not enjoying it. Pal Palek was mopping his rutted brow relentlessly and even Iru Zon, who tried *never* to appear ruffled, was being fanned by a small army of servants to stay cool. Krator knew they wanted to get this done, and quickly.

At last, Mar Malaan spoke again. "My lord," he breathed, sweating profusely, "perhaps it is time? He is like to return to the city if we do not send a man to answer his call soon."

Krator looked at the fat, silk-wrapped Sunrider with an empty smile on his lips. Men always said of him that his lips could smile, but his eyes did not know how. He liked that. He enjoyed being thought of as cold. "Mar, you do worry so. If he leaves he will only come again."

"Of course, my lord. I only…I wonder…"

Krator raised a hand. Silence followed at once. "You are an old maid, Mar. But have it your way." In the spirit of haste, he would get things moving. "I will go myself," he decided. "I am eager to hear what this herald has to say."

The others would no doubt caution against that, but their council meant little to him now. Palek had proven useful when he fled from the battle at Aram into Pisek, offering him safe harbour, and he had answered his summons when he was called upon to muster an army as well, but still…he did not like him, and never had. *To think I was going to give the hand of my cousin to that ugly little man.* And Iru Zon was even worse. *That arrogant fool thinks himself the rightful leader of this cause.* Iru was the descendent of Helio Zon, who had formed the Patriots of Lumara long ago when he was City Master of Solas. It was his birthright to lead them, Iru often claimed. *He forgets that strong men* take *power, they aren't given it. I'll make that clear to him today.*

Mar Malaan made to follow as he stepped away into the sun. Krator turned his head. "No, Mar. Stay here. I wish to go alone."

"My lord? But...there are archers on the walls, and...who knows what may be lying in wait beyond the gate. It may be a trap."

"I think not. The herald bears a peace banner, Mar. And I will have *Braccaro* with me. That ought to make them think twice."

"Yes, my lord...of...of course." Malaan drew back and made no further protest; the rest did not say a word. Braccaro made them uncomfortable, he knew. *And as well he should,* he thought.

Beyond the shade of the awning, the sun throbbed down upon him in blistering waves, unrelenting and still worsening, he had been told, with each new turn of the moon. Within the city there were sanctuaries against the heat, but even those could only offer so much respite. No doubt they were overcrowded and overwhelmed, harbouring the great masses of Lumos and many more who had fled here from afar. He could see signs of old refugee camps outside the walls, much as there had been outside Aram. They lay deserted, baking under sun and sand, and the dead were in great evidence too.

This is a graveyard, he thought, seeing the rags and rotting bones poking up from the dirt amid the broken shelters and tumbled lean-tos, the abandoned tarp tents blowing listlessly in the wind. The heat had claimed them, no doubt, and perhaps disease as well. The old and young were particularly at risk. *Poor souls. Did she not open the gates and let you in?* He laughed bitterly. The woman was weak, and not long for this world. She would be in there now, cowering. *I will make her kiss my boot,* he thought, *before I have Braccaro make her his meal.*

The giant sunwolf stalked along at his side, shaking the ground with his hulking tread. It had taken Elio Krator a bit of time to get used to his new form, he would admit. At first he had been horrorstruck to look upon him. The vast size. The twisted, muscular shoulders and hunched back. The unnatural, almost crooked proportions of the legs. The mane that had once been a great regal flow of golden hair was now a strange and fiery red, and the face was changed as well, turned savage and long and crazed, with fangs elongated and misshapen, jutting queerly from his mouth. Even his fur was different now, scaly and armoured, with tufts of gold and crimson hair splaying out like bristles from between the segments of plate.

It was the High Priest of Fire who had led Braccaro out from the deep mountain chamber where Eldur did his work. "Your new steed," he had said, grinning horribly. "How do you like him, my lord?"

Elio Krator had not managed to muster words. *Freak* came to mind. *Aberration.* "What have you done to him!" a part of him wanted to shout, and another part wanted to just turn and run, to wish he had never come, but he had. So he just stared, impassively, or so he had hoped, and nodded. "He is even better than I could have imagined."

The priest had laughed, a horrid echoing sound, full of malice and cruelty. He was a mimic of his master, and he spoke with his voice, a simple creature now filled with power. "He is nothing like you'd imagined," he had said, seeing straight through him. "You expected a larger version of Braccaro only. But here, you have a new breed. A sunwolf and a dragon, mixed and merged. Take heed, my lord, and watch him closely. He may yet continue to *change*."

He was nearing the herald now, a mere fifty paces away. Behind him the high walls soared, and archers peeked past the smooth rolling merlons that curved in the shape of half moons. The gates were still open, each door painted with celestial symbols, and the squares here in Lumos were not squares at all, but circles to honour the Mother of the Moon. The roads and streets too curved and arced and few but the main thoroughfares were straight. All was moon and sun and stars here, and the moon in particular was revered. The glass temples shone out with radiant light, and the great palace that sat at the very heart of the city was an orb of silvery stone, colossal in size and grandeur, with thousands of glass windows that peered out upon the world, gleaming as they caught the sunlight.

The herald's expression became visible as he drew near. Elio Krator smiled as he saw it…saw the disgust and horror in his eyes. "What…what is that *creature*?" he called out, cringing away and stepping back. "The *hellspawn* can come no closer. Keep it back, Lord Krator. *Keep it back*."

Good. They fear him, even on sight. He paused twenty paces from him and turned his head to the giant wolf-dragon. "Braccaro is my protector," he answered. "Consider him my white flag of parley."

"Bra…*Braccaro*?" The man was horrified. "You're to say that…that… that *thing* is your sunwolf?"

"Yes, though I understand your confusion. Braccaro has been through some…small changes of late." He put a hand to the giant wolf's hard scaly side, felt the hate and the heat running through him. The twin bulges that swelled either side of his back were pulsing, something moving beneath the plates of armour. That was odd, and not something he had yet seen. *Continue to change*, the priest has said.

The herald was gaping at the beast in dismay. "I will not parley with you until that *creature* is gone." He raised a hand. More men appeared between the flowing silver crenels, arrows knocked, crossbows cocked. Mounted scorpions were rotating on their turntables, loaded with long silver bolts, to aim down at them. "If that monster makes a move toward me…"

Krator's laughter cut him off. "A herald should be more composed, Mercalo." He smiled at the look on his face. "That is your name, is it not? Floris Mercalo. You were understudy to Herald Branis."

"I was. Now I am raised to Herald and Voice of the Empress in his place."

"Did you kill him to win that fine title of yours?"

Mercalo spluttered. "I would never…"

"What happened to him, then? He seemed in good health when I saw him at the warmoot."

"He was killed…by a mob." The herald glanced toward the ruin of a refugee camp. "He only ever wanted to help, to calm the people, but the heat…"

"A great shame." Elio Krator did not need to hear the rest; he could guess well enough what had happened. Branis came out to speak to the peasants with the empress's holy voice, and they turned on him. Very sad. "It can do strange things to people, this heat. A heat to drive one mad." He stepped toward him, waving for Braccaro to remain behind. The beast gave a consenting rumble, a much deeper sound than he used to make. *Even his voice has changed,* Krator thought. There was part dragon in that tongue now, but he understood it well enough.

The herald watched him warily. He looked terribly hot in those heavy ceremonial robes. "Feel free to take off a layer or two, Mercalo. She was cruel to make you wear all that."

"It is my honour to dress in this garb. The raiment of the heralds has a long-standing…"

"History. And not one I care to hear of again. Now speak. What does your empress bid you tell me?"

The man shifted his stance, affronted. "She is *your* empress as well, Lord Krator."

"No. She has never spoken for me, nor the many thousands at my back." He turned to present them, opening out a feathered arm, the legions drawn up from across the empire, by Palek and Zon and others besides, all in opposition to the woman's rule. "It is hot, I know, and this heat haze does cause a blur…but look hard and you will see them there, spread out across that plain."

"I see them," the man said. "I see a rebel faction, an insurgent army and no more. You made oaths, Lord Krator…"

"Then call me an oathbreaker, I will not weep. Your *terms.* Speak them."

"*Leave,*" the herald said. "Turn your host around and honour your…"

"Honour is dead, Floris. Strength is the only currency that matters now, and your empress is destitute, her coffers bare."

The man bristled at the insult. "She has riches enough, I assure you. And if you do not leave…"

"*I will not leave.* I have come a long way to be here, and won't be going anywhere without a crown. A crystal one, of the sparkly sort. It is owed to me."

"*Owed?*" The man almost laughed at him. "You are *Aramatian…* perhaps the Eagle Chair might once have been promised to you, but…"

"I will take that too. It will make a nice footstool." He smiled, rather enjoying this. For long years the rule of Aramatia had been his goal, with a greater one further in his future, but fate had shortened his course. He would see to Safina Nemati and Moonlord Hasham soon enough - *and Denlatis. Oh, Cliffario, I won't be forgetting you* - but for now his task was here.

The herald stared at him, incredulous. "This is sacrilege, Krator, even for you. And this wolf of yours. This...this monster. What you are doing is sinful, evil. You are dabbling in dark matters that…"

"Oh, I'm more than dabbling, Floris. I have made a deal with the devil, and there's no turning back now." He smiled, savouring the look of horror that paled the man's face. "Now, *my* terms. They are simple, easy enough to guess."

Herald Mercalo shook his head. Sweat was beading and falling down his forehead like rain. "She will not yield to you, Krator."

"Then her people will die. Every one of them. And her as well, most painfully."

The man was aghast. "You would speak of her death so flippantly? She is our holy empress, a pure vessel of light."

"No. She is just a woman, and a rather plain and uninteresting one at that." He was becoming weary of the man's empty piety. "Send for her," he said, more forcefully. "We can do this out here."

"Do this? You must be mad, Krator. She will never step foot beyond this gate with an enemy host at her door."

"I thought not." He did not imagine he would be invited in willingly either. "Then you give me no choice. Come sunset you can expect my return…along with a few of my friends." He flicked a hand behind him. "This host you see is but a portion of my strength. I have allies, *winged* allies, who will make quick work of your walls. You think it is hot *now*, Floris? Imagine how bad it will become when your city is aflame and all your glass temples are melting."

The man drew back. "You would *never*. Lumos is…"

"Dust. Or will be when I'm done." He looked at the fool as he would a bug at his feet. "It is her choice, Herald Mercalo. If I do not see her leave the gate by sunset, my hand will be forced." He let the threat settle for a second or two and then turned to walk away.

The man called him back. "A contest of champions," he blurted. "Choose your champion and she'll choose hers. The winner takes the city. The loser…"

"Yes, I know how it works." He was still half turned around, and his eyes were on Braccaro. *Hmmm*, he wondered. Thus far his new steed had not been tested, and the beast was desperate for a taste of blood, he knew. He smiled, seeing the wolf's eyes glow and light up, a mix of gold and crimson red. "So be it," he said, turning back to face him. "Return to your empress and choose your champion, Mercalo. We will reconvene here in an hour."

"We?" His eyes flittered to the beast at his back. "You mean to say…."

"Yes. I will stand for myself. Now choose well and choose wisely. I don't want to get dressed up for nothing."

He returned to his command shelter, where he found his minions eagerly awaiting him. It seemed Pal Palek did not think much of the plan. "A worthless risk, Elio," he said, in his gruff voice, once Krator had explained. "We don't even know who her champion is. Why would you put yourself in such a position?"

"My lord," said Mar Malaan. "There is a risk, I agree. And should you lose…"

"I don't intend to lose, Mar." His stink had only grown worse in the time he was gone. "Have my armour brought out and scrubbed down, and sharpen my weapons." It was unlikely he would be required to use them, but it paid to look the part, and his riveted, feather-shaped armour made for a striking sight.

"And if you win, do you truly think she will yield you the city?" Palek asked. "She's only doing this to buy time, Elio. Surely you can see…"

He waved him to silence. "We will attack at sunset regardless. I hate this city, and always have. I would see it brought to ruin."

"Along with all the world," hissed a voice.

Krator turned, seeing him. He had not realised the man was here, but this whispering priest had a way of creeping up on him. "Yes," he agreed, stiffly. "So you like to remind me, Val'kor."

The priest was an old and ugly man, cadaverous to look upon, pale-skinned and mad-eyed with spindly fingers with too-long nails and a twisting rope of red-and-white beard hanging from his jutting chin. The white was all his own, the red some sort of dye that he'd added to make himself look more menacing and peculiar. It was nothing like the great red horn that twisted from the High Priest's chin, no, but the effect was still unusual.

The old man curled his hands together. "It is *my* duty to remind you or *yours*, my good sunlord. Remember who you truly serve."

"I have not forgotten."

"Very good." The priest wore scarlet robes and a malevolent smile. "Then I will leave you to your preparations. My riders will be ready when you have need of them, Lord Krator." He bowed, smiling, and vanished as quickly as he'd appeared.

His departure left a sour feeling among the other men. "I do not like that creature," Pal Palek said, squinting as he left. "Bring the world to ruin, he says. No, this is not what I want. I like this world. It is all I know."

The man was a thunderous fool. This was the bargain, the deal that Elio Krator had made, and it would win him all he'd ever wanted. The others had flocked to his call. They had all seen Braccaro and all knew what he had done. What use in questioning it now? *If he continues to speak in this way, I will have to kill him,* the sunlord thought.

But he couldn't, not yet. Palek had the loyalty of many Piseki here, the same as Iru Zon with his Lumarans, and he needed them for now. "The new world will offer great opportunity as well," is all he said. "We can remake this empire as we please, my friend. When the dust of this war settles…"

"It won't settle," yawned Iru Zon. He was lounging in a chair eating a persimmon, his army of fanners hard at work. His eyes were deep purple, his hair bluish-black. Beardless, the hard planes of his face were clearly visible, and his smile was insolent. Krator hated him as much as he hated this city, perhaps even more. "You try rebuilding an empire when there are gods and titans running about." He bit into the fruit, chewing noisily. "Not so easy. Not so easy at all."

Elio Krator closed and opened a fist. "You have become a clairvoyant, Iru. I did not know."

"I have eyes, Elio, they're right here." He pointed, then shrugged. "And ears as well. They hear this priest talking about the end of the world and his fanatics all nod along. Dust, ash, cinder, smoke and fire. Those are the words they like to use."

"They're just words," Elio Krator said. "Do not let them unman you, Iru."

The man smiled at him. "Perhaps it is *you* who will be unmanned when the empress unveils her champion, Elio? You expect some armoured knight, yes? A famed paladin, perhaps a valiant Sunrider. No one to trouble you and your monster." He chuckled as he looked toward the city. "I think you will be surprised."

Krator did not deign to respond to that, lest he show concern. Yet Mar Malaan could not help himself. "To whom do you refer, my lord?" His fat face crinkled with worry. "You're not to say…"

"I *am* to say." There was a tone of mild triumph in the voice of Iru Zon. "There is a Moonrider within those walls, I do fear. He will not look kindly upon you or your *pet*, Elio."

A muscle rippled in the sunlord's jaw. "I was unaware of the presence of a moonbear here." He glanced away to the city. "Who? Ballantris and Tregardo are abroad."

"Ballantris, yes. But Tregardo has returned. It would seem that Empress Valura summoned him back to her side only a fortnight ago, my sources say."

"And you didn't think to mention it?"

"I did not expect you to agree to a contest of champions, Elio. Bullathor is a fearsome beast, we all know, but the priest's dragons would have taken care of him in battle. There are enough of them to over-whelm him, but single combat…well, that is different. There will be no one to help you should things go…wrong."

He could almost hear the moist sense of anticipation dripping from the man's mouth. *He wants me dead. He wants what I'm owed, and hopes to take it for himself.* Elio Krator would leave him sorely disappointed. He had asked for a test and he was to have one. *I will show them all what Braccaro can do.*

Away toward the city, the gates were groaning open. The sound rang out across the plains, the call for Elio Krator to come. It was too soon, far too soon. "I do believe Tregardo wishes to get this done," Iru Zon said, chuckling. "It's hardly been more than twenty minutes."

"You must make him wait," declared Pal Palek. "Only go when you are ready."

"I'm ready now." Elio Krator did not want to wait. "Mar, my armour." The fat sunrider quivered into motion, helping him dress, then fixed his feathered cloak. Its plumage was gold and silver and bronze, the colours of Aramatia, his armour gold and black for his house.

"My lord, must you do this?" Malaan fretted as he worked. "Bullathor and Tregardo make a brutal pair. Why not let another fight them in your place?"

Lord Elio Krator looked down at him, displeased. "And have them call me a coward? No. Braccaro matches Bullathor in size now. There is no creature in this land that can stop him." He would hear no more on it. "Go, and summon the men to watch. All of them. I want them to see."

He turned away. Braccaro was out beyond the shelter, panting feverishly beneath the blazing sun with a long forked serpent-like tongue. The giant wolf-dragon was already staring toward the gate, red-gold eyes alight with the promise of battle. When he saw Bullathor step out, he did not quell. The queer bulges on his back were moving. Puffs of smoke rose up through his teeth.

"Braccaro," the sunlord said. The monster turned to him, and a monster he was. *But mine. My monster.* "It is time." The beast went down onto his belly so that Elio could climb up the horns on his shoulder and mount up in his saddle, fixing himself into his harness. When Braccaro stood again the whole world rocked side to side and Elio's vantage grew high and higher still. Above his host he loomed. Calls were going out, shouted down the columns and through the ranks, as the men laboured through the heat to get a better view, spreading out across the dusty ridge. Krator's heart was thumping. He could see Bullathor stalking from side to side beyond the gate, Moonrider Tregardo tiny atop his back. *Do I look so small as well up here?* The moonbear paused, turning to face him, then stood suddenly onto his hind legs and gave out a thundering roar. Tregardo tore his blade from its sheath and raised it, bellowing, and beyond, in the city and upon the walls, Elio Krator could hear the cheering.

I will silence them, he thought, as he commanded Braccaro to advance. *I will silence them all.*

There was not much noise behind him. No more than a general hum of interest and some shouting here and there. He heard a few cries go out of 'Krator' and 'Aramatia' and even 'Braccaro'. One man with a foghorn of a voice was bellowing, 'Beast Braccaro! Beast Braccaro!' and he heard calls of '*firewolf*' too. But the chorus was not the same as in the city. *I am not loved,* he knew. *Not like Tregardo is.* It did not matter. *Fear is better than love,* he told himself. *And I will make them fear me.*

Braccaro's approach was slow and confident. Ahead, Bullathor slammed his forepaws back down to the ground, causing the hard dry earth to tremble and crack, then roared again, louder this time. His long white and silver fur was hardening, turning to crystal, impenetrable against all but the most powerful weapons. Though he could not see it from here, his claws would be extending, and his fangs as well. *I must be careful*, he told himself. A moonbear could bite through godsteel, all knew. *And a dragon's scale armour as well.*

The plains outside the city gate would be their battlefield. The sun would stand witness to one's fall. The land was broad and open, with no obstacles to trip or impede them beyond some patches of rough brown brush and a few scattered rocks and desiccated trees, their branches rattling softly in the hot wind. Bear and wolf came together fifty metres from the gate, standing thirty metres apart. One was white and silver, the other red and gold. Krator could feel the rage pulsing from his foe. Moonrider Tregardo's face was much as Herald Mercalo's had been, revolted by what he saw. He was a powerful man; oft as not Moonriders were. Big and bearded, he pointed his long curved blade at Krator and snorted in contempt. "You have found your courage at last, Krator," he mocked. "Where did you find this beautiful bear?"

The insult was cutting. For years men had whispered 'coward' behind Elio Krator's back for not emulating his Moonrider father and bonding a moonbear. Most who ever tried were slain, and often savagely, and only the bravest ever dared make the attempt. But it was more complicated than that. *I was an only child*, he thought, *my father's only son.* His own life he would have wagered happily, but the bloodline? No, that must be preserved, and his father demanded it was so.

He did not bother to explain that to the man. Why waste his breath when he was about to die? "I hear you returned only recently, Tregardo. Have you already lost your taste for war?"

"I like the taste well enough. Answering my empress's call, though? That is a sweeter savour."

He is trying to shame me. Elio Krator would have an end to this. "Shall we say the words?"

"I piss on your words, *craven*. And I'll piss on your corpse when we're done and have Bullathor do the same. We'll drown you in it." He laughed loudly. The sunlord could hear the scornful cheers ringing out across the battlements. "I hear that's Braccaro you're riding, somewhere inside that twisted freak. What you've done to him sickens me. Killing him will be a mercy."

Krator would hear no more from him. "I did not come here to trade taunts. If you don't honour the words of the contest, then…"

"You don't deserve to say the words, *traitor!*" And with that, the moonbear charged.

Krator had barely enough time to think, yet Braccaro was swift to action. In battle they had always fought with one mind, one purpose; now they were discordant, the link between them frayed. The giant fire-wolf sprung high at the moonbear's coming, and away to one side. Great chunks of soil and stone flew behind Bullathor's great clawed feet, and the hot dry dust was stirred up into a swirling cloud, half concealing them. The sunlord raised a hand to shield his mouth, but the dust had gotten in, and he was coughing, blinking, his body lurching side to side as

Braccaro swerved and snapped, ducking away from the moonbear's massive, swinging paws.

The world was a fog of noise and blurred movement. A hundred times he'd fought in battle atop Braccaro, but this was different, more thunderous and violent. Faintly he could hear cheering on the walls, men chanting for Bullathor and Tregardo and Lumara and Valura, yet mostly it was roars and the crash of rock, the bone-jarring thud of two giants clashing, and laughter, Moonrider Tregardo's trumpeting laughter as he exulted in the thrill of the fight.

"I see you, craven!" he was bellowing out. "I see you cowering atop your monster!"

Bullathor rushed through a drift of gritty mist, his huge head looming so close that Elio Krator could smell the reeking heat of his breath, see the infinite rage in his ice-blue eyes. His jaws snapped down at him, near-fatally close, and Krator felt all the hair on the back of his neck stand right up on end. For a moment the whole world seemed to stop…then in a great sudden *whoosh* Braccaro was springing away again, bounding beyond the bear's reach.

"A craven sits atop a craven! Fight us, freak, let me save you from this curse!"

Bullathor charged again, a whirlwind of fury and white-hot rage. Sand flew and billowed around them, spitting violently into Krator's eyes. Once more his sight was blinded. He could hear the monstrous bear approaching, and could do nothing to halt him, nothing to fight him. With another sudden and spine-snapping leap, Braccaro was retreating away once more. He seemed to have retained some of his nimbleness, even at his great weight, and was quicker than the bear and more agile. In a flash he was beyond Bullathor's swinging reach and the moonbear was bellowing, pawing wildly at the ground and bellowing pure white wrath.

So too his rider. "Is this how you would fight, Krator! You leap and run and fly in the face of us! You would try to tire us in this sun!"

It had not occurred to him, but perhaps that was Braccaro's plan? To tire the moonbear out? Sunwolves were more at home in the heat than their enormous ursine cousins. They loved the cool and silver glow of the moon. *But Braccaro, he is born of the sun and now…now there is fire in him too.*

"Fight us fair!" Tregardo roared again. "Stand and face us, coward!"

Krator smiled at him through the billowing brown dust. *Rage on*, he thought. *Let that red mist blind you.* "A clever warrior takes advantage of his conditions, Tregardo. You would scorn us for that?"

The Moonrider scowled. "A true warrior stands toe to toe. Do you think this heat will tire us? Bullathor can fight for hours like this. Hours! Show him, Bull!"

Another thunderous charge. Braccaro shifted once more in retreat, pouncing beyond a thrust of rock. It disintegrated as Bullathor slashed at it with a paw, raining stone across the plains. The moonbear reared up onto his hind legs, towering above them, roaring thunder. Elio Krator looked up as the great bear slammed his paws back down, but he met only rock. Braccaro was gone again, light on his feet for such a colossus, moving around the bear's back. Bullathor turned with him, but too late. Braccaro raised a front paw high and slashed down, raking a set of savage claws across the bear's hindquarters. There was the sound of crystal shattering, a wild bellow of anger, and Krator saw the blood. Bullathor had been cut.

"Your monster has claws, I see! But a scratch! A *scratch!*" Cheers echoed from the walls, Cheers for their city, cheers for their champion. "We are just getting warmed up, traitor. I will make this slow. A slow show for the glory of the empress!"

The man was boastful, a braggart, overconfident. *This is no true Moonrider,* Elio Krator thought. Oh, he *knew* Moonriders. He had lived through a great age of them in Aramatia, when Justo Nemati and Iziah Hasham and his own father Tullio Krator had reigned supreme. *What strength we had then, before the war. Before the Day of Death at the Burning Rock, when Justo took those wounds that would later kill him, and Hasham's bear Hothror died, and my father and Matharon were overwhelmed by a dozen Bladeborn Knights.* Only Agarosh the One-Eye lived through the war of those three famed bears, and yet even he was lost to his grief when Justo perished, returning to the mountain to live out his final years in silence and in solitude.

They were great men, all of them, men who won proud victories throughout the war. But Tregardo? Who was Tregardo against the likes of them? A true Moonrider did not boast. He spoke through his deeds, and what had *this* man achieved? *Nothing,* Elio Krator thought. Tregardo had only bonded his bear *after* the end of the war. He was young, no older than thirty, and what true battles had he fought? What threats had he faced?

Nothing like me, no. We are more than he is now. We are superior, different… evolved. A bark of laughter spilt from his lips as he realised the truth of it. "You're scared, Tregardo," he called. "You and Bullathor…both of you are scared."

"Scared?" the man roared back at him. "There is nothing a Moonrider fears! Fearless I went to the mountain that day, and fearless I returned with Bullathor bonded to me. You think this freak of yours unsettles me?"

"Scared," Elio Krator repeated, smiling. "You have no experience, Tregardo. But me? I have fought a hundred battles." It was so. A hundred battles during the war when Braccaro was just a wolf. Now he was more, so much more. He knew how to fight in a way Bullathor did not. Tregardo and his bear were green. *But we are dead-eyed killers,* Krator thought. *And he knows it now. He knows.*

The Moonrider hid in his boasts. "We will tear your creature limb from limb! When we catch you we will show you pain! A quick death for him, yes. Braccaro did not want this. Braccaro did not choose this. But you…Krator…*you* are the true monster. I will not kill you here, no. You'll be paraded through the city for the snake that you are. Humiliated. Shamed. *Tortured*, yes. I will make you wish you'd never been born."

Elio Krator yawned. "Empty threats, Tregardo. From an empty head. You never were the sharpest tool."

"A blunt tool, then! A blunt tool, I am! They kill just as well when you swing them!" Bullathor roared and charged, swinging his head side to side, shoulders bulging.

Krator smiled, watching. From the corner of his eyes, he could see that Braccaro's shoulders were bulging too, and the bulges were moving, rippling, *breaking*. The armoured plate split open with a sudden *hiss*, and smoke issued from the breaches, a strange steam of red and gold. Bullathor was thundering toward them, Tregardo standing tall in his saddle, his great curving khopesh sword raised to the sun in salute. A battlecry was pouring out through his lips. From the battlements the men were cheering.

But Braccaro did not move. There was a tension in him, a sudden grunt and rumble, and then from the widening breaches burst a pair of wings, unfurling and steaming, wide golden wings veined in red spreading to left and right. They flapped, stirring a dustcloud about them, one beat and two, three and four, five, six, harder and harder still. Tregardo shouted something out, but Bullathor rushed on, heedless. They surged through the cloud of spreading smoke, snapping and raging, but found no foe.

And in the air *above* them, Elio Krator laughed. *He is more,* he exulted, *so much more.* He laughed as Bullathor turned about in a circle to find them, and he laughed as Braccaro thumped his brand new wings and soared, and as the firewolf flew out across his army….as he saw the faces of the men below, of Iru Zon and Pal Palek and Mar Malaan and all the rest, saw their slack open jaws and wide staring eyes….and as he heard the stunned silence upon the battlements and the dying cheers for their champion, oh he laughed, he laughed like never before.

And in his head, a single thought.

Today I take what is rightfully mine.

23

___

Emeric

The sound of screaming awoke him.

It came from another room, the throat-shredding shriek of a man being tortured.

Emeric gasped and tried to sit up…only to remember he was strapped up against an old stone wall in a harness of ropes and rusted chains that rattled eerily in the dimness. He could see the outline of the door that led out of this dungeon, see movement passing, light flickering. A voice was pleading, begging for mercy. "No, no, please, no more. No, no…*noooo…*"

A wild cackle cut him off, deep and throaty, a demonic noise from another world. The sound made Emeric's blood run cold. He'd been dreaming…such a sweet perfect dream…and now he was here…back here in *her* lair…

"It's Willard," a dull voice said. Emeric turned his eyes to the side and saw him; Sir Ernold Esterling, chained up against a nearby wall as he was, no more than a shadow among shadows in the dark. "Poor lad. He's been in there a while."

There. The torture chamber. Emeric blinked and tried to recover his thoughts. The dark did strange things to him, and the foul sorceries in the air. He had no notion of how long he'd been strapped up here. Only that they'd *all* been here once; he and Ernold, Burk and Willard and Lambert and Torret, young Harey the Amadar squire. All but Raynald, who he'd not seen since the day the woman appeared… the beautiful woman who was not a woman at all, but a hag demon in human skin.

"How…how long was I out this time?" he asked. His voice was scratched and raw and dry, his head heavy, aching horribly.

"I couldn't say. I've been in and out myself."

Emeric swallowed to try to moisten his throat and tugged fruitlessly on his fetters. His bare feet dangled on the filthy stone floor, just enough for him to stand on his toes, his arms raised high above him, iron manacles bolted to the walls. He gave up his struggling as quickly as he started; he'd tried it before and the chains would not budge.

He scanned the room. Ernold was the only other shadow now. "Where's Lambert?" he rasped. The last time he'd been awake, the old man-at-arms was here with them.

"Dead," Esterling grunted. "That demon didn't bring him back this time. I'm guessing she's got all she could from him."

Emeric shuddered. *Blood*, he thought. He could feel the pricks and punctures in his back, feel the hard crusty bloodstains stained into his rags. *Varin blood sweetened by pain and fear.* Lambert was Bladeborn, the same as Willard and Ernold and Emeric. Those four had been kept alive for the hag's dark witchcraft, but there was only so much a man could take and Lambert had been old and grey, and his body must have finally given out. The others she'd had no use for. Torret, Burk, the Amadar boy…all had been taken and never returned, and no doubt they were dead as well. *Maybe they're the lucky ones*, Emeric reflected. *Their troubles are over, but ours…*

Willard was still shrieking hysterically in the next room. The sound was almost unbearable to listen to. Emeric grimaced against it, trying to shut it out, a part of him wishing he was still asleep, lost to the welcome refuge of his dreams.

Brewilla, he thought, remembering. He dreamed of her often here. They would wander through his estate beneath the warm spring sun, picking olives from the orchard and making love beneath the trees. In her arms he'd never felt such comfort. On his estate he'd never felt so whole. *We were to have a child*, he thought, his heart wrenching at the bitter memory. He had never told anyone, never spoken of it out loud, but in his dreams he would see his son be born and grow tall, see the future that fate had stolen from him. And there would always be a moment, a perfect pure moment, when he would lie with Brewilla and his son under the night sky, staring up at the stairs, speaking of brighter things. It seemed to Emeric that nothing could ever be better than that. Peace and plenty and a family to love. And just as that thought went through his head, he would awaken again into the fetid reek of this cell, and all thoughts of Brewilla would darken and spoil and he would see only *her*, the demon right there before him, the hideous witch grinning up at him through her soulless black-black eyes.

A high horrid shriek pierced the air, worse than all those that had gone before and suddenly Willard fell silent. A shiver went through Emeric Manfrey as he heard the hag muttering beyond the door in a low voice, shifting her sagging weight across the chamber to place some cruel tool on her table with a dull *clunk*. The sound of her ragged breathing made his skin crawl. His lips tore back in hate.

"We have to get out," he said in a harsh whisper. "We can't die here, Ernold. Not here." He looked over at his companion, at the shadow across the room. "Raynald may yet be alive. It's our duty to save him. *Your* duty as an Emerald Guard."

The man huffed listlessly. "I served that duty as well as I could. And it led us here. Raynald's dead, Emeric. We're *all* dead. It's just a matter of time."

"We don't know that," Emeric insisted. He would not let the knight give up. "Raynald may be in another cell…there are other cells down here." He could tell that from the sounds, the groaning of doors and low sinister muttering as the hag went about her work. "The prince's blood is richer than our own. If she's taking *ours*, then she's taking *his*. You know that as well as I do."

Even in the dark, Emeric could almost see the way the man cringed at that thought. This was his prince, the man he was sworn to protect by oath. The idea that he was being strung up and tortured and blooded as they were was like a stab of hot steel to his heart. "If that demon touches him…"

Good, he thought. *There's some fight in him still.* "We won't let her. The next time she comes…"

"*It,*" the knight cut in. "*It* comes. That creature's no woman, Emeric. It's a demon wife of Dhatar. A *stormhag,*" he spat.

"I know what it is. And I know it can be killed. When she comes…whether for you or me…if we can get our legs around her neck, then we might be able to…"

"To what? Break its neck? Strangle it. And what if we do? We'll still be trapped here."

I'm trying, damn you, Emeric thought. "Someone will come," he said. "Once she's dead her sorceries will clear. As soon as someone passes these woods…"

"That could be weeks from now. Or never. Without water we'd never survive that long."

"Then what do you suggest?"

"Mummery," he said. "We pretend to be unconscious when it comes for us. While it's strapping us down, snatch up one of its instruments and hack the bitch's head off. We'll see *it* bleed for once." His eyes gleamed balefully in the dimness.

He's got more hate in him now than fear, Emeric thought. It had not been so at first. Even the stoutest knight would fall to terror at first awakening in this dungeon. And the first time she came, showing her true self…the first time she cackled that demonic roar of hers and unhooked their chains and dragged them screaming into her torture chamber…oh, Emeric would forgive even Amron Daecar for begging for mercy then.

But time had toughened them, and their fear had dulled and hardened to hate. Perhaps that gave them a chance. Perhaps now they could think more clearly.

But he had his doubts, grave doubts about Ernold's plan. "She'll see straight through it," he said. "We should think of something else."

"There is nothing else. It comes for me again, I'm hanging my head and playing dead. That bitch is arrogant, Emeric. It'll never see me coming."

"And if she does?"

"Then so what? We're all going to die here anyway. Might as well go down swinging."

Emeric's lips twisted into a grimace. Would it work? Would anything work? His eyes moved through the dark of the room, searching for something, anything that might help them. The only light came from the thin gaps around the door, from the room where the hag did her work. He could see her shadow passing by, moving around the table where poor Willard was strapped down. The table was studded with a hundred little spikes and nails that would be embedded into the young man's back. The blood that leaked from him was collected into a vat and only the gods knew how many more of these rooms there were. She might be draining other Bladeborn even now for all he knew. There might be other hags out there, spread across a great underground network, all working toward some wicked end.

The shadow shambled past the door, muttering her inane babble. It was an ancient tongue Emeric did not know, some guttural language of the gods that had long since died, unknown to the mortal world. The stormhag was from that time. They were mages and witches, once wives of the battle god Dhatar, radiant in their brilliance and beauty and the envy of the other gods, the singers said. Yet when Dhatar died during the War of the Gods, overwhelmed by Agarath and his greatest captains, the radiance and beauty of the wives was stolen away, leaving them old and haggard and ugly, cursed to retreat to the edges of the world and hide from the sight of man. In that state they had festered, growing monstrous and cruel. Now they could only show their former beauty through magic and illusion, presenting themselves to weary travellers and wandering vagrants during storms to lure them back to their lairs.

There were new sounds now beyond the door. Straps being undone. A man awaking. "He's still alive," growled Sir Ernold Esterling. "I don't know whether to be happy or sad."

"Happy," Emeric said. "His troubles are over. That was his last time strapped to that bed."

The knight looked over at him, eyes shining in the dark. "Why do you say that?"

Emeric did not know. To cling to something, perhaps. To *make* himself believe it. "We're going to kill her," he declared, speaking now in a low voice. "Willard's not going back in that room, and neither are you or I. Hang your head like you said, Ernold. I'll do the same."

He frowned. "We're to play dead, then?"

"Unconscious. Make like we're still sleeping, dreaming those dreams she puts in our heads. Murmur and make pleasant noises if you must. It might be the only way."

"Then you're admitting my plan is better?"

Emeric almost laughed. How could the man compete at a time like this? "If I see a chance I may still try to strangle her. But you might be right…if no one comes by any time soon, we'll die of thirst chained to these walls." *Unless…*

Another thought came to him, sudden as a shooting star. *If I can get her to come over to me before she straps Will back up, maybe…maybe…*

He had no time to dwell on it. The old witch was muttering away, pulling Willard from the table, walking him toward the door. The bolts were drawn across with a rusted scrape, and the door flew open with a heavy iron groan. Light flooded inside, suddenly blinding. A pair of shadows stood at the threshold. One, a young man, barely able to stand, half the blood drained from his body. The other, bigger, a hunched hag of terrible power, thick at the gut and thin in the legs, great sagging breasts draped down to her waist. She wore nought but a breechclout, exposing the grotesqueness of her form.

Emeric saw that Ernold had hung his head, as agreed, but he had a different notion now.

"Hag," he said, loudly.

The creature stopped and looked at him. Her black eyes shone in the darkness. Behind her, her torture chamber was lit bright, fire blazing in braziers and hearths and from sconces on the walls. The sudden sensory change was another tool she used to disorient them and drive deeper into their fears. She was cruel, this hag, a master of malice. A bloody smile twisted on her lips. "Yeeees?"

"I want to know where my prince is," Emeric said. "I demand you tell me now."

"Demand." The hag tipped back her head and roared. Her face was a rotting white chaos of pits and scars and angry boils. Dried puss ran down from one horrid abscess and wild hair writhed like a thousand serpents from her head, stirring as though caught in a gale.

"Yes, demand," Emeric said, unbowed. "Where is he? Have you killed him? Tell me."

"Killed him," the creature said, suddenly innocent, suddenly quiet. Her voice went soft as a maiden's kiss and then just like that her face was beautiful again, as it had been the day she'd ensnared them. "No, oh no, I'd never kill him." She smiled sweetly. "I love him."

Emeric flinched at the word. The hag was toying with him, like a cat without a mouse. "Where is he?"

"*Here*," she said. "My love is here…with me." Her grin spread to the edges of her face, unnaturally wide, the beauty distorting and melting away to unveil the horror beneath. He had never seen such an unsettling sight.

"Let him go," he made himself say. He could feel his strength withering in the face of this evil. He must be strong. He must hold on. "Let him go and you'll be spared."

"Spared? *Spared*!" Her rotten laughter rang through the cell. "Spared by who? You?"

"They'll come for you. You kill a prince, and they'll not stop until you're dead."

"I'm not going to kill him," the hag said. She lowered her head; a swirl of blackness seemed to enshroud her, some demonic mist coming up from another world. She took a pace forward, letting Willard slump down to the ground. "I love him. He will return to me. He will, when he's ready."

He? Return? Emeric felt something darker at play here. "Who?" he asked. "Who will return?"

"*Him.* My love. He is my love. Always."

His chest clenched. "You mean...the blood, you're gathering it to..."

"*Silence*," the witch snapped. The word lashed at his ear like a whip. "*You* don't say his name. No man may say *his* name. He died for you...for all of you. He was the strongest, the bravest, the greatest of them all... and Vandar sent him out to die, to die so *you* could live!" Tears fell from her eyes, hissing and fizzing as they met the air and she screamed, suddenly, like a thousand wailing women all calling out at once. Emeric winced, trying to tuck his shoulders up against his ears. Willard was whimpering on the floor, curled up like a babe in the womb, hands clasped at the sides of his head. His back was stained and torn and scarred, the puncture wounds bleeding.

"Shut up! Just shut up!" Emeric cried. He could not take her earsplitting ululation any more. "Shut up!"

Silence returned in the blink of an eye. Just like that the hag went still. She stared at him, head cocked to one side, studying him. "You're braver than the rest. Defiant. Yes." She smiled at him. "That is your Manfrey blood."

He had not spoken of who he was. "You know me," he said. "You know my name?"

"I know you all." She moved, suddenly, lurching horribly toward him, and before he knew it she was right up in his face, head cocked and dead eyes widening. He recoiled, but there was nowhere to go. A hand reached out and cupped his cheek, long fingers and claws raking at his skin.

"You're strong," she whispered. "So strong, oh yes." A long black tongue extended from her mouth to lick at his chin, snaking along his jawline, back toward his lips, across his nose and cheeks...wet and rough at once, reeking of age and rot and death. She drew it back and tasted him, smiling. "I had thought the boy was best. That royal body...that royal flesh. What vessel could be better? But maybe... maybe..." She licked at him again; there was nothing he could do. Her tongue moved across the skin of his face, through his beard and down his neck. "Maybe a form like yours would suit him more. The other... he is just a boy, still young and soft...but you...you're harder, yes... stronger." She moved her tongue around her mouth, savouring the taste of him. "Yes, maybe you," she went on. "I could love you too, Emeric Manfrey. When his spirit fills you, I could love you too." She grinned horribly. "And I think...I think..." Her face changed, softening and darkening, the features shifting and suddenly he saw Brewilla before him, beautiful Brewilla, smiling her pure and perfect smile. "I think maybe you could love me too. Do you think you could? Could you love me, Emeric?"

Her voice was the same as the woman he had loved. But at the edges of it he could hear *her*, and he saw right through her mask.

He spat in her face.

"Demon!" he roared, and at once he was crunching at his core and lifting his legs, chains rattling as he wrapped them around the witch's neck, squeezing with all his strength.

The hag screamed in a deep foul voice. The sound of his chains clattered as she bucked, trying to escape him. Suddenly Sir Ernold was calling out loud and fierce, "Kill it, Emeric! Kill the bitch! Snap its neck! Kill it!" and Emeric heeded him, twisting his legs with all his strength… and he felt her neck go sideways, turning, felt the bone crack and snap… and his eyes widened in hope as Ernold screamed out, "Kill it! Yes, kill it!" in triumph.

But it was too easy. Much too easy.

Abruptly, *impossibly*, the neck cracked right back into place. The witch stood up straight before him, and on her face was a wide black smile, the flesh of her mouth stretching, broadening, lips thinning, curling. The mouth opened. Teeth jutted out from the top of her jaws, rows of them, sharp and small, brown and yellow and black. Laughter exploded, and then there was a surging sound, as the coming of a distant wave, and even before it came Emeric saw it, the black liquid bubbling and rising within, churning and spewing suddenly from her maw in a flood of bile and soil and crawling insects.

He turned his head from the splash, but the impact knocked his skull hard against the wall. His head fogged, but somehow he held on as she struggled to escape his grip, squeezing tighter with his thighs, trying to choke her. He could hear Ernold's voice across the cell. "Will, Willard… help him, Will! Damn you, help him! *Get up*, Will!"

Emeric could taste the putrid filth in his mouth, feel insects wriggling and crawling down his throat. He spluttered for air, spitting up, vomiting right back at her. "Die!" he bellowed, rasping. "Die!" The hag was laughing, even as the flood gushed out of her she was laughing. He squeezed as hard as he could and managed to drive a knee up into her chin. The jolt caused her head to snap back, the filth pouring up to the ceiling, splashing down in a wet black rain.

"Will…on your feet, Will. Yes, *yes*! Up Will, *up*!"

Through the black deluge Emeric glimpsed the man moving. He had found some strength, was rising to his feet, lurching and staggering back into the torture chamber. The hag's head spun all the way around like a nightmare, the skin twisting and rupturing sickeningly. Maggots crawled out from the broken putrid flesh. She tried to tug herself free of him, the flow of black vomit at last ceasing, but somehow Emeric held on. He could hear the clattering of tools, something falling to the floor. Then a moment later Willard was staggering back into the cell, propping himself up against the frame with his hand, breathing heavily. In his other he bore something, a long cleaver of some kind. Emeric saw the intense hate in his eyes, and the blazing fear. "Kill it, Willard," Ernold shouted. "Now! Now! Kill it!" Willard raised the cleaver and charged.

A shriek erupted from the lips of the hag that sounded something like panic. Her body was turned toward Emeric, her head twisted the other way. Her arms flailed wildly as they tried to swing at the onrushing man, but too late, and then Willard was there, hacking down at her. The cleaver bit into her shoulder where it met the neck, the flesh parting in an eruption of black blood and worms. The creature screamed and thrashed. Willard hauled back the hatchet, gouts of blood spraying, and swung again. The cut took her in the arm, through flesh and bone, detaching the limb. The howl she made was like nothing from this world. She twisted again, and Emeric's strength was spent. He could hold on no longer. The hag burst free.

Willard staggered back, slipping on blood and filth. Ernold Esterling was bellowing something Emeric could not make out. But Willard heard. He spun on the floor, scrambling over to the knight, the hatchet still in his grasp. The hag gave chase, a shambling freak, heavy breasts swaying side to side like a pendulum. Blood and worms were pouring from her arm.

Willard reached the knight and steadied himself, standing. He raised the cleaver and swung hard and high, hacking at Ernold's fetters. There was a flash of sparks and a sharp ring of steel, the sound of Ernold calling, "Again, Will! Again! Again!" Willard drew back, exhausted, aimed and struck. As he did so he slipped on the filth at his feet, his cut falling low. Ernold Esterling roared in agony.

And the hag was there. A clawed hand slapped down on Willard's shoulder and threw him bodily across the cell. The man stuck hard against the far wall, his right leg getting twisted and caught beneath him. Emeric heard the loud crack as his shin shattered, bone bursting out, white on red. Willard screamed, contorting in pain, shuddered and tried to stand. The hag lurched over, swung again to knock him down, her claws ripping through the flesh of his face. Willard hit the ground hard and went quiet. Then the hag started to gut him where he lay.

Emeric could barely watch. He struggled in his chains, screaming for her to stop as she tore Will open, entrails flying. She was savage, wild. "No…please…please, no…." Tears of hate and horror misted his eyes. Willard was dead and now they were too. They'd failed. *Gods forgive me, we failed.*

A figure moved past his eyes. A man in rags, broken chains at his wrists. There was blood all over him. He was missing half a hand.

In the other he had the cleaver. Willard must have dropped it when he was thrown across the cell. Quiet as a cat, he stalked her. Emeric watched with bated breath as Ernold approached and loomed behind her. The hag was still in a frenzy, stripping the meat from Willard's bones. She never saw or heard him coming.

Not until he said, "*Hag.*"

Then her head twisted right around, as it had before, and he buried the hatched right between her eyes with a soft wet crunch of blood and bone. The creature shuddered, jerking, but it wasn't enough. Her mouth opened wide and wider still and she rose, ragged red flesh hanging from her claws. "Die, demon!" Esterling roared. He ripped out the weapon and struck again…and again and again and again and again, hacking her head to a pulp, swinging through neck and breasts and belly all, screaming, "Die! Die! Die!" all the while.

Only when the witch was nought but a heap of bloody black mulch on the floor did he at last throw down the hatchet and drop to a knee, panting and shivering all over. He heaved, vomited, heaved again, drew several long deep breaths into his lungs then stood up and spat on her, and he spat on her again. "Bitch! You savage foul bitch!" He spat once more and kicked at the filth, unsteady on his feet. "Bitch! Monster! You demon whore!"

"Ernold, enough!" Emeric called.

The man turned to him, blinking. He was sprayed black from head to toe, blood pouring freely from his wounded hand. He'd lost his thumb and most of his fingers, his hand hacked through at the palm. Only his pinky finger remained, poking queerly from the ragged flesh.

"Your hand. We have to stop the bleeding. *Quickly*. Find the keys and unchain me. If you pass out first, we'll both be dead."

That got through to him. Ernold turned, wordless, and staggered away, returning a few moments later with his hand wrapped up in a bloody cloth and a ring of keys between his teeth. In his other hand he carried a wooden stool, which he set aside to step onto so he could undo Emeric's fetters. It took a little while working one-handed and the man cursed all the while, but eventually he got him free. Then they went through to the other room.

It was the last place the exile ever wanted to see again, but here he was. There were old bloodstains everywhere, on the walls and floor and the torture table, that most of all. Another table held a series of cutting and stabbing and probing instruments and the walls were draped with all manner of cruelties. It stank of terror and death.

Emeric set Ernold down on a stool and told him to hold the cloth hard at his wound, then stripped off a length of fabric from a bandage to make a tourniquet. Suturing the wound would be too challenging, he knew, so he needed to cauterise it. He found a flat blade and set it into the brazier until it was glowing hot. "This is going to hurt, but it must be done."

"Just do it. I've suffered worse."

"Bite down on this." Emeric gave him the wooden handle of an old knife to put between his teeth, then retrieved the blade and set it to the flesh. The stink of cooked meat rose at once up his nose and Ernold tensed and shuddered, crunching down on the wood. Tears leaked from his eyes, but somehow he stayed conscious, and when Emeric finally drew the blade away, he unleashed a terrible scream.

After that, the exile made a poultice from some of the hag's supplies and slathered it over the blackened flesh. He wrapped it all in bandaging. "At least it's not your sword hand, Ernold."

"Small mercies," the man managed, weakly.

The exile smiled. "Can you stand?"

"Stand? I'll fight if I must. Might be more of those hags lurking around here." He got to his feet, unsteady. Sweat was pouring from his brow, and he looked like he might collapse at any moment.

"Stay," Emeric said, easing him back down. "I'll go alone."

"Not on your life." The man stood again. "Just give me something for the pain. We'll find our things, find the prince, and then burn this whole place down. We can bury Will in the woods somewhere. Come, let's get on with it."

The dungeon was not as large as Emeric had feared. This was no great network of stormhag lairs, and they were not working together. Only the one, and she was dead. In a storeroom beside the torture chamber they found their armour and weapons…along with scores of other blades and spears, shields and axes, breastplates, gauntlets, pauldrons and helms, enough good godsteel to fit a full company of knights.

Esterling's face was twisted in pain and fury. "Dozens of men. Maybe even hundreds. All dead for that hag's mad scheme." He snorted as he looked at all the armour and weapons. "We should find Raynald first. We can dress after."

There were other cells in the dungeon. In some, skeletons hung down from chains in rags and in others were rotting corpses that gave off a foul ripe stink. It was too much for Ernold Esterling with his wounded hand, so Emeric told him to stand back in the corridor while he checked them. In one he found the others; grumpy old Burk, gap-toothed Torret, young Harey the Amadar squire. All had been killed days ago and the stench they made was overwhelming. Lambert was there as well, his body slung unceremoniously to the ground in a heap beside the others.

"You found them, then?" Ernold asked when he emerged. He could see it on Emeric's face. "All of them? Even the boy?"

"Even him."

The knight spat. "He deserved better than that, poor lad. They all did." He peered toward the cell with a snarl on his lips. "I suppose we'll have to bury them all. Gods, I could do without that, but what else is there? I won't leave any of them down here to rot."

Emeric sensed he'd have to take the brunt of that burden, wounded as Esterling was. "We'll see them properly laid to rest," he said, grimly. Then he gestured to a door at the dark end of the corridor. "There. It's the last place we haven't checked."

The door was iron, rusted and old, barred with a half dozen locks and chains. Emeric did not want to wait; he'd taken his dagger from the armoury, so cut down through them all in a single slice then put his shoulder to the door. It swung open with an echoing crash. The interior was dark as pitch and tasted of iron. There was a thick scent of sorcery in the air. "We need light," he said. "That torch, there. Grab it."

Ernold fetched it from its sconce and handed it to him. Emeric led them in, waving the light across the chamber. The space was large, the walls a queer metallic black and shaped like a dome with a low curved ceiling. War imagery flickered in the torchlight, worked in metal across every surface; scenes of battle and glory and death shimmering red and orange as the flame went by. At the heart of the room was a wide iron table. The prince lay upon it, naked, his ankles and wrists chained and fettered. Around him was a circle of large metal vats, each filled to the brim with Bladeborn blood.

"Gods above, there's so much of it." Ernold turned his eyes left and right, his butchered hand slung up against his chest. "There's blood enough for a thousand men here."

"Or ten men blooded a hundred times."

The knight snorted in disgust. "All that armour says otherwise. We've done a good thing here, Emeric, slaying that beast. No matter what happens in this war, that's something to be proud of."

Emeric struggled to feel pride here, in this foul place. Together they moved up through the vats and tubs to check to make sure the prince was breathing. Emeric put his ear to his mouth, then felt for a pulse. "His heartbeat is steady," he reported. He gave him a gentle shake. "Raynald, can you hear me? My prince, are you awake?" The boy gave no reaction. "He's out cold. The stormhag may have put him under with a potion."

"Or spell," grunted Esterling. "She might have had him under all this time." He nodded, as though that would be a good thing. "If we're lucky he won't remember any of this. We can be scarred by it, that's just fine. No sense in our prince sharing that burden."

Emeric nodded. A brief assessment of the prince revealed no further wounds, no pricks and cuts to his back or elsewhere on his flesh, no signs that he had been blooded. He ran fingers across the boy's gut, tracing the wound torn open by the dragon's tail, prodding gently at the flesh. "It looks well healed," he said. "How long do you think we've been down here?"

"Not long enough for that to have happened naturally," Esterling said. "The bitch must have healed him up to make him strong. All this blood…that was for sorcery, not sustenance. The hag was trying to raise Dhatar from the dead."

Emeric had figured that out as well. "She wanted to use his body as a vessel…"

"His, yes. Or *yours*." The knight looked over at him, his pale skin glistening in the torchlight. He gave a huff. "Well…maybe if we'd known what the hag was up to we might have let it happen. Would you give up your body for a battle god, Manfrey? All these pictures…" He thrust his chin toward them, across the walls and ceiling, "They're all Dhatar and his triumphs. All the great victories he won by the edge of his blade. He killed *gods*, you know. We could use someone like that right now, don't you think? Not even Drulgar would want to face *him*."

"There is no raising a god," Emeric said.

"You think? Tell that to Eldur."

"Eldur is no god." He was a lesser deity if anything, and long since made mortal when the true gods were gone. "No earthly body could sustain a god's spirit, Ernold. Not even a royal one like Raynald's."

"Well…none of that matters now." The knight looked close to passing out. He drew a deep breath and steadied himself against the table. "I need to leave this room," he murmured. "All the blood and smells. We should untie him. Quickly. Get him out of here…"

"You need to rest," the exile said. "I told you I'd do this alone."

"He's my prince. I need…need to…"

"To rest," Emeric insisted. "Go back to the armoury. I'll see to the prince myself and meet you there."

"Right." His breath was growing ragged. "Right, yes, I'll…I think I'll just…just…"

And he said no more.

Emeric saw it coming quickly enough and rushed around as the man collapsed, catching him before he might strike his head open. He checked his pulse and found it weak. The thrill was leaving him, and his blood loss had been great.

"Just don't die on me," Emeric said, hefting the man up onto his shoulder. He did not want to be left here all alone. He carried him through into the armoury, set him up against a wall, and returned to fetch the prince. After that he wiped himself down of all the black spew and soil that had erupted from the stormhag's guts and dressed in his plate, armouring himself from heel to neck and girding his waist in his trusty swordbelt, sheathed with the eagle-blade of Sir Oswald Manfrey on one hip and his common godsteel dagger on his right. He felt stronger at once, the touch of the metal driving away the worst of his fears. Then it was time to gather and bury the dead.

It was foul work. Willard in particular had been torn apart and fetching all the parts of him was grim. He carried the corpses up into the hag's woodland shack and heaped them outside in the rain. The forest was dark and gloomy and the wind was gusting and rattling at the branches. He chose a clearing nearby and began to dig, shovelling at the cold wet soil, grunting and heaving, grunting and heaving as he dug down deep past root and rock.

As he worked, he heard a great thunder somewhere off to the east, the sound of rock breaking and tumbling in the distance, and a faint high screech at the very far edge of hearing. He frowned and paused, a shiver moving up his spine, listening for more. But there was nothing. Just the falling rain and the keening wind and the rustling of the leaves in the trees. *Something awakes*, he thought, dourly. *Another ancient is stirring.*

He put it aside and kept on digging, grunting and heaving, grunting and heaving. It took him long hours, and by the time he was done a deep dark had fallen on the forest. The exile walked back to the shack and hauled the dead men over one by one, laying them gently in the grave side by side with their cloaks to cover their faces. "I'm sorry that happened to you," he said to them, sombre…though a part of him was thinking of someone else. "It was no way for good men to die."

And he was one of the best. Good, honest, true…

He saw to the burial alone, speaking rites to send them on their way. It ought to have been Sir Ernold Esterling - these were his men, after all, all but young Harey - yet his attempts to rouse him failed, so Emeric saw it done himself. After, he went back below and searched through the stormhag's stores for anything useful, finding ingredients and potions of a rare and arcane nature that he had never seen before.

Perhaps one might heal Ernold Esterling's hand or awaken the prince from his deep unbroken sleep, but if that were so, Emeric did not know which. The labels were written in words he did not understand, and the smells were queer to him too. Even the colours were strange, and the way the liquid swirled and moved in some of the vials made him think there was sorcery in their brewing. Unwilling to leave them, he decided to take all he could, packing up a pair of satchel bags he found in a dusty cupboard. In the woodland shack he unearthed cupboards of food as well; cheese, cured beef and salted pork, pots of nuts and sweet dried fruits, hard breads and sugary sweetbreads too. He sat for a short while, wondering if they were corrupted; just another of the stormhag's devious ploys. To bring men here and feed them, only to watch them fade into a deep and dreamless sleep, grinning that terrible grin as she slung them over her great hunched back and took them down to her lair.

He shivered to think of it. *It's over. Over.* He still felt tense and uneasy here, yet his hunger outweighed his fear. Tentatively, he tested the food, taking a strip of dried beef to chew on. When that did not send him to sleep, he cut a slice of cheese and ate it over a heel of bread. That too yielded no soporific effect, so he ate some more, and some more after that until his belly was full at last.

When he went back down to check on the others, Ernold was at last starting to come around. Emeric gave him a gentle nudge to rouse him, and confusedly the man stirred, groaning. "What…where…?"

"We're in the hag's dungeon, Ernold. Do you remember?"

"I…" His voice was thick with sleep and pain. He looked at his hand, bound and bloody, slung against his chest. A grimace crossed his face. "I…yes, I remember."

"The others are buried. I dug a grave and spoke the funeral rites. Can you stand?"

He nodded. "I lost a hand, not a foot."

Emeric helped him to his feet. The man looked utterly spent, his skin as pale as curdled milk and clammy to the touch. "There's food upstairs. You'd do well to eat something before we go." Emeric helped him into his armour, then led him up the stairs. "Here. Eat this while I dress the prince." He made him a plate of food and fetched some fresh rainwater from the well. When he came back he saw the knight frowning at something. "What is it?"

"I heard something. A neigh, I thought it was. Are there horses here?"

"Two."

"Truly? Bladeborn-bearers?"

"Yes." Emeric had found them earlier and tested them himself. "I suspect they once belonged to two unfortunate visitors." He thought of the skeletons and the corpses in the cells below. And one in particular. A ripple of grief went through him. "I doubt they'll be needing them now."

The man tore wearily at a bit of bread. He barely had the energy to chew. "That's good. I don't think I'd be able to help carry Raynald, not right now."

Or yourself. Ernold would be useless for a little while, Emeric suspected, and the days ahead would be telling. He had inspected the hatchet and seen spots of rust and old dried blood on the iron, and it was possible the wound would become infected. If it festered or he developed a bad blood fever, he could yet die of it. "We need to continue east," he said, as the other man ate. "I saw shadows out that way earlier, before it got too dark. Mountains, they looked like. Perhaps a few days walk away."

The knight chewed, swallowed. "Is there any wine here? For the pain, I mean."

"There's medicine for that."

"Is there? What vintage?" Esterling gave a tired smile and satisfied himself with a drink of water instead. "These mountains. The Hooded Hills, do you think?"

It was the only range high enough in these parts. "They must be. I say we ride there and find a way across. They're not high or hard to travel, I've heard. We'd have a better chance of finding a functioning town in the Lakelands."

"A town? You still think we need one? The prince is healed now, Emeric. We only need to wait for him to wake, and…"

"It's not just him. You may need specialist attention with your hand, and even if you don't, there's no saying when Raynald will awaken. It may require a mage or potion-master of some kind to revive him. Someone who understands spells and witchcraft. We'd have a better chance of that in a town or city."

The knight gave a nod and looked in no shape to debate it. The wind was gusting at the door and causing it to rattle in its frame and the rain was falling harder. "We can leave at first light, then. I don't fancy starting out in this weather."

Emeric nodded. "Fine," he said. "Eat and rest. I'll go see to the prince."

When morning came, it came wan and dull and the skies sat heavy with cloud. The rain still fell, though in a sprinkle only, and through the trees outside Emeric could see the shape of the Hooded Hills in the distance. He saddled and bridled the horses, packed their saddlebags with as much food and other supplies as they could carry, and lashed Prince Raynald Lukar to the back of the stronger of the pair, a large fine palfrey that looked very much a fit for a prince. Ernold took the other.

Before leaving, there was one last thing to be done. Emeric cut a flame with flint and blade and lit a torch. Then moving about the house, he set the flame to wall and door and roof, pressing up into the thatch to watch it catch and glow. Soaked with rain it took its time to spread, smouldering, smoking, but eventually the flames caught. They watched it go up, chugging out a black fume, and in the smoke Emeric imagined seeing the ghosts of the hag's victims escape, crying out in sweet relief as they rose and rippled away into the night…to pass at last into the Eternal Halls.

"Good riddance," Ernold Esterling said, scowling at the flames. He looked better after some food and rest; with luck no fever would take him. "I never asked. When you checked the dead in those cells, did you find that faithless Riverlander? What was his name? That great oaf who deserted us in that tower?"

"Ronson. No, I didn't find him."

"A shame. Hopefully those wolves got him instead. Or some other monster. That craven deserved to die for abandoning us."

Emeric gave no answer. He was tired, so very tired, and in mourning for a lost friend. Last night, as Ernold had slept, he had dug another grave near the others and marked it with a stone. His search of the cells had yielded a discovery he had seen no reason to speak of; a man he knew, a man he'd travelled with, and called friend, a man he had not seen since that day he left Jonik and the others at the Shadowfort, long months ago.

How he'd come to be here, Emeric could not say. *It was only the three of them left*, he thought. When Borrus came down the mountain with Torvyn and Mooton and the rest, Emeric had joined him and gone south. *I never returned to the Shadowfort, as I should have. It was Fhanrir's doing, some foul mage work.* That left only Jonik, Sir Gerrin and old Harden of the Ironmoors up there in the mountains. Emeric had not found the other two, *but Harden…poor Harden…*

"Well, are we going or not?"

He had been staring into the woods, toward the grave where the man was buried.

"You all right there, Manfrey? Don't tell me you sense some other menace out there?"

"No, nothing." *Just a ghost*, he thought. He took one last look toward the grave of his old friend, and continued into the east.

24

Pagaloth

Even on approach, the signs were not good.

From the air, he could see them, the mass graves dug outside the walls. The men who walked the battlements were cowled and cloaked and few, and half the tents and shelters inside the city were sunken and collapsed by the rain. Huge puddles riddled the stone squares, making pools among the rubble where some of the buildings had fallen, washing down the streets in restless grey rivers, and outside it was even worse. The coastal plains beyond King's Point had been a ravaged wasteland when Pagaloth left, torn and devastated and scorched by the Dread. Now it was a true quagmire, a sea of mud of filth, and the Steelrun River had grown so swollen as to burst its banks and flood the land.

"It's worse than you said it would be," shouted An'zon Graz, over the gusting wind. They were flying high, circling above the city just below the clouds, hair and cloaks rippling. No doubt they had been spotted by now. Pagaloth could see men gathering in the main ward within the River Gate, no more than specs from high up here. About the broken walls and towers some others were taking position with bow and spear, preparing to defend the city should they must.

"You said there were over ten thousand Vandarians here," Graz went on. "Where have they all gone? It looks half deserted."

Pagaloth did not have an answer for him. He looked down to where the prisoner encampment had been, just outside the eastern walls. That too was deserted, the ditches dug around the pens filled with dirty water, old shelters lying broken and ruined in the deep sticky mud. There was no one there that he could see. No prisoners. No guards. No one outside the walls at all. "The prisoners were being housed there," he called to Graz, pointing. "You can still see some of the debris. Hundreds of men and women from all across the south, there were."

"What happened to them?" Graz called out. "Were they killed, do you think?"

Pagaloth hoped not, though he could not rule it out given what he was seeing. Prisoners required food and food was scarce. "They may have been brought inside the walls," he said, scanning the city squares. "There, look…that could be them there." He pointed again. There appeared to be what looked like a camp within one of the southern squares, close down near the harbour. There were shelters sectioned off, tarps raised to keep off the worst of the rain, what appeared to be armed soldiers on guard and keeping watch.

They performed another high pass, scanning the lands below them, a vast mottle of black and brown and bleak greyish green; the city and coastland, the river and woods beyond, all pelted and battered by the relentless rains. The day was dark, much darker than it ought to be this early into the afternoon, the sky swamped and thick with swift-moving stormclouds that looked sure to unload another foul deluge at any moment. For the time being, the rain was light, no worse than a cold soft drizzle, but that looked set to change soon.

"So, where shall we land?" shouted Graz. "Do we drop right down into that square there? The one inside the gate?'

That would be unwise, though Pagaloth suspected the man knew that already. "We'll go there," he said, gesturing outside the walls. "Somewhere beyond the range of their defences."

"What? In that festering black bog? I'll spoil my pretty cape."

"They'll spoil more than that if we don't approach with caution." Pagaloth did not like the look of what he was seeing. The grim men on the walls, the abandoned and collapsed pavilions, the mass graves and headstones. There was a haunted air about the city, and he could see no sign of Amron Daecar either, no glowing white blade or swell of men following as the king made his way to the gate. Had he left? Returned to Varinar or someplace else? And if the king was gone, then surely Lythian had gone with him. He did not like the thought of that at all.

They stayed high in the sky until they were out of range, then glided down to land several hundred metres from the gate. They had little to worry about from ballistas and scorpions; those had been destroyed when the city was assaulted, and back then An'zon had been on the *other* side. He had fled during the battle, he'd said, following Garlath and Marak away east after the coming of the Dread.

"I'm starting to wish I'd not volunteered to come," he said, once the two dragons had landed in the mud. "Did you see that in the woods? There was something…something big, moving in there." He looked back; the Wandering Wood had its western border across the river, though there were still many hundreds of metres of mudland and floodplains between them.

"I don't see anything," Pagaloth said. "It's likely just the mists playing tricks on you."

Graz narrowed his eyes, still looking east. "Happy's not happy," he said. "You probably can't tell, but Lenny isn't happy either. There's something back there, I'm telling you."

"And it will stay there, I'm sure." Pagaloth was more concerned with what lay *ahead*. More men were appearing on the ramparts now, cloaked and hooded against the light falling rains, and the River Gate was groaning open. It looked like they'd worked to try to pile up rubble to seal the worst of the breaches in the walls, and there were some wooden towers erected to act as lookouts, he saw. Still, this was no true army, that was becoming clear, more a garrison left here to keep watch. He was eager to find out where the rest had gone. "We should leave the dragons here and go on foot. They'll never approach us otherwise."

"And leave us open to attack?"

"Yes. It's a risk we'll have to take." Sir Pagaloth Kadosk undid his straps and swung a leg over the saddle. He and Lendrathor had gotten along well these last few days, since the dragon gave him that cold wet dip in the lake, and the dragon lowered his wing so he could dismount more easily. Pagaloth thanked him for it, smiling up and resting a hand on his hard armoured neck. "I'd like you to stay here, with Hapthanor," he said. He had come to see that his choice of words was important. Demanding something of the dragon did not go down well, but when he asked nicely he seemed to be more amenable. "Is that OK with you?"

Lendrathor rumbled and lowered his head, to say yes. Then his eyes narrowed as they looked toward the gate, seeing the men appear from the broken city within, swirls of fiery breath rising and smoking through his teeth. The host came armoured, hands on the hilts of their blades and clutching at long tall spears, a strong cohort of knights and men-at-arms with a company of bowmen walking behind. None were mounted; the lands here were not suited for riding anymore.

"All will be well, Lendrathor," Pagaloth told the dragon, to calm him. "They mean us no harm. These are allies of ours now."

The dragon seemed unsure. Intelligent though the beasts were, they could not decipher complex political puzzles like this.

Pagaloth had been sure to bring a white flag with him as well, to better declare his peaceful intent. He withdrew it from his swordbelt, unrolled it and raised it high, then turned and began walking in the direction of the city.

An'zon Graz followed, though with a deal of reluctance. For all his pretensions of courage he was not a brave man, it seemed. And why should he be? He was neither a soldier nor a knight nor a true Fireborn rider, just a spoiled and flighty nobleman who had never expected to go to war. His first taste of battle had been King's Point, and look how that went. *I may have a craven on my hands,* Pagaloth thought. *He had best find his nerve and soon, else he won't make much of a wingrider.*

A white flag emerged from the opposing party as well, raised up high upon a pole to flap and snap in the gusty wind. That gave Pagaloth further comfort; the flag of peace and parley was a rule that most men followed, lest they be cursed to an afterlife of torment and pain. He could not see the king there, nor Lythian, which confirmed his fears. He was unable to find Sir Storos either, whom he'd travelled with for a long while and knew well, nor Sir Oswin Cole or any of his other men. Elyon Daecar was not present, nor was the scribe called Walter Selleck. He scanned for someone, anyone he knew, and then his eyes landed on the thin face of Rodmond Taynar, who had become lord of his house after his uncle's death. He wore blue and grey, and looked ragged and tired. The man beside him was familiar also.

"Those men," he said to Graz, who had caught up to him now. "In the front, wearing the armour."

"I see them."

"We can trust them. The one in blue is Lord Rodmond Taynar. The one with the silver and black cloak and pointed cap next to him is Sir Adam Thorley. He is the Commander of the Pointed Watch."

"The city guard?"

"Yes. Both are men of honour."

Graz was confused. "I thought House Taynar had another lord. This one looks young."

"They did. Lord Dalton, who was Rodmond's uncle. He perished during the battle." Pagaloth was certain he'd told the man that before.

Graz nodded; he seemed nervous. "Do either of them speak our tongue? This Lord Rodmond and…who was the other one again?"

"Sir Adam Thorley."

"Yes him. Do they speak Agarathi?"

Pagaloth did not know for sure, but had great cause to doubt it. Very few northmen spoke Agarathi well, and most did not speak it at all. "I only ever conversed with them in the common tongue of the north," he said. Pagaloth's grasp of the language was excellent, but An'zon? He looked over, wondering. In camp they only ever spoke in Agarathi, their own mother tongue, and did not dabble in other languages. "Do you speak it, An'zon? Their northern speech?"

"You mean that horrid butchery of words," he scoffed. "Well enough. I learned as a boy, though never liked it. My tutor was persistent, but I wasn't the easiest student, Pagaloth."

"Truly? I would never have guessed."

The man did not laugh for once. "I haven't tried to speak it in years. I'm not sure I'll be able to contribute."

Such a shame. Pagaloth was rather happy with this news, in truth. Graz would only intercede with useless quips and comments in any case, so it was probably all for the best. "Well, I'll be doing the talking anyway, so just listen and try to keep up."

He continued to hold up the white flag as they laboured through the bog, working around the worst of it where they could. It was hardly a straight path or dignified approach, and before too long the northern host stopped, only fifty or so metres from the city walls, to await them. Graz fretted again about them luring them into the range of their archers, but Pagaloth dismissed that fear. "We've been in range for a while, An'zon. If they wanted to shoot us they'd have done it already."

The man was slowing. "They look…*angry*, don't you think? Do you think they recognise me? And Hapthanor?" He glanced back at the drag-ons. "The white and green, it's striking. They may remember us from the battle. We may have killed some of their friends." He slowed further, then stopped. "Maybe I shouldn't be here. My presence may only cause problems."

"If it would make you feel more comfortable." Pagaloth stopped as well and waited. "It's your choice, An'zon."

The man took a long deep breath, blinking through the rain. The host did look angry…if you chose to see them that way. But that could be said for any company, heavily armed and armoured, staring menacingly from a distance. "I'm going to go," Graz said eventually. "I only came to make sure Lendrathor got you here, really. And I don't speak the tongue that well, so…" He nodded, making his decision. "If there's trouble I'll come with the dragons. Just…try not to be too long. Marak wants us back at camp by nightfall, remember."

"I remember, An'zon. I'll see you in a little while."

Graz nodded, turned, and marched very quickly away. Pagaloth continued on without him. Before long he could hear the muttering from the host ahead. There was a tension in the air, a stink of suspicion, but his heart said all would be well. *I have the white flag, and so do they. I can trust Lord Rodmond. He is a good young man.* When he got within twenty metres of the host the young lord broke out and began walking toward him. Sir Adam Thorley came as well, a pair of armoured guardsmen plodding to their left and right.

By then the voices of the men were audible. "It's that *dragonknight*," one was saying, "the one that went with Hadros." Another gave a shout of, "What happened to the others? Are they all dead?" while another barked, "How'd you get that dragon?" and a fourth said, "I know that one, the *green* one. He was here at the battle, the bastard killed Rodge…" and a big man bellowed out, "So whose side are you on *now*?" with a good deal of scorn. Then came the expected shouts of "Turncloak," and "Traitor," and only then did Sir Adam turn back and shout them to silence. Lord Rodmond was the first man to greet him.

"Sir Pagaloth," he said, pleasantly. "You'll excuse the men. We haven't had many visitors of late."

"They're all fair questions, Lord Taynar." *And accusations.* He had become a man of no nation now, he knew. *I'll be traitor and turncloak no matter where I go.* He gave a deep and deferential bow.

The lord smiled at the courtesy. "Can you answer them for us, sir?" The young lord had grown out a patchy beard, but it did little to hide his sunken cheeks or bony jaw. He looked pale, almost to the point of being sickly, and had bags beneath his eyes that aged him ten years.

"I would be happy to, my lord. So long as you answer mine."

"An exchange," Taynar said, nodding. His friendly manner helped put Pagaloth at ease, though many of the men were still squinting at him suspiciously, and others were creeping out from the city too, he saw, to see what the fuss was about. "That sounds fair, Sir Pagaloth. Let us go to my pavilion. We'll trade tidings there."

Pagaloth hesitated. "Would we not be able to talk here, my lord?"

"Your safety will be guaranteed, Sir Pagaloth," Sir Adam Thorley assured him. "You are Lord Lythian's sworn man still, are you not?"

"Yes. Until I should die or he release me from that oath." He frowned. "Did you say *lord*?"

"Now that would be cheating, Sir Pagaloth," said Lord Rodmond, with a smile. "We'll go to my tent first. Then we'll begin that exchange."

And so it was done. With a strong flanking guard under Sir Adam's command, the dragonknight was escorted into the city. He felt safe enough, though the cowled men on the walls and those lurking about the square did rather set him on edge. Through the ward tents and pavilions sat in soggy heaps of wood and waterlogged whaleskin. Some were still standing erect and in use; others leaning badly to one side or sagging in the middle, their flaps untied and billowing in the breeze, their interiors wet and abandoned. It looked like half of the lords and knights who'd raised their shelters in this square were no longer here, dead or left he could not say.

Amidst all that the young lord's pavilion was a palace. It was large and comfortable and pleasantly furnished. Braziers burned to keep it warm and there were rugs laid down on the floor. Tapestries bearing Taynar glories hung from the wall supports, helping to beat back the bitter cold, and a large desk was stacked with piles of leather-bound books on history and culture and art.

Lord Rodmond saw him looking and gave a modest laugh. "I'm lucky, Sir Pagaloth. Not everyone has such fine lodgings here as I do. I spend a great deal of my time reading, as you can see. There really isn't much else to do." He stepped to a drink counter. "There is even some wine left. Would you like some? Something to warm you on this cold dark day?"

Every day was cold and dark. "Thank you, my lord. But no. I would not want to deprive you."

"As you wish." Rodmond poured for himself and for Sir Adam. He handed the cup out and then sat down on a reinforced camp stool. "Adam, would you see that Sir Ralf is told of Sir Pagaloth's arrival? He will want to be here."

"Yes, my lord." Adam Thorley delivered the order to a guardsman outside and returned. The rain was starting to fall more heavily now, and the sound of distant thunder could be heard, a crackle and rumble at the edge of hearing.

Taynar gave a deep sigh. "It just won't stop," he lamented. "Sometimes we see a spec of blue through the clouds, but just as quickly it's gone. I can't recall the last time there was not at least a bit of drizzle in the air." He drank his wine. "Mostly it's heavy and stormy. We are drowned men here, Sir Pagaloth."

"I saw the tents," the dragonknight said. He waited to be invited to sit, and then sat. "Where has everyone gone?"

"Ah, now isn't that the question? We've suffered a spot of turbulence here, since you left. A lot of death and a lot of desertion. I'm ashamed to say my own people are largely at fault. Men mustered from Taynar lands."

"Kindrick," said Sir Adam Thorley bitterly. "Lord Kindrick was the worst. Did you ever meet him, Sir Pagaloth."

"Once, yes. I don't think he approved of me."

"Nor your kin," said Taynar. "Lord Kindrick caused a lot of bother here, with the prisoners. The Agarathi in particular. Put Lythian in a very difficult spot."

Lythian. Pagaloth was keen to unravel the mystery of his absence at once. *And what they'd said earlier....* "You called him 'lord' just now, Sir Adam. I only ever knew him as a captain and a knight."

"The title of 'lord' is granted to the First Blade of Vandar," Rodmond Taynar explained. "Lythian was raised to the post by the king, and granted the great honour of guarding the Sword of Varinar. It was the same day you departed, if I recall correctly. He must not have had a chance to tell you."

"No, he...he never said." Yet it made a great deal of sense, after Dalton Taynar had perished. Who better to wield the Sword of Varinar than the mighty and honourable Knight of the Vale? It made Pagaloth smile to think of it, his good friend and master raised so high after everything he had been through. "And this trouble with Lord Kindrick? This death and desertion..."

"Has been a terrible blight," sighed Rodmond, giving a weary shake of the head. "Lythian was put in charge of our forces when King Daecar went west. It started well enough...until Lythian brought the prisoners inside the walls. He was accused of being many things by Kindrick and his men and soon enough it came to violence. There was an attack on the Agarathi, and many were killed. Several Kindrick and Barrow soldiers were found to be the cause and strung up and hanged and it only got worse from there. At first a handful would desert each night, then a dozen, then a score, and before long hundreds were leaving. Lord Kindrick took off himself one night with some two hundred of his own men, and most of the rest have followed since. Sir Fitz Colloway was caught doing the same, and Lythian took off his head. That only inspired more desertion and infighting within our ranks."

He shook his head, and drank his wine. "There was a storm one night, a bad one. Hundreds fled, and dozens were killed. Sir Oswin...I know you knew him. He fell that night, along with many others. It was the same night Lythian was assaulted in his tent." He glanced at the Watch Commander. "The men Sir Adam posted to guard his door were slain, and Lythian...he..."

Pagaloth felt a stab in his chest. "Dead?" he asked, tensing.

"No," Lord Rodmond assured him at once. "No, he was struck down unconscious only, thank the gods, and was out for several days. There was no lasting damage." He looked to the flaps. "The Sword of Varinar was taken, Sir Pagaloth, by Brontus Oloran and some others. No doubt you heard of the man's obsessive longing for that blade. His petty complaints of how he was robbed of it? Well, the robbed has turned robber and Lord Lythian is out there now trying to track him down. He left some time ago, into the Wandering Wood. We believe Vilmar the Black went with him. He is no longer at his post."

"Post?"

"Yes. He was in put in charge of looking after the gruloks."

"*Gruloks*?" Pagaloth repeated. This was all very new to him. "You're to say there are *giants* living on your border?"

"A company of them, yes." Rodmond smiled. "I forget…you left here before they came. There are a fair few of them now."

It appeared An'zon had not been lying about seeing something in those woods. Pagaloth was slightly at a loss for words. "Are these giants restrained?" he asked.

That caused the young lord to laugh. "You see them up close and you'll realise the folly of that, sir. No, these creatures cannot be restrained. They are much too large and much too strong." He had a sip of wine, chuckling. "You're concerned about your dragons, I sense."

"The thought did cross my mind."

"Well you needn't worry. I daresay dragons move more quickly than gruloks, and there is quite some distance between where you landed and their camp." He smiled again, rather enjoying the look on Pagaloth's face. "They are not so primitive as you may think. They have a captain and a social hierarchy of sorts, a language of their own, and even make their own weapons. Some even speak a little of the common tongue, if you'd believe it. Though not well, it must be said. Only Vilmar was truly able to converse with them."

"And since he left?"

"Well, a few of us have gone out to see them. I went myself once, and Sir Adam has been as well. They take best to Sir Ralf, however. He visited them with Lythian once or twice and Hruum seems to like him."

"Hruum?"

"Their captain. He…"

They were interrupted by the return of the guard. "Sir Ralf of Rotting Bridge is here, my lord," he said, poking his head through the flaps.

"Ah. And right on time. Send him in, thank you."

The old knight entered, dripping wet from the rain. He was a very dignified man, upright in his posture despite his age, garbed in a beaten leather jerkin over a long shirt of godsteel mail, with a well-worn surcoat over the top, emblazoned on the chest with the broken bridge of his house. He saw Sir Pagaloth and smiled warmly. "The dragonknight returns a dragonrider, I am told. How can this be, Sir Pagaloth?"

"That is a long story, sir."

"And one it's time we hear," declared Rodmond Taynar. "A fair exchange, we did say." He stood and went to the drink's counter to pour Sir Ralf a drink and refill his own cup, though Sir Adam declined the invite for more. "Pagaloth, are you sure you won't have one?"

"I am sure, my lord."

"Very well then." The young lord passed the old knight his cup and then retook his seat. "So, Pagaloth. The floor is yours. Tell us of your time with the united company. Are they still out there gathering deserters?"

The dragonknight told his story. Of their early success and eventual failure, of the fire priest Ten'kin and the threat his kin posed. He saw old Ralf's brow tighten at that, as though he had something to say, but the man held his tongue. Pagaloth told them that most if not all of the company was likely dead, including their northern knights and men-at-arms. He told them how Sa'har had cut his own throat and how he had told Pagaloth to run, how he had been lost in the vastness of the forest for long days, hunted and tracked, before at last Ulrik Marak appeared to save him.

Rodmond blinked. "You're…you're to say Lord Marak is with us?" The youth's eyes were wide, mouth half open. "He…he no longer serves the Fire Father?"

"He serves the force of good, my lord, as he did before Eldur ensnared him. There are six of us in sum. Six riders and ten dragons."

"Ten?" Rodmond almost fell back off his chair. "Goodness. And they're all…these dragons, they are truly on *our* side."

"They oppose Eldur's plans," Pagaloth chose to say. "Others may too; we are still looking for more dragons and riders to join us." He saw something in Sir Ralf's eyes once more. "Rest assured our purpose here is aligned. Lord Marak is willing to combine our strength, and is waiting for my report." He paused. "I was hoping that King Daecar would be here. You said earlier he went west?"

Lord Rodmond had another swallow of wine. "We had word that the Twinfort was to come under attack. Great armadas heading for the Brindle Steppe and Green Harbour. The king took a host of our best men and marched to defend them. Reports have been thin on the ground since then, but we had a ship come in only days ago. One of Commodore Fairside's scouting vessels, I forget the name. *Kite* or *Swift* or some such. They told us that the port at Green Harbour was an ashen ruin, that they saw great plumes of smoke rising up from the Twinfort. Most likely it has fallen."

"You don't know for certain?"

"Certainty remains elusive, Pagaloth," said Sir Ralf. "No crows have come, no riders. Not from so far west, anyway."

"And elsewhere?"

"Well," said Lord Rodmond, "one man did come down from Crosswater, but only to say more refugees were fleeing from the Green-wood, making for the Vanguard and Varinar, and to tell us Lady

Brockenhurst and Lord Florian were doing well. Thin gruel I'm sure you'll agree?"

Sir Adam cleared his throat. "Sir Pagaloth, it seems your coming here is auspicious. You say you must report your tidings to our king. We wish to know what has befallen him. You have two dragons outside. Can you see where I'm going with this?"

It did not take much. "I would have to return to Lord Marak first, to seek permission to fly west. But I do not think he would stand in the way."

Rodmond Taynar clapped his thin hands together. "Well and good. Yes, this *is* good news. Perhaps we needn't rely on Elyon so much to bring us tidings anymore." He smiled. "Not to say your dragons are just over-sized crows, sir. No, not at all."

Pagaloth would have to choose his words with caution when he discussed this with Marak. The old dragonlord was nothing if not proud, and he would not want to be used to carry messages by these men. He paused a moment to think, digesting all he'd heard. This of Lythian was of paramount importance, that was clear, and perhaps he might be able to help in that as well. Oft as not the mists and fogs about the hills and valleys of the vast Wandering Wood made it hard to see much from the air, but that was not always the case. *Look for a glint of gold*, he thought. *If you see a fire burning below, swoop down and check who's there.* If he could find Brontus Oloran…find him and even kill him…well, he would prove himself a great help. *And I still have much to make up for.*

A rumble of thunder snapped him from his musings. The storm was growing closer, louder, and the dragons did not much like flying amidst thunder and lightning. He stood from his seat and straightened out his red cape. "I ought to be getting away," he said. "Before the weather worsens."

The others stood as well.

"I will report what we've discussed to Lord Marak. Expect my return soon." He gave a bow to Lord Taynar. When he turned toward the flaps he saw Ralf of Rotting Bridge looking at him.

"A word, Sir Pagaloth, before you go."

"Of course."

They stepped outside together. The rain was still washing down in black sheets and the clouds looked foul to the east. Sir Adam followed them out. He seemed to know what this was about. "You're to take him to the prisoner camp, Sir Ralf?"

The old man nodded.

"Then my guards will escort you. They will see you safely back to the gate when you're done, Sir Pagaloth." He gave the order, then dipped his chin and marched away.

Sir Ralf led Pagaloth south through the square. There was something sombre in the lines of his face. "I'm sure I missed much of what was said before I arrived, Sir Pagaloth. Pray tell, did you speak of the attack on the Agarathi?"

Pagaloth confirmed with a nod. "Lord Taynar said the culprits were caught and hanged."

"Some. Some others perished. And others were never caught at all, only to desert in the following days. Lord Kindrick was behind it all, we believe. Then he escaped as well, I'm sure you were told."

"With two hundred men, yes."

"Lythian would see them all dead," Ralf said, grimly. "He was growing dark here, Pagaloth. He spoke to me of his dreams. A harbinger of justice, dealing death on all deserters. A part of me does not want him to find the Sword of Varinar, lest it destroy him. Though I know it must be found."

They walked on for a time in silence, down waterlogged streets and past drowned and bedraggled men. More shelters built upon the ruins of the city looked abandoned. Pagaloth wondered how many men were left, but somehow he didn't have the heart to ask. *This city is cursed,* he thought. *The Dread has cast it in shadow.*

At last they wended down a street that opened into a large square. There was a broken statue at the centre, tarp shelters raised around it. To the left a set of stone steps led up to a temple of some kind, its broken entrance glowing with a blaze of firelight. Some guards were hunched here and there about the square on hunks of stone, or leaning on spears under whatever cover they could find. Each street in and out was being watched. The prisoners were much depleted from when Pagaloth had last seen them, the numbers of Agarathi in particular. They were being kept apart, the Agarathi and the men from the empire. The Agarathi were being guarded more strictly, that was clear.

"There are three men here I want you to speak with," Ralf told him. "Two you may already have met, from before you left. Another dragonknight like you called Sir Hahkesh, and a common soldier called Bah'run. They were both taken during the battle."

He had a faint recognition of the first name, but not the second.

"Were you told of Lythian's scheme to capture dragons, Pagaloth?"

He shook his head. "No, though he did make mention of it, before I left. He hoped to capture them to be bonded, by rogue riders."

"And here you return, a rogue rider yourself." There was something very sad in the old man's eyes. "Lythian's scheme ended only in failure. All involved are either dead or departed. Sir Oswin, Tucker and Marsh all fell the night of the mass breakout. Lythian himself is now gone, and Storos and Nathaniel as well. They followed him into the woods the morning after he left. Though whether they have caught up or not…" He shook his head.

"I will look for them," Pagaloth told him. "I will do what I can to help."

The knight smiled at him faithfully. "Perhaps Sir Hahkesh and Bah'run might help as well? They both volunteered for Lythian's scheme, but when it failed, they were brought back here. You have four dragons without riders, I understand. Perhaps these men will be of some use to you."

"I will take them with me," Pagaloth said. "So long as they are willing."

"They will be. I will have them prepared to leave."

Pagaloth looked into the square, toward the little camp of his kin. One man appeared to be separate from them, kept aside and watched over by a pair of tall guards. "And this third man?"

"You are looking at him. He…is different, Pagaloth. A man I have been watching for a while now. My suspicion was first raised the night of the disorder here. Lythian came to break up the violence, and during the fighting he told me he saw a man *smiling*, grinning at him through the bloodshed. The man had strange eyes, red-glazed he said. He had come alone, from the woods, only a few short days before, and been added in with the other deserters. A returned soldier from the battle, he claimed. Back then we had no cause to disbelieve him, yet now…"

"A fire priest," Pagaloth realised. "You think he was to blame for what happened?"

"In part. There is no doubt that the men we hanged were culpable as well. Weapons were stolen from the armoury, we discovered, and thrown down before the prisoners. They were urged to take up the weapons and fight…and when they did that gave Kindrick's men the pretext to kill them, and not just them, but others as well. Yet two things can be true at once, can they not? Our own men reported that the Agarathi were crazed and wild, biting and tearing at our soldiers during the fighting. And after what you said earlier of your own experience, of this Ten'kin and the others….well, I hope you might look into the eyes of this man and tell me if my suspicions are true."

Pagaloth was still looking at the man. "Lead the way, Sir Ralf."

He led him into the Agarathi pen, where the ragged broken prisoners and deserters were being kept. Beneath the tarp, the rain crashed down loudly. Mats and clumps of dirty straw and old clothes were laid out to make beds. Some were sleeping, others staring, vacant and half-starved. A few still had some life in them and were playing a game of dice.

And then there was *him*. The man Sir Ralf suspected. Pagaloth could feel his skin crawling even as he approached, feel the hair standing up on the back of his neck. There was a foul darkness about this man, and he need not look into his eyes to confirm it. He stopped a half dozen paces away and took Sir Ralf by the arm.

"Kill him, Ralf," he said, firmly. "Take him somewhere quiet…and *kill him.*"

25

Lythian

The entrance to the cave was tight.

Old scales littered the way, snagged and caught on the moss-covered rocks as the creature had come and gone. They were deep green and sometimes brown, the colour of the woodland. Their quarry was a master of disguise, Vilmar had told him. It had the ability to camouflage and blend into the world around it.

"I don't like this," Lythian said, as they watched from the branches of the oak. It was late morning and they'd been here all night. He was tired and grouchy, stiff and sore. His breath misted in the frigid air. "It's taking too damn long, Vilmar."

"Give it time."

"I've given it time."

"*More* time." The huntsman was watching the cave opening like a hawk, still as a hunk of weathered rock and he had not moved for hours. He was used to these long stakeouts in a way that the knight was not. "Patience. It's a virtue, they say."

"And a luxury," Lythian muttered. "Patience is not a currency I'm rich in right now." Every moment wasted here was a moment Brontus Oloran might be getting further away, and that thought was gnawing at him like a rat. But if they wanted to get access to Ramsey Stone, then they needed to first slay this monster. *If Stone knows where Oloran's gone, it'll make it all worthwhile*, Lythian told himself. He was hanging his hope on that.

Still, he wasn't enjoying it. There was a lack of certainty here that vexed him. "If I linger any longer in this damnable tree I'll start growing bark," he complained. "Another hour. Another hour and I'm going to have to go in there to find it."

Vilmar shook his head. "That would be unwise. There's a rule we huntsmen live by, Lindar. Never fight a beast in its lair if you can avoid it."

"We can't avoid it. It isn't coming out. If we go in there together…"

"Then we might die in there together. It'll be tar-black in that cave, and not even my eyes will pierce that dark. I prefer to stalk things I can see. The lure will work. Just give it time."

The lure in question was a juicy haunch of mutton, lying on top of a hempen rope net that they'd scattered with leaves to hide it. As soon as the *magradile* crept out from its lair, the net was rigged to close and trap it. That was the theory anyway. A simple trap and one Vilmar had used a thousand times before, though never with this particular prey.

This nightmare, more like, Lythian thought, recalling the huntsman's description. The magradile was reptilian, the size of a small flightless dragon, a spine-chilling monster that half slithered and half walked. It had a lizard-like face, a long licking tongue, inward curving arms that dragged along a thick scaly body, narrowing as it went toward a long thin serpentine tail. On the tip of the tail was a deadly spine, glistening at the tip with poison, and beneath the body were a dozen smaller sets of legs that would skitter its bulk along like a centipede. The pig farmer had said only bits and pieces of that, but Vilmar had not taken long to realise what they were dealing with. He'd supplied the rest of the detail and Lythian's blood had run ice cold. He had no idea such a creature existed, and this one Vilmar had encountered only once before during a ranging into the Darkwood several decades ago. An especially rare monster, and one of Agarath's making, he had failed in his hunt back then and it had been high on his hit-list ever since. When the pig farmer had described it, he'd all but licked his lips. "Finally," he'd said, with a big wolfish grin. "Always wanted another bite at that cherry."

But that bite was not forthcoming. Another hour went by, and another after that. By midafternoon the magradile still hadn't stirred and Lythian's patience was running parchment-thin. "If it's not here by nightfall, we return to the village," he said. "I'll speak to Gertner, try to reason with him that we tried. That should be enough for them to hand Stone over to me."

"It won't. Not without a magradile head. That pig farmer's a stubborn bastard."

"Then we'll track some other beast and pass it off as a magradile instead. Who are they to know? They only ever got glimpses of it, and mostly in the dark."

Vilmar's mouth narrowed as he considered it. "Might work. But that'd take finding another monster, tracking it, slaying it, and it'd have to be big enough to make the ruse work. Be quicker just waiting for this one to slither out. And you'd be risking that precious honour of yours too."

"It isn't so precious as it was."

"Aye. We all have our breaking points. When was yours?"

Lythian could think of half a dozen occasions over the last year or two. He'd been through a lot but didn't want to talk about it. "It's been a slow process," is all he said. "Not all rocks crack with a single swing of the hammer." He peered into the huntsman's deep dark eyes. "You never told me about your father. How you killed him. And when."

"Didn't I?"

"No."

"Then perhaps I don't want you to know. There's a darkness to kin-killing, even when they deserve it. That one I keep locked down deep. Best it doesn't see the light."

Lythian understood. All men had their demons and not all were for sharing. The gods knew he'd tried to keep his part in Eldur's rise from the ears of others. *And I failed in that as well,* he thought.

The wait went on. When the clouds thickened and a heavy down-pour fell, the woods grew dark and murky, as though dusk had come too soon. But Vilmar said it would not last. He had sniffed the air and sucked his finger and his forecast was right again. The rain waned. Some sunlight even pierced the clouds, an event rare as a blue rose and as welcome as the warmth of dawn. It shone down in glorious shards, spearing through the trees, and lit up the clearing outside of the cave. Lythian smiled to see it. "I never thought I'd take sunlight for granted."

"We take everything for granted," Vilmar growled. "Only when something's taken away do we realise what we've lost." He shifted in his stance for the first time in hours, sitting back against the thick trunk of the tree. "I'm old," he said, to Lythian's bemused look. "Once I could hold the same posture for days at a time. Guess I took that for granted too. My youth. Now it's the winter of my years and these hunts are getting harder." He clenched his massive bearded jaw. "This beast is trying me. Mocking me. It should have awoken by now. It's been days since it ate, they said."

That's what the old pig farmer Gertner had told them. The last attack had been five days ago and that was long enough for the magradile to rest and digest and come looking for more. Unless it had eaten something else, of course. "It's a big buffet out here, Vilmar," Lythian offered, looking out across the woods. "That village is just one plate on the table. It may have found some other prey."

The man grunted agreement. "Aye. Or else it's got a stockpile down there by now." He gave his thicket of beard a scratch. "Ancient hunter wrote about that. Maglor Monster-Killer they called him. Lived two thousand years ago, back when there were more monsters roaming about. Lucky bugger, I've always thought. I have to go deep into places men don't dare tread to find my prey, but not him. Vandar was still wild back then, leastways compared to now…"

"Now? Every ancient creature is crawling back into the realm, Vilmar. You have it better than Maglor ever did."

The huntsman glared at him. "You think? I've spent six decades stalking the wilds. A few good months doesn't change that. And what have I got to show for it anyhow? I've been sitting with the gruloks most of that time."

The man could complain with the very best of them when he

wanted. Lythian didn't care to hear his sour laments. "You were saying about Maglor finding a stockpile?"

The huntsman nodded. "Aye. He killed a magradile once. Tracked it, slew it, then entered its lair. Found dozens of bodies down there, both dead and alive. Claimed the creature was filling its larder up for winter."

Lythian's brow furrowed. "Why haven't you mentioned this before? Some of the villagers might still be alive down there."

"Doubt it. No one since Maglor has seen such a thing. That claim is disputed."

Still…Lythian would rather *not* have heard that. If there were innocents trapped alive in that cave, how could he not try to save them? "We need to act, Vilmar. Gertner said a child had been taken. A boy of eight. If he's still alive…"

"He's not."

"He might be. Some women have been taken too." Lythian's sense of honour was less concerned about the men. He looked down at the cave mouth, a tunnel only about five feet wide and four feet high. When first seeing it he'd wondered how such a large creature could get inside, but the magradile could squeeze through tight spaces Vilmar said. That only made it all the more disturbing. They could not say with any certainty what lay beyond that tunnel, whether it was a single open chamber, a series of smaller caves and passages, or a much larger system of caverns and shafts that went deep into the bowels of the earth. Any exploration was too risky and in that Vilmar remained adamant.

"Live prey," Lythian said, almost blurting it out. The thought came to him suddenly. "Might live prey lure it out?"

The huntsman looked at him. "You want to go down there and make some noise, be my guest. But it won't make a blind bit of difference. It'll come when it comes and not before."

It wasn't good enough. Not nearly good enough. "I have my full plate armour. My night-vision is excellent. I've fought and helped kill *dragons* before, Vilmar. Why should I fear a magradile?"

"I've told you why," the man said darkly. "And I don't care to repeat myself."

He didn't need to. Lythian remembered what he'd said. The tail-spine could paralyse a man with a single prick and it was strong enough to puncture armour if the strike was right. The creature had glands in his jaws that shot venom too. If one drop of that got on his skin the result would be the same. He'd go stiff as a statue and it would eat him slow. But Lythian had another end in mind. An end where he crept right up to the sleeping beast, lopped off its head, saved whoever needed saving down there and then strode on back to the village in triumph. He much preferred that version.

"Are you coming with me or not?"

When the huntsman gave no answer, Lythian started down the tree, clambering from branch to branch. Somehow he knew the man's pride would stir him to action and so it transpired. By the time Lythian's boots hit the sodden ground, Vilmar was scaling the branches just behind him. He landed as lightly as ever, barely making a sound. "You're a bastard, Lindar. And you wonder why I hunt alone?"

Lythian smiled. He felt a great deal better with the big huntsman at his side. "So how are we doing this?"

"My way," Vilmar said. He looked at the mouth of the cave, displeased. "We'll go in quiet and slow, wait for our eyes to adjust. Not a sound, do you hear me? It'll be sleeping somewhere, camouflaged against the rock. Even if there's light in there, we won't be able to see it until it moves. Magradile's not a scent I know well, so might take me a while to detect it. I'll have to sift through others, but once I have him..." He nodded, convincing himself. "If we can get close enough to strike this could go easy. But if he wakes before we reach him... it'll go wrong real fast." He studied Lythian's golden eyes a moment. "You sure you want to do this? We die, and it's done, you said. You think long and hard about what we're doing here. I can still find Oloran's trail again. We've lost a bit of ground, aye, but that's nothing we can't make up. And Stone...he may have nothing to tell us. You're wagering a lot on that traitor."

"It's not just about him." Lythian had reflected on what the pig farmer had said about honour, about the duties of a knight. He had always lived by those oaths and those codes, and here was a desperate village asking for help. That there might be innocent people trapped in there only made the risk more worthwhile. He had lost a lot of who he was of late. He had been drowning in the darkness back in King's Point but here he could do something good. However small, however insignificant, he knew it was the right thing to do.

He did not say any of that, and didn't need to. Somehow he sensed Vilmar knew.

"Very well," the big hunter said. "But if I hear anything out of the ordinary, smell anything I don't like, you do as I say, understand? I think that thing's creeping toward us in the dark, and I say run, you run. Yes?"

"I'll do as you say, Vilmar," Lythian told him. "On my honour as a knight."

The huntsman led the way. As they crossed the glade and crept around the concealed net, the last rays of sunlight withered and died. The world darkened, the clouds closing back in. It was a bitter omen, but neither man gave it voice. "No talking from here," Vilmar said. "Sound vibrates and the magradile will feel it. Same as our footfall." He looked him up and down. "You're light-footed as knights go, but in that armour...one heavy tread and you'll have that cave ringing like a bell. It'll be on us before we know it. So watch your step and tread softly. The boots will help."

Lythian wore leather boots over his sabatons and leather gloves over his gauntlets. The rest of his plate was hidden beneath his cloak and he kept his helm at his belt. He reached for it, fixing it to his gorget, completing the set as though ready for battle. Then he pulled up his hood for good measure, to help muffle any sound should he scrape his head.

Vilmar looked at him with only a mild amount of disdain. "Not your typical hunting garb, but it'll serve." He looked to the cave mouth. "We'll have to walk in a crouch. Breathe deep and slow, keep your heart rate steady. If you have to sneeze or cough, don't. It's got sensitive hearing and will rouse to anything unusual." The hunter drew his cloak tight about himself, fastening the buckles and straps. His great beard was almost like armour in itself. Over his head he pulled his hood, until nothing could be seen of him but a slit of skin about his dark eyes. Then he nodded and said, "Let's go."

And into the tunnel they went.

The dark swallowed them almost at once. Crouching, Vilmar moved forward, slow and silent, and Lythian followed his step. The man became a burly shadow within ten paces, bordered by the thick dark beyond him. Lythian could hear the air moving further down the tunnel, widening and opening out into a broader space. The floor was smoother than he'd expected. He ran a gloved hand gently along the wall and found the same was true. *The magradile,* he thought. It had smoothed the tunnel out as it came and went.

Blood. He could smell blood in the air, the tang of iron on his tongue. There were stains on the walls, darker patches where the creature's prey had been dragged inside. Other smells festered. It stank of damp and rot, of old leaves and flesh, the musty stink of wet wool from the poor souls taken into this hell. Rainwater dripped from the ceiling.

The going was slow. After some twenty-five feet, the tunnel opened into a much larger cave. Vilmar the Black stood to his full height. Lythian came through behind him, fingers wrapped about his sheathed dagger, his sight improving all the while. He turned his eyes around. The light was thin, pitch black to most, but to the Knight of the Vale the walls were visible. The chamber was large, shaped almost like an oval, the size of a middling feast hall. At the rear a soft glow of light spilled down from another passageway. *Another way out,* Lythian thought. He could see further caverns branching to his left, but the right wall was solid rock, draped in a coat of moss. It did not seem to go deeper, so far as he could make out. He turned to Vilmar the Black. The man's eyes were wide, drinking in the light, nostrils flared, mouth open. He was *tasting* the air, Lythian knew. He waited until he was done.

Then the huntsman turned to him and leaned in. His voice was a whisper of a whisper in his ear, soft as a butterfly's wing. "It's here," he said, words to send a shiver down Lythian's spine. "Rear of the main cave somewhere. I won't know until I get closer."

Lythian nodded to show he understood.

Vilmar went on. "Follow behind me. Step where I step. How are your eyes? Can you see? Nod if you can see."

Lythian nodded.

"Good. Perhaps we'll make a hunter of you yet." A glint of a smile in the dark. "Slow your heart rate, boy. I can hear it thumping."

Lythian drew a long breath to try to still it. He leaned forward and Vilmar turned his head. "I can hear someone in here. Those other caverns, to the left."

The hunter nodded. He knew. Into Lythian's ear he whispered, "After. We'll see to them after."

Them? Was there more than one?

"We kill the beast first. Walk where I tread." He drew away, eyes glistening with the thrill of the hunt, and turned to face into the cavern. Little by little the light was improving, the shape of the walls and floor becoming clearer. Moisture gleamed on the rain-soaked rock, patches of lichen spread palely across the stone. Vilmar the Black took a moment to calculate his course; after the smooth rock of the tunnel, the floor here was more rough and uneven, jutting with growths and outcrops large and small. Stalagmites rose up from the floor like fangs. On the ceiling their stalactite twins hung down, rainwater drooling like saliva from their tips. The cave was like some giant maw ready to crush down and devour them.

Vilmar set his route and stepped forward. Past the tunnel the ground sloped down. Each step was tested to ensure the rock would hold. One trickling pebble or crack of stone might awaken their quarry early. Lythian watched, breathing slow and deep, stepping where Vilmar stepped. His heart was hammering at his ribs, *thump thump thump*, beating loudly in his ear. *Calm. Breathe. Settle*, he thought. *Vilmar knows what he's doing. He's done this a thousand times before.*

They reached the bottom of the cave and stopped. All was silent but for the dripping of rainwater, the wind outside, the faint murmuring that echoed from the caverns to their left.

The huntsman's head turned slowly, left to right and right to left, searching. He drew out his hunting knife without a scrape or sound, and Lythian did the same. Slowly his dagger was withdrawn, its mists rising, swirling into the darkness. For a long while they stood, smelling, listening, looking. Then Vilmar stepped on, passing around a spear of rock and into the field of stalagmites. Some were large enough to soar over their heads, thick and craggy at the base. With each step more emerged from the darkness as it thickened and deepened, pressing in from all sides as though the whole interior of the cave was closing.

Calm. Breath. Settle, Lythian thought. He blinked, clutching hard at his dagger, looking to his left and right for movement. A soft tinkling sound rattled behind him and he turned on the spot, but it was nothing…just a fragment of rock coming loose from the wall. When he turned back Vilmar was there, staring right at him, a hulking shadow in the pitch of night. The huntsman met his eyes and then raised a finger, pointing to the rear left of the cave. Lythian looked, saw nothing. He shook his head. "I don't see anything," he mouthed.

"Look harder." Vilmar the Black pointed again. "*There.*"

Lythian followed the line of his finger, straining to see something in the dim strangled light of the cave. Some thirty paces away from them, past more stalagmites and spurs of jagged rock was a larger outcrop rising up from the floor. At first glance it appeared to be no more than that, but then all of a sudden he saw it; the faint shift of movement as something stirred. Folds and ripples of shadow in the dark, a seamless blend of beast and rock as it lay camouflaged upon the stone. The magradile was sleeping atop the shelf. He could see it now, see its chest going up and down. He turned to Vilmar and nodded. "I see."

The man leaned in. "We'll have to be quick," he breathed in his ear. "Come at it from two sides. We'll split when we get nearer the shelf. The closer we get, the clearer it will be. Then we move as one to kill it."

It sounded like a good plan to Lythian.

Step by step they crept toward their quarry, silent as its impending death. They had it in sight now, and that was half the challenge. If it moved they would see it, and could rush in and strike.

Ten paces from the creature Lythian sensed movement to his left.

He froze, eyes swivelling to the side. A large shadow slid out from another cave mouth twenty feet away, dragged on by a pair of inward-curving arms. Behind came the sound of skittering feet, a long tail slithering, a low menacing *hiss*. Lythian's heart leapt into his throat. "Vilmar," he whispered, voice choked in fear. "There's…there's another…"

"Kill it," the huntsman rasped. "The other one's mine. Go!"

All time for caution was ended. In an instant Vilmar was gone, rushing forth toward the shelf, leaping and clambering to slay the sleeping beast. The other one was stalking forward from the left, hissing as it came.

Lythian reached for his longsword and drew it from its sheath, shifting his feet to Strikeform. He saw the maw opening, widening unnaturally like a flower in bloom, webbed skin spreading, thin and translucent. *The glands,* he thought, turning his head just in time as the creature spat out a fine mist of venom, coating his cloak and hood, fizzing and burning. The knight shut his eyes tight, drew a step back, then threw up his cloak and stood to his full height.

The magradile was looming right ahead of him, a great strange shadow pressing up from the floor on its slithery bulk, rearing and rising fifteen feet high.

Lythian looked up at it and cast aside his fear. It was the dark he had feared, the creeping dread of the cave, the unseen terror lurking somewhere beyond his sight. But he could see it now. It was right there before him. A shape and shadow, no more, but that was all he needed.

He flew forward. The creature hissed and snapped down at him, but Lythian was quicker, swerving aside and swinging in a swift arc. The creature screamed and writhed as the steel bit into its flesh, camouflaged scales parting to unveil the soft, wet meat beneath.

Lythian hauled his blade out with a spray of black blood and thrust straight upward at the magradile's neck. The strike was true, plunging deep. Thrashing, the monster jerked sidewards, flinging its bulk wildly between the rocks. Lythian danced away, watchful of the lashing tail and the long sharp poison spine. When he saw it coming he jumped over it, landed and hacked right down, severing the tip. The monster screamed in a fearsome rage as though knowing its main weapon was disabled… then just like that it spun and ran, fleeing back toward the mouth of the cave.

I think not. Lythian went to give chase, but there was no need. An object whistled cleanly past his ear, trailing a thin pennon of silvery mist. The hunting knife struck the fleeing magradile in the back of the skull, sending its weight tumbling forward to crash into the stone wall. The monster jerked, twitching a moment, claws scrabbling at the rock…and then lay still. Vilmar the Black strode past Lythian and put his foot on the beast's head, tugging his knife out with a wet crunch of bone. He wiped it down on his cloak and turned. "That was kind of you, letting it run off like that."

Lythian was astonished. "Where did you come from?"

"I was right here in the cave with you the whole time."

"I know, but…" He peered out into the cave. "The other one…"

"Dead. I prefer to kill quickly. No sense in dragging it out." The huntsman stepped back toward him, opening his cloak as he came. He withdrew a torch from a pocket, took out some flint, and cut a spark to light a flame. The cave bloomed to life, every rock and every crevice, shadows shivering across the walls as Vilmar swung the blade around, scanning.

Lythian wasn't certain what he was looking for. "You think there's another one here?"

"No. These two were a mated pair. That was surprise enough for me."

"Then…"

"A nest. Reckon that's why they've been snatching away so much food. They're preparing to feed their young."

A shiver crept up Lythian's spine. "The people…" He turned to where the magradile lay dead. "They're through there somewhere. We need to get them out."

"Aye. I'll see to it. And I'll destroy the nest while I'm at it. You just see to fetching us a magradile head to take back to the village. It'll be easier with your sword."

He lit a second torch before he left, handing it to Lythian and then clambering away through another passage. The knight set to work, placing the torch into a nook in the rock, then beheading the beast with a single good swing. The amount of blood that came gushing from the neck was plenty enough to fill a bathtub to the brim, a sticky oily ichor that reeked of ammonia and copper. Lythian wrinkled his nose in disgust, let the blood pulse out until nought but a few weak squirts remained, then rolled the huge head into a bag, tying the end up tight. He did not spend any great time inspecting the dead beast.

One look at those skittering insectoid legs was more than enough for him.

Repulsed, he clambered briefly up onto the shelf to check on Vilmar's kill - he had slain his own foe with a single thrust to the side of the head, most likely before it had time to rise and realise the level of threat - then went to find a comfortable rock to sit on. The wait was not long; short moments later the tunnel leading left glowed with firelight and the huntsman came back through, leading two people.

Lythian rose and went over to them. Neither was the boy, he was sad to see, though one was a woman, the other a man. Both were stricken, shivering violently, so caked and covered in layers of oozy slime he could not make out what clothing they wore beneath. "Found them strung up by the nest," Vilmar told him. "Thought I would. Those mini-magradiles would've been hungry when they hatched."

The thought was appalling. "How many eggs were there?"

"Two dozen at least." He saw the look on Lythian's face. "I know. Imagine that many of them running about."

"I'd rather not." The knight turned to the others. "You're safe now," he assured them gently. "We're going to take you both back to the village."

The woman's response was to weep and stumble forward into his arms, her legs giving way beneath her. She shuddered all over, sobbing violently, inaudible words trembling through her lips. Gingerly, Lythian patted her back, very much aware that she was covering him in slime. "There there. You don't need to fear them now." Gently he managed to dislodge her, strands of sticky mucus stretching between them like some hideous spider's web. *Delightful.* "What's your name?" he asked her. "Are you Madeline? Sybilla? Rohese?" They were all names given by Gertner and his men.

"Sy…Sybil…Sybilla," she managed.

He smiled and wiped a hand across her slimy hair. "Sybilla. Your husband will be overjoyed to see you. He has been beside himself with grief, I know."

Mention of her husband had the woman breaking down all over again. "My Brendon," she sobbed, sinking to her knees. She clutched at Lythian's leg, planting slimy kisses on his thigh. "Gods thank you, good sir. Thank you, thank you, thank you…"

"Yes, well…I was only doing my duty as a knight." Lythian drew his leg away. "And you," he said, looking at the man. "Gernter spoke of many men taken from the village, and I regret I don't recall all the names. What is yours?"

The man was barely able to stand, swaying there on his spindly legs. His eyes were down, staring at the bare rock at his feet. *This one is broken,* Lythian thought. *Broken and starved.* He thought he spied some armour through the layers of slime. "How long have you been here?" Still he got no answer. "Can you speak? When was it you were taken from the village?"

"I…I wasn't…no, not the village."

Lythian frowned. "You weren't taken from the village?"

"No…I…I was…we were trying to find…to find…." He shook his head from side to side, squeezing his eyes shut. His hair was lank and thin, dark with filth. The man was a ghost, pale as curdled milk, gaunt and narrow…and yet there was something about him that Lythian recognised.

"Who are you? Raise your eyes." When the man did not heed him, Lythian reached forward to lift his chin. "Gods," he whispered, his suspicion confirmed. "*Sir Bardol*…is that you?"

The knight shifted his gaze and blinked up at him, as though seeing him for the first time. He reached out with trembling fingers, gently prodding at Lythian's lean stubbled jaw. "My lord…are you…are you real?" he quivered. "Are you…are you truly here?"

What has happened to him? Sir Bardol had left with Sir Hadros and Sir Pagaloth and Sa'har Nakaan several months ago. He was part of the united host sent out to gather deserters, bring them all together under common cause. None of them had been heard from since. Lythian had feared every one of them dead. "How did you come to be here, Bardol? The others…where are the rest of the men?"

"I…the others…I…" Sir Bardol's haunted eyes squeezed shut, trying to think. "We were…there was an attack. We'd gathered hundreds, my lord. Hundreds of deserters. We planned to return, to bring them back to the city, but…but…"

"But *what*, Bardol?" Lythian gripped his arm. "Where is Sir Pagaloth? What happened to Sa'har Nakaan?" He shook him. "Is Sir Hadros alive? Sunrider Bellio? Moro? Damnit, man, speak." He shook him again. "Speak."

"Give him a moment," Vilmar came in. "There'll be time enough to hear about that later."

"I want to hear now," Lythian said fiercely. He knew Hadros the Homeless but little, and the others as well, but Sa'har and Sir Pagaloth especially were dear to him. "You mentioned an attack? Who attacked you, Sir Bardol?"

"The…the attack, I…" The man's eyes blinked down at the rock floor. "I ran. My horse…I managed to get away, but…but…the others…"

"Are they dead? Are all of them dead?"

"I…I don't know, my lord." He cringed, shoulders drawn tight, and looked around the cave. "I don't want to be here anymore," he wept. "Please. Those things…they…if they come back…"

"They're dead," grunted Vilmar. "They can't hurt you anymore."

The man barely seemed to hear him. "I can't be here. I can't. Please…I have to get out…please…"

"We're leaving, Sir Bardol," Lythian broke in. "You'll feel better when we get outside." He accepted that he would get little from him here. But what else did he need to know? The campaign had been a disaster and most likely all the men were slain. He had feared as much when none of them were heard from but had always held to hope that they would return. *A faint hope. A fool's hope. I sent them all out to die.*

The way back to the village was not far. Lythian let Sir Bardol gather his senses as they went, stewing on his follies as they plodded through the rain. He could feel the weight of the magradile head knocking against his back as he carried it over his shoulder, but there was no sense of triumph in the kill. It was drowned out like the wood beneath these rains. Drowned beneath the deluge of his failures. By the time the village came back into sight, night had come again. They traipsed wearily through the dark and up to the log longhouse, splashing through muddy puddles in the road. The door swung open as they arrived, heat and light pouring out. Several men appeared with weapons in hand. "It's only them," one shouted. "They're back."

Gertner emerged. He pulled his cloak tight and scowled up at the weather, then saw the bag on Lythian's back and nodded. "You killed it?"

"Them," said Lythian. "There were two." He did not bother telling them about the nest. "We found Sybilla as well." The woman was ushered forward, shivering. When her husband saw her he let out a howl and ran down to sweep her up into his arms. It was a sweet reunion, but Lythian's heart was cold as ice. "Now for your side of the bargain, Gertner. I want Stone and I want him now."

"You'll have him," said Gertner. "Once I see into that bag."

Lythian swung it over his shoulder and tossed it into the mud. The pig farmer gave a nod and his son Jethro stepped down to untie the top. When the head was unveiled the crowd made their feelings known, gasps of shock and disgust filling the air. Several men stepped forward to spit on it and one little girl rushed through her mother's legs and began stabbing at the head with a knife. The mother snatched her hand and dragged her away, scolding the girl all the while.

"An ugly beast," Gertner remarked. "What of the other one?"

Vilmar growled. "Is one head not enough?"

"It's dead," Lythian said. "You have my word."

The pig farmer scratched his haggard jaw. He stared down at the head for a while, then he looked at Sir Bardol, frowning. "I don't recognise this man."

"He was imprisoned in the beast's lair as well," Lythian said. "He isn't from this village."

"These creatures…you're to say they were keeping live prey?" The notion was not to the crowd's liking. More spits went the head's way, and a big man stamped forward to kick it. When he did the tongue lolled out from the mouth, disturbingly long, dripping blood and venom. More screams rang out through the cold night air.

"You should bottle that," Vilmar growled. "Milk the glands and coat your steel. Be useful the next time a Brontus Oloran swaggers by."

Gernter nodded at the guidance. "We will." He turned his head. "Derik, Jeth, take the head inside and make sure no one goes near it.

Don't handle it without gloves." The two men saw to it. Then Gernter asked, "There was no one else then? In the lair? Just Sybilla and this man?"

He was wondering about the boy, no doubt. "No one," Lythian said. He looked into the longhall. "Now take me to Ramsey Stone. I have some questions I'd like to ask him."

The pig farmer dipped his chin and led Lythian and Vilmar inside, Sir Bardol stumbling along weakly behind them, unsure of what was happening. The rest of the crowd went about them like a wave being drawn in on the tide. They rounded the large smoky fire pit at the heart of the hall, passing more women with children huddled about their skirts. Several men stood guard by the iron cage at the rear in which Ramsey Stone lay sleeping in his rags and fetters, the bag tied about his head. "Get him up," Gernter said.

One of the men unlocked the cage door, stepped in and gave the prisoner a good strong kick to the ribs. He awoke spluttering, wheezing, and scrambled back against the bars, arms up as though to defend himself. "You've been beating him," Lythian said.

"No more than he deserves."

"How many did he kill? I never asked."

The pig farmer shrugged. "Not sure he killed anyone. Those other thugs saw to that, but he was with them. That's bad enough."

Lythian took some small solace from that. Cowardly as Stone had been abandoning Dalton Taynar during the battle at King's Point, he had not taken him for a wanton murderer. He was a Varin Knight. Even with cravens and deserters, that still counted for something.

"Take off the bag," Lythian said to the man in the cage.

The bag was removed and Ramsey's eyes squinted fearfully into the sudden light. His mouth was gagged. Lythian ordered that removed as well as he stepped inside the cage. The prisoner stank of his own filth, a pungent mix. His armour had been stripped from him to leave him in soiled rags. Lythian stepped forward and stood over him, drawing the man's gaze. His eyes bulged as recognition dawned.

"Lythian," he croaked, rasping out his name. He reached forward, straining against his chains. "You have to save me from these savages, Lythian. They're keeping me captive here…I'm a Varin Knight!"

Were, Lythian thought. "Tell me where Brontus Oloran has gone," he said.

The wretch blinked up at him. "My lord?"

"You travelled with him. Helped him steal the Sword of Varinar. Tell me where he has gone and I'll see your torment ends."

The man stared, struggling for words. "I never…I never helped him steal a thing…"

"Don't lie to me, Ramsey. I'm in no mood for it."

"It's the truth, I swear it! I wasn't with Oloran then. The Sword of Varinar, Sir Lythian. I'd never have…never…"

It made no matter. Perhaps Stone had joined them later. Perhaps he'd been creeping through these woods all alone and swore his oaths to Oloran then. Either way, he had deserted his lord and First Blade in battle, and that was crime enough. "I need to retrieve that blade, Ramsey. Do you know where Brontus has gone?"

The man gazed at him, eyes swollen in mute appeal. "I…he never said…"

"Then what good are you?" Lythian made to turn away.

"No, my lord, no! I saw a map. He never spoke to me himself but I saw a map, and the other men…Steelheart and the rest, they…"

Lythian turned back to face him. "Yes? What did you learn from them?"

"I know where they're going," the once-Varin Knight shouted. "I do, my lord, I promise you I do! He didn't tell me of it, because he didn't trust me, and he was right not to. I was not *with* him, not truly. When I saw the Sword of Varinar, I knew…I knew he'd taken it, my lord. I was only there to get it back. To bide my time and return it to King's Point, so Lord Dalton could…"

"Dalton Taynar is dead. Surely you know?" Lythian's eyes bored in him. "You abandoned him in battle, Ramsey. He bled out on the field. Had you stayed he may never have perished." *And I'd never have been cursed with that blade.*

The man's face was a blur of shame. "I know. I failed him, failed you all, but I've been trying to make it up. I have, my lord. You *must* believe me."

Lythian didn't believe him. Ramsey Stone was a liar and a snake and was only trying to save his own skin. "Tell me what you know and I'll see you're given a quick end. A knight's end. I'll swing the blade myself." *And add you to the rest.*

Stone's head sped side to side, frantic. "I never did anything to these people. I was only rooting around for food when the violence started. I never even had a chance to draw my blade before that boy struck me on the back of the head." He reached up to a patch of dried blood, grimacing. "I don't deserve this. None of it was my fault."

Lythian felt a small tug of pity for the man. He turned to Gertner. "Is that true?"

The pig farmer raised his grey-bristled chin. "He'd have joined the slaughter if he could. Don't believe his lies, Captain Lythian. He was reaching to draw his blade when my Jethro got him."

"To *defend* myself," Stone shouted. "Only to defend myself, I swear it."

Gertner snorted. Several others began shouting obscenities at the prisoner and some pebbles and worse were thrown into the cage. Ramsey cowered from them, tucking himself up into a ball. It was all far too familiar to Lythian Lindar. He'd been caged like this before, and for a crime he didn't commit. "Enough," he said, his voice cutting the air like a whip. "Control your people, Gertner. I demand it."

"They're angry. You can't blame them. They deserve their pound of flesh."

"Just control them," Lythian repeated sharply. He would not let this descend into a riot. "Stone is my prisoner now, not yours." The pig farmer grumbled out his complaints, but Lythian ignored him. He went down to a knee before Ramsey Stone. "You need to speak, Ramsey, and soon," he said quietly. "I won't be able to control these people for long."

The man looked at him pitifully. There were tears in his eyes and he didn't look quite so cruel like that. "My lord, *please*, you can't let them..."

"Tell me what I want to know, Ramsey. Now."

He shook his head. "I won't. Not until you free me. I'll tell you once we're gone. And I'll help you get the blade back."

Lythian trusted this man about as far as he could throw him. "You're in no position to make demands." But he was. In truth he was. He had information Lythian needed, and whether he was lying about that or not, Lythian could not risk it dying here with him. He thought it all through in an instant and then came to his judgement. "If you're lying to me. If I get a sniff that you're trying to deceive me..."

"No. I'd never...*never*, my lord."

"I hope for your sake you're telling the truth. Or I'll make you wish you were back in this cage."

"I will. Every word will be the truth. My honour...I sullied it, but give me a chance to make it up. I hate Brontus as much as anyone, and Steelheart too, you know it. I want them dead for what they've done. I..."

"Need to stop talking, Ramsey. You've said enough already." Lythian rose and turned to Gertner. The old man did not look happy. "I'm taking him with me," the Knight of the Vale said. He raised a hand before the pig farmer could protest. "You'll have to satisfy yourself with the death of the magradiles and the return of Sybilla. Do *not* try me, Gernter," he warned. "I am tired and have recently come into some bitter news. Raise a hand to stop us and you'll wish you hadn't. Do you understand?"

The man's mouth twisted. "Perfectly," he said. "You'll be wanting to stay the night, I take it?"

He would have. *Before.* Not anymore. It seemed prudent to put some space between Ramsey Stone and these men. "We'll be on our way at once. Tell your people to clear a path and that Stone is under my protection. If anyone should try to interfere, you'll hear the ring of godsteel again."

The threat was enough, and no one interfered. Through the crowd of grumbling, scowling men they went, and out into the dark of the night.

26

Saska

The eagle was circling high above them, its dark plumage stark against the hard white skies.

"You think the Elders are still watching you?" Leshie asked, trotting at her side. "Like they did in the south?"

There were always eagles then, perched on dusty spires of rock or old dead tree limbs or gliding high overhead as they made their way along the Capital Road. Much less so now, though. Saska could not remember seeing an eagle since she'd landed in the north, but true enough, she wasn't always looking. "Maybe," she only said. "It's been up there a little while, so…"

"It could be hunting," Leshie offered. She waved to the snowy fields. "I'll bet there are moles and voles and other things hidden in the snow. Just watch. If it plunges down then it's just a normal eagle. If not, and it stays above us, then it's one of the Elders' eagles watching you."

"The Elders' eagles still need to eat, Lesh. If it's hunting, that doesn't mean anything. It could be watching me as well."

The Red Blade chewed her bottom lip in that innocent way she had. "Yeah, you might be right. But I like my idea better. Let's watch it and see."

They rode on for a short while longer, following an old farm track through a region of farmland in the southwestern corner of Rasalan. A crop of spring barley had been growing here, Saska saw, and at any normal time would be ripe for the harvest. *Reapers would be working under the sun with sickle and scythe*, she thought, *cutting the crop and bundling sheaves as they worked up an appetite for their meat and mead*. That was how Master Orryn did it, anyway. Good pay. Good food. Good company. That was how he liked to live.

She was deep in the throes of those happy old memories when Leshie pointed at the skies. "What's it doing?" she asked, bemused. "I've never seen an eagle behave like *that*."

Saska looked up, squinting against the glare as the sun brightened behind the clouds. A frown furrowed her brow. The eagle was twisting, jerking in flight. "It looks like it's having a seizure. I didn't know that could happen with birds."

"Maybe it swallowed a fly or something? Have you ever done that? When flying with the Windblade, or riding horseback even? I have. I've swallowed all sorts of things."

"I don't need to hear about all the things you've swallowed." Lately, Leshie had swallowed Jaito right up and the young archer had grown besotted with her. Del had not been wrong in that.

"I'm just saying. When you swallow something it can get stuck in your throat. Especially if it's *big*." She grinned over at her, causing Saska to roll her eyes and sigh. "When that happens you will do anything to spit it up. So maybe that's happening now? With the eagle?"

"Maybe," Saska allowed, if only to stop Leshie from talking about swallowing things.

"It might be a bug as well," the Red Blade went on cheerfully. She was in a good mood today, though that could easily change. Leshie did have a habit of swinging wildly between extremes. "Not swallowed. I mean, in its brain." She thumbed behind them, where the Baker, Umberto, Jaito and the Tigress were riding single file a short way back. "Jaito told me about this beetle that crawls in through the ear of an animal and drives it mad from pain. It gets so bad the animal will do anything to stop it, even kill itself, so they dash their head on a rock or impale themselves on some stony pike. And when they're dead, the beetle feeds on their organs and lays its eggs in its heart. So maybe it's one of those."

Saska felt queasy all of a sudden. "Why would the gods make a thing like that?"

Leshie shrugged. "Who knows? There are all sorts of horrible things in the world. I'll bet some lesser god made that bug. Some evil one. Probably one of Agarath's underlings or something." She spat to the side, then looked back into the skies. "Hey look, it's diving. It's going to kill itself, you'll see. I'll bet I'm right about that beetle."

She was right, about the eagle killing itself at least. Maybe it was some brain-eating beetle, maybe not, but either way the sight was not one that made Saska feel very good inside. Spinning, jerking, shrieking its whistling call, the eagle plunged straight down into a rock amid the field and landed with a sickening *crack*. The noise was so loud they heard it from far away.

Saska cringed, but Leshie only hooted in triumph. "I'm right! Didn't I say? I knew I was right." She beamed broadly, turning her horse to the field. "I'll go fetch it. I want to see what this beetle looks like."

"No, Leshie. Let it lie."

"Why? I want to know what happened."

"Let it lie, I said. It's an eagle, a proud bird. You should give it more respect."

"I am. I want to know why it died, that's all. And if it *is* because of this beetle, I want to *kill* it." She snatched out her prized ruby dagger, a gift from Robbert Lukar. "We can't have it climbing into another creature's ear."

"And if you go over there, what's to stop it climbing in yours?"

"*Me*. I'll stop it. And anyway, what if Joy finds it? She went out that way hunting, didn't she? She might come back and sniff at it, and then the beetle will get in her head, and it would be like it's in *your* head too, because of your bond." She nodded to herself, firmly. "I'm only trying to protect you, Saska. That's all I'm ever trying to do."

"I know, Lesh." She would admit that much. Without Leshie she didn't know where she'd be, especially now Del was gone, and Elyon being so serious and dour. He'd been like that ever since he returned from Tukor.

"Then you'll let me go?" Leshie prompted. "I'll only go if you allow it."

"Fine," Saska said. "Go. But be careful." She glanced back. "Take one of the others with you to be safe. I'm going to check in with Rolly." Saska put her heels into her horse and left Leshie to it, riding forward up the track, though not quickly. With the Nightblade hitched at her hip, her horse was terribly overburdened and she had to swap over to other mounts throughout the day so they might have a chance to rest. Often she dismounted to walk as well, though quickly grew tired from the weight. Her bond was still young, though building. Before very long it would weigh nothing to her at all and she was longing for that day to arrive.

About fifty yards further up the track, the Butcher and the Gravedigger were riding abreast. When the big scarred sellsword heard her coming, he twisted his neck back and said, "Did you see the eagle?" with that grin of his, as though everything was amusing. "It burst its own head open like a melon. I think it must have been mad."

"Leshie says it's got a beetle in its brain."

"A beetle? Yes, this may be so. There is one in Aramatia, Pretty Princess. A horrid thing. It likes to…"

"I know. Leshie told me. Do you get that beetle here as well?"

"No. It is only in the south. Aramatia and Pisek, maybe some other places too. An ancient Lightborn sorceress made it, people say. She did experiments, this witch, and made new creatures with her magic. Pal Palek is of her line. It is why he has his menagerie. The beasts and men he keeps in his dungeons. Some say he has tried to cross-breed them before, but he does not have any gift for magic like she did." The Butcher laughed. "Palek is a weakling. I will crush his head if ever we see him."

We're not likely to see him where we're going, Saska thought. "Could there be another reason?" she asked. "Why the eagle killed itself."

"Of course, yes. His eagle wife might have left him for a handsome hawk. Or maybe his eagle children were killed by a jealous falcon. This would be enough, I think."

"I'm serious," Saska said. "Leshie's going to check for a beetle in its brain, but if she doesn't find one…"

The Gravedigger made a clacking sound with his mouth, then a hissing whisper that Saska didn't understand.

She frowned. "What did he say?"

"He says the eagle should be respected. Not *inspected*. He says it should be buried, and he will dig a grave for it. He likes digging graves, yes." The Butcher swung a paw into the Gravedigger's back, almost knocking him from the saddle. "All eagles should be revered. This is the way in Aramatia."

"We're not in Aramatia," Saska told him. "And men deserve to be buried too." They had passed many of those, dead men on the road and stinking out villages, corpses strewn across blackened fields and caught among the reeds of rivers. One river had been so choked with the dead that they'd formed a dam, flooding the lands. "We've passed hundreds of dead people, Butcher. And buried none of them. Why should an eagle get special treatment?"

"Because the eagle is sacred to Aramatians, and you are Aramatian."

"Half. And I never grew up there. I'm a quarter Rasalanian too, remember. These are my people we're passing."

"All are your people, then. Aramatian, Rasalanian, *Vandarian*, yes. That black blade of yours says so. The windy one too. But we cannot bury a thousand men. One eagle is easier. They are small, these birds."

The Gravedigger was looking at her through those unblinking grey eyes. He was a cadaver warmed up and rarely did he speak. When he did it was that queer clack-and-whisper combination that only the Butcher, Baker, and Umberto could translate. Clearly, this was important to him. And Leshie was fetching the eagle anyway, so why not? Eventually she gave a nod and said, "All right. There's no harm in it. Go out and tell Leshie to bring it back. We can bury it later when we make camp."

She swung a leg over her mare, dismounting. The mount was tiring, she sensed, and was well overdue a rest. "And take my horse, Butcher. I'm going to go on foot for a while."

She continued up the track in armour and cloak, drawing the Nightblade from its scratched leather sheath as she went, swiping it side to side in front of her. The mists were black and smoky grey and poured more densely from the steel than with other blades. With the Windblade the mists circled the sword, spinning in a swirling vortex along its length from crossguard to tip, but with the Nightblade they rose slowly, almost lazily, with a coldness and a calmness that its brother didn't share.

She watched them as she walked, fogging and rising, wondering what it would be like to *puff* herself and vanish in a cloud of smoke. That was how it worked, Elyon had told her. And the more one mastered the Nightblade, the more quickly and easily they could blink out of sight, even doing so without leaving a trace of smoke behind.

My grandfather could do that, she thought, as she hefted the blade higher, holding it out straight before her. She held it there as long as she could before her arm grew weary, and then dropped it back down to her side. *King Lorin. He could disappear right in front of a man even if they were looking straight at him.* Apparently Jonik could do the same, or near enough as made no matter. Leshie had said that in Elyon's hearing, and the prince had only scowled and begrudgingly admitted it was probably true.

But her grandfather was long dead now, and Elyon's half-brother was missing, and she had no one to teach her how that worked. There was no great rush, though, at least not yet. She still had to bond the blade properly first, so she could wield it weightlessly, and only then should she consider trying to figure out how to use it.

Up ahead, where the track reached the edge of the barley field, the Wall had stopped on Bedrock with the Surgeon at his side. They were talking, breath fogging, as she came up to join them. "What are you discussing?" she asked, in half a pant.

"The route," Rolly told her. "We must decide where to go." He looked at her, saw the blade fogging in her grasp. "You're looking stronger. The bond is building well."

"The second is always easier." Elyon had told her that. She slid the Nightblade back away into its scabbard - unlike the Windblade's fine silver sheath, the Nightblade's was plain and lacked ornamentation - and cast her eyes around. Here the track diverged at a crossroad. One path went left along some other fields, straight as an arrow to the west; another, less travelled and hardly more than an overgrown game trail, continued more or less the way they'd been going, winding northward into the undulating hills and through sinister misty woods of elm and oak. "So, which way are we going?" she asked.

"North," the Wall said.

"West, I say," put in the other man.

The Whaleheart shook his head. "North is better."

"West is quicker. And not so cold. It will be bitter cold up there." The Surgeon looked at her with those empty brown eyes. "Serenity, this road will lead us directly toward the coast so we might find a suitable crossing. It is a good road, as you can see. Neat and well-used. Unlike this one." He gestured to the game trail. "A poor track, I'm sure you'll agree. A horse-killer, I would call it. And there may be enemies in those woods."

"Those woods will offer us cover," the Whaleheart rumbled. "That has been sorely lacking so far."

"Lacking, yes, but we have not suffered from it. The dragons rarely fly here. How many have we seen?"

The Wall's jaw tightened. "It takes but one."

"The dragons are away," the Surgeon declared. "They are being drawn to the Ashmount for Eldur's sorceries and corruptions. The prince told us this. We must make use of their absence while we can and hurry west along this road."

Sir Ralston shook his head. "No. Further north it will be colder, as you said. That means the strait will be frozen over. We will be able to cross without the need for a boat."

The Surgeon frowned. "Folly. The strait will not be frozen for another hundred miles at least. We would be another week in Rasalan. Why bother? There are places to cross a short way west of here."

"Not safely. The water to the west is rough and will be full of floes of ice. Navigating the crossing would be perilous and we have our armour and horses. If our boat should capsize all of us will drown."

"We will use several boats. And wait for good weather."

"Which might take a day, or a week, or a month. No." The Wall was adamant. "We go north. It is the surer course, my lady. There is a crossing I know to the west of Harrowmoor, at the southernmost edge of the Oakwood. The Sibling Strait is at its narrowest there."

"And if the water is not frozen, as you promise?"

"Then we'll do it your way and find some boats."

"After wasting a week, and freezing half to death."

The Wall snorted like a bull, fogging the air. "Put on another cloak if you're afraid of a bit of cold. We have several going spare."

"Yes, from my dead companions. Four good swords I lost to the crab, Whaleheart. I have only the Tigress left and will *not* see her freeze."

"What about the Links?" Saska put in, to stop them arguing. "I suppose crossing the bridge is still out of the question?"

The Wall looked at her, impatient. "We have been over that. Crossing the bridge would invite too many questions, and there is always the chance it has been destroyed. We need to avoid major roads wherever we can. The enemy is searching for you, Saska. Any traveller we encounter could be a spy in disguise and we…"

"Need to stay away from prying eyes, I know. I'm just saying. It would be quicker that way." She wasn't sure about crossing the ice, not unless it was many feet thick and sure to be able to hold them. Rolly weighed a colossal amount with his armour and enormous twin greatswords and the Nightblade's tonnage was hard to judge. The idea of losing *that* through a crack was unthinkable. But crossing on a boat was hardly any better, not if the waters were rough and thick with treacherous floes. She gave a sigh as she thought about it. "Maybe Elyon could fly us over," she proposed, fumbling for a solution. "How far is this crossing west of Harrowmoor?"

"Too far. Miles."

"How many miles?"

"Seven. Maybe closer to eight."

She thought about it, wondering if Elyon might be able to fly them over one at a time. *All but me,* she knew. Elyon would not be able to bear the Nightblade across, so she'd have to do that herself, and that brought with it risks of its own. She chewed on it a moment longer, then said, "I'll talk to him about it when he comes back. Elyon will know best what he can carry in his harness, and how far."

The Wall gave no answer to that, which meant he disagreed.

"Have you seen him?" Saska asked. She scanned the skies, but saw only white and grey.

"Not for a while."

She nodded. There was nothing unusual there. Elyon only joined them to train her now, usually once they'd found somewhere to make camp. The rest of the time he spent flying a great ring around them, watching for threats, or simply waiting many miles ahead or behind when he needed to take some rest. Now that the Nightblade was here, it was critically important that the two blades be kept apart, he had said, for their own protection.

"They hate one another," the prince had warned her, that day he returned from the far north of Tukor. He had been away much longer than expected, so long that Saska had started to worry for him, but finding the Nightblade lying at his feet was more unexpected still. "Be careful of the whispers. If they both get in your head at the same time, they could start to overwhelm you."

That was one reason why they must be kept separate. Another was because of the aura they gave out, a power signature that might become a beacon to the enemy, drawing them to her location. "I will stay to train you, Saska," he'd said. "When I do, we'll fly out somewhere, away from the Nightblade. You'll have to leave it in camp, with Sir Ralston and the others. But the rest of the time I'll stay away. I don't want to. Know that. I'll do it because I have no choice."

She nodded, understanding. But the way he spoke disquieted her. "We saw a dragon landing," she said, confused. "It was Neyruu, Rolly told me." She had been further back down the road at the time, cresting a low hill, but Rolly had been out in the lead and had seen Elyon landing several miles away in the distance. He had taken a moment to remove something from Neyruu's back - the Nightblade, they only learned when they reached him - but the dragon had not stayed, and nor her rider. As soon as the blade was removed, they flapped back away into the westerly skies to vanish into the low scuttling clouds. "Why did Talasha have to go?" Saska asked. "I wanted to see her. And Ranulf? Cevi? Where are they, Elyon?" Rolly had said there was only *one* rider, not two or three, so it could only have been Talasha, and that meant the other two were not with her. "Did something happen to them, when they flew to find Ilith? Are they hurt? Not...they're not dead, are they?" She knew the girl Cevi but barely; it was Ranulf she was thinking of. Fear had twisted in her gut. The idea of losing him...

But Elyon stepped in and took her hand. "They're not dead, Saska," he assured her. "Cevi was wounded by an arrow to the leg, but she'll be fine, she only needs to heal. And Ranulf... he's going to stay in the refuge, to help Ilith. He wanted me to tell you sorry. That he would have come if he could, but there's something...something else he has to do."

"What?"

"I...don't know. That's not important now." He squeezed her palm, firming his eyes. "You have to focus on your training, Saska. We'll have to train hard and every night. I want you able to fly fast and far. It's critical you're able to fight in flight, to swing the blade without losing balance and direction. There are wind-blasts you're yet to learn. Other techniques I can teach you. We have a lot to get through, and you have to be strong. Bonding the Nightblade by day will tire you, but you have to save your strength for your training as well, and time…we don't have much time before…" He stopped, trailing off.

She leaned into him. "Before?"

"Nothing. Before the world ends. And Ilith…he's ageing." He tried to smile to reassure her, but it only made her more afraid. "But he'll be ready for when the time comes. All you have to do is focus on your training. Leave the rest to us. Can…can you do that for me?"

He's asking me not to ask questions. He's asking me to trust him. There were things he was keeping from her, she could tell. That had been the case all her life.

But she nodded anyway. "I can do that, Elyon." *I'd do anything for you,* she thought, unbidden. She had to turn away a moment, feeling the sudden blush warm the skin of her cheeks. "And…Talasha?" she asked, looking back. "I don't understand…why didn't she want to see me?"

"She did…she does. But…"

"But what? What is it? Does she have to go away somewhere? Is she returning to Cevi and Ranulf?"

"I don't…I don't know where she's going. She never told me."

"Never told you? I don't understand…"

"We were attacked," he said, turning his gaze away. "On our way back here. A dragon and some dragonknights, and…and a priest. Talasha thinks they were drawn to her by her blood…Eldur's blood. The priest said so…but, I'm not sure. It could have been the blades. I took him for a liar. But either way, she doesn't think it's safe for her to be here. So she decided not to stay. To protect you."

She watched his eyes closely. There was more to this than he was letting on. "She could have stopped for a few minutes at least. To say hello, or…"

"She said it wasn't worth the risk. And, she…"

"She what, Elyon? What happened? *Tell me.*"

"She's afraid to be seen," he said, almost blurting out the words. "She…took wounds, Saska. I was only trying to save her. I didn't expect…" He shook his head. "Her face. It is badly torn, and her left eye…" His chest sank. "I did what I could to stitch her up, but she refused to let me take her to Rockfall. I hope…when the swelling comes down…and the balms…she has healing balms with her…I hope…maybe, if…" He let out a breath, struggling to find the right words.

Saska had gone cold. "Will there be scarring?" she asked. Talasha Taan was the most beautiful woman she had ever seen. The most beautiful woman in all the world. It was a regal beauty, an exotic, mesmerising beauty. The idea of it being stripped away…thousands were dying daily, and the world was ending around them, so it shouldn't matter, not really, not with so much loss, but it did. It mattered.

Elyon only dipped his head. "Yes," he'd said, quietly, and in shame. "There will be scarring, Saska."

They had not spoken of it since. And the days had been long and hard. By day they kept to their course, crossing plains and fields and snowy meadows where flowers no longer grew. When they stopped to pitch their camp, Elyon would reappear with the Windblade in his grasp and fly her away somewhere for training. They trained for many hours every night, and sometimes they would train in the morning as well before they set back on the road.

It was arduous, gruelling work, but Saska was getting better every day. Flight was becoming second nature to her now. She was learning to swing the blade and not compromise speed or direction. Learning to slow and hover and pulse herself side to side with a variety of air blasts. Those were important when trying to outmanoeuvre a dragon, to dodge and flee as it snapped at her or lashed with its tail, to turn defence into attack in an instant. Now she only needed a test. To fight a dragon all by herself, as she had once before outside of Aram, but with the Windblade in her grasp this time. Last time it had not gone well. She would have died if it hadn't been for the coming of Agarosh the One-Eye, but this time it would be different, she told herself. *I killed that crab, and I'm better with the Windblade now.* She was ready to become a dragonslayer.

But no dragons had been seen, not for long days now. Elyon told her he would rush back to her if he spotted one during his daily vigil, to let her take up the blade and fly up to fight it, but that hadn't happened as yet. Instead he was glimpsed only rarely, a faint distant blur cruising through the clouds or hovering somewhere long miles away. Saska had asked Rolly if what he said about the blades was true. Could having them close together act as a beacon to the enemy? Or was the enemy only drawn to them because of Talasha's blood, as the priest claimed?

"Both things can be true at once," was the Whaleheart's answer. "The prince is right not to take the risk."

She accepted that, but wondered if this was Elyon's way of seeking penance as well, for what happened to Talasha. To isolate himself out there alone, like some tortured pariah, floating high above the world where no one could see his shame.

And now he was gone again, out there somewhere long miles away, sitting in solitude on a rock or hovering amidst the clouds, brooding on things he refused to say. It was midafternoon, and he would still be gone for long hours. If she wanted his input on which route they should take, she wouldn't get it. And in the end, what did it matter? One way or another, they would cross the strait into Tukor. Why bicker over where that would be?

"We'll go north," she decided, on a whim. It would take them longer to reach Tukor that way, she judged, and that served her. She still had reservations about making for this refuge at all, so the longer it took to cross to Ilithor, the better. "Yes?" She looked at the Surgeon to make sure he had no complaints. "Are you OK with that?"

The man bowed his head. "If that is your decision, Serenity, then who am I to argue?"

A man older and more experienced and wiser than I, she thought. His opinion was valid, the same as all her men, but in this she would trust her Wall. "Good. Then north it is."

They set off up the game trail, the others following up behind them. For a while longer Saska stayed afoot, withdrawing the Nightblade once or twice to watch the black mists puff and rise, to hold it out before her until it grew too heavy, to swish it side to side and practice her downcuts and thrusts. And imagine disappearing, yes. To walk unseen like her grandfather used to do and forget all the worries of the world.

She was swiping idly at a bush on the side of the track when Leshie rode up to her. "There was no beetle in the eagle's brain," she said, sounding disappointed. "Not that I could find anyway. But I might have missed it. There were bits of brain all over the rock and in the snow as well. It could have been hiding in one of those or crawled away before I got there."

Or it was never there at all, Saska thought, giving the bush another swipe.

"I stopped Joy from getting too close," Leshie added. "She came running in from the fields to sniff at it, but I warded her off. She growled at me for that...or maybe she was growling at the eagle, I don't know... but she doesn't scare me. I told her no and she went prowling away again."

Saska knew that already. She had sensed Joy's curiosity swell as she approached the dead eagle, sensed her sudden anger as she sniffed at it and Leshie shouted her away. The starcat had bounded off shortly after, scampering up the path and right past Saska, stopping only to lick at her cheek and get her head scratched, before continuing up the trail to where Rolly led at the front. She was there now, loping alongside him and sometimes dashing about and even beneath Bedrock in a bid to annoy the massive horse and the steel giant on his back. It was amusing to watch, Saska had to admit, and irritated though he appeared to be Rolly had warmed to Joy of late. He still did not entirely approve of her being here but accepted her as an important part of Saska now...and had even been known to pat Joy's head on the odd occasion when he didn't think anyone was looking.

She smiled to think of it. "Sorry, Lesh. About the beetle. I know you wanted to find it." She heaved the tip of the Nighblade up and shoved it back into its sheath with a dull scrape. "Do you have the eagle with you? The Butcher says we should bury it."

"The Gravedigger's got it. He'll bury it when we make camp some-where, like you wanted." She surveyed the skies, which were growing a little bleaker. "Have you seen the prince at all?"

"No. He'll be back later, when we stop." She looked over at her. "Why do you ask?"

Leshie shrugged as she trotted along. "Just want to talk to him, is all.

Before he takes you off for your training. None of us ever get to see him anymore."

"What do you want to talk to him about? Is this to do with what happened in the cave?"

The girl snorted. "No. What cave?"

"You know what cave. The crab cave, Leshie. You know, the night Savage and Scalpel died, and Gutter and Gore." Leshie had flown over with Elyon before the rest of them arrived that night, and there had been an odd energy between them when they joined. "You never said what you two talked about."

"Because it doesn't need saying. And he didn't listen to me anyway."

"Listen to you? Then you gave him some advice?" She peered at her. "Were you talking about me?"

The Red Blade laughed. "Not everything's about you."

But this was. That was clear. "What did you say to him?"

"Nothing. Just to stop trying to be like a mini-Wall. I'd call *him* Parapet if I hadn't already used up that name on Meshface. But did he listen? No. Unless you're keeping secrets?"

Saska was baffled. "Me? What kind of secrets."

"Well…you two do spend *a lot* of time alone together. Training, you say. Well…I'd hope you're doing more."

"More? You mean…"

"Yes, I mean. Well, do you?"

"No." She thought she knew what Leshie was talking about. "We don't go out there for that."

"But you wish you did. And he does too. You both wish it and neither of you are doing anything about it, and it bothers me…there, I said it, it bothers me. Gods, it's torture watching you two. All those secret smiles and longing looks and neither of you ever doing anything about it. I get it, you've got to save the world, but that doesn't mean everything has to be duty and dragons and *dread, dread, dread.* You deserve some joy along the way too, and I don't mean the cat. I mean a different kind of joy."

"Like you have with Jaito?"

The girl snorted. "No. That's just fun. Nothing serious. With you and Elyon, it's different; it's much deeper than that. Tell me at least he's more complimentary of you? He was trying to be too tough like Coldheart and Lady Marian, but that doesn't suit him, so I told him off. So? Does he praise you more?"

She supposed he did. Elyon always told her when she was doing something well and when she thought about it, that had started to happen a lot more since he'd returned from Tukor. "He's been more encouraging," she confirmed. "And is always trying to build my confidence. To make me feel more worthy." It was working too. The better she got the more worthy she felt and Elyon's encouragement had plenty to do with that. "So…you told him that, did you? To praise me more?"

"Yes. I told him. I said I know you better than anyone and that's true. Maybe I even know *you* better than you do, Saska. Or what you need at least. He's too stubborn to act on his feelings and maybe he's too scared as well, but you don't have to be. You have that power too."

"I...guess I do. But..."

"Look. I've said all I need to say. You're both adults and can do as you please, so I'll leave it there. That's enough from me." She was good to her threat. Putting her heels to her horse, she rode off up the track, splashing through a small icy stream and was gone.

Saska pondered what she'd said as the afternoon ambled on, passing across the snowy plains and through a foggy, haunted wood where the tree limbs creaked with every passing breeze and the canopy blocked out all the daylight. They kept tight through there, Rolly and the sellswords watching their flanks, Joy growling and hissing at every shadow until they emerged on the other side.

After another hour of open fields they came to a second eerie wood and decided it would be a good place to stop. Grand old oaks loomed about the edge as though guardians of the forest, while pale grey mist curled about their trunks and crept up to their lowest limbs. The Butcher and Umberto dismounted and ventured into the trees to check for beasts and bandits, while Rolly found a place for the Nightblade. He did that every evening, choosing some hidden nook where Saska could hide it, and would keep a watch on it while she was away. Today he found a large fist of rock punching up through the forest floor a little way into the trees, cut into its base a thin deep chamber and told Saska to put the blade in there. Then he covered the opening with dirt and snow to make sure it was well concealed.

The others pitched their camp all the while; each had a small tent of their own, except for Saska and Leshie who preferred to share. Gone were the days when they could all sleep in the open as they had done in the hot south. Here the days were cold and the nights were colder, especially when the winds picked up. As that was going on, a shout sounded from Jaito who had been asked to stand on watch. "I see him," the Aramatian archer called out, pointing. "There. The prince is returning."

Saska watched Elyon make his approach, wondering how far he'd flown today, and where, and how many times he'd cursed himself for that grim business with Talasha. He landed a little way out from the camp, some quarter mile or so, as he always did, waiting for her to join him. For a moment she didn't move. She was tired, more tired than normal, and had been holding the Nightblade for much of the day. Gods how she'd prefer him to come to *her* instead, for him to sit by the fire and spend an evening with the others, sharing in their company and not lingering out there alone. He even slept alone now as well, with only the Windblade to watch over him. It made her sad to think of it. She wanted to comfort him, and take comfort from him too. She wanted to do everything that Leshie had said.

She drew a deep breath and walked out to join him, wondering if tonight she would. She'd been thinking about it ever since Leshie berated her earlier, and how could she train properly with all of that on her mind? *I'm going to talk to him about it,* she decided. *It's time we cleared the air.* They hadn't spoken about their time at Harrowmoor at all, leastways not properly, and it was time they did. *Later, when we take a break.* She'd find some secluded spot for them and talk about it then.

He smiled as she neared him, which was nice to see. He hadn't smiled very much of late. "You've picked a good place to set camp," he said, each word coming out with a puff of mist. "Do you have anyone checking the trees?"

She nodded. "The Butcher and Umberto went in when we arrived. If there's trouble they'll root it out." She fidgeted her feet, crunching in the snow. "I have a request, Elyon."

"Oh? Of course…what is it?"

"Can we…have a light session tonight? It's been a long day and I'm tired. Less flying. Maybe there's a new technique you could teach me instead?"

He pondered, nodding. "There are a couple, yes, that I haven't taught you yet. There's one in particular…a wind-enhanced cut that will be useful for you later. It helped me kill that dragon, the night Talasha…" And he stopped, and his smile was gone. "It'll allow you to swing the blade much faster and more powerfully, and deal more damage." His voice was more businesslike now, more serious. "We can work on that if you want?"

That sounded good. She told him so, then added, "And…maybe we could talk as well. Later. There's something…" She scratched at her neck, beneath the gorget, awkward. "I just want to talk to you about something. Later, like I say. Once we're done for the night."

The conversation was terribly stilted. "Sure. If you like." He smiled again, though it seemed a little forced, and his eyes drifted past her as though searching for something else to comment on. He found it in the Gravedigger, digging his grave at the edge of their camp. The Baker was there as well, watching solemnly as his companion shovelled at the snow and hard frozen earth beneath it. A wrapped bundle was laid on the ground beside his feet. "What's going on there?" Elyon asked. "Are they burying something?"

"An eagle." Saska nodded. "It's custom in Aramatia to bury eagles, they say."

"An eagle?" Elyon wasn't understanding. "What happened to it?"

"It killed itself. We saw it jerking and shrieking as it circled above us. Then it flew down and smashed open its head on a rock. Leshie said it was because of some brain-crawling beetle, but she couldn't find one when she looked. I guess it was something else." She saw the look on Elyon's face, the sudden expression of concern. "What's wrong?" she asked him. "Do you know what happened to it?"

"It…might be nothing," he said, a little breathily. "But there's a chance that bird was being made into a spy."

"A spy? How? Only the Elders can…"

"There's something I didn't tell you about the Elders. Something the priest said. *New watchers of the world.*" He paused a moment in private thought, then said. "I fear the Everwood's been attacked, Saska. If the Elders have been killed or worse…taken captive. Then their eagles…" He drew a breath; his eyes were ripe with worry. "I'll tell you all about it later. But right now, we have to change course. Tell them to pack up and get ready to leave. We ride for the west at once."

27

Amron

The bellow of 'dragons' rang down the columns, the air fogging with the breath of a thousand men as they shouted out the warning call.

Spears were primed at once to throw, Bladeborn bowman drawing arrows to nock and draw. From the tip of the vanguard, Amron Daecar narrowed his eyes, watching the two shadows approach from the south-east. One was of not-instubstantial size, the other much larger, blurred by distance and the veil of falling snow. He could not see their colours as yet.

"Shall I order the scorpions unpacked, my lord?" asked Sir Quinn Sharp.

They had several of them here in the vanguard, more behind in the baggage train and others in the rearguard too, long miles behind. The scorpions were mounted on carts and could quickly be made ready to fire, if required. There seemed no harm in taking that precaution. "Go ahead, Sir Quinn. And send word to Sir Torus and the Ironfoot to do the same." Torus Stoutman had command of the baggage train, Lord Gavron Grave the rearguard, ably supported by Sir Reginald Hightree and his men.

Lord Styron Strand was riding at Amron's side on his powerful warhorse, the pair leading the army together down the High Way in the direction of Varinar. Their progress thus far had been slow, but steady, a ponderous procession battling daily through wind and snow. "They are both ridden," the lord said. "Unless my eyes mistake me."

"They are ridden," Amron confirmed.

"A duel, then," said the Strong. "Ridden dragons must honour the duel." He turned his head a little. "Sir Robin. Come forth."

Sir Robin Farrow rode up to join them. Robin the Resilient, they called him. A young knight, full of gusto and pride. "My lord," he said. "Do you have need of me?"

"You have always yearned to become a dragonslayer, Sir Robin. Now is your chance. Ride out and call them to challenge."

"Alone, my lord?"

"No, my son will go with you."

Amron almost heard Sir Gerald gulp behind him. "M-me, Father?"

"Yes, you. Rogen is sworn to the king's service, and not mine to command. Ride out with Sir Robin, Gerald. And the glory of House Strand."

"I...if...yes, Father. If that's your command, I..."

"Come, Sir Gerald," Farrow said in a stirring voice. He took his shoulder and shook it. "For death and glory. Ride with me!"

Sir Robin thundered forward with enthusiasm. Sir Gerald followed hesitantly, reeking of fear, but follow he did. They went from a trot to a canter to something approaching a gallop, putting good distance between themselves and the army. The men were cheering out 'Strand' and 'Farrow' and 'Robin the Resilient', though any calls for Gerald were lacking.

"My son is not loved," Styron the Strong said. "They call out 'Strand' but not for him. It is the glory of the house they care about. If he should fall, none will weep."

And you least of all, Amron thought. Styron despised his son for his weakness, the same as half the realm. "He is a proven traitor, Styron. All traitors are ill-liked."

"So are cravens. Alas that my son should be both." The big old lord snorted. "I hope he can at least die with honour. But I doubt he can even give me *that.*"

The distant shapes in the sky were not so distant anymore, though their colours were still obscured. Sir Robin led Sir Gerald off the road, taking charge as he made for a broad and open stretch of mostly flat land to the south. The dragons appeared to be veering toward them.

"They are engaging," said Lord Abel Darring. He was a weaselly man, hook-nosed and nasal of voice, and hard to like. "The big one looks...very big to me."

He wasn't wrong. Big and familiar, yes. Amron peered forward, wondering. Were those blue scales he could see? Was that not a faint shimmer of orange light steaming from the saddle? The realisation dawned on him quickly enough. "That is Lord Ulrik Marak," he said. "Riding upon Garlath the Grand,"

"Marak?" Darring spluttered. "But he's dead, I thought. The rumours from King's Point..."

"Are just rumours, Lord Darring. No one could say for certain what become of him after the battle."

"We must call them back," the weasel went on. "Neither will stand a chance against him. My lord..." He turned to Styron. "Your son..."

The big lord ignored him. "I had not expected to see Lord Marak here, I will confess. And this companion...do we recognise him?"

Amron didn't. The dragon looked to have scales in darker shades, red and copper it seemed, though the rider on his back was too distant to make out. The pair were nearing the two knights now, widening their wings to land on the snowy field a short distance away. Steam rose all about the dragons, from their mouths and necks and chests, even their wings. The beasts were fire-made-flesh, all knew. The snow melted and thawed about them.

"Gods, we need to muster a host to help them," Darring was babbling on. "We can ill afford to lose two good knights, my lord…"

"One good knight," corrected Lord Strand. "True, Sir Robin would be a loss."

There was a fog of noise behind them as the name Marak went from mouth to mouth. *He still inspires awe and fear,* Amron thought. He could hear a barked call of 'Make way, make way' coming from down the column and turned to see a small host bustling forward. He was unsurprised to see that Stegra the Snowfist was among them, flanked by his son Svaldar and wise old Wagga the White. Often did the Snowfist poke his nose in when he sensed trouble, or anything of interest afoot. With him was Lord Robert Borrington, joined by several rangers and guards - Robbert was very much the liaison now between Amron and the tribes - and Amara was present as well, wrapped up in a great grey cloak, accompanied by Sir Connor Crawfield who was wearing his new blue one proudly.

Amron was not happy to see that Amara had left the comfort of her wheelhouse, but could hardly call himself surprised. "Don't give me that look," she admonished him at once, tugging her cloak tighter as a stiff wind assailed them. "We heard the call of 'dragons' and I thought it safer to escape that prison you've put me in. It is wooden, and big, and a tasty target for our winged friends. I don't want to burn to death, Amron."

"She insisted, my lord," said Sir Connor. "Sir Daryl and Sir Penrose are with your daughter. They will keep her well protected if there is an attack."

There won't be, Amron thought. Not from these dragons anyway. He had seen a hundred duels between dragon and knight and participated in more than his own fair share. This was not going to descend into violence, no matter how fiercely Sir Robin Farrow bellowed for the dragonriders to engage. "Thank you, Sir Connor," he said to the new Varin Knight. "But I sense they're here to talk, not fight."

"Talk?" Stegra blustered loudly. Everything was loud with Stegra Snowfist. "Do dragons talk now?" His breath misted out from between the snow-bear fangs of his hood. "What is this language of theirs? The tongue of fire and ash?"

"No, Stegra. The men riding them will be doing the talking."

"This man Marak, yes, who has everyone squealing in fear. Who is he? Is he famous?"

Lord Darring gave the big tribal chief a sneering look. "These wildmen know nothing. He's the Lord of the Nest, you great fool. Scourge of Bladeborn. A killer of kings…"

Stegra looked around. "And who speaks? Who calls the Snowfist a fool?" He searched some more, then spotted him, looking down. "Ah, you. A little man with lots to say. Are you lost, little man? How did you find your way up here?"

Darring was baffled. "I'm a lord. Second only to Lord Strand among…"

"A lord? No. You are a Crowman, yes, with that hooked beak of yours. You have put on a lord's cloak and a bit of steel, but you belong with Narek and his people. You are very ugly like they are. Very ugly, yes." He wrinkled his nose. "And you reek. This man Marak has made you soil yourself." His son Svaldar started laughing and Amara looked most amused.

But the lord's eyes were hot with rage. "You dare…" he began, saliva spitting from his lips.

Stegra's big voice cut him off. "Dare? To speak truths to a little Crowman? Close your beak, crow. The grown men are talking."

Amron might have told Stegra that he was no grown man at all, despite his great brawny size, and that he was acting like an infant, but that would be a waste of breath. In any case, he'd heard enough. "Stegra, that will serve. Rogen, ride with me. The rest of you, remain here. I would speak with Lord Marak alone."

He turned Wolfsbane toward the two distant knights, kicked his spurs and rode away without further explanation. He did not want anyone else interfering, not Robert Borrington and not Lord Styron Strand, and certainly not the Snowfist. But Rogen was always with him, his eyes and his ears. "Tell me no one is following," Amron said, once they'd trotted away down the road.

"No one, my lord. They are all waiting behind."

"Good." Wolfsbane was snorting fog, stirring himself into a lather as though expecting a fight. Amron patted his powerful neck. "Not today, old friend," he told him. "They mean only to talk."

"Are you certain of that, my lord?" asked the ranger.

"Certainty is a hard commodity to come by these days, Rogen, but yes, as certain as I can be." They followed the tracks the two knights had made, veering off the road where Sir Robin had led them and across the snowy field. Before long Amron could hear Farrow's voice bellowing out in challenge, trying to goad the two dragonriders into a duel. *He is a belligerent one, this Robin Farrow.* Sir Gerald, to the contrary, was staying as quiet as a mouse, sitting stiff as stone in the saddle of his destrier a full horse-length behind his fellow knight.

Amron cantered right up behind them, hailing them as he came. "Sir Robin, hold your tongue. Sir Gerald, please be quiet as well." He could not resist the jibe.

Both knights pulled their reins and turned. Gerald's doughy face was a sagging mess of pale fear, collapsing in relief as he saw Amron and his younger brother Rogen approaching. Robin Farrow's was bright with the promise of a glorious death.

"Your Majesty," Farrow said, lifting his visor. His brow was knotted in a frown. "I was about to engage them. They…"

"Do you know who that is, Sir Robin?"

"Yes, my lord. It is Garlath the Grand, ridden by the Skylord Ulrik Marak. There would be no greater triumph than defeating the pair in battle."

Belligerent, and somewhat delusional. He would have next to no chance in such a duel, though it seemed discourteous to tell him so. "Stand down, Sir Robin. Lord Marak is here to talk."

"Talk? Why should he want to talk?" The man was confused. "He slew your father, did he not? And King Horris, during the last war."

Long years ago, yes, Amron thought. Much had changed since then and the time for vengeance had long since passed. "You may return to the column, both of you. I have no further need of you here."

Robin Farrow stared at him. "Sire? Ought we not at least stay close? If they should seek to…"

"Return to the column, Sir Robin. By your king's command. Go."

The man obeyed, though grudgingly, riding slowly back the way he'd come. Sir Gerald made a pathetic play of appearing reticent as well.

"They have recognised you," said Whitebeard. He'd been watching the dragonriders all the while.

"I should imagine they have, yes." Amron Deaecar was nothing if not recognisable, no less than Ulrik Marak was. He peered toward the pair, some eighty or so metres away. It did not take him long to realise who the second rider was, and quite frankly the sight astonished him. "Well gods be good, that is Sir Pagaloth Kadosk up there."

"The dragonknight?" asked the ranger. His upturned amber eyes showed as much surprise as they could emote. "I was not aware he was Fireborn."

Amron vaguely remembered Lythian saying that Pagaloth had a trace of Eldur's blood in him. Or perhaps it was Elyon who said it. He could not recall. "It would appear so, Rogen." He took a moment to let the shock of that sink in, wondering how it was the dragonknight had become a dragonrider, then swung a leg over his saddle to dismount. "We'll go on foot from here," he said. The snow was not so deep, a few inches only. Frozen grass crunched beneath his boots as he set off toward the dragons.

The Frostblade misted at his hip, sparkling white and silver and sometimes with melting motes of colour, his hand resting lightly on the pommel. Fine it was, made of a thousand snowflakes linked one to the next to form a perfect sphere, the crossguard and handle glittering with tiny, diamond-like studs that shimmered like crystal in the morning light. The blade was whispering alarm, as was common when dragons were near, thrumming excitedly, but Amron ignored and overpowered it, refusing to wilt to the whispers as they urged him into violence. *I will give it up,* he told himself. *I will. I will.* Ahead, he could see the two riders unfastening their harnesses and dismounting, the dragons lowering their wings to ease them to the ground. Pagaloth's dragon was a handsome beast, to be sure. A classic dragon if ever there was one.

The two parties converged on the open field between their steeds. Never entirely free of doubt, Amron kept his gaze fixed firmly on Ulrik Marak's eyes as he went, searching for those strange red swirls, but they were cast from him now it did seem. *He is in control, his own man again.* At his hip the Fireblade was steaming in the cold, leaving a trail of melted snow in his wake, and he wore his Body of Karagar armour, as impenetrable as the very finest godsteel. He looked fearsome in the craggy black garb, a man tall and powerful, with a wide jaw stubbled in a mat of stiff greying bristles and a head of hair cropped short and thinning.

The pair stopped no more than ten feet apart, Rogen and Sir Pagaloth remaining a step or two behind. Amron studied the dragonlord, and the dragonlord studied him back. A long moment passed like that, before the king claimed the first word. "You look better without chains, Lord Marak," he said. "How does that free air taste?"

"Cold." The skylord's voice was thick and well-spiced with the accents of Agarath. "I am told you are now king, Lord Daecar." He looked at the greying back hair on his head. "Yet I do not see a crown."

"It was lost when the palace in Varinar fell." It was the same day that Amron and Ulrik had seen each other last, when they'd duelled on the field before the coming of the Dread. *More a dance than a duel,* the king reflected. He had sensed then that Lord Marak was battling against his bonds and now it appeared he'd broken them. "I hope to retrieve it when I return. Though there is much rubble to sift through. We have your friend Drulgar to thank for that."

"The dragon is no friend of mine."

"And Garlath?"

"Is a power unto himself. As I am." His eyes burned with a fierce intensity, defiant and prideful. "You know my wingrider." He gestured and Sir Pagaloth came forward, boots crunching in the snow.

"A face I recognise." Amron favoured the dragonknight with a smile. "I confess myself shocked to see you at Lord Marak's wing, Sir Pagaloth. How is it you have bonded a dragon?"

"Bonded...no. That is a long tale, Your Majesty." The dragonknight bowed low, showing that accustomed courtesy. He still wore his black dragonscale armour and red cape, though the latter had been slashed and sewn with some new strips of copper silk as well, to match his dragon's scales. "And one I regaled only short days ago to Lord Rodmond and Sir Ralf."

That was a surprise as well. "You have returned to King's Point?"

"Briefly. And to bring a report to you, my lord. And Captain Lythian. Yet when I arrived I was told you were absent, away at war. And Lythian as well." He paused. "You have had no riders come? No crows bearing news?"

"From King's Point, no." Amron sensed poor tidings were afoot. "Tell me what you know, Sir Pagaloth."

"Yes, my lord," said the dragonknight, and he did.

When he was done, Amron's jaw was tight and his gauntlets were balled into fists. There was foul news there indeed. Mass desertions and betrayals in King's Point, the collapse of his army there under Lythian's rule. A great city fallen further into rot and ruin. The failure and destruction of the united host and this talk of a plague of fire priests crawling up from the south. Worst of all was the news of Lythian himself. Amron had wondered what had become of Brontus Oloran ever since Lord Randall Borrington told him he'd eloped from his duty, abandoning his five thousand men at the Twinfort. His concerns had been tickled when he'd heard of his desertion, and now the full scale of his treachery was exposed.

Damn him.

His fist closed tighter, near enough to sunder the steel. He had half a mind to make at once for the Wandering Wood himself and help hunt Oloran down, but had to trust Lythian and Vilmar had it in hand, and it seemed Storos and Nathaniel had rushed off in pursuit as well. He was too far away to affect any result there and he had too many responsibilities of his own to keep. *Damn him,* he thought again. *Damn that man to the Long Abyss.*

"I have flown several times across the wooded hills," Pagaloth was going on, "in an attempt to find him, but to no avail. The rain is still falling there, my lord, and the mists are too thick to see much of anything from the skies. I will try again when next I have a chance, but the area is vast, and I fear I will have no better luck the next time."

Lord Marak snorted. "Lythian let his guard down, and he is now paying the price. His fate is his own. He must correct this mistake himself."

Amron could not deny a word of that, though felt some sympathy for his friend all the same. *I left him in charge of that rotting ruin, as I left him in charge of that blade.* He knew how pernicious the Blades of Vandar could be. How they could change a man. Darken him. "But you understand our need, Lord Marak?" he asked. "You know the importance of the blades?"

"I was long in Prince Tethian's company," was his blunt answer. "I heard often his sermons, as I did those of Sotel Dar."

"Then you know the Heart must be reforged, and for that all five shards are needed. We can ill afford to misplace even the one. Only such a weapon can hope to defeat our enemy." He checked the dragonlord's hard dark eyes. "Eldur *is* your enemy as well, is he not?"

"He is enemy to this world. Yes."

That would have to be good enough. Ulrik Marak was not a man of many words. "Then we are allied in purpose, it would seem. I take it that is why you have come?"

"Is Pagaloth's report not enough for you?"

"For me, yes. It has proven most useful." Amron would have to send men to King's Point now, to secure the coast. And he would send more men to bolster Crosswater too, and make sure supply lines were improved down the river. "But that does not explain *your* presence here. Sir Pagaloth might have come alone to share these tidings. But here you are. Why?"

"A knight is not fit to deal with a king. Even a crown-less one." His craggy face showed something that might have been a smile and his eyes moved over Amron's shoulder, toward the sprawling force at his back. It snaked down the High Way for many long miles, bleeding far beyond the range of their sight. "You say you're making for Varinar. Are your borders not under siege?"

"Not in the west. Your kin were driven back and the dragon Angaralax was slain. They have retreated back south through the western gate."

"Then Axallio Axar is dead as well?"

"He died atop his dragon."

Marak nodded. "He was a gifted rider, if arrogant. I hope he gave you a good fight?"

"He fought well, yes," Amron lied. In truth the fight had not been close. The Frostblade had proven much too powerful in the snow, and the cold had hampered Angaralax's furnace fires as well. "So why have you come, Lord Marak? Are we to become allies now, you and I?"

The dragonlord stared at him. "I want this war ended," is all he said.

"An end with many paths toward it."

"No. One path. The destruction of Drulgar and the death of Eldur. Eight deaths," he said, with a hard bite to his voice. "The eight deaths of Eldur, Father and Founder. A number we consider sacred, upon which many of our customs are built...and a lie. We must make it truth. Only then can this war be ended."

Amron had no reason to doubt him, here and now beyond the demigod's reach, but later? Could he trust him then? "And if Eldur should ensnare you again? There is a risk to us in that. If we come to trust you, and you turn on us..."

"We shall not turn. Precautions are being taken." He waved a hand to Pagaloth. "Explain."

The dragonknight proceeded to do so, describing their base of operations in the heart of the Wandering Wood, the great rift that sounded suspiciously like something Brannatar had made, the use of the fire priests to build a resistance to Eldur's voice. "We are well protected now, my lord," the dragonknight finished. "Immune, you might say."

"To these priests, yes. But Eldur?" Amron still had his doubts. "A boy with a blade might struggle to put a dent in a suit of armour, but give that same blade to the King's Wall and you can be sure he'll hack right through it. Eldur is altogether more powerful than these priests."

"I know how powerful he is." Marak's voice had a snap to it. "We are doing what we can, and we know the risks."

"Then you cannot go near him. None of you can."

The dragonlord raised his chin. "You will not tell us what we can and cannot do. King you may be, but not to me. We know the risks, I said."

The two old warriors stared at one another. Frost and fire misted and steamed at their hips and they had matching scars as well, or near enough, savage wounds that marked their faces. *He is a mirror to me*, Amron thought. *That is what people say*. He would not let any fledgling alliance die by a few poorly chosen words. "I did not mean to cause offence, Lord Marak," he said, to assuage him. "I only fear you as an enemy as much as I would cherish you as an ally. You must understand…"

"I understand, and better than you do. Sa'har took his own life to keep those fetters off his feet, and we all commit to doing the same, if we must. We all know what it is to be enslaved. All would sooner choose death, than that."

There weren't so many things worse than death, though Amron supposed mental enslavement was one of them. To be used in the spread of an evil cause was unbearable for honourable men. "Very well. Then let us discuss how we can help one another." He looked beyond the two riders to their dragons, further back across the field. The snow had all melted around them now, showing patches of green and brown where they waited. Steam rose about them like vapour from a hot bath. "You have ten dragons, you say."

"As of now, yes."

"And eight riders?"

"Six. Sir Hahkesh and Bah'run cannot qualify as riders yet. But in time, yes. Eight."

Those two names were vaguely familiar to Amron. Pagaloth saw his frown and said, "They were taken from King's Point when I visited, my lord. Two prisoners from the camp. Lythian had been working with them."

His schemes. Those failed as well, Pagaloth had reported. "These dragons, then. I wonder if…

"I will not become a messenger service for you," Marak said at once, reading his intent. "We are Fireborn, not couriers. And we are helping to free your lands of this plague of priests."

"Which I am grateful for. And more than willing to support. If I could I would bring word to Crosswater and Varinar and Ilivar and Ayrin's Cross to send men through the Heartlands to clear this infestation out, but my means to do so are slow and ponderous and perilous besides. Any riders I despatch take weeks to reach their targets and many get killed along the way, never to return. Their horses break their legs in the snow or get stuck in a bog and their riders are left stranded, to be slain by bandits and beasts. And the crows are even worse. So few fly between our rookeries now, and even those that try are getting lost. The weather…it affects their ability to navigate. I am told that an eagle was sighted with a scroll on its leg only recently. An *eagle*. It was coming our way, my outriders report, but was killed before it could reach me, roasted in a lance of flame by a passing dragon. Where it came from or what it might have told us I couldn't say, but perhaps that is what we've been reduced to. Our crows are dead, so men are deploying eagles now. Eagles!" And he laughed bitterly.

"What's next? Sparrows and swallows? Shall we start training owls? Would that Wolfsbane could sprout wings and fly...I would happily go from coast to coast myself, but I can't, and my son...my son I have not seen since before I marched from King's Point, and who knows what has become of him. We were relying on him to spread tidings for a time, and if that is still the case, it would seem he has forgotten us. But you have *dragons*, my lord, *ten* of them, well capable of crossing these lands quickly and defending themselves from attack. I am not asking you to fly my messages all day and all night, only that you spare a dragon or two for the occasional pass. To bring me tidings from the east, and from Tukor and Rasalan if you can. Even south of here, in Agarath and the empire. It is asking a lot, I know, but...."

"Fine. I will help you."

Amron let out a breath. He had been going on, he realised. On and on and on. *I have beaten him down through boredom.* It had been his bane for so damnably long, this matter of crow-killing dragons darkening his skies, and a king could not rule or make war when blind, not as he should like. He still did not even know how his forces were faring in the east, or how many men they had left out there. Had Rustbridge fallen? Was Tukor being besieged? Rasalan? Had all the east been overrun now, as the Marshlands had? How could he prepare and plan to defeat his enemy if he didn't even know his own strength? *I've been blind, but now I will see again,* he thought. Of all people, Ulrik Marak, the man who had killed his father, was telling him he would become his eyes.

"You will?" he asked, needing to hear it confirmed.

"I hear your plea, Lord Daecar. And I understand your difficulties. Yes, I will help shed some light across these lands, but only where I deem it safe. We are dragonriders, and will be seen as a threat and an enemy during any approach. None of my riders are known to your people. If they are attacked..."

"My lord, if I may." Pagaloth drew forward, waited for Marak to grunt permission, then spoke. "Perhaps the king might be willing to share in this endeavour with us, by supplying trusted men of his own? Men well-known across this kingdom, who can perform the duty of gathering and trading tidings, while our own riders stay well back and out of reach of any harm? We only need to bring them close to a city or a fort, and they can do the rest. That would mitigate the risk to us, I think."

Marak considered it, giving nothing away. After a while, he nodded. "Could you supply such men?"

"I have many thousands to choose from. I do not think that should be a problem."

"No. We need no common men for this task. Trusted men, only. Men you value, to share the risk."

"I have plenty of those as well."

Behind, Garlath was stretching a wing, opening his great maw and yawning like some enormous grey-blue hound. Lances of flame speared out into the frigid air, and even away in the distance, Amron could hear the ripple go through his host, as if worried the great dragon was limbering up for an attack. He turned his head back to make certain no force was mustering to come to his aid and was reminded that Rogen Whitebeard was still with them, silent as a shadow.

"This man of yours," Marak said, seeing him too. "He is the ranger, yes? Sir Pagaloth has spoken of him."

"His name is Rogen Strand," Amron said.

"A man you trust? A man you value?"

Yes, on both counts, but Amron was not about to part with him. "People are not his strength, I fear. He would make a poor emissary, and is not well-known besides. I will think of some others."

"Then think fast. I do not plan to stand here in this snow forever."

"Of course." Amron was much enthused by this development. "How many will you take?"

Marak's thick neck twisted as he looked at Pagaloth. "Three," he said, deciding. "One can be taken to King's Point, to relay what we have shared. An oath was made by Sir Pagaloth to return there with news. I would not see our honour called into question."

Amron nodded, wondering....

"The other two I will take myself to our hideout," the dragonlord went on. "I will decide from there how best to deploy them and how far I will let them travel." He turned his eyes to the host. "Go, Lord Daecar. Make your choice and make it quick. The dragons are getting cold."

Amron pondered his choice as he rode back with Rogen Whitebeard. "You would you choose, Rogen?" he asked. "We need dependable men, and brave men. And men well-known as well."

"Sir Bryce, perhaps?" offered the ranger. "He was a Varin Knight for decades."

"And well respected," Amron agreed, "though not the most willing sort. I doubt he'd want to go, at his age." He rubbed the frost from his chin. "Stoutman is an obvious option. He's always up for a challenge."

"His sons all died at King's Point. He might not want to go near those dragons."

Amron nodded. It was a fair observation, though Torus had come a long way since then. War was no time to wallow in grief, all fighting men were taught. Loss was something to be buried deep down, and excavated and examined later on, once peace resumed.

"I will ask him anyway," he said, and should he consent, that would make one. *But who else,* he wondered, as he rode on toward the head of the column. *Who else...*

By the time he reached the head of the column, he knew. As he had expected, a hundred questions were shouted at him from the assembled lords and knights, but he was forced to wave them off for now. "Lord

Strand, Lord Borrington, Stegra..." He felt obliged to include the Snow-fist, who of course was still lingering around. "Rogen will update you on what was said. Rogen, if you would. Amara, a private word."

He took his good-sister aside. She seemed most confused. "And what's this about? I don't like that look on your face, Amron."

She won't like this either. "I fear I must steal Sir Connor from you, Amara. Not for long. And it might be dangerous, but..."

"What duty will you have of him?" Her frown was displeased. "You said nothing would change after he became a Varin Knight. Now you're to take him away from me?"

"Only for a short while. He will not be gone long."

"Gone? Where? Where are you taking him?"

"I'm taking him nowhere. He'll be leaving with Lord Marak."

She laughed out loud. "Marak? You must be joking."

"I'm not. We have come to an arrangement, and he has offered to be our eyes. But I need the eyes of my own men to go with him, and their ears, and they must be trusted. I trust Sir Connor Crawfield. Send for him, please."

When that was done, Sir Torus Stoutman arrived having been summoned from the baggage train. He gave a great big guffaw when Amron told him what he wanted. "Dragonflight? With Ulrik Marak, Bane of Bladeborn and Killer of Kings? Hell, why not? Can I smoke my pipe up there?"

Amron smiled. He had hoped for such a reaction. "You'll have to ask Ulrik about that. I sense he will advise you to spare both your hands for holding on tight. You will not have a harness, Torus. At least not until you reach their camp, where one will be made for you, I hope."

"I'll cling to some horns, then. I've got a strong grip." He closed a small meaty fist to show him. "So who's going too? Or is it just me on my lonesome?"

"No. There will be three. Lord Marak will take you and Sir Connor east atop Garlath. They have a camp somewhere in the high north of the Wandering Wood. Now play nice, Torus. I don't want you rubbing them up the wrong way."

"Me? Never." He gave a toothy grin. "Con will keep me in line, in any case. We're like salt and pepper, us two, though I can't figure out who's which." He guffawed again. That was partly why Amron chose them; the two men were hardly similar. "So who's the third? A bit of sweetness to go with that spice?"

Amron was not so sure he could be considered sweet. "I will be the third," he said.

28

Pagaloth

The dragonknight was confused when the king returned with only two men.

He knew one of them, the short wide one with the enormous thick beard and long rosewood pipe that dangled from one corner of his mouth. Sir Torus Stoutman, he was called; Pagaloth had met him during his time at King's Point, though would not say he knew him well. The other was introduced as Sir Connor Crawfield, a stiff-looking man of modest height and build who had a face made for sombre expression. He was the long-serving Captain of the Daecar Household Guard, Pagaloth recalled being told. Though a Varin Knight now, it would seem, to judge the new cloak he wore.

Lord Marak was equally puzzled. "Where is the other one?" he demanded of the king. "I asked for three."

"You have three," King Amron Daecar said. "I will be going with Pagaloth."

"You?" Marak's frown thickened. "You would leave your army?"

"They can do without me for a few hours, I think. I have a desire to visit King's Point myself and take account of the state of the city."

Marak looked him up and down. "You are a heavy man in that armour. Garlath could comfortably carry you, but Lendrathor may struggle. He is a much smaller dragon."

Pagaloth shared that concern. He gave the Vandarian king a passing look up and down and judged him tremendously weighty, armoured or no.

But the king seemed unconcerned. "It cannot hurt to try. If we fail, I'll choose someone else."

Marak snorted. "Fine. You may try. But on your head be it." He turned and marched away.

After that came the small matter of introducing the Bladeborn to the dragons. Garlath was no stranger to them, having borne Lythian on his

345

back a number of times before, but the same could not be said of Lendrathor. Younger and more cautious, he watched their approach warily, though the gentle rumbling sound that the Grand gave out suggested he was communing with his fellow dragon and telling him all was well.

Marak confirmed as much when Sir Connor Crawfield asked him. "He is explaining what is happening, yes," he said to the knight. "I have told Garlath that you are under my protection, and he has told Lendrathor. They understand what is required of them, but are still dragons, and you Bladeborn. The animus runs deep. Keep your hands from your weapons and give them no reason to harm you."

Sir Torus Stoutman waddled over and gave Pagaloth a jaunty poke in the ribs. "And you, lad? Can you chat with your big beastie the same way he can?" He gestured with his pipe to Lord Marak.

Pagaloth shook his head. "No, sir. Our bond is not the same. There is no telepathic connection between us."

"Oh?" The man took a puff and blew out a series of rings, widening as they rose.

"It requires a soul-bonding," the dragonknight explained, though suspected he must already know. "That can only be achieved with the Bondstone. Lendrathor and I share a different sort of connection."

"A big flying fire-breathing horse, is he?"

"Yes." It was a little reductive, but the imagery was compelling. "The bond could be described as much the same."

"Then I'd say you've got it lucky, lad. Why give up half your soul when you can fly a dragon anyway? We like our horses here in the north, aye, and grieve them when they die, but it's not worth living a shell of a man after now is it? You've got the best of both worlds there."

Marak snorted, overhearing. "Do not speak on things you do not understand, Vandarian. A true Fireborn rider is honoured to share his soul, and his dragon the same. There is nothing else like it."

"Aye. If you say so." Stoutman waited for Marak to turn his scowl away, then looked up at Pagaloth with a mischievous grin. "I still think you've got the better deal, lad," he said discreetly. "And you don't let that big grump tell you otherwise, d'you hear?" He grinned again and slapped Pagaloth on the arm, then shuffled away after the others.

The three of them set off first. It made quite the sight, watching Sir Torus and Sir Connor clambering awkwardly up Garlath's side as the great dragon swung his long neck around to look at them, rumbling and glaring, judging them much as a cat would do so, very critical and superior. When both of the Bladeborn knights were settled in place, as firm and fixed as they could be amid the deep ridges and high horns been Garlath's powerful shoulders, Ulrik Marak bellowed down a word of parting, telling Amron Daecar to watch the skies and that he would see Pagaloth back at camp, then left. Garlath was not a dragon to take off from a standing start, not at that size. He turned, facing east across the snow-draped field, widened his wings and began to run, the earth trembling and quaking beneath his weight as he thundered away through the pale wintry air. His wings thrashed, stirring a white wind as the snow swirled and stormed, and into the skies he went. Behind, amidst the northern army, a distant murmur of wonder buzzed in the air.

"Well then," Pagaloth said. "Our turn, my lord." He looked across at the king, who was watching the dragon depart with his two knights, deep in thought. Pagaloth wondered what those thoughts might be, though it was not his place to ask. "Your Majesty," he prompted. "We will have to test your weight first...before we risk a longer flight. And hope that Lendrathor accepts you. There is always the chance he will refuse to bear you."

The tall king turned, towering above him. His lobstered armour was silver, enamelled in azure plating about the border of his breastplate, his cloak rich blue with a silver stripe down the middle, his hair and beard black and grey, thick and regal. "Lord Marak just said otherwise, Sir Pagaloth. Lendrathor understands his charge."

"Yes, my lord, but I daresay I know Lendrathor. He can be unruly at times, and hard to control. Less now than when first I rode him, I will admit, but..."

The king cut him off. "You named him for your uncle, is that correct?"

He was surprised he knew. "Yes. My uncle Sir Lendroth. He trained me as a squire."

"And taught you all you know?"

All was too big a word. "I learned a lot from him, my lord."

"So you honour him by naming your dragon for this man. And now the dragon becomes the teacher, tutoring you in the skies." He looked into his eyes. "You trust this dragon, as you trusted your uncle." It was not a question. "And I trust you." He put a large steel hand on his shoulder. "As Lythian did. So come, cast aside those concerns, Pagaloth." He smiled ruggedly and stepped away.

Lendrathor was naturally suspicious, as could only be expected. He watched the Vandarian king through his shining green and orange eyes as they drew nearer, trails of smoke rising out past his teeth in a gesture to intimidate. It was not likely to work with Amron Daecar, who had fought and killed much larger dragons before, Angaralax being the latest. "He is not here to harm you," Pagaloth said soothingly, switching to his own native tongue. "We will be hosting him in flight, Lendrathor, as Garlath told you. We are allies now. Or have you not been listening?"

The dragon rumbled something that sounded like irritation.

"Enough of that. Now lower your wing, if you would, and prepare yourself. King Daecar will weigh a deal more than I do, and no, he cannot remove his armour."

It took a short while....partly because Lendrathor was nothing if not prideful and must of course make a fuss of it...but eventually the dragon snorted and submitted, permitting the king to climb up onto his back. His weight clearly came as a great shock, that was obvious from the way the dragon's bulk shifted to one side as the king climbed from horn to horn, Lendrathor growling confusion all the while. "I'm afraid my saddle is built for one," Pagaloth told the king, as he came up to join him. "If you would straddle him right there, just behind me. One leg between those horns, and the other right there, along that ridge. Yes, that's it. Hold the rear of my saddle, my lord, and you should remain firm in place." He thought a moment, wondering how he could better secure him. "We might be able to lash you up somehow," he said. "I have some rope, here in my saddlebag. It might be wise to take the pre…"

"No need, Pagaloth. I trust you to teach me where to shift my weight as needed."

Pagaloth had only just learned that himself, by the tuition of Lord Marak and Lady Kazaan and sometimes An'zon Graz as well. He said as much, and told the king the basic principle was to lean with the flow of the dragon himself. "If you watch me closely, my lord, and do as I do, we may be all right."

"We will be, Pagaloth. I have no intention of falling. And my armour will help protect me if I do."

But how much? The dragonknight did not imagine that even godsteel plate could withstand a fall from a thousand feet. "We will stay low," he decided, "at least at first. Once you and Lendrathor are both accustomed to one another, perhaps we can gain some altitude."

He performed a final check, looking over the king for a while. It seemed to him that the colourful mists that poured off the Frostblade were behaving oddly, shifting and moving in a manner he had not seen, an aggressive manner it did seem to him. He frowned. "My lord. Might it be forward of me to ask…"

"You fear this is unwise. To bring the Frostblade with me."

"I've heard it said the Blades of Vandar hunger for the blood of dragons, my lord."

"A remark I may have made myself," the king admitted. "Yes, they are hostile to the Children of Agarath, as is only natural. As echoes of Vandar, what else could we expect, but a strong man is able to control those urges. There really is nothing to fear, Pagaloth. Though if you would prefer, I could leave it here with my host."

Pagaloth did not think that would be a sensible course, given what little he knew of the king's pains and ailments. The Frostblade healed them, if temporarily while in his grasp. Without it the man was said to suffer a terrible limp in his right leg, and acute weakness in his left shoulder. Spasms of pain could grip him and overwhelm him, Lythian had confided, and they were only growing worse the longer he kept the blade. It was not something many people knew about. *He keeps it secret to show strength*, Pagaloth knew, and he was not about to deny him that here. In flight that strength would be needed to hold on and stay stable, and should a tide of pain seize him, well, there was a risk he might lose his grip and fall. "You had best keep the blade, my lord," he said.

Take-off was a little more laboured than was typical. With the burden of the steel-clad king on his back, Lendrathor was not capable of a smooth and easy lift, so had to run hard to build momentum, thrashing his wings all the while. Before too long he was skimming the ground, thumping his wings, climbing a little higher. He stayed low for a while, as though testing the king's weight, gliding along no more than fifteen metres above the plains, then gave a burst of wing-flaps, one and two and three, propelling himself higher, thirty, forty, fifty metres into the air. "That'll do, Lendrathor," Pagaloth said when he reached about seventy-five. "Maintain this height now please."

The dragon flattened off, turning in gentle arcs to left and right. The dragonknight moved with him and called back for the king to do the same, though gently. "At your weight, your movements must be subtle, my lord. Else you might overload him on one side."

The king understood. For a time they cruised, performing a series of steepening banks. Only once did Amron Daecar move his weight too much, and cause Lendrathor to lose his balance, yet that was quickly corrected. Pagaloth spoke to the dragon all the while, asking him to lift or raise his height, to shift further south or east, to be careful to not bank too fiercely or overdo his speed.

"You have the measure of him, Pagaloth," he heard the king say behind. "He seems quite willing to obey your commands."

"I would not use that word in his hearing, my lord. I ask, and nicely, and that seems to work well enough. We have built our bond on mutual respect. I suppose you would say the same of Wolfsbane?"

"A correct assertion, yes. Let us hope you and Lendrathor fly together for as long."

"I hope that is the case, my lord."

They soared in wide circles, staying largely to the south of the host. Pagaloth could see them all down there, gazing up in bewilderment to see their king and champion flying dragonback above them. *Not all will be happy about that, no doubt.* Lythian had been a forward-thinking man and they had cursed him as a dragonlover and sympathiser for it. Would they levy the same accusations at their king?

The army was larger than Pagaloth had first thought, snaking away in a great long procession into the far-flung distance to the west. It wended around low hills and descended through shallow valleys, passed snowy abandoned villages and farms and frozen thickets armoured in frost. Here and there it broke up, leaving open stretches between one segment or another. "They need to close those gaps," Pagaloth heard the king say. "I don't like those holes and breaches. Where are the captains? They need to get them in order." He raised his voice. "Take us west, Pagaloth, if you would. I'd like to look upon my rearguard."

He did as he was bidden. The king continued to review the formations of his army, muttering comments as they glided westward. Some walked and rode in rank beneath them, neat and orderly, spear tips and helm crests glinting in the sun whenever it should pierce the clouds, banners caught high in the stiff morning breeze. Others made for a disorderly sight, trudging along in ones and twos and little groups, pulling carts or driving wagons with oxen and goats and dogs running about them. It was not a trained force of soldiers alone, that was clear. There were many women down there, and children as well, and the old and infirm were to be seen in great quantity.

"We have a large militia force with us," the king explained, when Pagaloth asked. "Mustered from the high north by Lord Robert Borrington. Many brought their families with them. They're trying to escape the snow."

"And those?" Pagaloth pointed. One part of the host was queerest of all, made up of all manner of oddities. He saw giants down there over eight feet tall, and men wearing cloaks of patched animal skins, women with nesting birds in their hair. Some looked as light-skinned as the snow upon which they walked, with chalk-white hair and strange blue eyes, and many were dragging sleds made of bone, heaped with children dressed in seal-skin and whale-hide. "Who are *they*, my lord?"

"Tribesman, from beyond the Weeping Heights. They're fleeing the snow as well, Pagaloth. They call it the Endfall." The king's answer was somewhat perfunctory. He seemed distracted. "They need to move that cart," he said, again to himself. "It's holding everyone up. And that one…why have they gone off the road? The snow is too deep there. They'll only get themselves stuck." Lendrathor was soaring on, and with each passing moment the king saw another issue worthy of complaint. "This is the trouble of leading such a disjoined host, Pagaloth. Half of them are untrained and have no understanding of order. And no wonder we're making such slow time."

Yet further up the road, the sparkling north opened out, bands of mist blowing over the great white world like ocean-spray over the sea. The High Way rolled onward over those frozen plains, and the army with it, a great broken train in black and brown and green and grey that must be fifty or sixty thousand strong if the dragonknight was any judge. Eventually they came to its end, where a strong rearguard marched, greatly more orderly than the masses in between.

"Good," the king said, pleased by what he saw. "Lord Gavron has them in fine fettle today." The king spotted the lord in question, trotting on his warhorse with a host of men in black-grey cloaks arrayed around him. Their sigil was a misting godsteel scythe, fitting for a house called Grave. "That's good enough for a test flight, wouldn't you say?" the king called. "Could we land here, Sir Pagaloth? I'd like to speak with the Ironfoot."

"Yes, my lord. It will give us a chance to practice a landing." Pagaloth sensed that Lendrathor could do with a short rest as well. "There," he said. "We will come down by those trees." The trees in question were a clutch of oaks, big and old, a short way south of the road. It seemed wise to keep their distance and not come down too close. "Hold on tight, my lord. Lendrathor will swing his feet down when landing, so brace yourself and lean forward."

The landing was hardly the most gracious, but land they did, the heavy snow shifting and exploding beneath the dragon's weight as his clawed feet crashed down upon the hard frozen soil. Pagaloth smiled. It had gone well, better than he had hoped it would. He gave Lendrathor a good pat on the side and could feel his heavy breathing, the deep rumbling in his lungs. The exertion had taken its toll, clearly, but it was nothing a short rest would not solve.

"We may have to stop once or twice on our way to King's Point," he told the king. "For Lendrathor to rest. But I see no reason why we shouldn't make it."

"King's Point…yes." There was something doubtful in his voice. "That is good to hear, Pagaloth." The man looked over the side of the dragon. "You dismount down the wing, is that not so?"

"Most commonly that is the case."

"Well. I'll jump if that's all right by you." The king did not wait for a response. Standing, he leapt, landing with a thump near as loud as Lendrathor's, dropping to a knee and standing back up. The snow was thicker here and rose halfway up his thigh. "Stay here, Pagaloth," he said, brushing his cloak down. "I won't be long."

The king was good to his word. He stayed only long enough to relay some commands to the Ironfoot and some other men before hastening back toward him. Pagaloth stayed saddled all the while, watching through the wintry shroud. When the king was back in earshot, he asked, "Is all well, my lord? I hope the Ironfoot did not disapprove?"

"Disapprove? Of what?"

"Of this, my lord. His king sharing the back of a dragon with an Agarathi."

"With a friend and ally, Pagaloth. I spare no concern for such complaints. We're all trying to win this war, aren't we?" He climbed back up to sit behind the saddle. "Is Lendrathor well-rested?"

"Well enough, yes." He reached into a saddlebag and unfolded a small map, twisting back in his seat so the king could see. He tapped a finger and traced a route. "King's Point is some three hundred or so miles from here, my lord. I suspect it will take several hours to reach it, accounting for breaks. Lendrathor will win no prizes for speed, I fear. Not bearing your weight. We will take it slow, and steady, and…"

"I have not been entirely honest with you, Sir Pagaloth," Amron Daecar said, strangely.

The dragonknight frowned at him. "My lord?"

The king waved over to the road. There seemed to be some motion among the men of the rearguard, orders being shouted as if to call them to muster. "I've commanded the Ironfoot to make for King's Point," he said. "After what you told me, it must be relieved and restored. Lord Grave was there before and after the battle and understands its need. He will make this very day for Crosswater, and then head down the Steelrun River. His remaining men will go with him, a strong host. And some of my own bannermen too."

Pagaloth thought the plan sensible, having seen the desperate state of the city. "So you're to say you have no wish to visit King's Point yourself, my lord? Is there somewhere else you wish for me to take you?"

The king had a craggy and characterful smile. "You're sharp as a razor, Pagaloth. I would still like to share a cup of wine with Rodmond and Ralf, but only after. There's somewhere else I'd like you to take me first."

"Is it far, my lord? From King's Point?"

"Not so far." The king looked at the map and gestured with a steel finger. "Right about there, I'm told." He was pointing to a part of the Greenwood, right down amidst the southeastern reaches of the forest. It looked about a hundred and fifty miles from the city. "That's where the scouts say he was when they tracked him down. Though that was a while ago, it must be said, and it's possible he may have moved on by now."

Pagaloth was not understanding. "Who, my lord?"

The king answered that question with one of his own. "Have you heard of Brannatar the Boar?"

29

—————

ℜobbert

The lake that lay before his host had not been a lake only months ago, Robbert was told.

"Been watching it change daily," the tiny old marshman croaked, as they sat huddled in the damp little mud-and-reed shelter he'd raised beside its banks. "Every day I pop my head out my hole and I see the waters coming closer to my door. It's this rain, that's what it is, this rain that won't stop falling. I've had to move twice already, if you'll believe it. *Twice* in as many months! And now it looks like I'll have to move again." He snorted and shook his strange little head. "I'll go further this time, yes, yes I will…even further just to be sure. There's a good little place I got my eye on…been sounding it out already, I have, make sure it's safe, you know?"

"A safe place to call home is important," Robbert agreed. "Especially with all these monsters about."

"Aye, monsters." He bobbed his head queerly up and down. "Come in all sorts of skins, they do. All sorts of skins." And he snorted again, shaking his head at some bitter memory. He was very ugly, this strange little man, with wide flat lips and a sloping forehead and great angry groupings of boils and carbuncles spouting from his neck and nose. It all gave Robbert good cause to wonder at what point in his family tree a woman had coupled with a toad. His was an unsettling ugliness, the sort that made you want to constantly avert your eyes. Robbert did not want to spend any longer in his company than he must.

"So, this lake…" he prompted. "You were telling me how to get around it?"

The toad scratched at his lumpy chin. "Aye. Not easy, but I know a way. Would take you along the shore for a little way south, then through it."

"*Through* it?" Robbert didn't like the sound of through it. "Do you have boats for a thousand men, pray?"

"I got a boat, but it's the size for just me. Hardly more'n a tub, really. The sort you rich folk like to piss in, if you'll excuse my tongue."

"That's quite all right." Robbert found the image of this cantankerous little toad of a man floating about in a chamberpot rather amusing, actually. "But do explain to me how we're to cross this lake without any boats. Do you expect us to build them?" There was woodland here, spouting from the many islands that littered this sprawling swamp, but getting between those islands was dangerous work. Robbert had already lost several dozen men to bog lizards and marsh ghouls and didn't care to lose any more. *I have few enough as it is. They should be dying by dragonfire or at the edge of Agarathi steel, not dragged to their deaths in this endless bloody bog.*

"No need to build anything," the toad assured him. "You'd be walking. There's a way I know."

"Through it. You said." Robbert didn't like what this toad was peddling. "That sounds rather perilous, old man. Scant few of my men can walk on water."

The man made a croaking laugh. "More's the pity. I wish I could do that myself, but no…no, I'm talking about a road beneath the water, m'lord. A good timber road, raised and reinforced for you Bladeborn sort. I'm sure you've seen lots of those on your way here?"

They had. This entire region was crossed with these raised timber causeways, though many of them were underwater now on account of all the flooding from the torrential rains. "We've passed a few," Robbert said. "This road is beneath the water, you say? How deep?"

The frog flattened his long wide lips, thinking. "Maybe a foot or so, if I had to guess. Was always raised high above the swamp, that road, so it's still walkable even now that this lake's flooded in. Well, mostly."

"Mostly?" Robbert said.

The toad bobbed his head. "The road leads to an island, about halfway across the lake. There's a town there called *Bogroot*. Or *was*, in any case. A while back a dragon came by and burned it to cinders." He pointed with a knobbly finger. "It's right there on your map, you see. That line there, that's the road I'm talking about. And there's Bogroot too, you see it?"

"I see it."

Robbert had the map folded out in front of him as he crouched in the little mud shelter. It was the one supplied by Master Bartus at Winslow Point, well annotated by the old steward to help him navigate these treacherous lands. So far Bartus's advice had proven welcome, and Robbert had been able to steer his host safely, if slowly, through the marshes. But they were well beyond the bounds of Bartus's wisdom now and must rely on local knowledge. To that end, Robbert had sent out scouts to search for suitable swamp-dwellers, and that's how they'd unearthed this little toad when he emerged from his mud-hut to wave them down. A fortuitous find, that was. All the other scouts had come back shaking their heads and without this little gremlin they'd be lost.

"So, we take the road to the ruin of Bogroot," the prince said, tapping a finger on the map and trying his best to ignore how stupid that name was. "And then? Does the road not continue on the other side?"

"Well, it did. The dragon burned a large part of it down when he attacked the town. Or she. Might have been a lady dragon. Who am I to go guessing at its gender?" He grinned that long wide ugly grin of his.

Robbert was less amused. "So where do we go?" he asked, with thinning patience. "I don't care to find myself stranded on this island in the middle of a lake that wasn't a lake only months ago, marshman."

The man croaked laughter. "No, can't imagine you do. But good thing you found me, m'lord. There's another path off this island, you see, one that only *I* know about. A belt of higher ground between the bogs that's no more'n a foot or so submerged, same as that road. You'd never know to look at it. The water's so murky might be an inch or a mile deep, but I know where to put my feet, yes I do. So you just follow behind old Grimbel and you'll be fine."

"Grimbel," Robbert said. "That's your name?"

"Good one, isn't it? Grimbel Croakcloak they call me. Aye, I know what I look like. Awful toadish, yes, but that serves me well around here. Most of my neighbours tend to leave me be because of it." He grinned. "Mayhaps they see a fellow monster in me, m'lord. I know you do."

"No. I see an old man of the marshes, that is all. Well adapted to life out here."

"*Adapted*, aye. That's a good way of putting it." He wiped his hands together. There was webbing between his fingers too, Robbert saw, and for all he knew the man had gills. *Do toads have gills?* he wondered idly. He wasn't so sure on that. "I know the lay of the land better than anyone, oh yes. So you'd best trust me to know where I'm going. You need but follow, m'lord. Old Grimbel Croakcloak will lead you safe and true."

How had it come to this? That he must put his life and those of all his men in the hands of an overgrown toad called Grimbel Croakcloak? Robbert sighed. "And if I were to simply go *around* the lake instead?" He looked at the map again, wondering where the boundary of this lake might be. By his reckoning, this entire region was one vast basin, a lowland swamp that had made for a good collection point for all the recent rainfall. Small wonder it had become so flooded. "I suspect the edge of the lake runs somewhere along this course," he offered, tracing a finger to the northwest. The basin ended there, it seemed to him. "If we took that route we could avoid crossing the lake altogether and would intersect with the Mudway up here." He tapped his finger.

Grimbel Croakcloak shrugged. "You could…if you want to lose a week or two. And that'd be supposing the Mudway's not underwater as well up there. Which I'm guessing it was, further to the east? Elsewise why would you be here in my swamp?"

He had the right of that, did Grimbel Croakcloak. Robbert and his host had started on the Mudway from Winslow Point, but soon enough found it dipping through a flooded valley and had been forced to turn to another route. Bartus, mercifully, had anticipated that and given him sound instruction, so they'd veered southward along a different path, twisting here and turning there, sometimes having to backtrack or brave the low and muddy waters as they inched their way to the west.

It was painfully slow at times, and they had lost several days when they unwittingly found themselves walking a route they'd travelled before, only to realise later that they were going the wrong way. "This damned place is a maze," Lank had cursed. "A mire and a maze both, and full of bloody *monsters*."

That it was. They could always sense the foul denizens of this swamp lurking nearby, see the eyes glowing out there in the dark and hear the soft slosh of water as they tried to creep in and pull a man down to his doom. Bartus had told them to travel only by daylight to mitigate that threat, but it wasn't always enough. Some days were as dark as night when the rain lashed down, and not always could they find somewhere dry to rest either. Every day Robbert would send out scouts to search for places to make camp, but finding space for a thousand men wasn't easy.

They'd stopped for a night or two in abandoned towns raised up on stilts, and sometimes simply rested on the road if it wasn't underwater. When they did that Robbert made sure that a fifty-fifty rotation was observed, so that while one man slept, another would watch over him, and if they were lucky they'd get three or four hours each. The best nights were when they found wooded islands to sleep on, though, large enough to accommodate them all. That happened maybe one in three nights. The rest were tense, long, dismal and wet, and the men had learned to live in constant fear.

And from one creature above all. The bog lizards and marsh stalkers and swamp crawlers they could handle. Those were cowardly creatures in large part, ambush predators, and killable if they saw them coming. But *she* was different. *And this is her mire.*

Robbert withdrew from his musings and looked at his host. "How long have you lived in this swamp, Croakcloak?"

The toad moved his shoulders up and down. "Must be nigh on eighty autumns now, m'lord. Came here as a tadpole still suckling at my mother's teat and been here ever since. Might be a lake out there now, but I know all the lands that lie beneath it. The sunken islands and the drowned villages and everything else in between."

"And the creatures that live there? You know everything about them as well, I trust?"

The man smiled. "Well, I wouldn't have lived so long if I didn't. I know all there is to know about them, aye. Where they live, when they hunt, what they eat, when they sleep. I see a pile of droppings and know what made it, when, what they ate to give off that stink. I know every track and I know every sound. I could lay my hand flat to the ground right now and tell you if something was out there, lurking up close near your host."

Robbert looked at him. "Well is there?"

The toad pressed his webbed fingers to the damp earthen floor. "No," he said, with a smile. "There's a bog lizard off nearby in the reeds, but it's sleeping now and will be for a while. You seen any of those on your way here?"

"We have had our interactions, yes. A dozen of my men have been lost to them."

"Well, a host large as yours is always going to attract attention. Just the way it is around here. You pass this way and you'd best be prepared to pay the tax." He smiled again. "But you're past the worst of it now, I'd wager. So long as you follow behind old Grimbel, you'll have no trouble on the lake."

Robbert squinted at him. "How can you be sure?"

"Because it's too deep for most of them monsters. They prefer to lurk in shallow bogs and swamps, right up near the drowned trunks of trees. They come from the shadows, quick as that, and are gone. Can't be done around here, not anymore. Only the taller trees still poke out the water and there aren't so many places to hide."

"And Celaph?" Robbert asked, watching the toad's face closely. "We've heard stirrings that she's awoken, Grimbel. A man such as you might be able to shed some light on that."

The toad gave another of his wide, somewhat sinister smiles. "Awoken? Oh no. She can't wake up if she never went to sleep, can she? Celaph mightn't be seen for twenty years, but that don't mean she's not there. And when she sleeps for a century, that's just a little nap to her. The same as if you were to lay down now and wake five minutes later. She's *old*, m'lord, even older than this land. She came from out across the sea, some say, a goddess cast out from some other world and cursed to her serpent form. But before then she was beautiful, aye, and when the moon is just right she can still be seen as she once was, walking through the swamp at night, green-haired and radiant, so lovely it hurts your eyes to look at her knowing you'll never see such beauty again."

Robbert stared at the toad. "It sounds like you worship this beast, Grimbel." That thought gave him pause. "I was under the impression she was just another monster, raised by the gods to fight in their wars."

"A common misconception, m'lord. She wasn't made by the gods, she *is* one, and aye, most worthy of worship." He put his hands together. "This is a land of the old and the pious, young princeling, and we all live in the shadow of a god. So best not insult her with words like *beast* and *monster*. She might be close enough to hear you."

Robbert felt a shiver move up his spine. *He is toying with me, that's all. I'm an outsider and he wants to watch me squirm.* Well, Robbert Lukar would not show such fear. He turned his eyes down to the map again, agonising over his choice, but in the end he saw no other way. He wanted out of this marsh, and as quickly as he could, and crossing the lake was the fastest way. He made his decision and folded the map up, to tuck into his pocket. "This way of yours, then. What do you want in return for leading us?"

"I want these rains to stop so I can build back my home how it was.

Used to have different rooms and everything, but not here. This is only temporary." He slapped at the muddy wall. "Not sure you've got that power, though, do you? They say it's Vandar's tears for all the blood that's being spilt, this rain. You care to stop a dead god from weeping, m'lord?"

"When the war is won, his eyes will be dry. In the meantime, I can offer you riches…"

"Useless here. Coin. Jewels. I care for none of that. Nor anything you could give me. I'm a simple man of simple pleasures. I'll lead you across for free." He grinned another of his grins that Robbert didn't like. "Let me just fetch my stick."

Robbert crawled out through the door-hole, cutting a less than regal figure as he did so. Lank was outside with Bernie, waiting cloaked and cowled beneath the rain. Both of them stifled laughter to see him emerge on all fours, though Grimbel Croakcloak, minuscule as he was, was able to exit in only a crouch. He tottered through the reeds with a long walking stick in his grasp that he used to poke occasionally down into the wet muddy water.

"What's that about?" Bernie asked him.

"Feeling for things," Croakcloak said. He wore a mottled cloak of woven river reeds and cattails, good camouflage here in the swamp. "Things you'd be best avoiding."

"Like what?"

"Like that bog lizard I told your prince about just now. And the swamp lurkers off yonder, past them bushes." He drew out the stick and stabbed it deeper. Its end was sharp, Robbert saw, and where he held it was a wound leather handle that seemed to amplify his sense of touch. "There's a mire wraith out there too, but further off. That's not something you want to run into."

Robbert was getting a better idea as to how this little toad had survived out here alone. "Lothar, go and get the men ready to go. We'll be crossing the lake."

"*Crossing* it? And how's that? We'd need boats, wouldn't we?"

Robbert laughed and so did Grimbel Croakcloak, as two old friends sharing in a private jest. "Just get them ready, Lank. Grimbel knows where to go."

He watched the toadish little man closely all the same, keeping his suspicions to himself. That talk of taxes had given him pause and so too this mention of worship. As the men formed up on the banks of the lake, Robbert drew Lord Gullimer aside. "I want you to walk ahead with our guide, Wilson," he said. "Pose some questions about the creatures that lurk here. I want to see if you smell a rat."

The apple lord nodded. "You distrust this man?"

"I have minor cause to do so. You have a good nose for deceit, so I thought I'd call on you for a second opinion. It is probably nothing. But I want to be sure before we start out onto the lake." They had a bit of time before they reached this road the toad had mentioned. "Go walk with him and talk with him. I'll take command of the rearguard for now."

The march around the lakeshore was slow and wet. Men kept their blades drawn and primed, and spears were ever at the ready, to thrust at anything suspicious beneath the water. The mud was thick here, sucking at their boots with every step. Along their right ran the lake itself that wasn't a lake only months ago. To the left was open marshland, flooded beyond its usual waterline, but passable. There were some islands out there, shadowed in the fog, which was never far from thick. The rain fell lightly, a soft caressing sprinkle, and everything was dull green and brown overcoated with grey, as though all the world was veiled.

When they reached the road an hour or so later, the call went down the line. Robbert left Bernie in charge of the rear and marched past the men, nodding and sharing words of encouragement with those he thought might need it. He'd learned that from his father. Rylian the Brave always had a sense for a man's true fears, whether it showed on his face or not. A simple nod was all it took sometimes, the meeting of those steely eyes and he would give the man strength. Robbert tried to do the same, such as he could, though he knew he was not his father. Rylian had been a dragonslayer and a war hero and lived and breathed battle for decades. Robbert was no more than eighteen, just a boy to half these men. *And a one-eyed boy at that*, he reflected. Once before he'd harboured hopes of becoming a great hero himself, but those dreams had died the day Sir Wenfry Gershan put that dagger in his eye.

He closed a fist and opened it, still bitter about all that. *When I reach Raynald, we'll fight together*, he told himself. They were twins and shared a special sense with one another, and had always fought well back to back. *Perhaps neither of us would ever have matched Father alone, but together…maybe together…*

"My prince, the bridge is here." Sir Kestor Droyn showed him through to the edge of the lake where Lord Gullimer, Sir Lothar Tunney and Grimbel Croakcloak stood among the reeds. Lank soared about twice the toad's height and seemed very amused by that.

He pointed with a very long arm. "It's right here, *apparently*. This timber road the old man spoke of."

Robbert looked and saw nothing. Just more reeds and murky green water. Thick fog hid whatever might lie beyond; he could see nothing out there, and no sign of this island and the burned village of Bogroot upon it.

"It's there," Croakcloak said, waving his long sharp stick. "You check your map, m'lord, and you'll see. Or just watch me and I'll show you."

Robbert chose the latter, leaving the map in his pocket as the old man waded into the marsh, poking about with his stick. He walked in, a metre, two, then three and four and five and just kept walking. When he was ten metres from the bank he turned about, triumphant, and thrust his stick hard between his feet. Robbert heard the dull *clunk* as it drove into the timber decking about a foot down, just as he'd said. "You see. It's right here. Old Croakcloak will show you the way."

Robbert nodded. "One moment, Grimbel." He gestured Lord Gullimer over. "So?" he asked, under his breath. "Do you see any reason not to proceed?"

The apple lord rubbed his dimpled chin. "He's strange, there's no doubt there. But as to the rest, I saw no great cause to distrust him. There is nothing uncommon about a local population worshipping a greater power, Robbert. And he seems very knowledgeable about the native flora and fauna." He looked at him. "What concerns you?"

"Nothing. Just…he made mention of paying a tax. That a passing army is often going to lose men when crossing these lands. I am almost certainly being paranoid, but…"

"We'll keep a close watch on him to be sure," Lord Gullimer said, to assuage his fears. "If he does anything untoward, we can confront him on it." He saw that Robbert agreed, and called over Sir Lothar Tunney. "Sir Lothar. The prince wants you chaperoning our new friend. Droyn, you as well. If you see anything out of the ordinary, report it at once to either the prince or myself. Understood?"

Sir Kestor nodded at once, ever faithful to his lord. Lothar was rather less inclined to take orders from Gullimer, so looked at Robb, who dipped his chin, and then proceeded as he was bidden. "Fine. I'll be right behind him every step of the way. Droyn, come on. Let's go test the strength of this road."

Both men wore full godsteel plate, or near enough. The road creaked and groaned a little as they stepped onto it, but held. That was nothing new. Bladeborn were known to pass these lands often and thus the roads must be built to bear them fully armoured and ahorse. Once the two knights had joined Grimbel Croakcloak they set off into the misty grey heart of the lake. The rest of the men followed, walking along two by two. Robbert went beside Lord Gullimer, somewhere near the middle, leaving the rearguard to Bernie's command. It was a queer feeling indeed to feel the solid road beneath his feet but have a lake sprawled out about him. He watched the still waters carefully, his fist tight around the hilt of his sword, ready to draw and swing at whatever might come lurching from the murk. Gullimer did the same, and so did a thousand other men.

Before very long the shore was gone and only swirling mist lay ahead. The host marched and sloshed through the turbid water like an army of ghosts crossing some spectral land. Robbert had never felt such a sense of unease, not in himself nor among the men around him. It was silent but for the sound of their boots plodding dully on the submerged planks, the movement of the water as it eddied and splashed with every step, the soft drizzle of the falling rain. No one spoke, or laughed, or even dared cough. They walked solemn and unspeaking, praying the end was near.

They must have been almost a mile along it when Robbert heard a man squeak behind him. "What was that? I saw something…"

Men stopped and turned at once, stilling. "What did you see?" Robbert called out.

The man's voice was choked and tight. The thousand remaining men of Robbert's host ranged from grizzled veterans to callow youths, yet few were immune to fear. Even Robbert's heart was pounding.

"I don't…a shape, my lord. I saw a shape…out there…"

"Just a log," someone grunted. "I saw it too. Just a log floating on the water."

Lord Gullimer spoke up. He knew the names of the men better than Robbert did; many of them here were drawn from his own lands. "Is that the way of it, Finnegan?" he asked the first man. "Could it have been a log you saw?"

"I…maybe, yes, milord. It came and went between the mist, but…"

"Keep moving, then," Gullimer commanded. "Watch the waters, all of you. But no more calling out unless you're sure of what you see. We would be wise not to keep stopping here."

Silence resumed after that, but not for long. Soon enough shapes were appearing in the fog, the limbs of twisting trees reaching and grasping from the still grey-green waters. Sometimes they looked like creatures emerging from the depths and men would call them out, only to realise their folly a moment later. Several times that happened before at last they saw the dead body. From the mist it came, floating gruesomely toward them, bloated and pale. They stopped to watch as it neared. "That's no marshman," said one of the men. "Look at the cloak. Still got a bit of red in it."

Much of the colour had leeched away in the water, but he was right, there were streaks of red that remained. No sooner had they seen the first than the second appeared, floating on the same drifting tide. "There's another one." Sir Colyn Rowley pointed. "Look. And a third. They're floating this way."

At any normal time, the bodies would merely bump up against the road. Not so here. "Step away and let them pass," Robbert ordered. "Be careful not to fall off the road." One wrong step and a man could fall in; if heavily armoured, he would not come out. The prince could see more bodies coming from the mists. Five of them, ten, twenty, more. The cloaks all held colour, some more than others. Some were red and going grey, others still a deep dark crimson. A few had streaks of gold and black in them, and he saw armour beneath the cloaks, leather mostly, studded and tuned, but here and there some black dragonscale armour as well.

"That one's a dragonknight," Robbert pointed out. He stopped the man with his boot and turned him over in the water. The braided hair on the chin was soaked and frayed, but the eyes had been eaten out and the flesh of the face was soggy and soft, nipped and clawed at by crabs and other creatures. The stink was awful. "These men all died recently. Look how they're bloated."

Lord Gullimer nodded. "There must have been a battle near here." More men were drifting past, scores and scores of them, a fetid floating procession of the dead. "There's been a lot of fighting in the Marsh-lands, Robbert."

"Fighting, yes, but all these men are Agarathi." Something didn't smell right. No battle was so one-sided. "Look for northerners," he called to his men. "Check the dead for wounds."

The men called back what they found. There were no northerners among the dead, not one; all were from Agarath, and their wounds were not consistent with battle either. No deep cleaves as commonly made by swords. No puncture wounds from spears. None of the men had arrows lodged in them. All had perished by other means.

"This one's barely held together, m'lord," one big Swallow man said. He hefted the body, cringing from the stink. It was falling apart, the limbs all smashed and broken. Others reported the same, as though they'd been crushed to death. Another man had a foot-wide hole right through the middle of his body and others had lost limbs, which floated past inde-pendently, legs and arms and smashed torsos, even heads with empty eyes. Most of them had died horrifically, it looked. Only a few were phys-ically intact, their rotting faces fixed in a terrible rictus of fear. "It's like they died from terror," someone murmured. "Like their hearts exploded right inside them."

"I'm going to talk with Croakcloak." Robbert Lukar had a bad feeling here. Turning, he marched hard up the road, sliding past the men staring out at the bodies. More corpses were snagged on gnarled tree limbs; he saw at least a dozen accumulated in one, cradled in its black twisting branches. His boots surged through the filthy swamp water, and as he went he heard a splash behind him, as one of the men fell in. "Help that man out at once," he called back. "Be careful with your foot-ing. Don't let the dead take you down with them."

When he neared the front of the lines, he could see the end of the road ahead where it reached the island. The burned town of Bogroot was visible, no more than a charred and blackened ruin that sprawled across the island from one bank to the next. Some of the twisted heaps of buildings had collapsed into the water and he saw more dead men there, caught among the debris.

The first of his host had arrived when he got there, passing between the tall posts raised either side of the road. A sign was stretched between them, bearing the town's name. It was about the only structure here that was still standing. Robbert found Lothar and Croakcloak picking through the wreckage. "…died instantly," the little marshman was telling the knight. He prodded with his stick. "You see here. See these charred bones. That's what happens when a dragon blows its flame, though suppose you know that, don't you? Brave knight like you. Bet you've killed a few yourself."

"No…not as yet. But soon, yes, I'll…" Lothar broke off as he saw Robbert coming. "Oh. Robb. Thought you were further back."

"I was." the prince set his eyes on the toad. "Croakcloak. A word."

"Yes? What about?"

"These bodies in the water. Don't tell me you didn't see them."

"We saw them," Lank answered. "Smelled them too." He wrinkled his long nose. "And I thought this swamp was foul enough. An army of swollen corpses hardly makes it more inviting."

"They're all Agarathi," Robbert said. He looked at the marshman pointedly. "What do you make of that?"

The toad was bemused. "Same as you, I'd say. They must have come over from the west. Was a big army of them out there, I heard."

"Near Rustbridge," Lank said. "They might be deserters, Robb? Or maybe there's been battle there now and they're in retreat." He thought a moment. "Could have been heading toward Mudport or something? They've got ships there still."

"That doesn't explain how they died."

"Maybe some of ours chased them down?"

"And lost no one? They're *all* Agarathi," Robbert repeated. "Not a single northerner. Something else killed these men." He looked at Croak-cloak again. His eyes were narrow. "You know what killed these men, don't you?" he demanded.

"I might."

"Might isn't good enough, Croakcloak. This was Celaph's doing, wasn't it? *Wasn't it?*" he repeated.

The little toad grinned that horrid wide grin. "She doesn't like intruders, m'lord. The lady of the marshes has always been protective of her mire. And those that live in it."

"Like you? Is she protecting *you*, Croakcloak?"

"Oh, aye…I'd hope so. A good godly man is Grimbel Croakcloak. *You*, though? You did call her *beast* a little while back, lad."

Robbert snorted. "Stop playing games with me, old man. These men were killed only days ago, and that *monster*…"

"Careful now. Best be awful careful how you speak about her."

"Have you drawn us out here to die?" he demanded fiercely. "Tell me true. Are we to be some sacrifice?"

The man's smile lingered. "Now why should I want that?"

"Taxes. You spoke of taxes, earlier…"

"Taxes? And that's enough for you to accuse old Croakcloak of such villainy? I thought better of you, m'lord. You're *meant* to be a prince."

"A king," Robbert said, defensively. "And a king protects his people."

"By throwing about foul accusations? I said I'd help you, and that I'd do it for free, and *this* is the reward you give me?" He shook a webbed finger at him. "Well, I can do without it, same as those riches you offered. Old Croakcloak tries to do a good deed and he's made out to be some monster. No, it won't do. It just *won't*." He made to turn and shuffle away. "You can find your own way from here."

Robbert sucked in a breath and blew it out, battling to stay calm. "Stop," he barked. "Croakcloak, stop."

The toad tottered about to face him. He had another unpleasant grin on his lips. "Yes? Something you want to say to me?"

Robbert's jaw was so tight he felt he could bite through godsteel. "I apologise," he managed, with effort. "This way of yours. Where is it?"

"Oh. So you trust me now, do you?"

Robbert gave that no answer. He was still unsure. "*Where*, Croakcloak? You spoke of a land bridge beneath the water. Which direction does it go?"

The toad smiled and waved a hand vaguely toward the lake. The direction was somewhat westerly, so far as Robbert could figure. "That way. I'd have to poke around to find it."

"And it's straight, this bridge?"

"Straight, oh no. It's crooked as a dog's leg, and that's why you need me. I'm the only one who knows it. Or you can go back if you want."

Robbert didn't want to go back. If he did that he might be weeks longer in this bog and how many of his men would be dead by the time they finally escaped it. "Find it for me, then. Please," he added.

The little toad made an effort to bow, though it was smug and insincere. "I am your humble servant, good prince." His smile widened and widened further. "Old Croakcloak will show you the way."

Robbert let him waddle off toward the banks, trying to master his sense of agitation. He felt horribly unsettled here and was sweating despite the chill. There was something in the air that made his hackles rise. The dead Agarathi. The lingering stink of rot and dragonfire. The sinister flat water of the lake surrounding them on all sides. "I don't like him," Robbert said. "I don't trust him, Lank."

"Yeah, and he knows it. He's just playing with you, Robb. What else is there for him to do out here?"

"So he gets pleasure from toying with royalty, does he?"

Lank shrugged. "Who knows what these queer marsh-folk like to get up to. They live in a world of monsters, Robb, so they're bound to be a little odd. And that tongue of theirs…"

"Tongue? What tongue?"

"That marsh-tongue he was murmuring in earlier. Didn't you hear? All those clicks and croaks and low grunting sounds. He was doing that when we crossed the lake, tapping at the water with his stick. I guessed he was just feeling for monsters, like earlier outside his hole." He saw Robb's face. "What? What's wrong? You don't think…"

Robbert didn't know what to think. The old marshman had reached the edge of the island now and was tapping with his stick, just like Lank said. The prince reached to grip the hilt of his godsteel dagger, enhancing his hearing. He could hear the toad murmuring, *singing*, almost, some strange luring melody in an old tongue he did not know…

Suddenly, a voice called out nearby. "Thought this bridge was meant to be burned?"

Robbert swung his eyes to the sound. Almost directly across from where the road landed ashore, one of the men was standing in the water on the other side.

"Milord," he called over. "The bridge…it's right here." He walked along it, further into the water. "They must have rebuilt it, don't you think? We can go this way after all."

Robbert closed a fist. *Bastard. That lying treacherous bastard.* He turned to look at Croakcloak again; the toad was gazing over toward the soldier on the road. "No…you can't go that way…" he started.

"And why not?" Robbert thundered at him. "Why did you lie about the road, Grimbel?" He was marching toward him, drawing out his blade. "You told us it was destroyed."

"M'lord?" The marshman backed off, all innocent. "I never lied, never. There's a bit here near the shore that's still standing, is all, but further off…"

"You're lying. You don't want us to go that way. You want us to follow out onto the lake instead…"

"No, I…"

"That song you were singing just now…" It was all coming together at once, every foul little piece of the puzzle. "You're drawing her here, aren't you? You're summoning her here to kill us!"

"What? No, that's just a song. A song I like to sing…"

"You're *summoning* her," Robbert repeated. He pointed the tip of his blade at the little man's chest. "Why? Why do you want us all dead?"

"Dead? No…I don't want you dead."

He was lying. Robbert *knew* he was lying. "This is a sacrifice to your god. What is she to give you in return, Croakcloak? How long have you served her!"

The man's wide mouth opened and closed. "You're…you're mad… mad like your grandfather! Help, someone help, he's going to kill me!"

Then suddenly Lank was there, rushing up behind him. "Robb, stop, maybe he's telling the truth. That song was just a song. Put up your steel, Robb. You don't want his blood on your hands."

"I don't trust him, Lank. He's brought us out here to die."

"I haven't. I haven't. I promise you I *have*…"

There was a sound, then, a deep underwater groaning that shook the earth beneath them. Robbert spun and saw it, the movement in the water, the swollen bodies swept aside, the tree limbs snapping and vanishing as something monstrous surged toward them. "Gods," Sir Lothar whispered, taking a short step back.

"No," croaked a sinister voice. "Just the one god here."

Robbert's eyes flared open. "You…you…"

"Aye, *me.*" The little toad gave up on his pretence all at once. Croaking laughter, he threw off his woven-reed cloak. Beneath it was a body misshapen and hideous, squat and broad and sturdy with short crooked toad-like legs. *A monster,* Robbert thought, reviled, as the creature made that horrid wide grin and said, "I promise you I *have*. Didn't I just say? The tax, the tax, oh you'll pay the tax! The price of a prince! And at last she'll reward me! At last she'll change me back! The price of a prince!"

Robbert snarled and lurched for him, roaring, swinging down with his blade. But the creature twisted, suddenly quick, diving down into the water and vanishing with barely a splash. The legs opened out, propelling him away, one kick, two, and the toad was gone.

"Bastard!" Robbert roared. "I'll find you, Croakcloak! One day, I'll find you!"

"Robb, forget him," Lothar called out. "He was lying about the road. It's not burned like he said. We can go that way, Robb. *Now.* We have to go!"

"Flee?" Robbert Lukar wouldn't have it. "I'm not leaving the men. Half haven't made it to the island yet, Lothar."

"We have no choice. You're more important." Lothar took his arm. "I'm not going to let you die here, Robb."

Men were calling out, shouting in alarm. Some were already fleeing onto the road that led off the island, following the soldier out into the wet grey fog. Others were drawing blades to stand their ground. Lord Gullimer was there with Sir Kester Droyn, bellowing for the men to take up their arms and face whatever was coming. Robbert could see some men turning to flee back the way they'd come, knocking others into the water in blind panic.

And about that time, *she* appeared.

Out of the murky water she rose, forty metres from the bank, a colossal dragon-like head soaring up through the mists on an endless thick neck that twisted and heaped about it, coiling away through the depths of the swamp. Robbert could only stare in disbelief. *This is her mire,* he thought, numbly. Lank was shouting something in his ear, but he couldn't hear him. All was a blur of noise as men screamed and broke and ran, down one road or the other…as Wilson Gullimer pulled out his fine long godsteel blade and stood in challenge to the titan, raising up his sword. Some others stood with him, Droyn and Sir Colyn and Sir Gregory too, all calling for their men to gather. Then a voice roared out and across the island Sir Bernie Westermont came running as well, running and roaring and that was enough to break Prince Robbert from his trance.

"I'm not going to let them die without me," he said. He tore away from Sir Lothar's grip and strode away to face his doom.

30

Amron

The wind tore at his black-grey hair and his cloak was flapping loudly.

The cloak once worn by King Amron the Bold, it was, or so Lady Brockenhurst had told him after Walter unearthed it from the vaults beneath the Spear. He wondered what the Bold would say if he could see him now, clinging on tight as the dragon Lendrathor banked through the air, turning and slicing through a wet grey cloud.

You're a dragonlover, Daecar, he imagined him growling. *You're meant to slay those hideous beasts, not ride them!* In Amron's mind, the old king's face was twisted in contempt. *First you let my city fall, and now this? What depths will you plunge next, crippled king? How will you ever earn* my *name?*

Amron turned from the voice. The man after whom he had been named still came to him in his dreams, sometimes, taunting him with those insults and slurs - *You let my city fall. You have not yet earned my name* - but the reproaches were stale to him now, and like the whispers of the Frostblade, he had learned to ignore them. *Amron the Bold,* he thought. *Amron the Bloodthirsty.* Was he really such a great man to emulate, this king so mired in controversy? The conqueror who tore the world apart and all in the name of vengeance?

Sir Pagaloth interrupted his thoughts. "My lord," the dragonknight called out to him, turning his head to shout over the rushing wind. "How is this altitude? Should we not go a little lower?"

Amron looked out over the snow-draped world, the woods and rivers rushing by beneath him in a brisk white blur. It was magnificent, this dragonflight. Even keeping this slower pace he had never moved so swiftly, and the view…gods, the view….*No, higher,* he thought, exulting. *I would go higher and higher still.* "Only if Lendrathor is tiring, Pagaloth," he called out in answer. "Elsewise, no. I would claim a better view."

"Higher, my lord? Are you certain?"

He still worries I will fall. "Higher, yes. Let me see the length and breadth of my kingdom."

The man nodded ahead, if reluctantly, then spoke to Lendrathor in his native tongue. After a short exchange, the dragon flapped his wings and set into a smooth upward ascent. He was powerful for his size, no small beast by any means, strong and quick and agile Pagaloth had told him. *Rather less so with me on his back, granted.* Amron could feel the dragon's furnace heat through his plate armour, see the steam rising from him as they passed through the cold wintry air. Beneath them the lands were still cloaked in snow, but further to the south he could see it beginning to grow thin and patchy now, swathes of land showing brown and green amidst the white.

"How is this, my lord? High enough?"

"No, higher. I want to see the world, damn you."

"My lord..." His voice was edged with doubt. "A fall from here..."

Amron gave out a bark of laughter. "I can see why Lythian likes you so much, Sir Pagaloth. You two are just the same."

The dragonknight turned his eyes back. When Amron first met him, his beard had been recently shorn away by some loutish thugs serving at a place called Runnyhall and his hair had been savagely barbered. Now it had grown back out, thick and black, his beard as well, which he'd twisted into a double braid, albeit a short one. "How so, my lord?" he wanted to know.

"You're both vigilant and worrisome to a fault, Pagaloth, and especially as concerns me, it would seem."

"Well, I...I consider you my responsibility up here, Lord Daecar. It is not only that you are king, but the blade...if something should happen... the war..."

All valid concerns, Amron reflected. There was something slightly reckless about all this, he had to admit, and not entirely in his character, yet the temptation had been too much for him to bear. *I would see the world as my son sees it,* he thought. *I would know what it is to reach out and touch a cloud. And the titan, yes. I would look upon him too.*

His response was much more staid. "There is a part of dragonriding that is often glossed over in the north, Pagaloth," he called forward. "We all know how dangerous they are, how they are the foundation of your strength and power, but there is another side that is rarely discussed."

"And what is that, my lord?"

"This." Amron waved a hand, looking down at the snow-draped dales and icy steams, the thickets and roads and villages that marked and mottled the land. They were high now, yet the clouds were higher, and the air was free of mist and snow and rain, a rare spread of clear sky opening out before them. Amron drew a breath. It was the most astonishing sight he had ever laid eyes upon, a map brought to life before his very eyes with all its little intricate details. He took a long moment to indulge in the wonder of the view and then went on. "We barely acknowledge how much of an advantage this perspective gives you, Pagaloth. In battle, it is a rare gift to see the conflict unfold from up here. To be able to deploy your forces where they're needed most, pull back if they're under threat of being overwhelmed, or push for victory if a weakness is spotted. To be able to relay orders with such expediency is a boon we do not have. We rely on horse and runner and sometimes bird in battle, but you…no, you have these dragons."

"And now you have them too, my lord," Pagaloth said. "I know how much Lord Marak values these very things as well. If and when the time comes that we might share in battle, we will grant you the very same boon."

"I do hope so, Pagaloth," the king said, nodding. "Truly I do."

The test flight earlier had given him a taste. How many breaches had he seen as they flew over his host? How many carts and wagons stuck in the snow? How many groups trudging along too slowly, causing blockages for those behind? Amron had two dozen riders out there going up and down the lines to ensure these things did not happen, but apparently that wasn't enough. *A few dragons would serve me better,* he thought. *And in a battle, even more so.*

The winds were stiffer up here, and the air was colder besides. Before very long bands of mist and low clouds were sweeping back in to spoil the view and the dragonknight suggested they reduce their altitude.

"Very well." Amron raised a hand to shield his eyes as the wind rushed past his bearded cheeks, squinting toward the lands below. "There," he said, gesturing further to the west. "We need to follow the line of the forest, Pagaloth. We ought to be getting close now."

They peeled their eyes for signs as they glided southwest toward the woodland. A colossal boar-like titan was prone to make a disturbance when he moved, and the scouts had reported areas where Brannatar had lumbered headlong through the depths of the Greenwood, carving a path of toppled trees and trampled villages in his wake that Amron could only hope were already abandoned. The scouts had taken over a week to track him…and it was a week since they'd left him behind to return to the host. In that time he might have crossed to the other side of the world or burrowed down to some deeper realm. *He might be gone, or dead, or fled,* Amron thought. *Or not. He might still be here.*

"Rain, my lord," Pagaloth said. "Right ahead. The skies are darkening."

Amron looked forward, scowling. The dragonknight was not wrong. A silent curse slipped through the king's lips as he saw the gathering swamp of cloud brewing and thickening in the skies. He could not say this was entirely unexpected. On their march down the High Way from Blackfrost the snow never stopped falling for long and down here further south it was the rain that still ruled. He scanned the skies, hoping for some break in the clouds that might auger a dryer spell, but the weather of the world was rarely so kind. The winds were growing fierce as well. They roared like monstrous beasts and tore at the cloak of Amron the Bold. It had become very loud all of a sudden, loud and dark and the rain was already spitting at them. The wind gusted, buffeting Lendrathor from one side and then another, causing him to rock in flight. "Hold on, my lord. Flatten your weight and stay low. These winds…"

His words were cut off. Lendrathor was thrown suddenly to the side by a violent squall as though struck by some huge invisible fist, and for a moment Amron felt like he was going to be cast right off his back. But he held on tight and the dragon corrected himself, swaying left and then right, wobbling as he fought hard to stay straight. Pagaloth's voice was strained and alarmed. "My lord…we have to go lower," he called. "The air is too rough here." Down they went, cutting as steep an angle as Lendrathor could manage without losing control. Beneath the roiling stormy air the winds were not so turbulent, but still they howled and blustered, pushing the dragon this way and that as though these northern skies were bullying him to go back from whence he came.

Then the rain came down suddenly hard, a black deluge veiling all before it. All about them now the clouds were gathering, closing in grim and fearsome. It was as though Vandar himself was up there, frowning down at the king of his realm, displeased. *Do you curse me for riding drag-onback too, great lord? I am only trying to win your war.*

He was being overdramatic. This was a common storm, no more. They passed through a thick cloudburst, the rain leaping and bouncing off Lendrathor's wide red wings, a hard fall trying to force him down in submission, but the dragon proved a worthy foe. He pushed onward, bursting out the other side to where the rain thinned a little, and the gloom lifted a shade, and all of a sudden Amron could see the woods right beneath them, the lush verdant canopy of the Greenwood spreading forth in a thick green tangle. It went up and down here, with sharp ridges and deep rifts, wooded scarps and undergrowth so dense it required hacking tools for a man to pass. Through the rains and fogs the trees came suddenly, and Lendrathor had to bank sharply to the side, swerving around a sudden wooded upthrust.

"This is no gentle wood," Pagaloth called. More tree-clad crags and steep wooded slopes speared out from the broader wood around them, appearing abruptly from the fog, forcing the dragon to arc and weave. "I had thought the Greenwood flatter, my lord. Wild in the west, mild in the east, I've heard it said."

It was commonly known as such. Parts of the western side of the forest were so dense and dangerous as to be considered impassable by most. The east was much more forgiving in large part, sometimes hilly but gently so, good for hunting and even herding in places, home to many villages and woodsman's huts. But not all of it. "This part of the wood is known as the Green Masts," Amron called to him. "The people say these thrusts are like the masts of ships rising up from a grey foggy sea, each with sails in green. I confess I've never seen them until now. It is a place not often visited."

Lendrathor swerved around another of those masts, a great tall one reaching sharp and sheer for the skies. Beyond it several others poked up thin and shallow, a series of smaller teeth among the fangs. "We are nearing the edge," the king called. "The Green Masts cover only a few miles, Pagaloth. Beyond is where we need to be."

But where? The Masts spanned miles only, yes, but those miles went in all directions and the scouts had not been able to give exact instructions on where to go. They would have to fly a little higher again to give them a better view. Amron said as much and hesitant though he was, the dragonknight obeyed. Up they went, cutting clean through cloud and rain. Shortly thereafter the high crags and steep slopes withered and thinned behind them, and a more gentle undulating land opened out, densely clothed in beech and hawthorn.

"Fly a few passes around here, Pagaloth. Search for trampled trees and fissures. And a hole," he said. "A gaping hole of broken earth."

It was as the scouts had described it; a great breach where the boar had burrowed down into the ground, throwing up trees and great clumps of soil alike with his great powerful tusks. Even the rain ought not rob them of seeing *that*, Amron thought.

They flew for a while, turning this way and that. Amron could sense Pagaloth's growing agitation with each pass. "My lord, I'm not seeing anything," he called. "These fogs…it's hard to see much of anything. Perhaps we ought to turn back?"

"No. Not yet." Amron did not want to come all the way and give in so easily. "Fly a few more passes, Pagaloth. We'll see the tracks soon enough."

"As you say, my lord." The dragonknight's voice was thick with reluctance, though he was dutiful to a fault.

He's akin to Lythian there too. Amron was taking advantage of that, he sensed, though would not keep him here for long. He wanted only to glimpse the boar, to feel his power, get a sense of his might. *He's here. I know he's here.* The Frostblade was thrumming at his hip in excitement, a pulsing febrile energy. *It senses him,* Amron thought. The blade was a shard of Vandar's Heart and Vandar had given life to the boar. He'd felt something similar coursing through the Frostblade the night they felt the tremors back at Blackfrost. "There, Pagaloth." He pointed with his finger. "He's there, somewhere. I can sense him."

"My lord," Sir Pagaloth said, and there was a deep fear in his voice now. "I think we should go back."

"Go back? But Pagaloth, we're so close. There…fly there and we'll find him…"

"My lord. Lendrathor is anxious. He does not want to be here. I feel it. He's afraid."

Amron nodded, and he understood. "He can feel his presence too," he said. "Brannatar's. He is of Vandar's making, it's only natural. Tell him all is well, Pagaloth. There is nothing to fear. We are allies."

The dragonknight was shaking his head. "My lord…we *need* to leave…"

Amron gave a sigh. His eyes swung down beneath them and he saw what he was looking for. "There." He pointed to an open clearing below.

"Fly down there, Pagaloth. Land, and I'll go on foot. You can fly back and collect me later."

"Land? No…Lord Amron, Lendrathor, he…"

"May fly away and return later, Pagaloth. Please. We have come this far."

"My lord, you're not *listening*. We cannot be here. We should never have come. This is wrong. All of it is wrong." Pagaloth rasped something in Agarathi and in no time at all his dragon was twisting away, flapping his wings, surging back the way they'd come. Amron frowned, opened his mouth to shout something, and stopped. He could feel the deep shivers running through the dragon's plate. *He's trembling*, he realised. *Terrified.* There was an urgent desperation in the way he thumped at the air, his wings beating and thrashing, faster, faster, faster…

And then Amron felt it. The *change* in the air. All the hair on the back of his neck stood on end, and he heard it. The thump of wings, each one a thunderstrike getting closer, closer. His heart was in his throat and his eyes were on the south. A shadow, veiled by fog and gloom. Growing larger, larger, larger…

A rumbling erupted beneath them. Something was exploding up from the earth. Through the fog he could see nothing. He tried to speak but no words came. The Frostblade was shrieking now, shrieking in fear…

"My lord, hold on!"

Lenddrathror gave a sudden twist, banking hard and fast around a surging spire of rock. It came abruptly from the mist and the motion was fierce. Amron squeezed his thighs to try to cling on but to no avail. He felt his weight rip him free of his perch and away over the side of the dragon.

And he fell.

31

Jonik

When at last he stepped out into the daylight, Jonik collapsed to his knees and laughed.

Rain fell down around him, a soft light fall dancing off his cloak and armour, the sweetest smelling thing he'd ever known and the sweetest sound as well. His lips were cracked and broken, his body battered and bruised, and half the meat had melted off his bones, but none of that mattered now.

He was alive.

He was free.

He'd escaped the depths at last.

He took a long swig of clean pure air and pressed his face down into the grass. It grew thick here, thick and soft outside the abandoned mine that had turned into his salvation. The scent was intoxicating, the feel of the grass against his nose, his cheeks, his chin. He wanted to strip out of his armour and lie nude right here, to feel the touch of the grass against his naked body, feel the rain tip-tip-tapping at his buttocks and back as he lay there, smiling, drinking in the sights and smells and sounds of the world.

But he couldn't.

He must keep on going.

He'd been long away, far too long. And the clock was still ticking, tick tick ticking toward their doom.

Jonik stood on shaky legs. He felt weak, desperately tired and hungry, and his body was not without injury. His shoulder was still torn and painful from his tumble down the river, and only made worse when that hive collapsed all around him. His ankle was twisted too, sprained when he leapt out into the darkness and landed on the rocks below…though it could have been a whole lot worse. *Better than breaking a leg,* he thought. *Or snapping my spine in two.* Had he not jumped, he'd have been crushed in the collapsing hive as well, and shared in his grandfather's fate. A sprained

373

ankle was about the best he could have hoped for, given the dire set of circumstances.

The gods had been smiling on him then, to be sure. Not just with the minor injury he'd suffered, but the rest of it as well. As it turned out, the great black menace that had stalked him in that darkness had proven to be a most gracious help to him. When it tore its way up to freedom, it had brought down so much rock from above that it left a path for Jonik to climb out, conveying him back up into the luminous moss-lit underworld above, a veritable paradise compared to the dark desolate netherworld below. But that was as far as the titan's aid went. Winged as it was, the creature was able to soar up through some other enormous chamber and rip its way out into the daylight, screaming in glee as it finally soared back into the open skies above. But winged as Jonik *wasn't*, he had no means to follow. *I'm not my brother,* he had thought. *I carry the blade of mist, not wind.*

It had left him with no other choice but to find his own way out. It had taken days, many long days, through chambers and clefts and tight rock passages, down a long straight tunnel burrowed by a giant, ancient worm whose immense skeleton still rested in the deep. Further on, Jonik had found another smaller tunnel which in turn had brought him to the old abandoned mine. There were shafts and ramps and man-made passages there that wound back and forward, taking him up and up and, finally, back out into the open world.

And now here he was. Free at last.

He drew another big gulp of pure clean air and looked around, assessing his surroundings. The old abandoned mine was built into a shallow hillside, the old wooden door so cracked and broken and covered in grass and shrubs he might have missed it were he to walk by. Clearly it had been abandoned decades ago. Further off beyond the hill, he saw the shadow of larger mountains, obscured by distance and fog. They were hard to see from here, but he had a reasonable notion of what they were.

The Hooded Hills, he thought. When Jonik had abseiled down into that rift with Gerrin and Owen Armdall long weeks ago, the Hooded Hills had been away to their east. Now they were behind him, in the west; he could tell by the position of the rising sun. *I must have travelled right under the mountains,* he realised. *I entered the underworld from the Riverlands… and have escaped them in the Lakelands instead.*

The lakes would be further east of him, he knew. *I need to find higher ground to get a better vantage.* If he was lucky, he would be toward the northern edge of the Hooded Hills, and closer then to Tukor's Pass. That was where he must go, after all. *North,* into Tukor and back to Ilithor. North to the portal and the refuge, to bring the Mistblade to Ilith.

He set off wearily, limping a little on his damaged ankle. It was better now than it had been, but would take a little while longer to fully heal. Ahead of him, spreading eastward, lay shadowy foothills speckled in verdant trees, their trunks caressed by bands of wispy morning mist. He could hear birdcalls out there among the branches, the whistle of an eagle or a hawk soaring high overhead. A squirrel was scampering up an oaken bole and he sighted deer there too, a small herd of them prancing over roots and fallen logs as they vanished into the trees.

The sight of them made his stomach rumble. Venison. How he could do with a nice juicy haunch of roast venison to fill his belly. In the deep desolate netherworld where he'd awoken the nightmare, thirst had been his greatest enemy. That had changed when he'd scaled that path of tumbled stone and returned to the mossy underworld. Up there, water was plentiful, the heavy rains seeping down through the soil and rock to puddle and pool on the ground. But food was another matter. He'd managed to kill a bat once, but it was small and meagre and did not supply much meat. In one large pool he'd found some queer luminous fish, though they'd proven too elusive to catch. Insects he'd eaten, worms and beetles and bugs, and he'd chewed on some edible plants as well, but it was not enough.

I need a bow and a quiver of arrows, he thought. Would that he did, but he didn't. *Maybe there are roots here to forage, mushrooms, berries?* That would serve as well until he could find something more substantial.

He went in search of them; for food and higher ground both. The trees were well-spaced for the most part, though here and there they grouped in thickets where the light grew dim beneath them. Jonik held Mother's Mercy in his grasp as he went, keeping the Mistblade safely sheathed. From his armour glowed its reflected blue light, radiating out from his breastplate and gauntlets to dapple the trunks of the passing trees and glisten off the murky puddles.

The rain had fallen generously here and for a good length of time, he judged. In places the land was waterlogged, and dykes had turned to turbulent rivers that flowed away to the south, thick with branches and leaves and other runoff. Recent storms had brought down many trees and the deadfalls were numerous. He picked his way around and over them, sometimes cutting through with his blade where he must, searching at the base of trees for mushrooms, checking every bush for berries. Jonik knew how to forage well enough, but the pickings were slim and miserly. A few soggy blackberries and some half-rotted mushrooms were all he found. He wolfed them down hungrily but they barely made a dent.

Meat, he thought. *I need some proper meat.*

The going was slow. For the past week he'd been climbing, clambering, crawling through rifts and clefts and tunnels and all that toil had taken its toll without proper food to nourish him. He reached a slope and began to climb; the soil was soft underfoot, the mud sucking and pulling at his filthy godsteel boots. The rest of him was no better. His cloak was badly torn and rotted and ready to be discarded when he found one better. His armour, that godly armour forged by Tyrith to fit his frame and enhanced by Ilith with the properties of the Nightblade, was scuffed, scratched, and even dinted too from all his underground exertions. His hair was longer than ever, a flow of filthy black tangles, and a scraggly beard had started to grow out from his cheeks and chin. He'd seen his reflection in a still pool in the underworld and did not much like what he saw.

Meat, yes, and a razor would serve as well. A razor and a wash and a change of clothes, and maybe then I'll feel human again.

He continued up the slope, breathing heavily from the effort. The Mistblade was heavy to him, and his bond to it was insecure. That was necessary. Many times it had tempted him to use it when he found himself at some dead end in the deths. *Let me help you,* it would say. *Just focus…focus, and we'll walk right through the rock.* Jonik cast the voice aside and locked it behind that door. He imagined it now as some demon, scratching at the wood, hissing and howling at him to be let free, but he wouldn't. He had it trapped and kept his distance by refusing to further secure the bond. It was necessary, but it made it heavier. And without food it was even worse.

The slope continued for a long while. Along the way he found more berries and mushrooms and edible roots, ate some and stashed others away, and gradually he began to feel a little better. He wondered if Gerrin and Owen had escaped this way as well. *Maybe I'll find the old bones of a camp? Maybe they came out this way and went to some town on the shores of the lake?* It was all maybes with Jonik these days, and had been for weeks. Maybes were unavoidable when alone. What else was there to do, after all, than to think and fret and wonder?

He paused to rest for a short while, kneeling by a trickling stream to fill his waterskin, and then found a few more berries in a bush. Through the trees nearby he saw shadows watching him, and started, before realising it was only that herd of deer.

Follow me at your peril, he thought, glaring at them. *I may not have a bow but I've got a knife and know just how to throw it.* He considered stalking them, or laying a trap to lure them. *I could start a fire and feast on venison right here. Camp the night in these woods.* But he quickly put the thought aside. *Get your bearings first,* he thought. *You can make a plan when you know where you are.*

He pressed onward through the morning, step after weary step. The sun moved behind the clouds and the rain sprinkled down through the leaves. He had hoped the trees might thin out when he reached the hilltop but it wasn't so, and his view was still badly obscured by bole and bough. He began down the other side, moving through the muddy woods and beneath the spindly branches, listening to the sound of rushing water as some river raged away to the south. He passed a pretty waterfall a little later and wondered if there was a cave behind it where he might stop for the night, but there wasn't. He studied the pool where the waters crashed down, searching for fish, but couldn't see anything the way the water bubbled and churned.

On the other side, he reentered the trees and found himself climbing again. This hill seemed more promising, and soon enough the elms and ash were separating and the bushes were thinning and he saw an open hilltop ahead, and raced wearily up toward it.

At the summit, the lands opened out around him. He paused here on a broad grassy knoll, pulled out the Mistblade and shoved it into the soil. He felt better to be rid of its weight for a while. He stepped away from it, breathing deep, and searched the lands ahead. Obscured somewhat by the low-slung clouds though they were, he could still clearly make out where he was.

South, he knew. *I'm on the southern side of the Hooded Hills.* He could tell by the layout of the lakes, of which two were visible from his vantage. There were four great lakes that made up the Vandarian Lakelands, called the *Four Sisters* as a collective. The one that sprawled out to the east of him could only be the *Little Sister*, the most southwesterly of the four. He knew that because he could just about make out another lake beyond the Little Sister's northern shore, a slightly bigger one that was known as the *Young Sister*. The biggest, aptly named the *Big Sister*, was bigger than both of them combined and further to the east. He could not see it from here. Nor, of course, the *Old Sister*, more easterly still and away on the border of the Marshlands.

Jonik considered his position. He was disappointed, but only mildly. He had hoped to be a little further north than this, but he hardly had cause for complaint. The lakes were tightly grouped, the three nearest the Hooded Hills especially, and while he'd rather be looking out at the Young Sister than the Little Sister, she was only a few days to the north.

His eyes ran along the lakeshore down at the edge of foothills. The woods were sparse there, and he could see the faint shadow of a settlement in the distance, a small town or fishing village perhaps, a little further to his north. It could very well be abandoned, and that would be just fine by him. *Maybe I'll be able to scavenge some food. Or find a safe cellar in which to spend the night.* He had enough roots and berries now to keep him going, at least. *I'll make for that village*, he decided. *Spend the evening there.* It was a few hours away, it looked, and he'd reach it easily before nightfall.

He nodded, decision made, retrieved the Mistblade and on he went.

Hours later, he stalked through the last of the trees beneath a dusky sky. He had been observing the village for a short while and was satisfied that it was abandoned. The people here had likely left for Lakeheart, he supposed, and had packed up all worthy possessions before they left. He went from shack to shack and checked for food, found a heel of burned bread in an oven, a couple of half-rotten apples in a basket, a hunk of mouldy cheese in a cupboard…and made it into a feast.

For once it was not raining, so Jonik ate outside, beside the lake, watching the birds out there on the shimmering water as the colours of sunset shone on its surface. An eagle was circling high overhead and he saw herons, ducks, kingfishers too, some silly moorhens bobbing about. He smiled at the scene and ate his little feast, and sat there, relaxing, drifting off, as the last of the light drained away.

And when all was dark and the world was quiet, he stood, bone-weary, and ambled away into the shack. There was no cellar in the village he had found, so he would have to make do right here. Placing the Mistblade across the dingy little room, he found some old sheets and blankets and made himself a bed. He was alive, he was free, he'd escaped the depths at last.

Jonik had never slept so well.

32

Amara

She was dreaming of her husband when they woke her.

They wandered the flower-lined lanes of Varinar, strolling hand in hand beneath the high summer sun. Down toward the lake they went, past butchers and bakers, cobblers and costermongers, smiling and laughing, sharing pleasantries with those they knew. They spoke of old times and good times, perhaps sometimes bad times as well, but most of all they spoke of their unborn daughter. What she would look like. Be like. How strong she would be. Would she have Amara's once-golden hair or the coal-black curls of the Daecars? Would her eyes shimmer green as was common among Lukars or have that steely blue of Vesryn's house? And her name, her name…what would they call her? The rest would not be for them to decide, but her name was different. That was their choice.

"Elia," Vesryn said, as they ambled along the cobbles. "How about Elia, Amara? Do you like it?"

She looked up at him, squinting. "I know what you're doing," she said. "Elia? That's just a mix of Elyon and Lillia. You're not so crafty as you think, Vesryn Daecar."

"It's a nice name," he said, smiling. "Or would you prefer Lillyon?"

"I'd prefer you think of something original."

"Lillyon isn't original enough for you?"

She punched him lightly in the arm, and he spun her away down another alley and they kissed, twirling and dancing in a breathless blur. When they came to a stop they were in the midst of the docks and the lake opened out before them, sun-dappled and bustling with boats and barges. The quayside was alive with colour and motion and sounds, wonderful sounds, bells tinkling and children laughing and men calling out the catch of the day. Vesryn swept her along toward a skiff and leapt aboard, and before she knew it they were out on the lake, her husband heaving at the oars, the sun wheeling overhead as the gulls circled and cawed above them.

"We're forgetting Aleron," Vesryn said, suddenly. His face went dour, stripped of all humour. "We can't forget Aleron."

"Never," she agreed. "But he was always older. We didn't raise him like the others."

"And we did Elyon? He was twelve when his mother died. Almost a man grown, Amara." He looked toward the city, to the long bridge that went out to the Steelforge, and for a long while he sat in silent thought. "We should name her for Aleron as well," he said at last. He thought a moment longer. "Alya," he murmured. "What do you think of Alya?"

Amara tasted it on her tongue. "*Alya*." A bit of Aleron and Elyon and Lillia, all three. She smiled, rather liking it. Alya, tall and elegant, with dark shimmering hair and blue eyes flecked with green. Alya, strong and graceful, loved by the court and the commons alike. Yes, it was a good name. Alya Daecar. A good name indeed.

She was about to tell her sweet husband so…but when she opened her mouth to speak again her words were cut off by a sudden screaming gale…and beneath her the boat lurched and bucked. Her heart lurched too and she reached out to the side to cling on…and up the rowboat went, up and down and up and down, thrown about by the fury of the waves. Fierce winds blew about her, roaring like some monstrous thing, tugging at her cloak. She held on tight. "Vesryn…Vesryn…what's happening, Vesryn?"

The lake had become dark and terrible, the waves rising like cliffs above her. She looked up with wild white eyes and saw the black clouds gathering, and the gulls were no longer gulls at all but crows and vultures, black-winged and big, all screaming out as they caught the scent of death. "Vesryn," she repeated. "Take me back, Vesryn. Please. *Please*! Take me back to the city."

But when she looked at her husband she saw only a corpse in his place….a rotting corpse in crushed armour swaying with the motion of the skiff.

She gasped in horror and reeled away, and the water came up and grabbed her, and then she was falling, drowning, drowning in ash and cinder, thrashing and fighting to reach the surface. When she broke it she saw the city aflame and the shadow in the sky, the great shadow with a thousand smaller shades in his wake, and the whole world was shaking, shaking and breaking, shaking and breaking and ending…all the whole world was ending…

She took a sharp breath and opened her eyes.

There was a hand on her shoulder, shaking her awake, a torch blazing, shadows in the room. "Amara, wake up. You were having a terrible dream."

She grimaced, raising a hand against the sudden light. Sweat glimmered on her forehead and a bead ran down her temple. Her nightgown was soaked right through to her skin and her heart was pumping, *thud thud thud…* "Who…lower the torch…" she rasped. "I can't see."

The flame descended and she saw Artibus there before her, old and grey, wrapped in his worn motheaten robes. The man holding the torch behind him was Sir Penrose, and she saw Sir Talmer Hedgeside in the room as well, and Sir Ryger Joyce beside him. Carly was hardly more than a shadow on the window seat, watching like a cat from the darkness.

"What are you all…why are you here? Is there trouble? Are we under attack?"

"No, Amara." Artibus's voice was soft and soothing. "It is good news, in fact. The king has returned."

Amron. At last. That made her sit upright. "When?"

"A short time ago. No more than an hour."

"An *hour*?" She shifted higher in the bed. "Why on earth did no one wake me?"

Sir Penrose spoke up. "The king did not want to disturb your sleep, my lady. In your condition, your rest must come first."

Disturb my sleep? What sort of reason was that? "I've hardly been *able* to sleep for the stress he's put us through," she said. "Where is he now? I would see him at once."

"In Lord Gaston's audience chamber, my lady," answered Penrose Brightwood. "He is holding council. Perhaps you should wait for morning."

"Holding council? At this hour?"

"I understand he wanted to update his lords and captains at once as to his delay."

But not me, Amara thought, and not without a spike of bitterness. With an indignant huff she swung her legs over the bedside and threw off the covers, rising at once to her feet. The stone floor was cold and warmed by neither rugs nor rushes. Fat old Lord Gaston had always kept spare furnishings here in his modest little keep. "Carly, help me with my clothes," she said, already peeling away her sodden nightgown. "The rest of you, out. Artibus, you may stay."

The knights all left her, as was proper, filing out through the door before she might bare herself. Artibus had seen her nude many times before as the family physician, so this was nothing new. He took the torch from Sir Penrose first and placed it into a sconce on the wall, then set about lighting the candles. "Has Lillia been told?" Amara asked as her nightgown puddled on the floor. She stepped gingerly out of it, wiping herself dry with a cloth as Carly gathered her garments.

"No, Amara." Artibus set the taper to a candle beside her bed, then shuffled over to the side counter to light another. "Her father saw no sense in waking her."

This was ludicrous. "She is his *daughter*. She should be the first to know."

"He will be at her bedside for when she wakes. She will like that just as well."

Amara huffed and pulled on a fresh cotton shift. There was probably some sense in that if she cared to see it, but right now her ire was up. "If Amron told you not to wake me, why are you here? I am well and truly awoken now, as you can plainly see." Carly helped her with her gown, thick and woollen and warm.

"You were screaming, Amara. Your nightmare…"

"Ought not be enough to have half my company storm my bedchamber. It was a bad dream, nothing more. And screaming? Please. I made a whimper or two, I'm sure, but…"

"You were *screaming*," the old man repeated. "And loud enough to wake half the castle. Sir Ryger and Sir Talmer were first in to reach you, after which I came with Sir Penrose and Carly. It took you a good few moments to settle." He poured her a cup of water. "You were dreaming of Varinar again, I take it?"

She took the cup and drank. Her dreams had been vivid of late, sometimes sweet and sometimes sour, and oft enough they were one and then the other. Not always did she remember them when she awoke, but this one she did. "Yes. Among other things." Artibus had told her already that these disturbances could be common during pregnancy. Amara supposed the coming apocalypse might have something to do with it as well. "I saw the city burning again, from the lake. And Vesryn. He was in the boat with me. Well, his corpse was. Crushed armour and all."

Artibus nodded sympathetically. "Well…no one would blame you for having nightmares at a time like this. I will have to prescribe you something to keep you settled. A tonic, perfectly safe for the child." He looked down. "How are you feeling? The nausea…"

"Is an ongoing battle. The headaches as well." She had another drink of water as Carly helped her with her boots, then layered up in a large wolfskin cloak. "But elsewise I'm fine. I am carrying a child, not bearing a banner to war. I rather think I have it easy compared to most."

Carly gave a little laugh at that. "You wait for the day she comes screaming into this world, my lady. That's another battle right there. And a bloody one too."

She was fully aware of what awaited her, and the risks were greater at her age as well. But it was much too early to be thinking about all that. "Thank you for your contribution, Carly. Hopefully you'll have a few fights upon that battlefield as well in the years to come."

"Oh, I plan to. I'll refresh the ranks of the Flame Manes from my own womb, my lady. Just need some willing participants to lend me their seed."

"I should doubt you'll struggle to find volunteers."

"But not just anyone. Need good strong Bladeborn stock." She grinned. "When's your nephew going to fly back and pay us a visit? I still have a promise I need to keep."

"Soon, I hope." Amara placed down her cup and strode to the door, leaving any further talk of Elyon behind. To think of him only stirred her worry, and there was no use in putting herself through that. *He's busy doing something important,* she told herself. *He'll fly back west when the time is right.*

The three knights were waiting outside her door, muttering among themselves. *Discussing me and my condition, no doubt.* "You said the king was in the audience chamber, Pen?"

"Yes, my lady. Holding council. But…"

"But nothing. Come. The rest of you stay here."

Penrose bustled after her as she strode hastily down the corridor. This was not a large castle as castles went and only the very highest-born lords and knights had been permitted into Lord Gaston's halls, due to lack of space. The rest were in camp outside, a great sprawl that would soon be waking to pack and leave, continuing on their way toward Varinar. *Not long now,* she thought. The vastness of northwest Vandar was behind them and they had passed the western banks of Lake Eshina to their north. *Less than a week, and we'll be home.*

"You spoke to Amron yourself, Pen?" Amara asked as they went.

The knight had reached her side. His Daecar cloak stirred at the hem with each brisk step. "Yes, my lady. I was on the walls when he came down."

Came down. "Landed, you mean?" The thought was still bewildering to her. Amron Daecar, riding on the back of a dragon. She'd heard a deal of muttering about that, and not all of it good. The host was split, it seemed to her, and the debates rang long into the night. Some men said he must do all in his power to win the war, that they would trust him no matter what. Others were more old-fashioned in their thinking. To ally with Ulrik Marak was unimaginable, even unconscionable. And flying a dragon? That was even worse.

Sir Penrose Brightwood nodded and said, "Landed, yes. Outside the walls, far enough to be out of range of our bowman. It was hard to see the white flag in the dark. And they had to steer clear of the camp as well."

"Well I hope it was all worth it. Did he tell you why he was delayed?"

"No, my lady. But he looked somewhat…bedraggled. Like he hadn't slept much. And dirty. I saw mud on his cloak, some rips as well. And perhaps blood. It was dark, so I could not be sure."

Then he's been fighting, she thought. That concerned her. "Is it possible the Agarathi have invaded the coast again at King's Point?" That's where he had gone. He was meant only to speak with Lord Rodmond Taynar, share tidings with old Sir Ralf, and probably visit with these gruloks as well. Their captain had a funny name. Hruum or something of that sort. With Lythian gone and the Sword of Varinar taken, Amron was likely worried the gruloks would drift away, and he wanted them there, defending the mouth of the river.

Penrose was proving useless, though. It seemed he knew nothing at all. "I could not say, my lady. It's possible. And Lord Grave will not have reached the city yet."

Not for several more days, she didn't imagine. The Ironfoot had rushed away with at least two thousand riders shortly after Amron flew off, making for Crosswater and the road down the Steelrun River. Even riding hard it would take him a while to reach the coast, and the thousands more men afoot who had followed him would take at least double that time. If there was battle at King's Point, they would be too late to join it.

She spared the knight any further questions as she strode briskly toward the keep's great hall. There was nothing especially great about it, though it was a hall, spacious enough, and the tables and benches had been moved aside to make room for some of the men to sleep.

Amara and her company had dined in that very room when they rode west in search of Lillia. Poor fare, it was, though no doubt Lord Gaston had been saving his best for his own. She remembered how Sir Connor had requested Gaston give up his men for the war. "What fighting men you have should be marching to defend their kingdom, my lord," he had said, the same plea he'd made to ancient Lord Mandrake and truculent, one-armed Sir Barloff Terring and others as well as they went from keep to keep. None had been moved by him, though. They had been raided by outlaws and deserters and must defend themselves, they had said. Or they would argue a few more men would make no difference to the war. No king or greatlord had ordered these lands to muster, she distinctly recalled Lord Mandrake telling them. That he was under no obligation to supply his own men until an official summons was made.

Well, they would be marching past Mandrake's draughty old castle in a couple of days. *We'll see what he says then, when the king himself stands before him. And Gaston of the Girth as well,* she thought. *Perhaps he's already been told...*

She would find out shortly. Above the feast hall she could hear a faint murmur of voices coming from up the stairs. A short spiral stair led up to Lord Gaston's small audience chamber. "My lady, they are this way."

"I had guessed, Pen."

She let him lead the way; at the top, they found the wolfish form of Rogen Whitebeard at his usual place outside the door, tall and lean and all in black, guarding it like a faithful and extremely lethal hound. The door was ajar and a thrum of voices could be heard inside. "Lady Amara," the ranger said, seeing her. "Did the king call for you? I did not know."

"You did not know because it did not happen. But here I am." She stepped toward him. "Let me pass."

"My lady." His voice was stiff. "The king said he wanted no disturbances."

She'd heard all she could stomach of disturbances. "Just move. I want to see him." He could not very well restrain her physically...no, not in her condition...so she pushed right past and through the door.

The chamber beyond was crowded with lords and knights and trusted captains all talking over one another. The usual suspects were there. Strand, Borrington, Darring the Not-So-Daring. Sir Quinn and Sir Robin and Sir Bryce and Sir Lambert, who was the younger brother to her man Ryger Joyce. Lord Mantle was present in his bat-wing cloak, leaning heavily on a crutch, so too Sir Taegon Cargill who had wounded his knee during the fighting outside Blackfrost. His crutches were so large they might have been carved from the trunks of oak trees, but the knee was beginning to heal well, Amara had heard, on account of Artibus's excellent efforts.

Stegra the Snowfist was in the room as well, right at the heart of it in his snow-bear cloak, always wanting to be the centre of attention, while the Orca Lord stood marvellously to one side, quietly observing with those piercing blue-and-green eyes. He was as comely as Sir Gerald Strand was homely, and of course *that* turncloak had wormed an invite as well despite the fact that his lord father Styron clearly despised him. Seeing him standing there spoiled Amara's already sour mood. To think she was lower in the pecking order than *that* doughy, pock-faced craven.

Loudly, and pointedly, she cleared her throat. The room stilled and turned to face her.

"Oh. Am I interrupting?"

Through a parting between Stegra Snowfist and Sir Quinn Sharp she saw him, the king, sitting in Lord Gaston's oversized seat. He stood at seeing her. "Amara. You're awake."

No thanks to you. "I heard you were back. I wanted to see you."

He nodded. *Bedraggled,* Penrose had said, and he wasn't far wrong. Amron looked a fright, his armour marked and scuffed, his regal cloak hanging on a peg near the hearth, caked in grime and torn. It would need repairing, that kingly cloak of his. The Forgemasters might want to get to work on that armour too, when they reached the city. "You can see me now," he said, after a pause. He looked around. "My lords, return to your beds and get some rest if you can. We can pick up on any loose threads on the morrow."

No one seemed particularly eager to stay, though Lord Styron remained behind a moment for a private word. That did not surprise her. After Amron, he was the power in the room and in possession of their most orderly army. Remaining to leave last was his way of asserting that strength.

Amara waited until they were done, sharing words and nods with the passing men as they filed out past her. She told Lord Mantle that she was glad to see him up on his feet, wished Sir Taegon well with his knee, smiled at the Snowfist and Lord Robert Borrington, who she had always been very fond of, and stared perhaps a moment too long at the Orca Lord as he went by, darkly dashing as he was.

Before very long they were all gone and Lord Styron was appeased. With that oaf Gerald waiting like a dog at heel, the lord gave Amron a final word of parting and then marched away in his brown and yellow cloak, nodding at Amara as he passed, his son following. His *other* son was the last who remained. "Rogen, wait outside," the king said, and when he had done so, they were finally alone.

Amara was not going to waste either of their time. She set into her reproaches at once. "You told them to let me *sleep*? You didn't think I'd want to know the moment you returned? *Days*, Amron. You've been away for *days* when you said you'd come right back. We've been worried, all of us. We thought something terrible had happened to you. That you'd fallen, or…"

"I did fall. Why do you think I look like this?"

She lost her breath a moment. "You *fell*? You weren't…I thought you had been fighting."

"No. I would not call it that."

She looked him over, searching for fresh injuries. He did not seem to have taken further harm, though she could not be sure. His hand was resting on the pommel of the Frostblade. That meant he was driving away his pains and temporarily healing his wounds, old ones and possibly new ones as well. "You do not seem any more infirm than when last I saw you," she observed. "Filthy, yes, and there's a certain stink, but…"

"I was not injured. My armour protected me, and this." He tapped the blade. "I was able to encrust further layers of ice-armour as I fell. Those took the brunt of the impact."

"And how far was this little tumble of yours?"

"Far enough. I was not judging distance at the time."

The answer annoyed her. She wanted something more precise. Later, perhaps she would find the picture of Amron Daecar being thrown from the back of a dragon amusing, and would prefer to have a clearer image to accompany the tale, but not right now. Right now she was still well and truly of a mind to scold him. "I told you it was reckless for you to go, Amron," she said. "I warned you something like this might happen. Half the men think you have no business riding a dragon, and half of me agrees…"

"And the other half?"

"Thinks you'll do whatever you think is right and we must trust you, as our king. I go back and forth between the two. You could quite easily have sent another in your place."

"I did send another. I sent two, in fact."

"Yes, and neither of *them* are back either," she retorted. "Perhaps they fell as well? If Connor dies falling off a bloody dragon, I'll…"

"Mourn him for a man of duty, and move on. Lord Marak told me it might take some time for them to come back, Amara. Or did you expect Connor and Torus to return within a day?"

"I expected *you* to return within a day. Like you said you would." She shook her head at him, angry with his lack of contrition. *A bloody apology would not go amiss.* "So come, out with it. What happened to you, aside from this fall? Did you get drunk with Ralf, talking about old times? Did you go in search of Lythian? Or is there something *else* you're not telling me? Did you fly elsewhere, after King's Point?" She looked at him suspiciously. "Or *before*?"

He smiled wryly at that. "You always were perceptive, Amara. Yes, I flew elsewhere."

"I might ask 'where' but I already know." She peered at him. "Brannatar. You went to try to find him, didn't you?"

"Yes."

"And Lord Marak *allowed* it? I cannot believe that…"

"Marak did not know my intent, nor did anyone else. It was a private desire that I felt no need to share. And Pagaloth was willing."

"Was he? Or was he unwilling to deny you? There's a difference, you know."

"He was willing," he insisted. "Lendrathor had proven himself quite able to bear me, so long as he took regular rest. We were going to fly to the forest and then onto King's Point after…"

"But things went wrong," Amara said, gesturing to his cloak. "You fell. And not from a simple wobble or gust of wind, I would wager. Something caused this dragon Lendrathor to panic, is that not so? That's how you lost your grip." It was all starting to make sense. The dragon saw the boar titan and panicked, and in his frenzy to flee, the king was thrown. She tutted at him. "You might have considered that, Amron. How did you think the dragon would react upon seeing him?" She could tell from his reaction that she had the right of that. "Gods, so you truly saw him? Was he out in the open, or…"

"Brannatar is dead, Amara," the king said.

That shut her up. She stopped and stared at him, wordless for a moment. Then, "*Dead?*" she repeated, in a whisper. "*How?*" She could feel the blood draining from her cheeks. "Was he dead when you…"

"No. He was alive when we got there and right where the scouts said he would be. We did not see him at first, but we heard him through the fog. It was raining, dark, stormy. Lendrathor got spooked and Pagaloth called for us to turn back, and just as we did….*he* came."

He. She swallowed in a bone-dry throat. "You…you mean…"

"Drulgar. He arrived just as we did. I wonder…I wonder if that was not mere coincidence. I fear I may have led him there."

"Lead him?" She did not know what he meant. "You think the power of the Frostblade…"

"Yes. No. I…I don't know, Amara. The timing…Drulgar was already near. He had been sighted before, I found out later. In the area. Searching. *Hunting.* My presence, the Frostblade…it might have been enough to draw him to Brannatar's burrow." He sighed and shook his head. "I cannot say for sure, and what does it matter now? The boar is dead. The Dread killed him."

She drew a breath, trying to imagine it. The great clash of ancient titans. "You…you actually *saw* them fight?"

"I *heard* them fight," he told her. "The sounds they made…I have seen the Dread, fought the Dread, but this was something else. It was a clash from another time...I could not describe it if I tried."

"And that's when you fell? As Lendrathor fled?"

He nodded. "He was flying wildly. You know how the Green Masts are. Those rocky spires rise up suddenly in the fog and he turned sharply around one, and I fell. When I landed I was dazed, and may even have lost consciousness for a time, but otherwise I was unhurt. The titans were still battling nearby, how far I could not say. At their size they sound nearer than they are, yet I could sense they were close, and the Frostblade was thrumming...

"I drew it from its sheath. I had to help, I told myself. It was cold... not snowing, perhaps, but cold enough that maybe I could slow Drulgar so that Brannatar might skewer him. My skills have come on since I last faced the Dread, and the weather...the wintry weather...I thought maybe I could be of use...

"So I ran, lurching after them through the forest. It felt like the whole world was ending around me. The way the earth trembled and shook... the way the trees snapped and toppled. A half dozen times I must have stumbled as I went, tripped by a rock or root or thrown off balance by the tremors. I could hear them, beyond the fog. Once or twice I even saw shapes, monstrous shapes locked in battle, but just as quickly they were gone, and just as I thought I was drawing nearer, near enough perhaps to lend Brannatar my aid, the earth tore open in front of me and down I went into a rift...

"I hit a ledge, rolled over the side and fell another thirty feet. The bottom was all dirt and mud and filthy water, and I landed on my back, winded. For a moment I could only lie there, staring up as the rains came down, wondering if I might end up the same as Janilah Lukar. Just another fool king with a Blade of Vandar in his grasp, thinking he could face a titan..."

He snorted and shook his head. "But I was lucky. I was spared. The chasm never caved in and the battle moved off, and after that all I could do was try to find a way out. It took half the night. The walls were slick and sheer and the rock kept coming away whenever I tried to climb, crumbling to send me right back down to the dirt. Perhaps the gods were trying to humble me and show me my place? Well I got their message loud and clear. As the titans did their dance above, I was trapped in a ditch." He laughed a bitter laugh. "And you call *me* a saviour."

You are a saviour, she thought, adamant. She knew that right down deep in her bones, but right now he did not want to hear it. "What happened after? When you got out?"

He went over to the window and looked out, though there was not much to see. Just the shadow of the castle, the white of the snow against the black of the moonless sky. "I went searching for them again," he said, after a time. "It had been silent for a long while, though whether the battle had taken them far away, or one or the other had fled, I wasn't sure. But I feared the worst. During the fighting, the Frostblade had urged me on, drawn me toward them, but now…" He shook his head. "It was quiet, withdrawn. I think I knew it then, Amara, but I wanted to find him to be sure…

"The fogs were still thick around me, so I had to be careful in my step. It took hours more before I saw him, following the trail of destruction. In some places I could barely walk for fear of tumbling into a chasm; in others great swathes of woods were gone, trampled and toppled, and the air was full of ash and fume. It was much the same outside King's Point. The world changes at the Dread's passing, Amara. All he touches turns to death."

He gave a deep and sorrowful sigh, and she saw the woe in his eyes. "I have seen a lot of death in my life…men, mounts, creatures of all kinds, but this…to see a fallen titan…something that size, something that old. Brannatar was an ally to us, perhaps the greatest chance we had. And he fell like all the rest. Like Fronn before him, and Orthrand too. All the great titans of Vandar's making are dead. And now…now…"

She stepped toward him and took his hand. "This was always going to happen, Amron. No one truly thought Brannatar would stop the Dread." *We only hoped*, she thought. *Like the fools we are, we hoped.* "Did he at least wound him? Was there blood on his tusks, or…"

"It was raining heavily," he said. "By the time I found him most of the blood had been washed away, and Brannatar…he was savaged, his flesh rent and torn and burnt. The sight of him…" He sighed and looked at the white blade at his hip. Amara had never seen it so doleful; the mists were barely rising, as though enervated in their grief. "I could feel the pain in the steel," the king said, quietly. "Vandar…it was as though Vandar himself was mourning him. And…"

"And we'll avenge him," Amara said, pulling Amron into a hug. She wrapped him tight, tight as she could in his grand steel plate. "His sacrifice won't be in vain, Amron. All of them, we'll avenge them all." She drew away, looked up into the craggy lines of his weary face. "And Brannatar…at the least this may have given us time. Time to prepare. As I said back at Blackfrost. If Drulgar is truly wounded…as he was after Varinar…perhaps he may not return for a while. It may just be the window we need."

The king nodded at that, then looked back out through the window. "You may be right," he said, after a while. "And it is possible the Dread may yet be drawn to other foes. I said that he had been sighted already. It was Ralf who told me that. Drulgar was spotted off the coast by some of Admiral Fairside's ships only the day before he slew Brannatar. And he has been seen in the east as well, according to Lord Harrow. He had a crow come from the Lakelands…another of Lady Horsia's pen friends, like you. She shared few tidings of the war at large, regrettably, but this of the shadow she did mention. It was the Dread, she was certain. 'The shadow that haunts us is hunting' she wrote."

There was much to unravel from all of that. It seemed Amron had travelled to King's Point after all, and Crosswater as well following his misadventure with the two titans. That further explained his long delay in returning. The rest...this of the Drulgar sightings. "You think there's some other foe drawing Drulgar to the east?"

"It may be so. There have always been rumours that Celaph still lives. If that is true…"

There was a loud neigh outside, the sound of voices in the yard by the stables. Amara glanced down and saw men bustling forth to saddle their horses, grooms and stableboys stirring to attend them. "Your orders?" she asked.

A nod. "I asked that Lord Styron ride ahead to Varinar, to help prepare the city for our coming. He will take Darring with him, you'll be happy to know, and Gerald as well. I suggested they ride at first light, but Styron is not a man to wait around. The rest of us will follow behind."

"You as well?" She feared he would depart too, by dragonback even, now that he'd had a taste of it. *He says Styron the Strong is not a man to wait around? One might say the same of the Crippler of Kings.*

He smiled wearily. "I won't be leaving again, not for a while. Nor do I expect to travel by dragonback again, lest I must. I understand it divides people, Amara. Friction is the last thing we need right now."

She was glad to hear that. It would mollify any brewing dissent, if there was any, and the capital needed its king. From there they could make their preparations from a place of strength, and hope the Dread remained suitably distracted. *But not with Brannatar,* she reflected, grimly. His death was a blow, but might yet yield some fruit. *Be wounded,* she thought. *Be gored and bleeding. Return to your Nest and rest once more. Sleep so you do not see…*

The king needed to sleep as well, she realised. No doubt rest had come spare these last few days and they had a long day on the road ahead. "Artibus said you wanted to be at Lillia's bedside at first light," she said.

He looked at her. "Yes, that was my plan. The rest…" He glanced at the door. "I only called a council because I felt obliged to, Amara. As soon as some of Styron's men spotted me returning, I knew he would come to me, so I thought I'd kill a few birds with the same stone, and get it done. I would have preferred to wait, to speak to you first, and Lillia. But as king…"

"You have other obligations, I understand. You do not need to explain yourself to me, Amron."

He nodded tiredly.

"Go," she said. "You can take my bed. I won't be needed it…I think I've slept quite enough."

He gave no protest. "Very well."

"I'll wake you before Lillia rises," she said. "It will be nice for her to open her eyes and see that her father has returned." She kissed him on the cheek. "And wash, Amron. You stink. And bad enough to make a beggar recoil."

He chuckled softly, dipped his head, and left her, clanking wearily through the door and taking his torn cloak from its peg as he went. Amara paced for a short while, then planted herself in Lord Gaston's ample seat. Outside, she could hear the stirring as Lord Styron and his captains raised their men to muster. They were making a deal of noise out there, and no doubt waking the rest of the camp. But not Lillia, she hoped. *Let the girl sleep, and let her dream, and let those dreams be sweet.*

She reflected on her own. The dreaded shadow in the sky, the corpse of her husband in the boat. Sometimes she still found herself weeping for him, though largely those days were behind her now. She was proud of what Vesryn had done. Proud of how he'd restored his honour. *He cut the Dread,* she thought. *He showed us it could be done.* She would not, *could not* believe that a being the size and strength of Brannatar would not be able to do the same. *They fought long and loudly,* she told herself. That is how it sounded the way Amron said it. *If the boar was rent and torn and burnt, surely the Dread suffered too.*

She sat with that thought, and it gave her hope, and into her daydreams she went. It was not her husband in this one, no, but his brother, and the Dread was not haunting the city skies. Instead they soared above an open red plain with a battlefield far beneath them, and in his grasp Amron held not the Frostblade, but the Heart Remade, and it *glowed.* Light poured from it, and colour undimmed, and he soared and spun, encased in frost, and when the Dread gushed flame he shimmered blue and ghostly and the flame and fume rippled right through him. Around the great dragon he flew, invisible and unseen, as the beast snapped wildly and roared. And when the time came to cut him, cut him he did. Through his eye and into his brain he plunged, as a great golden sunburst erupted, blinding.

It was a dream, a fantasy, perhaps, and no more, but somewhere in that Amara saw truth. *He is the saviour,* she told herself firmly. *He and no one else. Keep your heirs and your bloodlines and your prophesies too…I'll take the one they call Varin Reborn.*

33

———

Robbert

Sir Bernie Westermont had been the bravest man he ever knew, the bravest and one of the very best, but now he was gone.

"Go to our fathers, Bern," Robbert said, kneeling beside the big man's body and reaching out to close his eyes. He felt a deep well of grief inside him, but would not weep, nor let out a sob. He must be strong now, stronger than ever for the few men he had left. "You go and tell Lord Marc you fought with courage. He'll believe you, Bern. You were always the best of his sons."

Sir Bernard had been the third-born son of an old and storied house long bound by blood to House Lukar. His grandfather Lord Morlay Westermont had been cousin to Janilah Lukar and his great-grandfather Lord Luthor was the king's uncle. As children Robbert and Bernie had grown up as cousins too. They were not just friends, but family. And Bernie, as ever, had died as he had lived. He had died saving Robbert's life.

Lothar was standing beside him. When he spoke his voice was cracked and broken. "He's gone, then?"

"He's gone, Lank."

"Took him…long enough. He was always a bit slow, wasn't he?"

Robbert almost smiled. "He was," he said, weakly. They'd carried him for days, in the slim vain hope he might survive, but at last his body had given out. The internal wounds were just too great; even his godsteel plate had not been able to protect him.

"Might have saved us the effort and just…just died there on that lake. *Stubborn.* He was stupid and stubborn and…and sweet. A great sweet fool and…and I'm gonna miss him." Lank sank to his knees, lowering his head in lament. Robbert could see the tears shimmering in the tall knight's eyes. "What'll we do with him, then? We can't leave him here, Robb. Not…not *here.*"

Robbert didn't want to. It was the very last thing he wanted to do, to leave his dear friend in this festering bog, but what choice did they have? Hauling him through this waterlogged hell had proven difficult for the men who remained to him, but they'd done it while hope remained. But now? Could he keep asking it of them now? "We've left others behind, Lothar. Far too many others."

He thought of the legions who'd fallen to the titan, the green boys and the greybeards, the grizzled veterans in dinted armour. It was not just common men who died, but warriors too, even Bladeborn knights. Sir Gregory Jarvis had been devoured right before Robbert's eyes and he'd seen Sir Colyn Rowley swept away into the waters as well. Hundreds were dead, hundreds more fled, scattered and lost throughout this dark unforgiving mire.

There were no roads now. No submerged timber causeways crossing this stretch of swamp. They'd entered a bog so dark and dreary that even Robbert's eyes strained hard to see. The willows here were old and sinister and bald cypress grew all over, their strange tall roots rising queerly above the waterline, canopies spreading wide to blot out the light. Everywhere they saw the glowing eyes, watching them from the dark, sensed the creatures lurking all around them. Yesterday four men had been taken by the bog and the day before that it had been seven. Sometimes there was only a splash, the sound of a quick struggle, then silence. At other times they would hear a man scream and would catch a glimpse of him being pulled into the murky water. Rarely did they arrive in time to save him; the creatures here knew who to choose and who to take, picking on the weak and the wounded, and almost always did they take their prize. It happened at night, when a man stood on watch, and it happened by day when they marched. One by one, the swamp was taking them. *My host grows smaller by the day.*

It was smaller now, and greatly so, for the loss of Sir Bernie Westermont. Robb wanted to take him home. If he could he would carry him all the way back to Tukor himself, but he couldn't, and they could not bear the burden. "We need to think about the living now," he told Sir Lothar Tunney. Much as he hated it, he had no choice. "We'll take him to the next dry island we find and bury him there. Somewhere memorable, if we can find it. So we can return to him, one day."

Sir Lothar had no fight left in him. "The next island," he said, sadly. "We can mark a tree or…or a stone, if there is one." A tree there might well be; a stone seemed much less likely here. "And the map. Mark the map so we remember."

Robb nodded. They did not know where they were, not exactly, but he had a vague idea. It would have to be enough.

They covered their fallen brother over with a spare cloak, and Robbert called over for Sir Kester to help carry him. "Take the rear, Sir Kester," he said. "I will carry him at the front."

Sir Lothar ventured forward. "Robb, you don't need to. I'll take him…"

"You've done enough, Lothar." Lank had been carrying the stretcher more than anyone over the last few days. "Lead on with Lord Gullimer and form a guard around us. We'll come upon an island soon enough."

It was early afternoon. The prince took the front of the charred-wood stretcher, made from some of the wreckage they'd scavenged from the burned village of Bogroot, and hefted Bernie's burly body up into the air. Two men went ahead of Robbert at his command, testing every footstep in the swamp to watch for hidden roots and perils. The rest formed a cordon around them, watching every ripple and listening for every sound.

The going was slow and solemn. The men at the front carried long thin poles cut down from trees, to constantly poke and prod at the murk ahead of them and judge its depth. It only made Robbert think of Grimbel Croakcloak and his stick. His fist tightened about the handle of the stretcher, cracking the wood. *I'll hunt him down one day,* he vowed. *If it's the last thing I do, I'll kill that treacherous toad with my own two hands.*

An hour passed before they found a suitable island to lay Sir Bernie Westermont to rest. Robbert found a place beneath a great looming willow that would serve as a good marking point, and the men began to dig. "That's nice," Lank said. "It's a good spot, Robb." It was almost pretty, if you looked at it right, the way the branches of the willow draped the gravesite. The canopy was a little thinner here too and some wan sickly sunlight pierced the shroud. "We should mark the tree." Lothar drew out his dagger and saw to it, carving the words, "Here lies Sir Bernard of House Westermont, Third Born Son of Lord Marc Westermont, Emerald Guard and Protector of the Prince. He Fought with Valour, and he Fell with Honour. This World is Lesser Without Him."

Robbert might have shed a tear were he alone. *Lesser without him, yes.* No truer words had even been carven.

When the grave was dug, the knight's body was lowered down, still wearing his crumpled armour. Robbert placed Bernie's sword across his chest and wound his stiff dead fingers about its hilt. He looked into his big characterful face and took a moment to murmur a private goodbye. "Thank you, Bernie," he whispered, steeling himself against his grief. "I will not let your sacrifice be in vain. I promise it. I won't." The tears welled, but he did not let them fall. Blinking to cast them away, he took a deep breath and climbed out of the grave to allow the men to cover him.

Words were spoken, but few. Sir Kester talked of Bernie's broad smile and unerring positivity, his indomitable fighting spirit. The lithe youth Martyn praised Bernie's training, his good heart, how he had taken the young lads under his wing and taught them to become true fighters. Lord Gullimer gave a fine eulogy, sparing Robbert the need. He told of Bernie's loyalty, his skill, his courage, his utter devotion to his prince. "And he was strong," the apple lord finished. "The strongest of us, and the most valiant. Not many men could stand alone against the King's Wall. But he did, in Aram. A rare warrior, he was."

Lothar nodded. "The rarest." Smiling tearily, he stepped forward and knelt to put his hand on the grave. "We'll come back for you, Bern," he promised. "One day, when the war's done and won. We'll come back and bring you home…back to the land of our fathers."

Those were the last words, a last vow to their fallen brother. Beneath the willow they left him, to rest and await their return.

They slept that night long miles from the gravesite on another wooded thrust of land. Hours passed in a solemn blur, but it seemed to Robbert that the marshes were starting to thin. The trees were fewer, the canopies less dense, the waters more shallow about them. *Are we past the worst of it?* he wondered. *Or is this just another false dawn, before it thickens and stews anew?*

He sighed, reflecting on the many tragedies they'd faced. The cruel collaboration of Krator and Kastor. The devouring fires of Aram that trapped and overwhelmed them. The terrible wrathful storms at sea that had splintered what remained of his fleet, and the betrayal of Lord Huffort when he took his vessels one dark rainy morning and fled for the sanctuary of his halls. Only days later Lorin's Bane had appeared from his slumber to come up from the depths and assail them, taking down *Blackthorn* before Elyon Daecar came and leaving Robbert with only three surviving ships and a thousand bone-weary men. *And now this,* he thought, too tired to even be bitter. The swamp and the titan and the toad who tricked them. From the forty thousand swords who sailed south an age ago…he only had forty left.

A dozen of those forty were set to guard the boundary of the island, and fires were lit around the perimeter to ward off any approach. If there was anything the denizens of this dark place did not like, it was light and heat, and their fires provided both. The rest of the men found places between the trees to rest, lying flat in the wet reedy grasses if they could or finding cosy nooks among the roots. A pair were commanded to climb into the upper branches and keep watch from there as well.

Robbert wanted to be alone. He found a quiet space and put his back against a tree trunk, pulling out the map to wonder where they were. They had barely stopped in the last few days and if their heading had indeed been westward, as they hoped, they might well be nearing the border of this land. He nodded, folded the map back up, and tucked it away. When his fingers emerged they did so holding onto a small grey hunk of coral, set in silver clasps, pitted and grooved and unspectacular, but meaningful all the same. He held it in his palm, wondering if what Saska said about it was true.

Luck, he thought. *Is this piece of coral really so lucky?* He'd lost hundreds of men and dear friends among them, and that didn't sound so lucky to Robbert Lukar, but maybe he was looking at it wrong. *Maybe we should all be dead, as Croakcloak wanted, and me most of all? Maybe it's lucky that any of us are still alive and that shadow…the shadow that scared the snake away…maybe we were lucky that shadow came too…*

The memory was still fresh to him. He'd been at the edge of the island amidst the lake, surrounded by the dead and the dying. Men thrashed in the water, tiny against the titan's bulk as the great serpent goddess loomed above him. Robbert stood there, panting, his blade lacquered in its green sticky blood. Half a dozen times he'd hacked at the hide of the beast as it snapped out at the men on the shore, or sent its great head down like a hammer to crush them where they stood. He'd cut at it and cleaved at it, but the creature barely seemed to flinch. Lord Gullimer was knocked down behind him, he remembered, and Lank had been brushed aside as well to go crashing through the ruin of the village. For a moment it seemed like Robbert stood alone. Just a one-eyed prince, standing against a titan, and up it rose, up and up, before all of a sudden the head came crashing down…

That's when Bernie appeared, running at Robbert like a bull and roaring as he smashed him aside. Robbert recalled flying through the air, his head rattling inside his helm. He remembered landing near the water's edge amidst charred wood and broken bodies….remembered the way the earth shook and trembled as the titan's head smashed down nearby…remembered staggering to his feet to find the great serpent's head rising back up, raining water and mud and blood…remembered the great deep depression in the earth it had left and Bernie…Bernie's broken body lying within it…

He vaguely recalled shouting out his friend's name as he ran back toward him, tripping as he reached the rim of the crater to go tumbling to Bernie's side. The earth was soft and the knight's armour was strong, but at once Robbert knew he would not survive. He had shaken him anyway, trying to wake him up. "Bern! Bern! We have to move! We have to go!"

Then something green splashed down onto his shoulder, green and gluey, and his eyes went up. There *she* was, watching with her clever red-green eyes. Blood oozed out from a hundred little wounds, buckets of it, barrels, but she didn't seem to care. It was nothing to her. Just drips. Robbert stood on weak and weary legs and raised his blade to face her. She was going to kill him, he knew. Robbert Lukar would die right there next to his friend.

But then he'd seen the shadow.

Something colossal passed the skies above her, moving swiftly through the misty air. The serpent's eyes had narrowed and her great head swung about, seeing it, and the hiss she made was of another world. The vast shadow arced and passed again, an immense winged nightmare giving out a terrible scream. Robbert had ducked and cringed against it, slapping his hands over his ears, and then there was the sound of rushing water, splashing, churning, more hissing and screaming and when next he dared to open his eyes and look, Celaph was plunging away through the lake, her immense long body slithering and swimming back into the murk from whence she'd come.

After that, they heard distant crashing, more screeching further off, as the snake titan fled and the shadow with her. Robbert had felt for Bernie's pulse, found him still alive, and called at once for a stretcher to be made to carry him. Everywhere there was groaning, moaning, the sounds men made when they died. Lord Gullimer had rushed up to him, telling him they had to leave, and Lank was shouting the same. More creatures were coming, they said. They were coming from the waters and swarming in at the scent of blood, creatures drawn to the slaughter, summoned maybe by Grimbel Croakcloak in the way that Celaph had been summoned. It was a feast for them, a wild crazed feast and the waters were churning and frothing everywhere.

The rest of it was a blur as the survivors fled across the bridge that Croakcloak said was burned. It had taken them out into this thick fetid bog on the other side of the lake, and along the way more men had been taken. Robbert might have had up to a hundred with him then, though by the time they plunged away through the mire, only half of them remained. Even now he could hear them in his head. Hear the screams of the men as they were snatched away behind him, hear the grown men sobbing and calling out for their mothers as the tide of terror overwhelmed them.

But that shriek most of all, he reflected, as he turned the coral necklace between his fingers. That was the sound that had stayed with him above all others; the piercing shriek of the shadow that had drawn Celaph away. Others had seen it too, rippling through the shroud, and said it could only be Drulgar the Dread. But Robbert Lukar thought different. The shape was not like a dragon, no, and the sound it made, that shrieking sound...

No dragon makes a noise like that, the prince thought. *No, it wasn't Drulgar. That shadow was something else.*

"What's that?" asked a voice.

Robbert broke from his reflections and saw that Lank was standing beside him.

"That rock in your hand. I've seen you holding it before."

Robbert reached into his pocket and tucked it away. "It's nothing. Just something Saska gave me."

"She gave you a piece of rock on a chain? Why?"

"It's not rock, it's coral. And it was important to her." Robbert hadn't spoken of it to anyone yet, though true enough he did find himself holding it sometimes, turning it over between his fingers, trying to feel its magic as Saska did. "It called to her, she told me. When she found it on a reef. She said there was an old man on the ship who could read the future in the grooves, and everyone had a piece of coral that called to them."

"Right." Lothar seemed unconvinced. He sat down beside him, stretching out his long legs. Both of them were filthy from their weeks here in the bog. "So what did this old man tell her?"

"He knew she was Bladeborn, even though she hadn't said so to the crew. He said there was a powerful blade in her future and that she was going to fight the darkness."

Lothar blinked at that. "He knew all that from a bit of rock?"

Robbert nodded. "He knew she was royal as well. Saska thought he was talking about her mother, but he wasn't. He was talking about her father." Saska had told Robbert all about it during her last days aboard *Hammer*. She didn't know who her father was then, of course, and certainly not that her grandfather was King Lorin, but it had been another part of the puzzle for her all the same. "She kept the coral as a totem," the prince went on. "She said it gave her fortune, or she believed it did anyway. You know how people have lucky charms? Well, this was hers."

"And she gave it away?"

"She insisted," Robbert told him. "I told her to keep it, but she wouldn't take no for an answer. I'm going to give it back to her, after the war."

"After the war only she can win," Lothar said, in a voice to suggest he was still struggling to accept it. "That blade the old man mentioned. He knew about the Heart Remade?"

Robbert doubted it. Saska had said the old man didn't see detail, only vague suggestions of things to come, and he'd seen something of great importance in her future. "He just knew she'd bear a powerful blade. I don't think anyone expected her to be Varin's heir or have to wield the heart of a god."

"Her grandmother did. The Grand Duchess. She knew all along who she was, and so did King Godrin." Lothar looked out into the marshes, frowning. "I wonder how she's getting on with her training. She'll need to learn all those blades if she wants to have a chance, Robb. I think we know that now, after fighting that snake. How many times did we cut her? Fifty? A hundred? And it was nothing to her. *We* were nothing. That weapon's the only thing that can kill these titans."

"Except other titans," Robbert said, thinking of that shadow again. He wondered if they'd come to battle somewhere. Maybe Celaph was dead, even? Maybe both of them were, and they were lying in a twisted heap long leagues away, sprawled out across the swamp.

"We can't rely on that. We can only rely on ourselves." Lank put a hand on Robb's shoulder. "Can I see it? This piece of rock?"

"Coral."

"Coral, right. Can I see it?"

Robbert withdrew it and handed it over, so Lank could inspect it. He did so with pursed lips, trying to find something interesting in it, then handed it back. "I don't understand magic. It just seems like a bit of rock to me."

"Coral," Robbert said.

Lank gave a weary laugh. "Coral, right. I'll have to remember next time." He gave a long deep breath, a weary breath, and sank a little lower against the trunk of the tree. "So, you want to get some sleep? Or maybe…if you're not tired yet we could talk of Bernie, just the two of us? You know, tell some stories like the Varin Knights do. That's how they honour them during their ascension. I've always liked that. Telling those stories so Varin will hear."

And grant the dead a better seat at his table, Robbert thought. The Emerald Guards did not go to that table, but to the Hall of Green, with its great open fields and mountains and waterfalls. It was meant as a calmer place to rest beyond war, but Robbert preferred the table, the feasting and the drinking and the singing and the storytelling. He had many stories of Bernie Westermont he could tell, adventures from their younger years and many since then as well. He smiled to think of them, recalling a simpler time. "I've got some stories, Lank," he said. "Do you want to start, or shall I?"

They spoke for hours, telling heroic stories and humorous stories, stories of Bernie's buffoonery and his bravery both. They laughed, though quietly so as not to disturb the other men, and Robbert felt on several occasions like shedding a tear, though he never did. He did not know at which point he fell asleep, though when he woke up Lank's head was resting against his armoured shoulder and Lord Gullimer was standing over him. "My prince," he said. "Wake up. Men have come."

Robbert shifted up and rubbed his eyes. It was dark still, though it seemed that a faint glow of dawn was shifting through the marshes. "Men? Some of ours?"

Lord Gullimer shook his head. "Not ours, Robbert. These men are Vandarians. A mix of Riverlanders and Marshlanders, as far as I can tell."

"Vandarians?" Robbert felt a swell of hope. If Vandarians had come, perhaps they were near the border of this mire after all. He pushed up to his feet, looking away through the trees. "How many are there?"

"Several hundred, it looks. Come, they're awaiting you."

Robbert rose at once to follow the apple lord across the small wooded island. On the other side, they found Sir Kester Droyn and several more of his men standing with a trio of strangers. Robbert did not recognise any of them. One wore full plate armour, badly scratched and battle-scarred. In the crook of his arm he held a helm with a faceplate wrought in the likeness of a smiling man. Another was massive; tall, barrel-chested and broad, he had an enormous black forest of a beard and the thickest neck Robbert had ever seen. A Riverlander, there was no doubt. They built them big and burly around there. The last of them was a Varin Knight, his rich blue cloak badly torn and frayed and filthy at the hem. As with the others, he was armoured in misting godsteel plate and seemed to be their leader.

Further off behind them, Robbert could see a sizeable host waiting among the marshes. Firelight burned among them, a score of little orange orbs floating in the morning mist. *Hundreds,* Robbert thought. The apple lord had the right of that.

The Varin Knight was the first to speak. He took a short step forward and then fell into a neat bow. "Your Highness. We are glad to hear of your return. Though here…" He had a plain, sincere face, grey eyes, a soldier's bearing. "We had not expected to find you *here*, my lord. You have come from the coast, Lord Gullimer said."

"From Winslow Point, yes." Robbert was still gathering his bearings. "And you are, sir?"

"Sir Gereon, my lord. Of Greyguard. And this is Sam Garrick, the Grinning Knight." He presented the man in the once-fine, battle-scarred armour with the smiling faceplate. "And lastly…"

"*Never* lastly," boomed the huge Riverlander. "The Beast of Blackshaw never comes last." He stamped forward and bowed. "Sir Mooton Blackshaw's the name. A pleasure, good prince. We all thought you were dead."

"Not yet, Sir Mooton. Though my enemies have tried." Robbert pointed to his eyepatch, but gave no further explanation. "And you? Have you come from Rustbridge?" he asked them. "Has there been fighting there?"

"Fighting?" repeated Sir Mooton, laughing. "I should damn well say! Never been a battle like it. It was the Burning Rock without the rock. Dragons, wolves, cats, camels, even a moonbear or two. I still dream of it every night. Desperate to have me another taste…nothing like it, I say, nothing sweeter in all the world…"

"You'll have to forgive Mooton's enthusiasm, Prince Robbert," said Sir Gereon. "He was very much born for battle."

Robbert Lukar looked the beast up and down. "I can tell." He had many questions circulating through his head. And one above all. "How is my brother, Sir Gereon? Did he acquit himself well during the fighting?"

The man's face curdled like spoilt milk. "Ah. Well, as to that…"

A terrible fear gripped at Robbert's heart. "Was he wounded? Not… he isn't…"

"We don't know the full extent of what happened to him as yet, my lord. He was gored by a dragon's tail spike during the fighting and taken to a tower so his wound could be examined. Sir Mooton himself was there, defending the tower."

The big man nodded. "We did what we could to hold the fire-folk back, but that dragon…same one as tore open your brother…it came and knocked the tower down. Word is your twin was taken out the back before then, though."

"He was spotted being taken from the battlefield," Sir Gereon said, taking the tale back up. "Sir Ernold Esterling was with him, and Lord Emeric Manfrey as well. None of them were among the dead when we searched for them after the battle. We think they fled into the woods to the north, but of your brother's fate…"

"You don't know," Robbert said. His voice went flat. "So he may be…be…" He could barely say it. Wouldn't let himself believe it. If Ray was dead he'd have felt it, he told himself. They had a sense, a sixth sense together. *I'd know*, he thought. *I'd know it.* "The battle," he made himself say. "How…what happened?"

Sir Gereon gave a grave shake of the head. "There is much to tell there, Prince Robbert. The cost of life was terrible on both sides; many tens of thousands perished, and Rustbridge was engulfed in flame. The fortress on the east bank of the river was primarily targeted, but the city suffered as well. The fighting began at dawn and went long into the night. I confess myself to have arrived to join only later, once it had begun. Sam Garrick and I had been tasked with…"

"The prince doesn't want to hear your life story, Greyguard," rumbled Sir Mooton. "You want to hear about the battle, lad, you hear it from me. I was there from start to finish and saw what sparked it off. Ven and Borrus and all that with his father's head. Gruesome stuff, it was. A cheap trick but enough to goad him. One minute the Barrel's giving out this fearsome roar and the next we're all ahorse, with steel in our fists, blowing the horns and charging into the dawn."

Robbert tried to imagine it. It was everything he wanted to be a part of, everything he had missed during his long days away. "The battle was won, then?" he said, hopeful. "Vargo Ven's host was destroyed?"

"Destroyed? No," said Sir Gereon of Greyguard. "When the battle turned against them, they fled in large numbers, breaking apart. That is why we are here. A host was said to have escaped into this swamp and Lord Kanabar ordered that we give chase. He is assembling the remainder of our forces in the west, and…"

"And we'll join him," Robbert said, at once. "How many Tukorans remain to you? I was told my brother had marched to Rustbridge with thirty thousand swords."

The Varin Knight shook his head. "I could not say with any certainty, Prince Robbert. The losses were grievous, as I have said, but no worse for your countrymen than our own. Half or more may yet remain to you, perhaps as many as twenty thousand." He looked over Robbert's shoulder. "And you? You left with tens of thousands when you sailed to the south, did you not? I see only a handful here among the trees."

"I have fewer than forty," Robbert said.

"So few?" The man was shocked. "What happened to the rest of them? Lord Kastor, is he…"

"A story for the road," said Robbert Lukar. "If you are willing, I would have you lead us from this swamp with all haste, sir. I have a strong desire to take command of my host."

"I do not doubt it, Prince Robbert. But we have an explicit command of our own. To hunt these Agarathi down, and…"

Robbert shook his head. "No need." He thought of all the bodies floating across the lake, scores of them, hundreds, all savaged by Celaph before she savaged his own. "The Agarathi are dead, Sir Gereon. There is no cause for you to continue into this mire."

Sir Mooton gave a laugh. "Well, looks like the good prince has done our job for us, Greyguard. Thank the bloody gods for that. I'm sick of this swamp already."

So was Robbert. More sick of it than he could say. He still had men out there, scattered and lost and rudderless, but would not ask Sir Gereon to send men of his own to try to find them. *They are on their own now*, the prince told himself. *If men are sent back into that mire, they may never come out.*

"The dead Agarathi was not our doing, Sir Mooton," he told the big knight. "There is a menace in this mire that none of us can match, and this many men…" He glanced back, fearing she would come again. "We must leave at once, and with all speed. Sir Gereon, how far from firmer footing are we?"

"No more than two days. By tomorrow night we will be beyond the worst of the swamp. The Marshlands become more bearable after that."

Two days. Only two more days. Robbert turned to Sir Kester Droyn. "Get the men up," he commanded. "See them ready to leave at once, Sir Kester."

"Yes, my lord." Droyn dipped his chin and stepped away.

Robbert turned back to Greyguard. "And Lord Kanabar? How far away is his host?"

"A week further by foot. The plan was to hunt down the fleeing Agarathi and regroup at Westmire. It is a fortress town on the border of the western marshes, north of Dragon's Bane. I would expect to find the bulk of our forces there. And yours."

Mine, Robbert thought. *Up to twenty thousand of them.* In a little over a week he would be standing before them, taking up in his brother's stead. The thought gave him goose pimples.

The men were waking and gathering their things behind him as Droyn's voice echoed out through the wispy morning fog. In the marshland ahead, the hundreds under Greyguard's command were stirring as well, the order spreading from ear to ear that their short time in the swamp was done. Robbert could sense the relief among them, as he could amongst his own. An auspicious meeting, it was, a lucky encounter for them all.

He reached into his pocket and took out the hunk of coral. Perhaps it was lucky after all.

34

Emeric

The stout knight was smoking a pipe and looking down over the edge of the precipice.

"Well met, friend," Emeric said, approaching cautiously up the stony slope from behind him. He thought it best to announce himself, rather than spring a surprise. "You're very close to the edge there. It might be wise to step back."

"I'm good on my feet, lad, no need to worry." The stranger sucked on his pipe, blowing out a series of pale smoky rings that widened as they rose. He was a very short man, wide-set and broad, armoured in a mix of studded leather and godsteel plate that must have been specially made. Few men met his proportions, to be sure. He bore a broadsword at one hip, a dagger at the other, and a battle-axe on his back as well. It rested atop a fine blue cloak showing an armoured knight on horseback worked in silver thread, a misting blade raised aloft. The cloak stirred in the cold mountain breeze, making that sigil look especially heroic.

And so it should, Emeric thought. He knew the sigil well; there were few who didn't. "You're a Daecar man," he said, motioning. "From which house do you hail, sir?"

The dwarfish knight turned to face him. His beard was most impressive, big and brown, sprawling down his dinted breastplate. Behind it peeked a line of teeth, arched into a grin. His brows were remarkably bushy as well. "I don't look like a Daecar to you?"

Emeric smiled. "Well, not meaning to be impolite, but..."

"It's the height, isn't it? I'm too short to be a Daecar."

"The height, yes. And..."

"And the looks. Are you calling me ugly, stranger?" He smiled and puffed on his pipe again, the breeze taking the rings away over the breach. Rosewood it was, a finely crafted thing, with a long handle and wide bowl. "Aye, mayhaps I am....though my wife never gave any complaints. Still, sure she'd rather have Amron in her bed than me.

Handsome bugger, that one. His father was the same, and his sons as well. Elyon," he whistled. "Now there's a looker. That lad's gods-blessed make no mistake."

"Yes, so I've heard," Emeric said. The Daecars were all famously comely and the best approximation of what Varin himself had looked like, people said. Lord Amron especially, grand and mighty as he was.

The stout knight looked him up and down. "You're not so bad looking yourself, you know. Nice beard you've got there, friend. I like that deep black. Very thick as well."

"If we're complimenting one another on our beards, I would be remiss not to mention yours."

"Oh, this old thing." He waved a hand through the great forest of hair, causing it to sway from side to side. "It serves me well on wintry nights. Makes for a good cushion for the wife." Another grin and twinkle in the eye. "So, Tukoran, are you? You got the accent. A good northern drawl."

"I was born above the Clearwater," Emeric said.

"Aye. Sounds like it too. So what are you doing up here on this hill?"

"The same reason as you, I would think."

"Oh, this little hole here." The knight waved his pipe over the abyss, which seemed to sink down into total blackness far beneath them. "Well come, don't be shy. Have a closer look. Let's see what you make of it."

Emeric took the man's invite and stepped up toward the edge. The breach had been made through a flattened ridge along the stony mountainside, some dozens of metres wide and roughly the same in length, a ragged, almost circular tear in the earth with a great deal of broken rock tumbled about its rim. Much more had fallen and crashed down the slope, some of the larger boulders ripping out trees and gouging great muddy tracts into the earth as they went barreling down into the plains far below. Emeric had seen the damage in the distance as he crossed through a valley with Sir Ernold and Prince Raynald, and felt compelled to come up and investigate. He had not expected to find anyone else here, though, and certainly not a Daecar man. They were all in the west, so far as he knew. There had been no Daecar men at Rustbridge that he recalled.

"Well? Care to share your thoughts, stranger?" The man grinned playfully. "Or ought we introduce ourselves first? That's the civil thing to do, isn't it?"

"I suppose it is." He reached out a hand. "Emeric Manfrey. Once lord, a lifetime ago."

That won him another smile. "Manfrey, aye, thought you were him."

Emeric frowned. "You know me, sir?"

"By reputation. It's said you bear the blade of Sir Oswald; eagle-winged crossguard and eagle-head pommel." He looked at the blade sheathed at Emeric's hip. "That's it right there. A famous blade."

"Middling fame. There are many of greater renown."

"Many's a stretch, I think. Not many blades have been used to cut down two dragons in single combat."

"No." Emeric could not disagree with that, nor would he wish to diminish Sir Oswald's deeds. Many still considered him the greatest swordsman of the age, a man raised up by Vandar himself when he travelled to his Tomb to seek a blessing from the Steel God's spirit. Oswald Manfrey had been a man of skill and potential only before he made that fateful pilgrimage. *He went into the mountain as an unfancied knight…and emerged to become a legend.*

"Karlog the Knight Killer and Bagazar the Brute," the dwarfish knight was going on. "Both as big as Garlath the Grand, they say, maybe bigger. Fearsome beasts who'd felled all who stood before them, but then comes Oswald Manfrey to put them in their place." He smiled. "Love that tale. Always have. It's a great pleasure to meet the man who shares his name."

His name and little more, Emeric thought. He had always felt uncomfortable by the comparison. "And you, sir. What do they call you?"

"Stoutman. Sir Torus Stoutman, the Knight of Steelvale." He dipped his head proudly.

"Steelvale. I confess I don't know it."

"No reason why you should. It's a small place up on the North Downs. Knightly house. We've been Daecar vassals since our founding."

"No one better to serve," said Emeric.

"Aye, I think so too. High and mighty though they are." He grinned another playful grin, then turned his attention back on the breach. "So, about this hole. I'm guessing some monster made it."

Emeric had suspected that for a while now, long before he'd even seen the breach. "I heard it emerge," he told Sir Torus. "Some days ago, while I was down in those woods." He gestured behind him; the forest in which the stormhag had lurked was a long way back now, away toward the western horizon. "I heard a great distant thunder during the night and took it for a creature tearing free of the earth. This breach stands as proof, I would say." He looked to the far side, a good fifty meters away. "Those ruts there. They look like claw marks. That was likely where it clambered free."

Sir Torus was smiling. "Clambered, yes, and then flew."

Indeed, Emeric thought. The claw marks only went so far, and then vanished. The creature must be winged.

"So, where you headed?" Stoutman asked him. "Crossing over into the Lakelands, are you?"

"That is the plan, yes. And you?" Emeric could see no horse nearby, no other men. This knight seemed to be all alone out here.

"Oh, I'm just passing through. Saw the breach from the air and thought I'd pop down for a closer look."

"From the air?" That didn't make any sense.

"Aye. The king sent me out to gather information. Me and Sir Connor Crawfield." He looked up. "This rain's not the only thing falling from the skies. There's been a black rain too, a rain of crows, and it's been turning us all blind as bats. The king bid me come out here and open his eyes. Question is, will he like what he sees?" He shrugged, smiling. "I guess we'll see."

Emeric was becoming confused. "You're talking about Amron Daecar?"

"The king. Aye."

"He is far to the west, I am told."

"True. You've not been lied to there, my lord. We were snaking on down the High Way last I saw of him. Some ten days out of Varinar. Might be he's there by now, and I'd best hurry back."

That would take weeks of hard riding, Emeric knew. Varinar must be nearly a thousand miles from here. *And this man has no horse...*

"This breach will require reporting on," the dwarfish knight went on. "Battles, betrayals, beasts, it's all happening out here. And now this. Another player in the game." He looked across the skies again, searching the clouds, and a smile touched his lips. "Goodness, look. A *dragon!*"

Emeric's heart lurched into his throat and he swung his gaze skyward. The man was right; a dragon was racing their way, plunging down from the wet white clouds, fleet and slim and quick. Greyish white and bright green were its scales, so too the cape of the rider on its back. Emeric reached at once to his left hip and the eagle-blade of Manfrey came singing from its sheath. "To arms, Sir Torus!" he called. "Take up your blade. We'll fight him together!"

The man made no move to draw steel.

"Sir Torus, come! It is getting closer..."

"Aye, I should hope so. How else will I climb aboard?"

Climb aboard? The man was making no sense. "Sir Torus, please. I am in no mood for this japing. Draw your blade. If I must face the beast alone, I will, but..."

"But you'd only be fighting a friend."

Emeric was exhausted. He blinked at the man. "A friend? You're to say...you *know* this dragon?"

"Aye. And the rider atop him. An'zon Graz is his name. I'm sure you know the house."

Emeric was well versed in the great houses of the south, and those from Agarath included. Graz, yes, he knew it. A storied house, old and rich. So far as he was aware, they had not had a Fireborn rider since Lord Mur'zon rode Klathnor to battle during the Twenty-Third Renewal, though. And he'd never heard the name An'zon.

Sir Torus seemed to be reading him. "He's of a lesser branch, is An'zon. A good-natured sort, quick with a grin like me. I'm supposing that's why he paired us in the first place."

"He?"

"Lord Marak. Sir Connor's with Lady Kazaan. A good pair too. They're both dour as a graveyard, those two. Couldn't buy a smile between them, not with all the gold from a dragon's horde." He gave a chortle. "Put up your steel, lad. They're getting near and Happy's not like to look well on it."

Just what on earth is happening here? Lord Ulrik Marak was involved as well? "You're telling me..." He could barely believe it. "You've been going about by *dragonback*, Sir Torus?"

"That's exactly what I've been doing. On Happy. Well, Hapthanor's his real name, if you want to know. Gods, I'll tell you...there's something about flying that really stirs the soul. Ah, who knows, maybe it's just me? When I'm up there I feel closer to my sons. They died, you see, at King's Point." He raised a more sombre smile. "You know about that, the day Drulgar came?"

"I know, yes." He softened his voice. "I'm sorry for your loss, Sir Torus."

He nodded. "My thanks. But they died heroes, all three of them, with swords in their hands and fury in their hearts, and what more could a father ask for? I'll see them all soon, in any case. I don't expect to live through this war." The knight drew the pipe from his lips and thrust it through his swordbelt. "Well, best be off, my lord. Mayhaps I'll see you use that famed sword of yours in anger one day, but that day's not now, so best sheathe it."

"Right. Yes, of course." Emeric slid the blade away as the dragon widened its wings to land. It did so back from the rim of the breach, some forty paces away, glaring at Emeric through narrow eyes. The rider, Graz, was looking over too.

"Stoutman, who is this person?" he called out, in a rough version of the common tongue. "He is making Happy not happy. Tell him he must go away!"

Sir Torus laughed. "You see, Lord Manfrey. He's got a good bit of humour about him, does Graz." He clapped him on the shoulder. "Be seeing you, then. Don't go becoming *too* much of a hero, now. Them Daecars won't likely thank you for intruding on their territory." And he laughed again as he left, the sound ringing out across the mountainside and down into the breach below.

Emeric watched him go, struggling to keep up with all he'd heard. The man went shuffling up toward the dragon with nary a care in the world, all but whistling a tune. Astonishingly, the beast even swung his head about to let the dwarfish knight give him a stoke beneath his chin. *Gods Above, what has this world become?* He watched the Bladeborn climb up into the saddle, watched him settle in and fix his harness. He spoke with An'zon Graz all the while, the pair laughing and tipping back their heads. *Bladeborn and Fireborn working together. A dragon carrying godsteel. The world's gone upside down.*

"Farewell then, my lord, been a pleasure talking!" Stoutman waved a fond goodbye and the dragon turned, beating its wings and gliding off down the hillside, before rising up, up and up into the clouds and vanishing into the afternoon gloom.

Emeric stared for a while longer, shaking his head. "I should have asked more questions," he muttered to himself. The man might very well have visited Rustbridge already during this information-gathering mission the king had given him. *He might have told me what happened after the battle. Whether any of my friends are still alive.* He closed a fist, opened it. It felt like a missed opportunity, to be sure, but there wasn't much he could do about it now.

He put it aside and began back down the mountain. A soft sprinkle of rain was falling and the air was bitter cold. His path took him over fields of scree and through brambly grass, across small mountain rills and stony rocks and patches of thick wet heather. The woods came up toward the foot of the Hooded Hills here, and between two prominences a valley ran eastward through the mountains. They'd been following it, taking an old goat track that ran up against a cliffside some halfway up. Below, at the heart of the valley proper was a true road, much wider and better travelled, but Emeric had decided to take the quieter course. He could see his two companions waiting down there. Sir Ernold had dismounted and was sat hunched on a rock as his mare munched at the grass that grew about its base. The palfrey that bore the prince was a few metres away, chewing idly as well.

A small trickle of stone announced Emeric's return as he half-staggered, half-slid down the steep slope above the track, dropping over the edge and landing with a rattle of steel. Sir Ernold Esterling slowly raised his head. His eyes were sunken, his flesh sickly pale. "You're back," he muttered. "Good." He stood weakly from his perch, his forehead dappled with beads of sweat despite the chill. "I thought something might have happened to you, Manfrey. There was a dragon, did you see it? Looked to me like it was coming down to land up there."

"Hapthanor," Emeric said.

"Haptha-what? What are you talking about?" His voice was brusque.

"The dragon's name. I spoke with its rider, or one of them. Though *passenger* would be more apt."

That did not do anything for Ernold Esterling's mood. "My hand hurts, Emeric. And my head is on fire. I have no time for these games." He looked up the steep hillside. "What did you find up there, then? Aside from friendly Fireborn?" He snorted, thinking he must be japing.

Well, let him. I'll tell him about it later. "There's a hole," Emeric answered. "A very large one. Something came bursting out of it, that night I dug the graves."

"Something? What?" The man's temper was short, his mood black. He was running a bad fever from his mangled hand, and that ought to make him fragile, but it only seemed to make him more hostile and blunt. *He fears for his life, perhaps that's why. If the fever gets any worse…*

"I don't know. A winged creature of some sort."

"Winged? How do you know it was winged?"

"There were no tracks, nothing but claw marks as it climbed out. It can only have flown from there."

"Great," Esterling snorted. "Some other monster to deal with. Aren't dragons enough? Isn't the *Dread* enough?" He kicked at a stone, sending it pinging away against the rock and into the side of the palfrey. The horse whickered, rearing. Emeric rushed right in to calm it, snatching at the bridle.

"Damn it, Ernold. He could have thrown the prince."

"An accident. Don't curse me for a bloody accident, Manfrey." He slumped back down onto his rock, pale and irritable. "He's lashed up, anyway. What's the worst that could happen?"

"The rope could come loose and he could fall. We're on a narrow goat path if you haven't noticed, with a sheer drop on one side. If he fell…"

"He wouldn't. And it's not sheer. And he's wearing his armour. Nothing would bloody well happen to him."

Emeric held his tongue. *It's the fever, that's all. That and his maimed hand.* The knight had displayed a warrior's bravado at first, claiming it wasn't his sword hand anyway and he didn't even need it, but Emeric could see that mask beginning to slip. He caught Ernold looking at the bound wound as he rode, scowling at the queer way his pinky finger poked out of the bandage. Two nights ago he'd spoken of hacking that off too. It looked stupid, he said. What use was that finger now? He might as well lose the rest of the hand and put a hook there in its place, like in those pirate stories men read when they were boys.

He doesn't like that he isn't whole, that is the long and the short of it. What man did? With the pain and the fever and the growing fear of death, it made him a poor travelling companion, and Emeric preferred the prince these days.

At least he's quiet. Still lost to the sorcerous sleep that the stormhag had put him into, the boy had not so much as made a murmur for days. Emeric had to spoon-feed him water and gruel to keep him alive, but elsewise his health was good. His heart beat regularly in his chest and his breathing was smooth and strong. It might take no more than a special word to bring him around, Emeric had thought, a secret word of the stormhag's choosing to break the spell, but if that were the case, the exile didn't know of it. Alternatively a potion might do the job. He'd taken as many potions and tonics and queer ingredients as he could from the stormhag's lair, but the labels were all in an old tongue he did not know, and if one was the cure for the prince's curse, he had no idea which one.

I need professional help, he knew. *A potion master, someone skilled in languages, maybe even a sorcerer or witch.* He looked at Ernold Esterling, sitting weakly on his rock. *And for him as well. He needs a proper healer.* There was only so much Emeric could do.

"We should get moving," he said.

Esterling nodded grimly, stood, and saddled up. They only had two horses, so Emeric walked ahead, leading along the prince's palfrey by the rope as Sir Ernold trotted behind. The track hugged the side of the mountain on the right; to their left fell a plunging drop that sloped away down the valley, not quite sheer but sheer enough. A killable drop it was, no matter what the Emerald Guard said. Emeric made sure to keep them close to the wall, though that had its dangers too. Some of the stone above them looked loosened by the rain and if a chunk fell away…well, best not dwell on that.

It had been mostly dry for several hours now, which of course meant a heavy rain was near. The clouds curdled and gathered close, turning light grey to dark with patches of black, and then came the sounds of thunder. *A storm. Wonderful. Just what we need.*

"We had best find cover before it gets too bad," Emeric called back.

He heard no response from behind. That was unusual. *Did he not hear me?* Turning, he looked back and found that Sir Ernold was slumped forward in the saddle, murmuring through some delirium. *The fever is worsening. He may need help sooner than I thought.*

The going was slow and fretful. When the rain came down, it came down hard and the way ahead became shrouded and perilous. "Slowly now, nice and slow," Emeric said. "Be calm, there's nothing to fear here. It's just a bit of thunder and lightning. Just a bit of rain." He spoke to the horses to calm them but perhaps did it partly for himself. He could almost hear the rock loosening above him, hear it crumbling and threatening to fall. "It's fine. Everything's fine." A flash of lightning cast the world suddenly bright, exploding against the goat track a mere two dozen horse lengths ahead. The thunder that followed was instantaneous and deafening, a great crash to bring some loose rock spinning down, leaping and bounding against the road and away into the abyss beyond. Emeric Manfrey could not say how he maintained control of the horses then, but he did. "Good, yes, just keep on going. That was the closest one. There won't be another."

More lighting flashed and thunder bellowed, ahead and behind them and down in the valley. Ahead, a figure slowly emerged from the shroud, a traveller leading a horse in the opposite direction. Emeric peered at him through the gloom. He seemed to be alone, so far as he could make out.

It was narrow on the track here, and the fall to Emeric's left was treacherous. The traveller drew his horse up toward them. "Foul place to meet," he said.

"Yes," Emeric agreed.

The man judged the fall, saw Emeric was leading two unconscious men on horseback, and said, "I'll go around. Get your horses up against the wall so I can get by."

Emeric eased the horses as close to the cliff as he could, one behind the other. The stranger continued toward them, leading his horse carefully past as the black rain tumbled down. He wore a large cloak that might be hiding armour beneath and had the bearing of a warrior.

"Heading east, are you?"

"We are," Emeric said.

"You're wiser than me, then. No war in the Lakelands yet."

"That's good to hear. Are you heading for the war?" Emeric asked.

"Might as well. I've got a blade going spare, so…" He shrugged, peering at the two unconscious men. "Your friends look unwell. If you're in need of a healer, take the Midsister Road toward Lakeheart. You'll find someone to help you there."

Emeric dipped his chin. "You have my thanks."

The man looked at the skies. He was about Emeric's age, he guessed, bearded and large. "This rain'll last the night. If you're looking for somewhere to camp, there's a shelf of rock about a mile further on. Not a cave, exactly, but it'll keep you dry. The storm ought to have passed by dawn. When it does, you'll get a good view of the lakes." He waved a hand backward. "When you reach the fork, take the path on your left. It'll lead down to the Midsister through some woods. Best take it when it's light. Don't be attempting that way in the dark."

Emeric appreciated the advice. The man seemed earnest enough not to be tricking him. "I'll do as you say." He could see the shape of a blade at the man's hip, amongst the folds of his cloak, the glint of armour creeping up his neck. There was a shield slung down his horse's flank too. "Are you travelling alone?"

"I am. Same as you." Emeric saw a grim smile through the man's ragged wet beard. "These two don't look much help."

"No," he admitted. "Not in their current shape."

"That's harder. Having to watch over two others. I don't envy you, friend." He smiled again. "Says the man riding alone into the war."

Emeric liked his bleak sense of humour. "You'll find plenty of that further south. I'll look for you when I return."

"That's a deal." The stranger dipped his chin and walked on by, leading his horse along the track.

Emeric continued the other way. True enough, about a mile further on he found the shelter the man had spoken of, and there they rested the night. Shortly after stopping, Sir Ernold emerged from his delirium long enough to eat and take on some water, and even keep watch for a short while so Emeric could get some much-needed sleep. It was not restful, nor was it deep, but it served to keep him sane. The storm raged on all the while, crashing around them before finally drifting off shortly before dawn. And in its wake came clear skies, a rare spread of blue, and the quick bright rising of the sun.

They continued into that confection of colour, the pinks and purples turning to yellows and golds as the sun climbed up over the horizon. When the goat track rose and passed the lip of a hill, Emeric got his first view past the mountains. The colour was reflected on the water, dazzling and brilliant, the great lakes spreading out before him to the far edge of his sight. Distantly, he saw the white and blue stone city of Lakeheart nestled between them, the Midsister Road leading toward it. *No fire*, he thought, *no smoke*. The man was right. The war had not come here yet.

There was a smile on his lips. A hopeful smile. "We're close, Ernold," he said, turning to look at him. "Only a few days away now…"

The knight was slumped forward in the saddle again, too weak to even answer. *He is dying,* Emeric Manfrey thought. *The fever is spreading too quickly.* He had taken a sniff of the man's bandaged hand and didn't like the way it smelled. *He won't last days,* he realised. *He needs a proper healer, and he needs him now.*

He could no longer remain afoot. Nor did he have the strength in him to run, not quickly and not for long. There was only one thing for it. Marching back, he vaulted up into the saddle behind the Emerald Guard, hoping that the mare could take both their weight. Reaching forward, he took the reins in one hand; in his other he held the palfrey's rope. "Hold on, Ernold," he told the knight. "I'm not going to let you die, not after all we've been through."

Ahead, the track widened; he could see the fork far below, leading left down into the woods. *Don't travel it in the dark.* It was dim still, gloomy beneath those trees, but by the time they got there the sun would be piercing the canopy. *If there are outlaws there, so be it. Monsters, I don't care.* He could no longer wander along at the slow pace he'd set; time was his enemy now.

He kicked his heels, driving the mare forward at a hard trot, to get her used to the extra bulk. A strong horse she was, a determined horse. "Good." He patted her neck. "Can you go a little faster? I'll let you rest soon, I promise. Just go a little faster for me."

The mare whickered a response, flickering her mane, and Emeric took that for a yes. He urged her down the path, faster, faster. And faster still they went.

35

———

Lythian

"You're certain?" Lythian asked, looking intently at the sheepskin map. "If you're leading us into a trap, Ramsey…"

"I'm not, my lord," the man protested, as he had a hundred times. He was growing quite irate about it now. "No, I've told you, I *only* joined Brontus to help get the blade back. For my…my crimes, my lord. To make up for my crimes. Oloran's there, I promise it." He prodded at the map. "Right there."

Lythian considered, rubbing at his raggedy bearded chin. "And if he's already left? You say Brontus was planning to go here, but you cannot know for how long. He may continue north, to his lord uncle. To Elinar."

"No, my lord, that isn't his intention. I've told you. He wants to kill *dragons*. He spoke about it openly…how he should have had the Sword of Varinar all along…how Lord Dalton was wasted with it. He didn't think much of Dalton Taynar. Said he was much the better swordsman, more courageous as well, and once he'd mastered the blade, he would do all he could to help win the war with it."

"How noble." Lythian's voice was blunt.

"He thinks so," Ramsey Stone went on. "I've never liked Oloran, you know that. He's boastful, arrogant, thinks far too much of himself. Him and Steelheart, those two, what they get up to…" His thin lips twisted in disgust. "But in this…"

"He believes he is doing the right thing. Yes, I know." Old Sir Ralf had said as much the day Lythian left King's Point. Brontus Oloran considered himself a liberator of the blade, and its rightful bearer. What he was doing was noble, just, a righteous act, and in time all the world would come to see it too. Lythian didn't care for such excuses. "The blade must be retrieved, Ramsey." He looked into the man's dark eyes. "Do you know why?"

He fumbled for the right words. "For *honour*, my lord," he said, imagining Lythian would like that word. "Yes, the sake of honour, and…"

"Survival," Lythian told him. "When Brontus stole the Sword of Varinar he put us all in jeopardy, unwitting though that was. The very future hinges on its retrieval, Ramsey. This is not about honour, nor my own sense of pride. I am here because of a puzzle, and Brontus holds a piece. A piece we need. One of five."

"Five?" Stone wiped under his sharp pinched nose. "You're talking about the Blades of Vandar?"

"I'm talking about the Heart Remade. About the only weapon capable of winning this war. Brontus may wish to kill a dragon or two, but lest he can slay the Dread, he is only serving himself. Now…" He looked at the map again, moving things on. He'd said enough. Quite enough for now. "You say Brontus has gone here. That there is something there. A fortress. Or a castle."

Ramsey's bony head went up and down. "That's what I saw on his map, yes."

But not this one, Lythian thought. Brontus Oloran's map was richer in detail, it seemed, or else showed an older version of the realm. Stone claimed to have seen a stronghold of some kind inked into Oloran's parchment, where Lythian's showed only a broad swathe of trees, yet another of the hundred separate woods and forests, large and small, that spread out across the vastness of the Wandering Wood. "And you're certain it was here?"

"I'm sure of it." There was some irritation in his voice. "I'm not lying, Lythian. How many times must I tell you?"

"I'm not saying you're lying. Only that you might be mistaken."

"I'm not. I know from this ridge line." He pointed it out on the sheepskin map. Faded though it was, most of the features were still visible; roads, rivers, dotted lines to show changes in elevation. "That ridge was on Oloran's map as well. I recognise the shape of it, the way it curves. This woodland beneath it…" His finger traced a line. "His map showed a stronghold here, right here, with a name, though I wasn't close enough to read it. Might have been the seat of some lord once, but I guess the woods sprung up around it, so people forgot, and it was never added to the newer maps like yours. That's what Brontus wanted. Somewhere secret where no one would look to find him, so he could train in peace. And game. There would be game to hunt in those woods as well, so…"

"More than game in these woods, boy." Vilmar the Black came prowling out of the morning gloom, making not a sound despite the weighty size of his frame. His dense black hair sparkled with droplets of water and dripped down through the wiry hair of his great beard. His eyes were dark and brooding. "There are older fouler things lurking here. Might be Oloran's already dead."

Lythian frowned up at him. "Did you find tracks?"

"Aye, though they were faint. Washed away. No more than a bolk on the breeze, here and gone in an instant. Not a soul in this world would have found them but me."

"And?" Lythian was used to his lofty talk by now, and to be sure, the man was worthy of the boasts. "Were they going toward this woodland, Vilmar?"

The huntsman nodded. "Aye, they were. Seems the craven's been telling the truth in that."

"Craven?" Stone surged up to his feet, mouth twisting. "You say that again, huntsman, and…"

"Craven. You want one more? Craven. You're craven, Stone." The huntsman was twice as large, twice as old, ten times as deadly. He gave a growling laugh. "Just own it, boy. You stand up on your tippy toes like that, and do nothing…only proves the point." He pulled a blade from his belt and scratched under his forested chin, dislodging twigs and bits of brush. No doubt he'd been snuffling about like a truffle pig again when searching out these tracks. "This wood," he said, ignoring Ramsey's stare. "It's still a good way off, half a day's walk from here. Best you three stay here in camp. I'll go see what's what."

Lythian turned his eyes across the current stretch of woodland where they'd slept the night. It was not long past dawn, and the rain was coming down from a bleak grey sky, drizzling through the leaves and branches. Thin shafts of strangled morning light dripped down with the rain, and the earth was soft beneath them, rotting, the roots struggling to get a grip across this soaked, waterlogged land. Everywhere trees had fallen, like old men unable to stay standing any longer as their feet were pulled from under them. The unceasing rain was killing the forest, Vilmar had said, drowning it. The Wandering Wood, with its hundred woods and thickets and forests of oak and elm and ash, was dying.

At last Lythian nodded. "Fine. If you think that's best."

"I go better alone, you know that. Be quicker that way." Vilmar gave the map a cursory glance. "Half a day to get to that wood, another half to get back. Add a good sniff and scour for this so-called fortress, and I wouldn't expect to be back before dawn."

"Very well. We'll keep a watch for you. But don't go getting distracted, Vilmar. I know you. If you get the scent of some rare beast, you're likely to go hunting it down for a prize."

"The prize is Oloran," the huntsman said.

"Yes. And if you find him, come right back. We'll take him together. Don't go trying to be a hero by killing him and his men on your own."

"Hero?" The hunter laughed like a beast. "I leave that sort of business to you knights. Well, not the craven here, but proper knights like you. There's no huntsman ever been a hero." He growled out more laughter and went to gather up his things; bag and belt, weapons and rations. In no time at all he was ready. "If I don't come back, figure I'm dead. Aye, there's *something* in this world that can kill me. Might be I'll meet it today."

"I'd rather you didn't. Do you need the map?"

Vilmar didn't dignify that with an answer. Turning, he stalked back into the trees as silent as a cat, and was gone.

Lythian stood from the little stump he'd taken for a seat, rolled up the map and returned it to his saddlebag. The black gelding that Vilmar claimed would not last long in the woods was indeed lasting, and proving a very reliable steed. Lythian drew out his brush to groom him, running the stiff bristles through his fine black hair and getting the tangles out of his mane. Sir Bardol was still sleeping, wrapped up in his furs beneath the cover of a grand oak tree. Sometimes Lythian wished they'd never found the knight in that magradile lair. He was more burden than boon, in truth, too unreliable to trust with the night watch and skittish of every passing shadow. Every day he would murmur and moan of some menace stalking behind them, and by night he would often cry out in his sleep, beset by terrible dreams.

"He's traumatised, that one," Vilmar had said, only a day after they'd left the village. "Might've been better to leave him with that pig farmer and spare us all the trouble."

Lythian felt compelled to disagree. "He is a knight, Vilmar. A *Bladeborn* knight. He is hardier than he may seem. He'll soon come around."

He had hoped so, anyway, though the days since had made him doubt it. So far as he saw it, Sir Bardol might prove a useful asset if battle broke out with Oloran and his men. They had entered the village as a two and exited four in number, but Oloran's host numbered eight, and all were Bladeborn as well, according to Ramsey Stone. During his days in Brontus's company, he'd come to know each man. Their size and age. Did they favour their left or their right in combat? Did any bear old wounds? What weapons did they carry? Longswords, broadswords, bastard swords, spears, throwing knives, daggers, morning stars, axes. All wore a variety, all forged of Ilithian Steel. "I watched them training as well," Ramsey had reported. "They sparred in the morning, sometimes, and at night when they set camp. I know their best stances, my lord. And what armour they're wearing under their cloaks."

It was useful information, the sort of detail that could prove the difference between success and failure, triumph and defeat. Most of all, Lythian had wanted to know about Brontus Oloran and his progress. Ramsey had seen him training as well, though only in glimpses and away through the trees. He would go off and train alone, Stone reported, though occasionally Sir Symon Steelheart would join him. "He was starting to swing it, last I saw," Ramsey told him. "I didn't see clearly, not from the camp, but I heard him. The grunts and the noises, and the trees falling down as he cut them through. He trained often, my lord. As often as he could. Sometimes he'd come back soaked in sweat and with this look in his eyes…it's hard to describe…an intense look, but also resolved. He had the look of a man possessed, Lythian. Like this was fate to him. Like he was doing Vandar's work."

He is lost, Lythian knew then, if not before. *The blade has enslaved him… there is no coming back.*

None of what Ramsey told him of the man surprised him. Brontus Oloran was always fastidious and obsessive in his training. Always one of the first to the sparring yard and always one of the last to leave, only Aleron Daecar had shown the same depth of dedication among the younger knights.

He will be fearsome now, Lythian reflected, concerned. He'd had the Sword of Varinar in his possession for long weeks, long enough to bear it well, if not weightlessly. Should he come face to face with Brontus Oloran in a duel, he could not afford to make a single mistake. *One wrong step, one wrong move, and he'll cut me clean in two.* It was not possible for him to fight evenly against the Sword of Varinar. His longsword would yield to it as easily as his armour, and only the other Blades of Vandar could resist its cutting power. *We will have to catch him unawares. Send in Vilmar to creep upon him in the night and kill him while he's sleeping.* If Brontus saw them coming…if he was armoured and ready, he might very well kill them all. He would not wish to, perhaps, but he would. If they came for the blade…he would.

Lythian pondered all that and more as the morning went by. The rain fell in a constant patter, tinkling through the leaves and running in little rills into the lower valleys. Here the lands swayed and rolled like ocean swells and many of the vales were beneath the water. Their camp was on a portion of higher ground, an island in the ocean, wet, yes, soaking even, but liveable for now. In truth, Lythian could not recall what a blue sky looked like; he could barely recall the shape of the sun. Dryness was an alien thing to him now, like an old friend, barely remembered, who'd gone away to a far-off land long ago and never returned. And to be clean too, to bathe and shave. He had vowed he would not remove his armour again, not until he had the blade in his grasp. *Soon*, he hoped. *Soon*, he prayed. He wanted to strip and scrub the filth from his body. And from his soul, yes, he wanted to cleanse his soul.

At the approach of midday, Sir Bardol finally awoke, crawling out from under his blankets like some starved bear after a long hibernation. "Sir Bardol. Nice of you to join us."

He blinked at him with those big broken eyes. "My…my lord? Did… did I sleep too long?" He lifted his shivery gaze to the sky, seen thinly through the canopy. Some of the green leaves were going gold now, and some a darker orangey brown, and across the forest floor was a matt of needles and acorns, of mulchy fallen leaves and mud all mingled and mashed by the rain.

"You always sleep too long," grumbled Ramsey Stone, hunched by the smoky fire. He was tending it grimly, throwing in twigs and whatever dry kindling he could find. "You'd sleep forever if we didn't wake you up. Time you snapped out of it. We need your blade."

Sir Bardol turned to Lythian again, confused. Always confused. He was a haggard-looking man, with thin dark skin beneath his drooping eyes and the dour bony features of an Ironmoorer. "My lord? Is this about Brontus Oloran?"

"Oh keep up, Bardol. What else do you think this is about?" Stone snorted angrily and threw a bit of wood into the fire. "He's got seven men with him. Seven, and all Bladeborn. Steelheart, Bullard, Waxen, Fish, Leatherbelly, Heggarty, Wormbreeches, I've told you all about them. We've got four, and that's including *you*. Or are you too *craven* to fight?"

"No, I…" Sir Bardol looked at Lythian.

"Don't look at him. Look at me." Stone stood up menacingly, every bit the mean little bully he'd always been. *He's sore from what Vilmar said,* Lythian knew. *And he's taking it out on someone weaker.* "You're craven, aren't you? Aren't you?"

"No. I…I'll fight when I must. I will." He swung to Lythian. "I will."

"Yeah. Sure. Sure you will. Craven."

"I'm not craven. I'm not."

"You are. Yes you are. I hear you at night, whimpering like a little girl. Calling for your mother. Moaning about the dark. It's over, damn you. You're not in that cave anymore! You see me moaning? I was caged, spat on, threatened all day and night. They didn't let me sleep. Gave me nothing but a few spoons of water. I could hear them all talking about how they were going to kill me. Whether they'd hang me or behead me or kill me slow. One man had a flaying knife and another a good blade for gutting, and they'd stand at the bars, just stand there, staring, and I've never seen such eyes, I've never seen such hate. You think that was easy? Wondering when they were going to come for me? I was dead in that cage, dead, and for something I never did. I killed no one in that village, not like the others. Bullard, he hacked men up and didn't care and Wormbreeches is as cruel as they come. But *I* was the one they caught, me. A dead man breathing, just waiting for the axe, I was dead in that cage the same as you were dead in that cave, but you don't hear me going on. Not like you, wailing and whining. And he calls *me* craven? That hunter calls *me* craven!"

"That's enough," Lythian said. Vilmar's words had cut him more deeply than he realised. "Calm down, Ramsey. Neither of you are craven."

The man took a sharp breath to recover himself, then slumped back down on his stump. "Maybe I am," he grumbled, scowling down at the fire. "I ran from battle. I'm a deserter, and deserters are craven, aren't they? But at least I'm *trying* to change. A man can do that, can't he? Change? A man's got lots of sides to him, different sides he can show. That's all I want, a chance to show it. That's all I thought about as I sat in that cage….sat in my own filth, soiled and stinking, with the spitting and the stares and the threats. Just a chance to set things right. To change, to help, to…"

"Reclaim your place at Varin's Table," Lythian said. He was under no illusions about the man's motivation. "You lost your seat when you abandoned Dalton Taynar, and you hope to win it back."

Ramsey Stone looked at him. "Yes. That's what I want." His mouth was tight. "Would you shame me for that, Lythian?"

"No," he said, fairly. "It is a worthy motivation…if a selfish one. You *are* selfish, Ramsey. There is no use in denying it to me; we served together for many years, and I know just who and what you are. But be honest with yourself. Do not pretend that you are doing this from the goodness of your heart. You're doing it for yourself, and yourself alone."

The man glowered at him briefly, but nodded, accepting. "So what if I am? Amounts to the same thing in the end, so long as I do my duty. I'm not a good true knight like you, Lythian. I'm limited, same as most. But so what if I want my seat back? If that drives me to do good, so what? I'm not long for this world, I know that well enough. But even if I was… even if I lived to be a hundred, what's that against an eternity up there?" He stared up for a long moment, through leaf and branch and cloud and sky, through the wetness of the rain and the cold bitter wind and beyond, to what lay beyond. "I always knew I'd have a lowly seat…way down west, ten thousand from the head. Knew I'd never hear Varin speak, or Ayrin, or Oswald Manfrey or Rufus Taynar. I'm no Daecar, no Kanabar or Amadar, I'm no hero, the huntsman had that right. But just to be there…to hear the songs and the stories of the men around me, to drink and feast and sit with my brothers…" He smiled, not a handsome smile, but there was hope in it, and something sweeter. "I ran from that battle through fear, but after…after a worse fear got into me. That I'd never get to take my seat. And that sat with me, worse than anything. It's a thing to ruin your life. But to ruin your *after*life." He sighed and shook his head.

A moment passed in silence. Then a sad voice said, "I never had a seat. You lost yours, yes, and maybe you'll get it back. But I never even had one. And it's all I ever wanted."

Ramsey regarded Sir Bardol curiously. "You wanted to be a Varin Knight, Bardol?" He was tactful enough to keep the mockery from his tone. The question sounded sincere. "I never knew."

Sir Bardol nodded and went to sit by the fire. His shoulders were hunched and drawn in, like a turtle in its shell. He stared down at his hands as he spoke. "Sir Hadros always spoke of it…getting a Varin cloak of his own. He said King Amron might grant him one if he went out and did his duty well…he would talk with Ruggard Wells about it, about joining Varin's Order. And sometimes even me as well. If we did our duty, and gathered those deserters, and returned them to King's Point, maybe…maybe…"

A deep sigh moved through his lips. Lythian could see the pain in his eyes, the glistening shimmer of the tears. "But we failed," he went on. "The deserters turned on us, and more Agarathi came through the trees, and when the slaughter began, I ran…I just got on my horse and ran. I left them all there to die." He hung his head low in shame. "I don't deserve a Varin cloak, not after that. There's no place for me at his table."

"No," said Ramsey Stone, denying him. "You ran, same as me. Fear can make a man do stupid things, but we both have a chance to make amends. You and your cave…me and my cage…we were both trapped, both dead, but Lythian's freed us and given us a chance." He looked over at him. "Isn't that right, my lord? If Bardol fights well, if he helps you get back the sword…there's still a chance for him. Isn't there?"

Lythian dipped his chin. "There's still a chance," he confirmed. He appreciated that from Ramsey, it was well done. "Fight with pride, Bardol, and I will tell the king of your valour. He will not give a Varin cloak out freely; it must be earned, through courage and deed, but if you serve me and fight for me, he may be willing to consider it."

The broken man blinked over at him, and suddenly he seemed a little less broken after all. A crack was healing, just one, but it was a start. "I'll fight, my lord," he said, in a small voice. "You can count on me, I vow it." And awkwardly, he slid from the stump and went down to a knee, drawing out his dagger to place it on the ground.

Lythian smiled at him, stepped forward and bid him rise. "If you're to fight, you'll need sharpening, Sir Bardol. I imagine the same could be said of you, Ramsey? And me." His eyes turned away to a nearby glade. "Come, let's have a swing. All this rain is causing us to rust. Best shake it off while we can."

And for some hours following, the glade rang to the sweet kiss of steel on steel, of grunting men, of the rush of boots across the forest floor and even, at times, the sound of laughter. Lythian had half forgotten the simple joys of sparring. The switch of stance. The ringing strikes. The cuts and thrusts and parries. He recalled the days of his youth when he would spar in the Steelforge yard with Amron and Borrus and Killian, enjoying the lick of the warm summer sun on his face, the taste of the salty sweat in his mouth, the smell of it rising, the heat in his armour, the crunch of sand and stone underfoot as he slid and moved, shifting forms, Blockform, Rushform, *Strikeform*. The others had always been friends to him, dear friends, yes, but Strikeform was *family*. Fighting in his favoured stance with Starslayer in his grasp had felt like the most natural thing in all the world.

And he was in it now, wearing it like a tailored glove, a perfect fit for him, each finger snug and secure. He felt warm in Strikeform, safe, happy. Each move was a memory, each sequence a song, a dance he'd done a thousand times before, in training and in tourneys and in the turmoil of battle too. The afternoon pulsed and hastened by as they worked off the rust beneath the rains, and each man felt the better for it. They puffed, panted, smiled, swung, stopped to rest and share their thoughts. Lythian gave praise where it was due, criticism where he thought it would help. Always fair. Always constructive. He felt alive again; this was the man he'd always been. Captain of the Varin Knights. Arbiter of the order. Well-loved by the men, a friend to all, honourable, noble, the famed Knight of the Vale who lived only for his duty, only for his service, only for his king and his countrymen and his kingdom.

I can be that man again, he told himself, as he stood by and watched the others duel. They were engaged in a bout, tournament rules. Shifting, sliding, splashing in the mud. The ring of sword on breastplate, vambrace, steel on steel. The mist of Vandar's Soul swirling about the glade. *Once we're done here, I'll be a knight again, no more.* He wanted to fight in battle again, in the great battle to end it all. To fight and die at Amron's side with the order arrayed around them.

Before long the light was thinning. Lythian looked around, saw the approach of dusk, the darkness creeping over the wood. It had come on quickly. He called an end to their training for the day and the others gathered around, smiling, panting. "You did well. Both of you." They were red-faced, weary-eyed, but *alive*. "We can go again in the morning, once we're rested," he said. "We'll sleep one man at a time, the other two on watch. Without Vilmar we are greatly more vulnerable here."

Lythian looked over to their camp. The fire was nought but a few glowing cinders now, long neglected as it was, and the night was going to be a black one. "Let's gather wood," he said, and they went off in search of it. When they got the fire going again, they tended it gently, whispering and blowing on it like lovers, and soon the flames were rising. It was true dark by then, a pitch-black night, as Lythian had thought. Ramsey slept first, a humped shadow near the flames, leaving Lythian on watch with Sir Bardol. The rain washed down unseen through the trees and the wind blew eerily, and distantly they heard thunder, though no lightning could be seen.

"You should rest, my lord," Sir Bardol said, after a long while had passed. "I slept too much, I know that. But you…" He must have sensed Lythian's fatigue. "Go. I can keep watch on my own."

He appreciated the offer, but it did not seem wise. "There must always be two, Sir Bardol. None of us is Vilmar the Black." That needed no explanation. Vilmar seemed to have the power to keep watch over himself, even as he slept. "I will give Ramsey a bit more time, then wake him."

"Yes, my lord. As you say."

Silence stretched between them. Lythian sat listening to the rain, the wind, remembering a night with Talasha under the storm. The night they had first lain together, the kindling of a secret romance that was not so secret, a romance that was fated to be doomed. He sighed, suddenly missing her. He wondered where she was, and with whom, and if she was still alive. The alternative made him grimace, a foul thought he refused to face. *Maybe I'll see her again, one day,* he thought. *After the war, when there is peace. Maybe…maybe we can still have a future?*

It was a sweet foolish thought and not one for these days. He put it aside, refocused on another. The task ahead, for that's all there was. Brontus. The blade. The Heart Remade. *Everything hinges on it,* he thought. *Everything.*

He took his rest some two hours later, swapping over with Ramsey Stone. Exhaustedly, he crawled beneath his covers, armoured still from heel to neck, with only his helm lying on the ground beside him. His swordbelt he removed for a modicum of comfort, propping it up among the twisting roots of a tree, keeping only his godsteel dagger to grasp, his fingers wrapped around its hilt as he lay his head down to sleep.

It came more easily than expected. To the patter of rain and whistling wind, he slipped away into his dreams. And there was Talasha again, smiling. In his waking state he could armour his thoughts against her, keep her at bay, but in his sleep he had no such defence. So there she was, radiant in her beauty, and her smile was playful, teasing. "You cannot lock me out in *here*, sweet captain," she told him in her sultry tone. Her hips swayed, left, right, approaching in silk and satin. "Do you miss me, my sweet captain? Do you miss the Western Neck?"

"I do," he breathed. He could never lie to her. "I miss those simple times."

"Simple?" she laughed. "Those times were never simple." She was at him now, and he could smell her scent of pine and jasmine and sandalwood, a heady mix, sweet and earthy, that stirred him, awakening a long-dormant lust. "But maybe they will be, one day? Peace can be simple, can't it, Lythian? Love can be simple, if you let it."

He looked at her, at all of her. Her beauty humbled him; he felt unworthy of it.

"Do you love me, Lythian?" she asked. Talasha was always like that, always direct. She smiled and spun, and her long rich hair swayed behind her, silk and satin fluttering, settling as she came to a stop. It draped her perfect body. She smiled through her perfect lips. "Do you, my sweet captain? Will you say it for me, if you do?"

He swallowed and said it. "I love you, Talasha."

"And now?" She spun again, once and twice and thrice, spinning more quickly, silk and satin and long hair flying. Lythian watched dizzily, as she went around and around and around, until at last he had to reach forward to stop her.

"Talasha..." He gripped her arms, took her shoulders. She slipped through them, still spinning, and he saw flashes of red as she spun. "Talasha..." His fingers tightened. "Talasha, stop..." They squeezed harder, harder, and finally she slowed and came to a stop, but her back was turned away.

"And now?" she said, and suddenly her voice was dull. "Do you love me now?"

He didn't know what she meant. "I'll always love you, Talasha."

And she huffed, "*Always*. There's no such thing as always."

He didn't understand. Her voice was darker. Everything was darker. It was closing in. "Talasha, turn to me." He tried to pull her around, but she wouldn't budge. "Talasha, look at me." She was immovable, fixed like stone. A wind was picking up, growing louder, fiercer. "Talasha..."

"No. It's over. It was never meant to be." Her voice was dead, empty. She stepped away from him, moving off into the void of darkness.

"Talasha, stop..." He staggered after her, remembering another dream. Of his first wife Talia, and his stillborn son, and the black wind rising to take them away. It was happening now. Happening again. "Talasha, stop, where are you going?" She was still walking, drifting away from him, but he couldn't catch her, couldn't reach her. "No, Talasha… no…stop…" The wind pulled at him, that same black wind. It swirled to form arms and tugged and grasped at him, and he tried to beat it away, tried to keep moving. "Get off, let me go…Talasha….TALASHA…!"

"Lythian," a voice said, insistent.

He was shaken by the wind, by the black killing wind. "No, no…" He beat at it. "No…"

It tugged again. "Lythian, wake up." The voice was a hiss, a low hiss near his ear. "There's someone coming. We heard talking, out in the dark."

He came around all at once. His eyes tore open and he saw Ramsey Stone over him, kneeling, his small eyes intense, thin lips tight. Sir Bardol was crouched down behind a stump, blade drawn, peering into the darkness. The fire had been beaten down, smouldering only, giving out a faint muted light. But around them blackness ruled.

"They're out there," Ramsey said in a harsh whisper. "I heard them, a little way off. We stamped the fire right out."

"Who?" Lythian sat up. His voice was thick. "How many?" He did not need to ask which direction. Sir Bardol would be looking their way.

"Not sure. At least two, maybe more. Unless there's one man talking to himself."

Lythian threw off his blanket, staying low. He still had his dagger tight between his fingers. He focused, blood-bond igniting, senses sharpening. The wind howled. The rain thundered. He searched through it, for other sounds. A slithering creature in the brush. Something skittering in the branches. A frog, croaking, in a bog nearby. Moving leaves and creaking limbs and a hundred other things, but no voices. "I don't hear anyone," he said.

"They stopped. Just past that gulley. Soon as we stamped out the fire they went quiet."

It wasn't Vilmar, then, playing some prank. The huntsman was likely on his way back, though wouldn't be returning from that direction. He'd gone northeast, but the gulley was southwest. Lythian squinted into the gloom, irises dilating like a cat, big and black. It was a lightless night. No moon. No stars. Just clouds swamping the sky. About the gulley the light shrivelled further where it descended into the ditch. It was a little brighter above, but only a little. He saw the shapes of trees, the tangled heaps of deadfalls. But no people. No men. "Did they go into the gulley?" he asked.

"Didn't see. Bard thinks they stopped just before. Took cover behind a fallen tree."

Bard. It appeared the two men were starting to get along. "Could it be Brontus and his men?"

"Might be, but not all of them. There weren't eight of them, that's for sure."

"Not there," Lythian said, staring southwest. His eyes flicked behind him, and to one side and then the other. "They might have us surrounded. Two on each side."

Ramsey's small eyes went big. "Gods. You think…if they caught that huntsman…" He breathed out, but slowly, staying quiet, staying calm. "If he gave us up…" He had his hand on his blade. Lythian heard the tightening of leather as he gripped hard at the hilt. "What do we do, my lord? If all eight are out there…"

"We rush them. Choose a side and rush them. Cut through and flee." This was no place to stand and fight. Against eight they would have no chance. "They'll give chase. We put distance between us, run hard. Work as a team. Pick off anyone if they break from the others, but otherwise… run."

"Right." Stone nodded. "Right. Only…"

"What?"

"Why'd they stop? If there are eight, why not attack? They have the numbers. No sense in…"

There was sudden movement ahead, right ahead across the gulley. From the black shape of a fallen tree a man popped up. "You there. You by the fire." The voice was familiar. "This standoff's gone on long enough, don't you think?"

"You started it," Ramsey called forward. "Creeping on our camp in the dead of night."

"Creeping? A fire's an invitation out here. We're only looking for a bit of warmth."

Lythian frowned. That voice…he knew it, he was certain. "You want a bit of heat, you can start your own fire," he said.

There was a pause. The shadow of the man seemed to face him. "Not wise to start a fire out here. Never know what it might attract." There was a note of knowing humour in his voice now. "There's a huntsman I know could tell you a thing or two about that. Grumpy old man, big black beard. You seen him hereabouts?"

Lythian chuckled under his breath. The tension in his muscles was melting into relief. Ramsey frowned at him. "You know him?" he asked.

Lythian nodded. "And so do you." He raised his voice and called, "You are terribly persistent, aren't you? I've been trying to outrun you since Runnyhall."

"Runnyhall?" There was an echo of laughter from the woods. "Oh, that old cell I found you in, Lythian. You remember that fool of a knight my father put in charge? Sir Clarence Fanning. He's dead now, I'll bet."

Lythian was standing now, standing and smiling, as Ramsey Stone watched on bewildered. Sir Bardol seemed similarly at sea. "Rest easy," Lythian said to them. "It's only Storos Pentar." He strode out of the camp toward him. "Let me guess. You've got Nathaniel with you?"

"Oh, how'd you know?" Storos waved a hand and another figure popped up beside him. Together, they hastened around the side of the deadfall, clambered down into the gulley and emerged muddily on the other side. Bardol was already at work re-lighting the fire, poking and blowing at the embers, throwing on a bit more wood. By the time the two knights came up to join them, the flames were rising again, throwing light upon them all.

"So," Storos said, striding up. "You've made some friends, I see." He looked at Ramsey Stone. "Surprised to see you've still got a head, Ramsey. Lythian's been beheading deserters for fun, didn't you hear?"

"I would hardly call it fun," Lythian said. He hoped those days were done. His soul was scarred enough. "Ramsey is helping us retrieve the Sword of Varinar, Storos. He's been providing useful information."

"For a pardon, is it?"

"That is the bargain."

Pentar shrugged. "Well, not like it hasn't been done before. Take Nathaniel here. Treacherous bastard, he is, an utter disgrace, but one of the finest knights in the realm for all that. Something about getting a reprieve that humbles a man. Maybe you'll be the same, Stone?"

The man nodded, though guardedly. He didn't seem able to decide if Storos was mocking him or not. "How are you here?"

"How are *you* here? Last we heard of you, you were fleeing from the battle at King's Point."

Ramsey seemed unhappy with the reminder. "I asked first."

"So you did." Storos put a hand on Nathaniel's shoulder. "We walked here. Well, rode at first, but then we walked. Our horses didn't last long. Since then we've been going afoot."

"You've been following our tracks?" Lythian asked. He could hardly believe it. He'd left from King's Point weeks ago. "How on earth did you find us, Storos?"

"Well, *you*. I wasn't looking for these two." He smiled over at Sir Bardol, recognising him. "I'll bet you've got a story to tell as well. You went off with that united host, didn't you?"

The man nodded, shamefaced. "It, um…it came to ruin, sir."

"I'll bet it did. Doesn't everything?" Storos Pentar looked half a ruin himself, as did Nathaniel Oloran. *They look like we do*, Lythian thought. To a man, they were filthy, shaggy, lean and bearded. Take off the armour and they'd all be as wild-looking as Vilmar the Black. "But how'd we find you? That'd be blind luck, Lythian. Not at the start, maybe. We left right after you, less than half a day behind, so were able to follow your tracks at first. Soon as we lost them, though, we were wandering blind. Came upon an old campfire or two, so hoped we were going in the right direction, but we've been going more in hope than expectation for a while now. We were about to call it a day and veer west for Crosswater before we saw your fire."

Sir Bardol was smiling. "A good thing we built it up, my lord. If we hadn't, they might have gone right by."

"Oh, we would," Storos said, briskly. "It turned us right around. We were heading away from it before, but just thought…well, best check on it first. I wondered if it might be you. Or Brontus, even. That's why we cowered down like that, in case it was him." His eyes roved the woods a moment. "Still haven't found him, then? Where's Vilmar? Don't tell me the huntsman's hunting days are done?"

"Not yet, no. He's hunting now."

"Oh? Is there some rare and dangerous beast around here?"

Traitors weren't so rare these days, though this one was certainly dangerous. "Brontus Oloran," Lythian said. "We may have a location for him. Vilmar is checking." His eyes flicked to Nathaniel, studying his face, wondering of the man's allegiance. He was cousin to Brontus, and the two had been close. Lythian wondered if that was good, or bad. He wondered if it could be used.

He would figure that out later. The fire was roaring brightly now, and they still had much news to share. Lythian stepped over to it and gestured for the rest to follow. And there they sat, and they ate, and they shared…

…until dawn brought the return of the huntsman, who emerged from the trees, nodding.

36

Amilia

The room was busy with scholars and scribes all scribbling and scratching in books. They stood at lecterns and sat at desks, and their faces betrayed a great serious concentration as though what they were doing here was the most important thing in all the world.

It wasn't. Far from it, in fact, though that wasn't to say it didn't matter. Much was done in this room to keep the refuge running smoothly. Records were taken, ledgers filled in, calculations rendered and registered by this scribbling army of clever little men. Seniormost and cleverest among them was, of course, crook-backed Archibald Benton. He shuffled about in his trailing grey robes as lord of this endeavour, very proud of himself and self-important in this setting, ruling over his little army.

He tottered over when he saw her enter. "My lady. A pleasure as always." He dipped his head in courtesy. Archibald Benton once had a great white beard, soft as snow and near long enough to bump against his crotch as he walked, but no longer. Now it was wispy and brittle and a little bit sad. On his forehead was a large wine-coloured birthmark shaped rather like the foot of a crow and his small nimble hands were positively brimming with liver spots. "Have you come to inspect the registers?"

"Insightful as ever, Archibald," she said. "Your percipience never fails to surprise me." She smiled to take the edge off the mockery, and Benton took it in good faith.

"Yes, of course. A silly question, of course." He chuckled to make light of it; he knew very well why they were there. "And how are you today, young man?" he asked of Amilia's companion.

"I'm…fine, my lord," mumbled Del. The boy was almost as crook-backed as Benton was, though not from age, but the curse of shyness. He was tall, but seemed embarrassed by his height, as though it was somehow unearned or otherwise useless, so he tended to go about in a stoop. "I, er…it is okay if I…"

"Of course. Yes, go right ahead."

The gangly boy dipped his eyes and moved timidly away through the scholars and scribes, toward the stack of shelves across the large open chamber where the population registers were kept. The names were not written alphabetically, alas, but sequentially. Every time a new man, woman, or child entered the refuge, their details were recorded and written into one of these books. Some of the scribes were working to order the names according to the alphabet, but it was a fearsomely long and time-consuming job and would take many months to complete.

"A determined boy," old Archibald observed. "Though I fear he is driven by false hope. The scribes are looking for his family members when they take their records in the tunnels, my lady. He knows this, does he not?"

"He isn't trusting," Amilia said. "He thinks perhaps the scribes might have forgotten, or that his family have given false names. There was some trouble with a lord when he last saw them. They may have taken on new identities to avoid reprisal."

"Then…" Benton pulled at his long brittle whiskers. Amilia half expected to hear them crackle like autumn leaves. "If their names are different, how does he expect to find them?"

"Other details," she said. "Height, age, notable physical quirks. His father had a limp, he says. Adoptive father, I should say." His name was Orryn, Amilia knew, and the man's daughter was called Llana. Del had last seen them half a lifetime ago when he was mustered for the war, and there was no telling what had happened to either of them since then. "I do hope we're not becoming an imposition for you, Archibald?"

"Oh no, of course not, no. So long as you vouch for him, he is welcome here any time." Benton smiled. He had always had a rather irritating obsequiousness to him that left her feeling a bit grubby. "Well, I will leave you to your search, then. If you need anything, I'll be right here."

He bowed and shuffled away, returning to his very important business of peering over shoulders and making young men uncomfortable. Amilia crossed through the room, attracting many a long lingering look from the spotty teens and unloved old men, and joined Del at his personal desk. So often did he come here, he'd been provisioned with his own little space and even had a helper on hand to fetch the latest registers for him. Several such leatherbound books were resting on the table. Del had sat and opened one about halfway through. That must have been as far as he got the previous evening before his eyes grew too tired to see.

She sat down opposite him and pulled over another of the books. "Today's the day, Del," she said. "I can feel it in my bones."

He peered up at her with a secret little smile. It was the thing she said every morning when they came here, and many mornings there had been. "Today's the day," he repeated, grinning, to complete the ritual. They met one another's eyes, nodded, and then turned a page together, and so their work began.

They read in silence for a while, turning pages, reading names and details to a backdrop of rustling paper and scratching quills and the murmuring voices of the clever little men. Archibald Benton went about like a very small pathetic dragon, swooping on his unsuspecting prey and pointing out deficiencies in their work. Sometimes he went off with a few other senior scholars to discuss something very important (to them, at least) and always were the scribes coming and going with books and ledgers and piles of papers.

It made for a pleasant atmosphere, all told, very relaxed and contented. Amilia liked it here with all these clever little men. She liked this room with its smells and sounds, the warm flicker of the torches and candles, the little twirls of smoke curling and rising. And she liked Del as well. He was shy, quiet, but slowly coming out of his shell, and he'd told her many stories of her brother Robbert too. She loved to hear them, loved to know that her brother was turning into a man, a king, that he was brave and protective and kind. *He is like Father,* she thought. *He's the king Father might have been.* Apparently, Del had even squired for Robbert for a day or two, and of all the crazy things happening in this war, that might just be the most absurd of them all as far as Amilia Lukar was concerned.

She smiled at the thought and turned another page, running her eyes over the names, glancing at all the little details. "I'm going to go and visit Cevi later, if you want to come." She turned another page and kept her eyes down, but could almost see the little smile on Del's lips.

"I…maybe, yeah. If…if she wants to see me."

"She likes you, Del. Why wouldn't she want to see you?" Now she looked up and saw the smile. And the shade of blush as well, of course. "She asks about you when you're not there. I think you're her only friend here, you know."

"You're her friend too, aren't you?"

"Sure," she said. "Though it's different with me." Amilia had made a promise to Lady Talasha that she would look out for Cevi, just as she'd promised Elyon Daecar she would look out for Del. Neither was particularly hard to keep, because both of them were young, innocent, kind, and interesting. Amilia's favourite pastime of late had been bringing the two together and watching a slow friendship and even affection build between them. Now she could even leave the room and go off on another duty, knowing they would tell each other stories while she was gone and not collapse into some awkward silence as might have happened at the start.

Amilia turned another page. More names. More details. She turned another and more of the same. This was a losing battle, obviously, though neither of them spoke of it. According to Lord Morwood's latest report, the population of the refuge had swelled beyond a hundred thousand now, and that flow did not seem to be slowing. "I'm going to walk the refuge before I see Cevi. You can come with me for that as well, if you like." She turned another page, kept her eyes down. It served with Del to keep things casual, she had discovered. Anything more direct and he would feel obliged to say yes, even if he didn't want to.

He chewed on it a moment. "Okay. I'll come." There was a pause, then, "Have there been any more riots?"

"Nothing too bad," she told him, casually. Her eyes moved past the words, the names. "Lord Morwood has everything in hand." There had been a big riot a few days ago and they'd almost been caught up in it. It was about rations, Amilia was told. Apparently not everyone was being properly fed, especially as the refuge filled, and some people were banding together and demanding the portal door be shut to any newcomers. "We'll have my guards with us, though," she told the boy. "No one would dare harm us with them around."

He nodded, eyes low, and turned a page in his register. "Tomothy said that some men tried to get into the armoury," the boy said. "They were trying to get weapons to start an uprising."

Amilia raised her eyes to look at him. "And who's Tomothy?"

"One of the scribes here." Del looked around for him, but he didn't seem to be present right now. "He's young and from near my village, so we get along." He turned another page. "Do you think that will happen? That the people will rise up?"

"No." She laughed at the notion. "Good gods, no." She'd heard about that little attempt as well, but it was nothing, a feeble effort by a few lackwitted men that was dealt with easily enough.

They relapsed into silence for a short while, turning pages and reading names. The chance of Del ever finding his family in these ledgers was about as likely as finding a man living inside the belly of a dragon, but Amilia humoured him anyway. She had her own men going about the refuge searching for them as well, and would much prefer for it to happen that way. She had a little fantasy of it. If Orryn and Llana were found, she wouldn't tell Del, but she'd take him on one of their walks and arrange for the reunion to occur naturally. That would be much better, she thought. For them to find one another like that.

She turned a page in her ledger, idly running her eyes down the names and descriptions below them. Where Del's face kept a stern concentration, and he would often go over the page twice or even three times to make utterly sure he'd read every detail, Amilia breezed along. Under each name was written their age, dependents, where they'd come from, their occupation, any notable health issues, lists of banned items they'd brought with them, and those that were permitted as well, along with other notable details. It was dull work mostly but served to pass the time. The names themselves could be amusing, though, or rare, or even beautiful. She had been quite fascinated to find that there were a good many Amilias here in the refuge, most of whom were her age or younger and had likely been named in the aftermath of her royal coming. It was common to get a glut of names like that in the wake of a royal birth. She'd seen lots of Robberts and Raynalds as well - more Robberts than Raynalds, of course, one being the heir and the other the spare - sometimes with different spelling, and there were some older men called Rylian out there too who were surely named for her father.

Sometimes she thought about going out to find them. To seek out these middle-aged men who carried her father's name, and look into their eyes. Would they look like him? Would they sound like him? Of course they wouldn't, but she had those thoughts anyway. Then she'd remember that while her father was dead, her mother was still living, and she'd feel obliged to return to Ilithor to spend time with her.

It was strange in the city now, though, different, almost eerie. The palace was empty but for a few servants and soldiers who still attended her lady mother, and she could walk for an hour at a time through the dusty halls and chambers without coming across another soul. Her mother was like a ghost there now, where once she'd been only a hermit. Sometimes, when Amilia spent the night, she could hear her mother's wild wailing echoing through the halls and a shiver would go up her spine. "You've been in these rooms too long, Mother," she would tell her the following morning. "You have to leave. You should come to the refuge where it's safe."

"Safe?" her mother repeated. "Nowhere is safe, nowhere, nowhere..." And she'd repeat the word a dozen times before snapping out of it. She'd grown deranged now, almost possessed. Her hair was wilder than ever, patchy and long and her scalp was riddled with bald spots. She didn't let the servants cut her hair or groom her, and her fingernails had become the stuff of nightmares. Her eyes made her daughter afraid. They stared and never seemed to blink and she would sit for hours, even days in the same place, staring, almost entirely unmoving, soiling herself in her chair. If the servants tried to get her to stand, she would come alive and shriek at them, scratch at them, spit at them. At other times, she would walk constantly, going from side to side in her rooms and adjoining chambers, muttering and murmuring until at last her body gave out from exhaustion. And then the sitting phase would begin all over again, the sitting and soiling phase.

Amilia had to brace herself every time she entered those rooms. Against the stink and the sounds and the sights. The windows were hung with heavy drapes and the balconies had been boarded over and the only light came from smoky candles. Her mother allowed only so much of it. It put her in shadow, in darkness and gloom. Sometimes Amilia would catch her mother at an angle in the candlelight and she would look demonic, like some inhuman creature crawled up from another world. She wondered why she still went to see her. She wondered why she saw her more now than she ever had before. That was curious and she couldn't understand it. *Am I a better person now? Am I trying to save her?* But then, she would often hope for news of her passing as well to spare her. Whenever she saw Lord Morwood marching heavily toward her down some corridor, a part of her would look at his face and hope to see a forlorn expression, a look of sorrow, would hope to hear the words coming from his lips, "My lady, I'm so sorry, but your lady mother has passed."

It's only a matter of time, she thought. That's what her mother believed. The last time Amilia saw her, Lady Clarris Kastor had been deep in a sitting soiling phase. Stiffly she had sat, stinking, staring, and Amilia did what she knew she had to do, and tried gently to coax her out of it.

"Mother, I'm told you haven't washed for almost a week. You need to stand, mother. You need to let them wash you."

"I'm going to die here," Lady Clarris had said.

"Mother?"

"I'm going to die here. Right here in this chair. I'll die."

Something angry came out of her, then. "*Mother!* You need to snap out of it. I warn you, I'm going to have you taken to the refuge by force if you say things like that again." Amilia had her phases too. Phases when she wanted her mother to rot here and phases when she didn't and she was in one of the latter. "It's been years since you've left these rooms for more than an hour or two. When was the last time? My wedding to Hadrin? Was that it? You have to go *outside*, Mother. There's snow all over the city. Do you remember how you used to like the snow? Back when you were young, in Ethior? Do you remember?"

But no smile raised her lips. No expression changed her face. She stared out through a mask of madness and said it again, "I'm going to die here. Right here in this chair. I'll die."

And Amilia switched phases. "Die, then," she said. "You've been dead for years anyway. If you're not living you're already dead."

"No. Not yet. I've seen my end in my dreams."

That unnerved her. The way she said it. The clarity and sudden consciousness. Amilia's heart began to pump. "It's just a dream, Mother. That's all, just a…"

"Soon," her mother said, staring into the darkness. "Soon, soon, soon, soon….it'll happen soon, it'll happen soon, soon, soon, soon…." And she collapsed into the word, folded into it, repeated it a dozen times, a hundred times, a thousand times until all the strength was spent of her, and she withered away into sleep…

There was a *clacking* sound behind her.

It broke Amilia from her daydreams and dark misgivings and coming around, she realised the room of scholars and scribes had gone silent, frosty, all the mirth of it sucked away. Men pulled in their shoulders and lowered their heads and fixated on their books and quill pens. Ever did the little mage strike terror at his coming.

Amilia turned on her seat. "Fhanrir, how are you?"

"Miserable." Even seated as she was, he was barely any taller than her. "Come, I want to talk to you."

She rose. Fhanrir's presence often meant news, and her thoughts turned quickly to Mallister, who'd been away on his mission for a long while now. "Is it…"

"No," he said, reading her. "Not him."

"Oh. Then?"

"Not here." He shuffled away toward the exit, clacking with his walking stick as he went.

Amilia brushed down her skirts. "I'll be back soon, Del," she told him. "Just keep searching, okay? Today's the day, remember." She smiled. "I feel it in my bones."

He glanced up to make sure the mage was moving away, then nodded briskly, a series of very short nervous nods. Fhanrir terrified Del as he terrified most. Not Amilia, though, not anymore. She had come to understand him now and even found all his petty meanness amusing. She wondered sometimes if they were even becoming friends.

Amilia moved past the desks and lecterns, past the scholars and scribes, past Archibald Benton as he bowed his head at Fhanrir's passing, fearing the little mage might turn on him with some scathing remark. He went silently, though, speaking not a word and everyone breathed a collective sigh of relief as he left. Amilia's guards fell in behind her, trailing a good way back lest they incur the mage's wrath.

They walked for a time in silence, then Fhanrir said, "My great-grandson's dead."

Amilia paused. "I'm sorry?"

"Didn't you hear me? I said he's dead. Vottur's dead."

"No, I heard. I only…I'm sorry, Fhanrir. What happened?"

"Ilith happened. Him and his pigheaded stubbornness. Vottur's been helping me keep the seals in place and it's drained the last life from him. He died this morning. I was there with him when he went."

Amilia hadn't knew what to say. "I…I'm so sorry…"

The mage grunted, *clacking* with his stick. "The seals will break anyway. We've been papering over the cracks, that's all we can do, and it won't last. Ilith…he's the only one who can restore those seals. This is *his* magic. *His* sorcery. But he won't do it, he says."

"Why not?"

"Doesn't have the strength. Needs it for his other work. The potions…"

"For the blades?"

"I'm talking. He's made two of them now. Essense of Nightwing and Seed of the Windwillow. It's made him old, girl. You'd know if you saw him. That's hard sorcery. Takes hours of precision and concentration. Very exacting. And only *he* can do it, before you ask. I don't know how… and Dagnyr, Agnar, they're useless. Might use them up holding the seals together a bit longer, but it'd only kill them like it killed my Vottur." He paused. Fhanrir sounded genuinely grieved by his great-grandson's death. "There's still three potions to make. Ilith says he's saving his strength for those now, but the way I see it, he's got enough juice for maybe two of them. And where would that leave us? Nowhere. We need all five and we need these seals fixed and we need him strong, strong so he can hammer the heart together. And you know what he tells me?"

"What?" Amilia asked.

"To be patient. Says to wait. *Wait!* Like I haven't been waiting for millennia…like I haven't been patient. I've cursed myself a thousand times over to bring us to the brink, and he says no, enough cursing, you're done…"

He's venting to me, Amilia realised. *Gods, maybe we are friends?* "What about the boys?"

"The boys," he spat. "Aye, I'd cut a thousand soft throats if I had to, I'd fill a hundred vats of blood and I'd see him strong for a century, but he won't let me. Might be he will when he finally wakes up, but now…" He shook his head. "So be it. It's on him. When he's lying broken in his bed and we still got work to do, he'll see sense. If he doesn't…"

"We're all doomed," Amilia said. "Is there…no other solution? Some other way to revive him?"

"It takes blood. Always blood."

"There's no potion, or…"

"Blood. There are ways of using it, but blood's the core ingredient. Bladeborn blood. And young blood's best. Death sweetens it, death and pain. Only powerful mages, sorcerers, witches can harness it. There are rituals, like I did with Hamlyn. And potions. The wives were good with that."

"Wives?"

"Dhatar's wives," he said. "They're old as me, some of them. Though not many left, maybe none." His face was hidden in the shadow of his large hood. "Ilith says something will come. Some solution. Don't know where he gets it. This clairvoyance. Might be blind hope. He was always hopeful."

They continued through the halls in silence. Amilia wondered where he was leading her, and why. They seemed to be making for the great door that led out into the Shadowfort, out into the mountains.

"Tell me of the registers," Fhanrir said, as they went.

The question stumped her. "What do you want to know?"

"Whatever you have to tell me. Anything unusual stick out to you?"

"Not particularly. There are lots of girls called Amilia."

"Unusual, I said."

"No, then. If you'd give me a hint…"

"Are you still walking about the refuge? Talking to the people?"

"Yes. Every day. You know I am." *Is this a test? Is he just passing the time of day?*

"There are too many men here," Fhanrir said. Maybe that's what he was getting at? The number of men. "Too many young and able-bodied men. I've spoken with Morwood and told him it's time for a muster. Don't worry, that boy won't be part of it. No one under the age of eighteen. We'll make it voluntary at first to ease them in, then turn it mandatory. This place is getting crowded. Not in space, in mouths. You ever been at sea?"

"Yes. I crossed Vandar's Mercy to…"

"How many aboard? Roughly?"

She couldn't remember. "I don't know. Say two dozen."

"Right. You got a raft aboard, can take a dozen. You capsize. What do you do?"

"Women and children first," Amilia said.

"Aye. Maybe a strong man or two to row and defend them, but mostly women and children. That's what's happening here. We got only so much food and there's too many people coming. It's a giant life raft and they're going to capsize us. I told Morwood to stop letting men in."

"None? Not even the old?"

"Especially the old. Why feed an old mouth when they're just going to die? Women and children. The young. Some strong men to defend them. This refuge needs a clearout and more men are needed for the war. We can send them down to join your brother. How about that? He'd like that, wouldn't he?"

"I'm not sure. Maybe not if they're not trained."

Fhanrir cackled. His walking stick clacked against the stone floor. The air was growing more chill and the torches were blowing on the walls which indicated that they were nearing the entrance hall. The great doors were kept open there by day. "Nothing unusual in the registers, then?"

"No." Her ire was creeping up. "Like what? What are you trying to say?"

"I'm saying we got some bad apples in the basket. I'm saying there's been devious work going on here. Pernicious work. I'm saying there are enemies within the walls."

Her mouth went dry. "*Enemies*? But only Tukorans and Vandarians are coming in. Are you saying some of them are working against us? That they're allied to…?"

"I'm saying some of them are Agarathi."

She shook her head violently. "No. Everyone who comes here is asked questions. Their accents, their features. They're all pale, northern."

"Blood thins, girl, and men are weak. Merchant goes to Agarath two centuries ago, time of peace, everyone's friends. He meets a girl, beautiful Agarathi girl, and times as they are he brings her home to Tukor. Their kids are half Agarathi. Grandkids a quarter. The blood thins down the line, but it's always there. A man looks Tukoran, speaks Tukoran, he *is* Tukoran. His family has lived here for generations. But there's a spot of fire in his blood, something he doesn't even know is there, just a little bit, but it's enough. Take Shackton. He's got a drop of Elder blood and it's enough for him to bond that eagle. Well, a drop's all it takes sometimes for a man to become a slave, and Eldur's good at that…he's good at making slaves."

Amilia's chest was rising and falling. She felt tingly as she walked on,

a little lightheaded even. Fhanrir led her through the great entrance hall
with the vats of melting snow, the lumbermen hauling wood. Guards
were waiting beside the great twin statues that stood either side of the
doors. Lord Morwood was there, and his face was cast grim. "Lord
Fhanrir," he said. "Your Highness." He bowed to Amilia and then
addressed the mage. "They're chained up below, as you requested."

"Good." Fhanrir led them out, cloaked and cowled and tiny. Amilia
pulled her furs in and shared a look with Morwood that said this was
serious. They went down the snowy, slippery steps, through the trenches
of ice, past the buried black buildings, and into the lower ward. As ever
the snow was cleared away here and the gate was open, men coming and
going gathering wood. There were many more guards than before. She
could see them at the gates, see them on the walls, see them stationed in
their huge woollen cloaks across the bridge and down the passes. "Why
so many?" she whispered to Morwood. "Are they all watching for
dragons?"

"No, my lady. They're making sure the men come back."

"Which men? The woodchoppers?"

"Yes. And the hunters and soldiers, everyone who leaves. Even the
watchmen are being watched, my lady."

"Then who's watching the watchers who watch the watchmen?" Her
pithy remark met silence. They turned a corner and saw them, the prisoners strung up against a wall, stripped down to their skin. So shrivelled
were their manhoods that they were almost not to be seen, and their
hands were raised above their heads and bolted to the icy stone. Each
had suffered beatings, it looked, by the blood and bruises about their
mouths, their chests, their shoulders.

There were ten of them. To Amilia's eyes each one was Tukoran or
Vandarian, pale-skinned, with brown hair or sometimes blond, beards of
a similar colour, northern features. All of them were staring out with dull
eyes, empty eyes. They seemed broken and uncaring. She saw neither
pain nor fear nor hate in them.

Fhanrir turned to her. "Northerners, wouldn't you say?"

"Yes. I'd never think otherwise."

The mage pointed at one of the men. "That one had a great-grandfather from Agarath. He came over here on trade almost a century ago.
Bedded a few maids and whatnot, maybe a whore or three. One had a
child and it went from there." His finger flicked at another. "He's got an
Agarathi grandmother. That's the nearest link and you can just about see
it. The shape of the eyes, bit of almond, no? Something in the skin tone,
maybe?" It was so, though hard to tell without looking for it. "The
grandmother was a servant down in Lakeheart," Fhanrir went on. "Her
master got her with child, she had a son, and that son had a son and
there he is." He pointed at the man again with his skeletal finger. "Same
for the rest. Great-grandparents, great-great-grandparents, even great-
great-great grandparents in his case." And his finger picked out another
of the prisoners. "These men are all common baseborn stock. In some

cases the Agarathi blood in them is rich, from higher bloodlines, lords and such, even Fireborn. That lasts longer. Just a few drops and it makes a man vulnerable for generations…so long as he's simple and weak. A stronger mind wouldn't submit, but these…" his hand waved dismissively. "They're chaff, cattle."

Amilia was looking at the men, wondering how many more there might be here. The scale of the problem was beginning to dawn on her. Over the last half-century, interbreeding was rare between northern and Agarathi bloodlines, but historically…well, if not common, it certainly happened, and there might be thousands, even tens of thousands of men and women across the north with a few drops of Agarathi blood in them from the generations and centuries gone by.

"This was the doing of the fire priests," she said. It wasn't a question. "Like the ones Talasha mentioned."

Fhanrir's little head bobbed up and down. "This lot were all refugees coming up the road, all broken, desperate men. The priests must have lurked among them in disguise. Picking them off like lions hunting lambs. They slither through unseen and unwatched and sniff out the Agarathi blood. And when they smell something they like, they strike. And onto the next victim. And the next. And the next…"

Amilia drew a breath. She felt suddenly terribly afraid. "Could there be priests *here*? In the refuge?"

"No. I'd know it. A priest is different, girl. Each one's got a bit of Eldur in him, bit of his power, and I'd know."

"But these men…"

"More, aye. Could well be more. They're dull-eyed, distant…I got men looking for the signs, but they can be hard to find here. Lots of dull-eyed broken men hereabouts. But all the while, these dull-eyed men watch and listen and learn, and once they've done all that, they come together and they act."

"Act?"

"Aye, act. You hear about the ones who went for the armoury? Who do you think *they* were, girl? They were trying to get weapons so they could get to Ilith. Well, they didn't get far. No, not with me here. No one is getting to Ilith so long as I live."

"Then maybe they'll try to get to you instead?"

He snorted disdain. "Let them try. You really don't know what I'm capable of, do you? I shuffle about and don't do much, but I've got a reserve of power if I need it. Got a sense I will, too, sooner or later. Why else would Tukor be keeping me around?"

"For your charming company?" She smiled nervously.

He flicked a hand. "This lot were trying to escape," he told her. "Take our secrets with them. They were snow-gatherers and lumbermen, good working men or so we thought. This location is a secret we'd best keep close. The seals are breaking, I told you, and this weather will only hide us so well. Soon we'll be exposed, girl. And if they find out…"

"They won't find out," Amilia said, defiantly. "You caught them all, didn't you?" When Fhanrir did not answer, she said it again. "You caught them all, didn't you? Fhanrir…you *did* catch them all?"

The mage stared at the prisoners. He stared and he stared and then he stared some more. And at last he said, "No. We didn't catch them all. There were more, quite a few more of them, girl. And we haven't been able to find them yet."

37

Elyon

They took refuge from the storm in a tumbled old tower that had fallen long ago.

Snow blasted and swirled through the broken stone walls and drifted down from the shattered roof, but at the rear they found a door that led into a cellar and the snow could not reach them there.

"We should build a fire," Elyon said, his voice echoing in the cold damp gloom. He drew a shard of flint from his pocket and cut a spark onto the head of his torch. The flame bloomed, throwing light and shadow across the room. Rough-hewn blocks of stone made up the weathered walls, spotted with nitre and here and there patches of moss where water had soaked through the cracks. The wood beams that crossed the vaulted ceiling were cracked as well, and rotting in large part. Elyon took a moment to inspect them more closely, fearful of a cave-in, but judged them strong enough to hold.

"We should be fine here for now." He swung the torch along one wall, unveiling wall niches bathed in shadow. There were some wooden crates stacked in one. "We can use that for firewood. Here." He handed Saska the torch, stepped over and kicked at the nearest crate, shattering it into two dozen shards. Gathering up the kindling, he stacked it at the heart of the room, then took back the torch and lit it. The flame took well, smoke curling up into the rafters. He could hear a pigeon cooing up there and the sounds of rats scuttling and squeaking.

"There's another door," Saska said, gesturing to the far wall of the basement. She made to step away. "I'll see what's behind it..."

"No." Elyon touched her arm. "Let me. Just in case." She was more important than him. "Just gather some more firewood from the crates. I'll be back in a minute."

The door was locked, but that wasn't going to stop him. He withdrew his godsteel dagger, swiped through the lock and pushed inside. He was greeted by a smaller cellar, walls stacked on either side with bottles and jars, a narrow aisle leading to yet another door further along. He sniffed the air. There were all sorts of scents here; the flowery aroma of lavender mixed with the sharper tang of mint; the must of old mushrooms and herbs; spicy scents of cinnamon and anise, a bit of pepper and ginger as well; the more unsettling metallic taste of blood, from bear and wolf and even…was that dragon blood in the air? There was more besides. Incense, sandalwood, the acrid unpleasantness of brimstone and sulphur, other smells and tastes that Elyon did not know. Dust coated all, covering every pot and jar. The room had not been entered in a good long while, he guessed.

He continued down the aisle toward the door. This too was locked. His dagger saw to that. The door groaned open eerily to show a long dark narrow stairway leading further down beneath the keep. Elyon Daecar gave a sigh. Why couldn't it just have been a simple cellar? It was too dark down there, even for him, so he turned back to find Saska rummaging around through some old boxes and crates. She'd already gathered a good pile of firewood and was searching for other supplies. "Find anything?" Elyon asked her.

"Not yet. Just some broken pottery. You?"

"A witch's lair."

"What? Are you serious?"

He shrugged, smiling. "There's a room full of potions and elixirs in there. And another door at the back leading to…well, I don't know. It's too dark. There's a stair." He went over and plucked out the torch that Saska had shoved into a crack in the wall. "I'm going to go down and check it out. *Alone*," he said, before she might ask. "If you hear me howling for help, don't. Just fly away and back to the others."

She looked at him flatly. "Not funny, Elyon." She peered past him. "Is there really a room of potions back there?"

"Well…ingredients for potions mostly. But they've been untouched for months, it looks, or even longer, so I don't think we need to worry. Whoever once lurked in this ruin left a good while ago."

She still didn't seem so sure, but Elyon gave her a reassuring look and then returned to the dark stairway. The stone was black and glistened with torchlight, and below he could smell the stink of damp and cold rising from some deeper place. "Hello?" he found himself calling, as he descended. "Is anyone there?" The only reply he got was his own voice echoing back to him.

About a hundred steps down he reached another chamber; this one branched into separate passages. He chose one at random, calling out as he went, if only to make himself feel less uneasy. Elyon Daecar might have fought titan dragons and demigods, colossal krakens and giant crabs, but always in the open and with the Windblade in his grasp. This was different. He didn't much like the idea of coming upon some decrepit old witch, an even-less-friendly Fhanrir without his sense of duty. "Hello…" he called out again. "If there's anyone down here, I mean no harm. I'm just having a wander. Don't mind me."

The tunnel ended in a door that led into a large open chamber. Inside he found long tables, benches, iron braziers covered in rust. The floor was hard-backed dirt with an overlay of planking. It seemed like a dining hall of sorts. Elsewhere, down other corridors, he found more storage rooms, a small library replete with crumbling, weatherworn books, a holy shrine to Rasalan and some other lesser gods, an armoury and rooms filled with bunk beds built into the walls, or at least what was left of them. Most of what he found was old and rotted and covered almost to the point of suffocation with spider's webs. The dead rats were multiple and the stink of their droppings clouded every room. It was a bunker, Elyon quickly realised. A refuge built by whatever lord or knight once ruled this castle long ago.

Once he'd completed his search he returned to Saska and told her what he'd found

"No witches, then?" she asked him, when he was done. She had taken off her cloak now, hanging it on an old rusty sconce on the wall, leaving her in the fine, fitted silver-and-blue godsteel armour that Robbert Lukar had given her. She looked magnificent in it, strong and fierce and beautiful. The firelight glittered in her radiant blue eyes and reflected off her olive skin, and she had untied her hair to let it tumble to her shoulders.

"No witches," he confirmed, admiring her a moment. "I might have been wrong about that."

"Let's hope. So when do you think this castle fell? It feels like it's been in this state for years."

He unclasped his cloak as well, hanging it on a separate sconce. "Might have been during the War of the Lowland Lords," he guessed. "That was a few decades ago, I think. Many minor keeps and holdfasts changed hands back then, and some were so badly broken as to be left to rot instead. This might be one of them."

Saska nodded. "I know about that war. When I first travelled down from Thalan with Marian and her men, we came across a village pillaged by Kastor's Greenbelts. There was a man there, Father Pennifor. He and Marian spoke of it. Pennifor said that Marian's uncle Lord Tandrick was the one responsible for ending the conflict. He intervened and saved many lives." She paused a moment. "I probably told you that at Harrow-moor, didn't I? During that time…in your tent."

"You did," he remembered. They'd both shared their life stories and unveiled their secrets to one another during those days. *Well, mostly.* Saska had never told him she might be an Aramatian princess. He only found out about that later, from Lady Marian.

She smiled at him across the flames. "We haven't talked about that much, have we? Harrowmoor, I mean. The time we spent in your tent."

"No." His throat felt a little dry all of a sudden as the memories cycled through his head. "There hasn't been much space for it. Not with your training, and…"

"There's space now," she said. "You know how I said I wanted to talk to you about something? That night when we changed course, because of the eagle? Well…it was all that. Those days we spent together. I wanted to talk about it…reminisce. But there hasn't really been a chance, not until now…"

She smiled at him, reaching down beneath her stool. "I found something while you were gone. In one of the crates." She drew out a clay bottle, bit at the cork and pulled it out with a *pop*, then spat it into the fire. She had a sniff. "It's good whisky, Elyon. Not spoiled or anything." She reached out. "Try it."

He took it from her, put his nose to the rim, raised his brow appreciatively, then drank. The liquor reached down into his chest with its sizzling fingers, burning his throat, and he coughed. "It's…been a while," he said hoarsely when she laughed at him. "We shouldn't have too much, though. That eagle…I still think…"

"It was just an eagle, Elyon. You're being paranoid, that's all."

Was that it? Was he simply worrying too much about things that weren't really there?

It was possible, he would admit, but he could not shrug off the nagging feeling that the eagle had been *corrupted* somehow…that maybe it had been bonded to an Elder, and that Elder had been captured by the enemy, and the eagle was being used as a spy against them, and that's why it had killed itself.

Right or wrong, it was not a risk he could ignore. If the enemy had used that eagle to spy on them, even for a moment, he knew he had no choice but to change their course. Their heading had been north, and their tracks led toward those woods where they were setting up camp for the night, so he turned them westward instead at once.

A long cold night had followed. Elyon flew behind the company at a distance, blowing away their tracks with the Windblade and watching warily for an enemy approach. Once or twice he felt like he had sensed something, some power surging up from the south, but by then they were far enough away not to see it. Come dawn, he found an abandoned tower nestled among some hills for them to rest in. "You'll be safe here," he told Saska. "Don't leave until I return." Off he'd flown, to spend all of that day on vigil. But it was a bleak day, a dark day, and no dragons had been seen.

He returned to the tower at dusk. Saska met him outside, leaving the Nightblade there in Sir Ralston's safekeeping. Leshie came out after her, and the Butcher as well. "I told them not to come," she said, shrugging. "They insisted."

"We want to know about this eagle," the Butcher had demanded. "The Pretty Princess says it is cursed. You told her this. That the Elders are destroyed."

"No. I said that eagle may have been corrupted."

"And the Elders?" Leshie asked him. "There was some letter, was there? To Ilith?"

Elyon had already told Saska about that letter. Now he confirmed it to the others. "From the First Elder, yes. He expressed a concern that they would be found. And the fire priest Rah'kin said something. Something that gave me pause. He called his order the *watchers of the new world.* I fear the Elders are dead, or captured, and that their eagles may be used against us. That's why we had to go."

The Butcher ran a finger through a deep scar on his chin. His face was horrific, a nightmare to behold. "Did you see any dragon today, Windy Prince?"

"No." Elyon would rather have said yes, if only to support his theory, but couldn't very well lie about it.

"And last night? Did this eagle spy give away our position before it cracked its head open on that rock?"

"It may have. I sensed something out there, searching for us. But too far away to see."

"Something? A dragon, was it? A thunder of them? Might Eldur have come himself?"

Elyon wondered if that had been the case. "I don't know," he could only conclude. "Perhaps."

"Perhaps? Then perhaps you are wrong about this thing you sensed? Maybe there was nothing out there at all. And this eagle was just an eagle."

That was possible as well. All the same, Elyon continued to counsel caution. "We'll have to forgo your training again tonight, Saska," he said. "I think it's best you all keep moving."

"Now? But it's nighttime," Leshie complained. "We're all tired from yesterday's ride."

You're tired? Elyon thought. *He* was the one who'd been flying for almost two days straight. He thought on that a moment, then realised another long night without rest would not serve him. He'd be likely to collapse from exhaustion if he had to follow behind them now. "Fine. Stay in the tower tonight. I'll return again at dawn and we can decide then what to do."

Saska took his arm. "You need to sleep, Elyon. Give me the Windblade tonight. I can watch the skies."

It was a thoughtful gesture, but he shook his head and told her no. "You need your rest as well. I'll find somewhere safe, as I always do. The Windblade will watch over me and alert me if there's trouble."

No trouble came to him that night except for the troubled nature of his dreams. He imagined a torture chamber in the dark of a mountain and Eldur standing with a bloody lash. He imagined ancient Lightborn bonded to birds strung up and broken down. He imagined eagles opening their eyes above to see northern lands below. And there beneath them, Saska on her horse with Joy beside her, and the Whaleheart and the Red Blade and the rest all in her wake. The eagles were watching, Eldur was laughing, and Elyon awoke with a start and knew what must be done.

"We continue west," he said, when he returned to Saska that morning. "And from now on we travel only by dark. We cannot take the risk of you being spotted."

The Whaleheart was with her this time, leaving the Nightblade with the others. "I had wanted to go north, Prince Elyon," he said. "To where the Sibling Strait is frozen. We may struggle to find a crossing this far south."

There was no helping that now. "We'll reach the coast and go from there, sir. With luck the weather will permit a crossing. If not, there may be no choice but to cross the Links."

The giant shook his head. "I have advised against that course."

"I know. And I know your reasons. When we get closer, I will fly there and see how the bridge lies. For now, we needn't worry about that. We are still long leagues from the coast and the dark will slow our progress. It will take several days before we reach it."

"And our training?" Saska asked him. "When will that happen now?"

"Whenever we can fit it in. It may be at dusk before you begin your nightly ride. Or at dawn, once you have completed it. We take it day by day for now."

"OK," Saska said, and so it was done.

The days since then had been slow and tense. They trained when they could, for an hour here and an hour there, honing the skills she'd already learned. By now there was little more for Elyon to teach her, in all truth. It was practice she needed. Practice and perhaps a test. "The next time we see a dragon, I want to fight it," she had said. He admired her courage and desire to prove herself. "I'm ready, Elyon. More ready than you were when you killed Ezukar."

"The lightning killed Ezukar," Elyon said. "There's no lightning here. Only snow."

"You've killed a dozen other dragons since then with your skill alone. I need to know what it's like to do the same."

He nodded, accepting that. "Very well," he said. "If we see a dragon, I'll let you fight it on your own. But only a smaller one. Anything large we must try to avoid."

But no dragons had been seen, not for long nights now, and soon the chance for Saska to prove herself would be gone. *Because I have to leave her,* Elyon thought now, as he sat gazing into the fire. They had reached the western coast of Rasalan two days ago, and the others were in camp nearby at a deserted village huddled at the base of the cliffs. He could not delay much longer. Her training with the Windblade was more or less complete and she could bear the Nightblade easily now. *When I go she can begin to learn its mysteries. She can focus fully on the black blade and won't have to split her time...*

Time, he thought. Yes, it was time. The Sibling Strait had been rough since their arrival. The waters were turbulent and full of treacherous floes and crossing by boat did not seem possible. Saska had asked if he could carry them over one by one but he would prefer not to risk that either. Earlier that morning, he'd done as he'd said and flown over the

Links and found the bridge intact and undefended. Some groups were crossing, vagrants and refugees and smaller bands of soldiers, but not the larger crowds or marching hosts the Whaleheart had feared. It was the best way, Elyon decided. *I'll see her safely across into Tukor, and then I'll go. I'll have no choice but to leave her then.*

Saska was looking at him strangely. "You seem distracted, Elyon. Are you still thinking about the eagle?" He withdrew from his thoughts and lifted his eyes. "I really think you're worrying too much. It's been a while now… and there's been no attack."

He nodded. He might well have it all wrong. *It was only a dream,* he thought. *Just a dream. Those other eagles might have died for nothing.* Three times now he'd seen eagles soaring too close for comfort and had seen no option but to kill them, just in case. That was something he'd kept from the others, something that caused further rot in his soul. Elyon had always loved animals. He hated that it had come to this.

"You've gone very quiet," Saska observed. "You should have another drink of whisky. It might cheer you."

He did as she bid him. The second swig was easier than the first.

"Here. Hand it back over."

He did that as well, and she had a drink as well. She coughed, wiped her mouth, and then took a second gulp.

"We shouldn't drink too much," he warned. "When the storm passes…"

"That mightn't be until morning. We have plenty of time."

They'd been training when the snowstorm came and decided to take refuge here to wait it out rather than return to the coastal camp. In such conditions, it was almost impossible to see, so they really didn't have much choice.

Saska drank again. And then again once more. "Leshie says we need to relax," she said. "Both of us. And maybe the gods think so too?"

Elyon frowned. "The gods…?"

"Well, why else would they bring us here? Just the two of us? Maybe they realise we need a break." She smiled at him and drank again then passed the bottle back. "Drink. As your queen I command it."

"My queen?" A smile touched his lips. "I wasn't aware you were wed to my sire."

"I'm Lorin's granddaughter and your rightful queen. You and your father bend the knee to me now." She smirked and the bottle passed between them again. "So, when are we going to cross the Links? I think it's pretty obvious that's the best way to cross."

He nodded. "I was just thinking about that."

"And?"

He felt a thick pump in his heart as he realised he needed to tell her. *I'm going to ruin it,* he thought. *We finally have a chance to rest, to talk, to reminisce about Harrowmoor as she wants…and I'm going to ruin it all.* He met her gaze. She could see there was something wrong.

"What is it?" Her eyes were soft, but hardening quickly. "Have you been keeping something from me, Elyon?"

I'm going to ruin it, he knew, even as he opened his mouth and said, "I…have to go away, Saska. With the Windblade. Not for too long, I hope, no more than a week, but it's important. It's…very important, Saska."

I've ruined it, he thought. That was obvious now. He could see it in her eyes. "Where?" she simply asked him. All the mirth was gone from her voice.

"The Icewilds. There's something I need to get, for Ilith. It's important. Without it he won't be able to bind the blades, so I have no choice…"

"You had a choice to tell me." She put the whisky bottle aside with a soft *clunk* and did not pass it back to him. "You don't think enough has been kept from me already, Elyon? You don't think I deserved to know."

"No, I…"

"No?"

"No, I mean…of course you deserve to know. But I told you, the day I returned, with the Nightblade. You need to focus on your training and leave the rest to us. I thought…you seemed to be all right with that."

"Don't try to turn this on me."

"I'm not. I'm just trying to explain…"

"Or find excuses? You should have told me."

"I know. I realise that now."

She stared at him. This was the hard side to her, the closed-off side with the carapace armour around her heart. "So that's why you brought the Nightblade back to me." It wasn't a question. "You knew you'd be taking the Windblade away, so didn't want to leave me without a Blade of Vandar to train with. Was that your idea, or Ilith's?"

"Mine. And it's worked." He would take some credit for that at least. "You bear the Nightblade easily now. And my plan to keep the blades apart has kept us from harm as well."

"So you say. You also said that the priest told you it was Talasha's blood that drew them to you. So maybe you were wrong about the blades."

"Both can be true at once," he argued.

"That's what Rolly said."

"Yes. And he's right. I've only ever tried to protect you and train you. It's all been for you, Saska."

"But not the rest." She turned her eyes away from him. A moment passed as he tried to riddle that out.

"The rest? I…"

"It doesn't matter." She snatched up the whisky and took another long drink. The air curdled to silence between them. Nought but the roar of the wind in the ruin above disturbed it, the faint crackle and hiss of the fire. He wanted to stand and move around to comfort her, but sensed she would just shove him off.

He let the silence linger on until at last he said, "You're talking about…us?" His heart thumped again, crawling up into his neck. *Of course she is, you blithering fool. Of course that's what she means.*

She gave him no answer. Her eyes were still steadfastly aside and she'd retreated into her shell.

"Saska? Will you look at me, please?"

She didn't. She didn't look at him.

"I've been trying to focus on your training. I feared the rest…well, I feared *this*. I thought if we opened that door…if we let ourselves give in to all that, then…" He paused, struggling for the right words. "This sort of emotion. It can be counterproductive to…we…we need to focus on… you can't let yourself be distracted and now…now look at us. Nothing's even happened between us and…"

"You should have told me, Elyon." Her voice was barely a murmur.

"I know. I know I should. But I don't have to go…not yet, not if you don't want me to. I'll stay for a while, Saska. I don't *want* to go. I want to stay with you, to *be* with you. But…I haven't let myself, because… because…"

Her eyes flickered over to him. It was all coming tumbling out now. "Because?"

"Because I'm *scared*, OK. I'm scared of getting too close to you and then losing you. Leshie had the right of that. Until the war's done, until there's peace, I…."

"Want to keep that door closed." She nodded. "I know. I've… thought the same, mostly…even though it's been hard. But now…to hear that you're leaving…." She looked at him with glistening eyes. "When? When do you have to go?"

"Not yet. I can stay…if you want…"

"*When*, Elyon? You had a plan, I know you had a plan. Was it to get me safely to Tukor first? To wait until I'd bonded the Nightblade?"

"Both," he admitted. "And the Windblade…your training…"

"Then when? We can cross the Links as early as tomorrow night. If we leave late afternoon we'll reach the bridge by midnight, and it's only ten miles across. We could ride that quickly if we must. So you'll leave then? In a day or so? Was that your plan, Elyon?"

His chin lowered. "Yes," he admitted, feeling so out of control. These emotions were unwieldy. *My blood-bond to them is weak.* "But, I don't…"

"You've said that already. I've heard you." She stood up suddenly, whisky in hand, and stepped over to collect her cloak from the wall. "Here, take this." She shoved the bottle into his arms and took the torch from its crack. And cloak in one hand, torch in the other, she left him there by the fire, alone, passing into the room of potions and closing the door behind her.

Elyon sank down on his stool, closed his eyes and let out a long sigh. "I've ruined it," he whispered to himself. "I should have bloody told her."

He wanted to throw the clay bottle right into the wall, to watch it shatter and spill…but chose to drink instead. He wondered if he should go after her. Would she want that? Is that why she left? Was it a test to show if he truly cared? For all the women Elyon Daecar had bedded, they remained hopelessly mysterious to him. His thoughts twisted in search of an answer, but in the end he couldn't find one. So he just sat, and drank, and cursed himself for being such a fool. This was the very sort of thing he had been trying to avoid, the very reason he'd wanted to remain just friends.

We haven't even kissed, he thought. *Not a single kiss, barely even a hug, and still we're bickering like a wedded pair. Damn Leshie for stirring the pot,* he cursed, drinking again. *Damn that girl for interfering…*

"Elyon?"

He looked up. Saska had returned and was standing before him in her cloak. How long had she been gone? The whisky bottle was much lighter than it had been so that suggested a while.

"I hope you haven't been drinking too much."

"No. Just a few sips." His voice was a little rough. He put the bottle aside and wiped his mouth. "I could always handle my drink, anyway. I'll be able to fly. It's fine."

"I wasn't talking about flying."

"Oh. Then there's some left for you, if you want it." He glanced over. "Not much, but…"

"I wasn't talking about drinking either."

He frowned, looking back at her. "Right. Well, I…about earlier… I…"

"Shut up, Elyon."

He blinked at her.

She took a step closer. "You say you have to go…"

"Yes, but…"

"Then we can't put it off any longer."

His brow twisted. He was hopelessly confused. "Put what off, Saska? I'm not sure I…"

Follow, he was about to say…before she removed her cloak.

It tumbled behind her to puddle on the floor and beneath it she was not wearing her armour; beneath it she wore only skin and hair and her perfect smooth anatomy, legs and hips and stomach and breasts, those breasts. *Gods.* His jaw went slack as he drank her in. "Saska," he managed to whisper. "What are you…"

"We've waited long enough, don't you think? The gods brought us here for a reason, Elyon."

She stepped toward him, the firelight gleaming off her skin, more calm and confident than she'd been that first time at Harrowmoor, and straddled him where he sat. He glanced down as her legs parted, looked up into her shining blue eyes. His breath was gone from him, and his codpiece was straining to contain him, and she knew it, she could see it. She smiled and leaned in, breasts pressing at his chest plate. "You had best take off your armour," she whispered, into his ear. "Quickly now…quickly, Elyon."

He had never undressed so fast.

38

Ranulf

It was a quiet night, with nary a breath of wind in the air, quiet and calm and bitter, bitter cold.

They had set up their camp at the heart of a small frozen lake, the ice four feet thick and strong enough to hold them. A fire flickered, under-laid with a foundation of rocks and logs, and they sat about it on blocks of carven ice, huddled in their furs, huddling close.

Around the lakeshore stood a black and sinister wood, of soldier pines and sentinels and twisted, ancient oaks, all armoured in frosted white cloaks. The men glanced into the forest constantly, fearing the emergence of some menace. They were an island of light here, of light in a sea of darkness; an island of goodness in a godless, wicked place.

"We'll leave just before dawn," Sir Mallister Monsort was saying, as they sat hunched forward, warming their hands by the flames. "We'll follow the river as best we can, but will have to cut through the woods *here*." He had the map on his lap, though it was crude and poorly drawn; the Darkisle was not a well-travelled place, a haunt of fearsome hunters looking for a prize kill and plucky adventurers like Ranulf Shackton seeking the ancient and arcane. "Kamcho will fly above us and keep watching for any threats, but I don't want anyone resting on their laurels. No slacking. No daydreaming. Eyes sharp, wits sharper. Yes?" He looked at his men.

The heads nodded.

"Good. If we cut from the river *here*, we should be able to avoid the thickest part of the forest. There is a ridge we can follow *here* that ought to be largely open, but after that there's no helping it. The forest it must be from *here* to *here*." He pointed at the relevant points on the map. Every word came out with a small puff of pale mist. "In all it will take a few hours to reach our quarry. We'll know then whether all this has been worthwhile."

"It better be," grunted Rufford. "Didn't come all this way for nothing."

"No. None of us did. But Ranulf assures me we'll find what we need."

The heads turned to him, the tired, wary eyes. Ranulf nodded and said, "The ice oak only grows in this location, right here in the depth of the Darkisle. It is a unique tree, very distinctive in its look and properties, and *not* made of ice, before any of you might ask." He looked at inquisitive young Darron, who looked like he was about to ask. "That is only a name people use due to its rare white colouring. When the early settlers came to this land, following the ending of the War of the Gods, they found it so prepossessing that they raised a monument to it and declared it sacred. The people believed that the tree is the living tomb of *Lady Lhara*, the wood goddess, who claimed the heart of *Hundrar the Huntsman*."

Simcock snorted. "Never knew Hundrar fell in love with some tree."

Ranulf smiled patiently. "No, the tree is only the last vestige of her, the casing of her spirit, if you will. Lady Lhara could once move between all the trees here on the Darkisle, it is said, but she liked this great oak the best of them. When Hundrar was killed by Eldur, as the legend goes, Lhara just happened to be sleeping inside it, but she felt the sudden withering of Hundrar's spirit from afar and woke up. Such was her terrible grief at his loss that the tree turned to stone around her, trapping her within it. Or so it is said."

"Why ice oak, then?" asked Rufford. "Why not *stone* oak?"

"It's not actually made of stone, is it, Master Ranulf?" asked Darron.

"No." It was Mallister Monsort who gave answer. "It's neither ice nor stone, it's just a tree."

"But a magic tree," Darron insisted. "That's why we're here, isn't it? To collect its sap. There's magic in it."

Ranulf pulled up a leg and laced his fingers together across his knee. "It's so. The sap is known as *Lhara's Tears*. Only once a year does it leak out through the bark, and that is the day that Hundrar died. On the night of the summer solstice, I believe it is. Lhara weeps this night, and only then can her tears be freely collected."

"But the solstice has passed already," old Gunter said, frowning. "How are we to get this sap, then? I don't want to wait around here for another year."

The other murmured and nodded.

"It's only a myth," Sir Mallister told him, dismissing it. "Maybe there's some truth to it, as with many myths, but it's not all to be taken literally. We'll get the sap through some other means. We need it, for Lord Ilith's potion. He wouldn't have sent us out here if he didn't think we could get it."

Ranulf nodded, to back up Mallister Monsort's statement and show the men that all would be well…though there was a concern in him all the same. He had seen enough to know that things once thought as myth were often true, and retrieving the sap might come with a cost if they must harvest it by some other method. What that cost might be, he did not know. *We'll face that when we must*, he told himself. Ranulf had never seen sense in brooding on the unknown.

"There are five, are there?" Stick Jym asked. He was a very thin man, was Stick Jym. "These potions, I mean? One for each of the blades."

"Five, yes," Ranulf said. "Each as essential as the last. Without Lhara's Tears, Lord Ilith will be unable to brew Tears of the Frostshade, so our mission is essential, a hinge on which all will turn."

"Too many hinges if you ask me," Simcock muttered. "What if one breaks? What if we fail?"

"You know what, Simcock," Sir Mallister told him firmly. "We all know what, and don't need to discuss it. We just need to do our job. We're a small part of something bigger, that's all. The rest isn't our concern."

Ranulf backed him up once more. He was the softer side to Mallister's hard, tough brand of leadership, and together they created balance. "We take it one step at a time, as we have until now," he told the huddled shapes around the fire. "When a man looks too far ahead, he can find himself overwhelmed. At the base of a mountain, he gazes up toward the summit and that is often enough for him to turn right around and go home, to quit before he even begins. But do not despair, I know the solution, and it's a very simple trick." He paused for effect. "*Don't* look at the summit. Take one step and then another, and another after that, and something magical always happens....the summit starts to *come to you*." He smiled at the group as he imparted his wisdom. "That, at least, is how I have always lived."

Mallister Monsort took it up. "Our summit is the ice oak," he said. "We're close now. Close enough to see the mists blowing off the snow at the top. And once we get there, the return journey is always easier. Isn't that so, Ranulf? Once you've made a trip one way, going back is the simple part."

"Yes, that is often the case," Ranulf agreed. "Psychologically, the outward journey is the harder leg. Going back is typically easier once you know what to expect."

He hoped it would be true of this journey as well, and so far it had been gruelling, a long, cold, dark and often frightening journey that started over a fortnight ago. The first stage had taken them five days, walking perilous paths past plunging drops, navigating snow slides and the risk of rockfalls as they ranged down through the Hammersong mountains north of the refuge in a bid to reach the coast. They had been stalked by wolves along the way, battled a fearsome snow lion defending her cubs, slain a great white python that lurked in a creepy wood. When they reached the northern coast, the next stage of their journey began, and they'd found the seas frozen over, as Ranulf had expected.

"We'll have to walk across," he'd said to the men. Mallister Monsort had gone out first, thrusting his longsword down into the ice to judge its thickness, then declaring it safe for them to travel in their armour. Ten of them there were in total. Ranulf Shackton, Sir Mallister Monsort, and eight good Bladeborn men under his command: Rufford and Simcock, big strong men-at-arms; Gunter, an older warrior who'd seen much and more; Stick Jym, skinny and fretful; Alyn and Darron, young and enthusiastic; Pecker, who had a very long nose; and finally the one they called Daecar, because he shared somewhat in their famous look. For a week they'd crossed the open ice, battling high winds and sword-nosed whales that tried to spear at them from the water below. Of seals there were plenty, some of them big and angry, and they'd come across a colony of walruses, too, gathered on a thrusting iceberg amidst that great white realm.

As they passed by, the walruses had been seized by a sudden panic, though not because of them. From behind the berg, a great white bear rampaged up and across the ice, scattering them as they honked and fled. The men had stopped to watch as it chose its target, ran it down, then mauled it savagely to death, staining that pristine white ice with great splashes of bright red blood. "That's a big bear," Simcock had said, pulling out his blade. "A snowbear, is it?"

"It looks to be so," agreed Ranulf.

"Thought you only got them in the Icewilds, them snowbears?" Stick Jym put in.

"Most commonly, yes, they are found beyond the Weeping Heights," Ranulf had answered. "This one probably crossed the frozen seas in search of better hunting grounds. And to flee the snow." The snow was coming down thickly there, Ranulf knew from his time with the Elders. It had been glimpsed from afar, this great unending snowstorm the tribespeople called the End-Fall. Many creatures were fleeing from that cold dark realm, and none were likely to be going back. *Well, except for a certain flying prince,* he reflected. *Not that he was particularly happy about the task…*

"Come, let's keep on going," Sir Mallister said. "The bear has no interest in us." He led them on, leaving the big snowbear to its feast, and the crossing was mostly uneventful after that. During the final three days they saw no sight nor sound of a seal or a snowbear or a whale moving beneath the ice. It seemed for a while as though the frozen sea would go on forever, before at last the shadow of the Darkisle appeared on the horizon, emerging through the morning fog like some spectre, dark and foreboding. The men had all stopped in their tracks upon seeing it. "Looks…uninviting," Rufford had remarked. "Maybe we'll just turn back after all."

"We've come all this way," Mallister told him. "We can't go back now."

"No, my lord. I wasn't…" Rufford sighed. "Just looks a bit sinister, is all I'm saying."

"It's called the *Darkisle*, Rufford. What did you expect? Sunshine and pretty waterfalls? We've all heard Ranulf's stories."

Only some of them, Ranulf thought to himself. Yes, he liked to tell tales to the men when they gathered by the fire at night, but he'd spared them some of the worst he'd heard of this place.

The men lingered a little longer, staring at the isle that was not a true isle. Some two hundred miles to the east a bridge of land connected it to the mainland, so that made it a peninsula, really. "Got a bad feeling here, m'lord," Gunter had said, in his grim portentous voice. "Feel like half of us ain't making it back out."

"Half I would take," Mallister said, stoutly. "So long as we get what we came for, that's a small price to pay." He stepped forward, unwilling to let his own doubts set in. All knew how important the quest was. All had volunteered, knowing the dangers. "Come on. We stand here too long and we'll freeze to death. The sooner we get there, the sooner we can turn back." Mallister Monsort led them on fearlessly. The rest trailed behind him, rather more reluctant.

That was four days ago now. Ever since then, they'd been creeping nervously through the forest, past tall looming pines and towering sentinels and those great strong oaks that Lady Lhara had so loved. They travelled by frozen river and stream wherever they could, always anxious, always wary, always watching the woods for the appearance of widow-makers and wild men with bark wrapped about their bodies and great long spears made from pinewood in their grasp.

Even Ranulf Shackton felt disquieted here, in this place, though he tried not to show it. He'd visited the Darkwood before, of course, but only on the mainland side where it clothed the northernmost lands of Tukor. But the greater part of the forest resided further north, on this peninsula, and there was no forest so sinister in all the world. Quiet it was, *too* quiet. The sort of quiet that said there were things all around you, silent things, nameless things, things with too many eyes and too many legs, primitive things that felt neither fear nor pain nor want, only hunger…hunger and the need to feed and here came prey, blundering by.

They made their camp each night at dusk and did not move again until dawn. That window was shorter than Ranulf would like, but Sir Mallister refused to travel in the dark. Always were their camps in an open space, even if one must be made. "I won't have the woods up close to us," Monsort had said. "We need a clear line of sight, clear land around us. If something's going to come, I want to know before it gets here."

On the first night they'd found a rocky clearing beside the river where the trees sat back some twenty feet, and on the second they'd managed to find a shelf of stone overlooking the woods that gave them a good open vantage. On the third, though, they were passing a thick stretch of brooding woodland and had to bring down several trees to make room. Ranulf stood back, listening to the crashing and the snapping, the rending of wood, the hacking and cutting. He had advised against making such a noise, but Mallister said they had no choice. The dark was coming upon them and he would not have the trees crowding near as they slept. So down came the sentinels, and down the soldier pines, and several large fires were built at the corners of their camp. The men took turns on watch, shivering against the fearsome cold, listening to the crackling flames and looking out for the glowing eyes.

That night came several reports. Darron swore he'd seen big spiders moving in the trees above them, and Pecker said he'd seen ghosts, shivery pale spectres drifting by and making a queer moaning sound. During his watch, old Gunter claimed to have sighted a giant lumbering through the woods nearby, and in the morning the tracks confirmed his suspicion. "Gods be good, it must be twenty feet tall!" The prints were hoof-like, almost circular in shape. Ranulf knelt down to inspect them and suggested it may very well be a grulok, one that had fallen asleep here thousands of years ago following Vandar's fall. He explained that the rock sentinels were rising now, to help in the war, and being drawn toward the bearers. "This one may be trying to find its way south," he said. "It could have sensed the Nightblade."

"It's being very slow about it," Rufford huffed. "Must have woken up recently or something. A very lazy grulok." He laughed to himself. "Hey, why not follow its tracks and see if it wants to join us? I'd sure feel better with a grulok on our side."

Ranulf smiled. "As would we all, I'm sure. Though I daresay we might find communicating with it rather difficult."

"We're not following any tracks," Sir Mallister said, all serious. "And I'm not sleeping in the thick of the woods again. Ranulf, let me have the map." He took it from his bag and handed it over. "That there looks like a lake. We can bet the ice will be thick, just as it was on the sea. It's a slight detour, but if we can make it there by dusk, it'll be our last camp." He looked at Ranulf. "What do you think?"

"I think this is your company to command, Sir Mallister."

The young man took his meaning. "Very well. Then we'll make for the lake and set camp there."

And so they had. And here they were.

There remained a long night ahead before they must set off in the morning. With shivering hands, the men took out their dinner ration from their packs and ate. The fare was poor - stale bread, hard cheese, some strips of chewy beef - but good enough, and they'd brought along plenty enough to last them. Alyn spoke wistfully about how he would move south after the war. He was an affable young man with a hopeful way to him that Ranulf found endearing. "I want to live somewhere *warm*," he said. "I know it gets warm in the south of Tukor sometimes, and Vandar can swelter in the summer in some places, but I want to sweat…not just sometimes, but every day. Every day until I die I want to sweat under the sun."

The others nodded, murmuring along. "I never thought I'd miss the mountains," said Rufford. "Thought I'd never feel a cold that went deeper than that, but here…this cold here is something else." He opened and closed a hand over the fire, wincing. "Think I've got frostbite in my toes. Can't feel 'em. Not for days now I can't."

"I'm afraid to piss," said handsome Daecar. "Every time I do, it starts to freeze before it hits the ground. One of these days it'll freeze up right inside me. My cock'll break off like a damn icicle, I swear."

"Aye, and the ladies of Ilithor will weep for joy," japed Gunter. "You're a menace with that thing, Daecar. Might be best for everyone if you lose it."

The others laughed, breath fogging the air. "Weep?" Daecar said, scoffing. "They'd weep, sure, but in lament, not relief. I've given half the girls of White Shadow a night they'll never forget on account of the Pleasureblade."

"Pleasureblade?" Mallister Monsort's voice was short. "That's what you call it?"

"Yes, my lord. A Daecar's got to have a famous blade, hasn't he?" The young soldier grinned, but not for long. It slipped away as he saw the look on his commander's face.

"You're no Daecar," the Emerald Guard told him. "It takes more than a bit of black hair and blue eyes." He spoke harshly and looked displeased. "It's unseemly, what you do. Going around pretending to be someone you're not."

"It's…it's just a bit of fun, my lord. Reckon the girls know I'm not really a Daecar, but for a night…" He shrugged, seeming embarrassed. "It's just play-acting, is all. Fantasy. No harm in it."

"You should pay the name more respect. It's a great name. It shouldn't be sullied by the likes of you."

"Ah, he's just a young lad looking to use every advantage," Gunter came in. "Can't blame him, m'lord. Some lads…all they care about is getting girls into bed and that Elyon Daecar…was a time he weren't so different, so I heard it. Used to run rings round the social scene in Varinar bedding ladylings and pretty young widows, a new one every night."

"Well things have changed since then," said Mallister, stiffly. "That is the old Elyon. It was peacetime. War has changed him. It's changed us all."

"You friends with him are you, my lord?" asked Darron. "Prince Elyon, I mean?"

"Yes, for my part. We've had our ups and downs, but we are on good terms now."

"Ups and downs," Pecker said, grinning. His long nose looked particularly pronounced when he smiled. "That's one way to put it."

The knight glared at him. "And what do you mean by that?"

"Well…just…all that with your sister." His eyes darted around, awkward. "I was there that day, milord, when you duelled him for her honour. First blood it was. A fight to first blood and the gods decide.

Well…you got him, milord. You cut him and you won, I saw the blood. So that with your sister…"

"The gods aren't always right," Mallister said. His voice was blunt and hard. "I think we've seen them err plenty of late, don't you?" He didn't wait for a response. "Elyon never slew my sister. I was mistaken in that. I know that now."

"How'd she die then?" Simcock asked, frowning. He was a big heavy man and had a brutish brow, a great ledge hanging over his eyes. "Was just her and him in that room, I heard."

"Just her and him," agreed Gunter, giving the big man a look. "Use your brain, Simcock. If it wasn't him, who'd you think it was?"

The man recoiled. "You're saying she did it to *herself*?" His face twisted at the notion. "That's a sin against the gods, that is. To take your own life. They frown on that…worse than frown. They send people like that down the Long Abyss…"

"Enough," said Mallister, almost shouting out the word. "Enough talking. Just shut up." He drew a sharp breath and looked from one man to the next. "We can't sit here jabbering all night. Rufford, Gunter, you take the first watch. The rest of you, sleep. We leave at dawn." He stood abruptly and marched away from the fire, bleeding out into the darkness where the lake met the wooded shore.

Simcock watched him go. "Was it something I said?"

"Something you said?" Rufford repeated, snorting. "You're a damn fool, Simcock, a proper bloody fool. Talking about sin and displeasing the gods like that. The Long Abyss? You're a great bloody fool." He looked over at the knight as he began a slow circuit of the lake. "You think he'll rest easy now with all that in his head? Damn you, Simcock. We need him strong and clear-headed tomorrow, and you've gone and buggered it up."

Simcock didn't enjoy the reprimand. "Just speaking the truth. He can't take it, that's on him."

"Some truths are best left unspoken," Rufford bit back. "You want me to tell you how your mother was a whore? Go on about all the men she…"

Simcock stood. "You take that back."

"Why? It's the truth, isn't it? Or can't you take it?"

Simcock drew his blade. Rufford rose and drew his in response. The other men stood as well, ready to step in as the two big soldiers glared daggers at one another. *There's a tension here,* Ranulf thought. It had grown and grown the longer they'd been in this haunted forest, infecting them like some plague. Was it just fear that did it, or something else? Some other more malicious force? He cleared his throat and said, "There are enough threats in this forest to worry about without making enemies among ourselves. Both of you, remember why we're here. Remember your duty and sheathe your blades."

The two men sneered, glaring, but relented. "Fine. But when we're back in the refuge, we'll throw fists over this, Rufford."

"Fine by me," the other man said. "Haven't had a good brawl in a while."

Simcock nodded at that, and Rufford nodded back, and it was done. The first man turned and stomped off to his shelter; the second sat back down to begin his watch. After that, the rest disbanded, moving off to crawl under their furs and try to get some sleep.

Ranulf stayed with Rufford and Gunter for a short while, warming his bones by the fire. Kamcho was circling high above them, floating on the frozen air. Ranulf shut his eyes and slipped into the bird's skin, seeing through his keen eagle eyes. The woods took shape below him, and the lake in its midst. He could see the little fire burning at its heart, the tents hammered into the ice around it, the shadows of the men inside. He saw Rufford throwing a log into the flames, saw Gunter chewing on a strip of meat, saw himself sitting with them, still as a statue, eyes closed as the other men paid him no mind. They'd seen him do this countless times already. It was nothing new to them now.

And lastly, he saw Sir Mallister Monsort, wandering forlornly around the perimeter of the lake in a slow, mournful tread. The eagle looked down at him, and Ranulf saw the shimmer in his bright blue eyes, the sheen of tears. "Poor man," he said, in a low whisper.

"What's that now?" Ranulf withdrew from Kamcho's sight and was back beside the fire. Old Gunter was looking at him questioningly. "You say something, m'lord?"

"Oh…no, nothing."

Gunter regarded him a moment. Then he moved his gaze across the lake, at the figure of Mallister Monsort, drifting by in the distance. "I knew a man once," he began. "Back home near Ethior. He had a son, good bright lad he always seemed…until he went and raped and killed a girl. When they strung him up, the boy was wailing and screaming about how he didn't want to die. The Long Abyss…it terrified him. The idea of falling like that in the dark, starving and screaming…forever." He gave a deep sigh. "The father…well, he was never the same after that. Condemned his boy for what he'd done, of course he did, but he still loved him despite it all. Thinking of him there, in that dark endless hole…couldn't get over it. It changed him, made him smaller, somehow, like he was only half a man. He used to laugh a lot, used to be friends with everyone, walked about with his chest out and his chin up, always smiling. But after…after he was withdrawn. Shoulders in, head down, a big buoyant man turned skinny and old, and there was no joy in him anymore…no colour, only grey." He watched Sir Mallister as he moved mournfully about the lake. "Our noble knight…he's going the same way, it seems to me. There'll always be a hole inside him now no matter what he does to try to fill it. He'll always be grey."

Rufford nodded solemnly. "I never believed in it, that Long Abyss. Someone should tell him. Tell him it isn't true."

"It's not about truth," old Gunter said, sagely. "And it doesn't matter what *you* believe, Ruff. This is about *him*, and he's always seemed a pious lad. *He* believes it, and that's all that matters; there's nothing gonna change that now." He looked across the lake, shaking his head. "Some men…they just love too fiercely. And Mallister…well, he's one of them. He loved his sister too much."

Yes, Ranulf Shackton thought, sadly. *And it will be the ruin of him.*

39

Lythian

In the thick of a forest of ancient elm and ironwood lay the fortress, long-forgotten.

It was a hidden place, an old place, a place raised at the dawn of man. Great blocks of tumbled stone lay scattered and strewn among the foliage, some so heavily overgrown with weeds and moss as to be indiscernible from the woods around them. Others poked out of the undergrowth, rising sometimes to form partial walls that hadn't yet fully collapsed. Around the wider grounds of the once-grand fortress lay many places like this; plant-clad parapets just two feet high, or four feet, or even up to six or seven feet here and there, with great earthy spaces between them filled with trees and shrubs and bird nests, burrows and bushes and blocks of rock that were once part of one building or another.

These were stables and storehouses, barracks and armouries, kitchens, pig pens, the bones of old towers. The curtain wall that once encircled the fort was crumbled and reduced down to its foundations, pulled down by the weight of time. There was once a gatehouse, a barbican here, with soaring towers and an iron portcullis. Little remained but for piles of heaped stone garbed in verdurous cloaks and the memory of metal - rust stains on rocks.

It was clear to Lythian Lindar why Brontus Oloran had chosen such a place for his lair. There were no roads that passed nearby, no farm tracks or woodland paths, and the forest was thick and tangly, with sudden defiles and ditches, bogs and scarps that made it hard to navigate. Were it not for Vilmar the Black, they may never have found it. Ramsey Stone knew only that Oloran had planned to come here to this wood, but could not give an exact location. It had taken the huntsman to sniff it out in the way only Vilmar could do.

He was with Lythian now, the pair crouched down behind a three-foot wall, watching. The night was black and cold and the rain was rattling through the leaves and the branches. Ahead, some fifty yards away, firelight burned at the heart of the ruins where a part of the ancient keep still stood. It was the stoutest structure remaining, largely collapsed but for one section where the walls still rose up some twelve or so feet, and a part of the ceiling remained. Inside was a chamber, large enough to accommodate Brontus Oloran and his men and provide sanctuary from the rain. Beside the keep the yard spread, some thirty metres by thirty, a quarter acre of space. The trees here had been hacked back, the bushes torn from the earth, the yard cleared for training. Torches marked the edge, thrust into nooks and cracks of crumbled bits of wall, flickering flame as shadows rippled across the forest floor and painted shapes on the trunks of the trees. Lythian saw men on watch, three of them, cloaked and cowled, walking a constant patrol. The rest would be in the cover of the keep, most likely sleeping, Brontus Oloran among them.

And the blade, Lythian thought. *So close…and yet so far.*

"Good night for it," the big huntsman said, in a low rumble. "This rain will cover our approach."

"Only until we reach the yard," Lythian returned. "Once we pass the torches, we'll be in the open."

"We'll have to cut down the guards nice and quick. Hope the others don't wake."

"I don't want to do this on hope, Vilmar. If any of them make a noise, or if one of the other five is watching from inside…"

"What choice do we have? We can't crouch here forever."

No. But he did not want to act on a whim either. They'd been keeping watch on Oloran's hideout for two days now, recording the movement of the men as they searched for routines and weaknesses, and their surveillance had yielded an unwelcome conclusion: Brontus Oloran was running a watertight ship. He had men on guard at all times, at least three of them whether night or day. No one ever veered from the yard that they had seen; they kept within the boundary of those fires, within that quarter acre of space and the shelter of the keep beside it. Lythian and his men had witnessed no one leave to forage, or to hunt, or to collect firewood. Vilmar said they would have gathered enough when clearing the yard, and had stored it in the keep to dry, and they had food aplenty too. Lythian knew that from the pig farmer Gertner; his village had been pillaged of as much food as Oloran could carry and they would not be in need of replenishing their stores for a while. In short, they had no reason to leave. They had shelter, food, warmth, and water; everything Brontus Oloran needed.

"So? What do you want to do?" Vilmar pressed. "Might be Oloran's sleeping like a baby in there. We've seen him training. He goes hard and long. Bet he sleeps soundly at night after all that. If we can get to him before he wakes up, while he's a bit groggy…maybe before he has a chance to fetch his blade…"

"It's not *his* blade," Lythian said. His voice spiked with anger. "It was never his."

"You know what I meant. Don't get sore." The huntsman's eyes were blacker than the wood, blacker than the night. There seemed no end to the depth of their blackness. "You're getting snappy again. Ever since we got here. You want to watch that, Lythian. There's still some darkness in you."

Lythian gave no response. Vilmar was holding up a mirror to him and he didn't like what he saw. Nor what he saw in Brontus. Yes, they had seen him train. And yes, he was looking fearsome. Strong, swift, powerful, he bore the Sword of Varinar well and didn't tire as quickly as Lythian would have liked.

"We'd have to get in close," he said, breaking the short silence. "Brontus will be wearing his armour, even to sleep. I think we can assume that is the case, given how cautious he is being."

The huntsman grunted. "Aye, seems likely."

"If we take out the three guards, that leaves five," Lythian went on, working through it practically. "We've got six. Three of us engage the other four men. Pick our targets and attack. The rest all go for Brontus. Best way would be to disarm him. Rush him and disarm him. Trying to engage him steel to steel would be folly. But if we can get to him while he's disoriented, as you say, still drowsy, we may have a chance."

Vilmar nodded. His sharp eyes scanned past the trees and heaps of overgrown stone. "The watches last four hours, give or take," he said. "I've been counting. They'll be changing over soon and that's the time to strike. So you'd best make your plans quick, boy. It's now or never. I say we go."

Lythian did not want to be rushed in this. "It isn't now or never. There's always tomorrow, Vilmar. Or the night after that."

"You're delaying. Why? Is it fear?"

He would not rise to the remark. "I want to consider all ends first. I still wonder whether we can climb up behind the keep. There may be a way down through the roof. If I could get in close..."

"Won't work," the huntsman dismissed. "Stone's not strong enough to hold your weight. Soon as a rock comes loose, they'll be onto you."

"Then we bring the whole thing down on top of them," Lythian said. "If we sneak in the back, we could hack at it with our blades. Bury them..."

The huntsman shook his head. "They'd hear. First whack of steel on stone, and they'd hear. All of them would come swarming out and you'd have an angry Oloran to face up to, wide awake and with that fancy golden sword of his to hand. Sorry, not *his*. Yours, is it?"

Lythian's jaw tightened. "I'm only its guardian, Vilmar. You know that."

The man grinned like a beast. "Aye, so I keep hearing. This heir, or some such. Well, where is he, then?"

"I don't know." Lythian didn't consider it the best use of their time to talk about that. He had one task here. Nothing else mattered. His eyes narrowed, watching the three watchers. "That's Fish there, with the spear," he said. "Leatherbelly further back, passing the torch in the southeast corner." He knew them from Ramsey's descriptions. Fish was the only one to bear a spear. Leatherbelly had his name from the fine leather brigandine he wore over his coat of godsteel mail. The last man on watch was Wormbreeches, so far as Lythian could tell. He was very much lacking in the size of his manhood, Stone had said, and had won the name on that account. "We need Ramsey here," he said. "Fetch him for me please, Vilmar. His input may prove useful."

Vilmar grunted and slipped away, returning a short while later with the crouching form of Ramsey Stone in his wake. "How are the rest of the men?" Lythian asked him, as he took his place beside him at the wall.

"Ready. They're eager to see this done."

Lythian nodded. It seemed the weight of opinion was against him, and they were unlikely to find a better time than now. If they delayed much longer, Brontus would only grow more proficient with the blade, and they risked being spotted as well. That would not do. They must act while they still had the element of surprise.

"We think that's Wormbreeches out there," Lythian said. "With Leatherbelly and Fish."

Stone squinted through the dark, watching the men for a few moments. "Yes. That's them."

"You said Worm has good hearing?"

"And sight," Ramsey confirmed. "Brontus would often use him when scouting. He's a good tracker."

"Then he's yours," Lythian said to Vilmar. "You're lightest on your feet and I've seen how you toss a throwing knife. He's lethal with it," he added for Ramsey's benefit, remembering the way the huntsman had taken out that magradile. "What armour does Wormbreeches wear?"

The man thought a moment. "Breastplate. Gauntlets. Maybe tassets, I'm not sure. That's all godsteel. The rest is beaten leather."

"No gorget?" Lythian couldn't make that out, not past the hood he was wearing.

"Not that I recall. Nor a helm."

"Well and good. Vilmar, a knife to the neck or eye should serve."

"You don't need to tell me," the huntsman growled. "You gonna tell the cows how to moo as well? The crows to caw?"

Lythian smiled. "The other two. Leatherbelly has a coat of mail under his brigandine, you said. What of Fish?"

"Scales. He's from the Tidelands originally. Was a hired sword out there for Lady Shark, if you know her."

"Lady Greyskin. Yes. I've heard the name." She was a notorious power in the city of Greywater, he recalled. "He doesn't wear godsteel, then?"

"Not that I saw. Though the scales are whalehide, like the sort the Rasal lords like to wear. Says Lady Shark gifted it to him for good service.

He claims to have killed over fifty men for her before he left looking for better work."

And ended up serving Brontus Oloran. This Fish was a sellsword, the same as Wormbreeches, Waxen, and Heggarty, who were both out of sight within the keep. Leatherbelly and Bullard were Oloran men-at-arms, while Sir Symon Steelheart stood out as the only knight in Brontus's service, long-serving vassals as the Steelhearts were to House Oloran. He was the only man among them who Lythian knew, though he didn't know him well. And he had met Bullard too, the night they stole the Sword of Varinar from his tent. Bull, or so they called him, was the big bearded brute who had thrown the table aside and stamped down on Lythian's back. *I'll thank him for not snapping my spine,* he thought. *Right before I kill him.*

"My lord," said Ramsey Stone. "I will take Fish, if you'll allow it. He is poor of hearing in his right ear. Says he heard a whale singing underwater once, when he was swimming, and it was so loud it burst his eardrum. I can get close to him. Kill him quiet for you."

Lythian had wanted Storos to be the third, but Ramsey Stone was no bad replacement. He would give him this chance to prove himself. "Very well. That leaves Leatherbelly for me." The man wore an axe on his back and a longsword at his hip. Lythian would see that he never had time to draw them. "We'll have to execute in unison. As close together as we can. Knife to the neck, hand over the mouth, no sound."

"And if someone's watching from in the keep?" asked Ramsey Stone. "There are gaps in the walls. You can see the firelight flickering in there. We'll have no way of knowing, Lythian."

"That's a risk we'll have to take."

"What about Nathaniel?"

"What about him?"

"We could use him. I know you've been thinking about it too. He could go in there and say he's there to join them. Brontus might believe him. Then, when he gets a chance…"

"I won't ask Nathaniel to become a kinslayer, Ramsey."

"He's a *king*slayer, isn't he?"

"Technically, no. Janilah Lukar did that. And he has worked tirelessly to restore his honour since then. The same as you are doing now."

Ramsey didn't care for the comparison. "I ran from battle in a moment of folly. He stood by and let his own king be killed. And as Commander of the Greycloaks too. That's another level of treachery and you know it."

This was no place for this discussion. "Nathaniel is Brontus's cousin, that's the bottom line. We cannot count that he would follow through and kill him. Would he join him? No. But if they see through his pretence, it will out us all and we will miss our chance." He had already decided against using Nathaniel in any such way. It lacked honour, that was the bottom line, and Lythian was trying to restore his own as well after those dismal days in King's Point, with all that desertion and darkness and death. "Vilmar, bring the others here. How long do you think we have before the changeover?"

"Ten, fifteen minutes I would guess."

"Then we must act quickly. Go."

The huntsman returned a moment later with Sir Bardol, Sir Storos, and Sir Nathaniel for company. They crouched down low in a circle, darkness around them, hissing in low whispers, making their plans. Lythian gave the update, then said, "Once the three watchers are down, we'll rush the keep. The focus is Brontus. Kill him and victory is ours." He checked Nathaniel's eyes, saw the merest flicker of doubt. "He must die," he said to the group, though largely for Nathaniel's benefit. "Brontus is beyond saving now. Even if he should throw down his sword and yield, we must cut him through. Understand?"

There were nods of agreement.

"Nathaniel?"

"Yes, my lord. I…accept he is already dead."

"Good. I will target him myself. Storos, Vilmar, I want you with me. The rest of you take down the others as quick and clean as you can. If the gods are good, we'll find them half asleep and unarmoured. But they're not. So we won't." That won him some grim chuckles. "The keep interior is small enough, and Vilmar says there's no undercroft or base-ment, so there's only one way in and one way out. In that space Brontus won't have much room to move."

"And if he's ready for us, my lord?" asked Sir Bardol. He looked nervous, but determined. "How will we defeat him if…with the blade… he could kill us all."

"We won't let him, Bard," said Ramsey Stone. "The plan's going to work. It'll go easy, you'll see."

Lythian nodded, hoping that was so. "Any other questions?" He looked around, at one man and then the next, at the apprehensive eyes and the defiant eyes and the frightened eyes. No one said anything. "Then let's get this done. Gertner told me they stole his private stocks of wine when they looted his village. When this is over, we'll toast our victory with it." He looked at them one final time, then swung back around to peer toward the yard. Vilmar had been watching the guardsmen all the while.

"Saw Leatherbelly and Worm share a word just now," the huntsman grunted. "Reckon they'll end the watch after a few more circuits."

"Then we'd best be quick. Ramsey, come here." The ex-knight crept in to join them. "You have your target. See that wall?" Lythian pointed it out. "Get in behind it. Stay low, down on your belly if needs be. I'll swing around through the woods and come in on the other side."

"What about you?" Ramsey asked Vilmar.

The huntsman snorted. "Don't you worry about me. This is my world, boy. There's no one gonna see me coming."

"No, but…I need to know where you'll be. For the signal. So I know when I act."

"It's a fair point, Vilmar. We'll go on your mark."

"No," said the huntsman. "I'm quicker than the both of you. So you'd best get a head start. Soon as you two enter the yard, I'll be right there with you."

"Fine." Lythian took a deep breath. "Ramsey, watch for me. I'll be across the yard from you. When I go, you go." He met the man's eyes. "Yes?"

"Yes." His voice was a little shaky. "I'll be ready, Lythian."

"Good. Then let's get in position." Lythian went left, creeping through the soaking brush as the rain pattered down through the canopy. He clambered over slick mossy stones and slipped between the tree trunks. Back from the yard there was plenty of cover, yet the shift of shadows could still be seen. Careful and quick, he was, quick and careful. Eyes darting toward the blaze of firelight, watching the watchers to make sure they weren't watching.

Before long he was around the other side, moving up close. A twisting old ironwood laid climb to what might once have been an armoury here. He stopped a moment, some ten metres from the nearest torch at the boundary of the yard. Peering around the edge, he saw Leatherbelly wandering by, turning away from him. Fish was further off, across the yard, Wormbreeches just now passing by the entrance into the keep. It was covered over with a woven net of vines and leaves and there was no way to see inside. There was a moment when Lythian thought Worm was going to pull the cover aside and enter, but he kept on going, plodding through the rain.

The Knight of the Vale exhaled, dropped low to his stomach, and bear crawled forward. The torch was fixed into a small corner of old wall, just tall enough to hide him. He slithered up behind it just before Worm came striding by, armour rattling, so close now, close enough to kill. But he must wait for Leatherbelly. Leatherbelly was his man.

He peeked out over the side, searching for Ramsey Stone. Nothing. He couldn't see him. Then a shift of movement, a shape behind the crumbled wall. *Yes, it's him. Good, he's in position.* He could see the ex-knight searching for him, hunkered low as he leaned out around the side of the rock. It took a moment before they met eyes, but meet eyes they did. *Good, good…*

He could hear the footfall coming now, the trudging boots against wet earth and broken stone. Fish would pass by first, then Leatherbelly. A *clunk* of something, the butt of a spear on the ground as Fish went by. Lythian stayed low, right up against the wall, sticking to it like a barnacle. The timing was working, it was going to be just right. Fish was walking away now, heading right for Ramsey Stone. He could hear Leatherbelly coming, a dozen metres off. A heaver step. A bigger man. His tread sounded tired, plod, plod, plod, his breathing weary. The man gave out a bored sigh as he neared…

…and stopped suddenly, still six metres away.

"Right," Lythian heard him call to the others. "That'll do now, lads.

Been long enough. Let's wake 'em." He turned and began to step away toward the keep.

Damn it. Lythian Lindar cursed under his breath. The man-at-arms was further away than he had wanted, but what choice was there? He had to go. He had to go now.

He surged to his feet, put a hand on the broken wall and vaulted over it. He was running at once, devouring the space, one metre, two, three, four....From the corner of his eye he saw Ramsey Stone doing the same, leaping the wall and racing for Fish. Leatherbelly caught the motion. His head turned sharply as he saw Stone emerge into the flickering firelight, and his mouth opened to utter a warning, but it never came. Lythian was on him. His knife slammed into the side of his neck, slicing through his vocal cords, and his spare hand slapped down over the man's mouth, pulled hard to one side to snap his neck for good measure. Fish heard, turning. Ramsey was rushing up behind him. The Tidelander's eyes widened as he saw Leatherbelly go down, saw the cloaked shadow at his back. His lips tore open. The beginning of a scream escaped him...cut off abruptly as Ramsey Stone reached him, punching his knife through the back of his neck.

There was a moment, then, just a moment, when Lythian thought no one had heard. A short silence, nought but an inward breath, as he looked at Ramsey, and Ramsey looked at him, and they hoped... hoped...

And then came the voices, the grunting voices, the sudden rush of motion inside the broken keep. Vilmar was standing across the yard with Wormbreeches lying dead at his feet. Lythian hadn't even seen him enter. "They're coming," the huntsman growled.

Lythian nodded. "Go." The man knew what he meant. In an instant he was bleeding away back into the night as though he'd never been there.

A second after that, the men came boiling out from inside, armoured and ready, pulling swords from their scabbards. They saw Lythian there, with Leatherbelly at his feet, saw Ramsey Stone standing over the figure of Fish as blood pulsed out from his open neck. "You bastards, you killed 'em," one of them shouted.

Lythian threw off his cloak; it would only get in the way. It was run or fight, and damn it, he wasn't going to run. He pulled his helm from his swordbelt and thrust it down over his head. "Men!" he roared. "For Vandar! For the king!"

"For the king!" came the reply, and from behind the trees and broken walls, came Storos and Nathaniel and Bardol, their drawn blades misting and glinting orange in the firelight as they charged the yard and engaged. It happened quickly, too quickly for Heggarty who was met with the full force of Sir Storos Pentar. Screaming, "Redhelm!" the knight surged ahead of the others and thrust his blade right up and through the man's guts. Blood spat from Heggarty's mouth as Storos pulled the blade back out, swinging in a side cut to finish the job. Bullard roared, swung a hand to knock the dying man aside, and pressed Storos back across the cobbles. Waxen followed him through, meeting Sir Bardol blade-to-blade as Ramsey Stone shouted, "Steelheart!" and drove toward him in Glide-form as Sir Symon backtracked, parrying and defending. In an instant the long-forgotten yard in the long-forgotten fortress was ringing to the sound of steel.

And then Brontus Oloran emerged.

Uncloaked he came, and fully armoured, godsteel misting from heel to helm. His faceplate was raised, and there was anger in his eyes. He held the Sword of Varinar. The glyphs that ran the length of the golden steel seemed to throb and pulse, as though it knew it was being fought for. *It wants him,* Lythian knew. *It wants me dead.* The blade knew Lythian's intention. But with Brontus, it was free.

"I wondered if you'd try to find me," the traitor said to him. "I spared your life that night, Lythian. You should never have come here."

"I have no choice, Brontus. You took something that isn't yours."

"It is mine. It's mine. Mine," he repeated. "You won't take it back from me. You won't."

"That blade is needed. And not by me."

"Who, then? Who? Dalton's dead, he died in the battle. And Vesryn Daecar. I heard about him too. He cut the Dread, that's what they say, but I'm the better man, younger and stronger. I'll more than cut him, I'll kill him, as Varin did. You shout out, "For Vandar" but you don't know *his* will. He wills I wield this blade, Lythian. He tells me. I hear him. I know it."

He's lost, Lythian thought. *The blade has driven him mad.* "That sword is one part of five, Brontus. It is needed, by the king. The heart must be remade."

"No. No. That isn't so, Lythian. The Sword of Varinar can cut anything. *Anything.* I can win the war with this blade."

"It cannot cut the Bondstone. That is the soul of a god. You must use your reason, Brontus. There is only one weapon that can end this war, and without that blade…"

"I won't give it up. It's mine. I earned it."

"Cousin." The voice was filled with sadness. Nathaniel Oloran stepped forward through the falling rain. "Please, cousin, heed me. Lay down the blade, Brontus. It's the only way."

"The only way of what? What, Nathaniel?" He looked at him, laughed at him. "You came too? Why? To restore your honour? You're a disgrace to our family, to your father. A *disgrace.*" And he spat at the floor, sneering at him. His eyes were full of loathing, twisted and hateful.

"Cousin." Nathaniel's voice stayed calm. "Please. Just lay down the blade and listen. There's much more to this than you know. What Lythian said, about…"

"I don't care what he says. It's all lies. You're lying to me, as that *letter* lied! Do you have the ear of a god, Nathaniel? Do you talk to Vandar as I do?"

"It isn't Vandar. It's just a part of his spirit, his broken heart. It's deceiving you, cousin. *Using* you."

"And what do you know of it? Nothing. Nothing."

"Please, Brontus." Nathaniel took a step closer. "Put the blade away and we can stop this bloodshed. It weakens us all. Put it down and we can talk."

"Talk? Talk? There's nothing to talk ab…." Brontus cut himself off. His eyes shifted suddenly to the side and he jerked his head backward. The throwing knife hissed past his face, cutting a thin line across his brow, and went flying into the forest. Oloran's eyes widened. Blood leaked from the thin long cut, dripping down past his eyes. He touched his face, saw the blood. Rage erupted in him. "You're trying to trick me, Nathaniel! Distract me, while…"

"No…" Nathaniel Oloran backed away. "Cousin, no. I didn't realise…I only want to talk, to talk with you. I…"

"A trick!" bellowed Brontus Oloran. "You would trick your own kin!" And he surged forward, swinging wildly. Nathaniel raised his own blade to parry the blow on instinct, but the Sword of Varinar cut right through it. There was a burst of mist, a clang of metal as a two-foot shard hit the ground. Nathaniel raised his broken longsword, stumbling away, but his cousin was on him. He swung hard for a killing blow. Nathaniel staggered back, but not far enough, and the tip of the Sword of Varinar sheared through the front of his godsteel breastplate, moving through the metal like silk. "A trick! A trick!" Brontus was bellowing, as he stamped forward, as Nathaniel staggered back, tripping, collapsing, blood streaming down his chest. The silver breastplate was turning red. "A trick! A trick! You'd trick me! Your own cousin!"

"No, please…no…"

"You're nothing, Nathaniel! Nothing! Nothing!"

"Cousin…" Nathaniel raised an arm to fend him off…

…and Brontus swung, severing it. Nathaniel screamed. The arm spun away. "A trick! A trick! You're nothing. Nothing!" Olaran swung once more, a savage swipe that opened up his cousin's belly to the spine. Blood boiled up, and his insides squirmed out. Brontus's lips twisted at the sight, at the stink. "Nothing. You were always nothing!"

"That's enough," shouted Lythian. "Damn you, Brontus, put him out of his misery."

The man's eyes snapped over at him. His face had turned crazed, chaotic. There were blood gouts spattered on his chest, his neck, his face. "You should never have come, Lythian," he shouted. "You made me do it. You made me kill him. You should never have come." He reached up and slammed down his faceplate, and with one last swing he took off his cousin's head.

Lythian watched the head roll away across the cobbles, watched the blood pump out of the severed neck in thick dark spurts. The sight was familiar. He'd taken many heads himself of late. "You're a coward, Brontus," he said, coldly. "Using that blade. A coward."

"It's *my* blade. I was born to bear it."

"Put it aside. Fight me fairly if you think you can."

"Fairly? It wouldn't be fair, not against you. I'm better. Better. I was always better."

"Then prove it," said Lythian Lindar. "We'll swear our oaths. To fight with common godsteel. And the winner wins the blade."

"The Song of the First Blade is done," the madman screamed back at him. "You never fought in it. You weren't there." He stamped forward a pace. "You were in Agarath, raising Eldur from his tomb. I heard about that, I know about your *woman*. You're a dragonlover, a sympathiser, a traitor to your people. All this is because of you, you! Raising the enemy! Bedding some Agarathi *whore!*"

The insult sent a ripple through him. Lythian's gaze narrowed, dangerous. He remembered his dream. Talasha asking him if he loved her. *And now? Do you love me now?* Her back turned and the black wind rising. The others were swirling around the yard in furious combat, but Lythian's eyes were only for Oloran. And his eyes were dark. "Say that again," he said.

He did. "Whore! Your Agarathi whore!"

And Lythian Lindar sprung.

Brontus bellowed and swung the heavy blade, trying to cut him clean as the Knight of Mists ghosted forward. Lythian danced away from it, shifting around, trying to get under and in, but Oloran was gone, backing off. He roared and came again. Lythian slid right, swung hard with his sword, smashing at the Sword of Varinar with all his strength. He connected against the flat of the blade. A great golden sunburst exploded from the steel and an echoing din rang out. For a split second, it was day, and then night was on them once more.

"You won't knock it from my grasp!" Oloran shouted. "You won't!"

Lythian barely heard him. He was already coming again, hacking this time at the man's wrist. Oloran raised the blade to deflect the strike. Steel kissed steel, silver against gold, but Lythian's blade did not shatter. The Sword of Varinar's power was in the cut, not the parry. It was an *active* power, not a *passive* one. Oloran didn't seem to know it. Lythian sensed a short hesitation in him as he whirled away in Strikeform. Brontus shifted into Blockform, turning as they circled, suddenly wary. Lythian was quicker than him, and he knew it. "That blade looks heavy in your grasp, Brontus. You'd fight better with one more suited to you."

"There is no blade more suited. I was born to bear it. Born to win the war." He watched Lythian carefully, turning, breathing.

Lythian scoffed. "I heard things too. I heard you were dismantled by Aleron during your semi-final of the Song. And Dalton defeated you too, at Crosswater. What makes you think *you* have a right to that sword? There are a dozen knights in Vandar who are better than you. And a hundred more worthy."

The man snarled inside his helm. "Dalton *cheated*. He cheated, cheated! There's no one better! No one more worthy!"

"Then show me. Kill me. It takes but one cut, Brontus. And you can't even manage that."

The man roared, goaded, and rushed at him. Lythian slid away, fleet of foot and nimble. His eyes flicked here, flicked there, checking the stone, the broken cobbles, the earthen grooves all choked with weeds. One poorly placed foot, one slip and he was done. The Sword of Varinar swung down in a gilded fog, slicing through the ground. Lythian swerved around the back of the man, swinging hard for the weak point where the gorget met the pauldron. His blade clattered fiercely into the plate, but not through it, cutting a line. Brontus pulsed back around, swinging in a fierce up-cut. The metal whistled past Lythian's face, too close. He jerked back and away just in time, putting some space between them.

A heavy breath rattled out of Oloran's helm. "Strikeform. Damn Strikeform," he muttered. "You're slippery as an eel, Lindar."

Lythian wasn't going to give him a moment to recover. He surged in once again, thrusting powerfully, anticipating Oloran's defensive parry, sidestepping away from it. He hacked down at his neck again, but the other man drew away, and at once he turned defence into attack, striding at Lythian, swinging, cutting, left-slice, right-slice, up-cut, down-cut, thrust and swing, step and slide and swing again. Lythian forgot hard-won instincts. He could neither parry nor deflect nor defend himself, not against those strikes. Left he went, sliding, right and ducking, spinning away, backtracking, only striking out once Oloran was through his swing, when the active motion was complete. Once and twice and thrice more he tried to knock the blade from the man's grasp, but his grip was iron, unyielding. *It's not going to work. I have to get in closer…*

A sudden shriek pierced the air.

Lythian's eyes swung across the yard. Steelheart was down, Ramsey Stone standing over him. There was a puncture in Sir Symon's armour, a thin cut in the plate at the abdomen. Blood leaked out from the wound. Steelheart raised his hand as though to ward off Ramsey's strike, and from his lips came a squeal of, "Brontus! Help!" and Oloran wheeled and charged at once. Ramsey heard him coming in time, backed out of the swing, and turned to face him.

"No, Ramsey," Lythian roared. "Run! Get away from him!"

He didn't. He stormed forward instead, for death and for glory, swinging at the approaching man. Brontus hefted the Sword of Varinar to parry the blow, turning it away. Another swing from Ramsey, another parry, swing and parry, swing and parry. Lythian was running up behind them, Sir Symon scrambling back to his feet. Ramsey's assault came to nothing, his blows ineffective. Brontus turned the momentum, driving him back, cursing him and laughing at him, calling him craven and weak, taunting him. Stone lost himself to the rush of the duel, tried to swing and deflect a blow, and his blade shattered as Nathaniel's had. "*Fool!*" Brontus thundered, mocking. "You were always so stupid, Stone!"

Ramsey snarled, swerving away from an arcing cut, then launched forward with his broken blade, trying to drive the shard up into Oloran's throat. Brontus moved deftly aside as he came, leaving behind a trailing leg to trip him. Stone's sabaton struck, and he stumbled forward, trying to arrest his momentum, failed and went crashing to the ground. Brontus laughed contemptuously. He turned, followed, spun the Sword of Varinar in his grasp and thrust it down through Ramsey's shoulder, through the misting godsteel and the meat beneath, through blood and bone and earth, pinning him to the earth.

The man's scream ripped through the forest. Steelheart was up and on his feet, moving to block Lythian's way. He held his blade forward. Blood leaked out from the wound in his abdomen. "Let it happen, Lythian. Stone deserves to die."

"Do we all deserve that, Symon? Are you as lost as your master?"

He saw doubt in him, the seed of uncertainty. The Knight of Nine-Hearth had once been pretty and primped, a pithy-tongued prancer with golden hair done up in ringlets and hairless, creamy skin. Now he was wild, filthy, ragged like the rest of them. He looked a different man entirely. "Anyone who denies the will of Vandar deserves to die."

"His will as Brontus sees it. You would trust him over your king? Over Amron Daecar." He sensed weakness in him. "Symon, *please*. Think. What you're doing here…"

Another shriek from Ramsey cut him off. Brontus was twisting the Sword of Varinar, staring down at him and twisting. His lips were twisted too, curling in glee. Stone screamed out as his flesh was torn and opened, as the godsteel armour strained and cracked and broke. "Weak," Brontus was saying, grinning. "Weak and craven and cruel, *cruel*. You were never a knight."

"That's enough," Lythian shouted. "Enough death, Brontus. Enough."

Ramsey was shuddering in agony. He turned his head, face down in the filth, and Lythian saw the appeal in his eyes. "Lythian, *please*…" he managed to whimper. "My…my seat, do I…have I…"

"You have done enough, *Sir* Ramsey," Lythian told him, acknowledging him again as a knight. "*He* is watching. Your seat awaits."

The man's eyes filled with tears. "My seat," he whispered, smiling. It was all he had wanted to hear.

But Brontus snorted loudly, ruining the moment, ruining it all. His voice was full of scorn. "Your seat? You have no seat, Stone! You'll go to the hall of cravens and deserters, the hall of traitors where my cousin now rests."

"*You* are the traitor," Lythian Lindar told him. "You, Brontus. And *you*, Symon." He met the man's eyes. "Neither of you will visit the Eternal Halls. It will be the void for you both, the Long Abyss."

Steelheart cringed at the name. "No, no, that isn't true…"

"Don't listen to him, Symon. He's only trying to frighten you. Our cause is righteous, righteous, Vandar wills it. We will be honoured guests at Varin's side."

Lythian sighed. "You are lost, Brontus."

"You be quiet, Lythian," Oloran raged. "And you…*you*…enough with your whimpering." He looked down, drew the Sword of Varinar from Ramsey's shoulder, and swished it right to left, cutting through the back of his head. The man quivered, convulsing, as his skull was split open, and then went still. Lythian shut his eyes a moment in silent prayer.

"Don't spare your care for *him*, Lindar. You'll join him soon enough." Brontus stepped up to Symon's side. For a moment Lythian wondered if he might have to fight them both alone. Then there was the sound of footfall behind him, and a figure came up to join him.

"Bullard's dead," Sir Storos Pentar reported. "Strong sword, but I got him eventually."

Lythian smiled. "I'm glad you're still with me, Storos."

"I've been with you since Runnyhall. Not about to abandon you now."

"And Bardol?"

"Dead. But he got Waxen first."

No Varin cloak for Bardol then, Lythian reflected. Still, he had done his part. *He can walk proudly now into the Eternal Halls.*

Storos saw Ramsey Stone lying still on the ground, Nathaniel a little further away. It was just the two of them, now. Just the two left in the yard. "You killed your own cousin?" he called out to Brontus Oloran. "The gods don't look kindly on that, you know."

"You don't know the gods, Pentar. Only I do." Brontus looked longingly at the sword in his grasp, the golden steel all slick with blood. It shone a light of its own, spreading to beat away the darkness. Oloran took that as some sort of sign. He smiled. "Vandar speaks to me. Mine is the way of light, the path to glory. That eagle brought only lies, more lies. I don't expect you to understand."

"Eagle?" Lythian said. "What are you talking about?"

"Like you don't know. Another trick. Just a trick. Trying to lure me away with your lies."

"I do not lie, Brontus. I know nothing of any eagle."

The man snorted and ignored him. "Symon, go inside. I will deal with them alone."

"Brontus? But…"

"I said go inside. You are wounded. You'll be no help to me here." He waved to dismiss him.

Steelheart glanced at Lythian, lowered his head, and drew away. A trail of blood marked his passing as he limped across the cobbles and into the cover of the keep.

"A shame it's come to this," Brontus said. He watched Storos step to the right, Lythian moving left. "You were a great man once, Lythian. I respected you."

"You had the potential for greatness, Brontus," Lythian returned. "Now you'll fall here, in this long-forgotten ruin, alone and in disgrace."

"No, no, you have that the wrong way around. The disgrace is yours. You brought about this war."

A big shadow slid out of the woods, past a chunk of wall. Silently it crept toward the keep, in through the woven door.

Brontus never saw it. "I will try to make it quick for you. Give you a knight's end, to honour the man you once were."

Lythian dipped his chin. He glimpsed movement within the keep, a silent struggle. "Thank you, Brontus. You are kind."

"It's more than you deserve," Oloran said, pompously. "But I am merciful, you will find. Pentar…well, I barely know you. Fifth son, are you?"

"Fourth. Tomos was fifth."

"Ah yes, Sir Tomos. Well, he was a Varin Knight at least. Unlike you." He gave a snort. "I'll give you a knight's end anyway, why not? Nathaniel…he betrayed me and deserved what he got. And Stone…that man was *vermin*. I'd hoped to take my time with him, give him a slow painful end, but alas…"

He stopped mid-sentence, sensing movement, and spun around. Vilmar the Black was stalking out of the keep with Sir Symon Steelheart struggling weakly in his grasp. The big black-bearded huntsman had the man's arm twisted up behind his back, a blade under his chin. "Found this inside. He one of yours?"

Brontus tensed. "You," he growled.

"Aye, me."

"That knife…"

"A poor throw…or maybe just a good dodge. I don't usually miss." The huntsman pressed the tip of his blade into Steelheart's neck, eliciting a whimper. A single drop of blood trailed down into his gorget. "Drop the blade or he dies."

"You touch him, I'll kill you."

"Already touching him." The dagger pressed harder. "Drop it, I said."

Symon Steelheart was weeping. "Brontus, please…just give it up. I don't…I don't want to die. Just give it up…"

Oloran was seized by an inner struggle. "I can't, Symon. You know I can't. How can you even ask it of me?"

"For me, Brontus. For *me*." His eyes were pleading. "Maybe they're right…maybe Lythian's right. That eagle, Brontus. The letter…"

"Don't tell me to give it up!" the man roared. "Don't ask that of me, Symon!" He was breathing heavily, voice thundering from inside his helm. He pointed the tip of his blade at Vilmar. "Let him go. Now! Let him go or I'll kill you slow!"

"No. Put down the blade."

"I can't. I won't."

"Guess he dies, then." Symon Steelheart barely had time to scream as the huntsman thrust the dagger deeper, sliding it into his throat. Brontus

Oloran gave out a blood-curdling roar and ran for him, but Vilmar only ripped the blade out of Symon's neck and threw him forward to the onrushing man. Brontus caught him in his arms as Steelheart stumbled, reaching for his throat, spluttering to draw breath. "Symon, no! No, NO!"

Then suddenly Storos and Lythian were there, coming up behind him, and Vilmar the Black bore down on him too. Six hands reached out, wrestling and wrenching at him, prying the Sword of Varinar free, and Brontus was roaring, in pain and anger and grief he was roaring, and from the blade the light was spilling, blinding, flashing against the ruins and the woods.

Their foe was freakish strong. The strength of Vandar was in him, the will of the blade. *It wants him*, Lythian knew. *It's afraid. Afraid.* He gripped at Oloran's wrist, twisting, as Vilmar prised off his fingers one by one. Storos let go and started slamming his closed fist into Brontus's head.

"His faceplate," Lythian roared. "Raise it, Storos!"

Storos reached in, pulled the faceplate up. Oloran's wild eyes were exposed, black with rage, wet with tears. He roared, grimacing, twisting, struggling. Storos threw his fist but Oloran turned his head, screaming like a beast as Symon Steelheart flopped down onto the ground, the blood pulsing weaker, weaker from his neck.

"You killed him! You killed him!" The man bellowed and twisted, throwing an elbow up into Storos's chin, knocking him back. Vilmar snarled, his big hands pulling at Oloran's fingers, but Brontus pressed forward suddenly, biting at him, teeth clenching down on the huntsman's neck. Vilmar howled, jerking away as the madman's mouth came back bloody, a hunk of ragged flesh between his teeth. He spat it out, ripping his hand back and away, but Vilmar clung on, and Storos recovered and surged back in and it was over, then, Lythian knew. He saw his chance and he took it.

His fist met Oloran's face.

The impact was savage, and Oloran's head cracked back. His body followed, and all the strength went out of him. He slammed down into the ground in his heavy godsteel armour. His jaw was shattered, mouth a bloody red ruin, nose crushed and bent out of shape. But his eyes were open, and they looked up at Lythian Lindar. Confused, they were, almost innocent all of a sudden. "Lythian?" he croaked. "What…what's…I don't understand…what's happening?"

Lythian pulled the Sword of Varinar away, setting it down on the ground beyond his grasp.

"I'm scared, Lythian. I don't…?" His voice was splintered, broken like his face. Spittle and bits of broken teeth bubbled up from his mouth with the blood. His eyes twisted in horror. "What…what did I do? You have to help me. The voice…the voice…"

"End him, Lythian," Storos spat. "He's trying to trick you. Don't you believe him."

Vilmar stamped in, one hand holding his bloody neck. "If you don't do it, I will…"

Lythian raised a hand to stop them. "Brontus," he said, going to a knee. "Your men are dead. Symon is dead. Your cousin is dead. You killed him."

"Me?" Tears rolled down his fractured cheeks. "No, please…I'd never…never…"

He felt a shred of pity for him. A pity perhaps only he could understand. "The blade took you, Brontus, twisted you. But you were a good man once."

"The blade…" His eyes blinked, quivering. He stared up at the sky, up at the rain. "The eagle," he murmured. "The…the eagle, and the letter…"

"Letter?" Lythian leaned in. He'd mentioned that already. "What letter, Brontus?"

"The map," he managed. "I…kept it, not sure…why. Inside the map. I…a trick, I thought…"

Lythian looked up. "Storos, find it."

Storos Pentar marched away. Brontus was still murmuring, his words growing increasingly incoherent. There was a sound of rummaging inside the keep, a few barked curses, then Sir Storos came marching back out. "Here." He handed Lythian the folded map. When he opened it out, a small scroll slipped out from within. Lythian caught it, unrolled it, read through the words.

Storos was watching him, and Vilmar the Black as well. "What's it say?" the huntsman growled.

"That we're not going back to King's Point," said Lythian. He tucked the scroll away, stood, and went to pick up the Sword of Varinar. He could feel its anger, feel its hate. The whispers howled at him, already trying to corrupt him, but he was deaf to them now, deaf. He knew where he must go.

"And what about him?" Storos asked, standing over Brontus Oloran. "We can't spare him, Lythian. You said it yourself. He's too dangerous to be left alive."

He had said that, and it was true. He took a final look at the fallen knight and turned to walk away. "Kill him," he said, "and make it quick. We have graves to dig before we go."

40

———

Emeric

He looked at the Emerald Guard anxiously. "Will he live?" he asked.

"If he's strong, yes, he'll live."

"Then he'll live," Emeric said. Sir Ernold of Esterling was nothing if not strong. "How long until he comes around?"

"The fever must run its course. Two days, three, could be longer. I have let out the bad blood and administered the required tonics and salves to halt the corruption." He raised his eyes. "You know this man well, is it so?"

"Well enough."

"Then you'll know how he'll react to the surgery. Some men…I have seen them react poorly, shall we say. They go to sleep intact and wake without a limb, and with some this heralds violence. I have been subjected to the same myself, once or twice." He turned his neck and pointed. "See here. The discolouration. Once I was required to amputate the leg of a renowned knight. When he came around and saw what he was missing, he put his hands around my neck and tried to throttle me dead for it. I was only acting under the orders of Lord Fullerton, you understand, yet he took it personally." He looked at Ernold Esterling, lying peacefully in his sickbed. "I would hope your friend has better manners when he wakes without an arm."

"A forearm," Emeric corrected. "You left him the upper half."

"Only by your insistence. I would have preferred to cut above the elbow to be safe. It is useful to keep the joint, it's true, but the risks…"

"Have passed, yes?" Emeric asked him.

"I will know by tonight. By morning at the latest. If the fever does not worsen, then he should make a full recovery. Less an arm, of course."

"Forearm. And he was already missing half the hand." He gave the old man a grateful nod. "Fear not for Sir Ernold's reaction, Master Alla-bor. If he tries to throttle you, just swat him away. It shouldn't be so hard. He only has the one hand, after all."

The small man smiled amiably. "I am feebly built, my lord, as you can see. One would be quite enough I should think." He slipped a hand up the loose sleeve of his light grey robes and withdrew a vial of blue liquid. He seemed to have many hidden pockets up those sleeves. "Here. The tonic you asked for. If this does not work then I'm not sure I can help you."

Emeric took it and held it up to the lamplight. "What's in it?"

"A good many things. I have a list over here, if you'd like to inspect it?"

"Please." The old man shuffled over to his stacked shelves of pots and potions and old leather-bound books, fiddled through a heap of papers a moment, said, "Ah, here we are," and returned bearing a scrap of parchment. He handed it over and Emeric ran his eyes down the scribbled words. In truth much of it was foreign to him, the sort of rare ingredients only masters of medicine and alchemists might know. But others... "There are some strong elements in here, Allabor," he said. "*Dew of the Dawnstone.* I've heard of grown men having attacks of the heart from taking just a few drops of it."

"Ah, this is true. But the balance must be just right. If the ratio is off..." He clutched at his chest and made a face. "Yes. The heart can be overly, um, *stimulated,* shall we say. The ingredient is commonly used to resolve matters of limpness between the legs. A common malady among older men, I'm afraid to report. They think an extra drop or two will keep them going all through the night, but alas no, it ends the night prematurely."

"And every other night to come," said Emeric. He handed back the sheet of paper. "I trust you to have the dosage right?"

"Of course. I know how to blend these ingredients, my lord. The balance, as I say, must be just so..." He did a little gesture with thumb and forefinger. "Few are able to negotiate the complexities of this sort of work, but I consider myself one who can."

"And if it doesn't work?"

"Then you must look elsewhere. I am richly trained in the practice of medicine, a man of science, you understand, but given the source of the prince's inertia, you may require a more...magical solution. In that I cannot help you."

Emeric nodded. "I am aware of the limits of your expertise, Master Allabor." His eyes surveyed the chamber. "Now, these other items I brought with me. Have you had a chance to study them?"

"Ah. Yes. They are right through here, my lord." Allabor led him into a smaller adjoining office where the items and ingredients Emeric had gathered from the stormhag's lair were laid out upon an old stained hardwood table. There were pots of murky liquid, vials of swirling mist, containers with animal parts inside them; teeth and claws, feathers and scales and tufts of hair, even organs. Some the scholar plainly recognised; he had little notes written beside each on scraps of paper, describing what they were. Others were foreign to him and came without such annotation. Those accounted for a good many of the potions and elixirs that Emeric had brought to him. On each, the hag had written labels so she knew what they were, though clearly Allabor was unable to translate her words.

"I had a master of languages pay me a visit today," he said. "This stormhag of yours. Whatever this writing is, it was not something he was able to translate, leastways not off the top of his head. He took down a record of each label and returned to his offices to conduct a deeper study. I have hope he will be able to decipher the words, in time. He is a very clever man, is Quillan, very fastidious. A good friend of mine, actually. He…"

"How much time?" Emeric cut in. The old physician could go on sometimes. "I don't mean to stay here in Lakeheart any longer than I must."

"Oh." The man sounded surprised. "Does our fair city not agree with you, my lord? Most find it beautiful."

"Its beauty is not in doubt. At another time I should like to stay longer, but there is a war going on, and I have a duty to rejoin it at my earliest convenience."

"I see. Yes. Of course. You can do much to help, I would think. In the war." He fidgeted with a vial. "Though surely you would wait until your prince awakens. You would not leave without him, my lord?"

"I swore that I would bring him to safety, and I have. If he fails to awaken, I cannot be expected to sit at his bedside forever. I am a soldier, not a nursemaid."

The little man bobbed his head. He was balding, very slight and quite short as well. Grey hair hung down from his temples and the back of his head, thin and brittle. "You must do what you think best, of course. Now, where were we…" He turned again to the table. "These I know," he said, gesturing to the items with notes. "We have some unusual artefacts here, to be sure." He plucked one up, a pot filled with little black flakes, hardened and crystallised. "This is *dragon ash*, if I am not mistaken. Not something I would use in my own medicines. No. It is commonly used in mage-work and…" He flicked a hand, dismissive, "…that sort of thing." He put the pot down and chose another. "This, I believe, is the feather of a *silver-wing*. It is a very rare and exotic bird found only in the…"

"Unseen Isles," Emeric said. "I have heard of the silver-wing."

"A fellow scholar?" The man smiled at him.

"An exile. I lived in the south for over a decade, Allabor. I encountered many people from the Unseen Isles during my time there."

"But you never went to the isles yourself?"

"No, unfortunately. I never got the chance." He looked pointedly at the table. "What else do you have here?"

"Well, many things. Here, *the widowmaker's silk*. It is a spider, the widowmaker, very large. Commonly found on the Darkisle, beyond the Darkwood Pass. A silly name, I've always thought. As a man of science, it irks me."

"Let me guess. You have an issue with the 'isle' part?"

"Don't you? That landmass is a peninsular, not an island. I do not like laziness in language, Lord Manfrey."

Emeric was more forgiving. "I rather think Dark*isle* sounds better than Dark*peninsula*, Master Allabor. But I take your point." He looked at the widowmaker's silk, knowing a little about that as well. "It is said the silk is as strong as godsteel when weaved in a special loom. The people who once lived on the Darkisle would make shirts of armour out of it."

"Yes. To protect them from the giant spiders, principally." Allabor gave a chuckle. "Have you heard the riddle about the chicken and the egg, my lord?"

"The cause and effect paradox? Who hasn't." Emeric wanted to move things along. "What is that one?" He pointed randomly, and the old man turned again, lifting another small container from the table.

"This contains *dried hollowberry skin*," he explained. "It has medicinal uses, a powerful agent. I took a pinch, in fact, for that blue elixir in your grasp. It was written on the list, did you not see?" Allabor waved to another pot. "That's *lightleaf*. Some say it is from the Everwood. The Twelve Trees of Aramatia. The leaves that grow are leaves of light, imbued with the ancient power of the goddess. There is a more scientific explanation, I'm sure."

"Of course," said Emeric, humouring the old man.

"Allegedly, lightleaf allows a man to see in the dark, but only when ground into a powder and mixed in the right measure of water. And the water must be the right temperature, of course. Too warm and nothing. Too cold and nothing. Too much and nothing. Too little and…"

"Nothing?" Emeric ventured.

Allabor smiled. "Quite. Such is the case in the brewing of potions, my lord, both magical and medicinal. It is a field with a thousand pitfalls. One wrong step and you go tumbling, never to regain your feet." His thin fingers poked out for another pot, and on he went, talking of this item and that: the tooth of a drovara, bovidor droppings, slime of a slytherak, an eyelash from a deep-sea mermaid. He picked out one little pot and raised it up reverentially. "Now *this*…well this is very special." It was a small pot, heavily bound up in layers of leather and linen from bottom to top, yet all the same Emeric could see the great golden light shining from within.

"Yes. I did wonder about that one," he said. "The light inside. What is it?"

"Well, there is always the small possibility that I am wrong…*small*, you understand…but I do believe this is the core of a fallen star."

"A fallen star?"

"An exceptionally rare element," Allabor explained. "And exceedingly hard to capture. You see, there are other worlds above our own, my lord, hidden beyond the sky. On occasion, a fragment of a passing star may come hurtling down from the heavens at tremendous speed, forming a crater where it lands. The rock that is left is astonishingly hot, far too hot for a man to handle until it has taken a long time to cool. But herein lies the issue. The core is found *within* that rock, you see, and the heat and the light are connected. As the rock cools, so the light of the core begins to fade. A man must break open the rock quickly before this happens. The quicker he does so, the brighter and long-lasting the light. And if done very earlier, the light may be inexhaustible."

He held the pot up again, smiling as he admired it. "This requires luck, of course. You must be in the right place at the right time. There is no knowing when or where a star will fall, and it happens very rarely, perhaps once every half century or so. There is also the matter of getting close enough to break it open. Not easily done for a common man. Oft as not, magic-users are the only ones capable. Individuals able to harness sorcery to protect themselves, like your stormhag. A fully armoured Bladeborn knight may also be able to achieve this. Or a rich-blooded Fireborn, better able to handle the heat."

He handed the jar to Emeric. "Now you must be careful with that, my lord. You see the linen? You see the leather? Your stormhag was wise to wrap it up so thoroughly; when unleashed, the light will be so strong as to make everything white and gold, blinding to mortal eyes. Only the very powerful can look upon it without averting their gaze. And this one…it would seem the *soul* was harvested early. The light may very well have been shining for centuries already."

Emeric frowned. "Soul?"

"A poetic flourish. Some call the core of the star its soul, or its spirit. I prefer not to myself, for the most part. It makes it seem rather more barbaric, does it not, breaking open a heavenly rock and ripping out its dying soul."

"Yes, I suppose it does." Emeric studied it a moment. Even with all those wrappings the light pulsed and beat against the glass and fabric, as though eager to escape. "What use could it have? This inexhaustible light? Other than being a very reliable lamp."

Master Allabor smiled. "You jest, my lord, but there is truth in what you say. There is a tale I know. Of an old southron warlord who suspended such a core high above the city over which he ruled. He reigned for a dozen years of day, they say, and never once was there a night." His lips betrayed him, flickering into a grin.

"I think it's you who is jesting, Allabor. Come now, tell me of its uses."

The old man returned to business. "In truth, these cores are typically used in sorcery. The brewing of potions and spells. Very powerful ones, of course. But as I've said, it isn't my field. Still, a fascinating item."

He smiled and turned his attention back to the table. "The rest… well, I could guess at what some of these elixirs are, but I would prefer to wait for Master Quillon's report. If he can decipher your stormhag's speech, we may find something that can revive the prince. An antidote, so to speak. That is assuming my tonic does not work, of course."

The exile smiled. "We can only hope." He tucked the blue vial into a pocket, already knowing it wouldn't work. "These items, then. Will they be useful to you?"

"Some will, yes. Others…" He shook his head. "They'd be better served in the hands of a mage or woods witch. I would be happy to take them off you, however. Circulate them as best fits their needs?"

"I will think about it," Emeric said. "And await your friend the language master's report. There may be tonics here that will prove useful when I ride back to war." He gave the fallen star a passing look. "And that I will take as well." The notion that it could blind mortal men was of interest to him. *Good in a pinch*, he thought. 'If surrounded, remove the wrapping and shut your eyes.' Maybe that's what the stormhag had written on its label? *And if not, I'll release it anyway.* No soul should be trapped in a jar, so far as Emeric Manfrey was concerned.

Allabor seemed disappointed. "Are you certain, my lord? It's such a rare item, and…"

"And your chambers are bright enough. You do not need an ever-lasting lamp, Master Allabor."

He forced himself to smile. "Very well. I will keep everything safe for you here, Lord Manfrey. Until such a time as you leave the city."

"See that you do, Allabor. I will return later to check in on Sir Ernold. Good day."

His escort was waiting outside the physician's chambers, ready to lead the exiled lord up through the tower. He held a torch before him as they twisted up the narrow turnpike stair, reaching a thick wooden door that led out onto an open walkway. The breeze was stiff outside, gusting from the east where the Big Sister sprawled in all her vast enormity. It was a dim day, the light poor. "It's wavy out there," Emeric noted.

"Always is these days, my lord. Always raining. Always windy." Sir Stafford was a dour fellow, a once-lowly Fullerton man-at-arms who'd been recently raised to knight. His cloak was white and showed a grey tower rising between three lakes, each in a different shade of blue, the sigil of the lord who'd anointed him. In his grasp was a long white spear that he liked to tap on the ground as he went, as though he was an old wizard with a staff.

Emeric had heard many stories from him. Stafford had been present at the Battle of the Bane and formed part of the retinue that rushed Lord Fullerton back to Lakeheart when he suffered life-threatening burns. That threat had not quite led to his death, however. Somehow the toadish Lord of Lakeheart had survived, albeit with terrible scarring across much of his body and breathing problems that kept him abed, wheezing all day and night. When Emeric met him, he wondered if death would have been better.

Still, Fullerton had been strong enough to climb out of his bed for long enough to lay a sword on Stafford's shoulder, thus knighting him Sir Stafford of the Bane. The name did not sit well with the man, Emeric had found. "I didn't do much, in truth," he'd confessed to him. "Not during the battle, anyway. Only after, when we got Lord Fullerton to safety." He'd shrugged. "He was delirious, from all the pain, but every time he woke up it just happened that I was the one beside him. It's like he thinks I got him back here alone, m'lord, but I didn't. There were lots of us. But he only honoured me."

"Then honour him back," Emeric had responded. "By becoming the best knight you can be."

Those words had sat with the man since, he knew. It was hard to be a great knight here, with little to do but watch over a dying man in his castle. *But out there?*

"How long does Lord Fullerton intend to keep you in his service, Sir Stafford?" Emeric asked him now, as they crossed from one tower to the next. Below, in the castle yard, a few old men were engaged in some training drills with sword and spear and a pair of archers who looked no older than fourteen were firing arrows at butts, and poorly. It was about all that remained of the sorry garrison here at Three-Lake Keep. "Would he release you if you asked him?"

"Asked him to…"

"To release you, Sir Stafford." The man was rather slow sometimes. "So you can win some glory of your own."

"Glory, m'lord? No…I…m'lord's protection comes first. That's why he raised me up. To protect him. If the war comes here…"

"It won't. Not after what happened at Rustbridge."

Emeric had heard at last of how the battle had ended when he reached Lakeheart some days ago. How the Agarathi and their allies had been driven back from the river, how they were broken, scattered, and fleeing south…as Borrus Kanabar hunted them down.

Emeric had smiled to hear the news. *The Lord of Rivers still lives, then.* Of the rest of his friends he knew but little. There were rumours that the heirs of House Amadar and House Oloran had fought valiantly, and word was spreading of the Warrior Woman of Rasalan who could only be Lady Marian Payne. It seemed Lord Rammas might have fallen…or not - it was hard to know for sure with all the conflicting rumours and reports - and Emeric had heard nothing of Torvyn or Mooton or the Blackshaws, nothing of the Silent Suncoat or Turner's men, Jack and Brax and the rest.

I will when I ride back to join them, he told himself. He was growing restless now, even after only a few short days in the city. But eager as he was to rejoin the fight, Allabor had the right of it. He would prefer to do so with Prince Raynald beside him. And Ernold too. To deliver the leader of the Tukoran forces back to his men, healed and hardy and ready to fight once more.

Sir Stafford of the Bane was deep in thought. When he reached the door leading into the Sapphire Tower, he paused to scratch his nose. A crooked thing it was; Stafford was not much to look at, in truth, with a paunch of belly and brutish brow and an unruly shock of brown hair. "You really don't think it's going to come here, m'lord?" he asked. "The war, I mean. I know people are saying it, but if the Agarathi rally, then…"

"Then they will rally elsewhere. Most likely at Dragon's Bane, where you made your name." He looked at him, saw the man dip his eyes. "I aim to ride from here as soon as I'm able, Sir Stafford. When I do, I hope to gather strong men to ride with me. I would like it if you were one of them."

"Me, m'lord? But, my oaths…to Lord Fullerton. I'm the only knight here now, in the keep. If I go…"

He's going to die anyway, Emeric thought. In a week, in a month, in a year, it didn't matter. Lord Fullerton's days were numbered. He wondered if he was dealing with a man of iron duty in Sir Stafford… or a coward. He couldn't yet be sure. "That is for you to decide," he said to him. "There is every chance Lord Fullerton will release you if you ask him." He would push the man on it no further. Turning the handle himself, Emeric stepped into the tower, the castle's central keep, and made at once for the stairs. The exile had been given private quarters toward the top, a floor below the prince.

It was the prince's rooms they made for. Two guards stood outside, both under oath to protect him. One was very young, the other very old and neither looked comfortable in their armour. *These are the dregs at the bottom of the cup,* Emeric thought, as he waved for them to open the door.

"M'lord, you'd best know…"

"Yes." Emeric turned on the older man.

"I tried to get rid o' them, I did, but it's like trying to herd cats with that lot. None o' them would listen to me, m'lord. They mean no harm, but…"

"They? And who are they?"

"The maids, m'lord. And serving girls. They all came barging in at once and we tried to stop 'em, didn't we Badge?" The younger man nodded. "We tried, m'lord, but…"

Emeric had heard enough. "Open the door. Now."

The door was opened and Emeric saw them; perhaps a dozen girls, most of them young, were all crowding about the prince's bed, giggling. Through the bustle, Emeric spied one right up beside the prince, not just by the bed but *on* it with him. She was crouching over him, brushing the wavy hair from his forehead, leaning down as though to kiss him…

Emeric cleared his throat. "Just what are you all doing in here?"

The girls spun at once, saw him, and scattered. Some rushed back to their duties as though nothing had happened. Others hurtled past him and out into the corridor, sniggering as they went. The girl on the bed was so mortified she went stumbling onto the floor as she tried to flee, hit her head on a bedpost, and two of her friends had to help her up. Only one of the gaggle had the gumption to answer.

"We thought it might help him, m'lord," she said, swaggering over and giving a little curtsy. She was young, pretty in a lowborn way, and had a coquettish way about her, a naughty way. "Dalabelle said if we kissed him he might wake up. He's our sleeping beauty, m'lord. There are tales of it. Princes in deep sleeps awoken by a kiss. Would only take one of us, Dala said. But we wouldn't know which unless we tried, so all of us had to have a go."

One of the other girls glared over and *shushed* her. *Dalabelle, no doubt.* "Nice try," Emeric said to the girl. "Would you do the same if he was ugly?"

She grinned at him. There was a small gap between her front teeth. "For a prince, we'd do anything, m'lord. But better that he's handsome. And he does have very nice lips." She ran a tongue over her own. "I should know."

The girl was so brazen he was almost impressed. "I'm glad you had your fun," he told her. "Now go. All of you. Sir Stafford, clear them out."

The man stepped up. "Right, you lot. Out, right now!" He began marching around the room, waving and herding them away through the door. Most scampered off quickly enough, though the girl who'd spoken took her time, smirking all the while and then swaying from the room in that swaggery way she had.

This place lacks leadership, Emeric reflected, as it was done. Such was only natural with Lord Fullerton laid low and so many of his knights and captains either dead, wounded, or away at war. It left the castle spare of proper fighting men and the women now ruled the roost. *Small wonder these girls go about as they please,* he thought. *Their numbers are overwhelming and the remaining men are weak.*

"They're all gone, m'lord," Sir Stafford told him. "Unless there's one hiding in the closet."

"Do check for me." He wanted to be sure.

He did. "No one, m'lord."

"That girl. The one I spoke to. What's her name?"

"That's Liza, m'lord. She's the kennel master's daughter."

"A confident girl."

"Yes, m'lord. Very much. Can be awful persuasive, that one."

"I would sooner you found men to guard the prince who were not so susceptible to those persuasions, Stafford. I cannot be having this again, do you understand me?"

"Yes, m'lord. Loud and clear. I'll talk to them."

"See that you do."

The man paused. "Now, m'lord?"

"Yes, now."

The knight left at once, stamping outside to administer the required scolding. Alone now, Emeric stepped over to Raynald's bedside and drew out the blue liquid vial. It would be their fourth attempt in as many days and would soon become their fourth failure, he knew. Each effort by Master Allabor raised the intensity of the tonic yet none had caused but the smallest stir.

Still, it was worth a try. Gently tipping back the prince's head, he opened his mouth and poured the contents of the vial right in. It slid easily down his throat. He pulled him up and plumped his pillows, set him down and waited. Nothing. Perhaps he wiggled his little toe or… *there, was that the smallest flicker in the eye?* Emeric did not sigh or shake his head or make any gesture to show his disappointment. He had never expected it to work.

Sir Stafford of the Bane re-entered the room. "M'lord, I've given them both a firm talking to. They promise they won't let Liza or the others in again."

Emeric nodded. "If they do, dismiss them. I cannot have all and sundry allowed into this room."

"Yes, m'lord."

Emeric drew the bed curtains to cover the prince and stepped away toward the balcony doors. It was windier up here than it had been on the walkway below, and the views were far-ranging. The balcony wrapped halfway around the tower, giving a view of all three lakes depending on where you stood. Each lake was a different shade of blue. The Big Sister was storm-blue, the Young Sister a bright cerulean, the Little Sister was closer to the colour of slate. Near the shore of each lake ran the city walls, shaped into a great triangle; each wall was painted to reflect the colour of the lake it faced. Between those walls sprawled the city itself. Lakeheart was not a tall city and had few great towers and forts, but it was broad. Filling the space between the three sisters, it spread far and wide, with many stone buildings painted in shades of white and grey and blue and large squares with bustling fish markets and holy houses to the gods.

There were three roads that led to Lakeheart. From the east, running between the Young Sister to the north and the Little Sister to the south was the Midsister Road, the path Emeric had raced along for a day and the best part of a night in a bid to save Ernold Esterling's life. He had reached the city just in time, Master Allabor had told him; another few hours and Esterling would have been beyond saving.

North went the Lakeland Way, between the Young Sister to its west and the Big Sister to its east. That road was branched, Emeric knew. From the city it ran northward up to the border at Tukor's Pass, but also eastward around the Big Sister and down the coast into the Marshlands. The same was true of the Mudway, which came up from the south between the sisters little and big. The main road ran through the Marshlands and all the way west toward Rustbridge. But along its route an offshoot branched up between the lakes as well. It was *that* road that Emeric Manfrey intended to take when he left, the road that would take him south, and back to the war.

He looked that way now; south toward the Mudway, south toward the war. Below, the city hummed and buzzed like a nest of far-off wasps, chaotic and thronging with a heaving population of refugees, but up here all was quiet. Emeric had not yet been into the city, not since the day he rode through it to reach Lord Fullerton's keep. In the days since he'd been here, with the prince and Sir Ernold Esterling, waiting for them to come around. But now…

"Tell me, Sir Stafford. Do you know of any mages here in Lakeheart?"

"Mages, m'lord?"

They should have named him Stafford the Slow. "Yes, mages. Those gifted in the magical arts."

The knight scratched his crooked nose. "Not that I know of, m'lord. There's a witch, though. Lives in some den down on the Big Sister side. People *say* she's a witch, anyway. Might just be because she's old and ugly." He shrugged, armour clanking.

"I would like to meet her," Emeric said.

"You…? Right now, m'lord?"

"I'm not doing anything else, Stafford." He had little hope this so-called witch would be of much help, but he could do with taking a walk all the same, giving his legs a stretch. "Come. Do you know the way?"

"I think so, m'lord. She lurks in some undercroft near the *Leviathan*. That's a statue, m'lord. Of Palaphan. People call it the Leviathan, though. It's in the old fish market down there. Not far from the Mudway Gate."

Emeric was already turning. "Take me," he said.

41

Jonik

The statue was old and cracked, the once-white stone gone brown and grey.

It rose from the centre of the hectic market square as though breaching above the water, twisting as it leapt, with splashing waves carved beneath it. Jonik should liked to have seen it when it had first been sculpted, before time and the work of wind and rain had worn the fine detail away. Now it was old and half in ruin, and some parts of it were missing: a dorsal fin, a large chunk from the tail, a section of its lower jaws.

Still, it seemed popular. As Jonik stepped closer through the filthy crowds he saw that many people were gathered about its broad stone base, looking at the writing scrawled into the stone. They were names, he realised. Hundreds, maybe even thousands of them, many with messages of love written beneath them. Some people were weeping. Others had flowers with them, in simple bundles and more elaborate wreaths, and were laying them up against the plinth.

"They died on the lake," a man said beside him.

Jonik turned. "I'm sorry?"

"The names." He gestured to the stone base. "They all died out there on the Big Sister." He was wrapped against the chill in a rich blue woollen cloak, an old man of short stature, lean of body and seamed of face. He wore a neat barbered beard on his chin, grey with streaks of white that contrasted well with his tan, leathery skin. His eyes were keen and his voice refined. "Most drowned during storms or were killed by sharks and sister serpents. People come here to remember them."

That explains the weeping and the wreaths. "Sister serpents?" Jonik hadn't heard of them before.

"They're like sea serpents," the old man said. "Only those found here in the lakes. So we call them sister serpents. We get them mostly in the Big Sister, though sometimes the Young Sister too." He pointed toward the names. "I lost a brother to one. And a cousin. Had a nephew go missing out on the water as well, though we don't know what happened to him. Might be a sister serpent sucked him down as well." He shrugged, as though he was long past caring. "Is it your first time in Lakeheart?"

Jonik nodded. "I arrived this morning."

"I see. Did you come in with some of them?" He gestured to the expanding population of refugees sprawled out all over the square. Some had come up from the Marshlands, by the look of them, though most were from smaller villages and towns around the lakes, like the ones where Jonik had camped the night on his journey here.

"I'm only passing through," was his answer. "I'll be going north as soon as possible."

"Back home?" the man asked. "You're Tukoran. I can tell from the accent." He looked across the square. "Well, perhaps you would be so kind as to take some of these others with you when you go? Half ought to do it. But if you can manage more…" He smiled, to hide his bitterness. "I've got nothing against them personally. Please don't misunderstand me. It's just the numbers. Once before this was a thriving fish market. Now the shelters outnumber the stalls by a hundred to one and food, well…food is becoming a real problem."

You don't have to tell me. Jonik's struggles in that regard were far from over and he'd decided to pass through Lakeheart for that very reason. "How many were there before?"

"Stalls? Oh, at least a hundred. And that was on a slow day. Often there were many more. I had several myself, as many as ten when the catch was good…I'm a fishmonger by trade, you see. Or *was*, before the lakes dried up."

"The lakes seem plenty wet to me."

"Apologies. I was speaking metaphorically. I meant dried-up of *fish*, not water." A sad sigh slipped through his lips. "See here…" He directed Jonik's attention to the statue's base, where a girl of about thirteen was scrawling a fresh name into the stone while her younger sisters and mother stood by weeping. "A sorry sight, but one that's all too common these days. Most years we might lose two dozen or so to the lake, but these days it's hard to keep up. Every day when I come by I see new names scratched into the stone. You can always tell by how white the markings are. See the older ones, they're grey, but the new ones are always white."

Jonik supposed there must be more sharks and sister snakes out there than ever before. When he put that forward, the man gave another solemn sigh. "Yes. Sharks, snakes, *storms*. It's always stormy on the lakes these days and half the fishing cogs that go out never come back. And even when they do, the catch is typically poor. I've lost three boats myself in as many months. And three dozen good men with them." He turned his head and grimaced. "Listen to that? Do you hear the prices they're calling out?"

It was loud in the old fish market, loud and unruly, and there was something in the air Jonik didn't like. Tension. Like a rope pulled too tight, fraying and threatening to snap. Cloaked groups prowled about with their hoods up against the drizzle and he glimpsed weapons hanging from belts and straps, axes and blunts and blades. *Hunger*, he thought. *It can make a man wild and dangerous.*

Through the din, several louder voices spoke up as the few remaining fishmongers called out their catch. "A silver spear for a pot of pickled herring," one man shouted. Another, in competition, bellowed louder. "A clay and five copper scythes. You won't get a better deal than that!" A third was offering fish one at a time, charging half a silver clay for a big cod and ten copper sickles for a small one. Eels were being sold, lamprey at exorbitant cost. The shark fin soup was eyewatering and not because of the taste. A few other sellers had only whitebait and minnows on offer, collected in buckets and barrels. "A copper for a minnow," one was hawking. "Just one copper a minnow. Won't find 'em cheaper nowhere else!"

"These prices are absurd," Jonik snorted. "How can anyone afford to eat?"

"They can't. That's the point. Not unless they're rich. I'll wager frog-faced Fullerton's doing just fine locked up in his castle, but he doesn't seem to care about his smallfolk." He shook his head. "I've got nothing against these poor people coming to the city where it's safe, but the numbers have to be managed. Every good waterman knows that it's folly to overload a raft at sea, but there's no sense left in this city now." He sighed in lament. "That frog-faced fool is going to drown us all."

Jonik frowned. "I thought Lord Fullerton was dead."

"No. Just badly burned. Part of me wishes he *was* dead, though. Terrible as that is to say."

"Why? Is he hoarding all the food, or…"

"He decreed everyone be allowed into the city. That the gates be opened for them to come flooding in here, no questions asked. A noble decree, you might call it, but an imprudent one as well. I went to the castle myself to try to talk to him about it, but he wouldn't see me. I was told he was abed, still sick from his burns, and there are rumours he's half delirious. Mayhaps that explains his ruling and lack of foresight? And his unwillingness to rescind the order." He seemed a deep-feeling man, this old fishmonger. "Tell me. Which gate did you enter through this morning?"

"The Midsister Gate."

"And were you checked on entry? Searched?"

"No." He'd been delighted with that himself, though understood it wasn't a sensible policy. "There didn't seem to be many soldiers. Not at the gate or on the walls. Are they all away at war?"

"Many are, yes. Lord Fullerton and Lord Shorton mustered many men when they went to Dragon's Bane to serve under the Lord of Rivers. A good many of them perished during the battle. Those who didn't continued to serve under their own captains when the army regathered at Oakpike Castle. Only a few returned; those who brought Lord Fullerton back here, principally. And now there has been battle again. An even greater one, or so it's said."

"At Rustbridge?" Jonik asked, eagerly.

"Yes. A great fierce battle on the plains and by the river. Much of the woodland to the east caught aflame; it could be seen from the Hooded Hills, they say. And the fortress as well."

"But not the city?"

"I believe the city went largely unharmed."

"The Agarathi…they were defeated, then?"

"Ah. But what is defeat, young man? What is victory?" He made a face like he was some sage old scholar. "Tens of thousands perished on the battlefield, we're hearing. On both sides. Can it be called victory to one just because the other flees, when they lose so many good men?"

"Yes," Jonik said. He was not interested in this old man's philosophical reflections on war. "If the enemy host was forced into a retreat then it is considered a victory."

"Yes, well…you'll forgive me for not seeing things in such simple terms. The glory of war fails to stir my spirit, as it does others. All that death and destruction…"

"Tell me what else you know. Is our army still gathered at Rustbridge?"

"Not that I have heard. Though reports do tend to clash, as I'm sure you understand. There is little reliable information coming from the south, only rumour and unqualified word. Most agree that the enemy forces broke eventually, however. And that the new Lord of Rivers is commanding a chase."

The new Lord of Rivers. Jonik had to laugh. *Well, Borrus, you got what you wanted in the end. Battle and blood and a great army of your own.* He wondered what had come of the others. Emeric and Torvyn and Mooton, Turner and Brax and Jack and the rest, Sansullio and his Sunshine Swords, the Silent Suncoat and the Blackshaws too. All had abandoned Jonik at the Shadowfort half a lifetime ago, and he'd lost Harden since, and now Gerrin and Sir Owen Armdall as well, leaving him all alone. *I was meant to be a leader,* he thought. *The Nightblade said so, when it squirmed into my dreams…*

But it was never meant to be so, and those days were long behind him. What had come of his friends he couldn't say. Had Harden left and gone for help when they didn't emerge from the depths? Were Gerrin and Owen still trapped down there? Were his other companions among the dead at Rustbridge? He wondered about Shade as well. He wondered if one of the men had ridden him into battle and the thought of it made him cringe. *He was never meant to be a warhorse. If ever I see him again, I'm going to set him free…*

The old man was going on. "A great host of your own partook in the battle as well," he said. "Thirty thousand of them, under the command of Raynald Lukar." He scratched at his neat grey beard, frowning.

"Though, one report I heard did suggest that the prince had perished, I do fear to tell you. Along with Lord Rammas of the Marshes. Though another…" He gave a bemused chuckle. "A fanciful thing, but there's a rumour circulating that Prince Raynald is in fact *here*, if you would believe it. In Three-Lake Keep. Someone recognised him, apparently. He was brought here wounded some four, five days ago. Or so they say."

Jonik couldn't understand why the prince would be here, so far from the battle. "Do you believe it?" he asked the old man.

"Me? No. It doesn't quite add up the way I see it, but you know how these rumours start. Idle minds, and all that. I daresay…"

Jonik did not hear what the man dared to say. A noise interrupted him, a high-pitched wail that pierced the din of the square. Jonik looked over at once. A fight had broken out at one of the fish stalls as someone took umbrage with the prices. Jonik spied a silver blade, the flash of blood. A cloaked man was staggering back, clutching at his stomach as a taller, bigger man loomed over him wearing armour, leather and steel. He swung his sword across the crowd. "Stay back!" he was bellowing. "Stay back or I'll cut you all!"

The wounded man was dragged away by two friends. Others did not back down. From nowhere, a stone went pinging into the guard's halfhelm, careening away into the throng. A woman screamed and a child nearby started crying. "Who threw that!" demanded the guard. "Stay back, I say!" He swished his blade nervously. "Stay back!"

He was a hired sword, a man paid to watch the stalls and make sure no thievery took place. Each stall had at least two of three such guardsmen standing by, Jonik had seen. But of official soldiers and city guards, he saw none. *This place is lawless*, he thought. He'd seen that when he first entered through the Midsister Gate, wandering in without checks or questions and no one seemed to care. The fishmonger hadn't been wrong there. The walls were poorly manned, the gates wide open, and this was not the first violence he'd seen either. Earlier, a brawl had broken out over a heel of bread as he passed through another square and he'd seen two women grappling on the ground in an alleyway as well, scratching and ripping at each other's faces, even biting one another he had seen. They were feral, wild, fighting like cats in the streets. Here in the market, it stank of fish and sweat and piss and rot, of the soiled reek of the unwashed in their crude lean-tos and tents. But earlier, he'd smelled *death*. There were corpses down some alleyways, he knew, thrown down where they were slain. Over what, he could not say for sure, but food seemed a likely thing.

He was smelling death again now. It was ripe in the air, the promise of it. "Stay there," he told the old fishmonger, in a low voice. "Do not leave my side."

"What…why? I don't…"

"Just stay there. These cobbles are going to get bloody."

The guard was still bellowing and waving his sword, but no one was backing down. Jonik could see those cloaked men prowling, encircling him. There were more of them, too, at the other stalls. A febrile energy spread across the square, thick with the threat of violence. *Any second now,* he thought.

"Back!" the guard raged. "Get back I say! I warn you! Back!" He turned his head, looking for support. There had been another guard with him, but his fellow was gone, slinking away like a snake in the grass. "Back!" He swung back around, swiping his blade from left to right. "Don't come any closer, or…"

Two men rushed him at once. He roared, slashing at one, hacking him diagonally open at the chest, but the other was on him in an instant. He was a weak ragged man, half-starved to death. The guard swivelled to one side as the man tried to spear him, pushed him away and pressed the tip of his blade through his back. A voice screamed, and the crowd pulsed and suddenly a dozen more were charging upon him. One moment the guard was swinging his blade, bellowing, and the next he was gone, trampled and overwhelmed, as Jonik saw the daggers and dirks rising and falling. After that, it was a free-for-all. Not just at that stall, but at the rest of them as well. The guards at each pulled their blades and started hacking wildly as a dozen others, two, three dozen starving men drew weapons from their cloaks and charged.

The fishmonger beside Jonik made a squeaking sound. "What on earth…what are they…no! No, they must *stop!*"

And who's going to stop them? More were joining in, the violence spreading; the whole square was erupting into chaos. He saw one of the fishmongers spin and run in an attempt to flee, but several men gave chase, hacking at him with axes. Another of the vendors climbed desperately up onto his stall, knocking buckets and casks of fish aside and clinging onto a support post, screaming. A muscular man in a leather apron came up behind him, grabbed his cloak and pulled him down into the throng; Jonik saw a blacksmith's hammer rise and fall and the screaming ended abruptly.

"Stop," the old man was weeping. "They have to stop. Stop!"

It won't stop, Jonik thought. *It has only just begun.*

Within what felt like ten or twenty heartbeats there was blood and carnage everywhere, from one side of the square to the other. The fishmongers were being hacked up and hunted, their guards overwhelmed by the starving hordes. Even their customers were being targeted and chased down as they screamed and ran. Old men and women in fine coats with guards of their own were being butchered and slaughtered for a few measly fish. The stalls were collapsing in the crush as the smallfolk swarmed like ravening rats, snatching up whatever they could. Jonik saw men feasting and ripping on raw cod with their brown rotten teeth, saw them opening their mouths like pelicans and throwing down handfuls of minnows to swallow them whole. Others were scrambling on the floor, gorging on whatever they could find, crawling about amid mud and blood in their desperate search for food. It was chaotic, feral. A crazed frenzy had gripped them all.

The old man was blubbering at his side. "I know these people. They are good people...friends..." He seized Jonik by the arm, as though begging him to help. "You must do something. You must....you must..."

He hasn't seen death like me, Jonik thought, seeing the tears streaming from the old man's eyes. He forgot sometimes how harrowing this must be for ordinary men. The blood and filth and screams and shouts, the sounds men made when they were hacked apart and killed. It was as familiar to Jonik as the cold kiss of the wind. He felt nothing standing there. No fear, no dread. Nothing.

"Please, *do* something. You have to do something." The old man was tugging at him desperately. "Please!"

Jonik looked down at him. *He has friends here. He is known.* The old man's garb was rich, and he'd spoken of his wealth. *The stalls, the boats. This old fishmonger fears for his life.*

Jonik saw an opportunity in that. "Where do you live?" he asked, keeping his voice perfectly calm.

The fishmonger blinked at him. "I...I'm off...up near the harbour. The Big Harbour. On the..."

"Big Sister?" Jonik guessed. *No doubt there's a Little Harbour and a Young Harbour around here too.*

The fighting was spreading out toward the lanes and alleys branching off the square. Big men were carrying off whole casks of pickled herring, swatting anyone aside as they came near. Jonik saw one smack down a child to crack his head on the cobbles. Another had a bloody sickle in his hand and was swinging out and cutting at anyone who got too close. A pack of street children went about with little blades and stabbing tools. He saw a boy no older than eight chase down one of the cask-wielders, jabbing at the back of his calf to send him sprawling. The big man bellowed and tried to stand, but the pack was on him at once, swarming and stabbing with their crude little blades at neck and ribs and into the back of his head.

Gods, Jonik thought. This was getting too much, even for him. He spoke to the old man again. "Stay close to me and I'll get you home," he said. "Which way is it to the harbour?"

The man barely seemed to hear him. He was looking left, looking right, in mute shock at all the violence.

Jonik took his shoulder. "Focus now. Which way to the harbour?"

"The...the harbour...?"

"Your home. I will get you safely home, but I want something in return." He opened his cloak to show him. The man's eyes went wet as they saw the misting godsteel, the armour and the blades, Mother's Mercy at one hip and the Mistblade at the other, wrapped up to hide its godly blue light.

"You're...you're Bladeborn?"

"Yes. What gave it away?" Jonik gave an easy smile to show him he was in good hands. So far as he could tell, he was the only Bladeborn in the square. "Now, which way? Show me and I will lead you home."

"It's…it's there…" He raised a shaking finger and gestured across the square. There was a good deal of fighting going on that way, Jonik saw.

"Is there another route?"

"Yes…Blackfin. It's a lane, over yonder…" He pointed it out, toward a slighter quieter side of the market. "We can circle around."

"The bargain first," Jonik said.

"Yes…yes. What do you want?"

"Food," he said. "And somewhere to rest for the night." He guessed this wealthy old fishmonger would be able to provide him with both. "In exchange for safe passage."

"Yes…of course. Anything you need."

"Food and rest will suffice." He paused. "And perhaps a new cloak. Do you have one that will fit me? Mine has seen better days, as you can probably tell. And smell."

The man gaped at him as though he was mad. *He wonders how I can be so calm. Well, I could tell you where I came from, old man, but it'd only give you nightmares.* At last he stammered, "Yes…a cloak, yes. I will find one for you. Any cloak you want."

Jonik paused to think if he needed anything else, but there was nothing that came to mind. "Lead on, then, and stay right beside me."

Across bloody cobbles and corpses, they went.

42

Ranulf

"Spiders," Sir Mallister shouted. "In the trees. They're coming."

Old Gunter cursed and spat. "*Godsdamnit!*" He ripped his blade from its sheath and held it up two-handed. "Knew they'd come for us eventually." The others were doing the same, forming a tight circle, back to back, facing outward. Ranulf was in the middle, defenceless as a declawed kitten.

"If they come near, cut them down," Mallister called out. "And watch for their fangs. They're venomous."

"Venemous?" Gunter groaned. "No one ever said nothing about venomous!"

The spiders were skittering down from the branches, knocking off clumps of snow as they came. They were big and black with red stripes down their bulbous bodies, sometimes one stripe, sometimes two, and each had hoarfrost glittering on the hair of its legs. Ranulf peeked past the men's shoulders to watch as the widowmakers went from branch to branch, leaping and scrabbling, crawling down the trunks. There were many of them, dozens, too many to count. An excited sound of chittering filled the forest as they finally made their move.

"Eight-legged freaks!" Rufford bellowed. He swung his blade as a spider came pouncing from a branch, splitting it in two. Thick blueish blood and entrails tumbled and splashed down upon them.

"Don't get it in your eyes!" Monsort called. "It'll blind you!"

Simcock spat out. "Tastes foul too." There was blue blood smeared across his lips and trailing down into his long brown beard. "Damn it, Rufford, you need to cut it in half like that?"

"Too violent for you, was it?" Rufford said, laughing. "You just wait for our brawl."

"This is no time for japing," Sir Mallister said. "Split them, behead them, gut them, I don't care. Just kill them! Kill them all!"

And the spiders came. From the branches above they came, and across the forest floor. Their too-many eyes gleamed hungrily and venom dripped from their three-inch fangs. The men swung and hacked and stamped as Ranulf stood impotent behind their backs. Being the relatively short man he was, the viewing was somewhat poor, but he could hear well enough what was going on by the soundtrack of screaming spiders and bellowing men. After a few minutes of furious noise and motion several dozen of the creatures were dead and the ground was no longer white, but black and blue, covered in blood and gore and twitching bodies.

An impasse ensued. "They're hanging back," Darron called out. "Look, m'lord, they're figuring some new plan."

"You give them too much credit," grunted Gunter. "They're *spiders*. Ain't got the wit to make a plan."

It did *seem* as though they were, though. The chittering changed, turning from excited to subdued, as though they were working things out. "They're afraid," Sir Mallister declared. "That's all it is. *Fear*." He took a pace away from the circle and swung his eyes around. "Ranulf, which way? I've lost my bearings in this fog."

Ranulf shut his eyes, focusing, and the world *changed*. Kamcho was circling high above them, up above the soaring treetops where the winds were blowing fiercely. It was gusty up there, and the sky was bleak and smothered, the light like dusk though it was not yet midday. He could barely see anything through the eagle's eyes. All was mist and ice and snow, grey and white.

"Ranulf? Come, which way?"

"I don't know. I can barely see anything."

"It's this wood," said Simcock. "This fog, it's *unnatural*."

"How are we gonna find the tree?" asked Alyn. There was a panic starting to edge into their voices now. "It's white, the ice oak, but *all* the trees are white in this snow…"

"We'll know when we see it," Sir Mallister said.

"But how? We'd have to get close before we do. All the fog and snow and…"

"We'll know," the knight repeated, firmly. "We'll feel it. Find it. We *have* to." He narrowed his eyes and scanned the trees. "We keep going. Away from the tracks we've made. Stay tight together and watch the branches." He led them on. The rest of the men followed behind him, their blades brandished outward. They moved like some eight-quilled porcupine with Ranulf Shackton snug in the middle. "Away with you. Away!" Sir Mallister swished his blade as they neared the spiders, driving them back. Heaps of snow fell from above them as more of the critters crawled through the canopy, following. "Back! We have no quarrel with you! You'll make no widows here! Back!"

The spiders clicked and chittered, moving with them. More seemed to be gathering, black shadows with red stripes massing and grouping and stalking. "There's so many," fretted Darron. "If they all come at once…"

"Then they'll die at once." Mallister Monsort was in a defiant mood, a hard mood. "Ranulf, how fast can you run?"

The question took him off guard. "I'm not Bladeborn," was his answer. Bladeborn could move at great speed depending on the strength of their blood-bond. That was not the case for Rasalanian adventurers with a few drops of Elder blood.

He saw Monsort's head go up and down, pondering something. "We might be able to outrun them. If we stretch a lead maybe they'll give up and move off."

"Or we'll run into some ravine," said Simcock. "Fog's too thick. We'd never see it coming. And there's rocks and roots under all this snow."

"Do you have a better idea?" the knight demanded.

"Maybe we go back," said Darron. "Back to camp. Try again tomorrow."

"No."

"My lord? Might be clearer tomorrow. This fog's killing us. Not even Kamcho can find this tree, so how are the rest of us to…"

"We press on," Mallister Monsort said, belligerent. "We're three hours from camp. The tree must be close. It's in this wood somewhere. The map said so."

"This wood is cursed," said Rufford. "I can feel it in my bones." He looked around. "We're in the heart of it here, and it's a black heart make no mistake. Maybe…"

"No." The knight didn't even let him finish. "It's a forest, untamed and unlived in for centuries. So the creatures have crawled here, thrived here. That's all it is." He glared out at the widowmakers as they went. Clustered eyes glowed in the dimness, watching, waiting, hungry. "The trees," he said. "Maybe we cut down the trees and make a clearing. Give them nowhere to hide."

"They'll only move on," said Simcock. "Can't cut down every tree in this wood." He paused, breathing out. "We should go back, as Darron says. It's folly going on in this."

"It's folly going back. Pecker's dead already. We go back, maybe someone else dies on the way. Then we'll only be weaker when we try again, two men down or maybe more." He shook his head. "No. We press on. We go back now and Pecker will have died for nothing."

It had been an icecat that took him, a slim long feline about the size of a starcat, white like the snow, silent as a shadow. Pecker had been walking at the rear as they went down the frozen river north of the lake, and the icecat had stalked him along the banks. They never even heard it, not until Pecker gave out a sudden high scream, and they turned to see the cat clamping its jaws down on the young man's throat and dragging him away into the trees.

"We keep on going and we'll *all* die for nothing," Simcock said. He'd been Pecker's friend, and knew him from back home. "This wood's worse than we feared. Maybe we go back…*all the way back*. We ought never have come here with so few men."

"All the way back?" Mallister stopped and turned on him. "Back to the refuge?"

Simcock jutted out his bearded chin. "And why not? We gather more men and return. Why ten of us? You wanted only ten, and one of them Shackton who can't even fight. Should have brought double that, triple…"

"Should have brought *nine*," Mallister Monsort said. "I shouldn't have brought *you*."

The two men stared at one another. Simcock's mouth gave a ripple, twisting. "You're not thinking straight," he said. "What I said about your sister last night…"

"Don't mention her again. *Never* mention her again."

"You're still sour about it. I never meant harm."

"I don't want to talk about it."

"No," agreed Gunter. "This ain't the time or the place, is it?" His voice was angry. "Look around you, damnit. They're getting closer every second."

It was true. The spiders were creeping in, little by little, watching, waiting, closing.

"We press on," Mallister Monsort said. "At pace. They'll leave us alone eventually." He swung about and kept on going. The men followed. Simcock was muttering under his breath all the while, his blue-blood-stained lips pulled back in a scowl. Ahead, the ground sloped down into a shallow basin, and the trees began to spread out just a little as the earth grew littered with boulders and rocks poking up through the snow. It was deep here, coming up to their thighs. There was a more excited chittering going on in the trees now, but Mallister Monsort pressed on, heedless.

"My lord," called Rufford. "I'm not sure we should go this way."

"The ice oak is this way."

"But my lord, the snow…"

"We press on." Their commander did not listen.

Rufford glanced at Gunter and the old man-at-arms said, "M'lord, he's right. We'd best find another route. The snow here's deep. We can't fight in this snow."

"They're spiders. Not dragons. We've faced worse up in the mountains."

"Never in conditions like this. It's getting deeper, m'lord. We should turn back."

"I'm *not* turning back, Gunter. We have to get to the tree."

"We should go *around* the basin," Gunter urged. "M'lord, you're not seeing sense."

"He's making poor decisions," Simcock came in. "Had Pecker in the rearguard alone, and he died for it. Now we're *all* going to die. I say we give Gunter the command."

That was it, the last straw. Sir Mallister Monsort wheeled about so fiercely he almost fell over. In a heartbeat he was surging between the men, knocking Ranulf aside, pressing right up into Simcock's face. Simcock was the bigger man, twice his age, but Mallister was the superior warrior. He wore armour from head to heel, a full set, even a helm beneath his hood. The rest wore only a patchwork, a mix of godsteel and castle-forged steel, leather and links of mail.

"Are you threatening mutiny?" the knight asked in a cold voice.

Simcock did not back down. "You heard what I said."

"The price is death," Mallister Monsort told him. His longsword was in his grasp, fingers tight. "Don't think I won't put you down right here. These spiders need to eat, Simcock." His eyes went up and down. "And there's plenty of meat on *you*."

"M'lord…" Gunter said.

Mallister raised a hand. His eyes were on Simcock and Simcock alone. "Well? Care to repeat what you said?"

"*My lord…*"

"I'm busy."

"My lord! The spiders!"

Mallister turned his head. The widowmakers had sensed their chance and were pouring toward them in a tide. The knight growled and broke away, and Simcock did the same. The world filled with squeaks and shouts and scrabbling feet as Ranulf stood in his cage of men, powerless to help. "There are too many," called Darron. "We have to run." Blades swished and slashed and cut, and the black bodies piled up around them. Ranulf could do nothing but stand and wait and hope, a common dagger in his grasp should any spiders creep through the cordon. He sensed Kamcho above him and looked up; there he was, high up in the branches, watching the fighting unfold. Ranulf squeezed his eyes shut and switched to the eagle's vision.

Gods. My gods. The spiders were unending. There were hundreds of them skittering across the snow and abseiling down from the branches on their thin silver webs. Ranulf could see more webbing in the trees, and sacks of eggs throbbing, and more were coming, more, more. Many were small, no bigger than squirrels or cats, but the largest were the size of wolves. *We can't stay here*, Ranulf knew. Darron was right. They had to run.

He blinked back into himself, into the shouting and the squeaking and the chaos. "They won't stop!" he called out loudly. "There are too many. We can't stay here!"

"Where, then!" shouted Mallister, swinging through one spider and another and another.

"Into the basin. They're coming from up the slope." The snow was thick but they had no choice. "We've blundered right into their nesting site. There are egg sacks up there. They won't stop coming until we're gone."

"Then we go." Monsort swung and swung again. "Rufford, you'll have to carry him. Simcock, up front with me. You're strong. We plough the snow, make it easier for the others."

"Right." Simcock nodded.

Carry him? Ranulf thought. He barely had time to process that information before Rufford was hauling him up onto his shoulder and charging after the others. Ranulf sucked a breath, stomach heaving as it smashed and bounced against the hard plate of Rufford's pauldron. The world flew by in a blur of rushing pine trunks and shouting voices, and the snow kicked up by their passing formed into a great white shroud. The widowmakers gave chase, squeaking and scrambling over the broken snow, pouring over rocks and boulders in a swarming black and red tide. Ranulf shut his eyes and went to Kamcho again, but it was too chaotic, too frenetic, and he couldn't focus. His head snapped up and down, up and down, and it was all he could do to stop from throwing up and vomiting right down Rufford's back.

He could not say how long it went on before they finally came to a stop. Rufford was panting hard, his chest heaving up and down. He swung Ranulf off his shoulder and set him down in the snow. "You're heavier than you bloody well look, you know."

There was laughing nearby. The sort of laughter that happens when you've come close to certain death and managed to avoid it. Ranulf blinked and managed to stand, unsteady on his feet. He counted out the men, standing and sitting about on rocks, panting and laughing, breath fogging the air. All were accounted for. All eight remained. He turned and looked back through the forest. A wide broken tract of snow faded off into the fog, but he could see no spiders in pursuit, hear no chittering nearby. "We lost them?" he said.

Sir Mallister wiped down his blade on his cloak. "Or they left us alone. Soon as we left their nesting grounds, they held back."

Simcock stepped up to the knight. There was a look of contrition on his face. "My lord, about before…"

"Think nothing of it. The tension can get to us all."

Simcock nodded. His cheeks were red from the cold and the rush. "You led us well, back there."

"And you ploughed like a bloody workhorse," Mallister said, smiling at the big man. "Couldn't have done it without you." He reached out and grabbed Simcock's forearm, shaking. "Well, Ranulf, how's your eagle?" He turned to face him. "Care to have another look, find out where we…"

There was a sudden choking sound nearby. Ranulf turned and saw Stick Thin Jym dropping down to a knee. His long face had gone chalk-white and his eyes were bulging, bug-like. He reached up, confused, and touched his neck behind the ear, and his fingers came back smeared in a thick black substance. "My…my lord?" He looked at Sir Mallister in mute appeal and then his mouth opened, and out came a sudden gush of blood, splashing horribly into the snow, bright red on white. He fell forward, seized by a terrible fit of convulsions, face twisting in pain, blood oozing from his lips, his nose, his ears. The men rushed in. "What do we do?" Alyn called in a panic. "M'lord Ranulf, what…what do we do?"

There is nothing you can do, Ranulf thought, sadly. He grimaced and shook his head. "I'm sorry, Alyn. He's beyond our help."

"No. There must…must be something?"

Ranulf wished it was so. He only shook his head again and looked at Sir Mallister. "You know what to do. It would be best to end his suffering."

The knight cringed at the thought, but nodded. "Step away. Move back." He drew out his sword as the others made room, all but Alyn who'd been Stick Jym's closest friend.

"M'lord, no, no! There must be another way."

"Step aside, Alyn. He is already dead."

Rufford came forward to pull the young soldier back. The venom of the widowmaker was fatal and unbearably painful, and there was no cure that Ranulf knew of. *He will suffer for long minutes,* he thought. *He'll buck so hard he'll spit up his own guts and his eyeballs will fill with blood.* Killing him was a mercy.

Sir Mallister Monsort saw to it. "I'm sorry, Jym." With a clean thrust, he drove his blade down into Stick Jym's hollow chest and pierced the thundering heart. At once the man went still, his jerking limbs falling down into the bloodstained snow. All that remained was the rictus of pain drawn across his lifeless face, the wide open bloodshot eyes, the red froth and spittle around his mouth and chin and cheeks. "We'll have to leave him here." The Emerald Guard's voice was empty. He knelt down and shut the dead man's eyes. "Alyn, you knew him best. You should have the honour of speaking the rites."

The young man was staring. "No, I…we have to bury him…to…"

"We can't. The earth is too hard and we can't spare the time. I'm sorry, Alyn. Speaking the rites will have to be enough."

Alyn swallowed. "I don't…I don't think I can."

"Very well, then," Mallister said. "I'll see to it my…"

Someone coughed. Mallister was cut off. Ranulf heard a splatter of something wet hit the snow. When he turned he saw the blood dribbling from Darron's mouth. "My lord," the youth whimpered. He wiped his lips; there were tears in his eyes. "I…please, I don't want to die…"

"It's all right, lad," said an older, gruffer voice. "You won't be going alone." When old Gunter smiled, his teeth were red.

Sir Mallister grimaced and stepped forward with his sword.

43

Emeric

They had heard the fighting from a long way off, though by the time they arrived it had largely simmered down.

Emeric looked over the old fish market, appalled by what he saw. There were corpses strewn everywhere. Ragged gaunt men in soiled cloaks made them up for the most part, though others in armour were to be seen as well. He saw merchants and vendors hacked up and slaughtered, saw women in fine coats bludgeoned to death. There were even children among the dead. One lay on the ground with his head cracked open like an egg, his eyes staring vacantly as blood oozed out onto the cobbles. Another had his throat slit open and several more had been trampled in the crush.

The exile gave a sigh. *Food,* he thought. *All of this was about food.* "Sir Stafford."

"Yes, m'lord?"

"See that the last remaining clashes are ended."

The man nodded. "As you say, m'lord." He took a short moment to recover his breath (they had run hard to get here after hearing the screams and ring of steel and seen the hordes of panicked peasants stampeding their way through the streets. Up until that point it had been a leisurely enough walk) then set off into the square, shouting out in a ringing voice and drawing his godsteel longsword as he went. "Lay down your arms. Surrender or you'll be shown no quarter! This is your only warning! I won't be giving another!"

Emeric followed him in, picking over the dead and the dying. If the dead numbered a hundred, the wounded were double or even triple that number, all moaning and crying out in pain. A grievous sound it was, a grievous sight and smell. From another lane he saw several city soldiers arriving at last and wondered why they hadn't been here all along. "You there," he shouted over to them. "Yes, *you.* Join Sir Stafford of the Bane in ending this wanton violence. And call more of your fellows. These people need help." When they hesitated, his ire exploded. "Now, I said! Damn it, *now!*"

The men broke. One spun and ran to fetch aid; the rest drew their blades and hurried in to break up the remaining brawls. As that was done, Emeric moved among the wounded doing what he could to help. It was little and less, alas. He tied a couple of tourniquets to staunch the flow of blood and set a splint to a broken leg, but that was all. By then more men were entering the square, soldiers and smallfolk alike. All across the market, the sound of wailing women erupted as wives rushed up to their dead husbands and mothers collapsed beside the corpses of their children, shrieking and shaking them and shouting for them to wake up.

"A grim thing," Emeric said sombrely, as Sir Stafford returned to his side. "To watch a mother lose her child."

The knight nodded. "Yes, m'lord. That's the sort of sound that lives with you." His fine white cloak was splashed with gouts of blood and he wore a grimace on his face. He had been required to use force, clearly, in deterring some of the more stubborn rioters. "Are we done then, m'lord? Or…"

"I think they have it well in hand now, Stafford. So…this *witch*. You said she lived around here?"

"Yes, m'lord. She's got a place down below the Winsome Whale. That tavern there." He pointed across the square. "There are stairs in the alley that lead down."

"Come, then, let's go and see her."

They moved through the square, past the carts of corpses and wailing women. There were broken stalls everywhere, bits of fish guts and gleaming scales, shelters and tents and lean-tos in their hundreds raised all across the square. Many of those had been crushed and trampled too.

Sir Stafford led him down the narrow stone stair just around the alley. The steps were slick from the rain. At the bottom was a small but sturdy wooden door. The knight rapped his knuckles against it and waited. When they had no answer, he turned and said, "Might be she was in the square, m'lord. Could be in one of those carts."

"Knock again, sir."

He did so, louder this time. A few moments passed. "The crone likes to visit the *Blue Traveller*, I heard. That's the Leviathan, m'lord."

"The statue of the whale?"

"Yes, m'lord. It's a monument, really. People write on the stone to remember the dead, those who died on the lake. The crone. She's old. They say she's lost a hundred loved ones to that lake and she goes to the statue every day. If was there when the fighting…"

They heard the door go. The slide of a rusted bolt. It creaked and pulled open and a tiny little woman stood there staring up at them in a frayed grey cloak. She was blind in one eye and the other was milky. She poked at Sir Stafford with a crooked walking stick. "Old, you call me?

How about ancient? I see you, Stafford of the Bane. You're the bane o'
me today, disturbing my sweet sleep."

"It's midafternoon. You shouldn't be sleeping at all."

She gave a cackle. "Live as long as me as you'll sleep when you
please. A thousand years ago I slept normal like you, but those days are
dead and done." She grinned toothlessly. "So what's this about some
fighting? I hear weeping on the wind."

"There was a riot, in the square. Over food."

"Food, yes, food's important. Scarce for some but not for others,
hey?" She poked her stick into his belly. "How's the fare at Fullerton's
keep? You're a well-fed boy, it looks to me."

"I'm a knight. It's wartime. Fighting men are prioritised during war."

"And the peasants go hungry. A story I've heard a thousand times
before across a thousand lands." Her milky eye whipped suddenly to
Emeric. "And who's your handsome friend?" Her long nose opened and
closed. "Got a sniff of lord about you. Tukoran, is it?"

"Once," Emeric said, wondering how she knew.

"And again, isn't that so?" Another smile. "A lost man needn't be lost
forever. Seems to me you've found your way home." She turned without
warning, hobbling along with her stick. "Well come on, you're letting all
the heat out. In, in." She waddled away.

Emeric followed Sir Stafford in as the knight shut the door behind
them. The interior was low-ceilinged and cosy, such that any man
more than six and a half feet tall would need to stoop. Emeric was shy
of that height, so too Sir Stafford, so they could walk unhindered. To
the crone the place was large, though. *She can't be much more than four feet
tall*, he thought, watching her waddle over to the fireplace to feed
another log to the flames. Candles burned everywhere, sitting in great
pools of wax on cluttered tables and in little niches in the walls. There
was no natural light, no windows and no way out but for the door
they'd come through. Everything seemed to be in one room, so far as
Emeric could see; bed and hearth, cupboards and stove and what
looked like an alcove toward the back where she kept her pots and
potions.

"Come, come, sit down." The witch settled into a little armchair that
fit her well, right up next to the heat of the fire. The flames worked
shadows across the deep wrinkles of her ancient face and little old hands.
Emeric and Stafford chose stools that were able to bear their weight. "So
how do you like my palace? Snug, isn't it?"

"It suits you well," Emeric said, with courtesy.

"Aye, so it does." The crone cackled. "Not *worthy* of the likes of you,
though. Fine brilliant *bird* that you are."

Emeric looked at her. "You know who I am?"

"Well, you're not Sir Dudley Reed, I know that much."

Sir Stafford was lost. "Who's Dudley Reed? You're speaking no sense,
witch."

"Only to the senseless. You're thick as rocks, boy."

"My castle was Osworth, Sir Stafford," Emeric explained, "and my sigil is an eagle battling two dragons."

"So…" The man looked puzzled.

"Os*worth*," Emeric repeated. "And the eagle is a brilliant bird, wouldn't you say?"

"Oh." He nodded, huffing. "You're a clever one, witch. And who's this Dudley Reed?"

"The man who took my castle," said Emeric. "Or rather, was granted its lands and incomes after my exile." It was Modrik Kastor who had conspired to see that done, of course. A final slap in the face, it was. Perhaps Emeric could stomach a man of valour settling in his old family seat, but Dudley Reed was a fat old fool and the honour was far beyond him. He turned to the crone. "How is it you know me? Do you have spies in Lord Fullerton's service?"

The old woman smirked. "I can smell it on you. When I look in a man's eyes, I can see his past and future. Give me a lock of your hair and I'll let you see it too. There's a potion I make. A portal to other times and other worlds. I knew who you were before I ever opened my door by your footfall. That day you came to the city, I knew it. I knew before you were born." She raised her little old hands to the ceiling. "He's here, he's here, the exile is here. I chanted it over and over like a loon that night and longed for the day you'd come see me." She smiled. "Or mayhaps that thing you said, about the spies? Could be that as well."

Emeric found that only partly amusing. "You're a playful one. Do you have a name?"

"What's wrong with witch and crone?"

"They are rather insulting, are they not?"

"Is lord insulting? Is knight?"

"They are official titles, granted by hereditary right and won through valorous deed."

"*Won*, aye. Like I won my titles too. Take crone. Means you're old, real old, and that takes some doing. Not many women get to be crones, you know. And fewer still get to be witches."

"And are you one? A witch?" He was less sure now, after that talk of spies.

"Why don't you ask your friend? He brought you here, didn't he?"

"He said he wasn't certain. I will not tell you the exact words he used."

"He called me old and ugly, didn't he?" The crone cackled wildly. "That'd be the crow calling the raven black, wouldn't it?"

The knight scowled at her. "You calling me ugly, woman?"

"Witch, crone, woman. And these are meant to be insults?" She flicked a hand at Sir Stafford of the Bane. There were many bands about her wrist, Emeric saw, bearing tufts of hair and little claws and fangs that jingled as they moved. "Be silent, Sir Slow. Or I'll turn you into a toad."

He huffed. "Like you could."

"I've done it before. Silly little man kept trying to get into my bed so I turned him into a great big toad and sent him hopping away down to the marshes."

Stafford snorted. "Why would anyone want to get into *your* bed?"

"And *that's* the unbelievable part!" The crone laughed out loud in unrestrained joy. "Because I was young and pretty once before, though that was ten thousand years ago. Back when the gods were nought but squalling babes and these lakes were dry as dust. I've seen a thousand worlds and I've lived a thousand lives and I've worn a thousand skins, and some of those skins were pretty. But skin grows old, that's how it works. I'll get myself a new one soon."

Sir Stafford snorted. "A new skin? What are you talking about?"

She ignored the question and asked one of her own. "How old are you, Sir Slow?"

He stared at her blankly.

"You age. Come. It's four and thirty, isn't it?"

"Yes," he managed, blinking at her. "How did you…"

"Spies, what else? And I got these too." She pointed to her wild white hair and the little ears beneath. "They're good for hearing if you care to listen and I've heard a million men speak in more tongues than I care to know. I could recite them to you now but you'd be dead by the time I'm done."

"There are only…there aren't that many languages in the world…" The knight looked at Emeric, as though in a plea for help, but the exile was more interested in what the crone was going to say. She was very curious, this crone. He was trying to find some truth behind her lies, for lies they could only be, lest she be a god.

"In this world, aye. Maybe a thousand across time. But a thousand times a thousand is what, Sir Slow?"

Sir Stafford stammered for an answer.

"A million," she said. "I could tell you their names and turn my tongue to them too. I'm fluent in many, maybe ten thousand or two." She grinned that gummy grin of hers. "Four and thirty, then? Yes? And five months and eight days if you want to be exact. You want the hour and the minute and the second too?" She laughed at the dumbstruck look on his face. "That's how long you've lived, Sir Slow, half a lifetime to you but a blink to me, no more than the flutter of a hummingbird's wing. The young should show their elders respect, you ever heard that? Well I'm so old even the gods call me crone, and was here before this land was born." She looked at him. "You don't believe me. Can't say I blame you. Half the time I don't believe myself."

The poor man looked utterly baffled. "You're a hundred years old, maybe…"

"*This* skin is, aye. You remember what I just said about the skins? Been lurking about Lakeheart for a century now, just waiting for all the fun to start."

"The fun? What fun?"

"The war," said the witch. "The Last Renewal, isn't that what you call it? I came here to watch the show and I'm still wondering who's going to win. That Eldur boy and his little pet dragon or the rest o' you lot all gathering up to stop him." She shrugged her narrow shoulders. Necklaces of shells and stones and animal bones rattled and clacked together. "Could still go either way, so far as I see it. Seen it happen a hundred times."

Sir Stafford was starting to get angry now. "Seen *what* happen? You're making no sense."

"The end of the world. Or its saving. I liked the last war. What do you call it? That one about the continents? Lots of good battles there, the Burning Rock, that was a fine one. I put on a soldier's skin for a day so I could see it all from up close. Was there when the Crippler crippled the king, though he was just a prince back then. Now the Crippler's a king himself…and a cripple. Isn't it funny how things work?"

"The only funny thing here is you, crone."

She smiled at him and went right on. "The stakes were low back then, though. Didn't seem it at the time, I'm sure, but it's true. It was just a warm-up act, a good clearing of the throat. You ever go to the Singer's Square, Sir Slow? With all them pretty shows they put on during the spring festival? Sometimes an act will come on, some peacock of a bard and he'll warble out a jaunty tune. He'll have a nice enough voice, aye, and the people will sing along and clap when he's done, but after he's left the stage the main act will come on. A better voice. A better song. He'll make the people weep. Well, that's what's happening now, with this war. Bigger armies, older monsters, demigods waking from their naps. The world's ending…or it's not. And I'm sitting here on the edge of my seat."

Emeric leaned forward on his. "Who are you?" he asked her. He was serious this time. "Tell me."

"Oh me? I'm just the crone. The old witch who likes to waddle about Lakeheart with a walking stick and go look at the Blue Traveller in the square." She grinned at him. "Twas me who thought up that name, you know. Had it once myself, in another land."

"That's Palaphan's name," Sir Stafford grunted at her. "People have been using it for a thousand years."

"Aye, since *I* gave it to them. Been here in Lakeheart for a century, as I said, but that doesn't mean I haven't popped over here from time to time before. I like to travel, see. That's why they call me the Blue Traveller some places…on account of that travelling, and the hair."

"Your hair's white not blue," said Stafford, snorting.

"*Here*, aye. In another place it's blue and another it's green. Here red and there black and sometimes it's all sorts of colours blended together." She gave another cackle and threw a log in the fire. "But enough about all that. I've said too much. My father doesn't like it when I talk like this."

"Your father?" The knight scoffed. "He must be dead, surely."

"You haven't been paying attention, have you, Sir Slow? My father can't die and nor can I. He is father to gods and forger of worlds and I'm his wayward son…"

"*Son!*"

"Aye, son. Then daughter. Then son again. And daughter and son and everything else in between. I've been wizard and warlord and crone and commoner, I've been goddess and gremlin and ghoul. In one land I fly, in another I swim, I can be small as a mouse or ten times the size of the Dread, a living mountain watching a world from its waking to its wake, from its dawn until its dusk. I've seen empires rise and fall and rise anew, I've met a hundred thousand kings. I've been one as well, a time or two. I've ruled and been ruled and killed and been killed, but never for very long. Sometimes I want to die for good, but my father will never let me. No matter how much I disappoint him, he says he loves me still."

She sighed wistfully and a tear ran down her cheek. "But that's enough. Enough from me. Any more and I'll get a scolding and *his* scoldings can be fierce. I've seen whole worlds shatter from his voice alone and even a simple stare can set the seas ablaze. You wouldn't thank me for that, I don't think. Not after all the hard work you've done to get here. Three millennia of war and renewal and silly old me says too much, so my father clips his finger and ends it all. No, oh no, that won't do. So that's quite enough from me."

At last the crone went silent, and that silence lingered a while. Emeric was trying to pick through what she'd said and decide just how mad she was. The alternative did not bear thinking about. Eventually, he said, "I came today to ask about…"

"The prince, yes. Our sleeping beauty. You want to wake him up."

Spies, he thought. *That's how she knows all this, the spies.* Perhaps that Liza girl was one of them? Or those men who guarded the prince's door? "Yes," he said. "Master Allabor's tonics have not worked…"

"Well of course they haven't worked. The boy was put under by a powerful potion and only a powerful counter-potion can revive him."

Emeric decided to test her. "I gave him one just before we came here. A tonic, that is. It had many ingredients…"

"And you want me to name them. Recite that list Allabor showed you? With the Dew of the Dawnstone and the dried hollowberry skin?" She yawned. There was no way she could possibly know that, unless Allabor was a spy himself. Or did he use a helper? Could there be a little peeping hole in the wall for one of the crone's cronies to see through? She smiled at the look on his face. "Spies, Lord Manfrey. Only spies. Think nothing of all the rest I told you. Best forget all that or it'll give you sleepless nights."

He wished he could. It was in his head now. "Allabor…" he said, in a slightly discomfited voice. "He had a visitor earlier…"

"Quillan, the language master. Clever man, yes, Allabor wasn't wrong about that. He'll translate the hag's speech for you eventually, though it'll take him a few days to do it. I know a quicker way, though."

She had his full attention now. "Will you tell me?"

"Why wouldn't I? Though I sense you and the good prince are going to part ways anyway. Once he's awoken, he'll be wanting to ride back south to the war. He'll take that one-handed knight along with him and you as well, Sir Slow, you'll go too."

"Me? I'm no Tukoran."

"You're a knight, aren't you?"

"I serve Lord Fullerton."

"The corpse," said the crone. "Not yet, but soon."

"I have every intention of returning to the war myself," Emeric told her.

"And a good intention that is. The sort that gallant men always like to have. But sometimes a wind will come along and blow you on another course. Not every ship docks at its chosen harbour, my lord. *Blue* sea and *misty* sky may have you veering elsewhere." She smiled at him, then cocked her head to the side, as though hearing something only she could hear. "Well now, best leave it there. He's coming and I want to take a look." She stood from her armchair and took up her walking stick. Emeric rose as well, and Sir Stafford of the Bane who had the look of a bewildered deer about him.

"Who's coming?" the knight asked. "I can't hear anything."

"You will. Those wings do bring a beat, Sir Slow. He's not the biggest I've seen, but close, and one of the meanest, there's no doubt. Very mean is the Fire God's favourite son."

"Now what are you saying? You're driving me mad, hag."

"The Mad Hag," she laughed. "Now there's a name. One I had elsewhere too, but that's another story." She shuffled off toward the door, leaving Stafford of the Bane in her wake.

Emeric followed behind her, moving past the knight. "You haven't yet told me how to wake the prince," he urged.

"Oh, haven't I?" She kept on walking, flicking a hand as she went. "The purple potion should do it. The one that looks like fog. You give him that and he'll wake right up."

Emeric wasn't certain if he could trust her. What if this was a trick? Some elaborate trick? There *was* a purple potion among the stormhag's stores, but still… "I may just wait for Master Quillan," he said.

"Suit yourself. You'll be gone by then anyway. That boy's not going to want to wait around."

"Boy? You mean the prince?" Emeric was confused.

The crone chuckled. "I suppose he *is* a prince…his father being a king and all. Oh, and take the rest of them too. Might come in handy later."

"The rest of them? You mean the potions and…"

"Aye, best take them all," she said. "But hear that? You hear that now? He's coming, come, quick, quick…let's go up and take a look…" She hastened for the door and the stone stairs beyond. And distantly, Emeric heard the roar.

Then the bells began to toll.

44

———

Jonik

He was dreaming of a beach on an island called Lizard's Laze in the southwest corner of the world.

The serving girl Sapphire was smiling at him and telling him of the Day of Dawning. "All the girls go naked in the sea," she said, her blue eyes twinkling in the sun. She had a grin that suggested she would too, and Jonik wished he'd been there to see her. He had never been with a woman, never even kissed one, and he'd seen few so pretty as her. "Maybe you could come with me," she said to him, in the dream. "Would you like that, Jonik? To swim naked in the sea with me?"

Even in the dream he was awkward. He averted his eyes from her, feeling the hot flush on his cheeks and neck, and when he dared look back, she was gone. Away she went with Jack instead, giggling as the brawny young Marshlander told her a joke and draped a muscular arm over her shoulder. They strode away from him across the soft powdery sand and toward a crowd of revellers further down the shore, and he could see young Devin there, with those girls he'd met, and Captain Turner and Brown Mouth Braxton rolling a barrel of ale. They stopped to prop it up and began pouring drinks for everyone, and there was music then, and gales of laughter spreading, and somehow to Jonik it sounded mocking.

They're talking about me, he knew. *It's about me. They're mocking me for being chaste.*

Suddenly, amid the mockery and the merriment, the beer barrel leapt up and came alive, and it had been Borrus Kanabar all along. A cheer went up for him, and Jonik saw that Torvyn and Mooton were there as well, and the rest of the Blackshaws too, who all looked much alike to one another, bearded and burly to a man. A drinking contest began between them as Braxton and Jack handed out the ale.

"A horn for the new Lord of Rivers," called Brax, smiling that rotten brown smile.

511

"And the Warden of the East," added Jack. "Hero of Rustbridge!"

A cry went up in echo of those words and the ale was handed around. Then they drank and drank and drank again, one horn and two and five and ten until only Borrus and Mooton Blackshaw remained. The two huge men stared at one another, glaring and grinning. "I'll drink you under the table, Barrel," shouted Mooton. "No man can outdrink me!"

Borrus snorted disdain and said, "Goblet or godsteel I'll slay you, Moot! I'm the better man in every way!"

And the drinking resumed. Some cheered for the Barrel, others the Beast, and Jonik watched on, alone. The sun arced away west and the sky filled with the radiance of a perfect dusk and the sea sloshed and lapped at the shore, reflecting its splendorous light. He saw the girls enter the water, disrobing as they went, their perfect golden skin and curves unveiled to the watching men. Teasingly, they splashed and frolicked and gave them inviting stares. And one by one, the men went to join them; Devin first, running and stripping, Brown and Grim Pete following behind, and the Blackshaws too, and old Gill Turner as well, and even Soft Sid entered the water, the gentle giant lumbering and laughing in the surf as the girls spun tiny and naked around him.

And Jack, who had been Jonik's best friend. Strapping Jack, confident Jack, kind Jack with his easy smile and quick laughter. He waded in after them, smiling that smile, and at once Sapphire squealed with delight and went splashing right over to intercept him. He lifted her up with his big strong hands, gripping her slim waist as he twirled her around, and she laughed, a sweet laugh it was, a laugh as pretty and delicate as she was.

And alone, afar, Jonik watched, standing in the distant darkness. The water ran off her smooth soft skin, off her buttocks and breasts and her long shining hair like droplets of sunlight in the gold glow of dusk. He wanted that, he wanted her, he wanted to be like Jack. The Marshlander laughed as he spun her, then lowered her down and took her in his arms and kissed her. And Jonik watched. With desperate envy, he watched. With lust and longing and desperate loneliness, he watched.

He could bear it no longer. Mouth twisting, he tore his eyes away from them and looked back at the beach. The drinking was still going on. Borrus drank and Mooton drank, one horn and then another and a hundred more after that, matching one another stroke for stroke. "You'll never beat me, Beast," Borrus declared, and Mooton laughed and said, "I'm just getting started, Barrel. Another," he roared, throwing down his horn to shatter on the ground. "Another! Another! Another!"

"Children," murmured a voice to his side. Jonik turned and saw Emeric Manfrey standing beside him, golden eyes staring forward. He had his arms folded and his gaze was judging. "Look at them, they're children." But he smiled a fond smile as he said it.

Jonik felt nervous all of a sudden. He swallowed; his heart was pounding. "You…never came back," he said, in a whisper. It sounded childlike, somehow. Scared. Weak. "You said you'd go down and fetch the others…but you left me and you never came back."

"I didn't want to come back," said the exiled lord, not looking at him. His voice was cold, distant. "Why would I want to return to you?"

"But…I thought…"

"What? That you were a leader?" And he laughed cruelly. "You were never a leader, *boy*. We followed the Nightblade, not you. You're nothing without it. And you're too much of a coward to use the other."

The other… "No, I can't. I'm meant to deliver it, that's all. I'm meant to…"

"Nothing. You're nothing now. You were a champion and now you're a courier. Just another no-name bastard without a home." He snorted disdain and walked away…away up the beach to join the others.

Jonik watched him go. He could see all of them there now, all those who travelled with him and served him, those who'd died for him and deserted him. Harden and Gerrin. Sir Owen and Sansullio, the Silent Suncoat and Sir Lenard Borrington. He saw Sir Corbray and Cabel and Kazil and Big Mo, even Vincent Rose was there. Ranulf, and the girl Leshie he saw. Hamlyn the Humble looked at him disappointedly, and Fhanrir was scowling his scowl. And his cousin Amilia was there, and his mother Cecilia, and there were tears streaming from her eyes as she looked at what he'd become.

"Bitch," said a different voice. "That bitch *deserved* to die."

Jonik's lips tore back in anger, and he turned. Before him stood his brother; taller, grander, glowing. A silver wind swirled around him. "Elyon…"

"Don't say my name."

"I've wanted to see you…to talk to you…"

"Silence." The voice was like thunder. "You'll never speak to me. Never look at me. You killed him. You killed my brother."

Our brother. And Jonik saw it, the body lying at Elyon's feet, armoured and cast in stone. There was a cracking sound, and he saw the stone split open at the neck, and a fountain of blood gushed up, rich and red.

"You killed him. You cut his throat. You're covetous, weak. You did it for the blade."

"No, I…I never meant…"

"We'll never accept you, bastard. My father hates you. He will hate you forever. You killed his son…"

"I am his son."

"No!" exploded the voice. "You're his seed, not his son! Crawl back to the darkness, bastard. You crawl back and never come out."

He could feel tears in his eyes. He was so small and weak. "I never meant…Aleron, I never wanted to kill him."

"But you did. You killed him. You killed him and you can't take it back."

The silver wind swirled, darkening, and all of a sudden Elyon was gone. Jonik reached out as the blackness closed about him, bitter cold and roaring. He stepped forward, but the earth gave way beneath him, and suddenly he was plummeting down, faster, faster, down through a bottomless pit as the screams rang out about him. *I'm dead*, he thought in choking terror. He would fall and fall and fall forever. Starving, shrivelled, in shame he would fall beyond time and space, down the Long Abyss…

He gasped and sat up, waking.

He could hear bells sounding out across the city.

Jonik heaved for breath and turned his eyes around, confused. It took a moment to recall where he was. *Lakeheart*, he remembered, as it came to him. *Yes, I'm in the fishmonger's home.*

A dream. It was just a dream.

His heart was pounding. There was sweat on his brow. He took in the chamber; a large bed and fine furniture, a high ceiling of crafted stone. A fire burned in a handsome hearth, throwing shadows across the room. His head felt as heavy as a hill, his thoughts muddled and thick. *How long did I sleep?* He could see a line of daylight drawn beneath the door, so night had not yet come. *A few hours, no more. Unless I slept all day and all night as well. Could it be morning? Are these the morning bells?*

He groaned and got wearily to his feet, armour scratching at the stone floor. The blaring of the bells was incessant and spreading and he could hear the sharp strains of panic outside, of people shouting and rushing about. Had the riots spread? The chaos had been ongoing when he led the old man from the fish market, but that was hours ago. Wasn't it?

He staggered wearily to the window and pulled apart the rich velvet curtains. Wan light flooded in, screened by a swamp of cloud. The view from the fishmonger's residence presented a broad vantage across the harbour and the restless waters of the lake. He glimpsed the glow of the sun behind the clouds, faint but visible. It had barely moved that he could see. *Not even an hour*, he reflected, dismal. *I didn't even sleep an hour.*

There was a sudden urgent banging on the door. Jonik spun as it opened, and the old fishmonger appeared, red-faced and panting. "Do you hear the bells?" he blurted.

"Yes, I hear them." *Does he think me deaf?* "Do you know what's happening?"

"No, no…but I fear…" Morlyn cringed and rushed to look out of the window. That was the name he'd given Jonik earlier. "Are they coming for me? Those men from the square? You will protect me if they do, won't you? Like you promised?"

Jonik's promise ended when they entered the man's home. Food and a place to rest for safe passage. That was the bargain and he'd fulfilled his end.

So too Morlyn, in truth. When they'd arrived here, he'd fetched him food at once and Jonik had gorged himself silly. After that, he'd been shown to this room and promised that a pack of rations would be ready for him to take on the road when he left, along with that fine new cloak that Morlyn had promised him. That he'd barely slept could hardly be blamed on his host.

"No one's coming for you," Jonik said. "They wouldn't ring the city bells just for that."

"You're certain?" He peered through the window, as though expecting to see an armed rabble marching up to his door. "But if they do…if they do you will protect me, promise me you…"

"Quiet," Jonik hissed. There was something in the air, a deep *pulse* like the beating of a colossal heart, low and distant. His chest tightened. *Wings,* he thought.

The old man was watching him. "What is it? What's wrong?"

Jonik didn't answer. Turning, he strode hard across the room to buckle on his swordbelt. The Mistblade felt heavier than ever after so little sleep, though the touch of godsteel helped revive him. The old man was watching all the while, looking at the scratch marks on the stone floor beside the bed. "Did you…sleep there, beside the bed? Why would you not…"

"My armour's too heavy. Your bed would not support me."

"But your armour…why not remove it? Surely it would be more comfortable to…"

Comfort was not a concern to him. "Did you find me a new cloak?"

"Yes, I…it's downstairs…hanging by the door. It's wolfskin, a fine garment…"

Jonik was already marching right past him, out through the door and down the steps into the entrance hall. The old man hurried after him, prattling on about things Jonik did not hear. He was listening to the wing-beats, the thunder getting closer. *It's coming this way.* Was it the creature from the depths? *It's found me,* a part of him was thinking. *It tried to kill me down there, but I got away, and now…now…*

There were half a dozen cloaks hanging on pegs beside the door. He ran his eyes over them. They all looked much alike at a glance. "Which one?"

"The wolfskin," panted the old man, following behind him. "That… that one…right there…"

Jonik saw it, took it, tried it on. It fit him well enough. Black it was. That fit him too.

"My son's," the old man explained. "He is tall, like you. He lives in Varinar now."

Then he's probably dead, Jonik thought. Varinar had been attacked already, many moons ago, and much of the city had been destroyed by the…

He paused. *Dread.* And the truth of it dawned. *Gods, it's not the demon. It's him. It's the Dread…*

And right then, right when the dark realisation dawned, the world broke open with a sky-shattering roar. The ground shook from it, and the walls and the ceiling, and dust sprinkled down upon them. The old man threw himself onto his knees, crouching as though the world was ending.

"Oh gods…oh gods…I'm going to die," he whimpered. Jonik kicked the door open at once, just in time to see the Dread soaring overhead. All the city seemed to be cast in his shadow as his bulk passed by, day turning to night, and a moment passed, another, another, until the shadow moved on, and the daylight rained back down upon them as night switched back to day. Then came the wind, the hot burning wind, and the crashing of wood and the collapsing of stone as the city cringed and cowered at his coming.

Jonik stood on the threshold and watched in awe. He could hear Morlyn sobbing behind him, hear the screams ringing out through the streets. The boats in the harbour leaned and twisted, bobbing on the water as it rose and fell. Waves splashed over the wharves and quays, washing away barrels and crates and even people too, who went tumbling away with their nets and rods. Horses were screaming and rearing and bolting, throwing their riders from the saddle. A dog raced past him like a bolt from the blue, and another followed behind. There was a crumbling sound, the breaking of stone, and a beacon tower teetered and fell down onto the harbour as the rushing crowds were crushed beneath it. High banners blew wild on the wind and one caught aflame, sending up fiery plumes of smoke to swirl off over the lake. *Fire, death, destruction,* Jonik thought. *And all from his passing alone.*

The Dread was already a mile away and going further still. Jonik stood there, staring at the shrinking shape. Never had he felt so small. The Mistblade was at his hip, calling out to him, begging and pleading to be taken up.

"Why?" Jonik asked it, bitter. "What could *you* hope to do against *that?*" He ignored any further appeals from the blade and turned again to the old man. He was still on his knees, hunkered down and weeping. "That food you promised me. Where is it?"

The fishmonger didn't hear him. Not over the bells and the screams and the chaos. "Morlyn," he shouted. "The dragon has passed. Stand up." When he didn't, he marched over and raised him by the scruff of the neck. "That food. Did you pack it up for me?"

The man's face was a mask of terror. "I…the food, yes, I…"

"Where is it? In the kitchen?"

The man nodded. Jonik rushed off. He saw the satchel on the kitchen table, performed a cursory check to ensure the rations were suitable for his onward journey, considered them generous enough, and swung the satchel bag over his shoulder. The old man was still standing in the entrance hall when he returned.

"Will he…come back?" he stammered, shivering all over. "He's gone…you said…did you say he's…"

"He flew over the lake." Jonik did not know if he would return or not, but if he did, he didn't mean to be here. He started for the door.

"You're leaving?" Morlyn cried.

"At once. Yes." *Before this city falls to further chaos.*

That was clearly the old man's fear. "I'll pay you to stay," he pled, desperate. "Not just food and lodging, but money as well. I have plenty of gold. And precious stones. Clothes. My son…he left many fine garments here when…"

"The cloak will serve." Jonik passed through the door and stepped out into the mayhem of the harbour. The black-red shadow was shrouded in the distance now, circling above the lake. He heard Morlyn blundering out after him.

"Please, I beg you. I have riches. I can make you rich…"

Jonik ignored him. "Which way is quickest to the Lakeland Pass?" That road would take him north between the lakes; it was the only way out of the city for anyone meaning to go that way. He turned. "Which way, Morlyn?"

"I…let me come with you and I'll…"

"You're not coming with me." Jonik would find his own way. Turning, he marched quickly away through the harbour, past warehouses and storehouses and tawdry inns of ill repute. Drunkards were lumbering out into the daylight, unaware of what was going on. They splashed out into several inches of floodwater. "You…you there…" one said in a thick voice, calling out to him. "What's all this? Was there some tidal wave or something?"

The waters of the lake were still moving turbulently, sloshing up and down from the pull of the titan's passing. Jonik raised a finger and pointed. "There's your culprit." He marched past them. A lane went west. People were rushing that way, away from the harbour. Jonik joined the flow. Above him, he could hear a man shouting from a balcony and pointing. "He's coming back! Run! Run! He's coming back! Run!"

The din grew louder. Screams and shouts rang all about him as the people pushed and scrambled up the lane. Jonik turned against the tide and looked back toward the lake, visible now as a banner between the buildings. Distantly, he saw the shadow of the Dread soaring above the water. He was veering their way, but his head was low, his eyes trained down, and all of a sudden he tucked his colossal wings and plunged, reaching out with talons the size of trees to snatch something from the water.

Jonik could hardly believe what he was seeing. *A kraken. It's…that's a kraken he's caught.* He could see the limbs, the long, wriggly tentacles, the bulbous black head and wide orange eyes. *I fought a kraken once.* It had been enormous to him, a colossal beast, but against the Dread it was nothing but a squirming little squid. The titan reached up with his claws and down with his long neck and started eating the creature in flight. The people were screaming and pushing past him as he stood at the heart of the lane, watching. He could not seem able to tear his eyes away. "Move! Move!" Someone tried to shove him, but he wouldn't budge in his armour. "Get out of the way! You're blocking us! Move!"

Jonik started stepping backward, but slowly, watching the dragon all the while. He ate the kraken in three great bites, tipping back his head to swallow. Then his head swayed, eyes roving. *He's still hungry. Still hunting.* Jonik was mesmerised. The scale, the size, the strength…

"Move! Get out of the way!" A woman this time, squirming past him. Others shouted at him as well, those who weren't screaming, and at last Jonik broke from his trance and turned, moving with them.

The lane ended at a branching crossroad. A small statue stood at the heart of the quad, some ancient Lakeland hero or another. Several ways led from here, though the buildings were too high for him to know which was best to take. He snagged a passing man. "I must make for the northern gate. Which way?"

The man blinked at him as though not seeing him at all, broke free and kept on going. Fear had addled him, the same as most. "North," Jonik shouted, to anyone who might listen. He turned fully around as people fled in a frenzy down lanes and twisting alleys. "Which way to the northern gate?"

"The Lakeland Gate," someone said. Jonik wheeled around again and saw him. A soldier, he looked. He wore oddments of armour, mostly studded leather though with a battered breastplate at his chest, and had a longsword at his hip, a worn white cloak at his back. "That's the north gate. Leads onto the Lakeland Pass."

"Yes." Jonik pushed through the people toward him. "Which way?"

"There." The man pointed toward a narrow lane with high leaning buildings to either side. "That'll take you direct, but that's a maze that way. And the streets are tight. Might run into a blockage with all these people."

Jonik could very well see that happening. People were squeezing that way already and the going would be slow. "Is there a better way?"

The swordsman nodded. "The way I'm going. To the city's heart. The castle. You can go north from there down wider streets…it'd be quicker for you overall." He said nothing more. Jonik followed behind as he rushed onward, jostling through the panicking crowds. They entered a wide road with balconies thrusting out over them on either side, filled with flower pots and little tables and chairs for sitting and watching the world go by. It was a pretty street, a summery street, with shops and winehouses lining the way, a wealthy street for wealthy people. Many of those people stood there, on their balconies, looking down at the people or away toward the lake. Jonik could see nothing but stone walls and sky and the panicking horde behind him. He thought he glimpsed old Morlyn among them, scrambling along in the tide, but couldn't be sure.

"That's Drulgar up there," the swordsman said, turning his head a moment. He was old, this soldier, past fifty and grizzled and a little crippled as well, Jonik saw. He had a shambling way about him, some issue with his hip. "I seen him before, bit way north of Rustbridge. Months ago that was. Flew right off to the west. Never seen anything like it."

"He's here to hunt," Jonik said.

"Aye, let's hope that's all it is. Nothing to concern him here."

Nothing to concern him. Jonik thought of the Mistblade and wondered.

On instinct, he drew his cloak over to cover it, lest the dragon should see it and sense it and come. He wanted to hasten his pace, but he couldn't. The crowds were thick and the city was overwhelmed; the fog of noise was deafening.

"You see that ahead?" the soldier called over. "The Sapphire Tower?"

Jonik could see the top of the tower rising above the buildings. "I see it."

"That's Three-Lake Keep. You want, I'll get you in through the gate. Sir Stafford's looking for good men to help watch the prince."

"The prince?" Jonik repeated.

"I mean the lord," he corrected, quickly. "Lord Fullerton, that is. The Lord of Lakeheart. He's abed, with burns." He glanced back awkwardly. "So? What do you say? You're a soldier, I can see the swords. We could use you."

"I'm going north," Jonik said.

"What for? We got food in the castle, plenty of room too. Wouldn't need to be squashed in with this lot or anything. It's good living there." When Jonik ignored him, he went blithely on. "Girls in the castle too, did I say? Lots of them. Liza, she'd be happy to have you join us. And others. That lot are living while they can, same as me." Jonik had a flash of naked girls with golden skin frolicking in the surf. Of a girl with a luring smile and dazzling blue eyes and the promise of something more. He turned away from it with a scowl as the man went on, "Food, a feath-erbed, a pretty girl to fumble with. It's good living there. You swear your blade and…"

"I'm going north," Jonik said, louder. "North. Do you not hear me?" He was getting weary of the man's temptations. "You said the prince is in the castle?"

"What? No? Who said that?"

"You did. There's a rumour that Raynald Lukar was brought here a few days ago." Morlyn had mentioned that earlier. "It's true, isn't it?"

"No. Don't know where you're getting that from. I said lord. Fuller-ton's no prince."

The man was vexing. Jonik was done playing games. He pressed up right beside him and gripped his arm as they drifted with the crowd. "You know what I'm asking," he said in a lower voice. "Just tell me what happened to the prince."

The other man hesitated, gave a pull to try to release his arm and seemed to realise what he was dealing with. Jonik's grasp was utterly unyielding in a manner only possible with Bladeborn. "You know him?" he asked.

"He's my cousin," Jonik said.

The soldier snorted in disbelief. "Your cousin? You don't look royal to me."

"I never said I was." They were still moving with the slow flow of the crowd. Ahead now, Jonik could see the road widening into a large central square. The castle lay across it, walled off from the rest of the city, a triangular fortress with high towers at each corner and a central keep, the Sapphire Tower, rising from its core. "What ails him? Tell me. I'm *not* going to ask again."

He squeezed tighter with his steel fingers until the soldier gave a grimace and said, "Fine, fine, I'll tell you. He's *sleeping*. That's all I know. Just sleeping."

"Sleeping? From what?"

"I don't know. Some deep sleep. There are whispers of sorcery, some stormhag, but I don't know more than that. He's been lying in his bed since he came here. I stand at the door, sometimes, that's all. I never go in. That exile's been trying to wake him with tonics, but nothing's worked. Allabor, he…"

"Exile? What exile?"

Jonik never got an answer. A great sudden groundswell of screaming rose up behind them and he felt the crowd pushing and shoving with more urgency. The guardsman slipped his grip and squirmed away through the press. He could hear the calls of, "He's coming! He's coming back!" ringing out around him. Wingbeats thumped like thunder through the air and then the shadow passed over, trailing a scorching gale. People were thrown forward off their feet and bits of debris went pinging and flying through the crowd. Jonik saw a great wooden shard impale a man through his neck, saw a woman turn at the wrong moment and take a dozen small splinters to the face. The Dread flew past with a deep rumble of motion, twisting in flight and diving down into the city's southern side. Jonik lost sight of him beneath the buildings, but he felt the tremors all the same, the heavy shaking through the stone as he skimmed the streets with his trailing claws, reducing all before him to rock and ruin. The crowd were pressing, screaming, scrambling wildly for the open square. The air had grown hot, it rippled and fizzed. Fires burst into life on banners and flags and wooden poles, and pot flowers withered and died. Old men and women were collapsing from the heat as loved ones stopped to try to revive them, only to be trampled by the merciless surge of the throng. He pressed on, stamping through the herd in his heavy godsteel armour, bursting out into the square. Hundreds, perhaps thousands were gathering at the castle, howling to be let inside, but the gates were shut and barred.

"Jaycob! Jaycob!" The voice was screaming behind him. Jonik glanced back and saw old Morlyn the fishmonger running toward him, red-faced and desperate. "Take me north with you, Jaycob! Please, take me north!"

"No." Jonik kept on going, studying the pattern of the streets. It was hard to see much of anything now with all the dust and swirling smoke, the heat haze brought by the Dread.

"Jaycob, please! Please! You have to he…."

Help, he was going to say, before the word collapsed into an imperilled wail as the dragon god passed by again. He was closer now, lower.

Jonik could see the red horns with their twisting black veins and the black horns with their red. He could see the ancient cuts and scars and wounds from a thousand battles over ten thousand years. His body was a tapestry that told a tale of time; it spoke of titans and heroes and gods. Two hundred metres in the air, he was, but he seemed close enough to touch. Darkness covered the square and terror spread among the crowd, and with one powerful wingbeat a thousand souls were scattered and blown like a heap of autumn leaves picked up by a gust of wind.

Something clutched at Jonik, an urge to tear the Mistblade from his belt and do something, anything, but he knew there was nothing he could do. The dragon flew by, turning in a wide arc back toward the south of the city, descending, dragging his talons across the ground, snapping with his colossal maw as if toying with them, playing like a cat with a mouse. The air was filled with rumbling, a low rumbling that sounded like laughter. Over the dragon went, and back again, crossing the south of the city three times and four, four and five, and each time more buildings fell down, and the high walls were shattered, and great plumes of smoke were thrown up as the fires took and spread through the streets and squares.

"Jaycob, please…" He felt something tugging weakly at the hem of his wolfskin cloak. The old man Morlyn was on his knees, blood pouring from a gash on his forehead to redden his teeth and soak down into his grey-white beard. "Take me north. Please."

"I can't." Jonik's voice was edged with pity. "I'm sorry. I just can't." He gave a pull of his cloak to dislodge the man, stepping away. Through smoke and flame Jonik saw the Dread again, passing the south of the city once more, though this time he did not dip or plunge to attack. With a pulse of his thousand-foot wings, he rose, up and up, half a mile into the air, and soared back out over the sprawling waters of the lake.

Jonik watched him go. Was he flying off to feed again? Would he come back to lay all the city to waste? He did not mean to wait and find out. Turning, he pressed north with the throng…

…and made it only two paces before he heard his name called out.

His *true* name, this time. Not the one his mother might have given him in another life, not the one he'd told the old fishmonger.

"Jonik?" The voice was familiar, deep, calm despite the chaos. Jonik recalled his dream; he'd heard the voice as he slept. He turned and saw him coming through the press. The black beard and golden eyes, the eagle-blade at his hip. "Gods, Jonik? Is that…is that you?"

Jonik stood, staring, as Emeric Manfrey strode toward him, accompanied by a man in a bloodied white cloak. He thought of his dream again, of the cold words and callous tone. *I didn't want to come back. Why would I want to return to you?* "Emeric. You…you're here…"

The prince, he realised suddenly. *It was Emeric who brought the prince.* That soldier had said it. *Exile,* he'd said.

Emeric came right up to him. He took him by the shoulders and looked him up and down, looked at him intently, looked deep into his eyes. There was a smile on his lips. "Blue sea and misty sky," he said, strangely. He lowered a hand, drew Jonik's cloak aside, saw the Mistblade at his hip. A laugh escaped him, sudden as a deer from the brush. "Gods, she was right. The witch, Stafford. She was right."

The man in the white cloak nodded. "Yes, my lord. She's strange, that one."

Jonik wasn't understanding. "What witch? Emeric, what are you saying?"

"Ships and harbours, Jonik. Nothing but ships and harbours and the uncertain blowing of the wind." A roar rang out, more distant now, as Drulgar the Dread soared far out over the Big Sister. The exile didn't even turn to look. "He's leaving," he said, as though somehow he knew. "And so are we, Jonik. So are we." He stepped in closer, then, and drew him into an embrace. "I'm sorry I left you," he said. "That was never my intent. I want you to know that."

"I know," Jonik said back, weakly. *It was just a dream,* he thought. *Nothing but a dream.* And he smiled and hugged the man back.

45

Ranulf

They trudged along in silence and sadness and all hope had left the group.

The fog closed in about them, and the trees loomed overhead. Alyn was sniffling, Simcock scowling, Rufford glaring as they went. "We'll never make it back," Daecar murmured. He looked around, racked by fear. "Even if we find this tree, how will we get back? With the spiders and the icecats and…"

"Panicking won't do us any good," Mallister Monsort interrupted. "We must be strong now, all of us. Once we find the tree, we'll go back by another route. We know where the spiders are. We'll be able to avoid them."

"But…what if they've got nests elsewhere? They might rule this whole forest…"

Sir Mallister had no answer for the man. "Focus, all of you," he commanded. "Look for white wood. We must be close." The strain was getting to him, Ranulf could see. "We have to find it. You all know how important this is. We have to succeed. We cannot fail."

"We can," said Simcock. He'd gone surly again, truculent. "We fail and they'll just try again. We don't come back, they'll know we're dead. Ilith'll just send another company. And a bigger one this time. Like he *should* have done before."

"Or the prince," said Daecar. "Prince Elyon could just fly here. It…it would be easy for him. He could fly here and back in a day."

Simcock nodded. "Should have sent him in the first place."

"Enough." Mallister Monsort flashed a glare at them. "Elyon has his own obligations. We can't rely on him for everything." He addressed Ranulf. "Does Kamcho see anything yet?" There was a small desperate quality to his voice now, and in the cast of his eyes. "Ranulf? Would you check please?"

"Of course." Ranulf did as the knight bid him, but the result was the same. Nothing. The soupy mist concealed all the forest from Kamcho's piercing gaze, and the eagle could be of no help. At least not from up there. Ranulf gave a high shrill whistle in the tongue of the Calacania, and the big eagle came plunging down through the fog. He landed on Ranulf's outheld arm and the two engaged in a short dialogue, whistling and clicking. Then Kamcho flapped his big blue and gold wings and flew off again, vanishing into the shroud.

"What did you tell him?" Rufford asked.

"To search lower. Fly between the trees and report back. He'll have a better chance of finding the ice oak down here." Ranulf could not communicate telepathically with Kamcho as the Elders did their eagles, but he knew the language, the clicks and cries. "I'll listen out for his call. If he finds it he'll guide us there."

Sir Mallister nodded, trying to remain upbeat. "Let's take another look at the map." It was retrieved from Ranulf's pack and set down on a frozen rock. The light in the wood had been weak all day, but it was beginning to thin yet further, withering like their company. "We should be on our way back by now," Mallister said quietly to Ranulf, as they crouched over the parchment. "I never expected it to take this long."

"These things rarely go smoothly," Ranulf said. "Take it from me, Mallister. I've been on enough adventures to know."

"Adventures." The knight sighed. "Four men have died today. I...I've had to kill three of them myself. To spare them, yes, but..." He spoke grimly. "That's not the sort of adventure I ever dreamed of as a boy."

"A poor choice of word," said Ranulf. True enough, adventure conjured a brighter image than this cold dark nightmare they were living through.

Mallister stared down at the map. He seemed conflicted, unsure. Nothing had gone well since they'd left the lake. Pecker, Stick Jym, Darron, and Gunter had been lost, and he had only four soldiers remaining to him now. "We may have to spend the night here," he said at last. "Even if we found the tree, we'd never get back to the lake in time." He looked around. The last of his men were all staring out in different directions, blades drawn. Daecar was shivering violently, from both cold and fear, and a pall of hopelessness had begun to fall over the rest. "None of us will be able to sleep with branches over our heads, not after those spiders. We need cover, Ranulf. A cave, if we can find it, or a clearing at least. Somewhere where we can protect ourselves."

Ranulf Shackton did not disagree, but if there was a cave anywhere in the dark heart of this forest, it wasn't drawn on the map. The details were too sparse and simple and worse, they didn't even know where they were, not after all that running. The fog was thick; there was no sun, and they had no way of knowing north from south, east from west. *There is a word for that,* Ranulf thought. He decided to just go ahead and say it. "We're lost, Mallister. This map isn't going to help us."

The knight seemed to know that too. "What do you suggest? You've been on a hundred quests like this, so…" He looked at him, hopeful. "What would you do, Ranulf?"

"The only thing we can do. Keep on going." He lifted his eyes, judging the faint pale patches of sky visible through the snowy branches. The air was still here, still and quiet, still and quiet and uncomfortably cold. He could no longer feel all his fingers, nor his toes, and night was coming on fast. "I doubt we have more than an hour or two of daylight left," he said. "Finding a place to camp should become our first priority now. If we do not find the ice oak in that time, we can resume on the morrow. A new dawn may bring better fortune."

Mallister dipped his chin. "Very well." He stood, and Ranulf stood as well, folding the map. He might as well have burned it for all the good it was doing, but stowed it away again as Mallister called the company to assemble. He updated them on their plans and on they went, Sir Mallister leading, Rufford and Alyn behind, Simcock and Daecar drawing up the rear. As ever, Ranulf went along between them, listening all the while for Kamcho's call and occasionally peering through his eyes. The trees here were older than the tall pines and sentinels they'd passed, older and broader, spreading their great limbs across the wood. It was a dark, brooding, tangly place, and the roots bulged and jutted beneath them, wrestling under soil and snow.

Alyn was looking around. "These are oaks," he said. "It's an oakwood, m'lord."

"It would appear so."

"And that white tree…that's an oak too, isn't it?"

"It's called the ice *oak*," Simcock snorted. "What do you think it bloody well is?"

"Then…it'll be here somewhere, won't it?" Alyn said. A small note of hope returned to his voice. "We've seen oaks, I know, but not grouped like this. It'll be here. Someplace around here. It *must* be."

"Why?" snapped Simcock. "Why *must* it? This forest's a hundred leagues across. There'll be ten dozen places where the oaks grow thick like this."

"But not here in the heart of the wood. The dark heart. This foggy part. I'll bet this is it. I'll bet it's right ahead."

Simcock scowled. "*Dark heart.* That's just Rufford's words. This fog might be all over the forest today for all we know. Not just here. In this 'dark heart'." And he snorted again, mocking.

Rufford was growing weary of him. "Or it might not be," he said. "Might be it's like this here every day. We don't know, and we're not going to know by guessing and complaining. So shut your trap, Simcock, else I'll shut it for you. I'm sick of your carping. I lost a good friend today."

"So did I. So we're even on that. You want to shut me up, make me."

Rufford spun about and stamped toward him. Simcock held his ground. The two big men came face to face, nose to nose, beard to beard, eyes glaring.

"Well come on, then." Simcock's lips twisted. "Back up your big talk, Rufford."

"All right." And Rufford swung. Simcock sensed it coming and leaned back, avoiding the blow. Rufford's big fist grazed the bloodstained beard that hung from Simcocks' chin, and his momentum took him on. Simcock's gauntleted fist swung up into his guts, though met only the godsteel breastplate he wore under his surcoat and layers of fur. There was a dull clang. Rufford reached out to steady himself and grappled Simcock to the ground and down they went together, tumbling into the snow. The others watched silently as they puffed and wrestled futilely on the floor. Even Mallister seemed to hardly care. For a moment Ranulf wondered if this was it, his breaking point. *Or perhaps he knows they have to get it out of their system.* He couldn't be certain which.

The men soon parted and rose back to their feet, puffing and panting, frosted from head to heel. "You fight like a woman," Simcock spat.

"Your mother was a whore," Rufford came back. "I should know. Had her a half dozen times."

Simcock roared and went again, spearing the other man to the ground and the bout continued. Ranulf looked at Mallister. "How long are you going to let this go on?"

"Give it another minute."

When that minute elapsed they were back on their feet again, panting even harder. "Your whore mother teach you how to fight like that?" Rufford taunted, between breaths. "She put up a better fight in the bedroom, let me tell you." He spat out a gob of blood. Somewhere in their snowbound scuffling, he'd split his lip and taken a gash above his right eye.

"Enough about my mother," Simcock growled. "She was a good woman."

"Good in bed, aye."

"Damn you!" And he drew his blade. He thrust the point in Rufford's direction. "She was a good woman. Sully her name again and I'll cut you."

Ranulf saw the internal struggle. He knew how these things went. If Rufford said nothing, he would feel as though he lost. If he said something, the fight would escalate. His eyes glanced over toward Sir Mallister and he seemed to come to some decision. "Put up your steel, Simcock," Rufford said, in a more temperate voice. "This has gone far enough."

"Not until you take that back. About my mother."

"I take it back. She was a good woman."

Simcock squinted at him, suspicious, then slowly slid away his blade. "Well...she was. A good woman."

"I know. I shouldn't have said anything." The corner of Rufford's mouth curled up. Ranulf groaned internally as the man-at-arms said, "And I only had her the *five* times, not six."

"Godsdamn you!" Simcock tore his blade back out and came rushing forward, swinging. Rufford's sword was free in the blink of an eye, rising to meet it. The ring of godsteel echoed out through the forest and Ranulf knew it was folly.

"Mallister, stop them." The men were going blow for blow, swinging, parrying, thrusting. "They're making too much noise."

The knight engaged, drawing out his longsword. Skilfully he got between them, knocking aside a strike from Simcock first, then spinning and deflecting Rufford's blow. "That's enough," he shouted. "Damn it, Rufford, know when to shut up." He spun. "And Simcock, your mother wasn't a whore. You know it, I know it, he knows it. So don't rise to the bait."

"Says you. You'd kill a prince for your sister's honour. Why can't I do the same for my mother?"

"That was different. My sister's dead."

"So is my mother! And I've got this smirking braggart befouling her name!" Their voices were too loud, far too loud. Simcock shouted out another curse, and Rufford shouted back at him, but Ranulf was no longer listening. Something tickled at the back of his head, and at the edge of hearing he heard a shrill cry. He shut his eyes and saw them. Men, big men, moving quickly through the trees. Kamcho was watching from a branch, staring right down at them. The eagle opened its beak and gave another piercing cry and Ranulf heard it almost at once, less than a second later.

"Be quiet," he hissed. "Quiet!" The men didn't hear him. They were still hurling curses as Mallister tried to break them apart. "Quite, I said!" Ranulf shouted, matching their volume. "Be quiet! Men are coming!"

That got through to them. "You what?" panted Rufford, breathless from his insults. "Men? What men?"

"Bark Men. I saw them. They're only a few hundred metres away."

"Which direction?" Mallister demanded, turning around. "How many?"

Ranulf didn't know. The sound did strange things here and he couldn't tell from where the cry had come. He put his fingers to his lips and gave a whistle, then moved to Kamcho's sight. The bird plunged down off the branch, flapping fiercely, weaving between the trees. The Bark Men watched the bird glide on by, heads turning as they went. They were towering men, hairy men, primitive men with old blood in them. The bark armour they wore was wrapped in widowmaker silk, strong as steel, and the long pine spears they bore had tips twisted and shaped from the silk as well, forming points that could pierce godsteel, or so the legends said. Ranulf would sooner that legend was kept a legend for now.

He opened his eyes. The others were looking at him. He heard the flapping of wings, another cry, and Kamcho came rippling through the fog so quickly he seemed to materialise before them. He flew about Ranulf's head in a tight circle, whistling frantically.

"What's he saying?" Mallister demanded.

"There are thirty of them. Three hundred metres and closing." He pointed the way the bird had come. "That's too many to fight."

He saw the conflict in Mallister's eyes. *He wants to fight. To stand and fight.* But the knight knew who he was dealing with. These were not common forest men. No one who lived here in this wood could be taken lightly and these men were half-giants, thickly muscled and hardy, and their armour was hard to piece. He came to a snap decision. "We go. On me, all of you, and stay close. Rufford, carry him."

Again? Ranulf groaned, accepting his fate as Rufford marched over and scooped him back up onto his shoulder, and they were running again, leaping over rocks and roots, weaving around boles and under branches, hurtling through the wood. Thinly, Ranulf heard the sounds of pursuit, the great grunting tongue of the Bark Men as they shouted out at one another and ran. Kamcho peeled off from the company and flew back behind them, and Ranulf shut his eyes and tried to focus. What he saw was only glimpses. Great beards twisted with twigs, thick tangled hair flowing back from broad, brutish brows. Many had exposed arms, densely covered in dark brown hair, bulging with muscle. Tree-trunk legs stamped through the snow, blasting it aside, and the mouths moved, shouting, and the narrow dark eyes roved, searching.

One of the men spotted the bird and seemed to know it was a spy. A spear came flying, a sizzling powerful throw, and Kamcho shrieked and flapped away. The spear plunged into the high broad limb of an oak, splitting it in two with a great resounding crack that echoed out through the forest.

Ranulf breathed out and opened his eyes. Rufford was puffing and panting, swerving around a huge oaken trunk. A gnarled root rose up from the snow and he caught it with his trailing leg, tripping and stumbling, and Ranulf went flying. He landed hard, the wind punched out of him. Before he could even gasp for breath, Rufford was there again, taking a fistful of his cloak and throwing him back onto his shoulder as though he was nought but a stuffed children's toy.

He wheezed, disoriented, fighting to fill his lungs. There was a pain there, a sharp pain in his chest and he suspected he'd cracked a rib. "They're gaining on us," Simcock was shouting. "Damn them, they're gaining!"

"Run faster, then!" returned Sir Mallister. "We're Bladeborn. Faster! *Faster!*"

The world became a rushing blur. Ranulf's head swung violently up and down and side to side and each snatch of breath came with a stab of pain. He tried to slip into Kamcho's sight again, but failed, his focus lost. He could hear the thunderous charge coming up behind them, hear Daecar shouting out desperately as he started to fall back. There were shadows in the trees now, big shadows in pursuit. He glimpsed Daecar trip on something, saw him fall and try to stand, saw him buck forward at the hips as he rose, saw the spear punch through the small of his back and out through his navel with a burst of blood. A moment later, the

Bark Men were there, stampeding past him. One slowed only to yank his spear from the man's back before running onward with the rest, and they were roaring now, roaring in anger and rage. The whole forest rang to it. *We're all going to die*, Ranulf thought.

He closed his eyes again, praying to Rasalan, to Thala, to whatever god or goddess or spirit might listen. Kamcho soared out of the fog, circling. The eagle was whistling at him, insistent, but through the din he could barely hear him. Around the bird went, around, around. Ranulf focused on the whistles, focused on the clicks. *Follow*, he thought, realising. *He's telling us to follow.* "Rufford," he said. "Rufford."

The man ignored him. Or didn't hear him.

"Rufford…" He spoke louder, shouting. "Kamcho…follow Kamcho…"

"You what?"

"Kamcho! Follow him!"

The big man nodded, filled his lungs and bellowed. "The bird! My lord! Shackton says to follow the bird!"

Mallister Monsort was a short way ahead, leading on. He nodded his head, hearing him, scanned for Kamcho and veered after the eagle in pursuit. The bird gave out a shrieking cry, weaving back and forward as they followed. Simcock was hard on Mallister's heel, Rufford labouring to keep up, Alyn right alongside them. The Bark Men were gaining, hurdling roots, hefting their spears to throw.

One came whistling by just as Rufford passed a tree and it *clunked* into the trunk, quivering. Another soared over his shoulder and into the fog. The man-at-arms glanced back, and Ranulf saw the fury in his eyes, the urge to stop and face them and fight. But it was fleeting, momentary. His head swung forward and he kept on going.

And the spears kept coming. Tips plunged into wood and earth and root and snow, and sailed away into the mist. One struck Rufford a glancing blow, ripping through his furs as it careened off his breastplate. The soldier staggered, grunting, but kept his footing, leaping a wide ditch, landing, running. A deadfall lay ahead of them, a great thick trunk all tangled in limbs. "Cover your face, Shackton!" he roared, as he charged right toward it, jumping the trunk, crashing through the branches. When he hit the ground on the other side, he went to a knee, heaving for breath. His eyes went left and right, searching. "Damn it, I don't see them."

"Here!" came a shout. "Here, Rufford!"

And he was up again, running again, running toward Simcock. "Let me have him," the other man called. "You're tiring. Let me take him."

"I can manage." Rufford gulped frozen air and looked right past him. Mallister was ahead, waving them on, Alyn behind, staggering, tiring. They could hear the barbarians shouting and grunting as they leapt the ditch, hear their heavy bodies crashing down into the snow. They sounded fewer now, as though some had been lost or given up the chase.

"Alyn, hurry!" Simcock bellowed. "Go, Rufford. Go, I'll help him."

"Don't die," Rufford said. The men nodded at one another. Rufford lurched on.

Mallister Monsort was waiting ahead, Kamcho perched on a low branch beside him. Beyond lay what looked like a clearing in the woods where the land rose up toward a shallow, snowy hill. "We have no choice," the knight said. "We'll have to fight from the higher ground."

Fog shrouded the hill, drifting by in torn grey banners. Ranulf glimpsed something back there, something solid, seen quickly and gone again.

Simcock and Alyn staggered up toward them. "M'lord," said Alyn, "Daecar, he…"

"I saw," Mallister said. "Their spears are formidable, and their armour. But on this hill we'll have room to move. We'll have the advantage here."

The Bark Men were emerging through the fog. The world misted in a shroud of heat around them and some of them were moving heavily, pausing to catch their breath, then lumbering on.

"They're tired," Sir Mallister observed. "A third have fallen behind, or may have turned back. We kill eight of them, ten, and the rest will flee. Show them who we are. For Tukor," he said.

The four men drew their blades. Ranulf slid down from Rufford's shoulder, unburdening the man. He winced as he hit the ground, holding his chest. Sir Mallister looked at him. "Ranulf, up the hill. Stay behind us. Find cover if you can."

They turned as a group and moved past the last of the trees and into the open air of the clearing. The slope was gentle, the snow hard-packed and firm, the earth frozen solid beneath it. Here and there were bushes and shrubs, but they were few. They reached a place fifty feet from the trees and the Bladeborn turned, facing their foe. Mallister Monsort stood in the centre, Alyn to his right, Rufford and Simcock at the flanks. "For Tukor," the knight said.

"For Tukor," the men echoed. They did not shout it out, as was common, not yet; their voices were subdued, restrained, determined.

"Ten," Mallister Monsort said. "Kill ten and victory is ours."

Ranulf stood a few paces behind them. He could not seem to drag himself away. He was one of them…Bladeborn or not, warrior or not, he was one of them. The Bark Men were nearing the edge of the forest now, stepping out into the open, breathing raggedly. They paused, seeing the men there facing them.

"They're big," Simcock said. "You weren't wrong about that."

"Big trees fall hard," declared Rufford. "And big men are slow."

Sir Mallister nodded. "Spread. We're too big a target for those spears." The men crabbed left and right, fanning out. A dozen or so Bark Men had gathered now. Some more were further back, approaching more slowly. They seemed more cautious all of a sudden. The biggest of them was truly colossal, a match for Sir Ralston Whaleheart in height and half again as wide. His beard was a thing of wild beauty, a magnificent brown flow that went right down to his navel. "That one," said Sir Mallister Monsort. "That one there is *mine*." No one had any complaint about that. "When I open his guts below that beard, they'll know what they're dealing with." He stared a moment, then turned his head. "Ranulf, why are you still here? Go. We'll be with you shortly."

He didn't want to leave. He wanted to watch, to see the clash of sword and spear. He wanted to see this young Emerald Guard show the gods what he could do. *They don't know what they're dealing with*, Ranulf thought. He had a good sense that Mallister Monsort was about to show them.

"I can hear you thinking behind me, Ranulf." The knight did not turn to look at him. "Go. Now. Find cover. Go."

And he went, reluctant, backing away up the slope. Then turning, he strode away more quickly, and as the shroud of fog closed about him, he heard a voice shout out, a great grunting bellow of a voice in a tongue he did not know. Then came the lumbering tread, the pound of heavy boots, and loudly now the Bladeborn shouted, "For Tukor! For Tukor! For Ilith! For Tukor!" as the Bark Men engaged and the fight began.

Ranulf raced away from it, every step sending tremors of pain through his ribs. The hill below rang to the sound of grunts and curses and bellows. "Kamcho," Ranulf called, and the bird was there, flapping down onto his shoulder. "That structure. Find it for me." The hill was larger than he'd thought, broad and open, but the fog was thick and the light was fading. The eagle soared again, shrieking, flapping swiftly away. Ranulf paused, looking around. When the mist blew by, he could see glimpses of the woods spreading around him, the great black forest covered all in white. It encircled them. This hill seemed like an island rising from the sea. Brutal noises echoed up from below. Ranulf hoped and prayed that his friends were winning. *They must win. I cannot survive here alone.*

A shriek and Kamcho was back, circling around him, once, twice, then plunging away into the murk. Ranulf hurried after him. The shouts grew more distant, swallowed by the fog. Then very quickly, a shape emerged, the stone structure he'd seen, and he knew at once what it was. *Gods, we're here…*

It was the monument, the stone monument raised up to Lady Lhara. Beautiful it was, if somewhat crude, carven from a towering block of stone in the likeness of Lhara herself. She stood there on the hill, thirty feet tall, one hand across her belly, head bowed low. There were tears on her cheeks, tears carven into the stone, and before her lay a body that could only be Hundrar the Huntsman. In death he lay, arms folded at his chest, his famous bow resting beside him. Snow had almost covered him over now, but Lady Lhara rose above it, weeping for her lost love.

Ranulf stared up at it for a long moment. Then a wind blew through, and behind the monument he saw it. The ice oak, another seventy feet back, rising grandly, broadly, brilliantly from the earth.

The fighting was ongoing below. He moved quickly past the lying figure of Hundrar the Hunstman, circling around Lady Lhara as she stood there, eternally grieving. The ice oak cleared before him, the biggest oak he'd ever seen. Ice glittered all about it, in the leaves and the branches, sparkling like ten thousand tiny diamonds. He pressed dizzily on. The trunk was enormous. Great thick roots bulged and surged and between them, at the base, he saw some sort of opening. Not a door, no, not large enough for that. More a window, a window shaped almost like a tear. Something was shining within it.

The sap, he thought. *The sap…it's right there…*

His legs felt weak as he drew toward it. The air felt suddenly thick and strange. In the back of his mind he heard what he thought was a whisper, a voice, away at the edge of his hearing. It was weeping, crying, calling out for a long-lost love. *Lhara*, he thought. *It…it is her…*

He swung the bag from his shoulder, threw it down into the snow. He dug into a pocket and took out a vial, pulling the cork with his teeth. The voice was growing louder. It wept of love…of sacrifice. Ranulf cringed and tried to get close, but some sort of force was holding him back. Some terrible disquiet, some unknown thing. *I need them*, he thought. *I need them. This is why we're here.* He pressed forward again, and his eyes were blurring. The sounds down the hill were no longer there.

He heard a voice behind him.

"Ranulf, let me."

He turned. Mallister Monsort was there, sprayed in blood. His faceplate was raised, and his eyes were fierce. He looked at the oak, looked at the tear-shaped window in the tree. He seemed to be hearing something, hearing the same voice that Ranulf was hearing.

"Give it here, Ranulf. Give me the vial."

"But…"

"Give it to me."

Ranulf lifted the vial. His hand was shivering. Behind Mallister he saw a shape coming up through the fog, but he could not tell who it was. The other two were nowhere to be seen. The other two were likely dead.

Sir Mallister took the vial from his fingers and moved right past him. Ranulf turned and watched as the knight walked up toward the trunk. He raised his hand to the tear-shaped window. There was a pause, as though Mallister was listening. A grimace passed his face, and a tear ran down his cheek. Then he nodded, accepting, and plunged the vial into the oak.

When he withdrew it, it was filled with light.

46

____

Saska

There were cloaked men ahead, barring the way onto the bridge.

"You want to pass, you got to pay," a gruff voice shouted out at them from the gate. "How many o' you are there? Eight, nine is it? 'Tis a silver clay a man…horses go free." He paused to confer with one of his companions. "And a piece o' gold for the big one. He counts for two at his size."

That made Leshie laugh out loud. "Only two? Parapet and the Tigress are big enough for two. Coldheart's worth three at least."

"It's that *stone* parapet above the gatehouse that interests me more," the Surgeon said, peering into the darkness. "Jaito, loose an arrow at their leader. Let's see how many more of them are hiding up there."

The young archer nocked his bow.

"Hold." The Wall's voice shook the air. "These men are Rasalanian. We will resolve this without violence if we can." He sounded thunderously displeased. This sort of confrontation was the very reason why he had wanted to avoid crossing the Links in the first place, but they were here now and there was nothing else for it.

"No violence?" The Butcher was appalled by the notion. "But we are built for violence, every one of us here. Rasalanian, Tukoran, Vandarian, what does it matter? They are craven outlaws and deserve what is coming to them." There were some murmurs of agreement from the others. "Let's send in little red to cut them all to ribbons. She is the smallest, so that will make it more funny."

Leshie nodded firmly. "I'll do it," she said.

"No," Saska told her. "Since when do you like killing northmen?"

"Since they tried to extort us. Meshface is ugly as sin, but he's right on what he said…they deserve what's coming. If not us someone else will get them, and how much robbing will they do before then? We'd be doing a good service."

The voice shouted over at them again, ringing through the cold night

533

air. "So? Do we have a deal or don't we? If you ain't got the coin, we can bargain. Jewels. We'd take those. Rings and bracelets ought to serve. Or if you got a good bit o' steel…"

"We have lots of *godsteel* here," Leshie shouted, unable to restrain herself. "You want us to remove our cloaks and show you?"

"Bladeborn, is it? We got Bladeborn too. Swords and spears and *archers*, aye. Lot o' them above the gate and in these here towers as well. Got an archer at every arrow slit, so you think twice before you do anything rash. We see any o' you take one step closer and we'll pepper you where you stand."

That gave them a little more pause. If they had Bladeborn archers with godsteel-tipped arrows then none of them were safe; such weapons could pierce their armour. Saska cursed under her breath. Elyon should have known about this; he'd flown over this way only shortly before they arrived to make sure the gate was open and the towers abandoned. Clearly he hadn't looked close enough. As soon as they'd ridden up within two hundred yards of the gate they'd seen shadows moving past the tower windows and several men had emerged from the gatehouse to bar the way. There were currently only four of them visible there, but who knew how many more were hidden out of sight?

The Baker was starting to grow impatient. "Let's just rush them. If there are archers, so be it. They won't be much good in this dark anyway, and we will close the distance quickly."

"I agree," whispered the Surgeon. He put a hand on the Tigress's arm. She was staring toward the gate with a crazed, wide-eyed intensity. Saska wondered if that was from this mention of Bladeborn in the ranks. *She wants a taste of blood,* she thought. *It's been a while since she'd had that savour.* "The Tigress and I will make for the gatehouse and see to whoever is lurking above. If there are archers there we will make quick work of them."

The Baker nodded. "I will take the left tower with Umberto. My brother and the Gravedigger will take the right."

"And what about me?" Leshie asked. "I want to fight as well."

"You are not ours to command," the Baker told her. "Go where you please. Just don't get in our way."

"None of that is going to happen," Sir Ralston Whaleheart said, ruining the fun. He had been quietly watching, intently listening, and seemed to have something figured out. "These men are simply trying to show strength where there is none. They have a single man or two in each tower, hurrying past windows and lighting fires to make their numbers seem more than they are. I judge their strength to be no more than ten, if that. And there are no Bladeborn here. They will scatter when I charge them."

"Charge them?" Saska asked.

"Yes." He swung a leg over Bedrock's saddle and landed with a heavy *thud.* "Stay here. This won't take long."

The voice at the gate shouted over at them again. "Hey now! I said don't move, didn't you hear me?" He sounded panicked all of a sudden. "You stay right there and don't take another step! We got bowmen here, Bladeborn bowmen…you move and they'll fire. This ain't no empty threat."

But it was. The Wall knew it was. Reaching into his cloak, he slid out a monstrous greatsword.

"Archers!" came the desperate cry. "Archers, nock! Take one step closer, *you*…one more step and…"

And then the ground began to rumble.

Saska had half forgotten what a fearsome sight the Whaleheart must make when charging his enemies in battle. It was not just his unimaginable size, nor the frankly enormous dual swords he carried, but his speed. Thundering forward, the would-be extorters broke and ran just as he said they would, fleeing into the night. Saska could hear them screaming. Two tripped in their haste and fell, scrambling back up onto their feet, desperate in their terror. But the Wall had no intention of hurting them. A simple jog in their direction was all it took for the giant to win the gate.

Once he'd done that, he raised a fist and called them over. The Butcher was laughing uproariously as he trotted up and dismounted. "They must have recognised you as you got closer, Coldheart. I think all of them soiled their breeches."

"They did," sniffed the Surgeon. "I can smell it."

So could Saska. It seemed the charge of her giant made for a good quick way of moving the bowels. "You're a walking cure for constipation," she told him, to laughs from the others. "We should search the towers for food. They probably have some stored away."

"And other things." The Baker had a hopeful gleam in his eye. "Mayhaps their efforts here have yielded some riches. I might find some new spectacles, even."

"If I find any spectacles I'm going to *crush* them," the Surgeon told him. "I will give you bits of glass and twisted metal instead."

The Baker scowled. "You have no heart. This loss torments me. Those spectacles…they were very dear to me."

"I'm sure. As were the four swords I lost. Gutter, Gore, Scalpel, Savage, all good friends…"

The Butcher scoffed at that. "They were not friends to you. You are not capable of friendship. Those spectacles meant a lot to my brother, but you care for nothing. Nothing but the cat woman."

The scarred sellsword offered said cat woman a placating grin, and where once she might have hissed at him, the Tigress only lifted her lips in return, which looked like her best version of a smile. They got on well now, such as they could with this limited form of communication. "I have tamed the beast," the Butcher had been heard to say…far from the Tigress's hearing, of course. "I think she even loves me, and I her. We will have many little children, yes, many mage-and-Bladeborn children with her wild beauty and my unstoppable strength and they will be giants, all of them, none less than seven feet tall and the biggest even bigger than the Wall. We shall start a new company of our own called the Scarredy Cats! You see…like scaredy cat, but I am *scarred* all over, yes, and so is she with the lash scars she hides, so it is *Scarredy* Cats instead." He was very proud of that name. "From our loins alone we will make the greatest sellsword company ever to live!"

He was joking, Saska supposed, though with the Butcher it was hard to know for sure. Not long ago the pair had been frothing for a fight to settle the score over Merinius's death. Now they often rode together and walked together and were in love, or so the man liked to claim. *Well, they're two sides of the same blade,* Saska reflected. *Hate and love.* Sometimes there was barely an edge between them.

She smiled, unbidden, thinking of Elyon. Sweet memories of the previous night flooded her mind and that only made her grin all the broader.

"So, it finally happened, did it?" a voice said.

She turned. Leshie was looking at her, not joining in with the others as they went off to search for supplies. "Sorry? Did you say something, Lesh?"

"That smile. I know *that* smile. You and Elyon…you finally did it."

Did it? How crude. "A lady doesn't tell, Leshie," she said primly….though she was anything but a lady down in that cellar. Something different had come out of her, some animal lust that she'd been suppressing for far too long. And Elyon too, the way they'd romped and rutted all night. The memories were so fresh they made her squirm for more. *Maybe I'll ask him to stay another day or two after all?* she thought. *Or will that only make it harder when he's gone?*

"You're *going* to bloody well tell *me*," Leshie said, in a voice that made it clear she would harass her until she did. "I want *all* the gory details, Saska. Every last little bit of it, and you won't leave anything out. I deserve that much at least."

"Fine. But not now, later."

"Why not now? You can tell me while we're crossing the bridge."

"No. This isn't the place." The bridge was unique; long and dark and straight as a spear, it stretched ten miles from coast to coast, linking Rasalan and Tukor, and was wide enough for a dozen wagons to roll along side by side. If they wanted privacy to talk, they would find it easily enough, but it wasn't just that. The bridge was something of a holy place as well, Saska had always believed. Ilith had built it, raising it up with his magic and his Forgeborn, an architectural feat of singular brilliance that no one else in history could have matched. To Saska, that made it sacred. It was no place to be discussing smut. "I'll tell you about it when we stop to make camp somewhere. And anyway, I'm too tired for all of that right now." She winked at her. "Elyon had me up all night…"

She rode off, ignoring Leshie's protests and accusations that she was a 'tease', joining Rolly beyond the gate where he stared out into the gloom. The wind was gusting in from the north and the waters looked rough, floes of ice jostling and crashing into one another as they poured down the strait and under the bridge to empty into the Redwater Bay. There were some wrecks down there as well, she saw. Splintered boats lying up against the shore or crushed amid the ice.

"That might have been us," she offered. "If we'd decided to cross the water."

The Wall's jaw was tight. He gave no answer.

"You're still sour that we didn't go north?"

"It was my preference, yes."

"Well, personally I'd sooner cross a four-thousand-year-old stone bridge made by a demigod than a bridge of ice, Rolly. One crack and we'd all be doomed."

"I would have tested the ice myself to make certain it was strong enough. Further north the route to Ilithor would be safer."

"You mean *quieter.*" That was the thrust of it. He wanted to avoid people as much as he could.

He nodded. "It will be busier on the other side. We have been fortunate these last weeks to have travelled such a desolate land, but at the far end of this bridge it will be different. We will try to keep to quieter paths, but more contact like we've had here will be unavoidable. We must remain extra vigilant. And the cat…"

This again. "Her name is Joy."

He gave her a judging look. "I know her name. You turn defensive whenever I speak of her."

"Because you undermine her at every turn." She blew out a breath. "I thought you were getting along better. She's playful with you, Rolly. Why do you hate her so much?"

"I don't hate her. She is a fine animal, but still an animal, driven by instinct. I fear for her, in truth. For what may happen when we reach the other side. What if she should kill a chicken or a sheep, and come afoul of a disgruntled farmer? Or be hunted by woodsmen defending their kin? She will be seen as an enemy to all across this bridge, you know that as well as I do. And if she should kill someone, or worse…*be* killed."

He worries how it will affect me. She knew that. He'd had that reservation all along and had wanted Joy to remain in Aram for that reason. But who knew what state Aram was in now? It might have been destroyed by Eldur for all they knew or overwhelmed by another power. Leaving Joy there with Elio Krator still alive and at large was not an option she was willing to take. "If she dies, then…she dies," Saska made herself say. "I have detached myself from that fear, Rolly. I've told you that already."

"So you say. But words are cheap. There are primal reactions you may not be able to control. True grief is not something you can prepare for, Saska. Why did you send the boy away?"

She frowned. "Del? You know why."

"Because you feared for his life."

"Yes. He's not a warrior like the rest of us. Not Bladeborn. And before you suggest I send Joy away too, I can't, and you know I can't. That's different."

"Why?"

"Because." She said the word before she'd thought of a reason. Her brow twisted. "Because Del's a boy and she's a starcat. What would you have me do? Send her away to the refuge as well? I can't imagine she'd enjoy being strapped up into Elyon's harness, Rolly, and I doubt he would either. It isn't made for cats."

"I wasn't suggesting that."

"Then what? Leave her here in Rasalan? To fend for herself all alone?" She saw the answer in his eyes. "No. I'm not doing that."

"She would be safer here," he rumbled. "These lands are deserted; there is no war here. And she is a cat, quite able to hunt and find warm places to sleep and hide from danger. It would be the wiser course."

"And not one I'm willing to take."

"Why not? Why won't you listen to reason?"

She said nothing. In matters concerning Joy she was irrational, she knew. If she'd been raised in Aram as the Lightborn princess she was, she'd have learned how to manage that bond, but she hadn't. It was not something she had ever expected to happen and she was doing the best she could. "I'll keep her close, I promise," she said, wanting an end to this conversation. "That's the best I can do."

"And when we reach Ilithor? Starcats do not belong in northern cities."

The man was relentless. "And snow does not belong in summer," she came back. "Nor should a slave girl from Tukor have to save the world. But that's the way it is. And there's nothing we can do to change it."

He stared down at her, unmoved. All the goodness that lingered from her night with Elyon was being swallowed up by his brooding doubts. "You carry a heavy burden, I know. Why make it heavier? Why take the risk."

He'll never understand. "I'm tired," she said, numbly. "If you want to keep talking about this, we'll have to do it later. This isn't the time."

She turned away from him. *He should have spoken of this earlier,* she thought. *Given me more time to consider it.* Maybe then she'd see the sense in it, but now...no, it was too late now.

The others were coming up behind them, talking about what they'd found. Some hard bread and salted fish, mouldy cheese and a few bags of nuts was the sum of it. The Butcher had found a freshly slain hare hanging up inside the gatehouse as well. "I will feed your Joy," he said to her, with a grin. "It needs fattening up. Too skinny is your Joy."

Is he talking about my happiness? Is he trying to be clever? She couldn't tell and didn't care for the Butcher's wit right now. "Thank you," she said, a little stiffly. "I'm sure she'll be pleased for the meal."

Once all the new loot had been packed into their saddlebags, Sir Ralston gave his orders. "I want two riding ahead," he said, grumpily. "To check for obstructions. There may be other bands of outlaws preying on this bridge and it would serve to be given warning of them."

"The Windy Prince would have seen them," the Butcher declared. "He would have reported to us any threats."

"He never said anything about those extorters," Leshie put in.

"Because he thought them no threat," the Butcher said. "Or he did not see them. They were hiding."

Saska nodded. "You can't hide on the bridge. But two should go anyway to make sure." She looked around. "Butcher, you seem to have a lot to say on it. Leshie, you too. Ride up the bridge together and report back what you find." She wanted rid of the girl so she didn't pester her about Elyon. If she could send Rolly away as well, she would, but that wasn't so easy. "But no killing," she added. "You come upon a band of marauders heading our way, don't engage. We'll handle them together."

"As the Pretty Princess says. Little red, let's race." The Butcher kicked his spurs and raced away, Leshie chasing hard after him.

The rest began their journey more sedately. The falling sleet was cold and wet and was soon soaking through their cloaks. The Baker seemed in a sombre mood. No doubt he failed to find any spectacles. "We'll find you some when we reach Tukor," Saska told him. "A golden pair, like before."

That made him smile, but it was fleeting. "It will never be the same, not really. Those spectacles...they had a special meaning to me, Sereneness. I do not talk of it much, but I had a wife, once before. She was clever and wise and loved to read....not beautiful, no, not in the way you are, but to me she was everything. She would wear those glasses when she read her books, and when she died, I wore them to remember."

Saska didn't know what to say to that. She never knew of the Baker's wife. "What happened to her?" she asked, softening her tone.

"She was taken by a wasting sickness, many years ago. At first she would still read in her bed, but soon she grew too weak, and I read to her instead. This is when I first wore the spectacles. I did it to make her laugh...we liked to laugh together, but that...that was the last time, I think. The last true laugh, when she saw me wearing them." He smiled sadly as he rode along the cobbles. "I still hear it, sometimes, when I think of her. That last laugh. Though since I lost the glasses..." He sighed and shook his head.

"We'll find you some new ones, I promise." It wouldn't be the same, she knew, but perhaps that weight...feeling it on his nose and ear, always fidgeting to rearrange them, perhaps that would be enough?

He rode on in silence a moment, then said, "And you, my lady? I have had my one great love, but yours is yet to come. You and the prince. Is there to be a future there?"

She couldn't possibly answer that, not with words, but her coy smile gave it away. "I don't know. We'll have to think about that later...after the war."

"After, of course. When the dust settles, we shall see who still stands, yes?"

"Yes." That only made her think of Elyon *not* standing, which caused her guts to twist, but she had to accept that was possible, the same as with Joy. She was hardly alone in that fear; didn't everyone have someone they feared to lose? Hadn't half the world lost loved ones already? How was she any different? *I'm not*, she told herself. *I'm no different at all. If I lose one of them or I lose them all I'm still going to keep on going. Like the Baker with his wife. I'll find some new spectacles and keep moving.*

It was an hour before the Butcher and Leshie came riding back through the darkness. Their speed suggested something was wrong, so Saska spurred her mare up to the front to be the first to greet them. "What is it? What's happened?"

"Elyon…he's back." Leshie pointed back the way they'd come. "He's up that way, waiting for you on the bridge. Says he needs to talk to you urgently."

"Right…" Saska swung a leg over her saddle and dismounted. "I'll have to leave the Nightblade with you," she said to Rolly, as she began unbuckling her swordbelt. "Stay here until I return."

Her guardian didn't like that. "What's this about?" he demanded of the others. "This bridge is no place to stop and hold council."

"The Windy Prince likes to keep that counsel to himself, Coldheart. He did not tell us anything, but to ride and fetch his Pretty Princess."

His. Well I guess they all know about us, then. "He may want to take me off for training," Saska said. That made Leshie snicker, and she realised how it sounded. "Training with the *Windblade*," she added, giving her a glare. "It might be our last chance, before…"

"Before? Before what?"

All of them looked at her, and she realised none of them knew. "Nothing. He's just…leaving, is all. For a bit. I'll tell you about that later." She turned to the Butcher. "Ride me out to him," she ordered. "If he flies me off to train, you can all keep going along the bridge."

"No we can't," Leshie told her. "We have to stay with the Nightblade, you just said."

"Take it with you."

"How?"

"Sir Ralston can carry it."

The giant gave a low rumble. "No. I have no bond to it."

"I'm sure you'd manage. Butcher, help me up." He gave her a hand and she vaulted up into the saddle behind him. With a kick of the heels they were off, riding through the night.

Elyon was waiting some five hundred metres away. Rarely did he let the two Blades of Vandar get any closer, and when he did it was not for long. "So you're leaving, Windy Prince," the Butcher called as he reined up. "This is sad to hear. Are you sick of my face?"

"Your face did not come up in the matter."

Saska climbed down and strode toward him. "So what's this urgent business? Are we going to train?"

"No. There's something I need to show you, but we must be quick."

Something to show me? She had an indecent thought of him carrying her off to some secret place to indulge their passions but was not getting that sense from him. This was serious, she could see.

"I'll need you strapped up in the harness, Saska. Come here." He drew her in and began working the straps and buckles. The Butcher lingered a moment until Saska dismissed him, then wheeled about and rode away with an order for the others to keep moving. She could feel Elyon's warm breath at the back of her neck as he worked. A ripple went up her spine.

"What's this about? Did you find a dragon for me to hunt?"

"Not to hunt, no." His fingers were working feverishly, pulling and tugging, making certain she was tightly lashed up to him. There was a tension in his body, his heart thumping through the steel of his breast-plate. Something had him excited and it wasn't her this time. *Excited and afraid,* she realised. "Ready?"

"Yes. Where are we going?"

"Southwest. There's an island, just off the Vandarian coast. Near the Lakelands…"

"The Lakelands? But they're hundreds of miles from here…"

"The Four Sisters are. The coast is closer. A hundred miles, maybe. The island's a couple of leagues offshore."

"And what's there? You're to say you've flown a *hundred miles* from us? I thought you were meant to be keeping watch?"

"I was. There was a dragon, Saska. It was coming too close so I chased it off and then…well…you'll see."

He was being mysterious. Whatever questions and demands she might have made were soon overwhelmed by the roar of the wind as he shot skyward at a blistering pace. He seemed in a race to get there, as though worried what he wanted to show her would be gone by the time they arrived. She watched the world widen as they went, broadening beneath them. Even in the dark the features were visible. The bridge, stretching east and west into the darkness. The little white ice floes tumbling down the strait. They spread out as they entered the bay, dispersing and melting as they met the warmer waters. Before very long the sleet was gone and a soft drizzle had taken its place.

The sea was rough. A storm was pummelling the waters much further to the southeast, but their heading was more westward, away from the worst of it. She'd wondered for a moment if he would take her there, into the storm, but no. Elyon always spoke about how alive he felt in thunderstorms, how powerful the Windblade became, but so far she hadn't experienced that. The only storms they'd had of late were *snow*storms and those were not the same.

Better for his father, she thought. *And me…one day soon.* She still got a pang of nerves at the prospect of dispossessing Amron Daecar of the Frostblade, no matter what Elyon said. To do so would condemn him to life as a cripple. *Can't we remake the Heart with just four blades,* she wondered. *Leave that one for him? Four of five is surely good enough, no?*

Elyon interrupted her musings. "We're getting close," he called over the wind. "Here, take the blade a moment. Just fly straight. I want to see if you feel it."

She didn't ask questions, just did what he said. Reaching out he carefully handed her the Windblade, something they'd done a thousand times before. Her blood-bond was initiated at once and she took control, keeping them on a steady course a mile or so in the air.

"Do you feel it?" Elyon asked her. "In the steel?"

She could not say what it was, but yes, she felt something. "The blade's frightened," she said. "And...excited." It was the same as she'd felt in Elyon, the same as she now felt herself. "There's something out there. Something...powerful."

"Immensely so." He reached out to take the blade back off her. She gave it up; her breathing was becoming more shallow as she sensed what lay ahead. Ahead she could see the Vandarian coastline emerging on the horizon, peeling back beneath the cover of night. Some islands could be seen off the rugged shore, most of them small and sheer, like the tips of spears poking up through the waters. One was bigger, though, perhaps half a mile across, flatter and broader and garbed in patches of dense green woodland that grew around a large central hill. That hill was craggy and black, unusually shaped, dominating the heart of the island. A curved ridge rose and fell. She saw sharp spines jutting out from it, reddish in hue, and steam...was that steam rising off it?

"Elyon, that hill..." Her heart was starting to thump.

"It's not a hill, Saska."

Not a hill. She tried to swallow, but her throat had gone bone dry. She could see it now, see what it was. "Elyon, why are we..."

"We have to keep our distance," he interrupted her. "He's sleeping, Saska, and we had best not disturb him."

She only nodded, wordless, and stared as they drew nearer. The hill that was not a hill took form before her eyes. The immense head, the long neck, the great colossal body with wings wrapped and furled across the flattened forest. The woodland had once clothed the entire island, she realised, before the titan had come down to rest, destroying all before it. She could see a great trail of destruction where the tail had come to land; the trees blasted on either side, blackened and burned by the terrible heat that wreathed him, steaming and warping the air around his body. Parts of the island were smoking, she saw now, pale ragged fingers reaching up to scratch at the sky. Here and there fires burned, nought but tiny flickers of candlelight against his bulk. One burned near the head, where a thicket of spruce had been smashed aside and trampled. *The trees are like pine needles next to him*, she thought, hardly believing what she was seeing.

The flames swirled and threw their orange light across his face, and she looked upon the enormous maw and spear-length teeth, the head as big as a war galleon with its crest of red and crimson spines surging and spreading behind it. She saw movement, the chest rising and falling, slow and steady. Even from high above she could hear the rumble of the breath, see the way the smoky air blew out from his nostrils and through his teeth to stir the ash and cinder, causing the bare trees to sway and lean, their leaves all scorched and gone. She saw another dragon down there too, sitting on a thrust of rock near the crook of the Dread's great wing arm. It was a worm to a python, a sapling to a redwood, dwarfed by the immensity of its master.

That dragon is the size of the one I fought in Aram, Saska thought. *The one that would have killed me had Agarosh the One-Eye not come.* The thought threatened to overwhelm her. Sometimes she still reflected on that failure and yet the dragon was nothing…nothing next to this.

Elyon brought them to a slow stop, hovering high above the island. The Dread filled its centre and she could see other dragons now, perched here and there, and a few were flying as well, circling about the coast beneath them, watching over their lord as he slept. She heard their high-pitched shrieks rising on the wind. "Elyon…if they see us…"

"We'll flee. I didn't bring you here to pick a fight with them, Saska."

"Then why?"

"To see him. To look upon your enemy. You need to know what you're fighting."

She shook her head on instinct. How could she fight such a thing?

"It can only be you," Elyon told her. "When the time comes. When you're ready. It can only be you."

Her breathing was quickening. "But…but…"

"No buts. Look at him. I fought him with my father and my uncle. I know he can be cut. And you're going to do more than cut him, Saska. So look at him and don't look away."

She did as he told her. Lower he flew, gently easing down, descending on a bed of swirling air. She wanted to tell him no, to take her away, far away, or to grab the Windbalde right out of his grasp and do it all herself, but she didn't. She only stared down at the Dread, trusting him. *Know your enemy,* she thought. *This is the power that will end the world if we let it.*

He brought them only as close as he dared, but even a half mile away the scale of the Dread was unthinkable. *It's like he's right there in front of me. How can such a thing exist?* She scanned, wondering why he was here, and saw what looked like scars on its body, cuts and gashes from battles of yore, yet some…some looked fresher, newly made. "Those wounds…" she said.

Elyon nodded. "He must have been fighting somewhere. There's been talk of other titans."

"Near here?" She looked out to the Vandarian coast. Faintly she could see a trail of destruction leading from the Lakelands. "He came from that way. Isn't Lakeheart out there?" She wondered if he'd been there, if he'd destroyed the city like he had King's Point and Varinar and maybe other places. "We should follow the trail," she said. "Find out if…"

"No." The word was final. "I came here only to show you him, Saska. We can't be drawn into anything else."

She knew he'd say that; he'd been saying it all along. She was about to answer when she heard a noise below, a deep grinding as though something enormously heavy was lifting. She looked down and saw that Drulgar was waking, raising his head. His great eye opened and looked at her.

He sees me, she thought. Her heart surged up into her throat. *He...he knows who I am.*

A powerful urge called for her to turn her head and look away, but she didn't. *Look at him,* she told herself. *See your enemy.* She drew a deep breath and firmed her eyes. From the nostrils of the Dread poured a thick black fume and fire spread out through his teeth, a hundred sheets of flame rising and swirling and crackling into the cold night air. She thought she heard an ancient laughter in that noise, a rumbling joy for what was to come.

"We had best go," Elyon said.

She nodded, breathless, expecting a sudden attack, but it never came. *He sees no challenge in us,* she realised, remembering something that Ranulf had told her. "Drulgar the Dread is his own master," the little adventurer had said, the last time she'd seen him in Aramatia. "He might not care even if he knew of you. More likely he would relish the challenge of facing the Heart Remade. Once all his enemies lie dead at his feet, what else is there? I do not think you need to worry about him. Not yet."

Not yet, the heir of Varin thought, wondering if Ranulf had been right.

47

Amron

The city streets were lined with well-wishers to mark their king's return.

Along the snowy, rubble-strewn roads they had all gathered, screaming out his name.

"They honour you," Amara said, riding alongside him. "I think many of them believe you're their saviour, Amron. You see. I'm not the only one."

Ahead, he could see Keep Kanabar rising grandly atop its flat wide hill, the only one of the greathouse keeps that had remained untouched during the city's destruction. It was to become their home here in Varinar for the foreseeable future, a palace by proxy until such a time as the true palace could be rebuilt.

"We've been working on digging through the rubble," Sir Hank Rothwell was saying over the din. "Amara mentioned to me when last she was here that it would be wise to unearth the throne from the wreckage of the Royal Palace, my lord, and have it set up in the keep. We are getting closer every day, though the throne remains frustratingly out of reach. Soon, however…"

"Only if it's safe," Amron interrupted. "I will not have men dying from collapses merely to recover that seat."

"That *seat* is the seat of Varin," Amara said, disapprovingly. "Of Varin and Ayrin and Amron the Bold and all the kings who followed in their line. We need it for your coronation. We can't have you planting your ample rump on any old chair now, can we? Symbols are important, I'll remind you. Varin Reborn must sit in Varin's seat."

He didn't respond to that either. Her ardent faith in him was heartwarming, though somewhat wearying as well. "And what of Keep Daecar, Sir Hank? Has the restoration begun?"

"Yes, my lord, though it is early days." Hank Rothwell was tall and spare, a humble household knight who'd spent most of his life running the defences of Snowhold, the seat of his cousin Lord Ronley. That he had been raised to a senior role in running the city of Varinar was quite the promotion, though he'd taken to it well. "I will take you there later, if you wish. Show you the extent of the damage, and what must be done to restore it."

"Tomorrow," Amron said. "Once I'm better rested." It was late afternoon and they had only just arrived, completing their long cold push down the High Way to the city. The tens of thousands who followed in his royal wake would still be passing the West Gate now; they had stretched for many long miles down the road, a great snaking fog of men and mounts, wagons and wains, to be housed and camped both within and without of the city walls. "We have been on the road since before dawn, Hank. I want a fire, a bath, and perhaps a cup or two of wine if there are any good vintages remaining in the keep."

The knight smiled faithfully. "Sir Miles has been sure to set aside his best, my lord, in preparation for your return. He awaits you at the foot of the hill."

Amron could just about see him and his men there, dressed in the Kanabar colours of silver, blue and green. One bore a banner showing the Kanabar sigil; a great powerful elk with misting, bladed antlers before a backdrop of river and mountains. *My new household.* He wondered what old Lord Wallis would make of seeing Amron set up in his keep. *Or Borrus,* he thought, smiling. *Oh, he'd have a good long laugh about that, no doubt.*

"He was expecting to prepare a feast in your honour," Sir Hank Rothwell was going on. "Nothing extravagant; I know you would not wish to waste the food. Just a small banquet for your senior lords and knights. A way to toast your return." He paused, glancing over at Amara, who seemed amenable to the notion. "What do you say, my lord? Should I have Sir Miles begin preparations?"

Amron shook his head. "Not tonight. If I'm to dine, let it be a small dinner with my family. I find myself in no mood to celebrate this evening."

"Yes, my lord. I understand. Seeing the city so…stricken. It does not stir the mirth of a man."

"Indeed," Amron agreed, looking around as Wolfsbane trotted grandly on, barded and caparisoned in the colours of the kingdom. There was a sense of desperation in the air, the cloying reek of rot and death and disease emanating from the ragged masses crowding either side of the broken road. A line of soldiers with spears stood to hold them back, as the people heaved and pulsed and shouted out for him, reaching forward with their scrawny hands. Most were tattered and filthy, their faces gaunt with starvation. No doubt half were screaming for food, not because they saw Amron as some sort of saviour as Amara would have him believe.

"Tomorrow, I wish for you to take me on a tour of the city," the king went on. "I have a pressing need to look upon her defences and walk among her people. To know the full extent of her suffering." He saw the big bug eyes, the hollow cheeks, the malnourished children hiding in their mother's dirty skirts. "How are the food stocks in the city, Hank? Many of these people look on the verge of death."

Sir Hank Rothwell cleared his throat. "Starvation has become a blight here, my lord, I fear to say. Sir Geofrey has taken a hard line on two things since he arrived with the Amadar forces: desertion and rationing. There are pot shops set up for the poor and needy, and every day wagons go out to deliver what food can be spared, but it's not enough, not nearly enough. There are too many people here and we have not the supplies to feed them. It is the same all across the realm, I know. Tens of thousands are dying of starvation and Sir Geofrey insists that the soldiers and fighting men must be prioritised."

Amron nodded gravely. It was a standard custom during wartime. "Are you sending people out into the lake?"

"Some, yes, though it is not without its dangers."

"The pirate lords are behaving, I hope?" Amara said. "The seneschal assured me he could get them in line."

"Yes, my lady. It would seem he has been true to his word on that, and these islands have been opened to us. That is not the problem, however."

"Then what is?"

"The cold, Lady Amara. This unseasonal snow has caused ice floes to form and often the lake waters are too rough to risk the crossing. The fishermen have all said the same. There remains a great abundance of food on the lake, but getting to it has proven difficult. With many of our grain stores destroyed during the attack, and the harvests being lost, I fear tens of thousands more will continue to starve in the coming weeks."

Amron rode along in private thought for a moment, then hailed Rogen Strand.

"My lord."

"Ride back down the column and summon Stegra and the Orca Lord to my private solar," Amron commanded. "Tell them to come in an hour, once I've had a chance to bathe and change."

Whitebeard nodded. "Yes, my lord." He wheeled about and rode away.

Sir Hank Rothwell wet his lips. "Might I inquire…"

"The tribes are accustomed to these wintry conditions," Amron explained. "Those who hail from the western shores especially. If anyone can fish the waters, it will be them, Sir Hank."

The old knight nodded his understanding. "A wise ploy, my lord."

"I would like to speak privately with Sir Geofrey also," Amron added. "See that he is brought to my solar later, Hank."

"Of course, my lord."

The heaving crowds thinned as they went deeper into the heart of the city. Here, inside the original city walls, the ten hills rose up south of the lake. In the western districts the destruction had been minimal, but here in the heart it was almost complete. Keep Taynar was gone, so too Keep Amadar, razed from the tops of their hills as though they were never there. Keeps Oloran, Pentar, and Reynar remained standing, though in varying states of disrepair. The great temple raised up to Vandar had been brought down to its foundations, just as the palace had been, the grandest, oldest building in all of Varinar reduced to ash and ruin. Faintly, Amron could see Keep Daecar now, standing upon its hill a little east of the ruin of the palace. It perched there a blackened husk, burned from the inside out, a shell of what it once was. *Yes still standing,* Amron thought, defiant. *Bowed, but not broken.*

Ahead, the Strand and Amadar escort was slowing and spreading out to form a cordon as they approached the gates of Keep Kanabar. It stood upon the shallowest of the ten hills, flat and broad, and the keep sprawled powerfully across it. Each castle was different, or had been, and was built in the manner of their lords and lands. Keep Taynar had been spare and grim and dour, Keep Amadar neat and elegant and beautiful. The Kanabars and their Riverland vassals had always been big and burly, so the keep was big and burly too, a robust castle, thick-walled and strong, with a bulky barbican and blocky towers encircling a stout and unpretentious keep.

Sir Miles came forward to greet them. He was a powerfully built man, with bull's shoulders bearing a thick neck topped with a heavy, stubbled jaw. A Riverlander through and through, as Amara would say. His hair was dense and brown, streaked grey, and his eyes were close-set and deep. He stepped forward as Amron dismounted and fell into a chunky bow. He wore plate armour and godsteel mail and a striped cloak in silver, green and blue. "Your Majesty. A pleasure to see you again."

"And you, Sir Miles." Amron knew him from previous visits to the keep. "I'm told you were tireless in your efforts to help during the aftermath of the battle. My man Artibus speaks well of you."

Miles Hewitt gave a good-natured smile. "If anyone was tireless, it was him, my lord. The old fella saved hundreds of lives during those days." He glanced behind him, to the mounted masses. "Is he here with you?"

"A little further back, in the wheelhouse. He'll be staying here in the keep so you'll have ample opportunity to see him." Amron helped Amara down from her horse, as Lillia leapt spiritedly down from hers. "You know Amara, of course. And my daughter Lillia."

"Of course." Hewitt bowed to Amara and Lillia. "You're the spit of your mother, Your Highness," he said to the girl. "And increasingly so as you get older. I'm sure you hear that a lot."

"I do." Lillia smiled graciously. "Though I don't have her spirit."

"Oh? And how's that?"

"She was a *proper* lady, unlike me. I'm trained with godsteel now, Sir Miles." She drew her dagger to show him. "Sir Daryl and Jovyn and Carly have been training me. Every day for months. I'm getting good."

"Well now, a rare thing. Not often do princesses have such prowess with the blade."

"Princess Iliva did. Varin's daughter. She bore the Windblade when she fought with him against the Dread." She had that look on her face, that look Amron didn't like. "I want to fight like she did. Not with the Windblade, maybe, but…" She glanced at him and then over at Amara. "They say I can't, though. Fight, I mean. I'm to stay here with the women and the old men and look after all the little children."

Sir Miles had not expected this disclosure. He dealt with it well, to his credit. "My lady. There is a reason why women do not go to war."

"Why? Because we're too *frail?*" Lillia's tone of voice showed him just what she thought of *that.*

"No, princess. There are many strong women. Is it only because you alone can bear the next generation. Men are expendable in a fashion that women are not, and princesses such as you are rarer still and must be cherished." He smiled at her. "I'm sure your father and auntie only want to protect you."

"Yes," Amara said. "And your father does not need the distraction of worrying about his daughter during battle." She gave Lillia a glare and then looked at Sir Miles. "My niece is of a quarrelsome disposition, you will find. Expect her to bend your ear on this issue often, sir."

"Yes, my lady. My ears are always open to the princesses' royal voice."

"Well put, but in this particular case, *close them.* Lillia will not stop until she finds some willing knight to stow her away in his saddlebag and ride her off to war."

The girl laughed at that. "I'd never fit in anyone's saddlebags, Auntie."

"No. I was being figurative."

Sir Miles smiled and turned to the king. "My lord, shall I lead you to your chambers?"

"Please. And see that your staff arrange accommodation for my captains. Lord Strand should have taken you through the particulars."

"He did, my lord. All is prepared."

"Very well, then. Lead on."

Through the castle they went, past the big furniture and large, open doorways. The stairs were wide and chunky, the statues grand and heroic. Amron recognised the many heroes of the Kanabar line as he went. Amara spoke of them, telling Lillia about each, as the others rustled along behind them.

"Lord Strand has taken up residence in the Westview Tower, my lord," Sir Miles said. "I'm sure he told you when you met at the gate."

"He did." Strand wanted a tower of his own to command from, Amron knew. His senior lords and knights were accommodated with him, his men in camp about the squares and buildings that bordered the hill.

"I understand the tribesmen are to take up outside the walls, is that so?"

Amron nodded. "We all thought it wise. They will camp up near the lake on the western side."

"Very good, my lord. Yes, I consider that the correct course, given the tension here. Lord Strand brought news of these tribesmen, and there is a fear running through the city at their coming. They have heard all sorts of tales of those who dwell beyond the mountains. They fear their children will be snatched away in the night, their pets eaten, their women raped, their…"

Amron cut him off. "The tribespeople are no more barbaric than we are, Sir Miles. Their customs may be queer, their manners a little rough, but they are a good kind people for the most part. Two will come here shortly with my sworn man, Rogen Strand. See that they are given every courtesy when they arrive." They reached a set of stairs and began to climb. "I will want my armour taken to the Steelforge as well," he went on. "Make sure that it's delivered at once to the Forgemasters so they can begin its repair and reinforcement."

"Yes, my lord. The Forgemasters are very busy, I know. Lord Strand has had them working night and day. His men brought much armour to them in need of repair."

"I trust all available smiths have been summoned to help?"

"No, my lord. The Forgemasters are working only with their apprentices. Common smiths have not been permitted to…"

"They are permitted now. Send men to find skilled smiths and armourers among the smallfolk. Tell them they will be given food and lodging in the Steelforge in exchange for work. If they have families, they may accompany them under the same terms."

Sir Miles was unsure. "The Forgemasters won't like that, my lord. They…"

"Can take it up with me when I visit them tomorrow." The Forgemasters had always been prickly about who entered their hallowed halls. "See it done, Sir Miles. Talk to Sir Quinn. He will help you."

The man hurried to keep up. "Sir Quinn. Yes, as you say, my lord."

They scaled another set of wide stone steps past walls lined with ancient tapestries. Staff moved about, shyly curtsying and bowing as the king marched by. His footfall rang heavily through the halls. The Frostblade sparkled kaleidoscopically at his hip as the ice particles met the warmth of the keep and melted. In the cold it misted mostly white, but here the colours were unleashed. Amron's time as its guardian was nearing its end, he sensed. He feared it and he welcomed it. He hated it and he wanted it.

"My lord, it's right along here." Sir Miles led him on. Amara was taken another way with Lillia. They reached the chambers of the lord of the keep, chambers Amron had sat in and drank in with Wallis and Borrus many a time before. Sir Miles would often have stood guard on those such occasions and had even joined them sometimes as well. "I've had some vintages laid out for you, my lord, the best we could find from what's left in the cellars." He pushed the big oaken door open, and there was a flicker of a smile on his lips. "I only hope there's some left."

"Left?" Amron wasn't understanding. "Why should there not be any…" And then he smelled the pipe smoke, and he saw the little man sitting in the chair across the room. He squinted at him. "Torus?"

"Who else?" Sir Torus Stoutman had one leg draped nonchalantly over the padded arm of his perch. He bore his pipe in one hand and a large cup of wine in the other. A cloud of pale smoke enshrouded him, and Amron could see the slightly drunken haze in his humorous little eyes.

"When did you get here?" he demanded. "We've been expecting you for days."

"Marak's cautious," was Stoutman's answer. "Had us training before he'd let us fly free. Like a big mother hen, he is, always clucking about." He grinned a wine-stained grin. "Got in overnight. Been in here ever since, waiting for you." He motioned with his pipe across the large, warmly appointed solar. "Crawfield's here too. We came back together."

"Your Majesty." Sir Connor Crawfield was standing beside the fire, dressed in his new Varin cloak that did not look quite so new anymore. "It was Sir Torus's idea to surprise you. I had wanted to come and meet you and Lady Amara at the gate, but…"

"But where's the fun in that?" Sir Torus laughed and stood and went to refill his wine cup. He poured one for Amron and thrust it into his gauntleted grasp. "A toast to your return, Amron." He clinked cups. "To the king."

"To the king," echoed the others.

Stoutman gulped his cup down to the dregs. Amron had a more measured sip. He was glad to see them, despite the ambush. And very eager to hear their news. "Sir Miles," he said. "Help me with my armour. You too, Connor." He would see that done first.

The two knights stepped in, sliding the plate from his body, as Amron unfastened his swordbelt and set the Frostblade aside. At once, he felt the dull discomfort bleed back into his shoulder and thigh, the deep penetrating throb in muscle and bone. Off came his pauldrons, his breastplate, his tassets, his cuisses and his greaves. Underneath he wore his padded leathers. Beneath those his sweat-stained linen shirt and hose. Before long he stood in only breeks, heavy muscle veined and rippling. His plate armour was packed into a sturdy trunk and carried out into the corridor. "Get that to the Steelforge at once, Sir Miles. I want it repaired and reinforced as soon as possible."

"Yes, my lord." The Kanabar knight gestured across the room. "There are clothes in the coffer there. Borrus's. Before he grew too portly."

"Must be twenty years old, then," laughed Stoutman. He gave his king an admiring study. "You want to leave some muscle for the rest of us, Amron? Gods be good, just look at you."

"Missing your wife, Sir Torus?" Hewitt japed. He smiled and said, "I'll see the trunk to the Forgemasters personally, my lord. Will there be anything else?"

"That's all for now." Amron went to the coffer and drew out some clothes; shirt, hose, breeches, a plain woollen tunic - simple garb, hardly kingly but warm - then settled into an upholstered armchair. There were many about the room, set against the wood-panelled walls where tapestries hung down between the windows. Across the chamber stood a huge oaken desk, the desk of Wallis Kanabar and his forebears, and ornaments and trophies rested on shelves and tables with piles of books on siege strategy and combat techniques and the history of warfare. The Kanabars were proud of their military past, proud of their millennia-long charge defending Death's Passage and the Bloodmarsh Isles, proud of their battle glory and prowess in tourneys, in the joust and the melee where they won so much acclaim. He sat, trying to remember the last time he'd been here, the last time Lord Wallis had ridden west from the Riverlands. *Years*, he thought. *Four, perhaps five...*

"Fond memories, Amron?" Sir Torus Stoutman eased himself down into a chair nearby, clutching lovingly at a freshly poured wine cup.

"Just trying to remember the last time I was here." Lord Wallis had been one of his father's closest friends, as Borrus was to him. "It feels strange, being in here without them. With Wallis dead and Borrus missing." He looked down. "And to wear his clothes..."

"Borrus isn't missing anymore," Stoutman said.

Amron looked up.

"He took up command at Rustbridge before the battle," the knight went on. "They're calling him Lord of the Riverlands now, Warden of the East, Protector of the Passage, all those fine lofty names the Kanabars get. The battle was *big*, Amron, brutal. Like the Burning Rock, men are saying. *The Battle of Bloodriver*, some are calling it, for all the blood that ran into the Rustriver. Others prefer *Battle of the Bursting Barrel*."

"The Bursting Barrel?"

"Aye, for Borrus. You know how he is with that temper. The *Barrel* Knight, *bursting* with rage. Well, Ven started dropping bags of blood and body parts over the ward, captured knights and such, good men, trying to get Borrus to react. And one bag...well, this is grim, Amron, but it had Wallis Kanabar's head in it. Newly cut off too. Seems he never died at the Bane like we thought, but was being held captive. Borrus took one look at it and...well, you can imagine how he reacted."

"Badly," Amron said. He closed and opened a fist. "Tell me of the battle," he said, gravely. He would take a moment to mourn Lord Wallis later. "How many men did we lose?"

"Somewhere in the region of thirty thousand, my lord," said Sir Connor. "From roughly a hundred thousand in camp. The enemy...they lost more. Somewhere approaching fifty or sixty thousand, it is believed."

"Is Rustbridge fallen?"

"Battered, but not broken," said Stoutman.

"And the city side?"

"Standing. A few dragons went and nipped at her. Killed some smallfolk. Took down a tower or two. But their focus was the fort. And the fighting."

"Death toll? For the dragons?"

"Eleven, I think."

Amron shook his head. "Once before that would have been unthinkable. Eleven dead dragons in a single battle. Now…now I find myself disappointed." He paused to reflect on that. "The captains?" he asked. "Killian? Rikkard? Rammas?"

"Killian's fine. Rikkard too. Broke some ribs, but nothing major. Rammas?" Sir Torus shook his head. "Made the mistake of challenging a moonbear, and you know how that usually goes. Not even your father could defeat one of them on his own, and him with the Sword of Varinar. Shame, as that bear had turned its cloak, as it turned out. Or fur. Turned its fur, I guess you'd say." He frowned, trying to puzzle that out. "Anyway. Rammas never knew about that, and he went and shouted that moonbear over and it said, 'all right then' and mauled him. He'll die, they think, though they've been saying that for weeks. And he's still hanging on. Hard to kill, that man."

Amron was too tired for a slightly drunk Sir Torus Stoutman. He turned to Sir Connor. "Connor, please translate."

"Yes, my lord." And he told him of the infighting among the Lumarans, the two factions under the rule of Sunlord Avar Avam and Moonrider Timor Ballantris, how the latter turned upon the Agarathi during the battle, how another Moonrider, the young Aramatian Risho Ranaartan had joined Ballantris as well. "It was Ranaartan's bear who mauled Lord Rammas," Sir Connor said. "Jahendroth. I saw the ruin of their work, my lord, when I flew over the battlefield with Lady Kazaan. Jahendroth slew a dragon himself, and Tathranor slew two others. It turned the battle in our favour, they say. That betrayal. Without them our host may have been overwhelmed."

"You're to say the Agarathi fled?"

"Yes, my lord. After a day and night of fighting they called the retreat and fled south. Lord Borrus has gone in pursuit of them. He is mustering his forces at Westmire, we're told. I wanted to fly south to find out for myself, but Lady Kazaan would not permit it. Only Rustbridge, she said, and no further. Lord Marak's orders."

Amron was hardly surprised. It had been clear from their parley that the dragonlord was not willing to risk harm to his riders. "Then neither of you spoke with Borrus yourselves? Or Killian? Rikkard?"

"No, my lord. I was granted an audience with Lord Lester Pentar, on the city side. Torus visited the fortress and took accounts from some of the wounded there. The others were long gone by the time we arrived. Lord Borrus had left a small garrison but took the great bulk of his strength with him. By now battle may be nearing again. Borrus…he is intent on slaying Vargo Ven himself, the men say. He was going about during the battle calling the dragonlord down, but Ven ignored him. Borrus wants his head, my lord. In exchange for his father's. He may pursue Vargo Ven all the way into Agarath for his vengeance…and if he should try to invade…with Drulgar the Dread still out there…"

"He will be annihilated," Amron said. He did not need to be told of the risks. The Dread was a roving apocalypse under whose shadow they all lived now. He was hunting his enemies, settling his scores, but if a northern host should march on Agarathi land, he would no doubt make them wish they hadn't.

The king pondered for a long while, sipping on his wine. It was welcome news, in sum. A victory, if it could be called such, to match their recent victory here in the west. There was fortune here, yes. In the west, the coming of Borrington's host had turned the tide. In the east it sounded as though the enemy discord had sealed their fate. Both cases had strengthened their cause and given them room to breathe, but the shadow of the Dread remained. Lest they should lift it, none of this would matter. Eventually, he would come for them. And they had not the power to stop him.

As he brooded over invasion plans, titans, and the small matter of the Heart Remade, there came a loud knocking at the door. Amron raised his eyes. "Yes."

Rogen Whitebeard entered. "My lord, the Snowfist and the Orca Lord are here." The ranger's amber eyes found Stoutman grinning at him, Sir Connor standing rigidly by the fire. He frowned. "If I'm interrupting…"

"No, Rogen, it's fine." He looked at the others. "We can continue later. Unless there's anything urgent you need to tell me?"

"Borrus and the battle not enough for you?"

"You've been gone a long while, Torus. I would hope you have other news to report."

"We do. Exiles, ancients, beasts and bastards, demon dragons, pyromantic priests, all sorts of things are happening out there." He grinned, knowing full well he was piquing the king's interest, stood, and thrust his pipe away into his belt. "But all that can wait. I need some food to soak up all this wine. Might go on a hunt down to the kitchens. Connor, you coming?"

"I had thought to visit Lady Amara and Princess Lillia."

"They're down the hall," Amron said. "I'm sure they'd be very glad to see you." Amron rose from his chair. "We'll resume later, then. Once I've settled my affairs."

The two knights bowed and withdrew and Amron moved to sit behind the desk. Then the tribal leaders were admitted, the Snowfist swaggering in wearing his snow-bear cloak, the Orca Lord approaching smoothly, cool and elegant, in his beautiful black and white whale-hide regalia.

"The summons of a steel king," Stregra hooted. "This is not to be sniffed at." He saw the empty cups scattered about. "Do not tell me the King of Daecar has been drinking sickmilk without me?"

"It is wine, Stregra."

"The Snowfist prefers sickmilk. Wine is for children." He poured himself a cup anyway and drank deep. "They are back, then? The steel dragonriders. Why did they take so long?"

"Lord Marak is a careful man," Amron said. "He made sure they were well trained before they were permitted to fly."

"Yes, training is good. Otherwise, you will fall off your dragon like the steel king did." He laughed uproariously, as though everything he said was the most amusing thing ever uttered.

Amron wanted to make this short. He did not have the energy for the Snowfist right now. "The body of water to the north of the city is called Lake Eshina," he told the two men. "Even in the fiercest of winters, the lake does not freeze, but right now there are floes on the water, and the lake can be rough and stormy. The local fishermen here are not accustomed to these conditions, but I know you are used to them. You in particular," he said to the Orca Lord. "And I know you want to put your people to work. If you will, I will set you the task of catching fish, as many as you can. Does that sound agreeable?"

The Orca Lord considered. "I will need to build boats. We fish in longboats, King Daecar. Sleek and swift and tough. Our methods are our own. For this I will need good timber, rope, nails, and other materials."

"You will have everything you need."

"And a place to build."

"There is a boatyard on the lake, outside the walls. Near where you're setting your camp. You'll be able to build there."

Stegra Snowfist crossed his arms. "So this is your need for us. To be your fisherfolk. Feed all these starving screamers out there." He did not look happy about it. "The Snowfist is no fisher. He is a father and a fighter, not a fisher."

"You needn't do any fishing yourself, Stegra. I will send my own people to help you. Lord Borrington will liaise." He addressed the Orca Lord again. The man's ambition made him eager to please. "Talk to Grella, my lord. There are places along the shore, little frozen rivers and inlets, where her people's expertise may be useful." Grella was the leader among the river folk of the Silver Scar. Expert fishers, they were, with net and spear. "Lake Eshina is mother to us all," he said. "From her bounty we live, and there is bounty enough for all in her waters. I will send local men out to tell you more of her perils. There are dangerous creatures that lurk on the lake."

"There are many fearsome beasts in the waters off the western shores," said the Orca Lord. "We know how to kill them, how to harvest them. And we learn quickly of new dangers when they come. Send your men, but do not fear for us. We will tame these waters of yours."

Amron liked this Orca Lord. He sensed the man would ask for something in return soon enough, though as yet he had held his own counsel. *He has a daughter,* Amron thought. *A great beauty from the cold white shores.* Stegra's son Svaldar had designs upon her, the king had been told, but he suspected the Orca Lord would want to use her to secure a better union, when the war was done and won.

He stood from his seat. "Thank you. That will be all for now. Rogen will escort you back to your camp."

The Orca Lord bowed low and proudly. Stegra filled his wine cup, drank it dry, filled it again and grunted, "I am not a fisher, Amron Daecar. When is your next war council? This is why I come here, to talk war, not fish."

"There will be much talk on that soon, Stegra. Now please. I have other meetings."

Stegra Snowfist left angrily, the Orca Lord following behind him. Amron sat and drank his wine, pining for his bath, but it would have to wait. Only a short time later Sir Geofrey Bannard was ushered in. He was a plain man, rigid in his discipline, very much the sort of captain favoured by Lord Brydon Amadar.

"Your Majesty." He gave a quick, low bow and stood to attention before the desk. He wore pink and pale blue, Amadar colours, with a field of flowers on his breast. "You wanted to see me."

"Yes, Sir Geofrey. Please sit." The man did so. "Tell me of your time here," the king said. "I hear you have taken a hard line on desertion."

"Yes, my lord. Those feckless Taynars were fleeing north after the coming of the Dread. The same is true of King's Point, I have heard. The rate of desertion there has been disgraceful."

It was a good word for it. Disgraceful. The men of House Taynar had not glossed themselves in glory of late.

"It was the same here, before I came," Bannard went on. "That is no slight on Sir Hank, of course. It was chaos, my lord, and he had not the numbers to stop them. There were some twenty thousand Taynar soldiers here, all left over from when Godrik was king. A good chunk of them died by fang and flame, or else were buried beneath the rubble, but far from all of them. Over half lived through it. Ten, twelve thousand men." He looked at him. "Do you know how many are left?"

"Enlighten me, sir."

"Four thousand. Give or take. The rest fled the city and went back north to the Ironmoors. They were still leaving in their droves when I arrived with my men. We even caught some on the road and marched them back. Had them strung up at the gates to deter the rest."

"And did it?"

"Not at first. So I strung up more and that got them in line. Tripled the watches and had men down at the harbour. Lots were leaving in boats, back then."

He'd heard that too. "How many did you hang?"

"Over two hundred. A small price to pay to stop the spread of the plague."

Fear was the plague here. Fear and hopelessness. That was the cause. "I want parties arranged to ride north," Amron said. "These men must be brought back beneath my banners."

Sir Geofrey frowned. "You'd pardon them?"

"I can hardly kill thousands of men, Sir Geofrey. It is time for us to muster our full strength. Not just trained soldiers. All who can wield an axe or a blade must be enlisted to the cause. It is a common cause that affects us all. You have five thousand men here, is that so?"

"Yes, my lord."

"Have two thousand of them split into companies of two hundred apiece. Gather food, fodder, and hardy winter wear. I have already compiled a map of destinations I would like you to visit. Lord Strand's men will ride in support."

"Support? But my lord, the Strands are Ironmoorers themselves, Taynar vassals. Surely they'd be better leading the operation?"

"It is their very position as Taynar vassals that forbids them, Sir Geofrey. They may be sympathetic. Even friendly with some of these men. No. I want a hard line drawn under this episode. You will lead yourself. Do in the north what you did here, sir. Get them into line."

The man was dutiful and hid his displeasure well. It was not a charge he wanted, not with the fierce cold and snow further north, but he would obey his king's command. "And if men say no? If they run and hide."

"A hard line, Sir Geofrey." Amron's tone of voice made his intention clear. "I would also have you visit Elinar. Make sure the Oloran banners are prepared to march. Lord Penrith has a wealth of power secured behind his walls, and it must be deployed when the time comes."

The knight paused. "He's near death, I heard. Half blind and half mad. And truculent. He may not permit me an audience."

"You'll have my seal. If he denies you entry, he will declare himself a traitor before the crown and his lands and titles will pass to his son, Sir Killian."

A tight smile appeared on Sir Geofrey's lips. "A clever ploy, my lord. We would all be the stronger with Sir Killian holding the Oloran helm." He paused for thought. "Lord Penrith may see it differently, though. Until you are officially crowned, he will say you have no such authority."

"As your lord does?"

Sir Geofrey stiffened.

"Brydon Amadar has always been a man to follow official protocol," Amron said. "He will remain sceptical of my kingship until he sees me crowned with his own two eyes, and with all the proper customs. Of course, I would not want to disappoint my beloved good-father." He smiled dryly. "Has word been sent to him of my return?"

"Yes, my lord. Sir Michael left the morning after Lord Strand arrived, to inform him of your coming. He should be reaching Ilivar any day now."

"Very good. Then I shall look forward to seeing my good-father and good-mother soon." There was nothing more to be said. "Begin your preparations, sir."

"Yes, my lord." Sir Geofrey rose, bowed, and left.

The evening was almost upon them by then. Sir Miles returned to inform him that his armour had been safely delivered to the Steelforge, and Rogen Whitebeard reappeared to stand guard at his door. The maids came and went, filling a large bath of hot water, and Amron soaked his tired old bones, enjoying the easing of his pain as the hot water worked at his muscles. As he lay there naked in the tub, Artibus arrived, shuffling along in his frayed grey robes. "I have your tonics, Amron. A stronger brew. Hopefully the effect will last longer."

The king nodded as Artibus set them aside. His tonics helped with the pain, but never for long, and still they had a dulling effect on his mental acuity, his speed of sense and crispness of thought. Had he been cut to the bone by a common godsteel blade, it would have been different. But the Nightblade left a lasting effect, a corruption in him that was growing, spreading. And he dreaded the day now that he would be without its brother. It was coming soon, racing toward him. *I will give it up. I will. I will.*

He dined with his family that night. Lillia was dressed prettily and Jovyn looked very handsome. They made a lovely pair, all who saw them agreed. "Will you let them marry?" Amara asked him quietly, as they sat watching at the other end of the table. "She is still betrothed to Robbert Lukar, you know."

"I never sanctioned that engagement."

"But it's a good one, don't you think? The Daecars and Lukars have a long history of marriage." She smiled softly. "It worked for me and Vesryn, despite a few…wobbles along the way." Her hand rested on her belly; a small bump was starting to show. "Amilia and Aleron made a fine pair as well, before…" She didn't need to expand on that.

Nor was it worth talking about. Robbert Lukar was long away at war in the south and the world was different now. "The future is shrouded," Amron said. "And Lillia and Jovyn are very young. They may yet outgrow this youthful affection. But for what it's worth, I'm glad they have it. To know what it is to love…before the world should end."

"End? Oh, it won't *end*, Amron." Her eyes shone as she looked at him. "You're not going to let it, are you?"

She did not smile, not this time, that sly smile she had, or tell him he was Varin Reborn. Her eyes were earnest, almost pleading, her hand resting protectively on the curve of her belly. He took her hand in his, a slim and graceful one entwined in his big, war-torn fingers. "No, Amara," he told her. "I'm not going to let it end."

And now she smiled, and had a very small sip of wine. And they shared a quiet, happy dinner, together as a family.

Later, hours later, Amron awoke suddenly in his bed. It was dark, the fire burned down low to its embers, and it took him a moment to recall where he was. He had taken one of Artibus's tonics to help him sleep, but it was wearing off, and his shoulder was aching. He sat up, groaning. The curtains at the door that led out onto the balcony were stirring, the door ajar, the wind whispering in. He sensed a presence there and tensed when he saw him. The shadow. A man, standing near the door.

"Who's there?" he demanded. His voice was a dry croak. "How did you get in here without…"

"Father, it's me."

The breath caught in his throat. "Elyon?"

"Yes, Father."

"How did…"

"I saw the banners. The royal banners. They're hanging from the keep." He went over to light an oil lantern, bringing a soft orange glow to the room. "I guessed you must be here…it's the last castle left in the city." Amron was still coming out of his daze. "When did you get here, Father?"

"Just…just today." He sat up and put his feet onto the stone floor. "We had dinner, Elyon. The family. If you'd come earlier…"

"I wish I'd been there. Lillia, have…have you found…"

Amron could hear the fear in his voice. *He doesn't know yet.* "She's here, Elyon."

"She is?" His tone leapt in relief. "Gods…gods, I've been so worried." He came forward, and Amron saw him in the light. The war-weathered armour, the tattered cloak. His face was leaner, harder, older. Elyon took a moment to indulge in the joy of that news, then his smile drifted away, and he said, "A lot has happened since I last saw you, Father. There's so much to tell." He drew a breath, straining to choose his next words. "Father, I need your help. I'm not here to stay…there's something…something I have to do."

"What is, my boy? What do you need?"

"Your sword, Father. Your *power*. I have to fly northwest, far to the northwest. There's something I must find, but I cannot do it alone."

"The Icewilds," Amron said. "You're talking about going into the Icewilds."

"Yes." He nodded his head briskly. "I have to."

"Elyon, it's the End-Fall there. All the Icewilds are buried in snow, and the cold…"

"Would kill me. I know. I know what's happening there. That's why I need you. You can protect me, protect us both. Form a shield of ice around us, or…"

"Tell me why, Elyon. Why must you go there?"

"For Ilith. Have you…heard of Ilith, Father? That he's arisen…the light against Eldur's dark. It's about the blades. He's the one who's going to reforge them, but first he needs ingredients, rare ingredients for his sorceries. Others are out there now, gathering them. Five blades, five potions, five spells. And one thing to bind them all. Something only *we* can find. Together." He stepped up to the bed and went to a knee before him. "Will you come with me, my king? To Vandar's Tomb? Will you come?"

My king. Amron reached out and put his hand on his son's cheek. "Of course, yes…if you say it must be done, then…of course I will come."

Elyon breathed out, lowering his head. "I feared…I feared you might tell me no." His eyes lifted again, and there was a smile of relief on his lips, a glitter in his eyes.

My son, Amron Daecar thought, looking at him. *My son is the one saving this world.* He had never felt such pride. "When do you want to leave, Elyon?"

"Soon. As soon as we can. Tomorrow, maybe. I have to get back…" He turned his eyes to the window. "I need to get back to her as quickly as I can."

"Her?" Amron asked.

His son was not a man to blush, but in the flickering lantern light, Amron saw it, the warmth on his cheeks as he smiled and said, "Father, I…" And his face went serious. "I have to tell you about a girl…"

48

Robbert

Westmire was no large city. It could barely even be called a town. Raised beyond the western edge of the Marshlands on an open tract of land, it acted as a border fort of sorts, a gateway and a garrison, and there was a stout castle at its heart, a classic motte-and-bailey.

Around the castle were muddy streets lined with wattle and daub buildings, a few shops, some taverns, a large traveller inn, some stables, barracks, a stone temple to Vandar…and thousands upon thousands of tents, pavilions, shelters, lean-tos, wagons and wains all sprawled out beyond the town's north and western sides where the sparse wet woodland provisioned some cover. The sight was enough to make the prince's heart sing, but he held the smile from his lips. He was a prince, nay, he was a *king*, and must acquit himself with dignity.

Sir Mooton Blackshaw had no such restrictions. His laughter was loud and thunderous. "Bugger me, that's a sight for sore eyes. I'm going to get stinking drunk tonight, see that I bloody well don't. If there's ale here, wine, I'm sniffing it out! And a woman! Must be a woman somewhere hereabouts."

"Not one that would fancy *you*," snickered Sam Garrick, the Grinning Knight. "You stink like a pigsty and look rather like a boar. Me, though." And he swished his hair. "I need only whisper to a woman and she goes weak at the knees. Did you ever see me compete in tourneys, Mooton? You could barely hear the announcers for all the screaming."

"Screaming, yes. From *little girls*. That's the sort you attract, Garrick. Little girls who don't know what a real man is." He laughed to prevent Garrick from responding, overwhelming the smaller man. Mooton Blackshaw was quite easily the loudest human Robbert Lukar had ever met, even accounting for the Butcher. He seemed to carry that loudness about with him as some sort of badge of honour, and showed it to everyone he could.

It was a bright grey day, though the rain was very light, and visi-

561

bility was good. The town was rather exposed, it seemed to Robbert, and did not have walls of its own; only the castle itself was raised behind battlements, and those were small, hardly the sort of grand stone ramparts that you found at other northern cities and forts. To the south of the town, Robbert saw that defensive lines had been drawn up. Twin ditches had been dug, stakes driven into the soil between them, and there were some wagons there as well, he saw, fit with mounted scorpions. Armoured men in cloaks wandered along on patrol, and firelight flickered off torches and in pits dug at intervals along the lines. The pits were protected by crude shelters to keep off the rain and each was attended by a ring of soldiers, warming themselves by the flames.

"A reasonable defence against a ground attack," observed Lord Wilson Gullimer. "If not an aerial one." He turned to Sir Gereon of Greyguard; the two men were much aligned in temperance and manner and got along well. "How many scorpions and ballistas do you have?"

"Not enough," the Varin Knight said. "We brought a dozen or so down from Rustbridge; mounted ones, I mean. The castle itself has perhaps a half dozen more on its walls. Fewer than twenty in total, Wilson. If we're discovered here it could go ill for us."

"How long does Lord Kanabar expect to stay?"

"Only so long as he must. This is a rallying point, not a long-term encampment." He gestured beyond the town and castle. "The trees offer some cover. If you look closely, you'll see that fireproof tarps have been raised between the branches. You'll get a better look later, my lord, when you visit with your men."

Robbert was becoming excited, and nervous. His own countrymen numbered some twenty thousand here, perhaps a thousand or two more, and he could see some of their pavilions now, and the banners in brown and green. He wondered if they knew that their new king was coming, and suspected they probably did. At the very least that information would be spreading right now; a little earlier, Lord Kanabar's outriders had come across them as they emerged from the marshlands and had been quick to ride back to announce their arrival. Robbert could not see the castle gate from here, not through the buildings, but the swell of movement was visible. A mounted welcome host was coming, he saw, all dressed up in full regalia as they rode through the town and out toward them. Robbert drew a breath to steady himself. This was a host to welcome a king.

He turned to Lank for a quiet word. "How do I look, Lothar? Presentable?"

"Depends who you're presenting to. If a privy, you're fine."

"Not funny." But he smiled anyway; a nervous smile. "Do I smell that bad?"

"We all do, Robb. There's no shame in it, the places we've been."

"But I'm a king now, Lothar. I should look like one."

"You do. You've got your armour and your cloak and everything.

Very kingly. And that eyepatch? I'm sure there were some famous kings who had eye patches in the past."

"That's pirates, Lank. You're thinking about pirates and maybe brigands."

"There are some, I'm sure of it." He thought long and hard about it, then gave up. "One will come to me. Just give me time."

The welcome host was fast approaching them. Borrus Kanabar led them in his striking green and blue enamelled armour, the blade-antlered stag of his house worked on his breastplate in tiny godsteel studs. They misted as he came, as though the stag itself was rising from his chest. The effect was very compelling, Robbert thought. With Lord Borrus were his captains: Sir Killian Oloran and Sir Rikkard Amadar, both greathouse heirs; Sir Torvyn Blackshaw, Mooton's older cousin and one of Borrus's oldest friends; Lady Marian Payne, who was more a man than almost anyone, Robbert had heard, and some other lesser lords, knights, and retainers. All had dressed in their best and looked magnificent; even their horses had been barded and caparisoned. Banner bearers went before them, bearing their standards. Among them Robbert saw his own, the crossed hammer and sword of Tukor. It looked like Sir Kevyn Bolt was the man honoured to bear it. With him rode Lord Malcolm Marsh, who had been put in charge of the Tukoran host after Raynald went missing following the battle. *And he is missing still,* Robbert thought. The outriders had told him that.

His heart was starting to thump with anticipation. Horns began to sound, giving out a great deep moaning. Robbert wondered how wise that was, how far that sound would carry, but he put aside those misgivings. *They are welcoming you as a king,* he thought. *They're honouring you. You should be proud.*

He tried to be, but it wasn't so easy given his lack of achievement. His tale had been one of trial, tragedy, and treachery, not triumph. *We left with forty thousand men, and return with only forty.* There were reasons, yes, explanations, but there was no way to spin a success out of that no matter how you looked at it.

Still, he smiled in a way a king should smile, and walked in a way a king should walk, and soon enough the welcome host was upon them. The horns blared out behind them, and there were some thumping drums as well, a buzz of excitement in the air. Borrus Kanabar, Lord of Rivers and Warden of the East, swung down from the saddle of his muscular destrier to greet him. He did not go so far as to drop to a knee - no, he wouldn't do that for a foreign king, and a boy king at that - but he did dip his head and bow in courtesy and smile and say, "Your Majesty, we're delighted to bloody have you."

Your Majesty. It was the first time Robbert had heard it, and coming from a greatlord too, a hero of the last war. He felt a little shiver go through him, a little shuddery breath, and the smile on his lips was both nervous and real. "My lord. Thank you. I'm delighted to finally be here."

The other luminaries were dismounting into the sticky mud. They came forward one by one, bowing and sharing their greetings, all going to Robbert first before moving along to the others. A murmur of voices filled the air, joining the drums and horns, the snorts and whickers from the horses. Robbert knew most of them from feasts and tourneys, though he'd been a much younger man then. *No, not a man, a boy.* He and Raynald would be bold and boisterous during such festivities, always drinking heavily and stirring brawls, but those urges had gone out of him now. He was serious, thoughtful, very different to how he once was. *Is Ray the same?* he wondered. *Has he been hardened on the anvil of life as I have?*

"You look more and more like your father," Sir Rikkard Amadar said, smiling at him handsomely. "*King Robbert Lukar.*" He tasted the sound of that on his tongue. "Has a nice ring to it, don't you think?"

"It will…take some getting used to," Robbert admitted humbly. His lips were in a smile as well. "How is your chest, Sir Rikkard? I hear you broke some ribs during the battle?"

"Dragon got me," the knight said, sighing. "Rather ruined my day after that. But I'm healing up well. Still hurts when I cough or laugh too loud, so I try to stay away from the Blackshaws."

"Emeric Manfrey slew that same dragon, is that so?"

"He did. Gallant one, is Emeric. Brilliant swordsman. I never saw it…no, I was thrown halfway across the field when that tail struck me, but some witnesses report a dragonslaying by single-combat. That remains a rare feat, Robbert. Even during such times."

Robbert might once have said something grand here, something bloated and haughty. That he would become a dragonslayer himself when next a chance arose and thus emulate his father and grandfather. But those days were done. His blinded eye made such a match unwise, and he'd matured beyond such bluster. "Mooton says the same. He slew a dragon as well, he claims."

"*Claims*, yes. There are a lot of things that Mooton Blackshaw claims." Rikkard grinned and glanced over at the hulking Riverlander as he shook arms with Borrus Kanabar. "Borrus refuses to believe it, of course. He cannot abide the thought that Mooton slew a dragon before he did."

"He was busy trying to call down Vargo Ven, I heard."

"True, yes. And all the other dragons flew in fear of him…he'll say." Rikkard smiled again. "The men of the rivers have always been generous with their boasts, Robbert. But I'll let the others greet you. We can talk more later."

He stepped aside, Sir Killian Oloran taking his place. The man was tall, slim, golden-haired, stern. His voice was a tone above a whisper, very soft and hard to hear. He spoke the required pleasantries and no more, then moved aside to do the same with the others.

Sir Torvyn Blackshaw was next. He was older, thinner, a lean man of ticks and sudden movements, lingering quirks from his long years interned in those Piseki pits. "Your father was a great man," he said. "The second finest blade I ever saw."

Robbert frowned, though playfully. "And who was the first," he asked, already knowing, and Sir Torvyn supplied the expected answer.

"Why Amron Deacar, of course."

"You knew him, sir? My father?"

"Of course, Everyone knew him." Torvyn Blackshaw took a moment to study his face, his features. He had a kind wise way about him, if a slightly strange one with those sudden winks and blinks and facial jerks. "I had thought I'd find a perfect reflection of Prince Raynald, but I see before me an older sibling, not a twin." He smiled a crinkly smile. "Perhaps that is only natural. Now that you are a king."

Robbert smiled and maintained eye contact. "I think it's probably just the eye patch, Sir Torvyn. And the beard, maybe. Though it's not much of a beard."

"We cannot all be like my cousin," Torvyn said. "Blessed in wisdom he is not, but the beard gods were very kind to him."

He gave another smile and stepped aside and Lady Marian Payne was there. She was taller than Robbert, much taller, very harsh to look upon and austere, though somehow beautiful as well, in a hard, fierce way. Her armour was smoky grey and perfectly fitted to her long lithe frame, her jet hair slicked back, face lean and pale, all angles and flat panes. "I hear you slew a dragon, my lady?" Robbert said to her.

"I care not for such honours," was her reply.

Robbert had heard this about her. She was not one to seek glory, though it seemed to come to her all the same. "I met your former charge in the south," the young king said. "Saska. And Leshie as well. I met them in Aram, and later travelled with them for a short time."

The woman's eyes changed. Not much, but enough. "That is a story I should very much like to hear, Robbert."

"You will, my lady. Later. This may not be the place." And his voice went confidential. "Too many ears," he said.

The woman understood. She lowered her head gracefully and stepped away, deep in thought, and Robbert could tell she was already figuring things out.

Lord Malcolm Marsh moved up to him and he *did* go to his knee. His head was bowed very low. "My king," he said. "I cannot tell you how happy I am that you have come home. I have so many questions. So many questions about your time away."

"The answers will come, my lord." Robbert was settling into things now. They were all making it very easy for him with their courtesies. "Rise, Lord Malcolm," he said, and he did. He was a middle-aged man, thickset and blocky, with thinning blond hair and cloudy blue eyes. Those eyes were moving across Robbert's tiny little host, searching no doubt for men he knew.

"So few," he murmured. "Is this truly all that is left?"

"Truly," Robbert said. "Though there may yet be some in the marshes. We were scattered, a short time ago."

"How many were you then?"

"A thousand."

"Only a thousand?" Marsh shook his head, disbelieving. "And your uncle? Lord Swallow? Lord Huffort? Were any of them…"

"I will speak of that later, my lord." Now wasn't the time.

The greetings continued and were soon completed and some of the welcome host were moving back to mount their horses. Borrus Kanabar stomped back over to him. "We'll have a room made up for you in the castle, Robbert. It's not much, but it'll serve while we're here."

"How long have you been here, my lord?"

"Too long. Waiting for the rest to arrive. We're not at full strength yet, but almost." He smiled, red-bearded and red-cheeked and bald as an egg. His beard was a little patchy and sparse, not a great forest of a thing like Mooton's. No doubt that irked him. Borrus's father had worn a stupendous beard as well, Robbert knew. "We're going to take the Bane back," the Lord of Rivers went on. "Clear the last of this infestation out. How does that sound?"

"Most agreeable," Robbert said. He smiled at the prospect, thinking, *at last…at last…* "How many Agarathi are there in the fortress?"

"Lots. They're still clinging onto that foothold, hoping they can use it to drive back north, but they won't. We'll send them back across the Bloodmarshes with the rest of them. But that's for later. Later. We'll have a quick council before the feast."

"Feast?"

"Oh yes. You think I'd welcome home a king and not lay out a spread? There's a hall in the castle fit to host two hundred. Not the biggest, but big enough. And we'll shake the bloody walls tonight." He gripped his shoulder, squeezing, smiling. Borrus Kanabar was a very large man. "Come, now, let's get you settled. You want my horse? Happy to let you ride him in."

"No, my lord, I wouldn't want to deprive you."

"Nonsense. A king should have a horse." Borrus whistled and the destrier trotted over and the lord wouldn't take no for an answer. So Robbert mounted up and the Lord of Rivers walked along just ahead of him, leading him toward the castle of Westmire.

The welcome was overwhelming. Horns, drums, cheers accompanied him and more and more men were flooding out of the woods and streets to watch the young king return. The Tukorans poured out with particular interest, and raised their voices loud and proud. Robbert smiled and waved and the calls went up for him. "King Robbert!" they cheered, and, "King Robbert Lukar!" and, "Tukor!" they roared, "Tukor! Tukor!" Some bellowed out other names. "The King of the Dawn," someone was shouting, and another was roaring, "Robbert the One-Eye! The One-Eyed King!"

Sir Lothar walked alongside his horse. "You see," he called up over the din. "There *is* a one-eyed king. It's *you*, Robb! You're the one I was thinking of."

"Very funny, Lank. What do you think that one means? The King of the Dawn?"

"I don't know. A new dawn, maybe, after your grandfather's treacheries? That would be my guess."

It was a good guess too. Robbert liked it very much. *The King of the Dawn.* The crowds were thick about the streets, hundreds of them, thousands, men battle-worn and bloodied and in some cases bearing wounds. Mooton Blackshaw stamped ahead of them, clearing a path with his thunderstrike of a voice, and some men joined him from the crowd. They looked rather like he did, though smaller, all burly and big-bellied and bearded and he greeted them as brothers and friends. "Blackshaws," said Sir Rikkard, riding alongside him on his fine, purply-black destrier. "A few died in the battle, but others have come down from Elmhall with Sir Arnold."

"Have lots of reinforcements come?" Robbert asked.

"Some. We've had men from the Lakelands and Riverlands march down to join us. Others are assembling at Rustbridge, we're hearing. The Rasalanians haven't suffered much from the war so far, Robbert. Lady Marian sent some of her men back to speak with the Lords of the Lowplains and Whaler's Bay. Only her uncle Lord Tandrick had provisioned us with Rasal support, but it's high time the rest did their part. Swiftwater. Merrymarsh. Buckland. Maynard. None have entered the war as yet."

"And they haven't been attacked?" Robbert asked. He knew Thalan was destroyed, of course, but that was all. "The cities along the Bay?"

"Not that we're aware. Of course, that could change at any moment with the Dread haunting the skies."

Borrus was listening as he led the horse. "We can talk about that later. You should be enjoying this, Robbert. Drink it in and soak it up and sup on it until you're full. All that serious stuff can wait."

They put it aside as the greatlord said, and Robbert basked in the adoring roars of the crowd. He sat up high in the saddle and hoped he didn't look too small in it, tilting his chin just right and setting his face to that expression his father always had. He knew full well that they were seeing a young Rylian, but that was just fine by him. *I'll be my father's ghost,* he thought. *I'll do my best impression.* If it stirred the men and inspired them, fine. That was his duty now, he knew. Personal glory was to be put aside in favour of the greater good.

The castle was surrounded by a shallow moat filled with spikes and filthy water. The drawbridge was down, the portcullis up, and before too long the lords and captains were leaving the heaving masses behind and passing beneath the walls. They dismounted in the lower bailey. Ahead, up the hill, the castle keep stood squat and grey before the bleak skies, firelight flickering behind the windows. Tukoran banners had been draped beside those of House Kanabar to welcome him, he saw. It was a nice touch. In the bailey were more barracks and stables, an armoury and forge and kitchens. Men in all sorts of cloaks and colours stood about watching and talking and grooms came forward at once as they dismounted.

"Give him a good brush down, Jack," Borrus Kanabar said, as Robbert swung down from the saddle. "Oh, and meet a king. This is Robbert Lukar. Robbert, here's Jack of the Marsh."

The groom bowed his head. He had red hair darkened by rain, broad shoulders, powerful arms. "Your Majesty. A pleasure."

"And you, Jack."

Robbert wasn't sure why he was being introduced to a common groom. Once the Marshlander had led away Borrus's horse, he asked him, and the big lord said, "He's not just a groom. He swings a sword well and he's learning the spear. Not Bladeborn, no, but a good brave lad. And a friend. A good friend of mine. We travelled together up from the south. It's a long story, Robbert. I'll tell you about it sometime."

Robbert was led into the keep, and granted a large guest room beside Lord Kanabar's solar. Due to lack of space, Robbert's men would be accommodated elsewhere. He invited Lothar to stay with him, of course, but the tall knight shook his head and said, "No, Robb, you're a king now, and you need your own room. I'll muck in somewhere else."

Servants came to fill him a bath, and he washed for the first time since his night at Winslow Point. His hair was trimmed, his beard as well, though he did not shave it completely for fear of looking too young. His undergarb was taken away to be washed and new clothes brought in. He removed his armour to be scrubbed and cleaned, and taken down to the forge where the armourers could get to work on it, knocking out the kinks and dents. They had brought men from Rustbridge capable of working godsteel. Robbert felt naked without the plate, but was assured it would be kept ready for him should he need to hurry down and put it back on.

The war council was held in the audience chamber above the feast hall. Men were already drinking below, smoking and laughing as they gathered. Mooton was down there, being thunderously loud as usual. Robbert could hear his laughter shaking up through the floor as he jested with the Blackshaws and Garrick and some other men.

"We'll make this quick," Lord Borrus said. "I don't want to keep you long."

"Meaning you don't want to keep *yourself* long," said Rikkard. "You're eager to get on with the feasting, Borrus. Some things never change."

Kanabar shook his head. "Plenty of things have changed, Rikkard. I'm a lord now, for one, and here we have a new king." He invited Robbert to sit and offered him wine, and Robbert accepted with kingly grace. "We're told you spent time with Prince Elyon, Robbert. I think we're all eager to hear about it."

Robbert sipped his wine, telling them of his days in the company of Elyon Daecar aboard his flagship *Hammer*. He spoke of Elyon's coming during the attack by Lorin's Bane and how he'd driven the great Kraken away. That led to whistles of wonder and appreciative nods, but men were quite used to Elyon's heroics by now. "Another glory to add to his growing list," Rikkard said. He seemed very proud of his nephew, as they all did; Elyon was widely loved here in Vandar. Naturally, Robbert's story led to questions about where their prince had gone, and Robbert could hardly discuss that without also rendering the story of Saska. So he told them of her as well and was met with the expected astonishment.

"The heir…Varin's heir….you're saying…it's a *girl?*" Borrus Kanabar stared at him, incredulous. "An *Aramatian* girl?"

"Tukoran, really. Even though there's no Tukoran blood in her at all."

Lord Malcolm was perplexed by that statement. "And how is that, my prince? King, sorry…my king. How is it that she's Tukoran if…"

"She was raised in Tukor, my lord. Up near Twinbrook. That's what I meant. She shares our accent and our customs of behaviour. But her blood is a mix of Vandarian, Rasalanian, and Aramatian, and she is descended of three royal and divine lines."

"A remarkable blend," said Rikkard Amadar.

"And we're sure of this?" Borrus asked. There was a thick frown on his reddish brow. "Absolutely sure? There hasn't been some mistake?"

"No mistake, my lord. It is certain."

Kanabar breathed out through his lips. "Well gods. *Gods.*" His head went side to side. "They rambled on about this heir when I was down in Agarath. That pious prince and his old liver-spotted tutor. They all expected a man, Lorin's son. But his granddaughter? Gods!" And he shook his head again, laughing. "Well, why the hell not? Marian's shown us how fierce a woman can be, so why bloody not I say!"

Lady Marian Payne was watching quietly from the side. The news that Saska was this prophesied heir seemed to extract almost no reaction from her. Nothing but a knowing glint in the eye and a small upturn of the lips, a look of pride, quickly gone. It was as though she knew all along, or had at least suspected.

"And you knew this girl, Marian?" Borrus went on. "You trained her?"

"I did. In Thalan. I confess I did not expect her to be so important when I first met her, but her aptitude for learning was always noteworthy."

"Noteworthy? We need something more than noteworthy from the heir of bloody Varin."

"She lifted the Windblade easily," Robbert said. "When Elyon presented it to her, she raised it right up above her head with the tip to the skies. It was…quite something, actually. Half the men went down to their knees before her."

"So they know? All of your men?"

"Yes. They know. Though Sir Ralston was always careful to try to keep her identity secret. For obvious reasons. I've sworn all my men to secrecy, and would prefer that this information not get out."

Lord Malcolm Marsh was realising something. "This girl…she's the one who you sent into our encampment at Harrowmoor, Marian? The one Prince Elyon had in his tent?"

"Yes."

"My son died chasing her down," Marsh said, unhappily. "Cleon. He was hacked to death at the docks in Shellcrest by the King's Wall. This girl…I can't believe it. She's the same one? The same one the Whale-heart escaped with?"

"If you want to blame someone for that, my lord, blame my uncle," Robbert said. "Sir Cleon was hunting Saska by *his* order."

"And where is your uncle?" asked Kanabar. "Dead, I hope. I never liked that man."

"He is dead," Robbert confirmed. "In Aram. The same night I met Saska. The same night he gave me this." And he pointed at his blinded eye. "He wished to remove me, clear his path to the throne. I was fortu-nate enough to lose only an eye. My uncle lost more."

"You killed him yourself?"

"Saska's starcat tore his throat out. Joy, she calls her."

"She has a *starcat* too!"

That news led to further befuddlement. Robbert paused to drink his wine and for a short time Sir Lothar and Lord Gullimer took over, describing to the others various events; the ill-fated battle in Aram, the odious alliance of Krator and Kastor, their journey by sea back to Eagle's Perch and the subsequent storms and scattering of the fleet. Within this the betrayal of Lord Huffort came out. "He abandoned us," Lank said bitterly. "*Landslide. Mountain. The Stone Maiden.* Took half our fleet and sailed home."

"*Mountain* was *my* ship," Lord Marsh said. His face was twisted in denial. House Marsh were vassals to House Huffort, and often that meant blind loyalty. "Lewyn Huffort was no traitor. I cannot believe…"

Robbert spoke over him. "He is a traitor before the crown, my lord. My orders were to sail west, for Vandar, and he didn't like them. So he slipped away one dark stormy night and left us." He was not going to let that treason go unpunished. It had weakened him severely at a time when he was already weak, and Huffort would pay. "I have sent orders with Sir Tamber Rickson to see that he is imprisoned, should he return to Rockfall. Sir Ronwyn rules there in his father's stead, I understand?"

Malcolm Marsh's face went grave. "Not anymore. Ronwyn died a few months ago. Killed on a hunt, as I understand it."

"Then all of Lord Huffort's sons are dead." Robbert mused a moment; in truth that made it easier. Sir Benwyn, his second son, had perished at Aram, and his third son Sir Edwyn had been torn apart by the mob in Ilithor. He'd been another of King Janilah's Six. "Well. It seems this is your lucky day, Lord Marsh," he said.

The man frowned. "My lord?"

"I'm raising you to Lord of Rockfall. House Marsh will take on the command of the city and all its incumbent lands and incomes from this day forth." It was a great seat, and made him a great lord. With one simple swish Robbert raised him high. "Do you accept?"

"I…my king, you honour me." He bowed his head. "Only…Lewyn is a good friend of mine, and…"

"It's likely he foundered at sea," Robbert said. "That ought to spare you your reservations, my lord. Send a crow…"

"We have no crows," Borrus grunted. "They're all dead. The skies are dark."

"Riders, then," Robbert went on. "Choose trusted men and swift strong horses. Send them to Rockfall to raise your colours in place of Huffort's. And see that all the strength of the city is mustered at once and marched south."

Marsh frowned. "My lord? They will never get here in time. It will take many long weeks for them to reach us, and surely we'd have laid the Bane to the siege by then."

"I'm aware. And I'm not thinking about the Bane. I'm thinking of what comes after. Blademelt. Skyloft. Eldurath. We'll need all the strength we can rally when we cross south and invade."

Borrus laughed. "I'm coming to like you, Robbert. You're direct like your father was. And I agree. We need to be summoning all our strength now, getting our pieces into place. Marian, what do you say? Will your own lords answer the call?"

"I could not speak for them."

"But you know them well. The Oakenlord, Browlan, *Buckland*…now there's a fighter. He and my father were great friends. Always liked to sit together at feasts and try to drink each other under the table. Gods, those contests were legendary." He laughed, remembering, and Robbert was remembering as well, remembering his sister's wedding feast to Hadrin, when Horus Buckland and Wallis Kanabar had sat together at their table, drinking and laughing and slapping their great bellies. That same night, Robbert's father had announced his betrothal to Lillia Daecar. He wondered if she was still alive. She was very pretty and would become a great beauty, but was too young for him right now. *Thirteen, maybe fourteen*, he thought. It was a good match, though, he knew that well enough. *She's a princess now as well. And I'm a king.* When he really thought about it, he wasn't sure a better match existed.

He put that aside. That was all for later…later, when the north needed healing. The discussion went on, moving from one matter to the next. Tidings were dripping in from the west. There was talk of victory there as well, of the Agarathi being driven back. Very occasionally a crow still raised the courage to cross the land and deliver news, and sometimes riders rode from fort to fort with letters and scrolls in their cloaks. There was a general stirring in the air, and Robbert could feel it. A sense that the tide was turning. Below, the clamour of noise only confirmed it, all the laughter rumbling up from below. *Men have hope again*, he thought. *They can see the light of a brighter dawn approaching.*

The meeting might have gone on forever had Borrus not called it to an end. He stood up suddenly. "We're missing your feast, Robbert. We can't be having that." He finished his cup of wine and plonked it down on the table. "Come, let's eat. We can talk more below."

So they filed out of the room and went down to join in, entering that great wall of noise. And at their coming, it only roared all the louder as they cheered out for Robbert Lukar, cheered out drunkenly for the Tukoran king. They took their place on the dais and the food was brought out, the soups and stews and platters of meat, the trenchers of bread and the mead that came with it. It was all very northern. All very East Vandarian. Hearty and big it was, big food for men big, and around Robbert the feasthall became a whirl of noises and motions and colours, a heady cloud of singing and shouting and yes, a bit of friendly brawling as well. Robbert watched on as an old man observing a child at play and thinking of his own youthful days. He sat in his place of high honour, with the rest of the lords and captains, wondering what would happen now if they heard the bells tolling and the warhorns blowing and the thump of wings in the skies. The Dread would consume them all if he wished. One pass, perhaps two, and the whole castle would be engulfed in flame.

"You should relax, Robb," Lothar said, striding lankily over to him. "You're sitting there all serious. Have some fun!"

"I need to be kingly, Lothar. I'm not a prince anymore." He sat in his chair and spoke to those who came to talk to him. At first it was Borrus and Rikkard to his left and right, but before long that familiar sense of chaos descended and men staggered and lurched about as they pleased. Malcolm Marsh came to thank him again for the honours bestowed. Sir Kevyn Bolt awaited his turn and went to a knee beside him. "My king. I wanted to say…about your brother…"

There was a stink of failure to him, of shame. It was unwarranted, so far as Robbert heard it. "I know what happened in the battle, Sir Kevyn. Raynald duelled a dragon and lost. That was not your doing."

"Yes, sire, but after…after…"

"You did all you could for him." Those simple words lifted a weight from the man. Once he'd been dismissed Robbert called Lothar back over. "I want a new order of knights assembled to protect me, Lothar. You'll be captain. Go out and find the best knights you can among our forces. Not now, Lank. You can start with that tomorrow."

Sir Lothar smirked. "How many do you want? Six?"

"No." Robbert would not want six. His grandfather had his six and he wanted no such association. "Ten, maybe. Or twelve." He shrugged. "We can talk about that later and think of a good name. I'll talk to Gullimer, see if he'll let Sir Kester join. And Sir Kevyn. Include him as well."

"Really? But he was one of grandfather's sworn swords."

"I'm aware."

"They killed your father."

"No, Lank. They were only following orders. I won't condemn them for that. And in any case, Sir Kevyn wasn't there that day. He and Sir Edwyn were absent."

"Fine. If that's what you want." Lank lurched back away into the maelstrom. For once, he was taking the night off from watching over him, releasing some of the tension built up over the last few weeks, and the grief too since Bernie's passing. Robbert smiled as he watched him move through the crowds, towering above everyone, singing and drinking and folding those enormously long arms over shoulders as he rocked and roared and got stinkingly drunk.

"You won't partake?" The voice was smooth and belonged to Lady Marian. She seated herself beside him. "There was a time you would be down there as well, I am told."

"Once, yes. Those days are behind me now."

She nodded. That seemed to impress her, and he liked that; for some reason he wanted to impress her.

"How wise is all of this, my lady?" Robbert swung an arm to indicate the room. "Every lord and leader in the army is here. And the noise… I'm not sure we'd even hear the warning horns if they started blowing."

She smiled at him. "Your time away has made you wary."

"Just sensible. I left with forty thousand men and returned with only forty. I know how quickly mirth can turn to misery. After Lorin's Bane. And Celaph…" He had spoken of the serpent titan during their council earlier. "I feel like this world is a playground for these creatures, and there's one worse than all the rest." He frowned, thinking. "I never said how Celaph was driven away."

"No, you didn't."

"The others think it was Drulgar. It was winged, colossal, no more than a shape above us. Not everyone saw it. Those that did only got a glimpse through the fog, but me…what I saw was not a dragon, my lady."

"No?" She smiled in a way that said she knew far more than she ever let on. "Tell me, Robbert. What did you see?"

And he told her, and she nodded, and they wondered together about it all, wondered whether it was good or bad, as the evening swirled around them, a cloud of smells and sights and sounds. And when Marian left, more came to pay their fealty to him, lesser lords and knights from the Tukoran host going to their knees and kissing the back of his hand. They called him 'king' and said his father would be proud, and some spoke boldly of the blight of his grandfather, how young Robbert would be the one to wipe it all away. And so the night went on, and not once did Robbert move. He ate well, drank little, and sat as a king before his host, nodding, smiling, and being very kingly.

It was hours later when Borrus came stamping over to flop back into his seat. He'd been away a little while, Robbert had seen, gone off with Rikkard and Killian to share in some secret meeting. He picked up his wine cup, drank it down in one big gulp, then waved for a server to refill it. "You're not drunk, Robbert," he said. "You should be drunk."

"I'd sooner keep my wits about my, my lord. If we should be attacked…"

"Life's too short for that," Borrus cut in. "Now especially. We've got to live while we can; that's what we Riverlanders think." He called the server to fill Robbert's cup and forced him to drink. Only once he'd seen that portion off and his goblet was refilled did the big lord say, "There's word from Ballantris. He wants to meet with you. Get the measure of you, maybe." He shrugged and drank. "He's in camp an hour from here, four of five miles, something like that. Did we speak about this earlier, in council? I half forget."

"Sir Rikkard spoke of it," Robbert said.

"Ah, yes, that'll do it. Sometimes I zone out when Rikkard drones on." He laughed and drank more wine. "Yes, well. I'm sure he laid it all out for you. Sometimes my mind runs ahead of me…I'm thinking of the next battle, thinking of Ven, how sweet it will be when I finally take his head off. I fought him two decades ago, you know? Cut Malathar a few times before he flew off. You can still see the scars on him, but I want more than that. I want him dead at my feet, Robbert. Both of them. I want both of them dead." He drank more wine. "But yes, yes, Rikkard's better at the planning, the strategy, him and Killian and Marian and Torvyn, they're all much cleverer than me."

"Moonlord Ballantris wants to meet with me?" Robbert prompted.

"Sure, yes. There's a new king about and he wants to see you. He's got about fifteen thousand men…and two moonbears. We could sure as hell use them when we tackle the Bane, but Ballantris is equivocating. Is that the right word? Equivocating? Sorry, I'm getting a bit drunk. Anyway, tomorrow…we can discuss that more tomorrow. That isn't what I wanted to tell you, no…there's news."

"News?"

"From the south. Lakelands." He turned to him and gripped his shoulder, and a big smile warmed his face, a big, slightly drunk, happy smile. "Your brother's alive, Robbert," he said. "We just had a rider come down from Lakeheart. He's there, in Three-Lake Keep. In Lord Fullerton's care."

Quick tears misted Robbert's eyes. "He's…is he well? His wounds…"

"Healed up, I'm told. Though he's in a deep sleep. There was an incident with a stormhag, or something. They're trying to find the right tonic to wake him up, but otherwise his health is good. So let's drink, Robbert. Damn it, let's drink!"

And Robbert drank. He drank a great gulp and then another and then he asked, "How…who brought him there?"

"Manfrey. Who bloody else! That great gallant fool is all over the place these days. You might have thought twice before giving Rockfall to Malcolm Marsh, Robbert. Emeric's more deserving. He's ten times the man."

Robbert was thinking of a better title for this Emeric Manfrey. He smiled, and then he laughed, and he drank down another great swallow. "He'll come, then? When he's awake? He'll come back here?"

"Sure, sure, why on earth wouldn't he? Seems Esterling's with him too, though he's lost half an arm. What a day, hey? What a day! Another reason to celebrate, Robbert. So let's celebrate, yes? Let's bloody well celebrate!"

And celebrate they did. Robbert drank and sang and maybe he even danced, but always did he hold back a measure of reserve. He was a king now, after all, and must be kingly. The men roared in laughter and sang in joy, and music rang out through the castle. Loud it was, so loud in that hall. Loud and raucous and wild and joyful.

And they never even heard the horns.

49

Saska

"You're getting better, you know," Leshie said. "I almost didn't see you that time."

"It's dark." Saska thrust the Nightblade back into its plain leather scabbard and the wisps of black smoke that enshrouded her fogged and faded away. Her form took shape. "That's the only reason, Lesh."

"Well, it's *one* reason. But not the *only* one." The Red Blade came up to sit beside her on the rock. She'd only gone off to make her water, and Saska had taken the chance to train. She took every chance to train, in truth. Every little chance she could. "Really, Sask, you *are* improving. Maybe you don't see it properly, but you are."

"A little," she admitted. "But not enough."

"Enough for now," Leshie came back. "That's all you can do. Enough for now."

Saska nodded. There *was* something rewarding in the process, she had to admit; a feeling of discovery, of self-taught pride, the same feeling Elyon must have had when he taught himself how to master the Windblade. But in large part the overriding reaction was frustration. *I'm fumbling in the dark,* she thought, *groping for connection.* Her bond was strong, yes, and the whispers were submitting to her, but the true essence of the Nightblade remained frustratingly elusive.

"You're too hard on yourself," Leshie said. "No one would be making progress any quicker, Saska. Just relax."

"Relax? That's your advice?"

"Yup." Leshie's head bobbed happily up and down. "You know how it is when you try to force something. Like when you're constipated…you just have to unclench and let it flow."

"Charming."

"Works for me," said Leshie. "You're all constipated up there, in your head. There's a blockage you're trying to get through and you're forcing it, trying to concentrate too hard. Maybe you just need to unclench, Saska."

"I'm not clenched."

And Leshie laughed. "You are. You're clenched up like a clam. We need Elyon back here sharpish. *He'll* unclench you, I know that much. Now that you've finally stopped all that pussyfooting."

Saska sighed. "We weren't pussyfooting," she began. "We were just..."

The barn door groaned open behind them. It proved a welcome distraction. Saska heard feet rustling across the frozen ground, heard murmuring voices as the Butcher and the Baker came up to join them. The bigger younger brother was yawning, stretching, and already complaining of the cold. The smaller older brother was chiding him for it. "If only you fought as well as you moaned, we'd have won this war already."

"I do fight as well as I moan. I am the greatest sellsword in all the world and the greatest moaner too." He thumped his chest, though it lacked the usual energy. "Too cold," he muttered. "My limbs are frozen and my cock doesn't work properly."

"It never did." Leshie grinned at him and stood from the rock. "Speaking of which, I'm going to go and snuggle up with Jaito. Get nice and *warm*."

"Make sure you do nothing more than snuggle," Saska called after her, as the Red Blade strolled away. "It's a communal barn, Leshie. *Communal*." She sighed and turned back to the others. "Can I stay out here with you?" she asked them, only half in jest.

The Baker smiled whitely at her. His breath puffed palely as he spoke. "Anything to report, Serenity?"

"Nothing. Well, we heard a fox screaming and there was an owl hooting at us for a while, but that's about it."

"An owl?" said the Butcher. "Are we sure it wasn't an eagle?"

"It was an owl. I can tell the difference, Butcher."

"Well, maybe they are evil too, these owls. Maybe *all* birds are evil. Maybe we should be killing them all." His tone was half mocking, half indignant. "The Windy Prince is a murderer. Eagles are sacred to us, yes, sacred to Aramatians. And he is killing them. Murderer, I say."

Saska was too tired for this. It had been another long cold watch and she was in dire need of rest. "You know his concerns," she said. "Valid or not, he's only trying to protect me." Before he left to fly west, Elyon had confessed to her that he'd slain a suspicious-looking eagle or two, fearing they may be enemy spies, and she'd been fool enough to share that with the rest of them. Those of Aramatian upbringing hadn't taken it so well.

"Then he must return, this murderer," the Butcher declared. "He cannot protect you from across the world."

"I have you for that." Saska didn't want to brood on Elyon's return. Her mind only conjured all sorts of tragedies, cycling between all the things that might have gone wrong, and what use was that? It had no utility at all to sit and mull on things she could not control. Rolly had told her that, and he was right. "I'm going to bed," she said. "I'll see you in a few hours."

She returned to the barn, Joy going along with her, ever now at Saska's side. The sleek black cat wanted to hunt, Saska knew, to prowl the night and stretch her legs, but Rolly's rebuke had gotten into her head, and she never so much as let her out of her sight anymore. Joy hated it, but obeyed. Sometimes Saska wondered if she should have just left her across the Links as Rolly had told her. She could have run free there. She could have hunted as she pleased and roved where she wanted. The cities around Whaler's Bay were teeming with life, they'd heard, but it wasn't the same across the Lowplains. They were quiet to the point of desertion, and Joy may well have been safe. *I could have found her after the war,* she reflected. *Maybe I should have listened to him. Maybe I should have seen sense.*

But she hadn't, and here they were. *What's done is done,* she thought. There was no sense in dwelling on that either.

She entered the barn quietly and shut the door behind her, trying not to disturb the others. She could hear whispering in one dark corner. Leshie, it was, crawling up next to Jaito. There was a soft giggle and then what sounded like kissing. *Leave it at that,* Saska thought, firmly. *Don't go any further, Leshie.*

The rest had taken their own private spaces among the beams and wooden pillars. Here the Surgeon, there the Tigress, the Gravedigger giving out his death-rattle of a snore somewhere, Umberto sleeping peacefully beneath his cloak. Saska could see no sign of the Wall, but that was hardly surprising. He seemed always to be on watch somewhere whether it was his turn or not. *He'll be on patrol, wandering through the woods and fields in search of danger. And eagles, yes.* Rolly had taken Elyon's concerns about the eagles seriously, certainly more than the others did anyway. He was always watching for them now, always wary. Always leading them to cover or down some different track if ever he should spot one.

She found a quiet space in a far, deep corner and sat with her back to the wall, drawing the Nightblade silently from its sheath and setting it across her thighs. Joy sat on her haunches and looked at it with her glowing silver eyes. She seemed mesmerised by the blade, by the curling wisps of smoke. It moved languidly, confidently. The whispers were subdued.

After a while, Joy settled down to sleep, stretching out long and lithe beside her and giving out a deep, rumbly purr. Saska could feel the plank boards buzzing lightly beneath her. *Relax,* she thought. *Just relax.* Leshie made it sound so easy, but Leshie was Leshie and she thought everything was easy...especially things she didn't have to attempt herself. Saska held the handle of the Nightblade loosely in her grasp, let the tension bleed out of her muscles. She took several long breaths in and out, in and out, in and out, closing her eyes and settling her thoughts. Then, gradually, she slid away into the Nightblade's world. A realm of shadows and shapes and shades of blackness. Of whispers in the dark.

Sometimes she wondered if some of those whispers were from past bearers. Talasha had told her that a part of Kin'rar Kroll's soul still resided *within* Neyruu, that he had helped to train her and guide her, to help her and Neyruu bond. Could the same be true of the blades? Elyon didn't think so. He'd told her the only whispers were from Vandar, the part of his broken spirit that still lingered within the blade, and she had to block them out and *never* let them in…but Saska wasn't so sure. She was Varin's own blood, Varin's heir. *Maybe that gives me a deeper access?* she wondered. *Something the other bearers cannot hear, or see, or know…*

She could hear the whispers now. They were heard as though beyond a shroud of fog, dull, muted, indistinct. There were many of them; different whispers, different voices. Faintly she percieved shapes, shadows, moving in the darkness. *Could they be bearers from the past? Echoes of them? Imprints?* She sat, wondering about all the other bearers gone before, the scores of men who'd mastered the Nightblade over the last three thousand years, and one man, in particular, came to mind.

So gently, oh so gently, she opened herself up and called out to him. *Grandfather,* she thought, projecting her voice into the darkness. *Are you out there, Grandfather? Grandsire, can you hear me?*

She focused her thoughts and tried to picture him, this king who'd died four decades ago, this king who was the last of his line. King Lorin had been magnificent, all agreed, a swashbuckler and perhaps even a bit of a scoundrel, fearless, flamboyant, and utterly brilliant with the blade. His preferred choice had always been the Nightblade…everyone knew *that* too. *Help me, Grandfather,* Saska thought. *If there's a part of you here, help me. Guide me.* She distilled her thoughts, willing him to come to her, and she drifted through the cold black world, the silent world, hoping…

She felt something, a presence behind her. She could not say how much time had passed. She started and turned and she saw him. A figure wreathed in shadow. The outline of a man, less black than the blackness around him. "Grandfather?" she whispered, and there was something small and childlike in her voice. "Is…is it you? Have you come to guide me?"

The figure moved, drifting toward her. "Child, sweet child." The voice was rich, deep, sonorous. "Yes, I am he." The border lines thinned and faded and the detail of the man emerged. Before her he stood, a towering wonder, black-bearded, blue-eyed, smiling at her warmly, a grandfatherly warmth. "Oh, you are so beautiful, child. I see a little of her in you. Not much, no, but a little."

There were tears in Saska's eyes. "Atia," she whispered. "Do you mean Atia?"

"Yes, Atia, my great love. My secret love. So few knew."

"I knew," Saska told him, almost proudly. Her lips were trembling, curling nervously at the corners. "Is…is it really you?"

"Oh child, who else would it be? I've been waiting for you, Saska.

Oh, for so long." He wore a cloak, she saw, a cloak pinned with a sword-and-mountain brooch, a great blue cloak with marks and scars from his hunts. He threw it aside and pulled out a blade, and it was the Nightblade, Saska saw. She blinked, just once, and imperceptibly the world changed. The dark quiet featureless world became a great open sea, surging with colour and noise and motion, and they stood on the deck of a rocking ship, lumbering across the waves. Men rushed and thrashed about them, pulling at ropes and rigging and the air was filled with the thunder of the ocean, the cawing of gulls, the shouts of seamen and sailors.

And King Lorin stood before her with the Nightblade in his grasp. "This is the day I died," he said, in a tone of sombre regret. He glanced over the gunwale. "He is down there now, the creature they'll come to call my bane. Ah, in another world it might have been different. They'd be down there now, all the krakens in their council, and they're calling *me* Kraken's Bane instead, but no…no, it wasn't to be." He smiled, but sadly. "I should never have died that day. Reckless I was, and foolhardy. With a little more poise, a thimble of wit, I'd have struck the squid down and returned to my sweet Atia."

And spared me, Saska thought. *Spared me all of this.*

"But it isn't the way, is it?" said the last of the Varin kings. "Fate is a map, child, a great tapestry hung in the halls of time. My thread did end, and thus did I, and the son I never met was born."

"Thalavar," she said. "My father." She looked out across the sea. "I never met him either."

"And so we are linked. Linked by a son and a father whom neither of us knew." He smiled at her and swished the Nightblade, and he blinked out of sight and appeared again. Saska stared in wonder at the ease of it, the brilliance. "A curious blade with which to kill a kraken, no? Would not the Windblade have been better? The Sword of Varinar?" He vanished again and this time he did not reappear. She heard a noise behind her and spun around and there he was again, smiling. "A curious blade indeed."

She fell to a knee before him. "Teach me," she blurted. "Will you teach me, Grandsire?"

"Here? Oh, no, this is not the place. He's coming, don't you feel it? He is coming up now."

And she felt it. The thrumming, thrashing, churning beneath them, the dark presence coming up from the depths. The men aboard the vessel roared and the gulls cawed and King Lorin gave out a great stirring bellow and called the men to arms. They charged and surged, pulling harpoons from stacks, running to man the scorpions. "Grandsire," Saska was shouting. "Don't do it. Don't fight it. Please…please…"

But he ignored her, he could not hear her, it was like she was no longer there. The ship rocked and bucked and she lost her footing, staggering forward to the gunwale, and a man came lurching past and bumped her, and before she knew it she was tripping, falling, tumbling over the edge of the ship and into the frothing sea. And the water came rushing up to meet her. She splashed into the frenzied white churn, saw king and kraken in battle beneath the waves, a dance of death, a beautiful brutal dance, then darkness swallowed her, and silence fell. And it lingered, on and on.

She opened her eyes and gasped.

Breath surged and filled her lungs.

She was standing on a lonely strand. A forest of pine ran behind the shore with rugged hills folding out into the distance in darkening tones of green and grey. Fine earthy smells moved up her nose. Of salt and sea and pine. The waves made a soft lapping sound as they washed against the shore. There was a boat pulled up the beach, a plain, simple skiff. Furtively, a youth came stalking out of the trees dressed in cloak and hood, a bag on his back. He rushed up to the boat and braced at the prow, pushing it across the shingly ground, legs driving, and when it glided into the crystal water he leapt aboard and threw down his bag and took up the oars to row. And fiercely he did row, cut and pull, dip and splash, cut and pull, heaving and puffing through the early morning mist, slicing out into the open sea.

"Your father," said a voice. "My son."

She turned her head. King Lorin stood beside her.

"He looks like me, don't you think? And you look a little like him."

Saska didn't know. The face was vague, too far away to see. It wasn't a famous face like his was. A face only a few ever knew. "Elio Krator killed him," Saska said. "*He* set me on this path."

"No. The path was always before you. Your father walked another."

"A short one," she said. "A sad one." *Thalavar*. The name was rich and royal, a blend of Thala and Varin, and that made it divine. Why name him so if he wasn't meant to do more?

"He did all he was meant to do," said King Lorin. "Siring you was his purpose. His path."

Saska looked up into his kind blue eyes. "Is he with you now? Up there, in the Eternal Halls? Will I get to meet him one day?"

"You'll get to meet them all," he said.

She looked back out to sea, and her eyes were firm and defiant. Her father was fading now beyond her sight, where he would founder in a storm as he crossed around the coast of Rasalan, to be taken in by slavers. And to Aram they would take him, as King Godrin had foreseen. To the safe care of the palace, and Safina Nemati, who would watch over him. *His path*, Saska thought. *His path that led to mine.* She wondered about all the paths that had come before, the thousands of them all twisting and turning through time, so they might reach this moment.

"Will you train me?" she asked again. What use was getting to this moment if she wasn't trained, wasn't prepared? "Here, where my father was raised. Will you train me here, in secret?"

"Secret? No, the secret is out, child. Everyone knows who you are."

Those words disquieted her. "E-everyone?" she repeated. Fear blew through her like a fierce winter wind. "You mean…"

"Yes. Did you think you could hide from him forever?"

Her mind conjured a shadow, the great shadow that had haunted her dreams. Even before she knew who she was, knew of her past and her blood, her rich royal blood, she'd *known*. Somehow she'd known what that shadow was, she'd known the fate that awaited her. "Train me, Grandfather," she said again. "I need you to train me. To guide me. To *help*."

"There is no help I can give you. I am dead. The dead cannot help."

"But…" She reached out and tugged at his arm. The sky was darkening, the wind picking up. "You're here. You're here with me. I have no one else. No one."

The features of his face were fading. "I am not here," he told her. "I am dead, child. This is all you."

"All me?" She didn't understand.

"You. Yes. You." The king turned a full circle, opening out his arms. "All of this is you."

And the world changed again. The waves retreated and the sea went with them and the mountains crumbled and fell away to ash and dust. The pines cracked and shattered and blew off in a sudden terrible wind, and the earth was scoured now, scoured and desolate, a great empty barren world of rock and fume. She could hear screeching in the sky, the song of dragons, see shadows rippling in the shroud. "Grandfather," she shouted, turning all the way around. "Grandfather, where are you? I need you! I need your help!"

But she was alone now, alone at the far end of days. *This is it*, she realised. *I have failed and the world has ended.* She felt the crunch of bones beneath her feet, bones in the ash and cinder. They poked out here and poked out there and the skulls stared up with their wide empty eyes. They were under her feet and ahead of her and behind her. They spread in all directions in a field of endless doom and death. She turned all about, searching for someone, anyone. She called and called, but no one answered, no one but the dragons screaming out through the skies.

She ran. Onward she ran, though where she did not know. Among the bones and skulls she saw faces now, fresh faces staring up at her. Leshie she saw, and she saw Del and Elyon and Rolly and Llana and Orryn. She saw Ranulf and Talasha, she saw Captain Rikki and little Billy and Old Hob and all the rest, she saw her grandmother and Lord Hasham and she saw Yasha and Milla and Koya, and she saw Marian and her men, Roark and Braddin and Lark and Quilter, and Astrid too, and Lancel and Barnibus, and the Butcher and the Baker and the other Bloody Traders, and she saw Sunrider Tantario and Kaa Sokari and Jaito and a dozen more men and women she'd known. All were dead, all of them. Everyone who had helped her, guided her, loved her, served her, everyone was staring lifeless from the bed of dust and ash as the dragons circled like crows upon them, exulting in their triumph…

Saska gasped awake.

Light spilled into the barn through the double wood doors, and the sounds of the morning came with it, the twitter of birds and the sighing wind in the trees and the soft crunch of footfall on snow. Joy was with her, sitting back and watching as though frightened. And the Wall, her Wall, Rolly was kneeling beside her too. His big hand was on her shoulder, a comforting, protective touch. "You were having a nightmare," he rumbled softly. "It's OK, Saska. I'm here."

She looked at him. There were tears in her eyes. "You were dead," she croaked, blinking the brine away. The others were outside, she saw, readying the horses to leave. She could see them passing the door, hear their voices, the fond voices she loved. "All of you…all of you were dead."

"No one's dead, Saska. It was just a bad dream."

But it started as a good one, she thought. Already it was fading, fragmenting, but she recalled enough. "I saw my grandfather," she said. "King Lorin. We were on his ship the day he died and then…then we were on a beach, on the Lonely Isle. I saw my father as a boy."

He helped her up to her feet. In her sleep the Nightblade had slid off to lie beside her on the floor, so she knelt to pick it up, guiding it away into its scabbard. She wiped the tears from her eyes and said, "It felt real, Rolly. Like I really met him."

"Who? Your father?"

"My grandfather. I think…the whispers in the blade. There's a part of him in there, I think. An echo of him. I asked him to train me."

"Saska…"

"I know how it sounds. And maybe it was just a dream…it probably was, but…" She looked away from him, from his doubtful stare. It was no use talking to him about it, she realised. He would not understand and would only caution against this, so why bother? She put it aside. "Are the others ready to go?"

He continued to stare at her. "You shouldn't open yourself to the whispers. If that's what you're doing…"

"I'm not. It was a dream, that's all." She stepped away from the conversation, from the deep frown and wary eyes. The horses were saddled and ready and the air was crisp with the bite of a wintry morning chill, winter though it wasn't. The Butcher and the Baker looked more tired than the rest having shared the final watch. That was good; it meant the Butcher would be quieter this morning, which tended to serve everyone except maybe Leshie, who thrived in their verbal jousts.

Even now she was trying to poke a reaction out of him, and failing. "You're dull today," she said. "What's the point of you if you're dull?"

The Butcher sagged in his saddle. "I'm the dullest sellsword in all the world," he said listlessly. "Yes, and the tiredest. It was a long watch."

"It was only a few hours," Leshie scolded. "I'll bet Coldheart was up all night again, and you're moaning about waking up a few hours earlier than everyone else?"

"The Butcher needs his beauty sleep. The Butcher hates this cold."

"The Butcher needs to stop referring to himself in the third person. It's ridiculous. And the Butcher needs to grow a pair." Leshie looked at him in disgust and then strode away to mount up. Rolly called them all to follow, and off they went into the bitter chill of the morning.

They passed through the woodland slowly, the hooves of their horses crunching on the film of frost that covered the ground. Leaves, twigs, and frozen grass yielded to their step. They followed a track that led from the barn where they'd spent the night through this pretty quiet land of thickets and hills and half-frozen brooks, open fields and picturesque little villages that were almost exclusively abandoned, they had found. After they'd crossed the Links, Rolly had chosen to lead them off the beaten path where he could, though this was a land well populated by these settlements and there were many traveller inns to be found as well. Still, the people were few. Almost everyone had retreated to the safety of bigger cities now, the farmers and crofters, the fieldhands and lumbermen, the little lords in their little keeps, the millers and foresters and ploughmen and carters…almost all of them were gone.

It was past noon when they heard the sound of rustling away to their south, a faint distant sound that suggested the movement of a great host of people. Rolly commanded they remain where they were while he dismounted and went to check. They stopped, watering the horses in a little stream that wended through the woods. Leshie came up to Saska. "You've been quiet all day," she said. "What did you dream of last night?"

"Nothing. It was just a dream."

"Was it a nightmare? You were making noises, Saska. And I saw your eyes when you came out. It looked like you'd been crying." Her eyes narrowed, glaring through the trees in the direction the Wall had gone. "Did Coldheart say something to you? If he made you cry…"

"He didn't. I just…I dreamt you were all dead. I saw the end of the world."

"Oh," Leshie said. "Yeah, I…I guess that would do it. Seeing us all dead." She paused a moment. "That….won't happen, you know? You do know that, don't you? The world isn't going to end."

Saska nodded. "I know, Lesh." But some of her friends would die, she knew that much. And depending on who and how many of them, it would be like the world ended anyway, even if it didn't. It was a grave thought, not something she wanted to dwell on. She wondered if she might talk to Leshie about her grandfather, and the whispers, and the rest of her dream that maybe wasn't a dream, but she decided against it. There seemed no point in talking about it, at least not until she'd had more of a chance to explore it. *Tonight,* she thought. *When I go to sleep tonight, maybe I'll try and see if my grandfather comes to me again.* Very carefully, of course. If this was just a trick of the Nightblade, she wasn't going to let herself fall for it.

The Whaleheart was not long in returning. Maybe only five minutes passed before he re-emerged through the wintry shroud and joined them by the little stream. "What is it?" Saska asked. "Are there refugees on the road?"

"Not refugees. It's an army."

"An army?"

"They're marching from Rasalan. Must have crossed the Links shortly after we did."

"How many?" Saska asked him. "Can I see? I'd like to see."

"Fine. Yes. It's not so far."

Rolly turned back the way he'd come and led her through the trees. Leshie followed behind. She was never one to miss out on anything. Saska heard her tell Jaito to 'stay' as a kennel master might talk to a faithful hound, and the Red Blade came hurrying up to join them. "He's starting to annoy me now," she said. "I can barely go off and take a piss without him following me out into the bushes."

Saska chuckled. "If that's what you're into, Leshie."

"Gross. No. That's not even funny, Saska."

"I thought it was."

They followed Rolly along, discussing how Jaito was absolutely in love with Leshie now and how Leshie absolutely wasn't in love with Jaito. "I'm going to ditch him when we get to Ilithor," the girl said. "Does that make me evil? I'm bored of him, that's the truth."

"It always happens, Lesh. You always get bored."

"Do you think that will happen forever? I don't want to *always* get bored, Saska. I want to find someone to settle down with one day."

"Let's leave 'one day' for another day, how about that?"

"Right. Sure. The ending of the world, and everything."

They could see the edge of the trees ahead where they gave way atop a sloping hill. A valley stretched out before them with a fine high view across much of the land to their south. The Wall halted them here. Very far to the east, they could see the Siblings Strait, days away now, and not quite so far, but still far away, the great towering statues of Tukor's Pass stood grandly to the southwest, standing their eternal vigil at the border.

And right ahead, moving along the road that wended through woods and around hills, was a great army of Rasalanians, marching stirringly along from the Links. Saska could see the colours, see the banners, hear the great clink and clank and rustle of their movement. There were thousands of them, maybe tens of thousands. It was hard to be sure, because many were lost from sight behind the hills and the trees, but it looked a considerable host.

"They're Buckland men," Saska said. She recognised the bear-and-stag sigil. "And Maynards. Those are the Oakenlord's banners."

Rolly nodded. "A strong host," he said, and his voice rang proudly.

He raised a finger, pointing out lesser houses and colours, both lord and knightly. "It appears that all of North Rasalan has mustered."

"This must be by King Sevrin's order," Saska said. A thought came to her. "Maybe he's seen something in the Eye of Rasalan?" Elyon had told them all about that. How he'd brought it to the new Rasal king.

"It's possible," Rolly allowed. "Or perhaps a call for help has come." His eyes moved away toward the distant statues at Tukor's Pass. "They'll be crossing the border. Going south down the Rustriver, would be my guess."

"Should we go and talk to them?" Leshie asked. "They'd be able to tell us best what's happening."

Saska nodded. "Lord Buckland will be leading them," she said. She'd met Horus Buckland at Northgate when she'd passed south with Marian and her men half a lifetime ago. She liked the big bear-like lord very much. *And Sir Francis Maynard*, she remembered. He was the second son of Lord Ferry Maynard, the Oakenlord. *Maybe he's there as well? And his father with him?* "What do you think, Rolly? We could go down and intercept them before they get too far ahead?"

The Wall did not have a chance to answer. From behind came the sound of approach, and the voice of the Butcher with it. "Bucklands. They are Bucklands, brother." He walked forward with the Baker at his side. The Butcher sounded very excited. "Maybe our father is down there? He was a knight. A Buckland knight."

"You don't know who your father was," Leshie said.

"Yes we do. He was a Buckland knight. He bedded our mother every time he came south." He grinned. "She was a whore, our mother, but a lovely whore. She only did it because she needed money. Our father was good to her, she said."

"But not good enough to give his name?"

"No names. No. Knights do not always use names with whores. But he was a knight, yes, this we know, and a Buckland, we know this too." He turned to his brother. "Shall we go down and ask them? Maybe he is there, with Lord Horus? He must be a great knight to have sired the two of us."

"You're not even brothers," Leshie dismissed. "Not full brothers, anyway. You look nothing alike."

"You're not going down," Sir Ralston told him.

The Butcher glared at Leshie and then at Rolly. "You would deny us meeting our father, Coldheart?"

"No one's going down," the Wall said. "If we want tidings, we'll hear them when we reach Ilithor. And we'll lose hours getting there and back. No. We move on."

He swung around to lead them back into the woods. Defiant as the Butcher could be, he did tend to fall in line more than he used to. His brother gave him an assuaging pat on the back and said, "We will meet our father another time. Once we are done in Ilithor, we will go south. We will find him then, brother. Yes? We'll find him then."

The Butcher nodded sadly and they began back into the trees. Saska followed behind. She made it about three steps before she felt the hair going up on the back of her neck, felt the prickles rising on her arms. She stopped, turning, and reached to take the Nightblade's hilt. And she knew it at once" "He's coming," she murmured.

The others stopped. Leshie stepped back toward her. "What? Who's coming?"

"Him," she said.

And he came.

From the south he came, a black shape growing quickly larger. His wings thumped thunder and the skies shattered at his approach. Distantly, Saska heard the buzz of terror running through the Rasal host. Horns began to sound, and men began to scatter. Those near trees rushed off into the woods, and those caught in the open turned about not knowing where to go. Horses bucked and threw their riders and ran in all directions, screaming, and those hitched to wagons began charging up the road, the wheels bouncing and breaking off, the drivers desperately trying to calm them. Some men were drawing swords for all the good it would do, and captains blared out orders, but mostly they went unheard. From the top of the hill, Saska watched as the entire army fell into a frenzy. And she saw it all in a blink. Because a moment later he was on them.

Drulgar the Dread dipped. His maw opened and he scooped up a dozen men, a score, a hundred in a single bite, gouging out a great tract of broken earth across the road. Fire blew from between his laughing lips, and the thunder of his joy rang out across the world. He pumped his wings and sent men flying. He pumped them and rose, arcing through the skies, diving again, exulting. The air was sizzling, the snow melting and steaming as it met his volcanic heat, and very soon the whole valley became a great white shroud, and in that shroud men were dying, crying out, scattering and screaming and running and burning. Saska stood at the edge of the trees, staring. She felt a hand come down on her shoulder. The Wall was behind her. "Saska, we should go."

She stared out, glared out, at the thing that was destroying the world.

"Saska. Come. We do not want to be seen."

He sees me, she thought. *He sees and he doesn't care.* "He's killing them for fun," she said. "Do you hear him, Rolly? He's…he's *laughing.*" The hate in her was fierce, fiercer than the fear.

"There's nothing we can do for them," the giant said. His voice was calm, but uging. He gently pulled at her shoulder. "Saska, come. There is no sense in standing here."

There is sense, she thought. *I must look upon my enemy.* She held for another moment as the Dread crossed the skies, and even from so far away she could feel the hot wind of his passing. But he seemed to be leaving. A few passes was all it took to scatter and sunder the host, and now he was turning, flapping away toward the southwest. "He's going for the border," Saska realised. "The statues. He's going for the gods."

"Come." The Wall drew her back. "Come, Saska, we must go."

She took one last look at the Dread, at her foe, as he grew smaller and smaller into the distance. And a short time later, as they moved back through the trees, they heard the distant crashing, the distant roaring, and the great echoing sounds of the twin statues coming down.

The gods were falling.

50

Amara

The pavilion was dank and made of pelts in shades of green and brown and black. It stank of death. Fires burned in queer animal-bone braziers, and the flames smouldered dull and low, throwing up tight ringlets of smoke. People lurked silently in the shadows, watching as she entered across a floor of dried leaves and twigs. She approached the throne cut out from the stump of a tree, old tangled limbs twisting and reaching up behind it. Around the walls of the shelter, branches had been stacked and woven, and the roof above her was a lattice of limbs, draped with hanging vines and carcasses. It felt like a forest in here. Like the Deadwood, from where these people hailed.

A herald stood beside the throne. An old man dressed in the patched skin of a hundred red foxes. "You come before Black Merryl," he proclaimed, "old blood of Shrikna the Watcher, the Prophet, who saw the End-Fall come to pass, who stood witness to the Red Storm's wrath and Orthrand's fall. State your name."

"Lady Amara Daecar."

"And what is your purpose here?"

"To speak with Black Merryl." She thought that must be obvious, but played along with their little game. "In private," she added.

"Black Merryl keeps no secrets from her people," the herald said. "You may speak openly before her."

"I would prefer not to. This is a delicate matter."

The herald made to speak again, but the woods witch raised her palm. "Go. Leave us." And they fled, all of them, scurrying out through the flaps and into the sting of the cold. This woman was more than a ruler to her people. She was near enough a god to them, and her line had ruled the clans of the Deadwood for thousands of years, Amara had heard. "Lady Amara," she said, once they were alone. "I welcome you to my humble home."

"It's very charming. I like all the tree limbs and branches."

"We brought them with us," Black Merryl said. "A woods witch is not a witch without a wood, is she?" She smiled, not unpleasantly. Her voice had a hissy, low quality to it, a voice that spread and reached across a room with nought but a whisper. She was not old, leastways not to look at. Amara put her at no more than fifty, though with these witches it was never so easy to tell. "What is it you wish to discuss, my lady?"

"The king," Amara answered. She glanced back to the exit. "Can I count upon your discretion?"

"That will depend upon what you tell me. If there is a risk to my people…"

"There isn't. It concerns the king's health."

"I see." The witch paused to look at her. Her eyes were fierce, the colour of moss, smouldering in the gloom that shaded her face. They were wise eyes, eyes that saw far. "You're speaking of his injuries?"

"Of his pain." Few knew the true extent of it, and Amara would see it stay that way for as long as she possibly could. *They must all believe in him, as I do*, she thought. *They must all follow him, rally to him, die for him.* If they saw Amron limping and shambling about, grimacing, struggling, they might lose hope. Amara wouldn't have it. The very future depended upon him.

"His pain," the witch repeated, thoughtful. "Pain kept at bay by the blade he carries."

"Yes."

"The blade he must give up?"

"Yes," she said again, more bitterly. "And soon. Without it, there will be no veil to hide his suffering. Our physician Artibus brews tonics, but their effect is becoming diminished and Amron says they addle him. He must be quick of limb and sharp of mind when it comes to battle. If the king falters, *all* will falter. He is the tip of the spear, the spear that will be driven into the guts of the enemy, and if that tip is blunted, then…"

Black Merryl cut her off. "You have come to ask me to cure him."

Amara drew a breath. "Yes. I hoped…"

The witch was already shaking her head. "I have no such power. These wounds…they were inflicted by a shard of a god's heart. A dark blade, full of ancient power far beyond my own. This pain is a blight that is not just of the flesh; it is a corruption of the very spirit. I am sorry. I cannot help you."

Amara stood before her, at a loss. "A potion," she said, grasping for something. "There must be some potion you can brew that can…"

"Ease his pain," the woods witch said. "Like your physician, with his tonics." Her head went up and down. "Yes, this I can do, but no potion I brew, no sorcery I conjure, will last. The blight is too deeply entrenched now. The power of his blade is the only cure, for it is a brother of the blade that cursed him. And as these blades grow stronger in the spreading dark, so grows stronger his pain. So the tonics fail to work, and the potions and the spells. I fear now that only one thing will spare him." She paused and then said it. "Death is the only release."

Amara found herself shaking her head. She would not accept it, would not believe it. "There must be another way."

"To cure him. No. There is no cure but the release from his mortal vessel. But I will do what I can to help him until that time." She motioned behind her; there was space beyond the stump throne in which she sat, private quarters they looked to be, partitioned from the rest of the pavilion by drapes. Smells emanated from there, strange smells Amara did not recognise, and it seemed to her shadows moved in the dark, rippling past the walls. "I have already begun," the witch said. "There are certain spell-cast potions that will help relieve him. They will be stronger than your physician's tonics, you can be sure."

"Thank you," Amara said. "I am most grateful. Truly."

The witch regarded her for a long moment. "You believe in him," she said. "I have heard his names, and one above all. You see him as your saviour, is that not so?"

"Yes. He is."

"And yet another will bear this weapon. This Heart Remade. It will not be him."

Amara wondered how much the witch knew. How far she saw. What secrets she kept. "It takes more than a single blade to win a war," she said, "no matter its power. The king is the one who binds us. Should that thread come loose, I fear all will unravel."

A smile from the witch. A nod. And her wild black hair shivered at the motion. "He is important. I have seen this too. A shadow stands before him, dark and eternal, and behind the shadow is another, immense and fading. I have seen this in my dreams. Glimpses. Shapes and sounds. Nothing more."

Amara leaned forward. "What does it mean? Dark and eternal. You're talking about Eldur? About Agarath?"

"That I cannot say. Dreams are fickle, and my sight is weak. I am not Shrikna, who saw clearly across time. No. I know only that your king is important. I know only that you have an ally in me, my lady. So go now and return to your business. I will do what I can to assist him."

She had more to ask, more questions on the tip of her tongue, but the witch's voice compelled her to leave. So she did.

Outside it was bitter cold, the wind coming in from the lake where the water was ice and white-caps and thin boats sliding through the floes. The fox-pelt herald and Black Merryl's other subjects were huddled outside in the frigid air looking frightened and miserable. A light snow was falling, misting the sky. "I'm done," Amara told them. "You may go back inside where it's warm."

They hurried through the flaps, back to the comfort of their wooded pavilion and all the decaying scents of home. Amara's escort was waiting nearby, some of her Knights Assorted led by Sir Penrose Brightwood. Sir Penrose saw her emerging and stepped away from the others. "My lady. Did it go as hoped?"

"Not entirely." She'd hoped for a cure, some spell to cast all Amron's pain away, but supposed this was as good as it was likely to get. "She'll brew a pain-relief potion," she told the knight. "Something strong, she says. She's already been working on it."

Sir Penrose frowned warily. "Then she already knew? Of the king's pain?"

"Apparently so. I'm given to think that the witch sees much, Pen." She could see the worry in his eyes. "What concerns you?"

"Well...she's a *witch*, my lady," he said, as though that fact alone carried great risk. "And from a cursed forest a world away. Her name is *Black* Merryl. I just...what if she has some ill design?"

Amara smiled. "I believe the 'black' is in reference to her hair, Penrose, not some aspersion toward the darkness of her soul. And witches have a frightfully unfair reputation for malicious work. As the saying goes, men fear what they do not understand. Ignorance is a common foundation of fear and hate, though hardly valid."

"It is sometimes," the knight said. "How can we be sure of her allegiance? She might be working against us, my lady. Whatever potion she brews...it could be poison...or some other device to control him."

"Or it could be the very solution we need so that Amron is able to lead our armies into battle." Distrust of witches really did run deep, Amara reflected, especially among certain types of men. "We will, of course, let Amron decide when he returns, Pen. Do you trust your king?"

The man went dutiful. "With all my being, my lady, yes."

"And me? Do you trust me?"

He nodded firmly. "I do, my lady. Of course I do."

She smiled. "Then free yourself of these concerns. I assure you, we have it all in hand."

That was enough to satisfy the knight. "Yes, my lady, as you say."

The others were called to assemble and took their places around her as they began back toward the city. The tribes were camped just beyond the western walls beside the lake, and despite being 'one tribe now', as Stegra Snowfist continually claimed, they still kept themselves apart, arranging their camps as the houses might in a northern host, lined up near and next to one another, though not quite intermingling. Through the dreary camp of the Deadcloaks they went, and past the Mole Men who dug their holes underground. The Crowmen of the Crag raised fluttery shelters made of animal skins woven with black feathers, and along the shoreline, the Orca Lord's people spread out in their whaleskin and sharkskin and sealskin tents, their longboats lined up along the banks. They were a most industrious folk. In only a short span of days, dozens of boats had been built, and many more were being hammered together by the sounds that rang out from the boatyard.

"They're nice, those boats," Sir Talmer Hedgeside remarked. "I was admiring them when you talked with the witch, my lady. Very sleek and sturdy."

"They can build them in less than a day," put in Sir Ryger Joyce, in his growly voice. "Makes you wonder how quickly they could knock together something larger. You ask me, it'd be smart to make use of them when crossing the Red Sea. Build them up with higher sides and we can even get the horses in."

Amara could not be sure if he was being serious or not. "You'd prefer to cross the sea in a canoe than a triple-decked galleon, Ryger?"

"I just might, my lady," he told her. "Big ships are easier to spot and I'd sooner not throw up a beacon for the Dread. We try to cross in a great armada and he'll have himself a good fun time of it, I fear."

It sounded like a valid fear. "And you think lots of smaller longboats would be better?"

"It's worth considering. You know what I'd do? I'd build a thousand of them, row them all down the Steelrun to the coast, wait for a bit of misty weather when the water's not too rough and then push on out one at a time. Spread our forces nice and thin until we can reassemble on the other side. We'd be easier to miss that way."

"And easier to kill," said Sir Montague Shaw. As a Rasalanian, his voice was worth hearing on any matter concerning naval warfare. "A few enemy warships come along, and you'll have no defence against them. Worse still should a few dragons get a sniff of you."

"Then we send an armada ahead," Sir Ryger said. "Each ship with a skeleton crew to draw fire. Once they're all sunk and burning the enemy will disperse. Then we sneak across after they're gone."

"Risky," said Shaw. "Though I see the thinking, Ryger." He rubbed his square chin. "I do not imagine the skeleton crews will favour being sacrificial lambs, however."

"Why not? They'd be doing a great service. We lose this war, we're all dead anyway. Might take a week, a month, a year or two, but it'll happen. Some men would rather die knowing they're giving their lives for something meaningful than live on without any hope at all. I know I would."

The same was true of all of her men, Amara hoped. That was why they'd joined her in the first place. To restore their honour and do something to help, not rot away in the service of a grotesquely fat, cruel, and perverted pirate lord.

The men continued to debate the topic as they passed through the tribal camps. Amara was no longer listening; her mind was elsewhere, with Amron and with Elyon, somewhere far now to the northwest. They had left the previous morning and planned to stop the night at North-watch. *The last hearth*, she thought. *The last bit of warmth and shelter before they go out into that great white wilderness.*

She feared for them. She did not expect to sleep well until they came back safely, but that was her curse as a sister and an auntie, the curse of her deep love and affection. *Keep him warm, Amron*, she thought. *Fly him safe, Elyon*, she prayed. Together they would make it there and back again, she knew. She feared for them, yes, but she trusted them too, and Amron would not let them fail. He may not be Varin's heir, but that did not mean he wasn't their saviour. She was too wedded to that thought now to believe anything else. *Let this Saska hold the Heart Remade. Amron will be the one to lead us to victory.*

She was interrupted by the sounds of arguing. "Well bugger you, Joyce," Sir Hugo Dain was saying. "We'll settle this with steel, how about that?" He clutched at his sword hilt. "A duel to first blood."

Sir Ryger frowned at him. "To prove what? We're talking about slaying dragons you great dolt."

"So you're too cowardly to accept? I see." And he nodded.

"By the bloody gods I'm not. I accept your challenge, Dain. First blood it is. Right here, right now." He turned, throwing back his long cloak, and drew his godsteel sword.

Sir Hugo drew his and at once the men moved out to form a widening ring around them. Penrose moved up close to Amara. "My lady? Are you going to permit this?"

She looked on, bemused. "Sorry, Pen, I was in another world. What's this about?"

"They were talking about dragonkilling, my lady. Dain said he'd slay one easily, and of course, Ryger took exception to that. You know how he calls him 'Dain the Vain'?"

"Yes, I've heard the name."

"Well, that's what sparked it. He called him Dain the Vain and now…"

"I get the picture." Amara pondered a moment. "Yes, let it play out." She sensed it was high time the men got it out of their system, and Hugo Dain could do with taking down a peg or two. His arrogance was starting to wear thin on them all. "Though I don't care to stay and watch, Pen. We are on a schedule, as you know."

She continued on toward the city as a crowd of tribesmen gathered around, Snowskins and Stone Men and Crowmen all wandering over to watch. Sir Penrose called a quick command to Sir Talmer Hedgeside to take charge of the men and make sure it did not descend into anything worse than 'first blood', then raced after her, escorting her alone toward the gate. A large contingent of Strands were assembled there. "I need a fresh escort for the Lady Amara," Penrose Brightwood called out, and a half dozen swordsmen came forward to walk them through the populated regions of the city.

And on they went, past the tower-topped hills of outer western Varinar, past the great masses camped in squares and yards and storehouses, past the Westview Tower where Lord Styron had taken his new seat, past the inner city wall of ancient stone sand into the rubble and ruin of the city's heart where Drulgar the Dread had wrought such widespread destruction.

They continued toward the ruin of the Royal Place, upon its high central hill. Huge great piles of rubble had been moved aside now, and the stairway that once led to the beautiful entry collonades had been cleared as well. Sir Penrose led Amara up the steps. At the top they found

Sir Bryce Coddington, shouting commands in his old, barking tongue. "You seem in a good mood today, Bryce," Amara observed.

He broke off from his barking - "You what?" - and turned to her. "Oh, Lady Amara. Didn't realise it was you." He straightened himself up. "Excuse the rough welcome."

"All is rough with you, sir. We wouldn't have you any other way." The man was an old retried Varin Knight, once brilliant, always grouchy, who'd settled down to wither away and die in his keep only for the war to drag him back into the fight, armour on and sword to hand. He was always angry, always sour, his lips were twisted into a perpetual scowl, and Amara had always liked him. "How are you getting along?"

"Me personally?" He snorted. "Same as ever. Bitter as a basket of grapefruits. This lot, though? Useless, every one of them. Well, some are all right, I guess, but most…" And he spat to the ground, strewn with great heaps of once-fine, ancient stone, carved and polished and perfect, now broken and blackened by ash and flame. "They're frightened of a cave-in," he told her. "Taking an age building out some support structure down there. It's bloody boring being here watching them, you know. I'd curse you for giving me this damnable charge if I didn't love you so much."

"You don't love anyone, Bryce. Come on."

"I do you. How could I not? You're the only one about this damn place with a bit of character."

"You should spend more time with the Snowfist. He has character enough for a dozen men."

"No. All that shouty bravado isn't character. He's a *caricature*, is what he is. Some boy's idea of what a tribesman is. Got no time for him. Got no time for any of them except you."

"Now Bryce, are you propositioning me? I am only recently widowed, you know, and not yet looking for another union."

The man snorted. "I'm old enough to be your father. And ugly as sin besides. Damn, I just want to die. When's the king coming back?"

"I don't know. In his own good time."

"And if he dies out there? Then what?"

"Well…then he dies, I suppose. That's what usually happens when someone dies."

His lips twisted from a scowl to a scowling smile. "Aye, seems to be the case. Dying does tend to cause death, doesn't it?"

She smiled at him. "So, how close are we to retrieving the throne?"

"A thousand godsdamned leagues," he grunted, motioning sharply down the wide, sloped tunnel that went into the depths of the palace ruins. It was lit by lanterns at intervals and Amara could hear hammering coming up from below, the sound of chisels at work, voices echoing. "We can see it, but can't get at it. The bloody thing's holding up a great load of stone and they're having to build these supports so the whole place doesn't come down on top of them. Might take a few more days."

She chuckled. "So not quite a thousand godsdamned leagues, then?"

"It's long enough. And still a boring bloody duty, babysitting this lot. Amron should have sent me north with the Amadars if you want the truth. I used to know Penrith Oloran well when we were younger. I'd have been better talking to him than that stiff bastard Sir Geofrey Bannard."

Amara smiled. "Isn't that the raven calling the crow black, Bryce?"

"No. I'm rough, not rigid. That Bannard's got a stick shoved so far up his arse he's like to choke on it. And we all know who rammed it up there too."

"Yes." Amara's voice went cold. "And he's arriving shortly. Might be he's already in sight of the gate."

"You'd best get off, then. Can't be having a greatlord arrive without a welcome."

She would sooner swallow her own tongue, but duty demanded her presence. "I'm to host him tonight in Keep Kanabar. A small dinner. Would you come?"

"I'd rather not. Never liked Brydon Amadar."

"For me? I could do with a friendly face."

"My face has never been called friendly. No. I'd only say something I'll regret. Our enmity goes way back. Best I don't make a scene."

It was a shame. Amara could do with a scene. Especially one that didn't involve her. "Very well. I'll come and see you again tomorrow, Bryce. Goodbye for now."

"Goodbye, my lady."

She pecked him on his rugged old cheek and stepped back down the hill. Sir Penrose fell back in beside her. At the bottom of the steps, he turned her eastward along Maple Way, a broad, wide road that went all the way toward the East Gate, through the inner city and the outer. The maple trees that lined the route were black and dead where they ought to be red and vibrant. The flowers that sat in their pots outside the shops and taverns and hung from baskets above doors and adorned every adjoining lane and street were black and dead as well. Varinar was a colourful city through summer and autumn, but the only colours now were shades of grey. This part of the city was utterly and unrecoverably ruined, populated only by rats and crows and little pockets of unwashed vagrants who lurked among the broken buildings, scavenging for bits of food. It was a bleak, silent, ghostly world of ash and fume, death and decay, a place accursed by the coming of the Dread. *And it's about to get worse still,* Amara thought, *with the arrival of that loathsome lord.*

She found Sir Hank Rothwell at the gate in the company of some Daecar and Amadar men, a little island of blue and silver and pink amidst the dull grey tones. There was to be no pomp and ceremony at the coming of Lord Brydon Amadar, no drums and horns and trumpets. It was not in his nature to crave attention, and it was not in Amara's desire to give it. She peered out through the open gate and into the snowfield beyond. Distantly, she could see the host riding toward them along the Lakeland Pass, a modest host of perhaps a hundred men. "Do my eyes deceive me, Sir Hank, or is there no wheelhouse in the company?"

"There isn't, my lady. The men on the walls have reported only riders."

"Then Lady Lucetia isn't coming," she said.

"No, my lady. It would not appear so."

She sighed. *Could the gods not at least grant me that?* It was bad enough that Amron was away and she had to deal with Lord Bastard herself. Now she wasn't even to have Lucetia here to soften the blow. Still, she would do her duty as a Daecar…which was more than she could say for her niece. Try as she might to persuade Lillia to come, the girl had refused. "I'll be *training* when he arrives," she'd said, in defiance. "He never let me train when I lived in Keep Quiet, so I'm going to train all the time he's here. That will show him."

The host made swift progress toward the gate. A cloud of fog accompanied their coming and before long Amara could hear the snorts of the horses, the whinnies and the neighs, the clopping of their hooves against the snow-clad hard stone road. They rode four by four in a neat tight column, banner bearers going ahead of them with the Amadar arms raised aloft. The Lord of Ilivar trotted imperiously at the head alongside Sir Michael Tunsen, armoured in his fabulous suit of godsteel plate with its scrollwork and adornments, the pink and pale blue lining around the edges of the breastplate and the pauldrons, a heavy cloak of grey-blue vair draped magnificently down his back. Amara scowled inwardly. Lord Brydon had always seemed much more youthful than his years and sat upright in the saddle, strong and fierce, his short grey beard cropped tight over his chiselled jaw. His hard, hazel-green eyes regarded her cooly as he approached. She stepped forward to greet him. "My lord, welcome. How was your ride?"

He frowned at her. "Forgettable." A glance over her shoulders, and his eyes returned. "I confess myself surprised to see you here, Amara. Where is Amron?"

"The king is currently away. He regrets he couldn't be here to greet you personally."

A muscle rippled in the old man's jaw as though it was an intentional slight. He was very prickly about his pride, was Lord Bastard. "Away? Where? I only came here for his coronation."

"He has gone to the northwest. On an urgent mission with his son." She smiled and said no more for now, knowing it would irk him. "We can talk about that later, Brydon. Lucy is well, I hope?"

"No. She's *unwell*. Lucetia is not as hardy as she seems and these times have tested her. She was too weak to come. She sends her regards." He spoke perfunctorily. "When is Amron expected back? I have much to discuss with him."

"I don't know. We can talk more over dinner." She performed a neat curtsey and ignored any further questions. "I have a fine meal being prepared for you, Brydon. You'll like it, I hope." She motioned to Sir Hank Rothwell. "Sir Hank will escort you and your men to Keep Kanabar. If you have further questions, direct them at him."

She left him there and began quickly back toward the heart of the city. The afternoon was moving along. Amara returned to her private chambers to take a short rest, as a soldier might before a battle, preparing and fortifying his strength of spirit for the challenges to come. There was a lot of noise in the keep. Necessarily, every room was occupied by this lord or that knight and never was it peaceful. The arrival of Lord Brydon didn't help. She'd made sure to have a fine chamber prepared for him, though the rest of his men would have to sleep where they could find space. *He'll hate this,* she thought. The Lord of Ilivar was all about neatness and order and contemplative silence. This castle would be torture to his prim and proper sensibilities.

Amara took some joy in that, petty though it was. She bathed, washed through the long locks of her silvery blonde hair, had some maids brush out the tangles and snarls, and let them garb her in the finest clothes they could unearth from the Kanabar stores. She permitted herself a very small cup of wine to give her courage. Lillia arrived, dressed in her armour and with a shortsword at one hip and dagger at the other. "I'm going like this," she declared, smiling. "It'll be funny, don't you think?"

Amara saw the appeal, but her better judgement compelled her otherwise. "Get changed, Lillia. There's no need to provoke him."

"Why not? I hate him."

"You don't. He's your grandfather. You don't hate him."

"I do," she said. "I wish he hadn't come. It's going to be horrible, I know it. Do I have to go?"

"Yes."

"But Jovy's allowed to come too, isn't he?"

She shook her head. "It would be best if he didn't."

"Best? For who? *Him?* I don't care about him."

"Lillia…"

"No. Jovy's coming, and that's that." She spun away and was gone before Amara could call her back.

The girl was not bluffing. The table had been set and the candles lit when Amara Daecar arrived. Sir Penrose accompanied her, taking his place outside the door beside Sir Michael Tunsen and Sir Miles Hewitt, who was diligently overseeing all goings on in the keep as the head of the Kanabar household guard. The family feast hall in Keep Kanabar was much the same as the one in Keep Daecar, with a wall of trophies along one side, pillars and doors leading to balconies on another, a grand pine table between them fit to accommodate fifty.

Brydon Amadar had already seated himself at the head. Lillia was present as well, sitting at the very opposite end, with Jovyn beside her.

She must have run to change and done so quickly, without washing, because she looked a mess, her hair dishevelled and ungroomed, her face dirty from her training, her garb poor. Jovyn seemed horrifically uncomfortable to be there as Lord Brydon stared down the table at them, a hard stare heavy with disapproval. The only other attendee was faithful old Artibus, who sat rather awkwardly midtable fidgeting with his small, liver-spotted hands. He rose to his feet as Amara entered and vented an audible sigh. Jovyn surged up too, Lillia turned and smiled at her in triumph, and Brydon stared coldly, then reluctantly stood as well.

"You're all here. Wonderful." Amara swayed into the room to sit opposite Artibus, all false confidence, smoothing out her skirts as she took her perch. A servant drifted in at once from the shadows to offer her wine, but she declined with a polite remark. "So, shall we begin with the soup? The chefs have prepared a fine broth to start. Haddock, I believe, with chunks of carrots, onion, leek and turnip. Well salted as you like it, Brydon."

He grunted acknowledgement as the bowls were brought out and set down before them. Lillia dug in eagerly, making all sorts of slurping noises and acting intentionally unladylike.

Amara looked at her. "Lillia, *please*. Whatever point you're trying to make, you've made it. Have a little more decorum."

"Decorum," she laughed. "I'm just enjoying my tasty soup, is all." She smacked her lips and looked up from her bowl, mischievous. "How do you like it, Grandfather? Delicious, isn't it?"

"It's pleasant," he said, spooning a measure into his mouth.

"The tribesmen caught it for us, you know. The people from the far western shores. They're ruled by a man called the Orca Lord. He's very noble, isn't he, Auntie? I think you'd like him, Grandfather."

"I'm sure." He had more soup, eating with stiff grace, and did not rise to Lillia's bait. "Sir Michael told me all about these tribesmen, Amara. You likely think I disapprove? Well, I don't. It sounds to me like Amron is making good use of his resources. It is the sign of a wise ruler to properly deploy his subjects to tasks best suited to their skills."

Amara agreed. "They are helping to feed the city," she said. "Their prowess as fishermen far outweighs our own." She had a taste of her soup. "How are you finding the lake over in Ilivar, Brydon? With the ice floes and rough waters."

"Troublesome. My fishermen are having similar difficulties as yours."

"Is starvation an issue?"

"Yes. Many are dying." He didn't sound like he cared all that much, and Lillia made that known with a snort of laughter. The old man ignored her. "Sir Hank tells me Amron mustered two thousand of my men to ride north. In the company of a thousand Strands." He had some soup and awaited Amara's response.

"The king is rallying all his strength," she said. "Many thousands of Taynars fled from the city after the coming of the Dread. From King's

Point also. He gave Sir Geofrey orders to bring them back under the banner of the crown."

"And visit with Lord Penrith, I heard?"

"Yes," she said. "A large part of the Oloran forces remain in Elinar. Barring those under the command of Sir Killian."

"*Lord* Killian now. Penrith Oloran is dead."

She paused in her eating and placed down her spoon. It hit the bowl with a *clink*. "You've had news? What happened?"

"It seems the smallfolk rose up in riot against Lord Penrith's policy of rationing. Starvation has been a problem there as well. Thousands rushed the castle and overwhelmed his guards." He had a spoon of soup. "I hear Penrith was unrecognisable when they were done with him. Not a tale I will elaborate on, with Lillia present."

The girl was staring down the table, big-eyed. "Please elaborate, Grandfather. What happened? Did they cut him open? Stab out his eyes?" She grinned. "Maybe it was like you and the Great One, Auntie. She savaged him, Grandfather. Did you know? The Great One."

His eyes were bored. "I haven't heard of any Great One, Lillia."

"He was some fat pirate on an island on the lake. I was taken there for a bit when I ran away from you." Speaking those words seemed to remind her that she hated him. Her goodwill vanished, and a scowl returned to her lips. "I've been training, you know," she goaded. "Every day. Hours a day. Jovyn teaches me, and Sir Daryl and *Carly*." She put emphasis on the final name, knowing how the old man disapproved of sellswords. "I'm good now. Really good. I'm going to go to battle with my father."

"I think not," Brydon Amadar dismissed. He raised a hand and waved over a server to take away his bowl. "Very nice, Amara. What is next, pray?"

The next course was brought forth. Stuffed pastries filled with egg, vegetables, and rabbit, along with a fish dish of fried salmon, and a generous offering of lamprey pie. Lillia scowled at her grandfather all the while, sore from the dismissal. They spoke in snippets, snippets spaced out by silence. Of the war, of their new alliance with Ulrik Marak, of the battle in the east, of Rustbridge and Lord Borrus Kanabar and Rikkard, Brydon's son, who had broken some ribs during the fighting there though was otherwise well, they had heard. Amara said nothing of Saska. She doubted very much that Lord Bastard would approve of Varin's heir being a girl, and a girl of mixed heritage at that.

I'll let Elyon tell him about it when he returns. Elyon was very fierce in his defence of the girl, and would never let his grandfather undermine her. Amara would be sure to be there to observe. She smiled at the thought, reached to have a sip of wine, realised it was water and returned to her pie.

Lord Brydon had a taste of fried salmon. "I hear you've done wonders for Sir Taegon's knee, Artibus," he said. He glanced down the table at the old physician. "Lord Mantle as well. And Sir Marcus Flint. All owe their strength to you."

The small old scholar smiled graciously. "That is generous of you to say, my lord."

"Brydon, please. We've known one another for decades."

"Of course." Artibus dipped his chin. "Sir Marcus and Lord Mantle were only ever likely to need time, Brydon, to rest and heal. Sir Taegon, however…" He nodded in a moment of pride in his work. "Yes, I am gladdened by his recovery. As Amron is. He feared the giant's fighting days were done."

"As he fears for his own." Lord Amadar had a bite of lamprey pie. "I hear he almost perished at the Battle of Blackfrost. Amron was overwhelmed before the tribesmen came to his rescue."

"The enemy vastly outnumbered us," Amara came in. She would not hear him sneer and cast aspersions like this, or suggest in some way Amron's prowess was diminished. *It isn't,* she thought. *Even when he gives up the Frostblade, he'll be as lethal as ever. I'll make sure of it.* "Perhaps you might join us in battle yourself next time? Lord Styron came south with all his power and fought bravely during the defence of the city. You are of an age, are you not? I'm sure your men would like to see you in the vanguard as you once were."

He ate more pie. "I function better as a commander than a combatant. Lord Styron the Strong must keep up appearances, I'm sure, but I care not for such honours. If I never again must draw steel in anger, that only means I am doing my duty." He put down his fork and took up his wine, swirling it, enjoying a moderate sip. "Sir Connor is away again, I'm told."

"Yes. And Sir Torus. They returned to Lord Marak's hideout this morning. Amron hopes he will permit them to fly to Westmire to gather news. Lord Borrus is gathering his host there."

"*Lord Borrus,*" the man scoffed. "That drunken oaf's no leader. It should be my son at the helm of that host. He has temperance. Wisdom. Rikkard would never have behaved so recklessly at Rustbridge."

"Borrus's recklessness led to victory," Amara said. "He was goaded, yes, but we triumphed all the same."

Lord Brydon scoffed again and drank more wine. Lillia, too, was drinking, and freely it seemed from the regular glances Amara gave her. Jovyn hadn't said a word all night. He ate quietly, eyes ever averted from the greatlord's strict gaze, slowly shrinking down into his shell as though wishing he wasn't there. Lord Brydon seemed intent on ignoring him. *Just as he ignores his offences,* Amara thought bitterly, touching the stump of her missing pinky finger.

The old lord had another bite of pie. "We ought not be allying ourselves to the Fireborn," he said, searching for another thing to complain about. "I even hear that Amron flew on a dragon himself." He shook his head, drank his wine. "What is this world coming to that a so-called King of Vandar would ride on the back of a dragon?"

"Much is changing, Brydon," Amara said. "We have entered an unprecedented time."

The greatlord scoffed at those words. "So, where *has* he gone, then? You still haven't told me. Northwest, is all you said. I hear whisperings of the Icewilds from my men."

"Yes. So far as I know."

"So far as you know? He didn't tell you?"

"That's all I know."

He stared at her. She could see the bones moving in his jaw, grinding side to side. "You're lying to me. You know more than that."

She smiled, ignoring him, and waved for the servers to clear their plates. "Bring out the meat," she said, and the venison was brought forward, the roasted boar, the fatty cuts of pheasant on beds of leaves with potatoes on the side, boiled and mashed and roasted. It seemed a lot, but none would go to waste. Any leftovers would be eaten by the household staff or else brought down to the knights and other men who ate in the feast hall below. "Try the boar, Brydon. It's very succulent."

"You won't distract me with boar, Amara."

"Try some. You'll like it."

His eyes were growing darker. "Is this about your hand? Is that why you're torturing me like this?"

"*Torturing* you?" She laughed, astonished. "Brydon, it was *me* who was tortured…"

"A poorly chosen word." He flicked a wrist to dismiss it. "You still hold to this notion that I betrayed you, I take it? That I somehow wanted this." He glanced at her finger, then away. There was more disgust in his face than shame. "I didn't. I was only trying to smooth over the mess you had made. What happened…it went too far."

She looked at him, expressionless. Her face was a mask. She said nothing at all.

"You're waiting for an apology," he said. "That's what this is. You want me to apologise." He paused, struggling to deliver the words. He physically grimaced in the attempt and then said, "Fine, you'll have it," in an angry, impetuous voice. "I'm sorry, there. I'm sorry for what happened."

"It's fine." She cut at a piece of pheasant, placed it delicately between her lips. Her voice was cold and distant.

He glared at her. "I'm apologising, woman. The least you could do is accept it with some dignity."

"Oh, I'm sorry. Have I offended you, Brydon?" She turned to look at him. Her hand was trembling. The hand missing the little finger. The hand from which all her nails had been torn away. "Have I hurt your feelings, my lord?"

He snorted and waved at her, a sharp brusque gesture. "Grow up, Amara. So you lost a finger and spent a few days in a dungeon. How long are you going to sulk over that?"

"Do I look like I'm sulking?" She spoke evenly. "I had only hoped for a word of contrition a little earlier. Some recognition of what I endured."

"Then I am in remiss," the old man said, loudly, making a show of it. "I should have said something earlier. Are you happy now? Can we move along?" He snatched up his goblet and drank a large measure, then shouted for a server to refill it. He drank again, losing his famous cool. Silence descended upon them as he began feasting on his meat, chewing vigorously on his venison, drinking his wine between bites. The muscles in his jaw were rippling, bones grinding. *And he tells me to grow up. He is acting like a petulant child.*

It was Lillia who broke the silence. "I *am* going to war, you know." She hadn't spoken since he'd disregarded her on that earlier. "I don't care what you say or anyone else says. I'm going, and that's that."

The old lord chewed his meat. "You're not."

"*Yes I am.* You think *you* can tell me no? You?" She laughed at him. She was empowered by the wine. "I'm a princess now, *royalty.* I can do whatever I please."

"You're *not* going to war!" Lord Brydon roared at her. His eyes lifted, blazing. "I've told you no. I'm your grandfather, and you will obey me."

She laughed again, heedless. "I'll never obey you."

"Then I'll have you carted back to Ilivar!" he thundered. He slammed a fist down on the table, rattling the cups and crockery. "You damnable *child.* This is your doing, isn't it?" And his eyes swung back to Amara. "*You've* made her like this. With all your drinking and defiance. That grotesque tart tongue of yours. You think it makes you witty, but you're just wanton, Amara. You're base. Low. And you've ruined her."

Ruined her. Amara's face was a mask, fixed with a smile, but those words cut deep. She could feel the tears welling behind her eyes. She clenched her jaw to hold them back and tried to find a response, but nothing came.

Lillia surged to her feet. "How dare you speak to her that way. *Ruined* me? How dare you! She's been an amazing mother! The only mother I've ever known. And she'll be an amazing mother again."

The Lord of Ilivar snorted disdain. "So it's true? You're with child?" He set his gaze on her. There was no hint of affection in his eyes. No softness. Nothing.

"I, yes…" Her voice was weak, a pathetic croak. "I am."

"Then we must hope you'll do a better job with this one. *If* it lives to term." He scoffed and drank his wine. "Though it might be kinder if it doesn't."

Lillia was spitting fire. She tried to run around the edge of the table, but Jovyn held her back. The tears were building in the corners of Amara's eyes now, building and sliding, sliding down her cheeks. She wiped them free and turned her face away. "Bastard!" Lillia spat. "I hate you. *Everyone* hates you. You're just a bitter old man who still thinks he's important, but you're not. It would be better if you just *died.*"

The old man regarded her with vast disappointment. "You're nothing like your mother."

"Good! I don't want to be! You've tried to make me into her, but I never wanted that!"

His lips flicked upward, disgusted, and he drank his wine and placed it down. The girl was still struggling in Jovyn's grasp, wriggling and struggling. "You're a disgrace, Lillia. Look at you. Unwashed. Ragged. *Wild.* You call yourself a princess, but you smell like a privy." His eyes moved icily to Jovyn. "Maybe you two belong together after all. You've brought yourself down to *his* level, it seems."

And Lillia shrieked. "I hate you! I hate you!" She struggled in Jovyn's arms. "Let me go, Jovy. Just let me go! I'll kill him!"

"You're to wed Prince Robbert Lukar," Lord Brydon went on coldly. "You set up that union yourself, Amara. Surely you'd want to see it through."

She still could not find her voice. Her eyes were turned away.

"My lord, perhaps you've had enough to drink," offered Artibus. "You'll excuse me for saying so, but you're acting rather cruelly."

"Am I? Oh am I, Artibus?"

"Yes. You are. Lady Amara and Princess Lillia are much loved here."

"In this cesspool of a city, that does not surprise me."

"Varinar? A cesspool?" Artibus had found his valor. "Perhaps you should leave, Brydon? You are only doing more harm."

"I'm *not* leaving until I've finished my dinner." He cut roughly at his steak, carving away a large chunk. He shoved it into his mouth and began chewing vigorously, gulping his wine. Lillia was still fighting her away out of Jovyn's grip, screaming drunken obscenities at him. Amara's eyes were down, and her hand was on her belly, and the tears were coming freely now, hot rivulets down her cheeks.

"You see what you've done," Lillia shrieked. "I *never* see her cry! Never! You've cut her you foul old man. I hate you! I hate you! Die! I want you to die!"

Amara heard the sound of choking.

Chair legs scraping on the floor.

Her eyes whipped around as Lord Brydon stood and he was clutching at his neck, fighting for breath. Artibus rose sharply. He hurried over behind the lord, thumping at his back, but Brydon Amadar's eyes were chaos, a black chaos of terror, and he jerked and threw himself forward, gasping, squeezing his craw, fingers digging in, face turning pale to pink, pink to purple, eyes bulging as he tore and scratched at his throat.

The door swung fiercely open and the knights flooded into the room. Sir Miles, Sir Micheal, Sir Penrose. "My lord!" shouted Sir Michael Tunsen as he rushed forward. Amara stood from her chair. Lillia had gone silent, white. Jovyn held her in his arms as she stared, sobbing. "I never meant...I didn't really mean..."

But Amara's eyes were dry now. She looked down at the man as he tore bloody lines across his neck. As his eyes bulged out, big and blood-

shot. As Sir Michael threw Artibus aside and lifted the old lord unceremoniously to his feet, as he started thumping at his back, squeezing at
him, thumping again, squeezing, thumping. Brydon's body bucked and
shook and she could smell his bowels give out in fear, the foul fetid stink
filling the air.

And she watched, saying nothing, doing nothing, just standing there.
He dies like any man, she thought. *The great Lord Brydon Amadar, defeated by a
hunk of meat.*

51

Robbert

The men had dull eyes.

There were over twenty of them tied, bound, and bloody, kneeling in the mud. They were Tukoran, all of them, men serving under the banners of the crown. But last night, for reasons as yet unclear, they had turned to bloodshed, the wanton slaughter of their fellows.

Robbert stood in the pale wet morning, bleary-eyed, bitterly tired, and nursing a fearsome headache. A light cold rain was drifting down from a sky the colour of slate, pattering softly through the leaves of the trees. "Water," the king said.

Sir Kevyn Bolt handed him a skin and he took a long swig to try to refresh himself. The morning had been a hectic rush so far and his head still swam with the noise of last night, the merrymaking and the singing and the drinking…yes, that most of all. He drew a breath, had another gulp, and handed the waterskin back. "Have these men been questioned yet, Sir Kester?"

"All of them," confirmed Sir Kester Droyn. "We've been interrogating them for the last hour."

"And?"

"And nothing, sire. They won't say a word."

Robbert breathed out. His head was pounding and he could feel the vein throbbing in his temple like some red hot worm that was trying to squirm free. *Too much bloody wine,* he thought. Whilst he was celebrating in the feast hall and toasting the news that his brother was alive, a plague of sudden violence was spreading through his camp. He looked blurrily at the bound men once more, trying to clear his thoughts. "How many others were there?" These men were only a portion of the aggressors, he knew; the rest had been killed during the fighting.

"A hundred or so," Lord Gullimer told him. "Though it's very hard to say for sure until the reports come in."

"And total losses?"

"Four times that number at least.

"Four hundred men?" Robbert was appalled.

"I fear so, yes, and many more wounded. They took them off guard, Robbert. Several of the larger barrack pavilions were tied and burned, with the men sleeping inside. They poured pitch on the canvas, and they went up quickly. Others were simply stabbed to death in their tents or awoke to find a friend cutting open their throat. What they *thought* was a friend, anyway. It was a bloodbath before the men even realised what was happening. When they started fighting back, it was hard to say who was who. It was their own brothers in arms they were fighting."

"But *why*? Why did they turn on us?"

"We're still trying to figure that out," Lord Gullimer said. His eyes were clear. He seemed the only man among them who wasn't still either a little drunk or transitioning into the state of being hungover. "Though I have a suspicion."

"Which is?"

The apple lord looked at the bound, kneeling men for a long moment. "I believe they may have been bewitched, Robbert. You need only look at them to know there is something…not right about them."

Lank snorted loudly. Lank was still very drunk. "Nonsense. Bewitched? *Nonsense*," he repeated. He swayed on his lanky legs. "These men are just…I don't know, anarchists or something. They were maddened by hunger, probably, and so rioted over rations. How's rationing here, Marsh?" he asked Lord Malcolm. "You've been running things. So….have you not been feeding these men?"

Lord Malcolm Marsh looked like a warmed-up corpse. He had indulged very freely last night after Robbert raised him to Lord of Rock-fall. "Every man has been fed according to their needs."

"Their needs? Men have different needs. Has there been trouble? Any trouble over the last few weeks?"

"No. There has been no trouble."

"Bollocks," Lothar said. "He's lying, Robb. You're a weaselly liar, Marsh, always were."

The lord looked up at him. "Always were? What are you talking about? We barely know each other."

"I've heard things. You're like Huffort, just a copy of him. I can still see the brown on your nose from all those years you spent with it shoved up his ar…"

"Lothar, shut up," Robbert said. "You're dismissed."

"Dismissed?"

"You're drunk, Lothar. Return to the keep and sleep it off. You're no good to anyone in this state."

"What state? We're all in the same state?" He swayed from side to side.

"Go to bed, Lothar. That's an order and not one I care to repeat."

Lank stared at him. "You're serious?"

"Yes, I'm serious. Go. Now."

"Fine." The knight swung a long arm and almost took Marsh's head off. "You're telling me to go sleep. I'll sleep. It's nothing to me." And he lurched away, moving back toward the keep, muttering remarks under his breath.

It was good to be rid of him. The man could be very argumentative and they needed clear heads here right now. Robbert asked for the water-skin again and drank, then handed it back. "You were saying the men were bewitched, Wilson?"

The apple lord nodded. "Yes. It would seem logical. We know the Fire Father is able to bewitch and enslave his own. But what of those of mixed blood? These men…" He turned to look at them, studying them, their empty eyes and dull expressions. "They may appear to be Tukoran, but I would not be surprised to learn that they have some Agarathi relatives further back in their bloodlines. This may be enough to ensnare them."

Robbert considered it. It sounded like a plausible theory. "Have they been questioned to that effect, Sir Kester?"

"Not yet," Sir Kester admitted. "Would you like us to try, my lord?"

"Do you think they'll answer?"

"They've answered no questions so far," Droyn reported. "We have beaten them, tortured them, promised them pardons in exchange for information, but so far none of them have so much as uttered a word. There are twenty-two men here, sire, and none of them have spoken despite all that. That's…unusual. At least one would have broken by now, and most likely quite a few, but none?" He shook his head. "That would suggest some sort of mental enslavement to me."

"Yes," Robbert agreed. "Try anyway."

"At once." Sir Kester stepped away and the questioning resumed as one man was plucked away from the rest and dragged away into the trees. He did not kick or scream or make any struggle, but went as though a corpse, a man already dead. The woodland began to ring out to the sound of shouting, punching, kicking, and all of it from Droyn and the two big men he took with him for the interrogation. Robbert looked at the other prisoners. Their faces were dull, their eyes empty, and not one of them gave any sort of reaction. A ripple went up his spine.

"Tell me of the Vandarians," he said.

They had suffered worse, Lord Gullimer reported to him. The Vandarian encampment here was much larger than their cousins from Tukor, and thus had their losses been greater also. Thousands may well have perished, and many more than that were badly enough wounded to remove them from the war, and permanently in many cases. In all, it diluted their overall strength at a time when they needed it most.

"Early word suggests that the aggressors came here recently," the apple lord went on. "There have been many reinforcements drifting here from the north and the west, and it would appear these men were among them.

Robbert nodded. "Water, Sir Kevyn." The skin was passed to him.

He drank and passed it back. *Gods, I feel awful.* His brain felt about two times too big for his skull, and he was beginning to feel a little bilious. He took a deep breath and then breathed out, slowly, to freshen his lungs, lest he vomit right here in front of them. *So much for appearing kingly.* He had kept his reserve as long as possible last night, though clearly not long enough. By the end the claws of celebration had gotten themselves into him and he was drinking liberally, while still thinking himself sober, as a man does when the volume of alcohol creeps up on him. Then, before he knew it, armed knights were rushing into the feast hall, and the music died, the singing ended, and they heard the sound of horns blaring out across beyond the castle.

The rest was still much of a blur to him. He'd been rushed back to his private room to keep him safe while the violence concluded. His armour, which the smiths had been working on overnight, was brought up to him. They had done a good job, though some work still needed doing. He'd armoured up anyway, taken a tonic to try to sober up, and watched the dawn rise from the window. He was told, then, that some men had been trying to get into the feast hall during the celebrations, and that helped sober him up as well. If they'd gotten in, who knows what might have happened? *They'd have come for me,* he knew. *Me, Borrus, Rikkard, Killian, they'd have tried to assassinate us all.*

He shuddered at the thought. Another man was being interrogated. Droyn had come and thrown the first one down, freshly beaten and bloodied, and a second was dragged away like a sack of spuds. The questions went unanswered and none of the prisoners reacted. "It makes me uneasy to look at them," Lord Malcolm Marsh said, disquieted. "It's like they're soulless. There's nothing there."

Gullimer rubbed his chin and turned to Robbert. "What would you like to do with them?"

"Keep questioning them for now, in the hope they break," he answered. "We'll give Droyn until tomorrow, then shorten each of them by a head."

Gullimer dipped his head. "Very well, then. I'll tell him." He stepped away to pass on the order, then returned to Robbert's side. He studied his eyes a moment. "How are you feeling, Robbert?"

"Unwell," the king said.

"Are you able to walk among the men? I feel it will hearten them to see their new king."

"In this state, I'm not so sure." Robbert lifted his chin, freshened his lungs, drank a little more water and said, "Fine. If I must, Wilson."

They set off through the trees. They were well spaced out here, mostly smooth grey beech and slender white birch, though with the occasional oak sitting bulkily here and there. In some places there were clusters of hornbeam too, and even some rowan trees to add some colour to the greys and browns and muddy greens, with their bright red berries and their fine feathery leaves. Between the trees, the pavilions and tents had been raised, the horse lines spread, the latrines dug, the wagons and carts lined up in their hundreds. Men milled about in their morning work, sharpening blades, fletching arrows, brushing horses, roasting meat. Some stopped to salute their new king as he went by. Others turned to watch him, many took no note at all. Robbert saw dull eyes among them, sad and distant eyes, and he wondered if they too might be under the influence of the enemy. Could there be another attack? Was that the first and only one?

"Are these men being vetted?" he asked Lord Marsh.

"These? No. They were brought down from Ilithor by your brother, my king. That seemed all the vetting we needed at the time."

"Times have changed," Robbert said. "I want every man questioned. The reinforcements in particular. If there are any more miscreants here, they must be weeded out."

They reached one of the burned-down barrack pavilions. The smell was horrific, of melted canvas and burnt flesh. The sight was no better as the dead were carried away, blackened and burned, to be buried in nearby ditches. Robbert took a moment to speak to the soldiers, sharing in the tragedy. There was a lot of confusion as to why their own men would turn on them like this, and that confusion led to fear. Robbert assuaged it as best he could, giving trite promises of vengeance and retribution.

"This was the work of Eldur," he told them, though it hadn't yet been proven or confirmed. It would serve them all the same, even if it wasn't true. The men must know the pernicious workings of that demon. They must hate him more than they feared him, and if they did it would serve them all.

He continued through the camp, visiting other sites of tragedy. One man reported to him that he knew one of the assailants from long years ago. He had an Agarathi grandfather, the soldier said. More men came to him with similar reports. They knew some of the attackers. They were changed from the men they knew, distant and quiet. Robbert asked if they had Agarathi relatives also, though mostly the men didn't know. "Not even sure they did," one soldier told him. "A man might know who his grandparents were, but you go further back than that and he's got no idea."

Robbert thought that was probably true. He knew his own, of course, but Robbert was the product of two greathouses and their bloodlines were famous. But the common man was different. His knowledge tended to end with his grandparents and didn't often stretch any further back than that.

He continued his tour of the camp until satisfied with his efforts, then returned to the castle keep at Westmire to take a short rest and eat some food. There was a knock at the door and Borrus Kanabar entered, looking as grim as Robbert felt. "Dour morning," he said.

"Yes," Robbert agreed.

"I just spoke with Gullimer. He said you lost five hundred men."

"Seems so. What about you, my lord?"

"Numbers are still coming in. But it's bad no matter which way you cut it. We think there might have been two or three hundred of these spies in our camp." He plodded to the side counter and poured himself a cup of wine, drinking it down quickly. "Hair of the dog," he said. "Better than suffering through a hangover." He poured again, two cups this time and handed one to Robbert.

"I'd best not."

"Drink it. You'll feel better."

Robbert supposed he should bow to the Barrel Knight's expertise on the matter. His first sip was bad, his second moderate, and by the third and then fourth his headache was starting to smooth out. They spoke of the risk posed by these men, of Gullimer's theory of bewitchment, and wondered whether this was the end of it. "Let's hope," was Kanabar's summation. "Anyway, we're wise to them now. It happens again and we'll be ready, but let me suggest something, Robbert."

"Yes?"

"Double your guard. Make sure they're trusted, loyal men with known lineages."

"I plan to build a new order of knights to protect me," Robbert said, nodding. "Lothar will start scouring for suitable men later."

"Later? What's wrong with now?"

"If you saw him, you'd know. He's less than useless in his state."

Kanabar laughed. "Still drunk, is he? Well, small wonder. He was stumbling all over the place last night, causing all sorts of bother. Made for an amusing sight, at his height. How tall is he?"

"Just shy of seven feet."

He laughed again and drank his wine. It was barely mid-morning. "I'm going to call a council this afternoon to talk everything out," Borrus said. His face went serious, because this *was* serious, despite the easy atmosphere between them. "When the dust settles here, we might have lost five thousand men between us, accounting for the dead and the wounded. But there's more. The men…they're unsettled. I walked among them earlier, and you could see it in their eyes. They don't know friend from foe anymore. They're distrusting, doubtful, and that's dangerous, Robbert. A man needs to know who he's going to battle with. If he's scared he might turn on him in the midst of a fight, then that's a real problem. It's a problem for us all…"

The door knocked.

"Apologies," said Robbert. He put his cup aside. "Come in." The door creaked open and Sir Kevyn Bolt entered, bald-headed and broad of shoulder. He wore twin blades with bull-head pommels and was cloaked in the colours of Tukor.

"My king," he said, and, "my lord," to Borrus Kanabar. "An envoy is coming. From the other camp. A Sunrider and some others."

Robbert went to the west-facing window. The lands were largely open there, patched in woodland, cut by streams, only gently hilly. He could see the host approaching in the distance, cantering through the falling rain. "I see them," he said.

"How many?" asked Kanabar.

"A dozen or so. Should we ride out to meet them?"

"Why bloody not." Borrus finished his cup of wine and clacked it down on a side table. They left the room at once, moving through the keep and down toward the stables. The Marshlander Jack was there with some other grooms. Borrus called for him to bring out his destrier and a horse for Robbert as well. As they were mounting up, Rikkard Amadar appeared.

"Some of Ballantris's men are coming," he said.

"We know. Keep up, Rikkard."

"You're riding to meet them?"

"No. I thought I'd take the king on a hunt. Of course we are."

"Then I'm coming too."

A few minutes later the three of them were trotting out of the ward, passing the portcullis, crossing the drawbridge, and riding down through the town of Westmire. An honour guard went with them, a mix of Kanabar and Amadar men, with Sir Kevyn and some Bolt men-at-arms. The rain lashed down sideways, growing stronger as they rode west across the plains. Before long the southerners were appearing over the crest of a small rise. The men peered forward.

"Looks like Pakavaro," Rikkard said.

"Yes, it does," agreed Borrus. He had a frown on his face.

"Who's Pakavaro?" Robbert asked.

"The Sunrider. One of Ranaartan's men. Strange that he's coming. Usually Ballantris sends his own."

"Why would they send anyone? You told me Ballantris sent a man last night."

Borrus nodded. "He did. Said the moonlord wanted to meet you."

"This is something else," Rikkard told them, and there was a note of concern in his voice. "We may not be the only ones to have suffered bloodshed last night."

The two hosts came together shortly after. Pakavaro barked a command and his men lined up behind him, then he swung down from the saddle of his sunwolf and strode forward. He was a well-built, hard-faced man with receding hair cut short and thick dark stubble on his cheeks and chin. Robbert, Borrus, and Rikkard dismounted and stepped forward to meet him. "My lords." Pakavavo's voice was as gruff as his appearance and his bow was perfunctory. He looked at Borrus, Rikkard, then Robbert and his eyes lingered on him a moment longer.

"The new Tukoran king," Borrus told him. "Robbert Lukar."

"Your Majesty." The man did not bow again. Robbert saw now that he had gouts of blood on his feathered cloak and spattered on his armour.

"What happened?" Borrus asked. "Did your own men turn on you too?"

The Sunrider frowned. His forehead was deeply rutted. "Too?"

"There was widespread violence last night," Rikkard told him. "Sparked by spies, we think, enslaved by Eldur. They burned barracks and killed men in their sleep, and when that was done, they met their comrades blade to blade. It was brutal. We lost thousands." Rikkard Amadar stepped forward. "Pakavaro. How many men did you lose?" When the man gave no answer, Rikkard said again, "How many?"

"We don't know." His eyes were dark. "Many…too many. Half."

"Half?" Borrus was aghast. "But you had fifteen thousand men. How could you lose *half*?"

"Maybe more," the man said. "The dead are being counted. We lost many captains, many Sunriders and Starriders." His jaw was tight. He lifted his chin. "Moonlord Ballantris was slain. The men came to him first and overwhelmed him in his tent, and when his heart stopped Tathranor roared. You could hear it across the whole camp. And then he came."

"Came?"

"*Rampaged*," Pakavavo said. "In grief and wrath, he rampaged. The men were waking to slaughter, and the bear only added to it. He did not see friend from foe. Only foe. And he killed and killed until Jahendroth stopped him."

"Jahendroth," Robbert said. "That is Risho Ranaartan's bear?"

The Sunrider nodded. "They fought. And a rare thing that is, for two moonbears to fight. Jahendroth was only trying to calm him, but Tathranor is the older bear, the bigger bear, and he could not be calmed. He mauled Jahendroth, wounding him, and then fled from the camp." His eyes ran across the open fields and woods. "He is a threat to you now. A threat to us all. There is nothing so fearsome as a grieving moonbear and when his bonded master is slain like that…in treachery…" He shook his head. "I came to warn you."

"Thank you, Pakavaro." Borrus Kanabar gripped his feathered arm. "What of Ranaartan?"

"Risho is the one who sent me to you. He has taken charge of our forces now, but we are severely weakened, and Janendroth will take time to heal." His head hung low. "We are broken from within, my lords. This is our punishment, for betraying Vargo Ven. We have little food, little fodder for the animals. Many of our stores were destroyed overnight, and…"

"Join us and you'll have all the food and fodder you need," Robbert Lukar said. He was sensing where this was leading, so might as well speed them there. "I am told Moonlord Ballantris was equivocating in his support. Tell me, Sunrider, what does Moonrider Ranaartan say?"

"Rider Risho is young and fearless," Pakavaro said proudly. "He is not yet twenty-three years of age and has ridden Jahendroth for five years already. That is rare, very rare, to compel a bond at such tender years. Only the fiercest of souls mount moonbears…they are born for it, it is said. They are the chosen of the gods of the south, Lumara's holy chosen, and they lead us in our wars. Timor Ballantris was a great man, but Risho will be one greater." He nodded, once and twice and thrice. "Yes, he will answer this call. Even if Jahendroth is not yet strong to fight, Risho will ride by the back of horse or camel, and he will battle the Agarathi with sword and spear. A skilled fighter he is, and a great paladin he would have made, but he stood up to a higher calling. Yes, yes," and he nodded again. "You will have his full support."

"Then join us here," said Borrus Kanabar, stirred by the man's speech. "Ride back and tell Ranaartan to add his strength to ours." He gripped his feathered shoulder and shook. "We'll take back the Bane together."

52

Elyon

The cold was in his bones.

It cut through layers of fur, through armour, through meat and muscle and into his bones. It cut through his spirit, his soul, his very thought, a dominating cold, an all-consuming cold, a cold that wanted to kill him.

Without his father it would have. He was the master of the Frost-blade, and he mastered the cold. Around them, he had formed a shield of ice to ward off the very worst of it, but ever it was there, creeping in and clawing at him, whispering its threats, hissing its hate.

It wants me dead, Elyon thought, shivering. The cold had driven all life from these lands. Man and monster, bird and beast had fled before it, or froze in the attempt. Nothing drew breath here now, nothing stirred. *There is death beneath our feet. The dead are buried deep.* From horizon to horizon, all was white, bare rock and wood drowned by the End-Fall. And the snow was falling still. Down it came, down and down, ceaseless, unending, concealing all.

"We should keep moving, Elyon," his father said, sitting up close beside him. He must stay close lest the ice shield fail. "Are you rested?"

He nodded, or perhaps that was just the shivering. It was a lie either way. The cold was in his bones and it sapped him, stole his strength, worked away at his very will. But they must go on. "I can fly," he said.

"You're certain? We can take another few minutes if we must."

"No. We need to get there, Father. The longer I sit here, the harder it will be to stand again."

They had stopped on a craggy upthrust of rock that curved up out of the earth like some monstrous claw. The snow climbed halfway up its jagged walls, a hundred feet deep his father had said, yet here at the summit the rock narrowed and thinned and the snow could only gather so high before it grew too weighty and toppled over the edge. Around them, other outcrops rose from the barren white world, but nought else was to be seen. No villages. No woods. Even the rifts had been filled in. *The very clouds in the sky seem frozen,* Elyon thought. *Inert, as though too cold to go on.* He understood that feeling.

"Then let us stand," his father said determinedly. "Come on. Up." He stood first, pulling his son up to his feet. The king wore the Frostblade at his hip, his gauntleted, gloved hand ever grasping at the hilt to channel its power. He released his grip only briefly, and together they began working the straps, harnessing father and son together once more to continue their long frigid flight into the north, into the whiteness below, the blackness above. Elyon's hands barely worked; his fingers felt thick and clumsy, fumbling at the leather belts and buckles. "Let me," his father said, and he finished the job alone, fingers working deftly, skillfully, quickly to bind them.

Soon they were ready. Amron Daecar reached at once to clutch the hilt of the Frostblade again, rebuilding the shield that had begun to thin and wither away. About them both it shimmered, an almost imperceptible film of ice, a sparkling orb, a protective bubble within which the the cold was bearable, survivable. Outside, no. Outside it would freeze a man in minutes, no matter how many layers of wool and wolfskin he wore. If his father should lose his focus, or faint, or fall asleep, they would falter, fail, and perish. "We must reach the mountain," the king said. "There will be cover inside. Perhaps even wood to start a fire."

Fire. Elyon smiled behind the scarf that covered his face. All but his eyes were shown. Frost clung to the fine hairs of his brow, and miniature icicles extended from his lashes. "How far are we, Father?"

The king thought a moment, looking around. "I recognise this land," he said, in a weighty voice. "The outcrops, I recall how strange they were. They're like talons, claws, fingers, the digits of dead gods reaching up from the earth." He paused and then went on. "There's an old legend, Elyon. It says that the Icewilds was once another land all of its own. A great island that drifted across the ocean from far away. Where it struck at our northwestern shores, the impact was so cataclysmic that the land was reshaped, crumpling and rising to form the range we now call the Weeping Heights. These outcrops. Perhaps they truly are the bones of gods. Foreign gods from this faraway land."

Elyon thought it an excellent legend, though wondered if now was the time to tell it. "Father. Which way? You say you recognise this place. Are we close to the mountain, then?"

He saw him nod, strapped up ahead of him, a towering form, taller than him, wider. Elyon had only ever borne those smaller than him in the harness. Amilia. Saska. Walter Selleck, whom he had not seen since the day he left him at the Tower of Rasalan. He'd carried Del in the harness too, a youth similar in height to him, though much slighter of build. No one like his father, though. It felt odd bearing a bigger man like this, a greater man. It did not matter what Elyon achieved, his father would always be greater than him, and he wanted it that way. *He should be flying, not me,* he thought. No doubt his father would learn to wield the Windblade quickly. *A few days longer in Varinar and perhaps he'd know how…*

"Close, yes," said Amron Daecar. "We are well north of the Silver Scar here, by my recollection. Were it not for this dark and snow, we would see it by now." He motioned forward. "Keep going that way, Elyon. I would hope to see its shadow soon."

The prince withdrew the Windblade from its sheath, and within that protective shield of ice stirred the wind that would carry them hence. They rose steadily into the sky, into the darkness. The clouds hung above them, suspended in the air, their borders sparkling with crystal frost. This world was a foreign land indeed, Elyon thought, reflecting on the legend. An alien land. A graveyard of gods. *Was that why Vandar came to rest here too? Was that why he made here his tomb?*

They flew on, deeper into the darkness of this queer white desolation. The sun did not rise this far to the north, not even to peek over the long horizon. *It's afraid,* Elyon thought. *It's so cold here even the sun fears to come.* His mind felt blurry, foggy, here, and his sight was dimmed and blunted. It was left to his father to guide them, to send his piercing gaze across the earth in search of the shadow of the mountain. "Veer a little right, Elyon," he called. "Right, good, that's enough. Now fly straight."

And on they went, the minutes following one to the next. Elyon's thoughts strayed to other lands, to other people and places. He wondered if and when he would return to the Tower of Rasalan. He wondered if King Sevrin had seen anything in the Eye. He pondered Lythian's whereabouts. Had he retrieved the Sword of Varinar? Was he on the way back to King's Point, even now? He thought of Rikkard, and Killian, and Marian Payne. He thought of the princely twins, Robbert and Raynald. He thought of Borrus back from the south. He wanted to talk with him, talk to him about his bastard brother. He wanted to stand in the ward at Rustbridge and say a prayer for Barnibus. To swear vengeance against Vargo Ven for taking his head as he had taken Lord Wallis Kanabar's.

He glanced up as he flew, imagining Barnibus there now, at Varin's Table, joining Lancel whom Ven had slain as well, joining Aleron to complete the trio. They had grown up inseparable, the three of them, and though death had separated them temporarily, they were back together again now, reunited in the Eternal Halls…

"Elyon," said his father. "Elyon, you're starting to drift."

He nodded, looked forward. "Yes, Father. Sorry, I…"

"You're tired. You need to sleep. That rest wasn't long enough."

"No…I'm fine, fine."

"You're not. You're starting to doze, Elyon. We can ill afford to crash."

"I'm not dozing. It's just hard to concentrate here. There's nothing to see but white." He had to raise his voice over the wind. "We'll reach the mountain soon. I'll rest then. You said it's close."

"I know. But even a mountain can be hard to find in this dark, son. If you fall asleep and we crash, all will be lost. It's what they want, the blades. Can you not feel it? Can you not hear them?"

"I hear them, Father." The blades knew their intention. They knew their purpose here. They wanted freedom, freedom above all, even if it meant being lost in this world of winter forevermore. Having them so close together was perilous also, Elyon feared, but they had no choice, not out here. "I…I just need a distraction," he said. "Maybe we should talk. What do you think of Lillia?"

"Lillia? What of her?"

"Her training. She's getting good, don't you think?" Elyon had watched her during his short stay in Varinar, which had lasted two days in the end so he could rest and recover from his last flight, and prepare for the next. Lillia trained every day, she'd told him very proudly, working hard under the tuition of Sir Daryl and Jovyn and Carly, who taught her the less heralded sellsword forms. "She wants to go to war, Father. She asked me if I'd let her come."

"And what did you say?"

"No, of course. Have you talked to her about it?"

"What?"

"The true face of war? The blood and screaming, the sights and smells. I tried to tell her, but she only smiled and said I was a hero. She doesn't understand what it's really like."

"No. She doesn't. Your sister holds her own beliefs and can be hard to convince that they're wrong. She sees the frescoes in the Steelforge and the pictures in her books, and it makes her think that battle is all gallantry and glory. She has taken to worshipping Iliva, did you know? You had better watch out, Elyon. When we get back you might just wake one night to find the Windblade gone."

He smiled inside his scarf, but his response was stolen away by a loud gust of wind assaulting them from the north, or what he supposed north must be. The winds became harsher, louder, and it drowned out all further conversation for now. The king had to shout out directions, telling his son to fly here, fly there, go lower, higher, but no sight of the mountain appeared. There was a thickness to this air, a wintry shroud, almost a mist of fine snow that concealed all. "We'll have to wait for this weather to pass," Amron decided, turning his head.

"And if it doesn't pass?"

"All things pass, son. And you need to rest anyway. I can feel you drifting again. Take us down."

"Down? But…the snow's too deep. It will never support us in our armour."

"The Seaborn master the sea, Elyon, as you master the sky. Yet I master the snow. Take us down," he said.

The prince submitted to his father's command. He brought them to a stop, hovering a few metres above the snow.

"Hold here," the king said. "Just keep us steady." And he went to work, bending the snow to his will, hardening it to make a solid ice floor, raising up a structure of walls, curved inward to connect at the centre in a smooth white dome. In a span of only minutes the ice chamber was formed. Around its base, the king secured the ice yet further, hardening it until it was metres thick, resting upon the packed snow beneath. He told Elyon to lower them down, to test their weight. The floor was solid, hard as stone, and held them well. "The tribes call it an igloo," the king said. "The Snowskins make them, sometimes. When they have no other means to erect a shelter."

Elyon nodded wearily. He felt suddenly very fatigued. "And…it'll be warm, in there? It's made of *ice*, Father."

Amron Daecar smiled. "Our bodies will warm the space within. Go. Get inside. I'll seal us off once we're in."

Elyon crouched to enter, moving down the short tunnel. His father followed him inside. There was just enough space for them to stand where the ceiling was highest. The king turned to the tunnel, held the Frostblade forward, and the air thickened, coalescing, turning clear to opaque as the ice hardened to block off the wind. He slid the Frostblade away, removed his outermost cloak, and laid it down on the floor. "Lie down, Elyon."

"Don't you need your cloak?"

"I am perfectly warm. Lie down."

He obeyed his sire, his king, and lay, bundled in his furs and pelts. He was shivering all over, his breath slipping through his lips in pants and puffs. "Will you sleep as well?" he asked.

"No. I have no need of rest." The king made himself a seat from the ice and perched down to watch over him. "You're safe here, son. Sleep. The air will soon grow warm."

Elyon nodded and settled down. His thoughts drifted, and the air warmed, and he was back in that cellar with Saska. Into his dreams, he went. Dreams warm and soft and safe, far away from this cold harsh land…

When he awoke, he was alone. A soft silver light emanated from the Windblade, sheathed in its scabbard and lying at his side. "Father?" He sat up, turning his eyes to the tunnel. It remained sealed, imprisoning him from the killing cold outside. The air was warmer now. Not warm, but warmer. He could barely even see his breath.

Where is he?

He propped himself up against the hard ice wall, staring at the tunnel, and waited. There was a tension in his chest, something lingering from his dreams. They had started so pleasantly, in the cellar with Saska, but shortly after they had turned dark. He recalled fragments only, feelings, sensations. There was a fear in him, a primal fear he could not place. *I need to get back to her,* he thought. *Father…where are you?*

It was not long before he heard the sound of steps outside, a heavy stamp on crunching ice moving past the igloo and toward the door. The seal began to disintegrate, and the king came through the tunnel in a crouch. The cold came with him, that unbearable murderous cold. Elyon drew his furs up about him as his father entered. "You're awake," he observed.

"For a while," Elyon said. "Where did you go?"

The king resealed the tunnel before the heat of their bodies could escape. "Searching," he answered. "For the mountain." He slid the Frostblade away and looked around, checking to make sure the structure was still secure. "I saw its shadow, Elyon, when the weather cleared. I was fortunate. The snow stopped and the stars came out. In their light I saw it. As a beacon in the dark."

A beacon in the dark, Elyon thought. *Vandar, calling us on.*

The king looked down at the white scabbard at his hip, at the pommel formed of ten thousand linking flakes. An icy mist rose, sparkling with pale colour as it drifted toward the domed ceiling. "This is my final duty as its guardian," he said, in a profound voice. "Getting you here. And getting you back." He nodded to himself. A smile curled the corners of his mouth. "A worthy end, would you not say? I'll give it up when we return to Varinar."

Elyon shifted higher, frowning. "You...won't fly east with me?"

"I have an army to tend, Elyon. Forces to rally, an invasion to plan. I have asked Sir Connor to speak with Lord Marak. He will entreat him to help us. To lend us the use of a dragon. Perhaps it will be Lendrathor? He has borne the Frostblade already."

"You *and* the Frostblade," Elyon said. "Father, you have to come. Saska will need you. You must train her as I have trained her. The Frostblade..."

"Will not be relevant in the fight ahead," he told him. "Drulgar won't yield to the cold no more than Eldur will. They are born of flame, Elyon, immune to it. You saw it yourself at King's Point. I was powerless against them."

"But Father..."

"The other blades are more consequential," the king said. "She must focus her efforts on those."

"It's not just that." Elyon got clumsily to his feet. His limbs felt stiff from the cold. "She needs to meet you as well, Father. You're the King of Vandar, our leader. I've told you of her doubts, how she has trouble feeling worthy. If you should give her your blessing..."

"She doesn't need my blessing."

"She does," he insisted. "She tortures herself at the idea of taking that blade from you. She knows what it means to deny you. Father..." He stepped forward. "To give the blade to her personally would mean the world to her. I wish she didn't need to bear this burden, but she does, and maybe you can make it easier for her. If only you..."

"Let me think on it," the king broke in. "I want to meet her, of course I do, but only if conditions allow for it. For now, we must focus only on the task at hand." He put his hand on his son's shoulder. "We will revisit this back in Varinar, yes? Once our minds are clear of this cold."

It was a fair compromise, Elyon supposed. He drew a breath, nodded. "So, how far are we? From the mountain?"

"Not far. Ten miles, perhaps. Come, let's get strapped up."

They set to it once more, fixing the straps and buckles. When that was done, the king summoned the shimmering ice shield to protect them, swung the Frostblade upward, and blasted apart their little dwelling. Blocks of shattered ice went flying and scattering and sliding across the tundra, and Elyon saw the open skies again, black with tiny flakes of snow falling and capering down. There were paths spreading out from the ruin of their shelter, icy paths that sparkled and gleamed on the surface of the snow. Elyon counted five of them, each striking out in different directions as though lances of light from the core of a star. "Was that you?" Elyon asked.

"Yes. I had to freeze the ground before I could walk on it." His father smiled wryly. "I will admit, I did err once."

"How so?"

"I fell in," he said. "Misjudged the strength of my ice bridge, and it broke beneath me. I must have gone forty feet deep before I stopped."

Elyon sighed. "That was reckless, Father. How did you get out?"

"I froze the snow. Cut steps and climbed." He motioned along one sparkling path. "It's that way. We should see the mountain very quickly in flight."

He was right. No more than a minute later the shadow of the mountain became visible, as a great vast ghost materialising from the shroud. From a certain angle it was said that you could see a face in the rock, the face of the God King Vandar peering out across his world. But if that was so, it must be by daylight, at another time of year, or perhaps their angle was wrong because Elyon only saw a lonely peak in a sea of snow, watching from the very edge of the earth.

It made him sad, somehow. There was a great desolate loneliness here. "Where's the entrance, Father?" he called out.

"There isn't one. The way in was blocked when I first came here with Stegra Snowfist. We'll have to search for a way inside."

They spent some time flying around the mountain, keeping up close to the crags and cliffs, the high ridges and rocky plateaus. At any place where snow could settle it was heaped high. Vertical surfaces and those fiercely sloped were grey and black, sometimes spotted with white where ice and patches of frost had formed. They passed the main door, the Godway Door, built by Varin's people when they first came to mine the mountain, but the great entrance was broken and smashed and the way was impassable. Elyon flew them a little around to where his father and Walter, Rogen and Stegra had found another way in, once before, but that was broken too. "There were tremors," his father called. "You remember how I told you? The whole mountain seemed to be coming down when we were here. It blocked the way."

Elyon remembered. His father had come here to restore himself, to seek out a blessing from the final fragment of Vandar that lingered in the depths of his tomb. Stegra Snowfist had called it folly but had accompanied them anyway, and no sooner had they found a way into the mountain than it began to collapse around them. They only made it out by the skin of their teeth. Only later did Amron Daecar unearth the Frostblade and fulfil the Snowskin's prophesy, laid down by the Sea-King centuries before. The king had never expected to come back. *No one ever expected to come back.*

But here they were again. And it was that final fragment they must find.

"We'll have to cut a way in," Elyon called. I don't see any other way, Father. All the entrances are blocked."

"There is too much stone. It would take days to cut a safe path."

"I'll use wind blasts, then. I'm better than I was. And you…maybe if the stone is frozen…"

The king understood. "Yes, *yes*. Perhaps I can move them." He sounded enthused. "The Godway Door, then. Take us there, son."

They swung back around to the front entrance and landed amidst ice and rubble. The snow had not fallen so thickly here, though Elyon hovered a moment to be sure, swinging the Windblade left and right, blowing the whiteness away. Soon enough, the bare rock was exposed. Elyon looked at the great ruin of the door. It was not like he'd seen in the pictures. Once it had been grand, colossal, a great arched opening of carven stone, chiselled with old glories from the War of the Gods, the victories of Vandar over his foes, the rise of Varin and his people.

But no longer. Now it was collapsed, broken, destroyed. The mountain was dead, and the doorway with it, and everything else that lay within. A gust of concern blew through him. "Father, what if…"

"We'll get in, Elyon. We must."

"I know, but…what if his spirit…the last of his spirit…what if…"

"It will be there, son. There is life in this mountain yet."

Elyon nodded. His father's word was law to him, unquestioned and immutable. "Do you want to try first, or shall I?"

"Let me. If I can pull the stone away, it would be better than blasting it further in."

They unharnessed and the king stepped forward, Elyon keeping close and within the protective shimmer of his shield. Raising the Frostblade, Amron focused on a large supporting block and drew the blade to one side. The rock shifted, bits of ice and stone fragments tumbling and breaking off. "Good. I think I can do it." He went again, pulling this time at the icy stone. The rock drew out, little by little, until it came free, rumbling away to one side. Elyon had expected a thousand tonnes of stone to come crashing down into the breach, but the ceiling held. "The ice has fastened it," his father said. "But I must secure it further to be sure."

Elyon found himself a bystander. He watched in fascination as his father unblocked the tunnel, stone by stone. After each frozen block was drawn out and moved aside he fixed the ceiling, icing it over, cementing it. When a stone was not iced enough for him to compel its movement, he dusted it in frost, hardening a film of ice about it, and that was sufficient for it to yield to him. He chose the biggest stones only, always those on roughly the same level. Once, and then twice, some loose rocks tumbled in to fill the gap, but those were little hindrance to him. He pulled and jostled them out of the way, one at a time, and continued his excavation. His father's power was astonishing here. *Would that the Dread came now,* Elyon thought. It might give them half a chance.

The rocks piled up outside the door and gradually the tunnel was cleared. When the final block was placed aside they entered together, father and son, holding up their blades to light the space within in a glow of white and silver. Together, they sent their power outward, and the light expanded to fill the room. Elyon almost lost his breath. "I never thought I'd get to see it," he whispered.

The ancient entrance hall to the mountain of Vandar's Tomb was colossal. Many parts of the ceiling had crumbled and broken away, and many pillars and supports had collapsed, but the effect was still stirring. The air smelled ancient. Elyon could almost detect the scent of unmined godsteel. Mist swirled from passages and tunnels, clouding and gusting through the still and silent rooms. Great statues lay fallen and strewn, statues of gods and kings and heroes broken off from their foundations. Elyon had seen this chamber depicted before, a hundred times before in paintings and frescoes and drawings in books, as he had the Godway Door and the Godway Road, the great forges and the armouries, the living quarters where the miners had dwelt, the places where visiting knights and lords and kings had stayed when they rode across the wastes for their appraisals. There was no place in all the world so grand and godly, no place so significant, no place so steeped in history. And though dark and broken and fallen to ruin, Elyon still gazed about in wonder. "It's magnificent," he said.

"Yes, it is." His father sounded similarly affected. "It is strange to be here again, in this great hall. And to see it this time…to really *see* it."

Elyon looked at him. "I thought you entered by another way?"

"We did. Though it still brought us into this chamber." Amron's eyes roved away to the high wall to their left, and a smile creased his bearded lips. "There," he said, pointing. "Do you see that balcony? We entered there, via a tunnel through the mountain. Rogen had to cut the way wider for us, but we managed to squeeze inside." He had a reminiscing look on his face. "We had to clamber down the stone to reach the bottom, and work our way through the scattered rock, the fallen pillars and statues." He swung the Frostblade, casting an ethereal white light upon the room. "All was dark, then. I did not even bear godsteel, no, I lost my blades in the Silver Scar. We had one dagger between us and I let Rogen have it. My eyes…I had no enhanced sight, no senses. I felt unnerved here, Elyon. I felt afraid. All of us were…all of us but Walter."

"Walter?" Elyon found himself only partially surprised. "You're to say even Rogen Whitebeard was frightened?"

"He was. Stegra as well. Walter was the one insisting we go on, the one determined to see my strength restored. He had been here before, of course. Had made it all the way down into the depths. Rogen fretted of creatures lurking here. He said he saw movement, heard things scratching about in the dark. Walter dismissed it. Dripping water, he said it was, and bits of falling stone. Nothing to worry about." He smiled, remembering. "He was the first to climb down and lead us on. Stegra spoke of some ancient malice that dwelt deeper in the darkness, some evil that feasted on the mists of godsteel, but Walter only dismissed that as well. He said that he had Vandar's light in him, the God King's blessing, and he went forward without any fear." He looked forward across the great chamber with a smile on his face. "We have that same light with us now, son. In these blades. There is nothing for us to fear here."

And with the Frostblade raised high, and the light of Vandar shining out, he led them deeper into the dark of the mountain.

53

Jonik

The gods are fallen, Jonik thought, as he saw the mighty monument to the God King Vandar sprawled out before him, face-down in the mud.

The statue had stood for millennia. A thousand foot tall it had soared….and now a thousand foot long it lay flat. Northward it had fallen, crashing down upon the Valley of the Gods with its great stone immensity, and beyond the wreck and ruin of the border town Jonik could see that Tukor too had been defeated and toppled, cast down to the east to lie smashed and strewn across rocks and woodland, his famed hammer broken off, the shield on his back shattered. The skyline once dominated by the twin statues here at the border was now bereft of them, bereft of that wonder, that magic, bereft of the greatest monuments in all the world.

Jonik stared forward with a tight grimace on his lips. "This was *him*," he growled, squeezing the reins. "Is there nothing he won't desecrate?"

Emeric Manfrey surveyed the destruction through his keen, golden eyes. "He must have come here recently. After he attacked Lakeheart, I would say."

Jonik nodded grimly. When last they'd seen Drulgar the Dread, he'd been flying eastward across the Big Sister, but that did not mean he hadn't swung back around this way some days later to continue his assault on the north. At his size he could cross from one end of the continent to the other in the span of no more than a day. There was nothing beyond the reach of his power now. No place, no person, he could not destroy.

"The Undercloak tooks to be standing," Jonik observed, peering through ash and smoke. "We should check in there. Lord Ghent may still be alive."

They struck their spurs and hastened their horses up the road. The land had been cast into shadow by the Dread's passing, the nearby woodland blackened and burned, the very earth broken and rumpled beneath them, and the sky was gloomy and nearing night. In the gathering dusk they had to pick their way carefully across the ravaged land lest one of their horses break a leg. Jonik cast his eyes toward the wreckage as they rode closer, to the fallen monuments and the crushed ruin of the town that lay between them. When last he had been here the border had been bustling, teeming, but no longer. The thick heaving crowds of people fleeing northward from the war had turned from a great swollen river to a sad little trickle, and he could see only a few lonely souls still wandering their way northward past the immense wrecks of the fallen statues. Many of those were refugees fresh from Lakeheart, like them. *They fled the Dread there, and now they come upon his work again.* Such as it was all over the north, Jonik did not doubt.

The Undercloak was so named due to its unique position beneath the great sweeping stone cloak of Vandar. Its walls were still standing, its gatehouse appeared intact, and only one of the towers had been pulled down when the colossal statue fell. For the first time since its construction, the Underloak was open to the elements above and deprived of its immense stone roof. The rain fell down upon it, a cold soft rain that was more like sleet in truth. When they reached the gatehouse they found a guardsman there, cloaked, cowled and miserable. He stood at the ramparts above the portcullis, peering down at them from the shadow of his hood.

"Good afternoon," Emeric said, amiably.

"What do you want?" the man growled down.

"To speak with your commander, Lord Ghent. Is he present?"

"Aye, he's present." The guard watched them a moment, and his gaze seemed to be on Jonik. "I know you," he said, after a pause. "You're that lad come by here a while back. The lord hosted you in his hall."

Jonik frowned, wondering. Then it came to him. *The old soldier,* he realised. The one on duty outside the keep. He'd spoken to him briefly, asked him a few questions. "I am," he said. "You're still alive, then?"

"Seems that way. One of the lucky ones, I guess. Hold there. I'll raise the gate." The old guard vanished from view. A few moments later they heard the winches go from within the gatehouse and the portcullis began to rattle and rise. When the iron spikes were high enough for them to lead their horses through, they crossed within and dismounted in the yard. The old guard came back out to greet them. "Never got your name before."

"Jonik. And yours?"

"Hugh."

"Well met, Hugh." Jonik clasped his hand and shook it. "This is my friend, Emeric."

Emeric stepped forward and performed the greeting gesture. "Well met."

"Aye, and you." The old man drew back his hood to let the sleety rain wet his balding head. He had a drooping, haggard face and tired eyes. "You came down this way with Lord Borrus, didn't you?"

"I did." Emeric had not entered the fort himself, Jonik knew, but had continued on down the road while Borrus and Torvyn Blackshaw spoke with the commander. The exile turned his eyes around the yard. Some blocks of stone had fallen from the cloak when Vandar fell northward, to lie stewn across the sleet-slick cobbles. One had come down on the stable and crushed a horse in its stall. The corpse was a spattered ruin, still bloody and fresh. "When did he come?" Emeric Manfrey asked.

The man scowled. "Two days gone. Came out from the east like thunder, he did. We all thought it was a storm, but was something much worse. Filled the whole sky in flame and fume and went crashing right into Vandar. Maddened, he was, like it was truly the god he was fighting, not some big statue. That first impact cracked the foundations, but didn't knock it over, and it only enraged him further. Went flapping about like a hurricane, roaring and scratching and biting at it, then flew off and came in for another charge. Knocked it clean over that time and it went and crushed the town. Then he went to work on Tukor after."

"Did you see all that?" Emeric asked.

"Me? Gods no. We only heard it from down in the cellars. Few of us managed to get down in time before all the air filled with that fume and flame I mentioned. The sounds, though…they were like to burst the eardrums and rattle the spine right out of your back. We all hunkered down, praying. Felt like the whole world was ending, it did, but a few of us lived on through it. The lucky ones, like I said."

Jonik nodded. Emeric Manfrey nodded. They both knew well enough what it was like to encounter the Dread. "How many are still here?" Jonik asked.

"In the Undercloak? Less than a dozen. Though can't really call it the Undercloak no more, can we? Under*sky* is all it is now." He sighed and shrugged. "Well, we're here, at least. That's more'n can be said for the Tukoran side. Fort there was smashed to pieces when the Forge God came down on them. Lord Hopham was killed, and near enough all his men. All death and ruin here now, and only a few stragglers coming through."

"Many of those will be from Lakeheart," Jonik said. "We were just there. The Dread destroyed half the city."

Old Hugh gave a snort. "Only half? What, he was in a good mood, was he?"

"It seemed no more than a game to him," Emeric said, rubbing at the dimple on his bearded chin. "Lakeheart had no defence. No more than you did here."

"Aye, and where does? He can take down Varinar, he can take down anywhere."

Jonik edged forward. "Has Ilithor been attacked?" If the Dread had come here, perhaps he'd continued north as well. He tensed as he awaited the man's answer, but his report was inconclusive.

"Not that I know of. Word is the dragon went south again after, but who knows? That menace might be anywhere." He scowled at the skies and then spat on the cobbles. "Anyway, let's get you out of this rain. There's a fire burning in the hall." They left their horses in a pair of open stalls and entered the keep. The warmth was welcome after many days of wet cold riding. In the feast hall a roaring fire was burning in the hearth, tended by a pair of women in threadbare robes. "You two. Out," Hugh said, and the two women beat a hasty retreat. "Lord Ghent snapped his ankle when the dragon came," he told them. "He's laid up in bed, but won't want you to see him there. I'll fetch him down." He made back for the door and stopped halfway. "You'll be wanting to stay the night, will you?"

Jonik and Emeric shared a look to consider, and silently conveyed their agreement. Emeric was the elected spokesperson. "That would be kind," he said. "We would be happy to stay here in the hall."

"No." The old man shook his head. "Ghent won't have it. We got spare rooms. I'll have them made up." He trundled back through the door, leaving a trail of rainwater in his wake. Jonik and Emeric drifted over to the fire to warm their hands and wait. There were some armchairs there, angled toward the flames.

Jonik looked at one of them. "Harden sat there," he said, remembering the night they'd stopped here on their way south. The hall was draughty, the rafters bathed in shadow overhead, and his words took on a sort of hollow, echoing quality as he spoke. "He told me he'd fathered three children by two of his wives that night. Two from his first and another from his third, I think. Did you know he had children?"

Emeric seated himself neatly. "No. I never knew. Where are they now?"

"Dead," Jonik said. "He told me all three of them were dead." He looked at the chair, recalling how morose the old Ironmoorer had been. How he'd spoken of service, of duty, how sad it made him to watch Jonik go from one master to another, always serving, never living for himself. *He wanted me to have a life and not just die in the name of duty.* Jonik stared at the seat, remembering the old man. Poor old Harden, tortured to death by a stormhag. A grimace rose on his face.

Emeric saw it. "His trials are over, Jonik," he said. "Be thankful for that, at least."

"Thankful? To die like that? Tortured and blooded, over and over again."

"Those things are now passed and I laid him to rest," Emeric told him. "In that we must take some solace." He looked at the chair as Jonik was looking at the chair, and it was as though both of them could see the grim old sellsword sitting in it. "He is with his children now. Some might call that a blessing." He looked at him. "You should sit. Try to relax. And best conceal the Mistblade, Jonik. We should try to avoid any awkward questions."

That was true. He wasn't in the mood for awkward questions. By the time he had removed his cloak and unbuckled his swordbelt, placing it against the hearth with his cloak draped over it, old Hugh returned with

Lord Ghent in tow. He looked hastily dressed, tired, and perhaps a little inebriated. Crutch under his arm the lord hobbled forward across the stone. "Well now, well now. Fancy seeing you two here. A fancy thing indeed. How are you?" He shook Jonik's forearm, then Emeric's. "How are you? Well met, Lord Manfrey. We didn't meet the last time you came by. Where is it you two have come from?"

"Lakeheart," Jonik said.

"Ah yes, yes, Hugh told me. Running from the Dread, so I hear it?" He laughed. "Aren't we all?"

"My lord," said Jonik. "Might I inquire as to the health of Sir Lenard? Is he still here?"

"No, no, not anymore. Borrington's gone, gone off with some others." The lord hopped over to the armchairs to sit by the fire, setting his crutch aside and raising up his broken ankle on a footstall that Hugh placed before him. "Thank you, Hugh. You're a good man. He's a good man," he said to the others.

"I can tell." Emeric smiled.

"Wine?" Lord Ghent raised his eyebrows. "Yes. I think we'll have some wine. Hugh, would you do the honours? It's about the last we've got," he told them. "It's swill, really, awful fare, but still gives you a headache in the morning." He laughed to himself as he settled in, putting his crutch aside. Hugh went off and returned with the wine, and that was when the big mastiff came loping through the open door. He saw Jonik and came charging, all but leaping up onto the chair in which he sat. Ghent laughed loudly, the sound echoing through the draughty hall. "He remembers you, Jonik. Good clever dog is this one."

The mastiff was desperately excited. His tail wagged so fiercely it shook his entire body and his great flappy jowls went flying along with him. Front paws up, he licked and licked at Jonik like he was some tasty treat to be devoured. Jonik was chuckling as he tried to fend him off. "Gods, enough! Get down, boy! Down!"

"Is that the dog from the Crabby Onion?" Emeric asked. He was frowning bemusedly. "You brought him here with Sir Lenard, Jonik?"

He nodded, still wrestling the dog away. "He was chained up outside by those deserters. Guess I had an impact on him when I set him free." He got the dog down at last, though kept one hand ready to bat him away if he must. "You said Sir Lenard left, my lord?" he said to Ghent.

"Yes, a week or so ago I think it was." Hugh served the wine and Ghent had a massive swallow, thinking. "Yes, about a week. Nice boy, he was, though he was left with some terrible scarring. Suppose being torn open by a grimbear will do that to you." And he laughed again, he drank and he laughed.

"Which way did he go," Emeric asked. "Was he planning to ride south to return to Lord Borrus?"

"South, yes, or maybe west. He seemed a dithery sort, to tell it true. Nice boy though. Very pleasant company. Told me he would make up his mind when he reached the fork in the road and decide then. 'The wind will blow me where it will,' he said. Might be he's racing down to join Kanabar even now. Or racing west to find his father. That was the other option. Said he wanted his father to know he was still alive. You know, after being lost in those pits all those years."

Jonik and Emeric were the ones who had saved him from said pits. "You sent he went with some others?" Jonik asked.

Ghent nodded his head. "Had a few willing swords go with him, yes. There's still power in being a Varin Knight, it seems, and still some good brave men about. Well, before the dragon came, anyway. Now more or less all of them are dead around here. But Lenard left long before that, so suppose he was the clever one. Left with maybe ten or twelve men, I think. Is that right, Hugh? Ten or twelve?"

"About right, m'lord."

"Were they Bladeborn?" Jonik asked. He knew how perilous it was out there now, and would prefer to know Lenard Borrington was well protected.

"Some, yes, I think some were. He picked up a few willing sellswords in the town, and managed to recruit a few Tukorans too. They seemed eager to get back into the war, ride south and join their new king." He scratched his chin. "Well, they won't like it if Borrington has decided to ride west, I suppose, so maybe he doesn't have ten or twelve anymore? Might be they split and went their separate ways. I don't know." He drank his wine.

"When you say king…" Emeric started.

"Robbert, yes. Robbert Lukar."

"Then he's returned from the south?"

"Ah, yes. Yes, let me explain." He drank a good gulp of wine and wiped his mouth. "We had a knight come through here a short while back, you see. Sir Tamber Rickson was his name. Rickety old knight out of Broadway, I think. He came from the coast, had a few hundred sick and wounded with him. Had quite the story to tell, did Rickson. He'd been in the south, you see, with Cedrik Kastor's host. The one that went off to Aramatia at the start of the war. The one no one's heard a peep from in only the gods know how long. Well, all sorts of things happened to them down there. He told me all about it."

"Like what?" Jonik asked.

"For one, Kastor's dead. Might be that'll put a smile on your lips, my lord?"

"And why is that?" Emeric asked.

"Well, it was the Kastors who threw you out, exiled you. That's as good a reason as any, no?"

"It wasn't Cedrik," Emeric told him. "That was his father's doing."

"Well, they're all the same, those Kastors. Rotten to the core and good riddance, I say." He drank more wine. "Prince Robbert's in charge now, Sir Tamber told me. Had some foul luck, they did, but they're back now. Not many left, though, sad to say. Prince Robbert had maybe a thousand when he went into the marshes."

"The marshes?"

Ghent bobbed his head. He was drinking between almost every sentence, which he did the last time as well, Jonik recalled. His cheeks were red, his nose a bulbous chaos of broken veins, and his eyes were becoming increasingly unstable. "He landed at Winslow Point. Harbour town north of Mudport. The prince sent Sir Tamber back up the coast with the last of his three ships. Said for him to take stock here at the border, to recover and then march back south when they were ready. Well, that's not going to happen now. Most of them died when the statue of Tukor came down. Crushed the fort there, you'll see it when you pass. All those sick and wounded were convalescing in the castle grounds. Almost all were killed, poor bastards. The few who weren't…well, I don't know where they went. North, maybe. Back to Ilithor." He drank more wine.

"And Sir Tamber?" Emeric sounded eager to speak with this old knight. Maybe he even recognised the name, though it wasn't one Jonik was aware of.

"Oh, gone. He was here at the border maybe a night or two before he left."

"Left? Where?"

"Rockfall. Robbert had orders for him. That was a while ago now, maybe two weeks, would that be right, Hugh? Two weeks?"

"Roughly that, m'lord."

Ghent drank and then held out his cup. "More wine, Hugh. If you would." Once refilled he drank again. "Swill, like I told you. Horrible stuff, isn't it?"

Jonik hadn't even tasted it yet, he realised. He did and found it quite disagreeable.

"Yes, exactly," Ghent laughed, seeing his reaction. "Horrible stuff, disgusting really, but does the job, does the job well enough…" He had another swallow. "I take it for the pain…well, that's one reason. My ankle was shattered when the Dread came, did Hugh tell you?" He scowled at the memory and his eyes were lit darkly by the fire. "That big bastard thinks he owns the skies….Gods, the noises he can make. I suppose you heard him, didn't you? In Lakeheart. You heard how he seems to laugh as he goes around destroying everything."

Jonik remembered that all too well. "He takes joy in it. The destruction."

Ghent nodded. "He's like a spoilt child…that's what I say. Daddy's favourite son and he thinks everything is his to do with as he pleases. He goes running around the yard picking up whatever damn toy he likes. And he shakes it and twists it and breaks it and throws it down, and then off he goes, running madly to the next toy." He snorted. "The statues were nothing to him. Thousands of years they've stood and he just knocked them down because he didn't like them. He's a bully. A giant bully and there's no one to stand up to him. You know he savaged an army that same day? The day he came here. Just for fun. Savaged them and burned them up just for fun."

"Which army?" Emeric asked.

"Rasals. Bucklands and Maynards mostly. The dragon caught them on the road before he flew here. Killed thousands. A few of the soldiers came by this morning to check if the road was still passable. They're in camp a two-hour march from here. Just trying to gather up their strength again before they continue south."

"Who's leading them?" Emeric asked.

"Horus Buckland. The Oakenlord died, I heard. Damn shame. Good man was Ferry Maynard. But Buckland's a stout old bastard and he'll get them back into line. The open road's dangerous for an army afoot, and if there's no cover, that bloody dragon might just get you…but what other choice is there? We all live under his shadow now, isn't that what people are saying?"

"He needs to die," Jonik said.

Ghent laughed. "Sure, sure, something we can all agree on!" He had more wine and wiped his mouth. "It's the how of it that's the trouble, though, isn't it? I don't know, maybe if we draw him into the open, we can get him with our ballistas. Takes but one arrow to kill a dragon, don't they say? Good arrow to the eye, and he's done for…so long as it gets into the brain. Well, the Dread's too big for an arrow, but a godsteel-tipped ballista bolt might just be about his size, don't you think?"

"The chances of a successful shot are slim to none," Emeric said to that. "If he can destroy King's Point, fight off three Daecars bearing Blades of Vandar, then go on to destroy most of Varinar in the same day, I'm given to believe that a few wagon-mounted ballistas are going to struggle to make a dent in him. No. That isn't going to work."

Ghent's head made that bobbing motion. "You're probably right. Yes, yes, you're probably right, my lord. Well, that's not for me to think about. I'm sure the king's got it all in hand." He nodded again, drank another large measure, and raised a hand to his mouth to cover a belch. "Excuse me, this wine…twists my stomach into knots. Poor fare, poor fare, just swill really. But it's all we've got." And he drank some more.

The evening descended from there. The jug of wine was refilled and emptied and refilled again and Lord Ghent packed it all away. They shared their own tidings and briefly described their tales, leaving out whatever important detail they preferred to keep to themselves. Which was more or less everything. They ate as well, Hugh bringing out bowls of soup and bread and cheese as they spoke, though Ghent largely forwent all that in favour of the wine. Eventually he got so paralytically drunk that he could barely form words, and Hugh decided that was enough.

"Come on, m'lord. Let's get you back to bed."

"Unhand me…you unhand me, you mean old bastard."

"Come on now. Come on, m'lord," Hugh coaxed. With a little more effort he got him up and out of the room, and returned a short time later, shaking his head. "I'm sorry about him, m'lords," he said. "A man needs a purpose and he's lost his. Was always fond of the wine, but…"

"We understand," Emeric said. "An unused tool will rust, Hugh."

"Aye, m'lord. I'll show you to your rooms." The man led them sombrely on through the quiet of the keep. In their rooms they found that fresh towels had been laid out and there were basins with which to wash, filled with warm water. "I'll have your clothes cleaned for you overnight," Hugh told them. "Just leave 'em outside the doors when you're done washing. They'll be ready for you when you wake."

Thanks were rendered and the men parted ways. Jonik went into his room, removed his armour, removed his leathers, set the stinking pile outside his door and washed himself as clean as he could. By the gods did it feel good to scrub himself raw after so very long in the wild, to wash the filth and fume from his hair. After that, he made a bed for himself on the ground - featherbeds had always been too soft for him - and somewhere along the way the big mastiff seemed to have gotten in. "I think you have the wrong room," he said, smiling. "Lord Ghent is down the hall."

The big dog licked his face, as if to ask permission to stay. *How can I say no to that?* "Fine. You can sleep here." Jonik grinned and rubbed him under his big droopy chin. "But no snoring. You have a snory sort of face, dog. If you snore I'm kicking you out. OK?"

He put out a hand and the dog raised a paw, and they shook on it. And lying down on his thin mattress of sheets and bedding, the mastiff flopped down right next to him and started snoring almost at once. Jonik sighed, smiled, and closed his eyes. He drifted quickly off to sleep.

The next thing he knew the door was opening, light was flooding in, and Emeric was standing in the doorway. He was dressed, armoured, washed and ready. "You two make a fine couple, Jonik." He chuckled at the sight of them, lying side by side on the floor. Neither mastiff nor man had moved all night.

Jonik blinked and rubbed his eyes, sitting up. He could not remember sleeping so cleanly or for so long.

"I'll give you a few minutes to get ready," Emeric said. "I'll be in the hall."

Jonik's clothes had been washed and dried and neatly piled outside the door, as Hugh promised. Jonik dressed quickly as the dog watched him all the while. He followed at his heel as he descended the steps to find Hugh and Emeric seated at a table. A breakfast of bread and cheese and ham had been laid out. Jonik ate ravenously, feeding the dog furtively under the table. "Is Lord Ghent not joining us his morning?"

"Best let him sleep," said Hugh. "He'll be better for it after all that drinking."

The sleet had ceased when they stepped outside, though the sky was still bleak and gloomy. Jonik and Emeric mounted up on their horses, and Hugh told them that both had been taken care of during their short stay, groomed and fed. They thanked him again and trotted out the gate, and of course the big mastiff was still loping along with them. "No. Go back now," Jonik said. "I told you last time. I can't take you with me."

He trotted on. The dog followed.

"No. This is your home now. Go back. Go on. Back."

The dog stared up at him in that way dogs did. Jonik could already feel his resolve beginning to weaken. "Damn you. Why do you have to look at me like that?" He raised his voice and called out, "Hugh, would you fetch him for me? He's trying to follow. We can't be having him along with us."

"Aye, m'lord, I got him." The old soldier came wearily out to take the dog by the scruff. "He's just fond of you, is all. Pined for you a bit the last time you left, you know."

"Really?" Jonik would rather not have heard that. He'd always had a soft spot for horses and hounds.

"Aye. Got up to a good bit of barkin', he did, though settled down a little after. He'll be doing the same again, I'd wager. They're good dogs, mastiffs. Protective and loyal."

Jonik nodded sadly. "Well...we'll see him again, the next time we come by. You keep him safe until then, Hugh." He gave the soldier a parting nod, smiled down at the dog, and turned his horse away.

Driving his spurs, he rode onward away from the gatehouse and along beside the great towering ruin of Vandar. Buildings were crushed beneath him; taverns, inns, pillow-houses, shops, the dwellings of mongers and merchants all smashed and destroyed. The stink of death was ripe in the air from all those crushed bodies beneath the timber and stone. Others were on show: men, women, even children and animals who'd burned in the fires of the dragon or suffocated from his fume. The rain had mixed with the ash to make a black filth beneath their hooves, clods of tarry sludge kicked up at their passing. They hastened along, past the legs and the hips, past the torso and the shoulders where the arm of Vandar, the arm that bore the sword planted at his feet, had broken away into a field of enormous chunks and boulders. They passed through and around them and even under them where they had fallen to form arches and tunnels. Past the neck they went, to the face with the magnificent beard, and those eyes...those eyes that always seemed to look at you, judge you, those giant lifelike eyes that seemed to follow you as you went.

The head was planted downward, the face smashed into the earth. Yet somehow...somehow the right eye *still* seemed to look at him, seemed to judge him, seemed to watch him as he passed. Jonik felt a shiver go up his spine. He was so close, so close he need only ride a little closer and he could touch the eye, touch the stone. There was a thick heavy pumping in his heart, a pulsing in the vein in his neck. He felt sick, seeing the fallen god so close. *It's stone,* he told himself, *just stone, that's all, made by hammer and chisel, this is no true god.* But the symbol disquieted him all the same. Vandar and Tukor, both toppled by Agarath's might. By Drulgar, his greatest weapon and favourite son.

But not his oldest son, Jonik thought, thinking again of the monster in the depths.

He rode onward, away from the judging eye. The air was heavy here, heavy and dark. Through the strewn stone they went, past the broken gates that barred the border into Tukor. The bodies here were thick as flies and there was no one here to bury them. Tukor's thousand-foot corpse stretched away to the east, obliterating the fortress, crushing the woods. Splintered trees rose up about it like pine needles and the crows wheeled and circled like black specs above its bulk, screaming their harsh calls.

Upon the shattered shield atop Tukor's back, Jonik saw an eagle. It was perched there, watching, following them as they passed. It unnerved him for reasons he could not quite explain. There was something queer in the way it stared. "I don't like it here," he murmured.

"Nor I," said Emeric Manfrey. "There's something sinister in the air."

They drove on through the last of the ruin of Tukor's Pass and beyond the ash-soaked earth. A little further up the path the black and greys gave out to browns and greens again, the air began to clear and lighten, and they even saw patches of white ahead where the snow had started to settle on the ground. Jonik paused to turn back. All was shrouded behind him, dark. It was a graveyard of dead gods now.

He was about to turn around and continue on when he saw the fume stir, saw the shape bounding up toward them. He smiled despite himself.

"He really does like you," Emeric Manfrey observed.

The mastiff loped up to him with a big smile on his face. "You're persistent, dog," Jonik said. "Is it really so dour in the fort?"

"He must have slipped Hugh's grasp," Emeric said. "Or found another way out past the walls."

Jonik swung down from the saddle to pet him. "We should take him back, I guess." The thought of passing back across the border didn't appeal to him much, but it must be done. "What…what do you think, Emeric?"

"I think he should come with us," the exile said, unexpectedly. "It's clearly what he wants, Jonik." He smiled. "And you."

Jonik could hardly deny it. "There's no war north of here," he said, trying to convince himself. "We can take him with us to Ilithor, and bring him back when we come south again."

Emeric agreed. "It will be nice to have his company. He does seem a very good boy."

"Aren't all dogs?" Jonik asked, philosophically. They debated that along the way.

The morning began dry, but before long the sleet had returned. It was soft and sludgy, the very worst form of weather the two men agreed, though the dog went along happily all the while. There was a dark feeling in Jonik, still, a feeling of disquiet lingering from the border. He felt ill at ease, prickly. They passed through a grim-looking wood, forded a swollen river thick with corpses. "Refugees," said Emeric, and Jonik nodded. They had died of starvation on their way north or been struck down by disease, and many were to be seen now, stiff and rigid at the side of the road.

Morning turned to afternoon and the sleet turned to snow. The white patches spread and merged until all the world was winter. They stopped at a stream to water the horses and saw bits of ice running along its flow. The men dismounted to eat some bread and salted meat, sharing it with the dog.

"What's his name?" Emeric asked.

Jonik fed the dog a bit of bread and smiled. "I don't actually know."

"How could you not know? You found him at that inn."

"Yes, but the owners were dead." He tore off another piece, and the dog ate it hungrily. "We should have asked Hugh. They'd have given him a new name by…"

He was interrupted by a flap of wings. A rattle of branches, a fall of snow, and Jonik looked up. The eagle was above them, watching from the tree. "I saw that eagle earlier," Jonik said.

Emeric glanced up at it. "A fine bird."

"It's following us."

"We have food, Jonik. It likely wants some meat."

Jonik didn't like it. Eagles, yes, he liked those plenty, but this one set his hackles to rising, and the dog's too, because the mastiff was growling at it. When he started barking the eagle opened its wings again and took flight. "Something feels wrong," Jonik said. "The dog wouldn't react like that to a common bird."

"It would if it felt like its food was being threatened. He's a mastiff, Jonik. They're a protective breed as Hugh said and make excellent guard dogs. It's a good sign, actually. We'll be able to sleep more easily with him watching over us."

Jonik remained unsure. There was something tickling at the back of his head, a sensation that felt somehow familiar. The Mistblade was at his hip, thrumming, trembling. There was a fear in it, a hate. Jonik lifted his eyes to the darkening skies, half expecting to see the Dread surging out from the clouds. But this was different. It wasn't hate for a foe, he knew.

And his brow twisted. It was hate for *family*.

54

———

Amron

The door was small and rimmed in light and an aura lay beyond it.

"This is it," Amron said, stopping. "That power, Elyon, do you feel it?"

Elyon nodded. His voice was thick. "I feel it, Father," he said.

It had taken long hours to get here. Long hours searching their way through the forges and the living quarters and the mines, walking, clambering, crawling, watching, yes, watching for hidden things in the dark. For there were creatures here, that was certain. Things that lurked and things that slithered, things that skittered and crept. Unnamed things and ancient things. Things long forgotten by the minds of man. *But nothing to threaten us,* Amron knew. This mountain was the body of a fallen god and they both bore a shard of his heart. *We are his servants, his champions on this earth. The creatures here bow to us. They watch us pass and bow.*

The route was long and arduous, and often was it spectacular. The old forges were grand and imposing. There was an armoury so vast that they could not see its end, with racks of weapons uncountable filling the high stone walls. One chamber was once used for a feasting hall, and it looked fit to host ten thousand men. Many rooms were filled with rubble fallen from the ceilings, and long corridors and passages were found to be caved in, forcing them to take other paths. When they at last reached the ancient mines, they found themselves in another world entirely, with great colossal rifts delving deep into the bowels of the mountain. There were veins of godsteel ore here that still shone and misted on the dark rock walls, and the scale was dizzying. There seemed no end to the depths.

"We should fly," Amron had said, and so they did.

Down they went, down and down, past broken stairs built into the sides of the mines, past collapsed bridges and fallen scaffolds where ropes and chains rattled eerily in the deep. These passages were once passable. Walter must have come this very way when he descended into the depths

637

of the mountain many years ago, but the recent tremors had caused many of them to fall apart, and without Elyon they would not have made it.

He flew them along the route Walter had once described, a route that all the pilgrims had walked when they dared venture here for their blessings. It led them to a tunnel, a simple rocky passage thousands of feet beneath the upper levels, and a little way into this tunnel, it transitioned into a stair, rough-hewn and crude, and they descended yet further down. A hundred steps they went, two hundred, three, and all the while the power of Vandar grew stronger. When it seemed as though the stair might go on forever it finally ended, levelling off again into a short corridor that had led them here, to this door rimmed in light, and to the great power that lay beyond...the power they were here to take.

"I hear a voice," Elyon murmured softly, as they stared at the doorway. "It isn't the Windblade, Father."

"It is Vandar, son. He is calling you on."

"Me?" Elyon turned to him. "Why me? It should be you."

"This is your task, Elyon. Ilith gave it to you."

"To us. He gave it to us."

"Did he?" Amron looked at his son intently. "Did he mention me, Elyon?"

"Yes," the boy said. "He told me it would require both of us to get here. So it's both our task, and it should be you. I'm tired from all the flying. And you're the king. Vandar would prefer it if it were you."

Amron smiled. "I know what you're doing, Elyon. You hope I'll receive a blessing. You hope I'll come out healed."

Elyon shrugged. "Well..."

"It won't happen, son. I had my chance once before, and I was denied. Vandar denied me."

His son shook his head at that. "The *tremors* denied you, actually. If you'd only continued on, as Walter wanted..."

"The tremors *were* Vandar, Elyon. *He* denied me. I was never meant to be healed." Amron Daecar held the Frostblade in his grasp, its pure white light enshrouding them. Motes of colour danced and sparkled as they rose up toward the rock ceiling. "This was my destiny," the king said. "Finding this blade was my purpose."

"And you'll have another," Elyon insisted. "Once he heals you..."

"No, son." Amron would not let himself submit to that hope, no matter how much he might want it. "The last of Vandar's power must be used to bind the blades. We have come for the final fragment, not miracles."

"But there may be power enough for both. You won't know unless you try." Elyon looked at him firmly. "What harm is there in asking? Maybe I'll go myself after all." He paused. "Yes, I think I'll do it." He took a threatening pace toward the glowing door.

"Elyon. Don't go doing something reckless now. My disability is not worth risking the world over, is it?"

"What's the risk? It's said you can commune with Vandar in his holy chamber. So, I'll just go and ask. If he says no, then he says no. I don't see how that's reckless."

"Because the blessing is often balanced by a curse, Elyon. Think of Oswald Manfrey. He entered this chamber an unfancied knight and went on to become one of the greatest swordsmen of all time, was granted a powerful lordship and became the First Blade of Vandar…only for his house to fall into ruin. Or Galin Lukar. We always used to think he came here to seek permission to invade Tukor. Now we know he made a promise to Vandar to win the War Eternal in exchange for a Table of his own. Look at what happened off the back of that, Elyon. The Ilithian kings ousted. Tukor conquered by a Vandarian house. A pursuit that led to Janilah Lukar and his many treacheries. There are many such examples. Finnebor the Fool wished to become the smartest man in the world, only for his expanding intellect and thirst for knowledge to drive him insane. Barren Marsha came asking for a working womb and went on to have a dozen children, then one of them murdered her. Darius the Daydreamer dreamed of sailing beyond the Stormy Sea and never came home. Lord Gallister…"

"Yes, Father, I know the stories," Elyon interrupted. "What about Walter? I'm not seeing much of a curse in that luck of his."

"Maybe it's still to show its face," Amron said. "Or maybe his curse came *before* the blessing when his entire family was burned to death. I don't know. But it's not worth discussing, Elyon. If there's a blessing to be made, then I rather think we should wish for something bigger than healing my little limp, don't you?" He stepped up to him. "I'll go," he decided, lest Elyon dart into the passage before he could stop him. "You're right, son. As king it should be me. Stay here until I return."

"I'm hardly likely to go flying off, am I?"

"Time can behave strangely in the presence of gods, son. I may come out in seconds, or hours. If it's the latter, do not be alarmed. Stay here. Don't enter the tunnel, no matter what you hear. OK?" He stood facing him, looking into his eyes. "OK? I need you to say it, son."

"Fine. I'll stay here until you're back. No matter what."

Amron nodded, pulled his son into a brief embrace, then turned and passed through the door rimmed in light before he might lose his nerve. The corridor beyond was just about high enough to accommodate him without having to crouch. He held the Frostblade before him, shining its light down the narrow passage, but before very long he didn't need it. The glow in the tunnel spread and brightened, and he slid the Frostblade away into its white scabbard, resting his hand on the pommel to give him strength.

Gradually, the walls seemed to smooth out, the rough grey rock becoming imperceptibly straighter, sleeker, the ceiling lifting a little, the walls widening, until he was walking along a much broader corridor, a corridor made of tiles of light. The change seemed very sudden, but also somehow natural. He paused, looking back, and to the far edge of sight the corridor of light extended.

He continued the other way. The light seemed to pulse down from his footsteps, rippling as though he was walking on the surface of a pond, and when he lifted his arm, a glittering mist followed his movement, like bioluminescent trails in the ocean. He smiled, looking at his hand as he swayed it left and right. He raised his other, clapped them together, and light exploded from the connection, moving in waves down the corridor ahead.

He wasn't wearing his gauntlets or his gloves, he realised. His palms were exposed, and he was dressed in a fine doublet now, with leather boots and a warm woollen cloak emblazoned in the sigil of Vandar. He wore no swordbelt, and he felt no pain. "This is a trick," he said, out loud. "A vision, nothing more."

A vision of the future, said a voice. *A future without war and a future without pain.*

Amron shook his head. "There is no such future." He was referring to the pain.

The voice knew what he was referring to. *There can be. Just take your blessing and heal yourself. Heal yourself and win the war. There is enough for both. Enough power for both.*

Amron looked around. "Vandar?" Could it be Vandar talking to him?

Yes, I am he. There is enough for both. For both. Take your blessing. You need but ask.

Something tickled at the back of Amron's neck. There was something wrong about the voice, something oily. "You're trying to test me. This isn't Vandar."

It is. You know it is.

"Only in part," Amron said. It was the voice of the Frostblade, grown louder and clearer than normal. That fragmented part of the God King's heart that had long since learned the taste of freedom. A savour it did not want to give up. "You would see the world fall before you went willingly," Amron said. He could almost see the spirit of the blade before him, a shimmering figure all in white. "You want your freedom, above all. You know there's no power for both."

But there is, there is, the white figure said. *You can heal yourself, restore yourself. You need but ask.*

Amron firmed his chin against it and continued down the glowing hall. The white drifted with him, never coming closer or getting further away no matter how slowly or quickly he moved.

Take the blessing. Take it and become great again. Take it and they will follow you. Take it and they will love you.

He hardened his jaw and ignored it. Onward he marched down the corridor.

Are you too craven? Is it fear, Amron Daecar? Expectation? The word was a long cold hiss. *You do not want to let them down. You like being the Crippled King*

It's an excuse, an excuse to hide your weakness. Because you fear him. Eldur. You live in terror of him.

Amron's lip flicked upward. "I do not fear him," he said.

The figure laughed. *Cripple, cripple, the crippled king. Amron the Broken. Amron the Fearful.* The laughter rang out. *But it doesn't have to be this way. Heal yourself. Restore yourself. There's enough for both…for both…*

"No," Amron said. "You're lying."

Then take it back, said the voice. *Take back the pain, cripple, it's all yours.*

A fit of agony assaulted him, ripping through his thigh and shoulder. His left arm dropped to his side, his fingers turning feeble, his right leg dragging behind him as he limped and shambled, dragging his bulk along. He looked for the Frostblade, but it wasn't at his hip. He wore the doublet, the boots, the warm woollen cloak.

The white figure was laughing at him, pointing now and laughing. *Amron the Broken. Look at your crippled king.* More shadowed figures appeared, multiplying to the left and the right, ahead and behind him, and they were laughing too, pointing and laughing and chanting his name, *Amron the Broken, Amron the Broken…*

He pressed on through the din, and the white figure was suddenly there, moving along at his side, whispering into his ear. *It doesn't have to be this way*, it said, as the shadows sang and chanted. *There's enough power for both, yes, for both. Heal yourself, restore yourself. Become the king they need…*

His sight began blurring now. There was sweat on his skin. The pain in his right thigh was unbearable, a searing heat flashing and pulsing. He dragged himself along, sweat pouring from his brow to patter against the floor in droplets of light. And that light was brightening further, brightening until it was blinding to him, and the voice was in his head now, screaming in his head.

Do you not want to save them? Do you not care if they live or die? There's power for both, enough for both. Heal yourself, you can have it all. There's enough power for both! For both! For both!

His breath grew short. The air grew hot. The noise in his head was deafening. He shambled on.

Why not? Why not? Why deny yourself? You can be one again, strong again, whole again. There is power for both, blessing and binding both.

Amron Daecar stumbled forward. He fell to a knee, writhing in agony, and clenched down on his jaw. His eyes were wet with pain. Sweat tumbled from his forehead and snaked down his scar. Spots danced across his vision and the voice was going on, on and on and on…

"Shut up!" the king bellowed. "Shut up! Shut up!"

He rose to his feet. Dizzily he lurched on, and there was laughter all around him. He found some strength, running now, stumbling and tripping and rising and running again, outrunning the shadows as they tried to keep up, as their chanting and their laughter faded behind him. And as he went, he sang out a chant of his own. "I will give it up, I will, I will. I will give it up, I will…"

He stumbled forward to the ground. The light was sucked away from the world like an indrawn breath, and all sound with it. Only his ragged breathing now, echoing through an open chamber. Only the sound of his armour scraping on stone as he struggled up to his feet. A small muted light was spreading from his hip. He reached to touch the hilt of the Frostblade, but his fingers drew back. *No. Take the pain. Master it,* he told himself.

He looked around. The chamber was faintly lit by a gentle ethereal radiance, something very soft and constant emanating from every surface. Circular it was in shape, with a cone-like ceiling that bled into a pool of total darkness at the centre, a darkness that seemed to shimmer and ripple like the surface of an oily pool. The floor was flat, completely flat. Amron turned around and saw that the tunnel he exited was not ablaze with light anymore, if it had ever been. *A vision,* he thought. *It was a test, nothing more.*

"I have been waiting for you to come," said a voice. It was different to before, grander, more godly, booming down from that pool of blackness above him. "Your name is Amron Daecar."

Amron collapsed down to his knees. "Great Vandar," he said, genuflecting before him. "I have come…"

"For a blessing," the God King said.

Amron sucked a breath. *A test. Was this just another test?* "No, I…your strength, my lord. It is your strength we need, to remake your heart."

"To bind the shards," said the voice, knowing. "The binding and the blessing. There is power enough for both."

Power for both. A test, a test…

"I do not care to heal myself," Amron called out. "I care for no selfish blessing, great lord. It is only the final fragment we need. Your power to end the war…"

"Then take it, Amron Daecar. Speak the blessing and receive the final fragment."

He shook his head. "I want no blessing." *It's a test. Just another test. A final test, that's all.* "Only your strength and your spirit, Great Vandar. Without it, we cannot end the war. Without it, Agarath…"

"Speak the blessing, Amron Daecar. Speak it and receive the final fragment."

"I do not need one," Amron responded. He was on his knees, staring upward in appeal. "I only want to help. To do what I can to help. Please, I beg you, as your humble servant…"

"Speak the blessing, Amron Daecar. Speak it and receive the final fragment."

"What blessing? I do not have one to ask of you. To risk diminishing your power…"

"The is power for both. Enough for both. Speak the blessing, Amron Daecar. Speak the blessing and receive the final fragment."

Amron shook his head again, straining to think, grimacing. "I want only to win the war," he said now, desperate. "I want no blessing for myself, nothing for myself…"

"For another," boomed the voice. "Speak the blessing for another. Speak it, Amron Daecar, and receive the final fragment."

Another, the king thought. *Speak the blessing for another.* His mind flashed, sudden as a thunderstrike, and he knew who it must be.

Amron Daecar stood up from the floor. He stood and he spoke the blessing.

55

Saska

"What's wrong with her?" Rolly asked. "She's tense. Her hackles are rising."

"I'm not sure," Saska said. They were riding two by two along a frozen mud track that wended through gentle forested hills. Joy had been loping along contentedly enough all day, but no longer. She was prowling now, her shoulders going up and down in that way of hers, glaring away into the darkening trees.

"She looks ready for a fight," Leshie observed, trotting behind them. "Maybe there's a grimbear or something out there?"

"Joy, stay." Saska could sense the cat was about to bolt. "*Joy,*" she said, with stern emphasis. "You're not allowed to run off anymore. You know that. You stay right there."

"She's got the scent of something," the Butcher said. "A deer, yes. She could catch a deer for us." He craned his neck back to the others. "Who wants venison? Joy will catch a deer for us."

"Quiet," the Whaleheart rumbled. "Be quiet so I can listen." He raised a hand and closed a fist, calling the company to stop. The clop of their horses' hooves came to a slow halt on the track, and a silence settled. He did this many times daily here in Tukor, always wary of what might lie ahead. His eyes narrowed and he went perfectly still. "There's someone out there," he murmured. "Further ahead. I hear horses."

"Men from that army," the Baker suggested. "Deserters."

"Why would they be here?" asked Leshie, keeping her voice low. "They'd go back the other way, wouldn't they? Back to Rasalan if they were deserting?"

"They may be trying to reach Ilithor," the Surgeon offered. "To go to this refuge."

"The road is near," the Baker told them. "The map said so. The road that comes up from Tukor's Pass..."

Saska ignored the chatter. The Nightblade was thrumming at her hip in a queer manner, an excited manner. She reached to grip the hilt, and sensed a want, a strange yearning, a dormant fondness. Her brow twisted into a frown. *It knows them,* she thought. *These men…it knows who they are…*

A sudden movement caught her eye. From the flank of her horse, a dark shape went running, long and lithe, dashing away up the path. "Joy!" Saska hissed. "Joy, stop!" The cat was whip-quick, though, and gone. In no more than a handful of heartbeats she was clearing the trees and speeding away out of sight, bounding toward an open field ahead. "Damn it," Saska cursed. She swung down from the saddle. This was no place to give chase on horseback, with all these frozen bits of mud jutting and surging from the icy earth, the roots and hidden rocks. It was a leg-breaker for horses and she'd come to like her mare. "Hold here. I'll fetch her." She set off running.

"Saska, wait," the Wall called. When she didn't, her guardian gave a loud grunt and swung down heavily from Bedrock. Others were dismounted too, but they were behind her now and she couldn't tell who. By then she was reaching the edge of the wood and breaking out beyond the trees. She entered a large glade, an open patch several acres in size encircled by woodland on all sides. Snow draped the ground, sparkling beneath the setting sun which peeked out beneath a thick bank of grey clouds in the west. Joy's path was marked by a track, her prints bounding away across to the woods on the other side. Saska could hear the sound of barking there, echoing out. She heard the shouts of men.

Fear erupted in her. If these men were deserters, or hunters, or just local villagers, they could kill her. *They have a dog. A hunting dog.* She burst away at once, racing across the snowfield, feet thumping the earth. The sounds grew louder, closer. The others were following further back, shouting out at her, but she paid them no mind. *Joy,* was her only thought. *Joy. Joy.*

As she neared the trees, she saw them. A huge droopy-skinned mastiff was standing and barking wildly as Joy stood facing him, hissing, her back arched and tail high. Saska heard a voice calling, saw a man riding through the trees on horseback. "Dog, stop! Get back!" he was shouting. Another rider was with him. Both were cloaked against the cold. Saska heard the rattle of armour as they dismounted and ran, the sound of swords knocking against their legs. "Dog, get away from that cat! It'll kill you! Get back!"

"Joy! On me!" Saska's shout was loud. The two men heard and slowed as they burst from the trees. Between them the animals were still staring at one another, barking and hissing. "Joy! On me! Now!"

The starcat finally heard her. She snapped her head around, but not at Saska. It was the younger of the two strangers she was looking at. She saw the long black hair framing his face, the hard jaw, the pale skin. Something nudged at Saska, some strange feeling emerging through the shroud of adrenaline. The Nightblade was exulting at her hip, thrumming like a hound reunited with its master. Saska looked at the man, *really* looked at him. She could hear the others coming up behind her now, the thunder of the Wall, the bluster of the Butcher, the fierce pant of Leshie.

It was the black-haired stranger who broke the standoff. "I know that blade," he said.

"What blade?" Saska came right back. She had the Nightblade well hidden, or so she thought.

"The one you're trying to hide. It led us to you. I can feel it. Who are you?"

"Who are *you*?"

"How did you come by it?" There was something tight in his voice, an accusation. "It was a long way from here the last I knew. Did you steal it?"

"No. It was given to me."

His eyes flicked past her, judging the others as they came running through the gloom. All were cloaked and not so easy to make out clearly in this dimming light, but the Wall was a rare structure of a man and not idly mistaken for another.

"It's the King's Wall," said the second stranger.

The younger man nodded. They turned their heads to confer with one another, whispering softly. The others were joining Saska now, who stood a dozen paces away. The dog and cat had stopped their barking and hissing, but were growling instead, glaring as animals do when they try to feel one another out. It would not go well for the mastiff should it come to jaws and claws. Big though it was, Joy was bigger and a cat besides. He'd have no chance.

Leshie put her hands to her knees, taking a few sharp breaths. "What's going on, then? Who are they?"

"I don't know."

The pair were still in conference, their heads turned inward, eyes darting over. Leshie caught her breath and stood up straight. She peered at the two strangers and gave out a sudden laugh. "Gods, no, is that…" She peered forward. "*Shadowboy*?" The black-haired stranger turned his head sharply. Leshie gave out a great whoop of surprise. "It is. My gods! It's the Shadowboy!"

"Who is Shadowboy?" demanded the Butcher. He was the only one who'd drawn his blade. "Another boy you've bedded?"

"No, no, I never bedded him." Leshie laughed in amazement. "It's the Shadowknight," she said. "The Ghost. Elyon's brother. Jonik!"

Jonik. Saska blinked and stared and blinked again. She could scarcely believe it. *Elyon's brother*.

Leshie was striding forward, right between the dog and the cat, waving them away as she went. "Gods, how are you? It's been so long."

"Hi, Leshie. How are you?"

"Good. Yeah, really good. You?"

"Yes I'm…I'm well."

"You were always shy." Leshie grinned at him and then made a half-turn. "I used to call him the *Shy Shadowknight*. Well, I did it once, anyway, and then Ranulf told me off. Apparently, he didn't like being called Shadowknight." She swung back again. "So where are the rest of you?"

"The rest…"

"Your crew." Leshie had an excellent memory when she wanted one, especially as concerned the many nicknames she'd thought up. It was a collection that made her very proud. She listed the names off. "The Plodder. The Ugly Crow. Bull. Nerves. Brown Mouth. Well, that one's not mine. Brown Mouth Braxton. Your captain called him that. Turner. Gill Turner." She turned again. "There was one a bit like you, Parapet," she said to the Butcher. "I called him Scarface. He had horrid scarring on his face."

"Maurice," said Jonik's companion. A man of forty he looked, perhaps a few years younger, noble and handsome, with a thick black beard, trimmed and neat, and piercing golden eyes. He seemed very calm by the meeting, very unflustered. "Or Big Mo."

Leshie smiled at him. "Yeah, that's it. Big Mo. He liked to eat nuts."

The man smiled. "He did."

"I know you too," Leshie said to him. "How are you, my lord?"

"As well as can be expected, given the times."

Another laugh from Leshie, who was relishing being the centre of attention in all this. She turned once more to perform the introductions. "It's Emeric Manfrey, the exiled lord. I owe him and Jonik my life. Ranulf does too, and lots of others. They saved us all from those pits."

"Palek's pits?" the Butcher asked.

"Yeah, those ones. We were only there for a bit, me and Ranulf, like a month or something. But others were there for years, even decades, and these two saved us. Say…" And she turned back once more. "What happened with Vinny…I mean Vincent Rose? He was the one who put us in those pits," she told the others.

"He's dead," Jonik said. "He was duplicitous, so I killed him."

"Rough justice, huh?"

"He had it coming."

"Damn right he did. I'm just angry I didn't get to kill him myself." She bit her lip in disappointment, then asked, "Where are the rest, then? There's only two of you. Or are there more?" She looked into the trees from where they'd come, but it was too dark to see much of anything in there now.

"Just us," said Jonik. "And you?"

Leshie swung an arm out to her companions. "That's the Butcher, the ugly one with the scarred face. He's a sellsword with the Bloody Traders and his brother's further back. You see…with the horses?" Jonik nodded. The others were moving across the open field now, leading the horses along. "They're all Bloody Traders too, except Jaito, he's an Aramatian archer. You know Coldheart, obviously. The King's Wall. And this is Saska. She's the important one."

"I can tell. She's carrying my old blade." Jonik had a good long look at her. *Elyon's brother,* Saska thought again, still reeling. She could see the resemblance. A harder, slimmer face, but similar. His hair was less full, longer, darker, and his eyes were more silver than silver-blue, but they were brothers, yes, that was obvious. "How did you come by it? You were given it, you said?"

"Yes. By your brother."

He paused, taken aback. "*Elyon?* He gave it to you? Why would he…"

"Because she's Varin's heir," said Leshie. "It's her blade. They're all hers."

Jonik widened his eyes and stared "You…*you're* the heir of Varin?" He gaped at her, temporarily speechless. "How…how can that be?"

"Believe me, I've asked myself the same thing too many times to count." She smiled, making light of it. It was better that way, she had always thought. To cover her discomfort in humour.

He stared at her for a long, long moment. "You're…not what I expected."

"No. I get that a lot."

"You're southern."

"Half-Aramatian. The rest is northern."

"And you grew up here? Your accent…"

"Since I was about a year old," Saska said. "Broadway, Ethior, Willow's Rise."

"Are you bonded to it?" he asked.

It took her a second to realise he was talking about the Nightblade. "Yes. For a little while now."

"And it's power? Can you use it?"

"No. Not yet. Not properly, anyway."

She regarded him, wondering what forces had brought them together like this. *Elyon's brother*, she thought again. *Jonik, who mastered the Nightblade.* He'd done terrible things with it, but for the most part those were forced. He was a slave, coerced and controlled, and she knew all about things like that. Even Elyon admitted that Jonik had been on a path of goodness since, a righteous path.

Her mind was whirling. *Maybe I don't need my grandsire to train me*, she thought. *Maybe it can just be a dream after all.* She had tried last night to find King Lorin again, to enter the Nightblade's mysterious realm and prove it was more than a dream, but she'd been too tired and had fallen right to sleep. *But he's here now. Jonik is here.* A smile flickered at the corners of her mouth, and Jonik returned the look.

"Are you going north?" she asked.

"Yes."

"Ilithor?"

He nodded.

She swallowed. "Then…will you come with us?" She knew Elyon wasn't going to like this, but she also knew he'd understand. "I need to be trained, Jonik. To use the Nightblade. You're the only one who can."

"That isn't true. Gerrin could train you, though…he isn't here."

Something glum came over his face, and he brooded for a moment. Then he asked, "You're going to see Ilith, then? Do you know about Ilith?"

"Yes, we…"

The Wall stepped forward. His voice interrupted her. "It's dangerous you being here," he said to Jonik.

The young man looked over at him. His eyebrows twisted. "Why? I'm no threat to you."

"You're carrying another blade. You have the Mistblade in your cloak."

Jonik's frown hardened. "So what if I do? If she's truly Varin's heir…"

"She is," said Leshie.

"If she's *truly* Varin's heir, then this blade is hers as well. I've been through hell and back to get it. And now you're to say I'm dangerous?"

"I'm not referring to you. I'm referring to the blades. Having two of them so close to one another is dangerous." There was a thick tension in his voice. His eyes scanned the skies. "We need to part at once. We can meet again in Ilithor. Prince Elyon warned us explicitly to keep the blades apart."

"The Windy Prince is an old maid," dismissed the Butcher. "He is the Prince of Caution, The Prince of Worry and Warriness, this Elyon Daecar. And he murders eagles. He is a murderer."

Jonik looked at him. "What do you mean by that?"

The Butcher snorted. "I mean what I say. He kills eagles, this windy brother of yours. He is the Prince of Eagle-Killing, yes, he…"

"Why? *Why* does he kill eagles?"

There was something in his voice Saska didn't like.

"Because he thinks they're spies," Leshie explained. "Not all of them, but some. He thinks the Elders have been captured and tortured and made to use their eagles against us. Do you know about the Elders of the Everwood? They can see through the eyes of their bonded eagles." She laughed. "Funny story, but Ranulf has one now. He's got Elder blood in him, Jonik. Maybe we'll see him when we reach the refuge. If he's back from his quest by then, anyway."

Jonik didn't answer. He stared out a moment, then said, "There was an eagle watching us earlier. There was something about it…something odd."

Saska's heart was thumping. "Where was it? When?"

"Just now, maybe twenty-odd minutes ago. Back through those trees." Jonik gestured the way he'd come. "And I saw it before as well, at Tukor's Pass. I thought it was following us. The dog…" He looked at the mastiff. "The dog was barking at it. And…"

"It's there," Sir Ralston said.

Everyone looked at him. They saw where he was staring, followed the direction of his eyes, and saw it. The eagle, standing in the branches of a tree, some fifty or so metres away, on the south side of the glade. It was watching them, staring, a glint of red in its eyes. *The sunset*, Saska thought. *Just the sunset, that's all*. But she knew it wasn't the sunset. A sudden dreadful fear was coming upon her, and she could feel it in the blade. A silence enwrapped them, and then the Wall spoke again.

His voice was a low warning rumble.

"They're coming," he said.

56

Jonik

They came from the south in a storm of wings.

Three of them there were, no, four…five…six…

From the darkening skies they emerged one and then another, flapping and shrieking out as the eagle watched on from the branches.

"To arms!" bellowed the King's Wall, his voice thundering out across the glade. Twin greatswords came ringing from his sheaths, misting. He marched forward and put himself in front of Saska. "Go!" he roared at her. "You have to go! Run!"

Saska backed away, unsure, her head moving left and right. The dragons were over them now, over and around them, dragons with thick chests and twisted tails and queer snouts long and short, demon dragons with great curving horns above their eyes and beneath their jaws, dragons that jerked and screamed in strange voices as though in eternal pain.

A song of torment filled the air. Around them they flew, three going one way and three going the other, and then Jonik saw a seventh approaching behind them, bigger than the others, fearsomely big, ridden by a man in robes of scarlet and ruby, red and purple, black and orange, the colours of flame. And his hair was flaming too, wild and flowing as it caught the wind, and from his chin twisted a great red prong, oiled and gleaming, twisted to a sharp point. His laughter cackled out across the sky.

There were cries coming from across the clearing. Horses screaming, whinnying, bolting in blind panic as Saska's sellswords lost hold of the reins. Half her company were only midway across the field. A dragon saw a chestnut horse gallop away and gave chase, descending, reaching with its long sharp talons, and the horse was taken, lifted into the air, torn apart in a wet gory ruin to splash bloodily onto the snow. Another dragon swept down suddenly in a fierce arc, reaching and snapping at

651

the sellswords as they drew their blades in defence, diving and leaping away.

One figure pulled a bow, nocked and loosed an arrow, but the shot was ineffectual, pinging harmlessly off the dragon's thick hide, and it saw him, turned and plunged down upon him, fire glowing in its chest, translucent, building and building and pouring out through its maw. The archer tried to run, to leap away, but he tripped in his haste and fell. The river of flame bathed him. There was a terrible scream, quickly cut off, and then another filled the air as Leshie gave out a shrill high cry and shouted a name Jonik didn't know, then ran that way, ran toward the archer as he burned and fell down and died. Saska shrieked, "Leshie! Leshie, no!" and gave chase, and at once the King's Wall thundered after her, and the sellsword called the Butcher made to follow as well, shouting, "Brother! Brother! We become dragonkillers this day, brother!"

It all happened in an instant. Before Jonik could react they were all converging toward the heart of the snowfield, the woods all around them, the dragons spinning and circling like vultures above a kill. They were entering a cauldron of fire and fume and death.

"Jonik, we have to get her away." Emeric was at his side, his eyes intense. "That girl is precious. She cannot die here."

Jonik nodded. "Dog, stay." He drew in a full breath, threw off his cloak, and tore the Mistblade from its sheath. A cobalt glow surrounded him and his armour took on the same hue. He could feel in the metal the tension, the terror, the thrill. He plucked his helm from his swordbelt and thrust it down over his head. Emeric did the same. "On me," Jonik said.

They dashed across the field. All was turning to chaos ahead, the earth churned by boot and hoof and claw. Horses surged in half a dozen directions and the dragons plunged down upon them, picking them off as they raced for the trees or fell trying, snapping legs and screaming. Lances of flame shot out at all angles, some high, some low, melting the snow, and the steam rose and spread and lifted, mingling ethereally with the red dusky light.

They sped for the melee as the dragons swept overhead, the men swinging their blades as they passed, ducking and diving. Some dragons bore riders, caped in their colours: black, brown, purple, red, gold and grey and green. Back and forth they rippled and whooshed, back and forth, back and forth. Leshie was staring at the burned archer as he lay black and smoking on the ground, and he was no longer recognisable as a man. Saska stood by her, pulling at her, shouting at her. The Butcher and some other men were roaring some southern warcry and the King's Wall stood alone, one greatsword at his side, the other pointed up at the seventh dragon and the fiery man atop it, turning with him as he circled around. "Face me!" the Whaleheart was bellowing at him. "Face me! I'm the one you want!"

Jonik ran right up to Saska. "You have to get out of here." He grabbed her shoulder, and she spun on him fiercely, almost tripping in the snowy mud. He steadied her. "You have to go. *Now*. You have to go."

She shook her head. "They'll chase me. It's me they're here for. We have to kill them or they'll chase me."

Kill them? It was unthinkable. "There are too many, Saska." He reached into her cloak, and she twisted away from him. "Give it to me," he shouted at her. "My blade. Give it to me."

"Yours? It isn't yours." She backed away.

He followed her in. "I can hide us. Give it to me. I can get us away."

Her eyes shone with fear. Fear for leaving, for losing her men. A sellsword had been snatched up by a dragon, and the dragon was climbing, climbing high into the sky. Two hundred metres up, he opened his claws and threw him, and the man came tumbling down, spinning uncontrollably, to land head-first on the hard, icy earth. There was a sickening crack. A tall woman hissed and shrieked wildly. She wore a striped cape in black and orange. She ran for the man, long strides taking her on, and separating from the group a dragon swung about and gave chase and dove down upon her.

Jonik did not see the rest. His eyes were on the heir. "Saska," he said, shaking her. "You have to go. Now."

"No, I…"

"Give it to me, damn you!" He surged forward again and took the Nightblade in his grasp and ripped it right out of its leather sheath. The feeling of power was automatic, intoxicating, *overwhelming*. He heard the voices in his head, both of them now, both fragments of Vandar shouting and screaming and hissing at one another. It disoriented him. He went to a knee, buckling beneath the dual weight of the twin blades. The noises of the world loosened and melted and blurred, folding into one another, and his sight blurred as well. He blinked and drew a sharp breath; his heart was hammering. He felt something on his back, a hand, shaking him. Vaguely he could hear Emeric Manfrey's voice shouting, "Jonik, fight them! You can do this! Command them!"

The voice brought to him a surge of strength. *Command them.* He blinked again and pressed up from the ground, rising powerfully to his feet. His eyes cleared. Everything sharpened: sights, sounds, smells. The whispers roared but behind the door now, behind the door in his mind, the door he'd barred shut. He had the Nightblade in his sword hand and the Mistblade in the other. Black mist and blue rose up side by side to mingle and merge, twisting and twirling, and they were as one; a deep midnight blue.

Jonik looked at the merging mists. His face was defiant. Summoning the Nightblade's power, he let his form ripple and fade and vanish, and he was gone from sight, invisible. He stood there a moment, turning around. The fiery man was still circling, cackling, ignoring the Whaleheart's roars. Leshie had stirred herself into action, joining the Butcher and the others. She'd thrown off her cloak to unveil a suit of fine red armour. Away to the north, the striped woman was still alive, he saw. She was battling the dragon blade to claw.

Jonik let the Nightblade's power pour back out of him. Instantly he reappeared.

Emeric stood observing him. "Your skills are still sharp," he said. He took Jonik's shoulder and leaned in close. "Get her out of here," he said, firmly. "Get her far away, Jonik. We'll hold them off."

Jonik drew back, and the two men met eyes. "I understand," Jonik said

Emeric smiled. It was a smile that suggested goodbye. He nodded, a single time. Then he spun and whirled away.

Jonik turned back to Saska. "Take my arm," he told her.

She was staring at him in astonishment. "You're...like my grandfather. The way you..."

"Take my arm, Saska. We have to go. Right now."

Her eyes cringed. They darted about, looking upon her friends, her company. *She loves them,* he knew. *She loves them and doesn't want to leave them.* He understood, but they had no choice. "Take my arm," he repeated, firmer. "The sooner I get you somewhere safe, the sooner I can return to help."

That got through to her. He saw her eyes change, saw her nod. "OK." She reached forward and wrapped her fingers around his forearm. He focused at once, fading, the black wispy smoke enveloping them, enshrouding them, sucking them beyond all sight. He drew a slow, controlled breath, to steady himself. It would require extra focus to conceal them both. "Don't let go, Saska," he said. "Whatever you do, *do not let go.*"

He turned back the way they had come. The snow was gouged and trampled here and if they made new tracks they might be seen. Quickly they went, leaving the fighting and the chaos behind them. Saska was craning her neck to look, her eyes twisted in desperation. "Turn forward," Jonik told her. "There's nothing you can do for them now."

The girl drew in a shaky breath. "Leshie," she said. "When you go back...please...make sure Leshie's OK. She's my best friend."

"I'll do what I can."

"Promise it," she said. "I'm holding your gauntlet. Godsteel. Promise me you will. Make an oath."

His jaw was tight. He knew what Emeric had meant. They were all expendable, all of them but her, and he must lead her far away, far away from here. It wounded him gravely to face that thought, but he must think of the bigger picture. She was essential. As were the blades. If the rest must die to give them a chance to escape, so be it. They would die for a worthy cause.

"Jonik? Why aren't you saying anything?"

"We can't talk. They might hear us." He stepped onward, keeping his feet in the prints already made. The trees were nearing. He could see the dog there, a dark shape beneath the boughs, and the starcat was there with him. The cat's eyes glinted silver in the shadows. "Yours?" Jonik whispered.

"My Joy," she said.

He frowned. "She's looking right at us. How can she…"

"She can't. She can only sense me." They took another step, another, and the starcat was sniffing the air, eyes moving, searching for them. She started moving forward, creeping out into the open. "Joy, no." Saska raised her voice. "Stay back, Joy. No…stay back…"

The cat stopped, raised her eyes and hissed. The dog started barking loudly.

Jonik tensed. There was a noise behind them. A deep roar and a heavy flap of wings. He froze on the spot, but Saska didn't; she was still moving forward, her hand slipping from his arm. The connection was lost and her body took form instantaneously, emerging from a puff of black smoke. It was like she stepped through a portal from another world.

"Ah. *There you are.*"

There was sudden laughter in the air. A cackle like the coming of a storm. It spread and stretched and a tingle went up Jonik's spine. The cat was racing out toward them now. "No, Joy! Go back, go back!"

Jonik turned. The seventh dragon was thumping the air with long wide wings. Black they were, and purple, webbed in dark orange veins. The monster was enormous, broad at the shoulder, thick in the snout, a tail lashing and snaking out behind it, wide at the base and thinning, thinning, edged with hundreds of long sharp spines and tipped with a point as sharp as a sabre. The tail moved like the tail of a cat, swishing side to side and sweeping through the snow as the dragon landed with a pounding thump that shook the very earth beneath them.

Jonik blinked back into sight. *Run*, he was thinking. *Saska, run.*

He stepped forward, drawing the fiery rider's eye. The rider cocked his head and looked down at him. He was a horror of a man, bone white and drawn and strange, and his eyes were red, a deep blood red. His great red prong of a beard caught the very last of the light, gleaming, and his hair was orange and scarlet and purple and black, rippling and stirring in the wind. There was a jewel at his throat, a great red diamond, pulsing with power. In his hand he bore some sort of sceptre, golden and encrusted with rubies and onyx.

He smiled. From the branches of the tree came the eagle, swooping and swirling around him. It landed on the shoulder of the dragon and screamed.

"Who are you?" Jonik demanded.

The man laughed from the summit of his monster. "I am Eldur's first and most loyal servant." And his lips tore open; he smiled proudly. "The High Priest of Fire."

Jonik glared up at him. He could hear Saska and her starcat further back behind them, hear the dog barking wildly from the trees. He held the Nightblade in one hand, and the Misblade in the other, and the mists were merging, mingling. *They're twins*, he thought, *twins.*

"Your name is Jonik," the priest said. "My friend here has been following you." He motioned toward the eagle, which opened its wings and shrieked again. And there was pain in that sound, as there was with the dragons, pain and terror somewhere down deep, and Jonik knew it was another slave. *They're all slaves. All of them.*

"I thank you for leading us to her," the priest said. His smile spread wide, wide and wider still, unnaturally wide. "My master wishes to speak with her."

"Eldur does not speak. He only destroys."

"Oh, you know him?" Laughter cackled from the priest's wide mouth. "Stand aside, boy. This does not concern you."

Jonik was not going to stand aside. From a standing start he surged forward, ghosting rapidly across the snowfield. The dragon roared, crouched, and swung, lashing out with its long spiked tail. It whipped around so quickly that Jonik barely had time to react. He dove down flat just in time. The tail rushed over him, spikes scratching at his armour, sparking. The tail went past, the dragon spinning back around to face him as Jonik pressed upward, bearing the twin blades. The priest was cackling laughter. "The boy has two, two silly swords! They will never be remade, never, my master will not allow it!"

Jonik vanished.

The priest's laughter ended abruptly.

The dragon's head went left, went right, nostrils flaring. Prints appeared as if by magic in the snow as Jonik surged forward unseen. The eagle was circling. It screeched as it saw them, and the dragon swung about, but too late.

Jonik was upon it.

He threw down the Mistblade, took the Nightblade in two hands, and swung upward.

The cut was true. It raked across the underside of the dragon's neck, shaving through knobbly black horns and spiny purple spikes and slashing a gash through the plate beneath. Blood gushed forth, thick and black like the blade that drew it. The dragon never saw it coming. He bellowed and flapped in sudden surprise, backing away, and Jonik pressed upon him, sensing his fear.

He cut again, another clean strike. Black blood boiled and spewed to the snow. The dragon emitted a red screech of rage, rising up and thumping its wings in a wild rapid storm. The snow exploded into a great white shroud as smoke poured and billowed up from the dragon's jaws and nostrils, spreading, and suddenly all was white and grey and Jonik was as blind as his foe. He drew a breath of smoky air and his lungs were tickled into a quick fit of coughing. The dragon heard him. There was a sudden pounding, quick tremors in the earth, and through the shroud came a great shape, charging him like a battering ram. Jonik scrambled away, diving and rolling as the monster stampeded past, its tail whipping behind as it went. Jonik was struck a glancing blow as he stood back up, and the dragon felt the connection, turning again upon him, and at once his maw opened wide and a great swollen surge of orange-red flame poured forth.

But Jonik was gone again, speeding beyond its flow, his cloak singed and smoking. He saw the Mistblade glowing nearby, but ignored it. *It's not my blade,* he thought. *No, this is my blade.* He spun again on his foe, the shadow searching for him in the dark, and skittered in, silent, swinging. The Nightblade slashed again through plate and flesh, jarring into bone, and the beast roared and twisted again, snapping out at him. Jonik ducked under the skiff-sized head, angled the Nightblade upward and thrust. The tip drove deep, one foot, two, three, almost right up to the hilt before stopping. Blood oozed out and down the handle, oiling over Jonik's gauntleted hand. He grasped the hilt with his other one as well, and pulled hard to the side, trying to open the beast's throat up, but the dragon thrashed, lifting its head quickly upward and it was all Jonik could do to cling on.

His feet left the ground, five feet, ten, twenty before the Nightblade slid free, and Jonik went tumbling back down. The earth was torn up and uneven where he landed, and his legs buckled beneath him, his whole body jarring as he pitched hard to one side, his grasp faltering. Before he even knew it, the Nightblade was slipping free of his fingers and falling into an earthen rut. He scrambled forward on hands and knees, but the ditch was deep, the blade beyond his reach…

Blood spattered against his shoulder. He looked up. Saw red eyes in the swirling smoke. Red eyes of beast and man. They were staring at him, and the High Priest was smiling. "Draknarak," he whispered. "Kill."

The dragon roared. Rings of jutting teeth surged down as it opened its great jaws to bite down on him. Jonik's fingertips brushed the Nightblade, but no more. It slid away, beyond his grasp, and the open maw was coming, coming, coming…

A sudden blue light blazed in the shroud.

The light was moving, speeding quickly toward them. Within its glow was a figure, and she was racing, surging, leaping. The dragon paused, turning its head.

Saska swung hard. The Mistblade cut down in a powerful arc and opened a rift in the dragon's left shoulder. The scales parted, and the flesh beneath, and more black blood poured forth. The beast thundered. Saska landed heavily, falling to a knee, and stood, trying to swing the sword again, but the cut was weak. She had not yet bonded the blade; it was a wonder she could even lift it. The dragon swung to face her and its eyes were wide and wild.

"Saska, run!" Jonik roared. "Run!"

He reached again for the Nightblade, scrambling down into the ditch. The eagle was circling overhead, watching. The dog barked loudly from the trees. Jonik took the blade at last, lurched back up out of the trench and saw that Saska was running across the field. The dragon lumbered after her as the priest screamed out, "Take her, take her, take her!" and the beast was closing…closing…

All of a sudden it swung its bulk, whipping its tail across the surface of the snow. Saska never saw it coming. The tip skimmed savagely across from right to left, tripping her, and she went tumbling forward horribly, heel over head, bumping and jolting and coming to a hard stop. Jonik could tell at once she was dazed. She tried to stand, stumbled forward again, scrambled back to her feet and fell once more…

"Saska!" Jonik roared, chasing. "Saska, run! Run!"

A black shape came racing through a whorl of smoke, leaping and scrambling up the dragon's flank. Sharp claws dug into divots beneath segments of plate as it scaled up the beast, making for the priest. The man saw the starcat snarling his way and smiled calmly, standing up in his saddle and lifting his sceptre. There was a pulse of power from the red diamond at his throat, a spreading wave that struck the starcat as she neared him, knocking her back, and her claws faltered and she flailed for a grip, tumbling, tumbling back down into the snow.

A great taloned foot came down atop her.

Saska screamed. She rose, started toward the dragon, dragging the Mistblade behind her. Jonik was running for them, running hard and unseen…

The priest's voice sang out across the glade. "Hold! Draknarak, hold!" He looked at Saska. "Stop, or the starcat dies."

She stopped at once, falling forward onto her knees, gasping. "Please no…no…" Joy was trapped in the talons, scrambling, hissing, but there was nothing she could do in that cage. "Let her go…"

The priest stood up grandly in his saddle, grand and triumphant, his cloak of many colours stirring in the wind. They whipped out behind him, licking like tongues of flame. "Tell the boy to drop his blade. We see him, we see his prints in the snow." The eagle was circling above, watching the prints appear, always watching. It let out a shriek and the High Priest said, "Show yourself, boy. Come, don't be shy."

Jonik slowed, grimacing, and then stopped. He let the power of the Nightblade bleed out of him, and he stood there, the blade in his grasp, the smoke rising from its edge, puffing and rising.

"Drop it," the priest demanded. "Now…or she dies." The dragon Draknarak squeezed and the starcat gave out a mewling whimper.

"Drop it, Jonik!" Saska shouted at him. "Drop the blade! Please!"

His mind whirred. His sword hand tightened. He judged the distance to the dragon, to the cat, but it was no use. One firm squeeze and she'd be crushed. He punched the Nightblade into the ground and his fingers uncurled from its hilt.

"Good, yes…a smart boy." The High Priest grinned that wide queer grin. "Now come, child, you will come with me. Come with me or she dies. Come or all of them die."

Saska hesitated. Her eyes were twisted in pain. The dragon squeezed again and the starcat yelped and Saska flinched.

The High Priest laughed. "Come, come, he wants only to meet you. The rest will be spared, this I promise." He looked across the field.

"Those who still live, yes. Give yourself up now and they will be spared. Do it not and every one of you will die."

The fighting was ongoing across the field. The dragons swooped and plunged down from the skies as shapes fought them off in the darkness, moving between bands of flame and smoke. Perhaps two of the beasts were dead, and some of the men, but it was not possible to know who from here.

"What say you?" the priest demanded. "It is a simple choice, live or die. If you do not come, all of you will perish." The fire priest raised his chin, and the red horn curved upward, gleaming. "Make it, child. And make it now."

And Saska made her choice.

In the end, what choice did she have?

Jonik watched on, impotent, hopeless, as she stepped forward and the dragon crouched down, as she scaled up the creature's flank, past the bloody wounds and shorn off scales, to take a seat behind the High Priest of Fire. The man smiled that smile, and the red diamond pulsed at his neck. He whispered a word and Draknarak was running, beating its broad wings, bearing them away to the south.

And from across the glade, the other dragons wheeled and followed.

And across the glade, a giant roared.

57

Amilia

She unwrapped from his embrace and looked up into his eyes. "Thank Tukor you're back, Mallister. I was so worried. I've been so worried for weeks."

"I'm fine, Amilia. Fine." He tried to smile and failed. Drew away from her, making room between them. "Who told you we were back?"

"Lord Morwood," she said. "He's gone to fetch Ilith now."

Mallister nodded. He seemed stiff, uncomfortable in her presence. *So much for a sweet reunion,* she thought. She'd almost run to be here when Morwood found her with Del and his ledgers, but Mallister was acting cold and distant. *Maybe I shouldn't be so surprised,* she reflected. It wasn't like they'd been spending much time together before he left, and it had been a long while since they'd shared a bed besides. *He's just tired, maybe, emotionally drained from his trip, that's it.*

"Do you want me to leave?" she asked him. "I can leave if you'd prefer to report to Ilith alone." When Mallister Monsort gave no answer, she turned from him and looked at Ranulf Shackton instead. "Is this a privy meeting, Ranulf? I would hate to intrude."

"By no means, my lady. You could never intrude." He at least had greeted her pleasantly when she entered the room. A bow, a kiss of the hand, a kind and merry smile. Even his big eagle, perched on the back of his chair, had opened out his fine wings as though happy to see her. "Please, come sit. Have you seen Ilith much of late?"

"Not for a while, no." She gave Mallister one last questioning look, then went to sit opposite the adventurer. "Fhanrir says he's much older now. Each time he brews a new potion, it ages him."

Ranulf rubbed his chin in thought, rough with a scraggle of beard. "How many has he made now, my lady?"

"Two…no, three, I think. He still has that 'soul' one left. For the Sword of Varinar."

"Light of the Soulstar," Ranulf said.

"Yes, that one. And your one, of course. I trust you got what you needed?"

"We did, my lady, yes." He withdrew a small vial from his pocket and placed it on the table between them. Within it shimmered a liquid light, a white living light that seemed to eddy around the glass. There was something mesmerising about it, and something terrible. She couldn't put her finger on what, but it disquieted her. "Lhara's Tears," he said, profoundly. "We paid a bitter price to get them, my lady, but it was a price that must be paid."

She looked at the vial, at the strange swirling light. *A bitter price.* "How many men did you lose?"

"Seven," Ranulf said, with a sorrowful sigh. "Seven brave men, and all on the day we discovered the tree. Pecker, Jym, Darron, Gunter, Daecar, Alyn, and Simcock. They all died in the discharge of their duty, and without them the quest would have failed. Thus did they all die well, my lady. Each will be remembered as a hero."

Amilia Lukar had never quite understood that phrase - to die well. It was a phrase often used when describing a noble, honourable death, even if the manner of that death was horrific. When a knight was burned to death by a dragon, he died well. When a warrior was savaged and mauled by a moonbear, or torn open by the jaws of a sunwolf, he died well. It was the lie told to boys so they took up arms and went willingly into the horrors of war. *Dying screaming and in agony is not dying well,* she thought. *Bravely, yes, with courage and fortitude, but well?* No, she'd never liked the phrase.

"I'm sure their losses have been keenly felt," she said, keeping those thoughts to herself. She glanced at Mallister. He was across the room now, standing beside a bookshelf, still dressed in his armour and filthy cloak. He seemed to be looking determinedly away from the vial.

"Yes, my lady," said Ranulf. "They were all fine men."

"You left with ten," she remembered. "Who is the other survivor?"

"Rufford. A fearless man and most defiant in the face of death." Ranulf's face was warm with gratitude as he spoke. "I owe him my life several times over, my lady. There were times when he had to carry me on his shoulder when fleeing one peril or another. But for his assistance, I would certainly be dead. And during the return journey as well, when it was only the three of us left, he was a pillar of strength for us all."

Amilia nodded. She did not know Mallister's men well, and their names were largely unfamiliar to her. Even so, she would be sure to find this man Rufford and give him a hearty embrace for getting them all home safely.

The sound of heavy footsteps outside augered the return of Lord Morwood. A moment later he plodded into the chamber, his chequered green-brown cloak swaying behind him. "He's coming," he told them. "Fhanrir is bringing him now." The jowly watch commander glanced back out through the door, then said in a low voice, "Be warned, all of you. He is…much older than he was."

A few moments later the proof of Morwood's warning was unveiled when Fhanrir entered the warm little library with a small, old, grey-haired figure, stooped and dressed in loose robes. Amilia's mouth fell open at the sight of him. He'd gone from a sinewy young man, lean and robust, to a crook-backed grandfather and looked old enough now to challenge Archibald Benton in a contest of age.

"I know, I know, I look a little different," Ilith admitted, as Fhanrir *clacked* in beside him with his stick. Even his voice was different. It had that grainy, croaky quality that came with age and had lost some of its silvery appeal. "We could be brothers now, don't you think, Fhanrir? I'll have to start using a walking stick too."

"It's not funny," the little mage rattled at him. "None of this is funny, Ilith."

"Not to you, no. You have no sense of humour anymore." Ilith chuckled happily and shuffled toward his motheaten armchair. He made groaning and grunting noises as he sat, then turned his eyes upon Amilia. "My lady. I had not expected to see you here."

"I told her they'd returned," Lord Morwood said.

"I wanted to see them." Amilia felt a little unwanted all of a sudden. "I can leave, if you…"

"Oh no, no, of course not." Ilith shook his head and his grey hair went side to side. "It's always a pleasure to host you here, child. I know you have been very worried."

"Yes, my lord. Very worried." She looked at Mallister, who did not look back.

"But our heroes have returned," Ilith proclaimed, and his old rumpled lips curled into a delighted grin. "Ranulf, Mallister, and let us not forget dear Kamcho. I am quite sure he was essential as anyone on your quest."

"He was, Lord Ilith," Ranulf confirmed proudly. He raised a finger and Kamcho gave him a fond nip, then opened out his great blue and gold wings in triumph. "Without Kamcho we never would have found the ice oak."

"But you did," Ilith said. "You completed the task I gave you?"

Ranulf nodded and gestured to the table. "It is right here, my lord. Lhara's Tears."

Ilith saw the vial. "Ah, yes, And there they are." He leaned forward to pluck it up, making those straining noises again as he reached to take it from the table. Ranulf had to stand and slide it closer to him. "My thanks, Ranulf. My limbs do not work as they once did." He took the vial in his grasp and sat back down, and those noises sounded once again. Settling, he took a moment to swirl the contents, raising the vial to his eyes, squinting at it, scrutinising it, then pulled off the stopper with his spare liver-spotted hand and took a quick sniff through his lengthening nose. The strange liquid light seemed to try to crawl up the side of the glass as though trying to escape, but Ilith blew on it and it retreated back down. He smiled another merry little smile and replaced the cork. "Excellent, yes. This should do nicely."

Ranulf breathed out. "That is good to know, my lord."

"Did you ever doubt it?" Ilith asked him.

"There is always doubt," Ranulf replied. "Doubt that we got enough of it. Fear of corruption, perhaps, during its extraction."

"Well, fear not. The sap is perfect and the quantity is just right." He swirled the liquid light again, nodding, then opened his cloak and stashed the vial away in a pocket. "Now, I would hear your tale. Ranulf, I know you fancy yourself a gifted raconteur. Or is the experience still too raw?"

"No, my lord. I am happy to speak of it."

"And you, Mallister?" Ilith regarded the knight for a long moment. "You seem very tired, young man. Do not feel compelled to stay if you would prefer to get some rest. You have earned it, to be sure."

"I am…very weary, my lord."

"Then go. Please. Ranulf can update us on his own."

"Yes, my lord." Mallister spoke as a man condemned. He moved across the room, making drearily for the door, then stopped. "My lord, if I may ask…"

"Yes?"

"The potion. When…do you plan to brew it?"

"Ah…soon, child, very soon. There is little time to waste and I am wasting away, as you can see." He gave a playful smile, then seemed to see that Mallister was very serious. "Well, I must first memorise the sequences and prepare the ingredients," he said, more thoughtfully. "Sharpen my mind for the trial and rest my body, brace against the rigours of the sorcery. That will take a little time. I would say I'll be ready by tomorrow evening."

"Tomorrow," the knight repeated, dourly.

"Yes. I would hope."

Mallister's face was fixed like stone. He lowered his eyes and gave a slow bow. "It has been the greatest honour of my life serving you, my lord," he said. Then standing again, his eyes flickered to Amilia…and away just as fast. He strode from the room.

Amiia watched him go. His manner made her feel uneasy. *Is it just tiredness?* she wondered. *Grief for the men he's lost?*

"He seems rather off-colour, Ranulf," Ilith observed.

"Yes, my lord. He's been rather…withdrawn of late."

The demigod stroked at the angular lines of his chin. "Well, let us hear your tale then. I would know of what happened to your intrepid company, Ranulf."

"Of course, my lord," Ranulf said, and the tale was colourfully recounted.

Amilia was only half listening. It was a tale of icecats and snowbears, gruloks and ghosts, widowmakers and wild men who wore bark. It sounded like the sort of dark adventure story that brave boys liked to hear in their youth. But a story, only. Not something anyone would want to live through. Even Ranulf seemed to have misliked it. He told them of the hunt for the ice oak, of the legend of Lady Lhara, how he'd heard a voice calling out from the tree. "It was Mallister who extracted the sap," he said.

Ilith rubbed the wispy white beard on his chin and said, "Did he speak much of it, after?"

"No, my lord. He has been somewhat insular since that day. Withdrawn, as I said."

The demigod frowned. "Was there some trial involved, Ranulf? A test he had to face?"

The Rasal shook his head. "The sap was given freely, my lord. There was a window, a sort of opening in the trunk shaped like a tear. Mallister only had to reach inside and when his hand came out, the vial was full of light. The tree itself was enshrouded in a great sadness, and a fog of magic suffused the air. I felt a terrible tugging at my heart as I neared, and my mind filled with the faces of those I have loved and lost. I suppose it was true for Mallister also. Perhaps that was the test, my lord...to face past griefs, to feel them again, so raw in one's heart. I saw his eyes when he gathered the sap. They were shining, I saw. He was weeping."

"Tears for tears," Fhanrir rasped. "That's the way with these sorts of things, Shackton. It's all give and take. He cries a little and Lhara cries and he comes away with the sap." He nodded, and his long dangly nose quivered within his hood. "No doubt the boy's sick with grief over that sister of his." His beady eyes swung over to Amilia. "Best you go talk to him about it, girl. She was your handmaiden wasn't she, the sister?"

"She was my best friend."

"Best friend who poisoned your betrothed."

"*Was*, I said. I didn't know about that until after Melany died."

Fhanrir snorted. "Well, see if you can smooth it over. Take some wine with you. You can drink it together, talk it out, maybe comfort him. He'll like that."

"Are you whoring me out, Fhanrir?"

"No. You do that well enough yourself."

"That's enough," said old man Ilith. "You are addressing a princess, do not forget."

"I'm addressing a mortal. I'm addressing *this*." And Fhanrir clipped his bony fingers, to demonstrate the brevity of her lifespan and importance in the world, or lack thereof. "And she can handle it, anyway. We're friendly now, the girl and I."

Amilia confirmed it. "He's like the great-great-great-grandfather I never had."

Fhanrir cackled approval at that. "You see. She gives as good as she gets, and I like that. But you know what I don't like, Ilith?"

"I could guess at a few things."

"You've still got two potions to make. You've got juice enough for one…didn't I say that, girl, a while back?" He did, she remembered. "Just one. Tomorrow, you say. Tears of the Frostshade. What then?" He didn't wait for a response. "You'll be bedridden, weak as a bloody kitten. The speed you're ageing, you won't be able to walk, talk, or think. You're turning senile already; I've seen it, aye, don't think I haven't. Your wits are deserting you, Ilith. Might be I'll have to invoke my right to take custody of you. There are ways, you know. I'll strap you down and do the ritual myself, see that I damn well won't."

"No, Fhanrir. You must preserve your strength."

"Me? It's *your* strength we need, not mine."

"We've spoken of this. Many times. Tender these baseless accusations of senility all your please, my friend, but my memory is still intact. I count this as the sixty-seventh time that you have raised this issue with me."

"Is that all? Thought we'd hit the century by now at least." The little mage snorted at him. "When you're bedridden after this next brew, I'll take charge of you. I'll do the blood ritual, and you won't be able to stop me. It'll be for your own good. For *all* our good."

"You're right," Ilith said.

Fhanrir was taken aback. "Well gods be good, you're finally admitting it!"

"No. Not that. You're right that I will be bedbound after this next sorcery, or near enough. That is a fair remark to make, my friend. This body is Tyrith's and it is mortal. How old would you consider it to be now? Eighty? Nearer to ninety? After the rigours of the next sorcery I might be one hundred and ten and you're right to question my fragility. So yes, that's settled it."

"Settled what?"

"That it is time for me to leave," Ilith said. "Before my body gives out entirely."

"Leave?" Ranulf asked. "And go where, my lord?"

"My city, Ranulf. It is time for me to return. I must make the journey while I can."

Lord Morwood cleared his throat. He seemed uncomfortable and confused. "My lord, might I ask…why? Your magical seals are no longer holding, I know, but surely you'd be safer here than you will be in Ilithor?"

"He doesn't have a choice," Fhanrir said. He didn't sound happy about it. "He's got to go there eventually."

Ilith nodded. "The heart must be remade in the same place where I unmade it. I must return to my mountain forge. Only there can that wrong be righted." He stood from his armchair, and those groaning sounds returned. "We have done what we can here," the demigod said. "The tides have turned our way, yes…and we may be interested to find what washes ashore." He smiled enigmatically. "We will leave late this evening when the refuge is asleep. Go, make your preparations. I believe I have some studying to do."

The meeting ended there. Amilia walked back through the refuge, returning to Del and his ledgers and the neverending search for the adopted father and sister who were almost certainly dead. The afternoon passed thus. Amilia sat at the table opposite the boy and flipped distracted through the pages. The scholars hummed and whispered around her, moving between lecterns and stacks of books, and that fine papery smell filled the air, with the incense and the ink and the pipe smoke.

Archibald Benton came over to her and droned on about the muster. Men were being recruited for the war now. And no more were being allowed in. That meant there were more going than coming to the refuge these days, and Benton loved to talk about it. Amilia barely heard him. Her mind was on Mallister Monsort. How much time had passed? Had he slept long enough yet? Was it time to go and see him?

She was nervous, she realised. His long absence had made her see just how much she cared about him, and she knew he cared about her too, despite how he'd acted earlier. *He was just tired,* she thought. *Tired and drained and maybe a bit grief struck from all the men he'd lost but once rested…once rested, he'll be my sweet knight again. We'll drink wine and watch the flames leap from the fire and make love…it's been too long since we made love.*

Benton was still going on. He spoke of the seals that were all but disintegrated, of the mages that were dying, of the spies lurking in their midst. Some more had been caught, Amilia already knew, and those who'd escaped were not all accounted for. "I fear they have been borne away south, my lady," the old scholar said, pulling worriedly at his beard. "I fear a dragon was awaiting them in the foothills below, and…"

"No dragons have been seen," she said. She'd spoken to Morwood about that earlier. "They don't fly this far north."

"No, not commonly, no, but if it was prearranged…"

"Then there's nothing we can do." She didn't want to talk about it. She didn't want him spoiling her anticipatory mood. "If you're worried, talk to Fhanrir. You two can worry together."

The man moved away. He was terrified of Fhanrir and was not likely to want to talk to him. Amilia returned to her ledger, flipping pages, scanning details. She sensed Del knew this was a lost cause now, but the boy still came here daily. It was a comfort to him, even if there was no hope. "Has there been word, my lady?" he asked her. "Of Saska and the others?"

"Nothing yet, Del."

He lowered his eyes. If there was one thing he wanted more than finding his family, it was seeing Saska again.

"They can't be far now, Del," she told him. "Any day now, we'll hear word."

He went back to his ledger for a while, scrutinising each page very carefully. With Del, hours could go by with barely a word being spoken, though the silences between them were always perfectly comfortable. "Are you going to see Cevi later?" he asked after a while.

"I saw her earlier this morning."

"Oh." He frowned.

"We could go again, though, if you want. You know, you might as well just stay in her room with her, Del, the amount of time you spend together."

The boy blushed. "We're just friends," he said quickly. "I don't think she likes me like that."

"She does," Amilia said. "I've already told you she does." She leaned across the table. "Perhaps you could kiss her tonight, Del? I know she'd like that, if you did."

He blinked at her. His neck had turned a dark shade of purple and his cheeks looked quite ready to combust. "Did she tell you that?"

"Maybe," she teased. "You'll never know until you try. I'm going to visit with Mallister later, so you two will be all alone. I promise I won't be spying on you from outside." She winked and turned a page. "We can go in an hour or so, how about that?"

He nodded, silent, and suddenly he seemed very nervous. For the next hour they sat and turned their pages, both of them now consumed by the same anticipatory, nervous mood. And when the hour was up, Amilia stood, closing the book and calling over an aide. "Put these back on the shelves," she commanded. "Del, come. It's time to meet your fate."

They found Cevi dozing in her bed, though she woke as they entered through the door. "Look who I brought," Amilia said, and Del followed sheepishly in behind her.

Cevi smiled sleepily at him. She was a sort of plain-but-pretty girl, not beautiful but very sweet to look at, with small, delicate features and a round, tan face. Her eyes were big and bright and brown, very curious about everything and very kind. "Hi, Del. I missed you earlier."

"You…you did?"

"Of course. I always miss you."

Gods, if that doesn't make it clear she likes him, the boy has no hope at all. "Well, I'll leave you to talk," Amilia said. "Some wine, maybe? Would you like some wine?" She went to a table and poured two cups from the jug she was carrying, leaving the rest for her and Mallister. "Enjoy."

There were two guards outside the room, always placed there to protect the girl. Amilia had selected them personally and had them on rotation. Today it was Sir Hammet and Sir Belligar. Both were Emerald Guards. "One of you escort Del back to his room if he leaves."

"If?" asked Hammet, with a grin.

"If, yes. I'm sowing seeds, Hammet. I want to see young love flourish."

"Reckon it's the boy who wants to be sowing his seed," Hammet chuckled.

"And you, my lady?" Belligar asked her. He was the more serious one of the pair. Amilia always tried to have one serious one and one more playful one on guard, if possible.

"I'm going to see Sir Mallister. He returned this afternoon."

Belligar nodded. "I spoke with Rufford. Told me he's gone a little distant, my lady. Sir Mallister, I mean."

"Distant, yes. I plan to try to pull him back closer, Bell."

She left them there, and a pair of other knights went with her. With these spies about, she could not move freely or alone, not even here in the unpopulated part of the refuge.

The halls were cold tonight. Colder than normal, it seemed to her, and eerily, achingly quiet. Her footsteps whispered along the stone floor and her guards trailed clankingly behind her. Mallister's private room was not far. When they reached it, Amilia braced herself, filled her lungs, and lifted her knuckles to knock at the door.

"Mallister," she said. "It's me, Amilia." She heard no answer. "I'm coming in, Mally." She turned the handle and entered. The door swung open and she saw at once that Mallister Monsort wasn't present. The bed sheets were undisturbed and looked unslept in and no fire was burning in the hearth. The room was cold, dreary, grey. She frowned, placed down the wine jug, turned, exited. "He isn't here," she said to her guards.

"Probably meeting with his men, my lady," suggested Sir Fendrel. He was the bland one of this pair. "After so long away, he'll want to take report from them."

"He's a restless sort," agreed Sir Mardon. "Always was. He probably slept already and went off, Highness. Someone might know at the entrance."

She nodded and paced on, her concern brewing. *No, it's fine, everything's fine*, she thought. *He never knew I was coming. He wasn't expecting me.* The air grew colder as they neared the great atrium. It was quieter at this time, and the lumbermen were no longer being sent down into the lower valleys. They had wood enough to last them now and did not want to risk further desertions. Some snow-gathers were still trundling in and out with their carts, but they were few, and half the water vats sat empty, no fires lit beneath them. Sir Fendrel marched ahead to speak to the guards at the great double doors, listened, frowned, nodded, and returned to her.

"What did they say?"

"He's outside."

"Where?"

"On the walls. Looking out over the valley, they said."

"He's taking the watch?"

"Seems to be, my lady."

Sir Mardon shrugged. "Restless, like I said."

"Stay here," Amilia commanded. She pulled her cloak tight about herself and pressed out into the cold. The wind was low, and the air was clear, and she could see the peaks of the mountains clearly against a sky strewn with ten thousand sparkling stars. It was beautiful. Beautiful and *dangerous*. With the magic seals broken, only the weather concealed them now. Clear skies like this could spell their doom.

The Shadowfort was quiet. From the courtyard beyond the refuge door, she saw only a few men standing on watch upon the walls. Her eyes scanned, searching, and then she saw him, away on the southeastern battlements and staring out toward the valley. She turned to her left, climbed a set of stone steps that led up onto the wall walk, and circled around toward him between the drifts of snow.

Mallister was wrapped in a black cloak, and she could see he wasn't wearing his armour or his blades by the shape of his body beneath the wool. His hair was unwashed, still filthy from his travels. It used to be a beautiful blond, but no longer. *He hasn't bathed,* she thought. Most likely he hadn't slept, either.

There was no one near him, no one nearby. He stood lonely and forlorn, his cloak stirring at the hem, facing away from her as she came along the wall walk behind him. Where he stood, the parapet wall opened out to a short stone walkway that ended in black oblivion. Amilia remembered Jonik telling her that executions were performed here. An endless chasm stood before him; he was near the edge, too close to the edge.

"Mallister," she said, carefully. "Why are you standing so close?"

He did not turn to her. He continued to stare out, eyes trained on the far distance. "You shouldn't have come, Amilia."

"Come inside, Mallister. Come inside where it's warm."

He did not answer her, did not look at her. He faced away toward the cold white valley.

"Mallister, please…just come inside where it's warm."

"I can't," he said. "If I come inside now, I…I may weaken. I can't weaken, Amilia. I can't."

"Weaken? I don't understand. Just come inside. Come to bed."

"He's going to brew the potion," Mallister said. "Tomorrow. I…I have to do it before then. She said so. Lhara. If I don't do it the sap will spoil, and the potion…."

"Mallister, what are you talking about?" She edged closer to him. "You're making no sense. Please, just come inside where we can talk."

"I can't." He shifted away from her. "Don't come any nearer, Amilia."

She stopped. "Fine, I won't, I won't. Just…come away from the edge. Come away and we can talk."

"I can't talk. There's no time. The sap will spoil if I don't do it. And Mel…Mel…"

"What about Mel?"

"I can save her," he whispered. His voice was shaking. "I can save her from the Long Abyss, Lhara said. If I don't do it…she'll fall forever. And the sap…the sap…"

"Mallister, please…" She dared to take a step closer, and he shied away, one foot sliding over the precipice, crumbs of ice breaking off and falling. "Don't do this," she pled. "*Please*, don't do this. Ilith won't brew the potion until tomorrow. Talk to him, please. He'll tell you it isn't true."

He shook his head; he would not listen. He turned at last to look at her, smiling, and there were tears in his eyes, she saw, glimmering in those beautiful blue eyes. "I love you, Amilia Lukar," he said. And he smiled again, a soft despairing smile…as he stepped backward into the abyss.

58

Lythian

The feast hall at Elmhall Hold was cold, dark, and dreary.

Two old women were working to light the fire while a small cluster of boys and grey-bearded men pulled an oak table from the stacks piled at one side of the hall and set it up near the hearth. Benches were laid down and jugs of mulled cider and spiced wine were quickly brought out, along with trenchers filled with hot cuts of roasted boar.

Lythian stood with his last two companions nearby, along with Alberfred West, the long-serving steward here at Elmhall. He had been hastily awoken at their coming and sped down at once to greet them.

"Sir Lythian," he said briskly. "A pleasure, a pleasure." He took his steel hand and shook it warmly.

"Alberfred," said Lythian, smiling back. "Nice to see you again. It's been a long while."

"Yes, too long. Much too long since last we hosted you here…and Lord Daecar, of course. Or king, I should say. He is king now we have heard."

"For a while," Lythian confirmed. He gestured to his companions. "This is Sir Storos Pentar, and Vilmar the Black."

The steward smiled. "Two names I know. Though we have not met." He shook Storos's hand, but Vilmar only glared at him and that deterred any such advances.

"Will Lord Devyn be joining us?" Lythian asked.

"No, the good lord is abed. He is very unwell, Lythian, I fear to say. Very frail now in the body, but his mind…" He shook his head. "He does not recognise me when I enter his chambers anymore. Sometimes he comes out in glimpses, but those are few, and largely he spends his time sleeping. When awake he is terribly confused and afraid. It has been very difficult to see him deteriorate."

"You have my condolences," Lythian said. Lord Devyn Blackshaw had once been a powerful warrior, but age and illness had stolen all his strength. "Does he have long to live?"

"Not long," said the steward, shaking his head dismally. "No, not very long at all I would not think, though I have been saying that for some time now. I believe he is trying to cling on, so he might see his son Torvyn again. He remembers *him*, if little else. Oft does he murmur of him in his sleep and pray he might embrace him, just one more time. But I fear...with the war...and with Torvyn so far away..." He shook his head. The rest need not be spoken. "Well, let's sit. We can talk more as you eat."

They moved toward the table, to sit by the fire. The flames were rising and bringing some light and warmth to the room and the rain was falling steadily outside. The boys and the greybeards left as the two old women moved about the hall, lighting torches along the walls, then left as well. Sir Storos and Vilmar attacked the food at once, wolfing it down ravenously, chewing and ripping and swallowing, licking at their fingers and sighing in sweet relief. Alberfred watched, bemused. "Hungry?" he asked, with a chuckle.

Lythian was dining more moderately. "We haven't eaten in two days," he told him, taking a bite of gravy-soaked bread. "The last of our food ran out north of Ayrin's Cross."

The steward frowned and poured the drinks; cider for Storos and Vilmar, wine for Lythian. He had a small cup of wine himself as well. "Ayrin's Cross is fifty miles from here, my lord. That is no small distance to travel afoot in such a time. I am told you did not come with horses."

"Only one," Lythian said. The black gelding that Vilmar had insisted would never last in the Wandering Wood had, in fact, lasted. It was a source of pride for Lythian and one of humiliation for the huntsman. "He is a fine horse, Alberfred. I'm sure you'll treat him well when we leave."

"My lord? You don't plan to take him with you?"

"No. Not the way we intend to go."

"And which way is that, pray?"

"North and then east, up through the Mistwood and across the mountains. We hope to take the *back door* to Ilithor, Alberfred. If we go the common way it'll take weeks. We'd have to cross east to Tukor's Pass and then turn all the way back on oursleves and we don't have the time for that. The way through forest and foothill is only sixty or seventy miles, I know."

The steward fiddled with his little grey chinbeard. "This is true. Though crossing the border by that route is technically illegal. Only sell-swords and smugglers tend to use it, Lythian."

"And knights and princes," Lythian said. "Elyon Daecar came down that very way with Sirs Lancel and Barnibus following his escape from Janilah's cells. And the Flame Manes did as well when they delivered the Windblade to this very hall."

The steward nodded, sipping his warm wine. "They were a queer sort, those Flame Manes. Everything red. Hair, clothing, weapons. Their sigil was monstrous…some flaming-haired skull, if I remember correctly." He fingered his beard. "But they know their way around, to be sure, I won't deny them that. Their leader…Carly I think her name was…she had used that route many times, she told me, though that wasn't the case for the prince. He and his companions found their way down through the foothills easily enough, but navigating the woods proved the better of them. Mooton had to go and find them himself. He…"

"I know what happened, Alberfred. Elyon told me the story himself."

"Oh. You have seen him, then?"

Lythian ignored the question. He didn't need to get into all of that right now. It was too late for it and he was too tired and he wanted this done quickly so he could rest. "We need a guide, Alberfred," he said, getting right to it. "Do you have someone who can show us the way?"

The man's wizened face went thoughtful. He tapped at his chin, *tap tap tap*. "Most of the men have gone away to war, my lord. Sir Anrold gathered them up and left. Do you remember Sir Arnold Claw?"

"Yes." He was the gruff old master-at-arms here, Lythian knew. He had also noticed a certain dearth of soldiers when they entered the humble woodland fort only a few minutes ago. Only two men had been at the gate when they drew it open and they looked disinterested enough.

"Well," said the steward. "Sir Arnold left a while ago with all the Blackshaws he could muster and went down to join Torvyn and Mooton in the south. It concerns me, my lord, to tell it true. We are very poorly defended here now and if there's an attack…with these rumours of Agarathi crawling across the Heartlands and the Wandering Wood…"

Lythian did not have time to spend on the man's concerns. A much more pressing duty drove him. "There must be someone who knows the way, Alberfred. These greybeards. Were none of them ever hunters? Did they not walk those woodland routes?"

"Most were crofters and cobblers and the like, my lord. All the guards here were never trained soldiers. They only took up their spears when the fighting men left and frankly, I'm not sure they know how to use them."

"They won't need to," Storos told him. "No one's going to bother attacking you here."

The steward looked at him. "I hope you're right, sir, truly I do. I know we are not much of a meal for the enemy, but I still have a duty to defend this fort, and…"

"Alberfred," Lythian cut in. "Think. Is there anyone who could help guide us?"

The steward frowned, thinking hard. It took him a moment, and then it came to him. "Ulf," he said, suddenly. "Yes, I think old Ulf might know the way. He was a prominent huntsman in his day, though those days are long since done. He would be your best bet, I should think."

"Is Ulf here now?"

"Yes. He has a small dwelling down in the bailey. If you would excuse me a moment, I will go and see if he is there." The man rose and left the bench, shuffling across the empty hall and out through the groaning door.

Storos stood as well, went over to the fire and began stirring at the coals. He threw on another piece of wood, removed his cloak and hung it to dry, then returned to his boar and cider. "We'll have a featherbed tonight," he said, as he ate and drank and ate some more. "Gods, how long's it been since we left King's Point do you think?"

"Too long," said Lythian. He rose from the bench, unbuckling his swordbelt, placing it aside. He still tried to put distance between himself and the Sword of Varinar where possible, to limit its corruptions. His cloak was removed as well to dry.

"Too *bloody* long," Storos agreed. He gulped down a huge measure of cider and wiped his mouth. "A bath as well. I want a nice warm bath, don't you? Maybe a maid or two to scrub me clean. Never felt so filthy in all my life." He looked down at himself in disgust. "I don't know how you do it, Vilmar. All this living in the wild for weeks on end."

"Try months," the big huntsman rumbled, hunched forward over his meat. He ate like a beast, protecting his food like a predator. "Even years. I was born in the wild, boy. It's home to me. The dark and the storm they call to me."

"Here we go," said Storos, smiling. "And I'll bet you'll find somewhere in the woods to sleep tonight, won't you? No featherbed for Vilmar the Black."

"Feathers are from kills. You pluck them from birds and then you eat the bird and the feathers are discarded. You don't plump them up in pillows for soft fat lords to sleep on."

"Well, you do. The world is full of fat lords and featherbeds, Vilmar. But you enjoy your mattress of mud. I'm sure you'll be very happy out there in the rain."

"I will go," Vilmar said. His black eyes moved from one side of the hall to another. "The only roof I want is that of the canopy, that of the sky."

"What about a cave roof?" asked Storos.

"Yes. Sometimes that as well. Rock, wood, leaf and cloud are the only ceilings that I need."

Storos laughed. "Gods, you're going to *hate* Ilithor if you can't stomach it here. This place is like a little forest shack compared. Those walls outside…did you see them, Lythian? They can't be more than twelve feet high and that gate…I swear, a man breaks wind in front of it and it's likely to come flying off its hinges."

Lythian smiled. He had a fondness for Elmhall, for its humble and modest design, its rustic woodland beauty. *And this forest,* he thought. Lythian had grown up in Mistvale, toward the very north of the Mistwood, and though Elmhall was in the south and hundreds of miles away, he still felt a strange affinity to it all the same.

Storos had another bite of boar. "So…we'll leave tomorrow, then, do you think?"

"Yes. Tomorrow," Lythian said.

"And if this Ulf turns out to be a fraud?"

"We'll make for the back door anyway. I have faith that Vilmar will find the way more quickly than if we were to take the alternative route."

"They have horses here, though," said Storos. "I saw horses in the stables and we'd only need two."

"I don't like riding horses," Vilmar said. "A beast should not ride another beast."

"Then stay. We wouldn't need you anyway if we took the long route." Storos grinned at him. "Might be just as quick if we rode hard, Lythian. What is it…four, five times as long a distance? If we galloped to East-watch, we'd get fresh horses there. Then again at Tukor's Pass. They'd have horses at the Undercloak for us. From there it's, what, a hundred and fifty miles to Ilithor? Two hundred at most. And we'd be in the saddle the whole way. We could even take fresh mounts with us and swap along the way to let them rest."

"If you're tired of walking, Storos, just say so."

"All right, I'll say so. *I'm tired of walking.* And jogging, running, barely sleeping, those too. I'll not lie, Lythian, I wouldn't mind enjoying a bit of saddle work for a while."

"You've had your time in the saddle, Storos." The pair had shared the use of the indefatigable black gelding. Vilmar, of course, didn't ride and so had been on his feet the entire time. Lythian decided to point that out. "Vilmar, how old are you?" he asked.

"Age is meaningless," was the big huntsman's answer. "How old is the storm, boy, how old is the darkness?"

He was playing up to it now. "He's in his mid-sixties," Lythian said to Storos. "And he has walked and run and jogged the whole way, and you don't hear him complaining." Well, not about *that*, anyway. Vilmar did like to complain about other things, of course. "We can rest properly when we reach the White City. And this talk of horses is speculative."

"How?"

"It assumes they have two Bladeborn-bearers here in the stables."

"One," Storos said. "Vilmar just said he doesn't like to ride. So we'd only need one."

"We both know Vilmar isn't leaving us, Storos. Not until our task is complete. So we would need two additional horses if we were to try to make good time. And three fresh mounts at Eastwatch and Tukor's Pass if we expect to flog them hard."

"Well…that's just an idea. We don't *have* to run them into the ground like that. We could just let them rest while we stay the night in the forts. Going through those woods and up into the foothills, even the higher ranges? It'll be slow going, Lythian. The rain. The *snow*. It's falling thickly up in the north, we've heard. It might be quicker by horseback."

"Or it may be much longer. And we do not know what we might meet along the way. The forest and foothills is the safer route."

"How do you figure that? Could be all sorts of creatures crawling about that way."

"And that's why we have Vilmar. To lead us from such perils, as he has done for so long." It was pointless discussing it. "Let's just wait and see, Storos. If there are no Bladeborn-bearing horses here, it's all moot anyway."

"There aren't," Vilmar put in. He slurped on his cider, dribbling some down into his thick black beard. "I knew Pentar would go on about this, so I had a good long sniff of those horses as we passed. Not a Bladeborn bearer among them. They're hobby horses, field horses, mountain horses, not warhorses."

"Then it's settled," Lythian said. He was glad to have that resolved. "We'll take the forest-and-foothill route."

Storos shrugged and refilled his cider. "Well, I'll have my featherbed at least. And my bath. A nice hot bath is some consolation I'd say." He drank his mug halfway down, then stood again. "I'm going to find those old women who lit the fire. Make sure they get some water on the boil for me." He finished his mug, refilled it, and went off searching, cup in hand.

Vilmar grunted as he left. "He's going to get drunk tonight."

"That's fine. He's earned it. We've been going hard for a long while."

"Aye, because of that letter." The huntsman snorted. "We've come a long way based on a whim, Lythian."

Was it a whim? Lythian didn't believe so. In fact, he believed in the contents of the letter wholeheartedly and had put all his faith in its instruction.

Bring the Sword of Varinar to Ilithor with all haste, it read. *Word is being sent to all the other bearers before its too late. You must go, and go now. Destroy this note upon receipt.*

And that was it; those were the words. Quite why Brontus had kept the letter Lythian couldn't say. Perhaps it was some small part of him that still leaned toward goodness, a part not entirely ensnared by the grip of the blade. Maybe that part even hoped Lythian would come, hoped he would release him, find the letter, and retrieve and deliver the blade. Or maybe it was all a hoax. Lythian could not be sure. Oloran had said the letter was delivered by an eagle and it was signed by a person who called himself the Second Elder. Vilmar told him that probably referred to these people of the Everwood, who bonded eagles once upon a time, but he didn't know much about that. Still, it was enough for Lythian Lindar to change their course. It felt right to him, somehow. *Vandar's Heart was broken in Ilithor*, he thought. It made sense that was where it would be remade.

Storos returned before Alberfred West, reporting that the women had been instructed to fill baths for all. "Even you, Vilmar. When was the last time you washed? During that storm you were born in?" He laughed and refilled his mug.

A few minutes later, the steward re-entered the dim-lit feast hall with a concerningly old-looking man at his side. "This is Ulf," he said.

"M'lords," said Ulf. He was of middling height, lean of build, knobbly and haggard as a tree branch, with smoke grey hair swept back from a thinning scalp. The skin folds and wrinkles about his face were many and deep and bristly grey-black stubble grew coursely from his cheeks and chin.

"You're a hunter?" Lythian asked.

"I was, aye. Long time ago." He pointed to a painted map above the hearth, depicting the Mistwood from top to bottom. "Used to go all over," he said, and his finger went all over. "Once I knew every tree in the forest and every bird in every branch. Had names for them too. Sure I could remember a few."

"Braggard alert," Storos said, a little drunkenly. He'd put back a lot of cider now. "He's one of yours, Vilmar."

"A hunter are you?" the man Ulf asked. He grinned knowingly. "Well, course you are. What hunter doesn't know Vilmar the Black? A pleasure to meet your greatness," he said to the huntsman, bowing to him as though he were a king. "Legend among us hunters, this one, m'lords. Most famous huntsman of the age."

"And the dozen ages gone before," said Storos, hiccuping. "Or so he likes to claim."

"Well, don't know about that," said Ulf. "Can't be forgetting Morrick now can we? Morrick the Many-Face, they called him. Used to make masks of the monsters he killed. And Skarf the Blind. Well, the name says it all. Was born without eyes, was Skarf, yet still hunted everything that could be hunted."

Vilmar grunted. "That's a myth. Skarf never hunted alone. He always had his four sons with him."

"Oh? Is that so?" Ulf considered that for a while, reevaluating. Then he peered at Vilmar and asked, "What happened to your neck there, m'lord? Looks a nasty wound."

"I was bitten by a dead man," Vilmar said. The flesh was still raw where Brontus Oloran had taken a chunk out of him, though thankfully no infection had set in. Vilmar couldn't get infected, he claimed, and was immune to all venoms and poisons. He narrowed his dark eyes and peered back at the man Ulf, judging him. "Tell me of your best conquest," he growled. "Every huntsman has a conquest they're most proud of."

"Oh, glad to, glad to," said Ulf. He bustled up to the table, reaching for the wine jug. "Mind if I...?" He didn't wait for permission, filling a cup to the brim, then drank. "Not sure I've got any stories to impress the likes of you, though, m'lord. All boar and bear around these parts, and not of the great or grim variety, if you follow me. I never hunted much for that, anyway. Tracking rare beasts, I mean, and taking trophies. Sometimes, aye, but that was never my main thing."

"And what was?" Lythian asked.

"Riches," said the man Ulf, shamelessly. "*Profits*, m'lord, that was my thing." He drank his wine and licked his lips. "Pelts, mostly. Bear and beaver, wolf and vair. Plenty of that in the woods hereabouts…back in my day anyway. Used to turn a tidy income selling them across the border."

"So you're a trapper," Vilmar said. He sounded disappointed.

"Aye, suppose you could call me that." Ulf smiled happily; his teeth were yellow and wonky. "Me and some buddies would hunt here in the Mistwood, then take the pelts across the mountains. Better that way, as we saw it. You go the long way around through Tukor's Pass and you've got to pay them tariffs. Daylight bloody robbery, I call that. Took big old bites out of our profits, so we thought, why not, let's take the back door."

"So you're a smuggler too," Storos said.

"Aye. Hunter, trapper, smuggler. I'm all three." He sounded very proud.

Lythian smiled at him. He liked the man's barefaced honesty. "Then you know the way?" he asked. "Across the mountains to Ilithor?"

"Aye, I know it."

"And you'll guide us?"

"Sure, why not? I'm just wasting away around here. And what hunter could pass up a chance to walk with Vilmar the Black?" He grinned at the big man and drank his wine. "So, when do you want to leave? Dawn works for me."

It worked for Lythian as well, though he suspected Sir Storos Pentar might appreciate a couple of hours of extra rest. "Shortly after dawn," he said. "We can reconvene here in the morning. Alberfred. I'd ask that you provide us with food for the journey. How long would you say it will take, Ulf?"

The man considered. "Well, that depends how quickly you want to get there, m'lord. You don't seem so interested in taking in the sights."

"No. This is a matter of great urgency." He looked Ulf up and down, wondering how quickly this happy smuggler could go. Old though he was, he looked robust enough and in fine fettle for his years. "So? How long?"

"A week," he answered. "That's going at a moderate pace. Can probably squeeze a couple of days off if we must, depending."

"On?"

"On what we find. Might be curtailed by some creature or find a route too badly laden with snow. I'd say pack up food for ten days, just in case. Might do it in half that time, but better to make sure."

"Very well then. We'll need food for four for ten days, Alberfred."

"Of course, my lord. I will see everything prepared. And…might I suggest also a change of clothes?" He wrinkled his nose. "Fresh garb can be provided. And warmer cloaks for the cold."

Lythian nodded. That would be welcome too. He stood from his bench. "Do you have a bedchamber ready for me to sleep in, Alberfred?"

"Yes, my lord. We keep several available for our guests."

"Show me." Lythian swung a leg over the bench, took up his cloak and swordbelt and bid the others goodnight.

Alberfred led him up the winding stone stair and to a south-facing bedroom with a bath-chamber down the hall. An old woman and two boys were coming and going with pails of steaming water, while another woman carried in a tray of soaps, sponges, and scrubbing brushes. Alberfred guided Lythian into the bedchamber and went to the window to close the shutters. It was dark and rainy out there, and the distant murmur of thunder could be heard far away.

"The bath ought to be ready for you soon," the steward said. They could hear the soft sound of sloshing down the hall as the tub was filled. Alberfred went to the bed and made sure it was freshly made. "How long has it been since you slept on a proper bed, my lord?"

"A long time," said Lythian. "Before the fall of King's Point."

"Well, it will make a nice change for you, then. You have the look of a man who could sleep for a week, if you don't mind me saying."

Lythian didn't mind at all. He could probably sleep for two. He looked at the bed. It was large and appeared very comfortable, but Lythian would find no comfort here. "Is that bed reinforced?" he asked.

The steward was plumping the pillows. He looked over. "Reinforced, my lord?"

"To bear godsteel," Lythian said.

The man seemed confused. "You…intend to sleep in your armour, my lord?"

Lythian Lindar had completed his vow. After the Sword of Varinar had been stolen from his safekeeping, he had told himself he would not take off his armour again until such a time as he held it in his grasp. For the last ten days, since retrieving it from Brontus Oloran, they had been making all haste across the kingdom, through rain and sleet and sometimes snow, beneath skies grim and wet and cold. They had stopped only to rest a few hours before moving on, never sleeping a full night, crossing open fields and plains by moonlight if there was any, beneath the stars when they briefly came out.

For those first three days since the fight with Oloran and his men, they had remained in the northern reaches of the Wandering Wood, but the last week had seen them emerge into the Heartlands and the vast openness of central Vandar. They had crossed fields and rivers, past abandoned farms and crofts, seen the bodies of Vandarians and Agarathi alike, some fresh, some old and rotted down to bones, and the destruction of the land was far-ranging. Sometimes they passed vagrants on the road, or saw hosts of soldiers moving here and there, but never did they interact with them. Lythian could not stop or slow, he could not be delayed. *Ilithor*, he thought. *I must get to Ilithor with all speed.* He wanted to be free of the blade once and for all, free of the whispers and the lures and the threats, and Ilithor was where he'd break those chains; in Ilithor, the curse would end.

So *that*, now, was his vow. *Ilithor. I'll remove my armour only when I get to Ilithor.* Perhaps he could do so tonight, here at Elmhall, if he wished. They were under no imminent threat tucked away in these woods, and he could dress quickly if he must, but that vow had been made now and could not be unmade. It had worked in his hunt for Oloran and it would work again now, he told himself. *Ilithor,* he thought. *I'll only undress when I get to Ilithor.*

"My lord?" Alberfred prompted. Lythian had been silent for a very long time. "You're not to remove your armour, then? What about your bath?"

"Forget the bath, Alberfred," Lythian said. "Storos can have two. Goodnight."

59

Amara

They returned to the city at dusk, flying out from the west beneath clouds drenched red.

Amara stood on a west-facing balcony of Keep Kanabar, pink-cheeked and panting, alerted at once to their coming. She'd had men on watch at all hours so she might know the very moment they were sighted, and had run hard down the corridor to be here. She peered out against the darkening skies, unable to see them as yet. "Where are they, Carly? Point them out."

Carly's Bladeborn eyes were keen and fierce. She raised a finger, "There, my lady. That shape there, do you see it?"

Amara squinted. It took her a moment and then she saw. To her eyes, they were hardly more than a dark smudge in the distance, easily mistaken for a bird at a glance, but they were coming nearer all the time. "Do they look hurt, Carly? Wounded?"

"No, my lady. They look fine to me. Though…" She paused.

"What is it? Tell me."

"Elyon is grimacing, my lady. But that's probably just from the effort. He looks very tired."

"They've come a long way," Amara said. She felt weak, suddenly, almost sick with relief. She breathed out, putting a hand to the stone balustrade to steady herself and Sir Penrose went quickly to fill her a cup of water.

"Are you well, my lady? Should I fetch Master Artibus?" he asked.

"No, Pen…I'm fine, fine." She sipped the cold water, catching her breath, and heard steel footsteps skittering up behind her. A moment later Lillia came bursting out onto the balcony, sweating and beaming, dressed in her armour. Jovyn was right behind her, and Sir Daryl Blunt as well.

"We just heard the call," Sir Daryl said, panting. "The little lady was running rings around us in the yard again, Amara. What's that expression? Saved by the bell." He laughed that famous laugh of his. Darly Blunt was no comely man, but he had the most handsome laugh in all the world, Amara had always thought.

"Why are they moving so slowly?" Lillia asked. She was pressed right up against the parapet, all but climbing up to get a better look. The pair were nearing the western city walls now and making for the direction of the keep. "Elyon can fly at a hundred miles an hour, can't he?"

"Only when flying alone," Amara said. "And in short bursts. Your father is a big man, Lillia." She wondered about the *fragment* as well, the very thing they had flown so far to find. How much did that weigh? The last little bit of Vandar's spirit? She had another sip of water and was starting to feel a little better. "Lillia, be a sweetheart and go and get changed into something pretty. Your father will want to see you more presentable."

"I don't want to look pretty or presentable," Lillia said. "I have to get used to wearing armour all the time now. Elyon said he didn't take his off for weeks when he was away. He'd sleep it in and everything. It'll be the same for me when we leave for the war."

The girl was incorrigible. It was as though she was trying to will into being this idea of her going to war by talking about it all the time, insisting it would happen. It was starting to get under Amara's skin and made her feel very uneasy. Many times she had attempted to describe to Lillia the horrors of war, and had even recruited old warriors like Sir Bryce Coddington and Lord Robert Borrington, who had terrible ugly scarring, to do it for her. But Lillia remained unperturbed and never seemed to hear them.

It was Brydon, damn him, Amara Daecar thought. *He told her no at dinner, so now Lillia simply must defy him, even in death.*

"Lillia, you are testing my patience. Do you want to give me an aneurysm? Because you will at this rate…you'll be the death of me, child."

"Don't be dramatic, Auntie. You're always so dramatic."

"Dramatic? I am quite happy to show you dramatic, little lady. You're not so old that I won't bend you over my knee and redden your rump right here." She glared at her. "Now go and get changed. Right now."

"Fine. Gods, fine, if it means that much to you." She whirled around and left, marching from the balcony.

"Carly, go with her, make sure she picks out something nice. Jovyn, you too." They left as well.

Amara returned her attention to father and son. She could just about make out their faces now, see the weary expressions and tired eyes, the great strain in Elyon's eyes as he flew them across the city. She raised an arm and waved for them, shouting, but they did not seem to hear. "Right, all of us," Amara said, and Daryl and Penrose raised their voices as well, and that seemed to get their attention.

"They're coming this way, my lady," Daryl said.

"I can see that, Daryl. Let's step back and make room."

They drew back from the balcony edge to open up space for them to land. Amara found that Artibus had appeared from his private study, and had come up to stand behind her in his plain old robes. "A red dusk," he observed thoughtfully. "What do we think? A good omen or bad?"

"Good. They're back, Artibus. I would call that good news."

"Only if they got what they went for," the old scholar said.

"They did," Amara told him.

"How do you know?"

"Because they wouldn't have come back if they didn't."

Elyon was bringing them down to land now, and the dismount was not the most graceful. Everyone moved away from the swirling winds as king and prince set feet upon stone, and were it not for Amron being harnessed to his son, Elyon would surely have collapsed. As it was, the straps and buckles held him up. Amara could see Elyon's eyes rolling exhaustedly inside his skull, see his features collapse from sudden paralysing fatigue. His arm fell heavily, and the Windblade slipped from his grasp to clatter and rattle on the stone.

"Help me with him," Amron said urgently, "Quickly. He spent all his strength to get us here."

The king began unbuckling his harness. Penrose and Daryl rushed in to help, and Sir Miles Hewitt appeared then as well, charging down the corridor to join them. As soon as the king and the prince were untethered, Elyon's legs gave way and he folded down to the ground, clinging to consciousness by a thread.

Artibus hurried right in, "Elyon, Elyon, speak to me now, Elyon." The prince was passing out, his eyes swivelling into the back of his skull as his head wobbled loose on his neck. Aritbus conducted a quick check of his vital signs. "He's going into shock," he said. "Quickly, get him up and into bed. Hurry, hurry."

Amara stood by barely breathing as the three knights heaved Elyon up into their arms and rushed him down the corridor to Amron's room. They piled in through the door, set him down again and began stripping him out of his armour. Artibus was there all the while, scurrying about, giving orders. He dashed away for a moment and returned quickly with a tonic, by which time Elyon had been placed in bed.

"Open his mouth," Artibus ordered, and Sir Penrose did so, pulling his jaws open. The tonic was poured inside as Artibus pinched the prince's nose until it was swallowed, then looked at him, appraising, nodded, and turned. His old face was furious. "My gods, what were you thinking, Amron? To drive him that hard? A man like you should know better."

The king stood back from the bed, cold with worry. "Will he be all right?"

"What did you give him?" Amara asked.

"Mint, sage, rosemary, among other things. It will help soothe his nerves and rehydrate him. And he'll be fine, after some rest." Amara breathed out, Amron visibly relaxed, and Artibus continued his tirade.

"You pushed him too hard, Amron," he scolded. "You should have stopped to rest somewhere. Why did you not rest?"

"I asked him to stop many times," Amron said. "He insisted he wanted to make it back by nightfall."

"Asked him? You asked him to stop? You're his father and his king. You should *tell* him." He shook his head angrily. "If this city was but a mile further away he may have suffered a cardiac arrest or collapsed in the act of flying. You should have *made* him stop, Amron. You should have seen the signs and demanded it."

Amron had nothing to say to him.

"Go, then," Artibus said. "All of you, go. Elyon needs to rest and I don't want any disturbances."

"How long will he be unconscious?" Amara asked, softly. Her heart was still thumping from the fear of it all.

"I don't know. Until morning, I hope. I'll monitor him for a little while, but all should be well. Now leave us, please. I will come if there is any news."

They filed out of the room, closing the door quietly behind them. Amara's hand was shaking, she realised. She held it up and looked at it, and then stepped right in and gave Amron a hug. "I'm sorry about him. You know how he gets."

"It's fine, Amara. He only does it because he cares."

She held him tight a moment longer and then let him go. His face was cast grim and tired as he turned to address the three knights. "We cannot leave the Windblade on that balcony," he said. "Go and bring it to Elyon's bedside. You should be able to move it together. If Artibus shouts at you, blame me. He seems quite irate with me anyway."

Amron turned at once and walked the other way down the corridor. Amara followed after him, her slippered shoes whispering on the stone floor. Torches lit the way, held in sconces shaped as muscular arms and armoured hands and sometimes the antler of an elk. Everything was big and bold and masculine in Keep Kanabar. "Where are you going, Amron?" Amara asked.

"The Steelforge," he said. "We have to keep the blades separated."

Of course. They'd done that before they left as well. Elyon said having two blades close together was dangerous and thus they must be kept apart. "Did anything happen?" she asked. "Having the two blades together for so long?"

"If you're wondering if we attracted any dragons or other dangers, no, we faced no such threat."

"But you fear we may here?"

"It's possible. Out where we went the world was dead and deserted. But here...no. We must take all precautions."

They marched on for a while in silence. There was a rather large dragon in the room that Amron seemed to be ignoring, but Amara could ignore it no longer. "So...did you get what you went for?"

"Yes. We got it."

"And? Do you have it with you now? Can I see?"

"There is nothing much to see," he said. "The fragment is not physical."

She had expected it to be some sort of magnificent jewel or something, a fragment of rock glowing in ethereal blue and silver, but perhaps that was stupid. Those were the colours of the kingdon, yes, but only devised by Varin after Vandar's fall. "What is it then? If not physical?"

"An essense. I have it contained in a pot."

"A *pot*? You have the last vestige of Vandar's spirit in a *pot*?"

"Yes," the king said. He was being frustratingly short on the matter, and very miserly with his descriptions.

"Well…how did you get it? Was it difficult? Did you do it or Elyon?"

"I did."

A small hope flared in her. She watched the king walk for a moment, studied the way he moved. His thigh, his shoulder. *Is he healed? Was all that business with Black Merryl for nought?* She saw that he was holding the hilt of the Frostblade, but maybe that was just habit. "Amron…" she started.

"I'm not healed, Amara."

Her enthusiasm sagged down into her guts. "So…there was no blessing?"

He ignored the question. "Gereth asked me to send his love," he said, moving things on. "We stopped at Blackfrost on the way back."

"Is he well?"

"He's fine. He had word from the Twinfort, Amara. Randall Borrington has largely recovered from his neck wound and is assembling what strength is left to him in the west. He says the Agarathi passed the Last Bastion and swarmed back out across the Briddle Steppe. They returned to their ships and sailed south, as we had expected."

"And no word as to where they'll invade next?"

"No, nothing. I gave orders for Randall to hold at the Twinfort for now, and the Ironfoot will be shoring up the Point. With our victory in the east we have given ourselves space to breathe…at least for now."

For now, yes. Until a certain dragon comes a-calling.

"How is the child, Amara?"

She smiled. "Fine. Horrible, but fine."

He raised a brow at her.

"Don't give me that look. You wait until *you* have a parasite growing inside you and making you feel all sorts of ill. A little horror, she is, but I love her. It will be worth it all in the end."

Amron looked worried all of a sudden. "Is there pain?"

"Of course there's pain. But it's nothing too unusual, Artibus says. I'm a hundred days in now, Amron. I could describe to you all the things that are going on inside me, but I daresay you'd rather not hear about them."

"Well…I'm sure Artibus has you in good hands."

They reached the main stair that curved down into the capacious entrance hall. At the door they found Sir Hank Rothwell dispensing orders to some of his men. He turned and saw the king and stepped right over, bowing. "Your Majesty. I just had a man tell me that Lord Strand is on his way here to see you. He had sentries watching the skies, my lord. I suspect he wants to be the first to hear your news."

Ah yes. Styron the Strong must always be first in the pecking order. Amara did not want that to happen. She was still waiting for a chance to tell him the grim news of Brydon Amadar's death and would not have Styron painting it any worse than it was. And that was bad enough, Amara knew, with all the rumours going around…

"Others will be coming as well, no doubt," she said. "They'll all want a bite of you, Amron. Are you sure you're up to that now?"

She could see his mind moving. The king was tired, drained, and clearly wanted to retreat to the sanctuary of the Steelforge before having to deal with the likes of Lord Strand. "Sir Hank, would you do me a favour?"

"Of course, sire. Anything."

"Please inform Lord Strand and anyone else who might come calling that I am resting after my journey. Tell them it's late and I will convene a council on the morrow, to share my tidings and hear their own."

"As you command, my lord."

Amron turned to Amara, "We'll take the back way out."

She smiled thinly as he led her away toward the rear of the keep, satisfied with her subtle manipulations. The way took them out of the postern gate, through the rear grounds, and down a stone path that led straight to the lakeshore, where a boardwalk ran east and west along the water. The dusk was setting in deeply by then and the shadow of the Steelforge could be seen out on its island, a little further to the east.

Usually, this stretch of shore would be bustling with little fishing vessels, but everything was being run from outside the city now, under the stewardship of the Orca Lord and his people. Amara spoke a little of that and informed Amron that the nets were now coming in full, that sharks, swordfish, and seals were being caught in great quantity, and that all other perils were quickly being tamed and overwhelmed. "They're astonishing," was her summary. "Every local fisherman I've spoken to says they've never seen hunters quite like them."

"Good," Amron said. "I had hoped as much. Has he asked for what he wants in return yet?"

"The Orca Lord?"

"Yes."

"My hand in marriage, hopefully."

He side-eyed her. "Are you serious?"

"Only partly. He is a remarkably attractive man, Amron. And near enough my own age. Who wouldn't want to marry him?"

He frowned at her, displeased. "Have you forgotten my brother so quickly?" he demanded.

That annoyed her. *More than* annoyed her. She was only being playful, but he was too blind to see it. She huffed and chose not to respond, marching on briskly ahead of him. *This is good,* she thought. *Be angry, yes. Maybe it will lessen the blow of his rebuke?*

She wondered if now was the time to just come out and say it. The shore here was deserted and there was no one else around. Rocks ran along the water's edge to their left and the city rose up grandly to the right, half broken upon its many hills. *Just tell him,* she thought. *Just get it done and tell him.*

She turned around and faced him. "Your good-father is dead," she said.

He stopped, staring at her for a long, drawn moment. The gulls were cawing as they flew overhead while some others bobbed on the water. It was as though they were gathering to watch, sensing the drama. "What happened?" he asked. "Did his company come under attack on the road?"

"He choked to death at dinner. Some in the city are blaming me."

His eyes were beginning to narrow. "And why should they blame you?" He could not keep the suspicion from his tone.

She was on the back foot at once; she could feel herself growing defensive. "They call it witchcraft," she said, speaking quickly. "I happened to visit Black Merryl that very morning and spoke with her alone in her tent. Rumours have circulated since, linking the two events. They say I went to the witch to get poison and planned to murder Brydon that night."

"And did you?"

She stared at him in shock. "Did I? Only in my bloody head, Amron! How can you even ask me that?"

"He conspired to have you imprisoned and tortured. You killed Godrik Taynar, Amara. Why not him as well?"

A hot fierce flush was rising to her cheeks. "And you think I'd be so stupid as to use a dose of poison at the dinner table? So callous that I'd kill Lillia's grandfather in front of her very eyes?" She was frankly astonished he would even suggest it. "The gods know I never liked Brydon Amadar, but I never wanted him *dead*, Amron." She was breathing heavily, staring at him, shaking her head. "Talk to Artibus if you don't believe me. He was there as well. He'll tell you what happened."

"I'm asking you."

"You're *accusing* me."

"Calm down, Amara. Take a breath."

She did. She took a breath and another and another, each one short and sharp. "Brydon was drinking heavily that night. He gulped down that boar like it was the last bloody boar on earth and he choked, that's it, he choked. Artibus tried to help but it made no matter, and then Sir Michael rushed into the room. He tried to save his lord, but he couldn't. He saw the purple face, the scratches on the neck, and Brydon…Brydon looked at me, just as he died. Sir Michael saw it. He read too much into it. And he stormed from the hall crowing murder."

Amron was frowning darkly now. The gulls were circling, watching, silent, like crows above a kill, sensing death. Amara felt a pain in her belly. "And?" the king asked.

She grimaced. "And he left," she grunted. "Took the Amadar men and left. They're gone, all of them. Back to Ilivar. They're gone."

He stared at her. "Gods, Amara, what did you do? We can ill afford to…

"What did *I* do?" she shouted. "What did *I* do? I didn't *do* anything, Amron! You're not listening to me, you're not listening. He just choked on his bloody boar…"

A fierce cramp seized at her. She was assaulted by a sudden wave of dizziness, and the world swayed and tilted as though trying to swallow her up. A grunt of pain slipped out through her lips as she doubled over, and there was a wetness there, a warm wetness between her legs.

"Amara, what's wrong?" Amron's voice was blurred. He was moving forward, rushing toward her, but too late.

The dusk was red, a deep blood red.

And the stone rushed up to meet her.

60

Talasha

She had come in the hope of finding help, but instead she found only death.

She had known it as she approached. She had seen it from afar, and smelt it.

They flew high above the burned and blackened forest, and into its holy heart. Towering tall were the Twelve Trees, once hidden by Aramatian's seals, but no longer. Towering tall they remained, but black and dead and lightless. *The light has left this wood,* she thought. *The power of the goddess is gone.*

Neyruu flew down through the fog of fume and the grey shroud that still lingered here. Below, the great glade came into view, once a place of trickling streams and pretty meadows, of laughing children and merry mothers and old women weaving baskets beneath the silvery light of the leaves. Now the old women were gone, and the mothers and the children, and only bones remained, bones and ash, and the streams had spoiled and gone brown and grey.

Neyruu came to land with a thick puff of ash billowed up by the pulse of her wings. All about them the colossal trees soared up, the Twelve Trees in which the Calacania had lived, and the Elders atop them, but no longer. The boles were burned, and the branches and the leaves, and the canopies were withered and thin. The wooden walkways had collapsed, and the ladders and the stairs, and the huts and the homes and the great carven platforms were gone, and high up atop the trees, the eyries were no longer there. *All is ash and ruin,* Talasha thought, forlorn. *I should never have come here. It was pointless to come.*

She dismounted all the same, climbing down from Neyruu's flank to go walking through this gloomy grey graveyard. Ash floated about her, eddying on drifts, and each footstep stirred death from the forest floor. Scorched bodies lay silent beneath blankets of soot and cinder, the bodies of the old and the young alike, of men, women, and children, scores of them, hundreds of them, all heaped in their little ash tombs. Most were in the south of the glade, she saw, where it reached the border of the Greater Everwood. *They were trying to flee*, she knew. *Did any escape? Are any still out there?*

She opened her mouth and called, "Hello? Hello? Is anyone there?" Her voice echoed dully through the shrouded glade, swallowed and smothered by the smog. She walked on, Neyruu following slowly behind her, past the great shadows of the dead trees, beneath the creaking lament of their limbs as they rattled in the wind above her. "Hello? Is anyone there? Hello?" She got no answer. No one heard or called back or appeared in the drifting fog. *We are alone here*, she thought, to Neyruu. *Still alone, as we have been for weeks.*

She walked on, further eastward through the glade. Beyond the cover of the soaring canopies and lightless leaves the clearing in the forest opened out to the east. She went solemnly, slowly, across the flowerless meadows and poisoned streams where the ashen water ran sluggish and grey. She remembered walking here before, during those days she'd stayed with these sweet simple people. She remembered how welcoming they were, how kind, how the little children would follow her through the meadows as she went, giggling and holding her hand, how the women would watch her, smiling and nodding their heads, how those who could speak in the Aramatian tongue would tell her how lovely she was, how radiant and beautiful. "You belong here," they would say to her. "A face like yours, so lovely and bright. You belong here among the light of the trees."

Talasha's lips twisted at the memory. She reached up to touch her face, that once beautiful face now blighted and destroyed like this glade. Elyon had sewn up the wounds as best he could, and she had used what healing balms she had, but there was little else she could do. Several of the cuts had gone deep, deep down to the bone of her cheek and chin, and one had torn a savage gash across her forehead, splitting it open to the skull. "My lady, I wish you would let me lead you to Rockfall," Elyon had said. "You will get help there, proper help. I do not have the skill to…"

"I'm not going to Rockfall," she had told him, emptily. "Do what you can, Elyon. It won't matter in the end."

It had been weeks since then, weeks since she had left the prince and the Nightblade on that open field in Rasalan, as Saska's company came riding over the hills. Talasha could not bear to be seen. Nor could she risk another priest finding her again, drawn by the scent of her blood. "Where will you go?" Elyon had asked her. His eyes were tortured by what he'd done, tortured by shame, but it wasn't his fault. *He only tried to save my life*, she knew. She did not blame him for that.

"Away," had been her answer. "Somewhere far away from here."

She had flown aimlessly after that, not knowing where she would end up. She had flown to lonely islands and crept into forgotten caves and taken refuge in abandoned hillforts, creeping across the world like a ghost. Sometimes she wondered if she might go south, back to the Western Neck, to walk those woods again and remember those days with Lythian, but she never did. It would be too painful to revisit something she could never have again. Too painful to think of their love, their sweet blossoming love, knowing her noble knight was maybe dead already, and if not, if not…

He will never love me now.

She cringed at the thought, at that terrible despairing thought, because she was a monster now, she knew. When she dared to look at her reflection in a pond or a puddle, she would see a broken creature staring back, a face to make children run and weep, a face to creep up in the dark of night and torment them in their sleep.

It will get better, she had tried to tell herself. *When the swelling goes down, and the scars knit tighter, it will get better.* She applied her balms daily. She kept the wounds clean as best she could. She tried not to look…tried to leave it days so there would be some improvement, but her heart sank whenever she finally gave in. *I am a monster,* she would only think again, quickly turning her eyes away.

She continued listlessly now through the glade, stirring ash with every stride. The thought had come to her a few days ago, a last desperate hope, if a faint one, that she might find her salvation here. The *Spring,* she had thought, as she sat in a cold damp cave on the Crescent Coast of Rasalan, staring out across the Stormy Sea. *Maybe the Spring of Aramatia can heal me? Maybe that holy water can restore my face?*

It had the power to strengthen, she knew, and the power to invigorate. The Elders drank from the Spring to deepen their bonds to their eagles, and Ranulf did as well, when he bonded Kamcho. She had not heard them talk of its healing properties, but in truth she had never asked. *I must fly there,* she realised, in that cave. *I must fly there and find out.*

So she had, she had flown in hope, and now that hope was gone. The streams were spoilt, and the little fishing pools were polluted, and what hope of the Spring being clean?

It was further ahead across the glade, down in the southeastern corner. She could almost see to the edge of the clearing now, see the trees coming and going behind the bands of broken mist, see the great redwoods and looming pines that soared to the sky. The Everwood was burned out there as well, and the air was dim and grey and gloomy. *There is no light,* she realised. Like the leaves in the trees, the Spring of Aramatia had glowed with an eternal radiance. But it was gone like all the rest. The light in that well had run dry.

"Sad, isn't it?" said a voice.

Talasha's eyes flashed quickly to her right. A figure was appearing from the gloom, a man of middle years, dressed in a tunic of roughspun wool and a cloak of ruffly eagle feathers. He had black hair pulled back in a sharp widow's peak, thick whiskers growing from his cheeks, but not his chin. His upper lip was shaven and drawn up in a friendly smile. It seemed very odd to smile here, with all this death and despair.

"I hope I didn't frighten you," he said. "You seemed very deep in thought."

"Who are you?" she asked. Her voice was rusty from lack of use, and hostile from lack of contact. It had been a long time since she'd spoken with anyone. "Are you one of the Calacania?"

The man smiled. "Well, sort of. *This* man was, anyway, before he died. Though I go by a thousand names."

That made no sense to her. "Did you hit your head?"

"Oh, oh no," he said, laughing. "It was the smoke that killed him. All the ash and fume. Choked him out, poor fellow. But me, no. I wasn't here when it happened. I was dying somewhere else, if you'd believe it. Over in Lakeheart. Though that happened a little later."

He's mad, she thought, backing away from him. She glanced at Neyruu, wondering why the dragon had not alerted her to the stranger's arrival, but she seemed more curious than anything and was not rumbling or growling at him as she might if he was a threat.

The man smiled at Neyruu, dipping his head courteously. "I like your dragon," he said to Talasha. "She's very pretty, much prettier than most I've seen, and I've seen many, believe me." He admired her a moment longer, smiling all the while, then his eyes were on Talasha again. "You are very beautiful as well, of course. I would not want you to feel left out."

Her jaw tightened. "Are you mocking me?" she asked him.

"No. I am not mocking you."

"You sound like you are mocking me." Talasha wore a cloak over her hunting leathers, a deep maroon cloak with a large hood, but currently that hood was resting at the nape of her neck and the terrible scarring on her face was exposed.

"I am not mocking you," the man repeated, earnestly. "The scars do not diminish your beauty. Truly. I believe that."

You don't, she thought. *No one could.* She retreated into herself a moment, reaching down to pull up her hood. Her face descended into shadow, where it now belonged. "I shouldn't have come," she said. "I'm sorry if I disturbed you."

"You didn't disturb me."

"I'm sorry anyway." She turned to Neyruu and motioned for her to lower her wing, but the dragon did not obey. *Now? Why now?* She was looking at the stranger still, looking at him in a way she'd never looked at anyone else. *Does she know him? Recognise him from when we were guests in this glade?*

"It's terrible what happened here," the stranger said, looking about solemnly. "This was a very lovely place before. One of my favourites, actually. And I've seen a lot of places."

Talasha nodded slowly. "Yes. It's terrible." *And here's me thinking only about myself,* she thought. She snorted in disgust at her own selfishness. Hundreds had died here, sweet innocent children among them, and the Twelve Trees of Aramatia were dead, her Spring corrupted. *The last bright light of a goddess is gone, and you are only thinking of yourself, of a few measly scars.*

"You're well within your rights to grieve, you know," the stranger said. "Do not condemn yourself for that. A woman's beauty is a sacred thing, I've always thought."

"Life is more sacred," Talasha murmured. "I still have mine."

"Do you?" he asked her, seriously. "One can walk and eat and breathe, but not live. When the shadow comes upon a person, are they truly living at all?" He let the question hang for a moment, then smiled more hopefully and said, "But such things can be ephemeral, don't you think? Beyond the darkness, there is always light, my lady, even if it seems dimmer than before. You need only find it."

"Where?" she asked, weakly. "I thought to find it here, but it's gone." *And in my heart, my soul, it's gone.*

"It may return," the stranger said. "Is that not how it works? Does the sun not set, only to rise again? Might it not rise again here as well… and in you?"

There were tears in her eyes, she realised. She felt hopeless with grief all of a sudden, and her guilt only made it all the worse. *Stop crying. Just be strong, damn you. There is so much tragedy and strife in this world, and you're not special. You're just ugly now, that's all.*

"How long since it happened?" the stranger asked softly.

She sniffed. "I don't know," she croaked. "A few weeks."

"Well, that's not so long at all to be in mourning. And you *are* in mourning, don't deny yourself that. Some seem to think only death can bring about a state of mourning, but that isn't true. It is *loss* that brings it, loss of any kind. And you have lost a part of yourself, my lady. It is only natural to grieve as you process it. It would be unnatural if you didn't."

She nodded gloomily. Perhaps that was true.

"*He* has been in mourning for longer. And will be for some time to come, I think."

Talasha looked at the man, confused. "Who?"

"Him," said the stranger, pointing to the east.

Talasha peered that way, through gloom and ash and shadow, and saw a great curved mound lying beside the blackened trees. It was near the Spring, a hill that shaded the woodland beyond, and not something she'd seen when she stayed here in the glade before. "*Him?* I don't understand."

"Look harder, my lady. Just let your eyes settle and look harder." He gave her a moment. "Now, do you see?"

And she saw. The feathers beneath the ash. The protective shape of a great curved wing. The beaked head, tucked in, as though hiding from the world. "Calacan," she whispered, exhaling in awe. "Is…is he…

"Hurt?" the stranger said. "No. Not physically. He was not here when that silly boy came with his dragons, else he might have driven them off, but *spiritually*, yes, in that he is hurt." He gave a sigh. "It is the light, you see. His mother's light. Her power has gone from this realm now and so his power is also fading. I suppose Eldur knew what he was doing with that. This wasn't just about killing and capturing the Elders. He wanted to drive the last light of Aramatia out of this world, and thus deprive Calacan of the source of his power. He is grey now, do you see? Not just the ash that coats him, no, but his spirit. There is no light in him anymore."

Talasha's heart was breaking for him. She felt desperately sad to see him lying there, alone, next to the spring of Aramatia, the light of his mother. "He saved my life," she murmured, remembering. Her eyes misted at the memory, as the sound he made, at the light he gave, at the sight of him soaring down from the skies to sunder and slay the dragon Paglar. "Both of us," she said, turning to Neyruu. "And Cevi. We'd be dead if it wasn't for him."

"Oh, he has saved many lives since his return. The south has been safe beneath his wing, but no longer. A menace stirs across the empire now, a great menace that goes about unchallenged and unchecked, and all under Agarath's will…"

"*Agarath*," he repeated, scoffing. "A nasty entity is Agarath. He brings wickedness wherever he goes, and I've never liked him, not even a little bit. So I'm going to give you a little nudge," the strange man said to her, nodding and nodding again. "Yes, why not? Well…I know why not. I'm not meant to interfere, only observe, and my father will be most displeased with me, but he's got other things to worry about right now. He probably won't even notice. If I'm discreet, I don't think he'll notice."

Talasha Taan was hopelessly confused. "Your father? I…"

"Don't worry about that, my lady," the man said. "I overspoke already with that eagle lord and Sir Slow, so best I check my tongue with you. There's no sense in overburdening you, Talasha. So let's just keep things simple, yes? I think it would be better to keep it simple."

"Yes," she agreed, bewildered. "So…"

"So I came to give you this," he said. And he took a step toward her.

Talasha watched warily as he turned over his palm. In it she saw a necklace appear, a little locket on a length of silver chain. He did not seem to be holding it a moment before and that made her wonder if he was some sort of mage. "What is it?" Her voice was edged with distrust. He could be some servant of Eldur, just another fire priest in disguise, here to lure her back into the Father's web. But if that were so, Neyruu would not be staring at the stranger in that way. She seemed transfixed by him, awed. There was wonder, not worry, in the dragon.

"It's a necklace," the strange man said. "I thought that was obvious."

"Yes, but…"

"But it has meaning," he said, nodding. "Well, of course. Of course. What use would there be in giving you a plain old necklace, my lady? I'm sure you've been gifted many fine jewels in your life, and those much prettier than this one."

She'd had her fair share of jewellery, yes. Her eyes were on the locket. "Is there something inside?" she asked him.

"There is," he said, reaching forward. "Take a look. There is a little pin at the back. You need only press it and the locket will open."

Her fingers moved forward tentatively. As they brushed the skin of the man's palm, she felt a strange power in him, an otherworldly power. She paused, looking into his eyes, and saw in them something unbound, something as vast as the starry night sky. "Go ahead, child. Go ahead," he murmured.

She drew the locket from his palm, lifting it. It was circular, plain, without pattern or adornment. Her fingers felt for the little mechanism at the back, and she pressed on it, and the locket opened. She frowned. Inside was a tuft of hair, bound in string and curved about its interior. Dark it was, though she saw lighter grey strands as well amongst it. She stared at it for a while. "Whose it is?" she asked.

"Mine," the stranger said. "Well, *most* of it is. The rest…" He didn't say any more than that. "Put it on. I would like to see you wear it."

She did so, closing the locket and drawing the chain over her head. It rested about her neck, in the hollow of her throat, and she wondered if this was about her face, about her scars. Gently, almost nervously, she lifted her fingers to her chin, hoping to feel the savage rut there smoothed away, the flesh made soft and new again, but no…no, her flesh was as torn and tender as ever. Her hope collapsed in her all at once. "What… what does it do?" she asked the strange man, confused. She looked up, frowning. "I thought, maybe…"

"Feel it," he said, reaching out to take her hand. He closed it around the locket. "Feel it, child, and it'll show you the way."

"Feel it? But…"

"That's all I can say. I will say no more." He drew back from her, moving away into the gloom, away into the fog. And with a smile, he was gone.

61

Elyon

He woke in an unfamiliar bed within an unfamiliar room.

A large fire was blazing hotly in a huge stone hearth and through a short passageway opened a separate chamber with a colossal desk and many large chairs. He felt light, almost weightless, and found that his armour had been removed. Slowly it all came back to him. *Keep Kanabar,* he thought. *We came down to land on that balcony, and then…and then…*

"You've been sleeping for almost eighteen hours," said a voice. A lithe shape shifted from the window seat and stalked over to him like a cat. "Hi, handsome. Feeling better?"

"Carly," he croaked, seeing her. "What…what time is it?"

"Late morning," she said. "It was my turn to watch over you. Not the worst duty I've ever had, I'll admit." She smiled coquettishly. "Your father didn't want you waking up with no one here."

Elyon sat up. He felt groggy still, even after all that sleep, and by the gods had that flight been taxing. It was even harder coming back than it had been going out, and those last miles…he barely remembered them. "The Windblade, where…"

"There." She pointed to the nearest wall, where the blade was propped up in its silver sheath. There were scratch marks on the floor to suggest it had been dragged there. "Your father took the other one to the Steelforge. They're well apart, before you ask."

He nodded, trying to gather up his bearings.

Carly was watching him closely all the while. "Artibus said you needed to stay in bed after you woke," she told him. "There might be some aftereffects of what happened. You need to wait for him to come see you."

"Nothing happened. I was just tired."

"No, Elyon. You collapsed from exhaustion and went into shock. You might have died, Artibus said." She went back to the window and drew open the drapes to let some natural light in. It didn't make much difference, dreary as it was outside. "How about some fresh air? It's awful stuffy in here." She turned the handle and pushed open the leaded glass window, and the cold air came drifting in. "There. Much better."

"Did I almost die?" Elyon asked her. "Truly, Carly?"

"You might have if you kept pushing yourself like that. You need to slow down, Elyon Daecar. You can't win this war on your own."

"I can't slow down. I need to go back east." He wasn't going to just lie here in bed. He'd been gone much longer than he'd expected, and needed to get back to Saska at once. "Where's my father? I need to talk to him."

"I don't know. I've been in here watching you."

"Fine. I'll find him myself." Elyon threw off the covers, shuffled to the side of the bed (it was a very big bed) and planted his feet on the cool stone floor. He was very clammy and felt very weak, but it was nothing a bit of food and godsteel wouldn't solve. He stood a little dizzily.

Carly came striding over. "Elyon, lie back down. You're to stay here. Doctor's orders."

He was dressed in nothing but his cotton hose. He turned his eyes around. "Where are my clothes?"

"I don't know. Why would I know that?" She bustled across to him, red hair and hips swaying. "Just relax, Elyon, and lie down." She went so far as to clutch at his bare shoulders and attempt to push him back down onto the bed, but he twisted away from her. "Don't make me wrestle you, Elyon. I will if I have to."

She lunged for him again, but he was gone, moving quickly across the room to a trunk. "Stop being weird, Carly. I feel fine." He flipped the lid open and saw garments inside, though they were all too big for him. *Borrus's*, he knew. He drew some out anyway, dressing in loose breeches and an oversized cream linen shirt, then crossed the room to fetch the Windblade. "Where's my armour?"

"Stop asking me things I don't know. And get that arse of yours back into bed, or I'll make you."

"Carly, just stop. Why are you so desperate to keep me here?"

She hesitated. "Artibus said…"

"I know what Artibus said." He looked at her and realised there was more to this than she was letting on. A slow frown creased his brow. "Something's happened," he said, and it wasn't a question. "What is it? Tell me."

She didn't tell him. She just stood there saying nothing.

"Damn it, Carly. Is it Lillia? Did she have an accident in training or something?"

"It's…not your sister."

"Then it's someone. Who?"

"Your auntie," she admitted, soberly. "Artibus told me not to say anything, in case it got you all riled up, but…"

"What happened to her? Carly, *what happened?*"

"She collapsed," she said, blurting it out. "Down by the lake. Right after you came back, she…"

Elyon was already moving for the door. Carly tried to call him back, but he was gone, through the door and into the corridor. He saw that Sir Talmer Hedgeside stood guard at Amara's room, alongside Sir Penrose Brightwood. The latter noticed him coming and started toward him. "My lord…"

"Out of the way, Penrose. I want to see her." He brushed the man aside as Sir Talmer moved back. Elyon turned the handle of the door and stepped within.

He took in the scene in a flash. Amara, lying unconscious in her bed beneath the covers. Her skin was pale and she had a bandage around her head. Lillia sat at her bedside, her face wan and stricken. Artibus was at a counter making some tonic while an old maid crouched down by the fire stirring at the coals and humming softly in a calming voice. The smell of lavender rose from a bowl of warm water and there was rosemary sprinkled on the floor. All turned at once as Elyon entered. Lillia stood, teary-eyed, and ran over to hug him. She was not wearing her armour for once. She was wearing a pretty dress.

Elyon hugged her back, holding her tightly. "It's OK, Lil," he said, without knowing if that was true. "It's all going to be OK." His eyes were over her shoulder, looking at Artibus. The old physician nodded his head toward an adjoining passage and Elyon gently drew Lillia away, brushed a tear from her cheek, and smiled to comfort her. Then he followed Artibus into a separate chamber. "What happened?" he asked him urgently, when they were alone. "Carly told me she collapsed?"

"Yes. Down by the lake with your father. She struck her head against the stone, Elyon." He paused, then said. "She has a fractured skull."

Elyon exhaled. *A fractured skull.* His eyes twisted in fear.

"It is a linear fracture, Elyon," Artibus said, to reassure him. "And there has been no displacement, so far as I can tell. That is good. It means the brain is unlikely to have been impacted, and the skull itself remains intact."

His face brightened. "So…she'll….?"

"She should be fine, in time. It may take her a couple of days to awaken, and the fracture itself will take several weeks or even a month or two to heal, but she should make a full recovery. There will be symptoms, of course. Dizziness, headaches, but those should also pass eventually."

"And…the child?"

The old man shook his head. "That is less certain, I fear. She felt pain, and there has been bleeding. That is a concern, though not unheard of at this stage. I will be monitoring her closely and doing all I can, but right now we can only wait. Much will depend on Amara's strength."

Elyon nodded, absorbing the news. He took a long moment to himself, then asked, "Where is my father? He should be here."

"He was. For a long time. But I told him there was nothing he could do and he was only getting in my way. He still has a kingdom to run, Elyon, and a war to plan. And after that business with your grandfather…"

"My grandfather? What business?"

"Oh. Yes, of course. You don't know."

"Know what, Artibus?"

The old man put a wizened hand on his arm. His eyes were very sympathetic and kind. "He is dead, Elyon. He choked on a piece of meat, at dinner, while you were away. In the aftermath, some blame was put on your auntie, and the Amadar men departed the city in protest. They took your grandfather's body back to Ilivar. Your father is trying to smooth things out, as best he can."

It was a lot to get his head around. "My…grandfather's dead?"

"Yes, my boy. I'm sorry."

He lowered his eyes. His thoughts went out to him, but only briefly. It was Amara who worried him more, Amara and her unborn child. "I have to see my father urgently. Is he in the Steelforge?"

"Yes, as far as I know." The old man peered up at him and seemed concerned by what he saw. "Elyon, I hope you don't intend to leave so soon."

"I have to leave right now."

"That isn't wise. Not after what happened. You need more rest, Elyon. Another day at least."

"I can't waste a day, Artibus. Even hours are precious."

He stepped back through the passage and into Amara's bedchamber. Lillia was sitting on her chair by the bed, stroking their auntie's hand. Her eyes were red from crying. Elyon pulled up a stool and sat down beside her. He laid an arm over Lillia's shoulder and pulled her close. "The baby will be fine, Lil. They'll both be fine. Amara's strong."

The girl sniffled. "But…what if they're not? What if she dies or the baby dies or they both die and…and, it's all my fault."

"Your fault? Why would it be your fault?"

"I've been stressing her too much. Saying I'm going to war all the time. And with…with Grandfather. He choked on the boar because of *me*, and she's the one being blamed for it. They're saying she's working with that witch. That she poisoned him, but she didn't…he only choked because of me."

"Lillia…"

"No. You don't know, Elyon. You weren't there. I wanted him to die…I did, I wanted him to die and I shouted at him to die and then… then he died, he did, and it was all my fault."

"Lillia…saying something or even wanting something doesn't make it real. We all think and say things we don't mean."

"But I did mean it. At the time. When I said it, when I thought it, I *did* mean it."

He squeezed her a little harder. "You'll do no good blaming yourself. None of it's your fault. And Amara and the child will be fine."

"You don't know that."

"Yes I do. I know it."

"But…how?"

"Because there's too much darkness in this world," he said. "Far too much darkness. And we deserve a bit of light. Amara had been so strong for us all for so long and she bloody well deserves it. And if anything bad happens to her, you know what I'll do?"

"No. What?" She sniffled again.

"I'll take the Windblade and fly all the way up into the Eternal Halls and I'll cause a real fuss, that's what I'll do. I'll tell off every damn god I see for what they did to her, and if I find her there, and her baby girl, I'll pick them up and carry them back down. *That's* what I'm going to do."

A small laugh escaped the girl. She rubbed her eyes. "You're so silly. Do you know how silly you can be sometimes?" She smiled at him and rested her head against his chest as he draped his strong arm around her. And there they sat, watching over their beloved auntie, until finally Lillia drifted off to sleep. Then he picked her up gently and carried her into the next room, laid her down in her bed, kissed her forehead and left her to rest.

"She was up all night," Artibus said, when he returned. "She hasn't left the room since Amara was brought here."

Elyon nodded. "What she said about my grandfather…"

"It was a very strained dinner, Elyon. Your grandfather…the way he behaved…" He shook his head angrily. "I am not one to speak ill of the dead, but his behaviour was appalling. I hope you do not think less of me for saying that. He was your grandfather, I know, but…"

"I could never think less of you, Artibus. And *you've* always been our grandfather, not him."

He left the old man there with a tear in his eye and went back to his father's bedchamber. Carly was still there waiting for him. "You don't hate me for not telling you, do you?"

"No. I don't hate you, Carly."

"So…what now?"

"Now I speak to my father. Did you have a chance to find my armour?"

She nodded. "It's right there, in that chest." She pointed. Elyon marched over and Carly followed. He began armouring up with her help, ignoring her sultry little looks and smiles, the way she touched him when she slid the plate into place. "Maybe later…" she started.

"I'll be gone later," he said.

"Oh. Right. Yes. You don't tend to stop, do you?" She seemed disappointed. "You remember my promise…"

"I remember, Carly."

"It'll never happen now, will it? Some other girl's stolen your heart."

Entirely, he thought, giving no answer. He finished armouring in silence, fixed his cloak with a Deacar brooch, then started for the door. Carly reached out and spun him around, and before he could even react her lips were pressing up to his and her scent was filling his nose. He drew away quickly. "Carly, I can't…"

"I know you can't," she said. "That was for luck, Elyon, just luck. Where you're going, you might need it."

"Luck," he repeated. "That was…a lot of luck, Carly. A peck on the cheek might have been enough."

She grinned at him like the born seductress she was. "Well, I'd want to give you a whole lot more, but it seems you're off-limits to me now." She went up close to him, as though to try to kiss him again, but this time her lips moved aside to touch his bearded cheek instead. "In another life, my prince," she whispered.

"In another life," Elyon agreed.

It was past midday when he reached the Steelforge, flying swift from the keep to land at the gate at the end of the bridge. Traditionally, only the Varin Knights, squires, the Steelforge guardsmen, Forgemasters and their apprentices and a few chosen servants and guests were permitted inside. Now all manner of armourers and blacksmiths walked the halls, and their families had been allowed to stay with them. The Forgemasters were furious, of course, but the king's decision had proven wise given the amount of armour and blades that needed mending. Much of it was piled up in the entrance hall, with repaired armour and weapons on one side and that which needed repairing on the other. It was being sorted by priority by some of the apprentices. "Where is the king?" Elyon asked one of them.

"Down in the crypts, Your Highness. He is taking some time alone."

Good, Elyon thought. He had no interest in seeing any of the other lords or captains right now. He withdrew the Windblade and set it against a wall. "Watch this for me. Make sure nobody touches it. I'll be back shortly." Elyon did not plan to be here long.

He walked the well-worn route down into the bowels of the ancient fortress. The newcomers were not permitted here, so it was quiet, dimly lit, and shadowy. The crypts were found down a very wide stone stair that plunged into the darkness below. Torches flickered at intervals along the walls and the air grew colder as he went.

The vault at the bottom was vast. Here were buried the knights of Varin's order, a thousand of them old and new. The stone tombs stretched out and spread into the distance with long aisles cast between them, each identical to the last. Here in the crypts, all men of Varin's Order were laid to rest in tombs unadorned and unspectacular, carven only with their name and the date of their birth and their death. An unheralded young knight who perished without glory or triumph would have no worse a resting place than a hero of a hundred battles. Here all were equal, equal in death. It was at Varin's Table where the labours of their lives were sorted, their placings granted, their seats attained.

Elyon stood at the bottom of the steps and surveyed the vastness of the room. Away in the distance, he could see a floating orb of light illuminating the figure of a man. He marched onward through the darkness, footfall echoing, and found the king just where he'd expected him to be. He was standing at the tombs of his father, and his son.

The king held a torch in his grasp, casting light upon his face. He looked weary, solemn. His eyes were fixed upon the twin tombs, at father and son. Father, who had lived long and glorious. Son, who'd been slain too young.

"I wonder if they ever speak," he murmured softly. "Do you think they speak, Elyon? Your grandfather and your brother?"

"I don't know, Father. We never really knew him."

The king nodded. "Aleron was only a young boy when my father died. And you little more than a babe in swaddling. It is a shame that you never got to know him. He was a great man. Greater than I am."

So say all sons about their fathers, Elyon thought. He believed the very same thing. "Father, we need to go," he said. Elyon had not come here to discuss the spiritual realm. He was not here to talk of dreams and tables, hopes and heartache. "I'm rested now and we need to go."

"Go?" The king turned now to look at him. He had not washed or changed since their return from Vandar's Tomb, and nor had he slept, that was clear.

"To Ilithor. We have to fly there, right now. I'm strong enough. I can carry you."

"No, Elyon. That last leg from Blackfrost almost killed you."

"So I'm told. But it didn't. I feel fine now and I'm ready."

"It's over five hundred miles to Ilithor, son. You cannot bear me again as a burden."

"We can stop at Ilivar on the way," Elyon said, trying to appeal to him. "Sir Michael might be there by now and we can talk to him ourselves, smooth things over."

"Then you know about Lord Brydon?"

"Yes, and Amara. I know it all, Father."

"Do you? All of it?"

"Yes."

"Then you'll know it was all my fault. You'll know Amara may lose her child because of me."

"No…I…"

"I was not tender with her, Elyon. I was too hard on her. This business with your grandfather…"

Elyon didn't need to hear this. *I've had my sister blaming herself. I don't need my father doing the same.* With Lillia, he would give comfort and reassurance, but him? *No.* He would simply move things along. "That's not important," he said, dismissing it. "What's important is getting the blades to Ilith at once. What's important is *Saska.* We have to leave, Father, and now."

The king shook his head. "We discussed this in the Icewilds, Elyon. I said I would think about it, and I have. I have to stay here. There is too much for me to manage, and your auntie…"

"Is in good hands. There's nothing you can do for her." He stared at him. "Is this about the Frostblade? Are you afraid to give it up, now that the time is so near?"

His father lowered his head. Elyon felt guilty at once for even saying it. "No, son. I have long since made my peace with that."

"Then come with me," the prince urged, stepping forward. "If you're not afraid, come with me, Father."

"I cannot, Elyon. I have told you why. You want me to meet Saska, but you do not even know if she is there. She may be long days from Ilithor still, or may have been waylaid. I cannot sit around and await her. I have the tribes to manage, and the lords. I have much and more I must prepare and cannot leave the capital at this time. There is too much at stake for me to go now. When Sir Connor gets back…"

"And when is that?" Elyon asked, loudly. His voice echoed out through the cold, dark hall, ringing from tomb to tomb. "Connor, Torus, they've been gone for days. You say you can't wait around for Saska. Well, *I* can't wait around for them either!"

"Elyon, lower your voice. We do not shout down here. We do not disturb the dead."

"The dead are *dead*, Father. They cannot be disturbed. It's the living that concern me more, and Connor Crawfield *isn't here*. You said a dragon could carry the Frostblade instead of you. Fine. You want to stay here, fine, I understand that, I do, but I need a dragon and there aren't any. So what do you expect me to do? Fly it myself?"

"No. You know that isn't possible."

"Then I'll fly to *them*," Elyon said. It was the only other choice he had and he knew it. "I'll fly to Lord Marak's hideout and bring them back myself. Connor made a map, didn't he? In case we ever needed to find it. Well, I can follow it. I know where they are and it's not so far from here. I'll be there and back within a few hours, and I want you to have the Frostblade ready for my return. Can you do that for me?"

His father nodded slowly. He was looking at the tombs.

"And the fragment," Elyon said. "Vandar's spirit. I'll need to take that too."

Again, his father nodded. "I'll have everything ready for you, Elyon."

Elyon closed a fist and opened it, trying to leech out a bit of tension from his arm. He was emotionally charged, frustrated, and his father was being as stony as these tombs. "I wish you would just come," he said. "It's not only the Frostblade, Father. It's *you*. Saska…I want you to meet her, to guide her, to help her…"

"I have helped her," the king said.

Elyon frowned. What did that mean? "How? How could you have helped her?"

The king did not give him an answer. He stood there solemnly, staring at the tombs, and Elyon could no longer delay. He gave out a breath. "Fine. Have it your way. I'll see you when I get back. And be ready." He had one long final look at him, grunted, then turned and marched back to the stairs.

62

The
Emperor

"Bring her forward," he said, and it was done.

The wagon came rattling up through the hot dusty dawn, drawn along by a large loping Piseki camel and mounted with an iron cage. Within that cage was a sparkling crystal throne, and atop that throne was chained a woman, half-starved and dehydrated, a husk of a human who had once called herself empress, a creature once seen as divine.

Elio Krator had shown the world otherwise. He had stripped her of her finery, stripped her of her crown, exposed her to the elements and the hard hateful glares of the men. Naked she was, fettered at the wrist and ankle, her skin burned and blistered, her hair bleached and made brittle by the relentless, baking heat of the sun. She had sat on that throne for weeks as they trundled along the Capital Road, only unfettered when they stopped to make camp so she might relieve herself and lie down. In that Elio Krator allowed her a small measure of mercy. He was not a monster, after all.

Alongside the wagon walked Herald Mercalo, dressed in his heavy hot ceremonial robes, denouncing her for the false ruler she was. "She is a woman, just a woman," the weaselly herald would cry out each day, as they rolled ever eastward along the coastal road. "Look, look at her. She is weak and too weak for this world, but our new emperor is *strong*, he is *divine*. Look, up there, you will see him in the skies. Beast Braccaro, Beast Braccro! Only a *god* could tame Beast Braccaro!"

He was a snake, was Floris Mercalo, a pitiful, faithless thing. As soon as Moonrider Tregardo had been defeated outside Lumos, and his brutish bear Bullathor thrown down and slain, Mercalo had defected at once to Krator's side, tumbling to his knees before him. "I serve only the crystal crown," he had proclaimed desperately. "Only the crystal crown, I swear it, my lord."

Krator had looked at him impassively. "Do you not have loyalty to your empress, Mercalo?"

"No, my lord, no, only to the *crown*." He had looked up pitifully from his knees. "It is yours now, my lord. *You* are the emperor, and it is your crown, so I serve you, Your Eminence. It is my duty, as herald, to serve *you* now."

"Then serve me," Elio Krator had said, and he had given the man his first charge.

So they had gathered around outside of the city gates to watch as the faithless herald stripped the clothes from the back of his former empress, as he drew away Valura's fur and feather finery and ripped off the silks and satins. Krator had watched, disgusted by him, reviled, as this man who was Herald and Voice of her Eminence had debased her and humiliated her to save his own worthless skin. Mercalo had tried not to weep as he did it, but Krator had seen the tears all the same. He had tried not to speak, but they could all hear him murmuring, "I'm sorry, I'm sorry, I'm so sorry," all the while. By the time the woman lay naked and stricken on the parched red earth, her crystal throne had been brought out from the burning ruin of the Glass City. Krator ordered it mounted onto a wagon, and told Floris Mercalo to chain the empress up himself. "But my lord… please…I have done as you asked…I have stripped her…please, that is enough, please…

"Do it," Krator had said. "Do it or die where you stand."

A part of him had hoped the man would deny him, but he didn't. Weeping and murmuring his pathetic regrets, he drew the naked woman gently up into the wagon and chained her in her iron manacles. When he climbed back out he went again to his knees before his new master, tear-soaked and desolate. "I have done as you asked, my lord," he'd said, in a blubbery, broken voice. "Please, do not ask more of me. Please, I cannot stand to…"

"You are the Herald and Voice of the *Emperor*, are you not?"

The man's eyes had come up, red and bleary. "I am, my lord."

"Then be my *voice*, Mercalo." And he had given him his second charge.

Ever since then, the herald had walked at Valura's side, walked beside the wagon and the crystal throne as it rolled endlessly along the Capital Road. Every day he would cry out his wretched denunciations, calling her a false ruler, calling her weak, decrying the Lumarans for hoarding power for so long. At every town and village they passed, the people who remained would crawl out of their homes and hovels and shelters and see this naked empress rolling by. Men of fighting age would be given the chance to join them as Krator's men went among them, handing out swords and spears, axes and maces and spiked morning stars. And all the while, Mercalo would bellow for him, like the snivelling sycophant he was.

"He is strong," the herald would proclaim. "Emperor Krator now rules both earth and sky, he is a man made a god, not like her…not like *her*…" And he would point and his face would twist in false disgust at the naked empress chained on her throne. "Look at her, look at her weak soft flesh and sagging breasts. And now turn your eyes up, yes turn them up, and you will see him, see our great lord and champion soaring through the skies." And, "Beast Braccaro!" he would roar out. "Beast Braccaro, Beast Braccaro, Beast Braccaro!" as the soldiers and guards around him took up the cry, and the men who followed after them, and those after them, until the chant had spread and spread for miles down the coastal road.

And that was how it went. That was how they had gone. And every day more swarmed to join them. From the towns and villages they had come, from the Sunlands and the Saltflats, from the deserts of Pisek. Krator had been sure to send out envoys far and wide and thus had their efforts borne fruit. Ships had come over from Solapia bearing armed men willing to serve. Cogs and fishing vessels struck out from the Twin Suns laden with fishermen holding harpoons and tridents. When they passed through Sutrek, the sprawling festering city had delivered to him many thousands more swords and spears. And onward they had gone, onward to the east, onward through the unbearable, oppressive heat. *To Aram*, Elio Krator thought. *Home.*

And now they were here. Now it lay before him once more. Aram, standing proudly against the pink dawn skies. Aram, his heart and his home.

Elio Krator smiled. "It's good to be back, isn't it, Mar?"

"Yes, my lord. Most certainly." Mar Malaan was smiling too. Smiling, sweating, and *stinking*, of course. *Already stinking*, Krator thought, wrinkling his nose. *Even overnight he sweats like a pig.*

They had arrived several hours ago, preferring to travel by night, as usual, than during the terrible heat of the day. By now the bulk of Krator's vast host had come rumbling up the road to pitch camp along the Amedda River. It was not the river it once was. The baking heat had turned it into a starved, sunken thing, and the broad brisk flow had been reduced to a meandering brook, hardly a tenth the size of what it used to be. Still, there was enough water coming from the west to service their needs for now.

"We will toast our victory later in the palace, Mar. It will be nice and cool up there." Even during the most unbearable summers, the pyramid palace remained cool inside due to the thickness of the stone walls. Elio Krator looked forward very much to being cool and clean again. *I will bathe in the pools,* he told himself. *Maybe Safina will still have some fine wine left. She can join us in our toast.*

"Yes, my lord." Malaan bobbed his head enthusiastically. "I would not object to a fruity Solapian red."

The wagon was still rolling up behind them; Krator could hear the wheels turning, the cage groaning, the clatter of iron and crystal. And Mercalo, of course, weakly bleating out his cries. *He knows I can hear him. He wants to impress me, the fool.* It would not save him. Elio Krator despised the herald for his disloyalty, in the same way he tolerated and even admired Mar Malaan for his faith, despite his obvious shortcomings.

Mercalo had performed his duties well, he would give him that, but soon enough his use would be spent. *Then I will feed him to Braccaro,* the emperor thought. *Beast Braccaro, who he sings for so sweetly.*

He smiled at the notion as the wagon came up to join them, then turned around and beckoned the herald over. Mercalo scampered at once to him, and collapsed to his knees, pressing his forehead to the dirt at Krator's feet. "My lord, what will you have of me?"

"I will have you stand up, Floris."

"Yes, my lord." And he stood up, hunched of back and shivering. He had the posture of a beaten dog, did Floris Mercalo. *If he had a tail, he'd tuck it between his legs.*

Krator looked at him for a long while, delighting in his fear. Then he smiled and said, "All those pretty things you say about me, Floris. I wonder...do you truly believe them?"

"My...my lord? Yes, I do...of course I do. Every word."

"Then why am I told that you whisper at night to Valura, telling her otherwise? You denounce your denunciations of her, Floris. You tell her everything you're saying is a lie."

"My lord, no...you don't understand." The man's eyes were wide with fear, deliciously wide. "I *do* mean what I say, I do. I only...I say all of that to give her comfort, that is all. Some small comfort, given her plight." He puddled to his knees again, all but kissing at his boots. "My lord, you *must* believe me. I do it only to spare her, to spare her, that is all..."

Krator smiled thinly. He enjoyed toying with this man. "Do not worry, Floris. Valura's troubles will soon be over." He waved a hand. "You may rise."

He stood again, shivering now violently. He may have evacuated his bladder, to judge the stain coming through his thick robes. "Now, Floris. I have one last charge for you."

"L-last, my lord?"

Yes, he thought. *Last.* Emperor Elio Krator gestured to the city walls. Many men had gathered on the battlements now with bow and crossbow, and of course the mounted ballistas and scorpions and other siege weapons were being manned and prepared. It was a fine pretty show, but would be for nothing in the end. Elio Krator wanted to take back his city without shedding any blood. *Enough of that was spilt in Lumos,* he reflected. But Aram was his home, and these his people. He would acquire it peacefully if he could. "Valura is to be taken to the city gates," he said to the herald. "I want you to accompany her, Floris, and bring with you my demands."

"Yes, my lord. I am honoured to serve you." He tried to smile, tried and failed. *He knows the end is near.* "What are your demands, Great Eminence?"

"I think you can guess, Floris, a very clever man like you."

"You...wish for them to yield," he said. "To open the gates to you, and..."

"I do not want another bloodbath, Floris. Lumos…that was different." He hated Lumos, hated it and always had, and had put the city to the torch. *The Lumaran Empire*, he thought, bitterly. Always the *Lumaran* Empire, but no more. It would be the Aramatian Empire now, and Aram would be its capital. "The gates are to be opened and the city is to surrender without a fight," he said. "Those who wish to join us will be welcomed. Tell them that we have men and women from every corner of the empire in our ranks now, and little to no dissent. It is faith that binds us, faith in our cause, faith in *me*. Tell them I will keep them safe in this harsh new world. Can you do that, Floris? Can you tell them?"

"Yes, Your Eminence. I can tell them."

"Then go." He waved a hand, and the wagon driver lashed his whip, and the giant camel honked and lumbered on. Herald Mercalo was pulled along by his invisible tether. The rest of the guards followed a little way behind in their scalemail armour and feathered cloaks.

The sun was just starting to climb now, and the dawn really was very pretty. *A rising sun for a rising sunlord*, Elio Krator thought. *The gods welcome me home as a conquering hero.* It had not been so when he last left. The night he fled the city, as the eastern districts burned, he had wondered whether he would ever return. His host was destroyed or captured, his alliance with Cedrik Kastor had proven false and ill-fated, and he had been forced to flee into the open arms of Pal Palek to take stock and consider his future. *My path changed that night. It shifted violently and beyond my expectations but led me to a more glorious road.*

He smiled, as broad a smile as Elio Krator could manage. It gave him immeasurable pleasure to return with such a vast host at his back. To return with the crystal crown already lain upon his head. Becoming emperor had always been his great ambition, but he had never expected it to happen so soon. *I was to become Grand Duke of Aramatia first*, he thought. *And to sit the Eagle Chair.* That he had done it the other way around was of great satisfaction to him.

The wagon was fast approaching the city gates. Pal Palek and Iru Zon were both with the emperor as well, invited up to watch, along with Mar Malaan and the other senior captains and commanders. "What if they don't surrender?" Palek asked. "Will you attack?"

"They will surrender, Pal. Safina is not stupid."

"Safina Nemati might not be in charge," the Piseki went on, gruffly. "She was sick when you were last here. Sick and dying. Might be she's dead already and if so Lord Hasham will be in command."

Hasham. Elio Krator considered Lord Iziah Hasham a great man… and a great bane to him as well. In that he respected him and hated him in equal measure. "Lord Hasham is of no relevance now," he dismissed. "It has been long years since Hothror died and he is half a man without his bear."

"Half of Hasham is still formidable," Iru Zon put in.

Krator looked at him coldly. "Does an old man frighten you, Iru? An old man on a barded horse?"

"No. I do not mean him, by himself. I mean his pride. He has always been prideful, and…"

Krator waved a hand to shut him up. "Hasham is proud, yes, but not so cruel as to let his people suffer for that pride. The gates will open, Iru. This city is already mine."

He was proven right in that. A short while later, the gates groaned and parted and a man came striding out to speak with Herald Mercalo, escorted by some men of the city guard. Elio Krator recognised the bald head and broad shoulders, the thick gut and stubbled jaw. He wore a shirt of interlinking rings in copper, silver and gold under a feathered cloak of the same. In the crook of his arm, he held his helm. Its crest was a soaring eagle with outstretched wings and an open beak.

Elio Krator went over to mount Braccaro, climbing up into his saddle. The firewolf was even bigger now than he'd been when he slew the moonbear Bullathor, bigger and fiercer and more monstrous. Krator enjoyed the silent horror that consumed the men on the walls as he walked closer. He enjoyed the looks on their faces as the firewolf thumped and thundered forward, gouging tracts from the barren soil with his long curved claws. Gouts of smoke and twisting tongues of flame rose up from the beast's elongated jaws, and his wings opened wide to flap and stir the air. There were audible gasps of shock then. From the walls, Krator heard the calls of 'freak' and 'aberration' and 'monster', but they were soon drowned out by the now popular refrain as his vast host called out from their camp along the river: "Beast Braccaro! Beast Braccaro! Beast Braccaro!" they roared.

The Strong Eagle, to his credit, did not quell. He was the head of the Aram City Guard, and had always been robust. He stared silently up at Elio Krator as he neared, stared silently up at the colossal dragon-wolf he rode. "What, no happy welcome?" Krator asked.

The Strong Eagle glared up at him. "The city is yours."

"Ah, even better." Elio Krator drew a deep breath into his lungs. "Kindly lead my men into the city and ensure there is room in the palace for my captains. The greater part of my host will remain beside the river, but many thousands will enter to take command of the walls. Order these men from the battlements." He waved a hand from right to left. "Have them assembled for inspection. As my good friend Floris Mercalo has said, all will be invited to continue in their service to Aram, and to me, their emperor. They need but swear me their oaths."

The Strong Eagle nodded his heavy jaw. "It will be done," he said.

Krator was happy with how this was going. A bloodless transition was better for everyone. "I will have you speak with Sunrider Malaan regarding the execution. Please see to the necessary arrangements." That part would *not* be bloodless, but it was necessary as a symbol. He could see the Strong Eagle's lips twist now, could see his eyes flick to the prison wagon, the throne, the poor wretched creature that sat chained atop it. "Mar will take you through the particulars. Is the Grand Duchess in the palace?"

The man took a moment to answer. He did so silently, with a hard nod.

"Then I will go and visit with her now." Elio Krator turned on Braccaro, and with a running start, the firewolf flapped his great golden wings and took off, thumping up and over the walls, across the city with its lofty hills where Krator had once had his estate, over the bridges that bustled with shops and taverns and whorehouses as they spanned the Amedda River, past the great dusty thoroughfares and the squares and the empty markets, over the harbour with its clots of abandoned ships all sitting listless at the wharves and piers.

He flew over it all, looking upon his city, at the blackened districts in the east where the streets and buildings had burned, at the hard-baked stone that was starting to crack and crumble in the killing heat. And lastly, he swung back to the palace, flying around and around the three-tiered pyramid with its poles and banners and balconies, its many statues and eagle-busts. At the top, the terrace gardens had been maintained, with the cherry trees and flowering bushes and the sparkling dipping pools. Elio Krator swung about the summit, smiling, yearning for the cool touch of that soft water on his skin, for the cleanliness of the rooms and the chambers set so high above the swarming masses below.

And as he came around once more, he saw her there, saw her shambling out from her apartments, grey-haired now and old, propping herself up with a cane as she moved toward the terrace wall. Once more they swung around, as Braccaro gave out that shuddering dragon-wolf roar of his, the howl and the scream all blended into one, and made loud and booming by his great size. Then flapping his red-veined wings, he swung forward with his forepaws to land, his hind legs following down behind him to shatter the stone at his feet. "Down, Braccaro," Krator said, "and carefully. Try not to make a mess." The beast lowered itself down so the emperor could climb to the ground, then sat up again on his haunches, folding in his massive wings. Elio Krator strode across the broad terrace to where the old woman stood awaiting him, leaning on her cane.

"You look well, Safina," he said.

"I'm dying," she returned. "I have been for a while." She looked pale, shrivelled, much older than he had last seen her. *She has become a little old woman,* he thought, and the thought came with a small measure of sadness. "What have you done, Elio? What have you become?" She pressed her wrinkled hand to his cheek. There was a deep grief in her eyes. "You were like a son to me once."

"I am still that man, Safina." He pressed his palm against her hand, and for a moment he closed his eyes. Then he opened them and drew her hand away. "But also an emperor now. *Your* emperor. My predecessor is down below." He led the old lady to the terrace wall and pointed down toward the western gate. By now his men were entering, and the prison wagon was being driven through the city to the foot of the palace. "I would like you to come down with me," he told her. "It's important that you're there."

The old woman's eyes were weak now, but she knew what he was saying. "Elio, must you do this? We can still oppose him. This host you have gathered, this great strength…"

"I cannot oppose him, Safina. I know the limits of my power."

She looked up at him, pleading. Her eyes were wrinkled with pain. "What is this crown to you if you are no more than a slave to another? Take it off, I beg you. It need not be this way."

He turned away from her. She did not understand. "You will be given every comfort here, Safina," he told her. "I do not mean to make an example of you or make your last months here unpleasant. We have differed in our ideology, but both of us love our country. I will see it made greater than ever, Safina. The Aramatian Empire. Is that not what we have always wanted?"

"It's what you've always wanted. What your Patriots have wanted."

"And are you not a patriot? A patriot of Aramatia?"

"Yes," she said. "Of Aramatia. Not Agarath."

He raised his chin. "I have kept us safe," he told her, angrily. "Had I not gone to Eldur, what do you think he would have done? He would have sent the Dread to destroy us all. Lumos. Sutrek. Aram. Every city south of the Scales would have burned. I did what I had to do, to protect us. Only in his service can we survive."

"Only in his death," said Safina Nemati.

"No." Elio Krator was weary of this. He had come to see this as the only way now. He was the saviour of the south, the only one who saw clearly what must be done. "This world is changing, and we must change with it," he said. "The north cannot hope to defeat the Dread, Safina. *Saska*…" And he shook his head. "Do you truly believe she can fulfil this prophecy? It is folly, it is madness. The north will not survive."

"And we will? Is that what you believe, Elio?"

"Yes. We will. It may be hard for a time, and many will continue to die, but this is the only way to guarantee our survival. We have no choice."

"So you would sooner eat the scraps from his table than fight for the feast?"

"I would sooner eat the scraps than *starve*. There is no power that can overcome that of Agarath. I saw it when I went there, I saw him in the storm. I *heard* it, Safina, the dark malevolence in the depth of that mountain. When he calls upon me to serve, I must serve. Or we all will perish."

She reached forward again. "Elio…

"No." He caught her wrist. "Val'kor. He says that even Calacan is gone. What hope could there be if even the great Eagle of Aramatia can be defeated?"

"A lie," the old woman said. She shook her head weakly. "Calacan will return."

He looked down on her with a measure of scorn. "Blind faith will not save you. It will save none of us. I have made hard choices, yes, but necessary ones. Look," he said, and he waved an arm beyond the walls. "Do you see it, Safina? Do you see the strength of my host? The numbers who follow me? They all see the dragons trailing us; they all see Braccaro in the sky. They know the deal I made to save them, and they revere me for it, they have come to worship me…"

"Worship you?"

"Love me, then. Use whatever word you want. They follow me, Safina, out of choice. Because they know only I can protect them."

"They are *slaves*, Elio. They follow you out of fear. This priest of yours. Val'kor. He is making slaves of them as he has made one of you. And you don't even see it, sweet boy, you don't."

He snorted loudly and thought to strike her, but she was too frail now, too brittle and weak. He closed a fist, squeezing hard to leech away the tension, then opened it again. For a long time he said nothing. "You don't understand," he finally told her. "How could you? You have been here for months, hiding atop your palace. You have not seen the world. You do not know what it has become."

"I know," she said. "Oh, I know."

"And yet you still condemn me. You condemn me for taking what I was owed. For following this path, the only path I could?"

"Elio, listen to me…"

"No. I have heard enough. You do not understand, Safina. You will never understand. I have always been ambitious, yes, but I have always sought power for the right reasons. I do not just do it for me, for my own vanity. I do it for my people. I do it to protect them. And I am protecting them now. Where is Lord Hasham?"

She looked at him. Her eyes were broken. "He isn't here," she said. "He left."

"Left? Where?"

"He did not say. We had word you were coming and he departed the city without telling me. He is gone."

"You're lying," he said. Hasham would never go without her leave. "Is he here, in hiding? Will he try to have me killed?"

"He is gone, Elio."

"If I am harmed, the city will come to strife, Safina. I will not be able to stop him." He looked over at Braccaro, sitting enormously on his haunches. His gold-red eyes were watching them, fixed with that rage and that hate and that anger. He was bigger than any moonbear now, as big as the grandest of dragons. *All but the Dread*, Elio Krator thought. "If I die Braccaro will show no mercy in his hunt for my killers. We are bonded, Safina, yes, still bonded even after the changes he has been through." He leaned into her. "So let me ask you again. Where is Iziah Hasham?"

"I do not know," she said. "He is gone, I know not where."

Elio Krator growled, and across the broad terrace, his firewolf growled as well. Smoke rose and curled out through his queer jutting teeth and he opened his maw, letting out a fiery yawn. "So be it. But if Hasham *is* here, make sure he is told. Nothing good will come of my death." He looked her up and down. "Now get changed into something better. I will see you in the entrance hall."

He left her. Climbing back into his saddle, Braccaro beat his wings and soared again, sweeping through the city as the emperor's host poured through the gate. He landed outside the palace steps to find the prison wagon arriving. As he looked up now, he saw several dragons circling high over the city, the dragons under the command of Val'kor. *He will be there too, watching me,* Krator knew. The fire priest was always watching, with his thin smile and skinny long fingers and that ugly red-white rope of beard that hung down from his pointed chin. Mostly he kept away, but every so often he'd wander into Krator's camp to remind him who he served.

I need no reminding, the emperor thought, as he watched the dragons circling. As emperor some might see him as divine, but it wasn't true, not really, no more true than it was with Valura. *Strip me and chain me and starve me half to death and I'll seem lesser too.* But Eldur *was* divine, he *was* eternal, and Elio Krator knew his place. Much as he did not like it, he knew it. *It is the only way,* he thought.

The prison wagon was positioned in the heart of the open square before the palace steps. Herald Mercalo stood beside it in his ceremonial robes, cringing and weeping, and now chained up to the iron bars. Krator felt no pity for the man, not a shred of it, none at all. If there was pity in him, it was for Valura. Plain though she was, a weak-witted woman raised up on the back of a powerful bloodline and no more, she had always had a good heart. Atop her throne she sat, nude and broken, her chin hung low, eyes distant. *It will be over soon, fear not,* he thought. *The pain will only last a moment.*

It did not take long for them to gather. Around the square they stood, the city luminaries summoned to watch. Krator knew many of them, the highborn nobles and powerful merchants, the rich shipwrights and once-great warriors. He was not so surprised to see that Cliffario Denlatis was absent, though hoped very much to see him soon. *I must thank him for his interventions,* he thought, smiling. *And ask him of my dear cousin's health.* She was not present either, the Lady Asherah Tamaar who had been the subject of all those suitors, though the Wise Eagle had come with his flock and the Strong Eagle with his captains. Mar Malaan stood at Elio's side, and Palek and Zon were invited to join him as well. Once Safina Nemati appeared, helped along by a pair of guardsmen, to stand with them on the steps, Elio Krator lifted a hand and called for the crowd to quiet.

His sermon was very short. He spoke of change, of the purging power of fire, of the rise of a new empire springing up from the ashes of the old one. In the silence between his words, they could all hear Mercalo's sobs, but Valura herself never made a sound. When Krator was done, he looked at Braccaro, and the giant firewolf rose and stepped forward. The crowd hushed in horror as the fire glowed in his chest, growing brighter, brighter as the flame moved up his neck, and then out through his opening maw in a fierce flowing gush. And all the while, Mercalo's screams rose higher and higher still, climaxing in a terrible wailing pitch as the fire came surging out to bathe him.

Krator watched the man writhe and scream in unbearable agony, his chains clinking wildly, his flesh blackening, melting…and then suddenly, he went quiet. He watched as the wagon went up in a blaze, and the iron bars glowed, and in her crystal throne, the fallen empress sat burning, dying, silent. And he watched as the wood of the wagon collapsed, and the iron cage glowed brighter still, and then they heard the cracking sounds as the crystal began to shatter.

And all the while Safina Nemati stood beside him, staring through desolate eyes. "You are truly lost, Elio," she murmured. "Sweet Valura… she deserved better than this."

"I needed a symbol," he replied to her, watching. "That throne, Safina. I always wondered what it would be like to sit in it, but I soon realised it wouldn't be right. No. The *Eagle Chair* will become my throne. The throne for the ruler of the *Aramatian* Empire. And this…" He looked at the crystal throne, as it cracked and broke apart, as the body sitting atop it slumped and burned. "I'll make a footstall out of it, Safina." He'd said the opposite not so long ago, but this was better. It made more sense. "It's time the Lumarans learned their place. We are the power here now. Us."

And she looked up at him, so sadly, and whispered it again, "You are lost, Elio. Truly lost," as a tear ran down her cheek.

Later, much later, when the city was dark, Emperor Elio Krator sat in the palace throne room on his eagle-winged chair, with a pile of blackened crystal at his feet. No particular part of it would make for a good footstool in this state, so he would see that someone made something out of it later. He sat there, waiting, until the door groaned open and Val'kor entered in his threadbare red robes. He had that sly oily smile on his face, that smile Krator hated. This priest was just a commoner given power. He was nothing until Eldur came along, a lowly holy man in some Agarathi backwater. *And yet he walks around with that smile, pulling my strings.* A part of him wanted to kill the man. Every time he saw him, he wanted to kill him.

"Your Eminence." The creature bowed, not low or with any sort of reverence. He was a corpse in robes, an insult to Krator's court. He could not help his lip from flickering in disgust at the sight of him. "I saw the show. Very entertaining, yes. I could hear the screams from the sky."

"Mercalo's. The woman didn't make a sound."

"Perhaps she was not so weak as this herald made her out to be?" Val'kor chuckled. He looked around the great chamber where Elio Krator had sat before as steward of the city, hearing the petitions of his people, passing his judgements. "Are you happy to be back?"

"Yes. What do you want?"

The priest looked at him with his strange red-flecked eyes. "A little gratitude would be nice. All of this, you have from us."

"From *Eldur*. Not you. You are just another herald, Val'kor, and you've seen what I do with them."

That won him another chuckle. "Oh yes, I would not want to get on your bad side, my lord." He spoke with utter disdain for him. Elio Krator squeezed a fist. "I have some friends joining me," the creature said, still admiring the hall. "Some more dragons, some more dragonknights, and some more *priests* as well. I hope they will be welcomed, my lord. They are very good friends of mine."

They're not your friends. You don't know them. You're a baseborn backwater preacher, nothing more. Elio Krator kept his thoughts to himself. "Fine. I will have somewhere in the city cleared out for you."

"Good. Very good, my lord. I am happy to find you in a helpful mood."

"It is my only mood," said the emperor. He wanted the man gone. He felt dirty in his company, slick with filth. "Was there anything else?"

"Yes. One more thing." He pulled at his rope of beard. "I am told that the Grand Duchess's health has somewhat stabilised, is this true?"

"It would seem so, yes." Elio had spoken earlier with Safina's physicians, and her condition had not deteriorated for a while. They seemed unsure of how long she had. Months and maybe even years seemed more likely now than days or weeks. "She is a strong woman."

"A woman you are fond of. She was once very close to you."

"Yes. A long time ago."

"And now?"

"We have…had our troubles. Don't pretend you don't know what they are."

"Oh, I know. I know so very much about that, my lord." He smiled that horrid smile again and pulled on his rope of beard. "I want her," he said. "Tonight. You will deliver her to me."

"*Want* her?" Something in Elio Krator came close to snapping. He rose to his feet. "If you dare lay a hand on her…"

"Oh child, *boy*, you misread me."

"Boy? You would call *me* boy. You!"

"*Sit down*, my lord," and his voice was different, rougher, louder, a harder voice full of darkness and malice that filled up all the room - it was Eldur's voice. Krator sat down, pressed back by its force. He blinked; the voice was ringing in his ears. "Go up to the top of the palace, now," Val'kor went on. "Yes, go, like a good little boy. Tell your sweet old mother to put on a cloak. I will be taking her away tonight."

Elio Krator wanted to reach for his blade, to call for Braccaro or his guards, but he didn't. He only nodded, quelled, and croaked, "Where?"

And Val'kor only smiled.

63

Pagaloth

Pagaloth drove his sword into the guts of a spearman, pulled it out in a gush of blood, sidestepped the swing of an axe and swung low, hacking through its bearer at the legs. The dragonsteel blade made it through one leg and halfway through the other, just below the knee, jarring into bone. The axman howled and fell as Pagaloth ripped the steel out, raised his blade to finish him off and paused. There was a shout behind him. He turned, saw a dragonknight pressing upon him in his black scale armour and long red cloak. "Traitor!" the man shrieked, maddened.

Pagaloth swung to face him, leaving the axman screaming and clutching at his stump leg. He met the dragonknight's cut with a ring of steel as the two red-black dragonsteel blades kissed and parted, kissed and parted, and the two men circled through the muddy field. Around them the battle went on, though skirmish would be more accurate, and it was ending. There were several hundred foemen only and most were already dead. The dragons had seen to that, with fang and flame. Pagaloth and the others had only dismounted after, taking to the ground to help finish them off.

"You are a traitor! A traitor to Eldur!"

"And you're a slave to him." Pagaloth had heard the same insult levied at him a hundred times before and it was becoming tedious. There had been many of these skirmishes now across the Wandering Wood, and parts of the Heartlands too, and he'd taken his share of life. It had not always been so. When the Agarathi landed at King's Point to siege the city, he had remained behind the walls, preferring to abstain from the slaying of his countrymen. That was no longer the case. They were slaves, and he was saving them. *Death releases them,* he told himself. *So give it to them. Break their chains.*

His foe came again. Pagaloth parried his swing, lunged to strike, and missed as the man slipped away. He was skilled, this one. "Where is Ten'kin?" he asked.

The dragonknight answered with a shriek of 'traitor' and hacked at his head with a savage downcut. Pagaloth swung to divert the flight of his blade and the steel sparked where their edges met.

"Ten'kin. Is he dead?"

"I know of no Ten'kin!"

That could be true, Pagaloth supposed. Ten'kin was one of many fire priests crawling across these lands, and further afield as well. *He is important to me,* he thought. *There is no reason this knight should know him.*

Their bout continued to the song of clashing steel. Their blades met and parted and met again. They were well-matched, well-trained, and Pagaloth wondered if he knew him. *Maybe I studied with him back in Eldurath? Served with him at Dragonfall? Maybe I knew him in my youth?* He could not see the man's face behind his visor, only the heat and the hate in his eyes. *Best not lift that faceplate when I kill him.* If Pagaloth knew this man, he would prefer not to know.

They passed a burning patch of grass as the rain began to fall. Smoke chugged up from the open field in a hundred places, filling the sky with fume. Dragon shrieks filled the air and their shapes rippled by, sometimes breathing down lances of flame, at others dipping to pluck men up from the ground to crush and dismember them. It was brutal, bloody, terrible. *But necessary*, Pagaloth knew.

He slew his foe at last, driving him back with a series of thrusts, cuts, and lunges until he toppled down to the muddy earth. The dragonknight snarled and spat out 'traitor' one last time as Pagaloth lunged in and drove his blade through his breastplate and into his heart. The thrust was clean and powerful. It had to be, to pierce dragonscale armour, and the man died at once, flopping down into the mud to lie still. Pagaloth stood over him, hating it. He took no pride in the kill.

"Nicely done," said a voice behind him.

Pagaloth glanced back. Sir Torus Stoutman was there, watching. He bore a godsteel battleaxe in one hand - double-edged and slick with blood on both sides - and his rosewood pipe in the other. Torus liked to smoke while killing and he did both very well. He plunged the pipe between his lips and took a puff.

"Nice and clean. A good quick death."

"I don't like to make them suffer needlessly." Pagaloth's eyes roved the field, searching for the others. Not far away, Connor Crawfield was battling against a few final stragglers, while Rhok, Sir Hahkesh, and Bah'run were already going among the dead, turning them over and looking at their faces. They were searching for fire priests, the true blight of this land. Not so easy, depending on how they were killed. Men burned to death in the flames of dragonfire did tend to look rather alike.

Stoutman wiped his bloody axe down on his cloak, then fixed it once more to his back. His pipe remained between his bearded lips, dangling to one side as little ringlets of grey smoke rose from the bowl. The rain was wetting through his great beard and dampening his hair. "Well, that's that, then. I killed fourteen, so you know."

"Thank you for telling me."

"Connor will be similar, I'd guess." He regarded his fellow Vandarian a moment as the Varin Knight put the finishing touches on the death of his foes. The swish of mist rose from his godsteel blade as he made quick work of them, and within moments he stood alone. "Maybe a couple more," Stoutman admitted. "He's a dead-eyed killer, that one. Though takes no joy in it. Same as you."

Pagaloth did not take joy in much of anything. He was a grey man, cold and colourless, and had been since the days of his youth.

"You'll tell Marak how we fought?" Stoutman went on. "Not sure I trust that dragonlady to paint us so pretty as you will, Pagaloth."

"I'll give an honest appraisal," the dragonknight promised. He smiled thinly, cleaned his blade against the cloak of his fallen foe, rather than spoiling his own, and sheathed it. Lendrathor was wheeling overhead with Hapthanor, and Pagaloth raised a hand to hail them. The two dragons banked together as the born wing riders they were and came racing down to land on the muddy field, stirring a nearby blaze with their wings as the flames erupted in a billow of black smoke. An'zon Graz was strapped up and saddled on Hapthanor's back. He was not one for battling blade to blade and had preferred to stay far above the action, the same as Lady Kazaan, when the others dismounted to fight.

"The skies are very dark to the east," Graz called down. "We had best get going before the rain becomes torrential, Pagaloth. Happy gets unhappy in the rain."

Pagaloth nodded. The clouds were big and ominous out there and nearing quickly on a stiff westerly wind. A foul deluge was on the way. "Did you see many of them flee, An'zon?"

"Some, yes. Maybe a score to two dozen, something like that." He stood up in the saddle in his green and cream cloak and pointed to the wooded valley at the far edge of the field. "They fled that way. South. Same as the others we've seen."

South. They saw many Agarathi moving south these days, when flying on their patrols and searching for targets and there was a growing sense that they were fleeing back to the Red Sea, back across the water to Agarath. Many had come over on dragonback, strapped to those structures, but not all. The majority crossed in boats, they knew. Pagaloth had seen them himself, scores and scores of them all huddled together in some broken harbour, or pulled up along some shore. The castles along the Black Coast were poorly garrisoned, and all had come under attack at some point over the last half year. Nightwell, Greyguard, and Chilgrave were the mightiest of the three, and so far as Pagaloth knew, only small standing forces of Pentar men remained to watch over them, if any at all. Any one of them could be overwhelmed and taken, and maybe they already had? *I should fly and check,* he thought. *When the weather clears, I'll go look.*

Now was not the time, though. The rain was already starting to patter harder against his helm and the dragons were looking suspiciously at the sky, judging its ill intent. Pagaloth peered across the darkening field as the big, slim dragon Tundrath came swooping down to land before Sir Connor Crawfield. Lady Adelle Kazaan sat awaiting him in the saddle, her sky blue and ochre cape quickly becoming sodden and sticking to her back. Tundrath hated the storm more than most and the dragonlady would want to be going as soon as possible. Once Connor had climbed up and mounted behind her, Tundrath turned their way, half running and half gliding, to join in their post-battle council.

"We are leaving," the dragonlady said. It was not a point of discussion, but an order. Kazaan was second only to Ulrik Marak in rank among their order of rogues. Across the field, the others were still checking the dead, but it was becoming increasingly difficult in the gloom. "Tell them to summon their dragons and leave. Now. I do not want to delay."

"There are still many bodies to check, my lady," Pagaloth told her. "If you'll permit it, I will stay a few minutes longer with them while you return to the hideout with An'zon. We will be fast on your tail."

"Fine," she snapped. The woman was very waspish and had a fearsomely short temper. "Mount up, Torus. We are leaving right now."

Pagaloth crossed the burned and boggy field as the others went from corpse to corpse, glancing at them only or turning them over to look into their faces before moving on to the next. He heard the thump of wings as Tundrath and Hapthanor soared off to the north with the two Bladeborn knights. Rhok watched them go, narrow-eyed. "They are leaving us?"

"We'll be right behind once we're finished. No fire priests, Rhok?"

"Not yet. But there is one here, I know it. I can smell the stink of him." His nostrils flared and he scowled.

"Find him," said Pagaloth. "Lord Marak will want to know for certain."

Pagaloth added his own eyes to the effort, though it was the living, not the dead, he was searching for. That was sadly the case for a good many of the men, who lay butchered and burned across the boggy field, still taking their last ragged breaths. He found an old man with grey streaks in his braided beard trying to scoop his guts up from the mud. "Do you know the name Ten'kin?" Pagaloth asked him. "Have you seen the Knight of the Vale?"

He had found that men flickered back to life in their last moments, like the final futile dance of a candleflame before it suddenly fizzled out. It was as though Eldur's hold on them faded and they were free again, if only for a moment, before death took them. The old soldier blinked and looked at him. "I...no, I have not seen him."

"And the name Ten'kin?"

"I do...not know it...no, I..." And he cringed, suddenly. "Where am I? Why...did you kill me? Why did you kill me? *Why?*"

"It was not me," said Pagaloth. "But I will ease your passing. Stay still."

He went around the field, asking questions and ending lives. The name Ten'kin was not known to these men, and no one had seen Lythian Lindar. Some spat at him in defiance, others answered honestly before they died. Not all were enslaved by Eldur's will. Some were here merely by coercion, through the deployment of fear, and others still by patriotism and the righteous belief that their cause was just. *They are just as lost as the rest of them,* Pagaloth thought.

By the time he was done, the deluge was coming down mercilessly upon them. Pagaloth hurried back over to the others. "Did you find any?"

"Two," said Sir Hahkesh. He kicked at a corpse. It was badly burnt, and one side of his face had been scorched and melted, but the other showed the remains of a beard and it was oiled and red and twisted. "And that one." He pointed out a second corpse, which was headless, though the head had been found and added to the body and together they made another priest.

"Good," Pagaloth said. Two dead priests made for a profitable afternoon, and a dozen dragonknights had died here too. He took no pleasure in it, but that was a dozen fewer to add to Eldur's armies. The two or three hundred others were common soldiers, and there had been a few northern defectors in their ranks as well. "We should go, then," Pagaloth said, scanning the skies. "Call your dragons and saddle up."

It was done. All of them mounted up as quickly as they could, and as the first flash of lightning crashed out of the east, they thumped away north, flying with all speed.

By habit, Pagaloth kept his eyes trained low, peering for firelight in the woods, for the movement of men below. He had flown across this land a hundred times now in search of Lythian, but the man remained frustratingly elusive. *No doubt he is long gone by now.* He may have returned to King's Point, or pursued Brontus Oloran all the way north to Elinar or some other place. *Or he may be dead,* Pagaloth thought grimly. That seemed just as likely by now.

They flew for an hour through the wind and the rain before the hideout came into view. Sometimes it could be hard to find when it got too dark and stormy, but all knew this land intimately by now, and were able to find their way home. Beneath the thick blanket of fog that hung between the rift walls a soft glow of light could be seen from the campfire. *Hard Place* plunged down first, stirring the fog and vanishing. He was a big dragon, thick and bulky, and much a fit for his rider, Rhok. The name, of course, had been thought up by An'zon Graz, and Rhok rather liked it once Graz explained what it meant, so called him Hard Place from then on. The dragonknight Sir Hahkesh followed behind on his serene female dragon *Madarax* and behind went baseborn Bah'run riding *Saminex the Small,* a pudgy but determined little dragon who'd had the last third of its tail cut off in some earlier battle. An'zon called them *Maddy* and *Sam,* much to Adelle Kazaan's annoyance. Dragons should not have pithy nicknames, she had said, and so Graz responded by giving them all pithy nicknames.

Lendrathor (Lenny to Graz) was the last to cut through the shroud and enter the great crack in the forest. The dragons screamed and landed on the broad rock shelf where they had raised their camp, waiting for their riders to dismount, then pumped their wings and went to settle on their private roosts, shaking the rain off their scales like overgrown dogs. Above them all, Garlath the Grand watched imperiously, master to them all, his silver and blue scales lit by the fire below. A deep rumble echoed from him, and trails of smoke rose through his teeth, and so followed a council of dragons as the newcomers gave him their reports.

It was being mirrored below as well, as Lord Marak took report by the fire from Lady Kazaan, An'zon Graz, Sir Connor Crawfield and Sir Torus Stoutman. Angrar, the tongueless cook turned rider, had prepared a stew and began ladling out bowls as Pagaloth, Rhok, Hahkesh and Bah'run went to join them. Lord Marak watched them approach. He sat on his stone block in his ancient Body of Karagar amour with the Fireblade steaming at his hip. His dark eyes met Pagaloth's as he neared, and he stood. "Pagaloth, come with me." He stepped away for a private word.

The dragonknight followed, wondering what this could be about. *Lythian? Has he found Lythian today? Or Ten'kin?* He was leading him toward the crack in the ravine wall where they kept the prisoners. *Could he be in there now? Will we kill him together, for Sa'har?* The storm could be heard raging beyond the rift, the rush of wind and slash of rain as it tumbled down from the broken skies. The dragonlord stopped just as he reached the crevice, then turned to him. The others were taking their places by the fire and being served their bowls of stew, chatting merrily about the battle. Graz was japing, Stoutman was smoking and japing, and Lady Kazaan was scowling. That was a normal day here.

"The dwarf says he fought well," Lord Marak rumbled. "He claims to have slain a hundred men."

Pagaloth smiled. "A slight exaggeration, my lord. He told me fourteen."

"It was meant as a jest, I am sure." He rubbed the greying bristles of his wide, dimpled chin, unamused. "Regardless, it is time to let them leave," he decided. "They have done as I asked, and fought for me. I must keep my end of the bargain."

Pagaloth agreed with that. "I think that would be fair, my lord."

Ulrik Marak had not wanted to be used without getting anything in return. His pride, if nothing else, had demanded that the two knights shed blood for him before he'd permit them to fly again on their scouting missions. They had done just that over the last week. It was time to let them leave again and bring tidings to the realm.

"Will you permit them to fly to Westmire?" Pagaloth asked. He knew that was where they wanted to go, above all other places.

"Yes. I will send one of them there, to see about this army under Borrus Kanabar. The other may fly further afield. I know that there has been little news from Rasalan. It would be wise to find out how the sea-folk fare."

Pagaloth nodded. "I would ask your permission to fly somewhere myself, my lord. South," he explained, "to give a study of the coast. I'd like to know if our kin are taking up in the fortresses there, or else fleeing back across the sea."

"Fine," Marak agreed. "You can visit the coast after."

"After, my lord?"

"I had a visitor earlier," the dragonlord said. "He wanted to stay and speak to you himself, but I told him not to wait. That you might be a time in coming back. He has returned to Varinar to await you. You'll fly from here before the dawn, Pagaloth, and land beyond the city walls. He will be awaiting you there."

"You're talking about Elyon Daecar?"

Lord Ulrik Marak nodded. "He will meet you outside the city with his father, and you will bear the Frostblade to Ilithor. It is time, it would seem, for the king to give up his crutch."

64

Emeric

The city of Ilithor stood before him.

Embraced by the mountains at the end of the valley, it was as grand and beautiful as Emeric Manfrey remembered it. *The White City*, he thought. It was named that for the pristine stone of its construction, but right now, it might have been because of the snow. It had fallen thickly here. Across the valley the grasslands were heaped in it, and the mountains that ranged out to the south and to the north were heavily laden as well.

The road, at least, was mostly clear, the snows swept aside and heaped in drifts by the travellers who had come this way. It cut a path through the valley, leading to the grand city gates, marked at fifty-metre intervals by posts. At the coming of dusk, lanterns would be brought out from the city and hung at those posts for many miles, to light the way home for weary travellers. It was a tradition that had lasted centuries, Emeric knew, and a tradition was no longer being observed. Dusk was upon them, and Emeric saw no lanterns. *The road to Ilithor is dark*, he thought.

Jonik was trotting listlessly at his side. They rode alone, just the two of them, with Dog loping along beside them. Ahead, some two hundred metres away, rode the last of Saska's company. There were only five of them now, following the battle in the clearing. The sellswords Emeric later learned were called the Surgeon, the Gravedigger, and Umberto were dead, along with the young archer called Jaito. The man called the Baker was badly wounded and sat uneasily on his horse with his brother close beside, though the rest were largely unharmed. Those were the Butcher, the Tigress, Leshie, and the Wall. The Whaleheart rode a gigantic horse and had been tasked with bearing the Nightblade. He did so solemnly, and his face was grave. A deep heavy sadness had consumed the whole company now. A sadness and a despair, for their shining light was gone.

It was a rarely pretty evening, and cruelly so, as though the skies themselves had expected a triumphant arrival. The twilight was red and gold and brilliant, and the slow-moving clouds were saturated in colour. Off the snow it shone, and the mountains and the city. Men stood atop the battlements above the gate, watching them riding closer. Emeric wondered how much they knew. Did they know of the blades, of the Heart Remade? Did they know of the heir who was meant to wield it? *When they learn that she is gone, what then? Will that same despair strangle them as well? Will it spread across all the north?*

"I should have used it," Jonik said, in a doleful voice. "I should have done more, Emeric."

"You did what you could."

"No. They're twins, the blades. Their powers are similar. I should have thrown down the Nightblade instead. I should have tried to use the Mistblade. If I had…"

"Then what, Jonik? Do you really think it would have made a difference?"

The man grimaced. "Maybe. The Nightblade didn't, I know that much. That *eagle*…it was watching me the whole time. If I'd used the Mistblade I might have cut right through that dragon. I could have killed it, and the priest as well. I could have saved her."

But you didn't, Emeric thought. *You didn't, nor did the Whaleheart, nor did anyone else.* Seven dragons had assaulted them. Seven, against a force of only a dozen men and women. Those were impossible odds no matter how you chose to look at it. "We should be thankful any of us are alive," he said. "Saska made the only choice that was available to her. We all would have died in that clearing if she hadn't given herself up, Jonik. There was no other way this was going to end."

And we still have the blades, he thought. There was some hope in that, at least.

Ahead, the gates were opening. Soldiers were coming forth from inside the city to stop the newcomers outside the walls. Emeric could see the remains of the vast refugee encampment in the snow, sprawled outside the walls on the city's northern side. None of the tents or shelters there looked occupied now. No doubt all had been let into the refuge, or within the walls at least.

They continued to ride slowly along the road as the dusk deepened in the western skies. A short conference was taking place at the gate. Then a moment later, they were waved inside and the Whaleheart led them on with a small band of soldiers accompanying them. Others remained outside, waiting for Jonik and Emeric to come.

They arrived a few minutes later. A big man with jowls and a chequered cloak of brown and green squares stepped forward. "Jonik. I'm glad to see you again."

"Lord Morwood."

"I just spoke with your companions," the lord said. "They are being led up through the city to the palace; we have rooms for you all." He glanced at Jonik's hip. "I confess myself surprised to see Sir Ralston Whaleheart carrying your old blade, Jonik. But I hear you have bonded a new one?"

"Only partly."

"Yes, I understand. You will want them taken to Lord Ilith, of course. I'm sure the voices have been particularly, um…poisonous, of late. As you have neared the city." He smiled uncomfortably when Jonik gave no answer. "Well, we'll see you to him at once. Come, come. And Lord Manfrey, well met. I know Lord Ilith is most keen to meet you."

Emeric frowned. "He knew we were coming?"

A laugh from Morwood, and a confused one. "I try not to ask too many questions. Most of what I hear comes through Fhanrir, and often he can be rather cryptic. And very mean, as Jonik will know."

"He's a bastard," Jonik said. "Though of a different sort to me."

Morwood chuckled. "Quite. Yes, quite. Very mean is the mage. But without him we would be rather lost as well, so I do suppose the trade is acceptable." He stepped to one side. "Well, in you come, then. You can dismount just here in the yard. I have men who can tend to your horses, and there is mulled wine if you want it as well. Something to warm you after your long ride."

Emeric could do with a spot of warming. Once he'd ridden through into the entrance square and dismounted, a stableboy came up to take his horse and a server approached with a tray of steaming cups. Emeric took one, thanked him, and drank. The wine was spiced just right and the perfect temperature as it trickled down to warm his chest. He sighed at the sensation.

Jonik did not partake, though a gate guard came out with a bone for Dog and the mastiff began chewing and crunching on it happily. "Where did you get him?" Lord Morwood asked.

"The Crabby Onion."

"An inn, is it?"

Jonik did not bother telling the story. "We had thought to take him south when we leave, but maybe he'll be better staying here with you. Are animals allowed in the refuge?"

"Some, yes. The cats have been helping to keep the mice honest, and the dogs are, well, they're dogs. Everyone loves dogs." He clearly did, by the big smile on his face as he reached down with a gloved hand and gave the mastiff a good strong pat. They looked rather alike, with those jowls. "Does he have a name?"

"Dog."

"Yes, the dog. Does he have a name?"

"Dog," Jonik said again. "That's the only name he's got."

"I see." Morwood frowned, puzzled. "Well, I suppose Dog's as good a name as any. I had a cat called Cat once."

"Did you?"

"No. Shall we get going?"

The watch commander led them on through the city. It was very quiet down in White Shadow, the lowest of the city districts, where typically it would be teeming. They passed up the sloping snowy streets, through squares and yards and sometimes up switchback stairs as they climbed ever upward through the tiers. Morwood spoke as they went, discussing troubles both old and new. He had plenty to say about the rioting at Galin's Post, about the latest squabbles and treacheries within the refuge. Men were leaving now, he told them, to be trained up and added to the war, and they were being kept here in the city for now. "They're being housed in the Sentinels," Morwood said. "We have many thousands now. Though they won't be much more than dragon fodder in any proper battle, I fear."

The city districts were each separated by walls atop which soldiers walked with bow and spear, watching the skies. There were many mounted ballistas on turntables, many trebuchets and catapults and mangonels. Some of the ballistas were set on rails that could move swiftly along the walls as well. That made them harder targets for dragons when they tried to plunge and dive to destroy them with fire and claw. Above White Shadow sat Many Markets, and above that the Sentinels. It was busiest here, with all the men being trained and armed. They could hear the ring of steel in training yards and the shouts of masters-at-arms bellowing orders. They heard the thud of arrows striking butts and the call of nock and draw. Beyond the Sentinels was the city's richest uppermost district, the Marble Steps, with its lofty mansions and high walkways, its covered bridges and balconies and marvellous views. Some of the more belligerent lords and gentry remained holed up in their stout stone strongholds, Morwood said, though by now, most had retreated to the safety of the refuge.

"Are any more being allowed inside?" Emeric asked.

"Allowed? Yes, they're allowed if they want to go. But only women and children now. No more men are being permitted."

"We didn't see anyone on the road," Jonik said. "Not for the last few days."

"No. There was a great flood some months ago, but soon the flood became a flow and then that flow became a trickle and now it's all but stopped. Though some are still coming down from the north as well. To escape the snow."

The palace sat above the rest of the city, grand, imperious, and beautiful. It was many-winged, with high towers and rich halls, and empty now for the most part, Morwood said. "Lady Clarris still lingers, though she never leaves her rooms," he told them, "and the princess returns often as well." He had a grave look on his face. "More so of late, I fear to say. There was a sad incident some days ago, involving a young knight called Mallister Monsort. He threw himself off the walls of the Shadowfort, for what reason I haven't been told. The princess has taken the loss rather hard. She was very close to him, very close indeed."

"Is she here now?" Jonik asked. There was a twist of pity on his brow.

"Yes. Though I understand she wishes to remain undisturbed. I would not call upon her yet, Jonik. Give her a little more time."

They reached the steps that led up to the palace doors and entered its capacious atrium. Ahead, a great stair swung to the left and right, curving up through many levels and crystal chandeliers hung down from the ceilings. The stone floors were laid with Solapian rugs in rich red velvet, bordered in gold and green, and each piece of furniture, each table and lamp and chair was exquisite and finely carved.

Emeric remembered the last time he was here. He had been summoned to the throne room to stand accused of his crimes before the great and good of the city. He remembered how they looked at him, and sneered at him, and scowled at him. He remembered Modrik Kastor's lies and Janilah Lukar's lazy dismissal. *One word from him was all it took*, he thought. *One word and my life was over.* He had been banished that day, dispossessed of his lands and titles and exiled beyond the borders of Tukor. He looked up the stairs, recalling how nervous he had been as he went up and how angry as he came down. *But I made a life,* he told himself. *I made a beautiful life in the south, and that was taken too.*

Morwood's heavy voice interrupted his musings. "You are both very tired after your long journey, I'm sure, but I know that Lord Ilith wants to see you as soon as possible. If you are willing, I will escort you through the tunnels. Sir Ralston has already been led there. He awaits us at the gate."

They turned right down a set of stairs, through long dark dusty corridors and open empty halls, before emerging to the edge of the palace where the mountains climbed away to the north. Sir Ralston was awaiting them there. His face was grim and drawn, as battered and scarred as his wartorn armour. *He lives in shame now,* Emeric thought. *His charge was to protect her, and he couldn't...not that night.*

The Nightblade was sheathed at his hip. The giant could carry it, but only with great effort, and refused to build anything but the most fragile bond to the blade. He looked weary, drained. For the last week he'd been sharing that burden with Bedrock, his horse, but the horse was down in the stables now and the giant must bear its weight alone.

"Can you carry it?" Jonik asked him.

"Yes. But it will be slow."

"I can help if I must," Jonik said. He peered at the giant for a moment. "How are the whispers? Do you feel them becoming more acute? More intense?"

"They are loud, in here." He tapped a steel finger against his head, and grimaced. "The things they are saying..."

"What are they saying?"

"They urge me to kill myself. For my failure." His lips twisted. "When we enter the mountain, they hope I will throw myself down some chasm."

"It is the last desperate grasp at freedom," Emeric said.

Jonik nodded. "They're afraid. I feel it too, Sir Ralston. We will go side by side, then, and watch out for one another. It will be easier when we reach the refuge."

"Oh," said Morwood. "No, no. Lord Ilith is not in the refuge. He is here, above the city. He returned to his old forge some days ago."

"Is it closer?" Emeric asked.

"A little," Jonik answered. "I climbed up there before, with Gerrin and Harden, when we came through the portal. We'll have to be careful on the steps. It will be the last chance for the blades to corrupt us."

Jonik shared a final look with Sir Ralston, nodded, and then the two bearers stepped forward through the gate.

The tunnels were dark as pitch. Morwood lit a torch, then strode ahead, igniting some of the lanterns fixed along the walls. The tunnels were closed at night, he said, for those coming and going from the refuge. They progressed down a long passage and into a wider chamber. Here Emeric took a torch of his own from the wall, waving it side to side as a broad cavern opened out, scarred with rifts and chasms that plunged away into blackness. Bridges had been built across them. Emeric watched very closely as first Jonik, and then Sir Ralston, passed over the first of them. He saw the giant grimacing, saw his eyes grow strained, saw him tighten his jaw against the urges. "Come," Jonik said, awaiting him on the other side. "Come, sir. It's this way."

The giant reached the other side safely. Emeric pressed on after him, glancing down over the edge. He could hear the wind moving strangely down there, hear queer haunting sounds drifting up from below. "It's always like that," Morwood told him. "Believe me, I've come back and forward through here a hundred times, and it doesn't get any less disquieting."

"Is something down there?"

"Just air, I think. Very ghostly sounding air."

There were more bridges to cross as they progressed through the system of caves, and over each Jonik went first, making sure his companion crossed safely. The King's Wall was panting from the effort, sweat beading on his boulder of a forehead. Before very long he was hunched and lurching, even muttering to himself, and sometimes waving out at things only he could see. Jonik coaxed him on all the while. If the voices were assaulting him as well, he showed little reaction to them. *He is used to them now,* Emeric thought. *He is in full control.*

It wasn't so for the Wall. Emeric could only imagine the terrible things the whispers were saying to him, the awful visions they were putting in his head. He could see the warped expression on the Whale-heart's face in the torchlight, see the wild look in his eye, see the lips moving as they murmured and cringed and fought back tears. It got worse as they went. The poor man was being tortured. At one point he sank heavily to his knees and started striking at the ground, sobbing. "I failed you, I'm so sorry…I failed you…I failed you!" The rock smashed and shattered beneath his gauntlet, and he lifted his head and roared.

"The cat! I told you to leave her! Why didn't you listen…why didn't you hear me!"

They could do nothing but let it pass. Jonik stood by with that pity in his eyes though Morwood's face was a puddle of fear. "What if he attacks us? Might…might he attack us?"

"No," Jonik said quietly. "He won't attack."

"But…if he does. We won't be able to stop him. He would kill us all…

"He won't attack, Trillion." Jonik edged forward very carefully. "Sir Ralston, hear my voice." It was calm, soothing. "It's Jonik, Sir Ralston. You're having a vision, that is all. The blade is showing you something that isn't there."

The giant puffed and wept and smashed at the ground. Pebbles began to come down from the rock ceiling above them. Emeric could hear that clattering away across the cavern. "I failed her, I failed her! The cat…the cat!"

"Sir Ralston," Jonik repeated, firmer. "Hear me. Remember where you are. We are going to see Ilith. *Ilith*," he repeated. "He will make the voices go away."

The giant's head swung side to side, weeping. His face was a chaos of shame. "I failed. I failed her. King Godrin, forgive me, I failed her!"

"You failed no one, Sir Ralston. Saska lives. She still lives. The blade is lying to you. It lies, that's what it does. It told me I was to be a leader, and it *lied*. Don't listen to it, Ralston. You're stronger than that. Be strong."

His words cut through to him. The Whaleheart smashed at the stone again, once, twice, gave out a great shuddering roar and then stopped. He knelt there, panting, and there was a great strain in his eyes. *He is fighting back*, Emeric knew. He could see it. See the conflict. Long moments passed like this until, finally, he pulled one leg up, so he was on a single knee, heaved a breath into his mighty lungs and pressed upward so he was standing. He towered above them all by almost two full feet.

He looked at Jonik. "Thank you," he said.

"That's all right. I know how hard it is."

The Whaleheart lifted a hand to his cheek and saw the wetness of his tears. He seemed confused by them, as though he'd never seen them before. As though he'd never wept.

"We won't tell anyone," Jonik told him. A smile touched his lips. "What happens in the tunnels stays in the tunnels. Are you good to keep going?"

"Yes. I…I think so."

"I can help if you wish."

"No." The giant shook his head firmly. "No. I must do this myself. It is my burden. My penance." He filled his lungs, setting his eyes down the darkened tunnel. And pace by heavy pace, he plodded on.

The way continued. The narrower tunnels had been opened out and reinforced by Morwood's men, and they began to see detritus along the way, things discarded by the legions heading for the refuge, and sometimes broken wagons or carts, even the remains of shelters from those who had waited in line. Where the ground was most uneven, plank decking had been laid down to make it easier for the carts to cross. In other places Morwood's men had used their godsteel blades to cut and shape the rock to make it flatter.

There was one final bridge to cross, spanning a broader chasm. Jonik went over first and turned to watch Sir Ralston follow. The giant moved slowly, looking forward. "Look at me," Jonik said. "Look at me and keep going." There was a moment when the Whaleheart paused at the heart of the bridge and looked over the edge into the blackness, and something seized in Emeric's chest. *He's going to throw himself off. The voices. He's going to kill himself.* But the giant wrestled his inner demons, defeated them, and kept on going. Once he was safely over Emeric heard Morwood give out a great sigh of relief.

"That is the last bridge," he said, breathing out. "From here it is only tunnels and chambers. Until we reach the stair."

And on they went, on and on, the King's Wall lurching and lumbering, struggling through every step, Jonik coaxing and helping him down every passage and through every cave. The young man must surely be fighting demons of his own, but he never showed it, never muttered or grimaced or cringed. Emeric Manfrey was proud of him. *He is a leader still,* he thought.

At last they came to a passage where the sky opened out above them, a band of black atop high white walls. It was true dark then and the stars were out, coming and going behind banners of tattered cloud. A wind was blowing fiercely and it was almost as though they could hear singing in it, the hum of a voice murmuring amid the storm. As they walked along the corridor, the left cliff wall began to recede until it was gone entirely, and the view opened out before them. Emeric saw the palace away beneath them now, saw the city spread beyond it, saw the great open valley and the road that stretched away as a thin line through the great white plains. They had come high, much higher than he'd thought, but must go higher still.

"The stair is here," Morwood said.

It was on their right, where the cliff face was cut with a treacherous switchback that went high up into the inky skies. There was a rope along the wall, hammered into the rock at intervals as it went back and forth.

"It looks worse than it is," Jonik said. "Sir Ralston, maybe I should take the Nightblade from here. I can climb up with one and return to fetch the other."

"No. I must finish this." The others shared looks, but the giant was defiant. He stamped straight toward the stair and began the climb.

Jonik went behind him, then Morwood, then Emeric. The stairs themselves were carved into the rock face and many were uneven and icy. Morwood turned his head and shouted something back, something about Ilith, but Emeric didn't hear him. The wind was blustering at them here, tugging and pulling at their cloaks and the bag of supplies that Emeric carried on his back. He peered up through the shroud, clinging to the rope, fearful that the Whaleheart might fall, but he never did. He seemed to be driving onward very quickly now, back and forth along the switchbacks, back and forth, eager to get this done. Soon the fog swirled in and there was only white beneath them and it felt to Emeric Manfrey like they were climbing up into some other world.

We're leaving the mortal realm behind, he thought. *Only the gods reside up here.*

He climbed up, up, up. The Wall was fading from view, and Jonik, and even Morwood, only a few steps ahead of him, was being swallowed up from his sight. It became a spiritual experience for Emeric Manfrey. *His forge,* he thought, *I am climbing up to Ilith's ancient forge. These are the steps that Varin himself scaled when he came to see the Five Blades. This is where they were born.* His heart was thumping with excitement, and his mind was whirling. Staid old Emeric Manfrey was beaming like a boy.

And then he reached the top. It came suddenly, the stairs turning to face the cliff and he was scaling the last few steps and up to the snowy summit. The fog cleared abruptly, and he saw the others standing there ahead of him, Lord Morwood, Jonik, and Sir Ralston Whaleheart all facing across the plateau to the mountainside. There was a large open doorway there, like the mouth of a cave, and beyond Emeric could see the anvil, the workbenches, the oven and the tools, he saw the bellows and the tongs and armour and weapons on the walls, the shelves containing hundreds of books and tomes and scrolls.

From inside, a little cloaked figure was shambling along with his walking stick. He clacked it as he came, *clack clack clack*, and the rotten features of his face were concealed with his hood. "You came. Good. Bring the blades inside." Fhanrir was not one for pomp and ceremony. He turned around, and they followed him across the snowy plateau.

To Emeric's left, the decaying body of a large dragon lay sprawled across the mountaintop. "That was the dragon my grandfather slew," Jonik said. "I saw it when I came here with Gerrin and Harden."

It was still partly preserved from the cold, though much of the skeleton was showing through the meat and it was well draped in a covering of snow. Fhanrir paused a moment and waved his stick at it. "I want rid of that thing. You. Whaleheart. You're a big strong lad. Think you can shove it off the mountain for me?"

The King's Wall seemed almost too exhausted to speak.

"Well, later," Fhanrir said, glancing at him. "We'll see to that later. Come."

The forge was a few dozen metres back from the stair, and firelight warmed the air inside it. Emeric felt like he was lost in a dream. He looked from one thing to the next, wide-eyed with wonder, trying to preserve his sense of calm. "My gods, is that..."

"The Hammer of Tukor, aye."

Emeric moved over to it as a holy man might approach the altar, gripped by a powerful reverence. The hammer rested upon a workbench, radiating a soft silvery-gold light, though it was plainer than the singers would have you believe. The handle was simple, wood wrapped in a leather grip that had seen much use, and the head was not so large or wondrous as it was depicted in sculptures and statues and paintings. Etchings and markings glowed on the metal, runes of magic beyond the exile's understanding. Plain enough though it was, he preferred it this way. *Ilith was always known to be humble,* he thought. It made sense that his hammer would be humble as well.

"Come," Fhanrir said. "You can put the blades here." The Whaleheart lumbered over, wordless, heaved the Nightblade from its scabbard and up onto the bench. It landed beside the Hammer of Tukor with a powerful and reverberating *thump*. Jonik removed the Mistblade more easily and placed it down there too.

"We've been trying to keep them separated…" he started.

"No need here," Fhanrir dismissed. "Not with Ilith nearby." He regarded the Whaleheart, lifting his eyes up and up and up to meet him. "Well now, you're a big'un, aren't you? Not sure I've seen anyone so large since Varin."

The giant looked like he might just topple over and crush him. "You…knew him?"

"Course I did. I *was* him, for a while." Fhanrir cackled at whatever that meant, though didn't explain. "Did the whispers give you any trouble on the way?"

"A little," Jonik said. "Nothing we couldn't handle." He nodded confidentially at the Whaleheart. "They're subdued now, though."

"Aye, 'cause they know it's over. This is where they were born and they know it's where they'll die."

"To be reborn again," Lord Morwood intoned importantly.

"Oh. You're here too, are you?" Fhanir snorted at him. "Don't try to sound grand, Morwood, it doesn't suit you. You three, stay here. You, with me."

"Me?" asked Emeric.

"Aye. Bring the bag."

Fhanrir shuffled to the rear of the forge. A door led through into a passage that branched into other rooms and living chambers. Emeric's heart was thrashing at his ribs. He glimpsed storerooms, an armoury, a library, a kitchen. He wondered if he should mention Saska; he wondered if the mage already knew. He was about to open his mouth to speak, when the little mage stopped, suddenly, at a closed door. "He's right in here."

He raised his stick to knock, waited a moment, then opened it and shuffled inside.

"Manfrey for you," he said, to a tiny old man who sat hunched at a writing desk, scratching at what looked like a crude hammer with a little metal tool. He was leaning close as he worked, as though half blind. There was a small bed to one side, some shelves bearing ointments and potions and pots. A large old painting hung across the wall above the desk, featuring what seemed like many dozens of separate scenes all muddled and blended together into a chaotic collage. The only light came from the candle by which the old man was writing, and a torch that was fixed to a plain sconce beside the painting, illuminating the faded details.

Emeric saw two winged creatures locked in a death embrace, a line of misting men standing against the storm. A burning city, he saw, and a figure in red and one in gold flying through the night sky. A dragon's face with a red tear falling from one eye. A cloaked man stood crowded by sinister shadows bearing something in his grasp…a hammer, maybe… and he was smiling beneath the cover of his hood. In the heart of the painting, an old man was standing next to a young one, staring forward at him and somehow there was a light in their eyes, a knowing light, and somehow they seemed to be *looking* right at him. *Just the paint*, Emeric thought. *Yes, that's it. The way the firelight hits the paint, that's all…*

The old man was still etching at the head of his hammer. It misted, like godsteel. "Ilith, did you hear me? I said I have Emeric Manfrey for you." Fhanrir raised his voice a little louder, sighing. "He's gone hard of hearing in his old age," he said, and shuffled forward to poke at the man with his walking stick. At last the demigod came out of his reverie, turning his head and frowning. "It's Manfrey," the mage said, once more. "You said for me to bring him."

"Yes…yes." Ilith rose from his chair unsteadily. He looked well past a hundred years old, a tiny twisted crookbacked thing, and Emeric was frankly astonished he'd made it up here. *The stairs. How could he possibly…* "Emeric Manfrey," he croaked. "How very good to meet you." He reached out a thin, liver-spotted hand, and Emeric took it gently lest he break a bone or two. The demigod had long white hair, a thin white beard dangling off his chin, narrow, rumpled lips and heavy drooping bags beneath his eyes. His head hung suspended on a pencil neck that drooped with sallow, wrinkled skin.

"And you…my lord. It's a…a great honour." Emeric tried to smile, but his thoughts were whirring. *How can this be Ilith? How can this man hammer together the heart?*

"Ah honour….yes, so they say." Ilith regarded him amusedly. "I daresay you were expecting someone different, Emeric. Someone younger, no doubt? Stronger, hmmm?"

"I…well…"

Fhanrir broke in. "How much do you know? What did Morwood tell you on the way?"

Emeric opened his mouth to speak, but the little mage waved a hand and said, "No, don't tell me. Just look at me. That's it. Look at me a moment, and…" A second passed as Fhanrir stared into his eyes, then he nodded, turned to Ilith and said, "He knows nothing. Morwood never mentioned the potions."

"Potions?" Emeric asked.

"There are five of them. One for each blade. They age him when he makes them. That's why he looks like this." Fhanrir went over and helped Ilith to his bed. "He's done four. Did the fourth a few days ago, after we came up here. Sad business, really, what with Monsort. Lad killed himself for fear the sap would spoil."

"Sap?" Emeric was hopelessly confused. He did not have the power to read a man's mind like Fhanrir did.

The mage didn't answer him. "The bag," he said. "Lay out the contents. Right there on the desk. Go on."

Emeric did as the mage bid him, removing the bag from his back and extracting the rare elixirs and ingredients he'd taken from the stormhag's lair and later from the workshop of Master Allabor. The little old crone in Lakeheart had told him to take *all* of them back, so he had, before he and Jonik left the city. He laid them all out, one and then another and then another, as Fhanrir stepped up and inspected them. Some he sniffed at. Others he peered at intently, or shook, listening to the contents within. Ilith sat on the bed all the while, a frail little thing, watching with a knowing smile on his lips.

"Anything interesting there, Fhanrir?" he asked.

The mage glared over at him. "You knew," he said, as though in accusation. "You knew he'd come?"

"I hoped," said the demigod, smiling.

"*Hoped?* This is too specific for hope, even for you. Is Tukor guiding you? Thala? Tell me."

Ilith smiled. "Perhaps it is Tyrith who guides me, Fhanrir. Did you ever consider that? I am he as well, do not forget."

The little mage snorted angrily. "Too many riddles. Too many damn riddles with you. Tyrith? What could that boy know of the future?" He made a series of little infuriated grunts and then swung back to Emeric Manfrey. "He's maddening," he told him. "Been telling me for months something will come along, and here comes some exile up from the south, and he's brought with him a bag of tricks."

Emeric wasn't entirely understanding. "Are some of these items going to be useful to you?"

"Useful? Try *essential*." Fhanrir reached forward and lifted up the item Emeric had found most prepossessing of them all. Light pulsed and throbbed from within the wrappings of leather and linen and the mage gazed at it, shaking his head. "You have any idea how rare this is, Manfrey? The core of a fallen star? And one of this quality?"

"I was told it was very rare by Master Allabor."

"He wasn't lying. He tell you about the light and the heat, how they're linked?"

"Yes. You have to reach the core quickly, before it cools, or you lose the light. That takes luck. And you must be able to bear the high temperature to get close." He paused. "I was going to release it," he admitted to them. "The core is the *soul* of a star, Allabor told me. I did not think such a thing should be contained in a pot."

"Many powerful elements can be contained in pots," said Ilith, mysteriously.

Fhanrir snorted at that. "The final potion is called *Light of the Soulstar*," he told Emeric. "Soulstar. The *soul* of a *star*. We don't make that potion, none of this matters. So a good bloody thing you didn't release it. If you had you'd have doomed us all."

Emeric swallowed.

Fhanrir cackled, seeing the expression on his face. "Aye. A lot to get your head around, isn't it?" He put down the star core and plucked up another container. "You know what this is?"

"It's…lightleaf," Emeric managed. He was becoming rather dizzy. "Allabor said…"

"From the Twelve Trees, aye. That's *Aramatia's* light. A goddess's light that's gone now, and we need this too. *Light* of the Soulstar. It's the second major element."

"We have been lacking both," Ilith said, in his croaky old voice. He was smiling very contentedly. "Thank you for bringing them to us, Emeric. They are the last ingredients I need. The rest I have already." He gestured to his shelves with the pots and containers and vials. "I shall now be able to prepare the potion."

"*Will* you?" Fhanrir rounded on him. "You're bedridden, like I said you'd be, weak as a bloody mouse. You don't have the strength for that sorcery, Ilith, or the youth. It'd kill you."

But the demigod only smiled that knowing little smile of his, looked at the ingredients laid out on the table, and said, "Check again, my friend. That one there, right there…"

Fhanrir turned, swung his eyes and dangly nose over the pots and vials that Emeric had brought with him, then stopped. He reached out almost tentatively, picking up a vial containing a sinister-looking red potion so dark it was almost black. His beady little eyes shone from within his hood as he drew it forward, pulled off the stopper with his skeletal fingers, and sniffed the contents within. "The wives," he muttered. "They were always good with their blood magic." He gave the potion a swirl and blackish bubbles popped and rose, fogging up into the room. "Sweetened by pain," he murmured. "And young. Aye, this should do."

"Bring it here, Fhanrir." Ilith held out his hand.

Fhanir shambled over to give it to him. "You knew," he said. "You knew all along."

Ilith glanced at the painting on the wall. "No, my friend. I only *hoped.*"

Then, standing up on his brittle old legs, he lifted the potion to his rumpled lips. He drank it down until nothing remained but a thin mist of reddish air.

For a moment, nothing happened. Then impossibly, incredibly, Ilith began to *de-age*. The white beard rose up and darkened and was gone. The white hair lifted and thickened and turned rich and golden brown, curling into soft little waves. The wrinkles on his face filled in and faded, smoothing, and his back straightened as he grew tall. The old loose robes tightened against his body, and through the opening at his chest, Emeric saw the lean, taut muscle, saw the light beginning to glow from his skin, glow from within him, spread out into the room.

He watched in astonishment as Ilith the Worldbuilder was reborn. And there before him he stood, now, the demigod he'd expected.

"Well," Ilith said, and his voice was young again too. "Shall we get going with that final potion, Fhanrir? I daresay I have the strength for it *now*, don't you think? For that and the final forging."

He smiled handsomely at the mage, towering above him now, but the mage did not smile back. He only scowled and said, "You'll be the death of me, Ilith. You know that? You'll be the bloody death of me."

Ilith nodded sadly. "Oh, I do fear you may be right." And he put a hand on the little mage's shoulder, glancing at the painting once more. "We have things to discuss, my dear friend."

65

Amron

The Frostblade was fixed to Lendrathor's back, strapped up behind Pagaloth's saddle. It was dawn, a beautiful dawn. In the east a pale glow of golden sunlight was warming the horizon, and into it they would go.

Amron crouched on the back of the dragon, making certain the Frostblade was lashed up tight. Pagaloth was helping with the knots, murmuring to Lendrathor all the while to stay calm. "It is different this time," the dragonknight said. "Last time he need only hold you, my lord. Now it's the blade itself he carries."

"Will he manage?" Amron asked.

"Yes, he will manage. He must, my lord, so he will. Lendrathor understands the importance of this."

When both king and dragonknight-turned-dragonrider were satisfied, Amron unclasped his fingers from the Frostblade's hilt for the final time, then climbed back down the dragon's flank to the snowy plains outside the city. He did not want to make a big show of it. He did not want to think about it, lest he err, lest he weaken.

Elyon was waiting for him. "I haven't seen a dawn like it in a while," he said, gazing out toward the horizon. It's almost as though its inviting us on. As though that light itself is coming from Ilithor." He smiled, and perhaps he was thinking of Saska. Maybe that was the light he meant.

"It's a fine morning," Amron agreed. The pain was already reaching into him, throbbing in his shoulder and deep in the meat of his thigh. He held the grimace from his face. He did not want his son to see it.

"Well…this is it, then, Father. I'm not sure when I'll see you again."

"Soon," Amron told him. He would not go with him now, but there seemed no reason why Saska could not come here. They could fly here together in the harness. Perhaps later, once the heart had been remade, she could bring that to him as well, to show him, and he could meet this young girl who carried it.

The king reached into his cloak pocket. "You'll need this as well, son." He withdrew the pot that would bind the blades. Within it was the last fragment of Vandar's spirit, the last vestige of his essence and earthbound power. It took form as a light, subdued and calm, and that light did not make a sound. There was no whisper, no voice, as there was with the blades. Only a sense of great weight…and purpose.

Elyon took the pot; it was the first time he had handled it. He raised it to his eyes and looked at it intently, then said, "Will it…try to fight me? Like the blades?"

"No. It knows what it is for, Elyon. It gave itself up willingly in the mountain, as I told you. I think it has been waiting for this day."

The prince nodded, looking at it a moment longer, then tucked it safely into his pocket. "I'm getting used to being a courier for these artefacts," he said. "I've carried the Windblade, the Nightblade, the Frostblade, and the Eye of Rasalan as well. And now this. Another part of Vandar." He smiled wryly at the absurdity of it. "What's next? Will I carry the Hammer of Tukor as well? Might Eldur be so kind as to lend me the Bondstone?"

Amron remembered that stone. He remembered the beams of crimson light that poured out of it, remembered how that light had screamed in that woeful clamour, as though every soul slain by Agarath was all crying out at once. He could not find the thought of his son bearing it amusing.

"Come. Let me look at you." Amron turned the boy to face him and looked long into his silver-blue eyes. "I'm proud of you, my son. Everything you've done…all your tireless efforts. No one has contributed more to this war than you, Elyon. I want you to know that before you go. Without you we would all be lost."

"Father, you'll make me blush."

"I'm serious, Elyon."

"So am I. I've always blushed easily, you know that."

And you've always hidden in humour when you feel awkward, Amron thought. He had said his piece, and it needed to be said. "Come here, then." And he hugged him, wrapping both arms around his son's back as a throb of pain went through his shoulder. He bit it back, fought it off. It was his new challenge now, to master it.

"Father, you're acting like we won't see one another again."

"I'm acting like a father who loves his son."

"We'll come back soon," Elyon said. "I'll come with Saska. She can meet you and Lillia, and Amara too."

"They'd like that," the king said. "As would I." At last they parted from their embrace. "You had best go, Elyon. I can sense that Lendrathor is getting impatient."

"Right. Yes." Elyon regarded his father's face for a long moment. *He sees it. He already sees it, the pain.* "I spoke with Penrose last night. He told me about Amara's visit to Black Merryl." He paused. "She's to make a new tonic for you? For the pain?"

"I won't be taking those tonics."

"But…"

"I can't, Elyon. After what happened with your grandfather, it would be ill of me to seek the witch's help. Many condemn her for playing a part in his death."

"But that's nonsense. He choked. The witch had nothing to do with it."

"I know. So do many others. But the fact remains, she is a witch and a wildling and is not trusted by most of the men. Some already look at me differently for flying by dragonback, son. I will not have them say I am colluding with a witch as well."

"But you're the king. They'd follow you whatever you do."

Oh, my boy. My sweet, naive son. Amron knew how fickle men could be. He knew how easily they could abandon one man and rally behind another, and Lord Styron the Strong was already positioning himself as his replacement if such a thing might come to pass. He would be crippled now, limping and shambling along, and that alone might give his men pause. He would not add any fuel to that fire. He had Artibus's tonics, and they must be enough.

He did not want to dwell on it, not here and not now. "You have to go, Elyon. Take advantage before the weather spoils."

"I know." The prince filled his lungs. "Tell Amara I love her when she wakes up. And Lillia…take care of her, Father. She's not in a good place right now."

"I will." He cupped the boy's cheek with his gauntleted hand, smiled, and took a step back. "Now go. Fly fleet and safe. And send Pagaloth back with news. I'll want to know that you've made it there safely."

Those were the last words spoken between them. Reluctantly, Elyon drew another breath, turned, and strode away. He called for Pagaloth to prepare for flight, then summoned the wind, raised his blade, and soared up into the air. Lendrathor turned eastward to the rising sun and Pagaloth raised a hand in parting, then off they went, running across the sun-dazzled snow, rising, rising, rising up into the air and bearing his blade to the east.

Amron watched them go. He was alone, with only Wolfsbane for company, Rogen and Sir Quinn Sharp and his honour guard waiting further back. There was a grimace on his face now, a grimace of pain and a grimace of grief. Memories came to him. Of his long days lost in that shrouded white wood far to the distant northwest. Of the visions and the voices, as he walked down that river. He remembered awakening on that lonely strand, remembered the cold icy sea roaring distantly, remembered seeing that great bright light pulsing from the shore.

The recollection was still as clear to him as if it happened yesterday. He recalled the pumping in his heart, the great sense of hope and purpose as he limped and hobbled to the beach, remembered seeing that rock, the block of stone in which the Frostblade had been planted long ago. *It was placed there, hidden there, and I was prophesied to find it,* he thought. *One great quest will fail, but one greater will light the way…*

And a great quest it had been, a great quest and a great adventure. He had slain with the Frostblade the famed dragon Zyndrar the Unnatural. He had stood before the Dread with it at King's Point when he fought with his son and his brother. Later, he'd fought with it in the Greenwood too, and at Blackfrost, where he'd battled and beaten Axallio Axar and his dragon Angaralax in single combat. He had never felt so powerful as in that battle. Never…until those dragons had come down and lifted him from the field, and the blade had slipped out of his grasp to tumble into the battle below.

Then the blessing had become a curse, and he became weak, broken, crippled. The longer he'd held the Frostblade, the more entrenched and terrible the pain had become when he was parted from its power. *And now we are parted forever,* he thought. *I will never be one and whole again.*

He watched his son and his blade depart until they were mere specs against the rising sun. Elyon carried with him Vandar's spirit now, and with that spirit Amron might have been healed. *Could I have taken the blessing myself? Was that the test, to grant it to another?*

He did not know either way, and he had no regrets over his decision. "I *have* helped her," Amron Daecar had said in the Steelforge crypts, when Elyon asked him to help the heir.

And it was true, he had.

In time, perhaps, he would find out how.

66

Saska

She felt something soft beneath her.

Sand, she thought, slowly coming around. *Yes, sand. It is sand.*

It was soft, powdery, and there was a pleasant warmth on her face. Her eyes flickered half open, flickered to slits against the fierce sudden brightness, and she saw the sun beating down atop her from a wonderful azure sky. Sounds came to her, the soft slosh of little waves lapping at the shore, the caw of gulls and sea birds, the gentle whisper of the brushing wind.

Where am I?

She sat up, her eyes breaking gradually open as she grew accustomed to the glare of the sun. The sea before her ran to the far horizon, to the very far edge of her sight, spreading out in many shades of blue. She could see fish in the water, shadows zipping about in shoals in the shallows. Further off seabirds were diving from the skies, terns and gannets tucking their wings as they cut through the surface to vanish without a splash. Cormorants and seagulls floated, preening, and a great wide-winged albatross was soaring majestically above her, surveying all beneath it like a king.

What is this place? she wondered. South. It could only be somewhere in the south.

"Do you feel well rested?" asked a voice.

Saska sucked a breath and turned her head. A man was sitting on a driftwood log nearby, a pale man in a fine red cloak. His hair looked almost white, but maybe that was just the gleam of the sun. He wore no shoes or sandals, and his toes were working at the sand, digging beneath it, letting it drift through the gaps, digging again, drifting.

He smiled pleasantly at her. "It's very nice here, isn't it? A paradise, would you not say?"

Saska got to her feet and took a step away from him. She wasn't wearing her armour, she realised. No armour. No cloak. No sword. Only a simple linen dress, tied with a leather belt.

The dress was half silver and half blue.

"Where am I?" she asked. Her voice was hoarse from lack of use. She swallowed to moisten her throat. "Who are you?"

"Just a friend, child. A good friend. That's all."

She took another step away from him. The man stayed sitting on his log. Her bare foot landed on something hard and she looked down to see her dagger there, her Varin dagger. She snatched it up at once, holding the blade forward at the stranger. Then she frowned; a deep frown. Something was different, something was *wrong*. There was no feeling rushing through her, no surge of power from the steel.

Her blood-bond did not ignite.

"What's happening?" she blurted, frightened. "Why…"

"Oh, that won't work here," said the pale man. "No, not here in this land."

This land? Her eyes swung inland, and her pulse was thumping in her neck. The world back there was broad and beautiful, unlike any world she'd ever seen. Beyond the long soft sandy beach lay verdant grasslands and jungly hills and high grand snow-capped mountains. She saw a great waterfall glinting in the sunlight, saw palm trees thick with coconuts. Banana trees and mango trees crowded around a sparkling pool and she saw animals there, happy animals drinking, saw flowers and plants and colours of every kind in lovely meadows and prairies and wide open fields.

She was breathing heavily. "Where…where are we?" Her eyes raced back to the man. "Tell me where we are!"

"Far away," the stranger said. "We are far away, Saska. They cannot hurt you here."

Hurt me? They? Her mind swam with a sudden flood of memory. The dog, barking, Jonik and Emeric Manfrey coming through the trees. The blades of night and mist and the eagle and the dragons and the priest. Her head filled with fire and smoke and darkness, and a sudden fierce terror gripped at her. She remembered scaling the back of that demonic dragon, remembered the murmuring voice of the high priest as he spoke to her, but after…after she recalled only snippets. The world moving below, the woods and the hills and the rivers. The rush of the wind in her hair. The dragons flapping and screaming about her and the priest, speaking to her, the voice lulling her into a deep sleep.

It was the last thing she recalled. *He was taking me south, south to his master…*

She looked at the man in the fine red robes and staggered back and away from him. "You're…you're…"

"Calm now, be calm. I am only here to talk."

"Talk?" Her chest was heaving up and down. She raised the tip of her blade, her powerless blade. "What do you want with me? Why are we here?"

The Fire Father smiled at her from his log and didn't make a move to follow. "I'm not here to hurt you, Saska. No, no child…I brought you here to save you."

"Save me? I…no…I cannot be here…" She shook her head fiercely. "I have to go back…go back…go back…"

"Calm, child. Take a breath. There is no reason for you to panic." Eldur stood, now, from his log, and brushed down the folds from his rich crimson cloak. "It is a lot, I know. Take a moment, Saska. I will speak to you when you are ready."

He turned to the beach and began wandering down to the shore, pressing his feet into the wet sand where the waves washed inland and smiling, all the while smiling that pleasant contented smile. He looked around happily, breathing deeply of the warm salty air, and continued into the water until it came up to his ankles, his knees, darkening the fabric of his cloak. His eyes moved as he watched the fish, watched the birds plunging and vanishing and rising again with fish and squid in their talons. Further off, a pod of dolphins were cruising along, leaping and twisting and playing. He chuckled as he saw them. And he smiled again.

Saska drew her eyes from him, turning them away from the shore, searching for someone, anyone, a village or even a hut, anything. She saw no structures, no dwellings, nothing to suggest that man had ever settled here. *Another land,* she thought, trying not to panic. This was a land unknown, a land beyond their own. She held her dagger in her hand, and it was nought but common steel. No mist rose from it. It held no light or power.

Eldur was still standing in the water, observing the delights of nature. She looked at him again and recalled her dream, recalled the looming shadow, the terror, but *he* seemed different here too. *Is this how he was meant to be? Is this Eldur, the demigod who helped build the world with the rest of the Five Followers, with Ilith and Varin and Thala and Lumo? Eldur, who was meant to rise benevolent? Eldur who was meant to help end the war?*

They said he had been consumed by the Bondstone, by the soul of his master, that he was a vessel of Agarath now, but maybe…maybe that wasn't true here? As she looked at him, he turned to her and smiled, and it seemed a kindly smile, warm and gentle. "Child, do not fear," he said, and his voice was clear, even though he was far away. "This is a paradise. Untouched by war. You can run free here. You both can run free."

Both? She didn't understand. The demigod reached down to touch the water, running his fingers across the surface, smiling blissfully all the while, then he stood again and began walking toward her. She wanted to move back, to turn and run from him, but she didn't. She waited where she was with her useless common blade held harmlessly forward as Eldur approached smoothly, confidently, serenely. He cast his eyes around, enjoying the wind in his white hair, the warm caressing wind, gazing inland now to the trees and the flowering meadows, the rich green jungle and high mountains beyond. "Do you feel an affinity with this land?" he asked her.

She didn't know what to say. No answer passed her lips.

"You are half Lightborn. Half *Aramatian*." He surveyed the wild beauty of the land once more. "This is one of hers."

One of hers.

"Aramatia raised it," he told her, smiling. "Our realm was too rough for her, child. She made her haven in the Everwood, but it wasn't enough, not nearly enough, so she left to raise lands of her own. And this is one of them. Unspoilt and untouched."

"A paradise," Saska murmured.

"And a beautiful one, don't you think?"

Yes, she thought. There was no use denying it. She had never seen such a majestic land, never seen such warmth and colour.

"Your grandmother is here," Eldur said.

She looked back at him sharply.

He was walking up to the log again now, sitting down, smoothing through his long crimson cloak.

"Would you like to see her again?" he asked, very casually.

She stared at him, thinking, *A trick. It's a trick. He's trying to trick you.*

"No? Your own grandmother. Your last living relative?" He smiled. "You don't want to see her again?"

She said nothing. Nothing.

Another little smile visited his lips. "I have something for you, Saska. A simple tonic, right here." He reached into his cloak with his long pale fingers and withdrew a small bottle. He placed it nimbly on the log beside him, resting it between a crack in the bark. "She is unwell," he said. "Do you remember? When last you saw her? Do you remember how unwell she was?"

Saska said nothing. She remembered her grandmother abed, remembered her slowly wasting away from the sickness inside her. The betrayal of Elio Krator had hastened it, deepened it, and Saska had left Aram expecting never to see her again. *He is lying,* she thought. *My grandmother is dead.* It was many months since she'd left the eagle city. *She is dead, she must be. He is only trying to trick me.*

The demigod was looking at her strangely. There was a glow of goodness about him, of warmth and comfort, but it was a lie. *It's a lie,* she told herself. *All of it. He is hiding his true face from me, deceiving me. He is evil... he is Agarath.*

"Sweet child, do you not want to see her again? She is your last living relative."

I want to see Leshie again, Saska thought. *And Rolly and Ranulf and Del. Elyon. I want to see Elyon again.* She wondered how long she'd been gone, how far away this strange land was, and where. *I will never get back to them,* a part of her thought, despairing. She was lost, alone, hidden beyond the borders of any map. *No,* she made herself think. *Elyon. He'll find me. With the Windblade. He'll fly over the sea and find me...*

"Look there," said Eldur, softly. "Child, look, do you see it?"

His pale finger was pointing inland, to where the fields and meadows gave out to jungly hills. Far away, far far away, a thin white light seemed to be coming down from the distant sky, as a falling star, the sharp line of its passage dispersing and spreading behind it as it plunged from the heavens.

"She is out there, child, waiting for you. Only you can save her. Will you not try?"

"Why are you doing this?" she groaned at him. She held the tip of her blade out, her powerless blade. The tip was shivering. "Why don't you just kill me? Is this fun to you? Does it give you joy?"

"No, no," the demigod said. "I want to give *you* joy. That is all I want. For you to be happy." His face was pained. "Oh child, you have suffered enough. But not here. You can have everything you want here. You can run free...both of you. Why should I not want that for you? Varin was like a brother to me, and you are the last of his blood. I could never end such a line, never, no, never."

He stood from his log, and he seemed taller now, grander. "Child, oh, my sweet lovely child. The things they have asked of you, the terrible things they have made you do. Do you not hate them for it? Do you not detest them? Do you not resent King Godrin for watching, for *knowing*, and doing nothing? All those things you suffered in Keep Kastor. The beatings and the whippings and the taunting and the threats. He *knew*, child, he knew and did nothing. He let you suffer to harden you, to shape you, to *forge* you. You are a weapon. A weapon to them only. But you don't have to be, not here. You can be free here. You can find her. She is out there, child, you must find her."

"Stop." Saska shook her head and cringed. "Stop. Just stop."

"You cannot bear to hear it, I know. They don't deserve you, child. You are too good for them. The blood of Varin and Lumo and Thala, born of steel and light and sea. You are a goddess, Saska...or so they want you to be. But it isn't what *you* want, is it? You want a simple life, you care for simple *joys*. And there are people here, simple people. They fish the water and hunt the woods and they are comely and generous and kind. You can live with them, be happy with them. Your grandmother needs you. Won't you go to her?"

She shook her head. "You're lying. She isn't here, she isn't. She's dead."

"No. She is alive and she is out there, out there all alone. She needs you. She has little time. Take the tonic, child. Take it and go to her. You can save her, Saska. Only you can save her."

But I have to save the world, she thought. *The real world. The world where I belong.*

Eldur the Eternal was looking at her. There was a light of red flame in his eyes. "The world you know will fall," he said, and there was a deeper quality to his voice. "It will fall so it can rise again, as is the order of things. Vandar's Heart will never be remade. I go to make sure of it, child, right now I go....so why suffer yourself? It is needless. You can be happy here. You can start again, with your family. You can live here with your joy."

My joy…

"Look, child, look." The finger was pointing again, pointing inland. "You can run free together. Haven't you dreamed of it? To leave it all behind and run free together. The both of you."

The both of us…

She stared across the flowing fields and flowering meadows, past the little streams and twinkling lakes. Something was racing toward her, something sleek and black and swift. Saska blinked the tears from her eyes. "I thought…I thought she was…."

"Dead? No. Oh no. I would never let them kill your joy."

The voice was close now, suddenly very close. Eldur loomed behind her and his long bloodless fingers came down on her shoulders, draping unusually down her chest. There was a whisper in her ear, the flicker of a forked tongue. "Ride her, child," said the voice. "Ride her, as you have always wanted. You wear no armour. There is no weight. You can ride her and race her across this land. There's nothing to fear here. Nothing to harm you. There is no envy or hate or suffering here. Only joy. There is only joy."

She was running hard, bounding past little rocks and over brooks. Racing, splashing, racing toward her.

"Your grandmother is dying," hissed the voice. "Take the tonic. Take your Joy. Run to her, find her. You can be a family here." A hand unclasped from her right shoulder and came strangely around the side of her. In the upturned palm was the tonic. "Take it," whispered the voice. "Yes, that's it, take it."

And Saska took it from the palm, from the large fissured palm, cracked like ancient stone, she took it.

The voice was exulting in her ear. "Yes. Good. *Gooood*," it said. "Oh child, child, you will be *so* very happy here."

She stood with the tonic between her fingers, and with tears in her eyes, as Joy raced across the land toward her. Her heart thumped and her lips lifted and she went to a knee as the starcat reached her at last, leaping and licking with her long purple tongue and from her chest rumbled a frantic purr.

Saska held her, kneeling, holding her tight, squeezing. The wind sighed and the waves lapped and the sun smiled down upon her. And when next she dared to look behind her…

…the demigod was gone.

67

Lythian

"Draw your weapons," said Lythian Lindar. He froze on the snowy path.

Ulf, leading on through the blustery gale, turned. "You say something, m'lord?"

"Draw your weapons," Lythian repeated, louder. He reached into his cloak and pulled out his dagger, leaving the Sword of Varinar safely sheathed. Storos Pentar was right behind him. Out came his longsword with a scrape of steel, his eyes quickly narrowing and looking around for danger. Further back, Vilmar the Black already had a throwing knife in his grasp and was sniffing at the air, sniffing and looking skyward. "Dragon," he growled.

Lythian nodded. "It's coming from the west." He had heard the shriek at the far edge of hearing, very faint beneath the wind. His eyes darted left and right, down the path and up. *No cover,* he thought. *Only snow. No rocks.* They were far beyond the woods now and no more than a two-hour trek from the city, according to Ulf. If the skies were not so white and foggy, they might even be able to see it further away through the mountains, see the Black Tower soaring from the rear of the palace. "Just stay still," he said. "If we're lucky it won't see us and will pass right over."

"Maybe we should lie down and pretend to be rocks," quipped Storos Pentar. "Hruum would be proud."

"Maybe you can jape the dragon to death," Vilmar rumbled at him.

"If japing kills dragons then Torus Stoutman is Varin Reborn. The Dread will quell before him."

"Quiet, both of you." Dragons had very good hearing, Lythian knew, so too sight and smell. They were rather good at killing as well, and Lythian Lindar would be damned if he died after coming so far. *A few hours more,* he thought. *If we're quick will get there by dusk.*

He clutched at his godsteel dagger, listening for the thump of wings, a high-pitched shriek, trying to determine the dragon's location and size.

There were no further cries, but wingbeats he heard. *Not too large,* he thought. *And certainly not the Dread.* He stayed very still, and low to the ground, hoping the frost and snow clinging to their cloaks would be enough to conceal them in this fog. Squinting from beneath his hood now, he peered up and saw it, the shadow in the sky approaching. It was fairly low, coming almost directly overhead, a mid-sized dragon of classic proportion. It appeared to be labouring hard, so far as Lythian could tell, beating its wings as though weary from a long flight or perhaps against the fierceness of the gale.

The Sword of Varinar was hissing at his hip. It was an ugly sound, violent, and Lythian blocked it out. He never touched the blade, never laid his fingers on the hilt, and had even gone so far as to wrap a scarf around the handle so if ever he reached to take it by instinct, he would feel the fabric and remember. *It grows more desperate every day. It knows the end is close.* Its attempts to seize and corrupt him were futile, however, and his will against it was iron. *I will not yield, I will not listen. I will not use it. I am its guardian only...*

"There's another one," whispered Storos Pentar, crouching at his side.

Lythian looked. The dragon was quickly being swallowed by the soupy skies now, labouring further away to the east. The bands of fog closed in to conceal it, and it was gone. "I didn't see it," Lythian said. He glanced behind them. "Vilmar?"

"No," the huntsman growled. "I only saw the one, though it was ridden."

"Ridden?" Lythian hadn't seen that either, not from below. "You're sure?"

The huntsman nodded. "I saw the saddle."

"A saddle doesn't always mean a rider. There have been lots of riderless dragons with saddles."

"This one had both. Saddle and rider."

"And you're sure there was a second dragon?" Lythain asked Storos.

"Pretty sure. It was much higher up, or maybe just much smaller." He shrugged, then stood up from his crouch. "Might be wrong. Could have just been a bird or bit of cloud or something." He slid his blade away and drew his cloak in against the cold. "You think they're scouts?"

If the dragon they all saw was indeed ridden, then it seemed likely. And that was concerning, given the direction they were going. A scouting party here could augur an attack on Ilithor, or even suggest the city had been attacked already. *Damn this fog,* Lythian thought. It was sure to conceal the rear of the palace from them until they got much closer to the city. "We'd best get going," he said. "Ulf, lead on."

They continued along the snowy track as the white wind blew about them. For a good long while they'd been climbing, all through the day in fact, though here atop the broad snowy pass the world began to flatten out. "Look there," said Ulf, pointing with a gloved hand. "Might be you'll get a glimpse of the Black Tower beyond that ridge, m'lord, when the fogs blow off."

"The way is straight from here?" Lythian asked.

"Aye. More or less. Used to be an old goat track I followed, but can't see it under all this powder. No trouble, though, old Ulf knows the way. He knows the way all right." And he nodded happily, pressing on through the wind.

Ulf liked to say that often, that he knew the way, and for the last five days he'd proven the right of that. Their progress had been swift since they'd left Elmhall Hold, ranging north through the Mistwood for those first three days and then veering eastward up through the foothills and then the lower mountain ranges since then. The duo of Ulf and Vilmar seemed a winning combination; Ulf showing them the way, Vilmar using those hyper huntsman senses of his to keep them away from the things that prowled and crawled and slithered and generally wanted to kill them. Storos complained, of course, that they were in another forest at all. "Didn't we suffer enough bloody trees in the Wandering Wood?" he'd asked bitterly, but over the last two days he'd become more cheerful as the trees thinned, the lands climbed, and up they went into the mountains.

And now the final stretch, Lythian thought, trudging on step by weary step. The skies were beginning to darken now, and the winds were howling ever more fiercely, but they were close, oh so close he could smell it.

I want to sleep, yes, to sleep for a week as Alberfred said.

He was exhausted. Completely and unrecoverably exhausted, and not just physically. No, it was the mental exhaustion that was getting to him more; it was the constant assaults by the Sword of Varinar, it was the scathing harassment he endured. When awake and walking, he could at least distract himself from all that; he could look at things and smell things and talk with Vilmar or Storos or Ulf, hear all the old man's stories of his days as a trapper and a trader and a smuggler…but that wasn't the case at night. At night he had no defence against it and it had gotten into his dreams, clawing at him and torturing him and trying to twist him into madness…

But not tonight, he told himself. Tonight he would set the blade aside for good and all. He would be free of it, free of its malice at last, and could become a simple knight again. The thought was exhilarating to him. *And I'll wash too, yes. I'll strip from this steel and wash and find a snug feath-erbed to sleep in.*

Gods be good he yearned for it. When they gathered in the feast hall following their night at Elmhall, Storos had arrived clean and shining, his face shaven, his hair washed and trimmed, all the filth scrubbed and scoured from his body. His clothing had been laundered for him, and even his armour had been given a polish. "Best night's sleep I ever had," he had declared, smiling broadly, and then he'd seen the state of Lythian and frowned. "Well bugger me, what happened? You didn't take a bath, Lythian?"

"Not until Ilithor," Lythian Lindar had said. And so it would be. *Tonight.*

The wind was unsettled, always changing direction as they crossed the snowy plains. It came now from the north, blowing down from the higher ranges that sat shadowed and grand in the distance. And now from the east, gusting right into their faces and tugging relentlessly at their cloaks as they struggled along. When it swirled around and came up behind them, Lythian felt suddenly light as a feather and old Ulf almost fell over when a powerful gale shoved at his back. "No, I'm fine, fine," he said, just about keeping his footing. He turned back with a wonky brown smile. "Fun this weather, isn't it?" he called. "You know what they say when the wind's like this?"

"No," Lythian said, "What do they say?"

"That there's change in the air, m'lord. Something big's about to happen around here."

Yes, I might sleep properly for once. I will bathe and feel human again. Lythian peered ahead as the wind pressed him along, and that…was that the Black Tower, out there? Glimpsed and gone between the swirls of fog?

Ulf saw him staring that way. "Did you see it, m'lord?" he asked.

"Yes. Just for a moment."

"Well, we'll be seeing more of it soon enough, don't worry." He led them on to where the open pass rose more steeply and turned them left along a shallow rock face. He seemed to be searching for something. "Ah, here we are." In the cliff was a narrow opening, covered in snow. He kicked it away and a path was revealed, a thin cleft in the rock about two feet wide. "We'll have to go in sideways," he said, entering. They shuffled along like that for a while, crabbing between the two rock walls that rose some thirty or forty feet above them. Eventually it opened out, but not much, enough for them to walk forward at least, their shoulders scraping at the rock either side. It was fine for Ulf, small as he was. Less so for a big broad-shouldered man like Vilmar the Black or the two Bladeborn men in armour.

"You smuggle your pelts through here, did you Ulf?" asked Storos.

"Aye. Sometimes. Good little sneaky way, this. Not many know about this little gorge."

"How far does it go?"

"Few hundred metres the way we're going. It's one big rock, really, all cracked inside. Lots of different ways you can take, depending on where you want to come out." They passed one such crack, opening to their right as they went along. "I used to take that one mostly. Takes you all through a series of tunnels and passages and out around the palace. Comes out in the Marble Steps. Up through a cellar and into some lordly mansion. Well, good thing I knew the lord who lived there, and he liked the glint of gold. Used to pay him to let us through. Even let us store our pelts in that cellar, sometimes."

"Who was this lord?" Lythian asked.

"Oh, no one you'd know," Ulf said.

"Meaning you promised he would remain anonymous."

Ulf grinned, which seemed like a yes. "Anyway, we could go that way, though reckon we'll keep on this path instead. It'll take us right up near the rear of the palace. Well, you'll see. Watch your step here. There's a drop." It was a pit where the floor fell suddenly away, though only a metre or so wide. Ulf hopped over it easily enough. The other three men followed. Further on, the cleft narrowed again to suffocating proportions and they were forced to squeeze sideways. "It's narrower than I remember," Ulf admitted. "Might be I've put on a bit of timber in my latter years."

It wasn't easy in their armour. On they went, scraping and grinding, until it finally opened out a little further on. All the while, the path began to descend, sloping away as the rift walls to the left and right maintained their heading, and maybe even continued to climb up a little, growing higher and higher above them. There were a few more pitfalls to navigate, several further occasions where the walls grew tight, and twice they had to crouch down to pass beneath a ledge. "These weren't all here last time," Ulf said, thoughtful. "Not that I remember anyway."

"Could the mountain have shifted?" Lythian asked.

"Aye, suppose it could. More likely my memory's to blame. Didn't take this route so often as the other."

"Are we close to the end?" asked Storos. He was starting to sound a little concerned. "I'm not seeing any light ahead yet."

"It turns, just up here," Ulf told them. "Goes around a little bend, then we'll see the way out." Thankfully, the bend was still there and had not collapsed or caved in. "It's tight here. Best take a big breath and suck in your bellies. I'm looking at you, Vilmar."

The huntsman growled. "I'll be glad to be rid of you, smuggler."

"Truly? And here's me thinking we make a wonderful pair." Ulf chuckled merrily. He was no true huntsman as he readily admitted, and had won no respect from Vilmar the Black. "Big breath now. Tight squeeze this one."

Ulf slipped through the rock, vanishing around the bend, and there was a short moment when Lythian wondered if this was all some great ruse and he'd led them into a trap. It was nonsense, of course, no more than baseless paranoia spurred by the sword at his hip. Easing himself through the gap, he turned the corner as well and saw that Ulf was right there, shuffling along sideways. He turned back to make sure all of them were able to fit, nodded, then continued as Lythian, Storos, and Vilmar the Black shuffled along in a tight little line. Some ten or so metres on, the passage ended in darkness, turning around another bend.

"This is the last one," Ulf said. "The way out's just around the corner." He moved out of sight, shimmying into a slightly wider passage, and the others followed behind him.

And there, at last, they saw the end. Only a short way ahead, the rift widened to permit in the last of the waning daylight and they moved quickly toward it, exiting onto a sloping hillside draped with frosted rocks that ran downward toward the rear foundations of the palace. Lythian breathed out in relief, smiling as he saw it. Storos Pentar and Vilmar came out after him.

"So?" said Ulf. "Have I won your approval yet, Your Greatness?"

"No," Vilmar growled.

"You've done very well," Lythian assured him. "We could not have asked for a better guide."

Storos was gazing at the construction ahead with a bemused frown on his face. "Not much to look at from here, is it? Pretty ugly if you ask me."

"The front is much prettier," Ulf agreed. "Though often the case, isn't it? The rear end of things ain't always so pleasant."

"Nor is the front," Vilmar told him. "You make a good example, smuggler."

Ulf laughed happily. "Aye. My gods did give me a good beating with the ugly stick, no doubt there. Though you see my *rear* end, Your Brilliance, and mayhaps you'll change that tune you're singing." He hooked his thumbs into his belt, as though to pull down his thick woollen breeches. "Want to see? I can pull my cheeks apart for you and everything. Tis a ruin in there. A ruin!"

Vilmar looked at him disgustedly, though Storos let out a bark of laughter that rolled down the rocky hillside. Lythian was ignoring them all, studying the construction laid out before him. He had never seen the palace from this angle either, and true, it was more functional than fair when looked upon from the back, all thick utilitarian stonework integrated into the craggy dark rock of the mountains. The front was the prize, the front that looked out over the city and the valley beyond, the front with its slim tall towers and fine curved balconies, the collonaded walkways and stone-carved platforms that linked together its many high wings.

The back was largely undecorated, unembellished, much less visually appealing, and the Black Tower itself had always been austere. Lythian could see it clearly now, at the rear edge of a snow-draped courtyard encircled with a low plain parapet wall. On the courtyard's other side, a cloistered stone gallery led eastward into the palace proper, spanning a drop, and to the south and the north rose up thick defensive walls and fortified towers, each armed with defensive weaponry, built into the bluffs.

Lythian could see no men on the towers or the walls here and supposed they were prioritising the front of the palace and perhaps the city itself. It seemed shortsighted. Dragons could come from any direction, and unless they were woefully short of men, all angles should be watched day and night.

"So," said Storos. "What now?"

"Now we enter," Lythian said.

"Sure. Where?"

"We have options." Lythian pointed them out. Down amid the rocks upon which the palace was raised he could see some thick doorways cut into the stone that likely led into rear tunnels and storehouses and armouries. He also suggested they climb up and over the wall into the courtyard where the Black Tower stood. They could enter that way, along the gallery. It would take them more directly into the palace at that level.

"Let's do that," Storos said, nodding. "I see a way up over those rocks. We can climb up easily enough."

Lythian agreed. The courtyard was built upon a platform of natural rock, though it did not look so difficult to scale. He preferred the idea of entering the palace through some grand chamber than sneaking up through its shadowy bowels like some assassin or thief.

"Right. Let's get going, then." He began down the slope, though only made it a few paces before the huntsman gave a low warning growl. He turned back. Vilmar's eyes were gazing up to their left, high up beyond the palace itself and away into the towering peaks of the Hammersongs. There was a very faint glow of light up there, far away. It shimmered in the distant fog, and in the shimmer, Lythian saw a shape.

"It's that dragon," Vilmar said.

His heart skipped a beat. It was a long way off, perched at the edge of some high ledge like a huge bird of prey, surveying the lands below. It seemed to be looking in their direction.

"It sees us," the huntsman said.

"You don't know that," Storos told him. "We're a long way off. It could be looking at anything."

"It's looking at us," Vilmar told him.

Lythian was wondering about that glow of light. He was given to think the dragonrider had built a fire up there, perhaps to stay the night and keep watch on the city, but it did not seem the right colour. It looked more silver to him, a soft silvery-gold light, more ethereal than elemental.

Then he heard something. A sound drifting down on the wind. He clutched his godsteel dagger to listen. *Shouting*, he realised. *A man is shouting up there.* He sounded angry, desperate.

Vilmar heard it too. "That's not an Agarathi voice," he said. "Sounds Vandarian."

Lythian nodded. The shouting went on a moment longer, then stopped, and a second or two after that, they saw movement: a tiny shape rising up from the mountainside and shooting swiftly down toward the front of the palace, disappearing quickly out of sight. Lythian frowned. No dragon moved like that. He was about to speak when the shadow of the dragon shifted as well, opening its wings and diving suddenly off the edge of the ridge. It plunged quickly down the snowy slope, then levelled out, coming right toward them.

"Oh bloody hell," spat Storos. "Now? The palace is right there!" He tore his blade out from its sheath. "We'd best get down there where it's flatter. Can't be fighting a dragon on this slope."

"We're not fighting it," said Lythain.

Ulf agreed to that. "We need to go back into the gorge," he said, briskly. "We'll be nice and safe in there until it goes away."

"We're not doing that either." Lythian was putting the pieces together, though the picture didn't make any sense to him just yet. Whatever was happening here, this dragon was not a danger to them. "It's friendly," he said. "That dragon is an ally."

"An ally?" blurted Storos. "And how on earth do you figure that?"

Lythian did not have time to explain. The dragon was soaring quickly down the steep mountainside, banking toward them, broadening its wings to slow. They opened like sails as the beast flapped hard and came down to land at the foot of the rocky hill some forty metres away. Scales of royal red and copper showed darkly in the dying light and the rider's cape was coloured the same. A voice called out to them, not the voice that was shouting, a different one, and a voice Lythian knew.

"Captain," it said. "Captain Lythian, is it truly you?"

"Yes." The word was small and choked. Lythian stepped forward, disbelieving. "*Pagaloth?*" He squinted, seeing him clearly now. The almond eyes and dark hair, the beard twisted in a triple braid. He wore his black dragonscale armour and his cloak, though it had been modified, slashed and sewn with strips of copper, to match his dragon's scales. *His dragon. His.* Lythian found himself utterly wordless.

"Lythian, I have been searching for you for weeks," the dragonknight called out to him, breathless. "Gods, I cannot believe it! We saw you… earlier we saw you. Prince Elyon…he sensed something…but said we could not stop. We had to come here first, and, and…" He snatched a breath. "Do you have the Sword of Varinar with you, Lythian? Do you have it?"

"Yes." He opened his cloak. "I have it, Pagaloth."

The dragonknight waved his hand urgently. "Then I must take you at once. Come, quickly. Lendrathor can bear your weight. Come."

"Take me where, Pagaloth?"

"There." And the Agarathi pointed up toward the mountain. "Ilith's forge," he said.

68

Jonik

He was dozing on his bed when he heard the noise. Dozing and dreaming of an island far away, and a simple life beyond this war.

It was coming from down the corridor, a heavy stamping tread and a raging voice. As he came around, he heard his name being called. "Jonik! Jonik! Where are you, bastard!"

Jonik pulled the covers off him and stood on the soft warm rug. His bedchamber was plush and decadent, and at long last he had removed his armour to sleep. The skies here were well watched, he'd been assured by Lord Morwood, and he could rest easy after so long on the road.

He wore hose and no more. He went to a chair beside the low-burning hearth and pulled on his linen undershirt. The voice was getting closer, louder. He could hear doors being kicked in down the hall, slamming open. "Jonik! Where you are, you wretched bastard! Show yourself!"

Jonik looked at his swordbelt, set aside, at the sheath bearing Mother's Mercy, at the dagger sheathed as well. He looked at them, but that was all, and did not buckle them on. His armour was in a chest by his bed, safely packed and polished since his arrival the previous night. He left that too, went to the door, took the handle and paused. His heart was hammering in his chest, and he felt suddenly lightheaded from nerves. He swallowed, drew a slow deep breath to try to calm himself, breathed out again and in and out. This was not how he wanted to face him. He wanted more time to rest and prepare and think about what he might say, but he wasn't going to get it. *If it must be here, and now, so be it.*

He turned the handle and stepped outside.

The corridor was dim-lit and quiet. Torches burned at intervals along the walls, fine paintings between them, and a wide red carpet ran the length of the hall, trimmed in Tukoran green.

Jonik turned to his right, taking a deep breath, preparing. His brother was several doors down, dressed in his full armour and cloak, windswept, wild, the Windblade in his grasp. His helm was looped about his belt, exposing the face and stubbly beard, the scar that cut through his brow, a new scar that was not there the last time Jonik saw him; no doubt he had many more besides. He looked harder, older, fiercer, a veteran now of many battles and a serial slayer of Agarath's spawn. He turned, hearing the door open, and his lip pulled back in a snarl.

"There you are, *bastard*."

Jonik stood his ground as Elyon came marching heavily forward. His arms hung down by his sides, and he was ready. Ready for whatever his brother might do.

Elyon was puffing and panting like a bull, coiled and dangerous. They hadn't seen one another since the night of Aleron's death. *The night I killed him.* Jonik lowered his eyes, silent, as he remembered.

"Pathetic," Elyon hissed, as though knowing. "Look at you. *Pathetic.*"

Jonik's eyes stared at the floor.

"Was it not enough that you killed my brother?" Elyon raged at him. "That you crippled my father? You had to let them take *her* as well."

Her. Jonik's gaze lifted. "You're…talking about Saska?"

"*Don't* say her name. Don't you ever say her name!" Elyon looked like he wanted to run him through right here in the corridor, and if that was so Jonik would let him. *I've done what I had to do*, he thought. *I found the Mistblade and brought it back. If he wants to kill me, so be it. I deserve to die. I want it to be him.*

"I didn't mean for them to take her," he said. "I tried to stop them, but…"

"But you weren't good enough. You were *never* good enough." Elyon drew a sharp breath into his lungs and blew it out, then thrust the tip of the Windblade down into the stone. "I left my father this morning. He gave the Frostblade up. He was trying to put on a brave face, but I saw it. I *saw*." He snarled at him. "You have no idea how much he suffers because of what *you* did. The blade masked his pain, but now…now it'll only get worse. He's living a nightmare because of *you*."

"I'm sorry," Jonik murmured. He could not look his brother in his eye, his grand gallant brilliant brother, so beloved by all who knew him. *Jaycob*, he thought. That was his closest version to Elyon, but it was a lie, nothing but a fantasy. The cold hard truth of what he'd done was staring him in the face.

"You're sorry? Sorry?" Elyon took a heavy step toward him.

"Yes." His voice was barely a whisper. "I wish I could take it back, but I can't. I've tried…"

"Tried what? What? To be good, to be noble? I know, *bastard*. I know all the good you've done. But it changes nothing, nothing. She's gone… she's gone now, and I…I…" Elyon cringed in despair, turned to the side and threw his fist into the wall. His gauntlet drove a hole five inches deep, causing the whole corridor to shudder. "I should never have been gone so long. If I'd only got back earlier…maybe…maybe…"

He loves her, Jonik realised. This is not about losing the heir, it's about her…about the girl. "We'll…get her back," he said, weakly. "We will, Elyon. Somehow…"

"Somehow? How? And who's we? You? Are *you* going to get her back? How? Tell me?"

"I…I don't know. We don't even know where…where she was taken."

"The Ashmount," Elyon said, gritting his teeth. There were tears in his eyes, Jonik saw, desperate angry tears. "She'll be there, I know it. I have to find her, bring her back. I'm the only one who can do it."

"No," Jonik found himself saying. "You can't."

"*Can't?*" His eyes sharpened again.

"The blade," Jonik said. "If you take it…"

"I have no choice," Elyon roared at him. "Without Saska none of it matters. Do you understand? None of it matters without her."

"You don't know that."

"I do. I know it. It's her. It was always her!" Elyon drove his fist into the wall again, and again, and again. Plaster and stone crumbled and crashed everywhere, and paintings came loose from their fastenings. He was breathing heavily, head swinging side to side. "I have to get her back," he panted. "Only I can do it." He turned around, suddenly, and ripped the Windblade back out of the stone floor. "Tell them I've gone to the Ashmount," he said. "Tell them I have to try." And he spun away, marching back down the corridor.

I can't let him leave, Jonik thought. *He isn't thinking clearly. He cannot take that blade.* He rushed after him, reached out and took his arm. "Elyon, stop. It's what the blade wants."

"Unhand me." The prince tugged violently away. "Don't ever touch me."

Jonik reached for him again. "You're not thinking. Just stop and take a…"

His brother spun on him, jamming hard with the heel of his palm into Jonik's chest, sending him reeling. He tumbled down to the carpeted floor, winded and gasping for breath. "E…Elyon…you can't…" He struggled up to his feet again, stumbling forward. "At least…at least let me come. If you're going to go, let me come. You have your harness. The Nightblade, I…"

"I'll *never* accept help from you."

"You're not thinking," Jonik said again. "With the Nightblade, I'd…"

"I want no part of *that* blade." Elyon spun and sneered at him and Jonik could see he was remembering, remembering that night in Varinar, that night in the alley when the skies broke and wept, remembering Aleron, remembering it all. "You should have killed me," he rasped. "I asked you to. You should have killed me that night as well."

"No, I…I never wanted that."

"You wanted the blade," Elyon hissed. "That black blade of yours. You killed your own brother for it. I hate it. I hate *you.*" His silver-blue eyes were burning, brimmed with sudden tears. "You took away his chance at greatness," he said, cringing. "At immortality. My brother...I wanted to go with him...to sit at Varin's Table with him...so he wouldn't be alone...but you...you *bastard*...you couldn't even give me that."

Jonik had no words. He felt sick to the pit of his stomach to think of what he'd done and there was nothing he could say to absolve himself, nothing he could do. He met his brother's grief-struck glare and went down to his knees before him. "It should be you," he said. "It should be you who kills me."

Elyon looked down at him for a long moment, temptation burning in his eyes. Then he snorted and shook his head. "I can't."

"I want you to. I want you to do it." Jonik raised his chin, exposing his neck. "Cut my throat. Take your vengeance. I deserve it, Elyon. Do it."

"No."

"Why not?"

"Because I made an oath!" Elyon shouted. "Amilia, she made me promise." He threw the Windblade down again to clatter loudly on the floor. "But I never said I wouldn't hurt you."

"Then hurt me," Jonik said. "Hurt me."

"Stand up. Off your bloody knees!" Elyon closed a fist and prepared to swing, then stopped, snorted, and began tearing off his gauntlets, one and then the other. He threw them down to smash against the floor, lying amid bits of broken stone, then began working at his pauldrons, his breastplate, tossing his plate armour aside. In that armour he could kill him. One good punch with a godsteel gauntlet could take a man's head right off his shoulders.

Jonik waited. It took a while. He could see some of the fire going out of Elyon as he undressed, his fingers working feverishly as they worked and tugged and pulled the segments of steel off his body.

"Do you want some help?"

"No."

"It might speed things along."

"I said no. I want nothing from you."

The wait went on a little longer. Then at last his brother pulled off his boots and slid out of his sabatons, and there he stood, in his padded underclothes, soaked and stained in sweat.

"You want this to be fair, you should remove those too," Jonik said.

"Fine." Elyon removed them, throwing the padded garments aside until he stood in only a pair of hose. "This good enough for you? Now *you're* overdressed."

Jonik nodded; that was true. He drew off his linen undershirt and dropped it at his feet and both brothers stood facing one another in that empty corridor in that empty palace atop that frozen city, each barefoot and barechested, bruised and battered and scarred. Elyon was the burlier man, his muscle thicker, broad in the shoulder and tight in the waist and abdomen. Jonik was all lean meat and sinew, the sharp lines of his muscles contoured against his frame. Paler he stood, though only a little, longer of hair, and darker. They were about the same height, about the same age, mirrors of one another, one dark, one light, one raised in the basking adoration of the north, the other a shadowy outcast raised by an order of bastards.

"You look skinny," Elyon said.

"You looked tired," said Jonik.

"I am."

"So am I."

"I've been flying all day," Elyon told him. "I've been flying for weeks, across the world and back."

"I've been in the wild for months," Jonik came back. "Trapped in the depths of the earth with a monster."

"The only monster here is *you*," Elyon snarled. He raised his fists. "You better fight back. Don't you dare go easy because of your guilt."

Jonik flexed his fingers. "You'd prefer it if I did."

"No. I want your best."

"You won't win," Jonik told him.

Elyon laughed. "You think?"

"Yes. I was raised in the Shadowfort. I had to survive."

"I was raised in the Steelforge."

"It's not the same."

"How would you know? You're all skin and bone, look at you. I'll snap you like a twig."

"You don't know how to fight like that," Jonik said. "You only know the forms."

"You have no idea what I know."

"Then show me."

"Fine."

"Fine."

Jonik raised his fists as well, and the two young men stood staring at one another, feeling each other out. Jonik knew he would not be the first to attack. He was delaying him only, that was his duty here. To delay him, milk the anger and the rage out of him. When the red mist was gone he might see sense. *And if I have to, I'll knock him out. He cannot fly off with that blade.*

A moment passed, another and a few more, and then suddenly Elyon bellowed in rage, as though to psych himself up, and charged forward. He looked like he was going to swing at him, but instead bent at the waist, tucked his right shoulder and drove hard, ploughing into Jonik's iron abdomen and spearing him onto the carpeted floor.

Elyon was quickly atop him, thrashing wildly with elbows and fists, grunting. Jonik fended with his forearms, twisting left and right to avoid the blows. One hammer of a strike came thumping down. Jonik saw it come, turned his head, and Elyon's fist dealt him a glancing blow, striking hard at the ground. He pulled it back suddenly, grunting in pain. Blood oozed out of broken knuckles, but he didn't seem to care. He struck again, swinging, but Jonik raised his arm to parry. More blows came, deflecting, missing, as Jonik twisted and moved on the floor, slippery as an eel. He waited, waited, and when he saw his opening, he struck, driving up with his knee and jamming it hard into Elyon's guts.

His brother was dislodged. He rolled off, gasping for air, trying to stand, but Jonik was too quick. In an instant he was up on his feet and leaping onto Elyon's back like a panther, folding an arm across his neck and clinging to his wrist to choke him out.

Elyon saw the danger. He stood, driving powerfully backward and smashing Jonik into the wall. He felt something crack against his back, the frame of a painting splintering as their weight went into it. Jonik held on. Elyon staggered forward a pace, and launched himself back again, reaching up with both his hands to tear Jonik's arm away. The strength in his hands and the force of the strike was enough. Jonik's arm weakened just a little, and Elyon drew it from his neck, gasped a ragged breath, and bit down.

Jonik howled. Elyon's teeth sank bloodily into the muscle of his forearm, and he slammed back into the wall again for good measure. Jonik let go, striking at the side of Elyon's head with his spare hand to open his jaws, then tore his savaged arm away. Blood boiled up through the pale meat of his muscle, oozing from the teeth marks, and he could feel a warm wetness on his back as well. "You're a savage," he said to his brother.

"Pot and kettle, bastard." Elyon spat a gob of blood from his mouth. "Nice move, though, with the knee."

"You too with the wall." Jonik wondered if that was it. Sometimes an impasse like this was enough to take the heat out of a fight. He reached around and touched his back, felt the blood and the splinters of wood lodged there. "You want to help me get these out?"

"I'd sooner drive them further in."

Elyon came again, setting his feet and swinging from the hip. Jonik groaned and raised his bloody forearm to parry, then ducked in and unleashed an uppercut. It missed Elyon's chin by a whisker as he leaned away, shimmied in a quick sidestep, and swung a swift right hook. Jonik swerved back, dropped to his knees and took Elyon's right leg, trying to twist him down to the ground in a crocodile roll. He felt he had the advantage grappling on the floor, but his brother saw the danger and dragged his leg fiercely away before Jonik could get a good grip. He took a second to rebalance, then swung a fierce kick for Jonik's face. A foolish move. Jonik took that leg instead, pulled him forward as he turned his body and Elyon went down.

Jonik scrambled atop him, wriggling once more behind his back. His arm was around his neck again and now his legs were coiling around him too, wrapping him up like a python. Elyon had nowhere to go. "Do you yield?" Jonik shouted into his ear. "Do you yield?"

"No...never..." Elyon spluttered. He jerked violently, trying to squirm free, throwing elbows into Jonik's ribs. The man was strong. Gods he was strong. Jonik's back was on the carpet. With each twist and jerk, he felt it rub and burn against his skin, felt the splinters driving deeper or breaking off, and he gritted his teeth against the pain.

"Yield," he rasped. "Just yield, Elyon."

"No!" Another elbow struck him, this time in the kidney. Jonik coughed and Elyon crunched suddenly at the core, making room, and his other elbow swung backward. It connected with Jonik's chin a half blow, but it was sufficient to weaken him, and Elyon scrambled back away again, rising unsteadily to his feet and planting a bloody hand against the wall.

Jonik got to a knee, panting. The whole corridor was a wreck of blood and broken picture frames, stained carpets and cracked walls and strewn, misting armour. "We're making a mess," he said.

"Your fault," Elyon returned. He took his hand off the wall and looked at his knuckles, wincing.

"That one's gonna hurt in the morning."

"You're worse. Let me see your back."

Jonik frowned at him, sensing a trap, but gave him the benefit of the doubt and turned. It was a trap. His brother came barrelling forward again and tackled him again to the floor, this time from behind. They went down in a weary tangle of limbs, thrashing, punching, kicking, rolling from one side of the corridor to the other. "Bastard," Jonik shouted at him, because of the trick.

"Crows and ravens," Elyon shouted back, getting a knee into him. "I hated your mother. I'm glad she's dead."

Jonik got on top of him. His fist crunched down into Elyon's face, striking at his cheek. He felt a crack. "She died for me. And Amilia. She died for us all."

"She died for herself. She was a self-serving whore."

Jonik roared bloody murder. He went to strike again, but Elyon rolled away and turned the tables. He fist found Jonik's jaw, a good firm hit this time, and his vision blurred. For a short while it was just colours and slightly muted sounds as Jonik blinked back into proper consciousness, kneeing and elbowing his brother away, and then all of a sudden he saw shapes running down the corridor toward them.

"Split them up! Split them up!" a girl's voice was shouting.

A big figure rumbled forward. "Come on…come on now. This is enough, I think." Jonik felt Elyon's weight pulled off him as a large, powerful man picked him up and dragged him away.

"Let go of me, damn you!" his brother shouted. "Butcher, let go!"

"Not until you calm, Windy Prince. The storm is for *outside*, yes. Not inside this corridor."

Jonik was still blinking and recovering when Leshie went down to a knee before him. "Hey, Shadowboy. Are you all right?"

"I'm fine." His voice was a grunt. He sat up on the ground, a little dazed, slick with sweat and blood and probably spit as well from all the shouting. Leshie offered him a hand to stand and he supposed it would be churlish not to take it. She was wearing her red armour and swordbelt, and in all that she was very heavy and very strong, despite her diminutive size. She pulled him easily to his feet. Elyon was still snorting and struggling as the Butcher tried to calm him further down the corridor.

"What happened?" Leshie asked. "When did Elyon get here?"

"Just now. He found out about Saska, and…"

"Oh. Right." Leshie chewed her lip, a sad mournful chew. "And he blamed you for what happened? That isn't fair."

"It was just a good excuse, I think. Not that he needs one."

Leshie understood. "He still hates you for all of that?" Her voice was soft.

"Still," Jonik whispered. "Always." He had no right to hope for anything else. His brother would hate him forever, as would his father, and he expected nothing less from them.

Leshie made a sympathetic face and patted his bare bloody arm. "He'll get over it eventually. It'll just take time." She smiled and then walked over to Elyon, pressing the Butcher aside and hugging him. Elyon was very stiff at first, and then his shoulders slackened and he relaxed into her embrace. They held one another for a long moment and then parted. It was about Saska, Jonik knew. Leshie loved her as well.

The corridor fell to silence. It was then that Jonik realised that the Butcher wore only his cloak, a tattered cloak in many hues of red…and nothing more. The terrible scarring that crossed his chest and shoulders and even legs was grimly exposed, and worse, he had not tied the cloak at the waist, so his terrible manhood was exposed as well.

Jonik sighed at him. "Your cloak is open."

"Yes. I know. Have you never seen a man's cock before, boy?"

"Close it, Butcher," Elyon agreed. "We're in the royal palace. You should comport yourself properly."

"That's a bit rich coming from the two of you," Leshie said, looking between them. "These paintings are probably priceless, you know." The Butcher was still standing proudly with everything showing, hands on his hips. He was a very well-endowed man, as he often claimed. "Parapet, cover yourself," Leshie told him. "It's disgusting, that thing. Put it away."

"It is very large, I know, but it is not disgusting. My sweet kitten enjoys it very much."

"No one wants to hear about you and your *kitten*," Leshie snapped. By kitten Jonik supposed he was talking about the Tigress; they were in love, apparently. "Just close your cloak."

"Fine." The Butcher pulled his tattered cloak closed and fastened it at his waist. "I did not know this was a palace of prudes."

Leshie looked at Elyon again, and then at Jonik, back at Elyon and at Jonik a final time. She was judging them, looking for injuries and any intent to keep fighting. "Are you both done?" she asked.

A glance between the brothers. "We're done," Elyon said. *For now,* he left unspoken. He raised his hand, studying his bloody knuckles, wincing as he flexed his fingers. Both of them were covered in cuts and burns and bruises, and Jonik could feel the splinters in his back, stabbing and biting as he breathed. His jaw also felt sore from Elyon's strike, and his forearm was pulsing with pain.

Leshie shook her head like a disappointed parent. "What were you thinking? You could have killed one another. Or caused serious harm. We need you both to be strong."

"It was nothing," Elyon said. "A scuffle."

Jonik nodded. "A scuffle."

"I don't want to see it happen again," Leshie told them. "Do you understand? *No more fighting.*"

"Fine," said Elyon.

"Fine," said Jonik.

"Good." Leshie nodded her head and looked over at all of Elyon's armour, scattered about, and the Windblade lying further down the corridor, fogging with a brisk swirling mist. Jonik wondered what it was saying to his brother. *Trying to get him to fly away south, no doubt, to the Ashmount.* The Nightblade had terrorised poor Sir Ralston yesterday, and the Mistblade had been raging in Jonik's head as well as they travelled through those tunnels. Leshie understood all of that. She looked at Elyon's face suspiciously and said, "You need to take that to Ilith *right now.* The Windblade, Elyon. You need to give it up."

"I will. After." His voice was hoarse.

"After? After what?"

"After I've found her."

Leshie shook her head. "You can't go."

"That's what he said."

"You *can't.* Ilith's done all the potions now and he's young and strong again. I know what you're thinking, and you know I'd want that too…but it's too dangerous. She'll come back to us, I know she will. Somehow she'll come back."

"But…what if…"

"She'll come back," Leshie said, in a voice that brooked no protest. "We need to focus on ourselves and take advantage while we can. Most of the blades are here now, and…"

"They're all here," Elyon said.

"*What?*" Leshie's eyes widened. "All of them?" She saw the answer in Elyon's eyes. "Even the gold one?" He looked at her, silent. Leshie's eyes sped excitedly to Jonik and then back at Elyon. "Then, if they're all here…Ilith, he can…"

"*After,*" said Elyon Daecar. "He can do it after. Once I've brought the Windblade back." He was backing away now, backing away down the corridor very slowly. The Windblade was close behind him. Its mists seemed almost to be reaching out to him, reaching out with silver tendrils, reaching to grasp him, enslave him.

"Elyon," Leshie said. "Stop."

He didn't. He took another step backward, keeping his eyes on them all the while. "Just tell Ilith I'll be back soon," he said. "I'll keep it safe, I promise it. Tell him I'll come back with Saska *and* the blade, and then…"

"You can't leave, Elyon," Leshie said firmly. She reached to her scabbard and withdrew her godsteel shortsword. "We're not going to let you go." The Butcher came up on one side of her, Jonik the other. "You take one more step toward that blade, and…

"And what? You'd fight me?" He looked at her, incredulous. "Would you try to *kill* me, Leshie?"

"Yes." She didn't hesitate. "If you take that blade away now, you'll doom us all. This is bigger than you. It's bigger than all of us."

Elyon was fighting some inner demon, Jonik could see. His eyes stared at them, at one and then the other, and his head swung side to side. "But…without her…without *her*…" He grimaced, eyes twisting, closing his fists into tight balls and blood dripped off his knuckles. *Fight it,* Jonik was willing him. He could almost feel the blade's influence in him, preying on his weakness as it had with the Wall. *Fight it, brother,* he thought. *Fight it.*

Leshie was creeping up to him. "Elyon," she said, softly now. "You know you can't go. You're not even wearing your armour. You think we'll just stand aside and let you dress?" She took another step, another. "You'd have to kill us. I know you don't want that. Just…let it go. The blades are here, Elyon. All five of them are finally *here*. We can't miss this chance. You *know* we can't. If we do…if we do it might never come ag…"

Again, she was about to say, when she stopped, mid-word, frowned and turned her head.

The hairs at the nape of Jonik's neck stood on end.

Out through the thick walls of the palace, far away across the southernmost fortifications and watchtowers, came the sound of warning bells.

The muscles tightened in Jonik's throat as he remembered the last time he'd heard that tolling. He looked sharply at his brother, and his brother looked sharply back at him. Elyon's eyes were suddenly clear. "Armour," he said, and Jonik nodded.

And the bells were ringing louder…louder…louder…

69

Amilia

Ignore them, she thought. *Just ignore them. They'll stop soon.*

The fire flickered warmly, throwing light across the table filled with empty cups and wine jugs. In a big armchair beside it Amilia Lukar sat embraced, her legs folded beneath her, swaddled up in wine-stained blankets and old stale tears. She used to curl up in this chair with Mallister Monsort, used to snuggle by the fire in it and make love in it and drink it in. *It still smells of him,* she thought. *It still smells of him in here.*

She had not expected to be so broken by his death. Maybe it was the way it was done. The way he spoke of Melany and the Long Abyss and how he had to kill himself to save her. The way he had smiled at Amilia across the snowy battlements, with those tears in his eyes, such a sweet despairing smile as he told her he loved her and stepped into the void. *Maybe that was it? That he loved me after all.* And the way he just *vanished* like that, dropping so suddenly, and how she'd screamed and scrambled up to the edge to see him fade so quickly out of sight…and how he seemed to be looking up at her as he fell away backwards, smiling at her still and mouthing, *I love you,* as the blackness devoured him.

She cringed at the memory. She could still see his face, still see his mouth moving, could hear his voice in her ear. The image was seared into her memory now and no amount of wine could blur it out. She'd been drinking for days to try, though, and trying very hard. How long had it been? Four days, five? Could she have been in this room for a week? The wine was her vice…and her crutch…and her curse. She knew it was foolish to start down this road, but she couldn't help it and the slope was slippery. One cup became two and two became ten and then she was truly lost.

She had her cup cradled in her lap. *Shut up,* she thought, to the city bells. *Just shut up and leave me in peace.* She scooped up her goblet and drank it dry, then reached over for a jug. She picked up one. Empty. Another. Empty. She snorted and reached for a third, stretching, and in doing so knocked it over onto the floor where it crashed into a hundred broken pieces.

Just like Mallister, she thought, as the red wine spread out across the floor like blood. *His body probably shattered like that when he finally hit the bottom. No, worse. It would have been much worse.*

There were no more jugs on the table. "Annabette," she called out. "Annabette, more wine!"

The handmaid was her only company now, if you could call it that. She lived in the little servant chamber annexed to Amilia's quarters and only came out when the princess called for her. Mostly that was to ask for wine, though the girl brought food as well. "You have to eat, my lady," she had said. "All that wine will not sustain you. You need to keep up your strength."

I don't want to be sustained, Amilia thought. *I want to drink myself to death, like before.* Only now it was worse than back then. Back then she'd lived in a state of decadence and indulgence, a state of selfish hedonism, drinking and singing and laughing and fornicating with her sweet dead Mallister Monsort. The world was ending, so what did she care? Then Elyon came along and shamed her in his nobility and she'd broken from that spell and started to help.

Now she was back…only without the singing and the laughing and the joyous fornicating…now she only sat and drank and wept and slept and didn't permit herself any visitors. "My lady," Annabette said, a few days ago. "I have heard that Gifford Gold-Tongue remains in the city. He sings for the soldiers, my lady, to stir their spirits and give them hope. Maybe…maybe he could sing for you again as well? I will go and bring him here if you want."

It was never his singing Amilia cared for, but the other fine use of that tongue. The notion was tempting if only to hide her hurt for a while, but she shook her head and told the girl no. "Let him sing for the soldiers still," she said. "They need him more than I do. More wine."

The days had merged one to the next, sticking together like some ugly amorphous wine-soaked blob. Annabette had suggested a visit to her mother might help, and Amilia wondered if that was true. *It might put my plight into perspective*, she thought. *Or maybe I'll just see a vision of my future in the deranged old hermit.* She was sure to become deranged herself eventually if she stayed in this room too long.

"Annabette?" she called out. "Anna, where are you?"

There was no answer. The girl must have gone off on some errand, maybe to fetch her some food from the palace kitchens, or hear what all the fuss was about with those bells. Through her drunken haze, Amilia could hear them getting louder and more insistent.

She frowned, sitting up now and shoving aside her blankets. Once more she thought of her mother, thought of her sitting in her rotting chair with her long nails and ungroomed hair. Thought of her demented mumbling, those repetitious things she would say again and again and again. One of them had disquieted Amilia Lukar more than the rest, and it came to her now, like a sharp spear through the shroud of her insobriety.

I'm going to die here, her mother had said. *Right in this chair, I'll die.*

Amilia stood up abruptly, enough to make her head spin. Those words echoed around in her skull, spinning too, lighting in her a sudden fear. She drew a deep breath to try to clear her head, looked around for a jug of water, saw one on a side table, stumbled over to it and gulped it down. A hot flush of sweat was spreading through her body, sweat glistening on her forehead. *It's happening again,* something inside her was saying. *Get out. Get out. It's happening again.*

The drapes were shut, the room in darkness but for the flicker of the fire. She staggered to the balcony door and pulled aside the drapes. It was dark outside; she hadn't even realised. Opening the door, she stepped out into the cold, and the sounds erupted loudly in her ears. The bells. The shouts. The groan and thrum of siege weapons. Shapes were slithering up through the southern skies, passing quickly over the city walls. She saw the shapes diving, saw bolts cut skyward, heard the groan of a catapult swing. Flights of black arrows poured up like pine needles. Orange-red lances poured down, one and then another and then another and then another, suddenly bright in the dark. She saw the dragons that blew them, lit from below, saw the men they bathed and burned, writhing and twisting and screaming.

Amilia Lukar backed away through the door in horror. *It's happening again. It's Thalan again...*

She spun, stumbling, cutting her foot on a bit of broken jug. Blood welled and oozed out into the spilt wine, but she barely even felt it. Blood-and-wine footsteps marked her path across the room. She went to a closet, threw open the door. The princess was dressed in a silken shift, green, light and flimsy and provocative, the garment that Mallister had loved so much, the one she always wore when he came to her. It was torn here and there from when he ripped it off her during their lovemaking and did not make for appropriate attire beyond the bounds of this bedchamber.

She pulled on a brown woollen kirtle, leaving it unlaced at the back, stockings, boots, and an overcoat of wolfskin trimmed with vair. As she tightened her belt, she heard footsteps outside, a loud banging on the door. That made no sense. Anna entered through her own door and didn't need to knock, and she'd sent all her guards away too, Sir Hammet and Sir Belligar and Sir Fendrel and Sir Mardon...all were still in the refuge to make sure Del and Cevi were well.

Morwood, she realised, suddenly. *It must be faithful old Morwood.* She hurried to the door and pulled across the bolts and drew it open. A girl with red hair stood before her. She wore red armour and had a red leather belt and clusters of little freckles around her upper cheeks and the bridge of her button nose.

"Leshie," Amilia said. She recognised the girl from Del's stories. Anna had also reported to her that the girl had come last night with her cousin Jonik and some others. She remembered that vaguely through her drunken haze.

"That's me," Leshie said. She did a quick curtsy, and Amilia realised something, then began laughing hysterically. The girl Leshie frowned at her. "Was it that bad?"

"No, no…it's not that…" Amilia was breathless with laughter, mad with it. "Astrid," she said. "You…you trained with Astrid…"

"Yes, I…"

"It was her, in Thalan," Amilia said. "The…the night the city burned. *She* came to me then. She came to my room. And now you… now this time it's *you*!"

"Right. I suppose…I suppose that's quite funny." Leshie did not seem to find it funny at all, because it wasn't, not really, it was just a wild coincidence. "My lady. Elyon said for me to come get you to safety. The city's being attacked. We have to go."

Amilia wiped tears from her eyes. "Elyon's here?"

"Yes. He arrived just now. I'll explain later, my lady. The tunnels. He said to take you into the tunnels."

Amilia Lukar shook her head. She was sobering up quickly now. "My mother," she said. "I have to get my mother out first." She could see the girl was about to try to deny her, but she wasn't going to take no for an answer. "This way. It isn't far."

They went briskly through the palace, Amilia leading her on, hurrying through the royal wing along a long carpeted corridor. They turned a corner and went down another corridor, reached some stairs and descended through a patch of darkness until they came out into another dim-lit hallway with suits of armour along the walls. The torches and lanterns were not lit as they used to be. Once before the palace blazed with firelight in every hall and corridor and chamber, but now only one in a hundred lanterns gave out a glow, and much of the palace lay in darkness. As they ran, Amilia spotted someone else lumbering toward them, no, two people, a man and a woman coming and going between pools of light.

"Small Wall," Leshie called out, seeing them. "I told you to get armoured and go wait at the tunnels."

"The Butcher does not wait. We came to help."

The two parties quickly converged. Amilia knew these others as well. The Butcher was the man in the slashed cloak of many red colours, and the woman beside him with the striped black and orange cape could only be the Tigress. Del had told her all about them too.

"Where's your brother?" Leshie asked.

"He went to the tunnels. I hope, anyway. He is a brave man, very brave and very strong, and maybe he went out to fight." He lifted his torn and tattered face, and the firelight filled his scars. He was horrific, utterly horrific to look upon. "I will go and fight as well, with the Shadow Prince. But first I will get you to the tunnels. You are the Drunken Princess, yes?" he asked Amilia.

"I see my reputation precedes me."

"Yes!" And he laughed loudly. "You would be Pretty Princess, but this is taken. But I think Drunken Princess is better. And you do not look so pretty right now."

"I apologise for him, my lady," said Leshie. "He has no manners at all." She kicked at his shin, godsteel clanging against godsteel. "We're going to get her mother first. Then the tunnels. My lady, lead on."

Amilia led on. It was a curious company of guards, to be sure. Leshie was so small she could probably fit her in her pocket, the Butcher was less a man with scars than a lattice of scars with a man attached, and the Tigress was as beautiful as she was tall, and as tall as she was strange, with those staring eyes and little hisses. Despite everything, Amilia smiled. *At least if I die now, I won't die alone.*

"Your mother is the hermit?" the Butcher asked, thumping along beside her.

"Yes."

"I hear she has claws ten inches long. I know how long ten inches is, yes." He laughed to himself. "I know very well."

"Hers aren't that bad." *But close enough.* "She's right along here," Amilia said, and they went through another open chamber and along the corridor where her mother's apartments were. There was rumbling by then. Shaking through the walls. *They're attacking the palace,* Amilia thought. It was the same as last time, just the same as last time…

She reached her mother's door and turned the handle, pushing, but it wouldn't budge. "Someone get this," she said, moving aside, and the Butcher was there, kicking the door down. A great stink came pouring out, worse than ever. Amilia braced herself and pressed inside. "Mother? Mother, are you here? Mother?" The apartment had many rooms, though Amila sensed she knew where she'd find her. "This way. Someone light a torch." She hurried through a side door, down a short dark corridor, through her mother's bedchamber and into an adjoining resting room where Lady Clarris would sit in her chair in her sitting-soiling phase, and no doubt she was deep into one of those phases now by the thick awful stink in the air. "Mother?"

The room was all dark but for the low glow of a single candle. It sat in a pool of wax on a little table beside her chair, melting down to the wick, giving out its final flickers. Lady Clarris Kastor was in her chair. The reek in the room was eyewatering. Her clawed hands clutched at the arms and her eyes were open wide, staring at nothing. Her lips moved. They moved and whispered. The words were too quiet to hear.

"Mother." Amilia rushed up to her. "Where are your servants, Mother? Your guards?"

The woman gave no answer. Her lips moved in and out, in and out, a hiss beneath a whisper, unheard.

"Mother!" Amilia grabbed at her arm to try to pull her up, but the woman's strength was iron. She felt the cords of muscle in her arm tensing, her entire body stiff and rigid, as though it was cemented into the upholstery. "Mother, I'll take you and the chair if I must." Amilia turned her head, saw the others coming through. "Someone get her up."

"She stinks," said the Butcher. "I will not touch her."

Leshie held a torch, throwing light and shadow across the room. The state of it was appalling. "Take this." Leshie handed the torch to the Butcher and stepped forward. She looked down at Lady Clarris, at the wild eyes, the moving lips, the wiry grey hair surging out in all directions. "Lady Clarris. Come now, we have to go."

"She won't answer that," Amilia said. "We have to force her." She gestured for Leshie to take the woman's left arm, reaching to take her right, and pulled. As soon as her mother's backside left the sticky soiled seat of the chair, she screamed, thrashing against them, kicking out and dislodging them.

"I'm going to die here!" she screamed. "Right here in this chair, I'll die!"

"No, Mother!" Amilia swiped across the woman's face, slapping her fiercely. "I won't let you die here, damn you!" She pulled her again, and Leshie pulled, and the woman screamed and raged as they wrenched her to her feet. Her long claws slashed out at them, raking at their faces, trying to put out their eyes. "Hold her!"

The Butcher stirred into life and came around her back, pulling her arms down to her side, and now the Tigress bore the torch as she led them back through the apartment, down the corridor and past the bedchamber and out of the main door, Lady Clarris Kastor spitting and shrieking and roaring obscenities at them all the while.

"This way," Amilia said, as they got her out into the hallway. "The tunnels, they're…"

A sudden shudder shook the world, throwing them off their feet, and the corridor behind them shattered, exploding, the walls and the ceiling and the floor ripping free as something monstrous, something colossal, something *impossible* surged by. A roar followed, deafening, world-ending. Down the corridor, the whole palace was crumbling, disintegrating to rock and rubble as the world opened up beyond. Amilia stared, breathless. An entire wing of the palace was gone, and in its place was open air…and beyond…beyond she saw the titan, saw the Dread, the immense shadow soaring out over the city, roaring that apocalyptic roar.

"My lady, get up! Get up!" Leshie was there, tugging her to her feet. "We have to go! Come on, come on!" She pulled her onward away from the devastation. The Butcher was sprawled on the ground further away, the Tigress helping him up. Amilia looked around. She could not see her mother.

"Where…"

"We can't save her," Leshie shouted, over the roaring, the rumbling, the crash of falling stone. "If she wants to die here, that's her choice."

"No, I…I can't…Where is she?" Amilia turned fully about. The door to her mother's chambers was still open. She tried to pull away from

Leshie, but the girl wouldn't let her go. "My mother…my mother's in there…"

"And she'll die in her chair," Leshie shouted. "There's no helping her, Amilia. You go back in there and you'll only die too."

She shook her head. How many must she lose? Could she not save her mother, at least? *I have to try…I have to try…*

And then she saw the storm. Out beyond the broken corridor, she saw it, the black storm with red lightning crackling and cackling through the sky. It surged upward, spreading from an orb of light, and beneath that orb was a tall black staff, and around that staff were clutched pale fingers, and she saw the eyes, the *red, red eyes*, as the demigod rode through the night on a demon dragon, and he was smiling at her, smiling as though he remembered her, smiling at her and laughing…

She backed away. *Those red, red eyes.* The demigod swished by quickly and was gone, and she could feel Leshie tugging at her arm, screaming over the noise. "We have to go! The whole palace is coming down!" Then a fierce pull, and Amilia was dragged, turning, losing her feet, stumbling, finding them again and running now, running as the whole world shook, jolting side to side, and she could hear it coming down, hear the corridor collapsing behind them, and she dared to look back and saw the ground giving way, the ceiling tumbling, chasing them, chasing… catching…catching…

Something hard and heavy crashed down upon her head.

There was a searing pain. A sense of falling. No life flashing before her eyes. No final thoughts. Just those twin lights in the night, the red eyes in the bone-white face, the demigod smiling, laughing as he passed.

And that was it. Then nothing.

Blackness.

70

Elyon

He surged in behind the dragonrider, weaving with the beast as it went left and right.

The city rushed by beneath them, the burning towers and steaming walls. Men teemed upon the battlements at every level, ducking behind the parapets and firing from the crenels as the ballistas rotated on their turntables and rushed along on their rails, launching their great bolts into the night.

One came for the dragon. It hissed by just beneath it, trailing mist from its tip as it went. The beast made a slightly panicked roar and flapped its wings to gain altitude, and Elyon went with it, closing quickly. *One at a time,* he told himself, *one at a time.* There were many targets to choose from here, but he must focus on one at a time.

The rider did not see him coming. With an extra pulse, he came up behind him, took a grip of the man's saddle to steady himself, and cut off his head with a swift side-cut. The head flew away behind them, and the body jerked, a jet of blood pulsing from the neck, and then slackened in the saddle. At the same moment, the dragon bucked in a terrible quivering motion, screamed in pain, and felt the point of the Windblade driving down into the base of its skull.

It died instantly, tumbling and spinning away to crash down into the snowy streets of Many Markets. At once Elyon launched himself off it, scanned for another target, saw a big bulky riderless beast soaring past right below him and gave chase. The brute trumpeted, seeing him, and tucked its wings into a sudden dive, whipping its tail defensively as it went. Men began firing up at it from the partition walls between Many Markets and the Sentinels, and a tower-top mangonel groaned around on its turntable, its arm loaded with a godsteel-weighted net. It took aim, waited, waiting a few moments more, then a man tugged at the rope, releasing the swinging arm, and the net was fired upward, opening out to embrace the dragon as it shrieked and tried to wheel away.

The net closed about it, tightening as it struggled, the weight of the godsteel barbs and spikes strangling any hope of widening its wings. The dragon thrashed, screaming, blazing out its flaming breath, but the net was oiled and fireproof. Down it went, crashing hard into the side of a stout defensive tower, then bouncing off to land in an open market square.

"Finish it off," Elyon Daecar roared, swooping past the nearest battlements. "You." He swung the Windblade at a company of spearmen. "Get down there now and finish it off!"

He kept low now, surging up and across the Sentinels, along the battlements and past the towers and the men who manned the siege weapons. "Fight!" he roared to them. "Fight for your city! Fight for your lives! Fight!"

He could hear them shouting, trying to summon their courage, could hear the clicks and low, heavy groans of the siege weaponry, hear the constant repetitions of 'nock' and 'draw' and 'fire' being shouted from a hundred positions. The dragons were many, but they could beat them off, Elyon knew they could. *If they hold their positions, they can beat them.* "For Tukor!" he found himself roaring out, to inspire them. "For Tukor! For Ilith! For the north! For Tukor!"

He swung upward, slicing at a passing dragon and cutting through its wing to send it reeling, then twisted away and chased another, gathering himself into a powerful wind-assisted thrust as he came up beneath his belly. The Windblade drove inward toward its furnace fires, juddering right up to the hilt, and with another great wind-surge Elyon pulled it sideways, ripping the dragon violently open. Fire and smoke and bloody gore gushed out as the creature moaned and fell and died, and Elyon was gone, spinning upward across the city as he heard the great chanting ringing up from below: "For Tukor! For Tukor! For Tukor!" they were roaring, and there was defiance in the voices, defiance and hope. *Yes, we can do this,* Elyon Daecar thought. *We can drive them off...*

And then, just then, he felt it.

The thrum in the Windblade, the sudden sharp change in the air. He slowed, stopped, heart thumping, eyes narrowing, and looked away to the west. The chanting trailed away like an outgoing tide, dying a death on a thousand tongues. And Elyon grimaced. He cursed the gods for their cruelties and grimaced.

Drulgar the Dread had come.

He cruised in from the southern skies, coming up over the mountains, banking and wheeling around casually to crash through a great wing of the palace. He laughed as he did it, that rolling huffing roaring laugh that shook the very bones in Elyon's body. Floating high, he watched as the Dread descended, trailing his curved claws across the stone bridges and quads of the Marble Steps, snapping at towers as a dog snaps at flies, flicking his immense tail from side to side, shattering stone strongholds and stairs.

At once, the city began devolving into chaos. He could see them far below, see the men abandoning their positions on the walls, see the bowmen and the spearmen throwing down their weapons and pouring for the stairs, scurrying like rats escaping the flood. A thick fog of fear rose up on the wind, and he could hear the screaming, the wild frenzied screaming as they fled from him, this Dread, their doom, this terrible titan that could not be killed.

And Elyon Daeacar breathed out. In sudden despair and desolation, he breathed out. He felt tired, so very tired now and he could not defeat this thing alone. The dragons were fleeing from the power of their master, flying upward to let him devour this great city alone, and down the Calamity came, casting a trail of disaster in his wake as he swept down past the Marble Steps and over the Sentinels, tearing through archery ranges and armouries and barrack buildings, laying waste to all beneath him.

I should lead him away, Elyon thought. *I'll make him follow me like I did at King's Point.* But where? Where? Where could he lead him and why would he follow? *I am an insect to him, nothing. There is nothing he fears, nothing that can stop him.* The monster was passing him now, passing close, and Elyon felt the great pull of his weight as he went by, the endless bulk, the soaring spines, the volcanic heat steaming and swirling from the ancient cuts and fissures in his body.

Elyon remembered the battle at the Point. He remembered landing on the titan's back and driving the Windblade down through his scales. It took several strikes, but he got through eventually, and when the blade punctured past the metre-thick armour and pierced the flesh, the monster had quivered and roared as a man does when pricked unexpectedly by a needle, and Elyon knew then he felt pain.

He is not invulnerable, he tried to tell himself. *He can be hurt, he can be killed. Vesryn cut him. He can be killed.*

The Dread was veering away to the stout defensive towers on the city's southern border. Each was armed with long-range ballistas and the prince could see the bolts whizzing out through the air. It would take the giant dragon turning his head at the exact right moment, take the perfect flight of a bolt to strike him in the eye to kill him, and even that was far from certain. *But it doesn't need to be a bolt,* he thought. *It can be me. I can be the bolt…*

Elyon did not need to consider it further. What other chance did they have? The dragon was already past his position. He swung around, wheeling swiftly behind him, through the vast trail of ashen smoke pouring in his wake. Over the forest of spines he flew, faster, faster, up toward the bulging shoulders as the wings spread out to his left and his right, out to the edge of sight, embracing all the world in darkness. And he could hear the deep pull of his breath, feel the mighty thunder of his heart, that heart as large as a greathall pumping that lava-like blood through his volcanic body. Above the beast, Elyon entered another world, a world of fume and flame and acrid brimstone, of surging black spines veined red and red spines veined black and over the old wounds made by the titans and the demigods and the ancient powers that Drulgar the Dread had destroyed. By Orthrand and Brannatar and Fronn the wolf, and by Brexatron the Bat who was Drulgar's older brother and by Varin himself, and by Varin's son Elin and his daughter Iliva who bore the same blade Elyon now bore.

All died by him, the prince thought. All but Varin who drove him away in his rage after his son and daughter had been slain. All had left their marks, but that was all, and how was Elyon to do any better? He surged through the spines, gritting his teeth, weaving through the drifts of burning smoke. *Try*, he told himself. *Just try. You have to try.* He would die if he succeeded, he knew that well enough, but it was a trade he was willing to make. *I'll join Saska in the Eternal Halls*, he thought. She was dead, he feared, no matter what Leshie said. *Dead and looking down on us now… looking down on me as Varin is and my brother and my uncle and my grandfather and my mother and all the rest. I'll do it for Saska. I'll do it for them all.* He raced onward, faster, faster, faster…

A sudden *crack* of shattering stone split the skies ahead. Elyon glimpsed a tower exploding through the eddies of smoke, the domed roof and windows through which the ballistas and bowmen were firing disintegrating into a rain of stone and wood and broken bodies. Elyon ducked away as the debris flew by. A moment later, a second tower was struck, and a great wall of stone came surging right for him. He swerved, desperate, diving into the forest of spines. The Dread was trumpeting out in triumph now; Elyon could feel the vibrations coming up through his body, buzzing through the steel of his sabatons as he landed on the titan's back, ramming the Windblade down tip-first into one of his great segments of scale armour that spread across his colossal bulk like tectonic plates across the earth. The blade made it two feet deep. Elyon clung on with both hands, bracing as a third tower was struck, and then a fourth and then a fifth, the entire line of defence along the city's southern side disabled in three dozen heartbeats.

The rain of grit and stone and death poured over him, and the Dread was laughing in exulting joy, steam puffing and hissing up from his fissures with each reverberating rumble. Out across the city, it rumbled, out across the night. And Elyon could only hold on, stay low, and wait for the monster to beat his mighty wings again and rise, turning toward another target.

Eventually, the stone storm cleared, and the air cleared a little with it. He felt the body moving, glimpsed the wings rising to left and right, rising and then lowering in a single great thump that had them soaring up, up, a hundred metres up, two hundred metres, three, high up over the eastern walls.

The Dread soared away across the open valley, wheeling in a wide casual arc over snow-cloaked woods and frozen streams and the wide fine rolling hills. It was quiet now, suddenly quiet but for the heaving breath of the beast, the thump and shudder of his heart, the sound his outspread wing flaps made as they rippled in the wintry air like giant black-red banners. For a short moment, Elyon wondered if the giant dragon was leaving, but no, he swung serenely around and made back for Ilithor. Beyond the neck and the shoulders and the warship-sized head, Elyon saw the city burning now in the distance, heard the din of chaos ringing out as the fires chugged and licked up into the night and smoke poured in a thousand black plumes.

It was time. Now was his time.

He braced his feet beneath him, stood tall, and pulled the Windblade out with a scrape of steel on scale. Then swinging upward, he flew, a dozen metres, two, flying quickly forward now, quick and quiet, as he made his final approach.

Don't hear me. Don't feel me. Ignore me. I'm not here.

The city walls were nearing again, tiny now beneath them. Each level of Ilithor was laid out, one atop the next, rising up into the mountains; the vastness of White Shadow, Many Markets above it, the Sentinels and the Marble Steps rising higher, higher up to the palace that perched above them all like an eagle on its eyrie…

But no longer, he saw. Half the palace was gone. The entire southern side had collapsed and more of it was crumbling away. Something tightened in Elyon's chest. Amilia was in there, Leshie had said so. He'd told her to get the princess out, but who knew if she'd made it. A part of him wanted to fly there and find out, to help if he must, but he couldn't. He was coming beside the titan's long neck now, past the jutting horns and folds of armour, and the great head was there, dozens of metres away only. The eye was enormous, near as big as a wagon, protected by a protruding great ridge of thick black bone. It glowed like flame within the black-red head, and even from behind Elyon could see the want in it, the wet eager joy in this wanton destruction and death.

It was looking forward, scanning for its next target. *He hasn't seen me. I am nothing to him. Nothing.* Elyon prepared himself. The dragon was moving more sedately now, taking a short rest. *A quick thrust,* he thought. *Wheel around and come from the side. Use a wind-assisted blast and you'll cut right through with the tip.* If he could sever the eye and get through into the brain, he could kill it, he told himself. He thought of that brain-eating bug that Leshie had spoken about, the one she said had driven that eagle mad. *I'll be that bug,* he thought. *I'm an insect to him, fine. I'll be the one that kills him.*

The Dread was speeding up again, veering toward the north of the city where another line of towers surged up from the rock of the Hammersongs. *Now. It must be now.* Elyon did not wait a second longer. Surging swiftly forward along the neck now, he swung outward in a sudden fierce arc, turning back to face the head. The eye was staring forward, and upward, looking toward something away up in the mountains. Hope flared in him. Elyon thrust forward. The wind propelled him onward. The tip of the blade glinted in the firelight. It neared the eye, closer, closer. He thought of Saska, his brother, his mother, his uncle…

The eye swung, seeing him. The pupil widened suddenly, dilating. The tip of the Windblade cut into the softness of the cornea, and Elyon felt it opening, splitting, seeping. Time was standing still. Deeper the Windblade went. Two inches, five, ten, twenty. *A little more, a little more…*

The eyelids slammed shut, sudden as a striking snake. One came down and the other came up and the Windblade was stopped in its tracks, trapped.

The Dread roared. It writhed in a sudden terrible motion and it was all Elyon could do to cling on.

He swung his legs up, fixing his feet, and pulled hard to haul the blade free with both hands. It wouldn't budge. The dragon's head was swinging madly side to side. Elyon tried something else. *In*, he thought, and he drove it harder with all his weight, sliding it a little deeper into the eye, and the dragon bucked again in pain, and a shadow loomed behind him. Elyon turned to his right. A huge taloned wing arm was reaching out to scratch him away. It filled all his view, filled all the sky, swinging down with colossal claws and Elyon could not avoid it.

He pulled back and this time the blade slid free, and he twisted, turning, trying to fly away, but one claw struck him, and struck him *hard*, and he was falling now, spinning and falling through the smoky night air, trying to command the winds, trying to arrest his momentum but he was dazed, too dazed, and the blade would not obey…

An open snowy square came rushing up fast to meet him. The cobbles bulged and broke as he landed, exploding to form a crater. All the breath was vaporised from Elyon's lungs. He could not breathe; he could barely think. Vaguely, he sensed the Dread flying in a terrible rage above him, and his roars were no longer full of laughter but of wrath. And there was something else as well, further up in the city…some great thundering crackling sound as though a god himself was bellowing.

Wheezing, he peered through his blurred eyes and glimpsed a black and red storm broiling up in the mountains. There was an orb of light up there, shining in the darkness. *Agarath*, he thought. *The storm…it is Agarath…*

He tried to stand. He needed to help. But his day was done and he knew it. No sooner had he got up to his feet than he collapsed again, back into his crater. And all the sights and sounds of the world went out.

71

———

Emeric

Emeric Manfrey stood at the edge of the high plateau, watching the Dread reduce the city to rock and ruin. His roars had turned to wrath now, and he was in a state of maddened fury. *There is no laughter left in his voice,* he thought. *This isn't like Lakeheart, he isn't here for fun.*

No. He is here to destroy us all.

From below, he could see the black storm rising up in their direction now, see the demigod standing between the bulging shoulder horns of his demon dragon, hoisting his black staff aloft. The Bondstone glowed atop it, and from the orb rose the storm, forming into a great fearsome face, and Emeric knew it was the Face of Agarath.

He drew a slow deep breath and gripped the hilt of his blade. *Deep breaths,* he told himself. *Stay calm. Deep breaths.*

He scanned the city a final time, wondering what had come of Jonik and his brother. The former he had seen rushing down from the palace into the Marble Steps shortly before the titan came. The latter he'd glimpsed more frequently, flashing through the night with the Windblade in his grasp and living up to his famed reputation. The last Emeric had seen of him, the young prince was chasing after the Dread as he swung away through the valley and then wheeled back toward the city, no more than an insectoid spec against his godly bulk. Short moments ago, the great dragon had begun twisting in flight, thrashing its head, emitting from its lungs a startled bellow, and Emeric could only assume that Elyon Daecar had something to do with that. Distantly…very distantly….he thought he saw a steaming liquid oozing from the titan's left eye, but could not be sure. Everything came in glimpses now through the great plumes of rising smoke.

And the storm was coming. *We have our own troubles to confront,* he thought. He could no longer stand observing. Taking another deep calming breath, he turned and strode back toward the forge. Sir Ralston

Whaleheart was standing outside, a hulking steel titan with a greatsword drawn. "He's coming," Emeric told him. "Be ready."

The giant nodded. Emeric passed him, entering the workshop. Reinforcements had been swiftly brought up from below courtesy of Sir Pagaloth and his dragon Lendrathor, who has since flown off without his rider somewhere. "He's coming," Emeric said again. "He'll be here in a few moments."

Sir Storos Pentar groaned, the big huntsman Vilmar the Black scowled, and Sir Pagaloth Kadosk stood perfectly still and gave a stiff assenting nod. There was a noise from the back and the door swung open and Sir Lythian Lindar stepped back through, briskly, and he had on his face a look of great purpose. He bore in his grasp the Sword of Varinar. Fhanrir followed after him, and then Ilith in his vibrant, youthful form, only partly dimmed by the brewing of the final potion. The demigod looked out through the cave opening and saw the black storm rising up now past the edge of the mountain, saw the features of the Fire God rendered in smoke and lightning.

He bore an expression that was not fear, or alarm, but something else, something knowing. It was a look Emeric had seen on his face before, and a look that fortified his own faith. The demigod turned his eyes upon the armoured men, one and then the next, to give them courage. "Do not be careless with your lives," he said. "We need only time. A short time only."

"For a spell?" Sir Storos Pentar asked. He was gaping at the demigod, still reeling from his unveiling. Lythian's party had only just arrived after a long, cold trek and knew nothing of Ilith's revival, nothing of the potions, nothing of the coming of the other blades. It was a lot to absorb in a few minutes only, and now this. Now the Dread and the demigod and the All-Father's face looking down on them from the red-black storm. "Will you fight him, my lord?" Sir Storos went on. "With…with your magic? Will you drive him away?"

"I have no magic to fight him."

"But…"

"My strength is in *creation*, not destruction, Sir Storos. One is light, the other is dark, and I tapped into the dark only once." He looked at the blade in the hand of Lythian Lindar. "When I shattered the heart of a god," he said. "And never again shall I walk that road."

There was a rumbling noise outside now, a thumping of wings and a crashing sound as the dragon landed at the edge of the plateau at the top of the switchback stair. Emeric turned and saw Sir Ralston stepping in front of the doorway, blocking it off, concealing those within. There was laughter, then, a great mocking laughter that seemed to come from both the demigod and the storm above him, a crackling thunder that spread and echoed out across the mountains, out across the world. Then a voice, a reaching, penetrating voice that blew into the forge like a hot burning wind and filled every particle of space.

"Come out, Ilith," it said. "My friend, come out. I wish to see you."

Emeric set his jaw against the voice. His fingers tightened around the eagle blade of Sir Oswald and he saw Lythian Lindar stepping forward, glancing at Ilith and at Fhanrir as he went, nodding and then moving straight past them. They had retreated into a back room only minutes ago, though for what reason Emeric didn't know. He didn't have time to think on it. "Storos, Vilmar, Pagaloth," Lythian said, stepping outside with the Sword of Varinar. He went to the huntsman and shared a quick private word, then to the dragonknight to do the same. *Orders*, Emeric thought. Lythian Lindar had been a captain of the Varin Knights for many years and was well-conditioned to lead men into battle.

The exile paused a moment before following. "I think Prince Elyon cut him," he said to Ilith. "The Dread. I think he cut his left eye."

Illith nodded. "A red tear," he said, sharing a look with Fhanrir. "Where is Elyon now?"

"I don't know, my lord. I think he might have been struck, after. I couldn't see clearly through the smoke."

Ilith considered it a moment longer, then said, "Go, Emeric. Join the others. *Time*. We need but time."

Time, Emeric thought, nodding. He swallowed to moisten his throat, turned and stepped out onto the plateau.

The air was growing warm outside, and the snow was melting now, steam rising to join the mists of godsteel, to join the bands of fog blowing across the mountains and the choking fume rising up from the city.

The men were spread out beyond the opening to the cave, a curious group: an exiled lord, two Bladeborn knights, an old huntsman and an Agarathi defector, with the First Blade of Vandar standing ahead of them. Something tickled in the back of Emeric's head. *A line of misting men, standing against the storm…*

Eldur the Eternal did not ride in a saddle. He merely stood where he pleased atop the dragon and tall he was, even taller than the Wall, turned grand and terrible in his power. He whispered a word and his demon dragon lurched forward, and the demigod stepped easily from one horn to the next, striding down as though they were steps until he was delivered to the steaming stone perch.

He wore robes that swirled, robes in red, and his skin was pale and broken, fractured and fissured like ancient stone. Abnormally long fingers wrapped about his tall black staff, white on black, and his long colourless hair was swept back from his high forehead to hang halfway down his back, stirring as though in a current of warm air. He looked at Emeric, at Storos, at Vilmar, disinterested, but to Pagaloth he smiled and even gave a soft chuckle and at Lythian Lindar he dipped his head. "I know you," he said, in that voice. "I have much to thank you for, son of Varin."

"I should have killed you when I had the chance," Lythian told him.

"And why didn't you? Was it weakness? Fear? Could it have been *hope*?" His chin was long, his nose thin, his eyes drawn to glowing red slits. There was something reptilian about his visage, something dreadful and dragonlike. "Hope," he said, once more, savouring the word. "You pin your flags to it, lean on it like a crutch, but what hope do you have now?" He opened out an arm, a long cloaked arm, and his clawed fingers twitched toward the city. "What hope do you have against him? Now that your *saviour* is gone."

Sir Ralston Whaleheart rumbled forward. His armour clanked and banged. "Where is she?" he demanded. "What have you done with her?"

Eldur looked over at the giant. He considered him a moment and then said, "You care for her…or claim to. But it is no different to how you care for those blades in your grasp. For that is all she is to you. A weapon. But a weapon no more."

"Where is she?" the King's Wall thundered again. Steam poured out from the vents of his buckethelm and mist puffed frantically from his greatsword.

"Beyond your power to hurt," said the demigod. "She is free, now, free of you all. She deserves more than what you have made her."

The Whaleheart stamped forward, heedless, one step, two, each thumping and shuddering through the stone. "Tell me where she is!" he was rumbling. "Tell me what you have done with her!" He thumped onward, onward, and Eldur let him come, towering tall, arrogant in his might. "Tell me!" Sir Ralston roared at him.

"No."

And the Whaleheart surged. Close he was now, no more than five metres away, and he rushed him at staggering speed, closing, closing, raising up his greatsword to strike…

Eldur tapped his staff.

A propulsive blast spread from the Bondstone, rings of red light spreading and screaming, and Emeric cringed, turning his head against the sound, an overlapping clangour of sorrow and woe like a million voices all calling out at once. The Whaleheart was struck in the chest. Off his feet he went, tumbling away across the plateau, landing with a great echoing thud. He struggled back up to his knees, shaking his great helm from side to side against the ringing, smashed a steel fist against the rock once, twice, thrice, and then rose back up to his feet.

"Again?" asked Eldur. And the black storm was laughing.

The Whaleheart surged. Eldur let him come, let him come, and as his greatsword swung mere inches from his cold white face he tapped his staff once more. Another pulse of power struck the giant and he went tumbling more fiercely this time, end over end, cracking sickeningly into the wall of the mountain. A great shudder filled the air. The Whaleheart stayed down, unmoving for a long moment. Then slowly, defiantly, he rose again, his armour dinted, scarred, sizzling.

"You have courage," the Fire Father observed. "You must truly love her."

"She…she is…everything…to me."

"She is a weapon to you," Eldur dismissed. "Such is not befitting for the heir of Varin."

The Whaleheart staggered forward once more, his greatsword

clutched in two hands. He heaved it up, lifting it to swing and this time Eldur *moved*. Strangely he moved, and quickly, like a banner of red fog with trails of white, and in an instant he was there, taking the Whaleheart by the neck and lifting him, lifting him. His fingers were closing, crushing, tightening, thick clawed nails cutting in through his godsteel gorget…and Emeric could stand by no longer. All of a sudden he was running, and so too were Sir Storos and Sir Pagaloth, closing from several sides as a throwing knife flashed out from the shadows, spinning end over end at blistering speed and whispering past the demigod's face, cutting through a lock of white hair.

It fluttered to the ground.

Eldur looked at it and his eyes sharpened. He threw the King's Wall aside, slamming him violently down onto the rock, slid back and raised his staff. From the Soul of Agarath came a shower of crimson light, sparkling like a waterfall caught in the glare of the sun. Emeric was there. His swinging blade struck the light. A sudden loud *crack* split the air, and there was a blinding flash of red, and the next thing he knew he was soaring backward, flying, tumbling, landing two dozen metres away where the edge of the plateau gave way to darkness.

The impact knocked the wind out of him. There was a fierce savage ringing in his ears, a deafening sound. His vision flashed, coming and going as bright spots of light danced before him. His sword arm felt heavy, dead, useless. He tried to close his fingers, but they wouldn't work. *My blade*…he was no longer holding his blade.

Gradually his vision returned to him, and he realised just how close to the edge he was. Another foot and he'd have gone tumbling over. Vaguely now he could see down into the city, see the flames rising and the smoke chugging up as the towers toppled and burned. The Dread was down there still, afoot now, swinging and crashing and tearing through the squares and markets and tiers, reducing all to ruin as his volcanic breath poured out of him, snaking as he swung his great head from side to side.

Jonik, Emeric thought, reaching out a hand. He was down there, somewhere. *Jonik*….

His ears were still ringing. Beneath the din he heard shouts behind him, that spreading voice and the crackling thunder-like laughter high above as the face of Agarath watched on.

He got to his knees, pulling a ragged breath into his burning lungs. One strike and that was it. One strike and he was done. His sword arm was a dead weight at his side, and he wondered if it would ever work again.

Across the plateau, Storos Pentar was lying dead or unconscious, and the Whaleheart hadn't moved since Eldur threw him to the ground. The dragonknight Sir Pagaloth was on his knees before the demigod, Emeric saw. A large pale hand came down to rest atop the man's head, and his long queer fingers curled beneath his chin. Eldur was speaking to him, murmuring, whispering.

A voice cut through the night. "Let him go," Lythian Lindar demanded. The First Blade stepped up to him, facing the demigod alone. "He is yours to command no longer. He has sworn his oaths to *me*."

Eldur smiled at him. "Oaths are air, son of Varin. Blood is richer. And his is *mine*."

"Let him go," Lythian repeated. He stood before him, noble, gallant, armoured from head to heel in his wartorn godsteel armour. The Sword of Varinar was glowing gold in the darkness, pulsing with swirls of gilded mist that seemed to protect him from Eldur's power. "You took Talasha from me once. I will *not* let you take him as well."

The demigod's slit eyes twisted upward in amusement. "Yes...yes, I remember. Sweet Talasha, who is my blood. Do you love her, son of Varin?"

"Yes. I love her."

Eldur laughed. And the storm laughed above him - they laughed together, the god and his vessel.

Lythian stood before them, unbowed. "Let him go," he demanded once again. He did not quell, did not weaken. His voice rang out loud and clear. "Pagaloth is not yours to torment."

"*All* are mine to torment." The demigod lifted Sir Pagaloth up, now, raising him by the chin with those long clawed fingers. Emeric caught a glimpse of the dragonknight's face and saw the strain, the terrible strain as his mind was twisted and overwhelmed and enslaved...though he seemed to be fighting, somehow, trying to fight him off. Eldur brought him close to his terrible visage, observing him closely for a long, drawn moment. "You have slain your own brothers," he whispered at him. His thin mouth twisted. "For freedom, you think? You kill your own kin to free them?"

The dragonknight squirmed in his grip. He was kicking, but it was futile, reaching with his hands as though to prise the Fire Father's arm away. The demigod was a giant to him. Pagaloth's feet trailed two feet off the ground, and his strength was leaving him, quickly draining away.

"Death is freedom to you, child," Eldur said. "Will you have it yourself, then? This gift you give so freely to your brothers? This gift that is not yours to give. Will you join them in the Eternal Flame?"

"No," Lythian said. He took a step forward, holding the Sword of Varinar before him. The golden shroud of light was a shield. It pressed against the darkness, pressed against the red screaming power that throbbed and pulsed from the Bondstone. "Let him go. If you must take someone, take *me*."

"You?" Eldur's slit eyes were disinterested. "You are nothing to me, son of Varin. You and your pretty golden blade...nothing. It had power once, when borne by Varin. Great he was, my brother, and it's my *other* brother I come to see."

"Then see me," said a silvery voice, as the Worldbuilder emerged from the forge. He wore his plain, stained, blacksmith garb and a brown wool cloak atop it. "Enough, Eldur. That is quite enough."

"Ilith. You join us at last." The Fire Father's bloodless lips curled into a smile. "How are you, brother? It has been a long time."

"Millenia," Ilith said. "And perhaps not long enough."

"You wound me. I have so longed for this moment. Ever since I heard that you had awoken, just like me. Oh brother, what a joy to see you."

"I do not share in your joy."

Eldur chuckled. "No. No, I understand. All this destruction…it pains you, I know. To see your creations brought to ruin. To see your city fall."

Ilith looked at him fiercely. "Command the Dread to leave," he told him. "Enough have died; let the rest live. Command him to stop and I will come with you willingly."

No, Emeric tried to say. *No, you can't. You can't.* The words were caught in his throat, caught there choking him and they went unheard. He only stared, wordless, sitting back on his haunches.

"Let Sir Pagaloth go and I will come." Ilith stood in the swirling fog, in the ash flakes rising from below. "Just leave my city alone, Eldur. I can hear them, you know I can hear them." He listened a moment to the terrible tumult, and a look of torment crossed his face. "I cannot bear it any longer. I will go with you. Just leave them be."

"You were always so sensitive, Ilith. I will leave your city, old friend."

Eldur's face lifted in triumph and a flash of red glittered in his eyes. He raised his staff and a great rumbling crackle was emitted from the storm that raged above them, the black storm that was the Face of Agarath. The Dread thundered an answer that rolled up from far beneath them, and the Fire Father nodded his reptilian head and said, "There. It is done. Your *city* is safe from him now, old friend. So come, come. We have much to discuss."

"Sir Pagaloth first. Put him down."

"Very well." Eldur flicked his wrist and sent the dragonknight tumbling away across the plateau. "Bring your hammer too. I may wish to make use of it."

Ilith paused, hesitating.

"Show it to me," Eldur demanded, and a pulse of red light flooded the plateau, shrieking. "*Now.*"

Ilith's head dropped. "Fine. Very well." He drew aside his cloak. "It is here, Eldur."

"Take it out. *Show it to me.*"

Ilith reached to the pouch at his belt, and drew the Hammer of Tukor into his grasp. He lifted it up, presenting it. A soft silver mist rose from the glowing glyphs and runes. Eldur looked at it closely, cocking his head to the side, then nodded, satisfied, and Ilith slid the hammer back away.

"Come, then," Eldur said, and Ilith walked nobly toward his fellow demigod, chin up, a smooth calm step, and together they scaled up to the back of the demon dragon. Emeric watched on, forgotten, desolate, as the dragon turned now and spread its wings. Eldur made a gesture, and then the beast reached out with a taloned foot and closed its claws around the form of Sir Ralston. "No," Emeric heard Ilith say thinly. "That is not the bargain. Leave him…"

"I want him," Eldur said, and nothing more. He lifted his staff once again, and trails of red light poured off the orb, forming into crimson ropes that swung around the Worldbuilder, wrapping him and binding him to a tall orange spine that surged from the dragon's back. "For your safety, Ilith. I would not want you to fall." The red light screamed all the while, a terrible torturous sound. It roped him and gagged him, cocooning him in that unbearable din and Emeric could suffer it no longer. He hunched low, now, holding his hands against his ears and cringed, praying, praying for it to end.

When next he knew, the screaming was fading and the demigods were gone, and he heard the thick powerful thump of wings as the Dread soared up into the black smoking skies. Emeric watched through bleary eyes as the titan soared out over the valley to the east, then wheeled, turning, and not south, but *north*, rising up, up and away across the mountains in a fearsome, thumping rage.

"The refuge," said a voice. Emeric saw Lythian Lindar stepping up to him through the fog. A glow of golden light came with him. "He is going for the refuge, Emeric."

The exile nodded his head. He knew about Ilith's broken seals. He knew about the spies who had escaped down into the foothills. "It's exposed," he said, still down on his haunches. Some small feeling was coming back into his sword arm now. He closed his fingers weakly, closed them and opened them. "He'll bring the whole mountain down on top of them, Lythian. He'll…he'll bury them all."

The Knight of the Vale looked inscrutably into the mountains. He seemed to know something that Emeric did not. There was something in his grasp. Hair, was it? A lock of white hair. "True blessings require great sacrifice, Emeric," he told him. Then he slid the Sword of Varinar away, reached out and pulled the exiled lord back up to his feet. "Pagaloth," he called out, turning his head. "Call Lendrathor back. We must find Elyon. And we must find him now."

72

———

Ranulf

"Is Lady Amilia coming back soon?" Cevi asked sweetly.

Ranulf took the girl's hand. "I hope," he told her, sitting beside her bed. "She has suffered a loss, Cevi. It may take some time for her to heal."

"I miss her." The girl looked at a chair that Amilia must have sat in during her visits. It was plush enough, to be sure, a good fit for a beautiful young princess. "It's so sad what happened with Sir Mallister. Do you think…what he did…do you think he needed to do it, Ranulf? With that sap, and…and his sister?"

"*He* believed it, Cevi. That is all that matters." Ranulf didn't want to talk about Mallister Monsort. It made him terribly sad to think of the young man's sacrifice and it was another reason that had brought him here, another tragedy…and one more troubling for them all. "I… have something I need to tell you both," he said, still clutching the girl's small fingers. He looked over at Del, sitting beside the crackling fire. "Put your book aside a moment, please. This will be difficult to hear."

The horsey-faced boy looked worriedly over at him. He had a population ledger in his lap and had been scrutinising the pages with great concentration. If those ledgers were filled with scholastic learnings, the boy would no doubt be a scholar himself by now, given the amount of time he spent with them. He closed the book, marking the page, and placed it aside on a table. "What is it, Ranulf? Is…"And his fear ripened further. "Is this about Saska?"

"Yes," Ranulf said, sighing. "I'm afraid…I'm afraid she has gone missing, Del."

"Missing? What…what do you mean missing?" He sat up abruptly in his chair.

"Taken," Ranulf explained, gently. "By servants of the enemy. She was taken, Del."

"*No*," he blurted. His head swung side to side in denial. "No, she *can't* have been. We need her, Ranulf. We need her."

"I know, Del. I'm…as upset about it as you are." He had only just learned of it himself, that very afternoon, when Lord Morwood came through from Ilithor bearing with him a fresh cache of tidings. There was news of Jonik. News of the Mistblade. News of the exiled lord, Emeric Manfrey, bringing with him some essential gifts. Much of that was positive, yet this of Saska's capture overrode it all.

Cevi was still clutching at his hand. She gripped tight. "How did it happen?" she asked, in a small voice. "Were there dragons, Ranulf?"

"Yes, child. Seven of them, I am told." It was too many, far too many for Saska's company to counter. "Saska had no choice but to give herself up, lest all of her friends be killed. She was taken, along with Joy. Some of them were killed, but…Leshie is alive, I know." That was some comfort to them. Ranulf had been through so much with Leshie, and cared a great deal for the girl.

There were tears shimmering in Del's eyes now. He stared at the ground, trying to blink them away and failing. When he sniffed and reached up to wipe them away, Cevi slid from the bed, limping over to comfort him.

"She will come back, Del," the girl whispered to him. "She will escape and come back to us…because she *must*." She wrapped her arms around the tall boy, holding him tight, and kissed him on the forehead. "Be strong, Del. We must be strong for her." Del held his head low, shoulders in. Cevi cupped his cheeks with both hands, lifting his face. "Be strong," she said, once more. "Be strong. She *will* come back." Then, gazing into each other's eyes, Cevi leaned in and kissed him on the lips, a firm but somehow soft kiss as well, a kiss in the blooming of an innocent young love and Ranulf sensed it was time for him to leave. He had more to say…he had to tell Cevi about Talasha, about her facial wounds and disappearance, but he could leave that for later.

He was about to absent himself when the door knocked, and Sir Hammet poked his head in. "Ranulf, a quick word," the Emerald Guard said quietly. He glanced at Cevi and Del, still kissing, smiled faintly, and then retreated.

Ranulf rose stiffly from his chair, following him out. He felt older since his trek to the Darkisle, older and stiffer and constantly cold as though something had been lost from his spirit, something stolen that he could not get back. Sir Fendrel was on guard with Sir Hammet today, and Rufford stood with them, breathing heavily as though he'd just run to be here. "Is there a problem?" Ranulf asked him.

The big man-at-arms nodded, taking a second to catch his breath. He was red-faced from exertion. "The beacons are lit," he said, between breaths. "I saw it, just now…the one up on Shadowlance Point. Means dragons, Ranulf. Means dragons are coming."

Ranulf knew the purpose of the warning beacons. Atop the mountains they had been erected to forwarn of an incoming threat, a device devised by Lord Morwood a month or so ago. They were spaced apart, raised upon the peaks, stretching for over a hundred miles across the Hammersongs.

"Where is Lord Morwood now?" Ranulf asked.

"At the main door," Rufford told him. "There's where I came from."

Ranulf turned quickly and went back into Cevi's room. "Both of you, stay in here. You're not to leave on any account." He stepped back outside before they could ask any questions. "Sir Fendrel, Sir Hammet, stay here. Make sure they don't try to leave, and if there's trouble, take them deeper into the mountain. You keep them safe, do you understand me?"

The two knights nodded. Ranulf and Rufford sped quickly through the halls and corridors, making for the main entrance hall where it opened out into the Shadowfort. The double doors were open, and outside Ranulf could see that the night was calm and clear and still. *No clouds,* he thought. *No cover at all.* Distantly, away on the high peak of Shadowlance Point, a glow of firelight was shimmering brightly against the starlit skies, throwing up a widening finger of smoke. The entrance hall was busy with soldiers, all standing there watching the flames, murmuring, fidgeting.

Ranulf strode up to Lord Morwood's side. "How long has it been lit?"

Morwood turned, saw him, and looked back out into the mountains. "Seven or eight minutes."

"Could it be an error?"

"No. They have been signalling us. The other beacons are burning. Something is coming from the direction of Ilithor."

Ranulf's breathing was growing shallow. He had mixed thoughts about the beacons. A useful tool in forewarning of an attack though they were, they might also lead the enemy right to them. "The night is clear," he said. "We have no concealment, Trillion."

"The mountain will protect us," the lord commander said, defiant. "This rock is thick and…" He paused midsentence, clutching at his godsteel blade as a light flashed up on the peak. The men there were signalling, trying to tell them something. "What are they saying, Bartram? I cannot make it out."

The man Bartram stood at the door. "I think…they're saying to retreat, my lord. For us all to retreat further back into the mountain." There was more frantic signalling. Bartrum paused to decipher the message, and then his face went pale. "My lord, I think…I they're saying it's the…"

His words were cut short.

The beacon fire exploded in a sudden great flood of flame.

Every man and woman in the hall leaned back, gasping, and some raised hands to shield their eyes from the light. The flames spread and widened across the mountain peak in a raging inferno, engulfing it, and from the blaze rose a great black swarm of smoke that poured up in rolling waves to fill the sky.

A silence followed. A sharp intake of breath. And then they heard the noise, the rush and force of it, a sudden storm, and a great heavy *thwump* of wings filled the air. The black smoke eddied and swirled and parted as a great monster burst through it, bellowing out into the night, soaring toward them. The roar was a crack like the breaking of the world and the whole hall shuddered as a shower of dust fell from the high ceiling. At once men were stumbling back, screaming and shouting. Several fell, tripping over their own legs as they twisted and turned and ran.

"Close the door!" Lord Morwood bellowed in his big commander's voice. "The door! Close the door!"

The men there surged into action. The chains were pulled, and the doors groaned shut, and every second the Dread drew closer. Ranulf could see him through the band between the doors, see the shape growing larger, larger, larger. As the doors finally came together, the dragon reached the fortress, and Ranulf had a final glimpse of his enormous feet spreading out as he landed.

The whole world shook. Ranulf spread his arms to steady himself, and his sea legs kept him standing. Others flew to one side or the other, knocking into one another as they fought to keep their balance. The Dread bellowed outside. Ranulf could hear the towers coming down, the walls and the buildings as the Shadowfort was swiftly razed. Great chunks of stone fell from the ceiling, crushing the water vats and the snow carts, which burst into shards of wood, and men were caught beneath them too. Heads cracked open like eggs and spines were snapped and legs shattered as men howled and screamed.

Ranulf turned this way and that as men died all around him. He saw another of Amilia's guards, Sir Mardon, flattened beneath one of the huge sentinel statues as it fell atop him. The soldier Bartrum was struck by a falling rock that caved the top of his head in. Rufford was dragging a man with a broken leg to safety when a chunk of ceiling fell on him as well, striking him hard in the shoulder and ripping a great gash down his arm. Lord Morwood was still bellowing orders, telling everyone to retreat to the very rear of the refuge. "Go!" he shouted, shoving at one man and then another. "Run for the living quarters! Tell them to retreat! Sound the horns!"

The horns began blowing, their deep moaning spreading out through the halls and chambers. The Dread was still thrashing away outside. It sounded like he was attacking the mountain itself, ripping and tearing at the rock like an anteater trying to get at its tiny prey, and the size differential was much the same. Ranulf backed away from the door, past blocks of stone and broken bodies. The floor was like that of a ship deck on a stormy sea, shaking and moving and going up and down. Men could hardly make it a half dozen paces before falling. Blood was spreading from split muscle tissue and crashed organs. Men were crying, limping, dragging themselves away.

Ranulf weaved through the chaos. He could sense Kamcho outside, flying high in the sky, but he had no time to enter his sight. There was a great sudden crashing at the door, and he turned to see several giant claws smash inside, saw the Dread's great bulk beyond, saw the head lowering down and turning as his glowing eye looked within. For a moment he seemed to look straight at Ranulf Shackton before the head rose again, snow and stone tumbling, and the dragon resumed his assault.

Ranulf blinked. He had never seen anything like it. *Calacan…he is so much bigger than Calacan…*

He felt a hand grip his shoulder. "We have to go, Ranulf!" It was Rufford. His right arm was torn open from the shoulder to the elbow joint, and Ranulf could see the white bone through the ragged red flesh, see the blood trailing to the floor. "We cannot die here! Not after everything we've been through!"

The entrance hall was coming down behind them. They ran together away from it, as echoes rang out from the halls and corridors, rock crashing, stone tumbling, men and women screaming. Rufford was losing a lot of blood, stumbling as he went. From ahead Sir Fendrel came running suddenly their way. "Hammet's taking the children further to the rear," he called, breathless. "Come, quickly…it's this way, this way…"

Another savage tremor went through the mountain, knocking them all to one side, and the corridor ahead came crashing down right where Fendrel had come from. There was no way forward…and no way back. "There….in there…" Sir Fendrel cried. He rushed toward a door, kicking it in with a loud wooden crash, and they poured inside as the corridor collapsed behind them in a great blowing cloud of dust. Ranulf was thrown from his feet. The only light came from the glow of the Bladeborn's blades, and it was faint, a gentle silvery blue wash that reached out only so far. It was a bedchamber. Sir Mallister's bedchamber, he realised, and just how he'd left it. Dead ashes in the hearth. The bed, neatly made. A jug of wine had gone crashing from a table to shatter and spill across the floor. "We're trapped," Fendrel said. "This…this is it. There's no way out."

The whole world was still shaking. It felt like the ceiling might come down on them at any moment. Rufford staggered over to the bed and collapsed, blood coming freely from his arm. Sir Fendrel's head swung about in a desperate panic. "This is it," he said again. "There's nowhere to go. This is it. We're going to die."

And Ranulf Shackton shut his eyes.

He drew a deep breath and shut his eyes.

If he was going to die here, he would look upon the thing that did it.

He slid into Kamcho's vision, and his world *changed*. He was high above the mountain now, looking down as the Dread rampaged. The whole of the Shadowfort was utterly destroyed. Drulgar stood among the ruins, ripping and slashing and biting at the rock, sometimes barging at it with his shoulder, swinging his head in a wild and terrible rage. His left eye seemed to be closed, bleeding. He could not see out of it….could not see that way…

…could not see when the vast shape *unfolded* from the darkness above him.

Ranulf's breath stilled in his throat. From a high mountain peak it came, flying silently down from its perch. Black eyes stared in unutterable hate, and the short snoutish nightmare of a face was hungry with anticipation. The wings were broad. From the thick, short neck to the legs, they went down the full length of the titan's body. Black it was, *full* black. No red like the Dread, no colour like its brother. Lightness, blacker than black, it was, and silent and unseen it came.

Ranulf Shackton remembered the greatbat, remembered the battle in the skies with Neyruu. *A preview,* he thought. *That was an appetiser only.* It was a feud ten thousand years old, a feud between brothers, a feud between titans, and Ranulf could barely breathe. He could feel the shaking in the refuge, hear the distant shouting of Sir Fendrel in the back of his head, but he would not return to them, would not open his eyes.

He stared, unbreathing, through Kamcho's sight, as the bat titan Brexatron plunged down upon the Dread. Smaller he was, but the surprise was his. Onto his younger brother's back he went, digging in with his sharp deadly claws, clinging on, and his teeth were ten metres long. A forest they were, a nightmare forest of needles that glistened wetly in the moonlight, and Ranulf saw them strike, he saw them strike and strike and strike again as the bat's head went savagely up and down, teeth plunging into Drulgar's shoulders and neck.

The Dread gave out a shuddering bellow. He thrashed back suddenly, crashing through the ruin of the Shadowfort. Ranulf felt the world tremble. He sensed the rock coming down around him in the bedchamber. But he would not open his eyes. He could not look away. The bat was biting, biting, biting. Lava-blood bubbled and rose up from the dragon's neck, steaming and gushing in rivers to either side. He stumbled and threw himself into another mountain to try to knock his older brother away, crashing through a thousand tonnes of rock, but the bat would not budge, he would not stop. His head went up and down, teeth stabbing, stabbing. Druglar's wings burst open wide and he thumped upward, upward, upward. A thousand metres he went, two thousand, three, up and above Kamcho as the eagle floated on the updraughts of air, watching.

And all the while the bat was biting, biting in hate and in vengeance, screaming out its terrible high-pitched shriek. Lava tumbled down in steaming waterfalls, hardening and darkening in the cold night air as it fell. Three thousand metres up the Dread stopped and tucked his wings. How he was still alive Ranulf would never know. *He is unkillable,* he thought. *He cannot die.*

The pair fell.

Quickly they fell, steaming, thrashing, locked in their death embrace. The mountains and the valleys and the rifts spread out beneath them.

And down they went, down and down, past the peaks and the slopes and past the fortress and the refuge, crashing down, down, down, into the mouth of a great yawning abyss. Ranulf saw them strike the sides and bounce from one wall to the next. Struggling, roaring, screaming, they fell…

…right down into the depths of the earth.

Ranulf Shackton opened his eyes, gasping.

The rumbling had stopped, the terrible violent shaking. He could hear bits of stone still falling, echoing beyond the walls of his prison. And a prison it was, a black prison full of broken furniture and tumbled stone. Faintly, he saw Rufford lying unconscious on the bed, lit only by the gentle glow of his blade. Beside the hearth, where Sir Fendrel had been standing, was only a great heap of stone now. Carefully, Ranulf picked his way to the bed, stepping over the rock and debris, feeling for Rufford's pulse. It was faint, weak. He glanced across the room and confirmed that Sir Fendrel was dead, crushed when the ceiling came down.

"Don't die on me, Rufford," he said, as he began tearing a length of fabric from his cloak, tying it around the man's arm to make a tourniquet. Rufford was the last of Mallister's company, but for him. He'd saved Ranulf's life too many times to count on the Darkisle, and damnit, he wasn't going to let him die. "They'll find us, Rufford, I know they will." The shaking was over, and the refuge was still. "Just hold on a little longer," he said. "And don't you bloody well die."

73

The High
Priest

The mountain rocked with triumph.

Within and without, the High Priest could hear it, the cheering of the legions that camped and crawled upon the slopes, the low strange rumbling of the fire giants and wyrms, the wingless dragons that lurked in the deep. In the main chamber where the Fire Father sat his godly black throne, the dragons were singing and shrieking as they wheeled over his head like crows and above, high above them all, the Storm of Agarath the All-Father cracked and crackled with approval.

High platforms and rugged rock balconies teemed with onlookers and the many walkways and bridges that crossed the central chamber like spokes on a wheel were crowded and packed full. Thousands had come rushing to see him, pouring from the many chambers of the Ashmount and even from the camps below, scuttling up the slopes like insects. Beneath them all, the fires that were the lifeblood of Agarath burned eternal, the lava moving in a thousand rivers through the vastness of his body. Sometimes, men fell from the walkways to plunge into those veins, but when they did, there were no screams, no shrieks of terror or pain, only great howls of glory as they were fed to the Eternal Flame.

The High Priest of Fire approved of that. He approved so much he liked to test men, sometimes, by *asking* them to jump, and never now did they disobey. *How many have I given to the flame?* he wondered. *How many have leapt by my voice and my word alone?*

But it was not *his* voice, not truly. *I am but a vessel of Eldur the Eternal, who himself channels the All-Father's will.* He wondered what he would do if *he* was asked to jump. *I would do it, yes,* he told himself. *Without hesitation, I would do it, I would jump.*

He nodded to that thought as he walked ahead of the procession, bearing his holy golden sceptre in his grasp. The red diamond that he wore at his throat throbbed with power and he had oiled the great crimson prong of his chin beard to make it perfect for the occasion.

Behind him came the dragonknights in their black armour and red capes, surrounding the two prisoners as they were brought toward the throne. They had only just arrived. Outside on the high mountain slopes Eldur had left them, handing them over to the High Priest's care. "Bring them to the main chamber," the Fire Father had commanded. "I wish for them to be paraded before my children."

The High Priest understood. It was better like this, to lead the *demigod* through the mountain, to let the men look at him and see him for what he was. *Weak*, the High Priest had thought, when he first saw him. Eldur had become tall and god-like in his might, grand and divine, but Ilith, no…Ilith was no taller than a common man, and the light that was said to glow from his skin was barely to be seen at all.

The giant was the greater concern. He had been left outside in his godsteel armour, and in one of the huge sheaths that hung from his swordbelt, a massive greatsword remained. The High Priest had ordered that he be chained and bound, his ankles placed in thick dragonsteel manacles and his wrists fettered together. A neckbrace was fixed as well, attached with half a dozen chains each held by a different man. If that was not enough to subdue him, the High Priest had ordered that he be drugged to ensure compliance, and that ought to be sufficient. He went along now, lumbering and rattling as the crowds spat and cursed and shouted obscenities at him, and at Ilith the Blacksmith too. Some tried to break through to get at them, so the High Priest flicked his sceptre, driving them back. "Away," he called out. "They are Fire Father's prize. Away!"

The masses parted before him, parted before his power. Many went low into crouches or even sank to their knees, because the High Priest was second only to Eldur here, he was his whip and his fist and his voice. "Move back," he commanded. "You…you are too close, move back." When the man in question did not move, the High Priest said, "Leap, go, leap to the Eternal Flame!" The man hesitated. "Now, I say. Do it now! Now!"

The man turned and shoved some other men aside and hurled himself to his doom.

The storm crackled, and Eldur nodded from his throne. *More*, thought the High Priest. *More, yes, more.* "Throw yourself to the flame," he called out. "To honour Ilith's coming. Welcome him with death, with death!"

Men threw themselves away over the edges, howling with joy. Five of them, ten, twenty tumbled over into the abyss, and *more*, the High Priest thought, as Agarath rumbled, *more, yes more*, and he shouted, "You, above us, welcome him! Welcome the Worldbuilder! Welcome him!"

From a dozen bridges now came a rain of men, flinging themselves from the higher walkways and platforms that jutted out from the great rock pillars. They cried out in squealing delight and rapture as Agarath thundered above them, and so more went over, more and more, feeding the mountain with their bodies and their blood and their bone.

"This is perverse," said a voice, behind him. "Is this what you call service? Mass sacrifice to your god?"

The High Priest turned, grinning. The dragonknights parted, and there he was, Ilith who had built the world...or so the northerners liked to say. When Eldur left him on the mountain slopes, he'd been bound up bodily in ropes of red screaming light, bound and gagged, but no longer. Only his wrists were bound now and in a common length of rope and no gag prevented him from speaking his mind.

"You seem very happy with yourself, priest," the blacksmith said. "Believe me, you won't be smiling soon."

He made his smile bigger in response, bigger, wider, *stranger*.

Ilith did not break eye contact. His eyes were more hateful than the High Priest had expected.

His smile withdrew. "They are honoured to feed the Eternal Flame," he said. "To bathe in the great glow of the All-Father's blood is a gift. A gift all welcome gladly." He looked left and right. Still more were jumping, leaping from on high. Their voices cried out in wild elation as they plunged through mist and swirling steam to vanish into the veins below. "Perhaps Great Eldur will grant you the same gift? Would you be honoured to receive it? To feed yourself to a god?"

"So that's why I'm here? As a sacrifice?" The demigod seemed almost amused by that notion. He looked around. Looked at the walkways and the bridges, at the pillars and the platforms, at the thousands all gathered here, hissing and snarling and spitting their curses, at the few who were still throwing themselves to their deaths. He looked around, and he did not quell; he looked around and he shook his head and said, "Slaves, that's all you are. Just one giant pit of slaves."

"Slaves? Oh no...no, all are here by *choice*, my lord. Did you not see them from the sky? The camps and the cookfires and the..."

"Be silent, cur. I care not to speak to you."

The High Priest swallowed his words. He was somewhat taken aback, in truth. He did not know Ilith to have such a curt tongue.

"Take me to your master, dog. Let's just get this done." Ilith stepped forward now, forcing the High Priest to turn quickly and stride ahead of him in order to maintain the structure of the procession. His cloak stirred at his feet and his fiery hair fluttered behind him and he was flustered, a little flustered all of a sudden. He raised his red-prong beard and took back possession of his composure. *He is a demigod*, he told himself. *That's all it is. There is power in his voice and his presence. You should respect that, yes. It is worthy of your respect.*

The teeming masses were still thick ahead of him. "Make away," he called, waving his sceptre. "Move, make way, make way." Far off the Fire Father's throne remained, eighty or even ninety metres away along the wide, central bridge. When a small clot of common men did not move aside, the High Priest told them to kill themselves, and they went willingly over the edge. That made him feel better again. Giving life to the Eternal Flame made him feel good. A low rumble crackled through the skies above, and he could see the black storm roiling now beyond the great open top of the volcano. The dragons slithered through it, entering and exiting and screaming out through the night, tiny against the swarming black clouds. He thought he saw his own dragon Draknarak moving up there, but he could not be sure.

"Make way," he shouted. "You, give yourself to the flame. And you… and you…" He swung his sceptre about at random. "You, yes, and you there, and you…the flame welcomes you, Agarath honours you, and you…and you…and you…"

"*Enough*," said Eldur. His voice reached out across the cavern, heard by the High Priest alone. It was as though the Fire Father was right there beside him, speaking into his ear. "That will do for now, my child. Great Agarath is quite satiated."

The High Priest was humbled. He lowered his head and his voice was much smaller now. "Make way…move…move aside, make way." They were still sixty metres away. Eldur was watching from his throne, red slit eyes always watching. The priest raised his chin and strode onward, briskly now, nice and briskly along the bridge. The people began to thin in number, the thronging masses spreading and separating. All followers were permitted to gather on the bridges as they made their pilgrimages to the holy mountain, but they were only allowed to get so close to the Fire Father's presence. Nearer to him were those closer to his trust: dragon riders, dragonknights, warriors of proven acclaim, priests. The scholar Sotel Dar still lingered in his shadow, but he was largely ignored now, a scurrying mouse whose use was spent.

It is time for him to join the Eternal Flame, the High Priest thought. *Perhaps I will ask it of him myself.* He did not like the scholar, did not trust him. He had been close allies with Talasha Taan and Ulrik Marak, and both had abandoned the Fire Father now. The High Priest wondered if the scholar might try to do the same. *I will tell him to jump one day, yes. That will test him. It will test his loyalty.*

The great platform was made from the summit of a huge rock pillar that rose from the lava lakes below. It was flat, stone-paved, roughly circular in shape and formed the central point of the chamber. In its vast heart was Agarath's crown-shaped throne, an enormous obsidian seat of soaring spines and barbs in which the All-Father himself had once sat… and even *worn* if the tales were true. Agarath could manipulate his size when in his truest form, in the same way he could manipulate the creatures that served him, manipulate life, manipulate matter and the minds of both monsters and men. He would wear the crown when he took his titan form, and then set it aside to sit in as he shrank down to a more moderate scale.

But still colossal, thought the High Priest of Fire. *Still forty or even fifty feet tall in that guise.* It was a wonder to him every time he looked upon the throne. To have worn it as a crown the All-Father must have soared a thousand feet high, as towering as the statues at Tukor's Pass that Ilith himself had carved. The High Priest had seen them when he flew to capture the heir, seen their great stone carcases strewn across the land beneath him, and he tried to imagine the statue of Vandar rising, standing up with his sword and his shield…he tried to picture in his mind how astonishing that would be.

Now the crown was set as a throne and no more, and within it sat Agarath's greatest servant, dwarfed in its embrace. Eight, even nine feet tall Eldur was, and yet he looked like a child in the seat of a giant up there, and must climb the short stair to reach it. He had his feet resting on the highest step, one arm draped across his lap, the other to his side and clutching at his staff. The Soul of the All-Father observed from atop it, and from the soul rose the storm, the great black-red storm that thundered out in a voice only Eldur and Drulgar and the other ancients could know.

The men and women on the platform were few. They stayed far back from the foot of the stair as the High Priest at last reached the bridge's end and led the prisoners forward. He stopped many metres away and went down to his knees, genuflecting. "Great Father, Eldur the Almighty, I bring to you Ilith, Forgeborn Lord of Tukor, and his companion, the King's Wall of Rasalan."

"Very good," murmured the Fire Father. "Rise."

The High Priest climbed back up to his feet. There, he fell again into a bow and then retreated away to the side, widening an arm to present the two prisoners, and his duty was done. Ilith strode forward willingly, his brown cloak stirring; the Whaleheart was dragged up, half-staggering in his chains. The dragonknights prodded at him with their long black dragonsteel spears, driving him down to his knees, spitting at him and cursing him.

"Now, children, that is no way to treat our guest." Eldur smiled and turned his eyes on Ilith. "Welcome, brother," he said, tapping his staff, and an echoing boom spread out through the cavern. "Welcome," he said again, and ten thousand voices repeated him. *Welcome*, they chanted. *Welcome. Welcome.* The din rose and fell away just as quickly. Silence was restored.

"Nice trick," Ilith said. "You might have just flown me here yourself, you know."

"And deny all my children the chance to see you? There is power in the show, old friend."

"Show," Ilith repeated, smiling thinly. He took a moment to savour some private thought, then looked over at the King's Wall, swaying on his knees in a state of semi-consciousness. "Why did you bring him? That was not a part of the bargain."

"I wanted to bring him," Eldur said. "Why? Well, that I shall think on. The way he fought with such passion for the girl…would you believe it if I told you that it touched me, Ilith? Perhaps I will reunite them. Or…perhaps *not*."

Laughter now, a sudden great gale of laughter that blew like a storm across the bridges. Eldur smiled through his thin pale lips, white skin crackling, crumbling, reforming. He raised a long-fingered hand and silence fell at once. Only the swirl of dragons. The gentle thunder of the watching storm. The bubble of lava and hiss of steam beneath them.

"Do not spare your concern for this man, Ilith," the Fire Father dismissed. "He is nothing, a plaything, a toy, irrelevant. It is *you* who we are welcoming here. So welcome," he called, and his children echoed him again - *welcome, welcome* - and again Eldur gestured for silence. Once it had settled, he opened out an arm and spoke loudly. "My brother Ilith has brought us a gift. Show them, Ilith. Show them the great tool you carry in your possession. Let them look upon the *Hammer of Tukor.*"

A murmur of anticipation rippled through the cavern, and the High Priest looked on keenly. He was most interested in these artefacts, these ancient gifts of the gods. Ilith just stood there, doing nothing.

"Now come, come, don't be shy. Show them, Ilith. Show them."

Still the demigod did nothing. He turned his head to his left, and to his right, observing the masses watching on all around him. Then, at last, he acquiesced, drawing aside his cloak and taking from a pouch the greatest tool of creation ever devised. It was surprisingly plain to look upon, the High Priest thought. Leatherbound at the handle, the head was not so large as he expected, and the luminance was pale and with-drawn. Mist rose from it, much as it rose from godsteel, puffing gently from the glyphs and symbols.

"The tool that forged the Fireblade," Eldur declared, for all his chil-dren to hear. "That raised fortress and statues and cities from east to west and north to south. That shattered the Heart of Vandar…never to be remade." He grinned and more laughter rang forth, spreading out across the cavern. "Come, Ilith, lift it up. Show them. They all want to see."

Ilith did as bidden. Up the hammer went, but briefly, then down again. He slid it back away and looked Eldur in the eye. "So, you wish for me to forge you another blade? Raise another city? What?"

"I need no other weapon than the one I bear." Eldur tapped his staff once again, and great rings of red light spread from it, screaming. "Your worldly gifts are beneath me, Ilith. But I have others whom you may arm."

The blacksmith looked at him, incredulous. "And you think I will? Are you truly so deluded?"

"You will," Eldur told him. "I have all you need here. Forges, work-shops, craftsmen to support you. You can experiment as you please. Do not tell me the delights of working dragonsteel do not appeal to you, Ilith. It will mark a new challenge for you. You always did like a challenge."

"You're thinking of someone else," Ilith said.

"I rather think not. By day you shall work. By night, we may talk. We have much to talk about, old friend. Thousands of years have passed since our last meeting. Oh, the riches we will mine together. From here we can observe the changing of the world. There will be bloodshed, yes, and battles, and we shall watch together the squabble of mankind. You will grow immune to their suffering eventually, my friend; perhaps you will even learn to enjoy it. We are above them, Ilith, above them. We are both gods, you and I, and…"

"Do you ever shut up?" Ilith asked him.

Cold silence flooded the chamber. The Fire Father's red slit eyes angled themselves into a frown. "Careful, now. Careful. You could be comfortable here…or you could not. Tread lightly, or…"

"Or what? You'll throw me to that lava down there? Like I care. I'm dead already, *Eldur*. I'm dead and you don't even know it." He looked at him disdainfully. There was a flicker of a cruel smile on his lips, and the High Priest was getting a queer feeling in the pit of his stomach, an ugly feeling.

Eldur's gaze sharpened. "Does something amuse you?"

"Much amuses me," Ilith said. "Your arrogance, your delusion, your *stupidity*, take your pick. It's all coming down around you and you don't even know it. You're as blind as a *bat*, Eldur." And he looked at the Bondstone, smiling. "A bat like your firstborn son."

There was a fearsome rumbling in the sky, then. The whole mountain gave a violent shudder.

"Do you know?" Ilith called up at the storm. "Do you know that they've come to blows, your sons? Do you feel it, Agarath, oh All-Seeing All-Father? Do you feel it? Do you sense it? Do you *know*?"

"Enough," Eldur hissed at him. "Ilith, enough."

"Ilith," the other laughed. "Ilith! Ilith! *Ilith*! I should thank you for that red rope you cocooned me up in, Eldur. Made an awful racquet, *aye*, but let me save my *power* too. Could relax a little, hidden away like that, knowing you couldn't *see* me." He grinned at him now, a horrible grin. "How long was the flight here? Four, five hours? Should be plenty, aye," he said. "Should be plenty if they've been quick."

The Fire Father's face was turning dark with realisation. There was thunder above, a loud bursting thunder that set all the dragons to screaming.

But Ilith was only *grinning*, grinning in what looked like victory. "One last great purpose, that's what he told me. And he was right, Eldur. Aye, he was right. My last purpose was deceiving *you*. You and *you*." He pointed at the Bondstone, pointed at the storm, turned a full circle and pointed at them all. "All of you. All of you," he shouted out loud, exultant. "I've deceived you all, deceived you all, great Fhanrir has deceived you all!"

And then, with those words, his form rippled and smoked, *changing*, as his brown wool cloak fell away from him, and the High Priest watched on in horrified confusion as the thing that was not Ilith at all grew small and stunted, shrinking away into a rotting twisted grotesque little creature no larger than a crookbacked child.

Eldur rose suddenly from his throne. He was quivering with rage. "Seize him!" he bellowed, smashing his staff. "Bring him to me! Seize him! Seize him!"

Men rushed in at once, bundling forward to the little cackling creature. The flesh was falling away from him. His bones were snapping,
breaking. They brought him violently to the Fire Father's throne, and
threw him down before him, but by then there was nothing, almost
nothing left of him but a sagging heap of broken bones and torn grey
flesh, a crooked spine and twisted neck and a skull spotted with bits of
paper-dry skin and strands of brittle white hair.

But somehow the creature was still alive. A little arm poked up from
the heap of dead flesh with the Hammer of Tukor in its grasp. Twin eyes
of black evil glinted in the firelight. "Keep it," the creature rattled, on a
wheezing, dying breath. "Ilith's got a better one. A better one, aye, a *better*
one."

74

___

Jonik

He could hear the hammer striking, *da-doom, da-doom, da-doom.*

It rang out through the forge. It rang out through the mountains. Through the smoking city it rang, through the valley, through the world, *da-doom, da-doom, da-doom.*

They stood outside in the cold night air, listening, waiting, hoping. Jonik's heart was pounding, pounding with every stroke. *Da-doom, da-doom, da-doom,* it went, *da-doom, da-doom, da-doom.*

The night was bright with stars, all crowding and glittering and gathering as though to watch, and a great full moon swung through the sky observing. They watched those skies relentlessly, watched for the return of the dragons. Hours had passed now and still nothing. *A little more time,* Jonik thought. *Just a little more time, that's all.*

Emeric Manfrey stood beside him, stretching his sword arm, flexing his fingers. "How's the feeling?" Jonik asked.

"Still returning," the exile said. He closed his fingers, opened them, closed them, then clutched at his eagle-pommel blade. "Ilith said I should get full feeling back in a day or two." His eyes roved the skies, scanning from one side to the next. "You can get some rest if you want. I can wake you if there's trouble."

Jonik thought it a terrible idea. He thought Emeric knew him better. "You think I'm going to leave *now*?" He glanced back at the forge. The night air was ringing, *da-doom, da-doom, da-doom,* and beyond the icy drape that hung over the forge door, he could see him, see the shape of the demigod within the shroud of godly white light, a faint shape working, striking at his anvil, hammering the blades, hammering the heart, *da-doom, da-doom, da-doom,* it went, *da-doom, da-doom, da-doom.* "You think I'd miss *this* for a bit of sleep?" Jonik asked. "You're many things, Emeric, but I never took you for mad."

The exile smiled tiredly. "It might take a while longer for him to finish, Jonik. Hours, even. He could still take hours."

Jonik hoped not. Fhanrir's power would only last so long, and eventually they'd see through his deception. He drew a deep breath to steady himself, scanning the skies, as his heart thudded to the beat of the hammer, *da-doom, da-doom, da-doom.* Strange things were happening within the forge, things no mortal man ought to observe, and thus had Ilith set that drape over the door to shield them, but all the same, they could *hear* it. And not just the booming of the hammer, either, but all the rest of it, too. The shrieks and screams and soothing words, the strange sounds the blades made as they tried to fight him and the calming noises the demigod gave out as he wrestled them back together. Every time Jonik turned back to look, he saw shapes through the drape, twisting and writhing and jerking in strange movements. *The spirits of the blades,* he thought. *They are fighting him, wrestling against his might. None of them want to yield.*

They were not alone on the plateau. Sir Lythian Lindar was with them, marching a patrol back and forth across the stone, his feet stepping to the strikes of the hammer, *da-doom, da-doom, da-doom.* The hulking huntsman called Vilmar the Black sat hunched on a chunk of broken rock, utterly still, staring at nothing in particular, while Sir Storos Pentar lay down on the ground staring skyward and sometimes murmuring or shaking his head in what seemed like disbelief. Every so often Jonik heard him huff or even chuckle as he went over everything in his head, and Jonik understood exactly how he was feeling because he felt just the same.

It would likely take a while for him to process it all. He was still reeling from a lot of what had happened, and even more of what he'd *heard.*

The painting, he thought. *Gods, I've got to look at this painting.*

Emeric had seen it, but only once, and Lythian Lindar had been shown it by Ilith and Fhanrir as well, just before Eldur arrived, so they might share with him their plan. Though…it wasn't *their* plan at all, not really. The painting was a portrait of the future. A chaos of seemingly unconnected scenes that were, in fact, visions of what was to come. They were often abstract, Emeric had told him, overlapping and spilling into one another, but in the chaos was a sequence, a sequence that foretold of one event after another, a sequence that had guided Ilith to this very moment in time.

And Tyrith, Jonik thought. The key to it all was *Tyrith.*

Tyrith, who had been imprisoned up here all his life.

Tyrith, who in his long isolation had come to know every scroll and book and tome in the forge as intimately as the ocean knows its death.

Tyrith, who had looked at the painting every night as he went to bed, who had stared at it and studied it, who had memorised every brushstroke and blob of paint. Ilith had never even seen it. No, it was painted long after his death. But that didn't matter, because *Tyrith* had.

And they are one and the same.

It was easy, sometimes, to forget that Tyrith was still a part of him, but when their minds were merged during the transference, all of Tyrith's thoughts and memories and knowledge became Ilith's as well. So it was that Ilith learned of the painting. So it was that he was able to *see* it in his mind, this painting that Tyrith had memorised. To Tyrith, it had been just a painting; a wonderful, chaotic, brutally beautiful painting, but a work of art and nothing more. Yet when Ilith learned of it, when Ilith saw it, he realised it was something so much more, a mystery that only his mind could unravel. Within the chaos, Ilith had seen a structure, and from that structure, he had divined a sequence. And it was that sequence of events that had brought them here. To this critical juncture in time.

Jonik breathed out. His head hurt just to think of it, and his heart was still pounding, pounding with the strike of the hammer. *Da-doom, da-doom, da-doom*, it was pounding, *da-doom, da-doom, da-doom.* He pressed his fingers to his neck, beneath his gorget, and felt his pulse thudding in time with the beat. Lythian Lindar was still striding back and forth, back and forth, and it seemed his steps were still timed to the beat as well.

We are all in sync, Jonik thought. He wondered if it was the same for the other bearers. Maybe his father was pacing in Varinar, moving back and forth through some moonlit courtyard, restless and aware of what was happening. Maybe his brother, recovering in his sickbed in the ruin of White Shadow, was dreaming of it too. Maybe his heart was thumping as he slept, thumping along to the sound of the striking hammer, *da-doom, da-doom, da-doom.*

Jonik was growing nervous now, increasingly anxious as time stretched on. "Tell me of the things you saw again," he said. "Just to pass the time. That face…"

"Which one?"

"The dragon's face. With the red tear. That was Drulgar, do you think? The tear is blood, from where Elyon cut him."

Emeric nodded. "The blinding of the Dread was followed in the sequence by the two winged creatures gripped in a death embrace, falling into the depths. It may be that the Dread did not see his brother coming in time. That would give Brexatron a chance."

A chance was all they could ask for, though the outcome…that was not yet known. "And me," Jonik said. "I'm in the painting as well."

"Yes, it is most likely you. A black-haired man surrounded by shadow, with a bat painted inside his skull. That sounds like you, don't you think? Down in those depths, waking Brexatron from his slumber."

Jonik remembered those days in the darkness. Remembered the colossal menace that stalked him in the dark. He remembered how he'd felt that stabbing pain inside his skull as the monster gave out that screeching roar, and perhaps that's what it meant. The bat inside the skull.

"Seems you were sent down into that underworld to do more than find the Mistblade, Jonik. You may have contributed to the death of the Dread. Or his imprisonment, at least. Perhaps that is all we need. Time beyond his shadow?"

Jonik nodded, thinking. "Does the eagle look like you?" he asked. Emeric frowned, taking a moment to puzzle out his meaning. "You said there was an eagle in the painting. Was it just an eagle or did it wear a green cloak or something?"

The exile chuckled. "It was just an eagle. With a glowing bag in its talons. I suppose that refers to the star core I brought, and the lightleaf. It might even represent the de-aging of Ilith. How the light erupted from him as he grew younger before my eyes."

"I should like to have seen that," Jonik said. He had been in the forge at the time, while Emeric was taken into Ilith's bedchamber. There, he saw the painting, and he saw Ilith turn ancient to youthful in the span of thirty seconds. *And the hammer,* he thought. Ilith had been working on his fake hammer when Emeric saw him, and that hammer was as much a part of the deception as Fhanrir's power of illusion. "Did you know?" he wondered. "When Fhanrir stepped out? Did you know it was him?"

"No. I wasn't told. Only Sir Lythian was aware of the ruse."

"How did he look?"

"He looked like Ilith, Jonik. That was the whole point."

"And Eldur didn't know? He wasn't even suspicious?"

"Fhanrir once deceived Thala into believing he was Ilith," the exile said. "If he could do that, then Eldur would be no challenge to him. And so far as I know, Eldur never even knew Fhanrir existed. The mage was no more than a boy when Eldur went into hiding following his defeat by Varin at the Ashmount. Sometimes you have to be searching for a trick to find one. And arrogance can be blinding, Jonik."

He nodded. That was true. Hubris was probably the best word, and their enemy was nothing if not hubristic.

The wait went on. After a while the steady pounding of the hammer paused for a short moment, before resuming, and Jonik knew that Ilith had completed striking one blade into another and had moved onto the next, following the sequence that Ranulf had memorised from that stolen page in the Book of Thala. It seemed to Jonik that a silver light was spilling out from inside now, and he could hear a great rushing wind in there as if Ilith was fighting a storm. *My brother's blade. Laquered with the blood of the Dread.* He was working the Windblade together with the others, and that meant only the Sword of Varinar was to come.

The storm was blowing loudly and the drape looked like it might even rip away from its fastenings. He could hear Ilith bellowing out in a commanding voice, could see his shape moving, his arm striking up and down, up and down. There was a great struggle going on, profound and powerful magic being wrought, and the striking must be perfect, precise; Ilith could suffer no distraction or interference lest he lose his rhythm to the ruin of them all.

"I might need to lie down," Jonik said. "Maybe Storos has the right idea." He could feel his heart throbbing in his throat, taste the bile in his stomach rising, rising. Across the plateau, Lythian Lindar was still pacing from side to side with a hard, thoughtful look on his face. Every so often he would go to the edge and look down into the city, or down the switch-back stair, glancing to see if someone might come up with a report. Mostly, though, he looked at the skies, always the skies, eyes turning here and there, scrutinising every star as though it might suddenly widen out a pair of wings and come screaming down atop them.

Eventually, a dragon did come, but it was a friendly dragon and a very handsome one with scales of crimson and copper. It came up from the city, landing on the eastern edge of the plateau, and the dragonknight Sir Pagaloth dismounted. Lythian went right over to take report from him, and Jonik joined them to give himself a distraction. Emeric came as well.

"What's the latest, Pagaloth?" Lythian asked. "Has Elyon awoken?"

"Not yet. He is still being treated by the nurses. They are fussing over him madly, Captain."

"Any serious wounds? Broken bones? Internal bleeding?"

"Nothing. His armour protected him from the fall. His worst wound is his hand. He has several broken knuckles."

Lythian gave a snort of laughter. "Seems you gave him more of a beating than the Dread did, Jonik."

Jonik felt awkward. He did not quite know how to speak to Lythian Lindar, and they had barely shared more than a dozen words thus far. The man was Amron Daecar's best friend and like an uncle to Elyon as well. *He probably hates me too*, he thought. *Though he's too polite to show it.* "The knuckles were *his* doing, really," he murmured. "He tried to hit me and I moved, so he hit the floor." He shrugged. "I wouldn't say I gave him a beating."

Lythian smiled, then moved things on. "What else, Pagaloth? Did you see anything on patrol?"

"Nothing."

"How far did you go?"

"I don't know in distance. Roughly to the southern edge of the mountains. I saw many rivers beneath me. And a large fortress among them."

"Tallriver," said Lythian. "It's the original seat of House Kanabar." He thought for a moment. "That's over a hundred miles from here, maybe closer to a hundred and fifty. And you saw nothing? Are the skies clear out there?"

"Clear, yes, clear to the southern horizon."

"They all want to watch," Emeric Manfrey said, profoundly. "All the gods in their halls. Varin at his table. The dead in the stars. Everyone wants to see."

It certainly felt that way. Jonik glanced again at the forge, though from this side he could not see it well. Still, the pounding was constant, *da-doom, da-doom, da-doom,* and it seemed as though Ilith was wrestling the Windblade into shape, dominating it with his will. The storm was not raging so fiercely now, and the drapes were only fluttering and not straining to rip free. Earlier, when Ilith had first begun, it had been as black as pitch in there, and Jonik had known he was starting with the Nightblade, using the Essense of Nightwing to make it more pliant and malleable so it would merge with the other shards. After that all went blue and there were all these queer hissing and spraying sounds, and Jonik had seen what looked like sea spray splashing and pattering against the drape. And after *that* the entire plateau had turned ice-cold, and a snow had started to fall, and the drapes had frozen solid like a thick white wall. Now this. Now the storm and the wind and sometimes the rumble of what sounded like thunder in there as he pounded the Windblade into the rest, into the shards of night and mist and frost.

And just one to go, Jonik thought. Gods, he felt so nervous he might just faint.

He turned back to the others, focusing on what they were saying. Pagaloth was speaking, telling them he would fly out again and keep watch across the mountains. "I should not be here long," he said. "This is no place for an Agarathi."

"It's a place for an ally," Lythian said, putting a steel hand on his shoulder. "We are all allies here."

"Still…" Pagaloth cast a glance toward the forge. "I feel less welcome here. I must go. Keep watch. If anyone comes, I shall bring warning."

"Very well," Lythian said, and the dragonknight mounted up again, plunging away into the night. They watched him dip out of sight beneath the mountain, then rise up in a soaring arc. He grew quickly smaller as he thrashed away south, and before too long, he was lost completely amidst the dazzle of stars.

They stood together in silence for a while, watching the dragon shrink away. Then Lythian turned. "Jonik," he said, "a word." He stepped away, and after a moment's delay, Jonik followed. They crossed to the edge of the plateau where it gave the best view of the city. Fingers of smoke were swirling to the sky and many little fires were still burning from the fallen towers and broken buildings.

It was unrecognisable, now, from what it had been. More thoroughly destroyed than even Varinar, perhaps, though it was hard to say for sure until the rubble was cleared away. Jonik had found himself almost entirely useless during the battle. What could a common swordsman do when the dragons refused to engage? What could he do against the Dread? The only ones who mattered were the ballista men and the soldiers who worked the siege engines, and sometimes the Bladeborn bowmen, too. All Jonik could do was hurry about, picking up spears from dead men to fling at passing shadows. But it didn't last long, in any case. Once the Dread arrived, the dragons all but fled, and then *everyone* was useless. *Everyone except my brother,* he thought. *My brother who blinded the Dread.*

"How do you feel, Jonik?" Lythian Lindar asked. He was looking at him. Looking at him while Jonik looked at the city.

"I'm…fine. Anxious," he admitted. "It feels like my heart's pounding with the hammer."

"I feel the same," Lythian said. He smiled evenly. "Do you feel better now that the Nightblade has been reunited with its siblings?"

"I…I suppose there's a feeling of freedom, yes. To be rid of the whispers for good and all."

"A feeling I am relishing," Lythian Lindar said, breathing out. He turned his eyes across the skies, thinking for a moment, then went on. "I wanted to talk to you about earlier. When we found Elyon down in White Shadow."

Jonik nodded, waiting for more.

"You were able to lift the Windblade more easily than the rest of us," the man said. "You have a natural bond to the Blades of Vandar. Having bonded two of them already."

"One and a half," Jonik said. "I never committed to a full bond of the Mistblade."

"That is still more than me or Elyon can boast. We have bonded a single blade only, and in my case…well, I have tried to maintain a modicum of distance from the Sword of Varinar as well. But you? Two full bonds…"

"One and a half."

"One and a half, then. And they say it gets easier each time. Certainly, it seemed that way when you lifted the Windblade onto Lendrathor's back."

Jonik barely even remembered. In the aftermath of Drulgar the Dread's departure, he'd rushed quickly down toward White Shadow in search of his brother, having seen him falling from the sky earlier. At the same time, the dragon Lendrathor was coming down from the forge with Pagaloth, Lythian and Emeric all aboard, and they were looking for Elyon as well. That was when Jonik learned of what was happening. They needed the Windblade brought to Ilith immediately, so he could begin the final forging, and Jonik had been the one to haul it up onto the dragon's back, with his brother lying unconscious. All that was much of a blur to him right now.

"What are you getting at, Sir Lythian?" he asked.

"I think you know, Jonik. Only you and your father have bonded two separate blades…"

"One and a half…"

"…and you bore the Windblade quite easily as well," Lythian went on. "Seeing as your father is far to the west, in Varinar, that would leave you as our best candidate."

Jonik shook his head at once. "Only the heir can bear the Heart Remade, Sir Lythian. The prophecy…"

"May be false, or incomplete, or open to interpretation. Eldur was said to rise benevolent as well, and I think it is quite safe now to say that has not turned out as the Agarathi masters predicted."

"Because they were lied to," Jonik said. "By Rasalanian mages and manipulators. They fed that lie into the wise masters' dreams. *That* prophecy was always false."

Lythian Lindar frowned. He did not seem to know that particular detail. "I was long in Prince Tethian's company. I heard often of the likes of Pullio the Wise and Quarl the Blind. You're to say they were deceived by the Rasalanians?"

"By Thala," Jonik said. "It was all a part of her puzzle." *Like this painting*, he thought. No one seemed to know who had painted it or placed it there, but Jonik was certain that the Far-Seeing Queen had a hand in it.

"Where did you hear this?" Lythian asked.

"Leshie told me. Saska's friend. Saska had it all from her grandmother, the Grand Duchess."

"Then I'd like to speak to her myself. If she here, in the city?"

"She was in the palace when the dragons came," Jonik told him. "Elyon told her to get Amilia out." He did not need to explain. Over half of the palace had fallen in on itself or been smashed aside by Drulgar the Dread, and it was possible Amilia and Leshie were crushed among the rubble. Men were searching now, though if there was any news it had not yet reached them here.

The Knight of the Vale was scratching at his scraggly beard, thinking it all over. But there was nothing to think over, so far as Jonik saw it. The prophecy was absolute. Eldur rising benevolent or not was not the same as the heir of a demigod wielding their godly gift. In that there was precedent. *And evidence*, Jonik thought.

"Only Ilith and his direct heirs have been able to wield the Hammer of Tukor," he said. "It's the same with the Heart Remade. Only Saska can bear it."

"Saska is not here."

"No. But…she will return."

"And if she doesn't? We must consider all ends, Jonik. Elyon returned the Eye of Rasalan to King Sevrin in the hope he would be able to peer into it. Sevrin is not Thala's direct descendent by primogeniture."

"We don't know if that's come to anything," Jonik said to that. "That whole enterprise might have failed."

"Or it may not. We do not yet know. As we do not know whether another…someone like *you*, who has bonded two blades…"

"One and a half."

Lythian smiled. "*Two*," he said, after a pause. "And a sprinkling of a third, as we saw earlier. So, when the time comes, I would ask you to *try*. That is all. To try. As I will try, and I'm sure Elyon will try, and anyone else who feels worthy of the challenge. Most likely you are right. Most likely, it will require that particular spark of primogeniture blood to ignite the bond, but we will not know until we have exhausted all other options."

Jonik knew who the best option was, if it wasn't going to be Saska, and he wasn't here. Still, he did not think anything would come of it. Without Saska none of this might mean anything. *The greatest weapon ever made*, he thought. *Sitting idle in a forge.*

They agreed to put it aside for now and revisit the topic later. Lythian dipped his chin at him, and resumed his patrol, striding back and forth to the beat of the hammer, back and forth, back and forth, always searching the skies. Jonik found a rock to sit on near the edge of the plateau, looking down at the city again, listening to the thud of the hammer, *da-doom, da-doom, da-doom*, thinking about everything and nothing in particular, his mind drifting from one thing to the next as the hammer sang into the night.

Gradually, the bluster of the wind died down and all went quiet and still. Jonik looked over and saw that the light inside was changing again, turning from silver to gold. He could see the shadow of Ilith there, placing down the Sword of Varinar atop the others, could see him taking up the final potion from the workbench, pulling the top off the Light of the Soulstar to pour atop the blade. There with a deep hissing sound, and a great golden mist poured up and concealed him, and as it began to fade Jonik saw the shadow of the hammer rising again, falling, and once more came the pounding sound, louder, fiercer than ever before, *da-doom, da-doom, da-doom*, it went, *DA-DOOM, DA-DOOM, DA-DOOM*.

Jonik sat, staring at the forge as the shadows and shapes twisted within, and amid the pounding were terrible sounds now, awful tearing, ripping sounds as though the very fabric of the world was being torn apart and reknitted and remade anew. Storos Pentar got up to his feet and backed away, Emeric was staring from nearby, Lythian had stopped in his pacing and even Vilmar the Black turned his head to look.

The stars were watching. And the moon. And the mountains. Time seemed to slow and stand still. Jonik found himself transfixed as the hammer went up and up, as the world boomed out, *DA-DOOM, DA-DOOM*, as the golden light within the forge swirled and rushed and pressed up against the drape, up and against it, up and past it and out of it. Onto the plateau it came bursting, spreading out across the mountain and into the sky and it seemed all of a sudden that night had turned to day, and all the while the pounding, the endless, ceaseless, powerful pounding, *DA-DOOM, DA-DOOM, DA-DOOM*, it went, *DA-DOOM, DA-DOOM, DA-DOOM*.

Jonik had to shield his eyes. He had to tuck his shoulders up to cover his ears. The light brightened and brightened and brightened some more, and the sound came with it, louder, louder, louder, louder, until all the world was those two things, that golden light and the pounding sound as the hammer rose and fell, rose and fell, and *DA-DOOM, DA-DOOM, DA-DOOM*, it went, *DA-DOOM, DA-DOOM, DA-DOOM*…

He did not know how long it went on for. Five minutes, ten, an hour, two? His thoughts seemed to stray out of time and place and when next he knew, the sound had been withdrawn again, and the light with it, and he dared to peek through his fingers and look again at the forge.

Ilith was withdrawing something from his pocket, glowing with a great new light, an ethereal light of whose colour Jonik could not place. He could hear the demigod murmuring, speaking, talking to the light, as he set the Hammer of Tukor aside. Then he nodded, as though some agreement had been made, and reaching out, he turned over his hand, upending the light upon the anvil, and it filtered down, sparkling, glittering, enrobing the blade, *binding* it. *The final fragment*, Jonik thought. *The final fragment for the final forging.*

The men were scattered across the plateau. All were down on their knees now, staring as a new, multicoloured glow throbbed gently behind the drape. Jonik watched with bated breath as the drape stirred, as though in a gentle breeze, and was drawn aside. An old man walked out. "Come," he croaked, weakly. "It is done. Come."

They rose and moved to the door. Jonik's heart was bashing at his ribs. His chest went up and down. Emeric was first to reach the drape. He stopped there, held a hand up to prevent Sir Storos Pentar from entering. "No," he said. "Bearers first."

Sir Lythian Lindar passed inside. Jonik followed behind him. Ilith was standing within, once more aged and grey and small and drained, the light from his skin withdrawn, his strength depleted. He was standing beside the blade.

It rested on the anvil, a longsword four feet long, single-fullered and double-edged with a perfect curve along its final third. Shimmering bands of colour shone along the steel from crossguard to tip, black, blue, white, silver and gold, and from each rose a mist of corresponding hue, puffing, fogging, sparkling, merging. Jonik looked at it in wonder, gazed at it in awe. There were no whispers, no voices, no temptations. Nothing but power. A throbbing, boundless power.

"The Heart Remade," Ilith murmured. He looked at it and a tear fell down his cheek, snaking through a wrinkle. "A great evil has been corrected this night. An evil I should never have agreed to." He seemed to be ageing, even as he spoke. "Come. We cannot leave it here." He lifted the blade. It yielded easily to him. Slowly, he led them through the forge and living quarters, to a room deep in the mountain, a circular room with a stone table at its heart. He placed down the Heart Remade and stood a moment, staring at it. "I presented the blades to Varin in this room," he said softly, reminiscing. "You must tell his heir it is here."

"My lord," said Emeric Manfrey. "What if the enemy should come? He knows of this place now, he…"

"I have raised seals against him. He cannot enter this room. Nor could he move it if he could." His voice was growing smaller, thinner. He reached into his cloak, taking something from his belt, and placed it beside Vandar's Heart. It was the Hammer of Tukor, cracked, *broken*. No light rose from it. The glyphs and symbols did not glow. "True blessings require great sacrifice," he murmured, so softly now, so weakly. His hand was shivering as it rested on the hammer. He ran his fingers lightly upon it, once, twice, then finally did he turn.

He was ancient. Truly ancient. Shrunken, shrivelled, dying.

Jonik did not cry. Yet a tear was snaking down his cheek. He felt it, warm against his cold dry skin as the demigod said, "Take me to my bed," in a voice so thin they could barely hear him. "Tyrith would like to see the painting…one last time."

And so they carried him through and laid him down and Jonik saw it at last. He saw the painting, but he did not care. No, not now. Could could he care about it now? "My lord," he croaked, kneeling by Ilith's bedside. "Without you…without you what…what are we to do?"

The demigod placed a wrinkled hand on his cheek, a cold hand, a shivering hand, and looked him deep in the eye. The light was leaving his own. Fading, dimming, as a once bright star giving out its final glimmer. And no star had ever shone so bright as Ilith who had built the world. He smiled and his lips whispered out a single, dying word. It was his last word. His last breath. And with it, the Worldbuilder passed.

"Prevail," he said.

EPILOGUE

Amron

He was armoured in his silver lobstered plate, repaired and reinforced and enamelled in Varin blue.

He gleamed magnificently, and his hair was washed and trimmed, his beard neatened, his shoulders draped with the cloak of Amron the Bold from whom he'd been given his name.

All of the city lords and luminaries had come, the best it had to offer. There were no greatlords present. Rodmond Taynar remained at King's Point, and Alrus Pentar was ruling from Redhelm. Borrus, Rikkard, and Killian, new lords of Houses Kanabar, Amadar, and Oloran, were far away to the east. The dowager queen, Elitha Reynar, had been invited with her daughter Lyriss but they had chosen to remain at Silverspear. Elyon was not here, nor Lythian, nor Torus. The Ironfoot was at the coast and Lord Botley Harrow had stayed at Crosswater. There were no foreign dignitaries. No kings and queens of Tukor and Rasalan, no princes, princesses, great lords and ladies from his cousins to the east. A poor communion, it was, to stand witness to the crowning of a Vandarian king.

But it is the best we have, Amron thought, as he stepped forward down the aisle.

The throne had been set upon the dais in the feast hall, the throne in which Varin himself had sat, the throne that Ilith had made. Mist puffed thickly from its arms and back and seat, fading and thinning as it rose.

He walked toward it alone, trying his best to hide his limp, trying his best and failing. He could hear them murmuring as he passed. He could feel the worried eyes watching. He kept his left arm folded across his body, touching at his ceremonial godsteel blade to give him strength. It helped, but not enough. Nothing was enough.

The hall was packed full. Grand it was, the feast hall of Keep Kanabar, and every inch of space was filled but the wide central aisle down which the king walked. His long cloak trailed just above the floor behind him, his footsteps rang proudly on the stone. He could see many faces he knew to his left and right, but he did not turn to them or acknowledge them or break his step. He wanted to get this done, in truth. He wanted it all to be over.

Only when he reached the front seats and saw Lillia there with Amara did he stop. He turned to them, bowing before his good-sister, kissing her pale cheek, and pressed his lips to Lillia's forehead.

"You both look beautiful," he said, softly.

Amara smiled up at him tearily. She had insisted she be here, despite Artibus's protestations that she remain abed. "I will not miss it," she'd proclaimed, with some of her old fire. "Not for the bloody world." Artibus had said it was a risk…not to her, but the child…but she had dismissed that as well. "If this child gives up on me because I attend her uncle's coronation, then perhaps she doesn't deserve to live at all." She had patted her belly, very gently of course. "But she is stronger than that, and so am I. I am *going*, Artibus, and that's that."

She was looking at him now, lovingly, proudly, and that made it all worthwhile. "Go," she said, cupping his bearded cheek. She wore a bandage around her head and was still very weak from her fall, but she looked graceful and elegant all the same. "You go get crowned, Amron. Let's make it official, at last."

He smiled at her. "Very well, Amara," and rose again, walking to the short stair that led up to the dais. Behind the throne great royal banners had been draped, and dozens of torches flickered around the walls. Amron stepped up before the throne. Forgemaster Merilore was presiding; Watling and Wainwood stood on either side of the stage. There was a long history of the Steelforge Forgemasters conducting the Vandarian coronations, a queer custom to other cultures who always chose holy men for the role. But the Forgemasters *were* holy, in their way. In Vandar, those who could shape and alter godsteel were often seen as the God King's vessels.

A large velvet cushion rested on the stone before the throne. "Kneel," Merilore said. He was all in red, to match his red eyebrows and red beard and red hair. Amron went down as gracefully as he could, and managed to do so without steadying himself with his hand. Kneeling was not a comfortable position for his right leg, though his pain was subdued by the tonic he'd taken earlier.

"State your name."

"Amron, son of Gideon. Lord of House Daecar."

Merilore stood beside him; Amron was facing the crowds. He saw Amara there, saw Lillia looking very proud and nervous. Jovyn sat beside her, and Artibus beside him, and beside him was the grand stately figure of Lord Styron the Strong, his own son Gerald beside him, then Sir Bryce, and Sir Quinn and Lord Mantle, and across the aisle Amron saw that Sir Taegon Cargill sat with Sir Marcus Flint and Lord Robert Borrington, and of course Stegra the Snowfist had muscled his way onto the first row.

Amron almost laughed when he saw him, but held his poise. Forge-master Merilore was going through the promises and proclamations, asking Amron if he would uphold the law and protect the realm, feed the hungry and educate the young. After every statement, Amron was expected to nod his head solemnly and say, "I will," or "I do," or "I shall." He wondered how many kings actually listened when the questions were asked. Truly listened to the holy vows they were making. Most just nodded and said the words, he did not doubt. Most kings were useless, that was the truth. He wondered what sort of king he would be, but then of course he didn't have to wonder. He'd been king for twenty years, they said. Vesryn crossed his mind, then. Vesryn who had ruled at his side. He cursed his brother for his treacheries and follies, but he wished he was here right now. *I could use you, brother,* he thought, sadly. *The gods know I could use you now.*

Merilore was still going on. Would he swear to unite all the people of his lands? Would he show all valour in the face of danger? Would he rule in wisdom and temperance?

Yes, yes, and…yes, he hoped. He wondered if his namesake had answered that last with a straight face. Amron the Bold was hardly known for his wisdom and temperance. *Will you make unnecessary war with your enemies?* he thought. *Will you cast aside your father's long peace and bring strife and suffering to the realm?* To those, Amron the Bold would have vigorously agreed.

The questions kept coming. Amron nodded his head and said, "I will," and, "I shall," and "I do."

"Will you do all in your power to maintain harmony with your allies?"

"I will."

"Do you promise to bring swift justice against your foes?"

"I do."

"Will you honour the accomplishments of your forebears with holy days and festivals?"

"I shall."

"Will you uphold all the traditions of the Steelforge?"

Merilore raised an eyebrow at that one. Amron had, of course, opened the Steelforge doors to common smiths and armourers, which was hardly upholding its traditions. Still, he answered in the only way he could. "I will."

Merilore gave a very light scoff, and went on. There were dozens of them, too many in fact. By the end Amron could tell that the hall was growing restless, and half of the spectators were probably wondering why they'd come.

When at last the promises and proclamations were over, Forgemaster Merilore called over the others, and Watling and Wainwood stepped in from the sides. Each was bearing a velvet cushion much like the one Amron was kneeling on. On Forgemaster Watling's cushion was a godsteel brooch shaped in the arms of the kingdom; a blade planted before the mountain. The blade was a representation of Vandar's Heart and the mountain was Vandar's Tomb, a representation of his body. On old Wainwood's cushion was a crown, newly forged to replace the one lost in the ruin of the palace. It too was godsteel, a plain circlet ornamented with two dozen miniature misting blades rendered in exquisite detail.

Merilore took the brooch first, stepped in front of Amron with his back to the audience and went down to his knees before him. He began removing Amron's current clasp, replacing it with his new one. "How am I doing?" he whispered as he worked.

"Very well," Amron said. It was Merilore's first time officiating. "Except for the scoff."

"Your fault. You've already broken that bloody oath, Amron."

He smiled. Merilore had always been his favourite Forgemaster.

Once the brooch was fixed, the Forgemaster stood, took the crown from its little cushion, and raised it high above Amron's head. The crowd murmured excitedly as it caught the light, gilding the silver mists. Then, lowering it down very slowly and importantly, he placed it upon Amron's head.

"In the sight of gods and men I crown you," he called out. "May you rule in justice and honour, in mercy and in strength, and uphold all the vows you have heretofore taken." He paused to wink at him. "Now rise, as king. Rise, King Amron Daecar!"

And Amron Daecar rose. He rose to applause, a spreading acclamation and the bellowing of Stegra Snowfist. He rose to smashing palms and stamping feet and he rose to shouts and cheers. He rose to beaming smiles and misting eyes, and loud and jubilant laughter. He rose to his feet and stood before them, their hero, their champion, their king.

And then came the name.

The name he so tried to shun.

Amron did not know who started it, or where it came from in the hall, but first ten, then twenty, then a hundred took up the cry, and before too long all the hall was chanting it. "Varin Reborn!" they called out loudly, and "Varin Reborn," they shouted proudly. From the seats they called it and the standing space in the back, from the galleries they sang to the rafters. "Varin Reborn," bellowed one and all. "Varin Reborn, Varin Reborn, VARIN REBORN!"

And in her seat, with her bandaged head, Amara was sat there, smiling. She must have felt terrible, and it was not wise that she be here with all this noise, but she was smiling all the same. He looked at her, saw the tear rolling down her cheek, and her lips moving along with all the rest "Varin Reborn, Varin Reborn, Varin Reborn," she said. "Believe it, Amron. You *are* Varin Reborn."

And so, at last, he nodded.

I will be who they need me to be.

Later…much later…after the festivities had calmed and the city was sleeping, Amron Daecar limped through the night into the ruin of the city. He passed the hills, passed the palace of fallen stone, passed the blackness and the bleakness wrought by the Dread. He came to the hill he'd scaled more times than any other. Atop it lay the shell of a castle, a ghostly apparition in the night. He began the climb.

Up the winding road he went, past the little tiered gardens that were dead and ashen, along the cobbled path he'd ridden along and walked along ten thousand times before. At the top he reached the castle gate; it was twisted and broken, he passed within.

The courtyard lay before him. The shattered pavestones sprouting with weeds. The collapsed bones of the stables and the storehouses. He had not been here since his return to Varinar. He had wanted to hold off until he could come alone, and now he was, he was all alone and the night was still.

He looked at the skeleton of Keep Daecar. He remembered his happy memories here. Too many there were, too many for him to count. His wife's smile. How beautiful she was when she danced. The sound of her laughter. Kessia laughed often. There was a time when the halls rang to it, and what a sweet music she made. He remembered how passionate she was in her work. How devoted she was to the poor and the needy. He remembered how much she loved her children, and how devoted she was to them too. *And me,* he thought. *And me.* She was so devoted to him that she had tried to give Amron another son…and the toil of it had killed her.

A tear was sliding down his cheek. He reached up and wiped it away. "I miss you, Kess," he murmured. "I miss you every day, my darling."

He moved toward the door, scaling the short stair and stepping inside. He could see his family in the entrance hall. See Kessia preparing to go down with her guards to the city. See Aleron and Elyon sparring with their wooden swords, *clacking* across the stone. Aleron in Blockform, of course, Elyon in Strikeform. Lillia sitting on the steps and watching, wishing she could join in. He could see Vesryn too, striding in wearing his Greycloak uniform to give Amron some report. See Amara coming gracefully down the stairs to either kiss her husband or cut him with her tongue, and Vesryn never seemed to know which he'd get.

He smiled, moving up through the keep, striding through a tide of memory. Lillia weeping on her bed after her mother's death as Amara held her and comforted her. Aleron, marching out every morning at dawn to train in the Steelforge yard and not returning until late at night, if he returned at all. He would sleep there, often, after Kessia's death. It was too painful for him here, the same as it was for Elyon. But Elyon stayed anyway, for Lillia. He was caught between the two of them, between his big brother and his little sister and he tried to make every-thing right. *He always tries to make things right.*

He wandered along on his tour of remembrances and memories, some happy, some sad, some crisp and clear, some fading. Kessia was gone, and Aleron and Vesryn, but he still had Elyon, still had Lillia and Amara. *I still have half my family,* he thought. It was more than many others could say, especially now, and didn't that make him lucky? More lucky than most, at least?

He came at last to the reason he was here. The family feast hall held a thousand memories of its own. He looked at the table and remembered Aleron's ascension, the day they'd buried him in the Steelforge crypts. He remembered Vesryn's guilt that night, remembered the songs they'd sung so Varin would hear. He remembered the night he sat with Amara and Artibus, discussing the blessings of Vandar's Tomb, and how Amara had encouraged him to make the pilgrimage to heal his wounds. Later, she had paired him up with Walter Selleck, and sent them both on their way.

She has always believed in me, Amron thought. *More than anyone, perhaps. Not once has she faltered in her faith.*

He would try to repay her for that. He would be the man she saw him to be.

Varin Reborn, he thought. They had called him that almost all his life. Even so long ago as the last war, when he earned his many names. *And now we reach the apex of another. We approach the peak of the Last Renewal.*

The final fight for the dawn was coming, and for that, he would need a new blade.

Or an old one, he thought, stepping up to the wall.

It was still in its brackets where he'd left it. A greatsword six feet long. A faint red mist rose from the steel, an old mark, like his scar, of the famous dragon it had slain.

It was the blade with which he had won his acclaim, the blade with which he'd earned his names. The Mercyblade, some called it, others called it Vallath's Ruin. But to Amron Daecar it had a deeper meaning.

It was the blade of his bloodline, the ancestral sword of House Daecar, familiar as family, featherlight in his grasp. He looked down the fine edge of the steel and swished it side to side. It was hungry, he could feel it, hungry for battle and blood.

"For too long you have sat here idle," Amron said. He gripped the hilt firmly in his grasp and somehow he felt younger, stronger, more hopeful again. He could almost feel Aleron in it, Aleron who had borne it himself, and his father Gideon, and his grandfather Balion, and the great men of his line going back thousands of years. He felt them behind him, felt them with him, felt them to his left and his right and around him. All looking at him. At nodding at him. *They are with me,* he thought. *All of them are with me.*

And steeling his eyes, Amron nodded right back at them. "We have a war to win, old friend," he said, as he looked down the length of the steel. "Will you ride with me, one last time?"

Vallath's Ruin misted accord.

THE END

The Bladeborn Saga is expected to conclude in book 8 - coming soon!

ALSO BY T. C. EDGE

THE ENHANCED SERIES (MAIN SERIES):

The Enhanced (Book One)

Hybrid (Book Two)

Nameless (Book Three)

Assassin (Book Four)

Captive (Book Five)

Renegade (Book Six)

Invader (Book Seven)

Avenger (Book Eight)

Defender (Book Nine)

Nemesis (Book Ten)

Sequel (to main Enhanced series, and Warrior Race series):

The Enhanced: Awakening

The Enhanced: Conquest

The Enhanced: Fractured

The Enhanced: Invasion

THE WARRIOR RACE SERIES (ENHANCED UNIVERSE):

The Warrior Race (Book One)

The Red Warrior (Book Two)

Angel of War (Book Three)

CHILDREN OF THE PRIME SERIES (ENHANCED UNIVERSE):

The Chosen (Book One)

Trial of the Chosen (Book 2)

Blood of the Chosen (Book 3)

March of the Chosen (Book 4)

War of the Chosen (Book 5)

Fall of the Chosen (Book 6)

Rise of the Chosen (Book 7)

Fate of the Chosen (Book 8)

VARIANT SERIES (ENHANCED UNIVERSE)

Variant (Book One)
Initiate (Book Two)
Survivor (Book Three)
Pathfinder (Book Four)
Legend (Book Five)
Prodigy (Book Six)
Worldkiller (Book Seven)

OTHER BOOKS BY THE AUTHOR:

THE WATCHERS SERIES:

The Watchers Trilogy:

The Watchers of Eden (Book One)
City of Stone (Book Two)
War at the Wall (Book Three)
The Watchers Trilogy Box Set

The Seekers Trilogy

The Watcher Wars (Book One)
The Seekers of Knight (Book Two)
The Endless Knight
The Seekers Trilogy Box Set

THE PHANTOM CHRONICLES:

The Last Phantom (Book 1)
Phantom Hunter (Book 2)
Phantom Legacy (Book 3)
Phantom Unleashed (Book 4)